The Camp-Fire

1918-1920

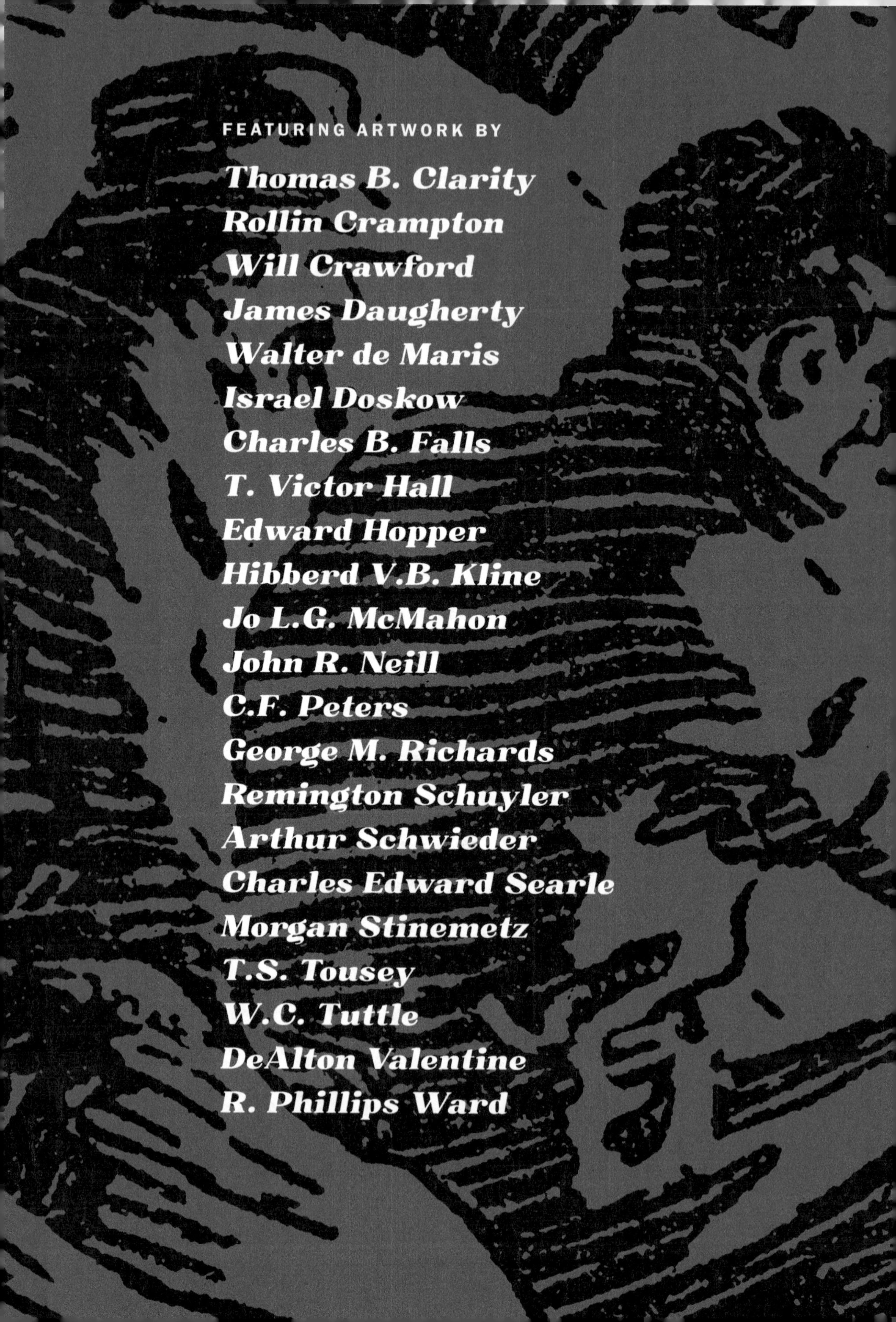

FEATURING ARTWORK BY

Thomas B. Clarity
Rollin Crampton
Will Crawford
James Daugherty
Walter de Maris
Israel Doskow
Charles B. Falls
T. Victor Hall
Edward Hopper
Hibberd V.B. Kline
Jo L.G. McMahon
John R. Neill
C.F. Peters
George M. Richards
Remington Schuyler
Arthur Schwieder
Charles Edward Searle
Morgan Stinemetz
T.S. Tousey
W.C. Tuttle
DeAlton Valentine
R. Phillips Ward

the Camp-Fire

The Complete Correspondence From the Pages of Adventure™

1918 - 1920

EDITED BY

ARTHUR SULLIVANT HOFFMAN

INTRODUCTION BY

TOM KRABACHER

COVER BY

EDWARD HOPPER

Steeger Books · 2023

ACKNOWLEDGEMENTS
Doug Ellis, Ed Hulse, Tom Krabacher, Walker Martin, and Sai Shankar

A NOTE ABOUT THIS BOOK

This edition contains facsimile images from actual vintage issues of *Adventure* pulp magazines, taken from several sources. As such, some images are in poorer quality than others. While there are only a few instances of lesser-quality images, we have striven to make these as legible as possible.

A MEETING PLACE FOR READERS, WRITERS, AND ADVENTURERS

BY TOM KRABACHER

In 1935 *Time Magazine* crowned *Adventure Magazine,* in recognition of the 25th anniversary of its publication, the "No. 1 Pulp" of its era. Today, it remains one of the most avidly sought-after titles by pulp collectors. This reputation derives in large part by the role played by its legendary editor Arthur Sullivant Hoffman.

Hoffman assumed the role of managing editor of *Adventure* in early 1912, less than a year after the magazine was founded. He would serve in that position until 1927 by which time he had built the magazine up into one of the most popular of the period. A key reason for its success lay in Hoffman's belief that adventure fiction and literary quality need not be mutually exclusive, and over the course of his editorship the stories he published regularly demonstrated that principle. In the early years, Nobel laureate Sinclair Lewis worked with Hoffman as an assistant editor, Pulitzer Prize winner T.S. Stribling published his earliest stories there, and the artwork of renowned illustrators such as Rockwell Kent and Edward Hopper graced its pages. Many of the magazine's authors from this period continue to be read and remembered even today.

In addition to the stories it offered, the magazine's popularity was due in no small part to Hoffman's commitment to the idea that *Adventure* serve not just as a provider of escapist fiction, but as a place where readers were "fellow adventurers," active members of a broadly-based community of readers, writers, and editors with a shared love of adventure. As a result, during the first few years of his editorship the magazine introduced a variety of features to promote this sense of shared identity. These included *Adventure* identification cards that were registered with the magazine so that "in case of death or serious injury to the bearer one should contact the magazine with details and friends will be notified." Readers were encouraged to establish and report on the activities of local *Adventure* clubs, and the magazine introduced departments such as "Lost Trails" to help readers re-establish contact with missing acquaintances, "Ask Adventure" where experts answered questions on exotic topics, and "Wanted—Men and Adventurers," which, as the name suggests, purported to serve as a recruitment site for individuals seeking their own "adventurous" opportunities.

By far, however, the most important of all these efforts to promote the shared sense of identity was establishment of The Camp-Fire.

The Camp-Fire was nominally a letter column that premiered in the June 1912 issue, four months after Hoffman took over the editorial reins. Letter columns were a common feature in pulp magazines of the era such as *The Argosy* and *All-Story,* where they gave readers the opportunity to comment on recently published stories, make suggestions to the editor, or respond to other readers. In turn, they provided editors a forum to promote the magazine's current contents and hype what upcoming issues had to offer. And no less importantly, they provided editors with free copy to fill the empty back pages of the magazine. Ultimately, the goal of letter columns was to establish a loyal reader base eager to purchase the next issue. In general, however, the letters of the time were brief and not particularly memorable.

Hoffman from the very beginning, however, saw *Adventure's* The Camp-Fire department as something different. As suggested by its subtitle, "A Meeting Place for Readers, Writers, and Adventurers." Eight months after its launch, when the popularity of the department was becoming apparent, the February 1913 issue described The Camp-Fire as:

> "... the one place in the world where every adventurer is welcome and where all who love adventure can gather to ask questions or to answer them, to talk over old times, or plan new tilts with fate, to make new friends or once more grasp the hands of old ones."

Throughout the years, Hoffman's personality dominated The Camp-Fire as its first-person host, but he was always careful to emphasize that "the thing... is not my department, but *ours.*" He frequently referred to readers as fellow adventurers, citing their "restless spirit," in an effort to create the sense that through The Camp-Fire, they were part of a special community, a band of brothers.

In terms of content, The Camp-Fire was not limited to letters and story comments but also included eye-witness accounts of adventurous experiences by readers and writers, discussion and debate of specific topics and current events, and technical advice for would-be adventurers; these often took up most of the space. Emphasis was on the outdoors, particularly exotic locales that were unfamiliar to most readers. In the first few years alone, The Camp-Fire contained reports on life in the British East Africa colonial service, a traveling elephant salesman caught in a Jamaican riot, recent political unrest in the Balkans and the Philippines, Amazon basin ethnography, the challenges of building a Central American railroad across an active lava field, and a rehashing of the *Marie Celeste* mystery. One correspondent provided sketches showing the different ways of rigging a schooner. In addition, Hoffman regularly selected for inclusion letters that encouraged debate on topics of interest; the Old American West was a popular area of discussion, and its personalities such Pat Garrett, Billy the Kid, Sam Bass and Wild Bill Hickok were common subjects.

DORIS ULMANN

Arthur Sullivant Hoffman

Hoffman made a concerted effort to bring the magazine's writers, his "writers brigade," into The Camp-Fire community. From the very beginning it was a regular practice for new writers to provide a brief biographical sketch of themselves on the occasion of their first appearance in the magazine (introduced with the phrase "Following our Camp-Fire custom..."). Not all writers did so, but rough count shows that approximately 110 writers introduced themselves to the readership during the column's first eight years. In addition, writers such Harold Lamb, Hugh Pendexter, and Arthur Gilchrist Brodeur would often provide background commentary for their stories. Writers' personal experiences, such as Capt. A.E. Dingle's, memoir "A Life on the High Seas" and Arthur D. Howden Smith's observations in the Balkans and Macedonia, were also to be found in The Camp-Fire.

By the end of its first two years, most of the basic Camp-Fire features were in place and would continue throughout the length of Hoffman's editorship. Beginning in 1914, however, its tenor began to change. In general, the pulps of the period offered their usual fare of escapist fiction and took little notice of current events in Europe leading up to America's involvement in the First World War. Even after the country's Declaration of War in April 1917, the pulps' acknowledgment of the conflict was often a token one—the occasional patriotic editorial or inspirational cover (and an increased tendency for villains to be German)—at best. The major exception to this was to be found in the pages of *Adventure.* With the outbreak of war in Europe, The Camp-Fire became a forum in which were debated many of the most important issues of the day, including wartime preparedness; patriotism, loyalty, what it meant to be an American; and ultimately the nature of democracy itself.

The country's wartime preparedness was front and center in the November 1914 The Camp-Fire, when Hoffman posed the question to the readers: *How about this?* The "this" in question was a letter from E.D. Cook in Costa Rica calling for the formation of a volunteer organization of able-bodied men willing to join the military and fight as a unit should the need arise. Cook suggested it be coordinated through the *Adventure* offices and called for the first volunteers to come from the magazine's readers. Hoffman was quick to take up the proposal; ultimately this gave birth to the American Legion, which still exists today.

Hoffman's ideas about what America should do to prepare for possible war were both educational and practical, and reader suggestions were common. At times, however, ideas bordered on the eccentric. In February 1916 he devoted an entire The Camp-Fire page to the idea that a regiment be created comprised entirely of red-heads, arguing "that red-heads have been known the world over and throughout history as fierce fighters, and their esprit would be strong." Readers never learned of what came of the idea.

Once America entered the War in April 1917 *Adventure Magazine* went with it: Camp-Fire discussions now offered enthusiastic support for the war effort itself. Hoffman argued the need for universal military service for all able-bodied men, maintaining that this would create a sense of discipline and focus in Americans that he believed was currently lacking. For other readers who wished to help, the magazine introduced a new department "How to Help Win the War" that suggested opportunities to that end.

The Camp-Fire was particularly proud of the members of its community who volunteered to serve. At one point the magazine listed 23 writers, many in uniform, who were serving on both sides of the Atlantic, and The Camp-Fire regularly reported on the experiences of its authors and readers in France. Accounts of the newly emerging aerial warfare were always popular. Occasionally, The Camp-Fire acquired a more somber tone when it reported on the death of someone familiar to *Adventure* readers. In May 1917 readers were greeted with the news that *Allan Quatermain was dead;* Captain Frederick Courteney Selous, Rider Haggard's inspiration for Quatermain, had died in combat against the Germans in East Africa.

Hoffman's most dramatic—and in retrospect, controversial—contribution to The Camp-Fire's wartime discussion appeared in the October 1916 in the form of the question *Are You American?* which appeared in bold, oversized letters in that issue's The Camp-Fire. He followed it with a 1500-word editorial explaining how the question must be answered. The answer, he insisted, lay not in the legal niceties of one's citizenship, but rather in one's personal loyalty to the United States of America. This, in turn, raised a subject that deeply worried Hoffman and one he would return to again and again over the next two years—foreign-born Americans and the threat of divided loyalties. Although initially he was careful to emphasize it was not aimed at any particular immigrant group, with Wilson's Declaration of War in Spring 1917 The Camp-Fire, like much of the America became virulently anti-German, insisting that Americans must forcefully deal with the agents of "Prussian militarists" operating in our midst. To address this, a new department was introduced, "Fighting the Hun Web," that encouraged readers to report what they saw as suspicious pro-German propaganda. Following the end of the war, the department was dropped and briefly replaced by the column "Looking Ahead for Democracy," although Hoffman continued to hold his anti-German suspicions.

WHICH BRINGS US to the book at hand:

The preceding overview reviews approximately the first six years of The Camp-Fire from its inception in 1912 and lays the groundwork for the present volume. The book reproduces the complete three-year run of The Camp-Fire from January 1918 through December 1920, some 70 installments in all, with each entry appearing in its original magazine format. This is the first undertaking of its kind; although references to The Camp-Fire frequently occur in pulp histories and excerpts are occasionally provided, few readers up to this point have had the opportunity to enjoy the actual Camp-Fire columns themselves without going to the time-consuming effort and expense of collecting the individual magazine issues. Steeger Books is to be commended for their time and effort in bringing about this collection and thus giving readers the opportunity to finally be able to do so.

As to why the years 1918 through 1920? Two reasons suggest themselves.

First, for many collectors, these years marks the beginning of the golden age of *Adventure,* frequently thought to have extended from the late 'Teens into the mid-1920s. Just a few months earlier the magazine's publication schedule had gone from monthly to twice-a-month as a result of its growing popularity. More generally, by that point Hoffman had built up a stable of authors, including Talbot Mundy, Harold Lamb, W.C. Tuttle, Gordon Young, Hugh Pendexter, Arthur O. Friel, and Arthur D. Howden Smith, that appeared regularly in the magazine's pages and were providing stories of the literary quality for which *Adventure* would become famous.

Second, the period also showcases The Camp-Fire at its peak: the entries from 1918 capture the flavor and intensity of Hoffman's war-related editorializing, and the 1919–1920 post-war years mark a return to Hoffman's original vision of The Camp-Fire serving as a clearing house in which would-be adventurers would find an interchange of ideas and reminiscences of interest, accounts of incidents from contributors' lives, practical advice given, and serious questions asked and answered.

Along those lines, readers of this volume will encounter:

- Ongoing war commentary including a detailed account of the death of writer William Hope Hodgson;
- Hoffman's vigorous defense of Negro soldiers against recent racist attacks, challenging the country to review its own history on race;
- Reports on death of Jack London, shrunken heads among the Jivaro, and death by volcano;
- More on the "spirit of adventure," this time its biological basis;
- More of the never-ending reader debate over personalities of the Old West, such as including George Armstrong Custer and William Cody;
- Additional new writer introductions, among them a colorful 5000 word, globe-spanning autobiographical essay by Talbot Mundy that, as subsequent research has shown, has the dubious distinction of being almost completely fabricated;
- More on *Adventure* ID cards, and the origin of the magazine's '71 ball' logo;
- The establishment national and international Camp-Fire Stations;
- Technical information on poisonous serpents, cacti, saddle types,

handguns, and sloops (the latter three accompanied by sketches from their authors);

- More than you could ever want to know about Gila monsters;
- Humorous sketches by W.C. Tuttle of the characters found in his stories;
- The announcement that *Adventure* cover art was for sale—*minimum bid $10 (!)*;
- And, in the true spirit of adventure, a report of a live Brontosaurus roaming the wilds of Africa.

BUT ENOUGH WITH introductions. Sit back, open the book, and become part of The Camp-Fire's "readers brigade": enter a meeting place for readers, writers, and adventurers "where every adventurer is welcome and where all who love adventure can gather." It may be a century later, but in these pages the "restless spirit" continues to thrive.

FROM E. A. Brininstool, of Los Angeles, comes further information he has gathered concerning one of the early pioneers of the West, some interesting data to be added to the information we of the Camp-Fire are gradually collecting about the old-timers before they slip out of the memories of living men:

For the benefit of those who may desire some further information about Frank Grouard, one of the greatest scouts and frontiersmen on the plains from 1865 up to and including the Ghost Dance War of 1890, I would like to add the following:

FRANK GROUARD'S father went to the Island of Tahiti in the South Seas along about 1845. He married a woman native of that country by whom he had two or three children, Frank among them. Frank was born in 1850. When he was two years old his father returned to the United States with his wife and family and settled at San Bernardino, Southern California. His wife, however, was unable to stand the climate, so she returned to her own people when Frank was about five years old, and neither Frank nor his father ever saw her again. She took the other children with her, but nobody ever knew what became of them. The elder Grouard learned that she had died, some years later.

Frank's father removed to San Francisco when Frank was a small boy, and finally placed the lad with a family named Pratt, who removed to southern Nevada, where Frank lived until he was fifteen years old. He grew tired of the life he was living and ran away, going to Montana and doing various things until he was nineteen, at which time he was a mail-carrier. On his route one day he was taken captive by a band of Sioux Indians. All but one were anxious to kill him on the spot, but the lone Indian stood out for taking him prisoner. It developed that this Indian was the noted Sitting Bull. Young Grouard's life was spared and he was carried away captive.

For nineteen months he was watched very closely by the Indians, until he saw that it was futile to try to escape, as he never was allowed to leave the camp alone. He then entered into the Indian life with real zest, and soon could outstrip every Indian in a foot-race, and was counted the best shot and game hunter in the band. He threw aside all the garments of civilization and adopted the breech-clout and moccasins of the Sioux, going with them on their wars against their hereditary enemies, the Crows, and other tribes.

Sitting Bull took a great liking to Frank Grouard, as did the great chief, Crazy Horse. For the next five years Grouard applied himself diligently to his surroundings. He learned the Sioux dialect until he understood it and could speak it as fluently as any Indian. The roving customs of his captors was also of the greatest benefit to him, for he grew to know every foot of the country around the Big Horns and through the Yellowstone and Powder River section, and as far east as the Black Hills. Gen. George Crook, the greatest fighter who ever went against the Indians, once said that he would "rather lose a third of his command than Frank Grouard." The scout's memory and wonderful keenness of the country were a constant marvel to Crook, for Grouard could go anywhere, day or night, with as unerring accuracy as if the country were laid out like a picture before him. He never used a compass, but one day he did smash one that an officer was using in a blinding snow-storm while leading his command. Grouard "borrowed" the compass and smashed it on a rock, then himself took the lead and guided the command straight to the spot they were destined for.

AFTER Grouard had been with the Indians six years, he came to the conclusion that he had stayed as long with his captors as he cared to, so one night he "lit out," joined the United States Army and took the trail against his former allies, the Sioux, and, it is needless to say, his services to the Government were of inestimable value. His knowledge of the habits and customs of the Sioux placed him in the front ranks of all the scouts with the army. He never made a mistake when guiding a command of soldiers on a scout. During the Sioux war of 1876 he performed his greatest services to the Government. It would take a hundred magazines to record the wonderful escapes and thrilling experiences which Grouard passed through in his capacity as scout. The Sioux were forever trying to capture him again, but Grouard well knew that it would be death by torture if he were ever taken alive—and he never was.

IN 1894 Grouard saw his father again for the first time since he was five years old. The old gentleman was living in Santa Ana, Cal., and learned that a Frank Grouard, well known as a frontiersman, was living in Sheridan, Wyoming. Correspondence followed, and the elder Grouard journeyed to Sheridan to see his son. After a visit of a month he returned to his home in California and died shortly after.

That is the latest date that I can give about this

wonderful man. I do not know if he is yet alive, but am corresponding with a friend of his in Denver, though I am under the impression that Grouard died in Wyoming some years ago.

The information I have here given is taken from a book written by Joe DeBarth, a Wyoming newspaper man, entitled "The Life and Adventures of Frank Grouard." It was published in 1894, and at that time Grouard was living near Fort McKinney, Wyoming.

Later: Just received from Grouard's Denver friend, who was very intimate with him at Sheridan, Wyo., imformation that Grouard died in St. Joseph, Mo., some four or five years ago.—E. A. BRININSTOOL.

ANOTHER of our number, now serving on an American ship in the European service, writes concerning two other pioneers:

> Concerning the statement in the August Camp-Fire regarding Amos Chapman, if it is the man that lived near Cleo, Okla., and frequently came into Watonga, I can positively certify that he is still alive as I saw him in the flesh—and an old lumber-wagon—in Cleo last Summer.
>
> As to Curley, I saw him in Coffeyville last Summer.
>
> Am still defying Bill and his tin fish with the same packet and hope to call on you pronto.

HERE'S an interesting idea from one of our comrades that might well be carried out by natives of other States as well as by those of Indiana:

> I am a soldier, a Lance-Corporal, in the regular army, having enlisted since war was declared. I am an enthusiastic reader of *Adventure* and of Camp-Fire and am greatly interested in the good work it does.
>
> I am a native of Indiana, therefore a Hoosier, and I am interested in all Hoosiers, especially Hoosiers in the Military or Naval Service of Uncle Sam, or of the Allies.
>
> Now I would like to organize a council whereby all Hoosiers of the abovementioned class could unite and communicate, etc. And I desire your cooperation; it would be an added service to Hoosier readers of which there are many in the service of Uncle Sam.
>
> MY IDEA is to organize an "International Council of Hoosiers" to be composed entirely of Hoosiers in Uncle Sam's Naval or Military Service, that to be the requirement for membership.
>
> Later we could be incorporated and have somebody design us nice membership badges and have Local Councils of Hoosiers on battleships or in regiments or battalions.
>
> Until we get permanently organized and can have an election, I will assume the duties of secretary-general. If you will help me in this object please write me soon.—CHAUNCEY D. JONES, I. C. H., Co. C, 54th U. S. Inf., Military Branch, Chattanooga, Tenn.

GENERAL BENJAMIN JOHANNIS VILJOEN has sat with us at our Camp-Fire. His was a well-filled past and out of its rich supply he told us things we found very interesting. When he died in January there was still in our safe another tale of his, not a fiction story but a bit out of his own past, and it is given to you in this issue.

He was born in the Cape Province, South Africa, September 7, 1868, a descendant of Francoa Villion, who, with other French Huguenots, fled France in the days of Louis XIV. He spent his boyhood in Tembuland, migrating to the Transvaal Republic when about sixteen, entering the Transvaal Mounted Police at nineteen. Several years later he was appointed chief organizer of the entire militia force. At twenty-four he led the successful two-year expedition against King Bruno of Swazieland. As an officer under Cronje he aided in the defeat of the Jameson expedition. A year later he was publicly congratulated by General Joubert for bravery against the revolting Mapoch Kaffirs.

WHEN the war with England started he was a member of the Transvaal Legislature but was made commander of the citizen forces of the Johannesberg district. He served at Elandslaagte, Moddersprui t, Ladysmith, on the Tugela, Spionkop, Vaalkrans. It is said that, covering the retreat of his regiment through a mountain pass with a machine-gun, he single-handed exterminated what was left of the Eighteenth Hussars.

In 1900, after the fall of Pretoria, General Viljoen was placed in command of the Boer army and proved a thorn in the side of the British. Two weeks before peace was declared he was ambushed and captured after being wounded. He has told us that tale himself, and many of you will remember "The Story of a Piebald Horse."

HE WAS banished to St. Helena for life. When England was pardoning all who would take the oath of allegiance he refused to take that step but England finally permitted him to accept Colonel Theodore Roosevelt's invitation to come to the United States. In 1903 he was in charge of the Boer exhibit at the St. Louis World's Fair, and in that city he met and married his wife. Shortly afterward he settled on a ranch near La Mesa, N. M., but he could not remain long inactive. In 1910 he became Madero's military adviser and was largely instrumental in toppling over Diaz. A year later he was made peace commissioner to the Yaquis, but illness forced his resignation and he was made Mexican consul in Breslau, Germany, visiting his old enemies in England. Still ill, he returned to New Mexico, and was made a member of the Governor's staff. In 1914 he went to Los Angeles and later settled in Sierra Madre, but continued ill-health sent him back to New Mexico.

Some of these things he himself told us, but his modesty omitted other things that history records. A full life bravely lived. Our salute to him.

THE side-lights and bits of Indian history, customs and psychology Hugh Pendexter gives the Camp-Fire concerning his stories of pioneer days are almost as interesting as the stories themselves:

> The plains tribes generally believed that the Pawnee were the first to possess the calumet, receiving it from the sun. This story is based on the fact it was the most sacred object known to the Indians north of Mexico. J. N. B. Hewitt, of the Bureau of American Ethnology, in writing on the calumet, mentions an occasion when a band of Sioux, "seeking to destroy some Indians and their protectors, a French officer and his men, presented, in the guise of friendship, twelve calumets, apparently of peace. But the officer, who was versed in such matters and whose suspicions were aroused by the number offered, observed one of the shafts was not matted with hair like the others, and that on the shaft was graven the figure of a viper, coiled around it." As this was the sign of covert treachery, the Sioux plot was frustrated.
>
> THIS incident suggested the hinge on which to swing the yarn. In building it I had to consider authorities on trade routes, trails, signaling, sign language, uses of the calumet, tipi structure, etiquette, buffalo hunting, ethnology of Dakota (Sioux) and Pawnee and Comanche, free trappers, fur companies, etc.

LETTERS have been coming in endorsing the little editorial "With Us Or Against Us" in our Mid-October Camp-Fire. So far there have been no outcries from the hyphenates, but doubtless some of them are cursing me. I hope so.

I want to give you here one of the letters that came in, for it contains some ideas that I had not advanced but which seem to me along the right line. It's time for all real Americans to show their colors, to exchange ideas and to begin to *act*. A country at war which allows newspapers printed in the language of its enemies to be freely published and circulated within its own borders surely *needs* help and action from its loyal citizens. If many real Americans are too much asleep or too much afraid to protest against and stop this and a dozen kindred practises, then those of us who *are* awake must do the work.

IT IS both weak and dangerous to allow the enemy spirit within our very midst to publish and spread itself broadcast in the enemy's language, or in our own. To see, here in America, a man with Teuton written all over him, riding in our cars, mixing freely with us, protected by our laws, and calmly reading a newspaper printed in the language of our German enemies, does that mean nothing to you? Most of us can not even read German, can not tell just how much the spirit of sedition and enemy hate is preached and fostered by the particular sheet in his hands, but we know from the facts of the past that too many of the German-language papers do foster these things and that *no* sheet of any kind published in German should be circulating in this country.

Every paper of any kind, whether printed in German or English, if it in any way, however indirectly, preaches treason to the United States, if it in any way fosters here in this country the German spirit instead of the American spirit, German tradition instead of American tradition, should be permanently suppressed. Any man or woman who reads one of them in public brands himself as an enemy of America and should be treated accordingly.

NOT only are too many of our politician Congressmen and other public officials so much afraid of the "German-American votes" that they do not act, but a few of them have practically openly espoused the cause of Germany in America. What can we expect of such self-seeking weaklings, such betrayers of our country when it comes to suppressing German propaganda in this country? But there are real Americans, too, among our public officers and it is up to *us* to get behind them, and against the others, with every ounce of energy in us.

When these same weakling or disloyal Congressmen and others come up again for election to any American public office *are the Germans and German sympathizers in America to give them these American honors? Is America to reward them for having served against America?*

AREN'T we at last getting tired of seeing the enemies in our midst handled with kid gloves, allowed to go on with their work against us? Aren't we tired of seeing Americans afraid to handle these enemies as enemies should be handled? The timid cry out that we mustn't alienate our German-American citizens, must bind them to us by kindness. Bah! We've given them every chance. Those of them who are citizens and have it in them to be loyal to America have already shown that loyalty, are of us and are to be treated like ourselves. Those who have taken oath of allegiance to America and already broken that oath in act, word or spirit have already made traitors of themselves. Those who are not citizens even in name are merely enemies in our midst. And these traitors and these enemies should be treated as traitors and enemies.

Don't make them hate us? Rot! They hate us already. Hate us, sneer at us, hold us in contempt, plot against us, do their utmost against us. If they had the power they would grind us into the dirt as their brothers have ground the Belgians; if German armies could land on our shores these Germans in America would join them on the instant and help in the Prussian work of atrocities against *our* women, children and other non-combatants, of destroying our towns and countrysides, of needless ruin and desolation and all the other outrages that have marked German conquest of other countries and that would surely mark the German conquest of the United States if the Kaiser could carry out his expressed intention of attending to America next. Treat them kindly, handle them with kid gloves! Let us not be impolite!

I AM no believer in mob-law but I am a most firm believer in the power of public opinion brought to bear in legitimate way. And it is you and I and the rest of us who make public opinion. A people who have produced the Minute Men, the Ku Klux Klan, the Vigilantes, the Texas Rangers can, when necessary, and by lawful means, make deadly plain to traitors in our midst that we too have iron in our blood even if it does express itself in the acts of a man, not the acts of a beast.

IN THE following letter I call your attention particularly to the points made concerning the teaching of German in our schools, to immigration and to the general status of enemy aliens after the war. Most of you know that whatever I, or any of you, say at our Camp-Fire has to be written nearly three months before you read it. Many changes in public affairs may take place in that interim; it is hard enough to keep up to date in these hurrying times, and infinitely harder to try to keep up to three months ahead of date. But certain truths remain truths at all times and I think what you find in the following letter will be as true when you read it as it is now in September.

Louisville, Ky.

As it is very probable that some of your pro-German readers will adversely criticize your editorial, "With Us Or Against Us" which appeared in your Mid-October issue, I am yielding to the impulse to write this letter, endorsing every word of your article.

UNFORTUNATELY for this country you have stated many truths and it is the part of every true American not only to endorse your statements but they should do all they possibly can to suppress disloyalty on the part of every one within our borders.

Any adverse criticism of the Government which appears in newspapers, magazines, etc., borders on treason, for this is no time for destructive criticism. Constructive criticism may be helpful if handled through the proper channels but we can not be too careful in making critical statements which we expect to be productive of good results in prosecuting the war to a successful conclusion.

American citizens of German and Austrian blood must bear in mind that the actions of many of their kin have caused us to regard with suspicion persons of German birth and while there are many true Americans with German names yet there are many of similar names who are traitors at heart, if not in act, to American ideals.

Therefore such loyal Americans with German names must be careful that no act or word of theirs will give ground for suspicion and they themselves should be zealous in preventing seditious utterances and acts on the part of any one. Only by such care will such Americans prove their worth and retain a place in our esteem and affections which was once held by the German peoples as a whole and which place has been lost forever by the Prussians and Huns.

THIS great country has and will continue to have many serious problems, but the adoption of your ideas will tend to eliminate many of those problems.

No man of foreign birth or of foreign ancestry can expect to become a true American if he attempts to maintain Old-Country customs, languages, etc.

The language of the United States and Canada is English and this only should be taught in our public schools.

I agree with you that the following should be done:

Stamp out every German Alliance Organisation of any kind in this country, local or general, social, athletic or political.

Stamp out every publication printed in the language of our enemies.

Stamp out English language publications which have been, are now or which may hereafter be guilty of seditious utterances or the publishing of any article calculated to hamper the Government in the prosecution of the war or to interfere with the manufacture, production, or transportation of any and all goods required by our soldiers or their dependents.

IN ADDITION I say that all traitors should be tried for treason and not let off with a simple admonishment. I also say that no man of enemy blood should be allowed to naturalize for the next generation or two at least. No subject of an enemy country should be allowed, after peace is declared, to acquire property, *i. e.*, real estate, in America.

In fact I believe that if all aliens were prevented from acquiring real estate in the United States some of our international problems would be prevented.

An alien might be allowed to lease property with privilege of purchase at a stipulated price after he had been a naturalized citizen for say five years.

Naturalization papers should not be granted to any alien who is unable to carry on an ordinary conversation in our language.

IN CONCLUSION I ask that our Irish kin remember that we are fighting autocracy and defending North and South America from German ambition as exemplified by the Hapsburgs and Hohenzollerns. I am an American of English, Scotch, French and Irish blood and the mixture boils at the thought of Hunnish atrocities as well as at American (?) traitors' actions in attempting to hamper our President in his fight for civilization and democracy.

I am with you and may 100 per cent. of your readers be also with you in thought and action.—W. R. Harris.

WE HAD a poem from Stanley Hofflund once but this issue contains the first story he has given us, so he stands up according to Camp-Fire custom and introduces himself:

My own adventures, I am afraid, would not be very interesting to a Camp-Fire group which has listened to intimate tales of African jungles and polar expeditions. Mine are of a more easy-going, home-loving character. I don't mean to apologize for them, for I have hugely enjoyed tramping through the Sierras—high and low—and Adventuring America First, so to speak, as a sort of preparation for greater adventures I dream of undertaking later.

I AM a newspaper reporter, with all the eagerness for "scoops" on police department scandals and grand jury graft probes which the very mention of my profession suggests. I like it much better than running a country store, a real-estate office, or anything else I ever tackled except ranching on a Southern California ranch. That last is—next to going to heaven—my idea of an ideal ultimate, provided, of course, that the ranch is in the mountains, is highly impracticable from a commercial standpoint, and sort of runs itself while the owner goes hunting and fishing or sticks a big pine log into a big stone hearth, sits in a big, soft chair, and writes stories about the sterling qualities displayed by others who endure hardships.

I WROTE the "Last Cup of Tea" while on the prettiest ranch in the world—near Alpine, San Diego County, Cal. The natural beauties and scenic wonders of that mountain ranch were hoary with age, but accommodations for properly housing human bodies were not yet born. You see, it was a new ranch so far as my friend, who had just bought it, and I were concerned.

And it was bitterly cold—yes, in Southern California. There was snow on the mountain nearest us. And we ran out of tea, dividing the last cup before retiring into our sleeping-bags.

It occurred to me that a last cup of tea, under severe conditions, can become of sufficient importance to be made the basis for a story. I transplanted the plot to Lundy, Mono County, having reason to know that to be a frigid region in Winter. I tramped through it once, and on over the divide into Yosemite. I had been working in a mine at Bodie. I remember that the entire galvanized iron shed of the Lundy Mine cyanide plant had been lifted up by a snow-slide and carried hundreds of yards up the mountainside across the narrow gorge, leaving the cyanide vats exposed, like a series of entirely uncalled-for cisterns. I know, you see, that it grows cold enough up there to be the proper setting for a story dealing with frigidity and the consequent craving for hot tea.

I WROTE "Steppin' on the Throttle of a Mountain Stage," a verse appearing earlier in *Adventure*, while marooned in the mountains between San Diego and the Imperial Valley desert, during the big floods of January, 1916, which caused death in Southern California through broken dams and flooded valleys. In attempting to drive my car through Morena Creek—about 200 feet wide from the flood, on a night so dark and squally that my searchlight would not pick out the approach on the opposite bank—I became unintentionally converted into a submarine commander. My craft was salvaged two weeks later. The actual heroism displayed by auto stage drivers, who made automobiles do stunts unbelievable, inspired the verses.

That's all I know about myself except that I am thirty-three years old, hale and hearty as a youngster, married, and like the Camp-Fire gang immensely.—Stanley Hofflund.

OUR boys are gradually going to the front and the Camp-Fire wants to keep track of them there, to know how they fare, to know as much about what is going on as the censor will permit. Also, if your comrades over there are lonely or want a correspondent back home, give your full military address and there'll surely be some among us to drop you a line of comradeship. If the letters of all can't be published we will, if you give the word, publish your name and address as one of our boys at the front who wants letters from back home in the good old U. S. A.

Our "Letter Friends" department had to be abolished, but we'll revive it for the sole use of Americans and Canadians at the front. I know that we back here will welcome the chance to write and that, besides letters, we can make some small individual shipments of tobacco, reading-matter and other little odds and ends.

Time for Our Annual Vote

ALL the 1917 issues of *Adventure* are in your hands, from January, 1917, to mid-December, 1917, inclusive, and the vote by our readers to determine the best ten stories in our magazine during this past year closes December thirty-first. This annual vote is the best means we of our editorial staff can devise for making *Adventure's* stories the kind that please our readers best. It's up to you, so go to it.

The voting is simple and easy. Any one, subscriber or not, is eligible to vote if he's read at least seven of the 1917 issues. Serials, novels, novelettes, articles and short stories included; poems and "Camp-Fire" barred. The same author may appear on the list as many times as you please. All you need do is write down your ten selections numbered in order of preference, giving title and author of each, sign your name and mail us the letter or post-card. If you like, add as many as ten more stories for complimentary mention.

Remember that no stories are counted unless they were published in one of the issues *bearing the printed date* 1917—January, 1917, to mid-December, 1917, inclusive. This issue in your hands is *not* included. However, a serial appearing partly in 1917 and partly in 1918 or 1916 *is* included in the vote.

The result of the vote will be published in a subsequent issue.

MANY of you will recognize the soldier on our cover this issue as one of that famous body of French troops, the Chasseurs Alpins of the 47th Division, better known to the Germans and to all the world as "the Blue Devils of France." You will remember that these same Blue Devils were among the French troops assigned to instruct General Pershing's men in modern trench warfare.

I CAN'T know what steps will have been taken, by the time this reaches you, toward suppressing German, German-American and American pro-German sedition in our midst, but it's pretty safe to say that the intervening two or three months aren't at all likely to see the end of this treasonable menace. The American Defense Society is making a brave and direct campaign against this evil and wants as many real Americans as possible to enroll as regular members, get the Society's button, service instruction card and certificate of membership. Their motto is a pungent one that bears thinking about—"You Need Your Country."

It's patriotic work they're asking of you. I'm sending my dollar and enrolling. How about you? And let's not let our part stop with the mere handing over of a dollar.

Here's the way they state their case:

> Serve at the front or serve at home. To win this war we must jail German spies. Will you give a dollar to help put them all in jail?
>
> *If you can't go to the trenches, serve at home, and stand by the man at the front. Telegraph, write or bring us reports of German activities in your district.* Aid in patriotic work by enrolling and serving as a regular member of the American Defense Society. Only Americans need apply for membership. Our service card will explain how you can serve your country at home. Advisory Board: HON. DAVID JAYNE HILL, Ex-Ambassador to Germany; HON. ROBERT BACON, Ex-Ambassador to France; HON. PERRY BELMONT, Vice-President, Navy League; HON. CHARLES J. BONAPARTE, Ex-Attorney-General, U. S.; JOHN GRIER HIBBEN, LL.D., President, Princeton University; HENRY B. JOY, President Lincoln Highway Association; HUDSON MAXIM, Member Naval Advisory Board; HON. THEODORE ROOSEVELT, Ex-President of the United States.
>
> Your dollar is needed. Make checks payable to Robert Appleton, Treasurer, American Defense Society, 303 Fifth Ave., New York.

YOU'VE noticed that all the headings in one issue of our magazine are drawn by one artist. If any of you have any marked preference for the headings of one or more of the nine or ten artists who do most of this work for us, drop us a line. We're trying to please *you*, you know, and every opinion from the readers helps a little in showing us how to do it.

NOT long ago we had a letter from our comrade Dean Ivan Lamb, American in the British Royal Flying Corps, saying that he hoped to get his discharge in order to offer his trained services to his own country and that maybe he'd be dropping in at *Adventure* headquarters before long. He did so last week. Had secured his discharge, was expecting the final papers in a few days, had landed in this country the morning of the day I saw him and was already on the job of connecting up with the U. S. service. He has been in the R. F. C. over two years, had sixteen months in France, a sergeant, and is officially credited with seven German machines —a man invaluable in training American aviators. And a clear-eyed, upstanding, modest fellow of whom the Camp-Fire can be proud. ARTHUR SULLIVANT HOFFMAN.

IT SEEMS that one of us, from whom I've heard from time to time, is a prisoner of war in Germany. In December, 1916, Pat O'Brien was in the Aviation School at San Diego. A while later I had a card from him saying he was in the British Royal Flying Corps and asking to have his mail forwarded to Canada. A bit later still he had risen from corporal to lieutenant and asked to have his mail forwarded to the other side.

In the Fall of 1917 I received the following letter:

September 17, 1917.

I write to tell you that I received word from France that my dear brother, Pat O'Brien, went out on a patrol on August 17th, and never returned. We are doing our utmost to get some information, but so far have not been able to.—MRS. CLARA CLEGG, Momence, Illinois.

Another of our American comrades in the Royal Flying Corps, Dean Ivan Lamb, had just landed here to give his services to the United States, and the next time he dropped in at the office I showed him Mrs. Clegg's letter. He had never met O'Brien, but sat down right there and wrote three letters to England that would probably get definite information if it could be had. A few days later came this second letter from Mrs. Clegg:

October 12, 1917.

Yours of the 8th at hand and will say that since writing you I have received word that a letter had been dropped by the Germans, to the effect that my brother (Pat O'Brien) is a prisoner in Germany, unwounded. Still I would be very thankful to you if you would put a paragraph of inquiry into the Camp-Fire department of your magazine, as the letter we received stated that its information could not be taken as accurate.—MRS. CLARA CLEGG.

Our magazine reaches out through the world along many thousands of threads, among us we have run down even more difficult trails that led to the firing-line, and perhaps some of us somewhere over there can supply the information wanted in this case.

ANYTHING having to do with lost treasure makes most people prick up their ears. Here's a pleasant little item about a cowpuncher digging up $400,000; but Mr. Harriman, who reports the report, doesn't suggest that you go a-digging:

Los Angeles, Cal.

CAMP-FIRE COMRADES:

You who have been interested in tales of buried treasure will be pleased to read this:

September 14, 1917.

H. R. Whitman of Solomonville, Arizona, reported at Phœnix that Jade Walsey, cowpuncher, had unearthed a cache of $400,000 in old Spanish gold coins and golden vessels. He was in the hills northwest of Solomonville, hunting strays, when he saw a shovel-handle sticking out of a tree-trunk. Digging brought to light an iron box containing the treasure.

It is supposed to be treasure left there by Spanish priests who left that section seventy-five years ago, while it was still a part of Mexico. The treasure has been taken to the county-seat, Safford, and deposited for safe-keeping.

NOW it will be in order for every dreamer in Southern California to get the fever and prospect the hills here for the treasure said to have been buried when Indians raided one of the missions. The story runs that two of the padres went with two neophytes and hid the church treasure but were all killed by the hostiles before they could rejoin the others. There may be a thread of truth in the story, but it is far more likely to be a canard. At any rate, with nothing to guide them, searchers would have a peach of a time hunting lost treaure in the thousands of likely hiding-places of our foothills and mountains. I'll bet I could hide a beer-keg there where Hindenburg's whole army could not find it in a month.—E. E. HARRIMAN.

WHEN our boys go to the front we want them to be in the best shape possible, minds as well as bodies, in their spirits as well as their spirit. We want this for their sakes, for our country's sake and for our own sake.

Here's one way we can help in getting and keeping them in the best shape possible. When they leave the every-day civilian life they've always lived in and go into camp they enter a new and strange world. But they don't cease being human. Most of them, however stiff they keep their upper lips, are likely to be homesick. Being human and young, most of them, left to their own devices when off duty, are likely to be more or less victimized at the hands of various human beasts of prey and to yield to the temptations that unfit them in many ways as efficient soldiers and sound, upstanding men. The more homesick or lonely they get and the more they are left to be strangers in a strange land, the more will they drift into various kinds of trouble for themselves—and us.

THEREFORE let all of us living anywhere near where our boys of any arm or branch of the service are stationed be among those who are opening their own homes to them and giving some of their own personal time and attention to making their off duty hours pleasant and interesting in wholesome and decent ways. Most of them don't care for pink teas and fluffy stuff in general, but most of them will appreciate from the bottom of their hearts any and every plain, ordinary, common-or-garden touch of simple, straightforward, man to man friendliness and friendship.

They are of all kinds and degrees. So are we. But they all have this in common—they are offering their lives in our service. Surely the least we can do is to show that, if they are our friends, we are theirs.

For example, why not get a few of them to help you with the Christmas or New Year's turkey? This is a season when they'll be particularly and everlastingly grateful for a touch of real home-life, friendly comradeship and good cheer.

WORD from a Camp-Fire comrade at the front. I've sent him some magazines, but that's no reason for not sending him more. Also he is one of those who want letter-friends.

Just a few lines to let you and the other "Adventurers" know how one of their comrades is faring.

I have been over here in this man's war for two years now—a year of which was spent in France. Believe me, it is a *war*, is this—no little "comic opera à la Mexicano." Until the attack and taking of Vimy Ridge I was fortunate enough to escape any of Fritz's "playthings," but there (Vimy) met my downfall in the form of eleven pieces of shrapnel in my back. Am out of hospital now and ready for another crack at old Fritz.

SINCE I have been over here have been unable to get copies of my favorite magazine, *Adventure*, with exception of old copies which I had already read. I would appreciate it greatly if some of the old Camp-Fire friends would send a few old copies.

Here with me are several of the boys I knew with Gonzalez in Old Mexico; would like to hear from more. Also from any one who would care to correspond. One gets a bit lonely at times. So if you will be kind enough to publish this bit am sure I could get some "letter friends" to whom I can write some interesting yarns of things that occurred "out there."—No. 264413, L. S. PHILLIPS ("Shorty").

25th Reserve Batt., Bramshott Camp, Hants, England.

AS STATED at our last Camp-Fire, we're going to revive our old "Letter Friends" department for the benefit of our boys in khaki or blue. Many of our comrades are where letters from "back home" are a god-send. For over three years appeals have been coming in for correspondents to help break the monotony of camp and trench life and to provide a thread tying the soldier to the old life and all it represents, and now that the United States is well into the war, the need is greater than ever. So we of the Camp-Fire are going to do what we can; and, judging from the number of responses the old department used to bring, we'll be the means of brightening things a bit for many a comrade who is fighting our battles.

Our past experience has shown, too, that a man advertising in "Letter-Friends" will probably get more letters than he can possibly answer. We should worry; he'll enjoy reading them just the same, and that's what we're after. On the other hand, it will take months to get the department under way (the magazine, as most of you know, has to be made up far in advance; for example, I'm writing this on October 16th), but once it gets going we may have more applicants than we can handle. These matters will adjust themselves as time goes on. Meanwhile we'll write letters, and if one man doesn't reply, that's all right, and we'll just send a word from home to some other chap.

THERE is too much possibility of good in the idea for it to be limited to one magazine alone, and I have written to the Committee on Public Information and other organizations suggesting that the whole question of providing personal letters and letter-friends for our soldiers and sailors could be easily and simply handled by asking all newspapers and magazines in the United States how many of them would be willing to give a little of their space to a department of this kind and then posting a printed list of those publications in all camp and field headquarters of Y. M. C. A., Red Cross, and similar organizations, at base hospitals, etc., telling each soldier to choose his own medium and locality but, in fairness to his comrades, to limit himself to one publication. I sincerely hope they will adopt the suggestion, for the need of letters from *anybody* at home is more keenly felt by our boys than most of us even dream.

LETTER-FRIENDS BACK HOME

A Free Service Department for American, Canadian, and Other Allied Soldiers, Sailors, Marines and Others in Camp or at the Front.

Any one in the United States or Allied service who wishes to brighten the time with letters from "back home," or wherever else this magazine circulates, and with the personal touch and interest of hitherto unknown friends, can secure these letters and these friends by sending us his name and military address to be published once in this department as soon as the present temporary censorship is removed. Among our readers of both sexes, all classes and from all parts of the world, he is likely to gain a number of friendly, personal correspondents. He is free to answer only such as he is comfortably able to answer under the conditions that surround him, and it is even suggested that the number of correspondents for any one man be determined by the needs of his comrades as well as by his own.

This magazine, of course, assumes no responsibility other than the publishing of these names and addresses as its space will permit. Experience has shown that the service offered is a very real and needed one, and all not themselves in service are asked to do their part in making the daily life of those fighting in our defense brighter and pleasanter through personal friendships across the intervening miles and by whatever personal, human kindnesses such friendships may suggest.

When giving your military address make it as permanent a one as possible.

(As the magazine is made up several months in advance, the above notice will appear with only such stray names as happen to come in to us until there has been time for it to reach the camps and the front and for names and addresses to reach us, be put in type and then reach our readers on publication.)

No. 264413, L. S. Phillips, 25th Reserve Batt., Bramshott Camp, Hants, England.

A. Tillemans, 2me Section, D 87, Belgian Army in the Field, Belgium.

MR. WADE ran across a book or something on Indian customs and found therein a statement that medicine men got their names from animals that live or walk close to the ground, while chiefs, on the other hand, took the names of higher animals and birds. George L. Catton sent us an Indian story and we sprung this bit of information on him in connection with the name of one of his characters. In the meantime we'd written to Hugh Pendexter asking him as an authority on Indians (he would deny being an authority on them, but he is) whether there was anything in this theory.

The replies from these two men, given below, seem to put that theory to sleep:

I used for my reference on that point Colonel Richard Irving Dodge, aide-de-camp to General Sherman, of thirty-three years' personal experience with the red men of the Great West. He writes:

"INDIANS have no surnames. . . . A man may have a dozen names, or no name at all. He may name himself, or be named by his companions. . . . On his initiation as a warrior . . . he has the right to name himself. . . . These names are intended to be expressive of some particular action or situation, and are generally adapted to a real or fancied resemblance of the actor to the known habits of animals or birds with which they are familiar. . . . The paint used on their expeditions (fights) . . . many names indicate the color of his paint—White Eagle, Red Dog, Black Beaver, etc."

Then we read: "Fifty years ago (1830) the office of chief was hereditary. . . . This, in most of the tribes, has been changed entirely. . . . It was fitting that the United States Government . . . should strike the first blow to free the Indian from hereditary despotism. . . . Now, *each chief of a band, or subdivision of a tribe*, no longer overawed by the Divine Right of a hereditary ruler, immediately sets up for himself."

THEN we read: "The position or office of medicine chief is not hereditary . . . and is not conferred by chief or council. A man gains it by general consent of the people of the tribe. . . . The medicine chief is dead. *A warrior* comes forward, who says 'I have found the proper "medicine,"' and after proving it to the tribe by and in actual combat—that point once conceded beyond doubt or cavil, and his character and standing being satisfactory, he glides into the coveted position by general acquiescence."

Then we find such names as: Little Robe, Spotted Tail, Big Mouth, Medicine Arrow, Lame Deer, Dead Arm—chiefs and medicine men.—GEORGE L. CATTON.

It might be that by coincidence in some isolated instance the medicine men bore names of creeping and crawling things, while the chiefs took the names as suggested in the article you refer to. But in all my reading I never found anything to substantiate such a belief. Always to the contrary.

I will condense from Dr. John R. Swanton's article on "Names and Naming" as published by the Bureau of American Ethnology:

"Among Indians, personal names given and changed at critical epochs of life, such as birth, puberty, first war expedition, some notable feat, elevation to chieftainship. Names divided into two classes: True names, corresponding to our personal names, and names which answer to our titles, etc. . . . The former define or indicate the social group into which a man is born, whatever honor they entail being to the accomplishments of ancestors, while the latter mark what the individual has done himself. There are characteristic tribal differences in names, and where a clan system existed each clan has its own set of names, distinct from all those of other clans and, in the majority of cases, referring to the totem, animal, plant or object."

I BREAK off to illustrate clan names, taking the Wyandot for example:

Man of Deer gens, *De-wa-ti-re*, Lean Deer; woman of Deer gens, *Ayajinta*, Spotted Fawn; man of Mud Turtle gens, *Sha-yau-tsu-wat*, Hard Skull; woman of Mud Turtle gens, *Yau-dac-u-ras*, Finding Sand Beach; man of Wolf gens, *Ha-ro-un-yu*, One Who Goes About in the Dark (a prowler); Woman of Wolf gens, *Yan-di-no*, Always Hungry; man of Bear gens, *A-tu-e-tes*, Long Claws; woman of Bear gens, *Tsa-man-da-ka-e*, Grunting for Her Young—and so on for Smooth Large Turtle, Striped Turtle, Porcupine and Snake gens.

TO RETURN to Swanton: "At the same time there were tribes in which names apparently had nothing to do with totems, and some such names were apt to occur in clans having totemic names. . . . The Kiowa, being without clans, received names suggested by some passing incident or to commemorate a warlike exploit. . . . Young men usually assumed dream names. The second name sometimes bestowed on account of bravery. The Pawnee did this during a public ceremonial. A similar custom seemed to have prevailed among Siouan tribes. After a man died his name held in abeyance for longer or shorter periods of time. If he were a Kiowa all the members of his family took new names. Among the Iroquois the official name of a chieftaincy, also official name of officer installed in it. . . . When names not taken from totem animal they were often grandiloquent terms referring to wealth or greatness of bearer. Names could often be loaned, pawned or even given or thrown away; on the other hand, might be adopted out of revenge without consent of owner."

FROM Garrick Mallery's "Picture Writing of the American Indian," B. A. E. (condensed):

"Indian names . . . when referring to an animal indicate an attribute or position of that animal. Whether objective or ideographic usually can be expressed in sign language. Receive several names in succession because of some exploit or adventure. All these names usually refer to material objects or actions. A warrior often changes his names many times after fights and hunting trips. The name he assumes for himself because of a dream or vision often is not the one he is habitually known by. Thus he is often known under several names. Deformities and peculiar adventures or mishaps are sure to fix a name. Several in the same tribe may have the same name, but seldom in the same band.

Example of some objective names:

High Back-Bone, Oglala, 1870; Broken-Back, Minneconjou Dakota, 1848; Long-Hair, Cheyenne, 1786; Big Crow, Dakota (he killed Crow Indian of unusual size); The Stabber; Red Shirt; Three-Stars (General Crook); Left-Handed Big-Nose; Spotted Face; The-Man-Who-Owns-the-Flute.

Some metaphoric names: Wolf's-Ear; Man-With-Hearts; The Tongue ("Tonguey").

Animal names: Bob-Tail-Horse; Two-Eagles; Bear-Looks-Back; Mouse; Badger; Spider; Spotted Horse; Spotted-Elk; White Goose; Spotted Skunk.

Vegetable names: Tree-in-the-Face; Leaves.

I append names of some noted warriors who also were medicine men: Sitting-Bull, Sioux; Crazy Dog, Dakota; Crazy Horse, Dakota; Black-Stone, Dakota; Cloud-Bear, Medicine Buffalo, Crazy-Head, Sacred Crow, White Elk, all Sioux; Sitting Bear (*Set-angya*), famous Kiowa chief and medicine man; The-Open-Door (*Tenskwatawa*), famous Shawnee prophet, twin brother of Tecumseh; The-Cock-Turkey (*Ah-ton-we-tuck*), Kickapoo, disciple of above; Four-Horns; Uncpapas; Lone-Horn, head chief and medicine man of Minneconjou. Elk's-Voice-Walking, same.

Names containing words of colors are thought to have mystic meanings. Some names of mighty warriors who were not medicine men: Little Turtle, Miami (in "Red Sticks"); Stinking-Saddle-Blanket, Kiowa; Little Crow, Sioux; Little Thunder, Sioux; Big Foot, Hunkcpapa Sioux; Big Bill, Paiute (led Indians aiding notorious John D. Lee at Mountain Meadow massacre; Black Hawk, Sauk-Fox chief; Black Fox, Cherokee; Black Hog, Shawnee; Blacksnake, Seneca; Two Strikes, Brule Sioux (and not a ball-game); The Rat (*Adario*), Huron; Broken Tooth, Chippewa; Cornplanter, Seneca; Crow Dog, Oglala Sioux; Curly Head, Chippewa.

J. N. B. Hewitt, B. A. E., in an article on "Chiefs" in part, says, speaking of Plains tribes: "Any ambitious and courageous warrior could apparently in strict accordance with custom, make himself a chief by the acquisition of suitable property and through his own force of character."

In nearly all tribes any man with sufficient force of character could assume the rôle of medicine man. Chiefs often did so. A. Hrdlicka, U. S. National Museum, in an article on "Medicine and Medicine Men" says: " . . . He announced or exhibited these attributes, and after convincing his tribesmen that he possessed the proper requirements, was accepted as a healer." Further on in same article: "If the medicine man lost several patients in succession, he himself might be suspected either of having been deprived of his supernatural power or of having become a sorcerer, the penalty of which was usually death."

I HAVE attempted to show by the above circumlocution that any warrior with a strong personality might become a chief or a medicine man, and often was both. That once a medicine man was not necessarily always one. His name had nothing to do with it. He could take a new name on becoming chief, like Little Turtle, the mighty Miami leader, or on becoming a medicine man, as Sitting-Bull. Many tribes had medicine women, namely, Pretty-Mouth and Captain Jack, Apache; Man-Who-Likes-Everybody, also Apache, but a mere male this time; High-Wolf was a noted Cheyenne medicine man. Nothing lowly or crawling about these.

This is an awful screed to inflict on you, but I am writing it in a hurry (and thereby overlooking much excellent material, no doubt) and I thought best to go into it a bit, even at the risk of being prolix. The examples are accumulative till they would fill volumes.

I'm very glad you wrote me and mentioned Brown Turtle, as I would desire, if not too much trouble or too late, to change his name to Black Turtle. In my haste to get away from the historical Little Turtle I forgot that few Indian tribes differentiate between black and brown, although I've found such names among Zuñi and Siouan lists. And few distinguish between blue and green, having one word for both colors. So, if there be some one supercritical, they might question "Brown."—Hugh Pendexter.

WITH his first story in our magazine William A. Shryer follows Camp-Fire custom and rises to introduce himself:

Detroit, Mich.

Born and spent my sweet young childhood in that contumacious community popularly known as "Terry Hut." After you have been to France you pronounce it differently, and as seldom as possible.

Am forty-one and don't look it, unless you sneak up on me from behind. Harrington Emerson once accused me of being a "convex blond," whatever that is. Am advised was a very engaging child. Consensus of intimate opinion at present refutes this interesting theory.

GOT a B. A. once. Said to be a more laborious process now. At the tender age of thirty-seven almost got an M. A. Spent three months at the University of Michigan in the interests of science, attempting to discover some possible relation between advertising phenomena and experimental psychology. Reported researches in *System* for six months. Concluded nobody was interested, much less science, so decided a year abroad more exhilarating than three months more for an M. A. Spent the cash and let the credit go.

In 1912 wrote a book on advertising. Weighs several pounds. One critic went so far as to say it was heavy in more ways than one. It proved a lot of advertisers were dead wrong, but few would admit it. Wouldn't have cared if more had bought. Think most of 'em went to the public libraries. They're an awful tight bunch.

Later wrote a two-volume business book. Got a number of people to contribute, which was a real bright idea. Sold a lot. Still moving. More money in fiction, though, if you want my advice.

WENT abroad in 1913. Visited Egypt, Syria, Turkey, Greece and one or two other places. Also saw Naples and managed to survive. Confess to a number of adventures, but protest wisdom of unexpurgated publicity relative thereto.

Met a lot of Italian Counts. Prefer a plain Wop any time. Also got chummy with the King of Greece's head gardener going to Corfu. Rode with a Greek bishop from Athens to Patras. He was a good scout. Let me test a set of bogus amber beads on his whiskers for electricity (in the beads, not the whiskers). Traveled from Patras to Rome with two smugglers of antiquities, winding up with a real adventure at Paris. Made a good story, but don't seem able to convince any editor it's worth the money.

HAVE spent a lot of time trying to demonstrate that William James was wrong. His theory that no man past twenty-five ever gains a single new idea outside his own business always annoyed me. Got married at thirty. Started a correspondence school at thirty-one. Still making the grade. Became an editor and publisher at thirty-five. James won a point, but I contend it should not be held against me. Successful publishers are born, not made. Learned the Egyptian written language at thirty-nine. Forgotten it since, so that's a half point each for James and me.

Wrote my first short story at thirty-eight and sold it. Laid off for three years and then wrote my first novelette. Sold it. Took heart and gave birth to "Old Josiah Simms, the Antiquarian Detective." He entered the arena at the ripe old age of sixty, *cap au jus*, just like the Pegasus, or was it Minerva? Parent and child doing well.

JUST sold my first story to *Adventure*. Hope to repeat, however. Too modest to send a picture. Spent thirty thousand dollars having it printed in the back of *Everybody's*, *System* and a lot of others less worthy, anyhow. Also, it cost $50 to get photo properly retouched, and it would be a shame to lose it. Editors are so careless about celebrities' pictures. Some say it looks like a Quaker preacher; others, like Jesse James.

Consuming ambition—to get as much per page for my stories as advertising managers have got out of me for space N. R. M. I'll have to go some, but what's the use of staking a good claim with a toothpick?

Last Call for Our Annual Vote

All the 1917 issues of *Adventure* are in your hands, from January, 1917, to Mid-December, 1917, inclusive, and the vote by our readers to determine the ten best stories in our magazine during this past year closes December 31. This annual vote is the best means we of our editorial staff can devise for making *Adventure's* stories the kind that please our readers best. It's up to you, so go to it.

The voting is simple and easy. Any one, subscriber or not, is eligible to vote if he's read at least seven of the 1917 issues. Serials, novels, novelettes, articles and short stories included; poems and Camp-Fire barred. The same author may appear on the list as many times as you please. All you need do is write down your ten selections numbered in order of preference, giving title and author of each, sign your name and mail us the letter or post-card. If you like, add as many as ten more stories for complimentary mention.

Remember that no stories are counted

unless they were published in one of the issues *bearing the printed date 1917*—January, 1917, to Mid-December, 1917, inclusive. This issue in your hands and the First January (1917) issue are *not* included. However, a serial appearing partly in 1917 and partly in 1918 or 1916 *is* included in the vote.

The result of the vote will be published in a subsequent issue.

ONE day last July I was planting beans in the half-acre lot that some of us out on Long Island had made into a "war garden." Suddenly a voice behind me announced:

"Honest, mister, I ain't a bum. I've been up against it."

That being an old story I decided at once that he *was* a bum and that it was I who was up against it. So I merely looked around to see a young fellow squatted down beside me and looking the worse for wear.

HE SAID he was a sailor from one of our ships then at Philadelphia, that he had come to New York on leave, gone joy-riding with a bunch of men and been drugged by them, robbed of a large roll and dumped in a vacant lot to come to in the morning.

That, too, was just a new variation of an old story, so I didn't take hold very hard. Asked him a few questions, however, about his ship and saw that at least he had once been in our Navy. Then he stood up and I saw his pants. Navy pants. He let his civilian coat come open at the neck and I saw the rest of his uniform. Also, taking a good look at his face, I saw that it wasn't just plain booze that he was recovering from; it looked like knock-out drops to me.

SO I QUIT planting beans, took him up to the house and did what little I could for him. If by chance one of his engineer officers sees this and happens to identify the case I'd like to testify for this adventurer. I gave him some stuff to settle his inside a bit and he drank some black coffee. He would take no food because he had no place to put it where it would stay. Incidentally, he wouldn't take anything in the line of strong drink when it was offered. His one idea and ambition was to get back to Philadelphia and report himself on time. He wouldn't lie down and rest, though he sure needed it, and he wouldn't wait for me to get a doctor, though he needed that too. He accepted just the few cents that would get him to New York where he had friends to send him on to Philadelphia.

I gave him his direction and watched him make his way up the street, pretty wabbly on his pins but losing no time whatsoever. If he didn't get back to his ship in time I'll bet it was not his fault.

What I want to know is, did he? I didn't ask his name or give him mine and I've gone and forgotten his ship, but if it happens that this meets his eye—and, so far as I can figure, *Adventure* reaches the eye of most men in our Navy—I hope he'll drop me a line to tell me how he made out.

GLAD to have the following on ants. Come across with more, any of you who have had personal experience with ant armies. Amazingly interesting little rascals, and they belong in the field of adventure, all right, as many of you can testify who are familiar with the pleasant little ways in which they are used as torturers and executioners by savage tribes, both black and white—white, at least, as to general color.

Miami, Fla.

It seems to me that there has always been a lot of bother about ants. My earliest recollection about them is a lot of uncalled-for talk on the part of an aunt (this is not intended as a pun) of mine, who used to hold forth on the habits of the ant as the antipodes of some person, or thing, called the sluggard. It has taken years (I am English) for this to filter through my ivory; I need not tell my age, but I have quit paying poll tax and wearing rosettes on my shoes, but I begin to think she had some reference to me. I have come in contact with ants personally, lots of times, and have wished the sluggard was there in my place. In the early eighties I punched cows in northwestern Iowa. I have gone to sleep on the prairie and awakened covered with them (ants, not cows) and used language which you camouflage in *Adventure*. But I want to tell you what I have seen in armies of ants.

TWO years ago I was living in Fort Lauderdale, Florida. One day my wife called me to the front of the house and showed me an army of ants. I don't know how long they had been marching. This was in the morning about ten-thirty, but they had worn a path about an inch wide and a quarter of an inch deep. They did not march eight abreast, but were in companies or regiments which were not all the same length. At the spaces between regiments there were some who seemed to be officers, part of these ran back and forth on the edge of the path as though they were delivering orders. They came from the south, passed the east side of the house and went to the north, and it was twenty-four hours before the last of them went by.

I did not follow them up to see where they went, as I have never been fond of them since my aunt said what she did, but after reading what you said in Camp-Fire, I wish I had. Anyway, I have told you all I know or have seen in regard to ants.

I know they do travel in armies or regiments, with some who seem to be officers, and I guess there are lots of people who have never seen them.—J. A. GAMBLE.

AT ITS first dinner of the season the Adventurers' Club, New York chapter, displayed a "service-flag" with 43 stars. Title to still more has been found, with others to hear from. Pretty good for 180 members of all ages and physical conditions, with some still unreported.

ARTHUR SULLIVANT HOFFMAN.

ADVENTURE'S FREE SERVICES AND ADDRESSES

These services of *Adventure* are free to *any one.* They involve much time, work and expense on our part, but we offer them gladly and ask in return only that you *read and observe the simple rules,* thus saving needless delay and trouble for you and us. The whole spirit of this magazine is one of friendliness. No formality between editors and readers. Whenever we *can* help you we're ready and willing to try.

Identification Cards

Free to any reader. Just send us (1) your name and address, (2) name and address of party to be notified, (3) a stamped and self-addressed return envelope.

Each card bears this inscription, each printed in English, French, Spanish, German, Portuguese, Dutch, Italian, Arabic, Chinese, Russian, and Japanese:

"In case of death or serious emergency to bearer, address serial number of this card, care of *Adventure,* New York, stating full particulars, and friends will be notified."

In our office, under each serial number, will be registered the name of bearer and of one friend, with permanent address of each. No name appears on the card. Letters will be forwarded to friend, unopened by us. Names and addresses treated as confidential. We assume no other obligations. Cards not for business identification. Cards furnished free, *provided stamped and addressed envelope accompanies application.* We reserve the right to use our own discretion in all matters pertaining to these cards.

Later we may furnish a metal card or tag. If interested in metal cards, say so on a *post-card—not* in a letter. No obligation entailed. These post-cards, filed, will guide us as to demand and number needed.

A moment's thought will show the value of this system of card-identification for any one, whether in civilization or out of it. Remember to furnish stamped and addressed envelope and to *give in full the names and addresses of self and friend or friends when applying.*

Back Issues of *Adventure*

Will sell: 1915, July—Dec. inclusive; 1916, all; 1917, all. 10 cents each, carriage paid—ED. S. RAHN, 1432 N. Allison St., Philadelphia, Pa.

Will sell: 1911, five issues; 1912, eight issues; 1913, Aug.—Dec. inclusive; 1914-15-16-17, all. H. C. DIXON, 1546 Woodward Ave., Cleveland, O.

Wanted: 1911, Nov.; 1912, Jan.; 1915, Dec.; 1916, Jan., Feb.—B. F. LEAVITT, 1040 Nicholas Bldg., Toledo, O.

Manuscripts

Glad to look at any manuscript. We have no "regular staff" of writers. A welcome for new writers. *It is not necessary to write asking to submit your work.*

When submitting a manuscript, if you write a letter concerning it, enclose it *with* the manuscript; do *not* send it under separate cover. Enclose stamped and addressed envelope for return. All manuscripts should be typewritten double-spaced, with wide margins, not rolled, name and address on first page. We assume no risk for manuscripts or illustrations submitted, but use all due care while they are in our hands. Payment on acceptance.

We want only clean stories. Sex, morbid, "problem," psychological and supernatural stories barred. Use almost no fact-articles. Can not furnish or suggest collaborators. Use fiction of almost any length; under 3000 welcomed.

Missing Friends or Relatives

Our free service department "Lost Trails" in the pages following, though frequently used in cases where detective agencies, newspapers, and all other methods have failed, or for finding people long since dead, has located one out of about every five inquired for. Except in case of relatives, inquiries from one sex to the other are barred.

Expeditions and Employment

While we should like to be of aid in these matters, experience has shown that it is not practicable.

Mail Address and Forwarding Service

This office, assuming no responsibility, will be glad to act as a forwarding address for its readers or to hold mail till called for, provided necessary postage is supplied.

Addresses

Order of the Restless—Organizing to unite for fellowship all who feel the wanderlust. First suggested in this magazine, though having no connection with it aside from our friendly interest. Address WAYNE EBERLY, 731 Guardian Bldg., Cleveland, O., in charge of preliminary organizing.

Camp-Fire—Any one belongs who wishes to.

High-School Volunteers of the U. S.—An organization promoting a democratic system of military training in American high schools. Address *Everybody's,* Spring and Macdougal Streets, New York City.

Rifle Clubs—Address Nat. Rifle Ass'n of America, 1108 Woodward Bldg., Washington, D. C.

(*See also under "Standing Information" in "Ask Adventure."*)

General Questions from Readers

In addition to our free service department "Ask Adventure" on the pages following, *Adventure* can sometimes answer other questions within our general field. When it can, it will. Expeditions and employment excepted.

Remember

Magazines are made up ahead of time. An item received today is too late for the current issue; allow for two or three months between sending and publication.

A LETTER from one of us at the front, one whose stories we've read in our magazine:

On a hill in France,
September 11, 1917.

Here I am in France, a land made up of color, odd characters and plot material. But, unfortunately, I have practically no time for fiction as my work requires almost every minute of the day. It is impossible to write here at night.

I LIKE this new life or experience. It is filled with the spirit of adventure. I live from day to day, wondering what is going to happen next. I can hardly realize that I am the same person who, a few weeks back, was turning out South Sea Island stories for *Adventure*. Indeed, I feel, at times, that Charles Brown, Jr., the ambulancier, is an entirely different individual from Charles Brown, Jr., the short-story writer.

Because of the strict censorship on all mail, I do not know what kind of letters I'll be able to get through to you for the readers of the Camp-Fire. However, I shall try to write you some descriptive stuff, the kind of material that does not contain information of military value.—CHARLES BROWN, JR.

I'VE learned more about the American Indians from Hugh Pendexter's stories and his Camp-Fire chats about them than I've learned from any other one source. That isn't saying so very much, but that's not Mr. Pendexter's fault. Here, for example, is some interesting "dope" bearing on his story in this issue:

The story is based on the tutelarism of the American Indian. J. W. Powell in his first annual report on the work of the Bureau of American Ethnology in part says (page 41), "Among all the tribes of North America with which we are acquainted tutelarism prevails. Every tribe and every clan has its own protecting god, and every individual has his *my god*. It is a curious fact that every Indian seeks to conceal the knowledge of his *my god* from all persons, for he fears that, if his enemy should know of his tutelar deity, he might by extraordinary magic succeed in estranging him and be able to compass his destruction through his own god."

McLean's experience is perfectly plausible. James Moony, of the B. A. E., in his article on scalping, page 482, part 2, Bulletin Thirty, in part says: "The operation of scalping was painful but by no means fatal. The impression that it was fatal probably arises from the fact that the scalp was usually taken from the head of a slain enemy as a token of his death, but among the Plains tribes the attacking party frequently strove to overpower his enemy and scalp him alive, to inflict greater agony before killing him, and frequently also a captured enemy was scalped alive and released to go back thus mutilated to his people as a direct defiance, etc."

Howo! page ii, interjection in Teton dialect. Translated *Come!* or *Now!* Dakota language embraces four major dialects—Santee, Yankton, Teton and Assiniboin. First two spoken by eastern Dakota bands, the last by those in northwest and Teton by western. The Oglala are the principal division of the Teton Sioux.

In the nineteenth annual report of B. A. E., page 431: "The Indian has always four as the principal sacred number, with usually another only slightly subordinated."

Mahopa, magic-power, is equivalent to the Iroquoian *orenda*. A warrior possessing a strong personal deity and at the same time blessed with a strong *mahopa* was well nigh invincible. There is any amount of similar dope along these lines and if I've skipped anything you'd like to know about please call on me. I always feel a bit embarrassed in inflicting data ot this nature, and have a fear of overdoing it.—HUGH PENDEXTER.

OUR "Lost Trails" is considered by many one of the most interesting things in the magazine. I rather think so myself. But, after all, its interest is a minor point. For consider the work it has done, the big changes it has made in many people's lives. Some of the inquiries, of course, are merely those of friends who've become separated and wish to find each other again. Even that is a thing of importance. But consider the grieving, anxious mother who has lost her son, the wives, husbands, brothers, fathers, daughters who have been lost or have lost a loved one. And our "Lost Trails" has found them.

IT FINDS one out of every five, and that is really an amazing accomplishment. It isn't just the United States and Canada that must be searched, but the whole wide, wide world clear into its most remote corners. And many of the cases are those that police, detectives, newspapers, private search and all the other means of finding the lost have already tried and failed to find even a trace.

Many are the heartfelt letters of gratitude that come in to us, giving us an insight into just how real, how varied and how great to those concerned are the human dramas always being acted out somewhere behind those small printed words on one page of our magazine. Maybe you'd like to read one of them, one out of many. The names of the people are, of course, taken out, for naturally it is a matter private and personal to them and not to be spread broadcast:

Lost Trails has again been the means by which mother and son have come together after months of separation. What a happy reunion, only those that have had the experience can understand. The Prodigal Son did not receive a better welcome than I. So it is with the greatest of pleasure that I thank you for your part in the reunion of two loved ones.

Your magazine has filled many a dark hour when at sea or on land, not only in the States, but out of them, for I have been somewhat of an adventurer myself.

I would like the pleasure of taking you by the hand and saying face to face what I can only say on paper. But nevertheless you have mother's and my own heartfelt hopes for the success of your magazine.

We ask the privilege of being called
Your friends, —— —— and —— ——.

FOLLOWING our Camp-Fire custom, L. Patrick Green, giving us in this issue his first story in *Adventure*, stands up and gives us an account of himself.

Boston, Massachusetts.

It's a dangerous thing to ask a modest man for his life history—something like holding a red flag before a mad bull. He hesitates a moment, pawing the ground, then rushes and there is no stopping him. Well, here goes.

I WAS born in a small English village in March, 1891, and a few weeks later was christened Louis Montague Greene. In after years the Louis Montague part was too much for me and so I changed it to Lewis Patrick. Do you blame me?

Went to a large boarding-school until I was eighteen, and then came the parting of the ways. My people wished me to study for the ministry, and I wanted to be an engineer. A compromise was effected, in which, be it said, my people had no voice. I had always loved to read stories of Africa, stories of the pioneers—Rhodes, Fletcher, Jameson and the rest of the Empire builders. Consequently, when, at this time, I read in a newspaper that men were wanted for the Rhodesian Civil Service, I jumped at the opening. Passing the examination, I was accepted, although three years under the age limit. So I was on the way to the land of my dreams shortly after my eighteenth birthday.

I WAS in the country almost four years and surely had my full share of "interesting experiences." I have been lost for two whole days—days that seemed like years—in the bush; that was my worst experience. Lions? Yes, I had adventures with them. On one occasion I had made my camp on the banks of the Shangani; it was in the lion country and so we made what is known as a scherm, a fence made of thorn-bush. The enclosure was made large enough to accommodate myself, the four native police and my own servant—also the animals. It was in the dry season and the river was quite dry, except for pools here and there. It was near such a pool that we made camp.

It was nearly an hour to sundown, and so I crossed over the river in search of game for the evening meal. I soon sighted and shot one of the smallest species of buck, a duiker. Not wishing to disturb the boys, who were busy building the scherm, I undertook to bring it back to camp myself. As it was quite heavy I dragged it most of the way, leaving quite a trail. Some of the buck we had for supper and the rest was hung up in a tree that formed one-quarter of the scherm.

IT WAS after sundown and all was pitch dark. The boys were seated around the fire, singing about the day's march. I was seated on my blankets, having a last pipe before turning in. Suddenly afar off we heard a low rumble, like distant thunder, followed by two harsh coughs. It was the indescribable, unmistakable roar of a lion on the hunting trail. The note of a lion on a hunt is petrifying—hypnotic in its influence. I know that my spine felt icy cold.

It had its effect, too, on the boys, for they huddled closely together. One, however, an old fellow, took a powder out of his pouch and strewed it round the outside of the scherm, muttering charms the while. This, he said, would prevent the lion from harming us.

MEANWHILE the moans—that is a truer descriptive word than roars—were coming nearer, ever nearer. Soon we could hear him down in the river-bed—the *swish, swish* as he went through the reeds, and the heavy crunch of big paws on the sand. Then came silence, and I, in the wisdom of twenty years, said "He is gone." I went to bed, but I did not undress and took care to keep my rifle close.

Next morning, awaking at sun-up, I noticed that the boys were not in the scherm, and hearing heated conversation outside, I went out to them. They were pointing to the ground and jabbering in an excited fashion. A heavy dew had fallen during the night, and there, plain as the nose on your face, was the spoor of a lion. We could trace it from the river-bed, following the trail I had made when bringing back the buck. We could see where he had come right up to the tree in which the buck was hanging, and had indeed stood on his hind legs, with his front paws on the trunk of the tree. In that position he could have looked over the scherm, and there was I sleeping just underneath him. He didn't touch the buck—and I am telling the story.

ELEPHANTS, giraffe, zebra, and, most dangerous of all the big game, the African buffalo, hippopotami, and the rest, I have seen them all, hunted most, and shot some.

Dealing almost entirely with natives, I learned to speak their language and came to admire them. They taught me many things that were good for a youngster to know. And always I kept in good condition. So when I was stationed at Bulawayo, one of the few towns in Rhodesia, I was selected to play on the team respresenting Rhodesia in the Currie Cup Football Tournament. Going south, we played all the other provinces—Natal, Cape Colony and the rest. When in Durban I did a little sprinting, training with Bobby Walker, who was at that time the one-hundred-yards amateur champion of the world.

MY CAREER was cut short by a sunstroke. I was riding a horse at the time, and fell with my back across a large rock. This happened about one hundred miles from the nearest railroad. I shall never forget the agony of the trip to the station, carried by natives on a poorly constructed stretcher. After six months in hospital I was sent back to England and finally given my walking papers—medically unfit.

England struck me as being too conservative and *small* so I decided to come out to the States (this was in the Fall of 1913), intending to go West, but Fate ruled otherwise. I have been a timekeeper for a New York construction company, life insurance agent, sold stock for a "shady" broker—though I did not know it at the time. Canvassed and spoke at open-air meetings under the auspices of the Massachusetts Woman's Suffrage Association, and for the last two years have been with a society for the care of children, in Boston, having charge of the older boys who are placed in homes throughout Massachusetts.

I am married. My wife *was* an American. (It's hardly fair that a woman should so lose her nationality.) My baby girl *is* an American, and I *will* be an American as soon as I can get out my second papers.—L. PATRICK GREENE.

WE WANT our readers to write to us whenever they have any criticisms to make on anything connected with the magazine. Naturally our object is to make *Adventure* suit them as much as possible. Even telling us which stories you like or don't like helps a great deal in choosing stories and authors for future numbers. But it helps still more when you tell us *why* you like or don't like them.

Also it helps when you point out the mistakes and discrepancies that occasionally appear in our stories, as they do in all magazines. No one of us here in the office thinks he knows everything about everything; if he did, he'd soon get over it in the face of the thousands of subjects *Adventure's* stories bring up. And when it comes to the very large number of subjects, each one of which at least some of you know more about than we do, why, we want your help and are grateful for it. If mistakes are pointed out we're less likely to make them over again.

AND I want to say right here that in the past practically all of you have called attention to mistakes in a way that was purely friendly. We appreciate that. Once in a while some fellow finds a slip, goes up into the air with a loud noise and cusses us out because the author made it and we didn't catch it, giving us to understand that he and we are therefore pretty nearly imbecile all around. It may have been a very unimportant slip, he forgets that while he may know more than the author and editors about this one subject they may possibly know more about a few other subjects than he does, and quite often he finds that he'd gone off half-cocked anyway and has to backwater. However, it's our general rule to pass any criticism of any value on to the author in question, and our writers have shown that they take criticism in the same spirit that we do. Also, thanks chiefly to our writers rather than to us editors, there have been amazingly few mistakes in our stories considering the great number of subjects and the various fields covered.

HERE'S a case, showing how easy it is to make a slip. Most of our readers didn't notice this slip at all, but there are always a few of you who have intimate knowledge of almost any subject that comes up. I've been in Cornwall, but I hadn't the faintest idea whether they use dories there or not, except that I'd always associated the dory chiefly with our own New England coast. As to where the Cornish gas-buoys might be placed, not an idea.

It's my fault about the dories. As Captain Dingle first wrote the story he gave it no definite geographic setting, but, at my suggestion, he gave one to it and in revising accordingly he missed the dories, which were, of course, entirely in place in the original version.

Captain Dingle in "The Avenging Sea" is trying to show that some of the people of Cornwall earn their living by wrecking. Such a story is false and brings discredit on the people of Cornwall.

THERE never was a gas-beacon or buoy on the northwestern part of Cornwall. There is a gas-buoy off the "Manacles Rocks," about twelve miles east of the Lizard Point. Ships coming from the south would open the "Wolf Rock Light" north, northwest of the Land's End about twenty-two miles, and if bound for Bristol would bear away for Hartland Point on the Devonshire coast. If coming from the Lizard they would (if sober) keep an offing until they opened the Longships which light is visible about fifteen miles. The next would be Godvery Light (with a light about the same radius), then Hartland Point (all these lights are visible one from another). Leaving Hartland, the course is altered for Portshead, for Bristol is on the River Severn. In case of fog all the lighthouses are fitted with automatic foghorns. The Longships and the Wolf Rock Lights were built about sixty years ago and at that time there weren't many steamers.

Now another thing, if Captain Dingle is going to have wreckers on the coast of Cornwall he shouldn't use dories, for the people there wouldn't know one without they were introduced to it. I hope you can see your way to publish this so people will know that the Cornish people are civilized and have been since the Phenicians bought tin there for Solomon's Temple.—JESSE D'ROUFFIGNAC, a native of Mounts Bay, Cornwall.

When I sent the above to Captain Dingle he replied as follows:

First conceding the point he undoubtedly makes, I acknowledge my error in using a dory. That was an oversight for which I humbly apologize to all Cornishmen.

As for the absence of gas-beacons—where such aids to navigation are known to exist at all it is surely a part of an author's license to place such a one (for the purposes of his story) in any other unnamed locality in order that he may not tread too harshly on the corns of those who live near, or know, the locality of an existing beacon.

MY OWN native place, Devon, is near enough to Cornwall to have given me a fair knowledge of, and a deep admiration for, the men of Cornwall. It also gives me the knowledge that wreckers were not always strangers to the famous duchy. What Cornishman or Devon man has not heard the story of the wreck near St. Anthony? This, happening just before churchtime on a Sunday, the clerk announced that "The Measter would gee them a hulladay, etc.," for purposes well understood by the pastor. Then, as the congregation prepared to rush pell-mell for the scene of the wreck, not on humanity bent, the pastor is reputed to have shouted: "Here! Here! Let's all start fair!"

Whether this particular tale is true or not, such stories do not gather around any community without some reason; and there are many such, and some of darker import.

AS FOR Cornish civilization, that is not disputed. But surely Mr. D'Rouffignac will admit that there never was yet a community so utterly civilized that it did not breed SOME brutal natures, some thieves, even an occasional murderer. Loyalty to one's native place may blind one to its faults; it doesn't render them non-existent. Many millions of people—good people—have until quite recently regarded Germany as highly civilized!—A. E. DINGLE.

I think perhaps Mr. D'Rouffignac has forgotten that fiction can not be judged at all points by the standards of fact articles. Even fiction mustn't make a people use a type of boat they don't use in real life, but in the matter of buoys the author was rather justified. And I fear his commendable patriotism has run away with him a bit in his last sentence. Cornwall has for centuries been "civilized," more than some countries, less than others; the Cornish, Welsh and Bretons, like the other main division of the Celtic race, have contributed much to the world. But if he means us to infer that Cornwall has been so civilized that there has been no wrecking by its people since the time of the Phenicians, he is asking too much. As a matter of plain fact, Cornwall stands out as a place where that pleasant little pastime was formerly particularly in vogue. The date of the story is not set, but its general tone makes it antedate the present day. "Civilized," too, is only a relative term, and I'm sure he'll admit, for example, that the civilization of the Phenicians was several eras ahead of that of Cornwall in their day.

FOLLOWING a Camp-Fire custom of years' standing, one of our number who has hitherto been a member of the readers' brigade and now joins the writers' brigade as well, stands up to give an account of himself. Men, shake hands with William Harper Dean. Mr. Dean, the Camp-Fire welcomes you among its writers and listens.

I'm afraid my autobiography will be just a bit disappointing to readers of *Adventure*, for until the last three or four years I have followed the non-adventurous career of entomologist, working my way by successive stages through the South and Southwest, in Government and State employ. And yet a field entomologist does find opportunity to assimilate fiction material if he is so inclined. To my mind the Texas drought and "norther," the Louisiana lagoon and bayou, and the unique life of the Mississippi riverman are all of them full of romance, ofttimes adventure.

About four years ago I set myself seriously to the task of writing, taking the job of Washington correspondent for *The Country Gentleman*, with free-lance privileges. I'm still at it and hope to be for the rest of my life.—WM. HARPER DEAN.

FROM the following do not get the wrong impression that E. E. Harriman does not hold in high respect all those of German blood who are loyal to America. It is the other kind he has in mind, those who pretended to be Americans, who, many of them, gave their formal oath to be Americans, but when the test came lined up against America and for her enemies. When his country goes to war Mr. Harriman is not friendly to her enemies, at home or abroad, and in either peace or war he hates a liar, a perjurer, a sneak, a hypocrite and a traitor. So do I.

Camp-Fire Comrades: If there is any doubt left in any of your minds as to the Germanic idea in America, read this.

"We have suffered long the preachment that 'you Germans must allow yourselves to be assimilated; you must merge with the American people,' but no one will ever find us prepared to descend to an inferior level. No! We have made it our aim to elevate the others to our level. We will not allow our two-thousand-year culture to be trodden down in this land. Many are giving our German culture to this land of their children, but that is possible only if we stand together. . . . Let us stand up for our good right and hold together. Be strong! Be GERMAN!"

These are the words of an official of a national German society in this country, spoken before ten thousand German-Americans in Milwaukee. Get it, boys? Don't be German-Americans or Americans, but BE GERMAN! And on top of that the liars say they are loyal to this country!

Add to this the words of another "American" of the same kind in Chicago:

"When the thousands and hundreds of thousands of those drafted for military service realize that their country is going to make them victims of a foreign adventure, there will arise a conflict between sentiment and duty which may threaten the internal peace of the republic. . . . We prefer to sacrifice ourselves rather than see the old Fatherland, after its glorious battles, done out of the reward of its victory."

Glorious sentiments for loyal Americans as they call themselves! If Germanic peoples do not intend to assimilate, why should they be permitted to take out naturalization papers? If they propose to be German forever, let them stay in Germany. I begin to think as a boy with whom I went to school said he thought. His parents were German. "They all think they are smarter than any one else and they are as dumb as the oxen. Just when they think they are smartest they are the biggest fools of all. I wish to God I wasn't full of German blood."

I thank God I have none of it in my veins, but the present actions of Germans in America make me think the boy was right about their "dumbness."

As Mr. Hoffman said in the Mid-October issue, "We must stamp out the language and every German alliance."

Think of what Dr. —— ——, a German-American, said to me long ago in Los Angeles when I asked him the question point blank, "Which land will you aid in case of war, your Fatherland or your adopted land?" He threw his right fist high and his face grew dark red and seemed to swell, as he gritted his words through clenched teeth: "*Hoch der Kaiser, bei Gott!* I vas Cherman furst! I shtay mit mein bludt, bei Gott!"

"Are you a citizen, doctor?" said I.

"More as t'irty years, but vat iss dat?"

"How about your oath to renounce the German Empire and its Kaiser?"

"Bapers undt schvearin', vat iss dat? I go mit mein bludt, I tol' you."

As Frank Huston said to me, "There are very few German-Americans in this country, but a —— of a lot of Germans living in America."—E. E. HARRIMAN.

SURELY we need not tell our boys at the front that we of the Camp-Fire are eager to have their letters with whatever of news they can give us. We all know they can send only such news as the censor permits—and all American publications have been asked by the Government to follow a long list of rules for suppressing certain kinds of apparently innocent information that might prove of value to the enemy and that might slip past the censors—but there are many legitimate things to tell. If you tell us only that you're safe and well, why, naturally, we're glad to know it, and there are always little odds and ends that may not seem much to you but that interest us back home.

And of course we always like to hear reports from those of us who, though not in the war, are in far places. It doesn't matter a bit whether you are a skilled writer; we don't care anything about that—what we like is men and facts and deeds.

ANOTHER of the three who in this issue join the writer division of our Camp-Fire follows Camp-Fire custom and introduces himself—Sidney Rittenberg.

Men of the Camp-Fire, you'll probably be yawning wearily before this newcomer has finished the spinning of his tame yarn. But—here goes:

BORN in Charleston, S. C. As a boy, was taken about the country quite a bit by my mother, who had to travel for her health. Always a studious little fellow, reading and thinking much beyond my years, but nevertheless managing to get into just as many fights and bits of devilment as other boys. Finished my schooling in New York City, where I lived several years. Incidentally, began my courting in high school there and, some years after leaving the Big Town, returned for the girl and brought her back South with me.

From New York City I went to a town of two hundred in the wildest part of South Carolina, Berkeley County, and clerked in a country store. A series of coincidences so improbable that they would never get by a fiction editor in a story got me into the newspaper game in Charleston. Octavus

Roy Cohen, whom most of the Camp-Fire folks know, had a lot to do with it, as he had with a number of other things that have happened to me.

I'M NOT yet twenty-five, but I've been earning my living at writing of one kind or another about seven years. I've done all sorts of newspaper work, from covering weddings and funerals to reviewing plays and writing editorials. For two years I had charge of the editorial work at a large agricultural college and just now I'm secretary of the publicity department of the Charleston Chamber of Commerce. I've also had a fling at the advertising game and have worked in various mercantile establishments.

For two or three years I've written magazine articles and stories. I've had articles in numerous periodicals of many kinds, but I've only recently begun to get my stories across.

EVER since I can remember I've hung about the water-front, and most of the simple adventures I've had have occurred there or at sea. I've talked with men of the sea so much that I feel as if I've been to many parts of the world I've never seen. For example, I believe that if I ever made a voyage from the West Coast through the Straits and up the Atlantic Coast, in the old way, I'd run into few surprises. Of course, this may be a silly belief, but—I have it.

And that's about all, except that I've been rejected by the army people on account of my eyes, but am trying to do my bit by serving as secretary of our County Council of Defense and working with numerous other bodies that are doing war work.

AS TO "Shorty's Letter from Home," my first *Adventure* story, there's little to say except that I got the idea several years ago from a yarn that was told to me by the mate of a British tramp that put into Charleston with nitrate from the West Coast. The big difference was that in his tale, which was about a Hindu prophetess in Calcutta, the chap who got the nasty prophecy had the hard luck to have it fulfilled by hearing of the death of his youngest child—a very gruesome narrative it was, probably invented by the mate for the edification of his young newspaper friend who, as I remember it, was importuning him for stuff of the kind during much of the two months or more that the ship lay in port.—SIDNEY RITTENBERG.

LETTER-FRIENDS BACK HOME

A Free Service Department for American, Canadian, and Other Allied Soldiers, Sailors, Marines and Others in Camp or at the Front.

Any one in the United States or Allied service who wishes to brighten the time with letters from "back home," or wherever else this magazine circulates, and with the personal touch and interest of hitherto unkhown frieeds, can secure these letters and these friends by sending us his name and military address to be published once in this department as soon as censorship of soldiers' foreign addresses permits. Among our readers of both sexes, all classes and from all parts of the world, he is likely to gain a number of friendly, personal correspondents. He is free to answer only such as he is comfortably able to answer under the conditions that surround him, and it is even suggested that the number of correspondents for any one man be determined by the needs of his comrades as well as by his own.

This magazine, of course, assumes no responsibility other than the publishing of these names and addresses as its space will permit. Experience has shown that the service offered is a very real and needed one, and all not themselves in service are asked to do their part in making the daily life of those fighting in our defense brighter and pleasanter through personal friendships across the intervening miles and by whatever personal, human kindnesses such friendships may suggest.

When giving your military address make it as permanent a one as possible.

(As the magazine is made up several months in advance, the above notice will appear with only such stray names as happen to come in to us until there has been time for it to reach the camps and the front and for names and addresses to reach us, be put in type and then reach our readers on publication.)

SOME straight talk on hyphenism from Theodore Seixas Solomons, whose stories we've read and enjoyed:

SOMETIME ago a few of your contribs of German and German-sounding names took occasion to record themselves as Americans, and it has occurred to me that the name Solomons might carry a suggestion of Teutonism, at least with some.

I know a lot of Germans and German-Americans. I hate hyphenated Americans—I mean I hate the hyphen and the nation names before it. There ain't no such animal as a French or Spanish or German American, any more than there is a cat-dog or a man of California-Maine birth or citizenship. That, however, is by the way. What I started to say is that there is nothing the matter with a good American, whether he was a German or not, or his parents before him. Nor with a present German living in America, if he is a good German, *i. e.*, a good man who is a German man. What we don't like is people that are not all right. And they are not all right if they can't see that we've got to look out for this country and what this country stands for—as we believe it does; and if they can't or won't either help or, if they are aliens, "stand from under" and not hinder by so much as a look! That's all there is to the alien question. This thing of allowing prejudice against a name to get under one's skin is all wrong.

NEVERTHELESS, I don't know but it is a good thing to make a confession of faith if one "sounds" German. So it will not do any harm at least for me to say that I am a pure-blooded Jew, with a little Polish strain of a hundred years back, and most of me British and Spanish blood of a couple of hundred. For that matter, of course it is all Jewish blood, but of a rearing originally in the countries stated. The Solomonses and Seixases antedated the birth of Washington, being among the first Jews to step upon the Western continents. And, ever since, they have been "doing their bit." They not only fought in the French and Indian wars and in the Revolution but they lent General Washington—or his Continental army—money, and their women folks used to dance with him, and they have handed it down to us kids that he was a stiff, ramrodish dancer, at that. One of my forebears helped found Columbia College, and his bas-relief, in which his Israelitish proboscis shines out resplendently, graces the walls of one of the buildings. And they have been doing things since, in a quiet way, in all the mix-ups.

Out here my father was a member of every Vigilantes Committee they had, and I remember him coming home mad one day and getting out the hickory club with the handkerchief loop through a hole in the handle to secure it about the wrist, so no rioter could wrest it from him, and bolting off again. That was when I was emerging from babyhood.

NO SENSIBLE examining board would take me for anything active at present, while there are millions of skookum young blades to draw into the mix-up—though I'm still in the prime of life, when it comes to that—so the next best thing seemed to be to take the place of some fellow who goes into active service. Hence I am now, and have been for some months, in one of the active industries upon which the Government largely depends, and hence also it is that I am not producing many stories for you or the other magazines.—THEO. S. SOLOMONS.

ARTHUR SULLIVANT HOFFMAN.

ADVENTURE'S FREE SERVICES AND ADDRESSES

These services of *Adventure's* are free to *any one*. They involve much time, work and expense on our part, but we offer them gladly and ask in return only that you *read and observe the simple rules*, thus saving needless delay and trouble for you and us. The whole spirit of this magazine is one of friendliness. No formality between editors and readers. Whenever we *can* help you we're ready and willing to try.

Identification Cards

Free to any reader. Just send us (1) your name and address, (2) name and address of party to be notified, (3) a stamped and self-addressed return envelope.

Each card bears this inscription, each printed in English, French, Spanish, German, Portuguese, Dutch, Italian, Arabic, Chinese, Russian, and Japanese:

"In case of death or serious emergency to bearer, address serial number of this card, care of *Adventure*, New York, stating full particulars, and friends will be notified."

In our office, under each serial number, will be registered the name of bearer and of one friend, with permanent address of each. No name appears on the card. Letters will be forwarded to friend, unopened by us. Names and addresses treated as confidential. We assume no other obligations. Cards not for business identification. Cards furnished free, *provided stamped and addressed envelope accompanies application.* We reserve the right to use our own discretion in all matters pertaining to these cards.

Later we may furnish a metal card or tag. If interested in metal cards, say so on a *post-card—not* in a letter. No obligation entailed. These post-cards, filed, will guide us as to demand and number needed.

A moment's thought will show the value of this system of card-identification for any one, whether in civilization or out of it. Remember to furnish stamped and addressed envelope and to *give in full the names and addresses of self and friend or friends when applying.*

Back Issues of *Adventure*

Will sell: 1915, complete; 1916, complete; 1917, Jan.—Aug. inclusive. Ten cents each, carriage collect.—H. J. SANDERS, 110 Todd St. N. E., Washington, D. C.

Manuscripts

Glad to look at any manuscript. We have no "regular staff" of writers. A welcome for new writers. *It is not necessary to write asking to submit your work.*

When submitting a manuscript, if you write a letter concerning it, enclose it *with* the manuscript; do *not* send it under separate cover. Enclose stamped and addressed envelope for return. All manuscripts should be typewritten double-spaced, with wide margins, not rolled, name and address on first page. We assume no risk for manuscripts or illustrations submitted, but use all due care while they are in our hands. Payment on acceptance.

We want only clean stories. Sex, morbid, "problem," psychological and supernatural stories barred. Use almost no fact-articles. Can not furnish or suggest collaborators. Use fiction of almost any length; under 3000 welcomed.

Missing Friends or Relatives

Our free service department "Lost Trails" in the pages following, though frequently used in cases where detective agencies, newspapers, and all other methods have failed, or for finding people long since dead, has located one out of about every five inquired for. Except in case of relatives, inquiries from one sex to the other are barred.

Expeditions and Employment

While we should like to be of aid in these matters, experience has shown that it is not practicable.

Mail Address and Forwarding Service

This office, assuming no responsibility, will be glad to act as a forwarding address for its readers or to hold mail till called for, provided necessary postage is supplied.

Addresses

Order of the Restless—Organizing to unite for fellowship all who feel the wanderlust. First suggested in this magazine, though having no connection with it aside from our friendly interest. Address WAYNE EBERLY, 731 Guardian Bldg., Cleveland, O., in charge of preliminary organizing.

Camp-Fire—Any one belongs who wishes to.

High-School Volunteers of the U. S.—An organization promoting a democratic system of military training in American high schools. Address *Everybody's*, Spring and Macdougal, New York City.

Rifle Clubs—Address Nat. Rifle Ass'n of America, 1108 Woodward Bldg., Washington, D. C.

(*See also under "Standing Information" in "Ask Adventure."*)

General Questions from Readers

In addition to our free service department "Ask Adventure" on the pages following, *Adventure* can sometimes answer other questions within our general field. When it can, it will. Expeditions and employment excepted.

Remember

Magazines are made up ahead of time. An item received today is too late for the current issue; allow for two or three months between sending and publication.

JACK LONDON. Surely he *does* deserve a tribute from all of us, as do the three other men Mr. Rollings mentions and many another adventurer who has passed out of the world in which he found so much life.

We must have a new Camp-Fire custom, some kind of fitting farewell and tribute to those of us who take the long trail, a toast to them, a salute as their way at last parts from our way. God knows there will be many to leave us in these bloody months or years to come. Stand, comrades of our Camp-Fire, hats off, heads bowed, and let each one of us send out his own inward Godspeed to London, Duncan, Davis, Smith and all the others of our kind who have gone. And with our Godspeed let us send out our silent thanks to them for the manly lives they lived in our sight.

And, now, our thanks to Mr. Rollings for leading us to stand up man-fashion and say the things that lay hidden in us. Here is his letter:

It is now almost a year since that master "teller of strange tales," Jack London, passed out on the "Long Trail." Since the daily press printed the sad news of his departure I have watched each issue of the "Camp-Fire" expecting to see some fitting tribute paid to one who (perhaps more than any other) brought to the modern reading public the savor and romance of the "Open Trail."

Among the world wanderers who gather 'round the Camp-Fire there must be many whose trails have crossed with ours, both here and in foreign lands. In my boyhood, among some of the Chippewa tribes, I remember a custom that when any noted "brave" had departed, they held a counsel and each man rose in his place and paid fitting tribute to the dead. Would it not be possible in some future issue to have each one, who had been favored with his acquaintance, rise in his place and pay some tribute of reminiscence to the tramp who wrote the "Call of the Wild"?

Some other men have passed out in the last three years that it seems strange were not "mentioned in passing." Norman Duncan, Richard Harding Davis and Hopkinson Smith, all were men who will be missed among the circles of adventurers, but, above all, it seems to me that London is certainly entitled to some "In Memoriam."—C. R. Rollings.

P. S.—Think too, of the buried stories that would be brought to light by such a page.

AN INTERESTING word from L. Patrick Greene on his story in this issue. You already know that Mr. Greene writes of Africa from intimate knowledge and personal experience.

In my story, "The White Kaffir," which by the way is the first story I ever wrote, *Dinabantu* is a composite portrait. *Dinabantu* is, I hope, still alive; he was a good friend of mine. The judgment of Dinabantu is indeed spoken of by the natives in his district. *Umglubu the Pig* might be any one of the white men, "gone black," that I met or heard of.

It may be doubted that any man could "come back" so quickly as I have made *Umglubu;* but it is a matter of record that during the Matabele rebellion one of these unfortunate men, a White Kaffir, was instrumental in saving a number of settlers in a certain district.

The song that the young men sing is the actual war chant of the Matabele race.

I THINK I told you that a sister of our comrade Lieutenant Pat O'Brien of the Royal Flying Corps wrote me saying it was reported he had gone out on patrol on the French front and not returned and asking me to try to get some definite information. Many strange things are asked of the editor of *Adventure*, and he is not always able to do what is asked, but in that case he was not only willing but saw a chance to get what was wanted.

Our comrade Dean Ivan Lamb had, as you know, secured his discharge from the Royal Flying Corps and come back to give his services to his own country after two years' service, most of it on the French front. The next time he came into the office I told him about O'Brien and he sat right down and wrote three letters. Last night, at the Adventurers' Club dinner, he handed me a reply stating that Lieutenant O'Brien is a prisoner of war in Germany.

BUT when I first spoke to him he said, "Oh, the Germans will drop a message over our lines if they've captured him or know his fate." And, sure enough, a few days later came word from O'Brien's sister that a German flier had done just this. In this brutal war it seemed a strangely kind thing to do, particularly for a Hun. So I asked Sergeant Lamb a number of questions.

It seems that the air service is the one service in all the war that has preserved the old traditions of warfare and even added touches of extra chivalry. The airmen in many ways fight like knights of old, with every courtesy to a worthy foe. It is the established custom, when an enemy plane is shot down, to notify his friends of the airman's fate.

A single plane bears the message. It must fly in a perfectly straight line toward the enemy lines, doing no maneuvering. Sometimes it displays a white rag of some kind, but this is not necessary. The enemy planes and anti-aircraft guns, recognizing the intent, leave the messenger plane unmolested. It is understood that it must carry no camera and do nothing except deliver the message. The message is dropped and the flier returns, again holding rigidly to a straight line and again entirely unmolested.

BOTH sides do this. And both make it a point to take care of any enemy airman brought down alive within their lines —protecting him from the crowds, seeing to it that, if hurt, he receives the best attention. One of our Camp-Fire comrades saw a Zeppelin brought down over London by an incendiary bomb from an English plane above it. He said the Zeppelin had hardly hit the ground before the English birdman had landed close to it, ready to give the aid that in this case was not needed.

It is good to think about.

OTHER experienced American aviators who have come home from foreign service to serve America have come into the office, all of them with stirring tales of the war in the air and, finely enough, always with tales about other fellows, not about themselves. At least so far as anything heroic is concerned; luckily for me they have talked a little about themselves and their every-day lives over there; but not at all about their exploits except unwillingly when cornered and pumped.

INCIDENTALLY, this is a good time to kill the many and circumstantial reports of the death of Tracy Richardson, famous among adventurers as a machine-gun expert par excellence even before the Great War began. Lieutenant Bond and Lieutenant Tracy Richardson, both in the uniform of the British Naval Air Service, having both served previously with the Canadian infantry and both here to serve the United States, were in the office the other day together and Richardson was very far from dead. He had risen to the rank of major in the "Princess Pats," then transferred to the air service and, first and last (I learned from others) had been pretty well shot up, but he was decidedly all in one piece and looking for more of the same. I learned (also entirely from others) that he had earned for himself over there a reputation as one of the best machine-gun operators on either side. I asked him to give me a word direct from himself for the Camp-Fire to reassure the many who know him that he was still alive, but he sort of shied away, so I'm telling it instead.

SINCE the above was written you have probably learned through the daily newspapers that Lieutenant Pat O'Brien leaped from a moving train one night after his capture and made good his escape. He had been made prisoner in a fight with four German planes, after accounting for one of them, had been shot through the upper lip, and his machine had dropped with him some eight thousand feet. Miraculously enough, he was not killed, being taken to a German hospital and then given three weeks in a prison-camp near Courtrai. The train from which he jumped, some sixty miles inside Germany, was going about thirty miles an hour, and, besides fresh injuries, the old wound was reopened and he was knocked unconscious. But it was not yet dawn and, by another miraculous chance, he was not retaken.

For seventy-two days he was a fugitive, traveling only at night, living on what vegetables he could find still in the fields, swimming rivers and canals, through

Germany, Luxemburg and Belgium. A Belgian finally gave him old clothes to put on over his uniform and directed him on his way. At the Dutch frontier, after a bridge he had built over the electrically charged wires had collapsed and let him in for a bad shock, he succeeded in tunneling under them with his bare hands, squeezed through unobserved and—was free. The nearest British consulate sent him on to London.

HERE'S a good look-in on Indian ways and character from Hugh Pendexter in connection with his story in this issue:

The Indian's eagerness for intoxicants, his loss of reason and self-restraint once he indulged, his precaution to usually choose by lot those who were to remain sober and protect the drinkers from killing each other, suggested this story. In "Account of Remarkable Occurrences," by Col. James Smith, a Pennsylvanian, taken prisoner to Detroit by the Indians, gives an account of how drinking bouts were policed, and in part says:

> —to conceal the arms and keep every dangerous weapon we could out of their way, and endeavor, if possible, to keep the drinking club from killing each other, which was a very hard task. Several times we hazarded our own lives, and got hurt in preventing them from slaying each other.

To elevate the incident above the plane of a drunk I have introduced Pontiac and find, now the yarn's finished, that he has "stolen" the scene from Red Jennet, the white ranger. Major Gladwin (spelled Gladwyn by some) like other commanders of frontier posts, was loath to believe the English were in any danger of an uprising once they had taken over the forts from the French. He was warned twice before he could give any heed, the second warning coming the night before Pontiac's first ruse to massacre the Detroit garrison. The ball-game, *baggatiway*, was used by the allied tribes to obtain entrance to Fort Mackinaw.

Making allowance for the barbarous manner of Indian warfare Pontiac was as much of a patriot as Kosciusko; he fought to deliver his people. I'll amend that a bit; in consideration of the Hun method of waging war Pontiac was chemically clean in his methods. Incidentally, scalping (derived from an old low-German word)— was not exclusively an Indian custom. The Scythians in Herodotus's time were given to the gentle practise.

Intertribal commerce, by means of transcontinental trade routes, east to west, was as much a part of Indian life as railroad traffic is of ours. Through these routes, plus the sign language and the various trade jargons, political alliances were speedily formed, such as Pontiac's which extended from the Atlantic to the head of the Mississippi.

Ensign Holmes, who reported the arrival of a "Bloody Belt" at the Kekionga village, opposite Fort Miamis (Fort Wayne) wrote he had obtained the belt "after a long and troublesome spell with them. . . . This affair is very timely Stopt." It was a queer twist of fate that Holmes, who was more on his guard than any other frontier commander, should have been decoyed from the fort by his Indian mistress, who urged him to visit a sick woman, and be shot from ambush.

When Pontiac and his warriors visited Gladwin with sawed-off guns under their blankets the signal for the massacre was to be Pontiac's act in holding up a peace belt in *reverse* position.

The common Indian term of "stinking water" for the ocean can be changed to "big water." "Grave posts" of the Algonquian tribes often had the upper half painted red.

Pontiac was murdered by a Kaskaskia Indian at Cahokia, Illinois, in 1769, who was paid a keg of liquor by an English trader. The late Dr. Cyrus Thomas, of the Bureau of American Ethnology, in an estimate of Pontiac says, "Pontiac, if not fully the equal of Tecumseh, stands closely second to him in strength of mind and breadth of comprehension. "When Pontiac met Sir William Johnson at Oswego in July, 1767, and, speaking for the western nations, renewed his assurances of friendship, he added, in referring to his recent revolt and defeat, "He who made the Universe would have it so."

I reckon I've touched on almost everything. I forgot the Algonquian custom of ransoming prisoners with three strings or belts of wampum. I have played that up correctly, "One to loosen the cord about the feet, etc."—HUGH PENDEXTER.

HERE is a sample of the kind of "Ask Adventure" question that will not be answered and ought not to be asked. Mr. Harriman was doubly justified in refusing to reply. A man who will ask such a question of a free service and then fail to include postage to carry the answer to him is beyond words.

Please send me literature covering California, Oregon, Washington, Utah, Nevada and Arizona, covering game, fur, camp, cabin, mines, minerals, mountains and homesteading.——— ——

Letters like this can not be answered, since they are fired at the general landscape, not at any one target or group of targets. I am always ready to do my best in answering any legitimate question, but the question or questions must be definite. This is too much like saying "Tell me everything you know and do it quick. I must catch a train in half an hour." Most men who ask questions like this carefully omit stamps, as in this case, and are therefore not entitled to answers.—E. E. H.

A LETTER from a man on the British front in France, a young friend of our comrade E. E. Harriman to whom the letter is written:

I was delighted to get your letter and am answering right away as we go into action again in a couple days. I took the liberty of showing your letter to my pals. They were "tickled to death" and our scouts will use your trick. Thank you much.

This is an Imperial and not a Canadian regiment. We're the chaps who came over at the very beginning, knowing just how big the job was and is proving to be. We're all from overseas and we have in our ranks quite a few from the U. S. I must thank you for writing my wife. It was a nice thought! As the war has lasted so long we are having simple "Hell" to make ends meet and keep our little home together on the army pay and allowance. Neither she or our little girl is in good health, so you see how I appreciate any cheering thought conveyed to her. I'm very much in love, I confess.

You're doing your duty, Mr. Harriman, stick to it! I knew those Boches in the States would give you trouble when you declared war. You have a big job at home, I know, but show them no quarter. Believe me, and I speak simply as a soldier ready at any time to face his God, they have proved themselves entirely unworthy of it. I hope you get this note and reply to it. I should like to keep up the friendship and make your acquaintance some day. . . . . Sincere regards and "carry on."——— ——

MAYBE the Camp-Fire might have some mild interest in how our magazine is made. Ours is a meeting-place for readers, writers and adventurers but we editors feel we are just as much members as anybody else, and maybe the rest of you would like to know about some of the things in our little field. I'll give 'em to you in small doses. There's nothing adventurous in them but, after all, the magazine belongs to all of us in a way and you may like to know more about its inside workings.

WHERE do our stories come from? It would take long to answer geographically and you already have some idea of that from what our writers tell us when they enter our writers' brigade. Our stories are selected out of a pretty large number of candidates. From 5,000 to 6,000 short stories, novelettes, novels and serials come to us every year. During 1917 they ranged from 358 to 598 a month. In addition there were poems to the extent of from 54 to 112 a month.

No, we don't read them all clear through. We can't. There wouldn't be time for anything else, and reading MSS. is only a part of the poor editors' work.

Personally, I seldom have time to read MSS. at the office. Take 'em home—nights and Sundays and generally Saturdays (the office closes at one on Saturdays) and, when they pile up, Wednesdays also are sometimes spent at home reading stories. Mr. Wade also reads a good many at home evenings and Sundays. Mr. Bittner and Mr. Clayton are kept too busy with copy-reading and proof-reading two hundred and sixty-odd thousand words every month and attending to other little chores like that to read MSS. except on occasion.

NO, WE can't read all of them clear through. Very many of them don't need more than a very little reading to show that they are unavailable. Some of these almost any one would know were unavailable; to detect the rest of these unavailables doesn't require any particular amount of brains but it does take considerable experience. Just as many of you can tell a poor horse without taking him all apart or a poor canoe without paddling a hundred miles in it. But on the other hand there are a good many stories that are read word for word from beginning to end, often by two, three or all four of us. I am the goat and all MSS. come to my desk first.

MAYBE some of you think life would be one happy dream if all the work you had to do were reading stories. I used to think that. Some of them it is a pleasure to read; even many besides the 4 per cent. we find available. But a large part of the unavailable 96 per cent., well, they become a bit monotonous after a while, even though a carefully worked-out system of informing writers as to our exact needs probably keeps some thousands of other unsuitable stories from coming in to us. In spite of all warnings and pleas and in spite of the masculine character of our magazine itself there are lots of women who are convinced we want stories opening with Miss Gwendolyn Panderbilt Tish in her boudoir or the well-known clubman and society leader Algernon Tryvial Tush being real haughty to his valet, or sweet Gracie or romantic Ethelinda hanging over the garden wall or something and talking a specially sickening version of love's young dream to some kind of adventurer that never happened.

But I didn't start to tell you our troubles. That's enough for this time.

SOME of you may not hitherto have come across the following bit of information:

To put "the fear of God" into Boche hearts, United States Marines in training here are practising the old-time rebel yell. Confederate veterans, who take keen interest in the activities of the sea-soldiers, are teaching the boys their battle-cry.

YOU AND DEMOCRACY

I DO not know whether what follows is for you or not. Probably not, for the test is a severe one and only a small minority can pass it.

For nearly ten years all my time and strength that could justly be spared after my regular work was done has gone to one thing. The only exception was that I put this one thing partly aside to work for national defense because the need for every worker was very keen.

The first stage of this work is now done. The rest of it is your work as well as mine. Some of you will not do your share, for there are always the shirkers, the unfit and those who sleep. That means that the rest of us shall have to do more than our share. For the work must be done, and there is no one but ourselves to do it.

IT WILL not be easy work. You will not be paid for doing it nor will you make money from it in any other way. You will find that it takes more time than you like to spare. It will raise up enemies against you, though only the kind of enemies a man can be proud to have earned. It will not bring you fame. None of you will live to see the work completed, yet those who take up this work must keep on with it all their lives. You will be working for others rather than yourself, and often these others will not thank you for it. You will be giving rather than getting. It will be a grim fight, most of the time dull and dreary, and we shall not be alive when the full victory is won. I offer you only the promise that it will be a good fight and that if we are strong and brave we shall die unbeaten, knowing that we have not fought in vain and that others will carry on our battle.

You adventurers who face death so bravely in all the nooks and crannies of the world, have you the guts and staying powers to take on another kind of adventure, one in which you carry no arms, in which you have monotony instead of change, in which there is little excitement and much work? You stay-at-homes, have you the spirit to accept an adventure at your own doors, an adventure that will change the placid current of your lives and give you much trouble where you had none before?

I DO not paint the work as easy. Nor do I wish to make it sound so hard that the reckless spirits will take it up in mere bravado. Only the steadfast are wanted. Only those who will forget themselves in working for something bigger than themselves. If the task is not to your liking, you need read no farther. Turn away now.

I can hardly even outline the work to you in this first brief presentation. It is definitely and fully mapped out, but it can not be compressed into a small space. I can not prove to you here and now that it has been correctly mapped out, but I ask nothing final of you until it *is* proved to your satisfaction.

Of the very few who know anything whatever about it and have endorsed it you know only these—Talbot Mundy, Henry Oyen, Arthur D. Howden Smith. It is the kind of work for which you would expect as sponsors the best-known men in the United States before it would seem worth your considering. It has none of them as sponsors. They may come later, or they may not. I have not tried to get any of them. I turn to you of the Camp-Fire first. There is no intention of flattery. You are of all kinds, good and bad, great and small. But I have come to know many of you and to feel much closer to you than to people in general, and I have found among you many who are the type wanted for this work. For years I have, unknown to you, been filing away very carefully the names of those of you who seemed most ready and best fitted, but I am presenting the plan to all of you at the same time.

I GIVE here only the general nature and purpose of the plan, without any attempt to make it sound as if it were assured of success or a cure for all ills. I believe in it with my whole heart, but if you believed in it before you had examined into it very thoroughly I should be sure that you were not the kind of man who is most needed for the work. I want volunteers to stand side by side with me and fight this thing through, but it's not mere numbers that are needed; it's the *right kind.* And the right kind are not those who go into a thing until they know just what that thing is. This isn't a joy-ride; it's hard, thankless work and I want the quitters to quit before they begin.

I want the plan to sound worse than it is, not better, and the worst sound I can give it is to call it a reform movement. We're all rather sick of reform movements and have pretty well lost faith in them. I want only those who still have faith enough to fight for what is right and who are so eager to fight for it that they will look carefully into every chance, however slight it may seem at first glance.

In the beginning I give you at least a few assurances. The plan is constructive, not destructive. It is evolutionary, not revolutionary. It begins at the bottom, deals with roots, not branches.

THE plan does not center about me. It will not be like most reform movements, for no part of its strength will be devoted to advertising its originator or any one else connected with it. The insane desire for personal prominence on the part of those who should have been bending all their efforts to further the work itself instead of themselves has been the rock that has wrecked most similar movements. There will be no such rock here. I use "I" freely, for that is the direct way of talking to a man and I am very much in earnest, but I'm asking you to help the work, not me. The plan has to do with public affairs, but I have no political ambitions. As to money, it is likely to leave my purse emptier, not fuller.

THE war has only intensified the growing unrest in the United States. What internal troubles will come to us after the war no man knows, but only a fool thinks there will be none or that they are not likely to shake us to our foundations. The war has already done us one service—it has forced us to see many problems and internal dangers that we could not or would not see before. That is all the war has to do with the following plan.

IF A man can not see the bad conditions in this country or the growing internal dangers that threaten us, if he is blind to the meaning of the increasing unrest among us, to the danger of our political corruption, to the menace of bitter class antagonism and of so much poverty in a country so rich, there is not time now to make him see.

But if you are not blind to the threatening problems that confront our country, I ask whether you can subscribe to the following creed:

WHEN people join together to form a nation or community they give up to it certain of their individual rights in order to get back from it things they value more than what they give up. They make themselves as a body supreme over themselves as individuals, always retaining the right to change or unmake, but only in accordance with the rules they have themselves laid down.

The American nation is the American people. Whatever it has we gave to it—liberty, justice, customs, land, property. Whatever it does is really done by the men, women and children who *are* the nation. Whatever it is or is not, it is we who make it so. If we are good citizens, it will be good; if we are bad citizens, it will be bad.

I am part of that nation, for I am one of the people. If I am a good citizen, I help make it good; if I am a bad citizen, I help make it bad. If I neglect to do my full duty as a citizen, I rob the nation of part of itself.

All the power of the United States of America, all control over it, really lies in the hands of the American people, in *our* hands. It is our own fault if we do not use our power and control and use them rightly.

OUR Government is only rules laid down by us and citizens chosen by us from among ourselves to manage our nation for us according to these rules of ours. Since we the people are the ones who make these rules and choose these officers, it is always we ourselves who are responsible for what they are and for what they do. If they are bad, it is always our fault at bottom and when we complain about them we are only complaining about ourselves, for we made the rules and chose the men and the real power over them is always in our hands.

We make our laws and choose our officers by majority rule, for democracy is rule by the people, and the will of the people as a whole can be determined only by following what most of the people want. Democracy is rule by the many, by the vote of the people as a whole. Whenever we allow the few to control the many, at primaries, conventions, elections, in Congress, State legislatures or anywhere else, or even to obstruct or postpone the will of the many, we have, by our weakness or neglect, injured our country and have struck a blow at the very heart of democracy itself.

A MAN or woman chosen by us as a public officer of any kind is merely our agent employed and entrusted by us to carry out our wishes and to protect our interests. If he fails to do this he is either inefficient or dishonest. If, in any matter great or small, he ever puts personal interest, party interest or any other interest before the interest of the people he represents, he has betrayed his trust. The public official who breaks his oath of office or violates the rights or property of the people is not merely a "grafter" or a "politician," but a liar and a perjurer, a thief, a prostitute and as much a traitor to his country as was Benedict Arnold. He has what is worse than the "yellow streak;" he has that infinitely dirtier and more shameful thing, the "black streak."

We ourselves are responsible for his treason, for we chose him. But ours is also the fundamental power and the everlasting duty to punish him. We have forgotten our power, but it is there. We have forgotten our duty, but it is there. His crime is against the whole people, against democracy, and is therefore greater than ordinary crime and deserves heavier punishment. "Graft" and "pull" and the "black streak" are not only the dirtiest words in our language but the most dangerous, for they mean rottenness in the very heart and core of our national being.

WE BELIEVE that the only permament and far-reaching remedy for our country's ills is better citizenship. You can not build a good house out of rotten bricks. Democracy, republicanism, socialism, monarchy, rule of capital, rule of labor, whatever form of government you please, will be rotten if the bricks from which it is builded are rotten, if its citizens are bad citizens.

We believe that citizenship can be systematically taught, in our schools and elsewhere, as easily as religion, manners, sociology, economics, Greek and physiology are taught, and that until this fundamental reform is put into operation all other reforms are but attempts to carry water in a sieve.

We believe that citizenship means obligation as well as privilege, and that the American citizen who takes without giving is a thief, a hog and a traitor.

We believe that all our country's hopes for the future are entirely dependent upon the establishment of clean, strong, alert citizenship among the American people.

We believe that the only way to establish this new standard of citizenship is through the union and concentrated endeavor of America's best citizens, working together along definite lines toward definite ends.

And we believe there are enough good citizens in the United States who can and will join in such a movement to give that movement a power and force that can not be resisted.

IF YOU can not subscribe to this creed, there is no need to read farther. But if you can subscribe to it, subscribe to it fully and earnestly, and are ready to work for it, I want you to say so and to send me your name and address by letter or post-card. It will not be published. It will bind you in no way. Word it in any way you please. All I wish is to know which ones of you are ready to work hard and faithfully for better American citizenship *if* I can give you a plan of campaign that meets your approval and convinces you that it can succeed.

Little by little, as space permits, I will give you the details of the plan. I make no large promises. I have no financial backing, no great men for sponsors. At this writing there is not yet even the nucleus of an organization. Just a plan, a definite, fully worked out plan that has grown slowly into final shape after ten long years of hard work and has won the endorsement of the very few who have seen it.

PERSONALLY, of course, I believe in it as firmly as I believe that 2 plus 2 equals 4, but most people believe in their own plans. You are not asked to believe in it or to subscribe to it in advance. You are asked only to register yourself as willing and ready to join in such a plan *if* it convinces you, to write down your name as an American who is ready to do his part for America's present and America's future as soon as he finds what seems to him a practical opportunity to make his work count.

I do not expect a great many names, but those that do come in will be the names of men worth while. And these are what is needed. Money, sponsors, organization, those will come easily enough. Almost any kind of movement can get them. But the names of worth-while men are hard to get, and they are the one solid foundation upon which to build. This will not be a paper organization. It will mean real Americans really united for real citizenship.

There are many of you to whom I could appeal on grounds of friendship or of service rendered, but I do not keep books against my friends and this is not a personal matter. It is primarily a matter between you and your country, between you and real democracy. I enter into it only if I am able to furnish a plan of action that you are willing to follow, and only to ask you to work with me, not for me.

AND even if there were no plan already mapped out, those of you who think most carefully will see the immense value and possibilities of getting anywhere a list of all those Americans, of all classes, who believe in the need of better American citizenship and are ready to band together to secure it for America.

To all such Americans, men or women, I do make earnest appeal. There is much at stake for us and for our children and our children's children. Every man of us is needed and already too much time has slipped away. Act, and act now! Get your friends to act. After all, it is very little that is asked and it pledges you to nothing but your duty, as *you* see it, to your country. Send in your name. But not unless you are in earnest. If you are fully ready to stop grumbling over conditions and start to setting them right and keep on setting them right, send in your name. If you are so opposed to political and economic corruption that you are willing to work and keep on working for better things, send in your name. If you know that the future of America and of democracy in America depends entirely upon what her citizens do for America and if you are ready to do not only your own share but that of shirkers as well, send in your name. You are needed.

ARTHUR SULLIVANT HOFFMAN.

SOME of you know "The Ace," but probably very few of you know who he is. Anyhow, he has been helping others and now he's asking others to help him a little. I've already put him in touch with one or two who can tell him something, but others of you can add still more and all of us of the Camp-Fire would like to hear as well.

In glancing over a few back numbers of *Adventure* I find some articles on some of our good old scouts of the earlier days. One of them refers to Wild Bill Hikok. Now I wonder if the gentleman who gave out the information could furnish me with a little more of Hikok's history? I would be more than thankful to him as I have an Indian tom-tom amongst my collection of curios, which Hikok got during a battle with Indians under the famous Chief Geronimo. It is the last tom-tom to which the chief ever danced a war-dance. It was presented to me by my father who was made a very good offer for it in Omaha, Nebraska. I wonder if some of our readers could furnish me with some interesting facts about Chief Geronimo?

I also have a pair of moccasins worn by Rain-in-the-face. Is he the man who killed General Custer?

P. S.—I wish you would furnish me with one of your Identification-Tags, which I think is a very good thing for a person to have on him at all times, although I still bear my U. S. Army tag. It was while in the service of our Uncle Sam, last Summer, that I had the name of "The Ace" attached to me. Of course this is rather a long story and I will probably tell it to you some other time if you are interested. There are a few little things that I am doing toward trying to make things easier for our boys now in service, therefore, I use the name of "The Ace" and I ask you kindly not to give out my true name, as I am not out for notoriety.—"THE ACE."

FROM Indianapolis comes a letter on Tiburon Island that isn't likely to lure anybody into going to that rather inacessible and much-discussed region. Just the other day one of you wrote in about Tiburon and I did what I could to discourage him from going there.

While looking through *Adventure* the other evening, in search of something that I might have missed, I ran across the plea from a Hollander for assistance.

Don't you know, Mr. Hoffman, that the average man is just like a cow? The grass is always greenest in the next pasture; the mines are always best in the next range of hills; in the most inaccessible places are the best placers, and so on.

I wish that it were possible for me to let the entire world know and that the people thereof would believe me as regards Tiburon Island. It would save a lot of unnecessary suffering. In the first place, there is no gold, silver or precious stones on the island. I have been over it from end to end, and in the party were ten Yaqui Indians, than whom there are no better prospectors in Mexico, and one Mexican, by name J. M. Villavecencia. We found nothing of value in any form on the island. We saw a number of the Seri Indians, and they are the most God-forsaken, degraded lot of humans that exist on this globe. We found quite a number of small white-tail deer, rabbits, quail and coyote and this completes the list.

If there are any that want to go to the island, let they go to Guaymas, Sonora; there they can engage any of the numerous Yaqui boatmen and go to El Baril, in Lower California; then across the Gulf of California (distance from El Baril about eighty miles). At El Baril they will find Villavecencia has quite a stock of goods, and he will fit them out at a reasonable figure, and the sail from there can be made in a night, and with safety. The trip from the Southern Pacific Railway in Sonora can, in this way, be overcome and, believe me, the trip across the Altar Desert is no child's play. Perhaps that trip is all that makes the adventurer want to see Tiburon. What think you?

Hoping that this may save some fellow a lot of trouble and worry.— ——— ——— ———.

THE Adventurers' Club of New York has improved its patriotic record since last reported to you. There are forty-five stars on its service-flag and the exact membership was a hundred and seventy-six, not a hundred and eighty.

ARTHUR SULLIVANT HOFFMAN.

PIRATES. Somehow we never lose our interest in these picturesque old hellions, and Stephen Chalmers's pirate story in this number gains extra interest from the man of God it pictures in their midst and from the fact that there really was a priest of the same name who became famous through his fearless handling of them, his immunity from harm at their hands and his remarkable influence over them. Hear what Mr. Chalmers writes us about him:

Like my Admiral in "Admiral of the Line," published in *Adventure* some time ago, Pere Labat is based on a real character. In fact, his name was Pere Labat—not Père, but a form, I think, of Pierre.

HE WAS the missonary-priest of the West Indies about a hundred years before the period in which I set him in order to bring in the anomalous position of the Gentlemen of the Sea and Knights of the Caribbee when Charles, Philip and Morgan turned the trick on them.

But he *was* the man I have tried in this tale to regalvanize into life. The description of his visit to the Isle of Santos is just the sort of thing he did all the time and, as I say, he was loved and honored by Indians, Spaniards, buccaneers, English adventurers, governors, slaves, etc., for the good he did. And he was absolutely without fear. The incident of the Mass aboard the pirate ship is true (it is referred to in Kingsley's "At Last" and Anthony Froude's "English in the West Indies") and, if I mistake not, it was held on this same Red Daniel's ship right in the bay of Los Santos. I did not think it advisable to use it largely, merely referring to the incident of the shooting of Jerry O'Chagres and substituting for the priestly ceremonial the marriage of a buccaneer to his mistress.

TOUCHING on the Catholic feeling of reverence for the priest in fiction, there is a priest in the Adirondacks with whom I am well acquainted. He himself is a modern Pere Labat. He recently celebrated his twenty-fifth anniversary; and you know what this region was twenty-five years ago—a wilderness full of trappers, lumberjacks and breeds. Father ...... won that element. Ten years ago his first real church was burned to the ground and what was built on the same spot is an edifice that seems rather to belong to a city than a backwoods village. The interior is that of a cathedral, and Father ...... is beloved of his mighty flock.

I took the tale of Pere Labat to him. When he assimilated it, he said to me. "I can well understand it. He was the sort of priest who was necessary in the time, condition and place. If your tale is based on facts, let us thank God there *was* such a priest and that he did what he did, even"— his eyes glowed—"to shooting the pirate who committed sacrilege. Anything to offend the Catholic Church? No, rather Pere Labat is something to be proud of!"

My priestly friend, however, had no personal knowledge of Pere Labat—had never heard of him, but he has since procured all the available data he can get on the subject, so great has been his interest in the man.

IT SEEMS to me right that he should be resurrected in a tale, for he is forgotten by all but a few. He wrote books, as I have described, but copies are rare. There is one in the Jamaica Institute (West Indies) highly treasured among the archives of the buccaneers. It was there I first made his acquaintance and later I had a personal hour or two with him while I sat astride an old, dismantled gun in the sand at Port Royal, close by Gallows Point. I am personally acquainted with Pere Labat!

There is also a copy of his work in the New York Public Library, I am told. It is in French, I believe; so was the one in the West Indian archives. Has it ever been translated, I wonder. If not, there's a great opportunity for somebody.—STEPHEN CHALMERS.

WHAT Michael Williams says about Tiburon Island will be particularly interesting to many of you. Also he is quite right in denying the second trip to Tiburon with which we credited him in good faith but erroneously:

New York.

I have recently returned to New York from California, and a friend has called my attention to a paragraph in your "Ask Adventure" department referring to Tiburon Island and quoting me as saying that I had recently returned from a second visit to that island, and that the island is entirely deserted by the Seri Indians. There is an error here. I did visit Tiburon in 1911, and many other parts of the Gulf of California, and in 1914 I returned to the West Coast as war correspondent with Admiral Howard's fleet during the Huerta-Carranza revolution, but I did not then go further up the Gulf than Santa Rosalia and La Paz. I do not like to be put in the position of appearing to claim knowledge (or adventures) which I do not really possess, and perhaps you will kindly correct this erroneous report.

AS TO Tiburon itself, as your Mr. Harriman says, the stories about the cannibalism of the Seris are moonshine, together with other weird legends concerning temples and strange tribes. The Seirs, like many savages, have eaten human flesh during famine times—but so have highly civilized folks, for that matter. As to the riches of Tiburon, that is still an unsettled question. On the Isla de la Guardia Angele, just opposite Tiburon, which I also visited, oil in huge quantities, I understand, has recently been struck. But I missed it—probably because I was looking for romance, not wealth. But what I sought after, that I discovered; and I'd rather have a life rich in real adventure than any amount of oil stock.

CURIOUSLY enough, just as I happen upon this reference to my visit to the famous island (one-tenth of its great romance has never been told), I am in the midst of a novel entitled, "The Treasure of Tiburon."

It deals with the vast wealth in pearls and church gold gathered by the brother of Oliver Cromwell, the Dictator of England, who, according to legends on the West Coast, was one of the most successful of the English pirates who once upon a time harried the West Coast, capturing the Spanish galleons. He buried this treasure on or near Tiburon Island, calculating that the infamous reputation of its Indians would serve to protect it. I believe I may claim, with all willingness to drop the claim if it is not true, that I am the only *professional* writer who knows the strange waters of the Gulf of California from personal observation.—MICHAEL WILLIAMS.

CONCERNING his tale of the North in this issue Robert Russell Strang gives some interesting facts. Also on some general conditions in Alaska:

The following incident was responsible for "Christmas Eve in Sulphur Flats." The real name of the camp is ——, on Lower Dominion Creek, and it took place Christmas Eve, 1905.

THIS particular woman, who shall be nameless because she is still living in ——, went into partnership with a man in a roadhouse on the trail between —— and ——. This woman, who was separated from her husband, had a beautiful daughter aged seventeen. She herself was not over thirty-six, was an artist and photographer, and an intelligent and broad-minded woman to boot. The man in the case I judge was close to forty. One night he and the girl got into a sled and rushed to Dawson and got married. This woman had spent a lot of money on her daughter's education, and she felt it badly. On discovering what had happened she threw a can of coal-oil over a corner of the roadhouse, threw a lighted candle into it and stood by while it burned to the ground.

SHORTLY afterward she formed a Klondike alliance with a man (she was afraid of her husband who lived in —— and who had frequently threatened her) and, of course, all the "respectable" women got down on her. A week before Christmas the committee sent her a letter telling her to stay away from future dances.

Christmas Eve came around. After the Christmas-tree was disposed of and the hall cleared for the dance this woman, dressed to kill, walked alone into the hall, took off her wraps, and there, pinned across her breast with nugget brooches was the committee's letter. For some time the air was electrically tense. But she had *Mrs. Hauksbee* skinned a mile, and the men fought to dance with her. She stayed pat on her victory. Understand, it was a woman's war, and—but, enough said.

IN THE Winter of '02 and '03 I was working a lease on No. 2 Goldbottom Creek (Bob Henderson's original discovery) in the Dawson country. I was in the bar of the Goldbottom hotel one night when ——, the lucky Swede, drove up in a double-horse cutter. He was on his way home to Whisky Hill, three miles farther up Hunker from where Goldbottom flows into it. He entered the barroom, made every man there a present of a bottle of wine, serving them himself, then had a case of Mumm's Extra Dry dumped into two water-pails, with which he watered his horses. Then he signed a check for $750 and resumed his way.

This was the same —— who gave a girl named —— her weight in gold to marry him. —— was a dance hall girl in Dawson. She stayed with him about a week after the ceremony. Last time I saw —— was over in the Tanana country. He was rustling a grub-stake. He could have got away with $2,000,000.

THEN there was Jerome C—— who had the millionaire habit—that is, before coming to the Dawson country he had made and unmade millions in other lines. He and another man controlled about thirty claims on Gold Run Creek. In the private poker games at night a white chip was worth $100, a blue one $1,000. Claim No. 27 was extremely rich. It was so rich that the creek storekeeper once remarked that "because of Jerome's men he couldn't keep a gold sack in the store." Hearing of this, Jerome C—— went down and told him "it was none of his —— —— business if the men helped themselves in the drift," but he drew the line at the sluice-boxes. Actually, I have known men to walk away from 27 Gold Run who were ashamed to ask for their wages. One man had the impudence to offer Jerome C—— $500 for a job for a month. The gold was "coarse."

Jerome is dead and, being a pioneer myself, I will not say what his financial condition was at that time. I could easily fill a book with such anecdotes.—ROBERT R. STRANG.

I PROMISED to give you a letter from W. Townend, written five years ago, explaining, so far as it can be explained, the mystery in his story in our last issue, "Mr. Harrington's Wife." Here is the letter:

Well, I scarcely know how to begin. But perhaps I'll ask you a question first of all. Did you ever read Kipling's story: "Mrs. Bathurst?" I suppose you know it. Well, have you a solution as to why *Vickery* went up country and never came back? I haven't. I've read that story many times and I am as far off a solution as ever. The story gripped me, puzzled me and interested me beyond any other story I have read for a long time. But why? I couldn't exactly tell.

SO SOME time ago I jotted down the outline of a story which was, if possible, to have the same effect on the reader as "Mrs. Bathurst" had on me. I wanted to try and depict the state of mind of a man whose marriage is the great mystery in his life. He does not know how it came about, or why the girl ever wanted to marry or for what reason she left him, and he broods and wonders. You see, *Harrington* knows the events of the few months of his married life as he saw them; the causes that led to those events he can only guess at vaguely.

What I aimed at doing was to try and transmit his feelings to the reader. In other words, I wanted the reader to put down the story, saying: "But why on earth did she want to marry him? Why did she leave him?"

Is this a legitimate aim?

THE idea of the story as it first occurred to me was this: The girl marries *Harrington* to prevent another marriage forced upon her by circumstances which are not essential to the story. The reader, however, knows about the man with the "shadow of hell on his face," the old gentleman, and the tall, stern lady who heard the news of the marriage with such anger and amazement, and also the old nurse who "never took to" *Harrington* and knew what he was.

The old gentleman and the stern lady want *Norah* to marry the other man; *Norah* refuses and finds *Harrington* only too eager to marry her; the old nurse despises *Harrington* as being of a lower "caste," yet falls in with the plan as being the lesser of two evils. The old gentleman and the stern lady are the girl's guardians.

NORAH did not love *Harrington* at first; she respected him, of course, knowing that he was straight and honest in spite of being more or less of a blackguard—tough, at any rate (his people were fairly good). So she marries him, reckless of consequences, glad to be able to checkmate the other three. Then gradually her feelings change; the baby is gone and she sees herself as unworthy of the man she married; she hates herself for what she has done, and in a kind of remorse at having made use of *Harrington*, with no feeling of love, vanishes. Later, when it is too late, love comes. She sees *Harrington* as the only man, after all; but she has thrust him out of her life forever.

This may absolutely ruin my chances of getting the story taken, because you may have had ideas of a different nature altogether. I hope not, of course. And I feel that it would be a great error, if not complete ruin, to explain anything more fully in the story than I have written.

NOT even to you, do I attempt to explain the real relations of the other man, the old gentleman and the lady, with *Norah;* nor the way in which *Norah* disappeared from the village near Cardiff, nor the hint of the other man, *i.e.*, the first man once more, and the shadow of coming tragedy.

But, I have added a few lines in *Norah's* letter which will explain things a trifle. So I have retyped page nineteen of the story—the last page—and in its stead enclose you pages nineteen and twenty, which please substitute, using your own judgment, of course.

I have not liked having to explain so fully, because I feel that I am spoiling everything. But, surely, if I have succeeded in making you and Mr. Olds wonder at the real mystery, haven't I done the same for the ordinary reader? If every story ended in a mystery, then I should say, "Mr. H.'s Wife" needed clearing up. As it stands, though, is anything else necessary?

Have not expressed myself well, I know. For this I am sorry and hope you will take into consideration the difficulty of the task.—W. TOWNEND.

AT THIS writing our comrade of both our readers' and our writers' brigades, Dr. J. U. Giesy, is in hospital recovering from an operation which will improve his chances of being accepted for service at the front. He had made two attempts and went under the knife solely to ensure the success of a third attempt. Not subject to draft, either. Just wants to leave a good practise and a fine opportunity in the writing field in order to serve his country. He is hardly what you'd call a slacker, is he? And for several years before we went into the war he was, as many of you know, working full steam for training camps and all other measures looking to national Preparedness.

WITH his first story in *Adventure* Samuel Edward Harris becomes a member of our writers' brigade as well as of our readers' brigade and follows Camp-Fire custom by introducing himself to all of us:

Born in Key West, I left for New York when I was twenty-one to reside in the "literary center" of the country. Shortly after my arrival, I started to do newspaper work, covering the Rockaways for several Manhattan and Brooklyn newspapers.

I HAVE had quite a few adventures traveling through the Florida Keys. One occurred six years ago, when a dingey, with a leg-o'-mutton sail, in which were Frank Roberts, who is now a local alderman; Claude Albury, who sells stamps for Uncle Sam, and I, capsized out in Caldias Channel, four miles offshore. We had aboard one hundred and fifty fish, including several large Spanish mackerel. Albury, a two-hundred-and-twenty-pounder and as good-natured as he is big, had hoisted the sail and was lumbering aft when he attempted to poke me in the ribs with his thumb. I drew back, Albury stepped on a mackerel and slipped, landing on the boom of the boat, capsizing her instantly.

Now, Albury couldn't swim, and as the boom and sail were carrying the boat to the bottom I took off my glasses and gave them to him to hold while I dived to unstep the mast. I went down four times before I succeeded in doing so. As soon as I removed the mast the bow of the dingey bobbed suddenly to the surface, and Albury, in his excitement, grabbed the stern with the hand in which he held my glasses. When I asked him to pass them to me, he held up, between his thumb and forefinger, a piece of lens about as large as a grunt scale. I don't believe in cussing unless circumstances justifies one in cussing. . . . I felt better afterward.

WE WERE overboard but a few minutes when scores of sharks began circling 'round us, devouring the fish we had caught. I think I'm safe in saying that sharks are the only things in this world that Roberts is afraid of, and the instant he caught sight of their dorsal fins he struggled to get into the boat. But his efforts were futile—the boat was filled to the scuppers with water. I consoled him somewhat by assuring him that the only thing necessary to drive away a shark was to clap one's hand upon the water, the resultant sound below the surface resembling the loudest thunder. Pretty soon Roberts was clapping his hands on the water every minute or two.

One big, sulky fellow, nearly as long as our dingey, swam drowsily near me. I pounded the surface, and he shot through the water like a torpedo, outlining his wake a few feet behind him.

We were in the water from at least 12:23—the time my watch stopped—until sunset, five hours later.

AFTER having been in the water several hours we succeeded in swimming the dingey to a bank about a mile and a half in back of Mangrove Key, which is a mile from the Key West shore, and using our hands and one oxford (we had lost our other shoes and our hats also) bailed out the dingey and started to scull for shore. Roberts had been sculling about ten minutes and we were still congratulating one another when Roberts espied on the bank the sail and mast, which we had cast adrift. We put the mast in place again and got under way for Key West, where we arrived bedraggled and well-nigh exhausted.—Samuel Edward Harris.

LETTER-FRIENDS BACK HOME

A Free Service Department for American, Canadian, and Other Allied Soldiers, Sailors, Marines and Others in Camp or at the Front.

Any one in the United States or Allied service who wishes to brighten the time with letters from "back home," or wherever else this magazine circulates, and with the personal touch and interest of hitherto unknown friends, can secure these letters and these friends by sending us his name and military address to be published once in this department as soon as censorship of soldiers' foreign addresses permits. Among our readers of both sexes, all classes and from all parts of the world, he is likely to gain a number of friendly, personal correspondents. He is free to answer only such as he is comfortably able to answer under the conditions that surround him, and it is even suggested that the number of correspondents for any one man be determined by the needs of his comrades as well as by his own.

This magazine, of course, assumes no responsibility other than the publishing of these names and addresses as its space will permit. Experience has shown that the service offered is a very real and needed one, and all not themselves in service are asked to do their part in making the daily life of those fighting in our defense brighter and pleasanter through personal friendships across the intervening miles and by whatever personal, human kindnesses such friendships may suggest.

When giving your military address make it as permanent a one as possible.

(As the magazine is made up several months in advance, the above notice will appear with only such stray names as happen to come in to us until there has been time for it to reach the camps and the front and for names and addresses to reach us, be put in type and then reach our readers on publication.)

HERE'S something for us from an old-timer. We surely like to hear from them:

You say "talk, don't be a clam." All right, listen. I have often wanted to talk when I saw some of the old-timers' names mentioned in *Adventure*, but I never can find any one to talk to about them. Now I am going to punish you, you're "it."

I WENT to Dodge City, Kansas, in '78; went to work for Bob Wright and Jim Langton; they were the "post traders," running the store at Fort Dodge. Bob Wright was good to me, consequently anything I read about him was interesting to me.

I was at Vernon, Texas, when it was called Eagle Flats. Ule Music, the first sheriff of Wilbarger County, was killed. The court appointed Tom Stewart in his place. Tom did not suit some of the people, so they had him ousted and A. T. Boyer appointed. Tom didn't oust worth a ——, so we had two sheriffs and everybody was a deputy.

I was one among the first boys (I was only sixteen years old) Mr. Boyer appointed deputy. We had a lovely time around that little frame court-house for a few days and nights. There was something doing all the time. The Rangers were the only hope of bringing order out of chaos. The nearest company of Rangers was on the head of Elm Creek, one hundred or one hundred and twenty-five miles northwest of Vernon. Some one had to go after them, of course it was me—I always was lucky.

WE DID not want Stewart and his boys to know I was going after the Rangers, so I had to make some kind of a stall to get out of town. I found two cowboys that were going to Done's store on Red River that afternoon and I saddled up and rode out of town with them. After I left Done's store on Red River it was about one hundred miles across the prairie "northwest on the head of Elm Creek"—that was all the directions they gave me, but I got there all right. Presented my credentials to Captain Smith, was given my supper and put to bed. Some time that night I was awakened, given another supper and we started back to Vernon. Did some riding, boy, believe me.

Things were pretty quiet when we got back to Vernon. Some of the boys told me later that they found out I had gone after the Rangers.

A SHORT time after this I helped Judge Riddle get out an issue of the *Vernon Guard*. While the editor, B. Wilson Edgel, was away on business, some of the Rangers guarded us while we were geting out the paper—in fact, some of them slept and ate in that little newspaper office. The editor wasn't very popular with Mr. Tom Stewart.

Oh, yes, somebody got killed once in a while, but that isn't so very long ago and it might hurt some one's feeling to mention names. Anyway we were "making history" and that's been the death of many a man. I will now offer my signature—the only one any old-timer in that country would recognize—"PEAS RIVER."

WE are all grateful to Hugh Pendexter for the "dope" he gives us on the American Indians of the early days in connection with his stories concerning them. There is much in what follows that not only adds interest to the tale he tells but gives us a far better understanding of the Red Man, who made our frontier period a long record of danger and heroic deeds:

In four of the various Winter counts (Dakota Indians' chronology) the year 1843-44 is designated by the recapture of the great medicine arrow of the Cheyenne. White Shield's Winter count for the Winter says the Dakotas captured the arrow from the Pawnees after a great battle, the Pawnees having taken it from the Cheyenne.

BATTISTE GOOD'S count for the same year (see 10th Report of Bureau of American Ethnology):

> "Brought-home-the-magic-arrow Winter. This arrow originally belonged to the Cheyenne, from whom the Pawnees stole it. The Dakotas captured it this Winter, and the Cheyennes then redeemed it for one hundred horses.
>
> "According to the Winter count of American-Horse, the arrow was recovered from the Pawnees by the Oglalas and Brules and returned to its rightful owners, no mention of any horses being made."

IN the enclosed story I have made the Arikara the thieves, as they traded corn to the Cheyenne for buffalo-robes. According to James Mooney, of the B. A. E., in his article on the Cheyenne, Bulletin 30, Part I, there were four of these medicine or magic arrows, each of a different color. The set "constitutes the tribal palladium which they claim to have had from the beginning of the world. The same authority says that when the two sections of the tribe separated in 1851 the arrows were preserved by the Southern Cheyenne. The public ceremony of "exposing" the arrows was performed as late as 1904, says Mr. Mooney. The arrows were "exposed with appropriate rites once a year if previously 'pledged,' and on those rare occasions when a Cheyenne has been killed by one of his own tribe, the purpose of the ceremony being to wipe away from the murderer the stain of his brother's blood."

IN James's "Long's Expedition" (expedition to Rocky Mountains by Major Stephen Harriman Long in 1819, compiled by Edwin James, 1823) mention is made of a semicircular row of bison skulls found on the Platte, left by a Pawnee Loup war band. The noses pointed down-stream. The skull in the middle had thirty-six red marks, showing number of warriors. Four parcels of bark on two rods signified four scalps had been taken. The war party was returning from a raid on western tribes.

The devices on Red Hawk's shield are borrowed with slight changes from Rev. J. Owen Dorsey's description of a Teton Dakota's shield, and quoted in "Picture-Writing of the American Indians," page 456, Bureau of Ethnology.

The Dakota word *wakan* expresses the idea of the supernatural, the mystic or unknown, or unknowable. In picture writing it is evidenced by a spiral line. In the sign language (which suggested the pictorial representation) the index finger is extended and pointed upward, back of hand outward, the hand (right) moving from in front of the forehead spirally upward, left to right, to arm's length.

AMERICAN-HORSE'S Winter count for 1821-1822 designates that Winter as Had-all-the-whisky-they-wanted Winter, and a barrel with a spiral line leading from the bunghole is shown signifying it contained *mini wakan*, or spirit water.

Good's Winter count for 1787-1788 is:

> "Left-the-heyoka-man-behind Winter." The man was mentally disordered—that is, *heyoka*—and advanced to a hostile war party while his own people fled. He was killed."

And so on indefinitely. A man who was *wakan* was the biggest kind of medicine, and if he were *heyoka* he was a nut. The *wakan witshasha*, or mystery man, had all the medals compared with a *pejihuta witshasha*, or "grass-root man" or herb doctor. The first possessed mystic powers; the last was skilful in the use of simples.

The old hunter's philosophy shows the influence of long acquaintance with the Indians and long separation from civilization. The Indian found a cause for every effect.—HUGH PENDEXTER.

WITH this issue the price of *Adventure* becomes twenty cents instead of fifteen. The reason is very simple—the increased and constantly increasing cost of practically everything going into the make-up of this magazine, including paper, inks and labor, etc. Those of you who know the paper field can very easily work out the problem for yourselves by computing the present paper cost of a fifteen-cent magazine and comparing it with the paper cost of the same magazine one, two and three years ago. If fifteen cents gave normal operating profits before, what has become of these normal profits now in the face of the greatly increased cost of paper?

But you don't need to know the paper field to see the reason. The increased cost of labor, material and transportation has raised the selling price of practically every commodity. Magazines are, of course, no exception to the rule. They are facing, in addition, the recent increase in postal rates on second-class mail matter.

We're sorry, but we have to. That's all there is to it.

There was, of course, the alternative of lowering the standard of *Adventure* and filling its pages with cheaper and poorer material. We rejected this alternative from the start. *Adventure* is *Adventure* and is always going to be *Adventure*. A cheaper magazine would be something else. If we can make it better, we will, but we refuse to lower its standard. And we know our readers will back this stand.

A WORD from our comrade D. Wiggins on Sitting Bull, Pat Garret and other notables:

Salem, Ore.

I noted with the greatest interest the letter from Mr. Rhodes on the death of Pat Garret. Also the reference to my opinions on the affair.

MY ONLY information on the shooting was the newspaper account of the killing, February 8, 1908, if I recall it correctly, and a short reference to the details of it by Emerson Hough, in an article on "The American Sixshooter," published in *Outing* in the Spring of 1909.

My ideas, gathered from these sources, are to the effect that Pat was riding in a buckboard with a companion when he met Brazee, who had leased a place from him. Pat was stated to have been unarmed, except for a shotgun in the bottom of the rig, while the killer is stated to have been armed with both rifle and revolver, the latter being the weapon used. Some quarreling was stated to have occurred over the running of goats on the land leased by Brazee, and after a few words Garret reached for the shotgun, it being loaded with quail-shot. Brazee went into action at once, and Pat is stated to have been shot in the rig, and once on the ground after he had fallen from it. I never heard anything after the notice to the effect that Brazee had been held by the coroner's jury. I understood that he was cleared at the trial.

This is not the best information upon which to base an opinion, but we used to hang people out here on a whole lot less. Mr. Rhodes is in a better position to judge the facts in the case, and I wish to offer an apology to any one whom I have unjustly criticized.

THE reference to the "folding gun" is of interest to me. I know of two of these weapons that have been on the market in the past—the one most commonly seen being a light shotgun, double or single barrel—and in addition the Burgess folding repeater.

The latter was a queer looking affair, and if a man attempted to pull a monstrosity like that on me I would probably do what the man in New Mexico did. It was hinged at the forward end of the receiver, and by some means unknown to me was capable of being folded up to a length that could be placed in a suit-case. Rumor hath it that they were in the habit of coming open when they were shot, also.

I've seen only one, and that was in a pawnshop in Ada, O. T. It was operated by sliding a casing over the grip back and forth. It was in very poor condition, so I did not purchase it. They have been off the market for a number of years now.

I think the other gun was of European manufacture, and .44 caliber. I used to see them advertised in the "Farmers' Bible," *i. e.*, the large catalogue issued by Sears, Roebuck & Co., of Chicago, Ill.

They were of fearful and wonderful construction, the idea apparently being taken from the guns used by poachers in the old countries. These weapons were used by the game thieves, and could be taken apart and carried in a coat pocket or similarly concealed.

BY THE way, William S. Hart, the film actor, is now packing a gun in his pictures that made history. It was presented to him by Otero Beeson, son of Chalk Beeson, old-time peace officer at Dodge City, Kansas (my birthplace). During his recent tour of the Eastern States he was at Dodge, and received this revolver, an old single-action Colt, from the son of the man who had taken it from the remains of a horse-thief. The late owner didn't need it where he was going, anyway. So Bill has now the real Western atmosphere.—D. WIGGINS.

P. S.—Just thought of a peculiar circumstance. A friend was talking with me a few weeks since, and we discussed the Custer fight on the Little Big Horn. He told me that as a child he had been in Sitting Bull's arms, and had felt an instinctive trust for the man. He still has a little neck-ornament that was placed around his neck by the chief. He told us that Sitting Bull had a most winning face, for an Indian, and was well known to his parents.

HE ALSO said that many people in the West believe today that Sitting Bull really went to West Point and was far more aware of what he was doing than the majority supposed. It will seem incredible, but it is by no means impossible. Did you ever try to run down a rumor and find that it really had some pretty good facts at the starting point? I did.

Whether it was really training, or just natural ability, the old Sioux showed that he was a good tactician. He was not the war chief, he was the statesman of the tribes. Anyhow, the old boy gave Uncle lots to worry over for twenty years.

I think the man whom Mr. Brininstool refers to was "Wounded Knee" (Captain George S. Bartlett), a demonstrator for the Peters Cartridge Company at the time of his death, six years since. He was the trader at the scene of the last battle with the redmen, and the vicinity was named after him, in reference to the stiff leg that an outlaw's bullet gave him. He had been a United States marshal there and had then a store at the scene of the battle. He found an Indian baby under the piles of dead three days after the battle; she was raised by General Colby, of Nebraska, and I understand still lives in that State. I understand that "Calamity Jane" was responsible for the saving of Bartlett's limb when the doctors wanted to amputate it after the bullet shattered the knee. This is only hearsay, however.—D. W.

YOU AND DEMOCRACY II

IN THE last issue I said I had been working a good many years on a plan in which I asked those of you to join who were ready to work for better conditions in America. But only those are wanted who are ready for hard, thankless work, without personal reward, without fame, work that for the most part will be dull and unexciting, taking your time and giving you trouble, putting nothing in your pocket and probably taking something out of it, work that is likely to make you enemies and often to bring you ingratitude from those you try to help.

I hold out no promises. I make no claims other than that I am sincere and in earnest. At this writing there is not yet even an organization. There are no names of national prominence as sponsors. There is no financial backing, no promise of any, no attempt to get such promise. Until the previous announcement to you only half a dozen people even knew what the plan is.

BUT if I make no promises, I ask none. You are not asked to pledge yourself to this plan. All that is wanted is the names of those who are ready to join in the hard, dull, thankless work of putting such a plan into practical operation if a plan is presented which seems to them worth their support. If you are expecting some miraculous remedy, some magic formula for curing all political and social ills, you are asked *not* to send in your name. If you are impelled merely by curiosity, there is no need to send your name; you will learn just as much by standing conservatively to one side. If you send it only through temporary impulse, you are not wanted.

Success is not guaranteed. The odds are against complete success. But I believe the plan is such that even failure would be success, that, however small the outward progress made, there would be a gain for the country that would be worth the effort. And the gain will be proportionate to the intelligence and selflessness and perseverance of the effort.

IF YOU are ready to face these hard facts and so eager to serve your country on the dull, unnoted battle-field of every-day routine that even the chance of a sane opportunity to do so seems worth while, send your name by letter or post-card. It will not be published. Word it to suit yourself. It pledges you to nothing. It may not even be acknowledged, but it will be carefully filed.

The plan can not be given in small space. There follows a brief general statement, given in the form of a creed, that can only partially indicate even its general scope and nature, but it holds most of the essentials. The details must come bit by bit as space permits.

A Creed

FOR SOME AMERICANS

WE BELIEVE that, peace or war, internal conditions in the United States are approaching a dangerous crisis and demand the active attention of every American who has his country's future at heart and who wishes to make democracy safe for the world.

WE BELIEVE in real democracy, real rule by the people.

THE American nation is the American people. As individuals we give up to it certain individual rights to get back from it things we value more, giving ourselves as a body control over ourselves as individuals but retaining fundamental control in our individual hands. The real power and control lies in our individual hands; it is our own fault if we fail to use it.

THE American nation is what we individuals make it. Our Government is only rules, laid down by us, and some of ourselves, chosen by us, to manage our nation according to our rules and wishes. Whatever our nation or our Government is, has or does is dependent upon us. If we are bad citizens, our nation and Government will be bad; if we are good, they will be good.

THE whole can not be greater or less, better or worse, than the sum of its parts. You can not build a good house out of bad bricks. You can not build a good government or a sound nation out of bad citizens. Democracy, monarchy, socialism, rule of capital, rule of labor, whatever form of government you please, will be rotten if the bricks from which it is builded are rotten, if its citizens are bad citizens.

WE BELIEVE that every political, economic and sociological reform movement now in existence is doomed to failure or to needlessly deferred success because of ignoring this simple fact, because of attempting to build a sound house out of rotten bricks. Their specialists plan brilliant campaigns, some of them sound, but they always forget that no campaign can succeed if its soldiers are not fit to carry out their individual parts.

WE BELIEVE in the reform upon which all other reforms are dependent. We believe that all reforms whatsoever have one first step in common—the practical awakening of the individual citizen to his individual power and control, his obligation to the people as a whole, his personal responsibility in whatever government the people choose, and the need of his loyalty, integrity and active cooperation in expressing and enforcing the will of the people as a whole.

WE BELIEVE we can serve best by uniting all good citizens on this first common step. Each of us is left free to follow whatever path he pleases after that, but we believe that general democracy, chosen by the American people but never logically developed and fully applied, will, if so developed and applied, automatically carry the nation along whatever path is best for it.

WE BELIEVE that good citizenship can, for practical purposes, be reduced to two essentials:

1. Active and honest participation in public affairs by each individual citizen. Democracy is rule by the people, by the majority, by the many. Whenever we allow, by our negligence or weakness, the few to control the many or to obstruct or postpone the will of the many, we sin against our nation and against democracy. And the fundamental power and responsibility lie with the individual citizens. Citizenship is obligation as well as privilege, and the citizen who takes without giving is a cheat, a thief, a hog and a traitor.
2. Patriotism is loyalty to the people. The rights of the people, or of their majority, are superior to those of individuals or of a minority.
3. Obedience to the will of people or majority, to their laws; laws must be obeyed till re-made.
4. The holding of public officials to the fact that they are the people's agents entrusted with carrying out the people's will and protecting the people's interests. If in any way he puts personal, party or any other interest before the interest of the people, he betrays his trust. His crime is against the whole people, against democracy itself, and is therefore greater than the same crime against an individual and deserves heavier punishment. The public official who breaks his oath of office or violates the rights or property of the people is not merely a "grafter" or a "politician," but a liar and a perjurer, a thief, a prostitute, an enemy to the people, a violator of democracy, a betrayer of trust and as much a traitor to his country as was Benedict Arnold. He has an infinitely dirtier and more shameful thing than the "yellow streak," he has the *black streak*.

WE BELIEVE that citizenship, centering upon these two essentials, can and must be taught in our schools and elsewhere, along with *true* American history, so that coming generations shall be better citizens than we have been. The first thing a democracy should teach is democracy. It is not enough to teach a child political economy, civics and sugar-coated history; the schools' duty is to make *him* a good citizen.

WE BELIEVE that, having proved ourselves unable properly to absorb the flood of immigrants pouring in upon us, this flood must be limited to such size as we *can* absorb properly, any economic demand to the contrary being only a temporary and surface need as opposed to the fundamental and greater need of the country as a whole. To such immigrants as are admitted, American citizenship should no longer be made a cheap privilege, either by ease of attainment or by *manner and ceremony* of giving, and it should be taught to them as systematically as to the children in our schools.

WE BELIEVE that the thousands of reform organizations will realize that in the long run the special aim of each will be best advanced if all unite upon ensuring the one first step that all of them must take in common, upon accomplishing the reform upon which all their reforms are dependent.

WE BELIEVE that we can build up an organization in which most other reform bodies can join for the common purpose, yet retaining intact their present independence, organization and aims.

WE BELIEVE that, with or without formal cooperation from other bodies, we can gradually build up among the people themselves an organization that will both teach and practise good citizenship, promote its systematic teaching and exert sufficient power to enforce its teaching little by little upon actual public affairs.

WE BELIEVE that we and the rest of the American people have let the specialists in economics and sociology do too much of our thinking for us and have suffered from the specialists' natural lack of general perspective. We need their help, but it is only one of the things needed. Most of all we need common sense and the realization that public affairs do not necessarily call for a special kind of thinking but chiefly tor the same kind of thinking we use in our individual affairs. Too many Americans feel that their Government is something apart from them and out of their control. It need not be and must not be.

WE BELIEVE that a first step in our work is to build up machinery for supplying, to the people at large, facts, not opinions, on holders of public office or candidates therefor, so that their actual public records, given without bias, may be placed before the people who are to vote for or against them at the polls.

WE BELIEVE that a citizen's allegiance should be given to the people as a whole, to the nation, not to any political party. No man can serve two masters. We believe in voting on men and principles, not for one party against another. We will cast our individual votes at all times as we please; as an organization we will strive to find how our votes will most further real democracy, without regard to party or persons.

WE BELIEVE that *public opinion*, expressed through the ballot or through standing laws, or expressed direct in conversation, print or on the platform, is a mightier influence than any force man can raise against it, that this force has been systematically used only by the few and generally by the worst, and that, by the right endeavor, it can be made a resistless weapon in the hands of the many including the best and wisest.

A. S. H.

BEARING on his story in this issue George Warburton Lewis gives us some interesting reading:

The three principal characters in the tale, *Tankersley*, the *Greaser Captain*, and *Nicholson*, are anything but figments of the imagination. Two of them probably will read the story. The third can not read (how fortunately), and even if he could, the story would not necessarily mean anything to him, for as a matter of fact the half-breed Captain was not a ship captain at all. In real life he commanded many and divers kinds of men, however, and from a long close-range study of him I can not doubt that, had he been the skipper of the *Pes Volador* (Flying Fish), he would have been much the same type of despot as the commander of the pest-ship.

OUTSIDE of fiction the *Greaser Captain* was a bully, but a bully without fear; and though a dangerous enemy, he was ever loath to fight fair. Once, two days after an altercation with one of his men, he treacherously struck the latter from behind with a pick-handle, and while the poor fellow writhed unconscious on the ground the Captain laughed at the wild chorus of threats and cries of protest that came from his victim's two hundred fellow workers. The Captain was of that distinctive type of outlaw that, once seen, sticks in one's memory.

NICHOLSON, in every-day life, was pretty much what he is in "Devious Are the Ways"—an average wandering Englishman, one of those fascinating vagabonds of nature whose stories you can listen to untiringly for hours at a stretch, day after day and week after week. *Nicholson* had, as he modestly expressed it, "knocked about a bit." When chance threw us together in one of the wayside places of the world he was the chief steward of the Canal Commission's hotel at Porto Bello, the historical Panamá stronghold so long ago sacked by a countryman of *Nicholson's*, Morgan, the buccaneer.

I had eventuated into the command of the Zone Police at Porto Bello, and *Nicholson* and I, having much in common officially, used to take our meals at a table apart after "the fellows who did the work" had finished. The awful aloofness of such places fosters mutual understanding and friendliness. I have found that the farther men are from the centers of civilization the closer they are brought together by the bonds of companionship. The intimate friendships of Broadway afford no such glimpses into human souls as do the solitudes of the waste places. *Nicholson* and I became friends, and it was from a yarn he told me over a third cup of coffee at one of our long-drawn-out luncheons one day that I evolved the framework of the present story. Quite in the same way, it was because of the unforgettable impression made upon me by the tramping dreamer himself that I worked him into the cast.

IN LOOKING over a carbon copy of this yarn, I felt not a little grouchy at having been unable fittingly to portray *Tankersley* as he was and is. I wish the readers of *Adventure* could know him. I had heard of men who could adapt themselves to all phases and conditions of life, but my skepticism as to their actual existence was never removed until, once upon a time, some whim of fortune side-tracked me into a job as second in command of the guard and secret service at one of our great American expositions. With a not unnatural curiosity as to the sort of personnel I should have to work with, I began gradually to widen my circle of vision over the tented expanse of the semi-military police camp, and then, all of a sudden—there stood *Tankersley*.

Between two wall-tents (at nine o'clock in the morning and on a work day!) dousing his head with basinfuls of cold water, I beheld for the first time the hero-to-be of "Devious Are the Ways." Not altogether a conventional introduction of a fiction hero, you may think, yet if you knew the man better you might think otherwise. He was only doing now the first of many unexpected things which were destined thereafter to establish him in short fiction.

"What's that for?" I queried, as he continued sloshing the water over his head, unmindful of my presence.

He paused, squinted out at me through the dripping flood, set the basin on the ground and slowly straightened. "For last night's indiscretion, Captain," and he smiled painfully, as though it might be his last.

I FROWNED, and as he rubbed his head gently with a towel, *Tankersley* gazed at me in calm contemplation out of wide, sky-blue eyes. He was a little under medium height and rather thin, though he looked hard and wiry. A column of dim freckles straggled like a routed army across the long high bridge of his prominent nose. He was lean of jaw and sunburned—and that was all. All, yet not all. Somewhere in the depths of the abnormally large, sky-blue eyes, barely perceptible, there was a merry twinkle, a half-hidden laugh.

"You see," he was explaining, "the chief detailed me last night to shadow a 'con' man, and getting drunk with him was all in the day's work. I finally got my man pretty well under way, all right, but by the time I had got him that far along I was unable myself to keep a very accurate record of his movements. I am quite clear, however, as to one important fact, and that is that he brought me home!"

That's how I came up with him, Detective *Tankersley;* one of the keenest analysts I have ever seen. Before breaking into secret service work he was a soldier in the Philippines. He was just good enough and just bad enough to be a very natural, human adventurer. When he reads this in his office in far-off California I hope it will remind him that he owes me a letter.—George Warburton Lewis.

ROBERT V. CARR first brought Wild Hickok into *Adventure's* pages some year's ago in an article on Wild Bill's death. From another of our Camp-Fire comrades, E. A. Brininstool, whose special interest for years in frontier matters has made him an authority, comes to us the following:

Los Angeles.

I have received through *Adventure* a letter from a party who signs himself "The Ace," requesting some information regarding a noted frontier character known as "Wild Bill" Hickok.

THE real name of Wild Bill was James Butler Hickok, and he was born in May, 1837, in La Salle County, Illinois. He was eighteen years of age when he first saw the West as a fighting man under Jim Lane of Free Soil fame, in the guerrilla days of Kansas, prior to the Civil War.

Before Wild Bill was twenty years of age he had made his mark, and was elected a constable in that dangerous locality. Later he developed into one of the most splendidly-physiqued men that ever trod the Western soil. Bill was not a quarrelsome man, altough he was a mighty dangerous one when aroused. His voice was low and even. But it was with the six-shooter that Bill shone, and perhaps no man on the frontier has ever surpassed him in quick and accurate shooting with the heavy "six-gun." The tale of his killings in single combat is the longest authentically assigned to any man in American history.

IT WOULD require too much of Camp-Fire's space to recount Wild Bill's many encounters. Probably his most noted fight was on the afternoon of December 16, 1861, when he was station agent at Rock Creek station, about fifty miles west of Topeka, Kan., one of the stops of the Overland stage route. Two border outlaws by the name of McCandlas (brothers) led a gang of notorious ruffians and tried to induce Wild Bill to join them. They wanted to run off the horses belonging to the stage company, and Bill told them to "come ahead and try it."

They came—ten of them—on the date above named. Bill was alone, his stableman being away on a hunt. He retreated to his dugout and got ready for the gang. His weapons were a rifle, two six-shooters and a knife.

TO MAKE a long story short, the gang battered in the door and attacked Wild Bill. He killed the first man inside with his rifle. Bill then grabbed up the six-shooters—with which he was as dexterous with one hand as with the other—and in three quick shots killed three more of the gang as they rushed in. In the smoky dugout Bill found he could not get a view of his assailants, so he dropped his revolvers and grabbed up his knife, with which he "waded in." There were six men to finish, and Bill proceeded to do it with neatness and dispatch, cutting, slashing, thrusting and parrying. To use his own words, "I just got sort o' wild. I thought my heart was on fire. I was cut and shot all to pieces myself."

They called him "Wild Bill" after that encounter. Two of the gang escaped when Bill fainted from loss of blood, but he had killed eight of them. There is no record of any fighting man to equal this. It took Bill a year to recover from his wounds.

BILL was successively marshal of Hayes City, Abilene and other tough frontier towns. Up to this time, according to some records, Bill had killed something like seventy-two men. I merely give the figures as stated by a well-known writer on Western frontier life.

Wild Bill took a fling at theatricals, but he was not a success on the stage, like Buffalo Bill. He says himself that he "got plumb scared" when before the footlights. When he saw what was expected of him he quit and went back to his beloved West.

I COULD enumerate scores of Wild Bill's fights with bad men on the border, but this is not the time nor place. His death occurred on August 2, 1876, at Deadwood, South Dakota, under the following circumstances:

Bill had won some money in a poker game from a hard citizen of Deadwood named Jack McCall, early in the day of August second. Later, as he was playing cards with some other men in a saloon, McCall slipped up behind him, placed a gun at the back of his head and shot him dead, before Bill knew an enemy was near. McCall was later arrested at Yankton, tried before a real court, convicted and promptly hanged.

WILD BILL'S body was buried at Deadwood, and "Calamity Jane," the noted frontier woman, lies by his side, as it was her request to be buried thus. Hickok was thirty-nine years old when killed, and it is said that he had averaged a little more than two men for each year of his life. He was well known among Army officers, and esteemed as a scout, being never regarded as a "tough man" in any sense. He was a man of wonderful personal beauty, being over six feet in height, and it is said that he had a waist as slim as a woman's and a hand and foot of the same feminine daintiness. Of him General George Custer said: "He was a plainsman in every sense of the word, yet unlike any other of his class. Whether on foot or horseback he was one of the most perfect types of physical manhood I ever saw. His manner was entirely free from all bluster and bravado. He never spoke of himself unless requested to do so. His influence among frontiersmen was unbounded; his word was law. Wild Bill was anything but a quarrelsome man, yet none but himself could enumerate the many conflicts in which he had engaged."

WILD BILL had killed a great many Indians at different times, but of these no estimate is accurate. Cutting out all doubtful instances, however, there remains no doubt that he had killed between twenty and thirty men in personal combat in the open, and that he was never once tried in any court, on a charge even of manslaughter.—E. A. BRININSTOOL.

JOINING our writers' brigade with his first story in *Adventure*, H. A. Noureddin Addis follows Camp-Fire custom and introduces himself:

Southeastern Ohio, the region of the early Ohio oil-fields, is the district that furnished me a birthplace. My earliest recollection is of an oil-well, and as a boy my first employment was in the oil-fields. My paternal grandfather followed the oil industry from Pennsylvania to Ohio when the first strike was made in the one-time famous Macksburg district, finally dying in that village at a fairly advanced age in 1909. There my father was born a few years after my grandfather's arrival, and in due course, myself.

OF ANOTHER strain my great-great-grandfather was one of the original Ohio settlers at Marietta in 1788-1789. His elder son was one of the engineers who surveyed the Ohio Company's Purchase. And his younger son, my great-grandfather, was born in the block-house at Marietta in 1794, being the first male child of white parentage born in the State. (At any rate if he had predecessors, history is silent on the subject.)

These things, and the fact that some of the early statesmen of Ohio were my near collateral relatives, together with the fact that the district where I was born was teeming with romantic historical landmarks of the State's early days, have given me a feeling toward my native State that is rather out of place in this country since the Civil War, but I have always felt that I was first an Ohioan. Yet, I am now a citizen of California.

I HAVE traveled some in most of the European countries, especially the Balkans; also Asia Minor. Those countries are rich in fiction possibilities, and constitute another rather extensive field of my literary endeavors. The eternal mystery and romance of the Orient are there; that is, to one who wishes to see it. To many, those countries are even duller and more sordid than the rest of the world. Of course in reality we're much the same the world over, and Ali ibn Youssouf, Hagop Krikorian, or Mirza Hassan Ali Isfahani, are virtually what John Smith would have been if brought up in the same environment. As proof I may say that I know Turks of whom the father and mother were English, born in England, who in adult life, being converted to Islam, have gone to Turkey, and their children are indistinguishable from any other Turks. In fact, in many instances it is almost impossible to distinguish the people of the older generation, who have themselves emigrated.

OF COURSE the English and Turkish temperaments are practically identical. Both are inclined to stolidity, impassivity. Both are essentially romantic, but would perish rather than knowingly allow an outsider to guess it. Being rather a Celt myself I haven't perhaps sufficient patience with these solemn humbugs, but rather prefer the Arab temperament which is perhaps the nearest analogy to the Celt that the Orient affords. While the Persian will, in my opinion, correspond more nearly with the Latin—philologists who connect Iran with Erin to the contrary notwithstanding. However, the Persian is not wholly Latin; he is the Latin tempered with blood of Celt and Teuton—the Frenchman of the Orient.

Yet I do not wish to be understood as depreciating the many solid virtues of the cool, hard-headed races. In their way they have contributed as much to the progress of the world as the others who enjoy an occasional laugh at them for taking themselves so seriously. Very possibly their contributions are of a more essential and enduring character than those made by the more brilliantly temperamental races.

AS FOR personal adventures, I have never had any that were startling. On the other hand, my entire life has been to a great extent an adventure—although for the most part prosaic enough. My nearest approach to real adventure took place some few years ago when I was closely associated with some of the leaders of a revolutionary party in an Oriental country. But as to go deeply into this would necessarily reveal certain secrets which, in the interests of others whose present political positions might not be improved by such revelation, I feel that I should not disclose.

Much of the romance and adventure in life rests with the mental make-up of the beholder. The point of view is everything. To some adventure is everywhere, to others, nowhere. One sees adventure in situations where another discerns nothing but the most casual of every-day affairs. Perhaps after all the whole difference in individuals is a questions of self-analysis, an ability to recognize and mentally catalog impressions. But this leads into deeper water, and I am neither psychologist nor metaphysician.—H. A. NOUREDDIN ADDIS.

A WORD from Harold A. Lamb on his story in this issue:

The germ of *Dorgan's Devil-Devil* came from an experience of an uncle who commanded a ship on the China station, and visited the Samoa and Fiji Islands. After one of these trips he brought home a collection of shark-tooth swords and curious tales of the South-Sea Islands. The next time he came home he was brought by his men, having died of sickness on the China station. Naturally, the islands offered many a tale to me of the Service.

In my opinion justice is seldom done to one of the finest types of adventuring men—the officers of the United States Navy. This is probably because the writers and public are not in touch with them, except in war-time. Newspaper men see a good deal of the Service, but their write-ups are confined to items of news value. Too much can't be said in stories or newsprint of the men who do their work outside the bounds of publicity with indomitable pluck, for the increase of efficiency in the Service. Just tribute is paid the English naval officer, but the best tribute I have ever heard paid the American officer—not in war-time—has been from Englishmen who have followed closely the work of the American Navy.—HAROLD A. LAMB.

IN OUR mid-February issue was the first call for the names of those Americans who are ready to unite for a more logically developed and fully applied democracy in the United States, for cleanness in public office and for the definite and systematic teaching of fundamental good citizenship. In that issue and the one following was given a creed or platform designed at least to outline the principles and work involved.

The ground could not, of course, be more than outlined in that small space. There was no attempt or desire to do more. The purpose was merely to get the names of those Americans who are ready to join a definite, comprehensive movement for the purposes named above, *if* that movement, when fully explained, meets with their approval. These names are not for publication and the sending of them involves no obligation.

AS ALREADY pointed out, no one is wanted for this movement who is not ready for hard, thankless work without other reward than the attainment of good ends for the people at large. There will be no "glory" in it; only dull, drab work day after day, work that would take, if all did their parts, no more time than every citizen owes to his nation, but, since many shirk, work that must fall on the shoulders of the comparative few willing to do extra duty until the shirking citizens can be taught to begin carrying their shares of the common civic burden. Men and women of all classes and degrees are wanted, but none except those ready and eager to carry more than their share.

The plan to be offered is not a magic cure-all. There are as yet no definite organization, no nationally known sponsors, no financial backing. But there is a very definitely worked-out plan of campaign, the result of some ten years' slow and careful labor. I believe very firmly, of course, in this plan of mine, but, equally of course, no one is asked to endorse it in advance.

I AM deliberately stating the case in discouraging form. I want all those who are easily discouraged to be eliminated at the start. Those of you who have read either of the former outlines of general aims are sufficiently informed at least to know whether or not you are in sympathy with the general purpose. Your name is wanted only if you are sufficiently in sympathy to want to know the plan in detail and, if it meets with your approval, to join in the movement earnestly and permanently.

It is not yet decided how the details will be put in your hands. I have embodied the plan in a book, but the book has not even been offered to a publisher. No, this is not a campaign for selling my book, but I'll try to convince you of that by deeds, not words. If you can see only a book-selling campaign in this, your recourse is a simple one—have nothing to do with it.

IF YOU send in your name you may not even get an acknowledgement. But your name will be carefully filed. For the present there will be no fuller statement in this magazine. I am writing this in December. The first announcement and call for names appears in our mid-February issue, which will be in your hands a month before you read this, but not until a month after I write this. The first names sent in can not reach me until the latter part of January; any names in reply to the second call, not until February. Until February, then, I shall not know how many names will come in, so until February there seems no need to go into further detail. That means that there will be little or nothing more on the subject in this magazine until the mid-May or possibly the first-May issue.

In the meantime there is work to be done in preparing the ways for the definite organization that will follow.

FOLLOWING our Camp-Fire custom, Edward Bellamy Partridge stands up and introduces himself on the occasion of his first story in our magazine:

My first adventure was sprung on me at Phelps, New York, on the 10th day of July, 1877. I don't remember much about the occasion except that my father said, "Another boy, eh? That means one more straight Republican vote."

THE next important adventure occurred at Lyons, New York, on the 13th day of October, 1903, when I dropped the wedding-ring on the floor and said "I do" in the wrong place until the minister became so confused that he said "A-men" instead of "Ah-men."

And in the meantime I had spent two years in a "prep" school in Norwalk, Connecticut, two more in Hobart College, and had then gone to the Albany Law School where I was awarded the honor of writing the letters, "LL.B." after my name. I had also lost cases for some of the best people in Ontario County, and won them for some of the worst.

FOR ten years I followed the law, writing intermittently, and hoping that some day I might be able to do it all the time. Then along came an attack of typhoid fever from which I was a long time recovering—and it was during the period of my convalescence at Atlantic City that I first learned of the charms of southern California life.

A few months later I sold out my practise, packed up the household gods and shipped them to San Diego (gods is what I meant to say), gathered together my wife and my faithful friend Fiji (a brindle gentleman from Boston), and, taking along two other friends for company, clambered into the family automobile and set sail for the Pacific Coast.

We pursued a westerly direction following the general course of the Lincoln Highway (although there wasn't any such thing in 1912) and after two months of leisurely travel—some of it not so leisurely and very hard walking—we reached our destination, sunburned and travel-stained, but happy and very much corrected in our ideas of geography and topography.

WE ALWAYS managed to sleep under cover except once when a sprained axle compelled us to spend the night in a lonely Wyoming ditch far from human habitation. During the night the ground squirrels ran over the top of the car, jackrabbits sniffed at the tires, and a coyote came near enough to eat the scraps of lunch which we had thrown away and for which we devoutly wished the next morning when one of the party was compelled to set out on a ten-mile "hike" with an empty stomach.

But a ranch was found not more than five miles away where the axle was straightened with the assistance of a forge and a giant cowpuncher who used the hub of an old wagon-wheel for a sledge-hammer.

EVERY day brought forth adventures of one sort or another. If we weren't being mired in an alkali bog we were running away from a sand-storm or sliding down a hill so steep that we kept right on going with the wheels locked.

On one occasion we ran twenty-five miles over rough mountain roads in the dead of night with no light except that of our tail-lamp which we had wired to one of the headlight brackets; and, when we chanced to plunge into a deep ford through which the road ran, we all thought our last moment had come. A little farther on I drove so close to a washed place in the road that I knocked down the danger signal. But we finally reached a town safe and sound and on all four tires—although one of them was flat.

LAST Spring I made several trips through the Mojave Desert with a party of miners, where I made the acquaintance of the taciturn sidewinder, and learned how to bathe, cook, shave, wash dishes and keep alive all on a pint of water a day.

After settling down to live in California I was not long in demonstrating to myself and several other people that I was not cut out for a successful real-estate operator. So I set to work to make a writer of myself—and I am still at it.

I think the most thrilling moment of my life was that at which I received the first letter telling of the acceptance of a story. And a moment that was a close second was that when I learned of the acceptance of my first book, "Sube Cane."

My motor wanderings which have, in addition to the trans-continental tour, carried me from Canada to Mexico and all through most of the Eastern States as well as on several camping-motoring trips through the West, are being gradually worked into the form of a book which I hope may be of interest to all lovers of the bark of a motor and the uncertainty about what is going to happen next.

SOME months ago a little coastwise steamer was wrecked off the Coronado Islands near this port (San Diego). In trying to launch their life-boats the crew had lost all but one boat which they lashed to the after deck, and in which they were sitting as they waited for the end, when a giant sea swept over the vessel and launched their boat for them. They made the shore in safety. And that part of "Rags" having to do with the shipwreck was based on the stories told by several of the survivors with whom I talked.

The diving-bell episode of the story came to me after seeing a local amateur diver remain over half an hour under thirty feet of water with an old soup-kettle over his head which was furnished with fresh air by a "Mex" on the dock who wielded a tire-pump.

INFORMATION as to the smuggling of the China-boys was gleaned from the Federal officers at this place who are in constant warfare with smugglers who receive so much a head for delivering a Chinaman on American soil. Several times Chinamen have been seen by picnickers, skulking about these islands which are uninhabited, and stories are told of how they have more than once been brought in by unsuspecting excursionists who have taken them for stranded fishermen or something of that sort.

Rags is a real dog. He lives not far from me. And while I do not know that he has done all the things he has received credit for, I know that he would do them if he ever had a chance.—EDWARD BELLAMY PARTRIDGE.

A LITTLE story passed on to us by D. Wiggins of Salem, Oregon, a tale recalled to memory by an old settler when he saw one of our covers, the old Kit Carson pioneer with his long squirrel rifle:

Salem, Ore.

I showed the picture of the old pioneer with his Deckard smoking to Uncle John McDonough, a neighbor of ours. You see, Uncle John is a direct descendent of Adam Poe, of the Ohio Valley in the days when to live there took as much hardihood as it takes to be a—well, a grocer and quote present-day prices to customers. Uncle is seventy-eight years young, and can beat ye scribe shooting with his long Kentucky rifle. He's done it.

"By ——," ejaculated Uncle John, on beholding

the cover, "that is just like I see old Injun Dave Sitler look; I knowed him in Ioway in the fifties." (You see, uncle was a frontiersman.)

HE then told me the following story: Sitler was a noted shot in the settlements where Fort Dodge, Iowa, stands now. There was in the vicinity an Indian, what tribe uncle did not state, who was a distinctly bad actor. And instead of scalps he boasted of having a string of ninety-nine human tongues. Why he preferred them to scalps I do not know.

At any rate, he was so ill-advised as to say on a certain occasion that he wanted one more tongue on that string, and that was the one of Sitler's mother. Dave heard of the boast, but bided his time. The country was so settled that the killing of the lustful one was not to be done in the usual fashion.

But at last the opportunity came. Dave, while scouting around on the banks of a little stream, came upon his man sitting on a log that extended into the stream, fishing. In telling of the affair he said:

"I just raised old Betty up and looked at him over the sights a spell, and thought how easy it would be to drill him. And pretty soon he fell off the log and drownded hisself. He never got my mammy's tongue."

"And," added Uncle John, "I reckon he told the truth; we found the Injun's gun on the bank by the foot of the log." He considers it a great joke.

WOULD we could serve some hyphenated citizens likewise; and some who are the native stuff also. We have very few of them here—have too many people here who are of uncontrollable tempers and ready fists. A German who insulted the flag on the Fourth was knocked down and joyfully walked upon by an unknown stranger. He is a model of loyalty since.—D. WIGGINS.

LETTER-FRIENDS BACK HOME

A Free Service Department for American, Canadian, and Other Allied Soldiers, Sailors, Marines and Others in Camp or at the Front.

Any one in the United States or Allied service who wishes to brighten the time with letters from "back home," or wherever else this magazine circulates, and with the personal touch and interest of hitherto unknown friends, can secure these letters and these friends by sending us his name and military address to be published once in this department as soon as censorship of soldiers' foreign addresses permits. In the meantime his address can be printed as "care *Adventure*," letters to be forwarded at once by us to the military address he gives us in confidence. Among our readers of both sexes, all classes and from all parts of the world, he is likely to gain a number of friendly, personal correspondents. He is free to answer only such as he is comfortably able to answer under the conditions that surround him, and it is even suggested that the number of correspondents for any one man be determined by the needs of his comrades as well as by his own.

This magazine, of course, assumes no responsibility other than the publishing of these names and addresses as its space will permit. Experience has shown that the service offered is a very real and needed one, and all not themselves in service are asked to do their part in making the daily life of those fighting in our defense brighter and pleasanter through personal friendships across the intervening miles and by whatever personal, human kindnesses such friendships may suggest.

When giving your military address make it as permanent a one as possible.

(As the magazine is made up several months in advance, the above notice will appear with only such stray names as happen to come in to us until there has been time for it to reach the camps and the front and for names and addresses to reach us, be put in type and then reach our readers on publication.)

PVT. C. F. WHITELEY, care *Adventure*.

WE'VE all learned a good deal about the marvelous running powers of Indians since the Camp-Fire took up the discussion a year or two ago. Here is a further interesting addition from Samuel L. Fegtly, Department of Law, University of Arizona:

Tucson, Arizona.

Last Saturday evening I attended an illustrated lecture by Dr. George Wharton James, noted writer, lecturer and student of our American Indians, on the Hopi Snake Dance.

DURING the course of the lecture Dr. James threw upon the screen a picture of an aged Indian who, Dr. James said, was personally known to him and was over seventy years old at the time the picture was taken. The day before the picture was taken this old man had run over the desert forty miles to his cornfield, worked there during the day (how many hours Dr. James did not say) and then ran back to his village at night. The day after this (the day the picture was taken, as I understood) he was on his way to a patch of timber twenty-seven miles away where he was to cut wood, returning to the village at night.

I remembered the discussion in *Adventure* and thought I would send this in to you to file with the rest of your information in regard to this matter.

DR. JAMES may be known to you, but on the chance that he is not I will add that, so far as I could learn from the people there who know him, he is an Englishman, came to this part of the country a good many years ago in poor health, has traveled over this Southwest extensively, is a "blood-brother" to several Indian tribes (among them the Hopi), has been present at the Snake Dance some dozen or more times, has assisted, or perhaps it would be more accurate to say, has been present at the washing of the snakes and other ceremonies preliminary to the dance, and in other ways has acquired a vast fund of information about these things.—SAMUEL M. FEGTLY.

COPIES of the first issue of *Adventure* are hard to get. Those who have them will not let go of them, and our office supply was exhausted years ago. But here's a comrade who wants one *hard*.

Leonard W. Barkley, Morrisburg, Ontario, Canada, has tried the second-hand dealers, has advertised in our "Back Issues" department, has written me a number of times, has tried in every way, but he can't get hold of a copy of *Adventure* for November, 1910. He has every other copy for over seven years to date and he wants this one. Many others of you have complete files and he isn't asking you to break yours in order to fill out his, but if any one of you has a November, 1910, and is not keeping complete files, maybe he'll drop Mr. Barkley a line.

INCIDENTALLY, a few copies of each issue of 1916—except March, which is completely exhausted—have been found in our sub-cellar and can be sold at the regular price. A few of 1915 and 1914 also came to light. At present they are held for possible needs of other departments but will, I think, soon be released for sale.

And *say*—when you write for back issues or about anything concerning subscriptions won't you please, as *Mr. John Wilkes* says, for G-a-w-d's sake write not to me or to the editorial department but to the circulation department? I have no authority in such matters and when you write me about them, all I can do is to send your letter with a memo to the circulation department and then write you a letter saying I have done so. I'm always glad to help when I can, but in this case I don't help any, and, believe me, I have more than plenty of work to do in order to keep my own job going. So far as we can estimate, from 8,000 to 9,000 letters and communications of one kind or another are mailed out from *Adventure's* editorial department every year. Also there are one or two other little chores to be attended to.

ARTHUR SULLIVANT HOFFMAN.

ADVENTURE'S FREE SERVICES AND ADDRESSES

These services of *Adventure* are free to *any one*. They involve much time, work and expense on our part, but we offer them gladly and ask in return only that you *read and observe the simple rules*, thus saving needless delay and trouble for you and us. The whole spirit of this magazine is one of friendliness. No formality between editors and readers. Whenever we *can* help you we're ready and willing to try.

Identification Cards

Free to any reader. Just send us (1) your name and address, (2) name and address of party to be notified, (3) a stamped and self-addressed return envelope.

Each card bears this inscription, each printed in English, French, Spanish, German, Portuguese, Dutch, Italian, Arabic, Chinese, Russian, and Japanese:

"In case of death or serious emergency to bearer, address serial number of this card, care of *Adventure*, New York, stating full particulars, and friends will be notified."

In our office, under each serial number, will be registered the name of bearer and of one friend, with permanent address of each. No name appears on the card. Letters will be forwarded to friend, unopened by us. Names and addresses treated as confidential. We assume no other obligations. Cards not for business identification. Cards furnished free, *provided stamped and addressed envelope accompanies application*. We reserve the right to use our own discretion in all matters pertaining to these cards.

Later we may furnish a metal card or tag. If interested in metal cards, say so on a *post-card—not* in a letter. No obligation entailed. These post-cards, filed, will guide us as to demand and number needed.

A moment's thought will show the value of this system of card-identification for any one, whether in civilization or out of it. Remember to furnish stamped and addressed envelope and to *give in full the names and addresses of self and friend or friends when applying*.

Back Issues of *Adventure*

Will sell: 1915: October, November, December; 1916: January, February, March, October, November, December; 1917, all except August. Any copy 10 cents plus postage.—MORTON H. SPENCER, Route 4, Wellsboro, Pa.

Manuscripts

Glad to look at any manuscript. We have no "regular staff" of writers. A welcome for new writers. *It is not necessary to write asking to submit your work.*

When submitting a manuscript, if you write a letter concerning it, enclose it *with* the manuscript; do *not* send it under separate cover. Enclose stamped and addressed envelope for return. All manuscripts should be typewritten double-spaced, with wide margins, not rolled, name and address on first page. We assume no risk for manuscripts or illustrations submitted, but use all due care while they are in our hands. Payment on acceptance.

We want only clean stories. Sex, morbid, "problem," psychological and supernatural stories barred. Use almost no fact-articles. Can not furnish or suggest collaborators. Use fiction of almost any length; under 3000 welcomed.

Missing Friends or Relatives

Our free service department "Lost Trails" in the pages following, though frequently used in cases where detective agencies, newspapers, and all other methods have failed, or for finding people long since dead, has located one out of about every five inquired for. Except in case of relatives, inquiries from one sex to the other are barred.

Expeditions and Employment

While we should like to be of aid in these matters, experience has shown that it is not practicable.

Mail Address and Forwarding Service

This office, assuming no responsibility, will be glad to act as a forwarding address for its readers or to hold mail till called for, provided necessary postage is supplied.

Addresses

Order of the Restless—Organizing to unite for fellowship all who feel the wanderlust. First suggested in this magazine, though having no connection with it aside from our friendly interest. Address WAYNE EBERLY, 731 Guardian Bldg., Cleveland, O., in charge of preliminary organizing.

Camp-Fire—Any one belongs who wishes to.

High-School Volunteers of the U. S.—An organization promoting a democratic system of military training in American high schools. Address *Everybody's*, Spring and Macdougal Streets, New York City.

Rifle Clubs—Address Nat. Rifle Ass'n of America, 1108 Woodward Bldg., Washington, D. C.

(*See also under "Standing Information" in "Ask Adventure."*)

General Questions from Readers

In addition to our free service department "Ask Adventure" on the pages following, *Adventure* can sometimes answer other questions within our general field. When it can, it will. Expeditions and employment excepted.

Remember

Magazines are made up ahead of time. An item received today is too late for the current issue; allow for two or three months between sending and publication.

FARNHAM BISHOP and Arthur Gilchrist Brodeur give us some interesting facts in connection with their story in this issue. If the period in which the tale is laid is as interesting and little known to you as it was to me, you will find the following facts good reading. These two men have given us stories laid in many places and in many periods of the past. Most of our stories "get by" uncriticized as to their facts and color, but it is one thing to have these correct in a story of modern times, and quite another thing to have them correct even as to details in tales laid anywhere from half a century to several thousand years ago. There are fewer who are equipped to criticize, but these few are zealous and exacting.

Berkeley, California.

Ironclads, breech-loading artillery and Japanese spies in Manila may seem a bit anachronistic in a story of the sixteenth century, but all three of those things were contemporaries of William Shakespeare and Henry of Navarre. The Korean "tortoise-boat" and the Dutch armored galleon are described exactly as set down in history, both as to appearance and actions. There is an excellent picture and description of the early breech-loading swivel on page 192, Vol. 20, of the Encyclopædia Britannica, in the article on "Ordnance." And Manila was never worse plagued with Japanese spies and the fear of Nippon than it was in the last decade of the sixteenth century.

JAPAN had not yet become the "Hermit Kingdom;" on the contrary, it was sending forth its adventurers to every corner of the Far East and even across the Pacific. The conquest of Korea was but the first step in the ambitious plans of the great Hideyoshi, when the tortoise-boat taught Japan a lesson in sea-power which it remembered in 1894 and 1904-1905. If the Portuguese had been willing to sell Hideyoshi those two war-galleons he had tried to buy from them, a few years earlier, there is no telling what the history of the Far East would have been.

Our having Hideyoshi try to capture a Manila-Acapulco galleon is fiction. But in 1596 the galleon *San Felipe* was wrecked and plundered in the Japanese port of Hurado, and six years later the *Espiritu Santo* was attacked there and fought her way out through a Japanese flotilla. Her captain, Lope de Ulloa, was a splendid sea-fighter—the *Diego de Torres* of our story. "Of persons of his quality and talent," wrote the Conde de Monterey, Viceroy of Mexico, to the King of Spain, "there is a great lack in the Southern Sea."

KURUSHIMA is as genuine a Japanese figure as the everlasting sneaky spy who is always being caught with the plans of Corregidor up his sleeve. Personally, I should like to see less of the latter in our magazines and newspapers, now that we and the Japanese are fighting the same foe. Let Hearst and the Kaiser do it.

The title is from the well-known line in Kipling's "Ballad of East and West:"

"When two strong men stand face to face, though they come from the ends of the earth."—FARNHAM BISHOP.

THE Chicago Chapter of the Adventurers' Club is entitled to an even prouder service-flag than the New York Chapter with its nearly fifty stars but larger membership. The Chicago membership at this writing is eighty-eight. Out of these thirty-six have gone into service, one is in France with the Red Cross, two are war correspondents and one is with the Council of Defense at Washington—forty in all, most of them commissioned officers. Here is the list:

Col. Henry A. Allen, 108th Engrs., 33d Div.; Capt. B. C. Allin, 108th Engrs., Co. B, 33d Div.; Lieut. Frank W. Alsip, U. S. A., Aviat. Sec.; Capt. G. H. Anderson, 18th Hussars, British Army, South Africa; Lieut. Frank Baackes, Jr., U. S. A., Statistical Div.; Capt. Edward Barclay, U. S. A., Truck Co. (Overseas) Port of Embarc.; John Bass, War Correspondent, Somewhere in France; Capt. Chas. L. Binno, U. S. A., Q. M. D.; Ben S. Boyce, U. S. A., Co. C, Signal Corps, 2d Fld. Battalion; Lieut. C. W. Brood, U. S. A., Co. B, 24th Engrs.; Leon Brokman, Russian Spec. Service; Ensign Otis B. Duncan, U. S. S. *Des Moines;* Lieut. Herbert H. Evans, U. S. Navy Yard; Maj. W. Robt. Foran, 17 Fordhook Ave., Ealing, W. London (now in India); Lieut. W. G. Hamilton, 1st Batt., Can. Black Watch (sick leave); Lieut. Wm. M. Hunt, U. S. A.; Capt. R. Hugh Knyvott, Intell. Off., 15th Austral. Inf., Base P. O., London; Capt. A. M. Lochwitzky, U. S. A., Asst. Post Q. M.; Major Lee A. McCalla, F. A. N. A., 164th Depot Brigade; Capt. Jos. Mattos (deceased—killed in colored riot, Houston, Texas); John T. McCutcheon, War Correspondent; Carl G. Macvitty, Red Cross (Somewhere in France); Capt. Edward Maher, U. S. A., Q. M. D.; Lieut. Barrett O'Hara, ———; Lieut. H. Nelson Orr, U. S. A., Med. Dept., Port of Embarcat., Surgeon's Off.; Capt. B. W. Phillips,

U. S. A., 31st Infantry; Lieut. W. Chandler Peak, U. S. A.; Maj. R. W. Patterson, 1st Oklahoma Engrs.; Lawrence R. Richey, U. S. Special Service; Dr. Daniel W. Rogers, U. S. Med. Reserve, 33d Div.; Philip Sawyer, U. S. Merchant Marine, S. S. *New York;* Lieut. Edson M. Steward, U. S. A., 78th Div., Regulars; Maj. S. C. Stanton, U. S. A., Med. Dept.; Capt. Philip Sampson, U. S. A., Instr. Bayonet Practise; James Sutherland, British Army, South Africa; Lieutenant Lloyd E. Thrush, U. S. A., Q. M. D.; Capt. Richard C. Travers, U. S. A.; Lieut. Warren C. Woodward, U. S. A. Aviat. Corps, Signal School; Col. Sir F. Younghusband, Brit. Forces, 8 Buckingham Gate, London, S.W., England; Douglas W. Clinch, Room 418, Council of Defense, Washington, D. C.

FOLLOWING our Camp-Fire custom, T. Nichols, with his first story in our magazine, stands up and introduces himself:

There are many kinds of adventure, but of them all Life is the greatest, the most fascinating, grim, uncertain.

LOOKING back over my own life, I am startled by the planlessness, aimlessness, changefulness of it; it appears to be a series of haphazard events, that only by a magic trick of fate has been redeemed, woven into a harmonious whole. It has been adventurous, more so perhaps than the majority of lives. Adventure was bred in me. Born by one of the prettiest of Norwegian fjords, where every knoll was a monument to some ancient hero, where every name was an echo of battle-blasts and songs of swords, I received as a legitimate heritage the roving spirit of the Vikings.

The intensest recollections of my childhood are memories of adventure and dreams of adventure. Clearly I recall the long Winter evenings on the farm when I sat on father's knee listening to tales of his adventures on sea and land in many countries and climes. They were exciting, breathless adventures, possible only under the more primitive conditions of half a century ago. Each tale was a tonic to my imagination, stimulated my mind to fantastic activities. At night, before going to sleep, I invented the most gorgeous careers for myself. I was not many inches tall when I had irrevocably decided to leave home "when I grew big."

LATER when I was old enough to consider it childish and effeminate to sit on my father's knee, other factors nursed my imagination and adventurous spirit. There were, for instance, the docks of the nearby seaport with their ceaseless activities, and the men-of-war, English, German and French, that each Summer dropped anchor, with much booming of guns, in the roadstead. Nothing could be more entrancing to a boy than these martial vessels, or the crews with their gay irresponsible ways and incomprehensible, strangely musical speech. Often of a Sunday morning my two brothers and I trudged the eight miles to town to marvel at them. At times the sailors would take us aboard in their steam-launches, and we explored the ships from keel to bridge. An enchanted fairyland they were, with their gleaming torpedoes, intricate quick-firers, immense turrets, and great sleek guns that seemed alive, seemed to long for something to destroy.

THEN there was school, of course, first public school, located about three miles from my home, and later high school in the city. The latter was a private afternoon school and caused me much inconvenience. As I continued to live at home, I had to go by railroad in to town every day at noon; and at night, because of a conflict between the schedule and my classes, I was obliged to wait until eleven o'clock for a train, arriving at my station half an hour later; and then after walking three miles along lonely roads, I could finally sit down to my supper and go to bed.

I WAS not yet seventeen years old when I left home one February evening. I remember vividly the train-ride, the dark desolate docks, and the shadowy background of the city asleep on the hillside, with a starless clouded sky overhead. Then followed a two-day journey down the coast inside a chain of bleak rocky islands forming a rampart against the ocean; then a trip across the North Sea in the steerage in a storm; a page of Dante's "Inferno." Then England, wonderfully interesting, and eleven days on the ocean; then America, and a train-ride into the heart of the country.

BUT this sketch of my life is becoming too long. Some day, perhaps, I shall write a fuller account, but here I can only hint at the happenings of the years that followed. I was a boy alone in a strange country, with only a smattering of the language, a hounding sense of my own uselessness, unimportance, and thousands of miles from home. There were years of restlessness, of grim adventure, doing odd work in odd places, searching for a position in the order of things. Half of the States in the Union are associated with memories in my mind; whenever I hear mentioned Nicaragua, Guatemala, Costa Rica, Panama, recollections are brought up; talk of the sea and sailing and I can relate personal experiences.

But throughout these first aimless years one purpose was my constant companion, to master the English language. It seemed a hopeless task but was too fascinating to be let alone. It was an adventure in itself the hunting through books for new words, jotting them down, and getting their meaning whenever a dictionary was within reach.

In spite of their harshness, however, those years were kind. I became acquainted with life, gained a greater knowledge of myself; and out of the chaos of my mind grew definite aims which in later less outwardly exciting years I have tried to realize. I have had a few hard lessons, and I hope I have profited by them. Life owes me nothing. Outweighing all disappointments, failures, is the gift, the grant of a tomorrow.

BEFORE I close this confidential but necessarily rambling talk with you, the readers of the "Camp-Fire," I wish to mention my work. I am new in the fiction field; but in the future I hope to devote all my time and energy to it. I do not intend to write stories because the work is easy. It isn't. I wish to write because I wish to justify my existence, to give something of myself to the world, to you. And I want to please you if I can; I want you to like me; you are necessary to me. And you may be assured I shall never try to impose upon you. Whenever you see my name at the head of a story, I want you to say, "This story may not be great, but it represents the best effort of a man who has had his tussle with life, just as I have, and therefore there must be something worth while in it."

AS FOR the story of mine appearing in this number I have little to say. It must speak for itself. Doubtless it has many faults, but it was the best I could do at the time. I trust I shall do better in the future; I trust I shall always do better in the future. Accept this first story, then, not as a finished, solitary product, but as a promise of a beginning.—T. Nichols.

DECEMBER thirteenth I received a letter from our comrade and member of our writers' brigade, Major W. Robert Foran, written in India September thirteenth, in reply to a letter written by me June thirteenth—the three being written three months apart to the day and all on the thirteenth. Glad I'm not superstitious, and the hoodoo seems not to have settled on him either, for he reports himself fit with nothing to kick about except heat. Here's more good luck to him.

EARLY in the Winter came a letter from "Canuck," which I've been unable to give until now, but which is as interesting and to the point now as it was then:

Ottawa, Can.

Am back again after four months in the north. I've had a wonderful time in the last north of northwestern Quebec, seen some grand game areas, directed probably the finest film of live game (moose) in action, etc., yet obtained, am tanned like one of my Indians and feeling tuned to a Winter's hibernation.

I HAVE followed with considerable interest your Camp-Fire talks on what all Americans owe the United States, and can only say I'm with you in all you've expressed—just as you've said it. The snake of treason—an ugly word but the only one that fits, unfortunately—must be scotched and done with absolutely no compunction; call them what you will—pro-Germans or anything else—they're all anti-Americans and their sub-rosa activities, to be squelched, must have radical application of the National knife.

The British, including the Canadian, have always been prone to allowing too much rope to treasonable citizens, and others calling themselves such, of this country and of the British Isles. Just in the same way is the ordinary American, as I know him, similarly unbelieving in his stand that "it's nothing but smoke." As I know the foreign element, whether the ignorant immigrant or the educated resident, while you can understand an out-and-outer, it is strange but true that many who should know better, who are actual citizens of the United States, having sworn allegiance to it, renouncing their former allegiance to any and all other States or republics, are the ones who at present have been and still are getting away with un-American actions.

AS I see it, applicable to Canada and to the United States, to Great Britain, to France, Italy or any of the other nations fighting in this war of democracy against the right of might, every one is either heart and soul for his own country and its allies or else he is an enemy. If the latter, why, in the name of common sense is he not promptly taken directly into the State's hands and treated as an enemy must be?

Cutting out newspapers and publications in any language other than the national one is a primary essential. Over here in Canada the danger of permitting any other is seen in French Quebec, where rabid anti-British, anti-French, anti-Canadian, anti-conscription, all are prevalent and all are fed and inflamed by the "Nationalist" French press. We have over here much anti-Ally underground work that will never be successfully disposed of with gloves.—S. E. Sangster.

IT IS seldom that one of our woman members joins our writers' brigade, but Lotta Adele Gannett, with a story in this issue, does so and in accordance with Camp-Fire custom rises and introduces herself. I know she will be warmly welcomed.

I never quite get used to the fact that so many women read *Adventure*. Yet it is not strange, after all. A woman does not necessarily prefer soft love-stories forever and forever. We all know plenty of women whose chief interests do not lie in that direction and it is natural that they, too, should like to turn to stories dealing more largely with other emotions than those of sex.

Also there are plenty of women who, though they like clean love-stories, do *not* care for the kind whose interest is dependent chiefly upon the physical aspects of sex. We keep our magazine as clean and wholesome as we can. We want the kind of reader who likes to look upon the world as it is but prefers not to look at it through sex spectacles that tinge everything in the world with one color, the kind of reader who cares most for the big, clean, fresh-air things of life. A magazine generally gets the kind of reader it aims for and, of course, there is nothing strange in there being many women who like exactly what our type of man likes. The women members of our Camp-Fire can be sure that they get from their men comrades exactly the kind of welcome they want from us, a frank, clean, "man to man" fellowship.

Chicago, Ill.

There is so little I've done that I'm afraid it will not be at all interesting. I was born of poor but respectful parents in the little old State of New Jersey—one of a large family who saw to it that I did not develop much conceit. I was born in June, married in June and my boy was born in June, the last-named event taking place while I was still well within my teens, the second, after I'd entered my teens by a very few years indeed. I don't know why I married so young unless some one whispered in my ear that men were getting scarce. So that now I have a boy who says he is big enough to eat pie off my head.

I TOOK a business course after my marriage when reverses came and finished the course in three months and three weeks. Have two records on the typewriter—nobody gave them to me, I took them myself. One is erratic touch and the other is the discovery of the greatest number of new ways to make mistakes every day. I might possibly do better work on the machine if I could bring myself down to less of a hurry in doing things. But—there is so much to do and be seen in this little old world and I've barely touched the edges.

I'VE been from ocean to ocean, dipped in one and rode on the other. Love Colorado and am going to camp out in its mountains before I'm many years older. I started to write five years ago—did three stories the first year, three or four the next and about the same the next, for two years I've been working at it fairly regularly for me.

I came to Chicago seven years ago, weighing one-hundred and thirty-three pounds—and look at me now, darn it! I'm American to the backbone and beyond. Dad served three years in the Civil War, entering when he was sixteen, and two maternal uncles served, one being killed in battle, so I'm not a bit neutral now—nor was I before we entered this war, and my greatest hope is that it doesn't end till the Kaiser is *licked*.

I think I shall remain at thirty-five years old—permanently, and I love to laugh.

AS I told you, the incident on the Atlantic City pier in my story "When Jim Came Into His Own" was taken from an actual occurrence. The man who did it is six feet four and weighs two hundred and forty pounds, and when the little event was finished the only thing to show that he'd been at all deeply interested, was that his cigar lay at his feet, bitten in two. He nearly converted me to spiritualism—or something—for he is the only person I ever knew who could materialize out of thin air. I'll take a vow that I've been on the street and no one in sight for two blocks in four directions and in an instant he has stood beside me, looking about like Billy Penn on the Philadelphia City Hall.

Here's hoping to our acquaintance being freely and long continued—LOTTA ADELE GANNETT.

WORD from our comrade, Harry C. Winters, now convalescent from hospital from England. Tommy need not worry. Our boys will, like the Canadians, come across with the deeds he's asking for. Hold up your end, Tommy, and our boys will hold up theirs. You've too many deeds behind you to let yourself get worried by other people's words. And I hope Comrade Winters, Australian, knows that one of America's—and Canada's—national games is kidding, and that when you play that game you don't let it worry you. Also, comrade, don't forget that the Australians rank as high as talkers as they do as blamed good fighters. Nevertheless your advice is sound and doubtless needed. Stick together? Of course. Live clean? You bet it's necessary.

Alnwick, England.

Evidently my last two letters miscarried, probably strafed by U-boats. Left hospital and am now in the running again, expecting to go back to the front shortly. I'm glad Uncle Sam has taken a hand. It should expedite matters. The first contingent got a very warm welcome; the people rose to the occasion. Seem men of fine physique; if they are as good as they look, should give a good account of themselves.

ONE thing I'd warn the boys of is this: Don't blow the horn too loud. Tommy is rather a queer chap and doesn't like to be told by new arrivals that they have come to finish the war. Of course it's only the —— fool youngsters that do so. What Tommy wants is deeds, not words. Let the men prove worthy by their actions and he'll find in Thomas a friend to tie to, who won't let him down.

The boys have a high standard to live up to. Personally, from my knowledge of the American, I know he can and will live up to it, but these few words of advice, from one who has had three years of it, may not come amiss. If we are to win the campaign, it behooves us to stick together, live clean. You know what I mean by that. And, above all, don't talk too much, act.

OLD Fritz is a hard man to beat and has put up a dashing fight and he's not beat yet. Please God, before next Spring we'll have him where we want him. These peace cranks want discouraging, when we have peace we want one on a solid and lasting basis and Fritz will not have the dictating of the terms. Best respects to the boys and tell them that, though perhaps unable to answer, would certainly enjoy a line from some of them. Incidentally, also a little Durham or some sweet chewing plug would come in handy.—PVTE. HARRY C. WINTERS, 48541, N. F. S., Command Depot, Alnwick, Northumberland, England.

THOSE of you on the front, land or sea, ought to know how much the rest of us are interested in your letters. Drop us a line. We know the censor limits you but there is plenty left to say and we surely want to hear from you. Write to the Camp-Fire and reach lots of friends at once.

BY THE time this reaches you the third Liberty Loan will probably be calling you. Answer the call. Buy bonds.

I say this to you not as blind, unreasoning patriots but as thinking men, and I practise what I preach.

Every minute of the war America needs *our* support. When the Administration makes mistakes America needs *our* support all the more. If the Administration asks less of some other citizens than it does of us, that does not free us from our obligation in full. We set up this Administration to lead and command us; it stands now for our country. We may not like it or approve it, but we owe it our loyalty and support.

LOYALTY to America divides sharply into two duties. Our first duty, at any minute, is loyal support of whatever Administration is at that minute in power, unquestioning obedience to whatever laws are at that minute in force. Our second duty to America is to see to it that whatever Administration we have chosen for her does its duty as fully as we should do ours, sees and corrects its mistakes when possible, sees and removes its incompetents always. These two things constitute patriotism, loyalty to America, to the people. But the second duty must wait upon the first; we have no right to point out the mistakes of the Administration if we ourselves have made the mistake of failing to support that Administration *as it stands*.

America needs money *now*. Buy Liberty Bonds. Don't just complain in advance about how the Administration is going to use that money. You have no right to any voice in that until you have done *your* part and furnished some of that money. *Your* duty *now* is to buy Bonds.

WE KNOW that much of our money must go to remedy the results of the Administration's stubborn or stupid refusal to prepare in advance for the war, that trying to do in months what should have been done in years means the loss of much extra money, time and effort without any extra returns. But that colossal blunder of the Administration's can not now be undone. We must not make a blunder ourselves by not doing the best we can *now*. Buy Bonds. *After* that, see to it that as many as possible of the Administration who were responsible for the tragic blunder of Unpreparedness are forced from office or at least never again entrusted with public office in America. But while they are in office, support them. Buy Bonds.

THROUGH the investigation by Congress we begin to know who are the incompetents responsible for national mistakes and delays. Our duty is to insist that power be taken from the hands of incompetents. We know, for example, if the head of the Ordnance Bureau is incompetent, that not only should he be removed, but that his incompetency argues the incompetency of Secretary Baker who retained him, either knowing his incompetency or else so ignorant of the condition of one of the most important bureaus of his department that he did not know of the incompetency of its chief, his direct subordinate for whom he is responsible. Secretary Baker's incompetency seems sufficiently established in other ways. A pacifist Secretary of War who for three years refused to prepare at all because "the war was three thousand miles away" is bad enough, but a Secretary of War who, after nearly a year of American participation, is still three thousand miles away from the war and three million miles away from any real comprehension of its needs is too limited mentally for the country's fate to rest so largely in his small hand. If you are convinced of the incompetency of officials, it is your duty to call for their removal. But that is only your second duty to America. Your first duty is to do your own part well and fully. Buy Bonds.

WE KNOW that Congress and the Administration have not equally distributed the financial burden of the war. There are those who believe there should be *no* excess profits from war or other industries when most of us are losing by the war, not profiting from it. In the present upheaval of economic conditions, with practical accomplishment dependent so largely upon individual effort and stimulus, an eighty per cent. tax, as in England, would seem wiser and productive of quicker, better and bigger results. But not less than eighty per cent. Most of us believe that the hundreds of millions of such profits already made should be the first money spent for Liberty Bonds, since what earned them is so large a part of what the war is waged to protect. It is our second duty to America to force Congress and the Administration to distribute the cost of the war more fairly and justly. But it is our first duty to support the distribution as it stands.

We know that politics and party have sometimes been put before patriotism and country. Our crisis calls for a leadership drawn from the whole people, not chiefly from one political party; from the brains and energies of the whole country, not half of it. It is our second duty to demand a coalition Government, but first we must guarantee our own full energies and support. Buy Bonds.

WE KNOW that, after two years and a half of warning followed by nearly a year actually in the war, great America, the richest country in the world, with a population of a hundred millions, is now contributing to the war much money and moral support, some brains, a navy smaller than it should be, and, at this writing in January, an army almost the size of England's casualty lists for six or nine months. We know that great America is not able to meet the vital demand of the crisis for merchant ships—which even a neutral and pacifist country is free to build—and that at the end of a whole year our contribution of ships is still chiefly plans and provision for the future. We know that great America was so unprepared and so incompetent in the actual test that she is not even yet able to equip the comparatively small army she has put into the field and has had to borrow from her Allies what they needed for themselves. We know now that William Jennings Bryan by his glib and silver-tongued prediction that "a million men would spring to arms between sunrise and sunset" has written himself down as the ass of history. We begin to feel now the whole long, bitter, tragic proof of the blunder of Unpreparedness. It is our duty to see to it that, so long as other nations carry arms, the advocates of unpreparedness do not again bring us to the brink of catastrophe. But we must think of past unpreparedness now only as a warning for the future. The damage will be repaired, so far as it can be repaired, not by complaint but by work, loyalty, support. Buy Bonds.

BEFORE our troops go into their first big battle they have begun to pay the toll of eleventh-hour preparation following three years of unpreparedness. But they who have died for unpreparedness are for a later reckoning. They have no bearing on our present duty to America. Our present duty continues to be one thing—to do *our* part *now*.

Buy Bonds. Buy all you can afford, and afford all you can by cutting out things you do not need. Buy Bonds. But do not stop there. By this time each of us knows what is asked of him, the ways in which he can help win the war. You know your duty, do it. In all things. And the foremost of these things is support and loyalty to our Administration, good or bad, so long as it remains our Administration, and to each man in it so long as he remains a part of it. For the Administration stands for America.

I KNOW that in speaking thus frankly I shall bring down upon myself from a certain type of American the charge of being unpatriotic. Another of the Administration's mistakes has been the building up of the idea that any criticism of itself is disloyalty. Purely destructive criticism of it *is* disloyalty, at least in its effect, but neither honest constructive criticism nor a frank facing of the facts is unpatriotic in the eyes of any one but fools.

Any man or institution that denies the right of constructive criticism is un-American and undemocratic. Only a fool or a traitor withholds one jot of his loyalty because of mistakes that can not be remedied, but only an utter idiot or a more subtle and dangerous traitor calls it "patriotism" to allow a present mistake to go uncorrected or fails to take steps against future mistakes.

We are at war, and war is facts. A war has never yet been won with mistakes. Or by incompetents. Or with excuses. If we are to win this war we can not listen to excuses, we can not leave mistakes unremedied, we can not retain incompetents.

IT IS truth and frankness we need. "Tell the truth and win the war." We want the facts, not the camouflaged facts. Whitewash is not war. Claims are not accomplishments. Sugar-coating does not destroy the bitter pill within. We have guts enough for facts, but not stomach enough for sweetened infant-food. Let us have a man's diet.

What disciple of fear and untruth can openly maintain that the American people will not fight better and make themselves better able to fight if they know the full need and danger? War makes necessary the suppression of information that will aid the enemy, if he doesn't know it already, but war also makes necessary the giving out of information whose *suppression* will aid the enemy.

I WILL make no appeal to any man's patriotism if the only kind of patriotism I am allowed to invoke is the kind that has neither eyes or ears or brains. And if any one finds disloyalty in what I have stated, I call attention to the fact that it is exactly the same kind of disloyalty that, from the Summer of 1914 to date, has been fighting for national Preparedness while certain other very good Americans were "too proud to fight" and too pacifically asleep to do more than watch waitfully behind the barn door until the horse had been stolen.

My platform now is very simple. First, let's all turn to and try to catch the horse. Second, let's see that the barn door isn't left open again.

In other words, let us do our immediate duty immediately. Buy Liberty Bonds. After that, let us attend to our next duty—see to it that the Liberty Bonds are used to America's best advantage.

ARTHUR SULLIVANT HOFFMAN.

ADVENTURE'S FREE SERVICES AND ADDRESSES

These services of *Adventure* are free to *any one*. They involve much time, work and expense on our part, but we offer them gladly and ask in return only that you *read and observe the simple rules*, thus saving needless delay and trouble for you and us. The whole spirit of this magazine is one of friendliness. No formality between editors and readers. Whenever we *can* help you we're ready and willing to try.

Identification Cards

Free to any reader. Just send us (1) your name and address, (2) name and address of party to be notified, (3) a stamped and self-addressed return envelope.

Each card bears this inscription, each printed in English, French Spanish, German, Portuguese, Dutch, Italian, Arabic, Chinese, Russian, and Japanese:

"In case of death or serious emergency to bearer, address serial number of this card, care of *Adventure*, New York, stating full particulars, and friends will be notified."

In our office, under each serial number, will be registered the name of bearer and of one friend, with permanent address of each. No name appears on the card. Letters will be forwarded to friend, unopened by us. Names and addresses treated as confidential. We assume no other obligations. Cards not for business identification. Cards furnished free, *provided stamped and addressed envelope accompanies application*. We reserve the right to use our own discretion in all matters pertaining to these cards.

Later we may furnish a metal card or tag. If interested in metal cards, say so on a *post-card—not* in a letter. No obligation entailed. These post-cards, filed, will guide us as to demand and number needed.

A moment's thought will show the value of this system of card-identification for any one, whether in civilization or out of it. Remember to furnish stamped and addressed envelope and to *give in full the names and addresses of self and friend or friends when applying.*

Back Issues of *Adventure*

Will sell: 1916, October; 1917, February to Mid-December, inclusive, except July; 1918, January and Mid-January. All stories complete. $1.25. Address—N. P. HUTSON, 613 Monroe St., Brooklyn, N. Y.

Manuscripts

Glad to look at any manuscript. We have no "regular staff" of writers. A welcome for new writers. *It is not necessary to write asking to submit your work.*

When submitting a manuscript, if you write a letter concerning it, enclose it *with* the manuscript; do *not* send it under separate cover. Enclose stamped and addressed envelope for return. All manuscripts should be typewritten double-spaced, with wide margins, not rolled, name and address on first page. We assume no risk for manuscripts or illustrations submitted, but use all due care while they are in our hands. Payment on acceptance.

We want only clean stories. Sex, morbid, "problem," psychological and supernatural stories barred. Use almost no fact-articles. Can not furnish or suggest collaborators. Use fiction of almost any length; under 3000 welcomed.

Missing Friends or Relatives

Our free service department "Lost Trails" in the pages following, though frequently used in cases where detective agencies, newspapers, and all other methods have failed, or for finding people long since dead, has located one out of about every five inquired for. Except in case of relatives, inquiries from one sex to the other are barred.

Expeditions and Employment

While we should like to be of aid in these matters, experience has shown that it is not practicable.

Mail Address and Forwarding Service

This office, assuming no responsibility, will be glad to act as a forwarding address for its readers or to hold mail till called for, provided necessary postage is supplied.

Addresses

Order of the Restless—Organizing to unite for fellowship all who feel the wanderlust. Entirely separate from Adventurers' Club, but, like it, first suggested in this magazine, though having no connection with it aside from our friendly interest. Address WAYNE EBERLY, 731 Guardian Bldg., Cleveland, O., in charge of preliminary organizing.

Camp-Fire—Any one belongs who wishes to.

High-School Volunteers of the U. S.—An organization promoting a democratic system of military training in American high schools. Address *Everybody's*, Spring and Macdougal Streets, New York City.

Rifle Clubs—Address Nat. Rifle Ass'n of America, 1108 Woodward Bldg., Washington, D. C.

(*See also under "Standing Information" in "Ask Adventure."*)

General Questions from Readers

In addition to our free service department "Ask Adventure" on the pages following, *Adventure* can sometimes answer other questions within our general field. When it can, it will. Expeditions and employment excepted.

Remember

Magazines are made up ahead of time. An item received today is too late for the current issue; allow for two or three months between sending and publication.

The:Camp:Fire

A Free-to-All Meeting-Place for Readers, Writers, and Adventurers

WITH his second story in our magazine Major Frederick S. Macy follows Camp-Fire custom and stands up to introduce himself to us. We bought the story before the United States entered the war, and Major Macy, then a captain, wrote to us from the U. S. Army Transport *Buford*, somewhere between the Canal Zone and San Francisco. Since then I've sat across the table from him at the Adventurers' Club when he was stationed at Governors Island. No one is supposed to know the whereabouts of any soldier nowadays and perhaps we're doing him an injustice in still giving his rank as major. I hope so.

Some time ago you asked me for a fairly full biography, and I prepared one; but by an inadvertence it was not mailed before this ship departed from New York.

However, I shall correct the matter now, in case you are still desirous of it, for it is only natural that those who read a story should ask by what authority the writer speaks or upon what experience he bases his narrative, in order to form a just opinion of the value of the picture.

THE early part of my existence began forty years ago in Detroit, Michigan, when I was formally presented to my parents as an addition to a long line of Colonial descendants, the first of whom found Massachusetts an uncomfortable place of abode for Quakers and removed himself to Nantucket. Whittier's poem, "The Exiles," celebrates the performance, but really contains more poetry than fact.

After the period of schooling, and growing up in a thoroughly domesticated way, as most boys do, I entered a prominent Boston institution for the preparation of physicians and graduated therefrom in 1897.

IN 1900 I entered the Army as an acting assistant surgeon, and my life, since then, has been filled with many things; with professional honors and education such as I, at least, could never have received in civil life. I have had experiences and trials of many kinds, as well as triumphs and the discipline of an ordered, active career, which is, I think, the secret of real happiness as well as of usefulness. I have felt the pain of long separation from those who are dear, and the unparalleled joy of reunion with them. I have faced death in many forms, and what is sometimes harder, life. I have felt the caress of my babies' hands and the blandishments of human foxes.

FOR nearly four years I hiked, as they say, with many different military organizations over the largest islands of the Philippines. I saw men conquer and I saw them die. I saw the natives of those islands under all conditions, peaceful and savage, in idolatry, cannibalism, and in what passed for Christianity. So, too, I have seen the soldier under all the conditions of his life, maligned and lauded, in peace and in jungle warfare.

In 1900 I returned to God's country, and after a service in our home posts went again to the Islands in 1907. This time I spent a little over three years among the head hunters of Luzon. There, two little sons came to me, and their nurses were two brown lads of the high mountain tribes, who loved them as tenderly as women.

In 1910 I came home again to America, back to the posts and the routine of barracks and quarters. During the last two years I have been wandering about over two oceans on a transport, and just now I am on a voyage from New York to Manila by way of the Panama Canal and Honolulu.

So you see I have been much of a traveler both in the Occident and the Orient, and in other countries than the Islands. But I speak of them particularly because of *Paddy*.

EXCEPT as a type, he had never an existence. But it is types which I wish to show; to show you the soldier as he is, your Army as it is. I want you to know it and to love it, its traditions, its honor, its privations and its joys; to feel that it belongs to you and your people, individually and collectively. I want you to live with me in it, to revere the noble, heroic women, the wives, who see their men depart for God knows what, and yet can smile at them a brave good-by—till the dust has settled again.

And I want you to believe that what I say of them all is true to the life as I have seen it. For I shall not distort truth to fit the play, nor endeavor to conceal the fact that they are just as human as others. I shall not always paint a rosy day. You must be patient with their faults. In any case you will be proud of them and glad to call them yours.

THE modern Army surgeon has many military duties to perform in addition to those that are strictly medical. So I hope to take you and yours with me through many adventures, though in the armor of the easy chair, and to listen to the men jesting in barracks as well as making light of their pain in hospital.

Upon my return from this voyage I expect to go to a post once more. There is many a story of the sea, I find, that has not yet been told, and I shall bring back some of them with me.—FREDERICK S. MACY.

HERE is a greeting to us from one of the real pioneers of the old West, just a friendly hello and handshake:

Los Angeles.

Dear old plainsmen, stage guards, horse-breakers, scouts or miners—greeting. I belong to your tribe. I am not a big chief or a big cheerful liar. Anyway, age has changed me a little from the old ways of the frontier to a mellow, thinking, contented man. I once roamed the mountains and valleys and the plains. Now in my little cottage my sweet old wife and I are enjoying ourselves. With love for all I ask you to listen to my story. First, I would like you Camp-Fire boys not to expect too much from one who never was very much. I passed through the frontier from 1856 until lately. I broke horses that were running wild over the plains of our California, Nevada, Oregon and Utah from the mountains to the sea. I did my duty as I saw it. Have no excuses to make, only am a poor writer. But my friend, E. A. Brininstool, has asked me to write the Camp-Fire. He, Brininstool, is a live wire. He can do justice to the old boys by story and verse. I knew Frank Gruard; Brininstool's story is very correct. So I will only introduce myself to you all as your friend.—CLARK B. STOCKING, "The Old Guard."

WE IN the office are trying an interesting stunt. Managed to squeeze out four or five bound volumes of *Adventure* from our office files and are going to turn them over to some library to be sent to some of our boys at the front. In each one we're writing a brief message from us of the staff, sending our greetings and good wishes and asking every man who reads any of the stories to write his name on the fly-leaves and, when they are filled up, on the margins of any of the pages, giving the unit to which he is attached. And we're asking, too, that when the war is over if there happens to be anything left of the books, any or all of them be sent to our office, at our expense, to be kept always as very wonderful souvenirs.

BACK in the Fall there came to me a letter from our comrade Basil D. Woon, one of whose exploits on the Mexican border we have heard from others. Several weeks later came the second of the two following letters, both from "somewhere in France":

France.

This is my first line to you since the war, I think. My last, I believe, was from Dallas, Texas, and the one before that from Mexico City. Well, this isn't Dallas, Texas; nor is it Mexico City; but I've been here long enough to feel almost at home. As a matter of fact, my home is in London, so I am nearer to it now than I have been for many a long day.

I SUPPOSE you have seen that poster—by Gibson, I think—"Don't Read History; Make It." I think it was as much that poster as my innate love of "butting in," combined with a bit of "wanting to do something," that caused me to enlist. I thought it would be great fun, making history. It is, but it isn't a bit as I had pictured it. Do you know, after seeing the way war is waged under modern conditions, I believe I'll take the Mexican brand for mine, and thank you kindly. There's too much precision, too much system, too much machine work for me. Why, half the fun of war as we played at it in Mexico was the joy of taking somebody by surprise, or being taken by surprise oneself. And a man *felt* some one down there. Here he is only one of a score or so millions, all doing the same thing. I have just put in a transfer to the Air Service, having at last scraped through the physical, and I sincerely hope that there at any rate one's individual self will count a tiny bit, anyway.

I SUPPOSE something like this is in the minds of most of the other boys, but outwardly we're all happy and contented and waiting for our chance. It's a great game, anyway. France has treated us well, every one has been most kind, our quarters are about four times as good as any of us expected, and the chow is better than we got with Pershing in Chihuahua. In fact, if there's any scarcity of food in France it isn't inconveniently noticeable. Prices are either about the same or slightly less than one pays in the States—which is not so bad when you consider all these wild claims Germany has been making. *I* haven't noticed any one hungry, and I've only met one beggar during the entire time I've been in France. He met me at the Place de la Concorde one afternoon in Paris and exhibited five distinct wounds gained in the war. *That* man had a *right* to beg. I felt ashamed to be the one handing it to him—he had given so much and I hadn't even begun to give anything. I realized then what a lot of lost time we Americans have got to make up for.

The trouble about a letter like this is that the censor has nothing to do except delete. It becomes a habit with him, and I'm afraid if I go rambling on I'll transgress some rule or other and this letter won't reach you at all.—BASIL D. WOON.

His second letter brings up the point of *Adventure* in France. We've tried hard to make it obtainable over there and are still trying, but the chief answer is that ship tonnage is needed for more important things than magazines. I've personally sent quite a few copies to Camp-Fire comrades over there, but not many of them seem to reach their destination. At this writing any public library in the country will send books and magazines, received in good condition, to our forces abroad for general distribution, and post-offices will send magazines carrying a one-cent stamp and, in some cases at least, I understand, with or without the printed line on the cover, but to put a magazine on sale over there in large quantities is a different matter.

France.

One of the fellows just came over to my desk and whispered: "Hey, there's a copy of *Adventure* on that table!"

"Grab it, for the love of Mike!" I answered, and he did. I have just been looking it over, and the result of the perusal is this letter.

AS I WRITE you, I'm in France with the American Expeditionary Forces, holding down temporarily a job as sergeant in the Quartermaster Corps. I say "temporarily" because I have put in for a transfer to the Air Service, and, having passed the physical, am expecting to be ordered away in a few days. Meanwhile I am learning all I can at the French aviation camp near here.

Some day I hope to have something real to write you about—some day when I've actually done something—but just now there's nothing particular that I can say. Our boys over here are in splendid spirits and aching for action. They'll get it, too, no doubt about that. They are working like beavers at the new game of war, and the French instructors say they're learning rather remarkably fast. This is easily understandable when one knows their officers—as fine a set of men as I have seen anywhere in the world. One instinctively knows that whatever these men set out to do that will be done, and no nonsense about it.

THE French people have met us very cordially and we have no complaints to make. By the time you receive this the news will be a trifle stale; however, I may interpolate that we have excellent quarters, good beds and plenty of first-class American chow. Nothing to kick about—not even the weather, which has just turned chilly after a long spell of Indian Summer.

There are just three things we need now—a constant supply of all three. They are: smoking tobacco (American vintage), plenty of mail, and *Adventure* every month. I'm going to give my copy to the Y. M. C. A. after I get through with it and ask them to padlock it to a table, so that every man in the outfit will have a chance to look it over. But I wouldn't give it up now to my best brother.

WE HAD a brush with a Sub coming over—missed us by ten feet. That was a long time ago, because I came here the 1st, so I suppose the censor won't find anything censorable in the information. I expect it's been printed in America, anyway. I happened to have just gone on duty as helper at Gun No. 4 when the thing happened. A little tow-headed Jackie startled the fits out of me by yelling "Torpedo!" in a voice that could be heard all over the ship. I looked to port and, sure enough, there was a wake, about three feet wide, and coming like Billy-be-damned right for my feet. I thought of a number of things in the ensuing seconds, I can tell you, and I think my bitterest reflection was that some other lucky son-of-a-gun would be writing the story. I wasn't sure whether I would come down on top of the gun or whether the gun would come down on top of me. However, the thing missed by a shadow and we got in a shot or two at the periscope. Some say we hit; some that we missed. I'm personally neutral.

WELL, I'll close with the personal assurance to you that America's "Old Contemptibles" are "doing themselves proud," and that you folks back home will be having lots of things to read before long. Hope to hear from you soon. With remembrances to all my friends in and out of *Adventure*.
—BASIL DILLON WOON.

IT'S mighty seldom you are asked to follow the fortunes of a woman as the central character in one of our stories. Our interests don't run much to boudoirs and other ladylike affairs. But the Lady Fulvia wasn't a lady, at least in that sense, and boudoirs meant nothing to her. She lived in an iron-hard age and held her own—ana then some—among the men of a race who have never been surpassed as grim fighters and adventurers par excellence. She could wear a sword, and use it, but most of all she could use her wits. And God help the hard man and grim fighter who crossed the path of this warlike, beautiful, courageous and very likeable and human young woman. Tougher men than you, my friend, have matched themselves against her and, one by one, you'll hear what happened to them.

I give Fulvia this careful introduction to you because I know she needs it. When the authors suggested her adventures for your reading, I shied away. I don't run to boudoir stories myself and view with deep suspicion any woman presented as being some one whose deeds would make good reading for us. But, having learned what she really was and did, I've surrendered as to Fulvia, and when you've got acquainted with her I don't think you'll blame me. The adventure given you in this issue is only one of several and, as most of you probably aren't any more familiar with the time and place she lived in than I was, the authors here give the setting, color and general understanding that make the picture living and complete:

Long ages before the shepherds of Latium laid the first primitive walls of Rome, forgotten peoples whose very name has almost vanished, were fighting desperate wars for the possession of Sicily. This loveliest and most fertile of islands, lying in the middle of the Mediterranean, was destined from the beginning to be the meeting-place and battle-ground of nations.

THITHER came the exiles, the fortune-hunters, the adventurers of all the world—the greedy merchants and luxurious princes of Carthage; the daring colonists of Greece, with their matchless military skill and their passionate love of beauty; the Romans, seeking universal empire; plundering Goths and piratical Vandals; the myriads of effeminate Byzantium. Thither came also the two fiercest of medieval peoples: the Arabs, at the height of their inundating conquests, drowning out the survivals of Roman civilization and enslaving all that called on Christ; and the half-viking Normans, who spoke French and lived like their Norse sires.

AMID the rich beauty of Sicily all these races ruled for a time, were absorbed, and fell before the rude vigor of the next conquerors. Yet one, more than all the others, held what it had taken and made itself the arbiter of Southern destiny.

This was the Norman folk. Never more than a mere handful, almost lost among thousands of alien blood, these Northern adventurers carved their way to empire through hosts of pagan Saracens, liberated the oppressed Greco-Sicilian Christians, and drew the island within the intricate network of their superb organization. On the ruins of a score of dead civilizations they set their throne; in the veins of their subjects ran the blood of half the world; their castles, churches, and palaces were rich with the blended art of Europe and Africa. Never the birthplace of a ruling race, Sicily was the glorious spoil of all who adventured by land or sea.

Law-givers though they were, the Normans were harsh and brutal to their captives, treacherous and ruthless to one another. The natives, Christian and Moslem alike, were driven to band together in secret, to plot in the dark against the conquerors, so that out of such obscure leagues the Mafia of a later time arose, with all its heritage of hidden treachery.

NOT till Roger the Great, himself the first of Normans, was crowned king at Palermo in 1130 did the land know justice and peace. Even then the wilder of his countrymen could be held in restraint only by the long swords of their more law-abiding kinsmen. So Norman baron fought Norman baron, on one side greed and lawlessness, on the other order and honor; till all were alike absorbed by the kindly motherland of Sicily, and became Sicilians.

IN THE middle of this strife between Norman law and Norman license these stories of Rocca Forte are set. The child of a Norman father and an Italian mother, Fulvia of Rocca Forte loves the land of her birth no less than the viking traditions of her ancestors. Born in the very year of King Roger's coronation, she regards herself a Sicilian, and considers the oppressed Sicilians her own folk, to be loved and cherished. She is sought in marriage by all who have seen or heard of her beauty and her father's well-kept lands; but she will not listen to the suit of the blood-stained robber-barons. Her own shrewd brain and her father's sword suffice to defend her against the strength and cunning of her disappointed lovers.

She lives in a time celebrated for learning and art as well as for its brutal savagery. The rich plains, the rugged mountains, the enchanted coast-line of her land is strewn with the shards of dead cities and forgotten ports, out of which her Greek and Moslem subjects create new loveliness in stone and metal. Her king welcomes to his court Moorish scholars and Byzantine artificers, and builds universities to house the wisdom of all lands and times.

THEN, into this varied, many-colored life, strikes the swift fervor of the Second Crusade. God wills the destruction of the unbelievers who threaten His sepulchre; men's hearts are set on fire with flame from Heaven. But cosmopolitan Sicily dares to resist the call of Heaven. Roger has Moslem subjects of his own, peaceful, industrious, faithful men; and he sets their well-being higher than the need of Jerusalem. Yet the Crusade will not let him rule his land in peace; when all Europe burns with religious enthusiasm, one little land can not remain unkindled.

Civil strife and rapine around her, the storm of the Crusade threatening from without, her people buffeted by the strokes of both, Fulvia of Rocca Forte has barely reached her eighteenth birthday when she must defend her people and herself. Before she is nineteen the disaster of 1149 sends the backwash of the beaten Crusade swirling in upon her. She is the storm-center of Sicily; Sicily is the storm-center of the world. From the bleak North, the burning South, the conquest-greedy West, and the gorgeous, colorful East, the tides converge upon her.

These stories tell the tale of her struggle to keep her people safe, to be true to her traditions and her ideals, to find happiness for herself, and for Sicily.
FARNHAM BISHOP and ARTHUR GILCHRIST BRODEUR.

FROM Peru comes word from our comrade M. R. Cuthbertson. The omitted part of his letter deals with several men whom many of us know, but, though there are only pleasant words concerning them, this part of the letter was probably not intended for publication. One episode I'm leaving in, but omitting, with regret, the man's name. I shouldn't think he'd mind having his name given in this connection but he isn't where I can get his definite assurance.

Tirapata, Peru.

Something tells me that it is a long time since I have given you an idea of my doings and whereabouts. The last time I wrote I believe I was in Arizona. Nothing exciting happened for a long time. I took a little jaunt to Arkansas and worked for a while in the mines and mills and a smelter of the Joplin zinc district of Missouri about a year ago last March to June, but the West called me and I went back to the same old hole eventually, then things took up the same old course until last January, when I was offered a chance to come down here.

SAW ——— ——— in Arequipa, Peru, a few weeks ago. He had a lot of trouble with the law in Lima a while back for tearing the can off of a German with one of his famous punches. The last I heard of him was that he had gone to ———.

That's about all the news I can give you, and I doubt if any of it is news by now. I haven't seen an old-timer for a —— of a while; guess they are all over in the "World's Series" by now. That is something that I am going to miss, I guess. But I have my reasons, which are good.

MYSELF, I am on the east side of the Andes and about one hundred and fifty miles from the railroad. We are down about seven thousand feet and the country is quite tropical. The camp is about six miles from the Inambari River which reaches the Amazon in time; it flows into the Madre de Dios, which empties into the Madera, and the Madera flows into the Amazon.

The trail goes on into the Amazon country and all of the rubber that is shipped from Mollendo comes through this camp. It would make a good story if it was written up right. I haven't the time or I would make a stab at it.

This is a gold proposition and a winner, but it is all work and nothing but the Victrola to play with. The fact that it is one hundred and fifty miles by mule and two days more by train to Arequipa, stops us from making many trips.

If any one should happen to ask you where I am just hand them the address below.—M. R. CUTHBERTSON, care of Inca Mining & Development Co., Tirapata, via Arequipa, Peru, S. A.

A WORD from one of us with the American Expeditionary Force "somewhere in France," one of the many of us, by the way, who was also one of the twenty-five thousand of our American Legion:

WE ARE billeted here in a pretty little rural town, the boys sleeping in houses, garrets, barns, etc. Am very fortunate myself in having a whole room with a real bed in it, the first bed I've slept in, by the way, since last July, when we were called to the colors.

Will write more fully later, when we are not restricted as much as we are at present. Would be glad to hear from any of the Camp-Fire crowd at any time.—C. F. WHITELEY.

A WORD from one of our women comrades who is doing her bit at home:

Montreal, Canada.

Hello, Camp-Fire! May the "female of the species" salute? I have only about a year's acquaintance with you, but many a lonely, dreary hour you have helped me pass. You see, "my pal" enlisted with the 73d Royal Highlanders of Canada and has been gone overseas over two years, and we have tramped many trails together, read much together, and now, while "little folks" and I keep camp-fires burning at home, waiting lonesome-like, you help much, and "The Big Pal" writes me he enjoys you, too, as he lies in the hospital at Aldershot, England, where he has been the last six months. So I send you greeting and best wishes.—MRS. ——— ———.

IT'S been a long time since we've had word from our comrade, Albert Kinross, whose stories we enjoyed in years past. He is in Egypt and in an interesting service. The photograph referred to is one, sent me before the war, which, as a newspaper correspondent, he had secured in Russia during a former revolution, and I had written asking for some forgotten data.

I wish I could agree with him that the war is over. Germany will be beaten, but now, writing in mid-Winter, the wise thing for us to do is to settle down to the understanding that it's going to take time and greater effort than we've yet put forth.

Egyptian Expeditionary Force.

Your letter of July twenty-eighth reached me here in the desert. My address is Lieut. A. Kinross, A. S. C., attached C. T. C., No. 1 Depot, C. T. C. Egyptian Expeditionary Force. C. T. C. stands for Camel Transport Corps, so you may imagine I am having a change from mules, horses and torpedoes. I had the dubious pleasure of assisting in a U-boat affair a short time back. Still it's all food for later on.

Now the photo depicts a band of Lettish revolutionists (1905-1906) who felt so sure of themselves that they had their pictures taken. This is one of the pictures. On the evidence of this picture many were executed by the government forces which suppressed the revolution. I hope above will do.

How are you and *Adventure?* I had a letter from *Everybody's* some time ago asking me for a story. No chance, unless I get to the hospital again, which I am not anxious to do, thank you.

The war is really over bar the killing. Germany is beaten, but how can the Kaiser and his friends admit it? I wish the U. S. A. could attack from the Russo-Rumanian side.—A. KINROSS, Lieut.

THE responses to "You and Democracy" exceeded my expectations by both their number and earnestness. Nearly a month's illness prevented a prompt reply to these responses and the movement will designedly advance slowly. The American League for Citizenship has been incorporated, its general work and certain of its specific tasks are definitely mapped out, but in these and in determining its further specific tasks the co-operation of all interested is desired. It is not a one-man, but a democratic organization. There will be as few officers as possible; it stands for the idea that office-holding is not opportunity for self-glorification and self-advancement, but the undertaking of extra work and extra responsibility.

Full information will be given slowly but as fast as possible.

ARTHUR SULLIVANT HOFFMAN.

FROM one of our Camp-Fire comrades, writers' brigade, comes a "bye" to the rest of us, written in December. Good luck to him!

My regiment, the —— Engineers, will leave —— and we expect to eat New Year's dinner at sea. Please say "bye" for me to the Sitters at the Camp-Fire.—HARRISON R. HOWARD.

OUR older readers will remember Captain George A. Schreiner's personal reminiscences of the Boer War published in some of our 1913 issues. Since then many things have happened and Captain Schreiner has had a hand in many of them, as witness his article in this issue.

When the Great War began, Captain Schreiner was one of the few correspondents who gave this country all its news of the first German rush and the overwhelming of Belgium. Being thus on duty inside the German lines he was continued there and, during the three years following, was an American correspondent on the French, Italian, Russian, Serbian and Rumanian fronts with the German and Austro-Hungarian armies. Probably the Americans who have seen as much of the war as he has can easily be counted on the fingers of one hand.

August 7, 1917, I received the following letter from him, written in New York—my first news of his having returned to this country some time before—he came home on our entrance into the war.

I have recently blown in from Europe. Greetings:

Having made Aguas Calientes, Mexico, and Deera, Northern Arabia, in a single jump, as it were, I have been able to gather a whole lot of most interesting stuff of an adventure character. It includes the Villa operations of 1914 and my eight months' stay in Turkey, not to mention some six months in the Balkans. Perhaps I should state here that what I have is not war copy, but just personal adventure connected with the war, which I may even say of my Dardanelles and Gallipoli experiences.

I do not consider myself competent to judge what the value of this copy to you would be, but I may say that most of it appears to me to be better stuff than my South African stories. At any rate, it is more actual.

Most of my notes were put in shape as I went along. I made the mistake, however, of using the pronoun I and lapsing now and then into the present tense, so that in all probability the stuff will have to be rewritten—though in personal adventure it is rather difficult to get away from the "I."

THE above is only part of the letter. In the remainder, however, he mentions material he had gathered in Mexico and Europe—at Zacatecas, in the bandit zones, campaigning with Villa, experiences in Galicia, Serbia, Budapest, Turkey, Bulgaria, Suvla Bay, Asia Minor. At Zacatecas, in Anatolia, Syria and Damascus he was the only American newspaper man present, and the only one who ever interviewed the Sultan of Turkey, Mehmed Rechad Khan V. (see the article in this issue) or who witnessed one of Armenia's "red caravans of sorrow."

Of Pancho Villa he wrote:

I was known in Mexico as the friend of "Pancho." On a passport he gave me he said so himself. At any rate, I lay claim to knowing this picturesque character as few do.

I may add that his "stuff" has *not* been rewritten by us.

Another letter, dated September 27, 1917, gives an interesting perspective on the events set forth in our article:

There are a good many other things which might be said in connection with the article. But I feel that you, and not I, should say them. A few of them I will briefly indicate. The operation was by far the largest of its kind ever undertaken, having but a scant parallel even in the bombardments and siege of Port Arthur. Had the operation succeeded, the European War would have been over long ago, since in that case Bulgaria would not have entered the war on the side of the Central Powers and in doing that permit Germany to ship into Turkey the means needed to fight the Russian and British troops in Southwest Asia. In that case Serbia might have carried out her plans against Austria-Hungary instead of being out of existence.

Success against the Dardanelles in March, 1915, would have averted the killing and wounding of some two hundred and twenty thousand Allied troops on Gallipoli, and that success would have come had the Allied fleet returned to the attack on March nineteenth.

Aside from the modification specifically noted here, I have not changed the copy, but improved it here and there.—GEO. A. SCHREINER.

THE modification he speaks of was a shortening of the account of his interview with the Grand Vizier. Just what things should be added by me I am not sure. The importance of the crisis at the Dardanelles is made sufficiently plain above and in the article itself. It is not necessary, I trust, to point out that Captain Schreiner was with the armies of the Central Powers during the nearly three years before this country entered the war and that he was stationed there by the American news agency that commanded his services. During the events set forth in the present article the United States was, of course, only a neutral.

Captain Schreiner, a relative of the famous South African writer, Olive Schreiner, was born in Avricourt of Alsatian parents. He is an American citizen.

FOLLOWING our Camp-Fire custom, Herbert Slocombe stands up and introduces himself on the occasion of his first story in our magazine:

I was born and educated at New Haven, Conn. How many thrilling adventures and hairbreadth escapes I had in my boyhood days I venture not to say. I remember a few instances of close calls in Long Island Sound. In one instance in a closed-cabin catboat during a Labor Day squall, when the combers swept us stem to stern, we were forced to turn and take refuge in a little cove far up between the innumerable reefs of the Thimble Islands. The big seas that boarded us broadside kept four men bailing while two manned the dangerously keeled-over boat. Being sidewiped in a leaky rowboat against an oyster stake by the bow waves of a large excursion steamer was another close call. Adrift on a raft, alone, and beyond hailing distance from shore, also threatened to end my adventurous career.

MY FIRST adventure in camp which stands above all others in my mind, was simply a matter of localized skill of a certain set of trained muscles. The event was a quoit tournament at the second encampment of the Fox Fire Outing Club, seventeen Summers ago, at Lampher's Cove, on Long Island Sound. I can recall that last full day at camp with remarkable clearness. It was the closing day of the quoit tournament in which I was a hard thrower. On that day the scores of the seven official preceding games were to be computed and the two pitchers with highest scores were to be pitted against each other to decide the championship. And for whom an appropriate medal was to be struck.

The tenderfoot games had been pitched in the morning, but we old-timers on the 'varsity bench held haughtily aloof.

Johnson, my opponent, held 201 points to my 203. We had made close scores all the week and betting was now fifty-fifty with no favoritism shown. I feared no opponent more than Johnson, for at times he would develop a brilliant run of play, an almost uncanny precision of aim that could not be beaten and seldom tied.

WE PLAYED the game by our own camp rules counting "ringers" 5 points, "leaners" 3, "touchers" 2, and the nearest quoit 1. Players led alternately, throwing both their irons in succession. These four throws we called a "heat." The game was for 21 points, the scores announced at the completion of each "heat."

The big game had started and I recall that we proceeded with almost tie scores up to the last heat. Sixteen to seventeen in my favor was the announcement as Johnson smirked one of his characteristic grins and bent to lead off for his last two throws. His first iron struck the peg, whirled, slewed off and rolled away. It was a lost throw. Undaunted, however, Johnson only grinned and bent his long supple body for his last throw. This time he landed a high "leaner," a dangerous play to follow because the least jolt threatened to jar it over the peg, in which case it would count Johnson 5 points as a "ringer," and that, with his previous score of 16, would count him out. As it stood, however he had only 19 points. Either I must throw wild and depend entirely on the next "heat" for a decision, or summon all my trained cunning to save the situation. I decided on the latter.

I DREW a long breath as I crouched for my first throw, gaging everything to a nicety in my mind's eye. I would play my irons to the left of the stake (Johnson's "leaner" was on the right) so that any collision would have the effect of shunting his quoit off and away from the peg. I uncoiled my arm and let go. But when the little cloud of dust from the dry dirt we had pulled about the stakes had settled, lo! Johnson's iron was ringing the peg! I had one throw left.

Rooters close in about the peg broke into lusty yells and whoops as my last iron dropped with a clang, with the usual spurt of dust partially obscuring results. When I recoiled from that crouched, panther-like position everybody was hooting—Johnson the loudest of all. I was about to congratulate him on his luck, though my heart felt heavy, when I noticed the referee clearing away the dust, exposing what I alone had failed to discern. Two irons lay encircling the peg! My last one, an oversized quoit which I always threw last, lay snug on top of Johnson's.

That "double ringer" scored me 10 and won me the medal with a score of 234 points for the eight official games we had played.

YES, I've traveled pretty well around the rim of this Union, and been in some out-of-the-way places, but most of all I've met and companioned with adventurers, confided and learned their life stories from their point of view. Particularly I have talked with sailors about the great docks on seaboard and lake. With river boatmen North and South and with railroad men of the West. But, most of all, I have visited with miners and prospectors—of mountain and Alaska fame. Several I have met, who have made big strikes on the borders of civilization, had returned only to drop their elusive hoardings. One old character, a Swede, a decade ago returned to Omaha to visit his folks with clock-like regularity every second Summer, returning to Nome, up the Porcupine, or over the Tanana Hills to his biennial tasks afield.

From all these sources, a combination of first-hand knowledge together with first-hand reminiscence from toil-worn adventurers I have gathered the materials for most of my stories.—HERBERT SLOCOMBE.

THE other day I had lunch and a long talk with our Camp-Fire comrade Lieutenant Pat O'Brien, the American of the British Royal Flying Corps who, wounded and captured by the Germans, jumped from a train and escaped after seventy-two days of hardship and danger—certainly one of the most dramatic and splendid individual adventures that have come out of the Great War. You will remember how our Camp-Fire helped get news of him after his capture. A fine chap, entirely unspoiled by his fame, and, I am glad to say, almost as sound as ever after his terrific experience. I'll not try to tell you more, for, by the time this reaches you, you can get the full story from his book or lectures.

A WORD from the authors on "The Iron Arm," the second of the tales of Rocca Forte and the warlike Lady Fulvia:

Arnulfo, Count of Rocca Forte, is about half historical. His achievement in rising from a sick-bed to hurl himself upon a numerically superior enemy was actually drawn from an exploit of Guillaume Bras-de-Fer, one of the Norman conquerors of Sicily. Forced to lead his seven hundred men out against ten thousand Greeks, when he himself was sick with fever, Guillaume watched the battle from a hill against the slope of which his men were being ground to pieces by the enemy. at the critical moment he rushed down the hill, waving his sword and calling out his war-cry. His men were heartened, and put the Greeks to flight.

We have moved up the date of the story to 1148, given Arnulfo a castle such as served the Normans in Sicily as fortresses and centers of oppression, and made him a better man than most of his compatriots were. The setting is strictly historic: Sicily under the Normans was most cosmopolitan in population, being peopled with men of many stocks, among which Greeks, Arabs, and Italians (then called Lombards) predominated. Tyranny was a matter of greed: King Roger tolerated all religions, and all the inhabitants preserved their native customs ntact, until the slow process of the "melting-pot" had worked. The scene is the north coast of Sicily, about seventy miles east of Palermo.—FARNHAM BISHOP and ARTHUR GILCHRIST BRODEUR.

CONCERNING "With Sharp Sword-Edges," Arthur Gilchrist Brodeur, speaking for himself and Farnham Bishop, asks to be heard at Camp-Fire and gives us some interesting information. He speaks with authority on these subjects.

Incidentally, remember one of our covers showing an old Norse galley? It was on the issue in which "Sword Edges" began. One of you wrote asking whether it were authoritative as to historical detail. It was. The artist, Dwight Franklin, suggested the idea by showing us a photograph of a model he had made in miniature. That model was one of many he has made illustrating scenes from various past ages and so accurate in archeological and historical detail that most of them go to the various museums of the country. The one in question is now, I think, in the Metropolitan Museum of Art in this city.

WHEN the magazine reached the authors they were amazed and delighted to find a cover illustrating their story, done by an old personal friend of theirs.

Another personal link in the chain is that recently Will Crawford, another of our artists, a particular favorite with you, took up working quarters with Dwight Franklin in the same studios where these wonderful models live until completed and disposed of. Some of them, by the way, are half a year in the making, for the amount of research required is immense.

Back to Mr. Brodeur's letter to you:

Some time ago, I read Lee M. Hollander's review of a story on a Norse subject by Maurice Hewlett. Dr. Hollander justly censured Hewlett for failing to admit his indebtedness to the saga which furnished him with his material. We don't want such a censure to fall on the magazine or on ourselves. I realize that "Sword-Edges" will be entirely published before any statement could be made in the magazine concerning our sources; but if you could find space, in the Camp-Fire of some future issue, for such a statement, it might disarm just and dangerous criticism. The statement might read something as follows:

"WITH SHARP SWORD-EDGES" depends, for its material, on "The Saga of Harald Fairhair," one of the divisions of Snorri Sturluson's "Heimskringla," or "History of the Kings of Norway," written about 1200. The authors have made a number of changes in Snorri's time-scheme and have slightly altered the relations of some of the characters. These changes are, for the most part, entirely justified by the large legendary element in Snorri's account, which makes Sigurd the great-grandson of Ragnarr Lodbrok and contemporary with Halfdan the Black, and makes Ivarr the Boneless the son of Ragnarr and contemporary with Halfdan's son Harald Fairhair. The poems in the story are, with one exception, genuine Norse productions: the verse attributed to Hornklofi was actually written by him; Ragnarr's death-song is genuine, and so is "The day has come up with din of cock's feathers."

THE statement concerning the changes made in Snorri's account is suggested on the basis of a letter Bishop and I received from Mr. H. Bedford Jones of Santa Barbara. Mr. Jones praised the story as a story, but objected strenuously to the changes. I wrote him, showing him the discrepancies and errors in Snorri's account, and I think I proved to his satisfaction that the changes were proper and necessary. But since *Adventure* numbers among its readers a considerable number of men who know the Norse sagas, it might be as well to disarm their possible objections by publishing such a statement as I suggest, if you can find space in some future number.—ARTHUR G. BRODEUR.

SOME of the letters that come in to us are delayed a good deal in reaching your eyes. In any case it takes two or three months to get it out to you in the magazine and often there's additional delay owing to the "exigencies of make-up." Also, some of these letters spend a month or more in the mail. The following from our American comrade, M. Logie, with the Salonika forces, was written October 29th and reached me December 20th—nearly two months on the way. The copy of our magazine I sent him must have been about the same length of time in the mails.

Here's hoping he was back in good shape again long before his letter reached me and that he is O. K. at this minute and now with our own forces. I haven't yet seen him in New York.

As you'll notice, the censor got busy on part of his letter, as said censor had done with an earlier one:

The Mid-September reached me just in time to act as a good stimulant and a pick-me-up. The fact is I'm down and out in a base hospital with dysentery and malaria, so you can readily understand how much I appreciated its arrival.

WELL, as regards my ailment, I'm getting on O. K. except for the malaria, which continues to give me a shake-up now and then, the "original seed" still in the system from former days below the Rio Grande. Well, it's no use kicking, this has meant a rest, peace, and a clean bed to me, with a change of diet which was most acceptable after fourteen months up in the "front line," which naturally gets a bit monotonous, although I can say we have had some bully times.

Well, to get on with the tale I received quite a surprise in seeing one of my letters to you in Camp-Fire. Many thanks for the same; it will keep some of my old pals posted as to my whereabouts, etc. Well, what the censor did obliterate was referring to —— troop, etc., in the —— of a certain —— and where the . . . . At any rate, all panned out well as regards myself, and of course, which is to be expected, did not for a good few other individuals; all in the game.

HAVE you heard this one? A big Jock (Scot) in a certain famous Highland regiment, who was one of the "first wave" in the attacking force, got his kilt full of the Bulgar wire (barb), failed to clear himself, stripped off said kilt, which was left hanging on the wire, and kept on going. Some sight! How would that do for a recruiting poster? And of course he used that bit of steel on the end of his rifle that does credit to his breed. All "gospel."

Well, as regards that transfer to the U. S. forces. I'm still in strong hopes for the same. I made a second application to the War Office for a transfer to the U. S. Army, either as an instructor or to join the force already in France. Still waiting; usual "red tape." At the same time the head guys at Washington D. C. failed to see where I'd be of any value to them. Too much trouble, I expect. Your reply to a grievance from a National Guardsman was O. K., straight from the shoulder. Some —— with the . . . 1914-15.

Well, I'll finish this long, dry spiel, wishing you the best of luck. I've got a hunch that I'll strike the old town yet, hoping it's before Christmas.

A YOUNGER brother of mine, a C. C. N. Y. man, has received his commission from Plattsburg, is at present over at Camp Upton, L. I. Expect he'll have a lot to learn yet; what do you say? All those new shave-tails will have to study "human nature" a bit, also themselves. At any rate I'm glad to see that everything is going O. K. and that "Old Glory" will soon show her weight "over yonder" and of course there will be another kind of weight back in the U. S. A. when the "Sammies" are in the thick of it.—Lance Corporal M. LOGIE, Black Watch, Salonika Forces.

BEFORE this reaches you you will know that our Navy is in urgent need of binoculars, spy-glasses and telescopes. These are things that money can not buy now, and our Navy must have its "eyes." If you have any, send them in; in this crisis, if you are a good American, they do not belong to you but to your country.

Here are the official directions for sending:

All articles should be securely tagged, giving the name and address of the donor, and forwarded by mail or express to the Honorable Franklin D. Roosevelt, Assistant Secretary of the Navy, care of Naval Observatory, Washington, D. C., so that they may be acknowledged by him.

Articles not suitable for naval use will be returned to the sender. Those accepted will be keyed, so that the name and address of the donor will be permanently recorded at the Navy Department, and every effort will be made to return them, with added historic interest, at the termination of the war. It is, of course, impossible to guarantee them against damage or loss.

As the Government can not, under the law, accept services or material without making some payment therefor, one dollar will be paid for each article accepted, which sum will constitute the rental price, or, in the event of loss, the purchase price, of such article.

HERE'S one of you doing a kindness to another of you whom he's never seen—except at our Camp-Fire. It's an indication of what our Camp-Fire is becoming more and more—a real fellowship and comradeship by no means limited to periodical meetings and talk on paper. As to Captain Drannan I have no direct personal knowledge. There is no question of there having been such a person, but there seems question of the authenticity of all the adventures attributed to him. Some go even further. I have seen a letter from a general, with whom it is claimed Drannan served, saying he had never heard of Drannan. But, be that as it may, he did write a book and the book is what we're talking about now:

Austin, Texas.

In your Mid-December issue, Mr. A. M. Buck wants to know where to get "Twenty-one Years on the Plains," by Captain W. F. Drannan, Chief of Scouts. Will you please tell Mr. Buck through Camp-Fire or otherwise, that if some one else doesn't beat me to it I will try to buy him a copy of this book in some of these Texas towns?

I met Captain Drannan in 1902 in Houston, Texas. He used to sit at the market in his picturesque buckskin coat, wide-brimmed hat and all, and sell his book. I met him again in 1906 in the Texas Pan Handle, on "The Plains." He posed for my kodak. I remember at the time thinking myself lucky in getting a first-hand kodak picture of this old scout before he passed out. The last time I saw him was in Mineral Wells, Texas, in 1913. He conducted a shooting-gallery there, but his health was bad. He was over eighty years old then.

Lots of men here in Austin knew King Fisher. A book, "The Life of Ben Thompson," will give a few facts about King Fisher. He is said to have been buried in Eagle Pass, Texas, 1884. I will be in Eagle Pass next month and will try to verify this.—Frank Caldwell.

AS TO "YOU AND DEMOCRACY"

AT SEVERAL recent Camp-Fires I've talked to you concerning something upon which I've been working for about ten years, a definite program and a definite organization for the definite work of building up in this country a definite conception of good citizenship, a definite realization of the vital need of good citizenship under any form of government or in any economic conditions, and the definite habit, practise and development of good citizenship and real democracy.

OF THIS definite work, however, I spoke in rather indefinite terms and did so purposely. In the first place, my object was to get, through these general and intentionally discouraging calls, the names of any of you sufficiently earnest in desire for better conditions in this country to investigate even a rather vague and unenticing chance to work for them and to work for them without promise of personal advantage, ease or pleasure. In the second place, it is the intention to move forward slowly and carefully, making sure of the ground as we go; there are various factors to be considered and it is only common sense that no one of them should be allowed to advance until all the others are ready to advance with it. In the third place, whatever I say to you at Camp-Fire is always written some two months before it reaches you, so always I must limit it to such things as have already happened or can be definitely foreseen.

I DID not expect, or wish, a great number of responses. A few earnest ones are of more value. The replies, in both quality and number, have been better than expected. Those who responded I ask to be patient; they can be sure they will be kept in touch with all actual progress. This is not a one-man movement; they will be asked to help in giving it its final shape. If sincerely interested and ready for hard work, not personal advantage or prominence, send in your name.

The American League for Citizenship has been incorporated. It is an organization without political, class or religious affiliation, advocating no new and startling theories of government or economics, devoted to just what it says it is devoted—the promotion and practise of good citizenship and real democracy.

ANOTHER inquiry on the West of earlier days from one of you who signs himself "A Reader." Before we're done our Camp-Fire will have collected and preserved quite a lot of pioneer material valuable to those who come after us. The clipping follows the letter:

Toledo, Ohio.

Enclosed you will find a clipping out of the Toledo *Blade* about some noted "bad men" of the Old West. Can some other reader give us some information on the old stages that were covered with sheet-metal and guarded by a young army of men? That was 'way back in the time of the rush to the Black Hills, I think.—A READER.

Tombstone, Ariz.,
Dec. 8.

"Boot Hill," the burial-ground for the men who died with their boots on when Tombstone was a lawless camptown, has been converted into a municipal waste-heap and is now fast being covered with tin cans and waste.

WHEN Tombstone was a "Bad Man's Town," back in the '80s and '90s, Boot Hill was a busy burying-ground. Dozens of men were buried there with the simple ceremonies of the times and no slab remains to mark their graves. Five men, who were hanged legally, and a good many more who were shuffled off less formally are buried there in what used to be known as "Scaffold Row."

There is nothing now on "Boot Hill" to recall the early days, but some of the "old-timers" recall a notable or so who lies on "Boot Hill."

"BAD JESS" SPRAGUE, noted in the early Arizona days as a gambler and gunman, was buried there after his duel with an Easterner named Bastian. Sprague and Bastian played poker for high stakes and Bastian won. Sprague challenged Bastian to fight it out and the duel was staged in what was known as "The Red Owl Saloon." Sprague was armed with two formidable-appearing six-shooters; Bastian's weapon being an innocent-looking Derringer of small caliber. Sprague lost his nerve at the stranger's coolness, fired wide and was killed instantly by a bullet in his heart. It developed later that Sprague had wronged Bastian's sister and that Bastian had gone West intent on getting Sprague.

HERE'S a job for us. Where can this comrade find adventure? What is it? What's in it? If you know, tell all of us, if it won't take too much space.

U. S. S. Vulcan.

For some time I have been studying a problem which I can't figure out. It is: where can I find adventure? Maybe you can help me out. I don't know where it is, what it is, or what is in it. At present I am serving in the Navy, but as soon as the war is over I will be free to do as I please. I have ten years' sea experience, having gone to sea at the age of thirteen. I have no education, have gone to school only three years. Hoping you can help me find what I have been searching for for ten years.—EARL J. TEETS.

NOW Edgar Young goes and springs something. Something pretty big. "What is the Spirit of Adventure?" And what he wants to know about is the *biological* side of it and what place does it occupy in the evolution of the human race.

That's a large one, and a very interesting one. How about it? Here's his letter. (It was written from Sayville, Long Island, but he's not there any more.) And what *is* the Spirit of Adventure in its biological aspects?

I am up against a hard proposition and I want to see if I can't get you to help me out, through the Camp-Fire. I have been trying for a month to figure out what the SPIRIT OF ADVENTURE is. I have arrived at several conclusions, but the more I study on it, the larger it becomes. Perhaps some of the comrades—men who have studied things out for themselves—have formed opinions on this subject and can give me a better angle than my own.

I HAVE rushed to the library and tried to find out from "the books," but they are strangely silent on this question. I wonder if it would not be possible through Camp-Fire to find out what ADVENTURE is, from a biological standpoint. And what place does it occupy in the evolution of the human race? Also, is there such a thing as INTELLECTUAL ADVENTURE?

I shall watch eagerly for any letters you print along this line and suggest that all the letters received be carefully preserved for future reference. —EDGAR YOUNG.

A LETTER from a comrade with the Canadians, telling about a little party they had between the lines:

WHILE my battalion was in the front line at —— I was one of the battalion bombers. One evening the section was ordered for a raid—I made the usual preparations—and about four o'clock we started over to annoy old Fritzie. Everything went as planned until when we were on our way back we met a party of Huns about twice our strength. We took cover in a shell-hole and prepared to give them a hot time. Imagine our surprise when at our first shot the lot of them raised their arms and shouted: *"Kamerad! Kamerad!"* Well, we took the bunch back. After our arrival we were talking to them and during the "confab" learned that one of them had lived in "little old New York" for quite a number of years, and he informed us that they were delighted at being taken prisoners. Sounds like they are about "fed up" with the war, does it not?—No. 264413, L. S. PHILLIPS, No. 2 Co., 25th Reserve B't'n, Canadians.

YOU, whoever you are, are a member of our Camp-Fire if you wish to be. We welcome all, without formality or red tape. By wanting to join, you at once automatically become a member.

ARTHUR SULLIVANT HOFFMAN

NOT so long ago I blew my own horn by saying that since our Camp-Fire had started I had not yet slipped up by printing a letter that the writer didn't wish published. I've got my just deserts for boasting, for I've gone and done it. Luckily Mr. Sargent had no serious objections, but he had not written for publication the letter I gave you about part of his journey in, through and around South America. He had not, of course, asked me not to print it, but he had not told me I might.

My apologies to him. He's already written me that "it's all O. K., but I wish you would say something in the Camp-Fire to the effect that I was not writing for publication. However, since the letter was printed, I wish you would say this much about the Inca Highway, as I do not wish to create a false impression." And then he gives us the following very interesting talk. He is writing from Peru.

Incidentally we have here again another example of the amazing running-power of Indians, which has been a subject of Camp-Fire discussion.

La Fundicion, Peru.

From Concepcion, Chile, to Quito, the Incas built roads that were fit to take their place among the wonders of the world. The main highways were from Cuzco, Peru, to Quito, Ecuador. There were two roads, the main highway over the mountains and the coast road which led through the valleys of the Chimu and other races and peoples conquered by the Incas. When a new conquest was made, a road was built so that the Inca could travel over it and visit his new domains. A thing which comparatively few people know is that, the ruler alone was the Rey Inca and the members of the royal house Incas. The great mass of the people were merely known by their tribal names.

FROM the river Maule in Chile, we find traces of the road, and it was over these pieces of road that my brother and I hiked. At times we would lose it for scores of kilometros, and then we would pick it up and follow it for many miles. It was about (in places) thirty feet wide, and mostly paved. All showed traces, except in certain parts of the desert, of paving.

Inasmuch as this is about the road, I will quote from my note-book:

At times the road was in perfect condition, and served as the *camino real* for the Indians of the present; then it would pass out of sight for hundreds of kilometros, only to "bob up" in the most unexpected places. Where it crossed swamps, huge blocks of sandstone were laid down, and the streams were spanned by all sorts of bridges. These and the causeways were made of huge monoliths, in many places. Many of these bridges especially in the far-out-of-the-way places, and "Off the Beaten Track," excite the wonder and admiration of the tourist who is lucky enough to behold them. Crossing some deep ravine or rushing rapid, we come to a very good bridge made of osiers, llanas, reeds, wire, twigs, limbs, and what not, all woven together, all in all forming a very safe affair for ourselves and pack-animals.

THE Inca roads (to return to them) were, because of their peculiar course, fitted only to the travelers of the day and time, *i. e.*: foot passengers, and llamas, but if they were not adapted to any other mode of travel, rapid transit was most assuredly performed over them by native runners, soldiers, imperial messengers, and other official delegates. We have absolute proof that the Peruvians had rural postmen long before they were known in Europe.

At the end of each stage, about two leagues or six miles, all along the road were small houses, wherein two Indian messengers were stationed day and night. One of these received the message to be carried from the preceding messenger, who shouted it while he was approaching the station, so that when the latter actually reached it, the other was on his way to the next post. Remarkable speeds were maintained by these carriers, and it is a matter of history that the ordinary time taken in the trip from Imperial Cuzco to Quito, some 1200 miles, was made in ten days! (Do I hear scoffers? Before you scoff, look this up and investigate.)

THIS road led through all sorts of wonderful places, and some of the ruins of the pre-Inca and megalithic people are considered by every one who has seen them to be far superior to anything Egypt can boast off. No one knows anything about these; their very traditions have been lost in the mists of centuries. At times we would be fifteen or sixteen thousand feet above sea-level and then way down in the valleys near it. Everywhere we found something wonderful, and the trip that all *Adventure* readers should make if they possibly could, is the trip from Antafogasta, Chile, up through La Paz and Tiahuanucu, Bolivia, across Lake Titicaca, up to Cucco, over to Lima, up to Cerro de Pazco, and then back home. There is but one place in the world that can show as many wonderful things that Nature has bestowed, as Peru, and that is our own God's Country, the "Good old U. S. A.," and even we are excelled in the wonderful ruins and traces of a long-forgotten people we find here in Inca land.

WE ARE leaving here next month for Huanucu Viejo, then on to Caxamarca, where Atahualpa, the last of the Incas was murdered by the Destroyers (whom some call the Conquistadores), then up through Quito into Bogota, as I wrote you before.

How much more of the road we will find I don't know, as we are taking the coast route from here passing through Truxillo and the wonderful Chan-Chan country, but shall hang on to its route, trusting in luck to pick it up here and there.

Since writing you, I have purchased a Panorama camera and a 5 x 7 Speed Graphic. We have films enough to take 1250 photographs. These with my Graflex and my Vest Pocket Kodak make a camera equipment hard to beat. Another thing I want to pay special tribute to is my little portable typewriter. I would not be without one for anything.

Shortly after I receive your reply to this, I shall enter the country of the bandits, and as the first seven days will be taken up in a trip through an exceedingly "bad" country, *quien sabe* what adventures will be met with?

I am not prone to write letters for publication, but inasmuch as the ambiguity of the statement in my letter to Mr. Hoffman was sufficient to cause a misunderstanding about the Inca Roads, I thought it best to write more fully.

Best regards to every one of you.—John Winthrop Sargent.

HIS story in this issue is not his first in our magazine; but, probably through my fault, Stanley Shaw has not yet followed Camp-Fire custom and stood up to introduce himself. He has been in the business end of the theatrical game, an advertising manager, literary editor and business counselor, and he has got most of his adventures from the day's work.

One of the most quietly exciting moments I ever knew was, as a police reporter, seeing four stolid officers take from one room sixteen of the worst crooks that ever lived, each with a country-wide record, and as indifferently herd them into two "Black Marias" as though they were so many sheep. It was the famous "Albany Street" gang. Another was when the head of a great advertising agency, about to go to the wall, was signing his lawyer's application for bankruptcy proceedings, with tears in his eyes, just as his partner rushed into the office with an exclusive contract, that meant business salvation, from one of the world's largest users of publicity space.

Yet another was once when the late Joseph Haworth repeated the curse speech from *Richelieu* before its natural place in the play, because a note had been passed to him stating that the engines were coming down the street for a fire in the next building. He knew that the two or three minutes of wild applause that invariably followed that speech would drown the sound of the approaching apparatus and, perhaps, prevent a panic. The theater was burned flat after the audience had gone quietly out.

Oh, yes, there is quite as much adventure in politics or business as there is in a shipwreck or a hunt for buried treasure, and the writer has been in all four.—Stanley Shaw.

THE following very interesting letter comes to us from Captain Achmed Abdullah, who, as some of you know, is an Afghan by birth and a British subject by naturalization and a recognized authority on India and the lands adjoining:

He refers to two points in one of Gordon McCreagh's letters printed in "Ask Adventure," saying that a certain dignitary was not, as stated, Regent of Tibet and that the Dalai-Lama did leave Lassa. When I wrote to Mr. McCreagh that Captain Abdullah had differed with two of his statements he replied as follows:

If I remember rightly, I answered this query from the Navy Aero School at Pensacola, where I had access to no books of reference and had to rely on only such information as I had on hand. . . . I bow to his superior knowledge in all things Oriental . . . It is a safe bet, since he has raised the question, that he speaks from facts which are not known to the general public.

Here is Captain Abdullah's letter:

Allow me to corect certain of my friend Gordon McCreagh's statements *re.* Tibet and the Dalai-Lama.

THE Tashilhumpo—so named after his capital which is also known as Shigatsé—is not, nor ever was, Regent of Tibet. He is a powerful abbot of the yellow-cap order, who formerly had the privilege of examining newly-born candidates for the Lassa Grand Lamaship and of ordaining the one finally selected for the new reincarnation. He is a Grand Lama by rank, and himself a reincarnation of the bastard Buddha known as *Amitabha*—"The Boundless Light"—(see Austine Waddell's "Buddhism" for details on this reincarnation). He has no temporal duties of any sort to perform, beyond supervising the immense landed estates of his monastery. The consequence is that he occupies himself altogether, or nearly so, with spiritual matters of faith, more so than the Grand Lama himself, has therefore a reputation, far superior to the latter's, in piety and learning and is generally called in consequence *Pan-Chen Rhimpo-Ché*—"The Re-Splendent Jewel of Learning."

THE Regent, at least when I was in Tibet as Intelligence Officer under Macdonald and Younghusband in 1903 and early 1904, was a Cardinal of the yellow-caps, known as *Kri Rimpoché*—"The Precious Enthroned"—and also as *Gahldaen 'Kri'disn-pá*—"Holder of the Gahldaen Throne"—a very learned and highly cultured gentleman who had complete authority over the great Tibetan State monasteries and also over all the yellow-caps who is not a reincarnation of any sort, but a man of "natural birth," who reaches his position through wisdom and scholarship. His Chinese name—if I remember rightly—is "The Noble-hearted Banner."

Furthermore, the Dalai-Lama *did* leave Lassa, besides his little trip into Sikkim. He did so in 1904. That was the chief effect of the Younghusband expedition. The Dalai left in a —— of a hurry, on the very day the British crossed the Tsangpo. Together with a retinue and Dorjieff, the Russian Buddhist and Intelligence Officer, he went first to Nagchuka, beyond the Tendri Lake, and finally to Urga, the capital of Mongolia, where, for many weeks, Buddhist pilgrims came to do him homage, chief of them Erettuyeff, the chief Russian Buddhist Lama of Eastern Siberia. The *Warsaw Gazette* in November, 1904, printed a detailed account of his arrival there. Too, the Indian Government, Survey Department, brought out a Blue Book to that effect.

IT IS not hard to reach Tibet. There are in Lassa, have always been there, Moslem and Nepalese Consuls. Christians, too, can go there. The easiest way would be *via* Baxa, in Northeastern Bengal, thence up *via* Tashi and Punakha, northwest to Chumolhari (all this in Bhutan), and cross the border there. It is quicker than the trip from Siliguri up the Chumbi. Not quite as cold, and more interesting.

Finally, the trade was *not* entirely carried on by Tibetans. For nearly all the so-called Tibetans, who traded into the North before the Younghusband intermezzo, were British subjects. Do you remember the Babu in Kipling's "Kim"? He is a conglomerate of several real characters, but chiefly is he meant to represent the explorer Krishna, known officially in the Survey (Intelligence) Department as A.-K. He was not a Babu, but a Tibetan, and a naturalized British subject. Others of the same sort, working for Britain, naturalized, and going freely into Tibet, were Lama Ugyen Gyatsho and Kuentuep, the latter having lived long in Darjeeling.

I believe that Krishna died recently, and that *Munsey's* magazine printed a charming obituary notice.

THE man who knew Tibet best, from an Intelligence Department point of view, was Babu Sarat Chandra Das of Bengal. From the Russian side the best was Dorjieff, above mentioned, and M. Tsybikoff, who brought some capital photos from Lassa in 1902. There was also a Japanese Buddhist priest, Kawaguchi by name, who went there the same year and had a rotten time of it . . . but all that—the last four—is another story, which I am going to put into story form some day.

I suppose you know that for many, many years the Jesuits had a mission, chapel and school in Lassa.

Pardon the lengthy letter. It got me going. Old memories, you know.—ACHMED ABDULLAH.

A WORD from Farnham Bishop and Arthur Gilchrist Brodeur on their story in this issue.

The Norman barons of the twelfth century ruled their conquered possessions in Sicily with savage brutality, plundering and exploiting their mixed Greek, Italian, and Arab subjects without restraint. *Gaimar*, the villain of our piece, is a much more accurate representative of his race than *Arnulfo*, the just Norman. But that there were a few just Normans is demonstrated by the fact that there was never a general uprising against them as a race. In making our heroine a girl of mixed Norman and Italian parentage, we have tried to give her a double inheritance: her Northern blood expressing itself in stern strength, her Southern blood bringing her into closer sympathy with her Sicilian subjects. She is neither Norman nor Roman at heart: she is Sicilian.

Arnulfo's castle is partly modeled on the ruins of Norman keeps in Sicily, and partly pieced together from descriptions of those keeps before they were ruined and looted. The builders were Norman; the workmen were the Greek and Arab natives, who put into their work all the rich artistry which was the peculiar property of their race.

SOME time ago, while he was still at Sayville, Edgar Young wrote the following letter to me but did not mail it till a month later. In the meantime we met, for the first time, had a long talk and got acquainted. I hope to meet him many other times.

He begins his letter by quoting word for word from the letter I send to every writer when he first joins our magazine, asking him to tell the Camp-Fire about himself so that we'll all be humans together instead of printed names. "So that your readers will feel they really know you." I made it strong, and now he turns it back on to Mr. Wade and me.

It has just occurred to me that you and Mr. Wade have dodged a part of your responsibility in this line. I used to think that an editor was not human—that he was a great Hocus-Pocus or something, back behind the scenes, but by constant effort of trying to get things straightened out in the niches where they belong I have finally come to the conclusion that editors and associate editors are, after all, human beings. I must have been suffering from embonpoint of the coco that it has taken me thirty-four years of my life to arrive at this conclusion.

ALSO, I will wager that this fact has never occurred to many readers of the magazine. The Camp-Fire section of *Adventure* is a strange place. The men who turn to this portion of the magazine first are all college men—with the various degrees given out by the Universities of Hard Knocks, of Adventure, of Experience. I have sat by camp-fires with hard-handed men who could jounce ahead the philosophy of Spencer, of Darwin, of Emerson, with men who could discuss glibly the trend of affairs after socialism had come and gone. To some of these men I owe more than I can repay. My education ended after a few years in free school and these men taught me the trick of thinking on my own initiative. Sometimes I don't make the hill but that's the fault of my motor. It wasn't built to take some hills "on high."

WE WILL forgive you if your college happens to be other than ours has been. The spirit of Adventure is big. It girdles the earth. It is the front rank of Life. There are many ways a man may qualify to step ahead into this front rank. In fact, I feel that both of you have qualified—and I never saw either of you personally. We want to hear about it. Start back about the callow age of ten or thereabouts. It's nothing but fair that you should do this. A good many of us have done so. People in this small village where I reside did not know that they entertained an ex-tramp and ex-filibuster in their midst, unawares, until I told about it in the Camp-Fire. Some of them right now don't know whether to run or make friends. But I have lived through it and they will live through it. Fitting this and that together we will all think and be better for having done so.

And if there is any one else down there behind the scenes—that fellow with the horn-shell glasses who reads MSS., that red-headed girl who holds down some desk or other, that young college chap who doesn't understand our bunch as yet—you can tag them and tell them they are "It," if you want to. A pretty good way to do is to *dare* them to. Down where I was raised they used to say that "a feller who'd take a dare would steal a sheep and eat the hair."

Gentlemen and Ladies of the Camp-Fire, we have with us to-night Mr. Arthur Sullivant Hoffman and Mr. Harry Erwin Wade, editor and associate editor of *Adventure* magazine.—EDGAR YOUNG.

It's fair. I'm fairly caught. I've managed to dodge it all these years, for I have no great adventures behind me and have felt that any account of myself would be dull reading for the rest of you. Some of you have asked me before and I sidestepped. Now it comes up square in my path. All right, let's have it over with, but remember I didn't start this.

As a matter of fact I'm glad to do it if it gets us better acquainted. I'm no hand for formality and haven't done it before only because there is so little of interest to say about myself:

Born, 1876, Columbus, Ohio. They've built a Y. M. C. A. building on the spot. I don't know why. My people on both sides were all Americans for some two hundred years; father the first (and unsuccessful) candidate for Congress the Republican party ever had in his southern Ohio district (around Jackson County); my maternal great-grandfather the founder of Franklinton, now Columbus.

COLUMBUS public schools; Ohio State University, '97; two years' teaching in Coshocton, O., high school; three as joint editor and owner weekly paper and job-printing plant in Troy, O.; 1902-3 a cub editor on the *Chautauquan*, Chautauqua, N. Y., and Chicago, with a graduate course in English at the Univ. of Chicago; 1903-10, assistant or managing editor of *Smart Set*, *Transatlantic Tales*, *Watson's*, *Delineator;* 1910 to date, managing editor or editor *Adventure*. Think of an editor of *Adventure* who has worked on *The Delineator* and the *Chautauquan!* Thank Heaven, those who know the game won't even grin; they know a job's a job. I understand the editor of the *Police Gazette* collects rare and beautiful objects of art, while I've known fellows off of church papers that were so tough—oh, well.

Adventures? Tame. Most of them while I was in my teens. Any devilment, author unknown, happening within half a mile of our house was fastened on to me as the most likely chance and I didn't suffer much from injustice. Except once when a policeman took pot-shots at me in the dark, thinking me a burglar. I've never been a burglar. At college I had a very good time but got through. Managed to play football eleven years, including four after college. The best game I know. As a kid, about 1889, had a wee taste of amateur cowboying; Kansas still largely open country then, neither wild nor tame.

HAVE traveled a little, but most of the time just in the ordinary way—U. S., Canada, Costa Rica, Canal Zone, Jamaica, Morocco, Spain, France, Holland, Belgium, Channel Islands, England, Wales, Ireland. In 1904 with two other fellows bicycled across Spain and France, keeping as much as possible out of the tourist track. Some pretty backwoods spots in Spain—places where a whole village turned out to see the fillings in our teeth, districts where neither bicycle or railroad train had ever been seen, where a camera couldn't even be explained, where they wore cowhide with the hair on. But all safe enough, except the Valdepeñas pass—which we went through on a train. A kindly and most polite folk, but giving us never a taste of real adventure, though there were times when we really suffered for water or food; there are some very dry stretches and sizeable deserts in Spain. And of course we were broke now and then.

Tried another wheel trip later—at least I'm spoiled for the ordinary tourist stunt—and had plenty of adventures but the —— wheel furnished them. There was one time when it was in four different places in Ireland and I in another. On the first trip, taken on four or five days' notice, I had a wheel that cost $17.50 but it got replaced piece by piece as we went along and must have been worth a lot more when I sold it for less in Normandy. It went over the Pyrenees tied together with rags and got down only by running into snow or a mountain torrent at intervals to cool hot-boxes.

THE only real tragedy we met was a preacher and some feminine satellites of his flock or family. One of these loud vegetarians. There aren't many vegetables in Spain except eggs, and, strangely enough, no chickens except a few pecking around your feet at table. Eggs, tortillas, everywhere, but no means of knowing who laid them. Vegetables, if any at all, used chiefly for garnishing meats. The first time we saw the preacher was in Tangier; only moderately thin; declaiming aloud over the Moroccan lack of vegetables. Next time, we saw him in Spain—Granada; still declaiming over getting no vegetables; still refusing to eat meat; markedly thinner. Third time, still declaiming and refusing, still thinner, the women satellites looking decidedly worried about him. Fourth time, so thin we could barely see him, too far gone to declaim. Last time, we saw only the women; he was gone entirely.

OF COURSE, like everybody else, I've had quick little adventures that sound bigger than they are. Four fires, a train wreck, an upset canoe, a tangle with a dead tree under water, a broken coal-mine car-cable, accidental or —— fool bullets that missed, the precipice you didn't go over in the dark, the horse that didn't come down on you when you were under his hoofs, etc., almost all of them having more scare than danger. One or two odd ones—was chased, caught and chewed by blood-hounds in Florida; aged six; rescued by my frail, delicate mother with her desperate bare hands, the same mother who, in a runaway, another woman having been thrown out, laid her baby down on the floor of the buggy, climbed out over the dashboard and along a shaft till she could pick up the dragging reins at the horse's collar, climbed back along the shaft with them and stopped the horse. I am proud to be her son. But they say family traits are likely to skip a generation.

Once, at college, when we were playing cards in an unpublic room of the museum, we were startled by a shriek from one of the assistants who leaped at an expressman opening a box of arrow-heads or something with a big hammer and a cold-chisel. The cold-chisel was a Civil War relic—a percussion shell which the professor had carried three miles in his arms to avoid the jarring of a trolley-car. Nope, it was rusty. But that didn't prevent all of us from going away at once and all at once.

Maybe I have one record. I was knocked down three times in three minutes by the same fellow, hit on exactly the same point of my jaw each time and lit on exactly the same spot each time and with exactly the same part of me, and didn't lose my pipe out of my mouth till the third landing.

HAVE hunted very little, fished much—the small-mouth black bass for mine; dabble with canoes, skis, snow-shoes; swim, skate, etc. Spend all my vacations on Maine lakes. In addition, travel over 5,000 miles during the other eleven months—*i. e.*, live out on Long Island and commute to the office! It does add up.

Am 6 ft. 1 in. and weigh only 160—15 lbs. less than when I left high school. Eat anything except liver, kidneys, tripe and brains. Nose crooked and one knee unsound (football). Am nuts on making things grow out of the ground; hate cities, hope to live in the country some day. Never play poker; once filled a royal flush from the middle, won two copper cents and quit forever. Used to be able to do 100 yards in under 11. Smoke Bull Durham, rolled or corn-cob. Married, one boy. Like lakes, open country, Westerners, chocolate, dogs and horses. Used to read a lot, but now almost nothing outside my work and newspapers. Too busy to do much except work, eat, sleep. The Camp-Fire is one of the best things I ever struck—has brought me many real friends.

ONE of the things I want most is to see our country get real democracy, cut off the flood of immigrants until she is able really to absorb them, make her political life clean instead of dirty, and attain the ideals of liberty, justice and equal opportunity she has so far attained only in small part.

I've talked a lot, but, having got started, I wanted to clean up the whole job and then close down permanently on the subject. Though my adventures are scanty, I'm with you in spirit. Drop in on me when you're in town. I'm always rushed, but I like to stop long enough at least to shake hands.—A. S. H.

And now I can pass it on to Mr. Wade, which I am very pleased to do:

The smoke is following around evidently to choke me off if I get to yarning. So it won't take long to tell how little has happened to me. But, seeing you've got me cornered, I'll stand up long enough to let you see I don't wear horn-rimmed spectacles, that I weigh 160, and hate the feel of a stiff collar.

HAVE been a traveling salesman; reporter; helped survey in the Alleghany and Blue Ridge Mountains; cut brush one Summer to keep a herd of sheep from caving in; tramped an eight-mile trap line half one Winter; taught both in a university and in a little worn-out lumber settlement on Buck-Tooth Ridge, to which I had to climb three miles every Winter's morning on snow-shoes. Was contributor to a few magazines, and for the past four years have been on *Adventure's* staff.

PLAYED baseball, basketball and billiards through high school, college, and play them now. Can't remember when I didn't prefer whipping a trout stream to seeing a World Series game or reading Stevenson.

Have fished and hunted from the Southern States to the White Mountains. My traveling has been confined to the U. S. and Canada—800 miles of it by canoe. Have been in three train wrecks, blown into the Hudson from a motor-boat, licked eight or ten times with gloves and without, know how it feels to be shot at, and have been butted into a barbed-wire fence by a buck sheep.

I HATE salt water, razor-back hogs, and every German soldier alive. Like Virginian mountaineers, most of the Camp-Fire crowd, and the Great Lakes when they behave.

The last three months I've been trying to learn how to clear a hill-crest and hit a Boche on the opposite slope with high explosive shell. Expect to be in an army camp playing a real game at last by the time this reaches you.

Some one give me a smoke.—H. E. W.

IN A letter the other day J. Allan Dunn spoke of the present war as "the Twentieth Century Crusade." I wonder the term hasn't come into general use. Particularly now that it has accomplished what most of the old-time crusades failed to accomplish—the capture of Jerusalem.

THE Gila monster has always been the subject of considerable debate but I don't think we've ever threshed out the subject at our Camp-Fire. Now, however, in connection with Major George B. Rodney's story in our Mid-November issue one of you brings the matter up. (It is, by the way, no longer Captain, but Major, Rodney and I know the Camp-Fire will join in congratulations.) Me, I'm no authority on Gila monsters and I stand from under, but the information sent in seems, to my lay mind, convincing and authoritative.

But I am considerable of an authority on liars, more so than some people suspect. I don't always recognize a liar when I see one, but I recognize 'em a whole lot oftener than some of the liars think I do. At any rate, I've known from the first that *Mr. John Wilkes* of Arizona is a liar. Every time he's appeared in one of Major Rodney's stories I've known he was a liar, an awful liar, and I'd taken it for granted that every one of you also knew it. That's one of the chief reasons Major Rodney, who created him, put him into a number of the stories we've read and enjoyed. *Mr. Wilkes* was such a picturesque, wholesale, habitual and free-handed liar that we thought you'd like to sit back and listen to him. Personally I wouldn't think of taking him as an authority on Gila mosters or anything else except lying, and I wouldn't trust him even on the subject of lying.

BUT our comrade who gives us the interesting facts on Gila monsters, though he undoubtedly recognizes *Mr. Wilkes* as a liar in general, seems to have taken him literally on Gila monsters. I can't blame him. *Mr. Wilkes* is a convincing liar, the kind that can let you know he's lying about some things yet make you believe him on others. That's real art. And highly dangerous.

As to our comrade's other criticisms I'm "agin" him on his criticism of "Gawd." I'm a poor speller, myself, but the Standard Dictionary gives "Navaho" as correct, giving it preference over "Navajo." Personally, I like "Navajo" better, maybe just because I'm used to it.

PRESCOTT, ARIZONA.

The Gila monster is a black (or very dark brown) and buff-colored reptile, has a thick stubbed tail and a warty skin. I never saw any spines along its back. Its nose and under jaw are black.

IT IS normally sluggish in movement and, unless angered, is generally considered to be harmless. It will not attack man on its own initiative as will a rattlesnake. It is poisonous. When poison-glands and fangs were not found in its upper jaw the question as to its being poisonous was raised, but a few years ago a naturalist who made a close study of the reptile found its poison-glands in the lower jaw and, I believe, that the teeth of the lower jaw acted as the poison ducts. When the Gila monster bites it hangs on like a bull-dog, to give time for the poison to exude and penetrate the wound.

Some years ago, here in Arizona, I saw a man bitten by one. He was holding it in one hand and striking its nose with the other, paying little attention to the possibilities. Suddenly the Gila monster grabbed his hand between the thumb and knuckle of the fore-finger and before its jaws could be *pried* loose his hand and arm began to swell and turn black. Only prompt attendance saved the man's life, as it was, he was laid up for several days. I knew of another case in Tucson where a half-drunken man teased one and laughed at those who warned him. The Gila monster grabbed his hand, also, assistance was delayed. The man died.

AS TO its breath being poisonous, that seems to be generally supposed—that the Gila monster uses its breath to stupefy its victim. I know of a case of a young man who claimed to have been poisoned by a Gila monster's breath when a child. At any rate he was always severely nauseated when near one in captivity and he claimed it was from its odor.

I have seen two fight and kill each other and when dead one or both would be gripping the other in its mouth.

NOW for the criticism. The horned toad does not hop. It runs. It is a lizard, not a toad.

Please have your authors spell Navajo correctly instead ot "Navaho." Why, when using the name of God as an exclamation or an oath must the speaker invariably be supposed to pronounce it as it is spelled—"Gawd?" 'Twere better not to use it at all; but no man in exclamation or in swearing pronounces it other than God.—— —— ——

Now I sent Comrade ——'s letter on to Major Rodney, it being only fair that he should be heard in his own defense. Owing to his intimate relationship with *Mr. John Wilkes*, he is, of course, in a delicate position, torn between his friendship for *Mr. Wilkes* and his knowledge of that gentleman's habits of mind and tongue. I think he has acquitted himself with credit. I should, of course, like to know his own opinion on Gila monsters, but as he didn't offer them in the story itself, he seems quite within his rights to leave the burden where it belongs—on the shoulders of *Mr. John Wilkes* of Arizona. And if I know anything about *Mr. Wilkes* he won't care a ——. He's just that happy-go-lucky and irresponsible.

It's just as well to brand *Mr. Wilkes* right now as an utterly hopeless liar, for in a recent number of our magazine he told us in "The Fire-Bug" one of the most G-a-w-d-awful lies I've ever heard and I'd hate to think any of you even tried to find a single word of truth in it.

And now for Major Rodney's letter:

As regards the Gila monster, its habits, manners, dress, etc., I respectfully submit that while Mr. —— is probably correct in the main in what he says about them yet this interesting family of *helodermatidæ* is so large and its habitat so varied that I doubt if he ever knew this particular one that *Mr. Wilkes* says he saw.

AS FOR its color, well, all I can say is that *John Wilkes* says it had yellow on it. If he says he saw red, he undoubtedly saw red. Mr. .... does not criticise the other colors that *Mr. Wilkes* says he saw. Personally I see no reason to doubt that he saw yellow if he says he did.

The African and the Asiatic elephants are both elephants, yet they differ in many points. If two animals of the same species, as big as elephants, can vary as to color why should we deny to one miserable little Gila monster a little yellow? God knows he has few enough pleasures in life!

I have known *Mr. Wilkes* for many years. He lives in many places in Arizona. I have served in various parts of the State for a good many years and I have run across *Mr. Wilkes* wherever I happened to be and, except in matters of life and death, morals and mundane affairs in general, I have found him to be more or less truthful. Shall I doubt him now?

IN MY spelling Mr. —— hits me in a tenderer point. "Navajo" is certainly spelt with a "j" and not with an "h," a mistake due probably to a typographical error, but shall two consistent readers of *Adventure* fall out over a jay?

As for the spelling of the word "God," Mr. —— does me scant justice. I have read many books sacred and profane in tracing that word to its lair and I find it spelled one way quite as frequently as the other. *Mr. Wilkes* invariably pronounced it as though it were spelled "G-a-w-d." One man may spell it one way; one another. The god of the Patagonians was spelled with an "S" if we can believe Pigafetti or Shakespeare—Setebos. I may quote as my authority for this way of spelling the following:

"How all the gawdless rising at a venture
Question the spelling of stories in *Adventure*."

taken, no doubt, from that well-known old play "The Printer's Error," written in 1733 by John Smith of London.

At any rate, even if I am in error in quoting my authority for the spelling the only real evidence of the correctness of a signature or a name is the testimony of the owner of that name—testimony that in the present irreligious state of the world can not be obtained save through the doubtful authenticity of a ouiga-board.

This doesn't settle any thing, but I will never believe *John Wilkes* again—entirely, that is.—George B. Rodney.

THE following letter from Captain James Moorhead, an old windjammer shipmaster, is not only good reading in itself but gives added interest to the complete novel in one of last Fall's issues. It tells of a real adventure, by one of those men who have made themselves a place in the history of the sea, on the very scene of a fictional adventure that we read a few months ago.

New York City.

As a steady reader of *Adventure* since its start, I have been deeply interested in your story "Wave Bound," by Samuel Alexander White, November 18, 1917, issue, as I spent several weeks on the Island of Amherst among those hardy fishermen, while salvaging cargo and wreck of schooner *Kocheko*, wrecked on point of Fortune Bay, while en route for Europe with cargo of birch timber from Campbeltown, Bay of Challeur.

I left Campbeltown November 15, 1892, bound for Queenstown for orders, with a cargo of fine, dry birch in lower hold and spruce deals in between decks and upper deck. Shortly after clearing Bay of Challeur I ran into one of the heaviest northeastern gales I ever experienced, and as I was carrying close-reefed lower sails to try to weather the Bird Rocks, I sprang a butt, the lower hold filling almost immediately and forcing us all to take to the rigging, where we were lashed for over twelve hours in a blinding snow-storm, the vessel almost awash, our only hope that she would hold together until the gale was over.

Forenoon of next day. As the gale was beginning to moderate I told one of the men to get down and see how it was in the forecastle, and he soon reported it perfectly dry. The cabin was entirely gutted out, as it was below deck, while the forecastle was secured on upper deck and safe by the deck-load all around it, so we all got in there and thought we had struck heaven, although our stores were all washed away.

We stayed there twenty-four hours, and as the gale had passed and changed to northwest wind and clear weather I sighted the "Magdaline Islands," and was surprised we had not drifted further south. After setting some sail on the wreck, I thought we could fetch around the point into Fortune Bay, but as we could not steer the wreck we grounded on the point, where we stood by until daylight. In the meantime the wind had shifted around southerly for another blow, and the pounding of the wreck on the bottom would knock you off your feet. I expected every minute to see the spars coming down about us.

As soon as daylight came, I went aloft and could see people running up and down the beach, but as they had no boats fit to stand such a sea as was running, I decided to make the attempt to land in our own boat, which was a fine able one and had been moored well astern of the wreck, all ready for such an emergency. About 9:30 A. M. we hauled her up as close as possible and watched our chance for a jump, most of us getting a good dip before reaching the boat. I jumped in last and cast off immediately on our perilous trip, getting the boat headed for shore and running before the terrible sea.

I watched my chance between seas and, urging the men to pull for their lives, I ran in on top of an extra large roller and the people on shore grappled the boat, helping us to hold her against the undertow and we were safe, almost by a miracle. The islanders took us in their carts, wet and hungry.

over to Amherst, where we were given the best the poor people had, and after a good warming before raging wood fires we soon forgot all our suffering and troubles.

About November 25th I managed to get all my crew shipped on the Pictou steamer for Boston, via Pictou, and stayed behind to salvage the wreck and cargo, if any should be left, and got billeted with a good old French fisherman and his wife and I shall never forget their kindness to me. I soon got acquainted with the lighthouse-keeper, the only man who could talk English and who was very useful to me as an interpreter, also the old Judge, who was the head and practically the father of the whole community (and who is so like the description of *Monsieur Boucher* (*Admiral Pellier*) in your story "Wave Bound."

After the weather moderated in a few days, we notified all the islanders to come in, as I promised them a salvage of fifty per cent. on what they could bring ashore. I had lots of volunteers and, as the weather kept fine for a while, we soon had quite a lot of our spruce deals on shore, put up in different piles, also the birch timber, and named a day for the sale.

This was the most unique auction sale anybody could imagine. I did my own auctioneering (snowing most all the time), standing on a pile of lumber calling for a bid and raising it with all the haranguing I could do, dressed up in my old French host's coat, pants and cap. I supposed I looked the picture, but I managed the sale O. K., even to the last of the hulk standing up out of the sand, which was my last call, and fared very well for a finish of as fine a little vessel as ever was built.

The night we returned to the old French Judge's house we all worked hard and faithfully together, taking in the accounts of sales, paying out salvages, etc., and when day broke we were far from being finished with our job. I was very anxious to get finished up, as the captain of the Pictou steamer told me on the previous trip that this would be his last for the season and for me to be ready when he came back, as he would not leave me to spend the Winter at Amherst if he could help it. So when he arrived, in a day or so, I was pretty well ready to come away with him, although he waited nearly three hours for me at that, whistling for all he was worth for me to hurry up; and as I did not want to spend all Winter on that lonely island, I was glad to find myself on board the Pictou packet, at last bound for God's own country.

Your story "Wave Bound" and its characters were so vivid to me that I could not resist writing you a kind of story of the shipwreck, where we all suffered so much from hunger and cold that I could not describe it. In closing I must not and never will forget the kindness of these hardy fishermen of Amherst, especially the old Judge and the lighthouse-keeper.

Arriving at Boston later on at about 6 P. M. and entering the office of my broker, J. J. Hall & Son, Mr. Hall took me for a tramp still dressed up in the old French fisherman's outfit, but after a good, square meal and some clothes I was soon myself again.

The Magdaline Islands are about the most desolate place, any time of the year, on the Atlantic coast. The couple of months I spent there were lonely enough, in the Fall of the year; what would it be in Winter? If the captain of the Pictou steamer had not waited for me over his time I would have had plenty of time in a long Winter to write a story of those lonely islands and the people who inhabit them.—CAPTAIN JAMES MOORHEAD.

P. S.—I might mention here, when we grounded on Fortune Bay, the crew wanted to land at once, but I told them they would have to wait until morning, and, taking the cook's ax from the galley, I climbed aft and gave all hands to understand that the first man that would attempt to get to the boat I would cut her adrift. So I had to sit there all night with a faithful colored cook and watch the boat, hanging away astern well moored with one hundred and fifty fathoms of good rope, but when we hauled the boat up next morning to leave the vessel I found a Greek sailor in her rolled up in the boat's sail. He got over and swam to the boat, thinking he was safer there than on board ship. It would have been better to have landed at night, as we landed in a heavy southeasterly gale, with a sea running like a mountain next morning, but it was unexpected.—Capt. J. M.

HERE'S word from an Australian comrade who helped take German New Guinea from the Huns, served later in Egypt and finally in France. We salute you, comrade. Yes, we know the name "Anzacs" all right. Everybody knows it now. Here's to them!

I omit the good things he says about our magazine but leave in a scrap about our Camp-Fire:

Ringwood, Oia Merriwa,
New South Wales, Australia.

Guess you can find room at the Camp-Fire for another comrade, hailing from the sheep country of N. S. W. I come amongst you not as a writer—but as a reader . . . . . . I like . . . . . and above all its bohemian readers and writers, who foregather at the Camp-Fire from all parts of the world.

I HAVE had all my adventures packed inside the last two and a half years. Enlisted with the Australian Expeditionary Force early in 1915, with the island force that captured German New Guinea from the Huns. Followed a few months of hell—midst jungle, malarial fever, earthquake shocks and a little snipe-shooting with cannibalistic tribes. Later, sailed for Egypt and lived like Arabs for six months out in the desert—sand, sand everywhere. Hardship galore—lack of water and food principally. A few skirmishes with small parties of Turks made life livable.

ON 12th May, 1916, my brigade sailed from Abscandina to Marseilles. French people enthusiastically welcomed us. Guess you comrades of the Camp-Fire have heard of the name "Anzacs." After three days' sailing through La Belle France we hit a town at the rear of the line and, after a preliminary few weeks of training, we sailed into our first big shoot with Fritz and Co. Some battle place. Flembaix, July 19, 1916, we lost 8,000 men in fifteen hours in casualties. Think of it! Waterloo and Gettysburg fade into insignificance.

It was during this battle in France I got my ticket back home to sunny Australia. German

5.9 shell exploded in trench my section was holding, buried us, and the end of the world came. Week later woke to semi-consciousness in a French hospital. Dazed, and paralyzed in both legs. Sent to England; five months bed; finally invalided home, after the most stirring adventures a man could wish for.

I AM pretty O. K. again now and am back on a station (we don't call 'em ranches here), sheep-growing and wheat-producing. Guess I am through with fighting abroad, but it's some job, crushing these Germans, and before we can do the thing properly every nation on the Allies' side will have to put forward the last man and the last dollar. German arrogance and tyranny must be wiped out. That's our job. It would make your heart ache to see the sights I saw in stricken Belgium. . . . . .

Well, I say, cheer and good luck to *Adventure*, to you, and to all comrades of the Camp-Fire.—Corporal J. W. Martin, late 30th Battalion, Australian Imperial Forces.

P. S.—Australia welcomes Uncle Sam and wishes her troops Godspeed on their departure for the greatest adventure of all—that of avenging the stricken countries of Europe and crushing German despotism and tyranny.

ANOTHER suggestion for preserving our Identification Cards. The card in question, sent me by Mr. Murphy, had been treated along its upper half.

Before long there may be an announcement that our metal cards are at last ready, but don't write in for them until there is a definite notice giving price and so forth.

Washington, D. C.

It was soaked in warm water for an hour and a half-then dried by rubbing it off with a cloth. The upper part of the card was twice dipped in a solution of one part flexible collodion to one part acetic ether. The so-called New Skin preparation sold in drug stores ought to answer the same purpose. I believe that three or four dippings, allowing to dry thoroughly after each dipping and using a heavy, hard card, make as nearly an indestructible record as any one could want. Have given this well over a year's try-out myself.

Hoping this will help out some of the brothers.—G. D. Murphy.

WORD from another old-timer of the West, with definite facts as to the death of Frank Gruard. These old-timers are of the kind of men we younger fellows particularly like to hear from and to give a warm welcome and a comfortable seat at our Camp-Fire. They can tell us wonderful tales, if they will, and we are eager for them:

Hudson, Wyoming.

In your issue of December 3, 1917, I notice a letter from the pen of E. A. Brininstool, author of "Trail Dust of a Maverick," in which he mentions two very warm friends of mine, namely, Mrs. T. J. Foster, of Sheridan, Wyoming, and Frank Gruard, one-time scout in the army operating against the Sioux.

HE ASKS if Frank is alive yet, and it is with sorrow that I have to answer no, that Frank has gone to that camp-fire from which none may return. Let us hope that his long years of faithful service for Uncle Sam have entitled him to a seat among the famous men who served so well in opening the now great State of Wyoming. Frank passed on over the last trail several years ago at St. Louis. As to where a copy of the book, "Life and Adventures of Frank Gruard," can be obtained I can not say, but believe there is a copy in the Wyoming State Library in Cheyenne. I do not know whether the author, Joe De Barthe, is yet alive or not. The last I heard of him he was selling patent medicine in Chicago, and that was about twelve years ago.

Mrs. T. J. Foster, so far as I know, is still alive and well at Sheridan, Wyoming.

Hoping Mr. Brininstool may secure some information from this scrawl, I am.—L. Davidson.

IT SEEMS impossible to explain too often that our Camp-Fire is open to all. There is no ceremony or red-tape of any kind to be gone through with in order to be a member. Likewise, all our free services are open to *all*. You do *not* need to be a subscriber. You are asked only to observe the rules. For abuse of these services three men are now barred. All others welcome.

SO LONG as mail and general transportation conditions remain unsettled we ask both our subscribers and our news-stand buyers, if the magazine is delayed, to wait a reasonable time after the usual date of delivery before writing in to inquire. We provide against delays as best we can, but the delays do not run on a regular schedule.

And if you write in concerning any circulation matter, won't you address the Circulation Manager, *not* the editorial department or me personally? Glad to help when I can, but if it's a matter that the circulation department can handle, one that falls within their field, not mine, why not send it to them direct? I have quite a few little jobs of my own to attend to and, well, you know how it is.

Arthur Sullivant Hoffman.

THERE'S a funny tradition still kicking around that each magazine has its "staff of writers." I don't expect ever to see that idea killed off. But it's a funny one. A very few magazines do have a kind of "staff" of writers in the sense that they depend almost wholly on them for their stories, and all magazines have writers whose tales they use more often than those of others for the simple reason that these writers can furnish the particular kind of story these particular magazines want. But what the tradition means is that magazines are not open to contributions from any one outside their "staffs." Rot.

OF COURSE some magazines fall into the rut of limiting themselves too much to a certain few writers, but generally they do so more or less unconsciously. Anyhow, that's none of my business. But as to *Adventure*, judge for yourself. Our Camp-Fire custom that whenever a new (to *Adventure*) writer joins us with a story he stands up and introduces himself serves as a pretty good index to the steady flow of fresh blood among our writers. I'm glad, however, that along with the new blood we retain some of the old and that we still have stories from some of the men who were giving us stories five, six or seven years ago. They made good with you, with us, and of course we stick to our old and tried friends. And one reason we don't tire of them is because of the constant addition of new writers.

Few of our issues appear, even now that it is twice a month, without at least one new writer to introduce himself to us and sometimes there are two or three. For example, of the eleven issues thus far in 1918 only one has failed to introduce at least one new writer and even this one gave us a story by a man from whom we'd had only one story before. In this issue there are two, and one of them herewith follows our old custom and introduces himself—E. S. Pladwell. I know he is mistaken in thinking we, his Camp-Fire comrades, might not be personally interested in what he has done and been:

Oakland, Calif.

I have decided that it's the only sporty thing to do to make myself acquainted *via* the Camp-Fire. I hesitated not necessarily from modesty but because one success hardly allowed me to classify myself as an author, because my life has not compared with many of your other writers for pure adventure, and because I feel that no one cares a hoot who I am outside my own warm friends, and they know all about me anyhow.

I AM a newspaper man. I have been so for several years. There are many adventures in this profession, but somehow they all seem second-hand. One is not living his own life, but that of his paper. The things I have got into have been through and for my paper. I have been sent into shooting affairs, stabbing scraps, riots and battles, but to me they are a matter of routine business. It's a good game and I like it.

Before that I was assistant construction inspector on the San Francisco water front, a railroad ticket agent in San Francisco and Portland, and a member of the party which established the elevation of Death Valley for the United States Geological Survey. I was assistant superintendent in a construction job on the Eel River, on a contract for building the Northwestern Pacific railroad into Eureka.

I WILL admit I was a poor engineer and surveyor. I was born with an inborn loathing for mathematics, and got much higher in the business than mere mathematical ability would warrant. I had some adventures in handling men in large gangs and perhaps I prospered at times because I early learned the one essential of the art of bossing: A boss should boss as little as possible. Unless there's shirking, let the men alone. I've seen dozens of good, expert men get in wrong for lack of knowing that one cardinal principle.

I WAS born in Brooklyn and educated everywhere. At fourteen I acquired spinal tuberculosis, which took many years to down. It made me weak in body and, as my bad temper kept well ahead of my physical condition, things became torrid for me. It's cured now.

In wandering about I obtained much local color which will, I hope, aid me in whatever writings I do. I learned to swim, row, box, play baseball and football, draw, dance, write, ride, drive, shoot, dive, and almost everything else, becoming master at none of these arts but a dabbler in all. I have even tried singing, despite certain frank comments.

MY MOST thrilling experience was a fool Mexican battle, where a lot of men were endeavoring to slaughter each other at Tia Juana. The spectacle was all right, but the smell was awful. Since then, battles have sort of paled in my imagination. It was nothing like a Meissonier picture. It was just bad smell. Since then I have longed to get to Europe, despite the much-advertised smell, but so far the Fates have not decided my way.—E. S. PLADWELL.

And here's a word on his story in this number:

Oakland, Calif.

Almost word for word, the first episode relates what actually happened on the Western division of the Southern Pacific Railroad between Sacramento and Davis some fifteen years ago. The mystery was never solved. Taking patches from other railroad yarns and transplanting the whole thing to the desert, I have managed to evolve a solution with enough climaxes for three or four stories. The first episode I will admit is a bit gruesome, but I think the rest of the yarn takes that all away.—E. S. P.

CONCERNING their story in this issue a word from Farnham Bishop and Arthur Gilchrist Brodeur. The former, after many previous efforts, is now one of the boys in khaki; the latter, after as many efforts, is still barred out by defective eyesight. Here's good luck to them both!

Berkeley, Calif.

Odo and *Sigismundo* are tolerably faithful portraits of twelfth-century Norman adventurers of the baser sort. Brutal, superstitious, eager to plunder the weak, yet even the worst of them were hard fighters and keen sportsmen. It was good medieval folk-lore that if a woman wore men's clothes she could work witchcraft, as you can read in the report of the trial of Joan of Arc.

Here, too, is a note on their story in our last issue, which through my fault didn't get to our last Camp-Fire, and an item to add to the information on a still earlier story, the tale of Japan in the old days:

History says nothing of any secret league of Sicilian serfs, such as described in "The Quest of Gaimar the Grim," in the Reign of Roger II. But there were such secret societies on the island in ancient times, when Eunus the slave suddenly revealed himself as the head of a wide-spread brotherhood that rose at his word against their masters and defied the power of Rome for six years, till the insurrection was finally crushed by Publius Rupilius, the consul, in 132 B. C. In modern Sicily, there is still the Mafia, now degenerated into a semi-criminal organization, but which was founded about a century ago, after Napoleon had driven the Bourbon King of Naples to seek refuge in Sicily. Feudalism still existed there till the British, in return for the protection of their fleet, made Ferdinand IV grant a constitution which abolished the feudal system in 1812. This deprived the armed retainers of the great land-owners of their livelihood, and most of them became brigands. Unable to surpress them, Ferdinand IV made them into a sort of mounted police, somewhat like the Mexican *rurales* of Don Porfirio Diaz, but without their discipline. In sheer self-defense, the poor people of the island founded the Mafia, which was at its inception just such a secret league as we have ascribed to *Gian the One-Handed*.—A. G. B.

I should like to add this note to our other short story: "*Two Strong Men.*" We got our information about the Manila-Acapulco galleon from the unpublished Ph. D. thesis of Dr. William Lytle Schurz, of the University of Michigan, who has brought together a great mass of information on the subject as a result of years of research among the original Spanish sources in the Bancroft Collection at the University of California. This acknowledgement should be made, out of fairness to Dr. Schurz. We changed the date of the sea-fight in Urado Harbor from 1602 to 1592, in order to make it coincide with the tortoise-boat and Hideyoshi's Korean campaign; also, we gave the galleon a bigger and better armament than was customary. We fought her according to the rules laid down in that most useful and spirited little volume: "An Accidence or The Pathway to Experience necessary for all young sea-men . . . written by Captaine John Smith sometime Governor of Virginia and Admiral of New England," printed in London in 1626.—FARNHAM BISHOP.

SCALPING. I don't know why we've never happened to get on that subject before, but here we are now:

Salem, Ore.

I read Hugh Pendexter's story with great pleasure and noted the allusion to scalping in the Camp-Fire. As nearly as I was ever able to ascertain, only two persons were ever scalped in the old days on the Plains and lived to tell about it. One was a chief of the Crows, if I recall rightly, and the Sioux lifted his hair in an intertribal war.

THE other instance was the famous one of James Thompson, the English railroader. This occurred near what is now North Platte, Neb., in 1867, I think. He was shot from his perch on a telegraph-pole by a war party of Indians, and his scalp taken. The bullet which hit him in the head stunned him slightly, but he described the pain of the operation as terrible. The brave who mutilated him lost the first piece cut off, and came back and got another one. Thompson saw where the scalp lay and crawled over and secured it. He was rescued by a party from the fort near by, and finally recovered.

His scalp was placed on a wigmaker's stand in one of those glass bells that you formerly saw the flowers under in Uncle Allen's parlor, on the farm. The gruesome trophy was placed in the Public Library in Omaha, Neb., where I saw it some years since. Thompson was alive in England, I think, in 1907. I got the principal facts from his story in the *Wide World* in the same year. I have also read the article in a Nebraska daily paper of the old-timer who saw Thompson carrying his hair in a pail of water down the streets of the town near the fort. It was later tanned, I heard.

THE reason that scalping was so fatal was the fact that blood-poisoning usually set in at once, due to the fearful lacerations and the condition of the knives used. The antiseptic treatment of wounds was of course not dreamed of in those days. It appears that it was, however, nothing unusual for a man to survive the actual scalping two or three days till the blood-poisoning had time to finish him.—D. WIGGINS.

FROM another of our writers' brigade at the front comes greeting to us. He's getting adventure at first-hand and on a large scale, and he seems to like it, but he's the writer still and while he does his bit he gathers grist for his "mill." I've sent him magazines, but he and his comrade can use many more.

I would have written you before this, but work of the most trying nature has prevented me from doing so. If the censor so wills, the next paragraph will go through to you, but if he says "No!" you'll then receive some ink-blacked lines instead.

Section 59-592, New York University Ambulance Company, U. S. A. A. S., is now officially attached to the French Army. Wherever our division, one of the most famous fighting divisions in the whole of the army, goes, we follow. Short stories and long stories, articles and books, poems and brief paragraphs have been written about the *poilus* of this division, and I am confident that they will hold a permanent place in the war writings of the world. For they turned back the Huns at the Marne. They were at Ypres. And their life-blood was spilled at Verdun. They have been at numerous other places, too, places made famous and never-to-be-forgotten by the biggest battles of this war.

And to think that we are a part of that division. Does that not sound like adventure?

Every other day I go out on an ambulance to a *Poste de Secours* (an infirmary) which is situated a short way behind the lines. I remain there with a driver until noon of the following day. We do little in the day, but are subjected to a great deal of night driving. And all of this without a single light—and within hearing of the Boches. More adventure.

I have one letter of twenty-one hundred words, entitled "Salvagers." So far I have been unable to mail the same to you. Censorship is the stumbling-block. Then, too, I am working on a new letter, "The Mad Adventure," in which I tell how a lieutenant, a section clerk, a cook who can not cook, an interpreter who did not interpret, a wheezy old Ford that coughed all the way, and a pay-roll that was all signed with the exception of two signatures, went up to the very mouth of the trenches—indeed, right into them—in search of two ambulance drivers who had gone promenading to the trenches, thus failing to sign the pay-roll. Some time I shall get this stuff through to you. Also, other letters, among them being "In the Red Cross House of François Lartigau."

I shall be glad to receive copies of *Adventure*, and I can assure you that it will be read from cover to cover by all the members of the section. We receive little reading matter here.—CHARLES BROWN, JR.

FOLLOWING our Camp-Fire custom, with his first story in our magazine, Kingsbury Scott stands up and introduces himself to the rest of us:

Grand Haven, Mich.

I have written many thousands of words since I first saw the light of day in a sailor town on the east shore of Lake Michigan, but very few of those words have been about myself. My task has been to write of other people and other people's troubles. Because of the fact that I am a newspaper man I have seen more of troubles than has been good for me, perhaps. I have rather lived on the rim of adventure all my life, without having tumbled in very seriously. Naturally I have had many interesting experiences, which, however, would have no particular place here.

BORN in a sailor town in the tag end of the lumber days, my first memories are of the craft which sailed the lakes in the days when pine was king. There were the old steam-barges, with their deckloads piled high amidships, and long clean-looking schooners, with green hulls and white upper-works and with their bewhiskered skippers, who were lords of their own domain. Men were pretty well the masters of their own ships in those days. They were the judges of wind and weather and no one asked them to risk their ships if they did not deem it wise to cast off their moorings and sail away.

My father was a sailor. My first recollection of him is the best picture my mind retains of him. He was chief engineer and part owner of a lumber steamer and, as a little boy, I made many trips with him. I knew every man on board by his first name and my parents trusted me implicitly in the care of any one of them, from a deckhand to the skipper. Many times I clasped a big rough hand tightly on excursions through the lumber-yards "above the bridges" in Chicago.

All my life I have been in closest touch with lake craft and the men who sailed them. Though the men and the ships have changed greatly in the years, the hearts of "the boys" have remained the same. The wild ones keep on firing or decking until age and weakness retires them, without pay, and the steady ones become the masters or chief engineers of better ships. I have had the opportunity of observing these men closely, and I will say the great majority of them are pretty good chaps, with some few similar characteristics and a great many differing personalities. They are the sort I like to write about. In these men I have found my adventures.

FOR many years after quitting the lakes my father was United States steamboat inspector of the Lake Michigan east shore district, and his wide acquaintance with marine men brought me likewise into touch with them. By some queer turn Fate made me a landlubber, with sailor blood in my veins. Both of my brothers started out on the lakes, one to continue until he, too, became a chief engineer with a license which would make him the chief of any size ship on any ocean, the other to become a mill and ship operator himself. I chose a profession new to the family. I became a newspaper man. Breaking in on a country daily, where shipping news was a feature, I went out at last for bigger game. I did the wharves for Milwaukee papers, and followed up with the shifts to other cities, a common trait of men of the game.

With the sea blood in me, with the memories of old time masters and mates and engineers stamped upon my brain, I had to have an outlet, so I began writing stories of the lakes and I discovered that there were magazines which would pay money for them. I have been at it more or less ever since.

I HAVE always felt that I knew intimately the men of the lakes, and the women who worried about them at home, when the Fall storms came. My father's house faced the harbor and I spent many an idle hour watching the ships slip past. From the upper windows I could see old Lake Michigan rolling in to the white sandy beach, and the roar of the breakers has sounded in my ears many nights as I lay staring into the darkness. One day I stood beside my mother in our upper lookout window and watched a fine big schooner come rushing in to her doom on the beach. I saw her spars fall as the combers conquered her at last and I heard my mother sigh for the poor souls whose lives were in danger. That was in the long ago, but incidents such as these, together with the traditions of ships, which surround every sailor's town, could not fail to leave impressions upon a young mind.

A LOVE for the marine has kept me always within the sound of the deep-throated steamer whistles. I have always come back to the water, because I have felt that life was not worth living away from it. I hope I shall always be able to see a ship when I want to. I like to smoke a pipe with the skipper up in his room in the "texas." I like to get down in the engine-room, with the chief or the assistants, where the oils have a comfortable fragrance, where the dynamos hum, and the fans pull the cool air down through the ventilators. I like the steamy smell of the place. I like to get a whiff of the galley, if the cook is good-natured. In fact, I like a steamboat or a schooner from end to end and she's like home to me even if I've never seen her before.—Kingsbury Scott.

IN CONNECTION with his story in this number, Thomas Samson Miller says "The Tailed Giants of the Pagan Belt are not fabulous creatures but are mentioned in the report of the Alexander-Gosling Expedition."

And it happens that, nearly seven years ago, when we were just beginning to get our readers and writers into touch with each other by asking the latter to give us full accounts of themselves, Mr. Miller was one of those who responded in good comradeship and was also one of two or three whose responses got into a cranny of my detail-laden desk and then into a cranny elsewhere and—has never been given to you, although I thought it had. (I must seem, from this and other instances confessed to, a careless kind of person. Well, maybe, and yet if you were to have a few weeks on this job I think you would judge me gently.)

Anyhow, here is Mr. Miller's account of himself, written back in 1911 for us of the Camp-Fire.

SEE a boy in class gazing, not at the blackboard, but beyond to the wall map—tracing out bays, continents, seas, capes, mountains—the big, wide world outside his little country village, and longing for that outer world—hungering for it. To fine poetry in geography; to devour stories of other climes and races; to find a hayrick and, sprawled on his stomach, give his soul to the wonders of Robinson Crusoe; or to climb the highest hills, to look at the world beyond—a glimpse of the English Channel—scintillating, silvery highway to that Beyond; perhaps a liner's smoke trailed against the sky, and, oh, how the heart followed that liner into the western horizon!

BUT how to escape the commonplace—in my case, tight, tamed, policed little England? Was there a chance I did not try, an advertisement I did not answer, a relative I did not bother? The disappointments of those early years—till I stood one day in the scrumptious offices of the Royal Niger Chartered Company and signed a contract (every clause of which spelled Romance). So eager was I that I bluffed two years on my age to fill the requirements of the contract. Read for yourselves part of those clauses that lured me from clean bed and roof for——

(9) Mr. Thomas Samson Miller agrees to communicate to the aforesaid Company any discoveries of pecuniary value made by him or any knowledge whatsoever that he may acquire directly or indirectly in the Nigerian sphere (as set forth by the Anglo-German, French and Portuguese treaties and boundaries commissions of the years. . . . That any presents given to him by emir, sultan, chief or lesser dignity shall be the property of said Company. . . .

(15) That he understands the wild nature of the country designated the Nigerian sphere and absolves the Company from all responsibility whatsoever for death or accident. . . That he understands and signs with full knowledge of the unhealthy climate and that the Company is not responsible for failure to provide, though they agree wherever possible, to transport, feed and house said Thomas Samson Miller as befits his station. . .

Africa! the very word spelled romance, adventure, glory.

I SIGNED blithely, and shook hands with a real earl, not to mention lesser lords on the directorate, and stepped aboard a West African liner at Liverpool with the emotions of a Raleigh, Columbus, Livingston concentrated in one bosom. Not even the doleful tales of the ship's officers of the palm-oil ruffianism, fever, savages and mosquitoes could damp a young fool's ardor for the unknown. Not even Mary Kingsley's taffrail-explored and deck-written book of horrors of West Africa could spoil dreams. I rather think my buoyancy got on the nerves of the Old Coasters, for they sure did sling it into me in that little smoking town—such stories of cannibalism, privations, savagery! It was their fun. Blessed was my armor of ignorance.

THERE are landmarks in all lives. That first sight of Africa! I was up at daybreak, waiting for the lookouts cry of "Land!" It was Mount Teneriffe, by the way, my first mountain. How foolish it made the home hills. And, oh, that landing! The chatter of foreign tongues, the little brown urchins who smoked cigarets as if to the manner born; the strange fruits and stranger flowers; the swarthy faces; the sun (later I was to know that bald, blistering African sun only too well); the curious customs. And the meeting in hotels and *patios* of men who did things—men of the outer world, who spoke in half-sentences and seemed to say more in a half-nod or elevation of the eyebrows than we stay-at-home mortals say in a laborious paragraph.

And then the slow voyage down the Gold Coast—the oily calms, splashed with flying-fish and dolphins, not to mention open-mouthed voracious sharks; the crazy little, smelling, barbarian villages on the bleached shore, until we steamed into the Niger Delta, and coconut trees, monkeys, pythons and hippopotamuses were not behind bars. Now the history of the next few years—its aches and pains, transports and adventures; its strange animals and stranger animal-men are set forth in my stories.

WELL, there it is, I have been writing and journeying ever since. A rolling stone gathers no moss, maybe, but it keeps shiny and clean. This globe-trotting is a disease; ever it is mountains and plains; sea coast and inland prairies; mighty rivers and mightier deserts, and new faces all the time, not to say new friends. Sometimes I hit the cities, only to revolt quickly from collars and cuffs, three meals a day and the daily newspaper.

Nor does it cost much, this bumming around, not when you know how—not when you ship overboard the prejudices for sheeted beds, clothes and accustomed foods—not when you learn to do in Rome as Rome does—to eat spaghetti in Italy, garlic and olives in Spain, tortillas in Mexico, the "damper" in Australia, manioc bread on the Guinea Coast, dates in the Sahara and flapjacks in a lumber-camp. Ship overboard the prejudices and superfluities of civilization and you know what real freedom is.

I LIKE the schooling of the outer world—am thankful for the medicinal value of hunger (by the way, and it is curious, one never hungers in a barbarian community; the mealie-pot and campfire are almost always free to the stranger of right approach; it is in the big cities of civilization that one hungers if he hasn't the price)—I like hunger for the dreams it brings; I like hardship for the ache in the bones and the deep sleep it brings; and am glad for the mighty poetry of tornadoes, sandstorms, madcap seas, cloudbursts, electric storms, meteors; the heave of the deep sea, and above all the still voice of the solitudes.

SO IT is I lay aside my writing for spells, an find myself hidden in the forest with the bark-peelers, or working long, laborious healthy days in a lumber-mill, and recently there was a trip to China in the engine-room, my friend the chief engineer having made an oiler of me pro tem. Then there were orange-picking days in Southern California, with a gang of Japs, where I discovered that there *is* a Jap Question. Picking oranges has a flavor of the poetical about it, but is tedious work and not to be thought of with cement mixing, which had fallen to my lot.

AND the stories these experiences have given me. On my left forearm is a scar where a turbaned mahdi up in Sokoto (on the caravan route to Timbuctoo) thought to rid the world of at least one Dog-of-a-Swine-Eating Christian. Up in British Columbia is a mine I staked—the stakes are there yet, perhaps, as are the two Chinamen still panning gold out of the Columbia with the infinite patience of their race, sometimes panning a dollar a day, sometimes three. From there I tramped through Oregon a no-account remittance man (it is a mystery to me however the remittance man was so long the hero of popular fiction.) In those days we found an alfalfa stack for bed, the blue sky for roof, a loaf of bread with "swiped" peaches to moisten it down for food, and snatches from Verdi with stanzas from Omar to feed our dreams. My fingers fairly itch to write the hobo's vindication.

I RECALL a peaceful month of Fall plowing on Manitoba's undulating prairies. The quiet joy of those open spaces are still. And how my team—four real Canadian horses—and I got to know each other. What frolic and character there were in those four, Jerry, Madge, Prince and Minna! I have ever been happiest in overalls, and always out-of-doors.

I WAS the other day crossing the San Francisco-Oakland Ferry at the hour of the evening rush of homebound communters. I saw an *Adventure* in the lap of a tired little stenographer, open at one of my own stories. She was rounding a day of key-pounding with half an hour in Africa. I watched her snapping eyes and glowing face as she followed the adventure and love to its climax, then closed the magazine and came back to the crowded, hustling every-day commonplace. Is it not a power and a pleasure to be able to take people out of themselves, and sometimes, in a sly way, educate, or proclaim some wrong? A writer dearly loves to preach; so look for the pill in the jam—the sermon under the love-story.

I BELIEVE one good story harvests more good than a hundred ephemeral sermons. I never met a lover of good reading who was a degenerate. Get a good magazine in your hands and you are getting more for the money than anything else offers.

WHEN Gordon McCreagh writes about air-men, as he does in this issue, he does so at first-hand, through experience in the U. S. N. R. aviation service. When you think of it, there is something startling in a change from jungle-tracking in primitive Burma to handling in America a flying-machine typical of the utmost advance in modern science and civilization.

ARTHUR SULLIVANT HOFFMANN.

THE CAMP-FIRE
A MEETING-PLACE FOR READERS, WRITERS AND ADVENTURERS

E. E. HARRIMAN writes of a curious coincidence in connection with his story in this issue:

Los Angeles.

I have a neighbor from Arizona, a sick man who came here to recover. Lives next door. I call on him now and then and one night I told him about Pap Gleason in my yarn and he laughed. Then he asked if I knew Pap Gleason of Arizona. I told him that the name just popped into my head and I had no idea that there ever was a rancher there of that name.

"Why, man," he said, "old Pap Gleason is one of my dearest friends and he fits your description to a T."

Funny, eh? Then he told me Pap Gleason had been ranching out there for forty years and is a well known character in the State.—E. E. H.

DO YOU remember the little discussion we had about the old whaler *Morning Star?* Here's the latest chapter in her sixty-five years of adventure—a news item from the New York *Sun* last Summer sent us by L. H. Haight who has given us news of her before:

A marine specimen of unusual interest has been added to the collection in the harbor. This is the former New Bedford whaleship *Morning Star*, which after a service of sixty-four years in the whaling fleet has been drawn by the war into the business of cargo carrying.

THE *Morning Star* is said to be the first of the whaleships to enter the cargo trade and she is thought to be the oldest vessel in point of years in New York harbor at the present time.

This vessel was examined by interested visitors recently at Brady's wharf, Staten Island. Outside of her square-shouldered, stanch appearance she does not resemble very much the old ship that for so many years put out past Gay Head on long whaling voyages.

LIKE many of the old whalers the *Morning Star* was bark-rigged. For present purpose she has been cut down to a fore-and-aft rig. All the old yards are gone, the topmasts unstepped and she is now a three-masted schooner as far as sail plan is concerned, with her original lower masts still in use.

Further to change the appearance of the ancient craft those heavy davits, which used to hold her boats always swung out, have been removed. Also that high, strange deckhouse aft, typical of all old whaleships, has been cut down to a more practical cabin. An auxiliary engine of sixty horse-power has been put in to help her along on windless days.

BUILT by skilled Dartmouth shipwrights of hardy oak, the *Morning Star* joined the whaling fleet in 1853. A vessel of 238 tons, 104 feet long, she was somewhat smaller than other famous whaleships. But for long years she successfully breasted the storms of the seven seas and brought her owners several fortunes in oil.

There is only one older vessel in the whaling fleet still in service. This is the *Charles W. Morgan*, built in 1841, which recently sailed from New Bedford on a whaling cruise.

IN A letter to me concerning his story in this number, L. Patrick Greene writes: "In the character of *Zari* I have tried to refute the unjust, at least to my mind, characterization of witch-doctors by Stewart Edward White in his Kingozi stories."

FROM one of our comrades, writers' brigade, at the battle-front in France, Charles Brown, Jr.:

In a Y. M. C. A. Hut,
Twelve Miles Behind the Lines,
France of the Bleeding Heart.

I am "in repose" with our French division, which has dragged itself out of the trenches for a short breathing spell. But strange to say, I do not care about being in repose. There's no adventure in this repose life.

COMEDY there is, however. For instance, the local "cinema." The picture-house is across the river. Before the war the city council met in it the first and third Tuesday of each month. Always the house is crowded. For the most part French soldiers attend. Last night it seemed that practically every poilu in the town was there. You could have cut the smoke and trench-stench into huge chunks. It was the most tangible stuff I had run into in weeks. And dialogue! The place flowed with it.

Most all of the soldiers brought their canteens of Penard (red wine) with them. Also, tin-cups were in evidence. The trench-weary poilus were not contented to sit in their seats and dispose of the red goods. Instead, they insisted on sitting on the backs of the long benches. Some of them were so "zigzag" (intoxicated, if you please) that they rolled off of the bench backs into the laps of their comrades. And the comrades reciprocated by shampooing the "zigzag" ones with Penard.

WELL, after thirty minutes of this "Keystone" stuff the show began. The title of the picture was "The Banker's Crime." I saw one reel and a half of the thrilliest thriller I ever gave both eyes to. It moved as rapidly as a German "Zep." In all probability I would have seen more of it, but the picture ceased to move.

"The —— machine has broken down," I said to Flitcroft E. Evans of Brooklyn.

"Then the grand performance is *fini*," Evans spoke up. And never did Evans speak more wisely. For, forty-five minutes later, the operator emerged from his little shack at the end of the council room. His face was flushed and he clung desperately to the stair railing. He put one foot before the other very slowly. At any moment I expected him to fall and roll to the bottom of the stairs. At once I realized why he had kept us waiting by turning the lights on and off, as operators have a way of doing. He was "zigzag"—not partly but totally "zigzag." In short, he was incapacitated for work that night.

I HAVE not yet been successful in mailing my "war" letters to you. Censorship is the stumbling-block. However, you'll get them sooner or later.

Write me a few lines, *bon comrades*. They will be appreciated on this side of the water.

In a few days I am going back to the lines. We may make a three-day auto trip across France before we return to our work.—CHARLES BROWN, JR.

"UNCLE FRANK" is Frank H. Huston of almost anywhere outdoors in California, whose inquiry some time ago started us collecting information on the pioneers of the Old West. I dare say many a future investigator or historian will refer to the back pages of our Camp-Fire to get data he can find nowhere else. The men who know are among our number and our work in gathering this knowledge before it is lost forever is not only interesting but a very valuable service.

"Uncle Frank" is a pioneer himself and if only we can persuade him to tell us some of his own adventures among the Indians we'll get some particularly good hearing. Let's put it up to him now. He started all this discussion and it's only fair that he should contribute his own share.

THE first name omitted in his letter is that of a prominent man, whom we spare through politeness; the second is *not* that of one of our own writers. The story he votes for is "The Secret Wolf," by S. Carleton, back in 1916. The "E. E." referred to is our comrade E. E. Harriman of Los Angeles, an "Ask Adventure" editor and one of our most enthusiastic Camp-Fire members; "Uncle Frank" has christened him, himself and me the "H Triangle," and we do quite a bit of talking among ourselves. I have to do mine by letter only, but, as a result of our three-cornered correspondence, the two other points of the triangle have hunted each other up personally and become good friends at first-hand. And some day, so help me, I'm going to get out there somehow and try to make good in the flesh as the third point of a triangle that exemplifies the real friendships that are more and more growing out of our meetings at the Camp-Fire.

And *will* you tell Camp-Fire that "Uncle Frank" says any one who will use an automatic shotgun or rifle a-hunting game is a black and white, bushy-tailed, odoriferous —— ——, or, to be exact, *Mephitis amcus*. Hoh, hah! now you know how to get the old man's goat—auto-guns, auto-wheels to hunt with. I can't swear; words fail me; can't even sputter.

WILL you tell Hugh Pendexter that he is the only writer I've seen who seems to really know anything about the Plains Injuns. Where did he get it, and how does he know about the ceremonial buffalo hunt? Yet ninety-nine readers out of ten wouldn't appreciate him (on that point, I mean). If they were all as correct in detail as he—or is he another B. M. Bower to fool me?—then we'd have some writers.

When I see more every issue *re* old-time West I feel like the man whose wife had triplets. "Gawd! did I do that?" Just my harmless little inquiry and what a wealth of information!

God labored six days and rested on the seventh. E. E. works six days and on the seventh goes to Catalina and repairs his house, so he tells me, and I tell him that house is like my britches.

I'M SITTING out back of the hogan before an Injun fire and writing by lantern-light—cold as it was in the snow-country, but that's the desert in Winter always. I just wish I had you and "Big Bill" (E. E.) opposite. There's a gallon of coffee on right now and half will be in me before I turn in—good old bootleg coffee—hat full of water, leg of your boot and a plug of tobacco b'iled together. Um, say Mister! that and the 44 cal. Win. and Colt won the West, naught else.

If you happen to be Mr. Benedict, tell Mrs. to mash fine some sweet potatoes and mix in the flapjack—"Cho-Noa (?) the griddle-cake" batter, and wear a golden halo.

Oh, —— ——, situated in a school for "writers" on the Hudson, makes a man just prior to the Battle of New Orleans pull a *revolver* on Gen. Jackson! . . . Finis! But then in "Julius Cæsar" Bill Shak. makes one character say "The clock strikes," so —— is in good company.

My vote: another gory but good tale from that woman who went to France, the one who was skeered to show up at the camp-fire because she wore skirts, and took her chance underground to kill 'em after smelling 'em up with wolf-bait. *No obstante* the buckets of blood, she can write, and not amateurish "eyethur."—"UNCLE FRANK."

I ASKED Kathrene and Robert Pinkerton about the curious disease that figures in their story in this issue because I thought that those of you who, like myself, were not familiar with it might think it a fantastic invention of the authors instead of a medical fact. Also, Indian conjury is interesting and the following letters from the authors make good reading:

We first encountered a case of this kind in the fall of 1916, at a Hudson's Bay Company post. An Indian woman had started to turn white, patches of white skin showing on her face, neck and breast. The next year we saw her again, and her entire face was white. The manager of the post told us he had seen the same disease twice before in other parts of Canada.

WHILE we were talking of it Mrs. Pinkerton found an article in a magazine describing it. She gave it to a sister of the Indian woman and we forgot about it. At your suggestion we looked it up and find that Stelwagon describes it something as follows:

"Vitiligo, sometimes called leukoderma, a disease involving the pigment of the skin alone, characterized by the development of several round or oval, circumscribed, smooth, milk-white patches, tending to increase in size, and exhibiting at their margin increased pigmentation.

"VITILIGO and leukoderma are synonymous and interchangeable terms, although some authors use the former for the acquired disease and the latter for the congenital, patchy loss of pigment.

"The malady may be extremely slight, only a few spots presenting, or they may be numerous and, exceptionally, may gradually invade the entire surface, as in instances observed by Levi, Hall, Hardaway, Simon and myself."

Stelwagon goes on to say that some negroes have turned entirely white and that at no time in the course of the disease is the general health impaired, the malady having no damaging influence.—R. E. P.

Morrison, Colorado.

Conjuring and the fear of conjuring plays a large part in the lives of all Indians, even the Christianized ones. We did not realize how large a part it played until this Summer. Of course, it is not logical for a Christianized Indian to fear conjury, but then nothing that they do is logical. I will quote a few instances.

AN OLD man, the son of a former Scotch manager and an Indian woman, is really the leader in the church and in the absence of the priest reads the prayers on Sunday. Yet when he was hunting with his son and they caught a beaver in hunting territory that belonged to another Indian, he told his son to hide the beaver lest the Indian would find out about it and conjure them. You see, he was sufficiently a white man to dare to take the beaver but enough of an Indian to fear being conjured.

A full-blood Indian woman, the wife of a former manager of the post, became, during her years at the post, most Christianized and adopted many of the white woman's methods, including having her breakfast served in bed and demanding two maids. When her son went to the war she consulted the priest and asked for his prayers. At the same time she had an Indian, who is supposed to have some influence with the spirits, make her some medicine which would protect her son from the white man's bullets. You see she played safe and tried both methods. When she is sick she has both the doctor and the medicine-man.

EVEN a better instance is the story of a woman who was at the post this Summer. Her father had grown jealous of another Indian who had caught a silver fox and killed him. After he recovered from his jealous rage he concluded that the Indian who had caught the fox must have conjured him into a *weetigo*, a cannibalistic evil spirit. He did not want to become one, but he thought his own desires had no weight against this conjury. He concluded that he had better die than become this fearful thing and he asked his children to kill him while he was asleep. His sons refused to do it, but his daughter, thinking that she was doing the right thing, cut off his head with an ax while he slept.

Samuel Hearne tells a better instance. After one of his expeditions, wishing to gain favor with one of the Indians he gave him a paper and told him that that paper would conjure one of the Indian's enemies. The enemy heard about this and became so frightened that he did die. Samuel Hearne in telling of it admits that he was really responsible for the Indian's death, but insists that he had never imagined such an outcome to the trick.

—KATHRENE GEDNEY PINKERTON.

FOLLOWING the idea of giving, for those of you who don't happen to know, a few facts about the actual home of our magazine, here are a few items that will make us easier to find next time you're in New York.

Adventure lives a long quarter of a mile south of Washington Square, Macdougal Street, being, under another name, the western boundary of the Square, and the Square marking the lower or southern end of Fifth Avenue. Extending west and southwest from Washington Square is Greenwich Village—pronounced "Grennich" and famous as the habitat of human beings who devote nearly all their time to being "bohemians." No two people, including themselves, agree as to just what a bohemian is, but the New York ones rather specialize on living in Greenwich Village, which, incidentally, bears no resemblance to a real village.

IF YOU want to stop off there and eat at the Dutch Oven, or Polly's, or the Purple Pup, or elsewhere, and see the natives and the ordinary humans who also eat at these places, all right. I generally eat lunch there myself, but I rise to remark that I don't live in the village.

The village fades away into an Italian quarter just south of the Square. The only English names I can remember offhand on Macdougal Street between the Square and our building are the Dutch Oven and the National Noodle Company, the latter having disappeared of late. Southern Italians and, I think, Sicilians. Shops and tenements both sides all the way; hundreds of children in the street. Once it was the aristocratic quarter; the park gates of Aaron Burr's estate used to be right across the street from where our office is now.

ADVENTURE lives in the Butterick Building, which rises up, white, above the surrounding buildings, fifteen stories. Three women's magazines live there besides *Adventure* and *Everybody's—Delineator*, *Designer* and *Woman's*. Twelfth floor. A big reception-room that makes us all feel poor when we go home. *Adventure* is down the hall in a big room with four men, their desks and other desks and tables, and quite a few souvenirs around the walls.

The windows face the east, toward lower Broadway and, a mile and a half farther, the East River, the bridges, Brooklyn and Long Island. Look down quite a few stories and see wagons and trucks kept on top of roofs five or six stories from the ground. Also the men and boys with poles flying pigeons from numerous roofs.

FROM the west windows, on *Everybody's* side, you can see the North River half a mile away, here about a mile wide, but partly filled with long docks up and down each side. Also, across the river, at Hoboken, several of the German liners the United States took over, or maybe they're gone now—I won't say which, though, of course, such facts can't really be kept secret. If you're lucky, maybe there'll be a camouflaged steamer just coming in, painted like a nightmare or a rainbow but not easy to see.

From the building's south windows, lower New York, for a mile and a half beyond, the Singer tower and most of the famous skyscrapers—a wonderful fairyland of lights in the early evening. Beyond, the Upper Bay, Statue of Liberty and Staten Island.

From the north windows the Metropolitan tower, over a mile away, the *Times* tower farther still and all the rest of Manhattan for a dozen miles and more—buildings and streets, bricks, stones, asphalt, steel—and noise, a humming, thrumming, vibrating noise that rises and falls but never ceases day or night, year in and year out.

THE aerial trail in his story in this issue, Robert J. Pearsall writes, has its replica in fact:

San Francisco.

Many a time I've seen the *tuba* men of southern Luzon—the most agile humans in the world, I think—running across those teetery bridges from bamboo top to bamboo top. Sometimes they use only a single pole, with not even a handrail to cling to. They splice hollow pieces of cane, called *songas*, into the bottoms of the flower-clusters; and the sap they obtain, when fermented, forms *tuba*, next to *vino* the principal drink of the Islands.—ROBERT J. PEARSALL.

IT'S long since we've had word from Donald Francis McGrew, whose stories the old-timers will remember. I knew he had volunteered with a Maine regiment and was in France, a commissioned officer, but had no direct word from him for some time. Yes, France is different from the Philippines:

France, January 12, 1918.

This is a great show, with distinct features quite unlike previous affairs. If I have luck with me, I'll have great material when I return. As it is now, I am forbidden to write stories for publication; and, besides, I have no time to write.

I have heard a great deal of talk about the idea of the Boche which seems to be prevalent at home—that is, that the Boche yells "*Kamarad*" P. D. Q. You can tell the boys that this is not true of Mr. Boche as a nation. He fights like ——. He's a dirty, treacherous, stinking fighter, but he can fight like forty whirlwinds and he does. . . . It's a tough job and a rough one. At least that's what we think over here. . . . One thing in closing—the *men are splendid*. If the drafted men are *half* as good as these volunteers, we'll trim Germany this year or next. *Voilà!*—MAC.

IT IS seldom that a woman joins our writers' brigade and so follows Camp-Fire custom by standing up and introducing herself on the occasion of her first story in our magazine, but we always have special welcome for them. And those who have thus joined us have proved to be good fellows. Gentlemen, Ruby Erwin Livingston of Arkansas:

The friendly glow of the Camp-Fire attracts me, yet I much prefer to remain in its shadow rather than in the light, for I am merely myself. My adventures have been only near-adventures; nothing startling or thrilling ever quite happened. Was on a Mississippi steamboat once when the deck hands mutinied and some of them got shot while making for the tall timber at a landing, but I slept peacefully through it all and had to hear about it next day. I've also had the experience of sinking in water the third time and mentally witnessing a speedy motion-picture of my life—but some one grabbed me.

But these and other instances where something "nearly happened" have served at least to keep life from being monotonous, and I've traveled enough to know and be interested in all kinds of people—good, bad and indifferent. I first broke into print with bits of verse, about seven years ago, but had no idea that I should continue to follow this alluring will-o'-the-wisp, the writing-game.

WITH regard to "The Luck of Forty-Four" let me say that the main incident of the story really happened. The negro, nicknamed Forty-Four, voluntarily made the daring attempt to row through the overflow, capsized, and nearly died of exposure, but would not rest until his errand had been attended to. As a reward, he was pardoned, but I preferred to change the ending a bit, as you will see. One coincidence is that, after I had written the story I chanced to have a talk with a warden of Forty-Four's camp and found that I had drawn characteristics, age and physique, all true to life.—R. E. L.

HARRY MOORE, now collaborating with our old comrade George L. Catton, rises and introduces himself, following our Camp-Fire custom, on the occasion of his first story with us:

Born in Renfrew, Canada, in October, 1882. Apprenticed to the printing trade in 1896. Have worked as printer, foreman, reporter, editor of weekly and semi-weekly papers all over Ontario. Also worked in lumber mills in Ontario and Quebec. Began the writing game as a lyric writer for a Toronto publisher. Got lots of experience but no cash. Have been writing short stories and articles for magazines. Have soldiered a little; am fond of hunting and fishing. Have two brothers in France, with Canadians, and am proud of them. Have always been identified with sport—played lacrosse for years. Interested in baseball, horse-racing, prize-fighting or anything that shows action. Have been publishing papers for myself for thirteen years. Married, no family.—HARRY MOORE.

IT LOOKS as if our magazine might possibly have acquired supernatural powers of prophecy, or maybe it's a few of our authors who have this gift. Anyhow some of our stories show that their writers knew all about certain actual happenings long before they happened.

For example there was David L. MacKaye's story, "Brothers in Arms," in our issue of October, 1916, in which an officer made a private salute him forty times by way of teaching him military etiquette. Only the officer forgot that the regulations provide that an officer must return a salute, so his superior made said officer stand up in front of said buck private and salute *him* forty times. Well, nearly a year after this story appeared in our magazine that very incident happened. Yep. Up at Plattsburg. Lots of the newspapers told about it. Only they raised it ten, from forty to fifty, truth being stranger than fiction.

Odd, isn't it? Maybe some officer read the story, stowed the idea away in his mind, laid for a chance to soak it to some other officer and finally got his opportunity. Maybe it just happened. Maybe Mr. MacKaye was a prophet. Maybe some conscientious newspaper man, knowing how often the papers turn truth into fiction, felt he ought to even things up by turning fiction into truth. Maybe the newspaper man was working on space rates.

THE other day one of us, R. S. Arthur of Greenville, Pa., sent me an article of nearly two columns from the Pittsburgh —— of December 31, 1917, bearing this head: "Pittsburgh Border Guard Tells of Tragic Results from Disobeying Orders: National Army Man Gives Story of Treachery at Night at Eagle Pass; Pretty Girl Decoy." The article tells how the same thing that happened to Sentry, Post No. 4, in Edwin C. Dickenson's story, "To Quit My Post," in our issue of December 18th, has really happened to a sentry at Eagle Pass on the Mexican border. The article says the teller of the story is —— ——, 41st Infantry, F Company, U. S. A., home on furlough, and gives his home address and the name of the man he used to work for, and prints his picture, too. It gives his name, of course, but I omit it because I'm sure he wouldn't like any more fame than he's got already. Also the name of the newspaper, for it was probably what you'd call an unconscious medium.

MR. DICKENSON'S story, says —— ——, happened to Private Dickson, Post No. 10. The number of the post was different and, no name being used for the hero of our story other than No. 4, of course we don't know whether the names of the two men were the same or not, but strangely enough the name of the real man is very much like that of the author of our story. And there are lots and lots of other similarities between our story and what —— —— tells about happening to Dickson. The plot is just the same in both cases, and Mr. Dickenson was so good a prophet that he could tell in advance not only just what was going to happen later in real life but also just what a lot of the words and phrases were going to be when —— —— told the newspaper about it. Some prophet, I call him.

Of course it may all be coincidence, but it seems more probable that Mr. Dickenson is gifted with second sight.

THE chronology of events is interesting, too. We bought the story June 7, 1917, so Mr. Dickenson wrote it no later than May, 1917, maybe considerably earlier. It was published in our Mid-December issue, out November 18, 1917. The —— printed their record of fact December 31, 1917, stating that —— —— had told it "recently." He says it happened when F Company of the 41st was stationed on the Mexican border. I don't know just when that was, but I'll bet anything that some of you belong to the 41st, very possibly to F Company, and I'm sure all the rest of us would like to hear about this remarkable occurrence from those who were on hand at the time. Write in, comrades. Tell us the date and everything—or as nearly everything as seems wise.

I've asked Mr. Dickenson about it, too, and you'll find a word from him below.

Another odd thing is the name of the "enchantress" in the newspaper story. In our story it was Nita, but —— —— says the lady who "had a date" with the sentries was Data. I wish I knew whether the newspaper man's face grinned or failed to wake up when that name was handed to him.

Hartford, Conn.,
January 7, 1918.

Concerning the origin of my story "To Quit My Post," I would say that the situation that has arisen is certainly a remarkable one. The only facts which I had when I wrote this story, which by the way, was in March, 1917, are as follows:

THERE was a certain Mexican girl, of perhaps thirteen or fourteen, at Arivaca, Arizona, (where my troop was stationed during the late border trouble) whose father had been killed by American soldiers many years before, on the ground that he, having been engaged to assist them in some earlier border affair, had turned traitor and attempted to betray them to fellow Mexicans. This girl once made the statement to one of our troopers that some day she would even things up by killing one of us. Let me set your fears at rest by stating at this time that she never did.

This incident, together with an impression that I got one night when I was sergeant of the guard and had just posted a young near-millionaire at Post No. 4, the street described in the story, went to make the foundation of the tale. The incident at the ford was entirely fictitious, only brought in in order to give strength to my hero in resisting temptation. Or, at least to show that the habit of discipline had so thoroughly seized him that he could not escape it.

I NEVER heard the story described in the Pittsburgh paper and I must say I very much doubt if its author in that paper ever did, until he read it in *Adventure*, as it appears to have been copied more or less literally.

I think, under Mr. Hoffman's ruling in the matter, we are to be "congratulated."

I might add that the situs of the story is taken bodily from Arivaca, Arizona, where you will find the street, hotel, ford and cottonwoods, exactly as I have described them.—EDWIN C. DICKENSON.

I WISH that there were space to reprint the responses to "You and Democracy." The spirit and desire of them would make even the discouraged realize that, despite all our faults and weaknesses and sins, there is still in America a leaven of real Americanism and real democracy that can save her from the internal dangers that threaten. But work is needed in addition—systematic, organized work aimed at a definite goal, and that is why the American League for Citizenship has been incorporated. It will move slowly until it is ready and full prepared to move faster, but it is moving all the time.

One of the responses came from Goodwin Lee, editor of the *Fire Engineer*. He, too, had seen the need, and, he has been doing his bit for better American citizenship. I want you to read this from one of his editorials:

You must remember that this is our Government, each man is individually responsible, each man is individually benefited, and, being a part of the Government, he must be prepared at all times, in all ways, to defend the thing he has helped to create.

No privilege without responsibility.
No responsibility without power.
No power without a full knowledge of the meaning of privilege and responsibility.
No Government without the realizing sense of each right citizen of privilege, responsibility and power, and—there you are.

That is good food for all of us to chew on. Our stomachs have not been nourished by enough of it.

ARTHUR SULLIVANT HOFFMAN.

The Camp-Fire

A Free-To-All Meeting-Place For Readers, Writers, And Adventurers

SOMETHING from Frederick J. Liesmann concerning the facts back of his story in this issue:

New York City,
Oct. 11, 1917.

A troop of U. S. Horse *was* thrashed by Mexican smugglers and rescued by Texas Rangers for the reason and in the manner which I describe. I had the yarn from a survivor, good old chief of native scouts and Medal of Honor man, while we were chasing Quentin Salas, Delgado and Jalandoni in Panay in the glorious days of the Empire. Also there was a Pablino, who was Winchestered "over the hill" in a mesquite thicket near the Mex. line by some Ranger or deputy sheriff. I named the smuggler chief after him, thereby conferring upon him a dignity and honor which he probably did not deserve. Of Palomas there has always been a healthy crop. We've all met them.—FREDERICK J. LIESMANN.

HERE is a letter from one of us who helps make our meetings interesting by "coming across" with a bit of personal adventure instead of staying closed up like a clam for fear of seeming to talk too much about himself. I hate a blow-hard and a liar, but the man who has something thousands of other people want to hear and holds on to it merely because he is afraid of what they'll think of him is open to criticism too. It's only that his sort of conceit is ingrowing instead of outgrowing.

This letter begins with a doubt over addressing me as "Art" instead of Mr. Hoffman when he has never met me. In replying I wrote him I didn't care what he called me just so it wasn't something I had to fight over. But that isn't entirely true. I can spare the "Mr." any time and I'd really like it better if you of the Camp-Fire didn't use it in writing or talking to me. When I write letters to you I nearly always address you as "Mr." But that's only because I write thousands of letters, some people would think me fresh or disrespectful if I omitted it, and it's nearly impossible to keep track of which ones would and which ones wouldn't. Also it's a small matter after all and in most cases neither side takes the trouble to speak about it. But please remember that even if you omit it and I use it in answering, nothing is meant by my doing so except that I slipped a cog. I'd much rather get along without any "Mr." on either side.

YOU see, the outworn tradition that an editor is some kind of very superior and superintelligent being dies hard. Nothing doing. We're just like all the rest—know more than some and less than others. You may not know what I know, but I may not know what you know. That's all.

One day one of our writers went to lunch with me. He made no secret of his awe over the impressiveness of meeting a real editor and appearing in public with him. We ate at a hotel where I've gone for years, but he didn't know that there was probably not a soul there among guests or waiters who knew I was an editor or who would have been much interested in that fact. A fellow has to be quite a large bug to attract much attention in New York. But the funny part was that I was feeling at least as much honored as he was. I haven't any more reverence for a writer than I have for an editor, but this man was a writer only in his spare time; his regular work seems to me very impressive and he had made his mark in it. While he was feeling impressed with the honor of lunching with me, the object of this deep respect was very conscious of a childish desire, such as most of us never get rid of, that I could stand up and tell all the other people: "Look here. This is —— ——, of the —— ——, who was the man who thus and so, and here I am actually having lunch with him!"

I told him, finally, just how I felt and I hope it has forever ruined his awe of at least this editor. Probably it hasn't, for the experience didn't entirely ruin my awe of him. That's the irritating thing—it's so blamed hard to be simple and human and friendly even when we try. I'm just as bad as the rest of you. But at least it helps to clear up the clouds a bit to make an effort in the right direction. I believe in every man's having self-respect and personal dignity, but if mine are the kind that are dependent on such things as whether people address me as "Mr.," then they can't be worth much and I don't want them. We're all very much alike. What's the use of pretending differently?

AND sometimes it hurts. The other day an engine-driver wrote to me about something and when I replied he wrote again to say how surprised and gratified he was that I had actually taken the trouble to answer an old engine-driver fully and personally. That hurt. Why *wouldn't* I answer him? There isn't time to answer all the thousands of letters personally, but every one that calls for a personal reply instead of a form letter gets it, and there certainly isn't any discrimination between rich and poor, high and low. As I told him, we're all driving engines of one kind or another, unless we're wasters or rotters, and it doesn't matter what the engine is so long as it is an honest and clean and useful one.

And he was an American, too. There's too much of that feeling in America, where there should be none of it.

IF ANY one thinks I'm saying all this merely as a bit of jolly and for policy's sake, I'll disabuse him. I reserve my right to pick and choose my friends—among the Camp-Fire or anywhere else. Most of you whom I've met or got acquainted with through letters, I like and want to be friends with. Some of you are rotters or fools and I have no use for you. Some of you doubtless have equal disregard for me. No, I'm not jollying anybody. Just trying to cut out needless formality.

And now, after talking so much, I'll call it off and let you read our comrade's letter. Needless to say I'm glad to be called "friend" when I believe it's meant, as I believe it is here. I think I've already registered in agreement with his idea that some women have as good a right as any men to claim a front seat at our Camp-Fire.

Cleveland.

DEAR FRIEND ART: I suppose it's all right to call you Art. I've been with you for about five years now. I *know* it's all right to call you friend. . . . You know I am pretty much disgusted myself tonight; I missed out on going "Over." I believe the last time I wrote you I had just received my discharge from President Madero and had left Mexico City for Arizona. Well, when Huerta killed Madero I went back to Mexico again and fought against the Huerta régime. But when Carranza got to quarreling over who was the big chief I got disgusted and quit and went back to Arizona again.

ABOUT that time Col. Roosevelt offered Congress a division of volunteers and your humble servant went about organizing a regiment out in Arizona to help make up that division. Well, that fell flat. So when the troops went into Mexico after our friend Villa, I went with them, and came out with them. And although that was just a pink tea compared to what we have on our hands now, still I've been in some *very, very* tight places—the kind of a fix where you haven't time to think. You ask us for tales, so I am going to give you one. Oh, it's true. That's why it's good, and it leads up to something that I have wanted to put up to Camp-Fire for a long time. And any of the bunch that has had any dealings in Mexico will know. Anyway, here's the tale.

It happened in Mexico, and José Inez Salazar was one of the chief actors, he and I and a woman. (I read a report of his death not long ago, may the devil give him special attention!)

SALAZAR at that time had a band of about two hundred ignorant, degenerate mongrels who termed themselves revolutionists. Yes, that's what they styled themselves. They didn't have nerve enough to be bandits. And they just sneaked around over the country, friendly through fear of them, and looted wherever they found a town defenseless. And one day they rode into San ——. There were at that time about twenty Americans living and working at San ——, and they didn't like the idea of being looted. But Salazar and his mongrels looted just the same. And then there had been quite a lot of talk of intervention by the

U. S. about that time, and Salazar was in an anti-gringo fury and had ordered his men to pay especial attention not to overlook looting all the gringoes, giving his men free rein.

I was staying with an American lady whose husband had been killed in one of their raids, and she had no love for a Mexican, bandit or otherwise, and knowing that I had served Madero's forces in Mexico, appealed to me to save her property from being looted and perhaps her from being brutalized (for this sort of thing happened quite frequently). I agreed to do all in my power to help her, and when the looting party came to the house and demanded entrance I went out to them and, showing them my commission as a captain of the revolutionary forces, told them that house and occupants were under my protection and not to be molested. The *'teniente* in charge, a big ignorant clod, read my commission upside down, looked me over, grudgingly decided that I must be some *jefe*, and ordered the men to enter the next house. But I knew it wasn't all over, for I knew *'teniente* was going to report to Salazar.

THAT afternoon Salazar made a fiery, denunciating, anti-gringo speech in the plaza, calling Americans by all the names he could think of, telling us we were low-lived cowards and afraid to fight. Some of the things he said would make a man's blood boil. He then ordered every American in the town to bring in his arms and ammunition under penalty of death and a relooting of all Americans' homes. I heard that speech, and I made up my mind there was one American's home in that town that wasn't going to be looted and there was one gringo that wasn't going to give up his arms, to Salazar or any one else.

I hurried back to Mrs. K.'s and told her just how things stood, and I didn't try to smooth it over, either. I asked her if she wanted to let me go ahead and protect her and her property or if she wanted to give up and let me go ahead and make out the best I could. She said "No, this is all I have in the world and I am going to keep it if I can." I'll tell you, Art, the odds were heavy, and I wanted to keep a fight down if I could. So I got my rifle, we took the floor up—that is a board in the floor—and put both rifles under the board. I had two belts of ammunition and one of these she put around her under her clothes. And I did the same with the other and my six-shooter, where I could get it quick and handy. And it wasn't long before they came.

THIS time another officer was in charge. They kicked the door in and fifteen of them crowded into the house. I asked them what they wanted. The officer spoke up and said General Salazar had issued orders for every house to be searched for guns and ammunition. I then told him I was a captain in the revolutionary army and showed him my commission. I told him there were no guns or ammunition concealed in the house and that the only gun around was my six-shooter and that I intended to keep that. I also told him that I vouched for the lady of the house as a tried and true friend of the revolution, and that even her husband had been killed for the cause; that I knew orders had to be obeyed, but that I would consider he had paid me an especial favor if he would order his men not to molest anything in the house in their search. That line of flattery got him, and he ordered his men not to help themselves. They searched, but they did not find the ammunition either.

But the other *'teniente* had reported my august presence in the town and, when the second raiding party reported, Salazar questioned the officer about the gringo captain and of course the officer reported that the house had been searched but nothing taken and that I only had a six-shooter that I refused to give up.

WELL, when Salazar heard that report, believe me, the game commenced to loosen up. He sent that officer back with twenty men to get that six-shooter and to loot the house. But I saw them coming blocks away and so did Mrs. K. She knew what it meant. We got the rifle out. She took one belt of shells, I the other, and I looked at her, Art, her face was as white as a sheet. But I knew she'd stick. She never said a word, just cried a little.

The officer and his men marched up to the door, I beat them to it, opened the door a little ways and asked him what he wanted and why should I be molested three times in the one day. Had I found favor with the general? He informed me that I was to deliver up my revolver and to accompany him to General Salazar. I shut the door in his face and politely told him to go to ——. Mrs. K. went to the front window and poked the rifle out just as cool as you please, and we waited. Art, it seemed just like a million years I stood just back of that door waiting for a volley.

THEN we heard some one ride up on horseback. Five shots were fired through the door. I was lying on the floor and I opened fire, and then Mrs. K. yelled at me to stop shooting, that they were all running away. I didn't know what to make of it, for I knew they wouldn't give up that easy when they knew they were ten to one. But finally I got up nerve enough to peep out of the window and, sure enough, they were running toward the plaza as hard as they could go.

In about half an hour one of Mrs. K.'s Mexican neighbors came over to the house and explained the thing. Escondone, another revolutionary chief and a bitter enemy of Salazar's, with about fifteen hundred men, had marched up to within three miles of San —— before Salazar found it out, and then Salazar beat it quick. Escondone came in the next morning and in a few days everybody forgot Salazar, which only goes to show that the devil takes care of his own.

NOW here's the idea: There was a woman with the real stuff in her, and she is not the only one in Mexico and elsewhere who are hoeing their own row. There are a lot of women in this world that are real true adventurers, women who are willing to and do take just as big chances as men do. Why not get them into the circle? Let them tell about where they have bucked the fickle goddess. Get the idea? Think it over and let's hear from it some time, eh?

Well, being as I know I've talked till midnight and ain't said much either, I guess I'd better throw some wood on the fire, chain up the dog, and crawl in the blankets. So will say "*Buenas noches, amigo.*"—E. A. TALBERT.

FROM Farnham Bishop and Arthur Gilchrist Brodeur an interesting word on their story in this number:

Modern military mining and trenchwork is directly descended from medieval siege-craft. To undermine your opponent's wall and bring it tumbling down in the manner described was a well-known and well-approved practise, long before Roger Bacon mixed the first batch of gunpowder. And a long projecting angle of wall or tower was the best place to sap, which is why square towers went out of fashion and round ones came in, in the later Middle Ages.

(N. B. to the editor: Please do not let mistaken zeal on the proof-reader's part change "Sicanian" and "Sicelian" to "Sicilian," for these are the names of two of the strange, pre-Hellenic races of the island, here mentioned to remind the reader of the many people who have fought one another for the treasure-island of the Mediterranean.)

HERE'S a letter from an American officer in France, a Camp-Fire comrade known to many of us. He didn't tell me what the souvenir was, but I can give a sort of guess—and a sort of a gasp. But his suggestion of putting a curb on self-elected heroes after the war is the important point:

If you can find a place, or think it deserves it, would you put the following suggestion in "Camp-Fire," on the chance that some one will take it up. We all know of the many Civil War "veterans," generals, colonels, majors and others, who never heard a shot fired. Will it not be the same after this war? We have a lot of limousine sports who will go home with more medals and get more glory than the lads who were up front. Why could they not make a national or state military directory, with every man's name who served and a notation of battles and wounds? Is it too big a proposition, or might the camouflage birds buck it?

ABOUT that souvenir now. The alcohol must have been poor stuff, or else I did not seal the bottle properly, because there is a very suspicious odor about it, and I'm about come to the conclusion that it will have to be chucked away. However, I'll be going up again soon and I'll make sure of a better job this time. If there is any part of Fritz's equipment that you'd care for too, let me know, but please don't say a helmet unless you mean one of the steel trench ones. The others travel too fast for a poor infantryman to catch.

AND still our collection of information on the pioneers of the Old West grows and grows:

Los Angeles.

In answer to "D. W." in a late issue of *Adventure* as to my probably referring to Capt. George E. Bartlett in one of my letters to Camp-Fire, I would state that such was the case. Bartlett was a very intimate friend of mine for several years prior to his death in this city about six years ago, and I had charge of his funeral, as he would not even see any one but me during his last illness. He is buried in Rosedale Cemetery here. I have his entire collection of Indian relics, from which the photos were taken which are to be shown in *Adventure* some time in the future.

THE inference is also correct about his finding the little Indian girl on the battle-field of Wounded Knee three days after the fight, and her adoption by Gen. Colby. The girl was married some five years ago to a man in Oregon or Washington. It is also true that Calamity Jane saved Bartlett's life on one occasion by nursing him through a very serious sickness. At the time of the Ghost Dance uprising in December, 1890, Bartlett was the only scout at Pine Ridge who had the nerve to visit the hostile camp of Chief No Water on White Clay Creek, at the instance of Gen. Miles, to secure some very valuable information. Both Buffalo Bill and Gen. Miles said when he left that they never expected him to return alive.

"D. W." refers to a horse-thief whom Bartlett shot. I have the saddle, cartridge-belt and knife which Bartlett took from the dead outlaw. A bullet-hole through the cantle of the saddle, which also clipped the top of one of the shells in the thief's belt, testified to Bartlett's marksmanship—together with the bullet-hole through the body of the outlaw.

Bartlett was well known and highly esteemed by the Sioux and, as he spoke the Sioux language fluently, he was of great service to the army officials as an interpreter at the councils and powwows with the hostiles. Later, he traveled on the road for the Peters Cartridge Company of Cincinnati, demonstrating their ammunition, and was called "the marvelous marksman" because of his dexterity with firearms. In the collection of Indian trophies mentioned above, I have the beautifully beaded buckskin suit which Bartlett wore at Pine Ridge about 1886, and several of the ghost-dance shirts which went through the war and which were supposed to be "bullet-proof" by the savages. I also have in this collection the finest and most beautiful war-bonnet I have ever seen in any collection of Indian trophies. Bartlett told me he had refused three hundred dollars for it.—E. A. BRININSTOOL.

HI! GEOLOGISTS, physicists, scientists in general, here's one of you asking the rest of you some questions. Thomas Samson Miller started it with some "Ask Adventure" information about the sound-communication system of West African and other savages:

In your magazine of November 3d I read of the Nigerian natives communicating with each other by drumming on the ground and I became greatly interested because I know of cases in my own experience, which have always puzzled me very much and I have never been able to solve the mystery.

I MAY say since childhood I have been tangled up with botany, geology and astronomy and have a fine telescope and microscope and am always "sticking my nose into this and that," at least sufficiently to be known as "an old crank" who sits up all night to look at the stars or spends an hour in cutting up a spider and magnifying its internal parts.

When I was a young man in England some of us would take a long walk on a Saturday night to a village three or four miles out of town, have some bread and cheese and a glass of excellent home-brewed beer and walk home again. About a half-mile from this village stood an old and big elm-tree beside the sidewalk, and, standing under this tree, one could feel the strokes of the blacksmith on his anvil in the village. The first time I felt it I found "Old Tom" was just closing up his shop and he told me he had been putting on a horseshoe for a traveler. Several times during the three years I lived in that town I have had the same experience and, though giving it much thought and consideration, I never solved it. Now put that in your pipe and smoke it.

I COULD give several other instances, but for fear of making this letter too long I will state only one more. On a ranch in Texas where I used to spend a week in Fall botanizing and picking up fossils, insects and plants, I had a room in a house about five or six miles from where a railroad crossed the country, and when a train passed, only one window in my room used to shake and chatter for three or four minutes. The country between was very rough and rocky, with hills, cañons, valleys—snakes, armadillos, tarantulas and other friendly insects in plenty.

Now I have no doubt you have many scientific readers in your family of subscribers so let them scratch their heads and ponder over these two facts and send you a solution of the mystery.

IF THE sound is carried down, it must be by a pillar or column, entirely detached from surrounding matter. It must then be imparted to a rocky layer of homogeneous formation, for by a crack or "shake" all vibration would be diverted and lost. It must then be carried up again to the surface by another isolated and solid pillar. There is a solid rock in the formations of West Texas rocks, which is solid and without cracks or shakes and which I have seen extending along the bluffs for several miles; this might answer for carrying sound along, but how about the descending and ascending pillars or columns?

Should your esteemed wiseacres solve this, then tell me how it is only one window in the house of six or seven rooms responds to the sound waves and all the rest are silent?

I am making this letter too long but some other time will send another dose—meanwhile let your peripatetic philosophers study over these two riddles and send me their solutions through your magazine. —"AN OLD CRANK."

CHARLES BEADLE'S story in this issue is not his first in our magazine but, though he followed our established custom and sent in his self-introductory talk to the Camp-Fire, the mails brought it too late to appear along with his former story, "The Christman," so here it is in the issue with "The Idol of It:"

My native heath is somewhere in mid-Atlantic. I was born rolling and have been ever since. No moss. My infancy was spent around Siam and the farther East: early memories, fire-flies, mosquitoes and ayahs. Educated at boarding-schools in England; hence no home life and consequent atrophy of the sentimentalities. Parental Government required me to become a consulting marine engineer; but a congenital dislike of work and a gaudy poster persuaded me to learn poker, to starve in Cape Town where I held down a waiter's job for four hours, and to join the British South African Police.

TOO late for big rebellion but kindly chief got up a small one to console me; saw Boer War in B. S. A. P., Morley's Scouts (unpaid Looting Corps) (if any of the Scouts should read this should be glad to hear from them) and Stock Recovery Dept. After Peace held various jobs from three days to a week—in a news office, a bar, hawker, insurance agent—and peddled cheap jewelry for three months (and made money!): served in Transvaal Customs and became Asst. Compound Manager to the Witwatersrand Native Labour Association.

Then I raised a syndicate to finance me for an exploring-trip on the headwaters of the Zambesi ("The Christman" scene). Returned to London to promote a company; failed—of course. A head on a coin sent me to British East Africa and Uganda; native trading, running transport from Victoria Nyanza to the Kilo Mines, Congo; shooting and various ventures. England again, company promoting; and failed again.

Went to Dutch Borneo, rubber planting. Afterward returned to go to Morocco; penetrated into interior in disguise during rebellion; met Pretender Sultan, Mulai Hafid; instead of cutting my throat or crucifying me as predicted he gave me a palace and an escort and treated me as an Ambassador; eventually I failed and Hafid lost his throne. We both had a royal time, anyway.

Until I came to America last year I have lived in France.

THE material of the "Idol of It" was gathered in the forests of the Upper Ituri district of the Congo when I was running caravan through from Entebbe to Kilo. As brothers of the solitude know, many strange things happen and stranger states of mind come to pass. The trick of chatting to a photo or a magazine cutting for the sake of companionship and hearing your own white voice is not uncommon. I've done it myself. In the Police I had a mate on an out-station who did go crazy. He was given his discharge later, started off to walk (!) to Umtali and encountered a lion. Apparently the lion was not dying for social companionship as poor old Denham was!

THE scene of "The Christman" is laid on the upper waters of the Zambesi; in fact, the exact village is indicated. The story was founded—or rather suggested—by an incident which happened on my trip. A bearded gentleman—as described in the story—arrived at Livingstone from nowhere in particular with a wonderful tale of hidden jewels and buried ivory in the southern Congo. A prospector named Poindextre fell for it and financed the *safari*. Just after they had gone we heard that our bearded friend was wanted for murder and robbery in Cape Town. The next thing was that Poindextre was found nearly dead with black water fever in a native kraal. His charming partner had abandoned him in the bush, taking guns and outfit. Natives had found him. He recovered, came down to Livingstone, had a relapse and died. "Miéville" was never heard of again.—CHARLES BEADLE.

HER story having been scheduled for an earlier issue and taken out at the last moment, in this issue you have Lotta Adele Gannett's story without her talk to Camp-Fire, just as you had, in the other issue, her talk without her story. I guess the blame is up to me.

OUR discussion of ants brings in another contribution of personal experience. I confess that when a kid I did the same thing Mr. Sleeper did as a kid. Though most kids are cruel and though I'm glad to say I didn't run much in that direction, I still feel shame over what I did to those ants. For one thing, they were so much bigger than I in their unfaltering bravery and tremendous tenacity, contending on the heroic scale because a brat of a kid wanted to amuse his very unheroic self. I didn't have brains enough, luckily, to try a general battle, but confined my experiments to individual duels. My ants, however, behaved, so far as I can remember, just as Mr. Sleeper's did.

Incidentally, if any kids read this I hope they won't be darned fools enough to try. A grown man oughtn't to need the advice. There's enough cruelty in the world just now without dragging the ants into it.

First comes the clipping Mr. Sleeper enclosed from the Boston *Globe:*

On a day that a great battle took place on the Western front in Europe I witnessed a fierce and bloody hand-to-hand fight in my garden. And over nothing but cattle.

A CERTAIN kind of plant-lice are the cows of ants; the ants stable the lice in their underground homes, and every morning they bring them to pasture in the gardens, where they feed on the plants. The plant-lice produce a sweet secretion which the ants drink; in fact, it is their milk.

The battle I witnessed was between armies of black and red ants. The black ants were the owners of the herd pastured in my potato field, and the red ants were rustlers trying to stampede and drive off the herd.

EVERYWHERE I saw red and black ants fighting to the very death. The ants clawed at one another, gnawing off each other's feelers and legs. There was no quarter—it was a fight to the death. The cattle huddled together in a group, helpless and apparently disinterested spectators of one of the greatest battles ever fought in the ant world.

I watched the battle till near sundown, and when I left it waged as fiercely as ever. Apparently the black ants were victorious, for the next day I noticed them peacefully tending their flocks in my garden.

Now for Mr. Sleeper's own letter:

South Hanson, Mass.

I was interested by the few lines concerning the habits of ants. A few days later I chanced upon the enclosed in a Boston newspaper and thought you or some of the Camp-Fire members would be interested in reading it.

I HAVE never been so fortunate as to be an observer at a battle of ants; but, I take shame to myself in telling this, when I was a kid I tried often to bring different tribes together on the battlefield. I noticed one day that individuals of different tribes, while apparently carrying on their regular, daily business, would occasionally come unexpectedly face to face. Invariably both raised the antennæ and remained motionless for a second or more, the antennæ touching. Then both would step back, and each would turn off about his business. It struck me at once that this must be the usual way in which stranger ants investigated one another, but it reminded me of the way in which two gentlemen might have met in some age past. It was almost as if two men had met, clashed their swords together, and then gone on.

SO I did a cruel thing in the hope of learning something further. I caught and injured a specimen of each tribe, and then pushed them together on a flat stone which was swarming with their fellows. They grappled without delay, and soon the surface of the stone was covered with fighting ants, some in pairs and some in groups of three or more. The loss of one or even two legs did not seem to sap the desire for fight. The chief object of each warrior seemed to be to get upon his adversary from the rear and sink the nippers into the "small of his back," or the junction of thorax and abdomen. Several hours after the start of this battle several of these groups were still holding whatever grips they had managed to place, and many of them died, still hanging on.

I am not a scientific observer, but I learned one fact concerning ants: the bulldog has nothing on the ant for gameness, or for holding on once he has closed his jaws in a fight.—MYRON O. SLEEPER.

IT DID not take you long to discover the drama and romance and adventure behind the human-story items of our "Lost Trails" department, but I wonder how many readers have realized the dramatic tales our Identification Cards could tell if they could talk to us. Here, for example, is a look-in given by one of the thousands who carry them. He begins by recalling the morning he dropped in at the office and got a card at 10:30 before sailing at 12, and goes on to say that since that day he "knows personally over five hundred persons, somewhere on earth, who are today (please God) holding them." And then:

Since the war started—I've tried to do my bit wherever I was most needed for Uncle Sam. Some weeks ago met one of the Japanese mission who was my room-mate in college, 1900-01, and exchanging my card with him he noticed my No. 1484 card, and produced a duplicate in all but number that he carries next his heart. A few weeks later had the same experience happen with one of H. B. M.'s officers on a special mission to this country, who obtained his card on active duty in India. The same week one of our own officers on his way to the front after several years active service in the Philippines was proud of his card and wanted to know how I had taken precedence of him in getting a lower number, one of the two-thousand class. A week later, in another part of the country, had some work which brought me in touch with a Russian M. E. (Mechanical Engineer), who told me he had taken his card after an afternoon in Paris.

THEN to finish: Scene, front of Café de la Paix, Paris; one of my friends whom I couldn't place bumped into me; proved to be (in 1897) our Broadway and Thirty-first Street traffic officer; on his way home as major of Philippine Constabulary on long leave. Talked cards and, through my talking up mine, bumped into me again last week—on his way to France and, he says, Berlin, and identified himself by the card which he had taken out as soon as he got in touch with you. And so it goes.—No. 1484, in care of *Adventure.*

THE following from the organized publishers and writers of magazines, addressed to the readers of magazines, is a strong presentation of the evils of the "zone system" postal law:

Do you wish to put a tariff on intelligence? Do you want to levy a tax on education? Congress does. Your Congress. What! You didn't know about it! Read:

AT THE last session Congress passed a law which establishes a postal "zone" system for magazines and periodicals. It passed a law increasing the postage on periodicals to you, the readers of this publication, from fifty to nine hundred per cent. And it did it by reestablishing a postage "zone" system that was abolished by President Lincoln in 1863. Instead of a flat rate, made as cheap as possible in order that there could be a chance for the intelligent consideration of public questions to reach the farthest limits of the country and the most remote habitation on an equal basis, the magazines containing all this discussion and all the best fiction and all the best art must hereafter pay an excess rate like so much fish or canned lobster or fabricated steel.

You are going to buy your education by the pound-mile now. It isn't a free flowing stream from which all may drink. It has been dammed and its flow checked. Congress did it. If it would bring any increase to the revenues of the country that would amount to anything, it would never be opposed. But it won't. It will drive magazines out of business.

WE WOULDN'T say that the discussion of public questions in the magazines, which sometimes calls attention to the delinquencies of Congress and public officials, resulted in the enactment of this law. We would not say that it is a form of censorship that is really prohibited in spirit by the Constitution, although the law has been so cleverly drawn that it probably can not be called unconstitutional. We simply call your attention to it because we don't believe you know it. And further than that, we don't believe you'll stand for it.

Write to your Congressman about it. And demand the repeal of this particular passage.

I may be prejudiced, so I do not ask any one to accept my opinion. But consider this matter for yourself. Magazines and periodicals amuse and entertain, but they do something much more important. They are educational in a very high sense of the word. How much of your knowledge of public affairs is due to magazines? If they are killed off, what other means is there of getting anywhere near the same amount of knowledge about public, particularly national, affairs? Books, newspapers, lectures, individuals. All are valuable, but all have their limitations—expense, rarity, localism, etc. Compare all these together with the periodicals alone.

THIS zone law, if not repealed, will cripple all periodicals. Those that can continue to exist must pay often nine times as much as at present in order to reach you. They may be able and willing to shoulder part of this extra expense, but who will pay most of it? You. Unless you give up your magazines.

To my mind the worst result of killing off the magazines would be the resultant growth of sectionalism. Our country is three thousand miles across. In union there is strength; in sectional development there is destruction. Do we need every possible medium that serves to draw us closer together by mutual information and understanding among the sections? Do we especially need the periodicals that give us a national, not a sectional, point of view?

Think it over.

IF YOU want to join in organized effort against sedition and enemy activity in our midst, join the American Defense Society. Among its objects are the internment of those who need it, the suppression of publications in the German language during the war, and the abolishment of the compulsory study of German in public schools. Address 44 East 23d St., New York.

ARTHUR SULLIVANT HOFFMAN.

ONLY those who don't care for it claim fishing is not adventure, yet both in our stories and at our Camp-Fire there's been very little said about it. Now, however, Harold Titus raises a few points in connection with his story in this issue that may start something.

He is not fishing this season, however. In the Army and trying hard to get to France. Today also comes a letter from Arthur Gilchrist Brodeur who, like his collaborator, Farnham Bishop, after many attempts and some special physical training, has finally got into the Army, though not so close to the front as he tried for. Roy P. Churchill, also with a story in this issue, is back in the sea service of his country, today's mail bringing word of his work.

THESE are only four out of many of our writing comrades who are in our country's service. I often wonder how we are able to go on getting stories up to our standard in numbers sufficient to our needs. On the face of things it looks impossible, but our magazine has been growing not only in circulation but in the number of writers who send us stories, enough, it seems, to keep things nearly normal in spite of the fact that our writers are particularly of the type which furnishes men for war. I have no facts for comparison but venture that our writers have furnished an unusually high percentage of men in service.

AND meanwhile here is that fishing story. We have need, in these times of tension, of amusements that temporarily relieve our minds and nervous systems of the strain under which labor all of us not too dull to understand the world-crisis slowly developing day by day. That is why our magazine is buying even fewer stories with the atmosphere of the present war than formerly. So far as we can be of service, the more closely we keep our minds on the war, the better. But when we have time for deliberate relaxation and amusement the more relief we get from the war-strain, the better able we'll be to carry our end of it when we turn back from relaxation to work.

At our Camp-Fire it would be both foolish and wrong to bar discussion of the war, but we make up the magazine well ahead, as you know, and events move too rapidly for current topics to be still current by the time written words have reached you in print. What I'm writing now will reach you in June, but I'm writing it in April while all the world is trembling on the issue of the great Hun offensive now under way. Yet, though it's hard to think of anything else, there is nothing I can say that would have any interest two months from now. No man now knows whether the Germans will be held and bled to death or whether they will be able to pound their way through to a victory that would damn the world for generations and doom it to years more of warfare, on our own soil as well as on many other bloody fields. Probably you will know when you read this. No one knows now. What a vast gulf two months can be!

AND while destiny unfolds we must keep our balance by meeting the strain intelligently, working as long as we can work effectively, resting and relaxing when we need to rest and relax for the sake of the work itself. So it is good to go fishing with Harold Titus, forgetting war a while so that we may come back rested, refreshed and better able to do each his own part in the grim task lying to our hands. As the author of this story is himself doing.

I suppose my home town, Traverse City, Michigan, is the "fishingest" place they could find with a search warrant. We are located on some of the best trout water east of the Rockies. In fact, the Boardman River, which flows through the town itself, has been one of the remarkable streams of the Great Lakes country, and we are within easy reach of innumerable rivers that offer splendid sport. A big proportion of the population fishes, too. I believe that some of the best fishermen that ever wore waders call this particular place home. You see, we have men here who have followed the sport through all its phases from the days when grayling were plentiful until now, when those varieties of trout that will survive warm waters are being planted in streams which drain settled country to keep them from being fished out.

THE catch which I describe in this story is one which was made by my friend "Pat" Hastings, who has hooked his share of 'em. It's a dog-gone good fish story (his, I mean) and may seem a bit incredible to a novice who reads it, but I'll vouch for its adherence to fact. Two changes I must mention, however; the first is that I have moved the time of the catch forward three or four hours for the purposes of the plot; the other is that the fish actually taken was not quite as large as the one in my yarn. Six-pounders and larger are taken from this water occasionally, but a fact which I have never had clearly explained is that these big fish, caught after dark, do not fight with anywhere near the vigor they display when hooked in daylight.

It is during the hatch of the caddis fly that the big browns are taken from the Boardman River in the greatest numbers. The best water is within fifteen minutes from town by automobile and each evening during the hatch of this insect you'll see a representative gathering of liars and fly-fishermen strung out along the stream trying to get the big one of the season.

THIS river, by the way, demonstrates what can be done by restocking. To a large extent it flows through relatively newly-settled country. Fifteen or twenty years ago it was alive with speckled trout, but as the timber was cut off, the water warmed, and the number of fishermen increased, these fish fell off. Rainbow were planted and did fairly well but, even then, the sport was mediocre. Then the State commenced sending up German Brown spawn and now the Boardman shows every sign of reviving and some regular old-time catches were made last Summer. We know that the speckled trout, like the grouse, can not stand up under civilization. Many men do not like the Rainbow, although it's a sporty fish. The Brown, however, is a noble fighter, good to eat and seems to withstand the clearing up of streams. Propagating this variety in quantities is going to keep rivers stocked indefinitely, it seems.

ONE attractive feature about this part of Michigan is the diversity of water and country offered. We have pond fishing in many places. There are trout streams, like the Boardman, almost in your dooryard. Again, given a Ford and three hours, you can strike streams like the Manistee or the Au Sable (that last will take an hour or so longer), which run through country as desolate as any white man could ask for. The upper waters of the Manistee are still well stocked with speckled trout, than which no better fish ever rose to a fly, and many other rivers still offer this particular kind. The Rainbow predominates elsewhere and the Brown is fast appearing in waters hitherto strange to it. Another interesting fact is that you can fish, say, one day in the little Platte River where the speckled trout has a bright steel-blue cast, the next in the Rapid where they color a rich orange with lots of red on the fins and again in streams farther to the eastward where they get the pink tint on the belly.

Lots of bass, too, in this country, but most of the natives go nutty over trout and the bulk of the bass fishing is done by men who come especially for it.—HAROLD TITUS.

GOD knows where Lieutenant Dwyer will be by the time your answer to his inquiry of January could reach him, but if you know what he asks, write him in our care and we'll forward to the best of our ability. He was in a U. S. camp when he wrote. Perhaps it would be safer just to print the answer in the magazine.

Wherever I have been among tropical tramps there is one poem always known. It begins thus:

"So, so, you're come to the tropics.
Thought all that you had to do
Was to be in the shade in a coconut glade,
While the dollars rolled in to you.

and ends:

"You don't go down with a short, hard fall;
You just sort of shuffle along
And lighten your load of the moral code,
Till you don't know the right from the wrong

Could you not reprint it; or tell where the entire thing may be obtained?—RICHARD M. DWYER, First Lieut., —— Infantry.

NOT the least interesting part of Hugh Pendexter's stories about our old Indian frontier days is the little chat from him at Camp-Fire concerning the history and real Indian customs upon which all his tales are based:

Norway, Maine.

The Skidi, a tribe of the Pawnee confederacy, believed in supernatural animals and located their underground dwellings, or Nahurac lodges, in the valley of the Loup River, Nebraska. In this belief of mythic animals holding councils they will remind you of the Cherokee myths. Guide Rock in Kansas was another Nahurac lodge.

WHEN the Siouan tribes entered the Platte valley they found the Pawnee there. Harahey was the name of the province which the Pawnee told Coronado contained much gold, the Wichita country of east-central Kansas. The confederacy had no totems and descent was traced through the mother. Each tribe had several secret societies, each based on the belief in supernatural animals. One writer gives the time of the last Skidi sacrifice of a human being as 1838. During the first quarter of the nineteenth century Petalesharo, a Skidi chief, rescued a Comanche woman, who was bound to a cross preliminary to being sacrificed, and carried her back to her people, some four hundred miles. This chief was one of the signers of the treaty at Grand Pawnee Village on the Platte in Nebraska, October 9, 1833, by the terms of which they ceded all their lands to the United States south of the Platte River. One authority (Powell) states they were least understood of any of the important plains Indians, and this, perhaps, because during the seventeenth and the greater part of the eighteenth centuries they remained outside the Spanish-French sphere of influence. Their prowess as warriors is established by their successful warfare against the many surrounding tribes.—PENDEXTER.

WHEN we read "On Short Allowance" I queried Mr. Pladwell about several points in it in order to be on the safe side, as we often do on our stories. My queries are of no present interest, but Mr. Pladwell's reply to them is worth listening to. The queries can be gathered from the context; they were intended to make sure of points that might disturb the average reader, not as comments from one wise in all the technicalities of nautical lore:

Oakland, California.

In the first place, the story was a growth of a query. I saw some rotting tubs in Oakland estuary. I wondered what might happen if one of them took a long trip. I got some yarns from old salts hereabouts, and gradually I evolved the yarn, pieced out of the other yarns. Then when it was finished I took it to some of the veteran mariners. I have mucked around the water a lot myself, but never on a three-masted schooner. So I needed criticism.

The mariners helped me much, and yet not one of them saw the points that you saw. They are, I think, debatable.

YOU will note on the map the long series of islands of the Aleutian group, stretching across the north Pacific. These islands as a general rule comprise the northernmost boundaries of the average sailing-ship course across the western ocean. Sometimes prevalent winds drive the windjammers very close to the Aleutians, often in sight of them. The Aleutians are bare, bleak islands, populated by sea-fowl, Aleuts, beach-combers, seals, and occasional wanderers. Many a ship's crew has deserted to take a chance on picking up seal illegally around these islands, and while there is not a real settlement on any of the islands except, I think, one lone mission church, a crew getting there in a small boat has easy chances for survival and, possibly, for profit.

AS FOR willingness to try such an alternative. The schooner in the story is cheap. The food is awful. The master is a martinet. The men are scum, with not a first or second class seaman among them. A few days of cheap food and unwelcome work is enough to make such a collection of men, I think, willing to take a chance, especially when a glib-tongued person is stirring up trouble and putting ideas in the men's heads. To make it more logical I might have put in something saying Big Frank had hinted at seal-poaching; but as I said, the mariners who saw the story took this desertion so much as a matter of course that it is safe to assume there is nothing new about leaving a cheap ship for the thrills of the islands' chances.

OFTEN in the dreary reaches of the night one can find helmsmen dozing at the wheel when the weather is calm. Why not? There is something about the sleep of a man on the job that does not let him make many bad slips. I have often dozed myself at the tiller or the wheel, but the instant the boat slewed off her course I set her right automatically. She can not fall off very badly without your knowing it. The motion of the ship tells you. Now, in the story the crew is desperately short-handed. In such a case it would be peculiar, perhaps, if the helmsman were not taking a cat-nap, especially with the weather calm. At least, he might not be wide-awake enough to observe a man sneaking up a hatchway from the after-cabin. On a liner, a tramp or a big four-master such a thing as a sleeping helmsman might be serious, but not on that old tub.

EVEN on the old scows sailing around San Francisco Bay the master's lone helper uses the "sir" to the blowsy old bird who happens to run the thing. But there again my story skids off the usual. With so much to contend with, could the average master induce such a crew of landsmen to observe this matter without possibly starting more grief aboard? They are landsmen, not sailor-men. And yet, toward the end of the voyage, I think he would. I believe that a few "sirs" might not hurt the story. And yet I've seen a drill sergeant in the United States Army work three weeks to make a bunch of rookies say "sir." It's the hardest word in the United States language, I think.—E. S. PLADWELL.

ONE of our comrades at the Camp-Fire, one of the writers of our stories, will no longer gather with us at our meetings. William A. Shryer is dead and I know that our sympathy goes out to the wife and little son he has left behind him.

Born in Terre Haute, Indiana, Mr. Shryer has made his home in Detroit. Well known as a writer on business subjects, he was equally successful with fiction and it was in the quest for material for future stories that he met his death. The news came to me from Honolulu, following by a few weeks a cheerful letter from him enclosing a newspaper clipping telling of a bad fall he had had in the crater of the volcano. March tenth he had preceded his family to a temporary home taken on the Glenwood-Volcano Road, met them at Hilo and on the return trip met his death in an automobile accident due to a nut that had worked loose in the steering gear, sending the car over a sixteen-foot embankment.

His wife and their Japanese maid were severely injured, the boy escaping unhurt. Mr. Shryer's neck was broken and he lived only long enough to tell his wife that he was "done for." The body was brought to Honolulu from Hilo on the *Mauna Kea* and was cremated.

Let us stand and salute him, our comrade, for a life bravely lived, then wish him God-speed on the Long Trail over which we all will follow.

LOUIS ESSON, whose tale, "The Pearl of Torres," you will find in this issue, introduces himself to the Camp-Fire according to our custom:

Most Australians are wanderers and adventurers. This roving spirit is a racial characteristic; for if their forebears had not possessed it there would never have been any Australia. All my prople are Scottish; but, though I was born in Edinburgh, I was taken to Australia as a child, and my first memories are of the Big Bush, an ideal playground for boys. There is an abiding fascination in the life of the Bush, with its great spaces, its sheep and cattle, and the quaint characters that meet in the township on market day, or for some great sporting event—a wood chop or race meeting.

I DUTIFULLY did an Arts course at the Melbourne University, studying Latin and Philosophy; but this brought me little credit with Billy Smith, the stockman, who refused to take me seriously at cattle droving, or even riding—subjects unfortunately not included in my academic curriculum. I wasn't up to the bushman's standard, so I drifted into journalism; thence the easy descent!

I have written for most Australian papers and magazines and worked for a year in London, beside publishing a volume of verse and having a play produced in Melbourne; but my best performance in this line was editing a little daily newspaper on the edge of beyond. Strange types would drop into the office—we called it "the office"—drovers and shearers setting out for far back stations, miners from the coal fields, selectors and cockatoo farmers, politicians, and what is called the "scrub aristocracy." It was an exciting life, especially when the worthy president of a wayback agricultural society dropped in to interview the staff with a horsewhip. I usually referred him to the manager, a burly man who had been an amateur pugilist in his early days.

LATER on journalism sent me to Asia where I had my fair share of adventure, wandering through many fascinating lands from Ceylon to Japan. I have seen the dawn rise near Darjeeling over the sacred Katchenjunga; I have been turned back from the Khyber Pass, for my own good; I have been in Peshawar after a raid by the Afridis and I have seen the beggars and yogis 'round the temples at Benares, the sacred cows and monkeys, and the burning of a body at the burning Ghat by the Ganges.

Once I traveled from Moulmein to Bangkok through Burma and Siam. My traveling companion, a forest officer who was going northwards, left me in the middle of Siam. With much difficulty I obtained a boat and a Lao crew who promised to take me down the Menam to Paknam-Po. This was a terrible journey. None of the crew could speak a word of English, and river traveling was slow. Stores ran out, and for three days there was no food except what the Laos had—gigantic bananas, rice suitable perhaps for elephants, frogs and larvae of bees—impossible, even curried. At Paknam-Po I discovered a friendly Englishman who put on a dinner that would have done no discredit to Delmonico's.

MANY Australian journalists are scattered along the Asiatic coast from Singapore to Yokohama. Among others I met at Hong-Kong Pratt, who has since drifted to Bangkok, and Donald, now representing a New York newspaper, both acknowledged authorities on Asiatic affairs.

All Australians are deeply concerned in the fate of the Northern Territory that lies close to Asia, and is perhaps the largest unoccupied territory in the world today. This is our land of romance, a land of pearl and gold, of the mirage, of our strange aboriginals, a more interesting race than is usually supposed, and of the great bushmen and adventurers from all the ends of the earth. My half-brother, Frank Brown, at present in Mesopotamia chasing Turks, has been thrice through the Territory, studying the elaborate native customs and making explorations in uncharted country. I have been through it only once, but I can never forget its subtle spell.

YET, after all, there is always romance at home. Before going to New York and London I spent two years in a cottage only forty miles from Melbourne. But the little clearing was cut out of the virgin forest, huge fallen trees and stumps were 'round our door, and down by the creek an old man, the last of the fossickers, was still puddling for gold. This Bush homestead is at present occupied by Vance Palmer, who is not unknown to readers of *Adventure*.—LOUIS ESSON.

BY THIS time—I am writing in May—I had expected to report considerable progress by the American League for citizenship, Inc., but I've been ill during most of 1918 so far and not able to be on my regular job all the time, so work on the League has had to tread water.

But the prospects are promising, and I expect to have things moving before long. It was never intended that they should move rapidly. Slow and sure and safe is the better method. There need be no doubt as to their moving when the time comes. I make no other promises or predictions, but before long I hope to be able to report practical accomplishments.

ARTHUR SULLIVANT HOFFMAN

DO YOU remember that several years ago we suggested naming regiments instead of numbering them, or in addition to numbering them? The idea is sound. Since we've enlarged our Army, regiments and divisions have frequently been given names. It makes for *esprit de corps*. Also it is a natural human impulse.

One of you who took up the idea was C. S. Edmiston of Quitman, Mississippi, who suggested a regiment of musicians. But he did more than that. He went ahead and by his own efforts organized a military band. That band was accepted for service and, when I heard from Mr. Edmiston, was stationed with the 114th Engineer Regiment. He himself was expecting a discharge because of physical disability (his third honorable discharge), but his band remains in service.

AN INTERESTING word from H. A. Lamb concerning his story in this issue. Mr. Lamb, like several others of our writers' brigade, is still able to furnish us occasional stories though in the Army.

> Alamut is not a creation of the author. It was one of the four castles of the Refik. The latter are more commonly known as the Ismailians, a sect that separated themselves from the other Mohammedans.
>
> A secret empire, wielding murderous power, more powerful than the Knights Templars, the Council of Twelve, or the Ku Klux Klan! The "Old Man of the Mountain" a master of the empire so feared by his subjects that two of them threw themselves from the high walls of a castle at the bidding of a priest in order to impress a foreign envoy! A paradise so devilishly ingenious that the warriors of the Refik threw away their lives readily in order to return, as they supposed, to the joys of the Ismailian paradise!
>
> THESE were startling particulars, even for the adventurous times of the thirteenth and fourteenth centuries. They proved, however, to be history and not legend. The dynasty of the Assassins, as the rulers of Alamut were called, holds its place among the kings of Persia. The Old Man of the Mountains, who should more correctly be called the Sheikh of the Mountains, was known to travelers and historians from Marco Polo to Mirkhond. As to the paradise, it is not known whether its power for evil lay in the effects of the drug hashish or in an actual scene of splendor and license.
>
> The power of the Assassins was broken by Hulagu Khan and his Tatars some two hundred and fifty years before the time of Khlit, but nests of the Ismailians survived until the end of the eighteenth century, and as a religious sect the Ismailians number many followers today—deprived, of course, of the secret terror of their ancient daggers.

ANY one who can tell just what our Camp-Fire is is wiser than I. On the face of things it is merely an indefinite something on paper only. Certainly there is no definite organization of any kind—no officers, no constitution or by-laws, no fees or dues. A few unwritten rules but no formalities of any kind. Any one belongs who wishes to and he doesn't need any help in joining.

Our Camp-Fire's general object is an indefinite kind of good-fellowship and it pretends to nothing except being the means of swapping interesting experiences. Of course our "Lost Trails," "Ask Adventure" and other free services are practical helps, but in each of them the magazine is a necessary factor. Our magazine avowedly tries to help its readers when it can, but the thing that always leaves me in doubt is the relationship among the Camp-Fire members themselves. Theoretically they are under no obligations to each other. Theoretically they only read or write the letters we have in our department of the magazine. Theoretically they are acquainted only on paper.

But the *facts* of the case? The facts knock the theories sky-high. Again and again and again I learn, here at this clearing-house desk, of real friendships created by our Camp-Fire. I am the richer by quite a number of them myself. And here is a letter from one of you which speaks for itself:

To show the Camp-Fire what its members are like I wish you would print this letter, without names or identity, of course. Just say a Camp-Fire-ist had his shack burgled and gutted, and got this letter from another Camp-Firer. I only wish it was good form to tell who he was. Of course, I didn't need the help, but oh, man! *What* a man he is to so offer! Any lodge would ask me "Are your dues paid up?" but he—I haven't the words to tell what he is. That is the old-time West exemplified in him.

The last sentence in his letter refers to three notches in the butt of my .45 that he noticed but was too tactful to ask about.

Following is the letter he enclosed and asked to have returned to him. The two men never heard of each other until they got acquainted through our Camp-Fire.

I am coming at you head on, square as a brick, with no evasion or dodging the issue. You would take me in and feed me and sleep me and divide your tobacco with me if I came along broke and down on my luck. Now you give your friends the same privilege.

SEND me a list of what you need most, with sizes, descriptions, etc., and send it at once. I'll be teetotally jumped up if I am going to have you left in such a plight. I have been studying how to help in some way that would not hurt your feelings and I have given up the struggle, believing that the best way is to come at you like one man meeting another. You and I are no women to hem and haw over things. If we were trapping in partnership or prospecting the same way, what one had both would have. It don't make a —— bit of difference if I am here in an upper room and you out there. We have got to look at this thing as though we slept under the same blanket and ate out of the same frying-pan.

What do you need most? If it is underclothing, what sizes? If it is socks too, what size? If it is grub, what would you rather have? I've got a few dollars in my kick and I'm not going to keep it there and have you hungry or cold. Come through, old man, come through!

IF THAT list does not get in here right soon I shall steal some fellow's auto and hike down there to wallop you. I went to the hospital for a big operation once, appendicitis, and had only thirteen dollars to my name and a wife and three children dependent on me. I was glad to have a man slip me a hundred and say, "Pay it when you get well." I took it, of course I did, for it was no worse to grab that than to grab a bit of plank some one hove to me when I was drowning.

Don't act squeamish now. If you had me as a pal and ran out of plug, you would say, "Here, you big stiff, whack up on that plug and when I get more I'll do the same." I won't eat an ounce less or have a mite less on my back for helping you out of a hole.

SO SPILL that list to me *muy pronto, amigo,* if you want to remain *amigo.* Underclothes, socks, grub, tobacco, whatever you need. I don't want you to do any funny stunt of letting pride get between us, any more than you would if we had bunked together all over the coast. I know one other man who feels just as I do and who will dig as deep, so you are to tell the truth about your need and quit your danged blushing like a kid girl. 'Taint your fault that —— robbed you.

S'POSE you rode along a road and saw a house burning down and some poor cuss in his shirt-tail beside the road, all his clothes gone in the fire. If you had some extra clothing along I reckon he'd get in them right soon. Well, the dirty ladrones were the fire and you are the victim beside the road. Now don't be dirty mean and refuse help that is offered as freely as you would offer an extra coat in such a case. If you do, well, just count that you have slapped a friend's face, and that without provocation. That list and the sizes, *pronto!*

I shall expect that list by return mail.

I wish I could get hold of that guy you think has your gun. I have a hunch that he would produce it and squeal on the rest before I hit him more than half a dozen times. If I had a car I would have gone right down there as soon as I heard and if I did go there I would sure labor with that cuss by force of arms. Don't you kill anybody unless you can prove self defense.

HERE is a letter with some big ideas. The general purpose is the *real* Americanization of naturalized citizens and the prevention of strong alien allegiance among those in this country who are not citizens, a general purpose which I indorse unqualifiedly.

As to barring the teaching of any foreign language in our schools, there must be limitations. If no Americans could speak French, Spanish and other foreign languages it would mean not only an immense commercial, social, literary and scientific loss but an increase in the provincialism that is one of our national weaknesses. Even from a military point of view a nation none of whose people can speak the enemy language is at a decided practical disadvantage, to say nothing of ability to speak the language of foreign allies. My own first impulse was a desire to sweep all foreign languages from our schools, but second thought convinces most of us that the remedy itself would be a calamity.

AND a needless calamity. Only the German language is now a danger. In its case I am for drastic measures. The other languages are a different matter, one that can safely be handled by wise limitations and a more gradual treatment. As a first step we might, for example, bar *all* languages as *compulsory* parts of any school course, forbid the use in schools of any foreign language as the *teaching* language in any subject except that language itself, and, perhaps ban the teaching of any foreign language in primary grades. These merely as suggestions; the subject is far too complicated for settlement in a few brief sentences.

BUT the German language is a case by itself, a case in which the one pressing necessity overrides academic arguments and even consistency in according German the same treatment as other languages. The issue of the war is, at the date this is written, still in doubt, but only a blind fool can deny that up to 1918 military success has been with the enemy. Their success has been due to only four things—(1) military and economic organization and preparedness, (2) unity of command in the hands of trained soldiers, (3) sacrifice of right to might, of humanity and decency to brute efficiency and, at least as important as any of the other reasons, (4) systematic *propaganda* at home and *abroad*.

We have been inclined to view this fourth reason, German propaganda, as bad but not as vital. Yet if you analyze the German success down to its very fundamentals and beginnings you find that systematic propaganda has been their *most important weapon*. It began several generations ago in Germany itself, the systematic, governmental education of the German people into efficient, carefully shaped cogs in the great Hun machine of brute force. The second step was the planting of Germans in other countries, notably Russia, the United States and Latin America, generally as citizens of these countries but always held to Germany and Germany's interests by the invisible steel chains of German propaganda. The third step was the building up among these hospitable peoples of sentiments advantageous to Germany's interests and particularly the fomenting and encouraging of any and all kinds of internal differences and strife among these peoples that would weaken them against the day when Germany would be ready to strike.

THERE was no chance in all this. No luck. No accident. Nothing but a coldly, carefully worked-out definite plan of tremendous size. And the whole sum and substance of that plan, the very heart of it, was Hun propaganda and education. Subtle, delicate, psychological, invisible and almost unsuspected. When sometimes we noticed a silken thread of the great Hun web we failed to realize that it was not silk but steel. Almost no one realized that the little thread was part of a vast, world-choking web of evil Hun ambition.

Even now Americans fail to give this web a hundredth part of its real importance. We are still enmeshed in it, our every effort more or less crippled by its barely visible throttling grip. It is not just a crude matter of spies and property destroyers in our midst. That is merely ordinary enemy activity—mere child's play compared to the less visible instruments, and not half so serious. Spies and bombs produce quick results; these more subtle instruments may not produce results for years or generations, but their results are infinitely more dangerous to us and—more permanent.

It would take years and volumes to specify all the tiny and various means employed, but as a whole they can be quickly gaged by considering the central Hun machine at Berlin that for years and years has been systematically spinning this silk-steel web. Do you know that at Berlin there is a regular and permanent government department officially called "The Bureau of Enemy Psychology"? Stop reading a minute and think what that means.

WE PRIDE ourselves on being a "practical" people. We believe in driving at main results by direct paths. We are commercial and industrial; labor, material, capital, transportation, these we consider the "practical" factors. We belong to the "want results," "show me," "ain't no such animal" class. It is *things*, not ideas, that we handle and believe in. The most patriotic thing I can say is that we are —— fools. No thing ever existed that was not first an idea or that can not be shaped and controlled by ideas. The average American business man believes nothing is "practical" unless he can feel it with his fingers or enter it on the pages of a ledger. And thereby proves himself an infant in swaddling-clothes, or an adult imbecile. And all the rest of us are a good deal like him. Wherefore the Hun, who, for all his brutishness, is intelligent enough to understand that ideas are more important and more practical than things, has been able to entangle us in a net whose strength is almost wholly psychological.

The Hun wove this kind of net because he

knew that to control the ideas of men is to control every concrete thing that men possess. We let him "get away with it" because we were too drunk with our childish delusion that only things were "practical."

THE Hun is so alive to the value of his psychological net that he guards from publicity its very existence; he has prevailed thus far solely because of it and he knows that if we begin to realize the importance of that net his immediate and his ultimate hopes are dead. I have heard that any one who sees the psychological net and tries to warn his fellows will be marked down by the Hun machine and quieted or—removed. Probably you and I differ because you do not believe that and I consider it very possible. God knows that if I knew more of the inside, definite details I'd gladly shout them from the house-tops. I do not know them, but I can see the web; the details are important only as a means for making *you* see it. If I can make any see it who have not seen it hitherto I do not mind seeming silly and childish to the rest of you by suggesting that, if any calamity "happens" to drop on me after this is published, said "accident" might be taken as tending to prove the very point I wish to make.

DOUBTLESS most of you will consider merely silly and fantastic the report that German thoroughness and understanding of psychological values has led them to install at Berlin a little corps of men steeped in the psychological wisdom of India, adepts in human "mysteries" laughed at by the "practical" Western world, and that hypnotism on an international scale is one of the weapons systematically used by the Hun machine. Personally I do not consider it silly and fantastic; it may not be true, and yet it may. Certainly it is in keeping with German methods, and I am not fool enough to laugh it off the boards merely because I can't pinch it with my fingers. In any case it is a perfect example of the *kind* of net they have been spinning for generations.

THIS (to come back to our letter) is why I am strong for drastic action against the German language in our schools, for that and publications in German are an essential part of the Hun web. The letter's suggestion that German be barred from all our primary schools seems to hit at the heart of the matter, but the remedy should go further. For example, no German course should be open at any time to any child of German parentage or birth.

As to the German press there is only one safe argument against suppressing it at least during the war—the plea that loyal publications in German can be of value in creating American loyalty among Germans. I do not belive this argument is sufficient.

IN GENERAL, Mr. Sexton's letter is based on the principle that no one is fit to be a citizen of the United States unless he is fully able to speak the language of the United States, fully able to transact all the business of a citizen of the United States in the language of the United States. A sound principle and a truth so elementary that we seem very stupid in being so long in seeing that truth. Any organization in support of this would be good, but it is to be remembered that there is already a strong organization working along similar lines—the American Defense Society, 44 East 23d Street, New York City, N. Y.

This is Mr. Sexton's letter; he can be addressed in our care.

DEAR SIR:—I propose the formation of "The American Language League." Objects: (a) Enactment of legislation (with concurrent development of public sentiment) to prohibit the teaching of any alien language in any primary school, whether public or private. (b) The suppression, so far as possible, of daily newspapers published in an alien tongue (whether or not they print parallel columns in English). (c) The Americanization of immigrants as quickly and completely as possible by providing facilities for learning the English language and encouragement to make use of said facilities. (d) Legislation limiting the rights of aliens to vote to such of them as can read and write and speak English fluently. (e) The development of a sentiment hostile to organizations designed to keep alive the interest of foreigners in alien governments, customs and institutions.

But the one weapon of sharp steel wherewith to fight alien intrigue is—*language*. It is because this is so true that the German Government through its agents in America fights so hard to retain the German language in the daily life of our people. Remove it and the Kaiser goes with its removal. You can not have a real American country unless the members thereof think exclusively in the American language and approach other languages as they approach Greek or Latin or as they learn some modern and unfamiliar language in the years of youth or manhood as an elective study.

If some of the "Adventurers" started such an organization I believe it would quickly acquire many thousands in members. Dues nominal.—A. R. SEXTON.

DR. ROBERTSON, our comrade in Honduras, tells me I am a stupid skeptic, only he uses more eloquent words of condemnation. Oh, well, all right. I'd be willing to let him call me nearly anything if only he'd go on talking. Skeptic or no, I'm ready to sit and listen. His letters are my idea of a pleasant time. I only regret that a large part of this one dealt with matters political and, though I pretty well agreed with him, it seemed best to omit it.

The —— referred to is one of our writers. Dr. Robertson hopped on to one of his stories and, as is our general custom, we passed the letter on to the author criticized to give him a chance to defend himself or plead guilty.

Galeras, Olancho, Honduras, C. A.

. . . Why did you not spend your holiday with me? I should have been tickled to death. We do not live so badly here that you need fear starvation, *por lo menos*.

Here's the menu of today's dinner:

MENU
Hacienda Las Lajas
28 Sept. 1917
Clear Turtle Soup, with Crackers
Baked Turtle — Cold Tapid-Quinta
Roast Venison — Roast Peccary
Boiled Beef Ribs
Venison Steak fried in Butter, with Onions
Baked Squash — Cabbage — Kale
Creamed Potato and Squash, with Mirliton
Aguacate, with Cheese
Chicken, adobado y estofada
Butter-Holland — Cheese-Stilton — Butter-Native
Pumpkin Pie — Guava Pie — Mango Pie
White Bread — Sweet Bread — Honey
Biscuits — Tortillas
Tea — Coffee — Chocolate
Oranges — Guavas — Mangoes — Pineapples
Music by the Las Lajas String Orchestra

This was a little more plentiful than customary, as the cook was *cumpliendo años* (birthday), and I fancy she was celebrating.

IN RE ROMANCE. That's everywhere, if one only looks for it. It is all in the man. Some men have a capacity for seeing it, and some others for making it, while many—drones in the hive of life—would not know it should they fall over it. Some of us can see only the pleasant lights, others gloom along in the dark shadows. All is in the viewpoint, the outlook. As I write, here comes an example. Here they come! Here they come! Before the tribunal appear—Johnnie Squat and Hipolito Orellana, both bleeding freely.

Johnnie cut the palm of his left hand when cutting a *carizo* with a dull machete. The *carizo* broke and pulled through his hand, making an ugly cut with its razor edge.

Polo gashed his big toe with an ax, and comes, very chastened, saying, "For God's sake, doctor, fix me up quick! I'm losing all my blood. *Ai*, doctor, will it lame me for life? *Quien sabe* when I'll be able to work again?" Johnnie, on the contrary, says to me, "Finish your letter, doctor, this is nothing. The loss of a bit of blood will do me a lot of good. I'm lucky it was my left hand."

And there you have an epitome of life. One always happy, always lucky, the other a poor afflicted being, mourning and moaning. A pessimist and a philosopher. The two extremes.

ROMANCE and Fun are all around. Yesterday, while riding off a bit of ill-temper, I ran across a house of sadness. A woman of some thirty years had lost her daughter, who was washed, clothed in her cerements, and awaiting the ultimate offices.

The grief-stricken mother was seated on the dirt floor, giving loud tongue to her affliction. A peripatetic pedler and I arrived simultaneously. I dismounted to condole with the sufferer, as is right and proper, and expected of every one. Meantime the pedler spread his wares on a temporary bench which he had erected, using a cedar plank, one end on an *abardo* (native saddle) and the other supported on the prone body of a drunk. A most satisfactory display counter indeed.

"*Ai*, Mother of God, *Virgen del Carmen, se me fue mi muchachila*, my child is gone. My poor heart is breaking. Have mercy, O God, on a poor suffering mother. *Cuanto vale la cinta rosada, señor?* (What price the red ribbon, sir?) *Ai, Dios, que dolor!* (God! what suffering!) I'll give you a real the vara. *Socorreme, Dios* (Save me, God!). Are you carrying silk handkerchiefs? *Ai, Madre Sanctissima*—" and at this juncture the outside leg of the bench woke up, gave a heave, in two senses of the word, upset the apple-cart and presented his breakfast—or supper, mayhap—to the reluctant pedler. About this time I made a hurried departure to save my face. And yet they say 'tis a solemn world.

I HAD a nice letter from ——, and I think we'll strike up a friendship after our little spat. You surely stirred up the dog when you forwarded mine to him. He gave me what for in style. He took me to pieces, and scattered them over the landscape. I'm still in a state of dislocation, and fear I shall never get thoroughly assembled again; such his fury. He seems to be a regular fellow under the professorial shell. That's a hard shell to crawl out of, I assure you. . . . *In re* the handicap of your rules—piffle! Most rules are more honored in the breach than in the observance, and, more to the point, 'tis the fate of all rules, from the original ten, on downward. Finite man may lay no plan for the morrow; all is subject to change. Can you formulate a rule for the mutations of the kaleidoscope? What else is life, pray tell me? Environment makes the organism, and circumstances alter cases, and as both are mutable, mutable also must be the rules. Q. E. D.

This is so long I expect you'll charge me for reading it.—Wm. C. Robertson.

STILL letters come from people asking to join Camp-Fire. No need to ask. The wish is sufficient.

Arthur Sullivant Hoffman.

12

THE American Legion, suggested and originally organized by us of the Camp-Fire, was turned over to the Government in December, 1916, and thereby went out of existence as a private organization. Only partial use was made of it, but that was not the Legion's fault and the work it was doing beforehand is the same work the Government has had to do since we went into the war. Military authorities considered it the most practical step taken for defense before the war, and it had high value as propaganda in a country that at the time certainly needed to be waked up to the peril that has since materialized. We need feel only proud of the organization we started.

Even after a year and a half men try to join it. Its mail still comes in and is forwarded from its old address to me. From its former secretary, Dr. John E. Hausmann, I hear frequently. He is a captain in the Quartermaster's Department, though he preferred the Medical Corps and is trying to get to France. From what I can hear the reason he doesn't get to France is that he has made himself too valuable where he is and they won't let go of him. Here's luck to him and may he see France. In several letters he has sent his regards to the Camp-Fire and I transmit them herewith.

I ADMIT I didn't even suspect the allegory in his story in this issue until Mr. Lyle told me about it. It might be well if those of you who are as dull as I would not read what follows until you've read the story. We took it because we liked it as a straight story. The allegory part, therefore, is velvet so far as we are concerned, but knowing about it beforehand might check the swing of the story itself.

I suppose you have noticed that this story has a stolen plot—that I stole it from the Great War, with Germany and the Entente fighting for Supremacy and Jonathan Sam standing by (at least he was then), and Supremacy changing from a brute physical creature to something more spiritual, endangered by the wolves of anarchy as Civilization begins to break down. But anyhow, if you don't enjoy the allegory, don't let it spoil the story for you, please.—EUGENE P. LYLE, JR.

HERE'S part of a letter from Frank H. Huston which I pass on to you. "Uncle Frank" knew the Indians intimately in the old days:

Some tribes scalped differently, as did individuals; occasionally (the latter) skinning whole head, again, with ears attached, or pieces from the side of the head, but the "lock" differed. Some Atlantic coast tribes shaved and left a piece extending to forehead like the dewdad on a Roman helmet or shaved all but the actual lock, the "whorl" at back of head.

Plains tribes did not shave head, being neither Mussulmans or Mongols.

BEFORE scalp dried it was stretched on a little hoop and cured, then trimmed and pared, and when attached to articles of dress the skin part was rolled into size and shape of pencil or little finger and attached. How do I know? Well, after having been called a "damned gowl" by an army officer I surely ought to know. Had not all my effects been destroyed some years ago by a fire would send you some samples, bona fide ones at that, but not as well fixed up as Injun cured. But greater honor than taking a scalp was batting a strike or "coup" with the hockey or shinny-shaped coup stick. Remember Many or Plenty Coups, Ty Cobb, as it were, of his day, or is it Honus? Any squaw could kill or scalp, but to hit a corpse or "blesse" with the coup-stick in the heat of action was a greater achievement and so honored.

SURE I got a medicine-bag, and have opened many a one, same as we used to open the skin-wrapped dead uns stuck up on pole platforms when lucky enough to find them. When the upright skin poles rotted and fell, or were blown down, the varmint cleaned up the rubbish, but sometimes a comparatively fresh one was found and even to windward was far from fresh. Those book or closet ethnologists, and some of the field variety, suffer from a species of strabismus, even can't see what is before their nose or distort it from their civilized view-point, sort of like English and French view of *our* customs, etc.—"them us an' us them."

Look into the political economy of Dakota Confederacy, its pure democracy, and find that "men of wealth" did not exist, or they gathered wealth only to turn over to the clan or tribe and so "acquire merit." Red Cloud, three separate times was worth or gathered Injun wealth to the value of an American equivalent of $20,000 and other "big chiefs" nearly as much, all of which was gathered, not for personal use, but for the tribe.

THE word Dakotah, meaning men, typifies "them people." They *were* men, except in the eating line. There was nothing an old-time plains Injun would not eat, except apples and fish. After one had seen a buck with a yard or two of milk guts hanging out of his jaw, a hunk of raw, hot liver in one hand, and a gob of the undigested contents of the critter's paunch in the other for a vegetable relish, one could understand why you could smell 'em a mile to windward. Summer camps were not bad, but Winter camps, Wooh! The trenches in Yoorup aren't in it. Every one stripped at night even at forty degrees below. Just naturally had to or be eaten alive. My skin crawls yet and it's fifty years or more. (A strange fact is that the Yankee troops had more lice than ours. Why? Never could reason it out.) A Texas law used (if not now), to prohibit Injuns entering or living within the borders of the State. Too much Comanche, and by-the-by, the Comanches used to have a queer scalp-lock, approximating the Pawnees' and Kioways', who were undoubtedly of the same original stock.

And the plains Indians or meat-eaters used to have a profound disgust for the N. W. tribes whom they termed "fisheaters," as an Englishman uses the term Hun, or an American, wop, dago, mick or hunk.

PLEASE don't say skunk-skin but "taft-skin." And "pipe" ceremonies varied, in some, presented with both hands, bowl to right or left. Pipe in council passed, if I remember, to left-hand party. Hard to remember after so many years. Any old pipe would not do, certain pipes for certain occasions, and "pipe-keepers" who guarded the same. Smoking was religious or ceremonial, as on occasion of receiving visitors, councils, powwows, and was sucked like a Chink sucks a dope-pipe. Everything per ritual; in fact, their whole lives were per ritual. Do you know the reason of the waddling shuffle of the squaws? Roping. And the law of the roping of the legs, and the many ways it was done and penalties for violation? Do you know the working of what whites would call divorce? That women were *not* bought as wives, except occasionally a captive? That the *home* pertained to the squaw; she could fire the buck out if she felt like it? Oh, heaps of things that nine-tenths of the book-writers never fathomed.

AND do you remember how the army and plainsmen roared in mirth when the Meeker outfit women protested that the Injuns had been Galahads with them? First thing done was to violate the person of a woman captive, sometimes even in a fight.

And do you know of the milliards of secret societies and how some went broke buying captives from neighbors and giving 'em their liberty? A bunch of Yanktonais adolescents did that right after New Ulm and Col. Chivington and his 1st Col. Cav. at Sand Creek started the war that ended in '91 at Wounded Knee by massacring the So. Cheyennes who came in for a council? That "dog soldiers" were the police and were the only ones who could strike or man-handle or legally "bump" a tribesman? The voyagers mixed up dog soldiers with Cheyennes, who were not Dakotahs but conquered and incorporated with the latter.

AND do you know what caused the big cicatrices on breasts and shoulder-blades of the bucks? The ordeal of the Sun Dance and Rain in the Face, through enmity to the medicine-man who "slit" him, endured longer and busted more muscle and flesh than any other ever known. That marriage went by clans, the laws being frequently unobserved, but the violation frowned upon, as when an Eagle took a Turtle to wife? That a band was not always all one clan, but various weaker bunches who joined some well-known astute chief, or followed a famous war chief? That government was by the "elders" and not by individual chiefs, and that obedience to any order of a chief was voluntary and optional?

HI HO, I wish I was young again and those days were back! I'd drag the buffalo-head or throw back from the Sun Pole and receive my accolade and gain the three feathers that no squaw could ever gain or wear. Squaws with feathers in their hair! Whoo! instant death by the dog soldiers should one dare. Did you ever "tootle tootle" with the flute and then the "Twa" wrap up and sit under a blanket? Were you ever given a "common" name, did you ever gain a special name, did you ever glaum a name from a deceased enemy, etc.? And did you ever hear of "The Young Man whose horse would not go," otherwise "Standing Horse"? (He was not an Injun by birth.) And did you ever trade booze for "cattriges" and sell 'em to the Injuns? If not, make the sign rapidly by moving the open hands, palms facing, an inch or two apart, up and down in a chopping motion (meaning "stop" or, done quickly, "shut up,") or wave your hand, palm outward, right and left in front of you (meaning "no"; also, "enough," "no more").

WITH their new serial beginning in this issue the following from Kathrene and Robert Pinkerton will be of interest.

Father Jacques Marquette is generally considered the discoverer of the Mississippi River. By most historians the credit is given to Louis Joliet, who was trained for exploration work through many years and finally sent out to find the "great water" by the Governor of New France. Marquette, who had spent several years on the southern shore of Lake Superior and at the north end of Lake Michigan, had the Jesuit desire to find new lands and new peoples to bring into the church. He planned the trip for several years and it is possible that it was arranged that he and Joliet make the journey together.

AFTER their return from the voyage of discovery, which took them far down the river and back to Lake Michigan by way of the Illinois River, Marquette remained on Lake Michigan that he might return to establish a mission among the Illinois the next Summer. He wrote of his voyage and drew a map of the northern Mississippi valley, which he sent to Montreal, but he died about two years later after a visit to the Illinois.

Joliet, with complete accounts of his discoveries and a good map of the great valley and its waterways, hastened to Montreal. When only a few miles from the city his canoe was overturned in some rapids in the St. Lawrence and he barely escaped with his life. His map and account had only his memory as a basis, but these were sent to Paris at once.

Because of this accident, Marquette's journal and maps were the ones to receive publication a few years later, and early historians in this century credited him with the discovery. Researchers now generally give Joliet the credit, at least equal credit.

HOWEVER, though there are no records of actual discovery, any historian who has dug into original sources of information, grants readily that there is no doubt that some of the *coureurs de bois* reached the Mississippi and even went beyond it before Marquette and Joliet reached it June 17, 1673. These Frenchmen, trading without royal license as many of them did, were forced to keep their journeys secret. Many of them were forced to trade with the Dutch and English at Albany, N. Y., where they obtained goods and sold their furs. They were a wild, daring, irresponsible class of men, and there were several hundred of them in the region about the westernmost of the Great Lakes. Nothing daunted them, neither Indians nor the immensity of the wilderness, and there is no reason to doubt that more than one of them crossed the "great water," but never mentioned that fact when he returned to the St. Lawrence. Nicolet was within three days' paddle of the Mississippi River when he was on the Wisconsin forty years before Marquette arrived, and any *coureur de bois* had the information necessary to reach the Mississippi.

REUBEN GOLD THWAITS, who knew more of the history of the first days on the upper Mississippi than any other man, said there was no doubt that several *coureurs de bois* were ahead of Marquette and that it was even possible that an Englishman from the Colony of Virginia had penetrated to the great river prior to 1673. It was this statement that suggested the story, "Before Marquette."

We had been impressed for several years by the romantic story of the first French in Wisconsin, Minnesota, Illinois and Michigan. It is a hazy story, the more alluring and romantic because so much is only suggested, because there are so few facts, and yet room, for reasonable but marvelous deductions.

THE life of the *coureurs de bois* is largely the basis for this. Few men have been given the opportunity for more wonderful adventures. Yet the very nature of their operations made publicity undesirable and historical allusions little more than imagination - arousing conjectures. There were, however, some able, upright men among them, as Nicholas Perrot, and in "Before Marquette" we have tried to show the worst and the best of the *coureurs de bois*.

Our information was obtained entirely from original sources, some works, as Perrot's, having just been published in English. The Jesuit Relations have long been known, but Perot, in what was intended as a confidential report to the Intendent of New France, told of his life of thirty years on the Great Lakes and Upper Mississippi River and gave minute descriptions of the Indians, their many inter-tribal wars, their migrations, and also their customs, habits, etc.

THE American public has never understood the Indian and has never known what he is really like. Fiction, massacres and the results of injustice had induced queer conceptions, and yet the Indian of the upper Mississippi valley before the coming of white men was far different than he is today. One reason for drawing a more intimate sketch of the Sioux was to show how vastly diferent he was from the man Custer met in Wyoming.

Another thing that has never been recognized in fiction, and by only one historian, and that is the effect of the fur trade on the spread of civilization. It was for fur and fur alone that all the first trails were blazed, and the story of the upper Mississippi, down to the fall of the fur trade less than a hundred years ago, has been duplicated in Canada and the history of discovery there.

WE WERE both born and have lived much of our lives in the region described in "Before Marquette." Many of the scenes are familiar to us, though it is hard to imagine Marquette Wintering at the forks of the Chicago River after seeing the man-made river of today. We have paddled many of the streams *Dick Jeffreys* traversed, have camped where he camped, and in writing the story have lived over again many of our experiences. We have sat for hours on the great bluff from which *Dick* first saw the "great water," and now we are confronted with the necessity of forgetting *Dick* and his journeys. If we don't, we'll really believe he did discover the "father of waters."—KATHRENE and ROBERT PINKERTON.

THE suggestion, by C. R. Rollings at a recent Camp-Fire, that we should pay our tribute to the late Jack London has met with such response that there is not room for all the tributes that have come in. Nor is there need of all of them in print; the fact that they came is the important one, and one or two can typify our Camp-Fire feeling for the great and loved adventurer who has left us.

Personally I never met him and our slight acquaintance is limited to a letter or two and to the fact that he was an interested member of our Camp-Fire. And yet even the few written words from him are sufficient to establish him as what he was—not just a famous writer and adventurer, but a real man. It is only this simple tribute that I can pay him from my own acquaintance with him, yet if you understand that simple tribute as it is given you will know it is high praise.

Let us listen to the words of our comrade of the writers' brigade, J. Allan Dunn, and to the poem he has written to his friend:

The Camp-Fire

HEARTILY in accord with the suggestion of Mr. Rollings at a recent Camp-Fire, I feel that the memoriam of Jack London is, in a measure, up to me. In all probability he and I were more intimate than was the case with other members of the Camp-Fire who personally knew him but this privilege but makes me feel the more inadequate to fulfil the task.

I think one of the greatest attributes of Jack London was the brave gentility of his spirit. In the beginning all things were against him, he trailed in the mire by force of circumstance, he saw the seamy side of the world, and, while his spirit revolted against the injustice, the inhumanity that he encountered, so that in youthful bitterness he accounted himself an outlaw, yet his inherent sweetness was unspoiled and when his full manhood was achieved, his soul used his harsh experiences only as a means to better sympathize and understand and to treat them as a flux by which his genius crucibled the real impulses of humanity.

MANY there are who have set Jack London down as a roughneck and a Socialist, little knowing the man. There have been attempts to show him as lacking in American patriotism, as a pacifist. A pacifist! Jack London was ever a fighting man. A biography of him might aptly be styled A Fight with Fortune. He was always fighting, against poverty, against lack of education; he fought for opportunity, he wrote for years before he achieved either recognition or a bare livelihood; he fought for years against sickness, with a body weakened in the very beginning by the lack of fair food and lodging, weakened yet more by stomach troubles, aggravated by the hardships of his travel in strange seas and lands under unfavorable conditions, his nervous system largely smashed by tropical sun-rays in the *Snark* voyage. His spirit maintained a false but vibrant virility. It was ever buoyant, ever generous. I have known many days when Jack London fought off sickness to accomplish his allotted task, and at the very end, he wrote until the final unconsciousness overcame him. *And he always fought smiling.* Obstacles to him were only things to be surmounted. He bucked his way to the mastery of words, he never ceased to study. When navigation was wanted he went at it while handling his own roving vessel and mastered it. *Smiling.* He was a magnificent fighter. He loved life and loved to live, and the pity of it was that one so truly vital, so eminently understanding of the prime motives of us all, should have gone in his prime.

TO ME he is not dead. He was on his way to visit me when stricken down and now the memory of him, the inspiration of him is so vivid, so enlivening that I know his spirit moves and has its being in some strong measure here. If I meet him on some stretch of Elysian sand he will be no stranger and the place will be no longer strange. If, according to certain creeds, he and I should meet in Hades, that spot will have lost much of its allotted terrors—and Jack London will still be smiling.

He was nearly read out of the Socialist party for his "Iron Heel" in which he conservatively—according to his own conviction—set the Socialistic millennium hundreds of years ahead and hinted that it must come from within, born of a universal desire. He separated himself entirely from the party when he found its trend was against the Democracy of America and the participation of that democracy in behalf of the rights and freedom of its citizens and their allies.

SOCIALISM to him was an ideal and, with maturer years and judgment, he did not always find himself in harmony with the actions of its more ardent propagandists. Yet always he welcomed those he had styled "comrades" in the days of his trampdom and social outlawry. Seldom was the little cabin on the ranch at Glen Ellen without some vagrom occupants, exploiting Jack London. It got to be so bad that, in sheer defense, Mrs. London and Nakata, most lovable and faithful of Japanese majordomos, conspired to stop the lavish food supplies and Jack was himself brought to see that his generosity was being abused. Yet Jack, in the dead of night, would steal down silently and rob his own cellar, burglarizing the lock and packing a sack of flour and a ham across the ranch to set it down outside the door where those ever-sleepy "brethren" of his drowsed content in their belief in Jack's easy hospitality. Besides this, he held out a sure hand of encouragement and employment for certain men who had served their time in San Quentin or Folsom.

Nor, with a hundred calls on him, with his words worth each one what would have bought him a meal in earlier days, did Jack ever hesitate to set aside his own affairs and help some struggling author or to welcome a boys' school or some such caravan that came to see Jack London. He was pre-eminently human. Adversity sweetened his spirit rather than soured it, and prosperity—self won—still further ripened it.

JACK rode fearlessly, he could sail his ship and guide it, he could swing a coaching-team skilfully across skiddy pitches and tool them with the utmost chivalry and appreciation of their efforts. He swam like a Kanaka and dived like Neptune. Apparently he never tired. He was a he-man who stood up and grinned at trouble, was absolutely frank in self-analysis and confession and held a charity toward the weaknesses and backslidings of others, coupled with the will and action to help, that made him a potent example of real Christianity.

A strong spirit and a sweet one. Unaffected, despite all rumors. Jack abominated a stiff collar because he felt better without one. Never was a man who posed less.

THE story-teller absolute, his tales echo with reality because he wrote only of what he knew, what he had seen, enlivened with his genius, his intuition for what a man must feel. And always he sought and traveled so that his store of knowledge, so largely unused, might increase. Absolutely lacking in conceit, he called his wonderful technique "tricks." He was the first to acclaim merit in others and the first to abominate charlatanry of all kinds, save as he might forgive it in his friends for the better sides of them he knew. "Brass tacks," he would cry, when guests spoke metaphysics. "We are living now, we can not get away from the 'now.' Get down to brass tacks. Let us argue along tangible lines."

Jack London was a living answer to that vexed question of whether an adventurer can ever forsake the camp-fire for the home-side hearth and whether the love of woman can ever take the place of the wander-love. Of the wonderful intimacy between

Jack London and Charmian London I shall say little. Its ties were and are sacred as they were perfect. I do not cite them as an example. Their unity was made up of an affinity welded and refined by understanding, sacrifice, unselfishness that is only too rare. But he showed that the true wanderer need not go mateless.

No one can analyze genius. London wrote of what he had seen and heard and lived, his *motif* was life and the red blood of him tinctures the ink in which his words are printed. Jack London the writer, lives in his books. Jack London the man, was, despite his differences with the propaganda of that party to which he felt himself intuitively affiliated, a true Socialist. He was plucky, he was generous to a fault, utterly unselfish, absolutely frank. To all who came in contact with him he was a true comrade.

AND man and writer are indissolubly linked. He called up the nomad spirit of his own Nordic race, the "vanishing blond," as he was wont to style it. He challenged, he challenges, in all of us the viking mood, the desire to go beyond the rim of things, to fight, to conquer if possible, or to go down fighting—and smiling. He lifted us out of the commonplace, he made the daily round less sordid for a while, he revived romance in hearts made dull by drudgery and this not less by the clear fire of his own fighting manhood as by the flame of his genius. By all the tokens he was a man.

A few of us who knew him very well, and know the deeds he did in secret as well as in the open, called him "Greatheart."

J. ALLAN DUNN.

To Jack London

FATE at the first thumbed down,
Ere he dreamed of renown,
Ground him in mire.
Still he vowed to achieve
Telling his soul—"Believe!"
Fanned spark to fire
Till it burst into flame.
The world thrilled with his name,
Filled with desire.

Sure was his genius' pen,
Writing of human men,
Telling of life.
Red blood ran in their veins,
Primal sap in their reins,
Masters of strife.

Hearts that were sore and dull
Read—and their lives were full.
Attics became a ship,
Routine a 'venture trip,
Coarse food a ration.
Sailed they the Seven Seas,
Faced they the tundra's freeze,
Dreamed 'neath an atoll palm,
Drifted in storm or calm,
Kings of Creation.

He left the memory clean;
Vesting things crude and mean
With touch inspired.
Sweet was his generous mind,
Kin he to all mankind,
As he desired.
Words are his monument,
Born of a good intent,
No idle fame!
So shall he rest content,
Love as his cerement,
GREATHEART his name.

J. A. D.

A RECENT letter from W. Townend showed him stationed in Ireland after going through most of the war on the French front. The following bears on his novelette in this issue:

The tale is not an effort of wild imagination. It is fiction, of course, but I did not write it without a good foundation of fact to build on. And, as I always say in almost every tale I write, in war the impossible becomes possible.

Story-writing is simply a matter of luck. It is difficult to find time and I am usually too busy to do more than a little work each day.

As you will see by the address I am now in Ireland. The weather is glorious, so is the country, the people are—well, beyond all understanding. I like them, but to understand them is quite another matter. Is there a solution to the Irish problem? I thought once there was. Now, having spoken to most classes of Irish, I am not so sure.—W. TOWNEND.

FROM twenty-five miles from a railroad and 5,000 feet in the air comes greeting from one of us with word about a bit of the Old West:

Cake, Oregon.

This is an interesting country, a part of the "real Old West," and while most of the old landmarks in this section have wholly disappeared, the halo of romance still remains, fostered by the tales and reminiscences of the few yet living who were here during the stirring times of forty or fifty years ago when the Malheur and Mormon Basin placer mines were in the heyday of their frontier glory.

IN THIS county (Malheur) was the town of El Dorado, one of the first and liveliest camps of the early days, of which not a vestige remains at this time. Where at one time lived 6,000 to 7,000 people, with nicely built, painted houses, a 75-room hotel, lots of stores, saloons, dance-halls, etc., etc., nothing is left, not a board or brick, nothing except the glamour of its remembrance. In fact in driving along the road one would never know that a thriving and prosperous community had ever existed there. Originally the town was the headquarters of the Eldorado Ditch Company, who constructed a ditch 160 miles long to bring the water to these rich places. Some idea of the magnitude of the enterprise may be gained from the fact that the rents for the privilege of using this water ran as high as $150,000 to $175,000 in the total, annually.

SEVERAL miles from the site of Eldorado is the town of Malheur, known in the early days as "Malheur City," which was also one of the principal headquarters of the early-day placer-miners. Here still remain a few stores and houses, and an Odd Fellows' Hall, reminiscent of the "good old days," inhabited by possibly fifty or sixty people, but all the "glory" of former days has long since departed.

Several miles beyond Malheur, right by the road and in the midst of the sage-brush-covered prairie, is a small bright green spot, enclosed by a fence, where the luxuriant grass still thrives from the adjacent spring—as it were, an oasis in the desert. Here, away off by itself, once flourished a prosperous brewery, located there on account of the water being particularly adapted to the manufacture of beer—good beer and, believe me, lots of people wish it were still there, but alas! nothing remains but the grass and the spring.

STILL farther on is the site of the old town of Amelia, where naught but a battered old out-house remains of a busy and populous community of forty years ago. A few miles beyond lies Mormon Basin, said to have been one of the richest placers in the world and originally located by the Mormons—tradition tells us they used to carry the gold away by wagon-loads. I have never heard this verified by any one who saw the "wagon-loads," but the fact remains that it was one of the richest districts ever known. Placer-mining is still carried on in a small way by one or two who employ the few old Chinamen yet remaining of the many who were brought there in the early days (Chinese were always used, preferentially, in this work on account of their inherent honesty; at least, it is said, a greater percentage of them were honest than of other nationalities).

MILLIONS of dollars in gold was produced from these big rich placers and we are told that the "mother lode" which fed them has never yet been discovered by reworking the old ground with more modern methods. We occasionally see one of the old-time prospectors, still searching for his "ledge," always cheerful and optimistic and will be until the end.

This whole section of country is replete with legends and traditions, romantic and interesting, dealing with the early life amongst the sturdy pioneers, the miners and Indians—a good field for the historian and story-writer, with ample room for the exercise of his talents.

The writer first came West as a boy in 1880, living on the Idaho frontier, where many exciting events happened, and is glad indeed to note the Camp-Fire's efforts to correct errors and preserve authentic records of those events and happenings incident to that stirring and strenuous period as well as of the people who participated therein and helped make history.—"Q."

THROUGH the courtesy and thoughtfulness of Mr. B. W. Denison, Sunday editor of the Chicago *Herald*, I received the following telegram:

April 17, 1918.

Arthur J. Hayes died Tuesday at Camp Grant of pneumonia.

He is the second of our comrades of the writers' brigade to die within a short time, and though he just as truly gave his life for his country as if he had died in the trenches, we know that he would rather have passed out fighting.

We will remember him for his stories, notably that fine dog story "The Epic of Silver King," but we remember him also as our comrade. Let us turn back to what he said to us something over a year ago when, according to our custom, he stood up and introduced himself to the Camp-Fire:

Chisholm, Minnesota.

Your forwarded letter was received in the Pelican Lake country several days ago. The half-breed trapper who obligingly brought it in from Orr was not returning, so I was unable to get my reply out more promptly. I have been on the trail of the vanishing lumberjack for the past week, endeavoring to tone up my local color for a series of stories. The old two-fisted, red-shirted calk-booted character of earlier eras has disappeared. The old tote-trails are grown in with grass, and the tar-paper flaps, a forlorn specter, on the ridge-pole of the camps that were. To-day they build with milled lumber, import "Jacks" who pack their belongings in straw suit-cases, and who have attained the effeteness of unions, labor agitation, and organized strikes, and drag the log-laden sleighs with caterpillar tractors. But to get to the autobiography:

WAS born in Duluth, Minnesota, in the early nineties. My earliest recollections are of that strip of strangely wild territory between the Mesaba Range and the Rainey River. Knew it when the Indians killed swimming moose with axes from canoes and shot whitefish endeavoring to leap Kettle Falls. Have vague recollections of the high ebb tide of the Seine River gold-rush, an aftermath of the Klondyke Frenzy, when thousands of gold-seekers poured into Mine Center in quest of an Ontario El Dorado. They poured out again, disgusted and disillusioned. The stamp-mills and shafts, long since abandoned, are among the show places of the Rainey.

It has been my lot, hitherto, to live rather on the fringe of things. Saw the only gold brick the Foley Mine ever turned out, and the troops that poured in after the Nett Lake fiasco in '99. Have ridden eight miles about one jump ahead of a forest fire, and witnessed the burning of Chisholm, in 1908, in the State's greatest conflagration. Knew most intimately, perhaps, all phases of the Minnesota lumberjack existence. Have seen him in his hey-day and decline. There are some corking good tales in the old mackinawed Vikings of the pine country.

HAVEN'T adventured myself, but have been rarely fortunate in meeting in the out-of-the-way places many a man who had. Have done cub-reporting, attended college, and instructed sundry classes in rhetoric. I like the lonesome trails and the men from the far horizon. Will annex an LL. B. in June, but aspire rather to journalism and fiction. The family have pioneered from my birth and have seen the older, wilder days of the Iron Ranges. Regret that I can not qualify with Camp-Fire's first-hand performers. Hope to break in later with something actually worth while.

Our salute to him, standing, hats off, and may his way be smooth over the Last Trail. ARTHUR SULLIVANT HOFFMAN.

AS IT happens, the former letter from "Peas River" read at our Camp-Fire brought an inquiry from an Army officer connected with some of the people mentioned in that letter—a kind of unintentional "Lost Trails" accomplishment such as happens every little while through our Camp-Fire meetings. This second letter, also dealing with Western old-timers, is self-explanatory. I leave in the part about our movement for good citizenship; it serves as sample of the magnificent response to the call to good Americans—the response that assures the practical success of the American League for Citizenship.

Clarksdale, Miss.

Concerning my letter in your first March issue I wish to correct a mistake. It was A. T. Boger (not Boyer) that was appointed sheriff of Wilbarger Co., Texas, when Tom Stewart was ousted. I am sorry I am such a poor scribe; some one will pick me up on that sure. That is why I hasten to correct it.

I read with pleasure D. Wiggins' letter, especially that part about Chalk Beeson, Bill Hart and the single-action Colt. By the way, that was the only kind of a revolver to be found in the West in an early day. If I see Bill advertised I will sure drop in and see that old Colt. May be it won't be the first time I've seen it.

The best thing I have read in *Adventure* or any place else is "a creed for Americans." That is fine. All we need is to get enough people educated along these lines and we can do the thing we want to do—build a good house out of good bricks—"PEAS RIVER."

FROM Thomas E. Webb of Camden, Arkansas, comes the suggestion of a monument in New York to the memory of Jack London. "What if old Jack could but look back and behold in the presence of a huge marble the esteem in which he was held," writes Mr. Webb. "There's not an adventure-loving man in all America, England or where not but would contribute his share toward such a monument."

That seems to me a good idea. How do the rest of you feel about it? If a guaranteed committee of some kind were formed I dare say the money would come in freely. Personally I'm already carrying all the work I can tote—more, I judge, from what it did to me the first few months of 1918—but perhaps *Adventure* could, if desired, serve as a repository for contributions, our responsibility ceasing when the total was paid over to the committee.

WHAT kind of monument? I should say something simple and solid. How much money should be collected? Where should it be placed? What inscription?

I do not know Mr. Webb personally, but perhaps it would be the best plan for all interested to write to him and shape up a definite course of action. There ought to be a monument to Jack London and from whom could it come more fittingly than from the adventurers who gather about the Camp-Fire from all over the world?

A LETTER from one of our American comrades with the Canadians in England. At the end of it was a postscript, which has gone into "Lost Trails," inquiring for Richard Granville, "Linderfeldt," "Captain King," "Lea," "Dad Biddle" and the rest of the "American Legion" that was in Mexico.

Salt Pons,
Sandwitch, Kent, England.

There are many Yanks in this camp, from Maine to California. We wear the Canadian uniform mostly. Not a few are very homesick, yet as an average they are doing their bit as men. Many of them are holding some office as N. C. O. and some have commissions as lieutenants and captains. We have enough to eat and good quarters, as soldiering goes—better than I had in Mexico under Villa or Madero—and no fighting yet. Plenty of amusements. Wet and dry canteens, cinemas or movies, concerts, as there is some splendid talent in the ranks. But I miss my "Java"; here it is tea or cocoa.

AND what a medley of dialects, Scots, Irish, Welsh, English of several varieties, Yanks from Massachusetts, Michigan, Texas, Colorado, California, Australians and negroes. This is a study in sociology or hobo-ology; any way it's interesting. Especially when I enter the dining-hut to hear a Welsh orderly say, "Two more mans up this way." And if you were to be transported to our sleeping quarters about nine P.M. and woke up you would wonder if you had fallen into a "Nut Factory" and whether they used chloroform on the poor things.

But they are a fairly good-natured bunch. I have many warm friends among both men and officers, and expect a raise in rank soon. I am winning it here as well as in Mexico, Honduras, the U. S. A. and some others, on my merits only. From the ranks up it is not so easy here. Lots of red tape, savvy?

I AM full of real news and copy but no use writing it to be torpedoed by the censor, but I can tell you something about the country. Its quaint old houses with tile and thatched roofs, old wind-mills, castles, with walls twenty feet thick—they all look like oil paintings—and canals, tall bridges, large pasture-lands filled with sheep, and they are in good condition as the Winter has been mild. I was out and picked some wild daisies to-day and was boating on the river—no, not joy-riding, just a part of my duty, in the "Salvage Corps" of which I am the originator. The women and girls of England are sure doing their bit in this war. Will tell you about them some other time. I am disgracefully healthy. So long.—"POWDER JESS."

A WOMAN comrade of our writer's brigade. They are few and far between but always assured of friendly welcome. Greeting to Louise Rice, who gives us a story for the first time and introduces herself according to Camp-Fire custom:

This matter of discussing myself bothers me a little. I've never done any self-exploiting, nor allowed any one else to do it for me. However, I guess there really is an excuse for it in this case, if I am to be admitted to ADVENTURE's family, for if I write about thugs and bums and longshoremen and tramps, etc., as I'm likely to do, some of your men readers will be wondering how on earth I know anything about what I'm writing about.

I THINK a little story will illustrate how I happen to know more about the rough life of the world than the majority of women. I was coming home from the opera one night and, as it was unusually mild, my escort and myself started to walk home through Madison Square Park. Coming the other way, from tending his boilers in a well known building on Twenty-third Street, came an acquaintance of mine. I would gladly have evaded him, but he planted himself before me, looked me up and down and inquired, in amazement:

"Fer th' love o' Mike, Lou, where'd yuh get them glad rags?"

HE KNEW me merely as a rather dingy person who had chatted with him, off and on, for a year, as he stood taking the air at his cellar steps, and, owing to a chance word of mine about running a typewriter, he had always taken it for granted that I was an underpaid and overworked stenographer. Be it recorded to his glory, and to the everlasting honor of what are known as "rough" men, that I have repeatedly made friends with them in just that way, and have yet to receive from one of them a word which would shame the finest so-called gentleman in the land.

I did not want this particular friend to see me in the "glad rags," because I did not want him to think that I had been anything but the real friend that I really was. So I had to explain, and, alas, I never got another entirely frank and unconscious word out of him! But thanks to my acquaintance of the previous year with him, I know, intimately and in detail, just what a man like him thinks and wants—and I believe I could tend his boilers, too.

IN FACT, I've known about every kind of man and a woman that there is, I guess. I've been a reporter, and a "rewrite" woman, and worked in a big advertising office, and in a motion picture "exchange" and run a restaurant and had a manicure shop, and got five dollars an hour for doing massage, and a dollar and a half an hour for running a gymnasium, where I had every sort of person, from kids of fourteen to old men of sixty, from shop-girls to society women. I'm really a pretty good farmer, and a well known graphologist (give you three guesses as to what that is!) and I love to cook and hate to sew, and if I've got a clean collar and cuffs on I think I'm dressed up enough to go anywhere.

I'm older than you'd think, and I can walk twenty miles, easy, and put my knuckles to the floor without bending my knees. Selah!—LOUISE RICE.

P. S. I forgot to tell you about the characters in "Skirts and Brats." All of them are real, and the story is mainly so. The names are correct. Red Jumbo, Smoky Mike, Blond Maggie, Chicago Bessie and Larry the Dip will probably be recognized if any of their old pals read the tale. Jumbo married Chicago Bessie, of course, and is the devoted step-daddy to the twins. Larry, brave fellow, died in trying to conquer his habit. There's rather a pathetic story about him which I may write, some time. I don't know what became of Blond Maggie, but I do know that she started out to earn her living in an honest way. The McGurk's where Jumbo lay up, in New York, waiting for his beard to grow, was the famous McGurk's, one of the best-known hang-outs of criminals in this country. On several occasions myself and an escort spent a long evening in that dreadful place, successfully impersonating habitués, and gathering all sorts of impressions, data and information about the underworld.

THAT was in the days when New York was "wide open." I spent nearly all of one year investigating the conditions of the lower East Side, for I could not believe that the stories which the newspapers were just beginning to print about it were true. I investigated, as long as I could stand it, and had to conclude that the half had not been even whispered.

And let me add just one word. You see a lot written about the "adventurous" life of criminals, about their "orgies" and their generally gay and daring lives. Well, believe me, the most dismal, gloomy, care-ridden people I have ever seen in my not exactly narrow life have been criminals. When they drink they fight, instead of singing. When they don't drink they fall into such depths of abysmal misery that even the worst of them would arouse pity. From which you can easily deduce any number of morals!

But in the above Miss Rice told so little of her real adventures that I wrote and protested. So she added what follows. But, even so, she hasn't really done justice to a life of adventures that would make many of the men look to their laurels. However, here's the bit more:

I have been out of town, which is the reason why I have not answered your request for more dope about what I thought I'd said more than enough about. I didn't mention the fact that I really can and have run an engine because that wasn't much of an adventure—a sewing-machine is more complicated! Any dub can do it.

I DIDN'T mention about roaming around with my friends, the Romanys, because that isn't much of an adventure, either. The safest place I know of for man or beast is a Gipsy wagon—also, you get splendiferous eats, and the roof is hail-proof, and the talk is beautifully absent. However, if you think it interesting to say to the readers of ADVENTURE that I've done those things, go right ahead. As an adventure, I have found making my living in New York by far the most exciting and hazardous undertaking I have ever attempted.

The Gipsies are really wonderfully interesting people, but they are not the murdering, knife-out, stealing, "wild" people of the usual fiction; not a-tall—which is the reason why editors uniformly refuse my stories about them!

I THOUGHT it was rather an adventure to shingle a house of mine, once—there was not the slightest danger in sitting on the ridge pole, but the battery of long range glances which poured upon me while I sat there was one of the most trying dangers I ever endured. I like to plow and harrow, too, which drew an interested ring of onlookers for several days of one radiant Spring. But my most unusual feat was to carry a new broom down three blocks of theatrical Broadway one day. It was not a stunt—a friend of mine, who had just rented a studio really needed it—but you would have thought that the Wild Man of Borneo Had Just Come To Town. Things like that leave me utterly bewildered. *Why* do so many people in this very interesting and natural world connive to make simple and natural actions so difficult? But that's nothing to do with me or this adventurous life of mine that you insist on, has it?

I COUNT as the really wonderful adventures of my life the many, many unusual and wonderful people whom I have met—not necessarily well known people, although there are a good many of them, but the rare human types, the man or woman who has been and gone and done things, and couldn't write a word about them to save their necks! If I ever write any *good* stories I'll deserve no credit. It will just be a rehash of what those big people have *done.* Come to think of it, I guess my friendships are my true excuses for cumbering this already over-populated earth—I'm a sort of licensed singer, like those bards of old who earned their board and room by reciting the deeds of those more worthy than themselves, and far, far greater—LOUISE RICE.

ORDER of the Restless. Wayne Eberley, its secretary, asks to have it bulletined that, because of the long interval between the announcement of the formation of the society and the date on which constitution and blanks were finally ready, nearly half of the letters he mailed out to inquirers were returned by the post-office. Quite plainly the inquirers are entitled to be ranked among the Restless, since an address reaches them for so short a time. If those who thus missed their replies from Mr. Eberley will write him again, giving their present addresses, he will be glad to write again in his turn. For his address, see "*Adventure's* Free Services and Addresses" on a following page.

FROM E. S. Pladwell a word about the real facts behind his story in this issue:

Oakland, Cal.

The real story was not much like mine. It was grimmer but rottener. The missionary cleaned up the natives, established law and order of a sort, learned to live among them, took a native girl as concubine, achieved a taste for the native ferment-juice, and finally left this pleasant world by means of a suicidal revolver. In newspaper parlance, there was "no story."—E. S. PLADWELL.

AN INQUIRY from our comrade E. A. Brininstool concerning Captain Drannan:

If there is any old Army officer who saw Indian fighting on the plains anywhere from 1860 to 1886, or who took part in the Apache wars or the Modoc war, or who knows the particulars of the rescue of the Oatman girls from Apaches, I would like to ask if he ever heard of a man named Captain Wm. F. Drannan, author of a book entitled "Thirty-One Years on the Plains." Drannan's photo, the frontispiece of the book, shows an old man about seventy-five, in a buckskin suit, and is signed by himself as "Chief of Scouts."

DRANNAN alleges he was raised by the celebrated Kit Carson, and that he was later a companion of old Jim Bridger, Jim Beckwourth, "Buffalo Bill" and other frontier celebrities. I went carefully through the book and counted the number of Indians alleged to have been slain either by him in person or killed by companion "scouts" and himself, or by troops for whom he scouted, and his own figures give the astounding number of 609 redskins. The book has 586 pages. I only counted dead Indians in fights in which Drannan says he took part.

Drannan says he also scouted for Gen. George Crook in Arizona, Gen. Conner, Gen. Wheaton, Col. Elliott and Gen. John C. Fremont. He recites that he personally captured Capt. Jack, chief of the Modocs, personally rescued Alice Oatman from captivity among the Apaches, and was more or less prominent in other Indian scrimmages and campaigns.

I HAVE read about everything of a historical nature that I can get hold of concerning all our Indian campaigns, but in no book, article, story or any written documents of Indian campaigns have I ever seen this man's name mentioned in any capacity—much less as "chief of scouts." I know a great many old-time Indian fighters personally and many Army officers who were on the plains from '66 to '90, and none of them ever heard of Scout Drannan.

If this catches the eye of any men who served in the regular Army from '66 to '90—whether private or officer, I would like to hear from them. Now then, speak up, you old boys! Who knows anything about Capt. Wm. F. Drannan, Chief of Scouts?—E. A. Brininstool.

IN A letter written in February Captain George Ash asks to have it announced to his friends that he is in Japan and Korea, doing well.

THESE stories of Hugh Pendexter's do more than entertain us. He has studied the American Indian for years and his tales not only bring vividly before our eyes the early years of our country's history but can be relied upon for accuracy in both detail and spirit. They make the Indian and pioneer of the past a living reality.

I find I'm breaking rules and praising at Camp-Fire some of our own stories, but perhaps you'll make allowance for the fact that I'm speaking of them not because of their fiction value but because they are doing exactly what some of you (I'm glad to say) are doing—telling us facts about the days of the frontier that has moved westward across our country three thousand miles in three hundred years.

ANOTHER story in this issue, "The Devil's Dagger," performs a similar service as to the Scotland of the old days. I like these stories of old times mixed in with those of the present day and, judging from your letters and talks, most of you feel the same way. But they must be dependable in fact and atmosphere or the value and interest are greatly lessened. Comrades Bishop and Brodeur, like Comrade Pendexter, know whereof they write. Both have for years been students of past civilizations, and Mr. Brodeur—well, he reads the old sagas in the original and little things like that.

Now here's a little "dope on the side" from Mr. Pendexter on his story in this issue:

Norway, Maine

The story was suggested by the sacred myth of the Cherokee concerning the Raven Mocker, which, according to James Moony in his authoritative work on Cherokee mythology, was the most dreaded of all wizards and demons. The Cherokee firmly believed in the Raven Mocker. Once when Mr. Moony was among the Cherokee he says (page 504, "Myths of the Cherokee") "A sick man was allowed to die alone because his friends imagined they felt the presence of the Raven Mocker." The same authority says, "The grewsome belief in The Raven Mocker is universal among the Cherokee and has close parallel in other tribes." And he cites as an example the Iroquois belief in the "cannibal ghost."

AS THE time of this story is about 1730, or after the Shawneee had been driven to the Ohio, the superstitious fears of the white traders are plausible. The execution of witches in New England was less than forty years away. In speaking of another myth of the Cherokee, Mr. Moony says, "The faith in the existence of the miraculous Little Deer is almost as strong and universal to-day (1897-98 ed. "Myths of the Cherokee") among the older Cherokee as is the belief in a future life." On commenting on the talismanic power attached to the consecrated down of the young antler of the deer the same author remarks: "So firm was the belief that it had influence over 'anything about a deer' that eighty or a hundred years ago even white traders used to bargain with the Indians for such charms in order to increase their store of deerskins by drawing trade to themselves." I cite this to prove readiness of whites to accept Indian beliefs.

The raven "dives" while flying by folding one wing close to the body, falling and, says Moony, "apparently turning a somersault." The cry given at such times is described as being entirely different from the ordinary cry of the raven.

THE old stage route between Knoxville and Harper's Ferry practically followed the Great Indian War Trail. The Cherokee and other Indians generally believed they would become what they ate.

Usunhiyi—"where it is always growing dark," is used in myths and sacred formulas to denote the West. The land of the dead, or "Ghost Country," is situated in Usunhiyi. It is called Tsusginai. The common word for west is *wudeligunyi*—"there where it (the sun) goes down."

It is told by the Cherokee that in 1747 two Mohawks killed more than twenty in stealthy attacks on the Lower Towns. During the Spring and Summer their adroit ambuscades caused the Cherokee to believe they were wizards or witches—Hugh Pendexter.

SOME time ago we had a letter from our comrade W. E. Brandon telling his experiences in a Central-American earthquake. Here is one written nearly a year ago, telling about the unique job of building a railroad on hot lava, and a third dated in 1918. These letters were written to our comrade W. C. Tuttle, whose stories are part of our regular diet—this friendship between a man in San Salvador and another in Spokane who have never seen each other being another sample of the personal friendships growing up through our Camp-Fire.

LA LAVA, KILOMETRO 69-72, SALVADOR, C. A.

DEAR FRIEND TUTTLE:—Your very welcome and interesting letter came in yesterday. I will try to make this a connected letter, old-timer, but can't say that I shall. I ate a lot of cucumbers yesterday and for a wonder that old stomach of mine reniged. I can generally eat anything that is too thick to drink, or drink anything that is too thin to eat. But this time it failed. I got a "tummy-ache" and then thought I would cure it by taking a good shot of "hootch." I don't yet know if it was the cucumber salad or the hootch that put me on the blink, but naturally I lay it to the former. Anyway, I happened to be down at a town named Sonsonate (pretty nearly like Cincinnati, eh?), and was staying at a hotel. I sure passed a hi-yu night of it, griping with what resembled a cross between a baby with the colic and a full-grown hombre with the ptomaine poison. But I dug myself out in time for the first train this morning and arrived here on the job and found out that one of my engineers had stolen my hand-car last night and had taken a bunch to a nearby town and got them all hi-yu drunk and they had a fight with machetes on the way back and disabled several, and what was worse, broke my hand-car. Oh, this life in the tropics is ——.

NOW, I'll go back to the start and tell you the news: I think I told you that after I had volunteered for relief work and had done quite a bit of that, after the earthquake, I felt the pressing need of a few simoleons. About that time the Red Cross asked me to construct their building for them at my own price. I told them that I had no money to offer for Red Cross work but that if they would buy the material and pay for the labor I would do the construction for them, donating my work instead of money. As the officers of the Red Cross knew that I was broke they mentioned this offer frequently, so I got quite a rep.

Then I began to get offers at good prices in construction work. I started in that business and took in a partner who had almost as much money as I had, but who was a good hustler. I began to make money. But I had to work, old top. I worked literally day and night. Many a night I spent making elevations and setting my blue prints for the morning sun, and then spent the entire day in managing my gangs of men and wondering where I would land the money for the pay-roll that week. But I got the reputation and the business. I enclose one of my cards.

WHILE I was at this business, the railway whose letter-heads I am now using, 'phoned me and asked me to come down to see them. I replied that I was too busy. The general manager then came down to see me and wanted me to take charge of a certain job for them. I told them that as it would take me out of the city I could not do the work for them—if they could get any one else. They tried and then they asked me to at least go down and see the work and give them a report on what I thought of it, they to pay any sum that I demanded for my time so consumed and all expenses for the trip. I agreed to that if the trip would not occupy more than three days of my time.

AND here was the job: When the volcano broke loose it opened several new craters. An immense flow of lava from one of these ran down and covered a portion of the railroad about a mile and a half long to a depth of from eighteen to thirty feet of hot lava. The right-of-way troubles, etc., allow them to occupy only their old right of way. In other words, the job was to build a railroad over hot lava—a stunt never before pulled off in the history of mankind. Well, I have never seen a job that scared me. I walked across the lava, over the proposed route. I smothered in sulfur fumes, I ran over white-hot rocks, and sprinted through blue flames. I felt the crust give under my feet and jumped for other points which also gave way—for all I knew into an inferno of molten rock below. But I went back and told them the road could be put across in three months. They then wanted to know if I would take the job. I told them I would not, on contract, but that I would do it for them if they would pay all expenses and for my superintendence would pay me a certain sum per week. They snapped at it. So there you are; I'm the engineer in charge of this work, and am making good. Instead of getting across in three months, I will make it in between six and seven weeks.

DID you ever see lava? Hot lava, especially? It does not look like I had supposed. When it first comes from the crater it appears to be a mass of flames. At that time it is, of course, in a molten state. But it partially solidifies rapidly. Then the pressure behind breaks up this partially solid rock and rolls and tumbles it forward in a rugged mass which might be likened to a badly plowed field of some mythological giant. Portions stay boiling and spout out flames and sulfurous smoke, like miniature volcanoes. Other parts partly cool, but have no grain like natural rock or granite.

I HAVE had my troubles. No one knew anything about such a job. I had to go it blindly. The only way I have succeeded is because I know how to work the people. I know their language, their viewpoint, the arguments that get under their skin, I know when to be severe with them, and when to treat them in a patriarchal, or better said, a feudal manner. In other words, I get harmony of action from the five to six hundred laborers and thirty to forty employees I am using. I will succeed. But the troubles have been many. I have run across rock so hard that it would turn the finest chisels; it was so hot I could not use dynamite. It would burn up before even the shortest possible fuse could reach the cap. Using a chisel for fifteen or twenty minutes, it would begin to glow dull red, lose its temper, and double over under the blows like a piece of iron just taken from the forge. The rock was so hot that the men could stand on it for only a short time per trick. At one time I had gangs shoveling white-hot stone, their shovels wrapped in blue flame, and the bed of lava thundering and cracking under their feet. It is a job the like of which will probably never be seen again.

Anyway, I have gotten the line over about half-way already and when the general manager and his staff came down last Saturday and looked it over they told me they were more than satisfied and intimated if I went ahead the way I was going that there might be a substantial bonus in it for me at the end. I wonder what will happen this time to break me again? If I ever get any money and live to spend it, I think the shock will probably kill me.

WELL, that is enough of my vicissitudes. I was tickled to hear that your honeymoon had passed so gloriously, and I hope that the rest of your lives will be only a continuation of the honeymoon. I don't blame you at all for raving a bit over your wife. You have ample reason to do so. If an ornery, sour-dough artist who admits beginning to get bald-headed can get a wife like that, I wonder what a good-looking fellow like myself might do? And I can tell you, from experience, friend o' mine, you'll never meet up with the good times in other parts that you enjoy in your own teepee. I often wish that my life had been laid in different lines, but —well, there is no use bewailing the mandates of kismet. I am doomed, like the wandering Jew, to keep always on the move, and suppose I shall eventually kick in, like a desert rat—with my shoes on (if I own any) and glorying in the life I've led, even if repenting the death I die. Anyway I know that when I do kick in I will have LIVED. I'm a bit like the old-timer who had soused up with hootch for years and was finally told by the doctor that he would have to quit drinking or go blind. His reply was: "Wal, derned ef I haint seen nigh all th' world I want to see, anyhow."

I DON'T get much war news down here. I used to when I was in the Legation, but here it is scarce. I want to get into that scrap, but I've got to get a few ducats together first for my two sons in the States. From all indications I will have all kinds of time to get into it yet. Although I am getting past the age I did not think I would have great trouble getting into it, for I believe I told you that I am an ex-regular soldier from Spanish-American war times. In fact, I am a member of the Post of Spanish-American War Veterans in Everett, Washington, where I resided for a time a few years ago. I think I told you about that, did I not?

Must end this for a time and do some work.

Here is the later letter:

January 8, 1918,
San Salvador, El Salvadore, C. A.

Have tried to die of Black-Water fever—the most pernicious of fevers—worse than the yellow jack. Then I had amoebic dysentery. But I finished the job! If I had given up I might have saved my health, but I am bull-headed. I am now on my feet again and shall probably go at once to Guatemala City at the request of President Estrada Cabrera, to take charge of the reconstruction of that city. Don't know how I happened to not be in that earthquake.

MY ILLNESS left me broke again. I made a few thousand out of the job, and finished in six weeks. The Company treated me all right, but doctors, nurses, hotels and special diet got it all. I knew I couldn't live to really enjoy all that coin.

But I shall be in the States soon—along in the Spring. If I am flush, look for me. If I am broke well, I may hit the back door for a handout.

Won't write much as I have an engagement in about an hour which means some filthy lucre and I am pretty weak and nervous yet. Will write again very soon and give my address.—Brandon.

A WORD from one of our comrades on the French front. And I wonder how many of us altogether are over there doing their bit? Here's our good luck to our comrade who writes us and to all the others.

Somewhere in France.

When we arrived in this country it was sure cold and it rained or snowed pretty near all of the time, which made it worse. When the weather got a little warmer we were greeted by mud. It was mud with a capital M, for every step we would take we had to be careful so it wouldn't pull our boots off it stuck so. But now we can't complain, we're having real warm weather and most of the mud is dried up.

FRITZIE gets real fresh sometimes and throws some shells over, but he quiets down quick when the Sammies start shooting back at him. Fritzie don't like to taste his own medicine.

I've seen a couple of air fights and, believe me, it's interesting and exciting. The way those aviators can handle their machines is simply wonderful. When I read about them I used to think it was impossible, but now I've seen for myself. A German machine was brought down not far from here the other day and if you could have seen how quick the boys stripped it of souvenirs you'd have laughed.

When the anti-aircraft guns start banging away we like to see where the shells break. It looks as if little puffs of smoke were following the aeroplane but it really is the shells breaking. I like to stand and watch how close the shells land. I think it's a lucky shot that can bring one down.—Gustave Schimelfanning.

TODAY comes news that two more of our writers' brigade have joined the colors. Dr. J. U. Giesy, having made attempt after attempt and undergoing an operation in order to meet physical requirements, writes me joyfully that he has at last been commissioned in the Medical Corps of the United States Army. And from Europe comes a post-card saying, "Greeting to *Adventure* from 'Somewhere in France.'—George Rothwell Brown."

I HAD a recent letter from our comrade Harold S. Lovett, the marine who was on *H. M. S. Agamemnon* at the Dardanelles. But this letter was postmarked at New York. A previous letter, which is coming to you at one of our Camp-Fires, had told me he was now gunner on a merchant ship with one U-boat credited to his marksmanship. The other day he appeared in person and we had a good visit together and I hope to be seeing him whenever he's in port.

Arthur Sullivant Hoffman.

A FEW Camp-Fires ago Harrison R. Howard, of our writers' brigade, sent us a brief greeting as he took ship for France. Here is a word from him, now a sergeant in the —— Engineers, written from the other side, with a couple of clauses clipped out by the censor:

It's been a long trail since last I had opportunity of writing you, a trail fraught with excitement and bizarre pleasures. . . . But there's an exhilaration in it all, even the drudgery, that makes for enthusiasm and gets things done in super-American style.

UNLESS one is among that chosen few who are said to "think internationally," as it were, it is impossible, back there in America, to realize the magnitude of this noiseless engine for general accomplishment, this American Expeditionary Force, which is working twenty-four hours a day "over here." To the neophyte, at his first glance to the white light, a breath-taker, as the West has it. Those magic letters—A. E. F.! They mean a world, a literal world, a buzzing hive of activity. But the censor commands that its song, in detail, must remain unsung—yet a while . . . to look into a Camp-Fire. Doubtless, things are going on as usual, back there in the States; but it's difficult to believe it from here. It seems that America must be in a feverish state of activity, so accustomed have we become to it over here.

Taps is sounding, so I'll have to close this note.—H. R. HOWARD.

AT ONE of our Camp-Fires Edgar Young "started something" by asking "What is the spirit of adventure, particularly as considered biologically? Also, another of our comrades, Earl J. Teets, said he'd been knocking around a good deal but had never met adventure and is there any such animal? One of the replies—to both inquirers—is given below, from Charles Beadle, who, like Edgar Young, belongs to our writers' brigade:

GRAND ISLE, LA.

MY DEAR CAMP-FIRE:—The question that Edgar Young sets is most interesting. I should rather like to have a shot at it. Yet it is such a mighty big question to propound the definition of the spirit of adventure that I am going to hedge by, as politely as possible, inquiring what may be the spirits of love (sex attraction) and hunger? For does she not hunt with the same pack?

BIOLOGICALLY, I should say, that adventure (not the magazine, with due respect!) is as important as her (I say her advisedly, because she is so entrancing to a male) two sisters in the evolution of man. The purpose of definition is best served perhaps, on the principle of a pound of fact is worth, etc., by a simile. It is easy to imagine that some primeval person of the crustacea family thoroughly enjoyed his meals whatever they were, also his mate whoever she was. Is it inconceivable that the sand crab owed its existence to that very spirit of adventure worrying innumerable ancestors into finding out what was going on in that interesting land, the beach, and in another element, air?

"There's something lost behind the sand-dunes!
Go and find it!"

sang the crustacean Kipling. Get me?

As for the second regarding intellectual adventure, is not this question answered by Edgar Young? The impulse which prompted him to ask the question is the lady herself!

AS FOR Earl J. Teets I would say, in all comradeship, that I suspect that he has sailed in consort with *U. S. S. Adventure* many a time and oft, but that he has mislaid his signal-book. Has he never for example, felt a thrill during "line of battle"—even at maneuvres? If so, let him know that that was a promise of the kisses to come. And for a recipe let him take, when he be free, this recipe, which, like the patent medicine "unsolicited testimonials," I may recommend from personal experience: Take one map of the world; and with eyes blindfolded stab seven times, note countries pierced; take a coin and toss and reduce same to one: GO to that One. Never mind how, but go. If he doesn't find adventure, the Lord help him, I can not!—CHARLES BEADLE.

WHEN he wrote the story and the brief letter in January, our comrade, W. Townend, was stationed at Queenstown, Ireland, a lieutenant in the Royal Welsh Fusiliers. In May, when I write this, he may be one of those meeting the big Hun offensive. In August, when you read this, I hope that the German offensive power may be broken and that at least the beginning of their end may have dawned. It may take years, but at least we can hope that months or weeks will do it. However long it takes, I hope no soft, temporizing peace will be made until the Hun's fangs have been pulled and he ceases to be a menace to democracy, freedom and real peace. And I'm wondering what the coming struggle has in store for Townend, who gives us this story. Good luck to him and God bless him, and all the others who are fighting the good fight. Here is his word about the story:

SPIKE ISLAND, QUEENSTOWN, IRELAND.
January 12, 1918.

The main facts are accurately stated—that is, the dugout, the blocking of the doorway, shell-shock and the trench rats. I can assure you I hated the rats in France as much as I ever hated anything. —W. TOWNEND.

ALL American citizens are drawn from two sources—children and immigrants. If you want clear water in a barrel there isn't much use in trying anything else until you've stopped or clarified any streams of dirty water that may be flowing into the barrel. To put the matter baldly, both the streams that fill the barrel of American citizenship are pretty muddy. There is no sense in blaming the streams for being dirty. It is *our* job to keep them clean.

What do we do to keep these two streams clean, to ensure good American citizens instead of bad? What have *you* ever done toward it?

THE American League for Citizenship has been incorporated to afford the means of united effort toward this end, to install the teaching of real citizenship in all our schools and to limit immigration to what we can really absorb and to what will not merely pollute the water in our barrel.

HERE is a letter from Stephen Chalmers, comrade of our writers' brigade. The following I pumped out of him in the course of a long conversation on immigration and citizenship in general. He was a British subject, a Scotchman. Even though he had lived in this country quite a number of years, he would not ask for American citizenship until he felt he had been here long enough to be really assimilated, sufficiently understanding of American ideals to be a really worthy citizen of the country to which he intended to transfer his allegiance. Do you get the full force of it? This immigrant would not accept American citizenship until he felt *he* was worthy of *it!* Our laws giving citizenship to many who are *not* worthy of it, this immigrant takes the responsibility and the ideals into his own hands and makes sure that in at least one case the United States of America does not get a citizen who is unworthy.

THAT is very splendid. But doesn't it make you, one of those who determine our laws and policies, rather ashamed that the vote of this clean American citizen, or of a native-born American, is nullified by the vote of some unworthy immigrant who should never have been given citizenship? Say, for example, some German who has since been using his American citizenship as a means of hurting America and helping her enemy, Germany, the perjury of his broken oath of allegiance to us not even being punished, his American citizenship not even taken from him.

Who determines whether such things shall be? The politicians? *No!* You and I and the rest of the hundred million Americans who hold the fundamental power *always*. The politicians can do only what we let them do. You can argue a thousand years but you can never shake that fact. You can fail to use your share of the fundamental control, you can dodge your duty and be a dead weight and parasite, but you can never free yourself of the responsibility.

If our immigration laws are faulty, if some of our immigrants pollute the water in our barrel, *you* are one of those who are to blame.

THERE are many remedies that might be applied. Mr. Chalmers' letter sets forth one of them that merits your serious consideration—if you are a real American, a real believer in democracy, not a parasite, a shirker, or something worse.

SARANAC LAKE, N. Y., March 1, 1918.

. . . You know my feeling in this matter. I object to the walk-up of illiterate citizens who get first papers without a deep realization of what they are doing. During the next five years their environment is not always conducive to proper thinking and when they get second papers they are too often under the influence of this environment and are worse than no citizens at all.

I would like to see the law changed to at least two years before *any* concession is granted, and then only under the strictest examination as to integrity, intelligence, understanding of citizenship, record in the interval (to be supplied by pastor, rabbi, district police—what you please). In short, even as somebody or other served seven years for Ruth—and then some—make prospective would-be citizens regard citizenship *as a prize to be won and worth winning!*

Every vote of a bad citizen is destructive of the vote of a good citizen, and surely the American born is entitled to have his franchise protected against the influenced vote of the illiterate.—STEPHEN CHALMERS.

IN CONNECTION with his story in this issue Hugh Pendexter gives us a little historical "dope":

NORWAY, MAINE.

I have taken St. Clair's (spelled Sainclair in the old ballads) defeat and Wayne's victory over the Northwestern Confederacy for the background of this yarn. The invitation to war was given by red belts, strings and red sticks, the latter commonly being used by the Creeks and their cousins the Seminoles, and radiating from them up the Mississippi valley.

A Hidatsa Indian, living in Dakota in 1865, was held by the Indians to be a mighty magician because of his trick of producing red, ripe cherries from his mouth at any season. It is supposed he preserved them in whisky. He was known as "Cherry-in-the-Mouth." As it's never to my knowledge been played up in fiction I have transposed the trick back to 1791 for a white man to play.

Little Turtle's speech, "I am the last, etc." is a matter of history.

I HAVE shown that Bund was ransomed without narrating in detail the fact. The Indian and historical dope is O.K. Papakeecha, *alias* Flat Belly, lived and had his being. I have tried within the limited scope of the short story to sketch the horror caused by St. Clair's defeat, and the terrible possibilities for lonely cabin or settlement anywhere north of the Ohio. The Indians' turning back with their white prisoner instead of pressing on to the Ohio is true to life, as their service was purely voluntary and they could quit at any time without losing caste or inviting punishment.—HUGH PENDEXTER.

ONE of the few unwritten laws of our Camp-Fire is that, when it comes to printing, we devitalize cuss-words by using dashes to indicate them, and the same rule holds in our fiction stories. But perhaps some of you noticed that in a recent serial, "For the Flag," we let one cuss-word go as it lay. The following letter to me from the author explains the exception:

RICHMOND, VA.

I want to ask, while I think of it, one special favor regarding the story.

In chapter 26 *Billy Smith*, in speaking to the German minister of the Kaiser, says: "To hell with him and all his brood!"

Now *Billy* means this with all his heart when he says it. He doesn't mean "To —— with him;" he means "To HELL with" the murdering scoundrel. I myself meant it when I wrote it, and I'm sure that it echoes your personal sentiments. So I beg of you —please—to let the word stand when the story goes to print, and thereby bring mild comfort to the souls of the men who read it, and who in concert with you and me could voice what they feel in far stronger terms if it were permissible to put them in type.

I understand why, as a rule, you don't let down the bars to maledictory expressions in *Adventure*, but here's a case when the exception cries aloud for admission, and with a world-wide reason to stand upon.—THOMAS ADDISON.

I don't believe you'll blame me for making an exception of this case, though even where the full strength of the cussing is so strongly called for we can't keep up this exception business. For example, personally I have no brief for the Kaiser, unless it is that maybe he's insane or the helpless tool of still worse men. I can, in his case, get along with nothing more than dashes. But when it comes to Ludendorff, the Crown Prince, Hindenburg and Tirpitz it strains me a bit to be limited by dashes. If Mr. Addison can fill 'em in for the Kaiser, why shouldn't I be granted exceptions in these other cases? So there it goes. Mr. Addison's exception mustn't be considered a precedent or all the rest of us will be claiming equal privilege.

IF YOUR magazine is late in reaching you, please allow for present unsettled transportation conditions before hopping on to us. Because of war conditions we're starting the magazine out a week or ten days earlier then formerly, but troops, ammunition and supplies rightfully take precedence over magazines and the general routine of shipping is necessarily disturbed in many ways.

ON THE opposite page are some old friends of ours. W. C. Tuttle, who introduced us to *Ike*, *Magpie* and the rest of their bunch, used to be a cartoonist on a Spokane daily. Last Christmas, through his kind offices, I received a snap-shot of *Magpie et al* by way of greeting. Along with my thanks I ventured a regret that *Half-Mile Smith* and *Dirty-Shirt Jones* had so conspicuously slighted me and later was delighted to receive, *via* Mr. Tuttle's pen, a photo from Piperock's leading photographer. It appears on page 184 and bore on its back this legend:

DIRTY-SHIRT JONES (standing) and HALF-MILE SMITH.

Being as they were not in Xmas group, they willingly posed for this photo. They both send regards. The negative was retouched a little too much but otherwise it is good.

I thought you might like to see just what these old friends look like.

RESOLVED THAT WE WISH ARTHUR S. HOFFMAN A MERRY CHRISTMAS.
SIGNED—
BUCK
TELESCOPE
MULEY
HEN
IKE
MAGPIE
CHUCK

FOLLOWING our Camp-Fire custom, Gladys E. Johnson, on the occasion of her first story in our magazine, rises and introduces herself to us, getting, I know, the friendly welcome we always have for the few women who gain membership in our writers' brigade:

It's a handicap, being a woman. That highly original remark is called into being by my nosing this little biography of mine in among the Indian fighters, the explorers and the "knights of empire" generally, whose histories go to make up the Camp-Fire.

THRILLING adventures have a way of side-stepping the female of the species, as a usual thing. It's most discouraging; all my life I have been trying to put myself in the way of thrillers only to have them jump clear over my head or burst into nothing at the most intense moment. But in spite of my efforts, the only thrilling adventure which has happened to me in the last two years was turning an automobile, containing five people, on its side, while driving at forty-seven miles an hour. Even here my diabolical good luck stayed with me, for, miraculous as it sounds, no one was even mussed up. But at that, my passengers on that occasion unanimously agreed that it was adventure enough for them.

Since then, though most of my spasmodic vacations have been spent in the mountains trying to trap adventures—and the mountains of California can be pretty wild—so far, the cougars and grizzlies have been gentlemen enough to overlook me.

I HAD the same good misfortune as a child. You'd think that a childhood spent largely in logging-camps could boast some dramatic moments, but all I brought away was an unsatisfied longing for excitement and a never-forgotten picture of that beautiful, wild California background.

I have found the dwelling-place of adventure many times, shortly after it moved out. Last Summer I trailed it, by the aid of gasoline, through this State down into Mexico. At a bull-fight in that country I almost caught up with it, but after the one dramatic moment, occasioned by the "toro" nearly hooking a matador, the bull-fight simmered down to a rather tame affair—and I'm not bloodthirsty either, as evidenced by my nearly turning the car over a second time to avoid a ground squirrel on the road through the Mojave Desert.

THERE was only one time when I was living on all six cylinders and having the thrills of my own heroes. This was three years ago when I was working on a San Francisco newspaper. Having too little patience and too much sense of the ridiculous, I graduated from "sob-sister" on the paper to a sort of female trouble-hunter. The paper embarked on several reform campaigns; the most exciting being an exposé of the fake fortune-tellers and clairvoyants in this city. As I was playing detective for the paper in an effort to obtain proof of their "bunco" methods, I, for once, had my fill of thrills, especially when I was trailed and eventually confronted with my real identity in a clairvoyant's office. For a moment I expected to have to do the movie stunt of kicking the window out and jumping on to an electric sign a story below, for I was pretty unpopular in that office right then. Afterward, I laughed to remember that in the excitement of the moment I thought with true stage newspaper loyalty, "Anyway, it'll look fine in the evening editions." Then once more Fate backed down and I was allowed to walk out of the door like any other mortal.

THE newspaper work was the best sort of training for the fiction writing, which I immediately afterward took up. I haunted the police-courts and the waterfront and came in contact with some curious and rather gruesome characters. Many an idea for a story was born while I listened to the strange result of tracing down a news story to make a "feature" out of it or stumbled over some novel and haunting situation which had no news value.

A year of reporting and I took the jump—left the paper and launched into the fiction game and now I am putting my "heroes" through some of the strange experiences I have heard, and introducing into my stories some of the queer people I have met.

AFTER all, it's pretty much of an adventure just living in San Francisco. It's the "story-book city," with its Chinatown, its queer, sordid Greek quarter, its waterfront, whose habitués are recruited from the Seven Seas, its Barbary Coast and its Kearney Street—the Rialto of the Adventurers, Will Irwin calls it.

And, Gelett Burgess says that anything can happen in San Francisco, so, who knows, maybe I will still bump into my hair-raising adventure!—
GLADYS E. JOHNSON.

A LETTER, written some time ago, from one of our comrades who is finding army life good for more than preparation for fighting:

LINE 82, SECTION E, KELLY FIELD, No. 1, TEXAS
March 31, 1918.

Have been transferred from the Medical Department to the Aviation Corps. The rumor had it that the Detachment at the Base Hospital was to remain until the end of the war, and I got busy right away, applied for a transfer and through special recommendation from my colonel received same in six days.

I FIND —— hot and desolate in a way, but we sure do not get a whole lot of time to worry. The thing that seems to worry the boys here is that they can't get to France quick enough. And I cheerfully second the motion.

Do I like the life in the Army? You bet I do. It has done me a whole lot of good. In civilian life you may be able to stay up nights and have a good time and all that, but I prefer this. There is nothing like getting up early in the morning, feeling real good. It is the best and strictest school in the world, this army of ours, and with the material we have on hand and with the training they get, to tell the truth I can't see how the Kaiser is going to win this war.

I am expecting to be sent across in a very short time. Trade tested for the Camouflage Section and passed the test. So I am expecting to get a pretty close view of the Huns.—CARL G. LINDHULT.

WHEN Frank H. Huston talks about Indians he knows what he's talking about. Here's a letter to us from him which "Uncle Frank" labels as follows: "On Roping the Legs and Other Maunders."

All squaws amongst the plains Indians, who considered virtue as an essential jewel, "roped" themselves. The manner varied according to individual taste and the necessities of the moment. At times a thong at ankles or knees allowing them to shuffle along and at others an elaborate arrangement from ankles to waist with variations. An analogy may be seen with the Oriental custom of spiked belts and padlock with this difference; the squaws roped for self-protection, as the penalty for violation of a roped squaw was death. No woman old or young would leave the teepee without roping. Should they do so it would be advertising that they were common property, and a husband, brother, father or son would stand by and see them used like soiled doves without redress.

IT SHOULD be understood that the teepee and all pertaining to it, even the *travois* and ponies of burden were the property of the squaws; all the buck owned was his war-ponies, clothes and weapons of war and chase. In the home the woman was superior and could throw out the buck, even a big chief, and chuck his possessions at his head, as was occasionally done, not, however, if the buck was a good provider. As a protection against abuse the squaw could and did, even before her buck's eyes, propose that some other buck make up her dowry and take her as his squaw.

WHAT the whites called buying a wife was really a form of the European dowry. In some tribes a suitor would tie his pony near his adored's teepee; if she fed and watered it it was equivalent to saying yes. In others he left game at the entrance of the teepee; if she took it in and cooked it he was accepted. In others he made a rude reed whistle and at dusk would tootle for his charmer. If she, like Barkis. was willing, she would steal out, roped however, squat alongside him and with a blanket wrapped around them pulled over their heads they would sit for hours in seeming silence.

Sometimes a dozen flutes would be going at once, but no maiden ever seemed to mistake the wrong buck. I once heard the squaw of a poor hunter telling a buck in front of her husband that she liked him better than she did her own man and for him to give her man the amount of her dowry and she would move to his teepee, while all the while her buck sat with passive face taking it as a matter of course, which it really was.

THE whites introduced buying of wives, but for a long time the Indians thought they were only complying with Indian customs and were sore when the whites would go away and leave their squaws and progeny for the tribe to support.

Love in its highest sense appeared to be unknown; the relations were purely sexual and the whole thing to the acute observer appeared like a partnership. His duties were to protect, obtain game and skins, and to war; hers to prepare food, cloth, house and bedding from the skins he obtained and to do what slight tillage was done, to furnish wood and water—everything, in fact, that would leave the buck liberty to perform his duties, and each was proud and jealous of his or her prerogatives, these being sharply defined. Both squaws and bucks despised the whites because the latter did work pertaining to squaws and therefore seemed to lose caste, as one might say.

THE dog-soldiers were a sort of police, at times under direction of the elders, but having a close relation to the medicine-men who also directed them at times. They appeared to be a sort of militant neophyte, if one may use that term, and were executioners, preservers of law and order, and had various other duties.

The Dakotoh being of the Algonquin stock (original habitat New York and Pennsylvania, driven out by the Iroquois Confederacy), carried with them many of the customs of their original locality. One may see the analogy between the dog-soldiers and the Eries (cats) of the Six Nations, but the Eries were more strictly of the medicine ilk than the dog-soldiers.

A buck could take a scalp, make a coup, steal a horse, kill a grizzly and get his feather, but to reach the full rank of brave he must undergo the ordeal of the Sun Dance, which, if he passed satisfactorily, gave him his three feathers, marriage, the seat in council and the right to form a band of his own and be a chief if he could.

A STRONG high post was planted with thongs depending from the top like a May-pole. Certain preliminaries being complied with, the medicine-men slid a sharp knife under the breast muscles and a skewer, being passed through, was attached to the thongs. The candidate then danced and threw himself backward, the object being to tear or burst the flesh and muscles and thus free him. Cut the flesh one could not; it must be torn by your own exertions, and if one fainted or succumbed otherwise to the agony, he was released, dressed as, and took his place amongst the squaws. Buffalo skulls on thongs were sometimes similarly attached to the muscles at the shoulder-blades and the embryo brave danced around, dragging them after him, until the tortured flesh ruptured and released him. Some took on both at once front and rear. It was advisable to placate the medicine-man in Tammany fashion in order that he should not make the slit too close to the bones but shallow so that by strong exertions the flesh could be torn in a few hours or a day at most.

THE wounds left horrible scars, as any old-timer can testify. Rain-in-the-Face incurred the enmity of the conjurer who "slit" him and the latter ran his knife close to the bone and made a very long slit, front and back. Old Rain, however, managed in three days to burst the last and gained a wonderful renown. Rain was *not* a chief, but had the standing of one through his famous feat of endurance and also his ability. He told Tom Custer he would take his (Custer's) heart out and eat it, which he did later, and young Standing Horse, for one, never blamed him for so doing. But Rain, like Bull himself, had no use for *any* white. Two wise, very wise, and far-seeing men.

The "noblest Roman" was, of course, Red Cloud, but he antedates the former twain. Red was never whipped but once and then quit for good and gave his voice for peace always. The spirit was willing but he saw the futility of further hostilities and bowed to the inevitable. Will some millionaire erect a statue of him? The Lee of the Sioux.

When George Custer busted Black Kettle's band in Winter many Indians froze to death during the "session" having run into the brush stark naked from their beds with only their weapons.

THERE were so many delicate shades in Indian custom that no outsider ever mastered them all as did those to the manner or manor born. Frank Gruard, perhaps, excepted. I wish I could remember the buffalo hunt, the watchers, the procession to the first killed, the pipe-bearer carrying the uncased pipe on extended palms to the carcass and the pipe's return in its case; the ritual on starting, at the carcass, and the word given and the hunters darting forward; the partition of the carcass according to ritual, and the squaws and dogs and pickaninnies following to skin and carve the meat. And the good feast afterward—hump, marrow, tongue, milk-guts, suet and, as a *bonne bouche*, an unborn calf boiled in a paunch with its contents. Everybody's face, hands, arms and front bloody and greasy, but all happy. And later the squaws pounding the dried meat and suet to powder and stuffing it into skin and gut casings like Brobdingnagian sausage; the pemmican that beat any soldier's emergency ration ever contrived; good cold and raw or cooled and hot, strong meat for a strong people.

BUFFALO by thousands here in the hills; elk, deer, black and white tail antelope; prairie chicks; underfoot, camas for the digging; fish in the streams; no game laws or wardens; a blanket or buffalo robe, bag of salt, and gun, flint and steel and "Paradise enow." All gone past, as though it never existed! In its place a bread-card, the factory whistle, the big bell at the home ranch, a dad-blasted Bostonese with his imitation English accent or a hunk or dago or wap with a stinking devil-wagon. Cheyenne "Ki ye yi yuii!!!" silence. "Hy yoh hy yah hyyyy!"—*Finis*—UNCLE FRANK.

A LETTER written some months ago from a Canadian comrade doing war duty off the Atlantic coast, a man who was among the salvagers after the Halifax disaster:

C. D. 13, care H. M. C. S. ——.

This life is dreary and montonous, drifting around day and night in a ninety-foot boat. Overcast skies, gray-green waves, all add to the dreariness at this time of the year and ice-covered decks make life miserable. And oh joy! when your shift is done, down to the eight-by-twelve cabin and, hugging the oil-heater and sprawled out in as comfortable a position as you can possibly get, you grab your old favorite magazine and follow the adventures of some unfortunate cuss toiling through death and gore and hairbreadth escapes!

Our boat is number thirteen and has thirteen of a crew, and our little Hotchkis six-pounder is number thirteen! So hooray for the hoodoo!—W. MCKENZIE HAINES.

AS TO the copy of our magazine that has had more adventures than any other copy. That's a hard matter on which to get full data, but it is certainly interesting to record the reports as they come in from time to time:

The first *Adventure* I read I found in an old hut not far from Mexico City. That was early in 1915. I also found one that I had read in an old mine-shaft in West Virginia. On the inside I found these words in pencil, "Barney Mack carried this book from China to Frisco, then here." A rather long trip if it's true.—ROY J. WILLIAMS.

WHAT about conditions in this country after the war? There will be big changes and there's already discussion of various problems. Good. But why talk about doing this and that if we're not fit to do them? It is merely building on sand to attempt betterments if we ourselves, through whom they must be put into practise, are not sound and trustworthy. No -ism or -ology or concrete improvement ever suggested can withstand the dry-rot of bad citizenship, of *our* bad citizenship. Why not begin at the foundation?—ARTHUR SULLIVANT HOFFMAN.

TWO interesting lines of information from a Nova Scotian comrade, in response to questions previously asked by some of you:

Antigonish, Nova Scotia.

A few issues back you had an inquiry as to the feasibility of crossing the Atlantic alone, in a boat. Some of your readers in Gloucester, Mass., can give you detailed information regarding "Centennial" Johnson, who did this in 1876, and Howard Blackburn, who made the crossing in 1900. Blackburn's journey is made especially noteworthy by the fact that he had lost nearly all his fingers from frost-bite while astray in a dory on the Banks some years before.

You also had an inquiry as to the meaning of the African "Tagati." Rider Haggard uses it in the sense of "bewitched." If you can locate Edward A. Owens, who worked at Drake's bakery in Roxbury, Mass., ten years ago, and previous to that served some time in the Rhodesian Mounted Police (this may not be the official name of the corps), he may be able to tell you something.—A. A. MORRISON.

SOME time ago I received from one of our New Zealand comrades an interesting letter intended for our Camp-Fire. Unfortunately, though I hate to say it about any man, our friend's handwriting is almost as bad as my own. So I held his letter till I could send him a typewritten copy for him to go over and correct as to our misreadings and doubts, particularly as to proper names.

Though I've waited some time, the corrected copy has not come and I'm risking giving you our very doubtful "translation" of the letter. Probably his answer or my inquiry has gone astray somewhere in the thousands of miles between us and, as another exchange would take a couple of months, here goes:

Masterton, New Zealand.

This is a yarn of the good old days before the *pakeha* came much to our shores—when we ate those we conquered in our tribal wars—and, when meat ran short and no fight was toward, we killed a fat and young slave for the larder—*Ai!* Those days are gone forever and our young men train no more to fight the tribes' quarrels, but sit in the shade of some totara tree and drink liquor. An occasional whaler seeking to fill up with mats, carved woodwork, dried heads or greenstone (jade) weapons or ornaments after an unsuccessful cruise was our only visitor from the blue seas and the lands beyond.

BUT to my tale—the greatest of all our Maori chiefs was Te Raupara, often called by the *pakehas* the Maori Napoleon. At the time of which I write he was installed on the Island of Kapiti just on the southwest coast of the N. Island of Te Roto Aaua (N. Z.) and had conquered all his enemies to the north and south with the exception of Taumaranui, a Rantira on Banks Peninsula where Akaroa now stands. Three times had Te Raupara's war canoes dared the raging straits in new endeavor to bring Taumaranui and his tribe to their knees, and three times had the vigilance of the scouts of the Southern Ranitira foiled their efforts by giving the tribe timely warning to retreat. Te Raupara had sworn by his *Atua* (God) that he would sooner or later make an example of Taumaranui, and his chance came thuswise:

ONE fine Summer's morning there sailed into the Bay of Kapiti, the brig *Elizabeth*, commanded by Captain Stewart and John McLean, first mate. Her holds were only half full, as the whales were not running, and she hoped to procure some trade from the natives to fill up her empty hatches.

On shore went Captain Stewart and had a long palaver with Te Raupara and the bargain was struck that for the use of the brig for six weeks, sailed by her own crew, the Maoris would give as much trade as Captain Stewart could take.

At dawn, five hundred dusky warriors, armed to the teeth, were in the hold of the ship and the vessel under way, heading toward Akaroa, with Te Raupara and his savage lieutenant, Te Kuiti, in the cabin. Taumaranui and his *hapu* (tribe) welcomed the appearance of the whaler, for did not the *pakeha* bring cloth and beads and guns and *waipiro* (strong drink) and exchange these commodities for what the natives had to offer in return?

THE first canoe that put off was welcomed on board and the crew were shown down into the hold. Soon after, the Chief Taumaranui, his wife, and daughter, a young girl about seventeen, were welcomed on board by Captain Stewart and shown down into the cabin. To them entered quickly, Te Raupara and Te Kuiti. Taumaranui knew then he was trapped. Te Raupara jeered at and mocked him, saying the wife would be thrown to the sharks, and the girl, after he had finished with her, would be given to the rank and file.

As Te Raupara and his lieutenant left the cabin to seek irons, Taumaranui spoke in a low tone to his wife, bidding her strangle the girl and hang herself, and, when Te Raupara returned, the room contained only Taumaranui and two corpses. Taumaranui was securely handcuffed and ironed and a hook with a string to the roof of the cabin put through the fleshy part of his throat so that only by standing on tip-toe could he ease the strain.

Te Raupara's five hundred warriors made short work of the defenseless and unsuspecting tribe, burned their *pah* and returned, the voyage back to Kapiti taking three days.

On arrival here the luckless Taumaranui was tortured to death with red-hot ramrods.

CAPTAIN STEWART, claiming his promised cargo as hire for the use of his ship, was consigned to the Hot Place and the brig *Elizabeth* sailed for home half empty. A week later a King's ship called at Kapiti for water and the story of Taumaranui's death was told. Eighteen days later the *Elizabeth* was summoned to stop by a shot across her bows from *H. M. S. Bon Adventure* and a boat manned by blue-jackets and a lieutenant boarded her. The lieutenant was precise and formal:

"This is the brig *Elizabeth*, Captain Stewart commander?"

"Yes."

"Are you Captain Stewart?"

"I am."

"Take him, men; also the mate."

And in less than five minutes Captain Stewart and McLean were swinging at the yard-arm. A fitting end for such dastards.—FRONTIERSMAN 6980 L. F.

HAVE a look at these figures showing what the American people are, based on the last census, 1910. Don't they give you something to think about? Doesn't it seem to you that, when we've earned peace by uncompromising victory, there will be some man-sized problems for us to handle here at home?

Native parentage, white . . .	.50,240,000	54%
Foreign " " . . .	.12,950,000	14%
Foreign born	.13,400,000	15%
Mixed parentage	. 6,000,000	5%
Negro	. 9,830,000	11

SCALPING. Here we are again. First some reports gleaned by D. Wiggins from old-timers in his vicinity:

Salem, Ore.

In regard to the scalping problem have been making inquiries.

Close to my home live three old frontiersmen, and I applied to all of them to learn whether they had ever heard or known directly of any one who had survived scalping. I refer to a complete recovery, of course, not a lingering death of several days.

MR. F. A. THOMPSON, who helped solve the Little Crow problem in the great massacre in '63 said he had seen one young squaw who had been scalped in an inter-tribal raid and had recovered completely. Mr. Tompkins, who was out in the Western Territories in the early and unsettled times, met in Pierre in '76 a man who had been scalped two years previously. He was all right then, however. Uncle Jim Hall did not know of a single instance that came under his immediate observation of a scalping victim living, but had heard of a few cases. He did not seem to have any great faith in them, however.

I am not able to get to any of the writers on the old frontier, such as Gen. Dodge, etc., so can not say just how they regard the matter. But I think it was a very unusual occurrence for any one who had been so pruned by the red brother to live to lecture on it.

Both men who are mentioned as having seen the persons scalped told me that a piece of skin about the size of a silver dollar has been taken from the exact top of the head, the scalp-lock being located there.—D. WIGGINS.

P. S.—The odd character of whom I recently wrote you, "Injun Dave" Sitler, lived in Ohio instead of Iowa, as I stated. He was drowned by the capsizing of his canoe in the 40's, I understand. I do not know what became of the peculiar string of trophies the Indian he killed had kept.—D. W.

DO YOU remember one of Edgar Young's stories, "A Spur for a Jaded Nag," published a year or so ago? About a down-and-out beach-combing American doctor in South America who, dragged part way back to decency by another American, manages to meet an emergency by performing a difficult operation though still a nervous wreck. Well, it stirred old memories in at least one of us and brought us the following letter.

Now it would seem, off-hand, as if our magazine must be responsible for starting a good many boys under eighteen or twenty out into the world adventuring. Doubtless it does help along in many cases, though in each one the tinder must already be there waiting for some final spark to touch it off. But I think that our magazine restrains as many of these cases as it starts. Particularly at our Camp-Fire and in "Ask Adventure" it is real adventurers who talk and the result is that the seamy as well as the glamorous side of actual adventuring is made pretty plain. We don't hold up adventuring as just a happy joy-ride.

AND I've noticed we do quite a bit in the way of pointing morals without doing any "preaching" and often without intention of even pointing a moral. For instance, in the old days when we had our "Wanted" department, do you remember how many expeditions carefully specified that they wanted no men who were "booze-fighters" and so on? The moral pointed had especially strong value because it not only wasn't "preaching" but was merely the businesslike statement of a lesson learned by hard experience—that booze and reliability don't generally travel far together even in adventurous undertakings, perhaps particularly in adventurous undertakings. You know how it is with boys—that kind of thing will register harder than sermons, especially when it comes from the real adventurers themselves.

TRUTH, I think, is always safe medicine in the long run and, since it gives the facts, instead of only the glamour, of adventuring, I feel our magazine need not worry. We keep it clean and we give facts and treat them as facts. Personally, I wouldn't give a hoot for the kind of virtue, or for the method of teaching virtue, that depends on keeping the subject's eyes blindfolded to facts, leaving him to meet these facts, as he *will* meet them sooner or later, ignorant, unwarned and unprepared. The ostrich system of facing the world is considerably lacking in common sense. And the tender and inflated virtue that tries to "shield" a young chap from sight or hearing of the dangers he'll surely have to face some day seems to me merely an empty bladder too full of wind for its own safety and for that of the young chap. Talking about evils and smacking your lips over them is one thing; treating them like any other facts is quite another matter.

Well, here's Captain Brand's letter and it happens that, when I asked him whether we could have it at Camp-Fire and over his own name, his reason for saying yes was that it might possibly help herd the young fellows away from some of the things the older hands have found don't pay.

La Crosse, Wis.

This is to congratulate Mr. Young and perhaps the following may be of interest to him:

TEN years ago I deserted the British bark *Randova* on account of the *pisco* that was given to me by the hoboes of the water-front. Having been apprenticed on his ship, Captain Ed. Shaw, a kind-hearted gentleman, tried his best to get me back. However, the beach-combers had their hands on me; their alluring tales of the gold so easily to be found in the mountains, together with the *pisco* that first fires you on and next makes you sluggish, seemed to me far better than the strenuous voyage on a windjammer homeward bound around Cape Horn.

However, to relate the experiences we had walking the railroad track before we hit Oroya would take too much space. In Oroya I was lucky enough to make a favorable impression on the train conductor, thanks to the little Spanish I had learned in school, thus securing a ride to Cerro de Pasco, leaving the rest of the party behind, for which I later had reason to thank my lucky star. Arrived in Cerro de Pasco, I got work but soon the altitude got me. If it would not have been for the kind-hearted American boys and especially for a German, named Schmidt, who ran a saloon in Smelter and passed the hat for me, I have my doubts about sitting here and writing this to-day.

However, on my return back to Lima, a kind-hearted lady who ran a boarding-house took me in and kept me until I signed articles on the liner *Setos*.

When I arrived home my father looked twice before he really believed that it was me, because my associates (the beach-combers) had found out that my parents were wealthy and had written blackmailing letters demanding five hundred pounds for my release. Dad had moved heaven and earth, besides the Consular officers, and had not found a trace of me.

NOW I have finished, it strikes me to know just what made me pick up the pen; however, it must be that Mr. Young, in writing fiction, struck almost one hundred per cent. of golden truth. Furthermore, it may give a little warning to the boys of the age from fifteen to seventeen, looking for adventure, to wait a little and consider hard if they hear anybody roar about the finding of gold, etc., and hear all you need to do is get there and pick it up. A little more thinking and a little less liquor will often save much worry and many tears.—CAPTAIN WM. R. P. BRAND.

I'VE heard that several hundred copies of our magazine go on board one American battle-ship every issue when she's where she can get them. It seems rather a large number for a crew, but of course I hope it's true. The man who told me is not a liar or even a fool, though anybody can get strung once in a while. On the other hand, it's certainly true that a large number of our Navy men, men and officers, are members of our Camp-Fire. The *Arkansas*, for example, seems to carry quite a few of us. I remember several letters not long ago from comrades aboard her and here's a greeting to Camp-Fire from one of her crew who had previously served on merchant ships. In a postscript he suggests that he'd be glad to hear from Camp-Fire comrades. We have his real name, of course, and will forward letters addressed to "Texas" in our care.

U. S. S. Arkansas.

I am writing you a few lines to let you know how I am getting along. Yes, I have been over and back quite a few times. It sure is an interesting game. playing with the subs. Yes, we lost in one game. It was the S.S. —— (can't tell you what ship it was), but we got away. Believe me, brothers, New York sure does look good. Now, that's saying some.

Well, I'll close now as there isn't much to say. Wishing you all the luck in the world for those that are to go across, I remain, Sincerely, a brother, ——

The Most Popular Stories in Our Magazine for 1917

IT IS late to be giving the results of our annual vote by readers on the ten most popular stories published in our magazine during 1917, but I've been out of the running on account of health during most of 1918 thus far and this is one of the things that didn't get done when it should have been done.

The prominent feature about the 1917 results is that the vote was far more widely distributed than on 1916, showing a much larger number of stories that registered hard with readers.

In the following a serial is indicated by (S), a novel by (N), a novelette by (n). In addition to the ten best are given, for honorable mention, the ten receiving the next highest number of votes:

1. Penitentiary Post (N)—Kathrene and Robert Pinkerton..... 11,550
2. Gaston Olaf and Big Business (S)—Henry Oyen..................... 11,319
3. Hira Singh's Tale (S)—Talbot Mundy.. 11,109
4. The Petals of Lao Tse (N)—J. Allan Dunn.................... 10,374
5. Longhorns (N)—William Patterson White.......... 9,954
6. A Man and His Name (N)—Norman Springer................. 8,148
7. Claymore (S)—Arthur D. Howden Smith 7,938
8. Dangerous Men (N)—Gordon Young.. 6,531
9. The Soul of a Regiment—Talbot Mundy 6,426
10. Fire Mountain (S)—Norman Springer.. 6,195

11. Finished (S)—H. Rider Haggard....... 5,922
12. Rotorua Rex (S)—J. Allan Dunn..... 4,662
13. The Ninth Man—Edgar Young....... 4,074
14. The Damned Old Nigger—Talbot Mundy.................. 4,032
15. From the Seas (n)—J. Allan Dunn 3,989
16. On the Account (n)—J. Allan Dunn... 3,528
17. Nobody's Island (N)—Beatrice Grimshaw............... 3,129
18. The Epic of Silver King—Arthur James Hayes.............. 3,066
19. The Wave-Bound (N)—Samuel Alexander White........... 3,045
20. Pikers Afloat (n)—Walt McDougall.... 2,814

Of course there are a good many factors that play a part in such a ranking of stories. A story read a month ago leaves on the mind a more vivid impression than does an equally good story read eleven months ago. A long story has the big advantage of size and weight over a short one. A story read next to an unusually good one is likely to suffer by comparison more than it deserves. But, all in all, such a vote as ours furnishes an invaluable guide in helping the editors make our magazine provide the kinds of story our readers want.

As last year, we give also a list of the shorter stories by themselves. Those marked with a star are of less than ten thousand words; the others are of ten thousand to twenty thousand.

1. The Soul of a Regiment*—Talbot Mundy.................... 6,426
2. The Ninth Man—Edgar Young....... 4,074
3. The Damned Old Nigger—Talbot Mundy.................... 4,032
4. On the Account—J. Allan Dunn...... 3,528
5. The Epic of Silver King*—Arthur James Hayes.............. 3,066
6. Precedents in Piperock*—W. C. Tuttle 2,793
7. Jack Grey, Second Mate—William Hope Hodgson............ 2,689
8. The Measure of a Man—William Dudley Pelley............. 2,688
9. The Blue Wolf*—Arthur James Hayes. 2,226
10. A Spur for a Jaded Nag*—Edgar Young.................... 1,974

11. Contraband Matrimony—Arthur D. Howden Smith........... 1,932
12. The Island of Changing Shapes—H. A. Lamb..................... 1,911
13. Nerves of Iron*—W. C. Tuttle........ 1,743
14. Honest to Doughgod*—W. C. Tuttle... 1,701
15. The Yardstick*—Edgar Young........ 1,659
16. A Little Song that He Knew*—Hapsburg Liebe.................. 1,639
17. Kinnickinnick*—Hugh Pendexter 1,638
18. Ritter's Pond*—E. E. Harriman...... 1,555
19. The Last Wire*—Russell A. Boggs..... 1,554
20. The Six Silk Shirts of Silver Sam*—J. Allan Dunn.................... 1,533

ONE fact in the above is noteworthy—"The Soul of a Regiment" ranks ninth among all the one hundred and seventy published during the year, and ranks first of all among all the shorter stories. And, as stated at the time, "The Soul of a Regiment" was *re*-published in 1917, having first appeared in our magazine some five years before.

The annual vote by readers is both interesting and valuable. Be making your selections for the vote on our 1918 stories. It's your chance to help in editing our magazine and to make its stories a bit more to your own personal taste.

AND now a letter from Hugh Pendexter referring in part to statements concerning scalping and other Indian matters that we've previously heard at Camp-Fire. Who knows who rode the horse with four white feet? Who knows anything about the theory that Romans landed at Pemaquid and built paved streets there? I had thought the Romans were among the few people who had not discovered America before Columbus did.

Norway, Maine.

"Plains tribes did not shave head." Pawnee shaved the head except for a ridge. They plucked out beard and eyebrows.

THE practise of scalping was originally confined to a small area in East and on St. Lawrence River, comprising, practically, region held by Iroquois and Muskhogean tribes; absent from New England and most of Atlantic coast, and "was unknown until comparatively recent times throughout whole interior and the Plains area" (James Mooney). "A small, circular patch at root of the scalp-lock, just back of the crown," usually taken (J. M.). The whole skin of head was removed only when the practitioner was not hampered for time, then it was cut into smaller scalps and used to embellish war-shirts, leggings, etc. After a scalp was cleaned of loose flesh it was mounted on a hoop, six inches in diameter, made fast with sinews and carried at end of rod or pole. The skin, when dry, was painted red, or red and black, half and half. Hair rebraided and decorated. Given to women to carry in dance. No particular value after that. Might be tied to bridle, used for "medicine," or thrown away. See Smithsonian Rep., 1906-1907, for treatment of whole subject. Probably the greatest achievement was to throw away arms and grapple barehanded with foe.

RED CLOUD was principal chief of Oglala Teton Sioux of Pine Ridge Reservation, largest band of Sioux nation. He was the most famous chief of the tribe. Born at Forks of Platte, Nebraska, 1822. Died at Pine Ridge, December 10, 1909. Father died of rum; son rose to fame by sheer merit. Surrounded Ft. Phil Kearny with two thousand warriors, killed Capt. Fettermen and eighty-one men December 21, 1866. Fought second battle in August, 1867. Not a wagon passed during all this time. In 1868 demanded that Kearny, Ft. Reno on Powder, and Ft. C. F. Smith on Big Horn be abandoned and no further efforts made to open Montana road. These demands were basis of the treaty, the Sioux fixing limits of their country. One of most notable Indian victories ever won. Red Cloud had eighty coups to his credit. He ranked high in military strategy and was deserving great renown as a statesman. Keynote to character was patriotism. Mooney writes of him, "most courtly chief and a natural born gentleman, with a bow as graceful as that of a Chesterfield."

IT WOULD be almost always correct in saying any Indian name of a tribe meant "those people," etc. But *Dakota* is translated "allies" in "Handbook of American Indians," issued by Smithsonian Institution. Kiowa, "principal people." Pawnee name for themselves was (God forgive me for doing it) Chahiksichahika, meaning "men of men." Cherokee called themselves Ani-Yun-wiya, meaning "real people." And so on through the list if you take the Indian name for himself. The traveler goes to tribe A and guesses at its name, going by sound, or gives it a name because of some characteristic, viz., Gros Ventres, "big bellied." He asks for name of tribe B, over beyond. If A is friendly with B it will give A's name for B, descriptive, "cave people," etc. If at war, "an adder." Traveler accepts that name, goes to tribe B and inquires for tribe C. Same process, B's and C's names for themselves often being ignored. But if B's own name for itself be learned it will invariably be translated to show they're the real guys.

IT WAS stated that Kiowa, Comanche and Pawnee spring from same stock. Kiowa presents distinct linguistic stock and gives its name to the family. Comanche is Shoshonean, springing from Wyoming Shohoni. A confederate of Kiowa since 1795, and this intimate relation at first led students, perhaps, to believe the two were racially related. The Pawnee belongs to Caddoan family.

Food habits depended on nature of supply. Northern part of continent living was three-fourths animal, southern part three-fourths vegetable. Where fish could be had the Indians ate fish. Where only snakes and lizards they dined accordingly. Religious customs sometimes influenced uses of certain foods. The Apache and Navaho would not (probably will not today) eat flesh of bear or beaver or fish, the same being taboo.

WHO knows anything about who rode the horse with four white feet at Custer's battle of Little Big Horn? Dr. McChesney, army surgeon, identifies the soldier as Captain French, Seventh Cavalry. Red Horse, in his account of the battle, thought it was Custer but was not positive. Said he was the bravest man the Sioux ever saw in battle after many years of fighting many brave men. I have Red Horse's whole story of the fight, but it struck me as remarkable any warrior of experience should fail to identify Custer offhand. My clinched fists are pressed ag'in breastbone, palms down, they separate in outward, downward curve to sides. "Done," "Finished," or "That is all."—PENDEXTER.

P. S.—Squaw and papoose from Narragansett. Learned from whites by West Indians. Skunk into Neg, from Abnaki. Latin, *pupus*, "child," similar to papoose. Recall the theory of Romans landing at Pemaquid and building paved streets? Maybe they brought the term in, to filter into English through Narragansett. What?—PENDEXTER.

ALREADY we have had at Camp-Fire some of the tributes to Jack London from various of our comrades. Here are a few more of those that came in. Jack London's hold upon the admiration and affection of men who themselves know the strong, rugged, struggling side of life is remarkable and striking—and deserved.

JACK LONDON
(In Memoriam)

Strong, virile, self-made, he was a man. Only a brave, dauntless soul could have succeeded in such a bitter struggle to rise from obscurity to the fame that was and is his. But once in a generation is there born a man with his indomitable spirit. Think of what he had to contend with—ignorance, and poverty, and the lowest of environment. Yet, single-handed and alone, he fought on and won! He conquered every obstacle that beset his path.

IT IS said that the years are but seconds as reckoned by Eternity's clock, so it is a fitting simile to say that Jack London flashed like a brilliant meteor across the literary sky and was gone. His passing is mourned from the little cabins on the bleak Yukon to the balmy isles in the South Seas. He will not be forgotten. His work will always stand as a light, an inspiration, to countless thousands and thousands of men for bravery and red-blooded manhood. He regained for them their lost heritage—adventure! His best book unwritten, yet written, is "The Call of the Strong."

He died young in years, but not in experience, in emotion, in travel, in knowledge of humanity and the world. He had seen more of land and sea, of life and mankind, at forty than have most of us at three score and ten years. So in that sense of the word it may be said of him that he was old, that his best work had been planned and finished. It is a comfort to think so, at least.

I fancy that he was ready, even eager, to take the long, long trail, to start on the "greatest adventure of all."—GUY M. STEALEY.

JACK LONDON

During the alluring hours of the night of December 5, 1916, the pale and silent messenger tapped silently, steadily and persistently upon the chamber door of the "house of clay" of our erstwhile friend and fellow-comrade, Jack London, issuing to him a sealed summons, carrying back the soul to the God who gave it.

TO HAVE known Jack London was indeed to have been bettered along life's highways—to have looked into those alert, yet sad eyes was an indescribable pleasure. I knew Jack London, and to him I was as a "struggler." In his own language, "I know your kind, boy—just digging like old Buck for a toe-hold; I know your kind, for I have beaten out the same pathway." I knew him when he, too, was "struggling for an existence," when he was in and out, up and down, and, in all the years, not once did I know of Jack London weakening, breaking down or reaching any point near the whining stage.

WITH him in good, in bad, in plenty and in want, I learned that within his dear old bosom there beat a heart as white and as big as the "all outdoors"; that within him tingled all that was good for his fellow man, that he would hunger that his companions might eat, that he would suffer cold that they might be warm, that he would take a drenching that they might seek shelter and remain dry and comfortable.

I was with Jack London a great deal at various times. I was with him here, there and over yonder.

I HAVE in my possession a relic, one worthy of being handed down to posterity—what is supposed to be the last or one of the last personal letters ever written and signed by Jack London. The letter is dated December 3, 1916, and while of but few lines, it is one that I prize and value above all other communications in my possession. It was in reference to "The Hussy," (see *Cosmopolitan*, November, 1916), an object that had interested him, and one that, had he lived, would have led him to form and finance an expedition into the Chilean mountain country.

Jack is gone! Not dead, just gone on before, to prepare and watch and await the arrival of the vast army of his followers and admirers; just gone as an advance into that great unknown region as a brave, red-blooded and fearless Adventurer will; just stepped over the border, where his camp-fires are burning bright and forming a guiding light for the traveler who follows in his wake, just as you and I will ere so long. Jack was a faithful old scribe, and his facile pen has been placed away—not to perish, but to live and live and to enlighten future generations of the magnitude of his wonderfully fertile brain. The great scribe has, in his demise, written his masterpiece, and received the honorarium of Jehovah.—WANDERING WEBB.

JACK LONDON

You sang of spirits bold,
Who dared to venture into no-man's land.
Brave souls and true,
Each one a noble type by God's command.
Adventure was their quest,
As far out in the frozen North,
Habitable neither for beast nor man,
In little groups they ventured forth.
Though dead thy spirit lives,
As those that blaze the trail,
All chant thy praises to the wind,
The snow, the rain, the hail.—JOHN MADDEN.

YOU will notice that our magazine opens three new departments in this issue. These are times when it behooves all of us to render every national service within our power. *Adventure* is an American magazine, its readers are Americans or citizens of the Allied countries. Two of the three new departments are devoted to helping win the war. The other department looks farther into the future. When we were at peace, *Adventure* was a strong advocate of preparedness for war. Now when we are at war, *Adventure* advocates preparedness for the peace that is to follow victory. The vigorous prosecution of the war demands all our energies, but there is left to us time for thinking and, the duties of citizenship demand of us that we do this thinking.

Even if *Adventure* were only a fiction magazine its duty would be plain. But it is far more than a fiction magazine. This Camp-Fire of ours has gathered together all classes and through a common interest become for them almost a class publication. The very character of its readers has drifted our Camp-Fire talks to more serious affairs; it has become a forum for exchange of views. These new departments are only a natural expression of the spirit and interests of our readers.

ARTHUR SULLIVANT HOFFMAN.

AFTER nearly four years at the front our Australian comrade, Harry C. Winters, has been knocked out and sent to recover in England. Our good wishes to him. Here is his letter, written from hospital in April. As I answered his letters regularly, my replies must have fallen by the wayside.

My letters to you, having had no replies, have evidently met with bad luck, torpedoed. Old Fritz is very busy these times. You will note I am no longer in Northumberland Fusiliers. Got knocked out so badly that the powers that be have transferred me to this unit and I look like finishing my time in Blighty. Between you and I, I have had a fair over and it is about time I got a spell.

Glad you folks are in the joke now. Have seen some of the lads, they seem a fine type and should go far. They have already had a taste of it so can form some idea of the game we have been up against now for nearly four years. I know they'll make good and their aid just now is very welcome.

Give my respects to the Camp-Fire and with all the best for yourself, hoping we shall soon make finis to this racket.—PVT. H. WINTERS.

AMHERST College men, please straighten us out on this. "Lord Jeffrey Amherst" is one of your most particular and famous songs. Was he the Jeffry Amherst of Hugh Pendexter's story in this issue? What connection had he with Amherst College?

Incidentally, the man who wrote the words and music of that song, James S. Hamilton, was for a time on the staff of *Adventure* and his is one of the five little service flags that hang in our room. I went down to the boat that carried him to ambulance work in France, May 14, 1917, and he has been doing his bit over there ever since.

OUR other service flags are for Harry E. Wade, at this writing in training-camp and probably destined for the 22d Regulars, the aviation section of its infantry brigade; E. C. Clayton, who, like Mr. Wade, left us in May, and is now at Ft. Leavenworth; George S. Olds who went across in December, 1917, saw the sinking of the *Tuscania* and is now a sergeant in the Medical Supplies Department; Theodore N. Pockman, who recently joined theMarines. All the rest who are or at various times have been on *Adventure's* staff are over age (one under age), all married and most of them with children, except one of the present staff who is both under age and ineligible through a physical injury.

And now to Mr. Pendexter's two letters giving us more of the historical background to his story in this number:

NORWAY, MAINE.

The only fictitious characters in this yarn are the trader and The Killer, and the latter's part was played by some messenger from the Three Fires.

SIR WILLIAM JOHNSON'S tremendous efforts to hold the Six Nations back from joining the allied tribes under Pontiac constituted one of the most valuable services any man ever contributed to the English provinces. That he succeeded, with the exception of the Senecas and a few Cayugas, should be his most lasting monument.

The figurative language of the Indians in making peace or allying for war contained much of a sameness; *viz.*, the expressions, "the whistling of evil birds," "hold fast the chain, etc.," being constantly used at various councils.

It is a historical fact that Etherington atMichilimackinac threatened to send as prisoner to Detroit the "next person who should disturb the fort with such tidings." This after a friendly Canadian had warned him the Indians were plotting to destroy all the English on the lakes. I could not resist citing a parallel case, Fort Mims massacre, 1813, when, "At the very moment of attack a negro was tied up, waiting to be flogged for reporting that he had the day before seen a number of painted warriors lurking a short distance outside the stockade."

SIR JEFFRY AMHERST not only wrote Colonel Bouquet that he "wished to hear of no prisoners being taken," but to the same officer he also suggested, "Could it not be contrived to send the Small Pox among those disaffected tribes of Indians? We must on this occasion use every stratagem in our power to reduce them." (Parkman's Conspiracy of Pontiac, Vol. 2, p. 39.) I think

Amherst must have been a Hun. There seems to have been some sad scamps on both sides, but the blindness was largely in English eyes. A grim touch of humor is found in Sir Jeffry Anherst's letter to Gladwyn, besieged at Detroit, in which Gladwyn is ordered to *reestablish* and *hold* the forts at Michilimackinac, Sault Ste. Marie and Green Bay! and this at a time when the Detroit fort was holding on by the eyelashes.

WHAT impresses me deeply in my reading is the constancy of reports sent to Colonel Bouquet in Philadelphia, and Amherst in New York, from the most isolated posts. It has attracted my attention to a class of men never, to my knowledge, played up in fiction—the express-riders, who got through and got back no matter how closely a fort was besieged. Of course many were killed. History treats them anonymously, the official papers merely stating that "the following was received by—by an express." There must be a good story in them. God knows they got no promotion or glory. When it was impossible for a man to raise his head above a rampart, walk a rod from the post, etc., without losing his hair, these unrecorded express-riders were constantly carrying correspondence from Detroit to Fort Pitt, from all smaller posts, and *getting back* again.—PENDEXTER.

NORWAY, MAINE.

USUALLY an envoy was granted safe conduct, although there are instances recorded when their sacred office was not recognized. Besse's conductor, acting on the Indian impulse if not because of his respect for J.'s agent, an envoy with belts, acted correctly even from the savage's point of view in telling him to beat it. That his action should be overruled and he himself should take part in the pursuit is but another characteristic of the Indian's inconsistency. After he fled, the young brave's act of picking up the belt was accepted as being the act of the tribe. Perhaps the killer urged the capture of the fugitive. The Indian mind in such matters was as changeable as that of a child.

I'M UP a tree *in re* your Lord Geofry Amherst. I never thought of the college in writing the truth about Sir Jeffry. In fact, I have nothing at hand to show that your man founded Amherst. T. P. Field (United States Bureau of Education, quoted in Larned's History Ready Reference) says Amherst Academy was incorporated in the town of that name in 1816. Two years later the trustees voted to raise a fund of $50,000. "This charity may be said to be the basis of Amherst College. . . . This for many years was the only permanent fund of Amherst College, and without this it would have seemed impossible at one time to preserve the very existence of the college. So Amherst College grew out of Amherst Academy." He continues to say it was not till 1820 that buildings for the college were erected. In the opening of his article he says "Amherst College originated in a strong desire on the part of the people of Massachusetts to have a college near the central part of the State. . . . .The ministers of Franklin county, at a meeting held in Shelburne, etc." Nothing about Lord Geofry so far. . . . Parkman, in his preface to the sixth edition of "Conspiracy of Pontiac," makes a point of "the proposal of the Commander-in-Chief to infect the hostile tribes with smallpox."—PENDEXTER.

YOU will remember how Captain Moorhead, having read Samuel Alexander White's novelette, "The Wave Bound," told us how he himself had been wrecked on the Magdalen Islands. Now comes further information on these interesting islands from another comrade:

Bass River, Mass.

I have been much interested in the letter you published by Captain Moorhead about his adventure on the Magdalen Islands, as it has been my custom to spend about four months on Amherst Island every year.

LANDING as late as he did on the island, after such a severe experience, I can well understand how bleak the climate must have seemed to him, and it is a fact that the islands are a menace to navigation. Four large steamers went aground in the course of a couple of months last Summer, and many schooners are wrecked annually because of the shifting winds and hidden shoals.

But Captain Moorhead's impression of the Island's desolation is altogether misleading, and I am sure memory fails him when he states that he found only one man who spoke English in 1892. English is now well spoken pretty well throughout the group.

THE "old Judge" of whom he speaks must be Monsieur Brasset, formerly factor in the old days tor the Coffin family who held the islands in feudal fee under a grant from George III, to Admiral Isaac Coffin of Nantucket for his loyalist services in the time of the American Revolution.

The islands are extremely fertile, though much of Amherst is treeless now. When Audubon visited the island a century ago, he found it well wooded. But it is now stripped, and the land is divided into many small but productive farm holdings. It is a curious fact that the islands are still held by the last vestige of feudalism in North America, and each landholder has to pay to the seigneury one shilling of tribute annually per acre.

There is an excellent inn now, as then in 1892, kept by the four venerable Shea Sisters, well known through the writings of many a novelist and traveler, and they continue the famous tradition of hospitality inaugurated by their mother over sixty years ago. Throughout the length and breadth of Eastern Canada their little hostelry is famed, and I am sorry that Captain Moorhead was not directed to it, as he would have found a warm Irish welcome there.

IT HAS been a secret meeting-place for many of us who are writers and artists for a number of years, and if a history of the islands is ever written, it will be a rich storehouse of legendary lore. I regard the islands as a mine of untouched material for those who write of adventure, and the history of strange and terrible happenings at Bird Rock Light alone during the past twenty years would be subject matter for many novels. You will be doing a service to the writing craft by dispelling the bleak impression left on Captain Moorhead's mind by his own hard experience, and suggesting the islands as a new field to wanderers in search of local color and strange experience—EDWARD J. O'BRIEN.

ANOTHER comrade of our writers' brigade has gone into khaki. After many attempts and after undergoing an operation to improve his physical condition, Dr. J. U. Giesy writes joyfully that at last he has been commissioned in the Medical Corps of the U. S. Army. Congratulations and good luck.

DURING 1918 I've been ill a good deal, but there wasn't supposed to be anything the matter with my brains. Just the same here are two mistakes I've made in "Camp-Fire." One is failing to get the following from H. A. Lamb into the issue that contained his story "Alamut."

CAMP WADSWORTH, SPARTANBURG.

Alamut existed, and its conquest by Hulagu Khan is history. Settlements of the Refik survived as late as 1700. I have taken the liberty of putting one in the ruins of Alamut, and giving it a good deal of political or rather predatory power. The organization of the Refik, under rule of the "Old Man of the Mountain," is historical. You have probably heard of the Refik as Ismailians. Marco Polo started me on the trail of the Old Man of the Mountain, and the trail led to a bit of hidden history that proved rather weird.—HAROLD A. LAMB.

THE second concerned the facts sent us by Robert and Kathrene Pinkerton concerning the "turning white" disease that figures in their story in this issue. I got mixed and put their letter in the number containing their former story, "The White Indians." The letter established the fact that there is such a disease and gave several authenticated instances.

IT IS seldom that an article creeps in among our fiction stories. The man who wrote the article in this issue has been dead over four years now—Harry Couzens. A good many of you remember him, were his friends, as I was. I have been going through some of his old letters for things that might interest you. The things are there, but somehow I do not feel like talking about them. Not, of course, that they are in any way to his discredit. His slate was clean and his adventurings were interesting. But, if you don't mind, I'll not even give the long letter he wrote concerning the foundation for the present article, except to quote one sentence: "Everything mentioned has appeared in print as news at some time or other and may be taken as straight stuff simply dressed up."

Toward the letter's end, too, he adds that he is not certain the *Norna* was sold under the hammer or that Weaver died in Samoa, though he had heard the first report from several people and the latter from one who was rather in position to know.

BEFORE the article was written—and I'm not quite sure myself why I've let it lie so long in the safe—before, I think, I even became acquainted with Couzens, I had heard of part of Weaver's exploits from a friend of mine whom we will call B. I know of few men who are more the man and more the gentleman than B. and I omit his name merely because his chance share in one of Weaver's cruises, though in no way discreditable to him, is his private affair.

My recollection of it is hazy enough. As I remember, B. was a passenger to Gibraltar on a ship that touched at the Azores when Weaver's yacht was there. On invitation from this strange character, who at the time seemed only the millionaire he purported to be, B., a priest and possibly one or two others left the steamer and joined Weaver in a cruise to the Canaries. Whether they remained with him on his cruise up the Adriatic coast of Italy I do not remember, but that bleeding of wealthy Italian villa owners through fear of a purely imaginary trolley line across their estates is the incident that stands out most clearly in my mind.

HE TOLD me the story of his cruise. I had never known him to lie or even to embroider and I think no one else has, either before or since. But it was a tall tale and I confess I wondered.

Well, B., who had had experiences worth lecturing about, decided to try his hand at that game in spare time. He was slated for a talk at some Catholic institution in Harlem. Being his first attempt, he was a bit nervous and asked me to go along as a straw of moral support. It was one of the coldest, windiest nights I've ever known New York to furnish and the transportation lines suffered; when one kind of conveyance broke down we walked till we found another. The coldest thing I ever did was to walk—and run, for we were late by this time—across some bridge over the Harlem.

But we finally arrived and the lecture went off well. Afterward the priests invited us to their own warm fire and right in the middle of the invitation one of them and B. suddenly recognized each other. It was the same priest who had taken the Weaver cruise with B. Certainly I heard much about Weaver that night and the tall tale became believable enough.

STILL farther back I had read in the newspapers of Weaver's famous plan to publish a magazine from his yacht as it cruised about the world, with Kipling and other famous writers as contributors. Doubtless many of you also remember the publicity the proposal received, and doubtless many of you will remember much more about the man than I do. A queer genius. I always wonder why people so gifted, so able to make their way legitimately, should prefer the almost-sure-to-lose-in-the-end games. There are so many other ways of getting excitement.

ANOTHER of our comrades of our writers' brigade has ceased to come to our Camp-Fires. William Hope Hodgson met his death on the Flanders front April 17, fighting for the same cause our own boys are fighting for. Our salute to him, and Godspeed over the Last Trail.

A brief letter from his wife brought me the news and an enclosure from an English paper. He had volunteered for the dangerous duty of observation officer of his brigade, set out at night with an infantry officer and a signaller, failed to return. It was found that all three had been killed by a shell.

Only a few days before his death he had written home of the fighting on April 10th. As stated in the English newspaper:

> The enemy had broken through right up to the guns and when most infantry and artillery had retried, the commanding officer, Lieutenant Hodgson, another officer and a few N. C. O.'s fought a rear-guard action across three miles of country amid a hail of machine-gun and rifle fire, hotly pursued by the enemy. Lieut. Hodgson climbed to the roof of a wrecked farmhouse as F. O. O. under very heavy shell and rifle fire. All of that gallant little band got away safely, but with the loss of all their kit, even their Sam Browne belts and their revolvers.

I give here his last letter to me, written November 17, 1917. Though we had never met, we had been friends by letter for several years before the war. He had served almost from the beginning, leaving his little châlet on the French Riviera to join up; before that, "eight years at sea, three times round the world, ten years an author."

> NOVEMBER 17, 1917.
>
> Just a line to wish you good luck and . . . I'm dropping you this brief note from the front, as I thought you might be interested to have a word from what one might well call the "present heart of things." I may not, of course, tell you where I am, but I can give you an address which will find me: 2nd Lieut. W. H. Hodgson, 84th Battery, R. F. A., B. E. F., France. If ever you feel inclined to drop me a friendly word, as of yore, this address will always find me—that is, above ground!
>
> . . . I've just come out of the firing-line for a few days' rest. It's been pretty hot work lately where I've been and one sees things, naturally, that are pretty dreadful; but I should imagine that on the Hun side of the line, things must be absolutely appalling (?spelling!!) Jove! if, I'm spared, and can write, I guess I'll have a few tales to write that will interest you, after this war is over. How are you all regarding the war over there? What do you all think about this Italian business?
>
> LORD, man! You'd like to be out here to see and hear some of the sights and sounds of war. I've heard the machine-gun fire rise into an absolute scream of sound, by hundreds, a devilish torment of shrill, abominable noise, impossible to imagine in the mass. And then again, at other times, I've heard a lonely gun in some unseen field at night tap-tapping its disconsolate death-message across some stretch of darkness. Do you get it? I could go on for hours giving sights and sounds from a literary point of view but I might forget and say too much, and then this might not get past the censor. Drop me a line some time and tell me how you and the magazine progress. Meanwhile, as always, let me wish you all kind things.
>
> Most sincerely yours,
> WILLIAM HOPE HODGSON.

WHAT is patriotism? We are beginning to understand pretty clearly what it is in war time, but when we were at peace we heard very little—and thought very little—about it.

It doesn't seem possible that, when the war is over and peace comes again, we can think so little about it as we used to do. Maybe we'll begin to see that voting and keeping the laws isn't enough by way of service to the country, that patriotism means good citizenship and that it's our job to find out just what good citizenship is and then to practise it and teach it to others.

That is what the American League for Citizenship, Inc., is for. Probably by the time this reaches your eye the League will have begun active operations. And the kind of good citizenship it is devoted to building is good for war times as well as peace times. Are *you* a good citizen? *How* good? Do you want to be a better one? Do you want to make other Americans better citizens? Do you believe we can any longer trust to haphazard methods of teaching and imbuing good citizenship or should we unite in organized and efficient effort? The League will furnish the means.

BY WAY of comparison in the matter of running powers of Indians, here's the white man's record for one hundred miles straightaway:

Bloomington, Ill.

I have noticed with interest the discussion pro and con regarding the alleged speed of the Indians of the Southwest. I know little about Indians but I do know that the recognized world's record for 100 miles is 13 hours 26 minutes and 30 seconds, held by C. Rowell.

With this performance in mind I have little difficulty in crediting the Indian messengers with equal or greater speed.—F. W. P.

THAT query of Edgar Young's—"What is the spirit of adventure, particularly in its biological aspects?"—keeps bringing in interesting replies.

Winnipeg, Can.

The Spirit of Adventure is that inheritance of so many of us through long generations of ancestors back to the man-ape of Jack London, who first watched the log washed down by the river and wondered where it went, till at last he found one large enough to go voyaging into the unknown. To his descendants he handed down cells in brain and body which are responsible for the wanderlust, which makes us hear the call of the wild, the new, the strange. The man or woman with the Spirit of Adventure as part of his inheritance can find friends anywhere, and romance will meet them in the crowded street as much as, or now-a-days more then, in the desert solitudes. Without appearing to go out of their way, those who have it will travel whether they will or not. They are never so happy as when on the move, meeting new people and seeing fresh places.

THE brotherhood of those with the Spirit of Adventure will make itself heard anywhere. Family ties may and do harness it, but the call is always there. Fortunately Canada gives one lots of elbow-room. But I can go into a restaurant for a meal and pick up a stranger and have him tell me his life story before he realizes it, and then they say we old countrymen can't mix.

AS FOR the intellectual side of adventure, of course, it exists. It is in the blood of every born adventurer. There is no great author who is without it. Those who are happy (or the reverse) to possess it, study or at least play with all the sciences, and all the religious and philosophical beliefs. You have to start out with a proposition that "there is a divinity that shapes our ends, rough hew them how we will." Secondly, that while God made man in His own image, man has ever since been trying to make God over in his, which accounts for all the mistakes in the churches. Thirdly, you have to accept the proposition that man can not create. For this reason man may distort truth, but he can not conceive anything that is not. Consequently there is some truth in all systems of theology. Truth is like a mountain top. The aspect may be different in every direction you look. If you persist in looking only one way, naturally some one who is looking in another direction is going to call you a liar because you deny what he can see.

ONCE you recognize that all the knowledge we possess—spiritual, material, or mental—consists merely of a few grains upon the sands of the ocean of the universe and of the sea of eternity it becomes evident how important all *thought* is. It opens up vast possibilities in physical science as well as in moral and mental planes of thought. It provides a key to all religions. It is yours to adventure thereon. No thought is too daring if you do not let it run away with you when half fledged. Nothing is impossible, because the human mind, being finite, could not conceive it if it were absolutely impossible.

So all the range of the past, the present and future, and all the ideas, wild and distorted as many of them are, that men have ever conceived, are there for the strong brain to go adventuring on. It is dangerous, of course. So is all adventuring. It is uncharted and unmapped territory. Most of those who adventure may be lost or suffer shipwreck and disaster. Many try to start new schools and proclaim they have found a wondrous new land, but later explorers find no traces of what they proclaim. That happened with the early adventurers in the time of Herodotus and those from whom he drew his alleged facts, and continued down till long after the Spaniards came to this continent. But the known area of the intellectual lands of adventure is smaller than the world as known to the earliest adventurers of mythology in our world.

TO ILLUSTRATE what I mean about the human mind being always on the right track when it conceives anything as possible we have only to remember how steam, wireless, flying-machines, and submarine craft were derided by scientists for centuries before they became commonplaces. It is difficult in a few words to define or explain anything so vast. I hope I have suggested what you want, however poorly.—RICHARD H. McDONALD.

OUR comrade of the writers' brigade, Charles Brown, Jr., writes (during the second phase of the big German offensive) that his section of twenty ambulances has been attached to the "ace attacking division" of the French Army. Of this body of troops he says:

> A division like this one never existed before. Practically every man had been decorated again and again. And now they have put a stop to the Hun advance in these red meadows.

DON'T forget to be listing your vote for the ten best stories in *Adventure* during 1918. If you like, add a list of another ten for honorable mention as you did for 1917 and 1916.

A WORD from S. B. H. Hurst concerning his story in this issue:

Seattle, Wash.

There has always been a fascination for me in wondering about the men who never come back—who for some reason or other leave a good home, never to be heard of again. The slabs over many family vaults have vacancies, which are filled only with guesses. About the endings of such wanderers there is for me a greater pathos, and a greater human interest, than there is about even those who die in battle. On the outskirts of the world we touch the edge of the great mystery, for in such lonely spots our interest is less distracted.—S. B. H. HURST.

A VERY interesting contribution is added to the accounts furnished by members of the Camp-Fire of lost or buried treasures, not included among the hundreds described by Stephen Allen Reynolds in his series of articles a year or two ago. These data are given by Wolcott LeClear Beard, now a major in the country's service, with whose stories in *Adventure* and elsewhere you are familiar.

I am impelled to write you a word of appreciation of the Lost Treasure series, just completed, in which, in common with all your other readers, I fancy, I was keenly interested. I was also impressed with the infinity of research which must have been the price paid by Mr. Reynolds for his material.

This being so, the fact that he may have overlooked a bet is in no way remarkable; rather is it remarkable that he has overlooked so few. It may also be that while I was away where neither *Adventure* nor any other magazine was to be had, I may have missed one of his articles. Still, so far as I know, he makes no mention of what may be one of the world's greatest treasures.

I REFER to Atahualpa's chain. Most of us have read Prescott's account of the last great Inca (that there are Incas still is a fact not generally known, but is, as Kipling used to say, another story) and of the circumstances under which Atahualpa, the Inca in question, died. Taken prisoner by Pizarro, and held for what is said to be the greatest ransom ever demanded, Pizarro, while this ransom was being collected, got an attack of what now would be called "cold feet," and had Atahualpa treacherously murdered.

When they heard of this murder those who were bringing the ransom hastily concealed the gold they were bringing, in order that it might not fall into the hands of the Spaniards. Most of it was thrown into Lake Titicaca, but much was hidden elsewhere. While I was in South America one lot, amounting, it was said, to about $540,000 was found. I believe that the find was somewhere near La Paz, and at the time I was leading an exploring expedition in the far interior of Bolivia. The questions I asked when I returned were met by an impenetrable reticence. Moreover, I was given to understand that I would be more popular with the powers that were, if I ceased to ask them; which, as it was quite useless, I did.

THE chain, however, is another matter. As the story was told me by not one, but many, it was designed to stretch, on ceremonial occasions, entirely around the Inca capital of Cuzco, and its links were made of bars "thrice the thickness of a man's thumb." This would bring its value—for it must have been about three-fourths of a mile in length—well up into the millions.

The chain now is said to repose in only about four feet of water in the bottom of a sort of well, communicating by a subterranean passage with Lake Titicaca, situated on one of the small islands near the larger island of Copacabane, where it was thrown when the news of Atahualpa's death reached its bearers.

THIS is not a secret. Many times I have heard it discussed openly and casually. But it lies on or very near the border dividing Peru and Bolivia. Neither Government dares sanction an attempt to raise it, as it is an object of veneration among the natives and such an attempt might result, it is feared, in an *indiada*—that is, a universal rising of the myriad Quichua and Aymará Indians, which never yet has occurred, but of which all people of European descent live in constant dread.

I do not, of course, vouch for the truth of the foregoing. I simply "tell the tale as 'twas told to me." But, so far from being at all improbable, it bears strong internal evidence of a degree, at least, of truth.

MR. REYNOLDS hardly could be said to have overlooked anything in the Philippines; yet those islands, and especially Luzon, probably contain more buried treasure than any spot of equal area in the world. But it is scattered in comparatively small lots, as it was buried by its former owners in the time of stress and Aguinaldo.

Just before I took over charge of the province of Pangasinán as its supervisor, an individual named Prado was hung in Dagupan for three or four out of fifty or more murders that he was known to have committed. He was a chief of *talisanes*, or, in other words, a thief on a very large scale. While awaiting execution he, it is said, offered to reveal the hiding-places of his treasure to the sergeant of his guard if the latter would connive at his escape, which proposition was declined. But a dying native, who was one of two, and the only survivor of those who had buried the treasure, did reveal the location to my master mechanic, a white man married to a mestiza—all of which, please note, is quite in accordance with the established methods of fiction in such cases.

MY MASTER mechanic told me. We could not recover the treasure for reasons not necessary to go into, and for aught I know it may still be where Prado placed it. It was said to amount to about $40,000 Mex. For the benefit of any who wish to have a try, I hereby reveal the secret.

The silver was buried in two parcels. One of them was almost within arm's reach of the gallows upon which Prado was hanged—that is, underneath what afterward was the band-stand, built in front of the convent in Dagupan when the troops occupied this convent as barracks. The other parcel is under a circular, turfed mound, about twenty-five feet in diameter, before the building that was used, during the military occupation of Dagupan, as Q. M. and C. S. stores, and near its center.

ONE buried-treasure episode took place in the compound of my own house in Lingayen. One of my servants, and a very good man despite the fact that he was a "trusty" prisoner serving a nineteen-year sentence for murder, was in the habit of sleeping outside my bedroom door, armed with an old gas-pipe Remington, 50-caliber rifle. One night the rifle spoke, and running out we met Soltiro—the "trusty's" name was Soltiro—returning to his post with a satisfied smile on his face and the smoking rifle in his hand. Asked what had happened he said that there had been a man outside who didn't "desire to speak"—that is, who wouldn't answer when challenged—so he, Soltiro, had shot him.

"Was he a white man, Soltiro?" we asked him.

"Oh, dear, no!" he replied. "Only a Filipino, like myself."

Then he returned to his *petate* and once more composed himself to slumber.

SOLTIRO had not shot the man, however. The range being at least seven yards, he naturally had missed him. The next morning we found that this unknown person, whom Soltiro suspected of having designs upon my chickens, had really come on quite another errand. In a hole he had dug was the impression of a pot that must have held two quarts or thereabout of what undoubtedly was a cache of silver Mexican dollars.

FOR the benefit of any who may wish to raise Prado's treasures, it may be as well to state that in all probability these Philippine caches have been lifted by my ex-master mechanic long since.

AS TO Atahualpa's chain—assuming, of course, that the stories of its location are true, and even assuming that it might be reached, which it could not—it lies, as I said, in Lake Titicaca, which is on the Interandean Plateau, 12,000 feet above the sea and hundreds of miles from salt water. In that vicinity the country is rather thickly populated, and the presence of a strange white man would instantly become known. It would be hardly more possible to remove any considerable portion of the chain by stealth than it would be to do the like by the Woolworth Building; and to remove it in any other manner one would have to fight not only either or both the Bolivian and Peruvian Governments but—what is infinitely worse—the countless hordes of Indians that would rise to protect this venerated relic.

Had it been possible to get away with this treasure, there are no end of men, many of them desperate and intelligent, who would have done so. But so far as I know, no attempt, even, ever has been made.

YOU already know that our old comrade, Harold S. Lovett, the marine who served on the *Agamemnon* at the Dardanelles, is now chief gunner on a merchant ship and that he dropped in to see me here at the office. For several years I've been referring to him as an American. I don't remember now how I got that impression in the beginning but it was a mistaken one, for he's an Englishman. He had never bothered to set me straight on it though he has been getting our magazine as regularly as distance and circumstances would permit.

Incidentally, he tells me the British sailors aren't so willing to ask for things they want as are the Americans and that he has seen men on the *Agamemnon*, who wanted to read a copy of our magazine but didn't like to ask for it, stand off at a little distance with a pair of binoculars and read it over another man's shoulder.

Before this reaches you I hope to see him again. I owe him a lunch. Had it all arranged for last time and, through another person's fault, I missed him.

Here is a letter from him that came a little while before he arrived himself:

Special Service.

Have had a little sport since last I wrote you. Was running down the Irish Sea in particularly dirty weather, aboard an old tramp, capable of doing 7 knots at a pinch. In St. George's channel our engines went on strike, and we had to lay to for six hours for repairs. We'd hardly been under way five minutes when Fritz handed us a visiting card in the shape of a 6-inch shell.

I'M CHIEF gunner on the old lady, have a beautiful new 4.7; oh, I *love* her! Well, we returned the compliment and settled down a nice little duel which lasted close on five hours. The squareheads had two-six-inch guns to our four-inch and when they got busy you can bet we found life a fair bustle. However, we had a very limited supply of ammunition so I just fired slow and careful, taking pains over my spotting and making as sure as I could of each round.

AS I said there was one ball of a gale blowing, and being empty we pitched and rolled some, and Fritz was a good 4,000 yards away on the weather side, so we had to face all nature could give us as well as Fritz. After about an hour and a half we scored a hit, about the 15th round, and then I opened up with high explosives, having found his range. Well, it lasted more than three hours longer but, to cut it short, I guess I'm about the only guy who can tell his relatives where to drop a nice wreath.

At present am in our English port loading for America, so, if there is a chance, I may see you inside a month. Of course nothing is certain, but in any case I'll drop you a line as soon as we get across the Western. Am hoping to pass a word with many old friends of trail and camp, sea and range, so here's luck to you and all the Camp-Fire boys.—HAROLD S. LOVETT.

WHY isn't citizenship taught in our schools? The first thing a democracy should teach is democracy. Why isn't citizenship made a definite part of home training? An American's duty is to make a good American out of his child as well as out of himself.

To bring these things to pass is a main part of the work of the American League for Citizenship, Inc., which should be in operation by the time you read this. If you see the need of these things, there is the chance to work for them efficiently.

SOME time ago I told you about one of our fiction stories that was later written up in a Pittsburgh paper as fact. Also how a newspaper story had been made exactly paralleling an incident in a story by D. L. Mackaye—about the officer who made a private salute him fifty times and then, having failed to return each salute, was compelled to do so by his own superior.

It takes quite a while for a letter to go to Hawaii and bring back a reply, but here is Mr. Mackaye's answer to my query as to the origin of the incident he used:

Honolulu, T. H.,
April 15, 1918.

I am squeezing out a line in an unexpected odd moment, having the reply to your last note heavy on my conscience. Have been on duty with the waterfront guard "in addition to his other duties" (which is the "goat line" of the army) and those other duties have been considerable in themselves. Expect to be transferred to the draft regiment expected to be organized in Hawaii shortly and am looking forward to something besides guard duty.

NOW in regard to "Brothers in Arms" which you queried me about. Two incidents in that story, so far as I know, were facts. My informant was Fred Nugent, formerly hospital steward at Fort McKinley, P. I., and now pharmacist at a local sanitarium, a former pal of mine when we were together in the medical service in the Islands here. Before he got his stripes and while on orderly duty, he was the victim of petty persecution (according to *his* account, you understand) on the part of a shavetail in the California field artillery. The incident of the flagstaff and the salute which you say has been repeated in the East occurred in the course of this and was exactly as related in the story, the other officer concerned having been Major ——, then, I believe, of lesser rank. He was in the Islands at the time I wrote the story but was later transferred to the border. The second incident, the smallpox patient and his troubles, was also related in the story exactly as it was related to me, except that five wardmasters were successively jugged for refusing to carry out the treatment. Nugent was the first, passing the word of the man's real state on to the others in turn. Actually, the smallpox patient was not the lieutenant of the flagstaff, but the two incidents worked nicely together in fictional guise.

I never heard before of anything approaching these two incidents, and if one of them was repeated in the East, credited to another camp, have a strong suspicion that it was cribbed. There is only one way to get local color for army dope, that is, to live alongside it or in it for a long time and I imagine that the reporters stuck on a training-camp story.—D. L. MACKAYE.

BEING blind in one eye, he was refused by the American Army, so, when I heard from him, he was following another path to the front. And he makes a suggestion to his comrades of our Camp-Fire—that we establish a password so that when one of us met another he would, even if he didn't know him, "know that he was with a friend. I am quite sure," our comrade, E. C. Johnson, goes on to say, "that if I met a 'Bo' or 'Boomer' in tough luck and he gave me the password, if I only had a dime I would give him a nickel of it."

THAT is a fine spirit, and there is much of it among the members of our Camp-Fire. I've often wished we could have something of the kind, yet there are disadvantages. A badge would be good, but just as sure as we had one a lot of people would think it merely a scheme for advertising the magazine. A number of you have suggested it and I've suggested that we adopt some emblem for our own, not as a badge but for use in our part of the magazine. Perhaps such an emblem, made into a very small badge, without a word or even a letter of printing on it, might solve the problem.

I'D LIKE to see such a badge in use, but not if it is going to seem merely a piece of advertising. Our Camp-Fire has been kept as free as possible from that sort of thing, the whole spirit of it is one of comradeship, not of exploitation, and I don't want to see it changed. It does help the magazine, of course, and of course I'm glad it does, but it doesn't spoil itself in doing so, and if a badge is going to put any "commercialism" in our Camp-Fire, then I'm against the badge.

Would a badge without any lettering on it do this? Or would it be an advantage only? Being the editor, I'm not going to decide. It's up to you. What do you think? If you're for a badge, what would make a good emblem?

A password or sign is hardly open to the same objection, but would it be abused by grafters at the expense of real members? And some, of course, are not strong for that kind of thing. Here again, what do you think?

And while we're thinking it over, let's send a "Good Luck" from the Camp-Fire to Comrade E. C. Johnson whose heart is in the right place.

SOME of you have already read in the San Francisco papers about Mrs. Catherine Casey's service flag and its four stars for her three sons and her son-in-law. The oldest boy, John Joseph, was an artist in France when the war broke out in 1914, put in three and a half years with the famous French Foreign Legion, declined a captaincy in the British army in order to stay with his old comrades, but later transferred to the American Army.

The original Legion and his comrades are gone and "Casey, the man with the charmed life," is one of the four survivors, says the *Chronicle*. Also, that a wound during the Champagne drive was the only one received during all his service, though he was four times cited for bravery.

The second and third stars are for Patrick and Terrence, our comrades of the writers' brigade, now with the Naval Reserve. The fourth star is for Lieutenant Homer Winfield.

DANIEL BOONE. It will always be a name to conjure by. Daniel Boone, Simon Kenton, Davy Crockett, Kit Carson, those names stand for an epoch of American history. In this issue we meet Daniel Boone and come to know him intimately. In coming stories by Hugh Pendexter we will come to know Boone still better, and, fighting side by side with him against the Indians in defense of the Kentucky frontier, that other great woodsman, more hated even than Boone by the Indians—Simon Kenton.

And, later still, it's likely you'll be meeting Crockett, and perhaps Carson as well.

Here is Mr. Pendexter's picture of Kentucky when it was the "dark and bloody ground."

Norway, Maine.

While not the first to visit the Kentucky country (first called the Transylvania Colony) there was none more persistent than Boone in taking families there to effect permanent settlements.

JOHN FINLEY, trapper, who incited him to go to Kentucky, had been there two years before the time of this story. N. S. Shaler's "History of Kentucky" states that the first authentic report of a trip to Kentucky was made by Dr. Thomas Walker, who crossed the mountains in 1750. The first white woman in Kentucky, according to Collins's "History of Kentucky," was Mrs. Mary Inglis, "who, in 1756, with her two little boys, her sister-in-law, Mrs. Draper, and others, were taken prisoners by the Shawnee Indians from her home on the top of the great Alleghany ridge, now Montgomery County, West Virginia." She was separated from her children, escaped. One child died in captivity, the other was ransomed after living with the Indians for thirteen years.

George Washington surveyed the northeast corner of Kentucky some time between 1770 and 1772. The historians lay stress on the great danger from the Indians that attended all these visits.

IT IS Shaler's theory that originally the eastward trend of the buffalo was encouraged by the Indians' destruction of the forests by repeated firing of the undergrowth. Thus he accounts for the five or six thousand square miles comprised in the "barrens," and adds that doubtless this same process was employed in deforesting the southwest; "only there the extermination of the woods was more complete." He also reminds that it takes some centuries of repeated firing to reduce beech and ash areas to conditions of treelessness.

Kentucky had no permanent Indian settlements, excepting some Chickasaw villages on the Mississippi, since the advent of the whites. The Cherokee drove out the Shawnees, once their neighbors and allies, and the two nations raised Cain generally in passing back and forth over the marvelous region.

The slight use I've made of the Cherokee sacred formulas is o. k. Every move of the Cherokees' lives, practically, was governed by some formula.—PENDEXTER.

LET'S have a look at another of the answers to Earl J. Teets who at one of our Camp-Fires complained because, though he'd led what you'd call an adventurous life, he didn't know what an adventure looked like. Comrade P. R. E. takes quite the opposite view of things, and probably more of us will agree with him than with comrade Teets.

DEAR SIR: April 8, 1918.

I feel sorry for Mr. Teets. To think that he has been to sea for ten years and has probably roamed a good portion of the waters at various times, and yet has not found adventure! Perhaps he has no imagination.

In my opinion you must have imagination to have adventure, and although I have never been to the so-called "out-of-the-way places" where one commonly thinks he will find adventure, I have a good imagination and I have adventures daily.

ADVENTURE, to me, is the unusual, the exciting, the unexpected, the humorous events or occurrences that come to you outside of the regular routine habits of your existence. In other words, an *ad*dition to an ordinary venture constitutes an *ad*-venture.

I worked for two years in New York at the very unromantic job of department-store clerk, and while nothing startling ever befell me while there, I experienced many strange happenings that I would term adventures, though they may seem prosaic enough to those who have them in their daily lives always. I visited the dens and the cheap saloons of the city nightly (and there are plenty of such places in New York yet) merely to get a glimpse of the characters who frequent them, and was mixed in several rather bloody fights, which though not serious, were at least exciting to an ordinary day-in-day-out living clerk. I have seen bums of the worst order kicked out of some of the fancy saloons along Broadway, and have followed these unfortunates, spoken to them, taken them to a less particular bar and heard many interesting stories from their lips. Tame, perhaps, but unusual to me at least.

WITH nothing else to do at night I have set myself to follow a certain unknown individual whom I chanced to pass on the street, just to ascertain where he or she was going and what that person would do during the evening. I was curious, that is all, and while not looking for trouble, I would not have run away from it had it come to me.

Once I remember following a fashionably dressed young woman from the steps of an uptown brownstone house, through a maze of streets via subway, L and afoot, to the back room of a saloon on the East Side, where she sat and sipped the rank beer and wine served there until she was so drunk they carried her up-stairs to bed. There was nothing exciting about this either, but I wondered who she was and why she came down to this place from her fine home up-town simply to get drunk. And I tried to imagine what sort of story was in her life. I never found out, of course, but I would not have had even the opportunity to try had I gone home after work, eaten my supper and gone to bed.

NOW I am a newspaper editor in a country mining town, and small adventures crowd quickly to me every week. A fight or a killing by a gang of "hunks," train accidents, strikes, divorces, family fights, explosions—these are all adventures for me to get into and investigate and I enjoy them. Of course they are small compared with what the real adventurers of the world experience, but they will do for me for the present while I am in a section where "big" adventures do not happen often.

SO I say to Mr. Teets aboard his boat: Keep your eyes and your mind open and you'll find adventure, small perhaps, but adventure just the same. In a fog, when your commander is worrying his head off, do you ever imagine what *might* happen if another boat chanced to get in your path? Don't you ever visit out-of-the-way places on your shore leaves? Haven't you ever mixed with the rot that hangs around the sailors' lodging-houses and bars at every water-front? In your ten years at sea have you never had a fight for some cause, a mishap, or an encounter with a woman that has thrilled you with one or more of the primitive emotions of man?

If not, I pity you, because I know that you have missed much and that unless you learn that the prefix "Ad" means going "toward" the venture you will never find adventure.—P. R. E.

And also there is that very large question propounded by Edgar Young of our writers' brigade: "What, biologically speaking, is the spirit of adventure?" That is, what is this force, this impulse, that has, since before the dawn of history, moved man so mightily? For how much of human progress is it responsible?

SOME time ago there came this letter from a comrade in the 63d Artillery who found an old friend in a character in one of our stories:

Fort Worden, Wash.

It has been a long time since I have written you and after reading "Maloney and Matotte," by Robert Russell Strang, I just have to write, as my old friend Hungry Mike is in the story.

OLD Hungry Mike is quite a character and at one time was one of the best mushers in the North. Many a story has been told of Mike and some of his mushes and of the outfit he takes with him.

At the time of the Shushana strike, Mike, who is about sixty years old, put a pack on his back that did not go over twenty pounds, and that included his blankets and made the long Summer trip from Fairbanks to the Shushana. He started long after the first rush and was one of the first to reach the diggings.

MIKE is about 6 foot 4 inches and don't go over 130 pounds. From the top of his head to his toes he is a perfect curve and to look at him you would think that he was about to cash in at any time, but he is sure a tough old bird. Last Fourth of July the business men of Nenana, where Mike has an eating-house, played a game of baseball with the officials of the commission and Mike was on first base. Mike never caught a ball, but he stopped them all, sometimes with his head and sometimes with other parts of his body, but he was the life of the game.

Mike runs Mike's Place, an eating-house at Nenana, the interior end of the Alaskan Government Railroad, and, as he puts it, wants to run the best first-class, second-class eating-house in Alaska. —FRANCIS ROTCH, SR.

I sent his letter to Mr. Strang and here is his reply:

Groton, Mass.

I am in receipt of your note and the letter from Mr. Rotch of Fort Worden in regard to Hungry Mike Noonan—I guss I am one of the few men who know his full name. I am very glad to know that Mike is still on top.

I FIRST met him on Gold Run Creek in the Klondike region back in 1901. We have crossed paths many times in Alaska since then. The last time I saw him was in the Summer of 1910. He worked for me for a few days in Chena at that time. One morning he jumped on board a down-river steamboat bound for the Iditerod.

Mike is a great stampeder and a fast musher as Mr. Rotch testifies. His success is due to the fact that he splits the air like an elongated razor-blade. I can see him now with his bony elbow on the lunch-counter, and hear him wheeze:

"Yes, sir, gentlemen, I've cooked in every State in the Union except Delaware, and I spent a week and went broke trying to land in *it*, but couldn't make it. Next time I go back East I'm gonna *walk* into it, so as to be sure I won't miss it."

I HAVE also heard him declare "Gentlemen, during the World's Fair in Chicago I ran the biggest hot-cake dump in the city. The floor was half the size of a city block and there were gas-heated hot-plates all around three sides of it. I had twenty wenches doing nothing but frying, and they were kept so busy doing that that they had no time to grease the top of the range, so I got a big buck who wore a size fifteen boot, and to the sole of each boot I strapped a side of bacon, first having cut the skin off. After that it was easy, for all he had to do was to skate from one end of the hot-plate to the other, the girls pouring the hot-cakes behind him."

I WAS in one of the first parties to leave Fairbanks on the Shushanna stampede. It was a bad one, about four hundred miles across country. Mike must have arrived there after I left, because I didn't see him. Anyway, the strike turned out to be a small affair. But there is sufficient copper in that district to keep the world going for generations. Mountain sheep and caribou are plentiful.

Mike deserves a rich claim, because he's been doing the pioneer stunt for forty years. I don't believe there's a mining-camp west of Cripple Creek, Col., that he hasn't taken a fling at. I hope he gets stampeding out of his head and sticks to his place in Nanana. Mike is a good cook and a white man, and one of these days I'll give him the center of the stage in a yarn.—R. R. STRANG.

WELL, Americans, how do you like this? And what are you going to do about it? What are *you* going to do about it?

Lordsburg, N. M.

My business takes me all over the entire Western States. On my last trip, which consumed two years from the time I left San Francisco until I returned to that city, I took in every village and hamlet of ten States, exclusive of British Columbia, and I want to tell you now, as I have told others previously, that I saw in some places things that make an honest, stanch, true, patriotic citizen sit up and take notice and ask questions regarding the whys and wherefores of same.

IN NORTH and South Dakota I traveled for hundreds of miles in entirely German communities, where few, if any, spoke the American language to say nothing of their inability to read it. The churches were German. The schools were German. The papers were German. The people of these communities were strictly and entirely German and pro-German in all their inclinations and activities.

I met hundreds and hundreds of prominent men —citizens of the United States—bankers, merchants, school-teachers, clergymen and doctors, who had lived in those communities for more than twenty years, who had raised families and amassed fortunes there, who could not speak or read English. Some of them were good Masons; most of them professed to be good, loyal and true American citizens; and yet I have found in my intercourse with them that they were out-and-out Germans—Germans in their talk and ideas, Germans in their sympathies and affiliations, and that they would fight at the drop of the hat for the German Kaiser and the German Fatherland. And mind you it was in many instances to get away from the hardships and penury of the one, and the impositions and restrictions imposed by the other, that these same men left Germany to come and settle among us.

Mind you, I am not saying that there are not a great many true and loyal patriotic German-Americans in this country. Without doubt there are hundreds of thousands of such. But I am simply drawing attention to the thousands of others who are not loyal and patriotic Americans, who are more German than American, who would be spies and traitors to this country to help out the Kaiser and the Fatherland, and who, as such, are liable to be classed in and take refuge with the others who are good and true. And therein lies one great big menace for us.

NOW I maintain that no foreign-born person should be admitted to the rights and privileges of American citizenship who can not intelligently speak, read and write the American language. To do this each one will naturally have to live here a certain length of time, and he will just as naturally have to associate with true Americans and imbibe in a measure from them American ideas and principles and American conduct and deportment. To this end we should protest against the general speaking of a foreign language in communities of foreign emigrants. We should particularly prohibit the teaching in the public schools of foreign languages exclusively in such communities, and the publication of newspapers in foreign languages. In this way these foreigners in our midst will be compelled to study our language and customs, and they will gradually be weaned away from former ideas and affiliations and imbued with new ideas of patriotism and loyalty to this land of their adoption—the land of the brave and the free.—T. W. DUNCAN.

ABOUT the time this reaches you the Fourth Liberty Loan will be launched. Whatever German propagandists, conscious or unconscious, may say, this is a war for the American people, for the safety and welfare of all of us. Therefore it is up to each of us to do his full part. Therefore it is up to each of us to buy all the Liberty Bonds he can. It is just as simple as that.

Metal Identification Cards Now Ready.

MANUFACTURER'S cost to us 20½ cents. Cost to you, including postage, 25 cents. State present card number, if any. For other requirements, see page 185.

WORD from our old comrade of the writers' brigade, Major W. Robert Foran, written months ago. He has had four years of war now, having served, as you will remember, on the French front before being sent to England, then India and finally Mesopotamia.

The Royal Berkshire Regt.,
Att'd 6th Bn. South Lancs Regt.,
Mesopotamia Expd. Force.

Letters to and from America do take an infernal age to reach their destination!

The show out here is practically all over. Johnny Turks bolt as we advance. We have had three or four small brushes with him since last Summer, but no show since early in December. It is deadly dull and quiet out here.

It is great to hear America is going so strongly into this war and I hope it will hasten the victorious end.

Have been keeping fairly fit out here except that I can't get rid of this beastly muscular rheumatism. At times I suffer very acutely from it. I have had about two years of it now and am very fed up with the continual pain.

My latest news is that my wife and the two wee daughters are very flourishing and well. I am longing to be with them again. It is near a year now since I left England.

Kindest remembrances to every one whom I know.—W. ROBERT FORAN.

ONE of our comrades of our writers' brigade has had hard luck. C. M. Cosby, a former soldier in the Philippines, wrote me the other day as follows:

The medicos got me on a potential disability in the last ten days of training, which accounts for the fact that I am writing from New York instead of an Army camp where I had hoped to be. The result was so unexpected that a recommendation for captaincy had to be canceled by telegraph.

STILL further reports of lost treasure come in from members of our Camp-Fire, this time from California. One of these corroborates the account we have had from Wolcott LeClear Beard of Atahualpa's treasure.

The wreck of the old side-wheeler *Golden Gate* lies where she was beached ablaze, some three kilometers South of Graham's Head and about forty-five North of Manzanillo, on the west coast of Mexico. Well up in the breakers, nothing showed, at the time of which I write, but a few ribs and the remains of one paddle-box.

HAVING been on the coast for a number of years I was of course familiar with the tale of the treasure safe, containing millions in gold, that was supposed to be hidden somewhere under the shifting sand that partly covered her timbers, as well as with the histories of the various unsuccessful expeditions that from time to time had tried to recover the treasure.

In May of 1912 I had occasion to visit the town of Zihuatlan, a few miles inland from the old wreck, and whilst there learned from a creditable source what was locally believed to have become of the ill-fated *Golden Gate's* treasure.

SEVERAL years after the ship was beached a simple-minded burro-driver, following after some strayed burros, came down to the shore one morning after a severe storm. Arriving opposite the hulk, he found that a portion of the cabins had been torn away and cast up on the sands. Rummaging about amongst the débris he came upon the rusted iron safe, its door gaping open and still holding several bags of gold.

Hurrying back to Zihuatlan, the *arriero* told his compadre, Juan Murgia, who was like himself a burro-driver in the employ of the richest man in the district. Next morning the two hurried down to the beach but, finding that the load was too heavy for them, decided, at Juan's suggestion, to bury the gold till the next day when they would return with burros to carry it away.

Arriving upon the scene for the second time they found their cache looted, not a single piece of gold being left.

FROM this point on Juan's *compadre* of the simple mind is automatically eliminated from the story while Juan's fortunes began to mend with leaps and bounds, so much so that in a short time he was the richest man in that portion of the state and had married the daughter of his old *amo*.

As to proofs, I can only say that I have known Don Juan and his wife and that occasionally the coast Indians were wont to bring into town American gold-pieces which they said were found on the beach after storms.

ANOTHER tale of lost treasure that might well rank with those told by Mr. Reynolds is that of the royal treasure of the Tesoreria of San Blas, Tepic.

San Blas, up to the time of the Revolution, was the principal Pacific port of Mexico and the Royal Treasury was the temporary deposit of vast treasures on their way to Spain. The sudden arrival of the Republican troops found a great many Spanish families, with all of their convertible wealth, waiting to embark, while the Treasury was fairly overflowing. There was no time to convey the treasure aboard the few small ships in the harbor, as the Mexican troops were fairly in sight of the city, so that such as were able were glad to flee with their lives, leaving their wealth buried in a thousand places about the city.

AFTER a savage attack and desperate resistance the city fell, but, to the bitter disappointment of the victors, little or no treasure was found. The story is that when the Royal officers saw that there was no hope of withstanding the attack, all of the Royal and Church treasure was collected and thrown into a drain that ran down through the solid rock beneath the Treasury to what was then the beach at the foot of the hundred-foot cliff upon which the building stands. The drain was then sealed up and all evidences of its existence destroyed, after which the Spaniards faced their assailants to the bitter end, neither giving nor asking quarter.

THE following years of bitter strife in Mexico, together with the deep hatred felt by the Mexicans for their erstwhile oppressors, furnish reason enough for most of the treasure so hurriedly hidden at the time of the city's capture remaining undisturbed by those who buried it, only two or three cases being known of descendants of the Spanish refugees returning to San Blas to recover the wealth hidden by their forefathers.

That considerable treasure is scattered throughout the ruins of the ancient city is an indisputable fact, as is witnessed by numerous finds, one of these being an earthen jar containing three hundred golden doubloons found by a boy, half exposed after a rain-storm.

STILL another lost treasure, regarding the existence of which there is little or no doubt, is a hundred slave-loads of gold that was being hurried from Quito to form a part of the ransom of Atahualpa.

When news of Pizarro's foul murder of that unfortunate Inca monarch reached the convoy, it was turned back by those in charge and hurried day and night back toward the northern capitol of the Empire. When within sight of the favorite palace of the great Huayna-Capac the treasure-train was halted and the gold hidden in a small cave, the opening to which was then obliterated and the slaves and escort bound by the most solemn vows never to divulge the secret.

Despite numberless searches, extending practically from 1428 to the present date the treasure, amounting to at least a million and a half dollars, still lies somewhere within sight of the present capitol of Ecuador.—DONALD WILLIAM PAGE.

WHAT was yours? And which one would you choose to spend an evening with? Stephen Chalmers, having paid his tribute in this issue to "adventurers of the hearth," asks a few questions of the rest of you:

It would be interesting to hear what adventures (in fireside imagining) other fellows have enjoyed most. Mine was going back to the little town in Scotland where I was brought up, after ten years of actual adventuring. That was a hair-raiser at every street-turning, at every familiar, half-forgotten gatepost. It was like walking through heaven or hell and meeting ghosts.....Of all the adventurers you have met in the last thousand years of your wanderings, with which, or whom, would you choose to spend an evening? Already I hear a chorus—Napoleon, Columbus, Mark Antony, Harry Morgan, but surely out of the raft would come one name, one figure, and the reasons for his election. And I wonder what these reasons would be? Ever read Hazlitt on "Persons One Would Wish to Have Met"? Lamb, I think, or Thackeray, wished to have been shoeblack to Shakespeare. Personally I would have liked to fish just one afternoon with Walton when they were not rising much, so he would have explained why they didn't and other things in passing. However— —STEPHEN CHALMERS.

THERE comes to us a letter from one of our comrades of the writers' brigade, Charles Brown, Jr., telling of ambulance work on the French front. Ambulance Section No. 92 of New York University was organized and equipped, chiefly through the efforts of Professor Haring, by the students and faculty of that college. Mr. Brown was one of the student volunteers. I've had to hold the letter some time, because of its length, and because it was not mailed till February eleven, but the picture it paints is none the less interesting. A few words were cut—not marked—out by the censor:

Ambulance Section No. 92, attached to . . . . . of the French Army, is quartered in an old French town. All towns in France are old, for that matter. I have been across the whole of this stricken country, most of the way in an auto-ambulance, part in a train, and I can not recall one town with the mark of freshness on it. This one had its inception somewhere back of the wine-and-women days of Louis XIV.

THE town is all interest and color. Those who dwell in it are kind, affectionate, and glad that the American soldier is here. Most of their houses have been shattered beyond all repair. Others have been shelled into ugly piles of débris over which the grass is growing—as if striving to hide away all this brokenness which is so horrible, and yet so sad, to look upon. For in the very early days of the war the boches were here twenty-one days.

There are dwelling places, too, whose yellow walls and red-tiled roofs do not carry a scar. In the front of all of these houses, broken and unbroken, past which limp long roads sadly in want of attention, the maple trees are turning to yellow gold in the late November sun.

I HAVE been up to the front many times. Tomorrow or the day after I am going back again.

I am sitting beside a pine fire in an officer's room, one moment writing, the next lifting my face to watch the red sun glide down, down behind the sloping tiled roofs into late afternoon. Four miles out the road, and just on the fringe of "No Man's Land," men are struggling in rain-lashed trenches, fighting, fighting, fighting. Many of them are going to be brought back in our clumsy blue ambulances—oh, ever so slowly over broken roads—to the base hospitals for mending. Others will be hurled into the nothingness of death as their fingers grip their rifles and their faces distort with pain and fear. While I write these lines, my ears are full of the faint-off day-long booming of the French 105's. It will run on into the dark blackness of night—on, on, always on until there is no saying as to when those guns will be quiet again.

EVERY other day I go out there—to one of the many *poste de secours*, and remain with a driver until the following noon. The *poste de secours* is a short ride behind the trenches and is in no way a soft berth. Neither is it a place for slackers—those with the broad perpendicular yellow streak.

On the down trip the driver and I lumber along roads heavy with camouflage. Overhead stretch brown and green brush strips, reminding me of the mardi-gras decorations back home. We continue out past old barbed-wire entanglements. Devilish contrivances are these entanglements with their stakes set as close as straws in a brush. To these meshes rush the wild hill-winds between the dusk and the dawn to strum their hymns of hate.

WHEN a French soldier is wounded on the field of honor, a message is telephoned to the nearest *poste de secours*.

"An ambulance at once, *monsieur*," an *infirmier* (infirmary attendant) interprets the call, laying the nickel-plated French phone hurriedly on his desk. "At once, *monsieur!*"

Only the day before yesterday I was given one of those verbal orders. It was the first I had ever received, and it thrilled me as nothing else has ever done.

I was on duty at ——, a straggling, shell-torn village that is slowly recuperating in the midst of the trench country.

With me was Charles ("Windy") R. Williams of

Mamaroneck, N. Y. Men as red-blooded and acclimatized to the winds of the open world as "Windy" Williams are not met with every day. Some time in the not-far-off future, after the scourge of bullet and fire has ceased and the world armies have been disarmed and scattered, I am going to put together a book in which will be sung the strength and valor of those who went out to do their bit so that the world "might be made safe for Democracy." And therein will be written for the eyes of all the name of "Windy" Williams.

WELL, I was at ——. It had been asleep all afternoon in a still blue haze. Near dusk it awakened to watch five German planes that were skimming down to —— to bombard the women and children. They flew straight and swift, humming viciously, like immense dragon-flies, while below them anti-air-craft shells broke with a soft *plop*, throwing out fleecy clouds as white as wool.

As the day began to gloom down to night and the thin streams of smoke from the supper fires rose up, the boches on the far side of "No Man's Land" conceived, for the thousand and first time, the idea of shelling the village. There was not a thing in it that would further their purpose, but to them that made no difference.

The shelling was their rosary. They threw their shells over one by one. Four plunged in the rear of the *poste de secours*, laying the ground open to bedrock. Three struck 500 feet off the shoestring of a street. They ricocheted through the shell zone with a horrible whine, then smote the tormented earth with a roar and a crash.

THE explosions almost stunned Windy and me. Never in all my twenty-eight years had I heard anything so appalling. I am writing nothing but the absolute truth when I emphasize that I could hear those death missiles slow up preparatory to dropping and blowing every adjacent thing into particles as fine as screened gravel.

As the first shell went wild of its mark, I looked hurriedly toward the *poste de secours*.

The excited *infirmiers* were spilling into the street, like ants running off a platter. Some of them fell headlong in their flight to the bomb-proof *abri* or place of shelter.

THE *abri*, a narrow passage burrowed deep under the road and full of the smell of underground things, was at least 200 feet long. Both ceiling and walls were heavily timbered, while on either side of the earth-wet board-walk stretched platforms the length of a man. On these are laid the sick and the wounded during an attack.

Half-way down the *abri* I squatted myself on a platform, sitting beside Windy's long, big-boned body, and waited for the inevitable, all the while feeling, as some men feel in their near-to-dying moments, that my destiny had been snatched out of my hands. No longer was I the captain of my soul.

The next minute (it seemed an hour to me) the French batteries opened. They vomited mouthful after mouthful of life-depriving lead and copper at the Huns on the far side of "No Man's Land." The earth rocked violently with the clatter of the batteries' iron tongues and the thundering and screaming flights of shell.

Neither then nor in the half-hour that dragged on did the boches respond. So Windy and I climbed back to the *poste de secours* and sat in the low white-walled kitchen while François, one of the detached divisional cooks, prepared our day-end meal.

FRANÇOIS, who marched out of the sun-warmed grape lands of the Pyrenees when "To Arms!" sounded on that fateful August morning of 1914, is a small, big-beaming Frenchman with black pupils lying far down in one corner of his eyes, like splotches of ink. His blue blouse and trousers are far too large for him, and the soft black cap that tumbles about his ears is again the size of a mess plate.

Whenever he crossed the rock floor, moving swiftly from the field range to the kitchen table, his muddy wooden shoes hushed the river of French talk which had begun to flow in the dining-room. And while Windy and I ate our tinned beef and French-fried potatoes, he stood near the range, chewing a piece of bread thoughtfully and muttering from time to time in an intense hate voice:

"Boche! Boche! Boche!"

Twice he spat disgustedly into the black gloom beyond the circle of the lantern that hung beside the doorway.

AS SOON as it had come to nine o'clock, Windy took down the lantern and lighted the way to a tent in the woodshed back of the *poste de secours*.

Immediately we sought the two blood-stained *brancards* or French stretchers he had converted into cots.

For a long time—so long that I did not care to hold the exact time in mind—I lay with eyes wide open, feeling lonely and cold in the darkness. I was not homesick. For I have been too long out in the open spaces of the earth for that. Neither was I thinking of a love-woman. There are none of those women in my life. I was lonely, that was all.

Windy wanted to talk, but I would have none of it. Once the French guns began barking far away in the weary hills. They stopped after a while, blowing out of the blue-black of the heavens, their boom going down in the wind. But for the wind and the monotonous croaking of the frogs in a rain-made pond between the yard and the road, all would have been dead calm. I felt lonelier than ever before—oh, terribly lonely. It was as if a cataclysm had swept the world and left only Windy and me to live on for no visible purpose whatever.

SUDDENLY there fell on the graveled path running up to the mouth of the shed the quick clatter of hobnailed boots. The following minute the darkness was parted in two by the broad yellow ray of a lantern and the tent flaps opened to let in a full, black-bearded face.

I raised on my elbow with a start, then, recognizing an *infirmier*, sat up inquiringly.

"*Blessé, monsieur! Toute de suite! Toute de suite!*" he said in fast, guttural accents. His eyes, shining like black buttons, lowered until I felt his garlicky breath burning on my face. "*Toute de suite, monsieur!*"

"A wounded *poilu*," Windy spoke up, throwing off his four blankets. And then, as two years' of high-school French came back to him, "We must go at once—as quickly as possible!"

WONDERING aloud how far he would have to drive and who the poor *poilu* could be, Windy slipped into his coat and shoes. From the packing-case, a makeshift table at the foot of the brancards, he took both his steel helmet and gas-mask, then hurried out to the shell of a house in which he had parked the Fiat ambulance.

I followed him, thrilled by the whole thing. It was our first call, the call we had crossed the sea to answer first of all, and I wanted to see what lay at the far end of it.

During the next quarter hour we found it difficult to turn over the motor. Not an inch would it budge. The radiator was cold—almost frozen. Twice I brought hot water from the kitchen and poured it over the radiator and the pump. Then I primed the radiator, flooding the four petcocks with essence. After that Windy cranked and damned the machine a full ten minutes before the motor came to with a hard spurt.

WHEN we took to the dark smear of a road—the stars, shining cold and a long way off, threw down but little light in which to drive—the *infirmier* sat wedged between us, wrapped in a long fur coat. He had the *ordre de mouvement* and the word which would carry us past the road sentries.

"Where are we going?" Windy asked him.

"Far down," the *infirmier* motioned, throwing his small gloved hand toward the trench country. "Far, far down."

Keeping the road was the hardest thing Windy and I have had to do since coming to these parts. The road was narrow, in places a thin scratch of path, and the strata of earth had peeled off like the skin of an onion.

Once Windy cried in a strained voice, striving to maintain the road, "I have no eyes to-night, kid. I can not see in this darkness. You'll have to guide me—to keep me on this —— road!"

IN THE eleven years that are coming to a close I have done all manner of things from going down to the South Pacific on a hell-ship to studying in college halls, and I have been to the weird and far-out places of the world, but never until then, away on the slope of the . . . . . did I stand on the running-board of an ambulance, without even so much as a pocket flashlight, to pilot a comrade along a battle-front we had never before seen.

"Let her have the right, Windy," I directed, swinging on to the running-board. And, after we had taken a curve in the road five minutes beyond, "Now, give her the center of the road. Take it easy. Good. You've got her there, Windy. Hold her."

THE Fiat climbed over most of the road in second, at times creeping, it seemed to me, a mile an hour. Worse, not once did Windy throw out a light. The boches would have shelled us immediately.

We were crawling over the crest of a hill when Windy all but ran into an ammunition train. The train, dark like the road, was making slowly ahead of us.

"You —— frog!" Windy shouted at a poilu straddling a truck horse almost at the tail of the train. He braked the car. "Give me part of the road so that I can get by, —— you!" Then he swore again and again, wasting his breath and tongue on the fool.

At the foot of the long hill we began running between two rows of dead trees. Through their thin black ribs we saw star-shells breaking over the front-line trenches less than half a mile away. The yellow shell-fire gave no report, but drifted slowly above "No Man's Land" for two minutes or more, then went out like a torch in the wind.

WHEN midway in the trees, a boche shell sped over the car with a menacing whine and struck near the summit of the hill. Instantly my ears drummed with the horrible scream of the flying-death thing as its entrails were torn from its belly. The man-flesh of the *infirmier* winced hard. I looked at Windy, my nostrils beating like a heart. His tall, big-boned body was hunched against the wheel. Nerved and unafraid, he was driving through the deep road-ruts.

An hour had passed since we left the *poste de secours* at ——. Just when we were beginning to fear that we were going to drive through all the darkness and cruelty of night, we dipped away down into ——, a shell-riddled town, and braked in front of a three-storied stone house that looked across the valley.

"It's the *poste de secours*," I remarked to Windy. And, oddly, I tasted several grams of relief in my voice. "The *poste de secours*."

FROM the narrow doorway, before which stood a whispering group of poilus, I made out a red river of fire wrangling toward the impenetrable blackness of the hills.

"The French fight hard tonight in those trenches," the *infirmier* informed me, turning slowly to go into the *poste de secours*.

I shifted my look from the trenches to the *blesse* lying on a brancard in a long drafty hallway.

The blessé, a middle-aged poilu with thin black whiskers and eyes that were blood-shot and tired, lay blinking at the bandaged foot which showed from between the blankets.

"Shrapnel. Shrapnel!" he spoke up slowly, answering intuitively the question I would have put to him. "Shrapnel!"

The foot had been split open to the bone. And for that he had received five cents a day.

WHEN two *infirmiers* lifted him into the ambulance a few minutes afterward, he neither moaned nor cried.

"*Mon casque*," was all that he said in a quiet way, taking the steel helmet an *infirmier* passed to him a moment before we closed the ambulance door. "*Mon casque*."

Then Windy and I, salvagers of human wreckage, carried him into a base hospital for more capable hands to mend.

And when we were done with him, we rejoiced. For just before driving away from the hospital the medical chief whispered to us:

"He is through with the war. He will not return to the trenches. After he leaves here, he goes back to his woman!"—CHARLES BROWN, JR.

IN MAY the United States District Court revoked the naturalization papers of a foreign-born citizen because of his admitted desire that America should not win the war against the land of his birth, Germany.

In other words, the man had sworn *full* allegiance to this country and had not given it; he had sworn an oath renouncing *all* allegiance to Germany and had been false to that oath. He had not paid, as agreed, for the citizenship privilege he received from us. Therefore, it was taken from him. Though he had for thirty-five years been an American voter, Frederick W. Wursterbarth, former postmaster of Lakeview, New Jersey, was deprived by the court of his right to vote, of his American citizenship.

IT IS said that years ago there was a similar case in the West, but the present decision, if upheld on appeal, is likely to mark a new era in our guardianship of the privilege of American citizenship.

I hope so. The man who gets citizenship by deliberate perjury or who breaks his sworn oath of allegiance to his adopted country certainly has no right to that citizenship. It is our own shame—and perhaps our own destruction—if we allow him to retain it.

ONE of our stories that interested you strongly was Norman Springer's "A Man and His Name" and it was centered on the fight of a man against the drink habit during a long voyage.

Adventuring as a cure for drink. How drink knocks you out; how to knock it out. How it crawls up on you; how to crawl away from it. Can you fight it better outdoors in the open? Can you fight it better adventuring or following the uneventful, routine paths?

For a good many men these aren't just general questions. Often enough they mean success or failure, life or death. Often these men want the answers pretty badly.

I WONDER. Would it be possible to take this subject up at Camp-Fire and get some valuable practical results out of swapping experiences without having any smell of preaching attached to it? It might mean a lot to some comrades. I don't mean that we should discuss any such questions as "Is it naughty to drink?" The discussion I have in mind would be pretty well centered on the fellows who know they drink too much, want to stop and find that stopping is a job that needs all the help a man can lay hands on. If they want that help, why shouldn't we try to give it to them?

There were at least several of you to whom Mr. Springer's story wasn't just a story but a practical personal help, so much so that they wrote in to express their gratitude. And that story didn't have any of the odor of preaching.

SUPPOSE we leave it this way:—If any of you can offer really practical help and facts along this line, send it in. If any want to get such facts, and help write to Camp-Fire. Names and addresses, if desired, need not be printed. In other words, let's leave the gates open a while and see how things work out. If nothing much happens, all right. If both demand and supply seem pretty strong, why, maybe we've found something else worth doing.

SOME more "dope" on the pioneers, particularly about the much-discussed Captain Drannan. Also an inquiry—and another example of the good comradeship among Camp-Fire members:

Denver, Colo.

Here is a little dope on Captain Drannan. In a showcase in the Colorado State Historical Museum is a beautifully embroidered buckskin suit and an old-fashioned, round-crowned sombrero to match. Accompanying these are a photograph, a lithograph and a crudely made dagger. The suit has the following information pinned on it.

"Captain W. F. Drannan took the skins this suit is made of in the raw state and made them into buckskin. The suit was cut, made, and embroidered by his wife, Mrs. Sybil H. Drannan. Donated by Mrs. Belle H. Drannan, Mineral Wells, Texas."

The knife has this with it. "Captain Drannan took this knife from Myers, the white desperado who hired the Indians to massacre the Gordon emigrant train in 1853."

THE lithograph shows an old man in a buckskin suit sitting on a settee. The original had evidently been taken in a studio. It is signed at the bottom in pencil. "Captain W. F. Drannan, Chief of Scouts." At the side, in the same old-fashioned writing, are the words, "In his seventy-first year."

The photograph shows him in the same attire sitting on a camp chair on a sidewalk holding a book on his knee. Hanging on a telephone-pole is a large banner with the legend, "Captain Wm. Drannan, the oldest scout now alive and the only living companion of Kit Carson that crossed to the Rockies in '47. Read his book and see what he has done for his country." The picture was taken parallel to the street and there are no objects in sight from which a stranger could judge where it was taken. There is a second telephone-pole near with a sign bearing these names on it, "Market, Barber Shop and The Burkhart Laundry." Maybe some of our Southwestern friends will recognize them.

A YEAR ago a friend of mine loaned me and offered to give me Captain Drannan's book, "Thirty-One Years on the Plains." I wish now that I had accepted it. After reading Mr. Caldwell's letter I phoned my friend and asked him if he was still willing to part with it. As it happens, he also is an adventure fan and, after reading said letter, he said he wouldn't part with the book for any consideration.

No War Baby ever rose in value any faster than the book did in his estimation. However another friend of mine runs a second-hand bookstore and he located two copies in his files, one of which I immediately secured. If Mr. Caldwell doesn't locate Mr. Buck's one let me know and I will see that he gets the other one.

LAST Fall, while working in a construction camp, I heard mention of the "Jackson Hole Gang" and also a bad man named McCoy and a woman rustler called "Cattle Kate." The "Jackson Hole Gang" I had heard of before, but I am curious as to the other two. All that I know is that they operated in Wyoming. Perhaps some old-timer can enlighten us.—LESTOR B. WOOD.

P. S.—I stopped in the library to see if they had Drannan's book. Imagine my surprise when I found listed a second book, a sequel to the first, entitled "Captain W. F. Drannan," by himself. Immediately called for the book and was informed by the attendant that it was out. I guess that some other fan beat me to it. The attendant told me that in the last few days there had been a number of inquiries for it and that she wondered what the reason was. I don't think it is very hard to guess.

L. B. W.

P. S. No. 2—Here I am again. Some time back you published a letter (I think Mr. Brininstool wrote it) that spoke of Frank Gruard. It cleared a mystery that had long been in my mind. In the museum is a picture of a dark-skinned man wearing white man's clothes, bearing the inscription "Frank Gooard a Kanaki," followed by a short history. I looked high and low for a tribe called the Kanaki. When I couldn't locate them I went back and took another look at the picture. The man had a most un-Indian countenance, the nose being broad and flat and the lips being thick and full, suggestive of the Ethiopian or Polynesian types. I rejected the former because of the straight shiny hair and thin sparse mustache hanging low on the upper lip (like on Mexicans you sometimes see) and the latter because who ever heard of a South Sea Islander fighting Indians? On the way home I started to read the "Camp-Fire." One of the first things I saw was an account of Frank Gruard, a Kanaka. The problem was solved. It's funny how things will connect up, isn't it?—L. B. W.

FOLLOWING our Camp-Fire custom, H. P. Holt rises and introduces himself on the occasion of his first story in our magazine. And I think maybe we'd all like to shake hands with Captain Jim Gorring.

I have wandered pretty nearly everywhere in tramp steamers in search of happiness and material for books and stories.

ONE day, about eight years ago, on a two-by-four little island named Tarkei, to the east of Fiji, I felt myself going under with malaria, which I had contracted in Africa. The only person on Tarkei with whom I could exchange five words was a Portuguese. He was never sober and had a lurid reputation altogether. I had nearly four thousand dollars in my belt—every cent I owned.

The Portuguese was a real beach-comber—about the worst kind of type for a sick man to lean up against. His shoes were worn to nothing. He grunted, looked at my shoes, which were fairly new, and sat down to wait till he could step into them. I omitted to speak of the contents of my belt, or he would not have done any waiting. I should have gone down the sunset trail within a few hours if a trading schooner had not dropped anchor off the beach to get water.

The skipper—a complete stranger to me—came ashore and, while I was unconscious, took a hand in the game. He stayed there for three days, entirely for my benefit, and pulled me through. He stripped my belt off me and wore it till I was fit to go aboard with him. Then I remained on his schooner for four months, pottering about among the islands, trading with blacks who were mostly only about one-hundredth part civilized.

HIS name was Jim Gorring, and I believe he lives near Sydney, Australia, today. Anyway, I took him for my model in "A Flutter in Salvage." Jim couldn't help helping others, but never could make money for himself because he was curiously ingenuous and an altruist. He always insisted on holding prayers, morning and night, whether the crew liked it or not, except when we were just hanging on to the old schooner with our eyebrows. Also he hated to see a man drink liquor. I met him in Sydney a couple of years after our cruise in the south seas, and found he had had a stroke of luck such as sailors hope for but rarely experience. He had salved an abandoned bark laden with a valuable cargo, and, after the settling up, had "dropped his anchor ashore."

DON'T forget to be marking down your selections for our vote on the ten most popular stories in our magazines during the year 1918.

WHAT is the candidate who makes a campaign promise to the people and, when elected by them, breaks his promise? Can any one make him out to be anything but a liar? And do you like a liar? And trust him? Do you like a man whose promise is worth nothing? And trust him? Do you consider him fit to hold a public office?

Probably you'll say no to all these questions, *but* do you make it a point never to vote again for such a man? Or even to keep close tabs on him and his promises and how he keeps them? If not, just how good an American citizen are you?

ARTHUR SULLIVANT HOFFMAN.

THE CAMP-FIRE

A FREE-TO-ALL MEETING-PLACE FOR READERS, WRITERS, AND ADVENTURERS

NONE of us wants to help the Germans. One way of helping them is to buy German-made goods. Even after the war there will probably be need of putting a ban on German products. The American Defense Society, 44 East 23rd Street, New York, which has been doing splendid patriotic work since long before we entered the war, has taken up this matter and is circulating pledges whereby individuals bind themselves never to buy anything made in Germany.

Of course, if some day the German people throw off the Junker yoke, leave out the Hohenzollerns, change themselves back from beasts to humans and do a few other little things like that, it would be time to reconsider or cancel that pledge. But it will be long years before the Germans can prove themselves humans again.

AND here's another phase, suggested in a letter from one of you:

As one of the old one-idead type I am boxing around to secure the feeling of comfort and mutual support gained in an organized crowd in view of cutting out all trade with Germany and with the many German sympathizers we have with us. When you start such a ball rolling, list me.

I told this comrade about the American Defense Society's work and I judge he's registered with them by this time. They're good people to get in touch with anyhow, for their patriotic work is of a varied nature and may offer you other opportunities you'd welcome.

A BRIEF word from H. A. Lamb on his story in this issue:

New York.

The lakes in extinct volcanic craters are found in several of the South Sea islands. The island in question is located northeast of Santo, in the New Hebrides group, near Ambrym, which was the "Island of Changing Shapes." You won't find the name Vata Lavum in any chart, because I christened it that.—HAROLD A. LAMB.

THE article on firearms by D. Wiggins and L. R. Brown at one of our August Camp-Fires is bringing in answers and queries and arguments, just as we were sure it would do and wanted it to do. Here, for example, is a query from Comrade W. C. Tuttle of our writers' brigade, who has an old gun he wants identified.

Spokane, Washington.

Was greatly interested in that article "Firearms, Old and New," and would like to rise up and inquire if somebody would tell me something about a gun which I own.

Digging through the rust on the barrel I find the inscription: "Savage R. F. A. Middletown, Ct., H. S. North, Pat. 1856."

THE gun is about fifteen inches long and I think it is a .38 caliber. It is a muzzle-loading revolver, with an extra high hammer, which cuts off the rear sight unless cocked. Six-shooter. It has a peculiar shaped butt, but which fits the hand in good shape.

The novel feature is in the action. Instead of having the cylinder turn from the trigger-pull, there is another trigger, or lever, if you please, behind the pull-trigger, with a ring to fit the second finger. You turn the cylinder with your second finger and pull with the index finger—and pray, I reckon. It will weigh about four pounds.

The man I got it from claims it was picked up in

Mexico. It has seen a lot of hard usage. My dad, who is an old gun-man, and who knows a lot about old guns, told me that it was a new one on him. As far as I can see—awful rusty—the rifles run straight down the barrel. Would like mighty well to have somebody tell me something about this style and make of gun, 'cause it looks like a killer.—W. C. TUTTLE.

THE other day I got word from Octavus Roy Cohen, one of whose stories appears in this issue, that he had successfully passed the preliminary examinations for a commission in the Signal Corps. He writes: "This is the first real chance for service which has come my way; and it is my sixteenth application." Sixteen attempts would seem to indicate sort of a desire to get to the front.

IT WILL be good news to you that his tale in this number is only the first of a series that Talbot Mundy is writing for us. Time was when he turned out his stories briskly and in large number, and you liked them better than any others of our tales. Nowadays he works more slowly and though his stories come at longer intervals I think you'll find them even more worth waiting for.

Here is a word to you from him. In it he fails to mention that many of at least the minor incidents are bits out of his own life. For example, the landing at Lourenço Marques.

New York.

This, and the stories that will follow, are all more or less reminiscent. The names of people have been so entirely changed that the originals are unrecognizable, except that the man Charles du Maurier under his real name made such a reputation on that countryside as to be undisguisable anyhow. Any one who lived in Lourenço Marques in the bad old days of monarchical government would need no spirit of divination to help him identify the original of du Maurier and his family, even if I had called him Jones.

AS FOR the Portuguese and their government of those days, there is this to be said for them: they were human. Murder was frequent, "justice" was purchasable and not to be had by any other means unless a man took law into his own hands—as he very well could do, if man enough, at almost any point thirty miles back from the sea. Where the coconut trees ceased from bearing fruit there ceased all but the shadow of the King of Portugal's authority. But the Portuguese, unofficial and official, were hospitable folk, as far as I was able to observe and quite devoid of the Spanish element of cruelty, very often brave, and frequently generous. They were frankly ashamed of their own misgovernment and ready at any time to talk of a republic with any one, but in almost every instance unwilling, or unable, to forego the chance of looting while the chance remained.

Of course this utter corruption of their government attracted to Lourenço Marques and the other towns (such as Inhambane, Beira and so on) all the undesirables from British territory and not a few from Madagascar; and their crimes were naturally credited to the Portuguese. That was not so unjust after all, for it was the Portuguese who made the rascality possible and whose highest officials set the worst example in the first place.

THERE were two or three peculiarities I especially noticed that are worth preserving from oblivion; and there is one conjecture I would like to offer. They were much more capable of deliberate cruelty toward a white man than a black. It is true that they were guilty of the most atrocious conduct toward natives, but they fed them, whereas they would let a white man starve (and frequently did) without compunction. They recruited slave-gangs on the East Coast for the West, and *vice versa*, and the cruelty inflicted on the "laborers" is best unwritten. Yet the Portuguese themselves were often the severest critics of the system and the guilty officials responsible for its continuance were a minority held in unqualified contempt. They did not permit flogging of natives by planters and private citizens.

The lower-class Portuguese invariably loathed the English. The better class invariably liked them. (I found the exact contrary to be the case in German territory.) The reason, I suppose, was that the riffraff of the population and the corrupt officials came in contact almost exclusively with blackguard Englishmen, as corrupt, as greedy and degraded as themselves; whereas the Portuguese gentlemen met English gentlemen and discovered ideas in common. Unhappily, the gentlemen of either race were rare in that afflicted land.

MY CONJECTURE is that the reason why the Portuguese find themselves fighting on the side of the Allies in this war is that the Portuguese, as a nation, were conscious of the shortcomings of their government and had not a good word to say for it. The German people, of course, have endorsed every action of their government; the more scoundrelly the atrocity, the louder their paeans of praise. Whereas I never once heard a Portuguese—not even a Portuguese official—praise his government. They denounced it first, last and all the time; and, although they took advantage of it with almost unbelievable cynicism, when their chance came at last they overthrew it. They were human. They did not care ten *reis* for efficiency without humanity, and they made no pretense at all to be supermen or demigods.

A LETTER from E. A. Brininstool, indefatigable gatherer of data and souvenirs of the old West:

Los Angeles, California.

I was in Santa Fé, New Mexico, two days last week, running down an old-time photo of Billy the Kid. It required time and some chasing, but I have it. I had the photo rephotoed and have the negative—the only picture that was ever made of this notorious cuss of but twenty-one years.

I also met and heard from his own lips, the story

of the capture of the Kid, from Don Romulo Martinez, who was sheriff of Santa Fé County when the Kid was captured the first time, and who delivered him to the authorities at Las Cruces, by whom he was sentenced to be hung, but dug out of jail a few nights later, being shot and killed by Pat Garrett soon after, as recorded in my story. Believe me—that old town has some lively stories. The Don told me many things about the Kid never put in print. . . . If you want to add this picture of the Kid to the others, I will send you a print. It is a rare picture, as it is the only one the Kid ever allowed to be made.—E. A. BRININSTOOL.

I WISH that some great voice could boom out across the distances and speak a certain message into the hearts of all our soldiers and sailors who are fighting our country's battles. Some of them already have the message. I know, for they have told me of it. Giving their all now, yet they are planning further giving in the future. Fighting for the protection of things held dear, they still have time and thought to plan how, when war is over, they can help make these prized things even more worth fighting for.

THESE millions of fighters will come back to us, after victory. Back to what they have fought to maintain. But they will come back with keener insight, with a new understanding of other things than war. They will ask "What is this we have fought for? Our comrades died for it. Is it fully worthy of all the blood and tears that have been shed in saving it? We have paid out the farthest price and what we have paid for must be worth that price. If it is not so strong and clean and good as it can be made, then it must be made so. It must be made worthy of its price. And *we* bore the brunt of the payment. We have become the doers and the makers. If others have not made democracy and our country as clean and good as they should be, then we will take up this new fight so that our other fight may not be in vain. We are a mighty force. What we will to do we can do. We can fight in peace as well as in war. We will go on in our fight for the best in democracy."

SOLDIERS and sailors, if you have not heard the message, hear it now. If you have not seen the need, see it now.

In the little book, "To Americans," issued free to all by the American League for Citizenship, Inc., there is this same message to our fighters, an appeal that the League knows will be answered:

The League makes supreme appeal to the soldiers, sailors, marines and non-combatants now upholding in war the American people's honor and safety. They will return to us with new vision and with a more living understanding of the needs of democracy. That for which they have offered their lives and suffering will have become to them something to be more treasured, something made more peculiarly their own, something to be made more worthy of their sacrifice. In the hands of these millions of voting citizens will largely lie the future of American democracy. To them the League offers itself as their instrument in the building of a better America. And upon them the League relies for cleared eyes to see real needs, for strength to enforce cleanness and for true understanding of the need of common cause for the common good.

LAST year our readers selected by vote the best ten stories published in *Adventure* during 1918. We want our readers to have as much say as possible in making the magazine, and this annual vote not only helps decidedly in choosing the writers and kinds of story *Adventure's* readers most want but also gives every last one of you a chance to say his say in the making of the magazine and to have his say count.

It isn't just a question of learning which writers and stories are best liked by you. Nearly all our writers receive at least some votes and the general result is a long graded list tapering from thousands of points each down to several or even, in a few cases, none at all. The editors learn something about which stories were *not* popular as well as about the preferred ones.

VOTING is simple and easy. On any sheet of paper write your list of ten stories (giving author's names), numbering them in order of preference. If you like, add as many as ten more stories by way of second choice or complimentary mention. Add your name and address. That's all.

Any one can vote provided he has read at least *seven* of the issues, for 1918 (First January, 1918, to Mid-December, 1918, inclusive). Serials, novels, novelettes, short stories, and articles all rank alike and may be voted for. Poems and "Camp-Fire" are barred.

A serial that laps over into 1917 or 1919 may also be included in the vote. The same author may appear in the list as many times as you please. No votes will be counted if they reach us later than December 31, 1918, though allowance will be made for those writing from long distances, particularly the war-front. A list of the winners will be published in a subsequent issue, as was done last year.

If you've not already begun marking down your favorite stories, better begin doing so now. Don't let stories in the later issues overshadow those earlier in the year merely because you read the former later and have them more vividly in your mind. And don't let the mere length of a serial, novel or novelette outweigh the value of the shorter stories.

AND this year let's add a new feature to our voting. As in past years, we're leaving "Camp-Fire" and other departments out of the regular vote. But wouldn't it be interesting to find out just what relative values are assigned to these departments by our readers in general? Suppose that, in addition to the regular vote, we add a special vote. Call the total value of an average issue one hundred per cent., including both fiction and departments; then write down after each of the following items the proportion of value each of them seems to you to deserve:

Stories (all together)
Poetry (all together)
Camp-Fire
Identification Cards
Fighting the Hun Web
Looking Ahead
Ask Adventure
How to Help Win the War
Lost Trails

The total for the list should, of course, be one hundred per cent.

Of course, "Fighting the Hun Web" and "Looking Ahead" are not really under way yet, since there has not been time for replies from readers in response to the first appearance of these departments to be received, put into type and be published in the magazine. So perhaps in these two cases we'd better make some allowance and try to value them according to what they will be when really going.

I HOPE by this time I don't need to tell you that the staff is always wide open to suggestions of any kind for making our magazine better.

If there's anything you want to suggest or criticize, add it at the end of your vote.

SOME interesting bits from "Uncle Frank" H. Huston on Gila monsters, rattlers, the king of all Western pioneers, Calamity Jane, and the pronunciation of "God." The last is in reply to a comrade at a former Camp-Fire. And the rest of you who knew the West of the old days, what can you tell us about Major North?

Camp 5, North of Marysville, California.

Comrade—of Prescott should be told once more that "God" is pronounced like "hod" in "coalhod" when done by linguists, but ordinary geezers drawl it like a darky, but never with an "*r*," *i. e.*, "gord." English lends itself poorly to phonetics, you know that, but resuming, I strongly suspect threshing this out with "Prescott" some two years since. Again, whites say "Návajo," accent on "nav," but Greasers say "Navájo," accent on "va" as per academic Castellano; as to spelling, either is correct, but j is original Spanish form.

GILA monster will vary in localities slightly, as does the rattler. I've seen 'em with dominant color now reddish, again yellow, again brownish, again clayish and, on very large ones, like a beaded moccasin. Natural History Museum, Washington, D. C., used to have some fine "specemints" of latter. Trouble is lots of tenderfeet, or near "sandfleas," see a chuckwalla and think it's a Gila. In the 80's I saw two separate men bitten by 'em in "Prescott's" own town and both died of lockjaw, and, by the way, Prescott a few years since had more "skippers" and "bobtails" than all the rest of the United States combined. That's one reason Miles said he would see "grass grow in its streets yet."

THAT little inquiry of mine *re* old-timers sure started 'em, but, with all the wealth of information sent in, not one word of the king of 'em all—Major North. Come on now, some one, and give us the saga of the chief of chiefs.

NOW I can not go into this very deeply for personal reasons, but I've seen and talked with Calamity Jane, the real original one (several tried to palm themselves off as her). I remember her, but right here, understand, it is only memory dimmed and obscured by time, not facts.

Jane had many stories told of her, one that her husband and family were killed by Injuns and that she smelled trouble ahead and never showed up except as a prophet of evil to come, hence name Calamity. Again that she'd had so much trouble that the name was appropriate to her. She was a tall gaunt pioneer woman. Pike County, I think, but am not sure. Rode, talked and acted like many others of her kind—I've seen 'em even today—but she never was the hell-roaring roisterer she is credited with being. She was in Ft. Sidney, Nebraska, one time, "across the track" (the shacks opposite the Post), and bawled a young chap out as a "—— —— rennygate," which he was to an extent but not wholly so. If I remember she had tried ranching and been put out of business so often that she gave it up. I never heard a word or whisper against her morality (chastity) but one look at her was enough to account for that and I think she had a "way house," sort of tavern and with her usual luck lost out on it by a raid and flames.—"H."

Illustration by Mr. Tuttle, the cartoonist, for the story by Mr. Tuttle, the writer—"The Hand of Providence," in a recent issue

---

OF THE last four stories, including the one in this issue, by S. B. H. Hurst, three have been "flotsam" stories, tales of drifters, of human wreckage, in the world's far corners. As our old-timers will remember, Mr. Hurst has covered most of this round ball we live on and in the years it is only natural that he should have met many and many a bit of human flotsam. Out of these meetings he has built the tales he is now giving us.

Here is his own statement of the case:

Seattle, Washington.

You find them at the far corners of the world, these men who do not speak of yesterday; a devil driving each of them from a past out of which faces stare inhumanly, as through smoke. But they do not linger, and respectable squaw-men do not seek their acquaintance and would be more likely to be polite to their women than to ask them their business.

But they have, of course, come from somewhere, and of that *somewhere*, as well as of *something*, they breathe in patches when breath is coming hard.

Out into the air of strange places their whispers go, as if to break trail for the souls that will shortly follow them. Their eyes look you a last "so long," and you ease the weight from your arms—and wonder. And being yourself kin to them you understand much that the whispers failed to tell you. And you hope the ground is not frozen as hard as it appears to be, for you dislike working with a pick.

It having been my fate to have nine such bits of drift die in my arms, I have a patchwork of their history—scraps torn from each of the nine. I have taken time and made me a crazy quilt of them. But it is more seemly—or, at any rate, I think so—to show it to you bit by bit.—S. B. H. Hurst.

IT IS said that a main reason for desertions from our Army and Navy before the war was plain homesickness. At the outset of the war in April, 1917, War Camp Community Service was brought into being by the War and Navy Departments' Commission on Training Camp Activities to attend to all the wants and needs of our soldiers, sailors and marines while they are on leave outside of camp—at the time when they get lonely and homesick. The consequent reduction in the number of desertions was amazing.

This service has an organizer in every community near a training-camp, cantonment or naval station, ready to provide anything possible from a baby to play with to a nice girl to talk to or dance with or an inexpensive room for a mother, wife, sister, sweetheart or the man himself. If you're in Army or Navy, look him up to get the service; if you're not, help furnish it.

FROM one of our comrades who belongs to both our readers' and our writers' brigades, Samuel Edward Harris, comes to the Camp-Fire the following shark story:

Key West.

A few minutes before, I had caught a whipperee measuring 4 feet 8 inches, when the shark ran off with my line and I exclaimed, "This is another, boys!" Before I tell about the shark it may be well to explain just what a whipperee is (I don't know its technical name).

THE whipperee resembles the skate, which is frequently the pest of anglers in New York waters. But there's this difference between the fish: the skate is harmless, while the whipperee is feared more than sharks by native swimmers in Key West. The whipperee's tail is not only longer than a skate's, but is composed of a substance that looks like a strip of dried cowhide. According to persons who have been swiped by a whipperee's tail, it's like coming into contact with a live wire. Years ago I saw a Cuban's leg which had been cut by a whipperee, and it had a ridge, colored like indigo and as big as one's little finger, half way round it. As some Italians and others in New York eat the wings of a skate, so some Cubans and others in Key West eat the wings of a whipperee. It is said the wings, made up into a salad, taste like crabmeat.

TO GET back to the shark: Sammy Thompson, Albert Sanchez and I were out in the motor-boat *Trio*, fishing in Mangrove Key Channel, a mile offshore. The tide was running out, and snappers and yellow grunts, for which we were fishing, were not biting well. I was using a hand-line (gruntline, it is called here), which was about the size of a drop-line used to catch fluke and flounder in New York waters. After I had caught, killed and measured the whipperee I baited my hook and threw it out again. A few minutes later I had a bite and hooked the fish, though I didn't succeed in turning it. It was then I exclaimed to Thompson and Sanchez that I had another whipperee.

My line was 180 feet long, with a white grunt hook (about the size of a fluke hook) fastened to the line with a brass wire leader. In ten seconds or so most of my line had sung through my hands and I added to my first exclamation, "This is a whopdoodle! Cube (meaning Sanchez), tie your line to mine." His line was the same length as mine.

IN THE meantime I had jumped up on the sternsheet and was gradually inscreasing the pressure on the line, but still the shark (we didn't know it was a shark until ten or fifteen minutes later) kept heading out to sea. A few seconds later the Cube cried out:

"It's nearly all out, Sam! Hold her tight, and let him pop it! That's the only way you'll save any of it."

I held the line as tightly as I could and brought the shark up. But that was only the beginning of the fight. I had pulled in less than a hundred feet of the line when the shark turned and headed out to sea again. And again I stopped him (we refer to all fish down here in the masculine) at the critical moment, and again, after he had come my way for a few seconds he turned out to sea. We had gone through that procedure for ten or fifteen minutes, when Thompson shouted, "Look! It's a shark!" We looked to where he pointed and saw the monster's dorsal fin cutting through the surface of the water.

I FOUGHT that shark for thirty or forty minutes (the Cube said it was more than an hour), and by that time he was more fagged out than a Marathon runner on the home-stretch. I could guide him to whatever place I wished. Several times he was at the side of the boat, but a few feet away, and that was how we judged he was at least nine feet long, for he seemed to me half as long as the boat, the length of which is 19 feet, 4 inches. Finally I got him up to the stern of the boat, his head but a foot away from the rudder, and we took a good look at him. He was then as docile as a pet rabbit.

He was mossy with age and the color of deeply tarnished copper. Six or eight remoras were stuck to him, and occasionally one of them left him, swam away a few feet and returned to him.

IN THE final stages of the fight a dingey, with four men in her, hove into sight about the easterly end of Mangrove Key, and Sanchez called to the men to come to him. When they got within talking distance he explained that we had a big shark hooked and asked if they had a large hook or a harpoon aboard. They had a shark hook, and one of them crawled up in the bow of the dingey with the hook in his hand, but when he saw the shark he yelled to the sculler to pull the dingey about. The man with the hook said he wasn't going to take a chance in a dingey with "that brute." Instead he stepped out of the dingey on the house of the motor-boat, intending to go to the stern-sheet to try to get the hook into the shark's mouth. The man was walking aft, when the shark, exhausted, turned over on his back and, in doing so, put a kink in my wire and broke it. We watched him drift off like a soggy log.

It was not until the excitement died down that I realized how severely my hands were cut. The skin had been rubbed off my right forefinger in two or three places, and the remainder of my fingers and the upper parts of my palms, particularly of my right hand, were crisscrossed with traces of the line, some of which had cut through to the flesh.

THE case of the Y. M. C. A. is a very simple one. It is all set forth in the following statements from American headquarters in France. In a letter to General Pershing, Lieutenant-Colonel E. S. Wheeler said:

> Give me nine hundred men who have a Y.M.C.A. rather than one thousand who have none, and I will have better fighters every time.

General Pershing directed that Colonel Wheeler's letter be sent to the Y. M. C. A. officials, and himself added this comment:

> The conclusions and opinions of Lieutenant-Colonel Wheeler are concurred in by these headquarters.

It's a very simple case. Here is something that increases the fighting effectiveness of our forces in France by more than eleven per cent. On the basis set by General Pershing the Y. M. C. A. ought to receive one-ninth as much personal and financial support as is given to the entire American Army, for to every nine men it adds one more.

Modern warfare recognizes the tremendous importance of maintaining health in armies and of maintaining good mental condition as a requisite of good health. The extreme importance of morale, a thing less tangible, is also recognized, though as yet it still lacks the full and systematic attention it should receive. The Y. M. C. A. builds up all these things—health, good mental condition, morale. That is why it makes every nine American soldiers equal to ten without it.

Being a good and loyal American, what else can you do than support the Y. M. C. A. to the fullest of your ability?

HERE'S an interesting contribution to our discussions on ants and ant battles from a comrade in Indiana:

Logansport, Indiana.

If you are not already fed up on stories of ant battles I could tell a story of a most prodigious battle which was waged between two parties or rather armies of ants, apparently of the same species, but rival colonies. The field of battle was the portico of the old State House at Indianapolis, in the year 1863, when I was a small boy.

HOSTILITIES were in full swing when I appeared on the scene early in the morning, and I immediately became interested and saw to it that the little fighters had the field to themselves, persuading people not to tramp on them. This benevolent occupation kept me busy all day, for I wished to see the end of the fight.

The combatants were large black ants, about one-half inch long. Wending their way through the mêlée were parties of laborers, distinguished by their smaller heads and mandibles, bearing away a lot of white eggs, which seemed to be the cause of the fight. They worked steadily and, unless nipped by some fighter, seemed not at all interested in anything but their duty of bearing away the eggs to a place of safety, which in this case was a patch of burdock, where they stored the eggs temporarily, while another party, working on the ground, took them to their storehouses.

THE big-headed soldiers ravaged about the field, accosting every ant they met, ant-fashion, coming to a clinch without ceremony if the one they met was an enemy. They always aimed for a hold at the junction of thorax and abdomen, though a neck hold or even a good grip on a leg was good enough. If the hold was good the enemy was cut in two. If it was bad, the enemy at once got his hold, and neither let go till one or both was dead. Once in a while there was a perfect Donnybrook fight with a half-dozen or more in a hopeless tangle. It was very business-like, indeed, as the survivor invariably sought another enemy.

Toward evening, when the forces were nearly exhausted and only about one-fourth of the fighters were alive, another phase of the battle appeared. The eggs had disappeared and the laborers were again on the scene to look after the dead. It was evidently a perfectly organized effort to dispose of the dead, as the workers picked up the corpses and dropped them to the nearest step below, and others would pass them to the next and so on till the dead were neatly piled under some weeds. Another party, apparently soldiers, went about the field making sure that none of the maimed survived, and I could not see that they made any distinction between their wounded and the enemy's wounded. The ant is a practical fellow, like the German, and a wounded ant had no place in their economy.

ONE feature of the combat which I did not understand at the time was the offensive odor noticeable in the immediate vicinity of the fight. I have since learned that this odor is formic acid, which ants are said to discharge when angry or fighting. So the Huns are not the first to use gas in warfare.

I stayed on the field of battle till nightfall and left on account of the demands of hunger. Next morning not a dead ant was to be seen, and the pile under the weeds had disappeared, I know not where. The janitor declared that he had not yet swept the portico and steps, so it is likely that the ants did a good job of cleaning up.

The affair seemed to me so very interesting that I made it the subject of a "composition" which was read in school, thereby earning myself the nickname of "bugs," which stuck to me ever after. Some of my old schoolboy friends who survive in Indianapolis still use the name in preference to my lawful name and title.—NELSON W. CADY, M.D.

WE HAVEN'T heard from our old comrade A. D. Temple, of Piedras Negras, Mexico, for quite some time, though he and I get into touch every little while.

Here's the good word from him, written a year or so ago. Also he tells of a sample of the many former German-Americans who are now all Americans and as loyal as our best.

Saludes. Considering that I'm in Mexico, it is shockingly dull from a news-letter point of view. Nothing doing in the way of shooting and killing except way down south, where the bandits did blow up a train, kill a few of the train crew and passengers, rob all hands and carry off two señoritas to an unknown but easily imagined fate. Here they only do by retail what our friends the *boches*, thanks to their much praised efficiency, do by wholesale.

IN AUGUST I had three boy friends that had answered the call to arms against the Huns. Now I've only two. One—I never met him face to face, but we knew each other by letter and he was a family friend—died on August 15th as gloriously as a soldier can. He was a lieutenant in the Royal Artillery, advanced step by step through two years' fighting on the Western Front, and only a kid, not yet twenty-one. He was "up" for a military Medal on his colonel's recommendation for having successfully commanded a wire-cutting expedition and returned without the loss of a man.

He was home on furlough in July and saw some of our boys in London and liked their looks to no end, as fighting men. On August 8th he wrote to America from the trenches: "I was wounded today, but not badly enough to go to the rear; am still on duty." On August 15th they had driven the *boches* back and were advancing the battery to retain the ground already won, when a German shell struck an ammunition dump, exploding it, and Philip Sydney Marshall of Birmingham, England, finished his "bit" for England, America, France and humanity and joined the ranks of the thousands of young heroes that had gone before him. That name, "Philip Sydney" fitted him mighty well, I think.

GEORGE and Rob are still left me. They were my comrades on many a shooting and fishing trip; and I will say for George that he was about the poorest fisherman that I ever saw; but by ——! he could shoot all right, like most of the boys raised on the frontier. He is a high-school and college graduate. I saw his "old man" yesterday in Eagle Pass, mailing him the local paper, to France, where he is a captain in the —— Infantry, U. S. A. He is an expert on bayonet drill and has a marksman's badge. How these kids grow up and sprout whiskers before one realizes it. His mother says she's sorry she hasn't another boy to send to the front; that's the kind of a woman she is—no pacifist about her.

And there is Rob. He is only nineteen and just out of high-school. His mother, a pure-blooded German and a sympathizer with the German cause at the *beginning* of the struggle, and many a fierce argument did Rob and I have over it, as my blood forced me to be strongly pro-Ally.

BUT the U-boats and the Northern France and Belgian atrocities changed their sympathies; when the country called for naval volunteers, his mother sent Bob proudly and promptly, to answer the call and now he is aboard the U. S. S. ——. He was brought up most of his life in Mexico, speaks the language like a native, and is used to war's alarms. When a young Mexican captain arrested him some years ago during the first years of the revolution because he was hunting rabbits with a rifle and had no permit to carry arms, he not only retained the rifle that was in danger of confiscation, but seduced the captain to going rabbit hunting with him, and beat him shooting at that!

In 1913 Rob and I went on a hunting and fishing trip without asking permission of the military authorities, and ran into a hornets' nest when a company of what we supposed were cowpunchers gathering up the horse bunch unexpectedly dropped their .30-30s and Colts on us and suggested pleasantly that we turn over our guns to them for the benefit of *La Patria*. We turned them over, of course. Logic ain't in it with a .30-30 aimed at your bean, for facilitating quick and correct action in an emergency. They got my pet deer rifle and the old six-shooter that had traveled all over Mexico with me, and Rob's 16-gage shotgun. He took it all as coolly as if it wasn't the first time he had a gun thrown down on him, and seemed to rather look on the humorous side of the incident, after we were permitted to retire with only our fishing-rods.

He wrote to me that he had been half way to France convoying transports with troops and Red Cross nurses aboard and in mid-ocean was met by destroyers from the other side, to whom they delivered their charges and returned, being out of sight of land for eighteen days and encountering a rather severe storm on their return voyage.

He says the "eats" are good and he likes the life. If he is not submarined and sent to Davy Jones before his time that kid is going to make his mark, I believe. He has the stuff they make *men* of in him.

TO CHANGE the subject, I had venison steak for dinner, and very tough it was, but a luxury you New Yorkers don't get very often. It was from a superb ten-point buck that a friend killed a few miles from town yesterday. It was a fine trophy but deucedly tough eating. Three weeks ago I had antelope steak, which is a rare meat, even here, although antelope abound on the plains near here, and of late they have run a number of them down in automobiles and shot them at short range.

It is quite an adventure to chase antelope over a prairie with no roads and full of badger-holes at sixty or forty miles an hour until the animals slack up their gait and come within range; if anything breaks something is going to happen, and *pronto*. I wonder if some of those speed maniacs that enjoy runnning over babies and old women would like to come down here and try it.—A. D. TEMPLE.

WHEN peace comes it must be no compromise peace. It must mean the end of Germany as a maker of wars. And Germany will be a maker of wars until it *can't* make wars. Let the snake live on the chance it may reform. But pull its fangs.—ARTHUR SULLIVANT HOFFMAN.

HERE'S word to us from one of the old-timers of the West, a man who knew and rode with Frank Gruard. One by one they are "coming across," these men who knew the early West at first hand, and among them they are helping us to see the old days as they really were and are building up a valuable fund of historical information, often throwing light on points that have been obscure to historians.

And if George Harris will, as suggested, tell us about the days before 1874, we'll surely enjoy listening.

Surf, California.

As to Frank Gruard, Government Scout, he was given a lifetime position as scout for his services in guiding General Crook's command out through Sioux Pass in the Big Horn Mountains some time in the 70's, and from 1889 to 1892 I met Gruard many times. His position then was Post Scout at Fort McKinney on Clear Creek, Wyoming, near Buffalo. I rode with him from Fort McKinney to Fort Robinson, Nebraska, the Winter of '90 on the trail to the Pine Ridge. In 1892, in April, he was yet there at McKinney, when the Rustler War was on; George Harris of Trabing, on the Crazy Woman's Fork of the Powder River, could give you many details *re* the adventurous days prior to my time.

A MAN with a more adventurous history than Gruard was one "Liver-Eating Johnson." Last time I saw him was on the Yellowstone, November, 1887, when Sword Bearer of the Absaraka (Crows) led his followers at Fort Custer in Montana. He was a Norwegian, six feet and odd inches tall, weighed over three hundred pounds. His history was published many years ago by X. Biedler, the leader of the Montana Stranglers.

IN THE old time I knew such men as "Yellowstone Jack," "Kelley," Jim Cook (who afterward settled on the Running Water in Nebraska). Edmeaux Le Clair, Post Scout at Fort Washakie, and myself rode together in the Owl Creek Mountains and the Big Horn Basin. I first hit the trail in the Northwest, 1874, and since then have followed up a roving existence. I have been packer, scout, prospector, cavalryman, doughboy, filibuster (Rough Rider, Troop H 1st U. S. V. Cav., 1898), acting interpreter and scout in Luzon (33rd Regt. U. S. Pr. Inf. '99 to 1901), since then, Alaska, Mexico, California and way stations. I am yet in harness as one of Uncle Sam's "dogs of war." Am now guarding bridge on the S. P. R. R. in sunny southern California, but would certainly be in front if age would permit. Perhaps if you should use this letter some of the old boys might look me up. If Brininstool or some of the rest of your authors would take the trouble to write to me I might dig up enough memories of old times, places and people to help out a little.

PERSONALLY, I have always taken the world as a matter of course, and did not consider that I was of any particular importance as a maker of history, for, in fact, a great deal of the history I have seen in the making is not fit for publication. Yet I have followed close in the footsteps of the "Wild West." (The Sioux, Absaraka, Nez Percé, Blackfoot, Shoshone, Arapahoe, Cheyenne, Umatilla, Piute, Modoc and Klamath, the Simcoe and Klickitat —and a few more scattering remnants of the Noble Red Man have had the pleasure or pain of "reading my sign," as I have passed carelessly along their traditional trails).—EDWARD C. ST. CLAIR.

IN TAKING us back to the days of Tatar power in Asia during the thirteenth century, Mr. Lamb's stories are giving most of us a new experience. I'm afraid he flatters most of us when in a note to me he says:

"One of the songs in 'The White Khan' is from Li Po, a Chinese poet of medieval days. I don't think it is necessary to mention Li Po's name in the notes, as he is more or less of a classic. . . . The other poem of the tale, 'The Men of W'ang,' is my own fabrication."

He flatters me, anyhow. Doubtless some of you already were familiar with Li Po, but if any one of you can prove he knows less than I do about that, or any other, Chinese poet, I'll pay his expenses to New York just for the privilege of looking at him.

BUT most of us have heard of Genghis Khan, Kublai Khan and Timurlane or Tamerlane, one or all of them, and few names can so magically conjure up the odor of adventure, romance and mystery. Little enough we know, so when Mr. Lamb turns his search-light back through the mists of history and makes the forgotten and mysterious ages a living picture before our eyes we are grateful to him for more than a good story.

In the early thirteenth century the Tatars, or Mongols, conquered most of the known world. The Tatar armies, advancing from their homeland just south of Lake Baikal, swept over Cathay (China), Black Cathay (Kara Kitai) Turkestan, and the Han or Kin Empire (Southern China).

This period of conquest, under Genghis Khan and Kublai Khan, was perhaps the most rapid and savage in the annals of history. It extended the Mongol Empire through Tibet, the territory of the Indus, the Kwaresmian Empire (Afghanistan, Persia, Turkey in Asia) up through the Caucasus to the Crimea, and Russia as far as Poland, as it then was.

Under Timur Khan (Timurlane) the empire embraced the Mogul lands in India.

LIKE the empire of Alexander, the Tatar conquest was purely military. It was rapidly broken up, the Mongol armies mingling with the conquered population. What became of Tatary proper? The man who tries to find out what happened to Tatary in the heart of Asia will discover that the book of history is closed, or nearly so. He will get a few glimpses of a stirring story. Decimated in numbers and continually torn by quarrels, the descendants of Genghis Khan defended their homelands against invasion. The Muscovites, or Russians, did not conquer the remaining khans. A Cossack adventurer paved the way for Russian rule.

WE HAVE all heard the expression "catching a Tatar." It comes from the fact that Tatars were bad individuals to get hold of. Like the Spartans and the present Cossacks—who are allied to the Tatars in blood—they were born and bred to fighting. And for sheer courage it is hard to find their match.

THE Tatar method of storming a town is a historical fact. A European traveler in China about 1620 said: "The Tatars do everything in taking a walled city in the opposite way from Europeans. Instead of using their cannon to make a breach in the walls, they attack the walls with horsemen at once, and do not cease their efforts until the city is taken. From the moment the assault is sounded they ply ladders, from the ground and their horses backs, until they have a foothold on the walls. They are reckless of life, which they are more than ready to lose in battle, and each horseman bears himself with the skill and hardihood of a captain."

ANOTHER characteristic of the Tatar army was the speed with which it moved. On a march every soldier had at least one extra horse; when food in the saddle-bags was exhausted the Tatars drank blood from the horses' veins and mare's milk; they seldom stopped on a march to sleep, and were accustomed to push ahead as much as fifty miles a day or more even in extreme cold or in snow.

Their regard for the horse was so high that their boots were fashioned like horses' hoofs, and their hair like a mane hanging down over one shoulder.

An incident relates that a Tatar who was sent to pursue an enemy returned empty-handed to camp when he had killed the other's horse, saying, "Of what use is a man without a horse?"

IN "THE WHITE KHAN" Khlit crosses the border of Tatary into China and encounters the power of the Dragon Emperor with interesting results.

The various personages are to be found in the reign of Wan Li. Li Jusong is taken from history, together with the Lilies of the Court, and the border warfare in which the declining power of the khans, torn by dissension, struggled with the rising sun of China.—HAROLD A. LAMB.

LET us not be hoodwinked by Germany at the last. There must be just one plank to the peace platform—"Prussian militarism must be crushed forever."

We Americans refuse to consider any end to the war but a victorious end, however soon or late it may be in coming. Good. But what *is* a victorious end?

Beating Germany on the field of battle will be a victorious end in a way. But what good will that victory be if it brings us nothing of lasting value? If it leaves the whole bloody struggle to be fought out again at some later day?

And if Prussian militarism lives instead of dies there will be another bloody war. Prussian militarism exists solely for war. It must be killed.

THE other day I received a printed postcard from St. Joseph, Missouri, sender unknown. It read as follows:

> Who ever heard of the descendants of the Carthaginians? Nobody! They never troubled any one after Rome got through with Carthage.
>
> How about the descendants of the Prussians?
>
> It took Cato eight years to convince the Romans that Carthage must be destroyed. How long will it take the civilized world to decide about Prussia? Or shall we listen to peace propaganda?

That is a cruel sentiment. It seems to ask for the destruction of the entire Prussian (not the entire German) race. Perhaps our minds approve it as logical and correct, but, not being Prussians ourselves, we can not even plan or wish the destruction of a nation, including its women and children, and including at least some men who have been driven against their will. But Prussian *militarism* must be killed. It is the world's only chance of peace and safety in the future. And so long as there is enough of Prussia, or of Germany, to keep Prussian militarism alive and dangerous, Prussia and Germany must be killed.

I AM writing in August and you will read this when Winter has come again. I can not predict. No man can predict. But it seems very likely that when Germany is driven to offering peace terms she will try hard to fool us by making large concessions in the west and doing little about the east.

If she tries that trick she must not catch us asleep. The greater danger lies along the Russian and Balkan border. She can restore and indemnify Belgium and Luxembourg, give back Alsace and Lorraine to France, yield up still more of her territory along the western boundary—and go home from the peace conference laughing in her sleeve. Valuable concessions, of course, but as nothing compared to what she does *not* concede.

HER dream for generations has been an empire extending southeastward through the Balkans and Turkey into Asia and on to the Suez Canal, India, China and beyond. Limitlessly beyond. If she emerges from the war with her grip still on Austria, the Balkan States, Turkey, Russia and the new states along the Russian border, she emerges a victor. And a victor with the makings of a greater, though later, victory in her grasp. To the extent that she retains *any* hold upon *any* of these countries she is, to that extent, a victor and a dangerous victor. No matter what concessions she makes in the west, unless crippling indemnities are exacted.

Prussian militarism must be killed. It can not be killed, or really crippled, if Germany keeps open her dangerous doors on the east and southeast.

STILL another interesting contribution to the discussion started by Edgar Young's question "What is the spirit of adventure, particularly in its biological aspects?"

Metaline, Wash.

"The Spirit of Adventure," eh? I can't say what it is, but perhaps I can give some inkling as to what it is not. When "The Spoilers" was published the Eastern critics said it was a fine piece of imaginative writing—of romance, if you please; but the newspaper men west of Omaha praised it for its realism. Except for the sex interest, it was photographic, and the views were taken with discrimination. I was in Nome the next year, and met a number of men who had been in the Noyes-McKensie deal. One of them, a harp by the name of Cullen, was killed by a fist-blow on the streets of Seattle a year or two later.

WILLIAM DEAN HOWELLS speaks somewhere about "the wild guesses at reality" in "The Red Badge of Courage," by Stephen Crane—and Civil War veterans have told me that it is a wonderful picture of a recruit's feelings in his first campaign. In an old *Atlantic* I read a solemn statement concerning Cutcliffe Hyne's "Captain Kettle" and "McTodd," in which their adventures were described as "highly improbable." I have met men cast in the very mold of Kettle and McTodd—lived and worked with them. The paper-collared, pasty-faced parasite who doubted their reality could not have an adventure if he tried—and he will never try, as such things are bad form in his set. Imagination and humor—fraternity with men worthy of it—mark the adventurer.

A DECADENT and degenerate Puritanism, with its hatred of Nature, and its notion that "existence is immoral and unnecessary," have done much to destroy the true Spirit of Adventure, without which we should still be back in Back Bay hanging Quakers and sending their children in slavery to the Barbados. He has the courage to force from the fingers of grim and malignant Nature all that life can give him. If he loses youth and health and life itself in the contest, if his "stake" be finally swept across the green cloth, he settles with the relentless cashier and passes out "into eternal silence and the dreamless dust" without a murmur. Unlike the "Wabble" and the Near-Socialist and a dozen other whiners, he does not holler that the game is crooked because he has not the nerve to play the cards that Nature gave him. I read Kipling's "If" to a Wabble, and he made oration that it presented an impossible creed—that "nobody could meet them conditions." Adventurers did not cry "I can't," and "Wait on me!" when they were boys—they do not put class above country—they never plead exemption from work and war because of religious belief—they meet the white-hot sword of Destiny like men.

"A DEAD game sport" does not necessarily frequent cheap saloons and poolrooms, waste his substance on the most deadly females of the species, combine in politics and labor and society and religion to graft on his fellows—he may be, and usually is as straight as a string and as game as a pebble. The "gunmen" of the old West would more cheerfully risk their lives for a friend than the curs who now wrangle in the room they left would risk their money. He who can "So live each day that you can look every damn man in the eye and tell him to go to ——" has no need to fear anything in this world or the next.—E. C. ROSE.

THE vote by readers on the ten most popular stories (short stories, novelettes, novels, serials) published in *Adventure* during 1918 closes December 31. Covering from the issue of January 3, 1918, to that of December 18, 1918. All the material, therefore, is now in your hands. Send in your vote.

All you need do is write the titles and authors' names of the ten stories you consider best, given in order of preference, and mail us the sheet of paper to reach us not later than December 31. If you like, add as many as ten more stories for honorable mention.

POEMS, Camp-Fire and other departments are barred from the regular vote as heretofore, but this year we're going to add a special vote to the regular one in order to find out what relative value the departments have for our readers. After you've listed your ten or twenty stories, write down the following list and put after each item the percentage of value you think it deserves. Call the total value of an average issue one hundred per cent., including both fiction and departments, and then divide up that one hundred per cent. among these items:

Stories (all together)
Poetry (all together)
Camp-Fire
Identification Cards
Fighting the Hun Web
Looking Ahead
Ask Adventure
How to Help Win the War
Lost Trails

In the cases of "Fighting the Hun Web" and "Looking Ahead" make allowance for the fact that neither one is really under way as yet, since there hasn't been time to receive and publish replies from readers in response to the first appearance of these departments. Try to value them according to what they will be when really going.

ADVENTURE is your magazine. We in the office are trying to put into it what you want in it. By "you" we mean, of course, the majority of you. But it's not always easy to find out what the majority of you want. This annual vote seems the best method of learning, though the opinions—praise and criticism—that come in from many of you all through the year are extremely valuable as guides.

It's up to you as far as we see any way of putting it up to you. If you can think of other ways, tell us. And meanwhile send in your vote.

FROM Herman J. Love, of Ely, Nevada, comes to us the following newspaper clipping concerning one of the old pioneers of the West. "Years ago," writes Mr. Love, "I was well acquainted with men who knew the 'Adventurers' who made the Adobe Walls fight."

WITH JOHNSTON'S ARMY

DIED—At Blackfoot, Idaho, December 20, suddenly and naturally, James N. Hanrahan, in the eighty-second year of his age.

And so old Jim Hanrahan—pathfinder, plainsman, Indian fighter and scout—is dead, and after sixty years of a running fight with Indians and gunfighters he died naturally. Well, he had a strenuous life and earned his rest.

HE CAME to Utah with Johnston's army; he fought through the Civil War for the Union; he was a "bull whacker" and a wagon boss with the ox outfits that pulled west from the Missouri with army supplies for frontier posts in '67; he was a scout for Custer in '69, and rode with that long-haired commander when, to the tune of "Garry Owen," the Seventh cavalry swept down at the Washita on Black Kettle and his band of Arapahoes; he was a buffalo hunter during the merciless four years that killed off for their hides the great herds that ranged over the plains between the Platte and Canadian border; he was one of the handful of men that stood off the Arapahoes, Comanches and Kiowas at the battle of the Adobe Walls on the Pala Dura, in the panhandle of Texas, in '74, when 250 Indians fell in a vain attempt to capture two little stockades.

THAT was a battle for sure. Fred Leonard was in it and can tell you all about it. I was not far away and saw the wagonloads of war bonnets, shields, scalps and trophies captured in the fight. When the savagery of men and nature left the plains, Jim went into mining in Colorado and afterward took up ranching in Idaho, where he finally died. Had some one said forty years ago: "Jim Hanrahan is dead," there would have been bowed heads all over the Middle West, but now none but the few yet alive of all those who knew him on the border will take note of his departure. He was an honest man, not for religion's sake, for he didn't have any, but just because he didn't know how to be anything else. He read much and remembered what he read, and once when he was in the legislature of Idaho it was remarked that Jim's ideas were worth consideration.

HANRAHAN was a man of peace, and he would have it if he had to fight for it, and he could fight, if it was necessary, with his fists, or a gun or any old thing he could lay hold of; but mainly he preferred a gun, and, as was said of Thompson, "light and free was his touch upon the revolver—great the mortality incident upon that lightness and freedom." Once when they tried to take the Midnight mine away from Jim in Colorado—a bunch of men with Winchesters—he killed two of them and would have killed the rest, only they got out of range.

Whenever there was a gunfighter hunting for trouble and he could not find it anywhere else, and was bound to have it, Jim would accommodate him, from which circumstances there are several graves here and there in the West. And there was never anyone ever heard to say that he wasn't justified, or asked for anything more than an even show. When he died there was none of us who knew him in the old days to say, as did the farmer to his dying son, "Well, good-by, Jim, take keer of yourself."—E. F. Colborn.

OUR new metal identification cards or tags are ready. Same size and lettering as the present cardboard cards, but made of some aluminum composition, thin but strong, with a hole at each end for fastening to belt or cord.

These metal tags cost us from the manufacturer 20½ cents apiece—20.44 cents, to be painfully exact. We give them to you at cost or below. Send us 25 cents and we'll send you the metal card, postage paid by us. We fix on 25 cents as a convenient amount, the balance of 3½ cents over manufacturing cost being more than taken up by foreign or domestic postage, clerical handling, stationery and general office expense.

If already a holder of one of the old cards, state its number when you write for a metal card. If you like, keep the old card; we'll keep you registered under both cards, their numbers being different. If you want to cancel your old card, tell us so.

But, except to those already having an old card, we will give either a cardboard card *or* a metal card (on receipt of price), but not both.

I KNOW just enough about the following mystery to be as eager to know more as is Comrade Roberts:

Bridgeport, Conn.

I have a question to put up to my comrades of the "Camp Fire." In reading a book published some years ago by a man named Walmsby, called "Zululand, Its Wild Life and Adventures," supposedly founded on facts, there is one thing that the author dwells upon all through the book, namely, "The Lost Cities of Zululand." Undoubtedly some of my bunkies have read this book and I know that a good many of them have been in mysterious Africa and the question I raise is whether the cities that were built in the time of King Solomon, for the transportation of gold and woods needed to build his temple, are anywhere near the Zambesi River. Also if in any part of that territory strange fruits or trees have ever been noted by any of our adventurers. Also if there has been noted any Arab strain in any of the people in that district.

In the book the people found old ruins such as have been found in Mexico and Yucatan of an old temple of stone, but were not allowed to renew owing to the hostility of the natives.

If you will put this up to the sitters-in of the Camp Fire you will do me a favor and will undoubtedly give us more information about Africa which I think we will all enjoy.—L. V. Roberts, Jr.

WORD from an old comrade who is happy over now doing his fighting under his own flag:

London, England.

Just a few lines to inform you that I have finally secured my discharge from the British Army and am pleased to say that I have rejoined the A. E. F. in the good old Infantry. Am off for Winchester next week to get fitted-out. After that, me being a "trained man," I guess it means and spells FRANCE; so much the better for that. Intend going after a commission, as I think I am eligible for same, if active service counts. At any rate, time will tell.

Best regards to all for the present, trusting this finds you O. K. and that another year will see the finish of this Hell, I remain.—M. Logie.

WHAT is going to be done to the men who cheat our Government on war contracts, deliver inferior goods, graft in various ways on the country's great industrial and agriculture machine that supplies and supports our boys at the front? We Americans have grown into the strange habit of looking upon graft as a thing to be expected, passed over with mild punishment or none at all, even smiled at.

Graft is *treason*. A grafter is a traitor to his country.

One of the chief purposes of the American League for Citizenship, Inc., is to teach Americans that the citizen who grafts on public funds or resources or in any way betrays the trust of a public office in peacetime is just as much a traitor as the citizen who betrays our country's Army in war time. But, God help us, we Americans do not recognize a traitor when we see him even in war time.

IF AN American at the front shoots an American soldier, or kills our soldiers by poisoning a well, we can see that he is a traitor and execute him. If he is caught tampering with our soldiers' ammunition at the front or distributing disease-germs among the boys in khaki, we can see that he is a traitor and deserves death. But let him kill our boys at the front from *this* side of the Atlantic. Somehow we don't think of him as a traitor then. *Why not?* In God's name, why not?

Is an American soldier in France any more dead if he died from poisoned well-water than if he died of pneumonia because his rain-coat was useless through graft back in America? Is he any more dead if he's shot in the back by an American on the firing-line than if he died because one of his fellow countrymen back home grafted on food supplies or munitions with the result that they were unfit when they reached the soldier?

In either case an American has killed an American soldier for Germany.

THERE are a thousand ways in which graft and greed at home can kill our soldiers and sailors at the front. And just because the cause and the effect are so far apart we aren't clear-eyed enough to see that these grafters are black traitors to their country with blood on their hands.

Our soldiers' safety, our country's whole cause, is absolutely dependent upon the munitions and supplies furnished our forces. How many millions and millions of times in the millions of diversified situations and crises of fighting do the lives and fighting value of our soldiers hang on the slender thread of difference between perfect weapons, equipment, clothing and food on the one hand and imperfect ones on the other! No human being can measure and record all the deaths and losses from little imperfections, but we know that they are there.

Yet these Americans back home who are responsible for those imperfections—we forget, somehow, that they are black traitors to America, that their hands are red with our soldiers' blood.

AND it is not only imperfections that kill. Delays also kill. Supplies and munitions that are not where they are needed mean dead American soldiers. Delay in building ships for carrying means dead American soldiers. The man who causes these delays for his own selfish profit, be he capitalist or workman, is a black traitor to America, a slayer of American soldiers at the front.

Compared to these grafters the German agent in our midst is a noble being, the traitor at the front a hero.

I HAVE called them traitors, but they are unworthy of even that shameful name. A traitor may be a brave man, but these jackals are not men at all. They take no risk comparable with their gains. They claim virtue, like a sewer that claims to smell sweet. A beast of prey, however hated, commands some respect; a vampire none. How Benedict Arnold, a brave man for all his treason, would look down in contempt upon these millionaires and workingmen, these contractors, purveyors, agents and laboring men who betray their country in so cowardly and mean a way!

Traitors? They are not fit to be called traitors. However great the harm they do, they are too small and cowardly and dirty to be called even a shameful name that has been dignified by custom with the risk and penalty of so big a thing as death. Traitors? No, only *eunuch traitors*.

DEATH is too good for them. Make it life imprisonment. Let them live with their shame and our contempt for sole companions. Make the sentence non-commutable, the offense unpardonable.

And if some of them, unfortunately, are given lesser terms behind the bars, let us see to it that when they try to come back to the country they have betrayed they find only shame and contempt to greet them. There is blood upon their heads, the blood of American patriots. You who have lost a son, a husband, a brother, a sweetheart, perhaps through the treachery of these same sneaking curs, can *you* shake them by the hand, greet them smilingly on the street, even let the hem of your garment brush against their outcast bodies?

PERHAPS some day I can be Christian enough to forgive. Now I can see only their hands dripping with American blood, hands infinitely more accursed than the German hands that kill our boys in open battle. It is right to forgive, and I who can not do right in this matter should not be urging others to unforgiveness. But mark this, even if some day we can forgive, *today our duty is to save our boys at the front from traitors and eunuch-traitors here at home.* If these reptiles know their bloody crimes make them social outcasts, they will go slower in their filthy greed. We can put that check upon their traitorous murdering, and it is our duty.

TO PERFORM their assigned war duties, the following now cooperate as a single unit: Y. M. C. A., Y. W. C. A., National Catholic War Council (including K. of C.), Jewish Welfare Board, American Library Association, War Camp Community Service and Salvation Army. That makes very clear and easy our duty and opportunity to back our firing-line. A. S. H.

DANIEL BOONE. That is a name to conjure by for any American who has ever been a boy. Most of us turned our kid hero-worship on Boone at one period or another. But it's only when we grow up that we realize Boone was a figure of great national importance, playing a tremendous part in the winning of a continent.

Hugh Pendexter's novelette in this issue gives us a living picture of Boone and of the early days when Kentucky was "the dark and bloody ground," a critical turning-point in the expansion of our country from a few seaboard colonies to a great nation. If as a story it interests you as much as it did me, you'll have a good time reading it. If you learn as much American history from it as I did, you'll pick up quite a little without any effort.

For our benefit Mr. Pendexter supplies some of the historical facts and conditions in and back of the tale itself.

Norway, Maine.

I've tried to give a picture of life at Boonesborough when Dan'l Boone stood off Shawnees and Wyandots. In 1777 Boone and Simon Kenton, second to none except Boone, did many hair-raising stunts. It was starvation time for Kentucky, and the two often sneaked out at night and traveled long distances, sometimes as far as fifty miles, before daring to bag game.

OF COURSE my first desire was to tell an interesting yarn; secondly, to make Boone a human being with the historic peaks of his achievements forming a background and revealing how this great pioneer was a true American when Americanism was in the making. In doing this I must not only show what Kentucky endured, dared and suffered, as personified by Boone, Kenton, Jim Harrod, *et al.*, but also play up what Kentucky stood for. It was the hinge on which swung George Rogers Clark's conquest of the Ohio country; it was the outer bulwark on which split all attempts to divide the Colonies and to lose for future America the whole interior of the continent. In this Boone recital I've fought against the inclination to think of fiction plot first and have presented a continuity of action on Boone's part that parallels fact. This at the expense of a cut and dried plot. The restrictions in the Boone story were arbitrary as he was a man of 43, a great defensive rather than an offensive fighter, constantly passing back and forth between the Yadkin and Kentucky, with the exceptions of 1777—78, the time of the present story.

BOONE spelled it "Cantuck." As he was unlettered and spelled phonetically I have assumed he called it that; much as other old-timers said "Kentuck." Regarding the "prodigal" supplies of munitions possessed by the Indians it is said Boone's men picked up 125 pounds of lead at the foot of the stockade after one siege, and estimated that as much more was buried in the stockade timbers. An attempt to mine the fort was made in 1778 under the direction of Lieut. De Quindre. The muddy streak in the water betrayed this maneuver and a counter-mine was started. I have placed the incident in 1777 for fiction purposes.

An ancient and hollow sycamore figured in Boone's early Kentucky adventures. His brother-in-law, John Stewart, his companion on Boone's first visit to Kentucky, disappeared after the two had gone through many exciting adventures, including capture by Indians. Five years later Boone found human bones and a powder-horn bearing Stewart's name in an old sycamore.

Before Boone was old enough to have a rifle, or less than twelve years old, and was living near what is now Reading, Pa., he became an adept in throwing sapling roots, trimmed into clubs. Boone spelled his name "Boon." Roosevelt follows this form in his "Winning of the West."

TATAHECASSA, or "Black Hoof," was about 37 years old at this time. Born near what is now Winchester, Ky. He was principal chief of the Shawnees and one of their greatest war captains at a time when they were at their zenith as fighters. History places him in the fighting at Braddock's Defeat in 1755—a very youthful warrior—and he was conspicuous at the battle of Point Pleasant, mouth of the Kanawha, 1774, when Lord Dunmore's troops whipped the northern Indians. He led the Shawnees in persistently opposing the white advance west of the Allegheny Mountains and fought against Harmar and St. Clair. After Wayne's victory over the northwestern Indians he continued famous as orator and used his great influence to preserve peace, realizing his people's cause was hopeless. Due to his efforts the bulk of the Shawnee tribe refused to join Tecumseh in his war against the United States. He died at Wapakoneta, Auglaize County, Ohio, in 1831.

Kenton's use of the shamanistic language of the Cherokees, *viz.*, "Black Spirits" and "Red War Club," would be perfectly appreciated by the Shawnees because of their former intimacy with the Cherokees. "Red" was symbolic for strength and victory among all Indian tribes, just as it was an emblem for power and success among Oriental peoples.

Unlita, a Cherokee chief. His name is translated by Mooney "(He is) long-winded." Called "The Breath" by the whites.

BOONE cut the Wilderness Road (Trace) for the Transylvania Land Co., commencing work in March, 1775, from the Holston settlements. The course lay in as straight a line as possible to Cumberland Gap. The real difficulties began after reaching the Rockcastle River in Kentucky. The Road made for the Blue Grass Region near the junction of the Kentucky and Otter Creek and encountered a stretch of dead brushwood, impenetrable even to buffalo. Necessary to chop and burn every foot of the way for twenty miles before emerging on plains covered with white clover. While engaged in this work Boone was joined by fifty men, including Abraham Hanks grandfather of Abraham Lincoln, and Benjamin Logan, celebrated Indian fighter and builder of Logan's Fort.

The caves of Kentucky were often used for mortuary purposes by the Indians, the dry air reducing the dead to mummified forms. They were also used as hiding-places to escape pursuit, but seldom, if ever, for dwellings.

"Nolichucky" Jack Sevier, also called "Chucky" Jack, with James Robertson, laid the foundations of the State of Tennessee six years before Kentucky was opened. He was prominent in defense of the Watauga settlements, in Lord Dunmore's war and throughout the Indian wars of the Revolution. He was the first governor of Tennessee, serving six terms.

"NIGHT-GOERS," Cherokee for "witches." According to the Cherokee belief they could be destroyed by planting four sharpened stakes at the corners of a house and by puffing tobacco smoke towards every trail leading to the house. The stakes flew up and in descending impaled the witch.

The Cherokee offer of white wampum, "showing one dish," was meant literally. One dish, picked out in the pattern, signified the two nations were as one and ate from the same dish. In describing the war medicine as made by the shamans, I have followed the sacred formula of the Cherokees as set forth by Mr. James Mooney, an eminent authority on that and many other matters pertaining to the red men. Mr. Mooney says that almost every man of the 300 Fast Cherokees participating in the rebellion went to water and chewed the charmed root, and adds: "And it is but fair to state that not more than two or three out of the entire number were wounded in actual battle."

There is much more to the sacred formula for destroying life than can be given in the scope of a story. To be exact the shaman must see his victim and spy upon him until he could procure some of his spittle. Mooney says this idea regarding spittle is found also in European folk-lore medicine. The spittle is put into a tube of wild parsnip, together with seven earthworms and a bit of a lightning-riven tree, and then buried in a hole at the foot of a lightning-blasted tree. Seven yellow pebbles are placed on top and on them a fire is built to conceal all signs. Then the shaman can pull off the ceremony of the red and black beads as shown in the story. Boone's use of the formula for finding that which is lost closely follows the formula.

A RUNAWAY slave served with the Shawnees in the 1776 campaign against Boonesborough. He was an expert rifle shot and did much "sniping" from tree-tops overlooking the stockade until Boone brought him down.

According to all authentic personal data concerning Boone he was a poor swimmer. That the incident of Boone's shooting two Indians with one bullet may not be considered overdrawn it is recorded as a fact that while on his way to upper Blue Lick in 1779 he was fired upon by Indians in ambush. He crossed the creek and stole through the cane, found two in line, and at one shot killed one and wounded the other.

It is believed that none of the southern tribes used salt until the coming of the whites (Dr. Walter Hough, U. S. Nat. Museum, in article printed in Bulletin 30, B. A. E.). But the Shawnees were famous salt-makers. The Virginia Indians as well as the Cherokees used lye. Some tribes believed the use of salt caused sore eyes. (Same authority as above.)

BOONE broke his leg while fighting outside the stockade during the 1777 siege. Kenton rescued him after killing three Indians, carried him to the fort, and then returned for more fighting.

The capture of Boone, while directing thirty salt-makers at lower Blue Lick, his leading the Indians to the camp where his companions surrendered, is history. After his escape from captivity Boone was brought before a court martial at Logan's Fort on the charge of surrendering his men without a struggle. He was not only honorably acquitted, but as an additional mark of commendation for the course he had pursued he was advanced to the rank of major in the Continental army. James and George Girty, brothers of the malodorous Simon, were at the camp when he was captured. The whole story follows history rather closely, the vote at Chillicothe on the fate of the prisoners being fifty-nine for torture and sixty-one for ransom.

Boone not only won the good will of his captors but succeeded in making Hamilton believe he would turn Tory. He was forced to play this card in order to escape the Indians. The lieutenant-governor in vain offered a hundred pounds sterling for him. Black Fish's refusal to accept this price evidences how successful the prisoner had been in disarming the suspicions of the Shawnees.

Boone accumulated a reserve supply of ammunition as described in the story. On returning from each hunting trip the amount of game bagged checked up, to the Indians' satisfaction, the number of shots fired. Boone's fear of torture should he be recaptured was natural to one who understood the Indian character as he did. To the Indian mind nothing could be more abhorrent than for an adopted son to cut up like this. It was about the most cussed thing he could do. Nor is his race to save Boonesborough to be belittled.

BLACK BIRD, chief of the Chippewas, afterward lined up with the American forces. History sometimes neglects to play up the part played by the red men during the Revolution and places over-emphasis on the employment of redskins by the British. We used Injuns when we could get 'em, and we got lots of them. They were our allies as much as allies of the British, only we called them "friendly" Indians. Those on the other side were "red devils," eke other hard sounding names.

Where Black Fish led his warriors across the Kentucky, panting to carve up his son Dan'l, was afterward known as Black Fish Ford, and may be to this day for aught I know.

BOONE'S finish would be pathetic if not for the lasting homage posterity has paid him. When about seventy years of age he lost his land grants in Kentucky, some ten thousand acres, through inefficiency in "business" matters. Still vigorous, he moved to Missouri and took up ten thousand acres, and again, because of ignorance of certain legal formalities, was stripped of his holdings. Then he turned to Kentucky and asked for aid and the State petitioned Congress, and once more the grand old pioneer was given title to ten thousand acres. It would seem he had learned but little of white men's wiles, although second to but few in understanding the red man. Litigation sent him landless to his grave; and he had helped win a continent! His Wilderness Road was the beginning of the road across the continent.

SIMON KENTON was hated more intensely, perhaps, by the Indians rambling round in Kentucky than any other white man. He was not a home-builder like Boone, but an awful meddler in affairs of the reds.

If the dense forests gave Indians and sudden onslaughts to the pioneers it also gave (to those who survived) the true spirit of democracy. Reckon that's what the forests were for, to instil democracy. Otherwise the All Supreme would have had the land growing up to boarding-houses. All the basic values this country possesses hark back to the woods, the conquest of which brought so much hardship and suffering, and (to be guilty in a bromide-degree) reminds us eternally that whatever is worth winning must be dearly paid for. Those behind us paid for it; it's up to us to keep it.—HUGH PENDEXTER.

As I was born and raised on the Scioto and later lived so close to the Miami that I could sit at my window and shoot turtles, I became skeptical when Mr. Pendexter in his story located Chillicothe on the Miami instead of the Scioto, the present town of that name being indisputably on the Scioto. The following will satisfy the doubts of any other Ohioans as they did mine.

Also I couldn't remember ever having seen the Northern Lights in Ohio, but I'm far from sure.

It's a historical fact that Boone was held prisoner at Chillicothe on the Little Miami. The accompanying excerpt will clear it up for you, I'm sure. And it might easily be that a modern town takes an old Indian name while located nowhere near the site of the Indian village. It happens that one of the four towns called Chillicothe, was, according to Mr. Mooney, "probably called" etc. But there is no doubt as to the Chillicothe on the Little Miami.

FROM "Handbook American Indians," Smithsonian Institution, page 267—68, vol. I. Chillicothe:—"One of the four tribal divisions of the Shawnees. The division is still recognized in the tribe, but the meaning of the word is lost. The Chillicothe always occupied a village of the same name, and this village was regarded as the chief town of the tribe. As the Shawnee retreated west before the whites, several villages of this name were successively occupied and abandoned. The old Lowertown, or Lower Shawnee Town, at the mouth of the Scioto, in Ohio, was probably called Chillicothe. Besides this there were three other villages of that name in Ohio, viz:

(1) On Paint Creek on the site of Oldtown, near Chillicothe, in Ross Co. This village may have been occupied by the Shawnee after removing from Lowertown. It was there as early as 1774, and was destroyed by the Kentuckians in 1778.

(2) On the Little Miami, about the site of Oldtown, in Green Co. The Shawnee are said to have removed from Lowertown to this village, but it seems more probable that they went to the village on Paint Creek. This village near Oldtown was frequently called Old Chillicothe, and Boone was a prisoner there in 1778. It was destroyed by Clark in 1780.

(3) On the (Great) Miami, at the present Piqua, in Miami Co.; destroyed by Clark in 1782. (James Mooney, B. A. E.)"

IN "Boone and the Wilderness Road," by Bruce Addington, or Addlington (I haven't the volume at hand but the title is correct. I am a bit hazy as to author's name), the author says Boone was sent with a small detachment of Shawnee to make salt "on a lick on the Scioto." In notes from other authorities I have more on this, but can't lay my hand to them. Another of their licks, I remember, was a large saline spring on Saline Creek in Ohio, below mouth of Walnut Creek.

In re Northern Lights. I think it was Parkman, among others, in writing of Iroquois Indians, who spoke of Northern lights being ghosts according to northern Indians' belief. The belief was general wherever the northern lights could be seen and I assumed they could be glimpsed occasionally in Ohio.—HUGH PENDEXTER.

DON'T forget to be sending in your vote for the ten best stories in ADVENTURE during 1918. If you like, add a list of another ten for honorable mention as you did for 1917 and 1916.

HER collaborator, Louise Rice, has already followed Camp-Fire custom and introduced herself to us, and now Anne Throop Craig joins the small number of women writers who have joined our fellowship. Perhaps what she says about the ancient races may strain our brains a bit, but those of Scotch or Irish blood will find it interesting reading:

The Camp-Fire

New York.

My collaborator, Louise Rice, tells me that I am graciously invited to join your Camp-Fire, and inflict the story of my life on the other bivouackers. I consider it a pleasant and novel privilege, being only human, but hope you will not find it too much of an infliction.

The plot and scheme of the tale are the fruit, in the main, of the soaking in of old saga lore that I have done ever since I was a little girl; Norse and Irish, most, with Saxon and German, odds and ends of Eastern and Indian and Gypsy and Finnish and so on, thrown in. But my collaborator is not only—may I be a little slangy, and say—a "cracker-jack" at spieling out a yarn, but she knows a thing or two out of musty old books herself.

THE story deals with the ancient Irish colonizers of the west regions of the present Scotland, anciently known at one time as Pictland in Alba, at another time as Dalaradia.

Picts, Norse, and the Erse from some distant regions of ancient Ierna, or Eriu (some of Ireland's early names), settled and conflicted here, in and about the West Highlands, for many centuries—the flux and mergence of them doubtless beginning considerably before, or at least near to, the entry of the Christian era.

Part of this population in the early centuries where approximately we place our story may have been made up of still rudely living survivors of the wholly primitive Stone Age men. These in the course of time were merged with the tribes grouped in Norse and Pictish and Gaelic divisions. That the Picts were wholly Stone Age men, or more advanced survivors from them, I do not think there is any assurance, and it would rather seem likely that the so-called Picts surmised by many archæologists to have been a swarthy, dark-haired and perhaps curly haired, people, were, while unmixed, of the race known as "Mediterranean," and the origin of this race is more obscure, the relics of its settlements also often indicating advance in many arts and customs far beyond Stone Age rudeness. But we may say as much as this: that there was probably in all the western islands an aboriginal substratum of Silurian Stone Age communities, left over from the glacial period. These I believe, are discovered to have been "long-skulled," short-statured or medium-statured, black-haired types, and there seems reason to believe that these contributed to the tribes later known as Picts. There are indications, also, that tribes were classed with the Picts, who—perhaps a later mixture with those akin to the Cimbri, or Belgæ of the Rhine's mouth region—were large, big-boned, red-haired types.

OUT of legends we get not fewer grains of truth, and often a truer race psychology, doubtless than we get out of dug up bones and other tangible relics. The legends of Ireland tell of early races attempting to colonize the country; their expulsion by aborigines, and their return again in several detachments, after variously long periods. After the return of a first important detachment, this remained, grew steadily powerful and built up and organized communities in a most orderly manner, politically and socially. This immigration is known in the traditions as that of the Firbolg—with subdivisions, and, by a thousand evidences in the saga lore, it would seeem they constituted the actual and permanent backbone of the original Irish nationality. The return of these on their second arrival, is spoken of in the legends as from the East, some of them coming from the ancient "Scythia," others from Greece, perhaps in the region of Thrace. To these lands they had fled, in two divisions presumably, after their expulsion from Ireland by its aborigines. Their story is told in the traditions of the "Nemedians," to be interpreted as solar-myth, or as having a plausible claim to human reality, according to the school of folk-lorists to which one belongs.

OF THE parties of "Nemedian" refugees, those who unfortunately landed in Greece were made slaves. The other party went to a land, perhaps "Scythia," where the people were said to be deeply versed in arts and occult lore and magic through their initiate priesthood. There, we are told, the refugees became learned and advanced in such culture themselves.

One may suspect it was a Finnish population with the fair admixture attributed to the Slav, and not only of the Tatar variety, which was the Scythic population with which the refugee "Sons of Nemed" from ancient Ireland mixed, for there is much in the Finnish lore to correspond with the druidic tradition surviving also in the Irish materials, and in Ireland this is associated with a "fair race"— of which we are told next. This was represented in a wonderful immigration of a "fair-skinned," noble people, almost divine in their powers, the people known as the Tuatha De Danaan (Tribes of the Gods of Dana). The personages of these tribes, as they figure in the legends, are doubtless actually gods themselves of some considerable colony invading ancient Ireland, or else their gradually apotheosized priests and heroes.

BUT the colony of immigrants to which this pantheon with its beautiful heroic legends is assigned is ethnically classified as made up from some branch or branches of the Goidelic (otherwise Gaelic) "Celts" and it does not seem far fetched to think that those branches which brought with them the pantheon of the gods of Dana were minglings of possibly ruder western tribes of Europe with the earliest Cretans and their strangely advanced civilization; also with advanced communities which existed in Alpine regions at a certain period, the ultimate origin of both of which is obscure; and with, also, precursors of fair Norse and Slav tribes in the Finnish region about the Baltic Sea, the region known as Scythia. Such a supposition would explain many things regarding the organization of the more ancient communities of Ireland which manifested an orderly political sense to an extraordinarily mature degree, and which by the evidence of tangible relics and a thousand indications in the traditionary lore seems assuredly to be akin, not to barbaric peoples alone, but to one or more of the most remote ancient nations which had attained to civilization and refinements centuries before the Christian era; which had begun to deteriorate and to pass, perhaps, at the period when their emigrations reached parts of Europe; and whose ultimate origins were beyond Europe; but whether in Mesopotamia, Africa or an extension of our western continent with its polished

Mayans and Incas, no one can perhaps ever say.

These traits of orderly political and social conditions, and the impress of intellectual cults in religion and even in science, seem to have characterized the community of the Firbolg clans, and their eventual harmonious mingling with the other legendary people known as the Tuatha De Danaan. These latter, indeed, it is said, also significantly, discovered to their amazement that they spoke the same tongue as the Firbolg occupants they came to conquer in the island, and thus they knew they had been once the same people, although the difference in their places of sojourn had created for them different cultural attainments.

ALL this rambling about races may not seem clearly relevant to my topic. But it was from these earliest colonies which laid an actually strong foundation for Irish development that there sprang the strong clans which built the great cyclopean coast fortresses and mountain strongholds whose ruins, many of them, survive to this day in the northwest and west of Ireland, on mainland and border islands, and who sent doubtless the earliest strong-armed chieftains to build the like again on the west coast and adjacent islands of what is now Scotland and the Ilan Manainn (pronounced Ee-lan Van-non, the Isle of Man). These people were, it would surely seem, the basis of Gaeldom, the true Gaels.

The "Milesians" of the legends were doubtless also offshoots of Goidels (or Goidelic Celts); in the main, perhaps those known as "Celtiberians" of Spain, whose trail is possibly left in the Basque remnants in the Pyrenees. But traditions indicate also other conquering invaders, or partially conquering ones, who came against the earlier Gaels, conquerors who seem to have adopted afterward much of the lore of their predecessors, and to have even become confused in measure, in the legends, with the Gaelic "Milesians" on this account. These seem rather to have been, not Gaelic Celts, but other tribes of doubtless partially Celtic origin, but mingled with Norse, rather than with Alpine, Iberian, or Mediterranean strains. Such tribes are classified as "Brythons," Brythonic Celts. They were likely in part comprised by the red-haired, tall, loose-jointed Cimbri, or Belgæ, of Cæsar and the Roman historians, mingled with the Norse, and also, very likely to some extent, with the people merged of several stocks already, and constituting the Gallic population proper. But the old Greek writers did us a bad turn when they dubbed all tribes north of the Alps "Keltoi," for it is that which has kept the scholars guessing to reconcile history, legend and archæology.

AS FOR the Pictish tribes in Britain and Scotland, which enter our story, no one can absolutely contradict us if we stretch our imagination a bit and believe that, if they did grow up on a foundation of crude Silurian Stone Men, it is not impossible that minglings of those Mediterranean races which contributed Umbrian, Samnian, and Etruscan problems of origins to ancient history wandered through Europe and added no inconsiderable share to the social advance and the developments in religious cults which existed in the kingdoms of even far Pictland, when Irish and Norse began to descend upon it for plunder or settlement. It is on such a supposition that I build up a measure of the story of *Tlaya*, the wicked and handsome; and her venomous priest; of the *Sons of Dubha*, and of the beautiful *Fedalm*, in whom is represented such a mingling of Norse and Pict as doubtless took place often in those old days. Any or all of these characters *might* have existed. The *Macduff* of Shakspere, the MacDuffees, McAfees, and the other varieties of the name, are of the "Sons of Dubha" (the Dark One)—of the Clan Alpine and its kindred clans anciently in the West Highlands, the islands, and the coast there. *The Red Sweynie* (in the Erse: *Suibhne Ruad*, and anglicized "Red Sweeney") is nearest to a historical character in the tale. A chief, of his name, expelled from Ireland by infuriated Irishmen for similar misdeeds, is written of.

SINCE you ask me politely for personal details, may I choose only some which relate to my interest in things Gaelic rather than tell my college and miscellaneously chosen education, my Ohio birthplace, my family tree of American pioneers, patriots and professors—to say nothing of my age? It has always fascinated me to imagine that this interest is atavistic. Which may be nonsense, but I like to believe—while I am calling myself daffy for doing so—that I once was somebody—a queen, a knight, an ancient bard, a druidess, or even a fairy person, in that enchanted old land, and that I have had to return somewhere to take up its story. Or else that some spirit from that old time has sometime whispered to me whatever it was—that long ago made me wish to read and write and think about it.

OF COURSE every American has strains of all sorts from the old world's past in him, and French, Scottish, Welsh and English I have behind me in most of the lines of my forebears. But they have been in this country since its first guns were fired and its first forests cleared, and only my father's mother bears a Gaelic name. Yet it is she, of them all behind me, that I look most like, and she was Irish, of the type we call Iberian, out of the west of Scotland, and marked in certain regions of Ireland to this day.

No fairy tales spellbound me as the Irish ones did, and certain of the Scottish ones. And when I was growing older I brushed aside most other things for all the old Irish saga volumes I could coax from librarians. When I came first to New York I hunted up the Gaelic societies, where I didn't know a soul, and stole in to their evening meetings to listen, a stranger waif, in a corner, to their Irish songs and talk.

At last I began to write and lecture about Ireland. A few years ago I had the satisfaction of bringing before a good many people in our city two of my epic plays (called fashionably that year, "pageants") which told episodes of two great heroic periods of Irish life in its golden time: the hero story of her pagan warrior and defender, Finn MacCool, and a no less heroic tale of the soldier-saint days of her royal priest, Columkill.—ANNE THROOP CRAIG.

FOLLOWING Camp-Fire custom, Thomas McMorrow rises and introduces himself. I think you'll grant his last request:

New York.

You fellows ever see Spring Street where this magazine comes from? Me, neither. I went down there one day last week to give the works the double-O, and maybe meet these men Hoffman and Wade who been writing me so many nice letters and enclosing my manuscripts, but I didn't see Spring Street. I went down a long narrow alley lined with Italian delicatessen stores and saw an enormous building about twenty stories high. As I looked up at it and framed a few well-chosen words a splinter of Spring Street lit in my eye. It preyed on my mind. I went into an Italian druggist's across the way and found him plotting a black-hand outrage with two friends. He told me to throw up my eye-lids and give him my handkerchief. I wouldn't do that, so he stuck his black hand in my eye, looked into my very soul, and guessed I'd better see a doctor. I needed one, then, and I blew before he put me in need of a glass eye. The doctor cleaned out my eye and collected a cinder, some finger-nails, a dollar, and of black-hand bombs a trace. I was all spoiled, and streaked with tears, so I had to pass up *Adventure* for the day.

ABOUT me? Now, look here, I'm all right. I never been bit by a lariat or got lost in the pathless chaparejos, but I work for a living, never been in jail, and got lots of bad habits. I was born right here on Manhattan, thirty-one years ago, and have been here all my life. No, I'm not a cripple; I'm an ex-ball-player, six feet and one hundred and eighty, but just a regular city hick. When I go out West to Hoboken I strap on my sombreros and call people "stranger." I'm a member of the Tammany Hall County Committee, Irish parentage, white, unmarried (write c. o. *Adventure*), a member of New York Bar, ex-school teacher, builder of apartment-houses just now, and I raise on two pair when I sit next to the opener.

All the wild animals I ever saw are up in the Bronx Zoo, which is welcome to my share of them, but I admit there are sights west of the North River. I like the quiet life, with a cop asleep on the corner, the elevated snoring overhead—where you know a con man by his speaking to you without being introduced, where they hang the wash on the roof, dine in the back-yard, and where you remark it's a small world if you meet anybody you know. It takes all kinds of people to make a world, fellows! Let me live.—THOMAS MCMORROW.

THIS meeting of our Camp-Fire is pretty much taken up by long talks, I being the guiltiest party, but at least there's room to say that we've had word from a good many of our comrades at the front, reporting their safety. Among them are Erwin A. Walser, W. Townend, Harry C. Winters, Harold S. Lovett, C. F. Whiteley, S. B. Moorehead, Donald Francis McGrew, Carl G. Lindhult, George S. Olds, William H. Parr, R. R. Robertson, Geo. R. Cochran, Jerome E. Kemmerer, Patrick M. Gallagher, M. Logee, Roy T. Yellow, J. E. Hausmann, Erwin A. Walser, Ove Nelson, J. J. Gibbons, L. C. Longstreet, J. A. Pringle, Eric Levison, R. R. Robertson. There are many more but I have not their letters beside me.

If there were not so long a period between the time a letter reaches us and the time it can be passed on to you in print we would give at each Camp-Fire the list of our fighting comrades reported safe. At least we can share the word from them as soon as conditions permit and, of course, the report of any casualty sent to us. If you know any of our comrades who is a casualty, send in his name to be added to the Camp-Fire's honor-roll so that his personal friends among us may know the facts.

Now waiting for print are quite a number of letters from Camp-Fire members in khaki or Navy blue, and many other letters on many subjects, particularly on characters and phases of the old West, from comrades all over the map, Honduras to New Zealand, snow countries to tropics. Also there's a lot more good "dope" from gun-sharks, called forth by our article "Fire-Arms, Old and New," which we'll hear at our first February Camp-Fire.

TO WRITE in September anything concerning the war which will not be read until three months later is uncertain going, particularly with the Allied offensive in a state of progress that makes almost anything at least possible. Perhaps I consider possible a more sweeping victory from that offensive that do most other Americans, but even so I believe there are three points to be held in mind in spite of any hopes or guesses.

(1) First, we must push our war preparations on the basis that the war may last for years to come. For over four years Germany has tried to throw her enemies off guard and lessen their zeal for adequate preparation by sending out false reports of internal crumbling and general weakening. We must not swallow that bait. Germany will be crushed when she *is* crushed. Not before.

(2) Second, we must not keep our eyes on the Western front alone. I think the Allied belief that the war would be decided there has been largely responsible for Germany's successes. Having given less attention to other theaters of war, naturally the result has been to center the final struggle in the West, but that may have been merely

making a mistaken theory come true by forcing it into operation. Certainly the losses on other fronts have been heavy, and certainly these losses have built up a stronger enemy for the Allies on the Western front. Perhaps a Germany soundly beaten elsewhere would have made a Germany far more easily beaten in the West. Perhaps it would have shifted the final struggle to some other front.

AS THINGS are, however, the decision is quite likely to come on the Western line. But who shall say that, though the war be decided *on* the Western front, it was not decided *by* the other fronts, or at least greatly prolonged by them?*

In any case, the second point to be kept foremost in mind is that, however important the Western front may be in the strategy of war, it is *not* the most important front in the strategy of peace. In other words, when it comes to peace terms the real danger to the United States and the Allies is *not* in Belgium and France, but east and southeast of Germany and Austria.

If a defeated Germany is allowed to make peace by restoring Belgium, Luxembourg and eastern France and returning Alsace-Lorraine to the latter country, that will be a *German victory*. And a victory that we Americans will some day pay for with our blood or the blood of our children.

GERMANY planned this war forty years ahead. She is still planning forty years ahead. Nor was this war the end of her first plannings. If she could in this one war sweep all before her and gain the world-dominion which alone will satisfy her iron ambition, well and good. If not, then she would see to it that this war at least gained for her a footing that would make success sure at the next attempt. And if she merely gives up land on the Western front *Germany will have the footing she planned for*.

Her chance to prepare for another bloody effort to conquer the world ten, twenty, forty years from now lies not along the border-line of France but in Russia, Finland, Lithuania, Esthonia, the Balkans, Turkey, Asia Minor. Nor are we to forget her admitted plan of building up a formidable central empire in Africa, her untold plans for other colonies or her grip on South America.

* Since this was written Bulgaria has collapsed, Palestine fallen and the crisis greatly shifted to the southeast.

Take from her what you will on the West but leave Germany *any kind* of grip on the lands to her east and southeast, and she will go from the peace conference grinning in her sleeve over the victory she won from those who beat her on the battle-field.

THOSE lands to her east and southeast are rich in all the raw materials most essential to modern warfare. She knows how to use and develop them. Those lands are crammed with man-power. She knows how to seize it and make it serve her. Most of all, those lands are *the* strategic gateway to her real ambitions for future world-dominion. She knows how to use gateways.

For example, steel and the coal necessary to make it are perhaps the first essential among materials necessary for war-making. In 1914 Germany controlled 49 per cent. of Europe's steel-making capacity; her European opponents 48 per cent. Now she controls 68 per cent.; her European opponents less than 29 per cent. Much of this gain, of course, comes from Belgium and northern France, but captured Russia and Russian Poland are heavy factors and their supply is, unlike the Western deposits, capable of enormous expansion.

Man power? What are the limits if Germany is left free hand to her east where all is in a flux that makes anything possible?

Strategic gateway? Give Germany her gateway to the east and southeast and God help the world!

Even deprive her of technical political control of Russia, the new border states between, the Balkans and Turkey, but leave her *any* chance for her agents and propaganda to work in these lands and, when the next crisis comes, you will find that these lands, their vast supplies of material and men and their limitless political and strategic opportunity *belong to Germany*.

AND this brings us to the third point to be kept foremost in mind:

(3) So long as Germany is Germany she —is Germany. She is evil organized. Organized for generations; trained from childhood to see crooked; shaped root, stock and branch for the gaining of her evil ends. So long as any power is left her she will organize and build up that power until it

is great enough for her next bloody effort. When it comes to peace terms we can not, we *dare* not, let any consideration come before the absolute necessity of self-protection for the future. Mercy is both stupid and wicked when it means the death of the merciful and the bloody success of the spared. When it is a choice between living with a snake and killing a snake, we kill it.

Take from her every inch of territory she has seized. Leave her only room to live, but not an atom more to grow strong upon for new mischief. She is a criminal, a dangerous criminal, and must be kept in jail.

BUILD all around her a sure rampart of enemies or neutrals and *keep her out of them*. Allow no German to remain in them or to settle in them. Otherwise her agents and propaganda will undermine them as they did to Russia and have been trying to do to every other country on the globe. Doubtless that sounds extreme, but Germany's real weapon is not brawn or brain but *propaganda*.

Take her navy from her. Make her pay ship for ship for the merchantmen her U-boats have sunk against the law of nations. Leave her just enough commercial and economic strength to keep her own people in simple comfort. Boycott her from foreign markets. A nation economically strong is strong enough for war. Therefore she must not become economically strong. Germany has made herself a criminal, a convict. She must be kept in jail. For she knows no repentance except that enforced by might.

ONCE, like many other Americans, I was a victim of the German propaganda that the German people themselves were forced into this war by the few autocrats who ruled them, that the German people as a whole were not in sympathy with the militarism of the Junkers, that the German people were at heart kindly, peace-loving people who were to be pitied because they were being made to fight against their will. Like many other Americans, I became an unconscious agent of the Kaiser's and helped spread that friendly and broad-minded idea. Probably you did the same. But now we've waked up.

Now we know that the German people as a whole were heart and soul with their Government in the great ambition of world-conquest, in *Deutschland über Alles*, in the theory of might over right, the policy of "blood and iron." They had been systematically trained to it from childhood. It is bred in their bone. They do not know how to think in any other way. They are to be pitied because Prussianism seized upon them in infancy and distorted them into the ugly products it needed for its work. But that does not alter the fact that they *are* these ugly products and must be dealt with as such. The leopard can not change its spots.

IF THEY suddenly "reform" when a sword is held to their throats, let us not be deceived. Let them first *prove* their reformation. It took them forty years to become a nation of brutes. Give them, then, forty years probation and see whether or not they can in that time make themselves into a nation of human beings. Until at least one new generation is born and grows up, trusting the German people will be risky business.

Suppose they have a revolution and throw off Kaiserism? *They can't.* They can throw off the Kaiser, but they can't throw off the Kaiserism they drank in with their mothers' milk. They made no effort to throw off the yoke while they were winning. To throw it off after they've found they can't win would be merely doing what they think will gain most under the circumstances. Not a change of heart; only a change in their ability to do evil.

ALREADY, with the tide only beginning to turn against them, they are busily and systematically at work creating sympathy for themselves so that, taking advantage of our soft-heartedness, they can gain easier terms of peace when their cause is lost. Oh, this wonderful German propaganda machine! As delicately adjusted as it is far-reaching and powerful. Have you noticed that when Germany's hopes have seemed bright there has been no sympathy-getting German propaganda but that the very instant those hopes have been checked the Hun propaganda machine at once has begun sending out sympathy-getters preparing a soft bed to light on if Germany should lose—letters "accidentally" found on captured prisoners, news reports from neutral countries, artistic touches furnished by German agents in our midst?

If, like me, you have a file of daily papers running back to 1914 you can prove this. Watch the *little* news items, those of seemingly minor importance. Do you remember that news report of how the Kaiser, *after* the German failure at Verdun, knelt amid the battle ruins and called God to witness that he had not willed this destruction? *After* the failure. Why didn't he do this dramatic little stunt amid the ruins of some previous battle when the German hopes were high? That one instance proves little, but you'll find it is part of an unfailing system:—while Germany wins, turn the propaganda elsewhere; when things look bad for Germany, set the propaganda to creating sympathy that will make things easier for her at the peace conference. A cold-blooded, calculating, effective system nicely adjusted to the job of getting the most for Germany no matter what the outcome of the war.

IT'S working full-blast now. In July, the instant the Hun offensive broke down and the Allies took the whip-hand, the Hun propaganda machine began grinding for sympathy. All of a sudden German prisoners were found to have an amazing number of unmailed letters on their persons, letters full of phrases about "poor Germany," "this awful war," "suffering at home," "these horrors," "hopelessness," "our bitter agony," etc., etc. In American papers here again began the flood of little news items featuring the hard times the poor Germans are having. In the paper I bought an hour ago is a touching report from Switzerland saying that the Kaiser "has greatly aged and that his hair is snow white and his shoulders stooped . . . eyes are feverish . . . gestures abrupt . . . face severely lined . . . general expression of a man suffering a great sorrow." Too bad. But there weren't any reports about the poor old fellow's white hair, etc., between March 21 and July 15 while the Germans were winning. Strange that this touching picture is sent out just when it is needed most for Germany's interests. Incidentally, it isn't made clear whether he's sorrowing over the hell into which he swept the world or merely over the fact that his blood-and-iron attempt to Germanize the world is crumbling.

In the same paper is another report from Switzerland, this time about the poor Kaiserin's serious illness. These two items are on page 2. A good antidote is to turn to page 3, nearly filled with one day's casualty list of 815 Americans killed or maimed by Germans.

THESE are only chance samples out of thousands. Watch for them. And cross your fingers when you read or hear. With the war well into its fifth year it's a little late for the Germans to talk loudly about gentleness and sympathy—for themselves. How about the terms of peace *they* laid down from time to time when things were going well for them? Any gentleness and sympathy then? Their plan is a simple one:—if the Allies are whipped, use the iron heel; if Germany is whipped, use gentleness. Very nice—for Germany.

The civilized world has gone through years of hell to defeat Germany; only folly will render those years fruitless by mistaken mercy at the peace table. Safety first—safety for our children from another such hell created by the same ambitious, evil-saturated people. Safety for democracy and decency. Self-preservation comes before mistaken sentiment. Be merciful when you can and dare, but not when mercy means keeping alive an evil force whose sole aim is to substitute brute force for mercy throughout the world for all time. Better one act of stern justice to a criminal than such a plunge back into barbarism. Be merciful? Yes, but let's be merciful to our own children first, not to the breeder of blood-lust who is now destroying them and who will rise again to destroy them if we leave him the strength to do it.

BE PROOF against the subtle, cringing sympathy propaganda of the Hun who in his success used to boast that all sympathy and mercy were weakness. Let us keep before our eyes those things that can furnish the real sinews of war for another Hun attempt to Prussianize the world, and let us see to it that these sinews are not left to him in the peace terms. A partly crushed snake has still the power to kill. Let us see to it that the German snake is wholly crushed before we leave him.

ARTHUR SULLIVANT HOFFMAN.

SO MANY of you have sent in more "dope" on guns since our Camp-Fire article "Firearms, Old and New," that at our next meeting we'll have an interesting bunch of them all at one sitting. Meanwhile here are a bit of gun information and a gun question from our comrade E. L. Cunningham, Chief Yeoman, U. S. N.

El Paso, Texas.

Being something of a gun crank myself, I studied this list rather carefully, and wish to call your attention to an omission noted. No mention is made, in the guns of from 1850 to 1860, of the Colt revolving carbine. This gun was manufactured somewhere between 1850 and 1865 for use of the cavalry and chambered for either the .45-70 or .45-90 cartridge. The breech action was the same as that of the frontier model Colt revolver, namely, a large cylinder. One of these guns is, or was in 1912, in the collection of ancient and modern firearms of Captain M. B. Lloyd, deceased, displayed in the Carnegie Public Library at Ft. Worth, Texas. This gun, I have been informed, played a fairly important part in the cavalry engagements of the Union army but was shortly replaced by the first Springfield repeating rifles.

I WISH to ask if the revolver listed among those manufactured by Colt as the "new service" is the same as the revolver patented in 1871, 1872 and 1875 and known (in Texas at least) as the "frontier" model? This revolver is made in the .32-20, .38, .44 and .45 calibers. It is sold under the name of "frontier model" in the shops with which I have had acquaintance in Texas. If you could print a discussion of these points I have made in Camp-Fire it would be greatly appreciated. I am sure that either Mr. Brown or Mr. Wiggin, whose lists were very complete indeed, could clear up these points with ease, and this letter is intended in no way as a criticism of either gentleman.—E. L. CUNNINGHAM.

ANOTHER old English comrade of our writers' brigade reports himself safe and sound and on the job:

Egyptian Expeditionary Force.

I am ——ishly busy in a climate like ——, getting out a weekly in English, Hebrew and Arabic. But nobody cares a —— about us with the present fighting going on in France. Your men, as I knew they would, have done splendidly and are going to do better still.—ALBERT KINROSS.

HERE is a letter from one of us, a physician, whose letter seems to bear out the claims of the much-discussed scout and Indian fighter, Captain Drannan. Some of you were asking for any evidence that would substantiate the record Drannan claimed for himself. All we are seeking is the facts, though naturally we'd prefer to see it established that this old man had merely told the truth about himself.

Atlanta, Ga.

As an old reader of *Adventure* I am interested in Mr. E. A. Brininstool's letter concerning Capt W. F. Drannan, in order to help establish Captain Drannan's claims as an Indian scout or rather Indian killer as he was known among old Western men. Place all this only as a bit of second-hand information.

I MET Captain Drannan years ago at a hotel in Seattle, Wash., was with him for several days, and he told me some of his Indian experiences that I have since read in his book, "Thirty Years on the Plains," which book I believe a correct story of Captain Drannan's actual exploits.

He was an old man twenty-five years ago when I met him, rather lame in one leg from an Indian arrow having cut a tendon. Captain Jack Crawford, the well-known scout, has often told me in my office in Atlanta (Jack was my patient and friend) of Drannan's exploits and while he admired him as one of the very best of the old-time scouts of the Kit Carson school (of whom he was foster son), he usually made it plain that Drannan hated Indians and would take any and every advantage of them and kill all he could, alseep, awake or any other way, and was not afraid to tackle a camp of a dozen single-handed and usually killed them all by crawling among them, killing with a knife until the disturbance stirred them up, then finish with two pistols as he was ambidextrous and seldom missed with either hand.

Buffalo Bill and Colonel Burke knew him well and told me in Atlanta some years ago that he was one of the old timers and —— in a hand-to-hand Indian fight.

NOT being a Western man and a poor judge of such matters, I would not be a judge, but to me Captain Drannan rang true and had all the earmarks of an honest, rough, fearless man, of rather prepossessing appearance, gentle and careful in his manner with not the slightest taint of bluster. Personally I liked him and feel like I could vouch for any claim he has made. I think the reason he is not heard of is that he was overshadowed by Carson,

Bridger and other great scouts with whom he associated and he was too old to figure very prominently in the last of the Indian wars.

The information I give may throw a little light in favor of the old fellow; if so, I am glad, for his like has gone never to return. I might add that Drannan told me that so far as he knew he had no relatives, as he was born at sea coming from France, but if he did they were in Kentucky, where he left his little sister when he was a small boy, his parents having died, he running away to St. Louis and by accident meeting Kit Carson who in a way adopted him. Drannan always spoke of Colonel Carson as Uncle Kit.—JOHN H. POWELL, M.D.

THOUGH a changed press schedule makes it possible to alter this page, I'm leaving in it the following, written early in October, since it explains why our magazine, along with others, has not been able to adjust its contents at once to the ending of the war:

Sooner or later the day will come when *Adventure*, since it is made up several months in advance, will appear with its "help-win-the-war" departments and so on still in full blast after peace and victory have been won. That will look rather odd, but, since no man can know in advance just when the war will end, it can not be helped and we'll all be feeling too rejoiced to worry over a little thing like that. *Adventure's* little job is to keep hammering away at its little part in helping win the war, and it's better to seem to hammer too long rather than not hammer long enough. We Americans have learned by this time that the war isn't won until it *is* won and that it is foolish to relax any effort, great or small, until then.

WORD from a comrade at the front.

"Somewhere in France."

No doubt you will have forgotten me, seeing the length of time that has elapsed since I last sat down and dropped you a note, but I just thought I'd sit me down with my sack of "Bull," my book of "Riz-la" and my pen and let you know I am still alive and kicking.

IT HAS been some time since I lit on this side of the pond but if I remember rightly this is the first time I have essayed to let you know of my whereabouts. The idea entered my head when I strolled into a "Y. M. C. A." recently and picked up a late copy of *Adventure*, and believe me it's not often you get a chance at one; they don't last long enough. . . .

Have you been noticing what the "Yanks" have been doing to the "Heinies" hereabouts lately? I guess old Bill has changed his mind about Uncle Sam throwing a bluff. I'll admit we, as a nation, have the world stopped for throwing bluffs, but when it's necessary to back it up we have the goods.

By the way, I have been trying to locate a pal of mine with the Canadians in various ways and as he is a reader of *Adventure* I think you can help me. His name is Clifford Todhunter and all I know of his whereabouts, or rather probable whereabouts, is that he left Philadelphia, April 19 or 20, 1917, for Montreal and enlisted in the Queen's Own Rifles. The exact number of his outfit I never knew.

I am now the Gas N. C. O. of our outfit and, believe me, it sure is interesting work. The folks at home and even the majority of the soldiers on this side do not realize the German High Command's dastardly crime of introducing the use of gas in civilized warfare.—Sergeant WM. A. FULMER, 112751, A. E. F.

WHEN we first read Charles Beadle's novelette that appears in this issue *Hayes* seemed such an exaggerated type of American that we wrote Mr. Beadle asking whether *Hayes'* extreme line of talk hadn't better be toned down a bit. He replied that *Hayes* really happened, that he was drawn from life. And yet, to many Americans, he will seem as exaggerated as he did to us in the office, so we're just playing safe by stating the fact that Mr. Beadle, an Englishman living in this country, didn't think he was drawing a typical American but knew he was drawing a particular and actual one.

It's the old business of truth being stranger than fiction. Many a story is rejected because, though really true, to the average reader it would seem more incredible than the wildest fiction.

WORD from comrade W. P. Jensen, who has been up against a "tin fish" and other things with a kick in them. I'd call this comrade a glutton for adventure.

Boston.

I started to go to sea in the year 1911 and the lure of the ocean has caught me for, as Tennyson says: "Only those who brave its danger, comprehend its mystery."

MY FIRST adventure was in Chile in 1913, when I and two other sailors got robbed by two bandits. They held us up with a gun and cleaned us out for everything we possessed; that was between Coquimbo and Guayacan. The ship was laying in Guayacan. By the way; two men died of beriberi; round the Horn, we lost another man from the gallant yard. In 1914 was in a mutiny; the less said about it the better.

IN 1916 was on the Russian Finn four-masted barque *Marborough Hill*. She was chased by a sub two hundred miles off the English coast. He hailed us in the morning and we hove to, the sub gave a signal to abandon ship and we lowered away our lee life-boat, but a heavy sea caught it and broke it up, whereby we lost two men and three wounded and fractured. The sub signaled us to make a raft and get away in that. We were loaded with lumber from Pensacola, Florida, so we had plenty to make it of.

The captain called all hands aft and said that it was no other chance to reach the shore than run for it. There was running a heavy sea and blowing a gale. Then we was send up two man in each top to loosen the sail or rather to cut the gaskets away, and the other was standing on the deck and hoisting away at once. The sub got not a single shot home, but we got a lot of damage from the heavy sea in which the sub could not ketch up with us and we reached Liverpool in safety.

ON the twelfth of January I foundered in the British schooner *Meyric* of Beauamaris in a cyclone off the North African coast. We went out of Cadiz with a load of salt bound for Rio Grande do Sul, Brazil. Two days out that got calm and about dinner, when I had watch below, I got thrown off my feet when the skip keeled over for a terrific wind-gust and we heard a crash and down came the gaff off the mainsail. After that we saw everything disappearing bit for bit, masts, bowsprit and all. The seas were washing over the deck with a terrific force and succeeded in pounding the lifeboat that was lashed on the mainhatch to pieces. These pieces floated around and cut a hole in the ——(?). This got bigger and bigger during the night and was impossible to get to for the seas were pounding us about the deck from one side to another.

At last we saw the ship would sink and we abandoned her and hung on for four hours where one man was terribly mauled and slashed of the sea. At last in the morning we saw a steamer bearing down. Later showed to be the *Panachi Vagliano*. There had been heavy damage during the cyclone. He launched his boat with big efforts and succeeded in rescuing us, but the sea was too heavy for them to run the boat alongside so we were hauled on board by lines and the boat set adrift.

I got landed in Gibraltar, went in an English ship, witnessed air-raids in Salonika and London, bombardment in Dunkirk.

GOT sunk by a sub the eighteenth of December, forty-two miles off the Irish coast in the Swedish barque *Bellville* of Landskrona. The sub fired first a torpedo, then went under the bottom. Then he came to the surface and ordered us to stop, what we did, and he came on board and removed all brass, like bells, and even the wheel he took with him that was brass bound and blowed us up. That journey in the boat was not at all very comfortable for that was very cold and the sailors had saved three cases of whiskey so they did not know what they was doing. Some wanted to go to France, others to England, then there was a fight and at last everybody but me reached Konigbeg Lightship in the Irish sea from which we was taken off by a submarine chaser. They landed us in Waterford. From Ireland we proceeded to Hull for going to Sweden; went out from there and got sunk by gunfire of two German cruisers and returned back to Hull and now I am over here and expect to go over again shortly.—W. P. JENSEN.

HE DID what, so far as I know, has been done only once before, and that several hundred years ago—sail a small boat single-handed over the seven hundred miles between New York and Bermuda. Our comrade, Captain A. E. Dingle, of our writers' brigade and "Ask Adventure." But he and his dog and his twenty-eight-foot sloop *Gauntlet* barely got through. A storm and a hurricane gave them twenty-six days of it, pretty well smashed up the boat, ruined instruments and supplies and left them for days without water.

I read the account of it in Bermuda papers and the tale is a dramatic one. Perhaps we can get him to tell us something about it.

SOME time ago one of our comrades at the front quoted a few lines of poetry and asked the Camp-Fire to give him the poem's name and the place where it first appeared. Responses have poured in for months, giving the poem in full, but no one could remember where it had first been published and I did not feel warranted in reprinting it without the consent of the original publisher. Yet that poem had made so remarkable an impression that many men all over the country had memorized it word for word. Truly a splendid tribute and proof enough for anybody that this poem should be passed on to as many as possible.

At last one of you "thought it had appeared in *Collier's*" and later another of you was sure of it and knew the year approximately. So I wrote to *Collier's* and they kindly sent me the full and correct text so that I could pass it on to you. It appeared on the inside back cover of their issue of August 3, 1912, and they as well as the author have placed many of us in debt for lines that live so strongly in the hearts of men.

THE DOWN-AND-OUT

by CLARENCE LEONARD HAY

SO, SON, you've come to the tropics, heard all that you had to do
Was to sit in the shade in a coconut glade, while the dollars rolled in to you?
They gave you that at the Bureau, you got the statistics straight?
Well, hear what it did to another kid before you decide your fate.
You don't go down with a short, hard fall; you just sort of shuffle along,
And lighten your load of the moral code till you can't tell the right from the wrong.
I started off to be honest, with everything on the square,
But a man can't fool with the golden rule in a crowd that don't play fair.

It's a choice of riding a dirty race or of being an also ran.
My only hope was to sneak and dope the horse of the other man.
I pulled a deal at Guayaquil, in an Inca silver-mine,
And before they found 'twas salted ground I was safe in the Argentine;
I made short weight on the River Plate when running a freighter there,
And cracked a crib on a rich estate without ever turning a hair;
But the thing that'll double-bar my soul when it flaps at heaven's doors
Was peddling booze to the Santa Cruz, and Winchester forty-fours.
Made unafraid by my kindly aid, the drunk-crazed brutes came down
And left in a quivering, blazing mass a flourishing border town.
I was then in charge of a smuggler's barge on the coast of Yucatan,
But she sank to hell off Cozumel one night in a hurricane.
I got to shore on a broken oar in the filthy, shrieking dark,
With the other two of the good ship's crew converted into shark.
From a limestone cliff I flagged a skiff with a salt-soaked pair of jeans,
And worked my way (for I couldn't pay) on a fruiter to New Orleans.

It's a kind of a habit, the tropics, that gets you, worse than rum;
You get away, and you swear you'll stay, but it calls, and back you come.
Six short months went by before I was back there on the job,
Running a war in Salvador with a black-faced, barefoot mob.
It was General Santiago Hicks at the head of a grand revolt,
And my only friend from start to end was a punishing Army Colt.
I might have been Presidente now, a prosperous man of means,
But a gunboat came and blocked my game with a hundred and ten marines.
So I awoke from my dream dead broke, then drifted from bad to worse,
And sank as low as a man can go who walks with an empty purse.
But stars, they say, appear by day when you're down in a deep, black pit.
My Lucky Star found me that way when I was about to quit,
In a fiery-hot, flea-ridden cot, I was down with the Yellow Jack,
Alone in the Bush and all but dead; She found me and nursed me back,
She came like the Miracle Man of old and opened my bad, blind eyes,
And upon me shone a clear new dawn as I turned my head to the skies.
There was pride and grace in her brown young face, for hers was the blood of kings;
In her eyes flashed the glory of empires gone and the secret of world-old things.
We were spliced in a Yankee meetinghouse on the land of your Uncle Sam,
And I drew my pay from the U. S. A., for I worked at the Gatun Dam.
Mind you, I take no credit for coming back to my own,
Though I walked again with honest men, I couldn't have done it alone.
Then the devil sent his right-hand man—I might have suspected he would—
And he took her life with a long thin knife because she was straight and good.

Within me died hope, honor, pride, and all but a primitive will
To hound him down on his blood-red trail, and find—and kill—and kill!
Through logwood swamps and chicle camps I hunted him many a moon,
Then found my man in a long pit pan at the edge of a blue lagoon.
The chase was o'er at the farther shore; it ended a two years' quest,
And I left him there with an empty stare and a "John Crow" on his chest.

You see those punctures on my arm; you'd like to know what they mean?
Those marks were left by the fingers deft of my trained nurse, Miss Morphine.
Perhaps you think that's worse than drink—it's possible, too, you're right;
At least it drives away the Things that come and stare in the night.
There's a homestead down in an old Maine town with lilacs round the gate,
And the Northers whisper: "It might have been," but the truth has come too late.
They say they give me a month to live—a month or a year's the same;
I haven't the heart to play my part at the end of a losing game.
For whenever you play, whatever the way, for stakes that are big or small,
The claws of the tropics will gather your pile, and the dealer gets it all!

—Reprinted by courtesy of *Collier's*.

YOU may remember that Samuel Alexander White's novelette, "The Wave-Bound," brought us a letter from Captain James Moorhead who had been wrecked on the Magdalen Islands, and later a letter from E. J. O'Brien, about his own experience on the scene of the story. Here is a further letter from Captain Moorhead:

New York.

I have read with much interest Mr. E. J. O'Brien's answer to my letter in "Camp-Fire" of recent date. Mr. O'Brien's article is very interesting, and although he agrees I must have had a very rough experience on the Magdalen Islands, he must have seen that part of the world in different light to what I did.

He says lots of people speak English there now, but I could find only the lighthouse-keeper at Fortune Bay, in my time. He also mentions three old ladies who kept an inn where I would have met with a hearty old Irish welcome. Perhaps Mr. O'Brien's experience in Amherst Island was at some other part from where I landed, and I only wish I could have fallen in with these old ladies' inn, I would rather have enjoyed my visit instead of the suffering I had, which I shall never forget.

However, I have been delighted reading Mr. O'Brien's article. Would like to meet him sometime to talk over the Magdalen Islands.—JAMES MOORHEAD.

SOME years ago, perhaps five, one of you whom I had never met sent me several specimens of chalcihuitl, which has good ground for being considered the rediscovered sacred stone of the ancient Aztecs. One of these stones, a beautiful specimen showing a distinct and almost perfect representation of the sacred beetle, he asked me to keep for him until he called for it. The others, some of them showing the rising sun image, he gave to me.

So his stone went into our safe and has lain there for years with never a word from or of the man who sent it. It seemed to me I had better bring up the matter at Camp-Fire and ask for news of him. But this afternoon he walked into the office and I turned over his stone to him.

ALSO I listened to some interesting talk about chalcihuitl and other things. I asked him to write down some of it for the rest of you, some of the odd happenings connected with the efforts of various people to establish this gem on a commercial basis, but he felt that they sounded too much like fiction and too little like fact. I still hope, however, that he will "come across" and tell you the tale.

There are so many of you with wonderful tales to tell, and so few of you tell them. Some of you tell them to me personally but, when I ask them to pass it on to the Camp-Fire in general, they find this, that and the other reason for not doing it. Of course some are all or partly—well, exaggerated, but there are plenty more that are true. And very good listening. Isn't it only fair that those of you who have only sat and enjoyed the talks of other comrades should play the game fair and even and hold up their own end of the telling?

THE gentleman who wrote the following letter accusing us of using "paid propaganda in disguise" does not seem inclined to back himself up:

Of all the dishonest and underhanded methods employed by the insane and pestilential advocates of National Prohibition, otherwise National Insanity, the use of the moving-picture screens and story magazines is the basest. This propaganda does not go after proselytes by showing even a reasonable view of the worse side. The picture-shows bought for this work deceive poor people, to begin with, who have paid their hard-earned money for entertainment and remain to have their prejudices and passions played upon by harrowing showings of things on the order of ten-nights-in-a-barroom, or some obsolete or imaginary happenings incident to the development of the Western mining-fields.

The *Adventure was* a good magazine; I have bought and read it for its entertainment in the State of —— and surrounding territory for many years, during travels annually amounting to about twenty-five thousand miles. But when you take in such slush as now offered by the Pinkertons, paid propaganda in disguise, as the "White Indians" appears to me in the June issue, my connection with you ends, and I shall do as much against the *Adventure* and every other such poisonous propaganda in hiding, as I have formerly done for them.

"The White Indians" is a foolish and preposterous story, of course, but it is no more so than the pictured failings of the *Rollin* of the story in the matter of drink. As a young man I drank everything there is that is good to drink, and quit in the midst of plenty during a Christmas week, twelve years ago. My stop was absolute, and final. And I know hundreds of similar cases, not necessarily involving unusually strong wills. Alcohol is not a disease. It is a blessing of the Creator, sometimes misused as is every other gift of God. Let some one tell of the *happiness* it brings, and the comfort it gives. No one is ever allowed to tell that side, these days of Pharisees and hypocrites.—— —— ——.

In reply I wrote, among other things:

You have accused this magazine of accepting disguised paid propaganda for publication as fiction. That is not true and you owe us an apology. What I want to know is, are you the kind of man who makes wild charges of dishonorable things without being able to back them up? If not, then offer reasonable proof of what you've said.

I'm quite willing to submit this case to our readers. Have you backbone enough to let me publish your letter over your name in Camp-Fire? You did not attach your signature to the letter, but merely typed the name —— at the end of it. Please stand right up to the mark in your reply and affix your signature to what you say, particularly if you are game enough to give me permission to publish this letter in the magazine. I shall, of course, not publish your letter in the magazine until I have obtained consent from the Pinkertons, since their personal honor is involved in the matter.

It's been considerably over a month and he's not offered any proof, reasonable or otherwise. Nor has he had backbone enough to consent to presenting his case to you over his own name. He has not been game enough even to reply.

His charge is both false and ridiculous and the incident would be only amusing but for the fact that this kind of person is dangerous and contemptible as well as silly. If a fellow wants to accuse a man—and, still more, a woman—of something dishonorable he ought to have some pretty solid proof before he talks, ought to be ready to back up his charges with that proof, ought to sign his name with his own hand instead of a typewriter, ought to be willing to submit the case over his own name to the judgment of those in whose eyes he tries to blacken his victims' reputation. Bah! The Camp-Fire, as far as my dealings with them are concerned, may not all be ladylike and pretty-mannered, but they're real people who, if they hit you at all, hit you in the face, not in the back with a rock thrown from a distant thicket. I'm glad this chap is no longer to be among us.

Here is the Pinkertons' reply to his silly charge. And an extract out of a letter from Mr. Pinkerton to me. As to this story's being "preposterous," you will remember that a number of you have written in giving other examples of the same well-established disease upon which the story hangs.

Denver, Colorado.

"The White Indians" was written as any piece of fiction is written, was offered for sale in the same way, and was paid for by *Adventure* only. Never in our lives has either of us ever had any connection with, communication from, or arrangement with, any temperance or prohibition organization. We have never received a cent from or contributed money to such an organization. We have no desire to contribute to prohibition propaganda and have never done so in any way. The question of alcoholism was used in "The White Indians" because we needed certain situations and elements in the story. That it might be construed as an argument against alcohol we never even considered until we received a copy of Mr. ——'s letter. We did not, moreover, garble facts for the sake of the story. Alcoholism is recognized as a disease by members of the medical profession who know. Jack London, who certainly knew what booze does to a man, in "John Barleycorn" classified all men as alcoholic and non-alcoholic. Science is back of him, and science is knowledge, not a personal opinion stated fanatically over a type-written signature.—Kathrene Gedney Pinkerton, Robert E. Pinkerton.

Denver, Colorado.

Dear Mr. Hoffman:

Your letter, with a copy of that from ——, just arrived. Mrs. Pinkerton says that if it will give the readers of *Adventure* as good a laugh as it gave us, to go ahead and print it, all of it.

SERIOUSLY, though, we think its publication would be really valuable. It is hard sometimes to understand how German propaganda could be circulated in this country, but when any one can read a letter like this it is clearly evident. It is this type of mind that is quick to seize upon anything and twist it into the grotesque opinions and stories that are circulated continuously. "Vox Poping" is the favorite pastime of a certain mental class, and any one who reads the "Letters from the People" in daily newspapers knows the type. Facts, logic, science, laws, either of man or nature, go by the board. Nothing counts but prejudice, misinformation, fanaticism and a complete willingness to believe that which it is wished to believe.

You know them all—Tumulty shot as a spy, the five-dollar bill in the sweater, ground glass in food, the entire American Army drunk in France, Schwab keeping the war going to make money. I've been told all of them, one man bearing the Tumulty story direct, he declared, from a United States Senator. In denouncing these stories I have immediately classified myself as mentally lacking in the eyes of the tellers. I guess it's a hard game to beat, for the same reason that you can't make bread of Portland cement, no matter how much yeast you use. It just won't rise.

I THINK that I, too, have consumed about everything there is in the way of alcoholic beverages, and sometimes in considerable quantities, and I haven't quit yet, though I have happened to live in dry territory for the last two years and am beginning to forget what Scotch tastes like. But I have merely considered myself lucky. Jack London, you know, in "John Barleycorn," classified all men as alcoholic and non-alcoholic, and I happened to be a non-alcoholic. But I have friends who are the other sort, and I know that physicians treat alcoholism as a disease.—Robert E. Pinkerton.

NOW here is a curious letter received by Thomas S. Miller, of our writers' brigade and "Ask Adventure," and, following it, Mr. Miller's reply and a second and fuller letter from Mr. X. W. Among us there ought to be some who can piece out at least a part of the mystery. It may, of course, be a hoax, as Mr. Miller suggests, but, if so, it has become venerable with age and should be treated with respect. On the other hand it may be no hoax. I do not think Mr. X. W.'s sincerity is to be questioned and it doesn't seem likely that he is the victim of a joke. We all know what strange things can be found in bottles.

It is to be noted that in one copy of the inscription as sent by Mr. X. W. the seventh word, "E T," is present, while in his other version he omits it.

Mr. X. W., by the way, has given us his full name and address but asks that his name be withheld. Letters addressed to Mr. X. W., care *Adventure* will be forwarded. If any translations are received we hope comrade X. W. will let all Camp-Fire see them in return for help from some of its members.

Springhill, Nova Scotia.

Reading in *Adventure* of your familiarity with the African Coast and having been told that the enclosed writing was a Spanish-Portuguese mongrel dialect, would you mind trying if you can translate it as I have sent it to various sources and haven't been able to get a full and complete translation yet. —X. W.

> **VELET MANGE PAR**
> **DIOS DET NORTE ET ELVENGE**
> **PIROT BURE DESIMGILD**
> **CAPITAN BLACKBURNE**
> **MDCCCXIX**

San Francisco, Cal.

DEAR SIR:— . . . I hated to be beaten by this thing. Unless some one is playing a hoax on you it must be a mixed dialect from Portuguese East Africa, for *velet* is used by the Boers for "will you." *Par dios* is Spanish—"By God." I submitted it to the professors of languages of two universities, to Spanish and Portuguese, to a man well versed in the lingo of the Belgian Congo, all without result. I do not recognize any West African dialects in it.

Perhaps if *Adventure* publishes this it may happen that, as the magazine goes into every corner of the world, some reader may be able to help you. A message that starts out, with "Will you, by God" looks as if it ought to be translated—that there is a despairing cry behind it.—T. S. MILLER.

Springhill, Nova Scotia.

I would be pleased to have *Adventure* publish that screed in "Camp-Fire," as it has been a puzzle to all whom I have referred it to. George Manion, who was one of De Wet's aids in the South-African War, was the first one to give me any idea of any translation. It has been in our family a good many years now. I will tell you its history. My uncle and his chum (sailors) were walking along the beach after a big storm and they had not been able to continue their voyage. His chum noticed a queer-looking object washing up and down on the beach and picked it up. It was an old-fashioned bottle — stoneware — and was all encrusted with marine growths and stuff. He threw it away and my uncle noticed it was corked and sealed or crusted over. He hit it on a rock and an old parchment paper fell out. On this paper is a chart of some region with anchorages, courses and land courses marked on it, and that writing, which must be the key to it. My uncle didn't have any education and was not able to find any means of translation, so it has never been solved.

I do not wish my name published. If any of our comrades can decipher it they could forward their version to *Adventure* to be forwarded to me, could they not?—X. W.

DO YOU think our "melting-pot" melts? Or do you think we've been getting millions of immigrants who haven't been so thoroughly Americanized as they should be? If it doesn't melt, what's the trouble with it? You're an American; it's up to you to know whether we're letting millions of people into America who don't become Americans at all or become Americans in too small a degree. If we are, it's up to you, an American, to find out how and why it happens and how to correct this grave evil.

What proportion of our total population is foreign-born? What proportion of our total number of actual citizens? What proportion is born of foreign parents? Probably you have no idea. But you ought to have.

To what extent are they really Americanized? There is a lot for all of us to learn by talking personally to the foreign-born American citizens with whom we come into contact. Of all nations. Try asking them some of these questions: Why did they come to America? What did they expect? Did they find it? Did we treat them well and fairly? Do they consider us good citizens? To what extent did we help them to become Americanized?

Get honest answers to those questions from a number of naturalized citizens from various other countries. If you do, you'll have a whole lot to think about.

Annual Vote

LAST chance to vote on the ten best stories published in *Adventure* during 1918. This annual vote by our readers helps us get into the magazine the kinds of story they want.

Voting is simple and easy. On any sheet of paper write your list of ten stories (giving author's names), numbering them in order of preference. If you like, add as many as ten more stories by way of second choice or complimentary mention. Add your name and address. That's all.

Any one can vote provided he has read at least *seven* of the issues, for 1918 (First January, 1918, to Mid-December, 1918, inclusive). Serials, novels, novelettes, short stories, and articles all rank alike and may be voted for. Poems and "Camp-Fire" are barred.

A serial that laps over from 1917 or into 1919 may also be included in the vote. The same author may appear in the list as many times as you please. No votes will be counted if they reach us later than December 31, 1918, though allowance will be made for those writing from long distances, particularly the war-front. A list of the winners will be published in a subsequent issue, as was done last year.

Don't let stories in the later issues overshadow those earlier in the year merely because you read the former later and have them more vividly in your mind. And don't let the mere length of a serial, novel or novelette outweigh the value of the shorter stories.

And this year we're adding a new feature to our voting. As in past years, we're leaving "Camp-Fire" and other departments out of the regular vote. But it will be interesting to find out just what relative values are assigned to these departments by our readers in general. So, in addition to the regular vote, we add a special vote. Call the total value of an average issue one hundred per cent., including both fiction and departments; then write down after each of the following items the proportion of value each of them seems to you to deserve:

Stories (all together)
Poetry (all together)
Camp-Fire
Identification Cards
Fighting the Hun Web
Looking Ahead
Ask Adventure
How to Help Win the War
Lost Trails
Letter-Friends

The total for the list should, of course, be one hundred per cent.

Of course, "Fighting the Hun Web" and "Looking Ahead" are not really under way yet, so perhaps in these two cases we'd better make some allowance.

SCALPING. How often did the victim survive the operation? Here is another item to add to the information already sent in, taken from a letter one of you in the Aircraft Division wrote to Hugh Pendexter in connection with his stories of the American Indians.

Lancaster, Pa.

Mother knew a man who wore very little hair on his head. Indians scalped him when a child and left him for dead.

Another child, a girl baby, of the same family, while lying in her cradle (by the way, the cradle was a large basket, much like a clothes-basket) smiled and put up her tiny hands to the Indian who reached for her to knock her brains out, and that Indian let her go without injury, nor would he let the two Indians with him touch the child.

METAL identification cards, 25 cents. See page 185. Can not give same number on metal as on old card. Holders of old cards can remain registered under both cards if desired.

BY A fortunate change in the printing schedule, our magazine is now not forced to make up quite so far in advance as formerly. It is particularly lucky because it gives opportunity to break into the pages of this issue, take out material that was valuable only while the war lasted and insert matter that bears upon conditions after Germany's signing of the armistice. "Fighting the Hun Web" and "Looking Ahead" are retained as departments, for they still serve useful purpose, but they are now turned upon the new conditions that have come with peace.

OUR magazine advocates the kind of patriotism that is active and alert in peace as well as in war. Our country has suffered because most of us let our patriotism sleep unless a war woke it up. "Looking Ahead" will be devoted to building up among us the kind of patriotism that stays awake.

The Hun has not stopped spinning his propaganda web. And he will go right on spinning it. So we will go right on exposing it in "Fighting the Hun Web."

"How to Help Win the War," of course, is no longer needed. It has done good service, accomplished many practical results and receives its honorable discharge.

AT THIS writing, in November, the tide of world events flows too rapidly for comment made now to be read a month later and still be pertinent. But at least it will be pertinent then as now to say "Thank God, the war is over!"

Many of us are at least half regretful that German soil has not been devastated as the Germans devastated the soils of other countries. We wanted to see our armed forces tramping the streets of Berlin in victory, wanted ruined German cities and countrysides to teach the Germans what war really is and give them a wholesome dread of it in future. But it would have cost us many more lives to attain this. The war has already numbered its 10,000,000. Also, because we are not Huns ourselves, we can not adopt Hun methods of victory. We must make the world safe by whatever severity may be necessary, but God knows there is room for much severity without sinking to the Hun level of brutishness. The armistice seems to ensure us. May peace terms keep the world equally safe.

The Camp-Fire

AND now our boys will be coming back to us. You who have fought at the front for your country and your people can not have given so much without having got much in return. You come back with broader vision and understanding. You have been living and doing things bigger than personal things. Even we who worked at home have gained broader vision.

With our broader vision, what are you and we going to do now that the war is over? Just slip back into the old blind, selfish rut of seeking personal gain and advantage? Or have we all grown big enough to see a little more clearly man's need of man? That democracy and brotherhood are not won by a single great effort, but by a life-long effort? That allegiance is to the *people*, to humanity, and to *all* the people, not to *any* class or part of them?—A. S. H.

ONE of the remarkable things about our Camp-Fire is the diversity of those who gather about it. And the good-fellowship and comradeship despite the diversity. We come from everywhere—from the rods and the pulpit, from desert and stifling office, from the beach and the university, forecastle and physician's office. All kinds and conditions are we of the Camp-Fire. Yet because in each and all of us is a love for the big, strong, clean things of life, for the out of doors, for the power of muscle and brain and nerve, we gather together on an equal footing here, companions and comrades. Incidentally, it is democracy, world democracy.

Some of you are so lacking in the technicalities of education that I prime your letters here and there to make them easier reading. Some of you speak familiarly of such learned things that my poor brain can't follow you. What matter? Each one of us knows there is some one wiser than he and some one less wise. Each of us is wise in some things; ignorant in others. The man who can conjugate a Greek verb can not swing a lariat. The man who can go alone through the wildest parts of the earth is helpless in a laboratory. Who shall say which is the better man?

NOW here is a letter from a comrade who probably knows more out of books in a minute than I and many of you know in a week. It happens, also, that he has seen life from the rough as well, a member of the Legion of Frontiersmen. He has it on a good many of us both ways from the Jack. But does that matter at the Camp-Fire, either to him or to us? Not a bit. Why should it? He's merely one of us. Last time he talked to us he told us a simple story of the rough early days of New Zealand and the South Seas. This time he hopes he can find among us some who will be intrested in his present scientific work in the folk-lore of an extinct race.

AND he can. A man can find among us at least a few who are interested in whatever specialty interests him, learned or of the earth earthy. Of my own personal knowledge I can name off a dozen of you who fairly wallow in folk-lore or the histories and customs of ancient or vanished peoples. One or two of these are recognized authorities in the learned world, though I can think of only one who has dabbled in the early ages of New Zealand. There must be hundreds more of you and perhaps some of you will write to comrade Andrew and maybe add to the many personal friendships that have grown out of our Camp-Fire meetings—often enough friendships between men who have never met. And here I've gone and talked more than W. Andrew has! I'm a poor toastmaster.

Wharemouku, Upper Plain,
Masterton, New Zealand.

Inventory of writer:

> "We come of a hardy Northern race
> For of Yorkshire Blood are we
> Where the Esk so brown, thro' Whitby town,
> Runs out into the gray North Sea."

Fathered in 1860 by a parson C. E., one time Fellow of Lincoln, M. A. etcet.; senior of his year at Oxford; winner of Champion Sculls—a man of theories and much mentality. Mother—York blood; educated in Normandy; musical; painter; French as native to her as English.

WRITER, eldest son, worse luck, as all the Dad's theories were tried over on my person, my younger brothers only getting those that succeeded. Result at ten years: the binomial theorem and differential calculus were intimate acquaintances; quadratic equations were an article of diet, the Eton Latin Grammar as a Bible; French was more colloquial than Saxon; fairy tales were unknown but one had reveled in Greek and Roman mythology and was on speaking terms with Plato, Virgil,

Æschylus and Herodotus, but multiplication, etc., and English grammar were not invented.

Subsequent eight years were spent in forgetting what one knew and learning stuff of every-day use. Was intended for a physician but shied. Shied worse at divinity and turned land surveyor. That brought me in touch with Nature—and one's earlier training came in useful. The native race of New Zealand attracted me. They, too, have their mythology, and it agrees with that of the Phenician. Now surveying days are over, sheep farming done; resting on one's oars and endeavoring to put on paper the folk lore of an almost extinct race. Camp-Fire can warm up one's feelings, and among those around and in the circle one will find sympathizers and well wishers.

The yarn of the brig *Elizabeth* was sent as an envoy—more to follow if it pleases you.

Remember it pleases the old man to relive some of his life again when the Dominion was young. Maybe his style needs polish, likely it is rough; be that as it may, he writes for the sheer love of writing. *Ave atque Vale.*—6980 L. F.—W. ANDREW.

PRESTER JOHN and Ghengis Khan—adventure, mystery. In this issue we—but read Mr. Lamb's story and see for yourself. Here is what he has to tell us about the legends and history back of his tale:

Judging by general experience it must be pretty hard to follow a will o' the wisp—whatever that may be. And it's just about as hard to get hold of the truth in the myth of Prester John.

ON ONE hand we have stories of the European travelers who declared that a Christian monarch in Asia ruled a kingdom of fabulous wealth. That was around the tenth to the thirteenth century.

Then we have the travels of Jesuit and Nestorian monks, among them Fra Rubugin, who visited one or two Asian rulers who embraced Christianity. We know that before the time of Marco Polo there were Christian centers in "Tangut" and Hsi'en fu. Also, it is curious to learn that Christian engravings were found on the stone ruins of Karakorum, the oldest city of Tatary. Abulghazi, the oriental historian, mentions a Christian monarch in Asia.

Next, history tells us that the daughter of A-Wang-khan was a Christian and married a khan whose father was "Great King John" in Chinese. Ghenghis Khan was surprised by the riches of the Gur-khan's "golden tents" and "golden dishes fit for an emperor." Marco Polo says this man was the one reported in Europe to be Prester John.

The legend has curious details—a scepter of pure emerald, a treasure guarded by trained animals, a castle by a sea of sand, and a river of stones.

LASTLY we learn that the descendants of the Gur-khan were last seen at Kuku-Khotan, some 300 miles northwest of Peking. This is in the north of the once powerful Kerait or Krit Horde. And Krit is a Mongol name for Christian. But as Kuku-Khotan locates itself in the Kobi (Gobi) desert, it seemed better to move it to Changa Nor, the "lake of stones by the sea of sand."

The legend of Prester John of Tatary is one of the hidden by-ways of history. But, like other by-paths, it rewards any one who explores it.

One other point. The hunting of Gurd is a fact, and is actually carried out by the Yakuts and Tungusi of today.—HAROLD LAMB.

QUITE a while ago we telephoned the New York post-office and were told that packages and second-class mail-matter addressed to *individuals* could be sent to those serving with Allied forces but not to our own men. Consequently I told some of our comrades at the front, who wrote me for magazines and sometimes other things, that I couldn't send them. Postal regulations had undergone various changes from time to time and naturally I accepted the ruling from the post-office direct. Inquiring around, however, I found that other people were sending things that reached individuals. Finally I wrote the post-office who referred the letter to the Chief Clerk of the Railway Mail Service and he wrote me promptly that there were no restrictions against sending second-class mail to individuals in the A. E. F.

But in the meantime I'd turned down some requests that I didn't want to turn down. All I can do now is to square myself with these comrades by explaining how it happened.

HERE is an interesting talk from one of the West's old-timers. As the writer suggested, I've sent his letter on to Uncle Frank and I'm willing to bet my last cent that Uncle Frank will have a good time reading it. I did. So will you.

If some of the words are spelled wrong it's because our friend's writing is nearly as bad as mine and I didn't know enough to guess from the context. As he hasn't specifically given me permission to use his name, I'm signing his letter "Z. Z." And I'm hoping Z. Z. will be giving us more of his experiences at future Camp-Fires.

In your August number I read Uncle Frank Huston's letter about Indians, and I have not made the sign of which he speaks, but I greet him and you with the tribal sign of the Sioux, i.e. the right front finger down across the throat. Also I have hammered my shirt front and passed the same finger high above my head and backward and down. ("I am a Big Chief.")

IT IS mid-August and dog days—no wonder we remember. Yes, I knew Plenty Coups, knew him too well. He was Peace Chief of the Absaraka (Crows). After the great Sioux war was ended, Plenty Coups, Two Bears and Red Fox, all three

Absaraka chieftains, did me the great honor to common name me "Costa Cot Echeeta Nocka," which in English means "a colt." Spotted Elk, who was a war chief of the Ogallalla Sioux, called me "Little Guts"! In the far northwest I was named—and called by all who knew me (of the Red Brotherhood of course) "Colee Cuetin," meaning "Race Horse."

To those who have any doubts whatever of Uncle Frank's veracity, I have passed the sign of both hands in front, with fingers passing through and through, which is war, commonly meaning "Come and mix it up with me." The custom of smoking per ritual is always opened by blowing first a little puff upward. It is to the Great Spirit, and then the pipe is passed to the next in rank or to the stranger. No good Indian is guilty of beginning a conversation in a hurry, sometimes sitting in silence for hours.

I HAVE danced the Dog-liver, the Buffalo, Bear, and the Medicine Dance, Clattawa Salmon, Clattawa Clam, Hiack Clattawa Boston Marn, many times amongst the "Hated Fish Eaters" or "Salt —(?)," who are Siwash pure and simple; but the sun dance of the Sioux, not I! As the Cockney said, it's too bleeding brutal for me!

Apropos "Roping the Squaws," Plenty Coups once asked me to be his guest at a dog-eating contest on Rocky Fork of the Yellowstone (which is also known as Clark's Fork, and Red Lodge in its head waters). Two Bears and his tribe from ——(?) Creek was there. A band of young bucks had just returned from a raid on the Piegans, who brought with them amongst other loot a pale-faced young squaw, who by her moccasins seemed to be a Blackfoot breed. Old "Plenty" led her out for my inspection, and said his son would marry her—his son was Cut Knee, a crippled medicine-man. The girl was "roped" above the knees with rawhide thongs and I had a notion to cut her loose, but even a Crow will defend his rights, so I decided on a little strategy.

WOLF-TOOTH SMITH, a white man, lived at Farewell Bend and I told Plenty that Wolf-Tooth was my friend and I would go get fire-water and tobacco for the feast. He let me go. That night I returned with two gallons of 40-rod whisky and a horse that was good for a hundred miles from sun to sun. The one I rode was also a long distance horse known as Ace of Clubs.

Old Plenty was a good Christian then, but he got full of the booze just the same, and when it was almost daylight I crawled out of my saddle blankets, and sent a boy to bring my horses, which were both picketed near by. The camp was sound asleep except a few who had eaten too much dog the night before.

I WALKED into the old chief's teepee, after my horse was brought, shook him up and got a drink of the whisky, then smoked a cigaret with him, puff and puff about. He had the squaw staked out in the teepee; in addition to the thongs above her knees he had added a rope around her neck. The old hog went to sleep again and I cut the hobbles and rope loose from her, and then walked out to my horse. She soon followed with some blankets and a big knife which she had taken from among Plenty's private possessions. Some two or three old squaws and a few boys and dogs tried to stop her but I used my rawhide quirt and she managed to mount Wolf-Tooth's horse. I slid into the saddle just as Cut Knee came out of his teepee and I yelled back at him, "You slept too late!"

PLENTY'S young men gave us a great old run, but the Blackfoot queen was game and more than half white. That day we swam the Yellowstone at Pease's Bottoms near Stillwater, then we followed up the Yellowstone to the Big Timber Creek, and camped that night in the Crazy Mts.

She was, so she told me, a Bitter Root Blackfoot from the Flathead country. The Piegans had stolen her, and then the Crows, but she said that never before had she been stolen by a white man and I of course tried to explain that my action was platonic but she never could understand. We had ridden a hundred miles or more perhaps, but she staked the horses, got the wood and then stood guard and guard without once reminding me of her troubles. Say, when I think of that squaw as compared to some civilized women I have known, I feel like Uncle Frank says, "Hi ho, I wish I was young again, and those days were back!"

BUT, alas, I am old and I sit here alone in my guard house by the side of the railroad track, and dream dreams of the olden golden days of youth when to steal a band of horses or a good-looking female was only a common amusement among us renegades from civilization.

I yet remember most of the sign language, also Hudson Bay or Chinook Jargon, which is the *lingua Franca* of the Northwest. . . . I would make you the sign of the Race Horse (or "to Ride"), but I am a worse artist than I am a penman; but place your left first and second finger astride of your right hand and then make the hand go swiftly forward.—Z. Z.

THAT whale steak this comrade offers me sounds good. My thanks to him, and I'd certainly take a chance if I could get at it. Also he gives us a recipe for cooking rice, and I've asked him to tell us his methods for smoking trout and for other camp dishes. The pictures he refers to are, of course, those Mr. Tuttle drew of the characters in his own stories.

Victoria, B. C.

Your letter of June 4th arrived at Port Alice on the boat I left on so I missed it. After following me for three weeks I got it at Kynvuot whaling station on the west coast of the Island. I was very sorry to hear of your illness and was wishing you were with me to see the beautiful sights along the northwest coast. I had whale steak for dinner that day. I couldn't help but think of the difference in the surroundings from you back in an office in little old N. Y.

A WHALING station sure has a flavor all its own. The little whaling boats brought in eight whale while I was there, and it is quite a sight to go through the plant.

They can parts of the whale for food, which very much resembles beef, and very tender. I have been through most of the salmon canneries along the coast which are working to full capacity now.

I am going to inclose a newspaper clipping of a typical old Western adventurer. I have had several talks with him and greatly enjoy his tales.

FROM where I sit I can look across the water and see Mt. Baker and I guess that fellow that was looking for adventure would still find it as wild as when David Ogilvy made his trip to the summit. I got my mid-September issue of *Adventure* last night and was sure overjoyed at the pictures. Ain't they the tough bunch, though, to all be alive after all the shooting scraps they have been in? *Chuck* sure looks like a liar, and *Telescope* has a conceited look.

BY THE way, I have noticed that when any one asks what to take in the way of grub on a trip to the hills, they are generally told among other things to take rice, but I have never noticed that they told how to cook it. Now every one in the West knows you can't tell an old sour-drug anything about cooking, as they all think they know it all, but I will give my recipe for a few camp-dishes for the benefit of any younger members of Camp-Fire:

RICE—Boil the rice at night. In the morning take half the cold boiled rice and fry in the frying-pan in bacon grease after taking up the bacon. Mix the other half of cold boiled rice in some dough batter and fry in pan. These make excellent flap-jacks and nourishing. I always take dried apples and seedless raisins with me. I mix half and half and stew together, as I find the raisins will sweeten the apples sufficiently without sugar. When a person is eating lots of wild game they soon crave sweets and tarts and these dried apples and raisins just hit the spot.

DESICCATED potatoes or onions can be bought from Hudson's Bay store at Winnipeg. They are put up in five-pound tins. A five-pound tin will last two men on a sixty-day trip. A table-spoonful will make rations for two men.

If any one wishes it I will give my recipes for smoking trout and other dishes for the camp. I would like to tell you some incidents concerning my work here, but can not at the present time, but want you to know I am trying hard to do my bit.—CARLETON F. CRIPPEN.

AMERICANS in the Canadian forces. Who is going to sing their song as it should be sung, the song of the men who did not wait for America to enter the fight for humanity and freedom but rolled up their sleeves and went into it on their own? We'd always rather see Americans fighting under the American flag, but these men, and those other Americans under the banners of France, England and other Allies, went ahead of the flag and it is no trouble to forgive them for it.

Many of them were veterans against the Hun before the first soldiers of our Expeditionary Forces landed on French soil. Veterans or lying under that same French soil. Thousands and thousands and thousands of them, many of them later in our own service, but many staying with our Allies. And all we heard about them was the little casualty-list the papers published every day of "Americans killed with the Canadians," the reports of friends, letters to our Camp-Fire from our many comrades among them.

And they have done more than fight the Hun. They have very particularly cemented the bonds of friendship among what we call the Anglo-Saxon people. Adventurers? Yes.

FOLLOWING our Camp-Fire custom, R. N. Wall rises and introduces himself. His tale in this issue is his second, not his first, story in our magazine, but it's not his fault that he did not speak on the first occasion:

Richmond, Va.

Thank you for your invitation to join the "Camp-Fire." I want to say that I enjoy that part of *Adventure* as much, or perhaps more, than anything else in it; but as for myself, I "never had no adventures much." Which reminds me that, coming downtown on the car the other day with a very distinguished lady whom I know slightly, she asked me where I was educated. I looked her woodenly in the face and said: "I ain't never had no education much," and waited for her to grin. She never cracked her face and then I did feel foolish.

However, it is true that my life has been humdrum compared with most of your writers, for it has been spent mostly in the plow business. Not but what there are any number of good business stories worth telling—I have told a number of them already in *Everybody's*, *Munsey's*, *Collier's*, the *Saturday Evening Post*, etc., but my trouble now is to find the time to write them down. My responsibilities have increased a great deal lately, I am away much of the time, and, while matching wits with big buyers is a lot of fun, after a deal is made it leaves one more in a mood for recreation than for writing. I don't know that this material would interest you much, anyhow, although most editors seem to prefer it to the stuff about burglars, bartenders and pirates that I should much rather write. Of course, I have sense enough to realize that, knowing more about the plow business than about the other vocations above mentioned, I am likely to do it more convincingly, but, all the same, writing the others is much more interesting and restful.—R. N. WALL.

IF SOME gifted statistician could find the number of miles each member of our Camp-Fire has traveled outside the land of his birth and could add all those miles together, well, he'd have to turn to astronomy to illustrate how long a journey it would make. I'm no astronomer but

I know that the little twinkling stars are quite a distance away. Once I heard a lecture on astronomy and all I can remember is this: The fastest traveler—faster than light or electricity—is the nerve message from any part of the human body to the brain, yet the distance between the earth and a fixed star is so great that, if a man's body were so long his head could be on the star and yet he could be sitting on a red-hot stove on the earth, he wouldn't know he'd been burned until he'd been dead two hundred years.

For example, here's one of us who's been around quite a lot:

Berkhamsted, England.

I have read our magazine for some years and in many places. Those "many places" include England, Ireland, the U. S., all Canada, Northern and Southern Siberia, Cuba, Jamaica, the small West Indian Islands, Canal Zone, British Honduras, Venezuela, the Orinoco, all of Colombia, British and Dutch Guiana, Curaçao, British Gold Coast, the Canaries, Newfoundland, and *all* the Central American republics. For one only thirty-five that is rather good going, don't you think?—T. G. Effrey.

ARKANSAS, Indiana, Kansas, Missouri, Nebraska, North Dakota, South Dakota, Texas. In these eight States aliens who have filed their first papers are given all the rights of citizenship, including that of voting for President and representatives in Congress. How nice for the Germans!

Incidentally, it must be a little hard on a loyal, American-born woman, who has sent a husband, brother or sons to the war against Germany and has done her own loyal bit of war-work at home, to see an alien enemy go through the "scrap of paper" first-papers formality and help decide by the ballot who shall rule America, when said loyal American woman is not allowed this privilege.

Somehow I'm glad I don't live in any of these States. Do you?

A COMRADE in Dutch Guiana sends us a poem by another comrade down there which will bring many a member of our Camp-Fire a grin and maybe a pang. I haven't the heart to mutilate it by taking the cuss-words out of it and am trusting you'll forgive this breach of our Camp-Fire rule.

Moenco Mines.
Paramaribo, Dutch Guiana.

Emboldened by listening to many tales while sitting around your Camp-Fire, I venture to say that however gripping may be the lure of the Tropics, or however thrilling the adventure in jungle or town, there is something in the feeling when you are going "back to God's country" that is like no other, and that more than one American in the Tropics will agree with Mr. Barnett in the enclosed lines he was kind enough to give me, and which seemed to me to be too expressive to remain buried among his business papers. They gave me a good laugh. May they bring a smile to your face.—Leslie Ashley.

HOMEWARD BOUND

by A. J. BARNETT, JR.

WIDE the waves are washing
  O'er the ocean green,
White the clouds are floating,
  Blue the sky between.

Porpoises a-playing,
  Flying-fish a-skim;
Dim the distant mainland
  At the water's rim.

Brisk the breeze is breaking
  From a cooler main,
Bless the ship that's taking
  Me to Home again.

Let us make a *festa*
  Order 'round a dram,
And to all the Tropics
  Drink a fervid "Damn."

Damn the stinks and fevers!
  Damn the heat and sweat!
Damn the yellow rivers!
  Damn the jungles wet!

Damn the gray savannas!
  Damn the endless rain!
Damn the damn mosquitoes!
  Damn them ALL—again!

Ah! the thought of parting
  Fills the heart with joy.
Once again the beakers;
  Quick about it, boy!

'At a stuff, old steward!
Hats off, fellows! now,
All together, standing:
BROADWAY!—BASEBALL!—WOW!!!

SOME more interesting information on the Navajos and Pueblos. When, in some later issue, you read Hugh Pendexter's novelette, "Carson of Taos," you'll be meeting the Navajos and some of these same facts again. Also that very stirring and historic figure, Kit Carson.

Gallup, N. M.

It has struck me that perhaps a little more information in regard to Navajo and Pueblo Indians might not be amiss, as many people seem to have rather hazy ideas in regard to them.

IT IS believed that the Navajo came into this country about seven hundred years ago, probably crossing from Asia by way of Bering Straits and steadily worked South in search of that warm country that legends told them about. Indeed the

Navajos have a legend to this day that they came out of a great hole in the world in the North, and good Navajos expect to go back when they die. Also there is said to be a trible of Indians in Northern Canada whose language is practically the same as that of the Navajos. (I have not been able to verify this report.)

IT IS a fact not generally known that the Apache Indians are a branch of the Navajos, (the fighting branch, I might add), who were separated about five hundred years ago. The Navajo never was much of a fighting man; in comparison with the other Indians of the West, he was a pilfering, marauding, petty nuisance, but whenever he met other tribes on equal terms he always got the worst of it. When Carson rounded up the Navajos in 1863 he defeated a party of them at Red Rock Springs, about twenty miles from here, and also a larger party at Cañon de Chelly, not far from here.

In all, about twenty-five thousand were rounded up and taken to Bosco Redondo, where they were kept for several years, but so many of them died from confinement that the medicine men (who are the chiefs of the Navajos) begged to be allowed to return to their home country and signed treaties with the United States agreeing to be good. There was, however, one chief who did not surrender but retreated into the wilds near Navajo Mountain, one Hos-ki-ninni (don't know if I have this spelled right but that is the way it sounds) and these Indians have never recognized the authority of the United States to this day, and believe me they are certainly wild, more like the Apaches of old.

THE Navajo does not take kindly to white men's ways, only in as far as his immediate gain is concerned. I have seen many young men and women, who had been educated in government schools most of their lives and taught housekeeping, farming, etc., who upon being married became more dirty and lazy than the rest and who pretended not to understand English.

The Navajo is a fairly satisfactory laborer, excepting that one never knows when he will show up for work, especially if there happens to be a "sing" or dance going on in the neighborhood. There are various kinds of these "sings," some for pleasure and others ceremonial or religious. The pleasure "sings" are merely Navajo parties, but the religious "sings," such as the Ye-bit-chia, are taken from the Pueblo ceremonials.

In passing, will say that the Navajo is intensely loyal to his religion or belief, and that I have yet to see a truly converted Navajo, many overzealous missionaries to the contrary.

FROM this you will no doubt conclude that I am prejudiced against Navajos, but such is not the case. I have met many tribes of Indians and of all the Navajo is the most interesting. Confront one with a broken promise, and he will give you a most ingenious and naïve explanation, at the same time smiling hopefully, and if you do not believe it he feels hurt. He has a great sense of humor, and does not hold a grudge for long.

NOW in regard to the Pueblos, I shall confine myself to the ancient people who were the ancestors of the present Pueblos, as their customs have not changed much in five hundred years.

Several archæological societies (of which I have the honor of being a more or less valued member) have made some very interesting discoveries, a few of which I will give here.

First, did you know that the first authentic written history of the United States was written less then forty miles from here? Fact.

Fra Marcos De Niza reached Zuñi in 1539 and wrote of his discoveries which was the cause of Coronado's expedition in 1540. He told of the seven cities of Cibola of which Zuñi was and still is one.

WHEN Coronado reached Zuñi in 1540 he heard of fabulous cities far off to the north and at once sent out an expedition of four men to take them in the name of the king. Think of it! Four men across hundreds of miles of hostile country! These men came to the present Hopi towns and the natives were so overcome at the sight of the "Iron-Shirts" that the places fell with very little fighting. This expedition afterward reached the Grand Cañon of Arizona an returned to Zuñi but did not find the rich cities for the simple reason that there were no rich cities such as they were looking for. The commander's name was Captain Tovar.

WHEN an archæological expedition were excavating the ancient ruins at Zuñi during 1917 they found undeniable evidence of three different periods, each ruin having been built upon the other. Assuming that each period of occupation was of as long duration as the one we have record of it would make this Pueblo nearly two thousand years old.

The pottery of the second period seems to show the highest point of development of the tribe, but at all periods they were pottery makers, basket weavers farmers and weavers of cloth from fiber plants. They have raised corn and beans and other plants from time of record, and much of the corn and beans they raise at present are of the same strain that was planted at first.

Their corn was ground on stone *metate* or mortars and some of them are still in use. They had domesticated the wild turkey and used them for food as well as ceremonial purposes. These and the wild game of the country constituted their food supply.

THE Pueblos were not afraid of their dead as is the Navajo but buried them close to the living place usually on the eastern side for they were and are yet to a certain extent sun-worshippers. The dead were always given dishes of food and drink to speed them on their way to the unknown.

They were the first to take up the weaving of blankets or rugs, also the making of silver bracelets and beads, although some people give the Navajo credit for this. The first blankets were woven from yarn secured by undoing Spanish shawls and capes, and are called Bayeta blankets. They are almost priceless.

THE similarity of customs and language leads me to believe that the Pueblos were originally of the same race probably of different clans and that the difference in language is due to local conditions.

Indeed the clan system is still in vogue and it is seldom that members of one Pueblo will marry outside of their own. There is no doubt that they were directly connected with the civilization of Old

Mexico but of course they had about the same relation to the splendors of Mexico as the desert has to the gilded palaces of New York.

In conclusion the Pueblos are loyal to their religion, and while they will go to the white man's church to please him if he is a good fellow, they still believe they are right, as witness any of their ceremonial dances.—H. W. Brose.

TO FIND at the end of a letter a signature that I can't read always irritates me. How can you answer it if you don't know who wrote it? No, don't laugh, any of you who've had letters from me, for I'm going to say it myself.

I write some thousands of letters of one kind or another in a year. My full signature seems to be legible enough, judging from experience. But a good while ago I fell into the habit, when writing to some of you with whom I'd already got acquainted, of signing just my initials. Saved time and was less formal. But the habit grew till I signed only initials in most cases.

Every little while comes a letter referring rather caustically to an unknown individual who signed some unknown initials to a letter from our office. And, when I look at my initials as I sign them, I don't wonder. I couldn't read them myself. I've seldom seen a worse signature. You can't say anything worse about them than I can.

BUT it does save quite a bit of time in a year, and it certainly is less formal, and a habit is a hard thing to throw off. Particularly, if you can't write very clearly anyhow. Also it's partly your fault that I haven't reformed, for some of you began opening your letters to me with "Dear A. S. H." and, well, I liked it.

So, while I own up that it's a poor signature, I'm not promising to reform. But I want to make it very clear that there's "no disrespect intended."

THIS comrade is wrong in thinking he does not belong to Camp-Fire as actively as any of us. Every one who sits down with us, every one who drops in at our meetings, is an active member in full standing. There are no formalities or requirements except the desire to join.

Where is Clifford Sands? I don't know. Do any of you? I know that, after his expedition fell through, he was in a Central American revolution, was badly shot in one or both hands, returned to the States and tried, through our magazine, to get into touch with all who'd been interested in the proposed expedition. I heard both from him and of him from others who had seen him in Central America or later in the States. But I haven't had word for a long time and would be glad to hear from him again.

Portland, Oregon.

Though not belonging to the Camp-Fire actively, I am heartily with it and would like to let you know some of my little experiences in the South Sea Islands in which I spent most of the last five years.

I ONLY wish I was endowed with the power to tell interestingly what I went through. Just the same I can refute quite a lot wrong impressions that most people have, from reading Jack London and E. Darling literature on Tahiti and surrounding islands.

About five years ago, or to be more exact, in July, 1913, a certain Clifford Sands of Seattle was organizing an expedition for Cuzco, Peru, and after getting acquainted with him through *Adventure* and binding myself to go with him, we lost track of each other as the police stepped in and declared the expedition filibustering. I took it for granted that I should go my way and instead went then to Tahiti and stayed there since. I have been through a lot there from the days the Germans bombarded the town of Papeete and certainly ought to know as much as anybody else on that part of the world. I shall be glad to answer any of the Camp-Fire who would like to know what to expect of those places, the Society and Pomotu groups. I read an item of Mr. Mills' answer on the South Seas out of which a man can get a pretty good introduction to the Islands.

AS FOR myself I think I shall be going this next week to Sydney, Australia, but friends here would forward anything that comes to my address as long as they can keep track of me.

By the way, I would be very grateful to you if you could give me a chance to get into communication with the Clifford Sands of Seattle of which I spoke above, not for money matters' sake, as I gladly let my share go, but to see if he turned out again on the same Peruvian adventure that he intended to start in July, 1915.—E. Mayes.

P. S.—Here is also a salute for the comrades who have made their way across the Great Divide.

CONCERNING his story in this issue Hugh Kennedy gives us the following glimpse behind the scenes:

Victoria, B. C.

The setting of "A Gentled Burley," is in reality laid along the right-of-way of the cut-off built by the C. P. R. around Ottertail Hill and along the Kicking Horse River, just west of Field, B. C. I saw it last August on my return from England. I helped to tamp the big charge in the coyote hole myself about fifteen years ago, and I watched it go off, too.—Hugh Kennedy.

METAL Identification Cards. When sending in your quarter for one please do not expect to get the same number on your metal card as you had on your old paper card. It can't be done, as you will realize when you think it over. For how could we know in advance exactly which of the old holders would want metal cards?

And it will simplify matters if you destroy your old card on receiving this metal one, notifying us to that effect. It is not required, but otherwise you'll be registered under two different numbers, which might bring about complications.

ARTHUR SULLIVANT HOFFMAN.

THE CAMP-FIRE
A MEETING-PLACE FOR READERS, WRITERS AND ADVENTURERS

Our Camp-Fire came into being May 5, 1912, with our June issue, and since then its fire has never died down. Many have gathered about it and they are of all classes and degrees, high and low, rich and poor, adventurers and stay-at-homes, and from all parts of the earth. Some whose voices we used to know have taken the Long Trail and are heard no more, but they are still memories among us, and new voices are heard, and welcomed.

We are drawn together by a common liking for the strong, clean things of out-of-doors, for word from the earth's far places, for man in action instead of caged by circumstance. The *spirit* of adventure lives in all men; the rest is chance.

But something besides a common interest holds us together. Somehow a real comradeship has grown up among us. Men can not thus meet and talk together without growing into friendlier relations; many a time does one of us come to the rest for facts and guidance: many a close personal friendship has our Camp-Fire built up between two men who had never met; often has it proved an open sesame between strangers in a far land.

Perhaps our Camp-Fire is even a little more. Perhaps it is a bit of leaven working gently among those of different station toward the fuller and more human understanding and sympathy that will some day bring to man the real democracy and brotherhood he seeks. Few indeed are the agencies that bring together on a friendly footing so many and such great extremes as here. And we are numbered by the hundred thousand now.

If you are come to our Camp-Fire for the first time and find you like the things we like, join us and find yourself very welcome. There is no obligation except ordinary manliness, no forms or ceremonies, no dues, no officers, no anything except men and women gathered for interest and friendliness. Your desire to join makes you a member.

IN HIS novelette, "When Kentucky Starved," and in some of his other stories, Hugh Pendexter gave us a living picture of those great frontiersmen and Indian fighters, Daniel Boone and Simon Kenton. In this issue he gives us in story form an intimate and carefully accurate picture of another great pioneer, Davie Crockett. Later will come tales of still others—Kit Carson and "Chucky Jack" Sevier (who founded the state of Franklin, now Tennessee), and still others of the hardy men who were not only frontiersmen but history-makers, and history-makers on a big scale.

Most of us have formed our idea of American history, if we have any real idea of it at all, from the dry and generally poor school histories that swamp us with dates and dull, lifeless, colorless statements of political progress, bald, uninteresting information on national events of moment, and so on. No wonder most Americans don't know the history of their own country!

AND yet what a wonderful history it is! A handful of whites put down on the shore-line of an unknown wilderness extending three thousand miles to the west of them, inhabited by an almost unknown race of savages. And now, only three hundred years later, behold! a world power of a hundred million people. A continent of wilderness fought over by Spain, France, Holland and England, and now that same wilderness takes a main hand in settling the fate of Europe and the world.

And who changed this wilderness to what it is now? Was it just the statesmen, politicians, governors and generals? Undo the work of Boone, Sevier, Crockett and Carson alone, and it might be that the United States would now be only the States along the Atlantic coast. In the real history of America the names of her adventurers, her pioneers, should be written side by side with those we now call our greatest. The writers of our histories have been poor assessors of values.

TO MOST of us Daniel Boone was "just a great Indian fighter." Hugh Pendexter's stories have shown us that he was also a history-maker, a builder of empire, a founder of America. The history of our country, the real history, is crowded with other men who did the work of giants in making America, yet whose names are, to most of us, merely names or forgotten or unheard of. Our history is rich in adventures that make a fiction writer's efforts tame and dull, adventures that as fiction would be smiled away as incredible. For example, later on you'll read Allan Dunn's "Salt of the Sea" in which ten men left from Drake's ship in California, walk and sail their way down to Peru, then across the Andes, down the Amazon on rafts, take a Spanish ship and five get back to England. Quite a journey even today and with a sufficient outfit. What must it have been in 1580 through unknown wilderness with only savages and hostile Spaniards anywhere along the thousands of miles they traveled? Ten men! As a fiction story it is just an incredible lie. That would be your verdict or mine on reading such a fairy-tale. But it happens these men of Drake's did just that.

American history teems with such adventures. But we have been given only its dry bones in the schools and in many of the books we have read since school-days. Why should we not have some of the red blood as well? Real history is not merely a collection of skeletons. Nor can an American, particularly a foreign-born American, learn the true spirit of America and Americans by reading dates and dull records of bare events.

THE purpose of the stories in our magazine is to amuse. We are not conducting a school. The many stories we've published that have made historical characters vivid, moving human beings, or given true pictures of actual life all over our country at all times in our history, were chosen on their merits *as fiction* and, after passing the fiction test of our editors, passed the fiction test of our readers. They were good as *stories*. And naturally no intelligent man objects to learning something of value when he can do so without effort and by the simple and pleasant process of being amused.

Our magazine is an American magazine and I know you are as glad as I am that we can have in it stories that meet our demands *as* stories yet at the same time make us more familiar with our country's past and give us a fuller understanding of the men, the deeds and the spirit that have made her what she is.

Here is a brief word from Mr. Pendexter concerning his story in this issue:

Norway, Maine.

I have selected that period of Crockett's life when he was making a new start on the lonely Obion, as it afforded the best opportunity for fiction. The shadow of Murel, the super-bandit, was over the Mississippi valley, and Crockett was at that interesting point where political ambitions were awakening—the threshold of his entrance into national prominence.

THE flamboyant speech I put in his mouth when he first meets the men at Skow's trading-post is practically what he did deliver in a Raleigh tavern when on his way to Washington in the winter of 1827. The crowd did not give way and allow him a chance at the fire. When a young man yelled "Hurrah for Adams!" Crockett answered much as I have described. He says of himself at that period, "I was happy, devilish and full of fun."

Some may object to his avowed fondness for the "creature," but in that he merely reflected the manners of his time. His Americanism was a hundred and two per cent. There never was a more honest, courageous man in Congress. He actually lived his motto, "Be sure you're right, etc." It was impossible to bribe or bully him; and his wonderfully shrewd mind made it well near impossible to deceive him. We need Crocketts at Washington today.—HUGH PENDEXTER.

A WOMAN member writes from her home in Australia, asking us to enroll her boys, D. Doherty and B. Doherty, in our Camp-Fire. There is never any need to ask. Any one belongs who wishes to. Of course her boys are of our number and, as I wrote her, they have numbered themselves among a far greater body than ours—the millions who have eagerly offered their lives to the defense of humanity.

Her younger son, Brian, after being blown up by a shell at Gallipoli and spending six months in a hospital in Egypt, served eight months on the desert and then, after three vain efforts to reach France, "threw in" his corporal's stripes and got there as a private in 1916, serving at the Somme, Bapaume, Bullecourt, Ypres, Menin Road, Messines Ridge, Paschendaele, the Ypres Winter of 1917-18, Albert, and at the time of writing was one of the remnant of two thousand men of his division still on active service. He enlisted at seventeen.

Here is a bit from his mother's letter. The "enclosed" refers to several newspaper clippings.

Do you think the enclosed entitles my boy to be a member? When war broke out August, 1914, he was a boy of seventeen out on a cattle station. He wrote to me to let him enlist but I thought him too young. He tried to get the owner of the station to write me and on his refusing, as he also said he was too young, he walked one hundred and eight miles to get to Sydney as they refused him any means of conveyance, thinking it put him off. He walked till his feet would stand no more, then sent to me for money for his fare to Sydney. I sent it at once and, when his feet were right, gave my consent for who could stand out against such persistence? When he was wounded at Lone Pine, Gallipoli, August 6, 1915, my only remaining son, his elder brother, went into camp (First Motor Transports, then Australian Flying Corps; now home after two years and a half). By Brian's latest letter, received yesterday, of June eighth he is near the Americans and says they and the Australians are firm friends and they mean business every one. Since that was written the boys under the "Stars and Stripes" have proved his words.

The following was printed in an Australian newspaper. It speaks for itself.

For Remembrance

A token of respect to the memory of the four manly men who were with me before we went "over the top" at Lone Pine Charge, August 6, 1915 (K. McPhee, J. Skinner, L. Buckley, and J. Collins).—From the only survivor that day of the five, Driver Brian Doherty, original D Co., 3rd Battalion, 1st Division, now with 1st Australian Siege Battery, France, still on active service.

"They owed their mother such a love
That only life could pay,
Who to Gallipoli bequeathed
The Freedom of the Clay."

AT THIS writing, November twenty-six, no one seems to know just what is going to be done with interned alien enemies and pro-German "American citizens." What *is* going to be done with them? Is our Government going to make welcome guests of the enemy aliens? Is the America they have tried to kill now going to become a happy home for them? Is the Government going to let perjured and traitor "American citizens" retain the citizenship they have betrayed?

The enemy alien has some excuse. The American traitor should at least be deprived of American citizenship.

OUR new metal identification cards seem to have "filled a long-felt need." But some of you haven't quite understood the terms. The paper cards are still free of charge but the asker must pay postage on his card, and is asked to enclose a stamped and addressed envelope, which also saves us clerical work at this end. The metal cards, on the other hand, cost you twenty-five cents but this includes return postage. To get a metal card, just enclose twenty-five cents and a self-addressed return envelope, no stamp being required.

I don't handle these cards personally and have just noticed that some of you are enclosing stamps in addition to the twenty-five cents. From now on the amount of such postage will be returned to the sender. But up till now this hasn't been done and our records would not show whether or not a stamped envelope was enclosed, so those who enclosed one will, I fear, just have to pay that small penalty for their mistake.

Those who send for cards hereafter will please remember this:

Pasteboard cards—free; enclose stamped and self-addressed return envelope.

Metal cards—Twenty-five cents; enclose self-addressed envelope, *not* stamped; no return postage necessary.

FOLLOWING our Camp-Fire custom, Robert Palfrey Utter rises and introduces himself on the occasion of his first story in our magazine.

Amherst, Massachusetts.

I feel very much at home at any camp-fire with a frying-pan and blanket, but with a typewriter—that's different.

BESIDES, I am an owl-eyed professor, and I never had a real adventure in my life. I never even broke my leg except on a croquet-ground (that's a fact). Next to my family I love nothing so much as old books, unless it is the out-of-doors (I'll spare you the quotation from Chaucer). But, I repeat, I am thoroughly at home with the frying-pan and the rifle. I have walked literally hundreds of miles just for the fun of it, mostly within a triangle between Denver, Steamboat Springs and Glenwood Springs, and also much in the Wahsatch about Salt Lake. Before the mountains were infested with Forest Rangers and Fords, my father, my brother and I would tramp for two or three weeks at a time with blanket-packs containing corn-meal and bacon, sometimes on the trails, more often above or beyond them—you know:

"Sometimes we go where the trails are, but mostly we go where they ain't;
We'd climb up the side of a sign-board, and trust to the stick of the paint. . . .
And the wind is as thin as a whiplash, that carries away to the plains."

I was born a bit more than forty years ago in Olympia, Washington, the end of the Oregon Trail.

I went to school in Kansas City, Chicago, Cambridge, and Salt Lake City. I was an amateur writer of fiction at eight years of age, and an amateur editor at sixteen. I practised editing in college, on the *Harvard Advocate*, *Harvard Monthly*, *Harvard Daily News*. After graduating, in 1898, I became a professional, first on the *Youth's Companion*, then the *New York Evening Post*.

Then I spent six months in the saddle trying to pretend that I was the foreman of a dairy ranch at Santa Lucia, Mexico. I had the costume all right, and learned to swear volubly in Mexican-Spanish, but I wasn't much help to the owner, so I traveled back and did editorial work for a Boston publisher for a few years. Then I went back to the university, where I taught and studied till 1906 when I took my Ph.D. degree (or else they were kind enough to give it to me). That year I came to Amherst, where I am now Associate Professor of English.—ROBERT P. UTTER.

WHEN I first read Talbot Mundy's "Up-and-Down-the-Earth Tales" I wrote him that I didn't like *Monty*, that he got on my nerves just as he got on the nerves of *Yerkes* the American, and couldn't he tone *Monty* down a bit? I figured *Monty* would rile other democratic Americans as he had *Yerkes* and me.

Here is the letter in which Mr. Mundy knocks me out of the ring so hard and far that no undertaker is needed. It sounds as if he were mad. He wasn't. He and I have a pleasant little habit of pounding each other over the head and like each other the better for it. In this case I might dig up a small comeback or two but the honors are all his, and I'm pleased as he is.

BORN an Englishman, he has become an American citizen. If you want to know how good an American he makes, read a certain article in a back *Everybody's* that tells what he and Hugh Pendexter and a few others did to make Oxford County, Maine, one of the banner counties of the whole United States in all kinds of practical accomplishments toward winning the war. I wish we had a million more Americans like him.

Yarmouth, Maine.

Don't consider my feelings; I simply haven't any left after reading what you say about my friend *Monty*.

SEE here—from first to last I have never pretended *Monty* is a democrat. I don't pretend he's right. He's a character; and the proof he is one lies in the fact that you hate him. You wouldn't hate a nonentity, would you?

(As a matter of fact Lenine and Trotzky call themselves democrats—so does Hylan—so does Hearst. I'm not in love with the word.)

Monty is the type of man who led the men who died in Flanders. Under the mellowing influence of *Yerkes* I rather expect he will undergo a lot of transmogrification, if that's the proper word.

BUT the point of the story, which you say *you get*, and which I observe with gratitude that you consider makes good reading, is—when free men and true have elected a leader, then they shall obey him!

In course of my observations of the development of this great and greater growing land I have seen many a fine fellow in khaki wrestling with this question, put to himself by himself: "Why should I, a free man in a free land, submit my free mind and body to the absolute discretion of a man with whom I often don't agree, whom I regard on many points as a damphule, and whose personal attitude toward life's problems is not at all my notion of democracy? Here I am—in khaki—bound to obey! How do I justify it?"

YOU ask me to think it over. Gosh! Did I do no thinking before I took out final papers? I'm an American from choice, because I'm convinced that this America of ours begins to think at about the point where the rest of the world leaves off.

So if your readers are able to be perverted from the true path by the story of the views and unregeneracy of an imaginary English nobleman, then their democracy is slack in the back—and to —— with 'em!

Democracy is not "my will be done." Democracy is "*Thy* will be done, as in heaven, so on earth!"

An English nobleman who takes his election to be gang leader so seriously that he actually dares to imitate Abe Lincoln's method is *no* argument against democracy, but PROOF OF IT! Hurrah!

As Whistler said, I'm not arguing, I'm telling you!

Besides—*do* get this: I'm no lay preacher. I'm merely a recorder of what I see, using "fiction" for a method. If I can write good reading, yet preach no heresy—can a man do better?—TALBOT MUNDY.

AMONG the letters to Camp-Fire are a number from comrades who when they wrote were serving at the front against the Hun. There has not been time to publish all of them and now the war is over. But several bits from them make good reading still, and we all want to know about our Camp-Fire comrades and what they've been doing over there. So here are some scraps from their letters and a word about the writers.

Francis Rotch left Nenana, Alaska, in the Fall of 1917 for the O. T. C. at San Francisco where he won a captain's commission only to lose it the next day on account of his eyes. After two weeks he couldn't stand it any longer and enlisted as a private in the Coast Artillery Training Camp at Fort Monroe; 57th Engineers, Inland Water Transportation; sergeant; second lieutenant; France; transport work on the

Seine, after trying to get to the front. His is a good motto: If you lose a captaincy, get in as a private.

Like Mr. Rotch, Charles M. Cosby of our writer's brigade, had had previous military training, having served as a private in the Philippines. After a course at an Atlantic seaboard training camp, the doctors found an entirely unsuspected weak spot and he was honorably discharged so suddenly that a recommendation for a captain's commission had to be recalled by wire. Our sympathy to him.

A letter from our comrade L. S. Phillips ("Shorty"), with the Canadians. He tells us of the death in action of an adventurer famous before the war, a man known to many of us:

France.

Of all the queer places from which to write this takes the cake. I am in a shell-hole in the front line of some of our newly captured ground, said shell-hole about three inches deep with mud and water. And it's raining like, well, like it *can* and does rain in this portion of sunny France. Still, there's no time like the present, and I welcome the opportunity of saying "How" to you and *Adventure*.

DOUBTLESS you have seen in the "dailies" of the work the Canucks have been doing. I have been in the thick of it. Believe me, I have had a few narrow shaves in my time, but until recently I never realized how close shrapnel and machine-gun bullets could come to one and leave him with a whole skin. And say, never let any one tell you that a boche won't fight; he will, especially his machine-gunners. Also some of his artillery. We captured a battery at the guns of which the crew stuck firing until put to the bayonet. Still, they are no match for *white* men. One real man can best any five of them. I have seen it proved over and over again. And when the dirty squarehead is wounded he squeals like a stuck pig. His animal nature coming to the surface, I reckon.

I always was proud of good old Uncle Sam, but now, say, he sure is putting his heart into the work of making the world safe for democracy.

BY THE way it might interest you to know that Major Rasmussen has been killed in action. He, if you remember, was prominent at one time in the Mexican troubles. After obtaining a commission in the C. E. F. and winning the D. S. O., he transferred to the American Forces with whom he met his end. A better fighter and squarer man never lived.—L. S. Phillips, Esq., C. E. F.

A. Judson Hanna, of our writer's brigade, has seen active service with Co. G, 30th Infantry, A. E. F. Charles F. Teske served on the U. S. S. *Arkansas*. Our old Australian friend, Harry C. Winters, went through about four years' active service in France.

When I heard from George T. Masury five years ago he was in Alaska, prospecting. After "wandering a bit" he arrived in the Philippines when war was declared and his last letter contains his kick because Co. M, 31st Infantry, of which he is sergeant-major, was held in the islands instead of getting to the front. He writes:

One of the old-timers here, left over from the Empire Days, died a few months back—"Old Kentuck." He went the way of most of the fellows—tropics and booze.

OF FORMER members of our magazine's editorial staff, George F. Olds has been in France a year with the Medical Supplies Dept.; E. C. Clayton has been at the front, but at this writing I don't know his regiment; Harry E. Wade, after passing up a commission chance at home so he could get to the front, was caught by the armistice before he had quite finished a special and second training at Camp Lee; T. N. Pockman is with the Marines in this country; James S. Hamilton has won his commission after being in ambulance work in France since 1917.

Erwin A. Walser served with Co. L, 23rd Engineers, A. E. F. Victor Hope was, or is, a lieutenant and the executive officer of U. S. S. *Winifred* under Admiral Sims. Jas. Jos. Gibbons ("Happy") is one of the Americans who didn't wait for America but joined up with the English, May, 1915. He wrote last Fall from hospital in England, recovering from shell-shock. (He wanted letters through "Letter Friends," and Bull Durham, but I suppose by this time mail will no longer reach 217484 Sapper Jas. Jos. Gibbons, 2nd Canadian Engineers, at 3rd C. C. D., Seaford, Sussex, England. But a little Durham did go to him.)

R. R. Robertson, 12th Canadian Siege Battery, B. E. F. Lieutenant William H. Parr has been on special service with the A. E. F. after previous front-line fighting with the Canadians before America went in. C. F. Whiteley, wagoner, F. Co., 101st U. S. Engineers, went to France in 1917 and after graduating from motorcycle riding was the "pilot of a little Dodge" at last writing.

Corporal L. S. Longstreet, A. E. F., one of the first thousands to go over before the draft, writes:

Many of the Camp-Fire are in the Foreign Legion. . . . I met one one who was at the Camp-Fires of many moons ago and who died in the Lafayette Escadrille with honor.

Probably he means our young comrade Edmond C. C. Genet, who, as we know, transferred from the Legion to the Lafayette Escadrille and died in battle. He has talked at our Camp-Fire many times.

A letter from a New Zealand comrade, who has certainly been through the mill:

St. Albans, Christchurch, New Zealand.

Am a returned soldier, having left New Zealand with the Main Body in 1914 for Egypt. I was in the fighting at the Suez Canal. Left there for the Dardanelles. Was in the landing; it was a sight I never want to see again in a hurry. So you see I am a real Anzac. Was wounded the third day, after some good fighting with the Turk. Returned to the front again to have another argument with the Turks. I had better luck this time—was fighting for five months before I got my second and last wounds. I had been out getting some water for our wounded boys at a little risk of a sniper's bullet when all of a sudden I heard a shell coming, as I thought, over my head. I woke up on my way to New Zealand. I had been blown over Walker's Ridge with a couple of wounds in my left arm and a few minor defects. I have lost the use of my left arm. So I think I got out of it very well, don't you? I am at present a sergeant-major on Home Service till the end of the war. I am now settled and married to the finest girl in the world.—Charles H. Graham.

Unable to get a stamp for return postage.

A line from our old friend, M. Logie, who served with the British on the Salonika and later on the French front in the famous Black Watch. We already know of his transfer to the A. E. F.

France.

You will note that I'm over here again, having received my discharge from the British Forces, thanks to the U. S. Military Attaché, London. Joined the old 9th U. S. Regulars. Took part in that grand counter-offensive on the Marne, July 18th—29th. Came out all O. K.

Being with the M. G. Co. of the 9th, we had some grand opportunities "at the retreating boche," as our English comrades would say. After that I had my chance to attend the Army Candidates School (A. E. F. of course). Was commissioned a 2nd lieutenant Sept. 19 and assigned to a negro regiment (U. S.) attached to the 4th French Army. Again went "over the bags."

On October 1—6 in the Champagne Drive—some old story of rear guard action with his Maxims. No need to mention the gunners—they either run, get stuck, or pull off the *Kamarad* stuff, which is only natural with the swine. Again pulled out O. K. At present we are away over on the right of the line. E. France. Things going fairly easy.

This outfit is composed of men (negro) mostly from the New England or North Central States. Good stuff.

Regards to all. Glad to report that I have made 1st lieutenancy lately. My regards to old New York; hope I'll see the old burg soon. Going on for four years since I left God's country to take my place in this affair.—M. Logie, Lt. Infy., 372nd R. T. A. S. M. G. Co. No. 2.

The above, of course, are only a small part of the comrades "over there" who have written in to us. Just those whose letters happen to be on hand at this writing. In our files are many other letters, often only brief "reports" of the writer's being at the front by land or sea, but those are older ones. A complete roster of all the Camp-Fire comrades who have served with the colors—well, it would be big enough for quite a few army divisions and quite a few full ship's crews.

To end with, here are parts of two letters from our comrade Donald Francis McGrew, an officer of the 103rd Infantry, written to Talbot Mundy more than half a year ago but still interesting. The writer, you will remember, had seen service as a regular in the Philippines.

France.

Just to let you know that I came through the last "trick," thirty-six straight days, in O. K. and am still kicking. We are behind the lines for a few days now, but of course we won't be out long. The regiments of the Yankee Division 126th never are.

While they have no great newspapers to spread broadcast the story of their every little deed, these quiet, clear-eyed chaps from the hills of Maine, New Hampshire and Vermont are second to none—not even the Canadians or the beloved "Ladies from Hell" as regards their courage and soldierly possibilities. Certainly I knew what I was doing when I came all the way from Michigan to rejoin a Maine regiment. And I would do it again, for these lads have fulfilled my every expectation. The great majority of them ring true as steel in action, and I've seen them stand fast time and again under the ——est artillery and minenwerfer poundings that Fritz could possibly give them. Neither has Fritz ever captured any of the 103rd so far, nor has he been able to budge them from a single position they have held.

HOWEVER, it's all in the day's work and whether these lads get the newspaper "blow-ups" or not, we chaps from other parts of the country who have been with them know what they can do and are *doggoned* glad to have them under our command when the pinches come.

France.

I am afraid that this is going to be rather a disjointed letter—not even as well connected as the one which I wrote from the Soissons front. It took four days of "time snatching" to write that.

THIS is my third trip since then, on another front, and I have been in so long this time that I no longer remember the date we struck here. At any rate we hit this pulverized neck of the woods the day after the 104th's 2nd Battalion finished its ten-day scrap, and we've been going to it at intervals ever since. She am a hot one, this hole, when we all get going.

The Camp-Fire

By this time you've probably read the casualty list suffered by the 104th. That one battalion had at least 60 killed and about 100 wounded in the two days' shindy, but they piled up as many more boche, and then some. All told, there were nine attacks and counter-attacks in the two days, with the heaviest sort of shelling by both sides; and the Massachusetts lads retook the trenches every time. They were holding all but one when we came in, and no one was holding that—it had ceased to resemble a trench.

I reconnoitered it next day, and it was a shambles with broken equipment, dead boches, and bits of soldiers here, there and everywhere. Some of our own dead were still out in the wire. Our outfit went out and got them that night. The trenches roundabout were flattened out or filled in and many of the dugouts were reduced to piles of tangled wires and crumbled rock. Those minenwerfer and 150's are bad eggs when they land near you.

OUR 3rd Battalion took over and we profited some by some of the mistakes we understood were made in the scrap. The ground is rocky here, and a man below the level of the shell-hits is practically safe unless it is very close. So "Old Man" Southard had the boys lay low when a bombardment started, save for the unnecessary sentries and they never "stood to" until called. Meanwhile our heavy artillery and my "little heavies" gave the Hun —— and a little bit more; and Fritz never got to first base. We suffered few casualties, too. He kept us all awake for three days and nights that trip, but we've not been worried so much since then, and have, so far, been able to give him more than he sent.

(Interrupted again.)

THE 2nd Battalion of the 102nd got into a nasty slew about the same time, losing quite a number of men. I can't mention the place, of course. But there were some of them surrounded by boche for twenty-four hours. The machine gunners died on their guns, and although some were at first inclined to criticize them for allowing themselves to be outflanked, the nature of the ground and the dispersion of their line at that time made it practically impossible for them to do any differently. As it was, they counter-attacked with great fury and retook their former first line.

We are no longer "in" as "students," though of course we are still students in one sense of the word. While there is nothing so very complicated about this game, we will not be a professional army for some time to come. A soldier is a soldier, and a civilian is something else. But we are "in on our own," and if Fritzy's initial bombardments and barrages leave anything of us, we won't want to lose much sleep about our chances with an even number of his infantry. These young New Englanders can stand up under a heavy "crump slew" without getting unduly nervous; and, though they are inclined to throw all their grenades at one time now and then, they are learning fast and are ugly customers with the rifle and bayonet.

I WAS thinking the other day of some observations I have made since I struck France, and I intended to make a note of them but couldn't find them. Anyway, some at random might interest you, as I remember them:

I have yet to see an intoxicated French soldier, though they drink *vin rouge* as we drink water.

The Huns use bear-traps in No-Man's Land. Our patrols have brought in, not one, but dozens of them. The jaws have spikes that sink into the caught leg over an inch.

Many boys of 15 and 16 are being taken among other boche prisoners.

The Belgians are the most unpopular of the allied troops.

French soldiers are the best of comrades. I have never seen two French soldiers fighting each other.

I've never seen an American soldier fighting with a poilu. (But, believe me, I've seen American soldiers fighting one another! Ho, yass!)

Our soldiers use a lot of profanity but many of them don't realize how much less *filthy* language they are using now as compared to their talk of a year ago.

There is far less drunkenness in the service now than there was in "peace times" years ago. "Pay day" sprees are a matter of course, but they are not production of service crimes.

I have yet to hear of, let alone report or arrest, an American soldier charged with insulting a French girl or woman. There have been some minor disputes over the price of wine in cafés and occasional arguments over billeting arrangements, but no serious entanglements have come to my notice. The people of the town in which most of the 103rd were billeted asked that we be sent back there when we came out of the line the first time.

Tales of depravity and of drunken riots here behind the lines are pure bosh, save in very exceptional instances. The billeting areas that I have been in are Y. M. C. A.'s in comparison to many cities and small towns in the States. These boys behaved themselves —— well.

Too much credit can not be given the Y. M. C. A. for the work they have done.

MANY things have happened since I started in writing this letter. Nevertheless we are still here, holding the line and not attacking, it is true, but here just the same. God, I'll be glad when the whole American Army can dig in on a huge offensive and fight as so many fond but unmilitary people believe the American Army would fight! Just waiting for Fritz's attacks is not pleasant, even when you can stave him off and knock him galley west with all you've got. These boys *want to go over the top!* Hurry up with that blinking draft army that we read so much about.

The home company stood up against a hellish gas attack "somewhere in France" some time or other. Can't mention time or place. Fritzie shot over huge shells with projectors in a perfect cloud. I once heard a bombardment come with such intensity many of the men had no chance whatsoever to don a mask. The shells smashed in the doors of the dugouts, leveled parts of the trenches and literally plowed up their whole sector—all in the space of three minutes. The concentration was instantaneous. Then Fritz followed up with high explosives and though our artillery came back at once, the boys caught quite a strafing. I can't give you the extent of the casualties, but the people at home will have been notified by the time you get this. In spite of it all the boys did not want to be relieved—a necessity, as gas clings to the clothing—but were crazy to go over the top and back at them. Poor kids! They didn't have a ghost of a show against that damnable fire that night, but they were absolutely *splendid.*

At last reports Sgt. Bill was O. K.

WISH you could have seen another "incident." More cheerful from our point of view. Oh, boy! If I ever get the chance to write the story of it! At some time or other somewhere in France we helped the French prepare a big raid made by the Madagascar "tar-babies." It was the best show I've seen. We gave Fritz intermittent barrages and bombardments on eight kilometers of front so they would not know the point where the blow was to fall, then combined all along just upon the zero hour, and kept it up for 45 minutes. Blowey—what a glorious racket!

And can't you see those black giants, most of them stripped to gee-strings, gripping their knives in their teeth and chanting in the trenches? They could hardly be held until the zero hour. Most of them had cut themselves a bit to smear their faces with blood, and when you consider that they are given to cutting their faces in youth to produce blood-scars, you can imagine how beautiful they looked. And when they went over the top—Oh, boy! Talk about the legion that went roaring down to die! They went at Fritz like a tornado let loose, breaking clear through to the fifth line. But I'll spare you the details. Suffice it to say that they did obey orders and brought back some prisoners—and some ears. Mostly ears. Perhaps I'm kind-hearted, but, when I saw them in the woods about nine in the morning, I could have hugged every one, ugly as they are. Huge, brawny, coal-black fellows, with gleaming teeth and laughing eyes—More power to their arms and good luck to 'em wherever they go. They are the boys to put the fear of God into the hearts of those sick wolves in front of us.

Must close now, as I have a lot of work to do.—MAC.

Our Camp-Fire came into being May 5, 1912, with our June issue, and since then its fire has never died down. Many have gathered about it and they are of all classes and degrees, high and low, rich and poor, adventurers and stay-at-homes, and from all parts of the earth. Some whose voices we used to know have taken the Long Trail and are heard no more, but they are still memories among us, and new voices are heard, and welcomed.

We are drawn together by a common liking for the strong, clean things of out-of-doors, for word from the earth's far places, for man in action instead of caged by circumstance. The *spirit* of adventure lives in all men; the rest is chance.

But something besides a common interest holds us together. Somehow a real comradeship has grown up among us. Men can not thus meet and talk together without growing into friendlier relations; many a time does one of us come to the rest for facts and guidance; many a close personal friendship has our Camp-Fire built up between two men who had never met; often has it proved an open sesame between strangers in a far land.

Perhaps our Camp-Fire is even a little more. Perhaps it is a bit of leaven working gently among those of different station toward the fuller and more human understanding and sympathy that will some day bring to man the real democracy and brotherhood he seeks. Few indeed are the agencies that bring together on a friendly footing so many and such great extremes as here. And we are numbered by the hundred thousand now.

If you are come to our Camp-Fire for the first time and find you like the things we like, join us and find yourself very welcome. There is no obligation except ordinary manliness, no forms or ceremonies, no dues, no officers, no anything except men and women gathered for interest and friendliness. Your desire to join makes you a member.

FOLLOWING our Camp-Fire custom, Terry Ramsaye rises and introduces himself on the occasion of his first story in our magazine:

> My story, "A Handmade Hero," comes out of a fact experience very close to the fiction version in the course of my newspaper career in the West. Our hero, whom I have called *Denis Kearney*, really made good and is now a chief of police out West.
>
> My experiences and adventures have been those typical of an active career in newspaper and motion-picture life—including a stowaway trip to Liverpool, a dip in the early Mexican trouble, the first aeroplane trip across the continent with the late Cal Rodgers, two months with a yegg gang in behalf of a bank syndicate, some larking about in the Northwest and sundry disaster assignments.
>
> My adventures these days consist mostly of what can happen over a flat-top desk in a motion-picture promotion office—"same of which is considerable" as Will Ritchey might remark.—Terry Ramsaye.

SO FAR as I can remember off-hand, the following is the first letter to our Camp-Fire from Papua, and even it was prompted by something Mr. Armit read in "Ask Adventure" concerning New Guinea oil-fields. But then, in a way, "Ask Adventure" and all our other departments belong to Camp-Fire—old timers will remember that the older ones were for a long time run merely as part of our general "Camp-Fire," and of course all of them are primarily for the benefit of those who gather round our blaze.

Incidentally, I have no way of knowing how many of those who read our magazine are members of our Camp-Fire, since any one belongs if he wishes to and there are no ceremonies to be gone through with, but, judging from letters and some direct knowledge, they must include considerably over ninety per cent. of our readers.

If letters from Papua have been scarce, Mr. Armit states in a postscript that our magazine is "very popular" there, so probably we have quite a few comrades in that distant land, though only one has written. His letter is dated August 21, and reached me late in November. Even allowing for war disturbance, that is a long trip.

Port Moresby, Papua.

You may be interested by a few details of this rather unknown corner of the globe.

NEW GUINEA is the largest island in the world—some 360,000 square miles—of which Holland owns the western half, Australia the southern and eastern side (90,000 square miles), and the remainder is the former colony of German New Guinea, which includes the New Britain Archipelago, Nauru, Admiralty Group, and the Marshalls and Carolines. Japan seized the two latter clusters of islands; but Australia sent a naval and military force under the late Brigadier-General William Holmes and captured the former possessions in early September, 1914. Australia administers the captured territory for the Allies, and has a garrison located there as her Occupation Force; the final fate of the colony is in abeyance until the end of the war.

THE southern and eastern side of New Guinea, with the D'Entrecasteaux Group, the Louisiade Archipelago and many other islands and atolls, form the Australian colony known as Papua.

Dutch New Guinea is not very developed, and the interior, with the exception of the Charles Louis Range (a mighty chain of peaks, snow-clad and crowned by enormous glaciers) and a narrow belt along the great rivers, is still unexplored.

Papua, the first oversea territory of the Commonwealth of Australia, has made a great advance in settlement and development since it was taken over by the mother continent. The planting industry has made great strides, and the export of agricultural produce is rapidly becoming of large extent.

The total exports for the year ended June 30, 1917, were valued at over $782,000—copra, rubber, sisal hemp, gold, pearls, sandalwood, bech-de-mer, copper ore, pearl shell, trochas shell, turtle shell, and miscellaneous products. The principal export trade is with Australia.

THE oil-fields are situated in the Vailala River country, some two hundred miles west of the capital and seat of government, Port Moresby.

The field is still in the development stage, and the Australian Government has a monopoly of the oil business; private enterprise has not, so far, been allowed on the field.

Upoia, on the Vailala River, is the scene of the enterprise, and about twelve or fourteen men comprise the staff, with Papuan laborers for the manual work.

The Department of Home and Territories, Melbourne, Australia, controls the enterprise, and has a Director of Oil-Fields resident at Upoia.

PAPUA is within the tropics—between the fifth and twelfth parallels South latitude—and extends from 141 to 155 East Longitude. The climate is trying to those unaccustomed to extremes of heat and moisture. Malaria is common, but with proper care, and quinin in prophylactic doses, it is not very dangerous. Temperance, a mosquito-net, gentle exercise, a good and varied diet of all the fresh food you can obtain (canned "dog" and other horrors is the staple menu in the territory) and a cheerful disposition are important factors in the maintenance of robust health in malarial countries.

THE mean temperature at Port Moresby is about 81.4 degrees, maximum temperature 87.5 degrees, humidity 70.5 per cent.; at Upoia (Vailala) 82.4 and 90.9 degrees, and humidity 80 per cent.; rainfall at Port Moresby 38.48 inches and at Vailala 121.40 inches.

From April to September is the best season—the period of cool southeast winds from the seas; the rest of the year is wet, and mosquitoes work overtime.

THE New Guineas are a paradise for the student of natural history. Every schoolboy is familiar with the birds of paradise, of which there are about fifty-six varieties known to science; and the history of the mysterious island is rich in stories of adventure—real-life tales of strange and weird peoples, cannibals, head-hunters and primitive folk still in the stone age.—L. P. B. ARMIT.

WITH his first story in our magazine, Ben F. Baker follows Camp-Fire custom and stands up and introduces himself:

San Francisco.

Along about the middle of the Klondike rush (the Summer of '98) I met up with the managing director of the outfit that was paying me a salary for running one of their trading stations. Here is how he introduced himself: "My name is —— ——. My time is worth a dollar a minute. Be brief."

The gentleman has since passed out, but I still have my first estimate of him—a chump misplaced.

NOW, from 1876 to 1918 is a long time; so, in order to be brief, let's skip the first eighteen years wherein nothing much happened except a lot of kid fun, residence in Kentucky, Indiana, Illinois, Colorado and Montana, getting the knack of riding pretty well, shooting even better and finishing high-school.

And now see what comes of reading magazines. I have forgotten the publication—even the writer—but an article on Alaska started me North in July, 1894, from the little smelter town of Anaconda, Montana, at eighteen. The article dealt mostly with the Alaskan southeast coast and the writer declared that Sitka, with a population of seventeen hundred, boasted eleven hundred Indians! Me for Sitka!

BUT the fool boat went straight to Juneau, which, even then, was a regular, civilized community; so a sadly disappointed but not discouraged kid eagerly put in with a party of eight Cheechakos, Yukon bound. And right here I would like to try to tell you of the Yukon Valley of that period, its men, their customs and the conditions under which they lived, all of which were changed in a single season when the Klondike was discovered.

For of all the many gifts Alaska made me—many of them she took back again—the one without price was the privilege of seeing a little of the great interior of the pre-Klondike days and of knowing the real pioneers who blazed the trail for the hordes who followed them. Sure, I know, the Klondiker was a real pioneer; but—no, I won't do it. I don't belong to the "I Was There First" club.

JUST the same, my party had to have an Indian guide over the Chilkoot, in September, mind you! Three years later that trail was as easy to follow as a county road. No Skagway for us. No mushers by the thousand camped from Linderman to Labarge to furnish shelter or even food, in a pinch. We met white men just once on the whole trip from Dyea to Fort Selkirk; two out-going miners with whom we camped for a night at Rink Rapids. And we ran the Cañon and Whitehorse and Five Fingers with loaded boats, in extreme low water. Lucky? Nix. Looney.

Besides, we were bound for the Land of Gold, and misfortune was not for us—yet.

We drifted for days with mush-ice freezing to the boats so fast that one man did nothing else but knock it off so that we might keep afloat. And clothes! Summer togs from head to foot, all of us. Oh, we were a wise bunch!

WE WERE finally frozen in at Selkirk, landing there with a few pounds of beans and maybe half a pound of tea. There the party split up, some of us Wintering at that post and the others going on to Forty-Mile over the first ice.

And there, from Arthur Harper, the post trader and later one of the founders of Dawson, I learned the rudiments of fur buying and trading, which knowledge was to land me, four years later, in the soft berth of local agent (manager) for one of the two, big pioneer companies that controlled the Yukon Valley.

In the meantime, I cut cordwood, "cut up" as mate on the old *P. B. Weare*, mined two Summers at Circle City (Birch Creek) and drove a freight dog-team there most of one Winter. Then Dawson, '97 and '98, and a pretty fair stake which was promptly lost. Then on to Rampart for four years as "Company man."

AND then, until 1910, mining, working for the Company, trading on my own hook, contracting with the infantry post at Fort Gibbon for cordwood, having a hand in the attempt to make the ill-fated Chena the head of navigation on the Tanana, etc., etc., etc. some more, with one trip to the Outside in 1907.

Made dog-team or canoe trips to Salmon River, Forty-Mile, Birch Creek, Ray River, Dahl River, Koyukuk, Nenana and many other tributaries of the Tanana, Novikakat, Tozikatat, etc. Rode my moccasins to every stampede I got wind of. Made a little stake on Sullivan Creek, Hot Springs District, in 1910 and left for the States same year. Have not been North since.

AFTER 1910, Arizona, New Mexico, Texas, Mexico as far down as Tepic, on the west coast and as far inland as Torreon on the east side. Mostly in the show business and mostly broke. Of course. But fun? Well, I should say so! Been getting better than an even break, right along, except for one thing. Haven't been able to break into the Army. Enlisting officers tell me my eyes are not good. Correct. Snow-blind too often. And now the show is over, over there.

BUT believe me, I can still hear mighty good—good enough to hear Siberia calling. And I expect to be there in time to see the geese come North. Maybe you'll hear from me. Anyway, I hope to have the chance to tell you a few of the Indian folk-lore tales as I heard them from Selkirk to Anvik. And if I succeed in telling them as they were told to me, you'll find them interesting.

Also, I have a hunch some of you will recognize them as blood brothers to the legends of the Siberian native; for the Yukon Indian and the Husky are Mongols as sure as the Sioux is an Indian.

SINCE "Mis-Deal" has been selected to bust into print, I would like to add a little note.

The tale is founded on a trip of four of the "real pioneers" referred to a while back. They made the trip from Tramway Bar to Rampart with an involuntary side trip to the main Koyukuk, as stated. They did eat a dog and they numbered among them the original of *Michael Joseph Ryan*. He is still north of 53, chasing the yellow rainbow. Good luck to him and to you—all of you.—BEN F. BAKER.

CONCERNING his story in this issue, one of his "Flotsam" tales, S. B. H. Hurst writes me:

Seattle, Wash.

By the way, *Tom Spritz* is real. I knew him very well. He was a wonderful rough-and-tumble fighter, but with the gloves he was a joke. Of course he was older than I was. The last I heard of him was that he was chased out of Polynesia, and . . . He was actually married to three women, and made no bones about it. He and the bos'n of the —— fought for over an hour on the sea wall in 'Frisco. It was shortly after Corbett licked Sullivan, and the row started about that fight. The papers wrote it up in great style, saying —— got them to kiss and make up. As a matter of fact, he was hiding in his room, very full—the same man I told you about leaving me on Pitcairn.—S. B. H. HURST.

LITTLE has been said lately about the American League for Citizenship, Inc. As stated in the beginning, it will move slowly. And bad health has prevented my keeping up even to the slow schedule planned. But it keeps moving.

When it has developed sufficiently to make its real start more will be heard about it. Meanwhile those who have joined are asked to be both patient and confident, and it is hoped that those who have formed or are forming tens will push their work. These local organizations are the key-stones of the whole, whose work is centered in them. Particularly in towns and smaller cities even a single ten of the right caliber can make itself a factor that will be tremendously felt.

Not a penny of the money sent in as dues or contributions has been spent, nor will be until the course ahead is more definitely marked out.

If ever a country needed the teaching and furtherance of real and practical democracy and of definite, practical and understanding individual citizenship, this country needs it now. That is what the League is for, and, when the right time comes, I hope every good American among you is going to turn to and do his part instead of letting things drift as in the past.

W. C. TUTTLE'S own pictures of the characters in his stories, reproduced at previous Camp-Fires, have caused so many of you to write their appreciation that I thought you might like a close-up of *Magpie Simpkins* by Mr. Tuttle.

"Tut" is no longer a cartoonist by profession but he can't quite free himself of the pleasant habit. The envelopes of his letters to this office are sometimes decorated with humorous, rollicking little sketches that must have brought happy grins to mail clerks as well as to the staff.

CAN you find this man another war? He is a Camp-Fire comrade and he's asking for help. Also, both he and his pal were invalided home from the French front, so they are not hunting for something they don't know about. The letter was written from a U. S. General Hospital in this country. I do not give the writer's name or identify him in any way, for his letter was written to me personally and not meant for publication, but I know he'll not mind its appearing in impersonal form.

I fell down on this job of finding him another war, though I suggested that Siberia, Russia and maybe Germany herself might be able to furnish something. And almost the next day the papers reported Peru, Chile and Bolivia on the verge of hostilities. Maybe they will do the trick for him, though they seem at this writing to have quieted down, but who, if his own country no longer needed him, would want better fighting comrades than the Czecho-Slovaks? But if they too have ceased fighting by the time these two pals have got their discharges, who will find them another war?

Theirs is the unquenchable thirst for adventure and I wish them well—and the many others like them; but I can't help hoping that they will find satisfying adventure of some other kind. The world has had so much of war. But you never can tell.

> I don't know whether I let you know it or not, but since you have last heard from me, I believe, I've transferred to the Quartermaster Detachment at this Post. In that interval, also, it has begun to look as though peace is here, despite the fact that myself and a good many others are not in favor of such an early one. However, it's our duty to fight like —— and let the executive heads do as they please officially.
>
> WELL, my reason for writing you is this: My pal here, who has been with me since I landed in this country from France, seems to be of about the same mind as am I in regard to certain things. He was gassed when serving with the French artillery. Realizing that this war is about through, we are desirous of finding another one. We are informed that as returned soldiers we will be among the first discharged.
>
> Now, to get down to business. I know your "Ask Adventure" Department very well, but I don't believe that it exactly covers what I'm after. To be brief, he (my pal) and I are looking for another war or disturbance of some kind where, after we are discharged, we may find recreation and enlist or get commissions as ambulance drivers, cavalrymen, dispatch riders, artillerymen, or anything else. In our brief careers in this service we have had so many different jobs and served in so many different ways that we're almost fit for anything. Can you put me on the track of another war? Or, if you can't, can you put me on the track of some one who can, and if possible, give me a little dope on it?—A. A. A.

AS SOME of us already know, William Hope Hodgson, a lieutenant in the British forces, whose story appears in this issue, is among those who perished in the war. April 17, 1918, having volunteered for hazardous duty, he and his two companions were killed by a shell. He has sat at our Camp-Fire and his story, appearing nearly a year after his death, makes his memory very vivid. Our greeting and salute.

IN OUR "Ask Adventure" department one of you stirred up the interesting question of the Jivero Indians and their little habit of drying and shrinking human heads as souvenirs. Here are two letters bearing on the subject:

Washington, D. C.

In the National Museum there are three specimens placarded thus:

"Dried Human Heads—The Jibaros and other tribes of Indians, living on the branches of the River Amazon, in the cordilleras, removed the skull from the head of a slain enemy in the following manner:

"A cut is made around the lower part of the neck and the skin turned up from the head, care being taken to preserve intact the nose, mouth and other prominent features. The skin is then turned right side out, the mouth sewed up with coarse cord, which is left hanging in a fringe below the skin, and the cavity filled with coarse white sand or gravel . . . until the head has shriveled to one-third its usual size, preserving the features. It is then suspended in the cabin, and upon special occasions maledictions are heaped upon the victim of the tribe."

This may be of some interest. The specimens are good, remarkably impish in their expressions as though malice had been the motive of those molding the features.—P. A. STRACHAN.

Havana, Cuba.

The Jiveros are of Ecuador and not of Peru. There are a number of tribes whose habitat is in the region of the Marañon River and it is all these tribes together that are generally meant when the generic term Jiveros is used, yet actually all these tribes are distinct and have distinctive names.

THE flow of trade goods to the Indians of southern Ecuador is mostly out of the city of Loja and down the Zamora River. The tribe of Jiveros proper is that nearest to this center of trade influence, so that the exchange of cotton goods, firearms and trinkets, for rubber, gold, etc., is with the Jivero tribe. That part of the produce that comes from other tribes is either captured in war by the Jiveros or acquired by barter in times of tribal peace, and in consequence all the tribes are referred to as Jiveros as that is the only tribal name known to the traders of the region.

In the same way the name "Chunchos" is used for all the tribes occupying the lower affluents of the Madre de Dios in southern Peru, and there is still another generic name for the tribes of central Peru pertinent to the Huallaga and Ucayali rivers.

THE Jiveros proper occupy the territory immediately to the east of both the Paute and Zamora rivers, but they do not go, except in tribal wars when invading enemy territory, south of the junction of these two rivers, the Paute and Zamora unite to form the Sanitago, which flows into the Marañon. South of the Jivero tribe, east of the Santiago River and north of the Marañon the territory is occupied by a tribe known as the Huambizes (Wam-beé-zes) and they range along the north bank of the Marañon from the Santiago to the Morona.

It should be noted that the Marañon River after flowing for nearly a thousand miles in a general north and south direction changes this direction, after receiving the waters of the Santiago, to one almost due east and west, making a right angle, and the waters of the combined rivers break through the last low chain of outriders to the Andes Mountains on the Atlantic side, through a box cañon with walls from a thousand to two thousand feet high, and this cañon is called the Pongo Manseriche and is a bar to any navigation of the upper river.

The east and south banks of the Marañon are held by a large and very intelligent tribe known as the Aguarunas (Ag-wa-rú-nas) and the west bank by a sub tribe of the Aguarunas known as the Antipas (An-teé-pas). These four tribes together are those usually referred to generically as the Jiveros.

THE Huambizes are constantly at war with both the Jiveros on the north and the Aguarunas and Antipas on the south, and also frequently with the Moronas to the east. Except the Huambizes, all these tribes maintain at times trading relations with the whites, being desirous of obtaining thin cotton underwear as some protection from the insects and mosquitoes and which they wear only at night, rifles, shotguns, steel spear-points, needles, thread, matches, knives, machetes, etc., and will give in exchange quantities of rubber and gold, the amount depending on the keenness of their desire for some particular thing. The Huambizes, however, are utterly savage, intensely ferocious, hostile to white men and absolutely unapproachable by them. The only way to find out anything about their country would be by an armed expedition in overwhelming force.

IT IS this tribe who are the head hunters and not the Jiveros, who have had to take the odium of the sins of their neighbors. That reduced heads come out through the Jivero tribe can not be doubted, but so also do they through all the other tribes that surround them. The heads are either captured by the other tribes in raids on the Huambizes' villages or acquired through barter during periods of tribal peace. The surrounding tribes try to get the heads as they are good material for trade with the Caucheros, who will generally give some much coveted article for a good head.

The Government of Peru has passed very stringent laws to stop the traffic, regarding it as putting a premium on murder of traders and explorers, but nevertheless any one desirous of getting such a head can obtain one in Iquitos for from fifty to one hundred dollars each, depending on the available supply.

NO ACCURATE information can be obtained from the surrounding tribes as to how the heads are shrunk. It is evident, however, that the ashes of some wood very strong in lye are used to dissolve the fatty and gelatinous matters from the bones. The brains could be easily washed out through the spinal-cord opening after rotting a few days, and it may be that the skull is kept filled with such a solution for months. The bones could then be broken up and pulled out in pieces.

Rumor in the locality states that the moisture is driven from the muscles of the face and skin by filling the skull cap, either before or after boning, with small hot pebbles, possibly also by burying the head in hot sand. It is also said that the curing and shrinking is done by slow continuous smoking in the acrid smoke of certain species of palm-nuts, similar to those burned to coagulate the *leche* of the *Hevea* or rubber tree. The smoke of some of these nuts is heavy with both acetic acid and gum resins so that it is conceivable that a slow smoking in such an acrid and gummy menstruum might accomplish the desired result.

THE Huambizes seem to have an especial aversion to white men. There are reputed to be extensive gold deposits up the Santiago River, and many prospectors, disregarding the reports about these Indians, have gone up there to see. But to date no one of them has ever come out alive, and it is equally certain that some European heads have come out to market from this tribe. The writer has seen two, one unmistakably Irish, the other appearing to be German. The Huambizes have declared it to be a closed region to white men.

THE use of firearms is understood by these tribes, but as a rule they do not use them in their tribal wars. Ammunition is too scarce and difficult to obtain to waste it in this way. It is reserved for the killing of big game such as tapirs and howling monkeys, for while the poisoned arrows are very effective with birds and small animals they are not so with large ones. From a hundred to two hundred darts are required to paralyze a tapir sufficiently for them to capture and kill it. And a howling monkey will not stay still long enough to get filled full of arrows; one prick is enough and he is off. The poison appears to act as a paralyzant; stopping the heart almost instantly with birds and very small animals but causing only some motor paralysis in the larger animals. I imagine that it would take a great many darts to kill a man. At any rate they do not use them in fighting with each other, using instead bows and arrows, spears and clubs.

ALL these tribes at times make war on the whites and even in very recent years have penetrated for a considerable distance into civilized regions, killing some hundreds of people. Punitive expeditions by soldiers usually accomplish but little in the way of punishment, for the Indians scatter all through the forest and no one but themselves can follow their routes through the tangled masses, as most of their paths through the bush are mere traces.

The rifles they possess are an early type of Winchester, model of somewhere about 1865. In the Aguaruna language a rifle is called a "Wunchustre." The derivation of the name is obvious. So also their name for a shotgun (most of those they possess are of the muzzle-loading Belgian "gas-pipe" order) which they call an "Escupe," from the Spanish *escopeta*, a shotgun.

MR. YOUNG, speaking of the darts used in the blow-guns, states that they are about the size of a lead pencil. This is true in so far as width and length is concerned; their thickness, however, is no more than a sixteenth of an inch. They are made of bamboo and have a very long sharp point. Before being shot the dart is almost completely sawed through about half an inch from the point. The teeth in the lower jaw of a young mnokey being used for a saw. A twist of raw wild cotton is wrapped around the end of the dart to close the bore of the gun and give the blown breath an effective resistance for propulsion. The idea of sawing the point nearly through is that the long shaft of the dart will break off when it strikes, leaving the point with the poison on it sticking into the skin with a length so short that the bird or animal will effectively rub it in further, in any effort to rub it out.

IN PREPARING the poison it is Aguaruna practise to cause snakes of the viper species to strike into a liver repeatedly so as to inject the snake posion all through it before starting to rot the liver out. The poison when finished is a black gummy mass resembling tar, and is carried in a short section or joint of bamboo, about three to four inches in length by an inch in diameter. A dart quiver, and a gourd filled with raw wild cotton are usually attached to the poison receptacle so that these three essentials are usually carried in one bundle.

The guns are twelve to fifteen feet in length, some of them lined with split thigh-bones of small monkeys or large birds to give a very smooth bore. They are made in two pieces, longitudinally, and held together by strips of cotton that the Indians weave themselves, soaked in rubber, so that they are firmly held together and the interior is always dry and impervious to the very heavy rainfalls of the region. The mouthpiece is invariably made of bone. They are very expert with these guns, and get birds on the wing almost without a miss.

IN MANY ways these savages are more intelligent and enterprising than their civilized brethren of the highlands and the coast. And if judgment be based on the houses they build, the premium must be awarded to the savage. They live in various sub or divisional tribes of from a hundred and fifty to two hundred or more individuals each. The various divisions generally live in villages of two or three communal houses, protected by a fighting-tower.

The houses are built in the form of large truncated cones, about fifteen feet to the cornice and thirty feet to the peak of the roof, which is built with a high pitch to shed the rain easily, the thatch being of interwoven palm-leaves, each leaf six to eight feet in length. The rafters and roof are supported by six chonta palm-trunks placed equidistant, three on a side. Each house will accommodate easily fifty to seventy-five people. The door or entrance is through one of the bays of the cone at the end of the house. Immediately in front of the entrance is placed the stand of arms, in which are kept the spears, bows, arrows and guns. The center and sides are occupied by the beds, and the opposite bay is devoted to the making and storage of pottery. Provisions are hung from the rafters in baskets, the fiber for which is obtained by beating out certain species of bark.

The walls of the houses are made of straight canes, standing perpendicularly (class, *Caña Brava*), stripped of their spines. The selected canes are as nearly as possible of equal size. The butts are firmly fixed in the ground and the tops tied to the frame supporting the roof with strands of bejuco, a fibrous plant or vine with long tendrils that is very flexible when green, almost unbreakable when dry, and does not rot. The canes are spaced approximately an inch apart, the light coming in through the interstices. There are no windows. The sole opening is the door.

THE beds are very interesting. They are built to hold from four to six individuals each. They consist of a rectangular frame surrounding a lattice work of bamboo strips. The strips in the lattice extend from head to foot, are half an inch wide each and separated the one from the other by quarter-inch spaces. They are bound together by interlaces of fine cord, the cord is twisted twice between each strip, so as to firmly hold it, the rows of cord being about eight inches apart from top to bottom. The strips are smoothed and polished till they shine, and when finally bound in position, the whole forms a very effective spring, yielding easily to any change in position of the body. The head end of the framework is at an elevation of about three feet, whereas the foot is only two feet from the floor so that the bed is on a slope. The length of the framed lattice is only to about the middle of the thigh; the ankles rest on a cross pole beyond which is placed eighteen inches from the floor.

Between the end of the lattice and the ankle pole there is no support, but on the ground under this space three smudge logs are arranged in the position of the radii of a three-cornered star, the three burning ends in the center and together. The logs slowly smolder while the Indian slumbers, the smoke diminishing somewhat the plague of mosquitoes and gnats. Unless some of the individuals are lucky enough to own a thin cotton undershirt, they use no covering at all at night but sleep absolutely naked, men, women and children all together.

DURING the day the men wear a loin-cloth which falls to just above the knee and which is held on by being tucked under a stout bark fiber string which is tied tightly around the waist. The women wear a similar loin-cloth, and some of them a sleeveless loose chemise as well. The children wear nothing. The cloth is woven by the women from wild cotton that grows plentifully through the forest and is fairly fine in texture, and as a rule is dyed maroon in color. They also weave long narrow strips like ribbons; these are not dyed but colored threads are woven into them in fairly good semi-geometrical designs. These they use for ornamentation of the hair and in the construction of ornaments for the person. The hair is worn banged in front, a straight line across the forehead; another square cut is made just below the ears and the hair at the back is gathered together and tied with ribbon or cord in the form of a queue. Some of the young bucks wear brightly colored flowers made of feathers at the top of the queue.

The body painting is in various designs, some limiting themselves to a mere touch of color here and there, others putting on weird patterns. The colors are usually red and black, but blue is also sometimes used. On the occasion of feasts, of which there are plenty when not at war, they bedeck themselves in gorgeous ornaments—crowns of scarlet, blue, yellow and white feathers, long pendents from the shoulders, also of feathers, long hanging breast and back bands of intricate design made of beads, bones of birds, parti-colored seeds all highly polished and intermingled with small but brilliant feathers, belt bands of similar design, pendents from the ears six to eight inches in length made up of dozens of golden bronze beetle wings, necklaces of monkeys' teeth around their necks, as well as beads, buttons and colored pebbles—all are piled on the person in profusion, the amount of ornamentation depending on the enterprise of the owner in making or collecting this form of wealth. The gorgeous plumage of the tropical birds gives them an endless variety of shades to select their feathers from.

THESE tribes do not distend perforations in the lobes of the ears to any great extent, as do the Orellenes of central Peru, in whose lobes a small saucer can easily be carried. Holes of quarter- and half-inch diameters, however, are common, but are used more for carrying small objects than for ornamentation. They take the place of a pocket as it were. Any one of them who is lucky enough to own a steel needle wraps it up in cotton and puts it in a little box made out of a bamboo shoot, and then carries the box in the lobe of his ear, it never leaving him either night or day. It is considered a mark of beauty that the teeth should be stained black.

They are very clean, not only as to their persons but as to their camps and houses as well. They live about half the time in the water. Anything obtained from a white man is instantly plunged in the river and washed, no matter what the article is. Any stranger approaching a camp is immediately hailed with the question *"Aschmon?"* "Are you well?" Nor will they allow any one ill to land on their shores, no matter what the illness might be, as in times past the tribes have been bitterly decimated by smallpox and measles, the latter disease seeming to be very fatal to them.

THEY are nomadic by disposition, seldom staying in one encampment longer than a few months; and when the spirit moves them they must go, no matter how much trouble they have been at in the construction of their buildings. They invariably have three or four plantations growing in different localities at the same time. These are cultivated by the women, of course. This provides them against starvation in case of being driven from an encampment by a sudden descent of the enemy, or when tiring of a location from overlong use they feel that they must move to a new location.

Their crops are mostly yuccas, yams, Indian corn and plantains. The corn is all small eared, and of the variety where the grains are scattered irregularly on the cob, the kernels not growing in straight rows. Many black kernels are scattered in with the yellow. Salt they mine themselves from extensive deposits in the forests. Some of the tribes do not use salt at all. They use a great deal of fish, obtaining them both by spearing and by traps. The hook and line they are unfamiliar with.

There are many other things that might be written about their beliefs, superstitions, canoe manufacture, means of communication, drum signaling, feasts, funerals, sickness and death and tribal life in general, but to attempt any sort of an intelligible description would extend this letter into book length and completely transcend the limits of an ordinary letter, even to a magazine.—R. M. WHITEHEAD.

ONE of you sent me a letter from some of his old bunkies now in France, men with whom he had served in our Army before the war. It was written long before you read this, back in the first half of 1917, but the spirit of America it breathes is not a matter of dates.

It is not a matter of the war alone, but of peace as well, of the whole future of our country. In peace we know that our country is ridden by political rottenness, by those who do not know the meaning of patriotism and whose one aim is their own selfish gain, cost our country what it may. Often it is disheartening to contemplate the widespread corruption—graft, pull, trickery, lies, greed. But then you get a glimpse of the thing you see burning in this letter. Inside, down underneath, buried deep but strong, you find this flame of real patriotism. Perhaps under a humble or rough exterior, perhaps under a gilded or a frivolous one. Often it takes a mighty war to make it show itself. But it is there. For peace as well as for war. And it is our country's hope and dependence.

AND we must keep those fires burning. They must not be allowed to die down out of sight when war is over. Peace needs them too.

God bless the Americans who wrote this letter and all others in whom burns this fire.

The "Fighting Freddie" (Funston) referred to is the bulldog mascot of their old company down on the Border. "Banjo" is the name the comrade who received the letter formerly gave to shovels, a comrade, by the way, who ached to join his buddies over there but stuck to the duty of taking care of his dependent mother. Some of you know how much courage that kind of duty takes. Here is part of his letter which enclosed theirs:

It brings out the feelings of those men who have gone to sacrifice their all for us, those men to whom we shall have to feel ourselves indebted for all time for the sacrifice they have made that our most glorious Nation may go on its way of Freedom and Democracy. It tells—— Oh, well, go on and read it; you'll find it more interesting than what I could write.

Somewhere in France.

DEAR FRIEND JACK:

We have found a little paper, which is very scarce, and time, which is very plentiful, so we will drop you a few lines from the boys who still remember you and your old line of talk, which same we wish we had floating around now. At times we are awakened from our peaceful slumbers by the *zis, zis, zis* of old "Jerry," as the "Tommies" call them, and when he comes he always brings a *big* basket of "*big hard-boiled eggs*" and doesn't give a —— where he drops them.

NIGHT before last M Co. lost her first man and two wounded, all new men. The wounded ones are now at the base hospital. Thirty minutes after the bomb landed all that could be seen were "banjoes" and the dirt flying.

As each day goes by they dig one foot deeper. Even now, eight o'clock, we can hear the big guns playing "Stars and Stripes Forever" with a bass accompaniment, and, Jack, there is nothing to compare with these 12-, 14-, and 16-inch guns in action. And as we lay in our dugouts at night and feel old mother earth tremble like a ball of jelly we get callouses on our backs from trying to dig deeper. Talk about Fourth of July fireworks, this Fourth will show the world a celebration that even the devil will tremble at, and believe me your old pals will do their part.

SAY, Jack, if we could get another trip like the one to the Border it would be like a vacation to this one. You, no doubt, have seen dogs run away from other ones; well, that is the way that the Huns run from us Yanks as we up and over. Jack, that is the time we wish that we had you here to sing some of your "wild and woolly" songs. The Yanks will show the world that they *are* all that they claim to be and will make Old Glory the flag to be respected forever.

AS WE left N. Y. Harbor at 4 P.M. all N. Y. was out to bid us a pleasant voyage and safe return. When we passed the Statue of Liberty little did we realize what it really meant to live under the Stars and Stripes, but that day that we return and pass that same statue we can look at it in a different light and see that after all there's no place like the U. S. A. Jack, when you hear the "Star-Spangled Banner" played, stand up at "attention" and say, "Thank God, I'm an American citizen!" With the first strains of that we throw back our shoulders and it makes us want to fight like ——. We may have lots of things to put up with here, but we never grumble nor care, as long as it is for our country and every one in it.

All we can see is to finish this and do it quick, so that we can all eat our Xmas dinner back in God's country once more.

Well, Jack, it is close to taps and all lights must be out, so with this goes our best regards to you and your mother and also our "Fighting Freddie."'

FROM ALL YOUR OLD PALS OF M CO.

P. S.—I, Black-cat, got the paper, Roy started the letter and got cramps, so Ed had to finish it.

SINCE "The Ace" sent us the above letter he received the following, telling of the death at the front of one of these comrades:

Chicago.

I have just received the information that Private J. Edgar Carroll, one of the writers, has just died from pneumonia, while in the service of Our Country, somewhere "over there." It certainly was quite a blow to me, as he certainly was a man's man —you know, one of those men that one can always depend upon, one that would share his last five-cent piece with you. I can never forget the favors that he has performed for me.

HE WAS an old member of the old "Tombstone Squad," of which I was a member and which quite a few will remember. He afterward was promoted to cook and he sure saw that we fellows got enough to eat, as soon as he got on the job. Nothing lazy about him. And no matter what time it was, why, he always had a bite to eat and a cigar for me, which the latter was considered a luxury.

Another little incident which I remember was on account of my eyes which did not fit in with the awful heat down there until I got used to it. He saw that I was getting headaches, so took off his goggles and gave them to me, saying, "Here, take these; you need them worse than I do."

Yes, sir, he was a soldier and a gentleman from the very first word and I know fully well that the boys are sure going to miss old "Toots" Carroll, for a better man was never a member of old M o' the First.

I thought that probably when that letter did come out you might want to add a few lines as a tribute to one who was a soldier and a gentleman.—"THE ACE."

P. S.—I also have that pair of goggles with me now, and I certainly am going to keep them in remembrance of my old friend.

IF, AFTER you've read the story in this issue by Eugene P. Lyle, Jr., you care to translate it into international terms you will find a double meaning in it. If you don't care to, just read it as a story and enjoy it.

It was written before the count was finished for Germany.

AT THIS writing late in November the Republican and Democratic parties furnish us with an amusing spectacle. Neither one of them can decide upon a general policy to adopt. They are anxious to find some fine platform that will bring them votes and power, but neither one can find it.

It's been generations since either one of them had a really fundamental and permanent platform to stand on. They've had to depend on hand-to-mouth methods in espousing principles and causes, have had to seize on this or that immediate issue and brand it as their own for a vote-getter. Generally their method has been to fight all new ideas tooth and toe-nail, then find some day that this or that new idea had gained considerable popular backing, then, one or the other, grab it and adopt it. The one that didn't grab it would, of course, take the opposite side. (Do you remember how they used to hoot, both of them, at the planks of the old Populist party? And now you'll find that between them they've adopted nearly all of those planks.)

BUT just now all the issues lying around look dangerous. Neither the Democratic or the Republican machine can figure out just which ones to pick up, or, if they did pick one up, which side to take. All they're sure of is that, whatever issue is picked up by one of them and whichever side of it is adopted, the other party machine will promptly adopt the other side of it. They're like two runners ready to run in opposite directions, but neither one can make a start in any direction, so they just stand there back to back and don't get anywhere. And incidentally they look darned ridiculous.

THEY *are* darned ridiculous. The only thing any more ridiculous in this country is ourselves—for taking them so seriously and letting them hold so much power.

THE other and smaller parties have, generally speaking, something more real and permanent to stand on. But they won't have if they become the leading parties. They, too, will fall victims to the party system as it exists in this country. By splitting up, if not by the usual development.

THE blame, of course, falls on the people themselves. Parties are necessary as instruments for forwarding different sets of at least comparatively fundamental opinions. But we have made them ends instead of instruments, too many of us falling into party-idolatry and giving loyalty to party even before country. As a result we have grown careless as to whether they represent fundamental opinions or not, merely voting on whatever assortment of issues they find it to their own interest to deal us. And as a result of that result, fundamental issues have a hard time coming up for decision or even for thought. We're too busy with parties to have time or thought for the really vital problems.

EVEN on the planks they do see fit to present to us we can't vote with any free choice or discrimination. We have to vote for one bunch of planks or for another bunch. We may not like all the planks in any bunch, but we have to vote for all of them just the same. We may be strong for some of the planks in the other bunches, but we have to vote against them just the same.

In fact, we have to do about what the parties want all around.

It seems sort of stupid on our part.

There are remedies, of course, but it's more comfortable and easy-going to let the parties handle everything, including us.

A COMRADE sends the rest of us his recipe for making an auto into a sleeping-bunk:

St. Charles, Mich.

The front seats in the Studebaker 1916 and '17 models are twin, removable, and are set on a bench about four inches high. I removed the bench from the car and sawed a four-inch section from the center of it; then fastened each seat in its place on the divided bench and then returned them to their place on the floor of the car, using a heavy screen door-hook to prevent them tipping backward.

I NEXT removed the rear cushion and the slats and then took out the metal front-piece, substituting a wooden one which fits in behind the cleats at either end. This wooden front-piece is held firmly in place when the slat and cushion are returned to place. This arrangement allows me to take out all the seats, leaving the entire floor space empty, but with an open space where the front seats belong. This I filled by fitting in a floor-board. Now, then, for why?

WHEN the good wife and I, or two of us fellows, want to go fishing we take a three-quarter width mattress in place of the rear seat. On reaching our destination it takes us just five minutes to unhook and take out the front seats and other duffel and make our bed in the bottom of the car. If there are any "skeeters" we pull the curtains. With this arrangement we can make or break camp in jig time. Also we don't have to carry a tent, to say nothing of sleeping on the ground. To this last I do not object, but to say that the wife does is putting it MILD.—Geo. C. Gilbert.

THE Treasure of the Incas, a tempting subject. Also, here's a bit of an argument for Uncle Frank Huston on the matter of "roping" Indian squaws. And a rousing cheer for South America.

Charlottesville, Va.

As there has been some discussion about the Treasure of the Incas in our magazine, the following may be of interest to your readers. It is taken from a recent book, "The Incas of Peru," by Sir C. Markham Gordon, 1911. (The author spent many years in Peru and in studying its history, etc. He is an acknowledged expert on Peruvian matters, and has written a number of books in the last sixty years on the subject.)

THE Spaniards required a ransom in gold to be paid for Atahualpa. "The roads were promptly traversed by the bearers of gold in all shapes and forms. On the execution of Atahualpa, the gold ceased to arrive. All that was on its way was concealed, but already an amount equivalent to seventeen million five hundred thousand dollars of our money had reached the Spaniards, chiefly in the forms of square or oblong plates which had been used to adorn the walls of houses. A far greater amount was concealed and has never yet been found, though the secret has been handed down and on one occasion a small portion was used in the interests of the people. When the old chief Pumacagna was about to head an insurrection against the Spaniards, he had no funds for procuring arms and ammunition. After obtaining from him an oath of secrecy, the then guardian took him blindfolded to the place where the vast treasure was concealed, and he was allowed to take enough to meet his needs. He was defeated and put to death. No one else has ever been admitted to the secret. My friend Col. Astete remembered Pumacagna who rose against the Spaniards in 1815.

"PUMACAGNA was shown the wealth of the Incas by an Indian who had inherited the secret. Led up the bed of the river Huatany for a long distance, blindfolded and in the night, he suddenly found himself surrounded by vases, cups, plates, ingots and great statues, all of pure gold, in incredible profusion. He only took what he urgently needed to equip his troops. Returning to Cuzco, he went straight to Col. Astete's house. The Señora Astete told me that she could remember his coming into the room, and wet through, to relate his adventures.

"In another part of Peru (the coast region) much treasure had been discovered from the ruins of Chimu. "Altogether gold worth twenty-seven million five hundred thousand dollars is recorded. The amounts are derived from the records of the fifth part that had to be paid to the Spanish King. Excavations were continued at intervals. In 1797 the treasure called the Pefe Chico was secured. The Peje Grande has yet to be found. As late as Squier's time a certain Col. La Rosa was excavating and had already obtained thirty thousand dollars. Altogether millions have been obtained in gold bars and ornaments."

MY CREDENTIALS in regard to knowledge of the Indians are these—I went West to the real frontier forty-six years ago. I have lived in the country of the following tribes and have been in daily contact with them for often a long time: Northern Cheyenne, Northern Arrapahoe, Southern Arrapahoe, Sioux, Red Cloud's bands, Shoshone, Ute, Apache, Pueblo, Kiowa and Comanche.

A statement was made about the Indian women being "roped" (to protect their chastity). I never knew or heard of such a case in all the years I was amongst them. The different tribes vary much as to customs, etc. The inference was that it was a usual Indian habit. This is not so amongst the tribes I knew. Again, instead of their women having a shuffling gait due to the aforesaid "roping," their walk was free and often graceful. The handsomest Indian women I have ever seen were Cheyennes.

SINCE you started "Ask Adventure" it's the first part I read and enjoy most. But oh! how pitiful and pathetic are the inquiries of some of the writers who ask about West Africa. The worst place in the world for a white man, when they have in South America the finest place left on the globe, for adventures of all sorts. Rich in minerals and precious stones. The grandest forests and rivers. It's the best place I know of for the man who wants adventure. Where on this earth is a more beautiful spot than the Bay of Rio? Plenty of elbow-room in the greatest part of South America for one who loves Nature and wants to get away from the crowd.—"VIELHO."

IN THE Mid-February issue Jack Bechdolt gave us his first story, "Last Man Out," in our magazine but, not through his own fault, it is with his second, in this issue, that he follows our Camp-Fire custom and introduces himself:

New York.

During twelve years of newspaper work on the Pacific Coast I saw most of the things I have written about and a vast number of things I hope to write about some time. This education included such interesting special courses as mountain-climbing through blizzards and avalanches; going underground into caisson work and overhead on spectacular skeletons of bridges; all the usual routine of fire and flood and murder and violence that makes up newspaper reporting, but no first-hand adventure of any sort—unless it was being sued for libel.

OUTSIDE of being hungry for several days at a time and extremely uncomfortable on various occasions, I have had to collect my adventures second-hand. For instance, the tunnel experience in "Last Man Out" was related to me by a sand hog I met one day underground. He told me the story in a very leaky tunnel such as I described in this yarn and, while no doubt his idea was to entertain me, he made me extremely uncomfortable by suggesting something that might easily have happened to us—but it didn't.

All these excursions into forest fires and shipwrecks and snowfields were premeditated. They were part of my job. Sometimes they turned out uncomfortably, but they always ended happily in a nice warm office, a typewriter and a few more columns of copy for the Sunday paper.

I got a bigger thrill when I first saw New York than I did out of any of them. There is more thrill in hitting on a really good idea for a story—which happens rarely—than in a book full of earthquakes, so far as I'm concerned.

You see, I'm a tame sort of guy. I'd rather perpetrate a split infinitive than commit murder, but I'm an awfully good listener and I confess I like to listen to this gang around the "Camp-Fire." They're regular fellows.—JACK BECHDOLT.

THIS Australian comrade joined us from a hospital bed and he talks to us from a remote and lonely corner of the world. Our welcome and greetings.

Earl J. Teets, you will remember, in response to Edgar Young's query "What is the spirit of adventure, biologically speaking?" said that, though he'd knocked around a good deal and done things others considered adventure, he had never met it and wanted to know what it was anyhow.

The disease mentioned in the letter was the rare one that causes an Indian to turn white bit by bit. It figured in one of our stories by Kathrene and Robert Pinkerton and we've had other Camp-Fire testimony establishing it as a fact, though this is the first time any of us have vouched for it outside North America.

Mornington Island,
Via Burketown,
North Queensland, Australia.

My introduction to it was in this wise. Was having a bit of a spell in a military hospital, and at the time not feeling too fit for anything, not even reading, as the doctors had just finished having a little game with me. It was a Sunday morning and some ladies of the Red Cross had brought round some books. I did not feel like anything heavy and was going to decline any when one said, "I think you would like to read one of these." And *Adventure* was handed me. I read it and asked for more on the next Sunday and have been reading them ever since.

Our mails at this end of the country are very infrequent and irregular—we have to go for them about one hundred and thirty miles—and by last mail received four of your magazines.

I FEEL almost inclined to agree with your correspondent, Earl J. Teets, and ask "What is adventure?" Some would probably think my present position would be or hold adventure, but all I can say is life is very lonely and monotonous. Am acting superintendent of an Aboriginal Station. The natives murdered the former superintendent and attacked the station, the inmates barely escaping with their lives. The police came and arrested all concerned. I was rushed up and for past nine months have been alone, with exception of one other white, and he goes out this boat. Was here before the war and knew people and their ways and have got along very well with them.

Am always very interested in the stories of the Red Indians, but they are far ahead of these Australian aboriginals in nearly every respect. The disease described by Mr. Pinkerton is also known here. I thought it was leprosy at first and had a man examined for such.—N. A. PAULL.

WITH his first story in our magazine, William H. Pope, by Camp-Fire custom, stands up among us and gets us all acquainted with him:

Bradford, Arkansas.

I deem it a real honor to be allowed a seat by the Camp-Fire where I can stretch myself out and warm my adventure-loving spirit. At the same time I am honestly grieved that I have no fagot to contribute to its flames. However, here goes my best.

HAS a camp-follower ever been known to give advice to the commanding officer? If so, I can't recall the instance, and I don't think I should break the precedent by relating a series of trivial occurrences to a group of old-timers to whom the winding trails of the vast solitudes are open books.

I have never had a real adventure. Somehow, the spiced wine of romance, adventure and peril has flowed past and I have been unable to wet my lips. But I have that vague unrest of the mind, that insistent desire to crawl from beneath that irksome crust known as civilization and plunge into the heart of a land that is still as God made it—in short, the wanderlust, and some day I hope to give it free rein.

I HAVE bottled whisky enough to make an excellent swimming-pool—before Prohibition could walk without help, of course, and I have mixed concrete in the hottest months in the year in the hills of Kansas City. I have also railroaded a little (as a section-hand, thank you) and once had the temerity to laugh when one of my fellow-workers "shot" a spike he was driving which hit the section boss right where he lived, and the section boss was built like a wash-kettle, too!

I have flatheaded in the pine hills of Arkansas and listened to big pine logs crash through the underbrush, as they would do occasionally if you gave them a little push on the stony hillsides; and I have drifted from there to the bottom-lands and cut five- and six-foot oaks that jarred the ground when they fell.

AND the Brotherhood of the Brakebeam is not a mystery to me, for I have sat before a leaping fire in the hoboes' "jungles" and listened to some "blowed-in-the-glass" tell a colorful tale of an encounter with a bull or a shack. And I was once chased off a speeding train by a half-stewed brakie with a murderous gleam in his eye, and a still more murderous looking knife in his hand.

Then, too, I have hunted and fished for days at a time and had that pleasant experience of taking an indignant skunk out of a trap and the equally pleasant experience of dropping a rifle in eight feet of icy river-water one frosty morning in October and having to dive until I retrieved it.

Possibly the most hair-raising ordeal through which I have yet passed was getting married. But I am glad to add that my fright was short-lived.

I FIRST saw the light in the limestone hills of Tennessee and now make my home in the sandstone hills of Arkansas, and, while I have spent many years in the city, I have found the woods and fields better suited to my temperament. Rejected for the war because of physical deficiency, I tried to do my little bit by pulling a plowline over old Beck.

But some time in the dim future I am going to try my hand at a real adventure and, as I am only twenty-two, I think I'll get my chance.—WM. H. POPE.

A LETTER from a Chicago comrade that ought to make any real American with a white skin drop his eyes in shame:

Chicago.

I wish to thank Clyde B. Hough for his story, "Two Calls in the Jungle," which appears in the Mid-November copy of *Adventure*.

It is no secret that an overwhelming majority of the American whites seem over anxious to see only the evil side of the Negro race—which is no worse than the evils of another race—due I am sure to their ignorance of that race rather than from malice.

During the many parades witnessed in this city on several occasions I have heard the remark, "Look at the Crap Shooters" or "Look out for your chickens," and other disparaging remarks when our colored boys went by. On one occasion, when a troop train was going through Milwaukee this Summer, every one cheering and waving, a woman suddenly shouted, "Huh! it's nothing but niggers," at which the cheering stopped almost instantly as far as her voice carried.

It is with heart-felt gratitude that I have read the works of the one *White Man* who has shown the true character of the average American Negro, and again, I, a member of that race, thank him.—D. MAXEY.

Whatever other cities may have done I'm glad to say that New York, when our boys in khaki marched its streets before sailing for France, gave our colored troops a rousing welcome and salute. Indeed, all I happened to hear speak of it said the black Americans got louder cheers than any others that marched down Fifth Avenue. If Chicago jeered instead of cheered—well, as between a stay-at-home white man on the sidewalk or in a window and a going-to-the-war black man marching in the street, it seems to me that, before the white man does any jeering, he'd better figure to himself a whole lot as to whether the black man may not be a better man and a better American than he himself. Maybe he isn't, but the burden of proof lies on the man who is *not* offering his life for his country.

YES, we have our "race problem," and only fools take an extreme stand on either side, but April, 1917, gave us a still bigger problem to face. In that crisis we asked the black men to help fight for America and they responded as loyally as did the white men. More so than did large parts of our white citizenry.

I am glad a story in *Adventure* earns their thanks. And I am glad I have a chance, openly and publicly, to pay my personal respects, as an American, to their loyalty to a country that has treated them none too fairly and to their war service for a democracy that has given them only the scraps from its plate. The man who jeers those black soldiers ought to be knocked down in his tracks.

And if any narrow-minded fanatic will write me a brief word of condemnation for my attitude I'll take rich pleasure in telling him, fully and in very frank detail, my honest and glowing opinion of him—so far as the use of the mails permits.

IT MIGHT be a good plan for any American to find out what troops, at the outbreak of the war, when there were few places where disloyalty might not be found, were entrusted by the Government with the posts where utter loyalty was most essential.

Also, here is a point of view worth considering, from Mr. Hough:

Oakland, Calif.

When one compares the time since the negro, a ring in his nose, was yanked out of his native jungle, with the time that the white race has been in the process of civilization, one must admit that the negro has been traveling the road of progress in seven-league boots.—C. B. HOUGH.

I wrote to Mr. Maxey, expressing more briefly what I have said above, and asking permission to print his letter. I mentioned Captain, now Colonel, Rodney as having commanded colored Regulars and having a high opinion of them. Here is D. Maxey's reply, and I ask whether any one of you, white or black, high or low, could have brought to this matter a finer attitude of mind, a higher type of manliness, a more splendid patriotism or a keener realization of the individual citizen's duty to the people.

Chicago.

Knowing how much correspondence, sane and otherwise, to which you must attend, I call it rather good of you to reply to my letter concerning Mr. Hough's story.

The entire U. S. knows the attitude of Illinois to the negro in general, and your generous comment on the colored soldiers is doubly appreciated at a time when I have just left the open grave of a negro private, my brother—and helps take away the bitter resentment that it is only natural for me to feel.

Capt. Rodney was one of my favorite authors. If anything I have written can be made of use in any way, take it, and welcome, so long as it does not stir up the old race question, for I fully realize this is no time to start a personal feud when a world's safety is at stake.

Thanking you for your personal interest in the soldiers of my race, I remain—D. MAXEY.

LIKE the other three new members of our writers' brigade, William M. McCoy follows Camp-Fire custom and introduces himself:

Los Angeles, Cal.

I have to admit that there isn't much of interest about myself to tell. But I like the Camp-Fire, and not only want to do my share, but assuredly appreciate the opportunity to become more closely acquainted with *Adventure's* crew, so here goes:

AFTER looking over the field, I joined my parents at Booneville, Missouri, in 1882. The place had a good, adventurous name, but old Daniel had been dead for so long that things had quieted down. After hanging around for about a year, waiting for something to happen, I took my parents by the hand and led them to California—and have never been sorry. My people on both sides came to this country long before the Revolution, and they have always liked room, so sort of kept in front of the westward parade. Uncles and other relatives on both sides had preceded us to California, several having crossed the plains in '49.

Grew up on a ranch with dogs, horses, Chink cooks and most everything, including all the room in sight, with plenty more around the edges. Also numerous old plainsmen who had been a part of the days of '49 and all the days following, fine old chaps who are now only bright boyhood memories Learned to ride, shoot, and the kindred arts before I entered grammar school—such things were sort of requirements for admission to the school I attended.

SINCE then I have gone fishing, skinned mules, gone to college, ridden the range, reported for newspapers—night police in a wide-open town, and also politics—and perpetrated editorials for other newspapers, prospected, written stories, worked, received money for my stories, gone sailing, turned out a number of movies, and even when the daily snack of flour and beans has upon occasion decided to depart from my vicinity, I have always been able to get my rope on its hind leg before dark.

Adventures? Mine always have sort of sneaked up on me. If I had known they were coming I might have had a date elsewhere. Have seen a little violence and sudden death, wore a gun for some years, and out of the whole time it only saved my life once. And even that was the result of a mistake. A crew of peeved individuals had decided to dispense with the presence upon this earth of a certain person for whom they did not seem to care, and in the dark they inadvertently mistook me for this *hombre*.

AT ANOTHER time a forty-five caliber bullet got inside the crown of my hat. It didn't seem to stay long—sort of went on out the top in a hurry. But that wasn't the bothersome part; what bothered me was that the blasted hunk of lead had sort of snuggled up to my right temple and squeezed between my head and the sweatband of my hat to get into what what you might call my attic. After it was all over the boys claimed, of course, that when I saw that gun wink at me my hair stood up on end, lifting my hat so high that a brick could have been heaved clear through without touching anything but my brown tresses. It would be easier for me to see the joke in this, if it were not for the fact that from that day on I have had to wear very strong and expensive glasses. Any man who is dependent upon a bit of glass in order to see knows there is no joke in it.

I HAVE been thrown off of horses in all sorts of places, and in the most undignified manner, and have gotten myself into trouble in several languages. Have been over, around and through thousands of miles of desert, the Rockies and the Sierras. Once I wanted to prove that I was born to be hung—that's what the crew said—and got swept overboard at sea. Another time, when I had wandered away off the range, I got extra reckless and got married in Boston. But that isn't why I crossed the Klondike Hills in the desert while the Coyotes, a crew of outlaws, wanted for eleven murders, were holed up there. I had approached the Klondikes from the Devil's Playground country, hadn't seen a soul, and didn't know the Coyotes were about until after I had safely finished the job.

If I have any hobbies they are sailing on salt water, fishing in fresh water, dogs, mountains and folks. I like all the "ings" except working. Have tried repeatedly to persuade my Uncle Sam to let me fight, but he won't let me have my whack at ole Tin Bill. I am now expecting to be sent over-seas in the transportation and post exchange department of the "Y." I'm going to have a share in the great adventure some way.—WILLIAM M. McCOY.

ANOTHER definition of the spirit of adventure, from some one whom most of us consider an authority:

St. Louis, Mo.

I have watched for all the replies to Edgar Young's interesting query, "What is the spirit of adventure, particularly in its biological aspects?" But here is one that takes the cake. It is not my own but that of a great adventurer:

"THE history of civilization is the history of wandering, sword in hand, in search of food. In the misty younger world we catch glimpses of phantom races, rising, slaying, finding food, building rude civilizations, decaying, falling under the swords of stronger hands, and passing utterly away. Man, like any other animal, has roved over the earth seeking what he might devour; *not romance and adventure, but the hunger-need*, has *urged him on his vast adventures*. Whether a bankrupt gentleman failing to colonize Virginia or a lean Cantonese contracting to labor on the sugar plantations of Hawaii, in each case, gentleman and coolie, it is a desperate attempt to get something to eat, to get more to eat than he can get at home.

"It has always been so from the time of the first pre-human anthropoid crossing a mountain divide in quest of better berry bushes beyond, down to the latest Slovak, arriving on our shores today, to go to work in the coal mines of Pennsylvania."

Here is the spirit of adventure in its true light, with all the romance and glamour taken off, written by that greatest of all adventurers, Jack London.—FRED. K. SCHWALM.

AS HE'D said something in a letter about suhuara ribs and I didn't know enough to understand, I asked Alex. McLaren for more information. He kindly gives it in the following letter which will interest others than myself. Also something about our old pet the Gila monster.

Ruby, Arizona.

I will attempt to elucidate—on suhuara ribs. The suhuara (pronounced *soo-war-a*, *a* as in and) is the giant or sometimes called "Club Cactus," and in its infancy is sometimes referred to as "Niggerhead." They grow to a height sometimes exceeding twenty feet, and set one to wondering, after chopping one down, how it is it offers so much resistance to the strong desert winds and so little to the ax. And they are not deep-rooted, either; I have often seen them clinging to a mere crevice in a vertical wall of rock.

A CROSS-SECTION of one shows it to be made up as follows. We will assume the cross-section to be eighteen inches in diameter. The outside, a corrugated circle or circle of corrugations, dark green in color, the apex of each of the corrugations (which run parallel to the line of growth) is covered with a row of spines (not intended to sit on) from the bottom to the very top. The outside is covered with about two inches of spines, corrugations and pithy matter, which, when dried has a fibrous appearance, but when growing is mostly water. Beneath that two inches and forming a complete circle is a row of ribs. These ribs (I daresay they can be classed as wood) are about one and one-half inches in diameter at butt, tapering like a fish-pole to nothing at top, and are interlocked with each other at intervals of a couple of feet for near their entire length, on about the same plan as our ribs interlock in the breast. Inside of this "palisade" of ribs is a mass of pithy pulp. The ribs when dry somewhat resemble rattan in porosity but are not near as flexible.

THE suhuara bear what I think is a very delicious fruit, much sought after by the Indians. The squaws gather it and often I have seen them with a couple of "ribs" spliced together pulling it down, from the top of the cactus where it grows, on to skins spread below on the ground. It resembles and tastes very much like a fig.

When the cactus dies, and after a year or so in the desert sun, the only substantial part left is the ribs. The Mexicans and Indians use them in building their mud *jacals* (*ha-kals*, shacks), in the construction of which they play much the same part as nature allotted them in the suhuara, viz.:—reinforcing bars.

Are also used in light fencing and have even seen them used in mining as "lagging." And the old desert prospector invariably uses one as a cane and burro persuader.

THE word *suhuara* is of Indian origin and, I think, Apache or Papago. And at the time I encountered the Gila monster (pronounced *hee-la*) I was using one as a cane or alpenstock. I am sorry I can not now get hold of one Gila monster to skin and send you, but I will yet, and the color you can see for yourself.

They are not so overly plentiful, but a person who knocks about the desert and mountains as much as I do runs on to them occasionally. I had often heard what deadly enemies the rattler and the Gila were, so for my own information I once caught one of each and placed them together in a box covered with wire netting, for observation.

Mr. Rattler, a large "diamond back," got off in one corner and Mr. Gila in the other and no effort of ours could induce them to notice each other. Next morning, however, on looking in the box we found both were dead. How they worked it I can not say, but neither one was chewed up, and they were lying in opposite corners of the box.

I HAVE taken the liberty of enclosing a few photographs, inasmuch as some of them bear on people and places I have seen mentioned in Camp-Fire. These places may have their dangers, privations and inconveniences but believe me, partner, I would not give them, with the solitude, quiet, and in turn, adventure they offer, for the Biltmore, Fifth Avenue with its gay throng, Broadway with its clanging of bells and blaze of lights, Riverside Drive, Central Park and the Bronx, with their artificial sylvan effects, pretty nursemaids and perambulators, etc.

But then, every coyote picks his own range or "*Cada maestro tenga sus libros.*" Of course I have punched cattle, hunted and mined all of my life, and one can't find room for the East although a couple years since I did try to negotiate a mining deal on a property within three hours' ride of where you are probably sitting reading this. That was at Roxbury, Conn., up on the Litchfield branch, on an old property with a rich historic as well as mineral value, but then that has naught in common with Gila monsters or a suhuara.

I AM now camped opening up a gold-silver property just a mile from the Mexican line near Casa Piedra, where the little skirmish took place, just below the Montana Mine, and very near (as distances in this country are reckoned) to Arivaca where Edwin C. Dickinson was stationed when he got the "dope" for "To Quit My Post," which appeared in *Adventure*. I am very familiar with Arivaca and want to go on record in saying the points mentioned in the story fit that little place in every respect, and I don't think, if there is any contention, that it would be very difficult for me to find "*Nita*," as I have been told by Mexicans of a girl whose life's story would not need editing to cast her for the part.—ALEX. MCLAREN.

P. S.—The suhuara bears the credit for having saved the life of more than one desert prospector from death by thirst. The scheme, I believe, is to tap it about five feet from bottom. Hang the canteen, then light a fire at butt. Heat, I believe, causes expansion or ebullition of sap and it oozes into canteen. I have tasted it and I guess "any port in a storm" is the prescription it is used to fill. Take my word, it is sickening in taste. Not Burgundy by any means.—MAC.

THREE more of our comrades have left us. Ira South, poet, died in the Marine Hospital at Portsmouth, Virginia, of broncho-pneumonia. Thomas Clarity, an artist who has done some of our covers, also died in a military training camp. Charles Campbell Jones, poet, died in Kansas City of blood-poisoning. Our salute to them, standing, and may the Long Trail be soft under their feet.

Two died for our country as truly as if they had stopped a German bullet in France. The third, run over by an engine eleven years ago, paralyzed from the waist down, could not die for his country, but he lived for his fellow-men. "I'll never write the kind of stuff that adds to human misery, or if I do I'll tear it up." And Charles C. Jones lived up to that. From his invalid's bed came only words that were brave, cheery, strong, sweet with a man's sweetness.

"I AM somewhat of an adventurer myself." Many a letter to us begins with that sentence and often "somewhat" is a very mild word for the case. In the following letter, "somewhat" is the right word, yet, even so, the writer of it is a kind of "fireside adventurer" in butterflies. If his own expeditions are gentle ones, at least, by his exchanges with them, he shares a bit in the adventures of those other collectors whose butterflies are brought in from lands where butterfly-catching is often enough a matter of life and death.

Brookline, Mass.

I am somewhat of an adventurer myself. Not among wild and dangerous beasts or in far-off lands, but right here in the New England States, among butterflies. In short, I am interested during my spare hours in making a collection of butterflies, and so far have been able to gather together several thousand of species.—JASPER STEWART, 103 Abbotsford Road.

No, chasing butterflies in New England doesn't come under the head of "perils by land and sea." But neither do the pursuits of many of us, and, if I may join in our Camp-Fire discussion about adventure and the spirit of adventure, I'm one of those who believe that the quiet places of the world have their risks and excitements. Perhaps adventure is only a break in monotony and altogether a matter relative to a particular case. One thing seems sure —it's quite an adventure to attempt to define adventure.

WHILE already known to us at Camp-Fire, especially as one of those who compiled for us "Firearms, Old and New," D. Wiggins, on the occasion of his first story in our magazine, follows custom and stands up to tell us about himself. He wrote his "talk" to us while he was still in the Army and before the armistice was signed.

Camp Lewis, Amer. Lake, Wash.

This letter is perforce a hurried one, as I am writing at the Top Sergeant's desk, and he may return ere I can fade.

Yes, I'm in. Company Mechanic for Arms of the "Suicide Club"; the Machine Gun Co. of the 75th Infantry is my home.

Born on Boot Hill, Dodge City, Kansas, thus inheriting thirst for blood and iron. Schooling slight; reading various, and no favorites played. Kansas, Nebraska, California, Oklahoma Territory and Oregon in turn have been honored? by my residence. Now facing the Greater Adventure "Over There." Will send Iron Cross with .45 through center to you after march down Unter der Linden. That's all of importance.—D. WIGGINS.

THE writer of the following wrote his particular admiration for the story in question, but being a loyal "gun fan," duty impels him to take issue on one point:

Baltimore, Md.

Apropos *Lerch's* Luger pulling to the left; this was not caused by the mechanism being "jolted a little out of alignment," as Mr. A. J. Hayes suggests in his splendid story ("Sirgarkh Rubies"), as the jolting of the mechanism would not cause the gun to throw out of true. The function of the mechanism is to start the ball by firing the cartridge, but the barrel takes care of its flight. The gun pulling to the left was caused by one of the two following ways:

ONE was that, when *San Kee* threw *Lerch* off the Sacred Parapet, he fell with the Luger under his right side, his weight falling on it so suddenly as to bend the barrel only slightly, not so as to be noticeable when looking at the weapon, but sufficiently to cause it to throw to the left when shooting at fifty yards or more.

The other and more likely cause was that *Lerch*, being in a sandy country, in some way or other got a little sand in the toe of his holster (probably scooped it up when he was thrown), which settled toward the right side, causing a slight wear on the lands, on that side of the barrel. Now when a ball is fired, it leaves the firing-chamber and is gripped by the lands, which give to it its rotary motion, spinning it straight, and to do this the lands at the end of the barrel must be micrometically even, so that when the bullet leaves the muzzle all the lands let go at exactly the same time and, if this is done, the ball is steered true on its course, while if the lands are not even, the course will not hold true, for no rifle or pistol is any truer or more accurate than the lands at the end of the barrel warrant it to be, these at this point giving the ball its parting direction. Assuming, then, that *Lerch's* gun had the lands worn on the right side of the barrel, these would let go the ball an infinitesimal part of a second before the lands on the left side let go, which would cause the ball to be blown to the left, or, as we would off-handedly say, "the gun pulled a little to the left."

IT IS a great pity Mr. Hayes allowed *Lerch* to die, which caused the loss of the rubies. His kind is too scarce. I wish he might write a sequel; having *Foy San* recover the remains of *Lerch* and *Muriel McAllen* and, with the aid of his herbs and ointments, revive them for purposes of revenge, and then *Lerch*, with his crafty mind, outwit him, escape with the girl and the rubies, and a fitting end would have him plant a shot from the good Luger between the eyes of *Foy San*.—WM. E. MEPHAM.

As we know now, there can be no sequel to the story, since Arthur James Hayes has given his life for his country.

ARTHUR SULLIVANT HOFFMAN.

KIT CARSON—Carson of Taos, that name alone is sufficient to ensure interest in Hugh Pendexter's novel in this issue. It's been a good while since most of us have read anything about this hero of our boyhood and it is good to see him again with man's eyes—and perhaps surprising to realize that he wasn't just an Indian killer but among the chief of those who hewed our nation out of the wild.

Norway, Maine.

The date of the story is 1838, middle of the period when Carson was hunter for Bent's Fort. He was trapper for eight years, hunter at Bent's for eight years, and then guide for Frémont, engaged in Mexican War, Indian agent, Indian fighter, with spasmodic attempts at farming.

Norway, Maine.

ACCORDING to the calendar history of the Kiowa, as given by James Mooney, in 14th Annual Rept. B. A. E. the first Winter count, 1832-33, is designated, "Winter they captured the money," and refers to Lame-old-man's coup in capturing a large quantity of silver coins from a small band of Missourians after a fight close to the South Canadian, near the present town of Lathrop, in the Panhandle. The Kiowas lost Black Wolf and killed several Americans. Ignorant of money, they wore it in their hair and called it *adalhangya*, "hair-metal." The white men had ten thousand dollars in specie packed on mules. Swung off the main trail and followed the Canadian to escape the Indians.

IN 1856 a border desperado (according to Abbott's "Life of Carson," also given in D. C. Peter's "Pioneer Days and Frontier Adventure") by the name of Fox plotted to murder Messrs. Brevoort and Weatherhead, who were bound for the States with a large sum of money to be used in purchasing goods. Fox organized the escort which was to "protect" the traders. Before starting from Santa Fé he visited Taos, Carson's home, to recruit a certain desperado. The man refused to go, but said nothing until the party was well under way, then blabbed. Carson decided the killing would occur on the Cimarron, between two and three hundred miles east of Taos. Inside an hour, accompanied by a small band of employees, he took the trail. Overtook the party, drove thirty-five desperadoes from camp and brought Fox back to Taos, where he was kept in prison for some time.

These two widely separated facts suggested "Carson of Taos."

THE item in the *Missouri Intelligencer* is not mentioned in Abbott's and others' writings about Carson. They state he had a chance to join a wagon train and travel to Santa Fé. As a matter of fact he was "bound out" to the saddler at the time, and, seeing an opportunity, he simply "shoved." According to a brief article on Carson in Vol. 80 *Century Magazine* (author's name I can not, unfortunately, recall), Carson's remark about making Indians run after him, etc., was made by him when an army officer of high rank met him at Maxwell's ranch on the Cimarron and said, "What, the great Kit Carson, who has made so many, etc."

THE Red Jaguar is drawn after a description of the infamous bandit, Espinosa, as given by Colonel Henry Inman in his "Old Santa Fé Trail." Espinosa killed his sister's American sweetheart and fled to the Sangre de Cristo Mountains. He was killed by Tom Tobin, a noted trapper, in 1864. Tobin trailed him single-handed and shot him down and brought his head in a gunny-sack to old Fort Massachusetts, later Fort Garland. Colonel Inman did not believe Tobin ever received the reward offered for the bandit's head. Espinosa's career lasted for nearly ten years.

WILLIAM WILLIAMS is described in all works I have examined dealing with the old frontier days. He was a Methodist minister in Missouri before taking to the plains. He lived with many tribes, knew many dialects, was better acquainted with the Rocky Mountains than any man in the West. Colonel Inman says his knowledge of the Rockies was never surpassed until Jim Bridger reached the height of his career. Williams' name is alive today on mountain pass and streams. He believed he was to turn into a buck-elk at death and begged his friend not to shoot the animal he was at pains to describe. Frémont nearly lost his life when Williams acted as his guide, some claiming the old man was in his dotage. Colonel Inman says, however, that old mountain men contended that had Frémont followed Williams' advice he would not have lost three men and his papers and instruments in trying to cross the mountains from the source of the Arkansas in dead Winter. According to the old-timers he warned Frémont it could scarcely be done, but was ignored, and a novice allowed to guide the party.

THE Osage stole the Kiowa *taime* in the Summer of 1833. No sun-dance was held that Summer because of this loss. The medicine was subsequently ransomed by Dohasan, greatest of the Kiowa chiefs. The Osage did not scalp those killed when they got the *taime*, but after their fashion beheaded them and left the heads in the brass buckets the Kiowas had procured in trade from the Pawnees.

In the Summer of 1868 the Utes captured the "man" and "bear" *taime*. Setdaya-ite (Many-Bears), nephew of Ansote, carried them on a warpath. Hornless-Bull, his friend, went with him, each carrying an image. A skunk, a taboo, crossed their path at the start. Their Comanche scouts had little mirrors, another taboo, and afterward killed and ate a bear. Many warriors turned back, knowing their medicine was spoiled. Only thirty Utes, yet they won. Both Many-Bears and the Bull were killed.

The Utes experienced misfortunes after this victory and grew afraid of the medicine. The two images were given to Maxwell, on the Cimarron, and stood on his shop shelf for a long time. Then they disappeared and the Kiowas never got them back.

HEART-EATER was wounded in the leg in a Winter attack (1838-39) against the Arapaho. *Young Mexico* is patterned after Charlie Bent, the educated half-breed who "went wrong."

The incident of a warrior rescuing a boy by carrying him in his teeth, in Chapter Four, was inspired by the feat being performed by a Kiowa warrior when the Osage massacred the village in 1833, when stealing the *taime*.

Heart-Eater's boast about the legging fringe of finger-bones is the reflection of the fact that a noted Apache war-chief, called Chico Velasques by the Mexicans, boasted such ornaments, one leg being trimmed with bones of Mexican victims, the other by American victims.

Once Carson was in council with some Indians and smoked with them. Then the chief said in Spanish that he was to be killed "the next time he takes the pipe." Carson thoroughly understood Spanish, learning it when a youth from old Kin Cade, famous mountain man, and was on his guard.

"O sun, you remain forever, etc.," the death-song of the Kaitsenko, was sung by Setangya (Sitting Bear), famous Kiowa chief and medicine man, when he was killed in trying to escape after being arrested for attacking a wagon train in Texas.

Ansote, "Long Foot," was fifth keeper of the *taime*, holding office for forty years, or until his death in 1870.

YAPAHE, "Warriors," resembled other military organizations of various Plains tribes, known to whites often as Dog-soldiers, but more elaborate than those found in other tribes. There were six grades, or societies, going to make up the Yapahe. The first was the *Polanyup*, "Rabbits," composed of boys from eight to ten years old. Their dance imitated the skipping and jumping of a rabbit. This left five grades for military service. Each grade had its own songs and dances. Grades two, three, four, five, varied little in rank, but the Kaitsenko (also given as K'oitsenko), grade six, limited to ten picked men, was the highest military position a warrior could attain. Owing to his vow never to retreat unless his warriors pulled up the arrow that anchored him to his position, a member of this grade was pledged to death on every warpath where the arrow was carried. The arrow was carried only when it was intended to fight to a finish. The leader chosen to carry the arrow was only an ordinary warrior when going out to fight without it. It was permissible to loan the arrow to a brave eager to prove his courage. In that case the owner stayed at home. But if a decisive battle was to be fought the owner of the arrow was disgraced and branded as a coward if he failed to carry the arrow.

LITTLE can be said of Carson that is not already known to the reader. In an old geography my father studied when a boy everything from the western border of Missouri to the Rockies is marked, "Great American Desert." Zebulon Pike did not cause the myth to vanish, nor does Irving's account of the Astors dispel the false belief, if I remember his chronicles correctly. Carson traveled this "desert" and found it filled with game and Indians, with teeming rivers and rich lands.

Carson, it is claimed by border historians, possessed the confidence of the western Indians to a greater extent than any other man, with the possible exception of General William Clark. He was one of the first to urge that the red man be taught to cultivate the soil and live on farms. Our Indian policy, wherever it has improved and progressed, has followed his suggestions in a general way. He lived in the time of giants, and was distinguished even above such men as the Bents, St. Vrain, Jim Bridger, Ewing Young, Fitzpatrick, Williams, Maxwell, and a host of other Empire-builders.

THE Kiowas differentiated between Texans and Americans, as they believed the former to be of a different nationality. Their name for Texans, *Tehaneko*, was derived from the Spanish *Tejano*. They incessantly made war on the Texans, even when professing friendship to Americans. The Civil War cemented this old belief, for the Texans were fighting against the North, i. e. Americans.—PENDEXTER.

THIS letter from a comrade who gives neither name or address but opens up a few large, fat questions. So far as American newspapers are concerned the Mexican border has been removed from the map for nearly two years. The lid will be off before this sees print, but go to it easy.

Can't some fellow around the Camp-Fire throw some light on this subject? I've been through lots of the West—Utah, Colorado, Idaho, Nevada, Montana, Wyoming, Northern Arizona, but I've never been along the Border. Not long ago a guy came along and told me the Border was still tough in some parts. Rustlers, killers and the like. The toughest things I ever found were a bunch of greasers trying to kick up a revolution or some such thing. A bunch of cavalry hove in sight. Greasers vamoosed *muy pronto*. What was he? Loco or a —— liar?—A COMRADE.

A WORD from William M. McCoy concerning his story in this issue:

Los Angeles, Cal.

The idea for "Limpin' Bob" grew out of what I learned while associating with a number of old prospectors in the Shadow Mountains. *Limpin' Bob* is not drawn from one man, but is a sort of combination. I like to build my characters that way, taking suggestions from this man's life and that man's experience, etc. But he comes nearer being old Joe, whose picture I am also enclosing, than he does any other one man.

I took this snapshot of Joe one Sunday; you will note that he is all dressed up. I worked with him in developing the Desert Dolly Mine, and no matter how long the day, or how tired we were, he shaved every evening and cleaned up. On Sunday he became the dude of the camp, in clean overalls, shirt, and a sacred black hat. Old Joe is "queer" about a lot of things—but anything on earth would be safe in his keeping, if dog-faithfulness and plain, unvarnished honor could make it safe. There is a good deal of his story in "Limpin' Bob."

The other snapshot is of myself, taken last December, beside the monument on the Desert Dolly claim. The altitude there is nearly five thousand feet, and in Winter it is cold—in Summer it isn't, and in Summer there is no water—and all the year there is cactus and yucca as far as two men can see. Several of us thought we had the world by the tail when we discovered the Desert Dolly, but if we had, the tail broke off in our hands.—WILLIAM M. MCCOY.

FOLLOWING Camp-Fire custom, Mrs. Grace P. T. Knudson stands up and introduces herself on the occasion of her first story in our magazine. You will note that she has had her full share of adventures.

Castine, Maine.

Though born in the small town of Castine, Maine, now my Summer home, I am familiar with many of the larger cities and towns, and some hamlets, of the world. In the course of natural human events I have three times circled the globe; have claimed residence in the Philippines fourteen years; made five trips to Japan; browsed in Hawaii, Borneo and Ceylon; been seasick in all oceans but the Arctic and Antarctic—and in this connection have a special intimacy with the China Sea, having been obliged to cross it numberless times. Also, I have been homesick on every continent but Australia and South America. Whether this is all because I was "born with two crowns" or of a race of seamen I have never satisfactorily determined.

IN THE aforesaid course of events I have taught school, done newspaper and publicity work and been a business woman. Much of my wandering was in the last connection and along the line of searching for and buying oddities and art goods for sale in this country.

My most extended adventure was ninety days from Manila to New York on the old British tramp *Melbourne*, in company with one other young woman. The casualties were a fire in the hemp with which the vessel was loaded, and a set of disabled boilers while in the Indian Ocean.

My most interesting business experience was a partnership with a white Chinaman—name forgotten—in Cagayan de Misimas, Mindanao. We underbid a native Filipino who was starving the provincial prisoners on a contract to feed them. There were some two hundred in the jail at the time. We fed them up a year. Then the old native recaptured the contract by underbidding us, one-fourth a *centavo* per head, and our partnership was dissolved.

PERHAPS the most thrilling moments—to me—of any one adventure were when I stood alone in a ravine on the top of Mount Apo, the highest peak of the Philippines, struggling with the conviction that the other two white members of our party had been murdered. Four thousand feet above the limit of habitation, I felt myself to be at the mercy of sixteen pagans who had mutinied in camp the night before. After twenty minutes of waiting, unable to stand the strain of further suspense, I went forward to meet whatever fate was to befall. A long, long hike of another twenty minutes, and I came upon my people hunting for me. They had merely lost the trail.—GRACE P. T. KNUDSON.

FROM one of the many of us who, after being real adventurers, have now joined the fireside contingent:

New Hamburg, Ontario.

I have at last decided to do what I have felt like doing for a long time, and that is to put in my word at the Camp-Fire. I've been a listener for a good many years.

You can see by my letter-head that I am no longer in the adventure class. I am married and settled down, and all the adventure I get now is out of your magazine.

But I've had my share of the real thing, although nothing to be compared to some. My partner and I were among the first to hit Cobalt and came near hitting higher at the time of the explosion. Since then I've traveled over most of Canada and the States. Beat my way over most of British Columbia, Montana and Washington on the bumpers, worked in lumber-camps for seven Winters, rode the ranch and even herded sheep, but not long enough to go crazy.

But now I'm a quite inoffensive business man with a wife and kid and take myself back to old times with *Adventure* and Camp-Fire.—RALPH R. GRIBBLE.

SOME five or six years ago, when our Camp-Fire was just starting, I asked some of the men who were giving us our stories in those days to tell us rather fully about their own adventures. Some of these got published; one or two, because of those famous "exigencies of space," never saw print. Here is Talbot Mundy's; with his present series of stories now running in our magazine, it has an added interest.

Since it was written he has, as you know, become an American citizen and a very good one, spending most of his time in Maine but now in New York again, and adding no chapters to the record of his outland adventures.

It happens very seldom in a man's life that he gets the opportunity to talk about himself to the people who are going to read his stories; and it happens still less frequently that he can do it without his victim's being able to talk back. So I'm going to make the most of this. Sit still, and suffer!

The Camp-Fire

Why shouldn't a man talk about himself? I know when I read a story I always wonder whether the writer of it has lived through the fear and the joy and the various mixed emotions that he portrays, or whether he is only guessing. If I know that he has seen it all, or something very like it, I enjoy the story; otherwise I don't. And I dare say I am not at all unusual in that respect.

STANDING at my own grave-side, and looking down into the grave that had been dug for me, was what actually started me at the writing game. Though I did not actually begin just at that time, it put the notion into my head that some of my experiences might make valuable copy. I made the usual beginner's mistake at first of writing the bald narrative of what had happened, instead of inventing new episodes and fitting men I had met into them.

Naturally nobody wanted to read the unvarnished experiences of a rolling stone, strung into paragraphs but quite devoid of plot; in fact the only excuse for talking about them now is to prove that I know more or less what I write about, for a man who has knocked about the world for fifteen years or so without getting rich has very little to boast of.

But I was born with a thirst for adventure, or at all events I developed it at a very early age; and along with it came an insatiable passion for finding out how people would act under given circumstances. For instance, one of the earliest things I can remember is sticking a pin into a man to find out what he would do; and what he did to me was a very small matter when compared to the satisfaction of finding out something for myself.

My people destined me for the church or the law, I forget which, but I know they gave me the choice of two evils and that I chose a third that they never even dreamed of. They cut off supplies to enforce obedience, and I went without supplies—to Germany. The method of choosing my destination was my own idea, though I have no doubt that many people have used it before and since; but it is so delightfully simple and devoid of detail, and I have used it with desirable results so frequently, that it is worth mentioning.

THE plan is to first count all your money and then, by consulting railway time-tables and shipping lists, to find out just how far it will take you in any direction. Then put just so much of a map of the world on the table as your money will cover, shut your eyes and make a jab at the map with something sharp. Make a note of the town or village nearest to where the pricker lands, and go there without further argument. My pricker landed on a place called Quedlinburg in the Harz Mountains, and I arrived there a couple of days later with an English five-shilling piece in my pocket, a fox-terrier dog on a leash, and a portmanteauful of clothes somewhere on the line behind me. I have often wondered who got the portmanteau.

There was a sort of mechanic person in Quedlinburg just then; his job was driving a traction engine that towed some vans belonging to a circus. He talked tolerable English, and, as I couldn't talk German, I was glad to make friends with him. He had only two ambitions. One was to keep his job, and the other was to get drunk—very drunk, and very often. I helped him to satisfy one of them the first night with my five shillings. The next morning he gave me a job. In future I was to drive the engine and he was to drink the beer; I was to get ten marks a week from the proprietor and eight more from him, but on the other hand I was to do all the work, take all the blame if anything went wrong, and sleep under the engine in all weathers, so as to be "Johnny on the spot," so to speak.

It turned out to be a good job, and I liked it, and I found out all there was to know about that traction engine in a very short time. We had a steam roundabout and swings and boxing-booths, and some wild animals in cages along with the circus; in fact, it was almost a traveling fair. My job at night was to drive the dynamo that was fixed on to the front of the engine, and I used to sit up on the driver's seat and watch the crowd and absolutely revel in the noise and glamor and confusion.

BUT one day my mechanic friend got more than usually drunk and killed my dog; and he got the worst of the battle royal that followed. Of course that ended our gentleman's agreement and I had to quit; and I tried my luck from end to end of Germany after that, working at any sort of job I could get, and usually hungry.

I got a good job at last—back close to Quedlinburg where I started. But it seems that in this extraordinary world a good job always has a handle to it; you've got to give your whole time and thought and energy to your boss. I was hired distinctly on those terms, and I made good, but I didn't like it. A man back in England happened to hear that I had made good and hired me at a salary that was absolutely enormous for a boy of seventeen, but on absolutely the same stipulation.

My new employer had a peculiarity that is not at all uncommon among men of his type in England; he loved buying expensive hunters, but he had not always the nerve to ride them; so quite a large part of my duties consisted in riding his hunters for him three days a week or so during the season. Besides being splendid sport and keeping me in excellent condition, the experience gave me a knowledge of horsemanship and wood-craft that has been invaluable since. I piled up money, though, because I hadn't a chance to spend it. As a matter of fact I piled up too much money, and that, and the fact that I was barely twenty-one and that my job had grown monotonous, got me going with the map of the world and the sticker again.

This time, though, I could afford steamboat fares, so I hadn't got to cut the map. I had the whole wide world to choose from at random, and the compass point came down bang in the middle of India. I asked my employer whether he hadn't any kind of pull that would secure me a job in that country, and, as good luck would have it, he had; he secured me a sort of hybrid Government job in a Native State, and I started off for India feeling something as Alexander must have done.

The first thing I saw in India was a bullock-cart loaded up with corpses—legs and arms sticking out from every side of it, and a fetid mixture of flies and aroma floating up above. That looked good to me; I thought that maybe I might really get interested before long, and I left Bombay with a heart full of hope and a boxful of Kipling's books in the railway carriage with me. Plague, of course, was the cause of the corpses in the bullock-cart; they were on their way to be disposed of at the burning-ghat; and, though I hadn't bargained for it, I had to spend the next fifteen months fighting plague and cholera and famine in turn—single-handed a good part of the time—in a temperature in the shade of anything from one hundred and twelve upward.

The only compensation that made the job in any way worth while was the pig-sticking; that, and fox-hunting, are the two finest land sports in the world, and I got nearly all I wanted of it, though I could not always get away. There was a sort of permanent tent club not far away; it was the one common meeting ground for the white men scattered through the district, and when the morning's sport was over and we were lounging under the double flies I had the privilege of talking to some of the most interesting men I have ever met—men who were giving up their lives out of absolutely unselfish devotion to their country.

I FOUND out no end of things of course, and it was very interesting, but I can't say that I enjoyed it. No doubt the impression that the experience made on me has come in very useful since, but I don't like to think about the details for very long at a time; the sight of all those thousands of people, good decent people, too, for the most part, rotting to death from various causes and suffering unspeakably would be likely to have a sobering effect on any one. The worst part of it was being able to do so little for them.

I went down pretty badly from malaria and overwork, and a sort of temperamental nausea, so when the plague had retired under cover and the famine had lessened sufficiently to give the Government time to breathe, I asked to be relieved, and another man was sent to take my job. I could have had another job straight away had I wanted it; but I had a sort of notion that I had been deep down into hell, and I had no desire just then to take the trip again. The prospect of a trip to Europe with a pocketful of money was much more alluring, and off to Europe I went to luxuriate and loaf and breathe clean cool air for six months.

But six months of Europe are enough for anybody at one time, and I soon got hungry for India again, for, after all, I had seen only a little corner of it, and that from only one point of view. This time I was lucky enough to arrange with a big firm of publishers to act as their occasional correspondent, and I walked on board the P. & O. steamer at Tilbury docks with the idea firmly planted in my head that I was going to set the Thames on fire at last. I didn't do it, of course; but I had a durned hard try.

A little native war broke out almost directly after I landed, and on the strength of the credentials I had with me I hadn't very much difficulty getting to the front as a sort of junior war correspondent. My word! When I walked out of the Government office at last with the signed permit in my pocket I wouldn't have traded jobs with anybody in all the wide world! I could see fame in the offing already, and fortune coupled to it. Even now I would rather make a reputation as a war correspondent than in any other way, so you can imagine what I felt like then with what looked like the chance in front of me. I remember I felt awfully sorry for all the unfortunate writer-men who hadn't got my opportunity.

But I started in to make a whole lot too much of the opportunity. The thing wasn't so good as I thought it was anyhow, and besides that I was much too keen. The General commanding the British forces was enjoying his first experience of the war game too; he hadn't felt his feet yet, and he didn't believe in war correspondents on any terms; but he particularly didn't want anybody there to criticize him during the early stages of the campaign. Of course his objection was perfectly natural under the circumstances, but it didn't suit me; he issued an order forbidding any one to leave the lines after dark, or at any time without permission; and as he never once gave his permission I disobeyed the order. Or, at least, he said I disobeyed the order.

WHAT actually happened was this. I kept pestering him for permission to visit the advanced posts, and he kept on refusing; and each time he refused he did it more violently and with less command of his temper. At last one afternoon I was particularly insistent, and he turned round and told me to "go to ——!" Well, I took that for verbal permission to go just where I pleased; a fellow can't go to —— until he knows where it is, and I set out to find it.

I didn't get back to camp until two hours after dawn the following morning because a Ghoorka picket happened to hear me, and they amused themselves by firing volleys at me at intervals from midnight onward, and I had to wait until the mist lifted and they could see who I was. I hid behind a rock, but they made awfully good shooting in the dark, and chipped pieces off the rock all round me. Even when you know you can't be hit, the experience of being fired at is not pleasant, and it is still less so when you are wet through and shivering with cold.

So I lay there and tried to console myself with the knowledge that I had secured some quite important information. It was important, too, because the General pumped me dry and made use of it. But he didn't say thank you. He censored my despatches out of existence, and ordered me back to the base for disobedience to orders. And back to the base I had to go, having seen both the beginning and the end of my career as war correspondent within a month.

I went tiger-shooting after that; and then on a trip up to Afghanistan, though I hadn't gone very far over the Himalayas before the Government turned me back. I had come to the conclusion by that time that the Government of India was a pretty difficult outfit to fool, so I had a look at China and Singapore and the Straits Settlements and gave them time to forget me. I thought that wouldn't take long. Then I took a trip up the Persian Gulf on a tramp steamer with a black skipper; we broke down half-way up the Gulf, and then I really did know what —— was like. On that trip I saw oxen being fed on dried fish. It sounds improbable, but I saw it with my two eyes.

I cooked up a gorgeous scheme then for a trip with another man up through India to Siberia, but the South-African war broke out and that put quite another complexion on things. Of course I hadn't seen anything like the whole of India; a man couldn't do that in a life-time. But I had seen and got to know Tommy Atkins at his best, and the men who lead Tommy Atkins "when the guns wheel into line," and my head was already cramfull of facts and fragments of facts that have since formed the foundation for such stories as "The Phantom Battery." If I have the ill-luck to live a hundred years, and keep on writing all the time, I may be able to exhaust half the stories that I know I can write about India; and though I have dived down deep into it, and seen it from several points of view, I know no more of it than a crab knows of the ocean. India is some country.

The Camp-Fire

I WASN'T tired of it yet by any means; in fact I have always meant to go back there again some day; but for the present there was a real live war to go to, and there were quite a lot of men in India besides myself who imagined that war was the one big picnic that should on no account be missed; so we made quite a strong regiment. We spent our own money on accouterments, and landed in Africa with only one regret among the lot of us—that it wasn't going to be a real war. It seemed to us an awful pity that such a fine regiment as we were should be wasted on a coconut-shy campaign against an enemy that hadn't any cavalry. We were cavalry—to begin with.

Barring a few prisoners, and mighty few of those, I never saw a live Boer the whole time. The picnic consisted for the most part of lying in the rain and being fired at, or lying in the scorching sun and being fired at. The rations were usually dead trek-ox or dead horse, dry biscuit, nice green water to wash it down with, and as a general rule no salt. There was no smoke to speak of, but every now and then you could see a flash somewhere on the hillside in front of you, and sometimes the man next to you would give a short sudden sob and lie very still. Or then again, sometimes he would sit up and scream, and go rolling over and over in agony. When the ground wasn't wet it was swarming with vermin, and most of the men who weren't shot went sick either from the vermin or the flies or the bad water or else exposure. I had the good luck to get hurt with a piece of shell before the relief of Ladysmith, and that meant Cape Town for me, and nothing more to do.

The people in Cape Town who weren't talking treason were all full of schemes for getting suddenly rich. I thought out a scheme too. So two months later I left Cape Town, broke to the world and very glad indeed to get a job before the mast on a big steel sailing ship. I did the same thing again not long afterward, but not from choice, and I have since left off wondering why men can be found who are fools enough to go to sea at all—I mean on merchant ships. We were short-handed, fed on offal that would not be good for pigs, ill-treated, struck, sworn at, overworked all the time, housed in a fo'castle that was swarming with rats and vermin, deprived of any kind of privacy, and, in fact, treated like animals. Only animals are never worked so hard.

BY THE time that we reached Australia another Englishman and myself had had enough of it, so we ran away from the ship, leaving our kit and our wages behind us. We neither of us had any qualifications that were likely to get us a job up country, but we hadn't any money either, so we couldn't stay in Sydney; we had either to walk or go to sea again. We walked.

The two of us tramped all the way to Brisbane together, asking for work at every place we came to, and never getting it. We got food, though, because in Australia they have to feed all "sun-downers," as hoboes are called; if they didn't, nobody would ever go on the road to look for work. Now and then we eked out a little money by singing songs in wayside pubs, but we arrived in Brisbane just as broke as when we set out.

There seemed nothing else for it but the sea again, and we finally reached Hobart, Tasmania, in the stokehold of a small steamer. The work was hard, but the grub was good, and the pay (ten pounds a month) was quite excellent. Hobart is a lovely little place, but I couldn't see any chance of getting rich there. Charlie (the other fellow) elected to stop, though, and I pulled out alone, before the mast again, on a three-masted barque loaded up with blue-gum piles for the new pier at Delagoa Bay.

There is no need to describe that ship; it is sufficient to say that she was worse than the first one. We were very nearly wrecked on the way across, and the crew went sick from being fed on salt fish; every man Jack deserted, including myself, at Lorenço Marques.

Lorenço Marques is a pretty easy place to go broke in; and when you are broke it must be nearly the hardest place in the world in which to get on your feet again. Before I succeeded in getting a job I got so low with fever, and so absolutely busted, that I was glad to accept the hospitality of a Chinese laundryman; he put me to bed between clean sheets, and fed me back to health again. Then he told me where to go and get a job! I landed the job at the first try, and it was a good one, too, if you reckon without the climate.

I had to run a big estate up the Limpopo River, and while doing it I am glad to say that I was able to help my friend the Chinaman. It seems that he was getting too prosperous, and the local officials came down on him for an extra big rake-off. He refused, so they trumped up two or three charges against him and put him out of business, fining him every cent of money he had and turning him out on the street penniless. Then he remembered me, and one day he arrived at my hut on the bank of the Limpopo, much more dead than alive. It was turn about then; I gave him a bed and fed him back to health, and then lent him money, and in about three months time he was in a fair way to becoming a prosperous trader, buying corn from the natives and shipping it to the coast.

THEN I went down with fever so badly that I had either to chuck my job or die, and, not being at all anxious to die, I did the other thing. The British East African Government had just finished the railway to the Lake, and the country was being boomed like wild-fire, so I decieded to go there and took the very first steamer with the idea of getting well again on the way up. Of course everybody knows now that British East Africa is a very much overrated country; there is neither mineral there nor anything else of much value except wild game; but I was one of the comparatively early birds who helped to find it out.

There were no jobs to be had, but there was some money to be made shooting elephants, although one had to ignore the Government regulations in order to do it. Off the beaten track, though, it was not very difficult at that time to keep out of the Government's reach; the job was to slip through into the open and, once outside the pale, to stay there until you had cleaned up what you were after. So I hired a native named Kazi Moto, who had just come out of jail, as my personal servant and took the train up country. Kazi Moto means "Work like ——," and he certainly did fill the bill. With his help I got a *safari* together and slipped through into the elephant country, where I joined a Greek of most blazing amazing courage but very doubtful reputation.

The hunting that followed was the hardest and most dangerous work I ever tackled; for excitement it beat war all to smithereens, and among other things it gave me an insight into the meaning of the word fear. I will take off my hat at any time to a man who can truthfully say that he is not afraid of a charging elephant.

I didn't get rich at the game, but I made enough money to pay my men and I got hold of a good big mob of cattle, which I drove down over the border into German territory. A marauding band of Masai tackled me not far from Shirati and drove off the whole lot. Naturally I resented it and, in the process of doing so, I received a spear-wound in my right leg. Kazi Moto killed my assailant with the butt end of a gun and then proceeded to suck my wound. He said he was sucking out poison and that he wasn't sure that he had got it all out. I didn't believe him, but he called up six other of my men, and among them they threw me on the ground and cauterized the wound thoroughly with firebrands. During the proceeding I bit Kazi Moto, who was sitting on my head, rather severely, but he never bore any malice about it.

The cattle being my only visible wealth and the cattle being all gone, all my men except Kazi Moto ran away, taking their loads with them in lieu of wages; and Kazi Moto and I set out to reach Muanza, a place nearly two hundred miles away, where the nearest doctor was. By the time I reached there I was naturally about all in, although, but for the fact that it was full of insects, my wound was not so bad as might have been expected.

The Germans were not at all pleased to see me, but, as I had developed black-water fever, they gave me a place to go away and die in. It was a dark and very dirty shed with a grass roof, which, besides me and Kazi Moto, had to shelter nearly all the rats in East Africa. Kazi Moto used to go out every day and steal things for me to eat, and once a day the doctor would come, look at me, give me a bottle of physic, grunt and go out again.

ONE morning he brought a sergeant with him and I heard him say to the sergeant, "All right . . . he'll be dead by this afternoon . . . you'd better send the chain-gang over to the burial-ground and get his grave dug, then we can get him out of the way before dark."

He didn't come in that morning, but just looked at me through the door; what he said to the sergeant, though, did me more good than all his physic. Up to that time I had not particularly wanted to get well; I had neither money nor prospects and was feeling much too ill to care, and I haven't the least doubt that if he had said nothing I would have died either that day or the day following. But I hated the man so, and was so utterly disgusted with his treatment of me, that I made up my mind to disappoint him, and from that minute I began to get better. When the chain-gang came with a sack to tie me up in I was sitting up with the aid of Kazi Moto. Two days later I leaned on Kazi Moto's shoulder and walked out to have a look at the grave; I was so weak that I very nearly tumbled into it.

Until then it had never once occurred to me that I had found out nearly enough for a young man of my age; but, looking into it, and back across it, I realized that, although I had done absolutely nothing to be proud of I had really acquired quite a lot of information. I sat there for about an hour, thinking; and at the end of it I pushed some dirt down into the grave as a sort of concrete sign that I had buried the old wanderlust at the bottom of it and would try henceforward to put my garnered knowledge to some use. I have not wandered more than twelve or thirteen thousand miles since.

I did a good bit of trekking about German East Africa after I got better, but this time always with a view to making money; and when I found that I could not make more than enough to live on, I decided to go up to British East again. So I took passage on a dhow, and that was another choice experience. The dhow was about thirty-five feet long over all and was loaded down with cargo. The cargo was covered with a sort of thatched roof, under which, and on top of the sacks of peanuts and drums of ghee, I and Kazi Moto, two native women, two babies, two goats, some chickens and eleven other natives including the crew had to exist. The voyage lasted ten days and it rained in torrents the whole time. When we made a smudge to drive out the mosquitoes the smoke was intolerable, and when we threw the smudge overboard the mosquitoes swarmed in like a hungry army.

ONE night the native who was sleeping next to me died (of pneumonia I think); I felt his back getting colder and colder but I had no idea that he was dead until the morning. They carried him ashore, and buried him in my blanket.

I did all right up in British East, for I secured a road contract, and, when I made good on that, the Government gave me an official job. But the climate where I was was awfully unhealthy; I had made up my mind by that time to write stories, and I had to work too hard to be able to find time for writing. In addition to that, people had a distressing habit of committing suicide there; they did it one after another, and that kind of thing gets on your nerves after a while.

I saw two native campaigns, but they weren't sufficiently exciting to make up for the depressing surroundings during all the rest of the time. A final dose of black-water fever convinced me that I had had enough of Africa, so I paid off Kazi Moto and sailed for Europe. Before I left, Kazi Moto stole my razors, watch, camp-kit and some of my money, but I don't grudge him any of it. I had intended to give him everything except the watch, so he didn't get much more than he was entitled to anyhow. He was a good man, and he saved my life four separate times.

EUROPE turned out to be as amusing and as comfortable and as unsatisfactory as ever when I got there. So I held the map and used the pricker. Others maintained that I made it come down in the U. S. A. on purpose. At all events I am glad that it did so.

Now that's a deuce of a long talk about very little, isn't it! But I've left a whole lot out. What I've tried to do is to prove that I've met real live men and seen them behave under all sorts of conditions, and that I've suffered with them and seen what they've seen and laughed with them sufficiently to be able to understand them and their motives. And consequently I claim that the people in my stories are real people who are worth writing about.

That is the only claim that a writer-man has any right to make. He himself, his private life, and his present possessions are matters of absolutely no importance; but his experience does count, because that is his only qualification, barring of course the technical knowledge that he can learn at school.

It goes without saying that there are different sorts of experience which are suitable for different styles of writing. Mine has been mixed and varied, and I try to write various stories. I have dined with a prince, who was afterward a king, and also at a Chinaman's table between my host and a buck Zulu; it doesn't matter which experience I liked best; the point is that I have sampled both. I have earned my living carrying sacks of potatoes at the wharf-side, and I have also had a very good time indeed in certain London clubs; and in between those two walks in life are an unnumbered host of others, many of which I have come into contact with at one time or another.

I claim to be nothing but a lineal descendant of the old-time story-teller, who spun his yarn and passed the hat round. Nowadays it is the editor who passes round the hat, and he is rather more particular than the old-time capper used to be; but the effect is just the same. The public pays, and the public calls the tune. I believe, too, that the public likes to know now, just as much as it did then, that the man who spins the yarn has seen the things he writes about. I have no other excuse for discussing myself and my wanderings over so many pages.—TALBOT MUNDY.

APOLOGIES for a break in one of our stories. In a poker game one of the characters "filled a bob-tail flush from the middle." I'm not that innocent. Neither is Mr. Noyes or any one else on our staff. Nor the author. But the mistake got by, just the same.

I don't usually "pass the buck," but at least I'd like to explain that I've grown pretty rusty as to poker, though not rusty enough to hunt for the middle of an ordinary flush. Once, in my early twenties, I sat in on an innocent little game of penny-ante, filled a royal flush from the middle, won two copper cents, decided that poker was not my game and have never played it since.

BETEL nuts. An answer of Captain Dingle's in "Ask Adventure" brought a letter from O. W. S., which follows. Also Captain Dingle's reply, of which I give only parts, since on most points the two seem merely to be saying the same thing in different words.

Ancon, C. Z.

I believe you wish to have any mistakes corrected which may be published in your magazine and I am taking the liberty of writing you regarding, what I believe to be, a mistake, in your issue of Sept. 3, 1918, regarding the betel-nut, as described by Captain Dingle.

In the beginning I wish to state that I have spent the last nineteen years in the Orient, principally in the Philippines, as soldier, hunter, and in public health work. I recently transferred to Panama. The betel-nut, with its covering, is as large as a hen's egg and resembles a small coconut when the coco-nut is green. The betel-nut grows on a palm which resembles the coco-nut palm, but does not grow as large nor tall. The natives prepare it for chewing by placing a paste made of lime on an aromatic leaf taken from a vine called *itchmo*, and this leaf and lime are folded around a small piece of the kernel of the betel-nut and all chewed together. Betel-nut chewing is a filthy habit and soon destroys the teeth and then the user is compelled to crush his betel-nut mixture, in a small bamboo tube made for the purpose, with a sharp-pointed metal blade.

I don't think I ever saw a betel-nut chewer over forty years of age who had many teeth left, and they were black and decayed from the filthy habit.—O. W. S.

Pembroke West, Bermuda.

I have Mr. S.'s kick about my dope on betel chewing, and have hunted up the only question and answer I have handled on this subject. The results are, that all Mr. S.'s complaint is due to the trifling mistake on my part in assuming that the betel-nut grew on the same plant which supplied the aromatic leaf.

I freely admit my error in that, and thank Mr. S. for his information. I was always under the impression that the nut was the fruit of the climbing pepper; the mistake was easy to make. . . .

As for the method of using, Mr. S. simply corroborates my own statement, but takes exception to the leaf used. He names the Philippine leaf *Itchmo*, simply calling it an aromatic leaf. As a matter of plain fact, this aromatic leaf is nothing but the leaf of the climbing pepper alluded to above, and is not called Itchmo anywhere outside the Philippines. It is a local name. But the plant, the Betel Pepper, is known wherever else the betel grows, all over the Malay Peninsula, India, and Borneo (to a somewhat lesser degree). . . .

One other point, the preservation of the teeth. This, too, is a moot question. I have seen a great many betel chewers with fine teeth, although the teeth were discolored black. As for chewers over forty rarely having teeth, I would add that non-chewers among Eastern natives rarely have many teeth after that age.—A. E. DINGLE.

IT'S been a long time since we've had a story from Charles Wesley Sanders and it happens that, not through his fault, he had never introduced himself to Camp-Fire as is our custom. Here he is now:

Madison, Ohio.

At the age of twelve ran away from school because the teacher insisted on attempting to make me sing the scale before the other pupils. Knew then that I could never sing, and am now more than ever convinced. The powers that held destiny in their hands thought work might make the schoolroom look more inviting, so a place in the general offices of the Nickel Plate Railroad at Cleveland was secured for me. By hovering over sounders when idle, which was a good deal of the time, became somewhat proficient in the telegraphers' art. The manager of the general offices died. The superintendent of telegraph wrote a letter a few days later.

"You'd better read that," he said to me, one of whose duties was the copying of such letters.

THE letter appointed one of the operators to take the place of the man who had died. I was made the operator at the bottom of the list—then fifteen years old. The next year was made night operator in the same office. One reason for this was that I was able to "set in" an old-fashioned Millikin repeater, which was the despair of most operators. Didn't know then just how I did the trick and don't know now. Suspect the repeater was like a balky horse that would consent to be driven only once in a while.

In this year began to regret running away from the vocalizing teacher. Saw that an operator, however, except those working heavy circuits, can go to school while he works. A gentle Episcopalian minister initiated me into the mysteries of Latin and English, so that running away from school didn't prove so disastrous as it might have done.

SOME years later went into newspaper work. Was blown into recognition. The second week was assigned by the city editor to cover a section of the city while a street railway strike was in progress. Cars were being blown up all over town. One Sunday night a reporter for a rival paper and myself were waiting for a car at a cross street. The car came along and innocently slid into an open switch. By the time it had been put on the track again a score of passengers were waiting. Did the passengers let this first car go ahead and run into whatever explosive might have been placed on the track? They did not. Every one of them piled upon this car. Three blocks away a lead pipe filled with nitroglycerin had been placed on the track. Just before the car came to the pipe the other reporter put his hand on my arm.

"Say," he began.

But he never said it. There was a roar that shook that section of the city. The floor of the car was blown out and the trolley-pole blown off. The motorman landed on his ear on the pavement and the car sped ahead, dust-filled and dark, till it stopped of its own accord. The other reporter and I had been sitting in a rear seat. We were not hurt, but men and women in front of us were screaming and shouting. After helping the injured passengers as much as possible, we scudded for telephones and sent bulletins to the city editor. The bulletins were in the offices a few minutes after the explosion. The city editors called it "good work," which is often another name for pure luck.

WHILE working in the telegraph office at a coal dock I once let a train get by and found myself in a situation much used in fiction, but no fictionist has adequately described the sensations that come to a man in that predicament. The despatcher had sent an order for a certain train. When the train had passed I found the order lying on the table, broke in on the train wire and notified the despatcher.

"All right," said the despatcher laconically, "the other train isn't by 'DK' yet."

"DK" was at the far end of a double track and the train which hadn't got its order reached the near end and safety before a collision was possible. I watched my mail closely for a week, but no letter concerning the incident ever came. The despatcher had kept his own counsel.

Since then have been city editor of all Cleveland papers but one, and night editor and managing editor of one of the three.—CHARLES WESLEY SANDERS.

A LETTER from Captain George Ash, written last Summer from Kuala Lumpur, Selangor, Federated Malay States, near Singapore, Malay Straits, stated he was "going into the interior of these Straits for two or more months" and asked us to "advertise" and hold any letters that came to him in our care. We try to be of service to this comrade but my private opinion is that wireless is the only thing likely to reach him. He hops all over the map and a forwarded letter has to have very long legs to reach him before the next hop. However, we've been trying to handle mail for him for years, he's very welcome and, as he continues to use our forwarding service, a letter must reach him now and then.

The letter before this one was written from Manila, whither he had come from Japan.—ARTHUR SULLIVANT HOFFMAN.

Our Camp-Fire came into being May 5, 1912, with our June issue, and since then its fire has never died down. Many have gathered about it and they are of all classes and degrees, high and low, rich and poor, adventurers and stay-at-homes, and from all parts of the earth. Some whose voices we used to know have taken the Long Trail and are heard no more, but they are still memories among us, and new voices are heard, and welcomed.

We are drawn together by a common liking for the strong, clean things of out-of-doors, for word from the earth's far places, for man in action instead of caged by circumstance. The *spirit* of adventure lives in all men; the rest is chance.

But something besides a common interest holds us together. Somehow a real comradeship has grown up among us. Men can not thus meet and talk together without growing into friendlier relations; many a time does one of us come to the rest for facts and guidance: many a close personal friendship has our Camp-Fire built up between two men who had never met; often has it proved an open sesame between strangers in a far land.

Perhaps our Camp-Fire is even a little more. Perhaps it is a bit of leaven working gently among those of different station toward the fuller and more human understanding and sympathy that will some day bring to man the real democracy and brotherhood he seeks. Few indeed are the agencies that bring together on a friendly footing so many and such great extremes as here. And we are numbered by the hundred thousand now.

If you are come to our Camp-Fire for the first time and find you like the things we like, join us and find yourself very welcome. There is no obligation except ordinary manliness, no forms or ceremonies, no dues, no officers, no anything except men and women gathered for interest and friendliness. Your desire to join makes you a member.

OUR "Lost Trails" department could furnish many a dramatic tale, happy or pathetic, if its service were not of so private a nature. Letters of gratitude come to us, of course, but they are generally evidently not meant for publication. Sometimes, though, a comrade who has found an old pal rejoices aloud and, there being no reason for not doing so, expresses his gratitude to the Camp-Fire at large for the service one or more of you has done him. Here, for example:

Schenectady, N. Y.

Sixteen years ago this Summer I parted from a comrade in San Francisco, after a comradeship of two years. I had to go to Panama, where there was a revolution pending. He had to go to Oregon. Letters to him were returned.

AS TIME went by, a longing to get in touch with him once more was frustrated by a lack of knowledge of his whereabouts. Then came *Adventure* and "Lost Trails." Skeptical, I put off from time to time making use of the department. I myself turn to Camp-Fire first, and as time passed and I met in those pages trail-mates of other days, and in fancy was carried back to other climes and countries, as well as our own "God's country," I realized there was a possibility of picking up my pal again and advertised in first May issue.

I was advised by you of his address, furnished by a reader. I immediately wrote and today received a long letter from him. My card had followed him through several cities, finally reaching him in Scranton, Pa., a bare 150 miles distant, after an absence of sixteen years and a separation on the other side of the Continent.

Long life to *Adventure* and regards to Camp-Fire bunch. I am with you in spirit, if absent in flesh, and who can say what time may bring forth? We live in hopes, and Wanderlust never dies in the heart of the true adventurer. *A l'outrance! Beneplacito!*—One of you, G. LESTER AUMIC.

ANOTHER view-point of Calamity Jane. Jane seems to have made a vivid impression on all who saw her, which is easy to understand.

Tacoma, Washington.

I was interested in the article *re* Calamity Jane. I met her several times when I was operator at Buffalo station. She waited there a week once for her "man friend" to come in from the south *via* the old Texas cattle trail that passed just west of the station.

MY IMPRESSION is that *he* was a member of Dutch Henry's famous band of outlaws. Brininstool gives her a clean passport as a trusted Government scout; it may be true, but I never heard of it. She was a well-known character of the early days on the frontier, but I never heard anything to her credit. I know of my own knowledge she was one of the most profane women that ever lived.

She had a hard, repellant face, and she was *not* a noticeably large woman. She was at home on a horse and with a Colt's navy, all right. I knew her before she went to Deadwood; her character may have improved later, but she was a woman desperado when I knew her.—W. A. STERNBERG.

HERE are a couple of letters about the "turning white" disease that played a part in a story by Kathrene and Robert Pinkerton. Also another letter suggested by the subject.

Berkeley, Calif.

Re the Pinkertons' "Vitelego"—my second cousin, —— ——, of Portland, Oregon (brother of the eminent Philadelphia physician —— —— and —— ——), had the disease, if it can be called that, about ten years ago.

The family on the —— side are of the old Portuguese Jews (earlier Spanish) and olive-complexioned.

I "stopped" over in Portland on a trip from Alaska, and was horrified. He calmly explained the thing. He was half "white" at the time; the change had been going on for something like a year, I think, and later on the process became complete. He is a man of about sixty at present.— —— ——.

Russellville, Ark.

Speaking of the "white Indians," a negro in our State turned white last year with that disease.—RUBY E. LIVINGSTON.

Schenectady, N. Y.

After reading the very interesting story of the "white Indians" by Kathrene and Robert Pinkerton, it occurred to me that it might interest *Adventure* readers to know that among the Maya Indians of Mexico there were many who had blonde hair and blue eyes, and in some respects the build and features of a white race.

THE Mayos were a big tribe who lived in villages along the upper stretches of the Mayo and Tuerte Rivers in Southern Sonora and Northern Sinaloa. They tilled the soil extensively and were said to have numbered as many as twenty thousand when the Spanlards first found them about the middle of the sixteenth century.

They have a tradition, that was still a tradition when the Spaniards came, that tells of an expedition a party of them once made to the mouth of the Rio Mayo, where it enters the Pacific, and there finding a lot of castaways who had been shipwrecked. They were very large men whose hair and beards were long and yellow and whose eyes were blue and who were thought to be superhuman. The "strange men," as they were called, were adopted into the Mayo tribe with whom they ever after lived. This tradition came to me from old Mayo Indians many years ago and I never doubted its truth.—DONALD F. MCCARTHY.

SCALPING. A bit about the knife that did the work. And bathing.

I am not an authority on Indians, though my nurse and foster-mother was the squaw of Spotted Tail, chief of the Ogallala Sioux, and was adopted by him into the tribe, according to the stories told me by my parents. This in introduction to the subject of scalping.

ONE of the principal reasons that scalping was fatal was that the scalpee was already dead or nearly so. When otherwise, the wound was decidedly septic. The so-called scalping-knife was often made of iron tires of burned prairie schooners and not used exclusively for scalping. They were used for all sorts of camp work, as the modern camper uses his knife. With the proverbial uncleanliness of the Indian and the porous condition of the iron, the knife absorbed the animal fats and substances and became very deadly in itself.

WHILE engineering in New Mexico and Texas for the Santa Fé Railroad in 1887 I came across a character known as "Tanglefoot," horse-herder for the big English Ranch, who had been scalped in the middle of the 70's. Don't know his story, but did see the wound, a rough circle of bare skull. Incidentally he participated one evening in a discussion on bathing and remarked "I always take a bath when indications point that a way."

"What are the indications, Tanglefoot?"

"When I begin to itch."

Pretty good reason.

Incidentally, though I have been unable through age and disability to get Over There, I have the honor to be the father of the first girl or woman commissioned by the U. S., Jeannette C. Mullikin, 1st Lieut. U. S. Med. Corps.—LOUIS C. MULLIKIN.

OUR Camp-Fire pet, the Gila Monster, comes up to the blaze once more:

Raledon, New Mexico.

I very often see in Camp-Fire discussion and mention made of old-timers of the passing West whom I have known years ago from Texas to Montana. I am no Spring chicken myself. Wilbur Hall dubs me "Old Buccaneer," for which I forgive him, he not being altogether responsible. I think, however, he will vouch for some of my wanderings.

WHEN I started to write, however, the foregoing was not the intended purpose, and to get down to it will say I have been for several weeks out west of Nogales, Arizona, in the Pajarito Mountains along the Mexican border and I got behind with our magazine. Got three in a bunch when I got to Nogales. Now I don't know whether the Gila monster discussion has closed or not but it did seem fairly well started. Now as a matter of fact when Gila monsters are concerned I am not scientifically inclined. But I do wish to say I have seen hundreds of them, caught a few, and have never been bitten by one.

Now I am going to side with Major Rodney inasmuch as if any person should have asked me the color of one of these reptiles I should promptly answer "black and yellow." I may be color-blind; then again my eyes may be such as to prevent me from distinguishing gentle, easy gradations in color.

THEY are slow of movement, said to live on bugs, bird eggs and such. Have a peculiar habit of puffing or blowing their breath at one when molested. Breath is said to have a sickening effect, but from personal experience can not say. They snap viciously at one and poke a stick at one and he will grab the end of it.

I remember the first one I ever caught. After poking a Suhvara rib at him he grabbed the end of it and hung on while I carried him thus a couple of miles to camp.

I had another experience on Cave Creek about forty miles from Phoenix, Arizona. I caught one and brought it into the assay office of a cyanide plant I was running at the time, and with the aid of a glass tube, put 20 cubic centimeters of 50 per cent. cyanide solution down him and he just licked his chops and acted as though more would be acceptable. It took an equal amount of strong nitric to finish him an hour later. So I go on record with the statement that K C N solution will not kill Gila monsters and recommend use of HNO_3.

YES, for the "love of Mike," insist on spelling Navajo with a *j*. Don't try to "Easternize" our beloved West. That's about all we have left of the old West, is the names, and if pen pushers and machine-thumpers switch the spelling of those around until they are no longer recognizable, we have naught left.

Apropos of the use of the *h* and the *j* in an Indian name, I will call your attention to the word "Mojave"—the name of a tribe of Indians, a famous (or infamous) stretch of desert, one county, one town and one river. The county is Mohave Co., Arizona, and, as you see, is spelled with an *h*. The rest of the trimmings mentioned as being called Mojave are in California and spells with a *j*. Why this difference in spelling I can not say.—ALEX MCLAREN.

A PHYSICIAN comrade tells us that a passage in one of our stories might conceivably make serious trouble. At least it is safest to publish his letter. Though the author's reply shows that he was sufficiently warranted so far as facts and the requirements of fiction are concerned, there is always the remote chance that the "remedy" used in the story might be tried in some real life emergency. The two letters follow:

Green Island, N. Y.

As a medical man I wish to utter a criticism of the action of the hero, as physician, who, to save the life of a diphtheritic child, inserts a glass tube in its throat and sucks out the "deadly mucus." It isn't the latter which suffocates the child, but the membrane, which forms and mechanically occludes the air-passages, causing suffocation and death.

THE only thing to do in a case such as the author describes is to puncture the windpipe just above the breastbone (with a jack-knife if necessary), making a hole big enough for free breathing. If this membrane extends the full length of the windpipe the case is hopeless; of course, I mean in the absence of diphtheritic antitoxin. Sucking the mucus from a diphtheritic throat wouldn't save the patient's life, but only kill the would-be good Samaritan. I wish to state the above emphatically just to prevent spreading misinformation and to save some misguided reader who might imitate the hero, while living in some out of the way place and confronted with a case of membrane tonsillitis or diphtheria.

Apropos of medical topics, most authors are guilty of using medical terms without knowing their exact meaning, in particular the use of the word "aphasia" to denote loss of memory. Any good dictionary will tell them that "aphasia" means loss of speech. "Amnesia" means loss of memory.—H. F. ALBRECHT, M.D.

Seattle, Wash.

During the dark ages of medicine, which is still to a large extent in a process of experimentation, many ways were tried of relieving sufferers from diphtheria—sometimes called "croup." My story was purposely dated to show its relation to those dark ages: the man *Hume* doing something which no one able to diagnose the case would now think of doing, which was often done before the subject was properly understood, the patient recovering when it would have recovered without the operation, because in ninety-nine per cent. of cases sucking at the membrane would have no effect but that of endangering the life of the operator. In conformance with the then state of knowledge, I used the words "deadly mucus."

I WAS greatly surprised at being criticized, as I thought I had made myself clear; and the critic himself errs more than I did in advocating the slitting of the windpipe with a jack-knife, without adding the insertion of a silver tube, without which the patient could not breathe. I protest against that suggestion of treatment, because the operator takes no risk himself, and would therefore not hesitate or think of the danger—almost certain infection and death from loss of blood. Unless the antitoxin can be obtained, it is best to leave the diphtheria patient entirely to nature, and keep it warm.

BUT I have made a discovery which, if made before I wrote the story, would have caused me not to write it. I find that Kipling, in one of his best known books, "Stalky & Co." has the schoolmaster save the life of a boy by doing just what my man *Hume* did, without losing his own life! Had I read that book, I would not have, as I said, written the tale. Now, since Kipling is so much more widely read than I am, would it not be well for my critic to write him, advising him to stop selling "Stalky & Co." because he is spreading so much misinformation? Of course Kipling's tale has to do with the era before antitoxin, as mine has. You will remember that I wrote that antitoxin was only just coming into vogue when *Hume* left England, implying he had hardly heard of it. And any one who knows how reluctant doctors were to try the new treatment will agree with my attitude in writing.—S. B. H. HURST.

FOLLOWING our Camp-Fire custom, on the occasion of his first story in our magazine Barry Scobee rises and gives an account of himself. Also he gives us an interesting word on the facts back of his story:

I never had a real adventure in my life. Isn't that some confession! That is, I mean, an adventure like getting lost at the North Pole, or falling into a mine full of snakes and being fished out by a dusky maiden who led me to a deposit of pure gold, or being pushed from a Chicago skyscraper through a skylight eleven stories below into a nest of counterfeiters. It seems I don't have any luck connecting with the thrillers. Maybe it's because I was born at Pollock, Mo., not far from the Iowa line on a farm, in 1885. Or, to be more logical, maybe my poor luck comes from the fact that my ancestors were Scots, Irish, English, Canadians, Virginians and Kentuckians.

AS A matter of fact, it does seem to me that what I have got into has been exceptionally bare of adventures that arrived at a climax. I've had lots of good starts, though. With two exceptions the things I have done have not had to do with promising fields, according to my mental make-up. I attended, but failed to get a degree—owing, I hope, mainly to a lack of interest—at the State Normal at Kirksville, Mo. Then I followed, off and on, the trade of printing, was with surveyors some in the Texas Panhandle, joined the Army and got to the Philippines in 1910, have done considerable newspaper work among the military and on the Mexican border, and for a year and a half helped another man gather material for a "popular" history of that part of Texas lying west of the Pecos and up to the edge of El Paso. Traveled 30,000 miles in a Ford, saw every road, and met nearly every man in that region, and went back in history to 1535 when de Vaca was out there.

BUT here's my luck. I was an attendant in a Keely Cure institute once. No, I wasn't working my way through. Staying in a room one night to watch a dopey, I was awakened from profound sleep by him standing over me brandishing a razor and a revolver and calling me the man who had run away with his wife. But nothing happened. He forgot me and went to shout out of the window at some woman he insanely took for his wife. I and another man drove an old tin car through the guard into a besieged town once, that being the only available way of getting in. We were taken before the general, who threatened to shoot us. But nothing happened. In an hour we were sipping cognac with the American consul. I was taking a man to military prison once in the Philippines, on a small steamer, and lost my gun. But nothing happened. The prisoner found it and returned it to me. I have been deer hunting and bob-cat hunting in exceedingly wild country. But nothing happened. The other men got the game. I helped to go to the source of the greatest lost gold-mine story that ever tempted the Southwest. Nothing happened. There wasn't any mine.

Now all that isn't any laughable matter, believe me. It means that when I concoct a piece of fiction I've got to slave like a printer's devil to work up a climax!

THE steer branded with the word "Murder" was a "sure enough" steer, so far as I know. A lawyer at Alpine, Texas, out toward El Paso, first told me the story; then I had it vouched for by a number of other men by their adding of details of which the lawyer was not cognizant.

As a matter of fact, nine deaths are said to be connected with the original killing over the calf, which took place before a cowboy branded it. The connection in some instances is hazy. It is thought that no one is still living who was connected with the killings. I talked with one man who claimed to have been in the poker game when a dead man's hand was originated. Other men substantiated this claim.

I took the main and subsequent instances and made fiction pure and simple, but there was one incident which I did not include because to get it in would have required, I thought, a digression of such importance as to lead the reader astray from the story I wanted to get by with. It is this, as I was told:

ONE night a cowboy, connected with the "murder steer" in some manner, rode out of the town of Alpine—many years ago, of course. There was a pouring rain. The cowboy carried before him on his saddle a pet cub bear chained to his wrist. At the edge of town next morning he was found dead, shot, and the bear sat on his breast, whining in the cold.

The next shooting in the series, as I recollect, was the one at the poker game. He who was killed then was supposed to have shot the cowboy.

But here is the dénouement. A few years afterward a Mexican revolutionist was arrested, I think at Fort Stockton. His name was Ochoa, a name well known in, broadly speaking, the El Paso country. He told a story to this effect: He and a companion, journeying from the Mexican border northward, approached Alpine one evening in a downpouring rain. At the edge of town a voice called out in the darkness for them to halt. The voice was that of a drunken man, and Ochoa's companion, thinking that he heard the click-clock of a gun being cocked, fired. There was silence, except for a whimpering like that of a child. Ochoa reproached his comrade, saying that his hastiness seemingly had caused the wounding of a child. Cautiously they struck matches and examined, to find a dead cowboy, his horse nearby, and a cub bear tugging at the wrist of the corpse.

This story made it plain, it seemed, that the man in the poker game had been killed without being a deserving party—in other words, won undying local fame under false pretenses. But some coincidence, wasn't it?

THE Big Bend country, which lies south of the Southern Pacific railroad to the Rio Grande and extends roughly from Sanderson to Sierra Blanca, is full of such yarns. The country has been very little exploited by writers, but a friend of mine has claimed it for his own now. He and I spent a year and a half out there, traveling in a flivver back and forth, covering 30,000 square miles, making 35,000 linear miles, collecting material for a history of the section. The history goes back 400 years, but the fiction possibilities antedate that by a few more centuries.—BARRY SCOBEE.

The Camp-Fire

AT OUR Camp-Fire I said that Americans who sold inferior war supplies to our Government or who grafted in any way on the materials that meant the efficiency and life of our soldiers and sailors at the front were lower and more contemptible than an ordinary traitor. My vocabulary is not equal to my contempt and hatred for these cowardly vampires who are now enjoying their ill-gotten gains.

It was bad enough to prey on and betray other human beings before we entered the war, but to sell the lives of their own American countrymen for money, bah! such as Judas Iscariot and Benedict Arnold will not let these swine into their part of Hell.

HERE is one of the letters that came in and I know that the good American who wrote it joins with me in the fervent hope that these eunuch traitors, each and every one, great or small, may be damned and accursed to their dying day with the acid knowledge that they sold the lives of their fellows for money, that, three thousand miles behind their backs, they knifed those Americans who were fighting for the safety of the country and institutions which made it possible for these maggots to live in peace and plenty.

I mean *all* of those who in *any* way grafted on *any* kind of war supplies for American fighters—who put through inferior goods, who grafted commissions, who sold at unfair profits, who in *any* way made the country's need a means of personal profit to the country's loss. Some of you who read this are guilty, excusing yourselves on the idiot ground that it was "only a bit of graft" or not even excusing yourselves at all. If you have not yet seen the black shame of what you have done, may you be given to see it, and may the seeing of it keep you in the hell you have made for yourself—for money. May you, and all others like you, never spend a dollar or a dime or a cent of that stolen money without feeling in your heart that it is wet with the blood of men and the tears of women and children. May you never see your hands without knowing that they are red and black—black with your own filthy treachery and as red with the blood of murdered Americans as if your fingers had touched the bleeding wounds you have made. May you never know peace or happiness, justice or good fortune, respect of men or love of women until you have paid your full price and have made what restitution and atonement lie in your power.

Berkeley, Cal.

Your denunciation in the current issue of *Adventure* directed at *eunuch-traitors* strikes a responsive chord in my breast, but why make it so mild!

A HUN is born one; he shakes off the veneer of civilization at the bidding of his Kaiser and the surging up in him of his congenital instinct to trample toward his goals—other people's rights and property. He's the tiger or the rattlesnake described in one of James J. Montague's cleverest verses. The poet therein states that, while he holds no brief for these killers, he is obliged to admit that they merely satisfy the demands of their natures in a forthright sort of way. But the mosquito, on the other hand just eats and eats and eats, until he's wabbly and falls over. He says there's nothing to that brute but venom. Somehow the comparison applies to the American contractor-profiteer-privateer. He knows better, has no passion in the matter—just cold-blooded, low-down, sneaky lust of gain, let the tragedies of his acts strike where they may, far away from his home town and his respectability and local reputation.

THOSE choice spirits that economized in the quality of the explosives, or the fulminating mechanisms of explosive bombs, we sold to Great Britain before we entered the war left those gallant fighters without defense under a rain of very effective ninety-nine per cent.-exploding shells and shrapnel of the Germans during the first vital retreat across Belgium and Northern France. Who shall say what the result was in terms of subsequent casualties to the British and French? Proof of guilty knowledge of the results of that "economy" on the part of those manufacturers ought to be followed by punishments by compraison with which the fate of the paranoiac Kaiser should be as a slap upon the wrist. These eunuch-traitors ought to be roasted as "martyrs" to the suppression of that sort of thing for all future time, for Hell has no pit deep enough and no torture dire enough for them. A man who for lucre to buy automobiles or lobster dinners, or even new churches (for the flattering of his vanity and the getting of a reputation as a humanitarian) condemns his fellow men—and women and children—to the tortures of Hun gas, to rent bodies, to rape and slavery—such men hit the bottom of human turpitude. Below them the imagination finds no space in which to rank fiends of the darkness. Theirs is too dangerous, too fell a strain to be permitted to taint the general heredity of the race. Extinction—and not too painless at that—should be meted out to them in common justice to the race of men. Actually I could weep with pity for an influenza germ I was about to deluge with carbolic acid before I could utter so much as a sigh of regret at gibbeting these vampires.

So please, if you have occasion to revert to them again, put a little pep into your remarks and oblige this constant reader. You thought you did it, perhaps, but by the side of their real deserts your roast really "paled its ineffectual fires." Go at it right. Tell the whole truth of how unspeakably low they are and what they deserve. Try to ape them in the matter of mercy, and give them what they give others.—THEO. S. SOLOMONS.

THIS is more than the usual amount of adventure that falls to the lot of a woman, even a woman who has covered a good deal of the earth's surface:

Waterville, Maine.

My father was a sea captain, and with my parents I have traveled all over the world. I have had hair-breadth escapes from drowning, from epidemics of yellow fever and Asiatic cholera, and from small-pox. I was on board when father ran a blockade with a load of refugees, during a war between Chile and Peru. We were fired on, but escaped. I have been to Australia four times, and I have been shipwrecked out in the Solomon Islands, while bound, coal-laden, from New Castle, N. S. W., to Manila, P. I. For two months we lived among the cannibals, on one of the islands, Ugi. I have sketches of the place, drawn by the surgeon of the ship that rescued us, the *H. M. S. Lark*. The work of that same little ship is mentioned in Encyclopædia Britannica.—L. B. R.

A BELATED item—belated not through the writer's fault—on King Fisher, written from the Kingfisher Hotel, Kingfisher, Okla., by a traveling comrade:

Kingfisher, Okla.

King Fisher is buried at Uvalde, Texas, his old home, where he was a deputy sheriff. The house he lived in is there and I was told by a citizen of Uvalde, Texas, that a daughter of King Fisher is now living at Crystal City, Texas.—F. CALDWELL.

P. S. This town, Kingfisher, is the home of the Dalton boys. The name of this town reminded me that I had a little unfinished business with Camp-Fire.—F. C.

AT LAST we have our gun department. In "Ask Adventure" you'll find a new division, "Firearms, Old and New," with D. Wiggins and J. B. Thompson in charge, both of them already known to many of you as authorities on this subject. Address all gun letters to them.

ARTHUR SULLIVANT HOFFMAN.

Our Camp-Fire came into being May 5, 1912, with our June issue, and since then its fire has never died down. Many have gathered about it and they are of all classes and degrees, high and low, rich and poor, adventurers and stay-at-homes, and from all parts of the earth. Some whose voices we used to know have taken the Long Trail and are heard no more, but they are still memories among us, and new voices are heard, and welcomed.

We are drawn together by a common liking for the strong, clean things of out-of-doors, for word from the earth's far places, for man in action instead of caged by circumstance. The *spirit* of adventure lives in all men; the rest is chance.

But something besides a common interest holds us together. Somehow a real comradeship has grown up among us. Men can not thus meet and talk together without growing into friendlier relations; many a time does one of us come to the rest for facts and guidance; many a close personal friendship has our Camp-Fire built up between two men who had never met; often has it proved an open sesame between strangers in a far land.

Perhaps our Camp-Fire is even a little more. Perhaps it is a bit of leaven working gently among those of different station toward the fuller and more human understanding and sympathy that will some day bring to man the real democracy and brotherhood he seeks. Few indeed are the agencies that bring together on a friendly footing so many and such great extremes as here. And we are numbered by the hundred thousand now.

If you are come to our Camp-Fire for the first time and find you like the things we like, join us and find yourself very welcome. There is no obligation except ordinary manliness, no forms or ceremonies, no dues, no officers, no anything except men and women gathered for interest and friendliness. Your desire to join makes you a member.

ANOTHER inquiry for the "gun cranks." Who can tell our comrade about the old gunsmith, H. Pratt?

Belvidere, N. Y.

Who can tell me anything about an old-time gunsmith who made very fine flint-lock rifles and marked them "H. Pratt"? Would like to know where and when he lived.—C. E. WHITCOMB.

FOLLOWING our Camp-Fire custom, E. S. Pladwell rises and introduces himself. Though we have had stories from him before the one in this issue, his stepping forward has been delayed till now.

Oreana, Nevada.

I was born on a ranch in eastern Oregon, Oct. 9, 1892. The only breaks in the continuity of my existence since then occurred when I stopped a quick-breaking in-shoot with my solar plexus, and again when I ducked into a right hook and had my nose pushed across to a painful position under my right eye.

NATURALLY, having passed the greater part of my life in a cattle country, I have seen branding-irons smoke and heard the hoarse bellows of calves put under the knife and hot iron ever since I can remember. I have seen horses, with the fear of the wild captured thing in their eyes, struggling against the ropes, and have seen them go into the air under the terrifying saddle and rider. Though personally (the demands of truth force me to an unwilling confession) I am no better rider than the imaginary *Spike Ellis* in "The Silver Saddle," I have a pretty thorough first-hand knowledge of the thrills incidental to the mounting of a cayuse. I also know what it is to lose step with him, fall a jump behind, reach for leather, and grab two handfuls of sand or bunch grass—or anything that might happen to constitute the earth formation in that vicinity.

I GOT through high school at Baker, Oregon, and had my fling at scholastic athletics, also long-winded old Cicero and that brain-staggering invention of Euclid called geometry. I attended the University of Oregon for a year and a half before deciding that I knew enough to make the old world sit up and take notice of me. Then I quit school and got married, and soon, like George Ade fastened my fraternity pin on my undershirt and admitted to myself that there were several things that had not come thoroughly under my notice.

AT VARIOUS times I have done other things besides ranch, go to school and wonder how O. Henry and Jack London could get so much kick from plain facts. I worked for a while with a topographical engineering party, and with a railroad engineering party. I bucked wood for a donkey at a big lumber camp near Kelso, Washington. I mucked for two weeks with a railroad construction gang, and though I then had plenty of that way of earning an honest living, I saw more disillusioning facts in the every-day events of those two weeks than a year at college could build up.

One incident in particular convinced me that the Mexicans might under certain conditions be hard to beat. It was one morning at breakfast. A big American and a little Greaser got into a senseless dispute about the passing of a plate of bread. The Mexican slashed out with a knife and laid the big fellow's face open. His opponent caught up a gallon-capacity granite-ware pitcher of condensed milk by the handle and tried to beat off the Mexican's head. All he did, however, was to spoil his appetite. The Mexican worked that day. The other called for his time and left the camp so as not to furnish more temptation for that knife.

I SOLD enlarged pictures in Oregon and California, and quit because I couldn't lie convincingly enough to satisfy my own conscience, though I was doing fairly well with the "gullible public." I have never ridden the rods, but have made several hundred miles on top and on the blinds. If any one doubts that clothes don't make the man, let him get his coat turned wrong side out (to keep the conventional exterior of it clean) and his eyes rimmed with coal smoke, and look from the rock bottom up into our social order.

I have mucked a good many thousand dollars' worth of ore for various mining companies. One night, on the graveyard shift in an incline shaft, I stepped back to roll a smoke. Three seconds afterward a ton of rhyolite fell out of the hanging wall and crashed down on the spot I had recently occupied. The edge of the cave-in caught the machine man's leg. I lifted a few boulders off his foot. He looked up and grinned. "Uncle Sam came —— near losing a good soldier," he said.

IT IS needless to say that my unconventional and floating-laborer activities were confined to my pre-nuptial days. Since Dec. 19, 1914, I have been rather unflaggingly busy trying to get by. It was partly through a desire to escape the menace of the muck stick (shovel being used symbolically for all manner of tools designed for the use of those of us who haven't both hands full of the Top Rung), and partly due to an ardent desire I have always had to learn to tell a good story well, that I began trying my hand at writing a few months ago.

I have felt humble when reading in the "Camp-Fire" of men who have lived more in a year than I have in ten. And I have felt humble while talking with men over real camp-fires whose experiences dwarf my pitiable ones to kindergarten affairs in comparison. But I must admit, with a trace of shame, that my "ardent desire" aforementioned always appears, corrupting my humbleness, which has been divinely commended, with covetousness, which is condemned. I covet that man's experience and think, if I had seen so much, felt so keenly, read so deeply in the "open books of life and death," what glorious tales could I tell! And yet, strange to say, I often doubt if I should endanger O. Henry's place in the story world, even if I had seen the Klondike stampede—E. S. PLADWELL.

IT HAS frequently been suggested that our Camp-Fire should have a simple emblem or badge whereby we might know one another when we met. Finally I brought up the matter at a recent meeting, but presented the two objections that it might be taken advantage of by dead-beats and that it might be taken by some as a cheap attempt to advertise the magazine.

Quite a few of you have written endorsing the idea and objecting to the obligations. I suppose the first one can be dropped. After all, the badge would merely indicate that its wearer was a member of our Camp-Fire and would carry with it no obligations to any other member. Merely a sign, so that if two members, strangers to each other, met in some far place they could use their own judgment about getting acquainted but would at least know that there was a common ground between them.

The second objection is, I think, removed by the following suggestion from a comrade who was serving on a Medical Advisory Board when he wrote:

White Plains.

I am detailed temporarily at the above board—rotten old clerical work, Uncle Sammy declaring in his superior wisdom that I am not qualified to wrestle with our Germanic neighbors across the water.

THE idea about the badge stuff certainly should go through. You wanted suggestions as to what it should be. Here's an idea. Old stuff, nothing original about it, but it's a plain sort of a badge and we'd all know what it meant. Here you are:

A	D	V	E	N	T	U	R	E
1	4	22	5	14	20	21	18	5

Taking each letter in the alphabet and numbering it you get the above. Now add all together, making a total of 140 in all, and use this number for the badge emblem. Have the pin small.

Let me know what you think of this, will you?—PRIV. JACK HYATT, JR.

Yes, it does the work. Only, instead of using the word "Adventure," why not use the word "Camp-Fire"?

C	A	M	P	F	I	R	E
3	1	13	16	6	9	18	5

Added, these figures gave 71 as the emblem. Nothing but the number 71 would appear on the button—a small, neat, well-finished button in inconspicuous colors. No advertisement about it. Those who were members of our Camp-Fire would know what it means; those who were not would know nothing.

The button would, of course, be issued to any member of Camp-Fire and any one is a member who wishes to be. A charge would be made to cover manufacturing cost and postage. I think I'll go ahead and order a limited number, letting you know when they're ready for delivery.

THE Fifth Liberty Loan is about due. Here's what one comrade did on previous Liberty Loans. How many of us are as good Americans as he?

San Francisco, California.

Please put my name on your list for Democracy.

Been a hobo, sailor, soldier, business man, horse owner, stevedore, laborer, socialist, I. W. W., R. R. policeman, captain of ex-Army and Navy men, sent or helped to send over 300 "over there." Two of them decorated by the French Government.

Took your advice; bought 2d and 3d issue of Liberty Bonds. Compelled to live in a fifteen-cent house to do it, and sure made four others in the same house get them.

Started young boys and girls with Thrift Stamps. Started children with War Gardens.—J. JUNEMAN.

PIPEROCK again sent Christmas greeting to *Adventure* through the kind offices of W. C. Tuttle, ex-cartoonist and non-ex-teller of tales that make us laugh. This time it's *Judge Steele* that delivers the greeting.

Guns Again

SOME more about guns. It will take some time for letters to reach comrades Thompson and Wiggins and for their answers and comments to appear in "Firearms, Old and New" in "Ask Adventure," so in the meantime we'll have some of the letters that came in before our new department was announced.

Hereafter all letters concerning firearms in any way should be sent, *not* to the magazine, but direct to either Mr. Wiggins or Mr. Thompson, according to whether it belongs in the field of one or the other. They'll be the doctors from now on.

Phoenix, British Columbia, Canada.

I have been reading with lively interest the article, "Firearms, Old and New," in the first August number by D. Wiggins and L. F. Brown. As I know all are welcome to the Camp-Fire, I can not here resist "butting-in." The article purports to be "a complete history of the principal types of firearms, etc.," and I read it with keen anticipation in the hope of learning why the only shooting instrument of precision built on truly scientific lines, namely the Whitworth "rifle," was never universally adopted.

Unfortunately I am not able to speak with authority concerning this superb weapon, and, writing from hearsay only, I am asking for publication because the matter is one of universal interest to most all of *Adventure* readers. Some of them, no doubt, reading this, will be able to give us the information needed

I HAVE the story from an old Indian army veteran, one who has seen strenuous service under both the British and American flags, who, being an enthusiastic soldier (albeit a Socialist), is necessarily a gun-crank. This, indeed, is his main hobby, and I understand he has amassed quite a collection of the better sort of firearms. This is what I can recall of his story to me concerning the Whitworth "rifle," and, as I have to depend on memory only for the details of a narrative told to me some years ago, I shall doubtless make some mistakes, which, I trust, some of our members will correct later on.

SOME time before the middle of the last century, the British Government offered a substantial prize, perhaps fifty thousand dollars, for the best type of rifled small arms. There were a number of competitors, among whom was Sir James (?) Whitworth, who submitted a type built on a totally different principle to that of all the others. The latter embodied the style in use today, namely, the round bore, choked or straight, channeled with the customary spiral grooves to produce the boring, twisting motion in the bullet. Whitworth's gun had no grooves, but, instead of having a round bore, was hexagonal in section, the bullet hexagonal also, and instead of the rifled grooves, the bore had a spiral twist inside—built on a mandrel, I think.

ALL the different types were tested at the Government butts, and the result showed that the Whitworth weapon was far superior to them all, inasmuch as with a given charge of explosive it had a greater velocity, flatter trajectory, greater range and heavier striking force. Moreover, the barrel was easier to clean, and that bane of all rifles was eliminated—it could not get "leaded," that is, the grooves, being non-existent, could not get choked with metal left by the projectile. Again, it is necessary in all the present rifles, I believe, to make the bullet larger than the bore in order that the bullet's sides may take hold of the rifling, thus expending an unnecessary amount of force, whereas, with the Whitworth, a close fit is all that is needed to prevent the escape of gases ahead of the missile. Theoretically better, and proved better practically by testing at various ranges! Yet the British Government failed to adopt it, and gave the preference to another weapon.

MY INFORMANT told me the reason for this was the same as the reason for the prevalence of inefficiency among British staff officers today even in this hour of urgent need—favoritism and "pull." Here I must digress a little: Caste saved the perpetrators of the Dardanelles shambles. Caste saved the murderer of the British wounded in the Mesopotamia campaign, and Caste did its best to damn those who exposed the abominable neglect. To hell with Caste and all its votaries!

But to return to our muttons. The few Whitworth weapons that were manufactured were speedily snapped up, and I suppose that the magnitude and multiplicity of his other interests prevented him from continuing their manufacture as a private venture. Very likely disappointment was a factor, but I have ever since wondered why he did not give the enterprise in charge to some one who had the leisure to develop it. Nowadays collectors are very willing to pay fancy prices for isolated specimens, for I am told that, even judged by modern standards, it is a good, accurate tool.

TO BROACH another subject I would like to say that I became acquainted about thirty years ago in this country (B. C.) with an old-time trapper and hunter, one who made his living that way and knew nothing else. He would have nothing whatever to do with the modern Winchester and Marlin of that date, and from his point of view he was right, I think. He used, I think, a bored-out, breech-loading rifle (don't remember the make; bolt action, I think) and used to mold all his own bullets, round ones, probably 50 caliber.

His argument was: "See here, there ain't no place in this country where you can do any long-range shooting; if you see anything to shoot it's always at point-blank range and through bushes.

"Now suppose a grizzly's comin' at you under them circumstances?

"You shoots at him with a 45-90 Winchester, and the bullet hits a twig and glances off and where *are* you? Better have a shotgun." Here he fondled his old smooth-bore. "Well, young feller, I takes this here weapon and shoots a round bullet at him, and it hits a twig, but it don't glance, and I gets him first shot."

It struck me as a pretty good argument, though I've never followed his advice. Anyway, while he knew nothing else, he *did* know his business.

I HAVE read your remarks on the German Bureau of Enemy Psychology, and my views are identical with yours. We Britishers have had it drilled into us from childhood about the decadent condition of the English-speaking race. German propaganda, of course.

It is a lie dangerous and insidious. In a sense it is absolutely true, yet relatively, in comparison with other races, the German, for instance, it is entirely and wholly false. The trouble with us British is—I don't know that this applies to Americans—that our faults loom so large in our own eyes that we overlook those of others and fail to compare our virtues with those of foreign nations.—W. H. BAMBURY.

Kansas City, Mo.

I have read the letter of Mr. S. H. Prockter of Vancouver, B. C., in the November issue of *Adventure* with considerable interest and, I must confess, a great deal of surprise. Mr. Prockter states that the Colt .45 automatic is so much lighter than the Webley .45 automatic that he can't shoot it with any satisfaction. This is odd, as the Colt .45 automatic weighs 39 ounces and the Webley 39½ ounces. He says that he could shoot the old Colt .45 revolver very well as it was heavy. I presume he means the Single Action Army, which, with 4¾-inch barrel, weighs only 37 ounces and with 7½-inch barrel weighs 41½ ounces. The .32 Webley automatic which he says weighs more than the Colt .45, weighs 20 ounces. The difference in the balance of the two makes of guns is probably what has misled him.

MR. PROCKTER asks advice as to an effective pocket arm. To my mind there is nothing answers this want as nearly as a Smith & Wesson .38 military with a 4 or 5 inch barrel, and I prefer the 1902 model with the round instead of the square butt. The round stock doesn't make as big a bulge in the clothes as the square one.

It is a little thinner than the Colt in every direction, which makes it come between the Colt Arms Special and the Colt Police Positive Special. It uses a very effective cartridge and, if the bullets aren't of a destructive enough nature as they come, if Mr. Prockter will take a small saw and saw them back from the point about half-way or a little more between the end of the bullet and the shell I think he'll be satisfied with their action. They will surely open anything up that they hit.

I NOTICE that one of my above statements is a little ambiguous. When I state the Smith & Wesson is thinner than the Colt, I refer to the Colt Arms Special. It isn't, of course, as thin or small as the Police Special, but the Police Special is a trifle light for most men, though I can use it very satisfactorily.

A soft bullet would without question be better for stopping purposes than a hard one. I have demonstrated this to my own complete satisfaction so many times on different kinds of game that there can be no doubt whatever.—LLOYD F. BROWN.

THE next is from a comrade in China. It was written before the end of the war but there are still chauffeurs "over there" and perhaps some of them will drop him a line. What he says about the old Chinaman is like the proverbial small boy with a pin and a worm who catches more fish than the fully-equipped sportsman. Here are we arguing over the fine shadings in the best weapons that modern skill and science can produce, and there are those Mongolians with crude but treasured heirlooms bringing down the birds. Oh, no, I know that doesn't mean they can shoot better than we can, but, well, it's sort of amusing. And if all of them hit everything they shot at, as did the old Chino, well, that's about all there is to hit, isn't it?

And it suggests something that has always interested me: How did Boone, Kenton, Crockett, Carson and the best shots of their day compare with the best shots of ours: (1) With allowance for the difference in weapons then and now, and (2) without allowance for that difference? Have Americans improved in marksmanship or deteriorated since the use of a gun is no longer a necessity throughout most of the land?

Tientsin, North China.

DEAR SIR:

Just a few words from a comrade who is out on the rim. I have just been reading an article in Camp-Fire and found it quite interesting.

LAST week I was out hunting snipe and met an old Chino with a gun that I think is worth while mentioning. The gun itself was, I should judge, between a six and an eight caliber shotgun, and looked like it might be older than China. It was quite long from the butt to the muzzle, about seven feet, and the barrel was at least five and a half feet of that. The stock was very short. I can not understand how the old man managed to shoot with it, because it did not seem to have any balance at all, but the old man seemed to make out all right with it. I stayed with him more than an hour during which time he scared up six snipe and he never missed one of them.

The gun was an old muzzle-loading flint-lock, and after every shot he would set it down before he went after his bird. He tamped in his powder and shot and he sure was an expert at that; I don't believe that it took him a minute to get through the whole process.

I had a Remington 12-bore automatic and thought that I was doing good shooting when I got two out of three birds, but the old Chinaman got them all. I asked him how he would trade, but he said that his gun had been in the family for two generations and that the ammunition for mine would cost too much, while he made his own.

I have been talking with some fellows who were up in Mongolia on a hunting trip last Fall, and they said that the native hunters and trappers up there all used those kinds of guns for big game.

Well, here's to all Camp-Fire friends.—E. S. GAGNIER, Quartermaster Corps, U. S. Army.

P. S. Would like to hear from some of the chauffeurs "Over There." Address: Ft. Wm. McKinley, P. I.

Visalia, California.

Not so many years ago makers and users of rifles insisted on weights from ten pounds to and above fifteen pounds, while today rifles of many times the power, and of equal safety, weigh below eight pounds. The same facts hold true in shotgun evolution.

THE reluctance of manufacturers to change patterns, true English conservativeness, and the demand of many customers for something like grandfather had probably explains the excessive weight of the arms M. Prockter refers to, and not the necessity for either safety or endurance. The very lightest modern pistol or revolver of standard make is amply safe for the ammunition for which it is designed and will endure the "grief" of continued hard usage equally as well as the excessively heavy foreign made weapons.

In my own case I know how difficult it was to become used to the "feel" of the modern muzzle-light (shotgun-like) rifle after years of use of the stocked-crowbar pattern with which I began, and for several years I weighted the barrel of my Smith & Wesson target-pistol to give it the "feel" of the muzzle-heavy revolvers I was accustomed to, while the balanced weight of the more modern automatic pistol is still awkward for me and tends to slow down my shooting of it.

REGARDING the use of jacketed or soft-point bullets or even the nicking of pure lead ones, I have made sufficient experiments to convince myself that Dr. Newton (I think) was correct when he said that no projectile with a less velocity than 1,200 feet per second would deform or mushroom unless it struck a very hard substance.

I tried 32-20 W. C. F. smokeless with jacketed hollow-point bullets in a six-inch barrel Colt and secured a penetration of six to eight inches of clear, soft dry wood without indication of deformation (and then sold the gun and went back to the .45).

CAL. .32 Colt Police Positive cartridges with two thin saw kerfs made at right angles to each other and extending from 1-3 to ½ the depth of the exposed (soft lead) bullet were fired through six and eight thicknesses of woolen cloth (old breeches) and through one inch of pine board and recovered in the cloth in the rear of the board without any sign of deformation or mushrooming except where they encountered a hard knot or nail.

Colt .45s sawed as above and fired with full 40-grain charges of black powder penetrated the same thickness of cloth, then five to six inches of dry redwood fence-post, then the same amount of cloth on the far side of the post and some were recovered in the soft ground beyond and none that were recovered were mushroomed in the least degree.

OF THE regular pistol or revolver cartridges marketed in this country I rate the stopping power in the following order: Colt .45: S. & W. Russian .44; Colt .41 with the 200 grain, blunt, outside lubricated bullet .38 150-grain flat-point bullet as made by the Ideal people, and I doubt if any sawing, nicking or boring will greatly increase their respective stopping capacity.—G. L. CHESTER.

Baltimore, Md.

Mr. Prockter's inquiry interested me very much. In the first place there are two kinds of hand-guns, one for target work, with long barrel, belonging to the holster class, and the other shorter, for pocket packing, and the long barrel weapon always has it over the shorter one.

THE pistol, however, is primarily intended for close work, and one of the finest pocket-guns of today, for easy packing, is the .38 Pocket Model Colt automatic. This gun is only 7½ inches long with 4½-inch barrel and weighs 32 ounces, and the man that can stand up against the blow of its bullet is a real man.

The finest gun made today, in my estimation, is the .38 Military Model Colt, which has a 6-inch barrel, weighs 38 ounces and is 9 inches over all. In Mr. Himmelwright's work, "Pistol and Revolver Shooting," this gun is shown to be the strongest in the world. Both of these .38 guns shoot an 130-grain ball, which in the latter model develops a velocity of 1,175 feet per second at 50 feet from the muzzle, strikes a blow of 398 pounds and has a penetration of 10 inches in soft white pine. The only other pistol that exceeds it in any way is the 7.63 M. M. Mauser which strikes a blow of 373 pounds, which is less than the Colt, but owing to the shape of the bullet, has a penetration of 11 inches of soft white pine.

AS FAR as any of the Colts being safe is concerned, there is not the slightest danger of them blowing up as Mr. Prockter seems to fear, and this is probably his reason for not being able to handle one of them as well as he did his old Webley—fearing it will blow up, he flinches and of course does not score. For his benefit, in the Government tests a .45 Colt was fired more than 5,000 times without a misfire, jam or single broken part. A wonderful record.

The Luger is also a fine gun and he should have made good with it.

As to nicking the ball to make it mushroom, there is not much in this, as a pistol ball does not, like a rifle ball, get up sufficient velocity to make it mushroom.

I WISH to add one thing, and that is that the hold of the automatic is different from that of the revolver. I had three revolvers and sold them all, as they had seen much service, intending to get new ones, but in looking around the automatic came to hand and I bought one. I could do nothing with it and turned it in and got a new revolver, but an acquaintance, who had worked at a Government arsenal, whom I told of my experience, told me I had made a mistake, so I bought another automatic, shot it as I had been directed and the automatic is the only gun for me. I have a .32 which I feel sure is a pretty good "stopper" if needed, and a .22 for target work—both Colts.

Mr. Walter Winans has just put out a work, or is just about to put out a work, on automatic pistol shooting, and I know it will be good, but at this time I can not give the name of it.

Just why the Webley people made their guns so heavy I have never been able to learn, except that possibly, when the designs were gotten out, it was considered necessary to have the gun as heavy as it is, but if this is the case, the idea was dropped long ago.—W. E. Mepham.

Detroit, Mich.

The English Webley-Scott automatic pistol .455 caliber weighs two pounds seven and a half ounces, with a five-inch barrel, eight shots. Taking the general perceptive view of it, it is not by any means a neat-appearing arm, awkward both as to looks and to handle; furthermore is not positive in action on account of the large number of working parts poorly made and constructed. The material, no doubt, is excellent, but the lines on which it is made are not coincident with its working qualifications.

The English can not as yet make side-arms, and their market is at all times flooded with a grand and various assortment of foreign-made guns, ranging from the cheap one-shilling Belgian guns and German derringers and Flobert system single shot b. b. cap-pistols to the British bull-dog pocket arms. Clumsy, inaccurate, non-reliable and not fair to gaze upon, and all are overburdened with lots of scrap iron, steel, etc. The countries across the creek can not, it seems, conceive the idea of turning out a good reliable arm that is as consistent with looks as it is to weight.

One reason is the lack of interest shown in pistol and revolver shooting—the British army and navy and other branches of the service were not, at the time I have in mind, equipped with a side-arm, but I know personally of three that were, and this only in the case of certain non-coms and officers, and, at the last practise I saw at Birbright Camp, an American, who was an officer, with a Colt revolver, certainly did some shooting, both mounted and on foot. The others were using a Webley-Scott .455, 4½ barrel, weight 2 pounds 3 ounces, heavy, clumsy to handle, accompanied with a kick like a Texas jack and extremely inaccurate even at short distance. Their later W. S. model is constructed on better lines, weighing with a 7½-inch barrel, same caliber, 2 pounds 7 ounces.

The art of making side-arms by our good English cousins and allies has not gotten to the fine point where they can turn out a real fine pistol or revolver. If they have, I have not seen any up to the present time, and I am open for criticism. They all set too high in the hand, painful sprains, etc., resulting from heavy recoil and poor balance.

The trigger pull is way up in the pounds, ranging anywhere from four to eight, and in the case of European arms this, in almost every instance, is more.

AND, to answer the other portion of the question of Mr. Prockter, would say that from his letter I think he is a little gun-shy with a side-arm. Note he says "I find myself expecting it to blow to pieces." All the Colts and W. & S. guns are tested with overloads at their respective factories, and if one takes good care of his arm there is nothing much to fear, provided, however, one uses factory loaded ammunition that is suited for that particular arm, or reloaded ammunition by one who knows how.

He says that the Colt Company made their good name by the older "killer .45." Yes, that's where they got their start, and they have been climbing steadily ever since old Sam Colt first made and put on the market his revolver over three-quarters of a century ago, and to my idea they are the gun for a man who knows. This is only for side-arms. The Colt .45 auto stood the most severe test that was ever given any arm that was to be issued to any service in the world—some record. When the United States saw the value of automatics as side-arms for our boys, she called a board that passed judgment on the Savage and Colt .45s, and, as we know, the latter broke all records. And we had the choice of numerous foreign-made arms.

THE shooting of six-guns by our best shots and even when done by ordinary persons has always excited the interest and comments of our English cousins, whether this be at tin cans or regulation targets. We have this art down fine; there is no question about it, and I think, in fact I know, that if Mr. Prockter will stick by the Colt auto .45 he will find it the gun that is a gun.

The Savage I do not like; it does not function normally. It sticks, jams, etc., and it is not the fault of the ammunition. One thing, though, with any automatic, there is a tendency to jam, and the only cause that I know of is stale ammunition. Smokeless powder, we are told, deteriorates with age, length of time unknown to me at present, and, again, the grains of powder vary when seen under a strong glass, and if left in belt or carried in one position the larger grains shift to the surface, naturally causing the explosion when the primer is struck to take longer time, thereby losing power whereby, although the bullet is forced out, the recoil is not strong enough to eject the empty and reload. Hence, a jam.

So bear in mind—fresh ammunition for the automatics, or an occasional shaking up or around; keep them clean and there won't be any kick coming. For cleaning, a small, flat, enamel paint-brush, three-in-one oil, is recommended, and attention must be given to the right-angles of the grooving of the slide and receiver.

Here is a table of ballistics for W. & S. revolvers:

TABLE OF BALLISTICS FOR W. & S. REVOLVERS

W. & S. .455 Auto Revolver

7 grains of cordite, diam. of bullet .455, weight 220 grains, R. N. (round nose), muzzle velocity at 50 ft. 750, energy 280.6 ft. lbs. Penetration in pine 4¼ inches.

W. & S. W. S. Model

5.5 grains of cordite, diam. of bullet .455, velocity 265, R. N., 700 ft. at 50 ft. 288 ft. lbs. 4¼ in. in pine. This with a 7½-inch barrel.—C. RYAN.

P. S. A tip that might be used in regard to an automatic. When I come home I let my retractor spring out to full length and let the hammer down all the way instead of keeping both tense for months at a stretch. The spring is a main part, so baby it along. I find in carrying the gun that a shoulder holster is O. K. for carrying around, tied down by a whang string to the belt to prevent coming up when gun is lifted; or a good, well-made belt holster is O. K. Both of mine are hand-made and are "fitted" to the gun. There is no binding of leather around the trigger guard, and further, they are cut away to facilitate a guide draw by cutting the leather to permit my trigger-finger engaging directly with the trigger.

If Mr. Prockter so wishes I would be pleased to furnish him with a pattern that has been tried and tested by myself and proven its worth.—C. R.

A COMRADE, now a minister, joins our other comrades who have come forward with their own experiences in breaking away from the "booze habit" on the chance that such experiences may be of practical help to others who also want to break away. No, Camp-Fire is conducting no prohibition campaign. Our Camp-Fire considers that a matter for every man to decide for himself. But if a comrade has decided against drink and wants to get away from it, that is a different thing. If we can help him, we ought to and we're glad to. Hear this comrade:

AT ONE time I was rather successful as a newspaper man. I held a position as financial editor of a certain division of a certain newspaper syndicate. Because of my work I had to be a good fellow—or because I was a good fellow I was successful in my work. But, because of my youth and laws of nature that what we sow must be reaped in a greater quantity, my health broke. Insomnia. Weight 110 pounds. Walking early one morning when it was oppressively hot, the notion struck me to walk till I was tired. I did.

I left the city behind me about two miles, and became gloriously sleepy about 4 A.M. at a crossing of the road I was on and the railroad. As I was wearing "palm beach" which could be laundered I lay me down under an adjacent water-tank.

The next thing I knew some grizzled human shook me into wakefulness and said: "Come on, bo, here we are."

The humor of the thing struck me and I went—on to the side door pullman. I expected to telegraph back that I was taking a vacation, but the thirst hit me the first day, and I decided to stick it out with some two bucks in my pocket.

WE WENT into dry territory. I had to work or starve. I let my beard grow so none would recognize me. I left the railroad and struck right across country. The railroad was dangerous for me—communication was too easy. Money gone, I got work. Harvest hands were very scarce. I offered to work for my room and board. I pulled broom-corn the first day of work and fainted from trying to keep up with a ten-year-old girl. At the end of two weeks I could nearly do a day's work.

One of my arms was covered with scabbing sores. It puzzled me and hindered my work, as one as long as my hand was right over my elbow. I had never had any blood disease, and wondered what it could be. An "old-timer" asked me if I used to drink. I told him a little. He snorted. Then he confided that it was the booze coming out. Rather peculiar diagnosis, but the only probable one I could think of. I never asked a physician.

In six weeks the scabs were gone. In a year the scars. Two months after "embarking" I could do a man's work. Six months after, I returned, weight 165. A punch in either fist. Browned so my sometime boss didn't know me. Turned down my old job at $200 a month because of the temptation. Took work at $85 a month. Got married. That was six years ago. I have not yet reached my old salary but I will pass it in two years. In ten I will double it. If I had stayed I would have been dead by now or mooching enough to buy a drink and living on my past glory. Selah.

A WORD from Louis Dodge concerning his story in this issue. There is no "if" as to whether any of our Camp-Fire comrades have served in the Philippines and pretty surely his letter will put Mr. Dodge into touch with some of his old bunkies.

St. Louis, Mo.

The story, "A Fight to a Finish," is mainly true. The soldier called *Flynn* (this was not his real name) belonged to either the 18th or 23rd U. S. Infantry. I belonged to both regiments at different times back in the Spanish-American days. *Flynn* was actually driven to bay under a bridge, just as the story relates. And he was rescued by something like a miracle, combined with his own pluck and persistence, from a small band of natives. It was down in the Sulu group of islands, where the natives are Mohammedans. I have added a few "trimmings" to the story for the sake of proportion.

IT MAY be that there are among those who gather round the Camp-Fire some who served in the American army in the Phillipines around about 1899 or 1900. If so, any from the 18th or 23rd are likely to recall the story of *Flynn*.

I was in Manila in 1898; in Iloilo in '99; in Sulu, Siassi and Bongao in '99 and 1900. I'd like much to hear from others of those times and places who remember me.

We didn't do a great deal of fighting, but I think we constituted a "Watch on the Rhine" far more sinister and strange than anything the boys are facing in Europe today, now that the fighting is over. The weird silence of the little islands, the loneliness, the sense of being in a lost world—these constituted a situation altogether unique.—LOUIS DODGE.

FROM S. B. H. Hurst of our writers' brigade comes another answer to "What is the spirit of adventure, biologically considered?" I give only part of it and so do not do justice to Mr. Hurst's argument. Personally, though I do not agree with him, I think the world would be better off if it frankly discussed sex like any other fact of life, instead of leaving it to work its way half unseen, less than half understood and with the lure and mystery of attempted secrecy. But even those of you who feel as I do will agree that, popular attitude being what it is, our Camp-Fire is not the place for full and frank discussion of the subject, no matter how sane and decent the discussion may be.

So I merely present the outline of Mr. Hurst's main point, as a theory that deserves place among the others advanced. And I give warning that no other letters on this theory will reach Camp-Fire.

Seattle, Wash.

By the way, the answer to your repeated query in the magazine—what is the *spirit of adventure*, considered biologically—may appear unpleasant to many minds. Because, of course, sex is the answer. Adventure is such because it stirs up a greater amount of emotion than the ordinary. Probably the earliest form of adventure, except the mere hunting for food, was the cave man taking his club to take away from his rival the woman he wanted—the gratification of the sex instinct being the motive, as, indeed, it was in most of the hunting. The quests set upon knights had always some woman's scarf about them, and even the Holy Grail was in line—as a negation of sex, thus proving the theory. But you can very easily furnish illustrations for yourself.

Probably you will not like this answer. Unfortunately science is against you. You can not avoid your subconscious inheritance. But there are those who will say this is a nasty subject. So is embryology.—S. B. H. HURST.

FOLLOWING Camp-Fire custom, William David Ball, on the occasion of his first story in our magazine, rises and introduces himself:

Los Angeles, Calif.

All my life I've been waiting for a chance to blow my own horn. Now that you have invited me to tell something of myself, I find the blowing difficult. I'd like to flavor this letter with the glamour of far places, weave a thread of romance into it that should leave you marveling at what a really wonderful fellow I am. But when I glance over the list of bare facts in my life, my conceit goes out like a a candle doused with a wet gunny-sack.

I WAS born in Denver, Colorado, where I grew up like most other boys—playing hookey occasionally, reading of my favorite heroes (Diamond Dick and Jesse James) behind my geography, and dreaming of the time when I should adventure into the blue, cloud-kissed ranges of the Rockies rising to the west. When I had finished my schooling, at twenty-four, I left Denver. (I must not lose the opportunity here of bragging about my two degrees, lying tucked away somewhere in a trunk. I never mention them to my relatives, but to you, who do not know me so well, I may speak of them with pardonable pride.)

THROUGH Wyoming and Utah I went, landing finally in the sagebrush country of Idaho. For a year I worked on ranches along the Salmon Creek, saving my wages like a good fellow. South of the Snake River and nestled close to the hills that divide Nevada and Idaho, there was a Mormon settlement called Oakley. Oakley for twenty years had grown and prospered, a little world in itself, sixty miles from a railroad. I rented a ranch close to Oakley, with the firm purpose of making my fortune.

Things happened to me on that ranch, and they've kept right on happening ever since. I made my way back to Colorado without my fortune. I worked as a bookkeeper, I handled paper routes, I spun strings for musical instruments, I taught school. Finally, I drifted back to the sagebrush, where for six years I held down a desert farm under a worthless irrigation project. Just now, I'm running the "Flu" ambulance for the city of Los Angeles, interrupting for a while my chosen profession of writing short stories.

THE story, "The Affairs of Men," was suggested to me by an incident I witnessed in a cow-camp near the White River district of Routt County, Colorado, before the Moffat Railroad went through.

A cow-puncher rode up to the Silver Dollar Saloon, dismounted, and began looping the reins around the hitching-rail. The saloon door opened to let out a chorus of yells and laughter. The bronco reared back on the reins, sliding the puncher's right hand along the splintered rail. The man jerked his hand free, turned, and drove the toe of his boot twice into the horse's belly.

It was pitiful to see the animal slowly spraddle its four legs outward with grunts of agony. For an instant there was neither sound nor movement from the dozen men standing round. Two dance-hall girls, a moment before, had stepped from the saloon for a breath of air, carrying the billiard-cues with which they had been playing. Before we had quite realized what had happened to the horse, one of the girls had jumped to the edge of the platform, swung her cue twice around her head, and landed it across the face of the cow-puncher. The cue broke. Also, incidentally, the puncher's nose broke.

NOW, this was justice, prompt and satisfying, but the incident as it stands is not a short story. It was not until I had lived for a number of years in the desert, and had seen some of the ways in which the desert works out the law of compensation, that I conceived the story of Bartholomew Webb and "The Affairs of Men."—WILLIAM DAVID BALL.

P. S. I love horses, guns, and the open places. I smoke, I swear, and I'm always in need of money. This last condition, I feel, well fits me for the profession of letters.

Finish the job with the Victory Liberty Loan!

SO FAR as it could, our magazine has always leaned toward stories built on a sound basis of fact and it is gratifying to learn, from an authority, that two of our writers' brigade have not only made good in the groundwork of a story laid some thousands of years back in B. C., but have made a valued contribution.

Certainly all kinds sit at our Camp-Fire. Of the last three letters I've picked up, one is from a college professor, another from an ex-hobo, a third from an old-timer of the West, and among those just coming to my hand I see letters from a mining engineer, another old Westerner, a real-estate dealer, a U. S. Post-Office official, a merchant, an adventurer and showman, a physician, a woman writer, a paymaster in the Navy.

And now back into B. C. and archeology and obscure history:

I have been a reader of your magazine for a number of years, and I enjoy each issue immensely. It is a great relief to turn from the daily grind of life and get on to the rim of things.

I AM a professional man, a college professor of the classical languages and a professional archeologist. I have followed Bishop and Brodeur in their stories, especially the one entitled "In the Grip of the Minotaur." I may say that I believe they have solved the puzzle. As one who is very familiar with the site of Homeric Troy and Knossos, allow me to extend to these gentlemen my congratulations. You will find in my latest book, "Studies in Vergil," that I give them the credit of solving the puzzle of the first scene in Book VI. of the Æneid. The book is published by The Aryan Press, Point Loma, California.

. . . . I have spent my life in archeological and anthropological research round the globe (having circled it three times, among all the strange, savage peoples of the world) and in editing the oldest archaeological journal in America, written books and articles upon these subjects.—J. O. KINNAMAN.

Own and keep Victory Liberty Bonds.

THIS is not the first time we have had a story from the Baroness Orczy but the following is none the less interesting on that account. It was written before the war and came to us on the occasion of the appearance of "The Laughing Cavalier" in our magazine.

I think it is pretty generally known by now that England, though very dear to me, is only the country of my adoption. I was born in Hungary, at a place called Tarna-Ors, which is in the very heart of the most magnificent corn-land in Europe.

The Camp-Fire

MY PARENTS only came to England when I was almost grown up and I never spoke a word of English until I was fifteen. Within three months I was acting in a school play and within six months I had passed first-class College of Preceptors exam. with honors and a special prize for languages.

My theosophist friends tell me that this all fits into the theory of reincarnation—they declare that in one of my previous existences I was an English-woman.

Be that as it may, I certainly am an English-woman—in all but blood.

MY FATHER, Baron Orczy, besides being a distinguished diplomatist in his own country, was above all things a musician to his finger-tips. His beautiful opera, "Il Rinnegato," dedicated to the late Queen of the Belgians who was a Hungarian princess, was performed in London at the old Her Majesty's Theater with great success. He also on more than one occasion conducted his own compositions at the celebrated Philharmonic Concerts of the early '80s, and had also the honor several times to conduct the Royal Amateur Orchestral Society of which the late Duke of Edinburgh was the most distinguished violinist.

The great musical geniuses of the late nineteenth century were intimate friends at our house: Richard Wagner, the Abbé Liszt, Charles Gounod, Massenet, to quote only a few names from among those men who in those days used to pat me on the shoulder and ask me if I meant to be a musician like my father. Whereat I always answered, "No!"

THUS I was brought up in an atmosphere of music rather than of the sister arts. Nor, strangely enough, did I show in my earlier life the slightest tendency, talent or even desire to write. As I had no overwhelming talent for music, I wanted to be an artist. I studied art for years and achieved no small measure of success in it. I was at one time a constant exhibitor at the R. A. My picture, "The Jolly Young Waterman," illustrative of the old English ballad, "He eyed the young rogues with so charming an air that this waterman ne'er was in want of a fare!" hung on the line in the "gem room" of the Academy was quite one of the features of its year.

I was greatly encouraged in those days in my art studies by my old friend Edwin Long, R. A., the creator of those wonderfully popular pictures "Diana or Christ" and "The Babylonian Marriage Market."

WHILST studying art at old "Heatherley's" in Newman Street, I met my husband, Mr. Montagu Barstow, who already then was a well-known artist. For a few years after my marriage I joined him in doing numberless illustrations in black-and-white for books and magazines.

I have no hesitation in saying that—though during the period of my art-studentship I had of course no thoughts of becoming a novelist—that same art-training has been of incalculable value to me in my career. It taught me to see the scenes of my books and of my plays pictorially.

I BECAME an author almost literally in the turn of a hand. This was but a very few years ago. My husband and I were house-hunting, or, rather, studio-hunting, and in the interval we were staying as paying guests with a family whose chief recreation consisted in writing stories for magazines. These they would read out loud to one another and also to us before sending them round on their weary way to various editors, and, as they were not very brilliant, they were for the most part returned with the usual thanks. But one day one of these products of none too fertile brains was actually accepted for publication, terms were discussed and agreed upon, and altogether there was in the atmosphere of the Kensington house that delightful sense of excitement which comes only from artistic success. Some of the excitement also crept into me. To be quite frank: though there was neither hatred or malice in its composition, there was quite a good deal of jealousy seething inside me, and later on in the day I said to my husband:

"Look at these people who have never been outside their own limited circle. They not only write stories but have them accepted and paid for. Why shouldn't I, who have been all over Europe and have known so many people who are worth knowing, write stories too?"

"Why shouldn't you?" was my husband's simple comment.

AND that was the beginning of my literary career. Until then I had never even thought of such a thing. I had never taken up a pen for any other purpose than writing letters—and as few of these as possible. But now I set to with a will and wrote two short-stories which I sent to *Pearson's Magazine*. They were accepted and paid for at the rate of 10 guineas each.

But my first novel was "The Scarlet Pimpernel." I saw the whole story first, the scenes of the French revolution and the dandy-hero.

The novel was offered to a round dozen publishers who would have none of it.

Finally, going to less and less well-known publishers, the MS. at last found its way to Messrs. Greening & Co.

Close upon a million copies of the book have been printed and sold. The novel has been translated into fourteen different languages, and in Brazil it forms a portion of the library for the blind.

My third romance, called "A Son of the People," is descriptive of my old home in Hungary. The house which is described so fully in the novel is the house in which I was born. The life of the territorial magnates of that part of Europe was the first life which I knew.

As a matter of fact, the agrarian riots in connection with the setting up of a steam-mill, and the total destruction of a magnificent crop of wheat, occurred on my father's estate, and he it was who was the victim of that outrage. The peasantry was furious with him for introducing the grinding of corn through an agency which they could not understand, and one night just when the corn was ready for harvest and the weather so dry that not one atom of moisture was there to check the flames, they set fire to the four corners of a twenty-acre corn field.

I was a tiny girl at the time but I remember seeing the red sky, hearing the shouts and the tramping and being told that the corn was burning and that the horses and cattle were in danger in their stables. —Baroness Orczy.

Buy Victory Bonds and keep them.

INSTEAD of running "Fighting the Hun Web" occasionally, as previously stated, it seems best to discontinue that department entirely. The Hun Web is still working, but there are many other dangerous webs and the only way to fight them all is outlined in "Looking Ahead for Democracy."

THE last buffalo living at large in a wild state. What is the latest date on which one has been seen? Here is the testimony of an old-timer to June, 1882. A smaller man or a less real sportsman would have shot those poor last specimens of a vanishing race merely because he had the chance. It was probably a matter of food and skins for the Sioux. The writer is the brother of Major Frank North, inquired for at a past Camp-Fire by "Uncle Frank" Huston. At the end of his letter he said something about being afraid he'd talk too much when he got started on Indian fighting days. Not a chance. He is exactly the kind we most like to listen to and we hope Captain North will tell us a lot more about the old times.

Columbus, Neb.

I saw in the *Adventure* of December third an article headed "The Last Buffalo," by William Francis Hooker. The date he gives as 1879.

NOW I was riding range on the Cody and North Range sixty-five miles northwest of North Platte, Neb., at the head of the Dismal River, and in June, 1882, I ran across a herd of buffalo. There were twenty-eight head of cows and bulls, and seven calves. They were about seven miles from the ranch and my brother, Major Frank North, his daughter, a girl of twelve, and a nephew of ours, Mr. E. W. North, all rode out to where they were and, getting as close as we could before they saw us, we dashed out after them. They spilt into two bunches, and my nephew and I followed one bunch and cut out a live young bull and Ed killed him. I might have killed a half-dozen if I had felt so inclined, but I had killed many buffalo and so didn't care to.

MY BROTHER and his daughter Stella were both splendidly mounted and they cut out a cow and calf and tried to drive them to the ranch, but didn't succeed in doing it. He (my brother) said if I had been with them we could easily have roped the cow and calf, but he had no rope and so let them go, of course. He could have killed them, but didn't care to. Many years before that I saw him kill eleven buffalo with twelve shots from his revolvers. But that has nothing to do with the last buffalo. This band was all killed by a hunting party of Sioux Indians from the Rosebud Agency the following Fall, 1882. It is my belief that this was the last buffalo killed north of the Platte River in Nebraska, but I think there were one or two killed near the Republican River in the late eighties.

I ALSO saw in this number an inquiry from Frank H. Huston about my brother, Major Frank North. I am no writer, but if Mr. Huston will journey this far east some time and stop here for a few days as my guest, I can tell him many things about the chief of chiefs.

Does Mr. Huston know that he was named that by the Pawnee Indians? *Pawnee La Shano* which means "Chief of the Pawnees," and that included the chiefs of the Pawnees. No Indian and only one other white man ever bore this name among the Pawnees. The white man was General Frémont. Mr. Huston seems to know the Old Sidney pretty well. I wonder what year he was there. My brother was with General George A. Crooke (with two companies of his Pawnee Scouts) when he made his Winter campaign in the Powder River Country in 1876-1877. I was with him and was captain of one of the companies of Pawnee Scouts. We left Sidney Barrack in October and, after going with General McKenzie down to Chadron Creek where we rounded up Red Cloud and his band and took them into the reservation, we joined General Crooke at Fort Laramie and went with him to the head of Powder River where we fought the Cheyennes under Dull Knife. Killing many of them and completely destroying their village, we then returned to Sidney, Neb., about the first of February, 1877, I think, and were camped on Lodge Pole Creek just below the post till the following Spring.

I am the last one left of the officers of the Pawnee Scouts.—CAPTAIN L. H. NORTH.

AND another reply about Major North.

Los Angeles, Cal.

Major Frank North's celebrated company of Pawnee Scouts did wonderful work in the Middle West between '64 and '70. His name is a very familiar one to Army officers who were on the plains during that period. I have an old friend, now close to eighty years of age, living in the State of Washington who was with North at this time.

Later, Major North was in partnership with Bill Cody in the cattle business on Dismal River, sixty-five miles north of North Platte, Neb. Major North was greatly esteemed and beloved by his Pawnee scouts. At one time his outfit were guarding construction trains on the U. P. Ry., until its completion to Ogden, and they had many a warm scrap with the Sioux and Cheyennes, who "jumped" the construction camps at every opportunity. North was born in New York State in 1840.—E. A. BRININSTOOL.

WE'D like to explain to Mrs. M. A. Monsen that this office di not answer her several letters for the simple reason that she gave no address in any of them. This is particularly regretted as her object was to send letters and comforts to our boys in France.

OUR aluminum identification cards have met with such favor that we have far more demands for them at twenty-five cents than for the pasteboard cards given free.—ARTHUR SULLIVANT HOFFMAN.

A GOOD many of us already know David A. Curtis through his excellent poker stories—of *Old Man Greenlaw* and other interesting characters of Mississippi River life in past days. But on the occasion of his first story in our magazine he follows the Camp-Fire custom and introduces himself:

Somewhere in New York.

If I have a weakness, and I suspect I have more than one, it is a craving for companionship of good fellows.

You ask me to introduce myself by sending a "fairly full autobiography," but to be fairly full it would be too long to hold the interest of anybody but myself. There are, however, a few things I would like to have everybody know—especially my comrades of *Adventure's* Camp-Fire.

I AM a pronounced pacifist, detesting all wars and all fighting that is not absolutely necessary in defense of oneself or of others who suffer wanton injury. Holding this view, I hopelessly regret two things. One is that I was just a little too young to fight in the Civil War. The other is that I could not get into this one. They looked at my white hair and turned me down. I hate "Who's Who," because long ago I told them when I was born and they printed the damning fact.

Adventure? Well, I've had some. I've been married twice. Generally I have played the part of the innocent bystander. A man could not be a newspaper reporter and correspondent for twenty-five years in the olden days when we had newspapers, without seeing a lot of exciting incidents and sometimes getting mixed up in them.

I remember being run out of town by the Molly Maguires on one occasion and stumbling along for some two miles, over dead bodies and wrecked cars in a coal mine after an explosion on another day, but both times I was with Julian Ralph, and he wrote both stories, so it's hardly worth while to retell them.

I'M OFTEN asked how it comes that I know the Mississippi River and the people of the Mississippi Valley so well. If you will notice, you will find that I never write about them as they are to-day, but long ago I spent some years out there, living on the boats a good part of the time, so I really have some first-hand knowledge.

"Tall aches from little toe corns grow." If any one had told me, when I sat in at the poker game in Old Man Greenlaw's saloon in Arkansas City, that I was getting the material and laying the foundation of a dozen years of work, it would have sounded foolish to me, but I made a pretty good living for at least that long out of that poker game. Incidentally a good many thousands of readers have made the acquaintance of the old man and his gang. The game itself was not specially memorable. My losses were not heavy. I had a run in with Joe Barrett, though, that—but that story has been told, too. I don't want to get garrulous.

MOST of my personal adventures don't make stories. I think I have been fired out of more newspaper offices than any other man living, since I went on the *Sun* staff in '73. Some editors have fired me three or four times. And I've made business ventures—been burned out, frozen out, robbed and financially ruined more times than I have toes. Also I've wrestled with Azrael eleven times on the operating table. It was touch and go each time, but I've had perfect health now for some seven years.

Moreover, I've drawn two capital prizes in the lottery of matrimony, and I've held a jack-high straight-flush twice inside of an hour.

Aside from all this, my life has been calm and uneventful, but I like to read about other people's adventures, and I enjoy writing about what I've seen and heard.

I strongly suspect that the most of your writers are imposing on you when they sell you their "stuff" as fiction. It is too improbable. For one, I find it hard to write fiction so preposterously incredible as the actual facts I've witnessed.—DAVID A. CURTIS.

AS A result of an inquiry at Camp-Fire by one of you as to the whereabouts of Clifford W. Sands, several have sent in a clipping from the Seattle *Post-Intelligence* of Jan. 5, 1919, which says that he has been given the Distinguished Service Cross for saving the lives of three of his men during heavy fighting in the Argonne forest, Sept. 29, 1918. His rank is given as captain, attached to the 2nd Cavalry. Congratulations to an old Camp-Fire comrade.

AT OUR Mid-February Camp-Fire I gave a list of former members of our magazine's staff who had been serving with the colors. I gave also a longer list of comrades with the colors, but did not mean to imply, as I seemed to do, that these also had been members of our staff. Only the first five came under that classification. I didn't see the chance for misunderstanding until a soldier comrade in Canada wrote asking when his soldier brother serving in Belgium had been connected with our staff. Sometimes I wish we had as large a staff as that longer list would imply.

AS SOME of you already know, we have had to discontinue our "Letter Friends" service, so far as our own soldiers and sailors are concerned, because of a ruling of the War Department against encouraging general correspondence with our men.

AT OUR First-May Camp-Fire I said that, as your interest seemed to warrant it, I'd go ahead and order some Camp-Fire buttons that could be worn by those of you who like the idea of something that will distinguish Camp-Fire members without hanging an advertising sign on them or making them conspicuous in any way, so that when they chance to meet they can recognize each other as having at least one common interest and get acquainted or not as they see fit. Well, I've done so. That is, I've talked to the manufacturer and am now waiting to see the final working design.

The button will be enamel in gold-washed edging, small and neat—only about 3/8 of an inch in diameter, screw-back. It will have nothing whatever on it except the number 71 which, as you will remember, is the number obtained by numbering the letters of the alphabet and adding those of the letters spelling "Camp-Fire." The buttons will be divided into three plain fields, the middle one carrying the "71" and the fields being blue, brown and green, representing sky, earth and sea respectively.

THIS is being written February twenty-first and it may be that the buttons will be delivered to us by the time you see this in print, but I refuse even to predict until the buttons are actually in hand. After they do arrive it will be some two months before I can notify you in print.

As to price. The estimated cost of manufacture is about 20 cents in thousand lots. Some kind of carrier will probably be needed, adding slightly to the cost. Add postage to this. There is also the cost of office handling, but this will be added or not added according to how it figures in an effort to put the selling-price at a figure convenient for mailing. Probably a button will cost an even quarter with or without stamps included for postage. By the time of our next Camp-Fire I hope to have definite data.

NOW that we've actually "gone and done it," I like the idea more and more. It will be a button of the best quality, neat and small, such as no one need hesitate to wear. It carries only the number 71, which is sufficient for those who understand its meaning, tells nothing to those who do not and is free from the charge of advertising that would justly be raised if the word "Camp-Fire" or "Adventure" appeared anywhere on the button. And it ought to do a whole lot toward getting us better acquainted among ourselves, with especial usefulness for those who wander into the far places.

OUR old friends, members in highest standing of our Camp-Fire, the citizens of Piperock, Paradise and Curlew, have joined with the Cross-J outfit in sending a photograph to all the rest of us. Since it is difficult for all the rest of us to gather in one place to pass resolutions, I'm venturing to act as our spokesman and to state that every last one of us is now fully convinced that these esteemed friends are really on the map; and further to elucidate that if Fortune ever guides our footsteps near Yaller Rock County we'll sure take a chance and drop in on their hospitality and other things in the hope of getting still better acquainted.

To all ye readers of *Adventure* who have laughed with us or at us, we send a greeting from Yaller Rock County. Some skeptical hombre said: "There ain't no such animal," and for his benefit, or for the benefit of any who might feel skeptical in the future, we send this photograph.

Piperock, Paradise, Curlew and the Cross-J outfit held a meeting to devise ways and means of sending you a greeting. Magpie Simpkins suggested sending a picture to prove to you that we are honest-to-gosh folks. "Hassayampa" Harris suggested that we elect four delegates to be photographed.

"Sad" Samuels moved and seconded a motion that we elect four alternates, to be used in case there was any casualties among the delegates. Every suggestion was passed. Then "Scenery" Sims opined that the four alternates might as well get into the picture, which was passed by the four alternates. The delegates agreed to this, providing that we set down on the ground in front and remain passive.

Hassayampa didn't want to appear belligerent, so

he took off his gun and belt and held it out of sight. Just about the time that the photographer got ready to show us the birdie, "Telescope" Tolliver, "Old Testament" Tilton and "Doughgod" Smith has to horn into the picture. There would have been a killing if we'd 'a' knowed it. Reading from left to right, back row—not taking notice of them three aforementioned snake-hunters:

"Jay Bird" Whittaker, Cross-J; Magpie Simpkins, sheriff, Piperock; "Hassayampa" Harris, Curlew; Mike Pelly, Paradise. Front Row: "Scenery" Sims, Paradise; "Sad" Samuels, Curlew; Ike Harper, Piperock; "Chuck" Warner, Cross-J.

Folks may get the idea that we're a hardened lot of hombres, but we can point with pride to the fact that there ain't been a violent death in the county since Sitting Bull got up and walked away. Maybe at times we skate close to the cemetery; maybe we show absolute ignorance at times, but there ain't a community on earth that gets more fun out of life than we do, and if we can make you folks laugh once in a while—hurrah for our side.

Yours with the peace-sign,

YALLER ROCK COUNTY.

THE lost cities of the Incas. Here is an extremely interesting letter from a comrade living in Lorain, Ohio, at the time of writing.

S. S. *Thomas F. Cole*,
St. Mary's River.

Dear Congenial Spirits of the Camp-Fire: I noticed with interest the exchange of letters between Mr. Johnson and Mr. Young. I'm deciding to bring my Log and my yarn to sit in. Leaving Mollendo in Peru during the Spring of 1906, I traveled by way of Titicaca and Cuzco over a pass in the Cordilleras into the upper Amazon country. I stayed there two years, traveling by compass and the correct judgment of distance of land-marks in a wide half-circle to the land east, then back south until I reached the main Amazon some 500 miles down-stream.

I WAS lately under the impression that railroads were being built through there, but I see from Mr. Johnson's letter that this is not so. There are two large towns inhabited by the genuine Inca tribe and ruled by a daughter of the sun in the fastnesses of the Futahy hill region. The houses are built from square hewn rock with grass or bark roofs. Their temples are hewn into the rocks, each subterranean hall decorated with symbols of the sun and a curious kind of picture-writing. All their burros and guanacos live in one large community corral.

THE people claimed to have come from the coast where they were driven out by white men dressed in white metal. The name of the one town is Itzuatl; the other name I have forgotten, also the name of the reigning chieftainess. The people are friendly and good natured upon closer acquaintance. I had no trouble with them. Their weapons are blowpipes and feathered darts and short lances with bronze heads, also bronze daggers, used to rip up. Sorry I haven't my old Log at hand or I would give you the approximate longitude and latitude of these cities.

You might tell Mr. Johnson that if he finds these places he'll find an old Irishman there, very much married and very happy to see a white man. Possibly I'll beat Mr. Johnson down there; it's too noisy around here by day and too quiet by night.—George W. Brunke.

P. S—Looking through my Log-book I find that the name of the Aztec prince who engineered the exodus of the Inca tribe over the Andes is Cuscama. Also I might mention that Itzuatl is situated on the banks of a lake, shallow but very clear water, the circumference being about 21 miles.—G. W. B.

IN CONNECTION with his story in this issue, a word from Hugh S. Fullerton on steamship navigation on the Great Lakes:

Navigating steamships on the Great Lakes differs from salt water navigation. The cities and towns are not builded on the shores, in most cases, but are situated a short distance inland on smaller lakes separated from the big lakes by sand dunes and connected with them by narrow channels. The small lakes themselves are usually the distended mouths of rivers, held back by the sand dunes, and in almost every case the mouths of these rivers are guarded by shifting bars of sand.

PASSENGER boats plying the inland seas are operated by minutes and seconds. A vessel, clearing Chicago at 6 P.M. lays a course "one point off" for Ludington, the first stop on the Michigan coast. The captain orders the chief engineer to "turn 103," having figured that, with the existing wind and sea conditions, 103 revolutions of the screw per minute will bring the vessel to the entrance to Ludington harbor at 6 A.M. Leaving Manistee, for instance, a vessel, stroked at 97 revolutions, will hold one course for four minutes, another for forty seconds, due north for thirty-two minutes and, in densest fog, will turn and enter the narrow dredged channel leading to Portage Lake.

Going through Georgian Bay the plot of a vessel's course resembles the lines of an eccentric corkscrew. Twisting in and out among the ten thousand islands of the bay, a vessel runs by the watch, the time chart reading: twenty-seven seconds, one minute forty-three seconds, fourteen seconds, three minutes nine seconds, eleven minutes, one minute ten seconds and so on.

Even in dense fog or on the darkest nights scarcely slacking speed, the helmsman steers by chart and watch, depending upon the engineer to maintain a regular speed.

THE vessels are not light draught (nearly fifty per cent. of them were taken to the Atlantic for war work), nor have they the weight of ocean vessels. It is the marvelous skill of masters in handling the vessels that is astonishing. As Johnny Mack, the steward, remarked as we watched Captain Stufflebeam make a particularly delicate landing:

"On a heavy dew the old man could make a landing at the post-office and get his mail."—Hugh S. Fullerton.

WHO was T. Hutter, U. S. Scout No. 7, 1832, Fort Wa.? And I wish we knew the history of those thirty-two notches on his rifle-stock.

Richmond Hill, N. Y.

While wandering through Flushing, L. I., I found an old muzzle-loading rifle, the stock of which bore the following inscription:

"T. Hutter—U. S. Scout—No. 7—August 27, 1832—Fort Wa." The name on the barrel would indicate H. Gibbs of Lancaster, Pa., as the maker. Any information concerning this scout and his activities will be greatly appreciated. There were thirty-two notches in the stock of this rifle.—Anthony M. Voelker.

HERE'S another old friend of ours, the Gila monster. Unfortunately I don't know just which of several Camp-Fire letters the writer of the following is answering. As is our custom in these discussions we hear all sides of a case, so far as we can get them, and then every fellow forms his own opinion. It doesn't matter which letter it was; this one can stand on its own feet. But, comrade Williams, don't hold me personally responsible for all the opinions you hear at Camp-Fire.

I never said they smell bad, or sweet either, for that matter. In fact, I never said *anything* about them at Camp-Fire, either for or against. I've just sat back and listened like the rest. I never wronged a Gila monster in my life. But if some one else wants to wrong one at Camp-Fire, he has a right to.

Newark, N. J.

Having read the description of the Gila monster in the Camp-Fire, I wish to ask this gentleman personally just how many Gila monsters he has ever seen, and also if the one that has a liking for hands is the one on a slab in a drug store on Congress Street. I also suggest that the War College experiment on them in place of poison gas. Now for your information: my handle is W. P. Williams. I have prospected, punched cattle and hunted in the country where this pest lives, not on the streets of Tucson, Arizona, or in the lobby of the Santa Rita, only for the general "misinformation of tenderfeet."

His color, like any other creature, depends on his geographical location, and I have seen them almost yellow, and then again, in a hilly, wooded country, almost black.

NOW for my criticism. Rattlesnakes or Gila monsters never attack man or anything only their natural food. Reptiles shed their skin in the early Fall and at this time are almost blind and will strike at the least sound. This story of a man playing with one sounds to me like a fish, and as for the idea of one poisoning a man with its breath in the open that reminds me of the story of the bottomless lake (there is one in every State), or the hoop-and-joint snake that grabs its tail and rolls down hill and flies to pieces when it hits a tree, later to wiggle together again.

The writer wishes to call your attention to the Museum of Natural History in New York where you can obtain more real information in a minute than native sons of any place can give you in a year.

I wish to tell the editor that personally I am as well acquainted with the reptiles referred to as he is with dogs and cats, that a Gila monster doesn't smell any worse than a copperhead, and it very, very rarely bites, that when it does bite, the gentleman from Tucson has the right dope, it bites to die.

AS FOR spelling, I am a poor one but most Navajos speak Spanish and you can't spell it any other way in that language. I personally am not acquainted with Rodney but I am for him strong and wish to ask the major if the word Gila was ever spelled Gilla? In connection with a town, river or a monster? The word is always pronounced "hele" by natives. There is an "l" and "ll" in the Spanish. I don't know what I am talking about now—'tis information I want. I have seen the word printed Gilla. For the major's information I will say I speak, besides United States, three Indian lingoes and Spanish.

We are strong for the Camp-Fire but Mr. Editor give it to us easy.—W. P. WILLIAMS.

Who will give comrade Williams the information he asks for? Major Rodney is now Colonel Rodney—he was a captain when we first knew him—and a very busy colonel at that, so some other comrade may have to be called on.

BUT how about the statement that a musuem can give more information in a minute than native sons can give in a year? Personally, I think they can and, then again, they can't. I'm all for scientific knowledge. Encyclopedias are fine, scientific experts invaluable. But on a small scale I've been trying to learn some practical farming lately. The experiment stations and the books by scientific experts help me a lot, but somehow I keep finding all the time that if some of the neighboring "native sons" didn't give me the benefit of their "ignorance" I'd be in a mess most of the time instead of only part of the time.

But it happens, too, that we'll soon be having some reliable, scientific "museum" information on treating snake-bites and that just the other day I wrote for the scientific facts on the Gila monster.

WE'VE had a lot of authoritative dope on fire-arms. Here comes some on cowboy equipment, which should be of particular value to writers of Western stories. Mr. MacManus, in his just complaint about authors, is not aiming at our writer's brigade but at all magazines and movies in general. Our people make mistakes, too, of course, but in most cases those of you who know the West give them a comparatively high grade, often even praising them in this respect. Most of our people write from various degrees of first-hand experience.

I know the following will be of interest to many of you. And very likely it will call forth discussion on various points. Our thanks to comrade MacManus.

Michigan.

When Messrs. Brown and Wiggins wrote concerning firearms they certainly pulled the trigger and let fly a hammer that had been held in leash entirely too long. If writers would carefully observe the dates they give, also calibers and models, there would be fewer fiction heroes of the 60's armed with .38 automatics and other impossible things.

I THINK that criticism surely tends to improve the work of story writers and, following this thought, I wish to say a few words concerning the wild and woolly Western stories which seem to be very popular. I am sorry to say that a great share of these stories are too impossible and in small details give readers a very poor impression of our West and life there. Some few writers know the West and its people, but far more of them guess at things, and their stories, to people who know, are, to say the least, obnoxious.

Beginning with horses: There never was such an animal as a trained bucking-horse. Some may argue this point, but in the end we will all shake and agree that this is true. A horse may have been spoiled in the breaking or otherwise turned outlaw, but trained bucking-horses are unknown. By bucking-horse I mean a real "wampus-cat." Outlaw horses have various methods of making a rider "reach for the horn and get a handful of grass." They "sun-fish," "spin," "crow-hop," "fence-row," "side-wind," and other things not classified. Many "twisters" discover new antics very often and sometimes to their sorrow.

ANOTHER terrible blunder is made by referring to the manner in which the rider controlled the actions of his favorite mount by the pressure of his knees. In a heavy stock saddle the average man can not exert enough pressure in this way to make a horse pay any heed. However, many horses "mind the spurs," so to speak.

All well-trained Western saddle horses are "neck-reiners" and a rider does not jerk the right or left rein sharply as is so often told. The reins are grasped and held at even lengths and if the rider desires to turn to the right, he swings his hand to the right which draws the left rein taut along the left side of the horse's neck, and you might say "pulls" him in that direction. When turning to the left the above is reversed. Owing to the fact that good horsemen unconsciously lean in the direction they are turning, most old saddle horses can be turned by leaning in the saddle.

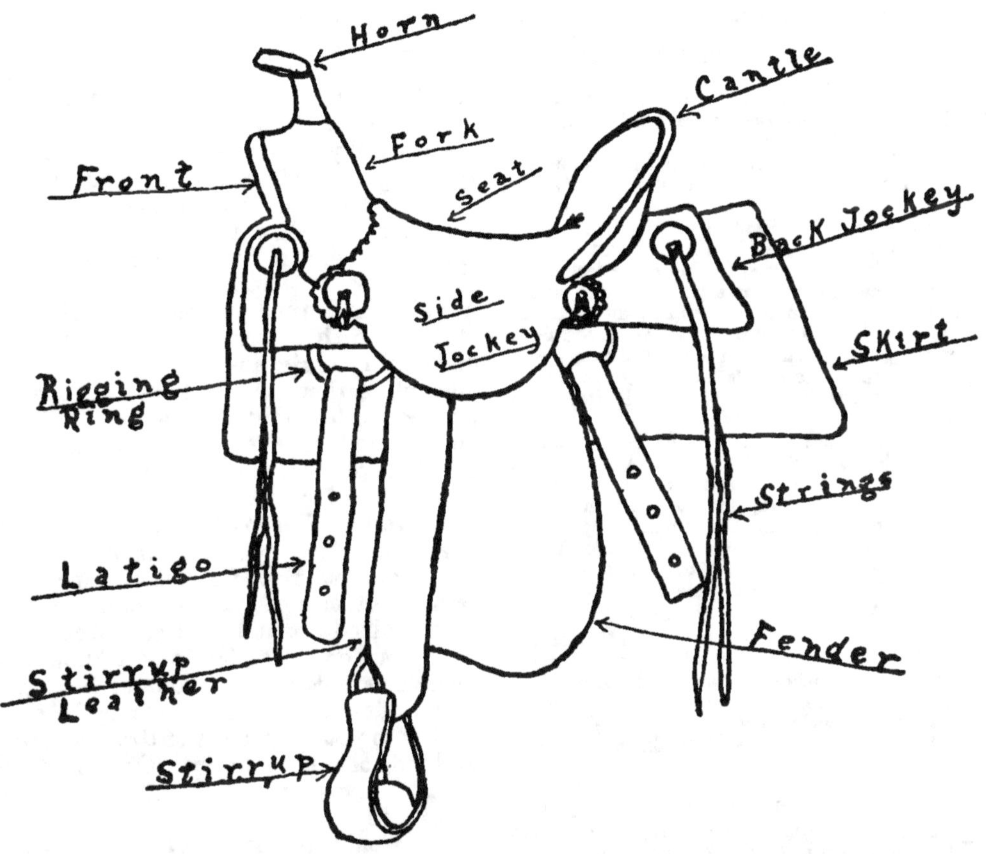

OTHER heroes of Western fiction have ridden pet mares. Please give them horses and let the mares run to rais' em horses. The reasons for cow-men invariably riding horses are too many to enumerate. The best way to learn them all in a bunch is to ride a mare with any old outfit. Not even Billions Shart rides a mare in his most chivalrous productions.

THE Western stock saddle also receives much abuse when certain writers refer to its different parts. The part most frequently mis-named is the "horn." They persistently call it "pommel," but in the West it always has been and is now called the "horn." There is no such thing as a saddle "flap," but a saddle pocket may have a flap.

Stock saddles are "double-rigged" (two inches), "three-quarter" (single or double); "three-quarter single," "center-fire," "five-eighths" and "Spanish." The article called a "girth" in the East is invariably called a "cinch" (from Spanish *cincha*) in the West. A saddle is often called "kak" or "hull."

THE words "lasso" and "lassoed" often appear in stories, but the punchers say "rope" and "roped." Ropes are of several kinds: rawhide, *maquey* fiber (Mexican), manila, sisal, cotton and linen. In the Southwest fiber ropes are often called "grass-ropes." This term originated when fiber ropes first broke the long reign of rawhide ropes. The small loop or eye through which one end of the rope passes to form the large loop is called a "*hondo*" (Spanish). They are made of brass, zinc or rawhide, but in late years the favorite hondo is made by tying or splicing a loop, so forming a tight hondo. Professional ropers make use of such terms as "heeling," "spreading a loop," "tying on to 'im," "heaving the hemp."

WHEN a roper makes his "catch," he holds by dropping a loop or double-bowline knot in the back end of rope over the saddle-horn, or by taking "dallys" (turns) on the horn. I have heard the former called "hard-hold" ropers. Trick and fancy roping is probably the most artistic work done by cowboys. A description of it would fill a good-sized volume, so shall have to pass it by.

A standard throw-rope is about thirty-five feet in length. "Slim," the hero of a well-known book, threw one hundred and fifty feet, but that was on paper. It can't be done. I know a man on the Pine Ridge Reservation who can make wonderful catches with sixty feet, but such men are scarce, tall, and long armed. When a man can "pick 'em up all around him" with thirty-five feet he is a roper, and some of the best ropers I know use thirty to thirty-three feet.

WRITERS often refer to the cow-man's side-arm as a "revolver," but on the range it is a "gun" or a "six." As stated by Brown and Wiggins, much impossible gun-play is described in fiction. In the movies, too, a gun-man is often shown with the drop on twenty or thirty men, but he can thank his lucky stars that it isn't the real thing. We read now and then that the hero "returned his gun to its 'scabbard.'" The contrivance in which they pack guns in the West is called a "holster." A rifle or carbine is carried in scabbard slung from the saddle.

The "leggings" worn by Western horsemen are called "chaps" (soft *ch*, from Spanish *chaparejos*).

WHAT I had intended to be a short letter has grown long and no doubt will weary some readers. It is without intent to injure the feelings of any writer that I have written the foregoing and I sincerely hope that it may serve somebody in need of such information. The use of accurate expressions in any story surely makes it a joy to the reader who happens to know the people and country which it concerns, and certainly can not injure its import to the uninitiated.

Caroline Lockhart in her famous Western story "Me—Smith" proved her thorough knowledge of range life in one short sentence: Smith, originally from Texas, after holding up the Englishman (in Wyoming) left him with the remark: "Just the same, I admires your nerve—ridin' a double-rig in a single-rig country." Enough to make any ex-rider forget to braid a cigarette and read on.—ANGUS MAC MANUS.

Michigan.

Received your letter acknowledging receipt of my information concerning horses and cowboy life.

I am writing this short note to say that the drawing of a saddle I enclosed was made hurriedly and I remember one part which is not shown as I had intended:

THE two straps marked "latigoes" hanging from riggings rings appear in drawing to be short billits. I intended to show these straps hanging in rolls, for latigoes are generally five to six feet in length and in "circling" are passed from rigging-ring through cinch-ring up through rigging-ring, then down on inside and again through cinch ring, receiving cinch ring tongue when drawn tight. This operation forms a block and tackle action which makes it possible to cinch even too tightly.

The above are used on the "near" side. Those "off" side are looped through rigging-ring and reach double through cinch ring and tongue passes through both thicknesses. These short latigoes are changed in adjustment only when necessary, as happens when using horses of various girths.

In some sections softer latigoes are used and are tied in hitches on rigging-rings, but their use is surely falling away in favor of the much quicker buckle-tongue latigo.

As it was my wish to make the information in this article absolutely reliable and as easily understood as possible, I hope this letter reaches you in time to publish with it.—ANGUS MACMANUS.

ONE of the most valued things in my life is the acquaintanceships and friendships that have grown up during the more than eight years of our magazine's life. I won't slop over about it, but I mean very fully what I say. It would take quite a little while for me even to list them over in my mind. I don't want to lose any of them.

It has always been a regret that in writing to the many of you who write to me I often could not write so fully as I felt like doing. But I've done the best I could. I don't believe any of you has ever written to me or to the magazine without getting an answer, and generally a personal answer, if his letter even faintly called for a personal reply. If he has, there has been an accident.

IT TAKES time. Often a short little letter with a seemingly simple request and getting a brief answer takes an amazing amount of time. It isn't just the strictly business letters that kill the hours. They are generally the easy ones. The other kind? I couldn't tell you about them if I tried, and I haven't the right to try. For they pretty well run the gamut of human affairs in one way or another. A good many of you may remember some little thing or other, not magazine business, that we've talked about by letter. Well, multiply your own case by I don't know how many hundreds or thousands and then figure that while some of the others may be cases similar to your own most of them deal with all kinds of other matters. Oh yes, it eats up a lot of my time. But I'd hate to have it stopped.

The trouble is that there are only twenty-four hours in a day and a fellow has to use part of them for sleep and food and getting from place to place. Most of the remainder of the time goes to my regular job, the necessary work on our magazine, which is very, very far from being confined to office hours only. Then there's my family. And me myself, but by the time it gets to me there's just about no time left at all. Well, no use going further into detail.

THE point is that as the magazine grows the work increases steadily in volume. We estimate our incoming first-class mail of all kinds, including manuscripts, at about 10,000 a year. And I'm likely to have the added job of another magazine besides ours. It's begun taking my time already and there's even a chance that it might be publicly announced by the time these words reach print. I'm hoping to meet a good many of you through that magazine too, though there will be no "Camp-Fire" in it. But it's going to mean lots more work for me. (What will it be like? Well, it won't be fluffy or unclean and it will try to give its readers a good time. It will have one kind of story that some of you won't like. Others will like that kind. I think most of you will like most or all of it, but don't take my word for that. Try for yourself.)

Of course there'll be plenty of others with me on the two jobs, but just the same I've had to give myself a severe efficiency once-over and plan out every minute of my time pretty carefully. I can see very plainly that I'll have to hold my letters down to brass tacks far more than ever before.

I don't want to. I like to be friends with people and to talk with them in friendly manner—not just snap a few words at them and run away. But—there are only twenty-four hours in a day.

I want you to remember how I feel about it. If my letters sometimes seem short and impersonal, I want you to remember that the spirit of them isn't impersonal—that I'm merely doing the best I can to make my time reach as far as it can in *all* the many cases.

There's one good thing. Harry Wade is back with us after his Army service. If I've been with our magazine over eight years, Wade has been with it five years. He's about as much a part of it as I am, and many of you are already in personal touch with him, not only because he's in charge of "Ask Adventure" but through his general identification with the magazine's affairs. Those of you who know him know he has no more use for conventional, formal relations with you than I have. And between us we'll do our darndest to see to it that no such formal relations creep in between our magazine's headquarters and its readers.

Well, that's all. I just wanted you to understand. I'm going to like the new magazine, but I served on five other magazines before I came to *Adventure*, and *Adventure* has always been first with me and always will be. As a magazine the new one will be fully as good as *Adventure*, and I know it will make real friends as it goes along. But it won't begin with eight years of friendships behind it.

THE following came from a hospital in Spokane. Probably he could write a better hand than I (which isn't saying much), but a man of seventy-seven in hospital isn't expected to do any copper-plate work with a pen. Anyhow there was much of his letter we couldn't make out, so had it typewritten and sent it to him, asking him to correct our mistakes. Our letter came back marked "Party no longer there."

So I'm giving you our haggled version anyway. The blanks indicate words we could not make out. Blame us, not Colonel Gardner, for mistakes. I hope this will reach his eye and that he'll tell us more about the old days on the Plains.

Spokane, Wash.

I read with much regret of loss of a — friend, Scout Jim Hanahan. Dated Blackfoot, Id., Dec. 20, 1918. Knew Jim in person from service with our Regiment, Custer's 7th U. S. Cavalry, which I was with as packer and scout, and I am the oldest living scout to-day — 77 years old. My name has not been in the lime-light like my brother scouts, but the record of myself stands the acid test. I am sick here and don't know when I will be able to get out till Spring again, so a letter will get me here.

You tell W. C. Tuttle that I hope to have the Citizens of Paradise and Pipe Rock, Montana, with myself and—train next Summer. Also will —— — — — written by me, how Arizona Bill saved Custer's rear-guard on that terrible day, June 22-24, 1876, the day of the historic fight, the Little Big Horn battle, and how many and many a time I have heard the famous 7th Cavalry band play "Garry Owen" and march to it —. It only seems like a few days ago. Yet there's no more — and — — a gas-wagon (as we say Devil-wagons), well, that's the way of the — —. Also I knew Captain Bull Dannon (?) and Uncle Kit Carson was one good (Arizona) friend. It all seems like a dream to me. I guess the bum hand write for an old timer, so I will quit. Happy to hear from you soon. Right; you may use this in Camp-Fire if you will.—COL. RAYMOND E. GARDNER.

THE other day our comrade M. Logee, from whom we've had so many interesting letters, dropped in at the office and we got acquainted at first hand. A big, strapping man, looking none the worse for wear during nearly the whole war, on the Saloniki and French fronts, with the English and then with our own Army. Among other things, he won his commission.

ALL letters conerning fire-arms should now be sent, not to the magazine, but to J. B. Thompson or D. Wiggins, editors of our new department, "Firearms, Past and Present," under "Ask Adventure."

ARTHUR SULLIVANT HOFFMAN.

AT ONE of our Camp-Fires W. C. Tuttle asked whether some of us could identify an old muzzle-loading revolver that had come into his possession. Quite a few replies have come in and some of them are given here. First Mr. Tuttle's letter:

Digging through the rust on the barrel I find the inscription: "Savage R. F. A. Middletown, Ct., H. S. North, Pat. 1856." The gun is about fifteen inches long and I think it is a .38-caliber. It is a muzzle-loading revolver, with an extra high hammer, which cuts off the rear sight unless cocked. Six-shooter. It has a peculiar shaped butt, which fits the hand in good shape.

THE novel feature is in the action. Instead of having the cylinder turn from the trigger-pull, there is another trigger, or lever, if you please, behind the pull-trigger, with a ring to fit the second finger. You turn the cylinder with your second finger and pull with the index finger—and pray. I reckon it will weigh about four pounds.

The man I got it from claims it was picked up in Mexico. It has seen a lot of hard usage. My dad, who is an old gun-man, and who knows a lot about old guns, told me that it was a new one on him. As far as I can see—awful rusty—the rifles run straight down the barrel. Would like mighty well to have somebody tell me something about this style and make of gun, 'cause it looks like a killer.—W. C. TUTTLE.

THE replies follow. Others were received by Mr. Tuttle or at this office, but the following seem enough to do the work:

Visalia, Calif.

The revolver you describe is the Civil War "Savage" revolver, caliber .3625, 5500 of which, at twenty dollars each, were contracted for by the United States Government in 1861.

The advantage claimed for these guns was the gas-tight joint formed between the cylinder and barrel by the reaming out of the front of the cylinder which allowed each, in turn, to fit over the rear end of the barrel, the action of the ring trigger being to first slide back the cylinder, then rotate it while cocking the arm, which was fired by the second or plain trigger.

Owing to its excessive weight and awkwardness as well as to its complicated mechanism, the revolver never became popular in competition with the Colt and other simple actions.

HENRY S. NORTH of Middletown, Connecticut, to whom, in 1856, was granted the patent covering the toggle or reciprocating joint between the cylinder and frame, may have been of the Simon North family who were celebrated gun-makers and inventors for at least three generations.

In 1859 patents were granted to North and Edward Savage of Cromwell, Connecticut, who may have been of the family of the present Savage Arms Company, these patents covering the rings or thimbles forming the gas-check at the front of the cylinder.

In 1860 Savage and North took out further patents for the improvement of the arm and in that year assigned their rights to the Savage Revolving Firearms Company of Middletown, Connecticut.

In my little collection of about fifty pieces of American made pistols and revolvers, I but recently added one of these Savages, it being a gift from a captain friend now in the service.—G. L. CHESTER.

Cumberland, Md.

Anent that old revolver of W. C. Tuttle's, my father (seventy-four years old) says it is one that the Government issued to soldiers in the Mexican War; that two neighbors each had one; and that they were highly dangerous to fire.—CLIFFORD E. DAVIS.

Middletown, Conn.

The gun he describes with the double pull, one for hammer and loop or ring for revolving chamber, could be identified by a number of the old residents of this town, as a good many of them were made here in about 1856. North was the inventor and I am told their factory was in what is known as the Rockfall district of this town. My informant, who knew it well, says it was known to him as the North Savage Company.

Another party here, who is a veteran of the Civil War, says he has one of these revolvers and that when Company A, 2nd Reg. Mansfield Guard, the local company, marched away to war each man was presented with one of these guns.

May it not have been so that as long as then, some of these guns got down into Mexico?—AVERY T. ELMER.

Boston, Mass.

The Savage Revolving Firearms Company did business at Middletown, Connecticut, prior to and during the Civil War. They manufactured North's and Savage's patents.

I am enclosing you two pen-and-ink drawings of two types in my collection of firearms. I assume from your description that yours is of the type marked "2."

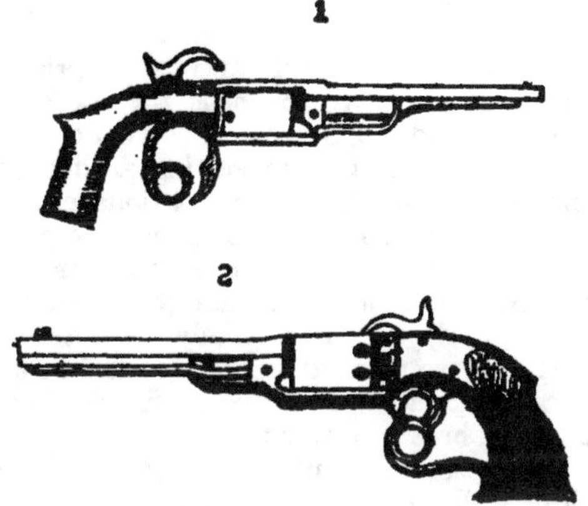

No. 1 is a Savage Navy Revolver, early pattern, marked "E. Savage, Middletown, Ct., H. S. North patented June 17, 1856." Length fourteen inches, length of barrel seven inches, caliber .36, number of shots, six.

No. 2 is a Savage Navy Revolver, developed pattern, marked, "Savage R. F. A. Co. Middletown, Ct. H. S. North Patented June 17, 1856, January 18, 1859, May 15, 1860." Length of barrel seven and one-eighth inches, caliber .41, number of shots, six.

In the attempt to get a gas-tight joint between barrel and cylinder each chamber is reamed at the mouth and fits, in its turn, over the rear end of the barrel. Pulling with the second finger on the ringed lever draws back the cylinder from the barrel, rotates and also cocks the hammer. Releasing the lever lets the cylinder move forward to fit over the barrel and also leaves the weapon cocked.

Although rather a clumsy way of self-cocking, the weapon is not a bad one and shoots very well. Both of mine are in good order, and I have fired them both, although I should personally use in preference a Colt .45 of the patent of 1871, '72 and '75, which, indeed is the gun I carry when I carry any. To my mind it has never been improved upon, and I much prefer it to later and more modern patterns.—Lewis Appleton Barker.

FROM R. A. Sutliff, Portland, Oregon, comes the information that the gun is listed and described in Bannerman's catalog and that he thinks it was made for a New York cavalry regiment during the Civil War. There is a good general suggestion for gun-cranks. Francis Bannerman, 501 Broadway, New York, is the largest dealer in second-hand arms and ammunition in the world, as many of you know. His store is like a museum and on an island up the Hudson he has an arsenal that could keep quite a number of revolutions going. His catalog is large and unique, crammed with information, and is almost as much text-book and treatise as it is catalog. It costs 50 cents and is worth many times that to any gun-crank not already possessing it.

ANOTHER gun inquiry. Gun cranks please rally to the call. But please remember that all communications concerning firearms are to be sent, *not* to the magazine, but to one or the other of the editors of our new "Firearms" department under "Ask Adventure."

Concordia, Kansas.

Can any one give me some information concerning an old pistol which came into my possession some two months ago?

THE gun is about seven inches long; having a huge curved handle or butt made partly of a hard, straight-grained wood and partly of iron. There is a very strong spring in the butt, which controls the hammer.

The hammer is curved and high, and it is set in such a position as to interfere with sighting unless cocked.

There is no trigger guard and the trigger is short. From the hammer on to about two inches the barrel is octagonal. The rest is round. Just in front of the rear sight is the inscription, "Arston and Knox, New York, 1854." And on the under side of the barrel is the number 142.

THE gun is put together in two pieces by two screws, one in the butt and one in the barrel just below the hammer. The rear sight is wide and flat and the front sight is merely a small bead. The rifling runs straight down the barrel. The pistol is, I think, a .32 caliber.

It is of the muzzle-loading type, and is fired by a cap. It is awfully rusty and has been knocked around quite a bit. It was plowed up in a field near this town about two years ago. It was in part of a rotten box, the box being banded by heavy brass bands.

I would be very much obliged if some one could tell me about this "Old Timer."—Byron E. Cook.

FOLLOWING Camp-Fire custom, Romaine H. Lowdermilk stands up and introduces himself on the occasion of his first story in our magazine:

Wickenburg, Arizona.

For a long while I have looked forward to the time when I could come before the Camp-Fire and tell you fellows what a nifty bird I am. So I'll start right out and point with pride to all my own achievements and possibly deplore the outrageous conduct of everybody else.

TO BEGIN with I am an argumentative cuss possessed of an earnest belief that whatsoever is done so and so could and perhaps should be done in another way. Then, too, I am addicted to egotism and recklessness which, coupled with a disorderly inclination to delve into human nature and find out what makes the other fellow "tick," keeps me pretty busy. Already my friends view me with alarm owing to various adventures I have got them into while in search of knowledge.

Speaking of knowledge, I will take this opportunity to touch upon my schooling. Indeed, I shall touch so lightly upon that subject that the tinkle thereof will scarcely be heard. My only approach to the real thing was during the year I spent at Baker University, Baldwin, Kansas. However, I will add in conclusion that throughout my school life I studied hard and really made an honest effort to learn.

IN LOOKING backward I can see some incidents that stick out as turning points, or at least points that to me appear as important. The first occurred twenty-nine years ago down near the Indian Territory line—I was born. Eleven years later came a trip into Oklahoma where I learned to ride a horse and eat watermelons. Then, while in public school up in northeastern Kansas, during vacations I worked for a building contractor who paid me real money for the fun of taking chances with his team of rapid-fire delivery ponies and threw in sound advice and encouragement together with consistent opinions on thrift and industry that I find still remain in good working order. His men took it upon themselves to take the conceit out of me and I hope they did a good job of it. Although several people have given me direct aid at different times in my existence and I am in no wise forgetful, still I feel that this contractor had more to do with molding my future (my father having died when I was three) than any other man. No one ever associated with old Joe Spurgeon and came away without spiritual and material benefit.

Later, at sixteen, I got in a year on the cow-ranges of Texas and New Mexico, which gave me the impetus that finally led to my settling, nine years ago, at my present location in Arizona. Which brings me down to my immediate status: I am a rancher—not a writer. But, sometimes, I write.

IN BETWEEN these mile-posts I have had time to learn to walk the wires, slack and tight, and ride inverted and otherwise upon a horse. Following this bent I spent a few months with the circus and in vaudeville. I also sang a season with a musical comedy company and was the mold of fashion all along the kerosene lamp circuit. Outside of this and during vacations from school I have worked in the timber, at construction jobs, and on newspapers. Also waited table, decorated windows and park benches. All of which I enjoyed immensely because I treated it in the light of adventure.

The only conclusion I can see—if any—is that I don't amount to much and don't think I ever will, and anybody can do everything I ever did if they want to, and try. My adventures have all occurred just around the corner, just modest occurrences anybody can find any old place in the United States, and I regret there haven't been more of 'em.

In closing I wish to repeat I am glad to have met up with the Camp-Fire and I hope you'll like my story. And, if you don't like my story, I hope you'll say so and thereby help me and Hoffman learn what you like and why you like it.—ROMAINE H. LOWDERMILK.

WHO can supply the best sub-title or characterizing line for our magazine, such as could (but probably won't) be printed on the cover along with the name "Adventure," or used on the first pages, on office stationery and wherever such a line would be useful and appropriate? Anywhere from 2 to 10 words, the fewer the better. Glad to send a five-year's subscription to any one suggesting an acceptable line. No rules or regulations except that the offer ends whenever we get what we're looking for. Try as many times as you like, but remember that the fewer the words used, the more likely you are to score. It would need quite a wonderful idea to warrant more than five or six words at most. Three is nearer the mark.

There is one rule, after all. Please address all letters on this subject to Harry E. Wade (who is back with us after service in the Army). If you wish to write about something else too, please keep this matter on a separate sheet.

A WORD from J. Allan Dunn on his story in this issue. And concerning this interesting question of pre-historic races in South America we have, waiting for an opening at our Camp-Fire, two other interesting letters from Edgar Young and H. A. Lamb.

There may be those who will cavil at the bringing in to the Peru of the Sixteenth Century a golden-haired, blue-eyed maid as a representative of pre-historic, or at least, pre-Incan, inhabitants. Such a question has already caused much controversy. I suggest that her origin and her survival were not impossible, emphasizing the fact that all Incan legends agreed that the men who built the astounding, and apparently unfinished, buildings on the shores of Lake Titicaca and elsewhere, were not Incan and were long-bearded white-skinned and blue or gray of eyes. And beards, to an Incan and others of his latitudes, were as strange as light-colored eyes. Anthropologically, it is your Nordic man, your long-skull, your blue or gray eye, who is hairy of chin and chest.

NOW bear with me a moment and see what Prescott says in his "Conquest of Peru," for he was a most thorough historian:

"Another legend speaks of certain white and bearded men, who, advancing from the shores of Lake Titicaca, established an ascendency over the natives, and imparted to them the blessings of civilization."

Also:

From "authorities contemporary with the Conquest, the story of the bearded white men finds its place in most of their legends."

We may, therefore, reasonably conclude that there existed in the country a race advanced in civilization before the time of the Incas. Who this race were, and whence they came, may afford a tempting theme for inquiry to the speculative antiquarian.

Ranking (Historical Researches on the Conquest

of Peru, etc., by the Moguls, London, 1827) finds it highly probable that the first Inca of Peru was a son of the Grand Khan Kublai.

Why not a Norseman or a Dane, the greatest viking races of all, or their descendants setting out from Crete? Such things are as much mysteries as the carving of the great statues on Easter Island and on other islands that form a chain all across Polynesia and Micronesia along the course of the migratory currents and which resemble, as much as anything, the statue of Memnon attempted by less skilful sculptors.

NEXT, as to the crossing of the South American continent by Trevennion and his company by way of the Napo and Amazon. It was done before his time and after. Let me quote for those of our readers who are sticklers for probability. More power to 'em.

Again from Prescott: Though not literally:

Pizarro appointed his brother Gonzalez over the territory of Quito with instructions to explore the western cinnamon-producing country. In carrying out orders, Gonzalez Pizarro and his men suffered terribly but, eventually, after finding the cinnamon woods, were tempted farther by reports of much gold on the Napo. They found the waterfall but not the gold. His men were weakened by fevers and lack of food and Gonzalez constructed a boat from the forest timbers, using nails from the shoes of his horses that had died, gum from the trees for pitch and tattered garments for oakum. He gave the command of this first European vessel to float on those inland waters to one Francisco de Orellana, a cavalier from Truxillo, and sent him down the Napo in this brigantine (*sic*) to where it emptied into a still greater river that flowed toward the east. (The river of the Amazons.) There was to be found a rich district and a populous nation and Orellana was to procure a stock of provisions and bring them back for the relief of Pizarro and his men and to condition them for the march, since the vessel could hold but half the company.

ORELLANA reached the Amazon confluence in three days. Supplies were non-existent. The tales of riches and populous communities were fables. The current was too strong for him to hope to return against it and he decided—with much commendable valor and much detestable cowardice in the desertion of his comrades with Pizarro—to sail down the Amazon and so to Spain. Sanchez de Vargas, a cavalier of good descent, objected to the abandonment of Pizarro and Orellana left him in the wilderness to shift for himself. And Orellana, without compass or pilot, did descend the Amazon and, after touching at Cubagua, reach Spain, where he wrote his statement (preserved in Spanish archives still), and was rewarded by a royal grant upon the realms he had discovered on the Amazon. But he died on the outward voyage and Portugal eventually got the lands. Pizarro got back to Quito after a year:

> "their horses gone, their arms broken and rusted, the skins of wild animals instead of clothes hanging loosely about their limbs, their long and matted locks streaming wildly down their shoulders, their faces burned and blackened by the tropical sun, their bodies wasted by famine and sorely disfigured by scars—it seemed as if the charnel-house had given up its dead as, with uncertain step, they glided slowly onwards, like a troop of dismal specters!"

IN 1769 a woman, described as a delicate female, a Madame Godin, attempted to descend the Amazon to its mouth in an open boat. With her were seven persons. The boat was wrecked. One after another all but Madame Godin died of hunger and disease and she was left alone in the howling wilderness. Friendly Indians at last conducted her to a French settlement, her hair perfectly white from terror and hardship. M. de Condamine in his history of a personal trip, "Voyage dans l'Amérique Meridionale," quotes this experience from details given him in a letter from the husband of Madame Godin.—J. ALLAN DUNN.

The next is part of an argument between Mr. Dunn and Mr. Noyes, at that time on our staff. Only part of the argument. It was a wonder, and, when the dust of good-natured battle cleared away, I gathered up some of the scraps for our Camp-Fire. I don't yet know just what it was all about, but the following pieces from one of Mr. Dunn's letter's make good reading:

Let me tell you why I was so anxious to write a "Westward Ho" story when Hoffman first mentioned it. I am Devon born. My own forebears sent out their ship to join Drake and Hawkins in the Armada. In our little village of Duncombe there are at least five families proud of having some forefather either sail with Drake or against the Armada. Small wonder that when I went to Winchester and afterwards to Oxford I revered the name of Drake and gobbled all that I could find. In the Bodleian Library is a chair made from the planks of the *Golden Hynde*, in the library is the original MS. of Chaplain Fletcher of the expedition and many other early writings anent Drake, including "Drake Redivivus" by his nephew. In the Greenwich Hospital is a model of the pinnace *Minion* (Mignon).

"SAILORS will object to pinnace as used." If they do they are not sailors. I have been at times criticised for my navigation by readers who did not hold what I do, a master's certificate, and who have not sailed, as I have, hundreds of leagues in the South Pacific in an eight-ton sloop. Please listen for a while to what others say. Remembering the model of the pinnace *Minion* in Greenwich Hospital the while.

Century Dictionary, last edition—Pinnace. a. A small vessel, *generally with two masts rigged like those of a schooner*, and capable of being propelled with oars; a galley; so called because built of pine wood.

Stow, Elizabeth, an. 1595. "A pinnace in Leaden Hall, being of burden about five or sixe tun."

Pope. "Swift as a swallow sweeps the liquid way
The *winged pinnace* shot along the sea."

Winthrop. Hist. New England, I. 67. "There came from Virginia into Salem a pinnace of eighteen tons, laden with corn and tobacco."

Webster's Dictionary, last edition—Pinnace. A

light sailing vessel, often schooner-rigged, sometimes also using oars.

Remember here that even the big galliasses and galleys of Spain and nearly all the vessels of that day, save galleons, were merging from the sail-and-oar period into sail alone.

LET'S take Clark Russell next. Few will dispute with him. He writes in the *Daily Telegraph* of London of June, 1888, a commemorative article on the tercentenary of the defeat of the Armada, an article accepted by all England, and writes as follows:

Concerning the bringing in to Plymouth of the sighting of the Armada in the channel by Master Thomas Fleming, a smuggler, who came in "his pinnace, a sailing craft of perhaps 100 tons."

I refer also to: "Drake," an English Epic by Alfred Noyes, American edition, F. A. Stokes Co., N. Y., surely a standard work; to "Drake and His Yeomen," by James Barnes, Macmillan, N. Y., and to the older MSS. and printed writings of Hakluyt, Purchas, Fletcher (Chaplain of the *Golden Hynde*), Pretty, and "Drake Redivivus" (by Drake's own nephew).

Mention is made of the pinnace *Minion* at Guadalupe, the Isle of Pines and San Juan de Ulua on Drake's voyage previous to his round-the-world trip. She is thrice mentioned as having landed *114* men.

I ADMIT that the word "pinnace" is now generally used as any small boat or ship's tender, but *it was not then*. The word "cutter" is similarly twisted in modern phraseology but I can't help that. There were small pinnaces, Drake carried what he termed "tiny pinnaces" in sections, but a vessel of 100 tons (W. Clark Russell), one of eighteen tons (Winthrop) or even six (Stow) can not be styled a small vessel. The word "pink" meant anything small in old English, yet the vessels styled pinks made trips across the Atlantic and around the Cape. I will not, at all willingly, give way an inch in this matter because I am right and have with mine own eyes seen the original MSS. in the Bodleian. I can give you the Clark Russell American reprint if you want to look it up.

NOW we come to "pavisade." There must be something wrong with the Standard Dictionary. I haven't got one, relying on the latest Century and Webster's. Both give considerable space to "pavissade" or "pavesade" which in broad sense means—any extended or continuous defense of a temporary nature as a screen, parapet or the like used in warfare. The Century quotes from

R. Eden, travels of Peter Martyr (First Books on America— "Owre men had bynne in great daunger (from Indian arrows) if they had not byn defended by the cages or pavisses of their shyppes and their targettes."

AS TO the hidden rubies of the English mariner. Chaplain Fletcher sets down the incident as I have related it. Alfred Noyes uses it the same way. It is history. I have tried to smooth it over in the change I shall make in the MS. when it reaches me.

I KNOW that the Doughtys seems a bit commutative. I don't know why Drake let the one off—but he did. Alfred Noyes ascribes Drake's belief in Doughty as coming from his own simple nature. I have tried to suggest otherwise—that Drake stood it as a matter of policy, knowing his own peculiar mixture of jack-tars and gentleman adventurers.

I am sorry there were two Doughtys who might get mixed up a bit. But there were and the main reason I am writing all this stuff to you is because I want you and Hoffman to understand thoroughly that I do not undertake an historical novel lightly. Up to the time that Trevennion leaves Drake every incident is *historically correct*. As I say, I have plugged up hard in Philadelphia, in Boston and in New York for modern notes on old commentaries.—J. ALLAN DUNN.

READ the following news report from a New York *Sun* last Summer. It happens that the measure under consideration was one for prohibition during the war, but that has nothing to do with the point.

The defeat of the recess plan has changed the situation regarding this legislation, inasmuch as senators who would have opposed its consideration if it interfered with their plans for a recess will have this excuse to offer and are expected to vote with the drys now that Congress must stay on the job.

The point is that it is given out as an ordinary news report that some of our United States Senators vote yes or no on an important national measure according to whether they get their vacations or not. The emphasis is on the word "ordinary." In other words, it is merely a matter of routine news that members of the United States Senate, instead of voting according to their understanding of the people's interests, vote according to their own personal interests—and extremely petty interests at that.

MAYBE the news report isn't true. But that doesn't affect the main point that we Americans accept such things as a matter of course. Just ordinary news. No outcry. No indignation. Not even comment. Just ordinary news.

But I say that such voting is black treason. If any Senators did change their vote on any national measure because they weren't allowed to go home on vacation, then those Senators are traitors to their country and betrayers of democracy. And a people who can permit such things to drift by as ordinary news have poor understanding of civic responsibility and real patriotism.

AMONG such a people there is great need of civic awakening. Patriotism that exists only in connection with war is good only during war and not good enough even then. There is need in our United States of the American League for Citizenship. And one of the chief offices of the League is to point out and condemn and rectify just such violations as this matter of "ordinary news" above. We need to be taught just what real citizenship and real patriotism are. We have need to be clean, and we can not be clean until we know very clearly and definitely what cleanness is.

HERE are some more letters concerning Captain W. F. Drannan. There is no other body of men and women like our Camp-Fire for investigating subjects connected with the history of the old West—or, indeed, any of the subjects within our general field of interest. And now it would seem that enough of us had had our chance to express opinion on this topic, so, what next? There are already a number of subjects up for investigation and data but there are a lot of us and we can always take on a few jobs more.

Some of the letters are addressed to the magazine, some to Mr. Brininstool, who not only printed his inquiry but wrote to various old-timers for information.

Fort Huachuca, Ariz.

E. A. BRININSTOOL:

I saw Captain Drannan in Douglas, Ariz., and heard him talk and talked with him. I came to the conclusion that his adventures were very largely the result of his imagination and, in support of my belief in this matter, will say I have been about forty years on the frontier (or what is known as the frontier).

I was personally acquainted with W. F. Cody (Buffalo Bill), Frank Grouard, and several other of the old plainsmen and border scouts who helped to make history in the sixties, seventies and eighties, besides a number of officers of the old Army, who were stationed at or near forts and places mentioned by "Capt." Drannan.

Now I have never heard of them ever mentioning his (Drannan's) name, or even say they had heard of him. I served one five-year enlistment in the First U. S. Infantry from 1878 to 1883, was stationed in places where Drannan claims to have been Chief of Scouts, and never heard of him.

Captain Dan Ming (an old frontiersman for fifty years) lives near here and, like the others mentioned, does not know the redoubtable "Captain Drannan."

According to his book, in which he tells of his Indian fights and killings, he was sure some bad *Hombre*. It is too bad that Uncle Sam did not have a company of scouts, all like him, with his faculty for mussing up Indians. They would have settled a vexed question very quickly.

I, of course, do not pretend to know all the old scouts of the West, but do know some of them, and they do not know "Captain W. F. Drannan."

There is no question but what he lived, moved and had his being in the places he speaks of in his book, but that he was the famous scout and frontiersman he claims to be is a matter open to argument.—J. W. BAKER.

New York.

I read your letter in Camp-Fire. Some years ago I read Drannan's book—found it in a library somewhere.

Like yourself, I've wondered who he was. I never met any one that ever heard of him and I was from April, 1866, until 1884 "on the plains." Was at old Fort Reno on Powder River until Feb. 20, 1867. Got my discharge that day and went up to Phil Kearney with reinforcements after the "massacre" of Dec. 21, 1866. Got located with Gen. Dandy, Q. M., and came down with Maj. Van Voast and party in April. Indians galore. We found the mail scattered in brush that Van Valzeh, Gen. Carrington's mail carrier, and Pte. Dickinson had started from Ft. Laramie with, but we never found their bodies.

At Bridgers Ferry I found Lieut. James Regan, who two years before had been my "bunkie" on Governors Island. He died in Manila a few years ago, a colonel, U. S. A. Put in some time at Ft. Laramie. A man named Brown had started a "hotel" on south side of Laramie River and could get a good meal for $1. Had a good time at Fort L. Once or twice a week used to ride down to Jules Coffee's ranch, five miles south, and pay $1 to play a game of billiards on a rotten table. More than once rode like —— going back 'cause we saw Indians. Had good times there. Those were the good old days. Nick Geneese, the scout, kept us well entertained.

Later rode over through Cache la Poudre and down to Denver. Took in all the Territory and down on the Trinity in Texas. Came back to Colorado in 1879 and was with McKinzie and 4th Cavalry in San Luis Valley. In all my wandering through that country and among the old-timers I never saw or heard of any one that had ever seen or heard of Capt. W. F. Drannan, and I thought I'd heard of them all.

Somewhere I got hold of another book on the order of Drannan's. It was written by a Capt. Brennen. Did you ever know or hear of him? Did you ever meet "Gov. Beale, Ex-Gov. of Wisconsin, sir," who had a ranch in 1866 a few miles west of Cottonwood Springs, old Ft. McPherson?—A. B. OSTRANDER.

IT LOOKS as if the next comrade hadn't herded sheep long enough to hurt him any. And cattlemen have been telling me that sheep are the thing nowadays anyway.

Douglas, Wyoming.

According to our friend, Mr. Tuttle—without whose stories life would not be worth living—sheepherders are crazy or are affected mentally in some way. While I am only a common sheep-herder at $65 a month and, I claim to have a small amount of gray matter in my dome, I am writing this letter in reference to one in which Mr. Brininstool asks information concerning Capt. Wm. F. Drannan, "Chief-of-Scouts."

I have read his book and have asked my grandfather about this great Indian fighter. My grandfather was an "old-timer" on the plains, although he never rose to such heights of renown as an Indian fighter as to become famous.

He was well acquainted with a great number of the "old boys," and he said that he had never heard of Drannan outside of the book. He had the same opinion of the "Chief-of-Scouts" that Mr. Brininstool seems to have.

Grandfather worked for the old famous freighting concern of Majors Waddell and Russell, and was one of the first men to go into Solomon Valley in Central Kansas, so he ought to have some knowledge on the subject.—DECATUR K. REIS.

Greenwood, Nebraska.

I served in the 2d U. S. Cavalry from 1866 to '69 and we were scouting all over the country between Omaha and Salt Lake during that time. I was in L troop. I have seen, and my troop has been with, Antonio La Due, John O. Janese and Buffalo Bill and Little Buckshot, and in the Summer of '66 with Gee Conners looking after a stray band of horses that got away from Ft. Ellsworth, Kansas, but in all our travels up the Platte and through the Bad Lands to Salt Lake over the proposed route of the U. P. we never heard of such a person as Captain W. F. Drannan. I was discharged for expiration of term of service as corporal at Ft. D. A. Russell, Wyoming, May 16, 1869.—EDWARD BUTTS.

Kelsayville Lake, California.

I thought (like yourself) that I knew something about scouts, but, my word, I never "learn, see or hear tell" of Drannan. I was in Arizona, New Mexico, Western Texas and Colorado from 1864 to 1866. Know all about the Fort Phil Kearney massacre. Have fought the Apaches, Navajos, Arapahos, Cheyennes, Nez Perces, Bannocks and others. Was in the Sam Creek fight where so many redskins were made permanently friendly those days. After the Nez Perce and Bannock campaigns, I finally settled down, or was virtually chucked into the newspaper business in Walla Walla. I was shot at three times, had six libel suits, a scrap any time. Never apologized to any one but a woman once who got on the war-path on account of an article my reporter wrote. She came in to horsewhip me, but before she left she subscribed to the *Daily Statesman* for six months—paid her $5.00 like a little sport.—FRANK J. PARKER.

Navy Mobilization Sub-station,
El Paso, Texas.

I have seen Drannan in the flesh many times, but know nothing of his history. When I was a kid in Fort Worth, Texas, Captain Drannan used to draw my gaze every time I traversed Main Street. He had a chair, shaded by a large wago -umbrella, in the street next the sidewalk, and here he sat all day long, sometimes accompanied by an old woman. He was then selling his book, "Thirty-one Years on the Plains," and an amateurishly painted sign announced that he was the only living scout who had crossed the plains with Kit Carson. All this in the Summer of 1910. Later on, perhaps six months after, it was rumored that admirers had purchased him a house and lot in Mineral Wells, Texas, to which he had moved.

Sorry I can't say more concerning this old-timer. He seemed to be accepted at his face value in Fort Worth and dressed the part—buckskin suit, low-crowned Spanish sombrero and the rest.—EUGENE CUNNINGHAM, Chief Yeoman, U. S. N.

WHEN I asked Alex. McLaren for permission to pass his letters on to Camp-Fire he made the kind of reply that rings the bell. Fair play, good comradeship, give and take—that's it in a nutshell. There are some who turn just as eagerly to our Camp-Fire—to listen; who are always ready to take beans out of the common bag but who never put any beans into it. Some have no beans to contribute. That's all right and they're just as welcome among us as those that have. But there are some whose pockets fairly bulge with beans yet who go on taking beans out of the common pot without ever contributing any.

No, they are not holding out on us through intentional meanness and it has never occurred to them that they are open to the charge of being sponges. Some, with good experiences to relate, good information to pass along, hold back because they think it "wouldn't be interesting." Why not let *us* judge as to interest? Some mean to, but just never get to it. Some think they "can't write." This is no literary society!

If you know strange things and strange places, come across with a word about them. We don't care how you say it; what we want is the facts. Particularly if you are an old-timer, with knowledge and memories that no one nowadays can get for himself.

Quincy, Calif.

Camp-Fire is the first I always dig into. That's one place where we old stiffs, flotsam and jetsam, "desert rats," etc., can get together even though miles separate us materially. So any way that I can help enliven the Camp-Fire gathering I wish to. Most of my life has been spent in the open, in the wilds and out of way places, so a Camp-Fire is one of the "home fixin's" for me. May good luck strike you all over.—ALEX MCLAREN.

YOU'VE probably noted the three new departments added in the last issue to "Ask Adventure." South America is a large piece of map, but the two men now in charge are particularly familiar with the ground and from a good many angles. The new Canadian department is in charge of a resident Hudson's Bay Company factor, which should be sufficient guarantee of dependability.

—ARTHUR SULLIVANT HOFFMAN.

A LETTER from one of us who served in Palestine:

Birmingham, England.

Any mail happens to come for No. 7,847 please hold until called for or I send for it. I just arrived in England via France from Palestine. Was out there for the big rush last Fall and believe me it was a farce. But I think there were more men died of dysentery and malaria than were killed in France. The advance was so swift that the Medical Staff could not keep up with us; men were just lying down to die by the wayside.

And grub! It was scandalous. Biscuit and bully-beef, stewed dates or raisins, formed the menu; a quart of water a day to drink, wash and shave. It was worse than in the Philippines in the last insurrection.

I am off for Russia again as soon as I get my discharge from the outfit I am with at present. There is some chance of grub over there anyway, but things are rationed over here. It's impossible to get decent tobacco, and sugar is out of the way algether.

My regards to Camp-Fire.—No. 7,847.

ON THE occasion of his first story in our magazine W. P. Lawson follows Camp-Fire custom by rising and introducing himself:

Morristown, N. J.

I don't at all mind entering the field of autobiography. Most of us have a sort of sneaking fondness for reminiscence, I think. Lots of things are funny after they are softened by years, which at the time they happened were considered anything but droll. On the other hand there is always the danger that a person who gets talking about himself may forget the fact that his history, if detailed at too great length, will not furnish to his audience the peculiarly intense joy its relation affords himself.

AS TO my own existence, I'll state briefly that after a few early years of school at Richmond, Va., I moved to Montclair, N. J., was graduated at the Montclair High School, went two years to Cornell and one to Columbia, and three years to New York Law School, with a year's reporting on the Evening *Sun* sandwiched in. After which a kindly disposed medical advisor prescribed a change of scene and I went West as a young man should.

I landed in Albuquerque, New Mex., and for a time essayed various local lines of effort, among which it may be sufficient to mention clerking, bookkeeping, ranch-cooking, cow-punching, vegetable peddling and mining. I also loafed considerably between jobs, which perhaps accounts for my versatility. I liked loafing best, largely on account of the fact that I appeared—to others as well as to myself—to be more proficient in that occupation than in anything else I attempted during that period.

FINALLY I got an appointment as Forest Guard, taking the Ranger examinations in the Fall of the same year. For several years thereafter I worked with the U. S. Forest Service in various States, but chiefly in New Mexico and Arizona.

My first real assignment in the Service was a six months' cruising and mapping expedition as one of a party of ten that covered the Black Range division of the Gila National Forest. We cruised during the season about 300 square miles of timberland and made in all some 31 camps, in rugged country varying in altitude from 7,000 to 12,000 feet.

IT WAS during this trip that chance, in the shape of our camp cook, led me to commit my first literary effort. The cook had a penchant for strong coffee. His method of obtaining it was to leave the coffee grounds in the pot all through the week, emptying them each Saturady night. He claimed that it stuck to a feller's ribs.

Very few of us attempted to test out the theory with proper thoroughness. You will perhaps recall the lady who asked her escort if oysters were healthy, and his reply that he didn't really know, but that he'd never heard them complain. In one respect we were like the oysters, because we didn't complain. Camp cooks are too hard to get. We just drank water instead of coffee.

Then we ran out of tobacco, and I quit smoking and coffying for some months. As a result I found that I could do a day's work and still feel energetic enough to want to sit up till ten or eleven each night.

So to fill the tedium I started writing a sort of glorified account of our trip, working in bed after supper by the light of a candle-stub stuck near the head of my sleeping bag. The result was "The Log of a Timber Cruiser," which later I found a publisher rash enough to bring out.

DURING that same reconnaissance I got together a good deal of material, worked up later into short stories. One of these is "The Hunting Party," the incidents and characters in which, by the way, are all based on actual events and persons.

I would like to say that that trip, and the following years in the service, were among the best I have known. And I'd like to say also that if at any time a member of the Camp-Fire is desirous of information concerning any phase of the Forest Service of the 183 National Forests, I'll be glad to give it to him or tell him where he can get it.—W. P. LAWSON.

CLEARING UP FRONTIER HISTORY

"Wild Bill" Hickok and Others; The Custer Massacre

WE OF the Camp-Fire have been doing our bit for some time toward clearing up obscure points in the history of the Old West. Scattered here and there are men still living who themselves took part in the making of that history, and still more who are or have been in touch with the pioneers. Many have been members of our Camp-Fire from the start and our investigations into Western history are bringing more and more of them within our circle.

With some of you the study of those old days was already a hobby. These were already in touch with many original sources of information and for years had let no man or book escape if there were chance of further knowledge.

Take it all in all, we of the Camp-Fire are in position to perform a unique service and one of considerable value to the full and exact writing of our country's history.

THE following contributions by members of our Camp-Fire deal with Geronimo, Sitting Bull, Custer, Miles, Crook, and many others of the soldiers, Indians, scouts and pioneers who made Western history. The information is of various kinds and covers many points, but through all this particular bunch of letters runs mention of "Wild Bill" Hickok and for that reason they are given here together instead of having them a few at each Camp-Fire as has generally been our custom with letters pertaining to the Old West.

Let us begin with a letter from a comrade in Canada:

Victoria, B. C.

Coming over on the boat from the mainland one night I noticed a letter in the Camp-Fire wherein somebody wanted to know more about "Wild Bill" Hickok. I was born and brought up in the Black Hills and among some of my recollections are those of Wild Bill, and stories that I have heard of him. The following information may be of interest.

J. B. Hickok (Wild Bill) was born in 1837 in Illinois. When but a lad he worked as towpath driver on a canal and when still a young fellow he drifted West into Kansas. He served on the frontier as wagon-boss, pony-expressman and guide and scout. He was assassinated in Deadwood by a fellow named Jack McCaul. There is a monument erected to his memory in the cemetery on the hill overlooking Deadwood.—Fred T. Evans.

So that none of the old-timers among us may begin saying to themselves "G. L. Chester? I don't remember any such scout back in the 80's," I'll state that this is not his real name but a sort of pen-name he types to his letters, writing his own name under it and using printed letter-heads bearing his own name. I know him not only through correspondence but through others.

California.

Some time ago "The Ace" told of being possessed of a curio coming to him from Geronimo by way of Wild Bill Hickok. I have failed to hear any one give friend "Ace" the information he asks for and I take it for granted that the Geronimo he refers to is the late Apache chief of that name.

I saw Wild Bill a couple of times prior to his death in (I think) 1876, and had some unfinished business with Geronimo after his Huns had wiped out the family of my friend Meadows (Arizona Charlie).

While in the Southwest I never heard of Wild Bill being engaged in Arizona hunting Indians nor of Geronimo being out of that territory unless driven into New or Old Mexico, until nearly ten years after the death of Hickok when Geronimo was driven north and captured.

I can not be certain that Hickok was not engaged in scouting in the Southwest, but I did not hear him talked of among the other scouts as being there, although many were the tales told of him around the scouts' fire in 1883 and 1884 when I drew pay and sustenance from our Uncle but wore no uniform.

Geronimo was a "second string" chief long after Wild Bill was killed and did not become very (in)famous before 1880.

My candid opinion is that there was slight possibility of an exchange of trophies between Hickok and Geronimo.—G. L. Chester.

A letter from "Uncle Frank," Frank H. Huston, who was himself one of those who knew the Old West at first-hand and played a part in its making. I could not be sure of several words, so they are queried.

In Camp (at southern foot of Fremont's Pass, now known as Newhall's Grade).

Now then you tell the "Ace" that Bill Hickok never saw Geronimo, as latter was only a kid when Bill reigned and Bill never was in 'Pache country and Geronimo was war chief of the White Mountain Apaches. Old Billy, who was with Crawford when he was killed in Mexico, was a scout of Grant and also a White Mountain 'Pache. He sold me "'Pache" a—(?) of a horse the only (?) in United States outside of old City Hall in San Francisco.

RAIN-IN-THE-FACE killed Tom Custer. Geo. Custer killed himself rather than be captured, which they tried to do, and that is the reason his body was not stripped and mutilated, as no Injun will touch a suicide under any circumstances and they avoid the place where the act was committed.

I never knew the 'Paches to war-dance, at least not like the plains Injuns, and the 'Paches are the most superstitious of all; as a French trooper in 4th Cavalry remarked in '84, they are the bravest cowards in existence.

Tell "Ace" to write Andy Mills, Wilcox, Arizona, who was in that country before the first (?) and hunted game for the posts. Andy has the leg-irons made for Billy the Kid when he did his first killing at Bonita three miles form Ft. Grant.—UNCLE FRANK.

Here is another interesting letter which the writer wants to appear over other than his real name, though he, too, signs his letter to me with his right name and writes on his regular printed letter-head. The principal reason, I judge, is a kind of ingrowing modesty about appearing in print. But talking at our Camp-Fire is different; no need of talking to us from 'way back in the shadows; why not come right up close to the blaze and talk where the rest of us can see as well as hear? However, that's their business, not mine, and though we'd rather have them use their own names we're glad to hear from them under whatever conditions their modesty imposes.

Iowa.

For the benefit of "Ace," would say that I have every reason to believe that "Wild Bill" never was in the country where Geronimo roamed. I can find no record of it in books. And as he was killed August 2, 1876, and the Geronimo trouble did not start till April, 1885, it is not likely that he took much part in that trouble. His true name was James Butler Hickok. He was born in May, 1837, in Illinois. He was the prince of all the border men, a wonderful shot, and the most coolly desperate man of them all. He was marshal of a number of "bad" towns, and while in that capacity killed a number of men. He was killed by a tinhorn gambler named Jack McCall, who was afterward hanged. I can obtain an original photograph of Wild Bill if the "Ace" should like one; they are very rare, and I do not know of any others.

Geronimo was a half-breed Mex. They chased him over 2,000 miles in 18 months, and when he surrendered he had only 22 bucks left. He was sent to Florida, then transferred to Ft. Sill, where he died a few years ago.

RAIN-IN-THE-FACE was supposed to have killed Custer, but I have his personal word that if he did he was unaware of it. He acknowledged and gloated in the fact that he *had* killed Tom Custer, for he had sworn to not only kill him but "cut his heart out and eat it" (which he did) for ill-treatment received at his hands. Custer had just returned from Washington, where he had trouble with Secretary of War Belknap and President Grant. He had been reduced in rank, had his long hair cut off, and went into the fight with no insignia of rank, and wearing a buckskin jacket. He was not "the last man to fall," for a horse and several men fell on top of him, and it was not known at first what had become of him. He was not "the only man that was not scalped," for there were very few that were. The Indians could hear the firing of Reno, and went while the going was good.

HAD Custer lived he would have been court-martialed, for had he used the least precaution he would or could not have walked into the trap as he did. He was disliked by his men, for the reason he was always "playing to the grand-stand" and would sacrifice men for a little glory for himself. He had won a number of battles by dash and bravado, but the "pitcher went to the well" once too often.

That "Curly the Crow" stuff is half buncombe. He started with Custer all right, but was either sent back or flew the coop when the doings started. I read the other day where Curly said "Custer died in his arms." Oh, bubbles!

My authority for making such statements comes from such men as Buffalo Bill, Captain Jack Crawford, George Fritz (the first man on the field after the battle), Rain-in-the-Face, and others. I, like the "Ace," have reasons for not wishing to sign this with my proper name, so for a *nom de plume* just sign it—DIRTY DEUCE.

A copy of the above letter was sent by me to E. A. Brininstool, whose keen interest in the old West is known to all of us. Here is his reply:

Los Angeles, Calif.

I have yours of the 20th with letter from "The Dirty Deuce" relative to Wild Bill and Chief Geronimo. I agreed with him that Wild Bill had no part in the Apache campaigns, for I, too, never have seen anything in books or newspaper articles regarding Bill as having taken part in those campaigns.

I HAVE read every scrap I can get hold of regarding the Sioux campaign of '76 when Custer was killed, and, to sum it all up, nobody knows who killed him—and further, nobody knows for sure that it is his body that is buried at West Point. The consensus of opinion seems to be that he committed suicide at the last minute, as he was shot in the right temple and the bullet-hole was powder-marked, showing that a weapon must have been held very close to his head when fired. He was also shot in the side.

An entire book might easily be written about Custer's last fight, his getting "in bad" with President Grant just prior to the '76 campaign, together with other personal affairs in which the public probably is not interested. There is no question about Custer not being liked by a great many of his men, at least. I have had that right from reliable sources. His fight with old Black Kettle's band on the Washita is well known to have amounted to about a massacre itself, and on a close par to the disgraceful Chivington massacre in Colorado—one of the most disgraceful acts ever committed, when the Indians were right under the protection of Fort Lyons and flying the peace flag.

I have been all over the Custer battlefield in company with "Curley," the Crow scout who was with the Custer command on that fatal 25th of June. I believe his story just as he tells it—that he escaped from the battlefield in the smoke, dust and general confusion by disguising himself as a Sioux, and made his way down to where the supply steamer *Far West* in charge of Capt. Grant Marsh was awaiting further orders, near the mouth of the Big Horn River. "Curley," when I saw him in 1913, was 56 years old, and I took his photograph in front of his little log cabin on the banks of the Little Big Horn and bought the buckskin coat he had on his back at that time.

THERE is no doubt at all about Custer having disobeyed his orders regarding the time he was to meet with Terry and Gibbon. At a conference aboard the *Far West* the night before Custer started on his scout, he was told to "not be greedy but wait for the rest of us." To which he is said to have answered, "I will." Instead of making a leisurely march which would bring him into the valley of the Little Big Horn on June 26th, he made a forced march, part of it in the night, arriving in sight of the Indian village on the morning of the 25th. His men were weary and so were his horses. However, he divided his forces into three detachments under himself, Major Marcus Reno and Capt. F. W. Benteen. Custer was to attack the village at the lower end, and Reno at the upper end, with Benteen under orders to "pitch into anything he came across." Reno was told that "the whole outfit will support you."

Reno charged the upper end of the big village, but instead of pressing his attack—right at the time when he had the Indians completely flabbergasted, so say their own chiefs—he retreated into a patch of timber and dismounted his men. Here, to make a short story, they became demoralized and a retreat was begun which ended in a genuine stampede. Here fell Charley Reynolds ("Lonesome Charlie"), one of the greatest scouts the Western frontier ever knew—quiet, modest, unassuming, but with a reputation as a mighty hunter and a wonderful plainsman. "Bloody Knife," Custer's favorite 'Ree scout also was killed here. Reno simply lost his head and went "while the going was good."

HAD Custer won this fight, it certainly would have been a big feather in his cap, and personally I believe that is just the way he had it all figured. There are a great many "ifs" in this Custer affair, but, boiled right down, neither Custer, Terry nor Gibbon had any idea at all of the immense number of warriors the former was attacking. His highest estimate, the previous night, in a council with his scouts, was 800 fighting men, while as a matter of fact there were between 2,500 and 3,000—some say even more. The entire village is said to have been the greatest assemblage of Indians ever gathered together on the American continent, and numbered, including men, women, children and old men too feeble to fight, over 15,000; therefore 2,500 is a very conservative estimate, counting all boys of 15 as fighters.

I HAVE seen paintings and pictures of the Custer fight showing the General in the center of a little fighting band, with his long yellow hair flying in the wind, wielding a saber. There was not a saber in the entire command on this campaign. They were all left behind at Fort Abraham Lincoln—in Custer's column, at least. Neither did he wear his hair long at this time. He formerly had done this at different times, but had it cut short just before starting on what proved to be his last battle. It is not correct to refer to the Custer fight as a "massacre," for it was nothing of the sort. It was a straight up-and-down fight to the finish, in which the troops were simply overwhelmed by vastly superior numbers, vastly better armed in every way than were the Seventh Cavalry. One of the reasons given for the defeat of the troops has been the fact that their Springfield carbines, single-shot weapons, had poor cartridge-extractors and the men were often obliged to open a knife and dig out the fired shell before they could reload. The Indians were armed—great numbers of them, anyway—with Henry and Winchester repeaters of the first model made, firing 16 shots without reloading.

Custer was not scalped nor mutilated. Neither was Capt. Myles Keogh—the latter from the asserted fact that he wore an Agnus Dei on his breast which the Indians respected as "big medicine." I have heard that a very few others were not mutilated, but most of them were.

BY ALL odds, the best account of the Custer fight is the one written by Gen. (then Captain) E. S. Godfrey, now living at Cookstown, N. J. He was with the Reno division. This article appeared in the *Century* for January, 1892. The next best is that of Major James McLaughlin, for years Indian Agent at Standing Rock reservation, who knew, personally and with much friendship, every chief who led in the Custer attack, including Chief Gall, Crazy Horse, Crow King, Two Moons and others. His story is contained in his book "My Friend the Indian." McLaughlin had the very best chance in the world to "get the inside" of the fight, and, as there was no white man's side to it, we must depend very largely on what the Sioux and Cheyenne leaders have to say.

Reno was besieged in the hills four miles from where Custer met his death. He was too badly "rattled" to make an attempt to assist Custer, although begged to try by his captains and lieutenants. The real fate of Custer and his men was not known until the afternoon of June 26, when Terry's and Gibbons' detachments arrived. The Indians retreated as soon as the dust-clouds announcing the arrival of reinforcements were seen. Most of them under Sitting Bull—who had no part at all in the fight, contrary to all statements that he did—fled across the line into Canada, and remained there five years.

I have Rain-in-the-Face's personal story of his part in the fight, which was printed in *Outdoor Life* some years ago.—E. A. Brininstool.

Los Angeles.

It may be well to print a verbatim copy of Custer's orders from Terry when the command left the steamer *Far West* a few days prior to the battle. The question is—did Custer disobey these orders or not? Most historians contend that he did. Anyway, here is a copy of these orders, taken from a life of Custer:

Lieut.-Col. Custer,
Seventh Cavalry.

Colonel:—The Brigadier-General commanding directs that as soon as your regiment can be made ready for the march you proceed up the Rosebud in pursuit of the Indians whose trail was discovered by Major Reno a few days since. It is, of course, impossible to give any definite instructions in regard to this movement, and, were it not impossible to do so, the department commander places too much confidence in your zeal, energy and ability to wish to impose upon you precise orders which might hamper your action when nearly in contact with the enemy. He will, however, indicate to you his own views of what your action should be, and he desires that you should conform to them unless you shall see sufficient reason for departing from them. He thinks that you should proceed up the Rosebud until you ascertain definitely the direction in which the trail above spoken of leads. Should it be found, as it appears to be certain that it will be found, to turn toward the Little Big Horn, he thinks that you should still proceed southward, perhaps as far as the headwaters of the Tongue, and then turn toward the Little Big Horn, feeling constantly, however, to your left so as to preclude the possibility of the escape of the Indians to the south or southeast by passing around your left flank. The column of Col. Gibbon is now in motion for the mouth of the Big Horn. As soon as it reaches that point it will cross the Yellowstone and move up at least as far as the parks of the Big and Little Big Horn. Of course its future movements must be controlled by circumstances as they arise; but it is hoped that the Indians, if upon the Little Big Horn, may be so nearly enclosed by two columns that their escape will be impossible. The department commander desires that on your way up the Rosebud you should thoroughly examine the upper part of Tulloch's Creek, and that you should endeavor to send a scout through to Col. Gibbon's column with information as to the result of your examination. The lower part of this creek will be examined by a detachment from Col. Gibbon's command. The supply steamer (*Far West*) will be pushed up the Big Horn as far as the forks of the river are found to be navigable for that space, and the department commander, who will accompany the column of Col. Gibbon, desires you to report to him there not later than the expiration of the time for which your troops are rationed, unless in the meantime you receive further orders.

Respectfully, etc.,
E. W. Smith, Captain 18th Infantry,
Acting Assistant Adjutant-General.

FOR one thing Custer did not examine Tulloch's Creek, nor send the scout (George Herendeen), lent to him by Terry for that purpose, back with a report. Herendeen was with Lieut. De Rudio when the latter, with Bill Jackson, a scout, and Tom O'Neil, were left in the river bottom at Reno's flight and made a most marvelous escape—worthy a story in itself. There are many other points to be considered which have no time to discuss. Custer *knew* Terry would not arrive until the 26th and was told to "wait for us." History shows how he "waited."—E. A. Brininstool.

The next letter deals Wild Bill's reputation a body-blow. And the writer gives us another case of "pen-name," exactly like the two others—printed letter-head and signature both giving his real name.

Springfield, Missouri.

Concerning one Bill Hickok, a left-over product of the Civil War more widely known as Wild Bill.

It is evident that "Ace" holds this man in some esteem, but I fear that much I have to say will shake it. In this town of Springfield, and during the latter part of the Civil War and for some years after, Wild Bill was best known, and it is here that he began to establish his reputation as a bad man.

IF EVER Wild Bill was an Indian scout none of his old-time intimates here know of it. For a time during the war he was attached to the Union forces as a scout, but his propensity to shoot up saloons and bully inoffensive citizens and to otherwise advertise himself rendered him useless as a scout. The duties of a scout required a quiet, stealthy and alert life; a man seeking such notoriety as did Wild Bill could not fulfil the duties of a scout. Because of this his employment by the Army officers was rare, as they only used him as a last resort.

The close of the Civil War left at Springfield much of the flotsam and jetsam that had been its natural attributes. In that day this country was a frontier country and all along its line similar characters were left adrift and had no mind to turn their swords into plowshares. It was of this class that Wild Bill came. He was merely a product of the war in a locality 'more or less lawless, where prejudices ran high for a period following the close of the war.

IF "ACE' will look a bit into history he will find that in 1876 Geronimo, the Apache chief, went with other chiefs into Mexico and did not return until 1882. Therefore, if Wild Bill ever came into contact with Geronimo it had to be at a time previous to 1876.

The reputation of a bad man is highest where he is least known. Wild Bill was known as a brave man only where he was unknown, or at places along his orbit where he flashed in and out like a shooting star. There are those now living in this community, survivors of those turbulent days, who will testify that aside from his long hair, his ability to shoot straight and to ride well there was nothing to Wild Bill.

FROM the beginning of 1864 until about 1876 Wild Bill made his principal headquarters in this town. In 1864 he shot a man on the public square in Springfield. The man he shot was an ex-Confederate, or, rather, was a rebel sympathizer. Prejudice against such men served to shield any Union man who oppressed them. Wild Bill was tried for murder, but his trial was but little short of a farce. As is often so nowadays, the facts of the case were one thing and the evidence at the trial quite another. The want of space forbids the detailed account of that incident, but I will be glad to furnish "Ace" with all the details, warning him that his idol will be shattered.

AFTER his acquittal Will Bill lingered for several years around Springfield engaged in horse-racing, gambling and kindred diversions. He had a pleasant way of riding his horse into our saloons, shooting up the place and otherwise adding to his reputation as a bad man. It was observed, however, that he used great discrimination in his selection of saloons for this purpose. This was no doubt due to a mishap that occurred to him when he attempted to perform in the saloon of a man named Philidor (but better known as Phil Dor). It was Philidor who slapped Wild Bill first on one cheek and then on the other; then turned his back and dared him to shoot. There are other instances similar to this, well known in Springfield but never given sufficient importance to be particularly noticed.

ABOUT this time the services of bad men were badly needed in some of the towns in the cattle country. Wild Bill's reputation had extended into that zone, and he was selected to be the marshal of one or two of those towns. It will be recalled by old-timers that he did not live up to his reputation, and moved on. He drifted back to Springfield and married a widow of a circus man named Lake, whose husband was murdered in the mining camp at Granby. He sought as he had been seeking for some time, a sort of affiliation with Buffalo Bill, whose appearance and mannerisms he sought to affect. But Buffalo Bill had the power of discriminating between real bad men and bogus bad men, and consequently Wild Bill Hickok was left to wrestle with his own reputation.

WILD BILL killed many men, but he usually had the drop. He had the drop on a cowboy named McCall and killed him. The avenging brother of McCall followed him to Deadwood and there shot him much after the fashion that Wild Bill had shot his brother. Wild Bill's death occurred several years before Geronimo ever returned to the United States. As a small boy I frequently saw Wild Bill and he was a hero in my eyes. His knack of putting two holes into a tin can by the wayside while riding at full speed with a derringer in each hand would inspire any youth of that period with infinite awe. But this idol was shattered for me, as he surely will be for "Ace," when the truth was known.

Since "Ace" withholds his name I will do likewise, and you may subscribe the name of "Deuce" to this letter. My real name appears upon my letter-head.—DEUCE.

It is difficult to reconcile the above letter with the others, but it makes the case of Wild Bill all the more interesting. In a letter to E. A. Brininstool I mentioned briefly that I'd had a letter painting Hickok as a four-flusher. He replied:

Don't you ever believe it. I know many men (Clark Stocking among others) who were intimate with him in Deadwood and Kansas frontier towns and who *know* he was the real thing and not a four-flusher.

Mr. Brininstool, however, had not seen the letter in question. It's hard to trace the path of truth in such matters, no matter how honest and sincere the reporters. Perhaps, since all men are both good and bad, both strong and weak, the facts lie on both sides of the line.

Our older comrades will remember "Wild Bill in Deadwood Gulch" in our July, 1916, issue, in which Robert V. Carr told us, in semi-story form, of the death of Hickok. Here is the letter that accompanied the manuscript when it came to us:

Gray, California.

The story of "Wild Bill in Deadwood Gulch" is, in all main points, as I got it from Doc Peirce. Doc told me several little side yarns, however, which I did not include in the story of Wild Bill.

FOR example, Doc mentioned the Mexican and the Indian head. About the time Wild Bill was killed a Mexican came riding up the main street of Deadwood, shouting and whooping, the while he swung a gory Indian head. As there was a bounty on Indian heads, the miners paid the Mexican for his trouble. Later it developed that the Mexican had not killed the Indian, but that the red brother had been shot by a white man. Doc said that some thoughtful Deadwooder later downed the Mexican on general principles, but largely for passing off a second-hand Indian head on the camp.

AS NEAR as I can ascertain from the various accounts given me by old-timers, the story of the killing of Wild Bill is correct in all details with one exception. I have never been able to learn positively whether Jack McCall was in that game of poker in which Wild Bill drew the black card or not. Doc says that McCall was in the game, but left after a hand or two and re-entered the saloon through the back door. I think Doc's account is correct, as it is reasonable to suppose that McCall must have been posted on the position of Wild Bill at the table. Other old-timers of Deadwood have told me the same thing. I recall Otto Uhlig. Uhlig was working on a hillside when the cry, "Wild Bill is killed!" came to his ears. Uhlig told me that McCall had been in the game with Bill a few moments prior to the murder.

I BANK a great deal on Doc Peirce's accuracy. Doc has a great memory, and has the history of the early days in the Black Hills down pat. A great many old-timers get things twisted after thirty-five or forty years, but Doc Peirce is not of that type. He can recall a man's gestures after forty years, and never forgets an expression. If you ever get out to the Black Hills—and, by the way it is the most beautiful spot in the United States—drop into Hot Springs and look up Doc Peirce. Like enough you'll find him at the post-office looking for his copy of the *Sioux City Journal.* He's a good old scout, and as full of humor as an orange is of juice.

AS FOR the motive back of the killing, I had so many stories regarding that point that I concluded to let it rest on what Doc told me McCall said at the trial in Deadwood, and Doc's conclusions regarding those remarks. There is no doubt that McCall killed Wild Bill just for the sake of being pointed out as the man who turned the trick. And there is no doubt but that, as Doc says, the lawless element of Deadwood encouraged Jack in that ambition.

ALL the characters in the story are true characters.

Preacher Smith was well known in the Black Hills, and was wont to hold forth on a soap-box in the street and give the miners samples of the old-time shouting religion.

Doc tells a story of a chap who had tried every game in Deadwood—and there were many kinds in those days—and lost. Presently he came to Preacher Smith, who was holding forth in his usual arm-waving, shouting fashion.

Thinking the parson was running a game of chance, the eager gambler broke through the circle and offered to try the preacher's game.

"Salvation is free," the parson informed him.

"Well," came the instant reply, trimmed with a string of flesh-colored adjectives, "if salvation's free, it's the only thing in this rippety-slam camp that is, by and so forth!"

Then he proceeded to take up a collection, placing therein his last piece of money, for the heart of the nameless chance-taker was in the right place.

AS A last word, I do not want you to take the story of Wild Bill as a report. The facts are there, but I have attempted to make a story of it. With the valuable aid of Doc Peirce—indeed, without his aid I could not have written the story—I have tried to give you a picture of the famous warrior as he went his way up and down the streets of Deadwood, or, rather, the clearings and trails that were in time to know pavements and the jangle of the trolley-car.

SOME of these days I am going to get Doc to tell me about Calamity Jane.

The last time I saw Jane was in the shop of Mac, the Saddler, in Deadwood. The old girl was about at the end of her string. She had left an old hat in Mac's place, and was worried about the set of a feather on that same decrepit lid—the eternal feminine. Also, she wanted a little money. MacDonald and I 'came through" with a little change. I could scarcely believe that the shabby old woman, husky with the bad whisky huskiness, sick and broken, was the famed Calamity, she of the buckskins, profanity and reckless ways.

"But," said Mac, the Saddler, a little sadly, "this is Jane."

My great regret is that I did not live in those red days. Deadwood was in full blast before I was born. I only caught the echoes of the shouts of the gold-seekers, although I did live some of the cowboy life.

But it's all gone now. Deadwood is a sedate town, with clubs and the moral uplift. And few of the old-timers remain. Every letter Doc Peirce writes me is a sort of an obituary.—ROBERT V CARR.

Next, a very interesting letter from an old Regular who saw frontier service in Geronimo's day. Will any other former members of the old 4th or 6th Cavalry or the old 13th Infantry tell us more about the taking of Geronimo?

I am an "Old Regular Army Man." I was in New Mexico when Geronimo appeared on the scene in 1883, but did not assist in his capture, as my term of enlistment (five years) expired in July, 1884. However, my old company assisted in capturing him in Mexico in 1885. After his capture Geronimo was sent to Florida, then to Mt. Vernon Barracks, Alabama, and after was eight years transferred to Oklahoma, where he died. An old comrade of mine remained in the Army until he was brought up from Porto Rico on that "Pest Ship" *Relief* during Spanish War and died on Bedloe's Island from starvation and dysentery. This comrade told me of hardships undergone in chasing after Geronimo and incidentally mentioned that I was lucky in escaping that terrible march over the lava beds.

I WAS sent to New Mexico in 1880 from Mt. Vernon Barracks, Ala., to help 9th U. S. Cavalry (colored) protect the people from Apache raids. The last Apache raids were from 1880 to 1885—Victorio in 1880; Nana, 1881; Juh, 1882; Geronimo, 1883 to 1885.

The scouts used against Apaches were regularly enlisted Indians—enlisted for six months and led by West Point officers. Those Indian scouts received pay and allowances of Regular Army soldiers but wore their own clothing and lived by themselves as they had been accustomed to. I never heard of scouts of the Buffalo Bill and Wild Bill variety being used to round up Apaches.

ALTHOUGH living in New Mexico I never heard of Geronimo before Victorio, Nana and Juh were put out of business. Victorio killed about four hundred men, women and children on his raid in '80 and '81 and quite a few "Buffalo Soldiers" as he called the members of the 9th Cavalry.

I feel certain Geronimo's record never equaled Victorio's. Vic, Nana and Juh were first started on their raids by white men of New Mexico. I never heard who started Geronimo. I do know that, when he started, the whites were incensed at our inability to protect them from Apache raids. General Crook was sent to take command and see what he could do with the Apache. Three times he induced Geronimo to come in under a flag of truce, but, as General Crook could not give his word that the lives of himself and band would be safeguarded, Geronimo refused to surrender—preferred to die in the hills, fighting. Washington had given orders to capture Geronimo dead or alive.

WHEN General Crook came to New Mexico the citizens claimed they would make him President of U. S. Because he let Geronimo go and respected the flag of truce they had pull enough to have him transferred to Leavenworth, Kansas, and his transfer took place before I received my discharge.

General Miles captured Geronimo, but I have always been under the impression that he disregarded the "dead or alive" order.

THE Apache was the finest skirmisher this world ever produced. They could go up a mountain in fifteen minutes that it would take any white man two hours to climb. They could live a week on an oil rag. Had a splendid system of signalling by smoke and broken pieces of mirror or looking-glass. A soldier rarely saw an Apache, but felt the effects of a couple of volleys, though when the soldier got where the smoke had been Mr. Apache had melted into thin air.

Even today I have great respect for the Apache

and would rather face one hundred Germans than one of them. If you could get in touch with any old members of the 4th and 6th Cavalry and 13th Infantry they could give fuller information of the chase after Geronimo. The 9th Cavalry suffered most under Victorio and Nana. They were sent out of the Territory and the 4th Cavalry relieved them afterward; 4th Cavalry was relieved by 6th Cavalry; 13th Infantry served with the three outfits. Cavalry did the chasing. Infantry guarded water-holes.

IN REGARD to "Wild Bill" I can only quote newspaper accounts. Some time about 1875 or 1876 "Wild Bill" came East as far as Rochester, N. Y., with a troupe of Indians, cowboys, etc. The first Wild West Show in the East. I saw the show in Albany, N. Y. It was called "Scouts of the Prairie," "Ned Buntline" (Judson) the author and principal character in the play. Buffalo Bill and Texas Jack were stars. Wild Bill was a U. S. scout when "Judson" brought him East. At Rochester the Government recalled him. He left the "show" and went back West.

I AM under impression it was a year or two later that he was killed at a gambling table. An enemy of his had been trailing him for a couple of years for revenge. He shot Hickok in back of head, killing him instantly. Escaped, captured after a year or so, tried and hung. The exact places of Bill's death and his murderer's trial and execution have slipped my memory. All papers in U. S. published the murder of Wild Bill, as Judson had brought him to public notice along with Cody and Texas Jack. Look up newspapers of the late seventies, or, if he was a U. S. scout when killed, write to Adjutant-General, U. S. A., Washington, D. C., and the date of his death will be sent to you. Geronimo and Wild Bill never saw each other. Bill was dead before Geronimo appeared on the horizon.

SCOUTS like Buffalo Bill, Buffalo Chips, Wild Bill and, in 1871, Kit Carson, whom I saw in Albany, N. Y., were used against Indians like Sioux, Utes, etc. Those Indians stood up and fought, the Apache was never seen but often felt and he appeared on the scene when you thought him one hundred miles away. Dana of N. Y. *Sun* published an editorial while I was in New Mexico stating that it cost the U. S. Government one million dollars to kill one Apache. As he had been the Secretary of War and as I know how difficult it was to catch one or even see one, I agreed with him.

THIRTY years ago the good people of the U. S. had no earthly use for an enlisted man of the U. S. A., and the citizens of New Mexico and Arizona had still less use for us. Get your Congressman to hunt up and send you the debates on bill to raise cowboy regiments to police those territories and remove the Regulars. When I get thinking of my Army experience I am apt to wander into many side trails.

FOR thirty-one years I have been a professional nurse and for eighteen years connected with a nurses' home and registry and would be pleased to have you keep my name and address out of magazine. You can convey this information to "The Ace" in any manner you think best and if he desires to communicate with me by letter I would be pleased to hear from him. There are four members of my family who are ex-Regulars and the four of us are sorry we can not answer the "Call to the Colors."

The authenticity of value of that tom-tom can be easily verified by finding out when Wild Bill was murdered and then comparing it with time when Geronimo was first heard of, 1883.—— ————

P. S.—Newspapers stated Rain-in-the-Face was the man who killed General Custer. As only a solitary Crow Indian escaped from the battle-field, the only evidence that he killed Custer was his own word that he did.

Though I can see no reason therefor (except in the case we've just heard), I think we've never had a discussion at Camp-Fire in which so many withheld their own names. However, we're more than glad to hear the things they tell us, leaving the method to them, though there's no cause for bashfulness when one of us speaks up at our Camp-Fire.

Here's an interesting side-light on Wild Bill. And, if Joe Beal and W. S. Harvey are among us, won't they tell us their tales of the old days?

New Kensington, Pa.

The following may be and may not be true, but I received it from a U. S. A. surgeon by the name of Albert Barnes. This was twenty-five years ago and he was an old man at that time and I suppose him dead now. At that time he had a son practising medicine in Indianapolis, and a son by the name of Albert, first lieutenant in the U. S. I.

WILD BILL had an arrow wound in one of his hips and it would not heal and he couldn't get along with it in this condition so he came to Chicago. Arriving there some time in the night, he went to this surgeon and told him that he wanted an examination of the hip, which he made, and told Bill that the bone was affected and would have to be scraped. Bill asked how it would have to be done; he told him. Bill told him he had no time to go to a hospital and asked him if he could perform the operation. He told him he could but he had no one to hold the light and no one to give the anesthetic. Bill replied that he did not need an anesthetic and that he would hold the lamp. The surgeon saw he would have to do something to satisfy him, so he got him on the operating-table, gave Bill the light to hold in a certain position, and commenced to operate.

He made the incision and scraped the bone and fixed everything O. K. Bill got up, walked to the depot, took the first train for the West, and this was the last he ever saw of him.

He told me that in all his practise it was the only man he ever saw that had no nerves or no feeling of pain.

THERE are two men living at Belle Vernon, Pa., who were with Custer for five years. They were with him at the Battle of the Wichita. One of them, Joe Beal, killed the Chief Black Kettle, and took from his body a medal which he has in his possession today. The other is W. S. Harvey. By writing these men you might get a whole lot of information.— ———— ————.

This comrade, who went to the Western frontier forty-six years ago, gives us the following:

Charlottesville, Va.

There have been many mistakes about the Custer massacre.

Reno was not dismissed for the reasons given by a writer. The record of his court-martial will show that. I knew several who fell with Custer. I knew Lieutenant Harrington well, and doubt the story of his suicide. For his relatives spent much time and money trying to find our his fate. If the suicide story was true, it would have been learned at that time. Search was made not only in our country but amongst the Indians across the border in Canada. His was the only officer's body not found. It is believed that he was shot crossing the creek, and his body fell in the water.—"VIELHO."

HERE are the results of the readers' vote on the ten most popular stories in *Adventure* during 1918. As in previous years, we give also the ten ranking next in the vote. (S) stands for "serial," (N) for complete "novel," (n) for complete novelette, those unmarked being short stories.

Of course a vote of this kind is only a partial expression, being cast by only a minority of the total number of readers, but nevertheless it is both interesting and decidedly useful in helping us in the office fill the magazine with the kinds of story our readers like best.

The vote on the relative value of fiction and the various departments was so scattering that we have not tabulated the results. "Camp-Fire" ran very strong, with "Ask Adventure" a good second. But no formal vote was needed to show that "Camp-Fire" is a favorite.

1. GABOREAU THE TERRIBLE (S), *Gordon Young* 6,237
2. HIDDEN TRAILS (S), *William Patterson White* 6,111
3. GABOREAU (N), *Gordon Young* 6,090
4. ALIAS WHISPERING WHITE, *W. C. Tuttle* 4,956
5. HIGH POCKETS (n), *William Patterson White* 4,788
6. THE MIGHTY MANSLAYER (n), *H. A. Lamb* 4,200
7. THE SURVIVOR (N), *Robert V. Carr* 3,885
8. ALAMUT (n), *H. A. Lamb* 3,360
9. THE BELLS OF SAN JUAN (S), *Jackson Gregory* 3,255
10. 021 (n), *Wilbur Hall and Cecil Haig* 2,919
11. WITH SHARP SWORD-EDGES (S), *Farnham Bishop and Arthur G. Brodeur* 2,772
12. BEFORE MARQUETTE, (S) *Kathrene and Robert Pinkerton* 5,262
13. TURQUOISE CANON (N), *J. Allan Dunn* 2,499
41. THE SIGN OF THE SKULL (N), *J. Allan Dunn* 2,247
15. GHOST ISLAND (N), *Courtney Ryley Cooper* 2,226
16. THE HOUSE OF HIDDEN FACES (n), *H. A. Lamb* 2,016
17. CHAPLAIN TO THE BUCCANEERS (N), *Stephen Chalmers* 1,890
18. THE RAVEN MOCKER, *Hugh Pendexter* 1,848
19. MAN TO MAN (n), *A. D. H. Smith* 1,785
20. AMBUSH (N), *Samuel Alexander White* 1,596

Because shorter stories labor under a disadvantage in a vote of this kind, those under 20,000 words are listed separately, those under 10,000 being marked with a *.

STORIES UNDER 20,000 WORDS

1. *ALIAS WHISPERING WHITE, *W. C. Tuttle* 4,956
2. *THE RAVEN MOCKER, *Hugh Pendexter* 1,848
3. *SIRGAREH RUBIES, *Arthur James Hayes* 1,470
4. TAL TAULAI KHAN, *H. A. Lamb* 1,365
5. *THE GOOSEYOKE RETURNS A CALL, *E. E. Harriman* 1,209
6. *MAKING GOOD FOR MULEY, *W. C. Tuttle* 1,155
7. *BLAZE, *Warren H. Miller* 1,092
8. OAKES RESPECTS AN ADVERSARY, *Talbot Mundy* 1,071
9. MISTER CASSIDY, *David Douglas* 1,050
10. *SALT OF THE EARTH, *W. C. Tuttle* 1,008
11. *BLOOD MONEY, *William Dudley Pelley* 987
12. WOLF'S WAR, *H. A. Lamb* 946
13. *THE HAND OF PROVIDENCE, *W. C. Tuttle* 945
14. HIP SHOOTIN', *Earl Ennis* 904
15. *THE WAYS OF MOUNTAIN MEN, *Hugh Pendexter* 903
16. THE COLOR OF HER SOUL, *S. B. H. Hurst* 883
17. *MR. HOBBS, *Hugh S. Miller* 882
18. *LOCO OR LOVE, *W. C. Tuttle* 861
19. *TIED UP FOR TOMBSTONE, *W. C. Tuttle* 840
20. A LEADER OF MEN, W. *Townend* 777

Bear in mind the coming vote on this year's stories and be marking down your favorites as you go along.

Camp-Fire buttons now ready; 25c covers button and postage.

MANY letters come in from our comrades with the Army of Occupation and I wish we had space for all of them. Also that those used could see print in less than two or three months after their receipt. Anyhow here's one from Sergeant Albert J. Cook of the Engineers, with news of various other comrades. The shell-tags arrived O. K.—the first any of us here had seen.

We are planted up here on the Luxemburg border and wearing our young lives out trying to find something more interesting to do than squads right and left. The 6th Corps is now composed of the 5th, 7th and 33rd Divisions, the 5th occupying the lower half of Luxemburg, the 33rd the upper half and the 7th lying along the Moselle River near Pont-à-Mousson, in reserve. The only excitement left is the destroying and detonating of the German gas and H. E. shells which number hundreds of thousands, many of them so deteriorated by the weather and electrolysis that a person can't even wink at one of them. However, they are being rapidly put out of the way and soon will be off our hands.

HAVE heard from quite a few of the Army and Navy Club boys. Ben Praeger, old-timer of the insurrection, Mexico, and stopped five M. G. bullets at the crossing of the Vesle which same was stopping his company's advance. He was top-sergeant so he put the whole outfit of boche out of business with his automatic after he went down; and his company leap-frogged over him. He pulled out of the hospital in time to take up the white man's burden on the lower edge of the Argonne at Dommartin and Fresnes, where his division, the

28th, fought like the —— till 11 A. M., November eleventh.

Bob Woodside, formerly treasurer of the club and now Captain of Co. M., 38th Inf., the hardest boiled regiment in the line and called by the French the "Rock of the Marne," got three or four punches in the anatomy at Montfaucon but up to armistice day was getting along fine. Bob was with the "Fighting Tenth" in the Philippines during the battle of Manilla and is the idol of every soldier in Pennsylvania. Buck Stehle, sergeant in the 122nd F. A., was bumped across the brow with a chunk of shrapnel while his battery was supporting the 1st Division in front of Montsec.

Have heard from quite a few of the other fellows and, so far, no report of casualties, so, if things break the same way we are hoping the old gang will still foregather in the club-rooms before long and there will sure be some barrage put up—minus the festive and alluring cocktail and the amber brew that made Milwaukee famous. Say, it will be rather hard for us hellions to sit around the big table and order some soft drink that we can't even pronounce. I suppose we'll have to move the club to Nogales or Naco on the Border.

SOME of the fellows have written me about organizing a platoon to volunteer if we go up into Russia, so I suppose if we do go it may be some time before we are back to the States. It's getting rather monotonous over here with no action at all except slinging a rifle around and worrying about a leave of absence to Paris. Went down myself for three days the other day and it felt good to see the old town again and feel real cobbles under my feet and see the white lights.

Am sending you some of the tags the Boche tied to their gas shells. On account of shape of tags they could tell in the dark what kind they were; also a little chart of Army Corps and Divisions, several Insignia that might help you out along Broadway.—SERGT. ALBERT J. COOK.

PIGTAILS—a word on them from H. A. Lamb in connection with his story in this issue:

New York.

By the way, in the future drawing for "The Star of Evil Omen," I'd like to voice a warning. Chinese of all classes, of the Ming period—up to 1643—who are in the story, did not wear pigtails. The Manchus did.

There are Manchu hunters with long hair in the story. But the Emperor and his court had short hair.

THE history of the pigtail is interesting. The Tatars—including the Manchus, who were and are of Tatar blood—worshiped the horse. They let their back hair grow and shaved their foreheads in imitation of a horse's mane.

The Cossacks had a lot of respect for the Tatars, and imitated them. Up to the present century the Cossacks grew a "scalp-lock," as Schweider has very accurately drawn.

When the Manchus conquered China proper, about 1640, they issued a dictum that long hair—pigtails—was the fashion. The adherents of the defeated Mings then had to wear pigtails or be beheaded. Most of them wore the tails.

Up to the present day a long pigtail was a sign of a valued citizen and official of China. Lately, the Chinks have left them off, more or less, like the binding on the feet of the Ming women.—Harold Lamb.

WHO will furnish the comrade inquiring with information concerning Benjamin Blockburger, Mexican War veteran and old-timer of the West?

Paterson, New Jersey.

I thought probably some of the readers might be able to give me a little information about Benjamin Blockburger who died in California in 1916. He was a veteran of the Mexican War—in fact, the last one alive at the time I knew him. According to the tales he told he fought the Indians, crossing the prairies several times in prairie-schooners, made a number of stakes in California and led a generally adventurous life in the West. He is distantly related to me and it was just lately I learned of his death. Any information would be greatly appreciated.—H. M.

ONE of the inquirers to "Ask Adventure" asked for the text of an old sea chantey entitled "The Flying Cloud." For once Captain Dingle was stumped; neither from his own memory nor from any of the book or magazine collections of chanteys could he draw the text of that particular one. But an appeal to the readers of our magazine did the work.

Complete versions came in from several of you and the chantey is given here in full. The versions differed among themselves in minor points; we have here followed, in the main, the version furnished by Captain J. A. Payne, Sapulpa, Oklahoma, but have in some dozen places substituted words, phrases or parts of lines from the version furnished by James McIntyre, Johnson City, Tennessee, where it differed and seemed better.

LATER we'll get a list of all published chanteys, pass that list on to Camp-Fire and ask for any other chanteys, title and text, that have not been preserved in print. There is no other agency in the world better adapted to getting results in such a matter and if we of the Camp-Fire can save from oblivion some of the chanteys that began to pass out of use with the passing of sailing vessels, we shall perform a very worth-while service.

And, meanwhile, here is one that, so far as we know, is not elsewhere preserved in print. (In the last stanza Captain Payne's version had "Madrid" instead of "Newgate.")

THE FLYING CLOUD

An Old Sea Chantey

My name is Patrick Hullahan, as you will understand,
I was born and reared in Waterford, in Erin's happy land.
When I was young and in my prime and fortune on me smiled,
My parents doted on me, I being an only child.

Now my father bound me to a trade, in Waterford's fair town.
He bound me to a cooper there, by the name of William Brown.
I served my master faithfully for eighteen months or more,

Till I shipped on board the *Ocean Queen*, bound for Bermuda's shore.

Now when I reached Bermuda, I met with a Captain Moore,
The commander of the *Flying Cloud*, just out of Baltimore,
And he asked me for to sail with him, on a slavery voyage to go
To the burning shores of Africa, where the sugar-cane doth grow.

Now it was but a few weeks after, that we reached the African shore,
And it was five hundred of those poor slaves, from their native homes we bore.
We marched them on our quarter deck, and placed them well below.
It was eighteen inches to the man, but they were forced to go.

Now in a few days we set sail, with our cargo of slaves,
'Twould better have been for those poor men, had they been in their graves,
For the plague and fever came on board and swept them half away;
We would drag their bodies up on deck and heave them in the sea.

Now it was but a short time after, that we reached the Cuban shore
And sold them to the planters there, as slaves forevermore
To lead a hard and wretched life beneath that broiling sun,
The rice and cotton fields to hoe, till their career was run.

Now when our money was all spent, and we were out to sea again
Then Captain Moore he came on deck and said to us his men:
"There is gold and silver to be had, if you'll remain with me;
We'll hoist aloft the pirate flags and scour this Spanish Sea."

Now the *Flying Cloud* was a clipper ship, five hundred tons or more;
She could easily sail around anything sailing out of Baltimore.
Her sails were like the driven snow, and on them not a speck,
While twenty-four brass nine-pound guns she carried on her deck.

Well we all agreed except five lads, who asked to go on shore.
Now two of them were Boston boys, two more from Baltimore,
While the other was an Irish lad from the County of Tramore—
How I wish to God I had joined those men and with them gone on shore!

Well we robbed and plundered many ships, down on that Spanish Main,
Made many the widow and orphan there, in sorrow to complain,
For we forced them all to walk the plank, gave them a watery grave,
For the saying of our captain was that dead men tell no tales.

We cruised around that Spanish Sea, till a warship hove in view
And fired a shot across our bow, 'twas a signal to heave to.
We heeded not that warning shot, but flew before the wind,
Till a chain-shot struck our mizzin mast, and we soon fell behind.

So we cleared our decks for action, as the larger ship hove 'long side,
And soon upon our quarter deck, blood flowed like a crimson tide.
We fought till Captain Moore was killed, and eighteen of his men,
Till a bomb-shell set our ship on fire, we were forced to surrender then.

So back to Newgate I was brought, bound down in iron chains,
For the robbing and plundering of many ships down on that Spanish Main.
It was whisky and bad women, lad, that made a wreck of me,
So beware, young men, of what I say, and shun bad company.

WITH a story dealing with them in this issue, William M. McCoy tells us how he comes to know about Chinamen:

Los Angeles, Calif.

I always liked Chinamen. When they want to carve up some one they pick out another Chinaman for the carvee. That ought to suit any one who is not a Celestial. When I was the small boy problem of a California ranch, female "help" was unknown, and the Chink ranch cook was sort of *ex-officio* nurse girl. I am afraid one or two of them were rather busy, but everything I did was always just right. Later one of our cooks retired from the kitchen and opened a gambling-house in Chinatown, Los Angeles. There was plenty going on in Chinatown in those days, and I used to look Wong up every once in so often. He naturally took me over, under, and around Chinatown, and just as naturally I gained a little insight into how the Chinks feel, act, and work their schemes. They were always mighty white to me.—WILLIAM M. MCCOY.

YOU will remember that at our Mid-January Camp-Fire one of you appealed to all of us for a translation of a manuscript found in a bottle picked up on the seashore. Here are some of the responses that have come in and that should help to solve the mystery:

Yreka, Calif.

Since a few of the words are unquestionably Spanish, it is reasonable to suppose it all intended for Spanish, or its sister language, Portuguese. Sailors often have a smattering of both. It seems to have been written by a person who did not speak the tongue and spelled phonetically from dictation of one who could not write. Such combination was common enough in 1819, the date of the MS. Any one who has heard an illiterate speak in the foreign tongue, clipping many of his syllables, can hardly wonder at the spelling, if taken down from dictation, by a writer who did not understand what he was writing. From the account in *Adventure*, it appears that you were not sent the MS. itself, and that the two copies sent differed slightly. It might be that the letters of the MS., after a century, are not easily decipherable.

Original copy

VELET MANGE PAR DIOS DET NORTE ET ELVENGE PIROT
BURE DESIMGILD CAPITAN BLACKBURNE MDCCCXIX

Letters corrected

DET, possibly DEL
BURE, possibly BURKE
VENGE, possibly VENCE

Notes.

In such a MS. one would naturally expect a call for help or a story of lost treasure, and the idea might be misleading.

In such a language as Spanish, vowel sounds might be uncertain, but the consonants must be accounted for. In this translation the pronunciation will be considered that of an illiterate:

par Dios, *norte*, and *capitan*, are all plain Spanish properly spelled, and are such words as any one might be familiar with, whether he spoke the language or not.
mange and *venge*, words not easily mispronounced, are almost as plainly Spanish.
velet and *desimgild*, the first and last words, are the most obscure.

Taking the easiest words first:
par Dios, 'By God' A common oath.
del norte, 'of the north,' or "from the north.'
et, 'and.' Old Spanish form.
el, 'he.' Used for 'it.'
mange, for *manga*, a ' waterspout.'
venge, possibly *vence*, for *vencio*, 'vanquished,' 'overwhelmed.' The verb of the sentence.
The *o* would hardly be heard.
pirot, for *pirata*, 'a pirate.' The sound is represented almost perfectly, since it would be pronounced 'pirat,' the last syllable being clipped.
buke, for *buque*, 'a boat.'
velet, a word very difficult to make out. To the writer of the word it was probably velet, with the accent on the first syllable.
For *vuelta de*, 'a turn of,' pronounced 'velt'd,' the *d* assimilating with the *t* sound.
desimgild, for *d'-s'-m'-gell*, an illiterate's pronunciation of *de San Miguel*, 'of San Miguel.' The *d* at the end of the word may be accounted for by the accent on the last syllable, a consonantal strengthening of a doubtful sound.

Literal translation

A turn of a waterspout, by God, from the north, and he vanquished a pirate boat of San Miguel.

The last phrase sounds as though the MS. had been written by an observer, and not by a participant. Since an observer could hardly have cause to put the account into a bottle, while a participant might have such occasion, the last phrase is probably intended for "the pirate boat, San Miguel."

Translation

A whirl of a waterspout, by God, from the north, and it overwhelmed the pirate boat, *San Miguel*, Captain Blackburn, 1819.—J. B.

The next letter was addressed to Thomas Samson Miller of "Ask Adventure," through whom the mystery was brought to our attention. We have readers in at least one of the Guianas and have already heard from them at Camp-Fire.

Well, now he does not say that the bottle was found on the African Coast, and even if he did, that is no reason for supposing that it was written somewhere near Africa. The influence of the Spaniards extended all over the world. Now, to find some place where there is also Dutch influence, English influence and African dialect.

There may be many, but I think the most likely place is Paramaribo, capital of Guiana (Dutch), called Surinam. The natives there speak a dialect called "Taki-Taki," which is a mixture of English, Dutch, Spanish, Portuguese, French, and some trace of African dialect. Doesn't this make your letter possible? If your magazine has any kind of a circulation in South America, or if Mr. X. W. could locate some one from South America, perhaps even from British Guiana, they could probably translate it for him.

If you care to find anything out about Dutch Guiana you might read the article in The National Geographic Magazine for June, 1907.—7999

The next came in handwriting which I'm not sure we in the office have deciphered correctly. It seems to be based on the idea that the message was written in script, for first this solution gives the words written in an illiterate hand and then, under each, the clearly written word which might have been intended instead of the one given in the form handed to us. But my understanding is that the message was printed out by letter. Here is the solution arrived at by "Thalatta," as he signs himself:

Follow Congo past divided mouths of Ubangi. Perish here Isangila.

He adds:

See Encyc. Brit.—Congo (exploration), Captain Tuckey's expedition, 1816.

So, knowing nothing about Captain Tuckey and little about the Congo, we looked it up. The encyclopedia says, in brief:

In 1816 the British Admiralty sent Captain J. K. Tuckey on an expedition to explore the Congo, sometimes known as the Zaire. The expedition reached the mouth of the river on the sixth of July, 1816, and managed to push up-stream as far as Isangila, beyond the lowest series of rapids; but sickness broke out, and the commander and sixteen other Europeans died, and the expedition had to return. Captain Tuckey and several of his companions are buried on Prince's Island. . . .

But Mr. Cox, who did the investigating, did it pretty thoroughly. Here are his findings:

This makes "Thallata's" solution seem extremely plausible. But other accounts of the expedition, chief among them Captain Tuckey's own journal, persuade me to believe for several reasons that the message is still unsolved. These reasons are:

1. Tuckey did not know the name Isangila, which is modern. In his journal he refers to the place as Sangalla.

2. The expedition began and ended within the year 1816. The date on the message was 1819. Thalatta passes gracefully over this.

3. Nor does Thalatta have anything to say about "Capitan Blackburne." No one of this name with the expedition.

4. No account of the expedition shows that it was ever in such straits as to make necessary the sending of messages in bottles. The party traveled mostly in a boat, with the best equipment that Europe at that time could furnish. Though seventeen men died, thirty-nine others came out alive. If need arose to communicate with the outside world, better means than bottles were at hand. So far as can be found, the only use Tuckey had for bottles was in dealing with the natives, who demanded these and many "fathoms" of cloth in trade for a scrawny chicken or two.

(Tuckey's exploration, by the way, was the first since the discovery of the river by a Portuguese, three centuries before.)

The next is an ingenious re-division of the words used:

Washington, D. C.

See page 181 "Camp-Fire" in *Adventure* of 1-18-19 as to "Velet Mange Par Dios Det Norte Et Elvenge Pirot Bure Desimgild Capitan Blockburne. MDCCCIX."

VE (we) let man Gepar di (die). O. S. Detvortee tel (say) VE (we) N. G. (no good). E (he is a) Pirot (Pirate). Bured (buried) Es (he) im (in) Gildcap. I tan block-Burne MDCCCXIX (probably some instruction as to numbers).—I. A. M'Therent.

Here are some helpful suggestions:

Chicago.

As my wife has command of several languages, I asked her if she could help any. The following is the result. Hope it may help some.

Velet Mange Par
weather hurricane by
Dios Det Norte Et Elvenge
God. Within north and altitude

Velet, we think, is Spanish for "weather," but should be spelled *Veleta;* a poor speller could very easily make the mistake. *Mange* should be *Manga*, supposing it to be Spanish. *Par* should be *Por*, to mean "by." *Dios* can also mean farewell. (I am not refering to *Adios*.)

Det Norte et elvenge.

The above four words are taken from Portuguese; the word *Elvenge* has the same meaning in Spanish ("Elevation").

Pirot Bure Desimgild pronounced as *Perowt Bwhoray Day-seem Khill* (as in "kill") my wife tells me is a man's name. The word *tempo* is Spanish for "weather," but among seafaring people *Veleta* is used. Hoping this will be of some assistance.—Walter F. Sullivan.

No, the riddle isn't finally solved, though at least one of the offered solutions goes a long way, but certainly progress has been made and perhaps, with the clues uncovered thus far, some others of you can run it down.

CONCERNING his story in this issue a word from Barry Scobee:

San Antonio, Texas.

The story "The Rawhiders," was written on the foundation of actual characters and interpretations of my own. I knew two men in the U. S. Army, in my company, who were pals yet were in real fear of each other. This fear came from their eternal rawhiding of each other. Each longed to hand the other the stiffest kind of verbal punches yet were afraid to go beyond defined limits. One threatened to smash the other in the face so as to leave a mark, and the other retorted that he would kill the person that smashed him in the face. They actually kept arms handy, and watched each other—except when they went out together, or were journeying with a third person, then they stood by loyally.

I TOOK those two for the story, and added this: A man who takes himself too seriously, pours out the things in his heart, then can't stand a little joking about it, is in the way to be ragged and rawhided. If he can't stand joking he shouldn't pour out what's in his heart. Let him keep his innermost thoughts to himself, or let him be able to laugh with others at his idiosyncrasies—let him see the humorous side of things, even himself. A man should cultivate the practise of taking jibes lightly, answering good naturedly, never quarreling. He can do all that and still have his fine convictions, his good character—in other words, be a man. To quote the truism, it is what a man does and not what he says that counts in the long run.

I KNEW a man in my company who had been a railroader before he enlisted. He served three years, then "re-ed-up" in the company I was in. He told windy stories of times when he was a freight brakeman running big trains out of Omaha. His refrain was, "And I gave 'em the highball." Men of company got to singing out in his presence, "Give 'em the highball." The man couldn't take it lightly. He had put himself in a ridiculous position by his too-much talk on a subject that lay in his heart. He took himself seriously. He couldn't turn the rawhiding aside, and he couldn't stand it. So he went over the hill—became a deserter and I haven't heard of him to this day.—Barry Scobee.

A WOMAN comrade, with the spirit of adventure strong in her and an interesting word to say about it:

Birmingham, Ala.

How I enjoy the Camp-Fire letters! I feel as if talking with friends, for I love adventure, but for the last seventeen years have been a hearth-stone adventurer.

In regards to Indians, Chief Red Cloud was a dearly beloved friend of my childhood and girlhood days, also had the honor (?) of partaking of heap good dog stew at the teepee of Sitting-Bull. I have photos of several Indians and my mother has in her possession photos of the battle-ground of Wounded Knee, of Red Cloud, Chief Sitting-Bull, also Jack Red Cloud.

I think the spirit of adventure is one of the greatest gifts of mankind. As it gives one the ability to be happy with very little of this world's goods, a courage to face trouble and to be unafraid of death. At least I have found it so.—Mrs. C. Meyer.

THIS comrade tried for four years to get into the Army but like many others was barred by physical disability. However, that's not what he's talking about. He's speaking very frankly and on a subject worth listening to:

Detroit, Mich.

When I first came to "the States" three years ago I didn't appreciate the privileges this country allows strangers.

WHEN one is raised in one of England's colonies one is generally very, almost rabidly, I might say, pro-English and, with the narrow-mindedness peculiar to those who have seen only one thing all their lives, I couldn't see what you Americans saw in this country that was so very wonderful. One of the reasons, I think, that made me antagonistic to America was the fact that at that time German propaganda was spreading round to the effect that England was fighting with Frenchmen and using the men of her Colonies to fight with, while Englishmen stayed home and drank tea. Of course, being British, I couldn't see that for a minute.

When I'd go to the theaters and hear the Stars and Stripes applauded with cheers and hand-claps I used to wonder what you people could see in a flag like that. You see, I didn't know what it stood for then and it looked tawdry to me, being used to the Union-jack.

ONE night at my rooming-house some one asked me if the wheat produced in the Canadian Northwest compared favorably with American wheat. I said it did, in fact it was a better grade than can be grown here. It wasn't a boast about Canada but simply a fact as I understood it. An old Kentuckian was at the table and he put down his fork and glared at me and said:

"You seem to think a lot of Canada?"

"I do," I said.

"Well, why in —— don't you go back there, then?"

Of course I didn't have any answer, but that question made me think some. I met a number of good Americans shortly after that and I came to understand what the Stars and Stripes really stands for. I began to ask myself questions like this "What right had I to take the protection of the United States flag, unless I stood up for it when it needed me?" "What right had I to live here and bawl out the country that was feeding me?" Well, there was no answer, and I can say that I felt pretty —— cheap, a rather rotten variety of carp.

SINCE that time, I've seen things in a new light and I'm glad to say and proud to say that the Stars and Stripes looks good to me and I'm willing to scrap for her any old time when she needs me, if she'll take me. I think a citizen of any country should place that country before all and until such time as I can put the United States before all I shall not take out my papers. I can stand up and say truthfully that I'm not a backbiter any more. I think the reason I was at one time was because I didn't look at things from the American point of view. I also think foreigners grab at the idea that this is a "free country" and that their support to the Government isn't necessary. I think that each one should be made to understand that he should give that support.—Allen Stuart Reid.

WHEN I wrote Mr. Reid to make sure he would have no objection to my using his letter in "Camp-Fire" I received the reply given below. Though there are at times good and sufficient reasons for not signing one's own name to a published communication, in general I'm inclined to agree with the old hunter:

I'm afraid my letter will prove a very poor "article," for my ideas, as I remember, were very badly brought out. That is the only objection I have to your publishing my letter, and if you do, you may sign my name, of course.

As the old hunter said: "If a man ain't got guts enough ter stand up fer his own principles, he ain't worth a ——."—Allen Stuart Reid.

AS SEVERAL of you have asked Camp-Fire to tell you about old pistols or guns in your possession, it occurred to me that some of you might be able to tell me about a small sword that a friend found in a second-hand dealer's shop in Piqua, Ohio, and gave to me some eighteen years ago. A cut follows, showing general shape, and another showing design covering base of blade for about six inches, same design on both sides. The words above the figure are "Vivat Bandur," but I have never found any one who could tell me who Bandur was, or when and where the weapon was used or anything else about it.

It is 22½ inches over all, the blade being 17½ inches in length. The handle is some strongly and straight grained wood, mounted at the ends with what looks like brass; brass hilt and butt of handle decorated rather crudely with a running design of flowers, one of six pointed petals, the other consisting of two concentric circles with whole flower covered with dots, an evident attempt to indicate a densely double flower of some kind. A small decoration on each side of middle of hilt (both

sides) seems a conventional design indicating nothing in particular. Butt of handle is shaped to imitate a deer's foot.

Can any of you identify it?

HERE is a bright thing done by me. In the May third issue I gave you the autobiographical talk of Everett Saunders and tacked on to it the name of E. S. Pladwell. Don't know how it happened but it did. In the proof Mr. Saunders' name was at the end while my introductory paragraph mentioned Mr. Pladwell. Possibly the printer's proof-reader noted the discrepancy and changed one name to agree with the other. More likely I did it myself. Those of you who've read proof know how easily such stupidities creep in. I didn't realize my break until I received the following from Mr. Pladwell:

Oakland, Cal.

Since reading my biography in the latest *Adventure* my friends are now convinced that I am leading a double life.

APPARENTLY I have become a remarkable example of the transmogrification of souls. That is, while being an Oakland newspaper man, my soul or alter ego or something was prowling about Oreana, Nevada, and this second-soul has among other things become married without my knowledge or consent, leaving me somewhat upset, naturally.

I am more than interested; I am excited. Have I any children? Can the wife sue me for non-support? If so, can she collect for many years back? Is she blonde or brunette? How has she worried along while my real self has been on the Great White Way of Oakland, California? Has my spectral self run up any debts? If so, can they be traced to Oakland? More important, has he made any money? If so, can I collect?

Kidding aside, though, I was much surprised to see this biography, which must have had names switched somehow. Mine was in *Adventure* many moons ago. I will gladly subscribe, however, to some of the thoughts in the article, as I think them rather good. I wonder whose biography it is?—E. S. PLADWELL.

THE best way I know of squaring things is to give you Mr. Saunders' talk again, but this time over his own name. Here it is. With my apologies to all concerned.

Oreana, Nevada.

I was born on a ranch in Eastern Oregon, October 9, 1892. The only breaks in the continuity of my existence since then occurred when I stopped a quick-breaking in-shoot with my solar plexus, and again when I ducked into a right hook and had my nose pushed across to a painful position under my right eye.

NATURALLY, having passed the greater part of my life in a cattle country, I have seen branding-irons smoke and heard the hoarse bellows of calves put under the knife and hot iron ever since I can remember. I have seen horses, with the fear of the wild captured thing in their eyes, struggling against the ropes, and have seen them go into the air under the terrifying saddle and rider. Though personally (the demands of truth force me to an unwilling confession) I am no better rider than the imaginary *Spike Ellis* in "The Silver Saddle," I have a pretty thorough first-hand knowledge of the thrills incidental to the mounting of a cayuse. I also know what it is to lose step with him, fall a jump behind, reach for leather, and grab two handfuls of sand or bunchgrass—or anything that might happen to constitute the earth formation in that vicinity.

I GOT through high school at Baker, Oregon, and had my fling at scholastic athletics, also long-winded old Cicero and that brain-staggering invention of Euclid called geometry. I attended the University of Oregon for a year and a half before deciding that I knew enough to make the old world sit up and take notice of me. Then I quit school and got married, and soon, like George Ade, fastened my fraternity pin on my undershirt and admitted to myself that there were several things that had not come thoroughly under my notice.

AT VARIOUS times I have done other things besides ranch, go to school and wonder how O. Henry and Jack London could get so much kick from plain facts. I worked for a while with a topographical engineering party, and with a railroad engineering party. I bucked wood for a donkey at a big lumber camp near Kelso, Washington. I mucked for two weeks with a railroad construction gang, and though I then had plenty of that way of earning an honest living, I saw more disillusioning facts in the every-day events of those two weeks than a year at college could build up.

One incident in particular convinced me that the Mexicans might under certain conditions be hard to beat. It was one morning at breakfast. A big American and a little greaser got into a senseless dispute about the passing of a plate of bread. The Mexican slashed out with a knife and laid the big fellow's face open. His opponent caught up a gallon capacity granite-ware pitcher of condensed milk by the handle and tried to beat off the Mexican's head. All he did, however, was to spoil his appetite. The Mexican worked that day. The other called for his time and left the camp so as not to furnish more temptation for that knife.

I SOLD enlarged pictures in Oregon and California, and quit because I couldn't lie convincingly enough to satisfy my own conscience, though I was doing fairly well with the "gullible public." I have never ridden the rods, but have made several hundred miles on top and on the blinds. If any one doubts that clothes don't make the man, let him get his coat turned wrong side out (to keep the conventional exterior of it clean) and his eyes rimmed with coal smoke, and look from the rock bottom up into our social order.

I have mucked a good many thousand dollars worth of ore for various mining companies. One night, on the graveyard shift in an incline shaft, I stepped back to roll a smoke. Three seconds afterward a ton of rhyolite fell out of the hanging wall and crashed down on the spot I had recently occupied. The edge of the cave-in caught the machine man's leg. I lifted a few boulders off his foot. He looked up and grinned. "Uncle Sam came —— near losing a good soldier," he said.

IT IS needless to say that my unconventional and floating-laborer activities were confined to my pre-nuptial days. Since December 19, 1914, I have been rather unflaggingly busy trying to get by. It was partly through a desire to escape the menace of the muck-stick (shovel being used symbolically for all manner of tools designed for the use of those of us who haven't both hands full of the Top Rung), and partly due to an ardent desire I have always had to learn to tell a good story well, that I began trying my hand at writing a few months ago.

I have felt humble when reading in the "Camp-Fire" of men who have lived more in a year than I have in ten. And I have felt humble while talking with men over real camp-fires whose experiences dwarf my pitiable ones to kindergarten affairs in comparison. But I must admit, with a trace of shame, that my "ardent desire" aforementioned always appears, corrupting my humbleness, which has been divinely commended, with covetousness, which is condemned. I covet that man's experience and think, if I had seen so much, felt so keenly, read so deeply in the "open books of life and death," what glorious tales could I tell! And yet, strange to say, I often doubt if I should endanger O. Henry's place in the story world even if I had seen the Klondike stampede.—EVERETT SAUNDERS.

FOLLOWING is a drawing made from a photograph of *Gauntlet*, the sloop in which our comrade Captain A. E. Dingle made his adventurous single-handed voyage

from New York to Bermuda, as narrated in his article in this issue.

Camp-Fire Buttons

AS BRIEFLY announced at our last meeting, the Camp-Fire buttons are now ready for delivery. Any one who wishes belongs to our Camp-Fire, the only requisite being an interest in the things in which the rest of us are interested. The buttons are designed to indicate this common interest so that we can recognize each other when we meet in far places or at home. Any one with this common interest is entitled to apply for a badge.

They cost us a fraction over twenty-one cents each in thousand lots from the manufacturer and one will be sent to you for twenty-five cents, which covers handling, stationery, pasteboard container and postage on the button to any part of the world. In other words, we are charging, only what is practically the cost price and making it a round number.

AS ALREADY explained, the button is enameled in gold-washed setting, screw-back, round, three-eighth inch in diameter. Three bands of color—blue, brown and green, for sky, earth and sea. The number seventy-one appears in gold on the middle band, representing the letters of the word "Camp-Fire" when each is given its numerical order in the alphabet and the results added together. Nothing else appears on the button.

We here in the office are immensely pleased with it, for it seems to us neat, in good taste and the kind of thing one can wear anywhere. We hope—and believe—that you will like it as well as we do.

So pretty soon you can begin keeping an eye out for men with the "seventy-one" button showing in their lapels.

ON RECEIPT of his first letter I hoped he would keep his threat and send us some of the interesting tales he has tucked away in his memory. And he did. After an extract from his first letter comes a later one with interesting data on the Custer massacre:

Merrick, Okla.

The story of Jesse James being alive in Los Angeles, reminded me that I was one of the first dozen people who saw him lying dead with a hole through his head from the assassin's bullet. This was April 1, 1882, in St. Joe, Mo. I have since lived neighbor to Frank James. I expect to be in Abilene, Kansas, this Spring and hope to be able to correct Robert V. Carr's description of Wild Bill's personal appearance. I have wandered up and down some distance from the creek's mouth and sometimes, if time and inclination should synchronize, I may hand in something that might be of interest to *Adventure's* readers.

Merrick, Okla.

During several years of my knocking about I had the job of buying horses for the Cheyenne Indian Agent located at Colony, Okla., and became well acquainted with John Otter, a full blood Cheyenne. He was and is foreman of the Indian farm at Colony, Four years before the opening of Oklahoma to settelment he was on the Indian Police force working out of Ft. Reno, located six miles Northwest of the present city of El Reno, Okla.

During one of our trips he asked me if I had ever heard the Indian version of Custer's last fight. I had not. I give it here just as he told it to me:

EVER since Custer's massacre of the Cheyenne band—men, women and children—on the Wachita River about ten miles from the present town of Strong City, Okla., the Indians had lived in hopes of sometime meeting him in battle, and, contrary to general opinion, they not only had no fear of him but longed for the opportunity to get at him. It came when their outriding scouts reported that Custer (Long Hair) had detached himself and a small company from the main command and was riding their way. The Indians sent a small band instructed to ride into plain view of Custer and, if Custer attacked, to retreat. They bet on his doing just as he did. The band led him into the center of 5,000 Sioux and Cheyenne. Each and every warrior engaged was instructed under no circumstances to kill Custer. He was to be taken alive and reserved for torture, which was to be skinning alive. To this day no Indian has ever been heard to make the claim of the killing and their tribe lore is that Custer finding his life spared seemingly miraculously, sensed the why and ended his own life.—F. K. Willis, M. D.

HERE is a dramatic personal story from history, sent in to us by D. Wiggins a long time ago, before he went into the Army, and, like many another good letter, left in the big pile of Camp-Fire correspondence till I could dig down to it and find a place for it in our pages:

Salem, Oregon.

Yes, there *was* "A Man Without a Country," and he was likewise the Father of Oregon.

DOCTOR JOHN McLAUGHLIN was the factor of the H. B. C. (the boys call it the "Here Before Christ") in the Northwest territory in the days when the first of the pioneers were pushing the borderland to the Coast. He had more power, in all probability, than even our President possesses today. His word was law in Oregon, Washington and a large part of Idaho, Montana and Wyoming.

When the gaunt, hollow-eyed Yankees came drifting down the river and tied up their boats at the bank under the trading-post at Oregon City, which the Doctor founded, his duty to his employers was to have sent them out of the country with all speed, encouraging the red men to harrass them a little to encourage their going. But he was a man before all else.

Although he well knew that this was the forerunner of the horde that was to win the Northwest land for America, he gave the newcomers welcome; he sold them the food and the supplies they needed to begin the task of carving a home from the wilderness. (And right here I am going to say most emphatically that "carving" is the right term. Out here a man has to remove from thirty-nine to four hundred and seventeen stumps from every acre before he can put a plow point into the soil. A man pays for this land and then works for it.)

WELL, Doctor John, as he was familiarly called, was a close friend to the new-comers, and but for him I don't think Doctor Whitman's famous ride would have been of much value.

And then the Hudson's Bay Company learned of what their factor was doing. And the ax fell with vigor. Doctor John was ousted from his high estate, and was not even recognized as a British subject by the majority of his countrymen.

He never took out American citizenship papers, but lived and died as did *Philip Nolan*, but regarded in a far different light. We of the Northwestern States consider him as standing alone among the great men of history—he threw away wealth, position and power for the sake of a few ragged, privation-worn Americans. For he certainly knew what his employers would do to the man who did not eject the invaders of their empire.

HE PASSED away in his home in Oregon City, and lies under the wall of the Catholic church in that town. It's a sleepy, drowsy old town, lying along the river bank, but no town of the Northwest, except Astoria, has such glorious memories.

Doctor John's home still stands on the hill, and I was recently in the room that served as his office, where he passed over to his reward. No foreigner he, but a true American.—D. WIGGINS.

A LETTER from G. A. Wells, of our writers' brigade, with a word about New Zealand and Haiti:

New Albany, Ind.

In "Ask Adventure," issue of February third, I read with great interest Mr. Finnegan's letter of inquiry concerning the opportunities in New Zealand, and also Mr. Mills' reply. It appears that the latter gentleman is very enthusiastic about New Zealand, and from what I know of the place he is right in being so. I was lucky enough to make the cruise with the battle fleet that went around the world a dozen years ago, and we stopped several days at Auckland. I was writing travel articles for several newspapers at the time and naturally it was my business to "get next" to all that was interesting about the places we visited.

I WOULD like to add my unqualified approval of Mr. Mills' attitude toward New Zealand. Of course he knows much more about the country than I could learn in the few days I was there, but I saw enough to make me think of it as an annex of the so-called God's country. I should say that there is as much opportunity there as there is here in the States, though success in any line and in most places depends almost altogether upon the efforts of the man seeking success. If the sheriff ever chases me away from here I think I shall go to either New Zealand or Hawaii, with Colorado as a third choice.

And by the way, just outside of Auckland a few miles is an extinct volcano that stands alone in the midst of a beautiful farming country. It is shaped very similar to a gigantic bowl, and the sides and bottom are covered with grass that would, I believe, shame Kentucky's famous blue grass. It was this hill that gave me the idea for the location of my story, "The Madness of Johnny Dyer," that appeared in an earlier issue of *Adventure*.

THERE is also another letter of inquiry in this department and in the same issue that interests me. Mr. Bent wants to know about Haiti, and Captain Dingle makes haste to reply in effect: "Good ——, man! Don't touch Haiti with a thousand-mile pole!" My actual acquaintance with the island is limited to reading extensively about it, though I have been close enough to it two or three times to hit it with a rock. However, I have a brother who is marooned in the jungles of Cuba with half a dozen soldiers of fortune, one of whom is an engineer and who spent several years in Haiti. This gentleman speaks of it as a "—— of a place for a white man." A white man has no more chance there than a mongrel at a bench-show. All advice to the white man is to stay away. If one hasn't a black skin one is a pup with the mange. This knowledge, of course, comes third-hand, but I think it is sound. I merely wish to add what little I know of the place to keep a compatriot from getting stung in a foreign land, for I have been stranded thusly myself and know what it means for a man to be several thousand miles away from home among strangers and have but a few dollars in his jeans.—G. A. WELLS.

THE CAMP-FIRE

A Free-to-all Meeting-Place for Readers Writers & Adventurers

A WORD from Clyde B. Hough concerning his story in this issue:

Oakland, Calif.

At one time I spent a little over eleven months on just such an island as is described in this story. The size of the island, the reef completely around it, the birds and eggs and the method of obtaining water, are all statements of facts. The island in the story is a true, accurate and complete reproduction of the one where I was located.—C. B. HOUGH.

HERE'S an answer to the inquiry about "Cattle Kate" from one who knew her and the circumstances of her hempen departure. Here's hoping he tells us other incidents of the old days of the West.

Denver, Colo.

Used to ramble around the map a little myself, putting in about fifteen years of my life looking for the place where the other fellow "wasn't."

SINCE settling down I get a lot of fun out of our magazine and frequently read of men I have whacked blankets with in various parts of the West. Was acquainted with a lot of the old-time gun-fighters, who, as a general rule, were quiet, unassuming men and the best of partners.

Have been intending to write a few lines to Camp-Fire for some time but kept putting it off until in a recent issue some comrade inquired for information of "Cattle Kate," and as I happened to know her and a little of her history I thought you would be interested.

KATE MAXWELL was born north of Des Moines, Iowa. Her father died when she was a little girl, her mother married again, and died when Kate was about fifteen. She continued to live with her step-dad, who abused her something shameful, until she was twenty, when she ran away from home, tackling one job after another, until she wound up in a dance-hall. Kate arrived in Wyoming and got to running with a bunch of rustlers of which she was soon the recognized leader.

I met her at her hang-out on the Sweetwater several months before she was lynched. Was about forty-five years old, with a face burnt the color of old brick, black hair streaked with gray, flying loose to the wind, a man's coat and hat, and two big forty-fives and the grit of a wildcat.

Was living with Jim Avery, who, I believe, was post-master at Sweetwater. Six other hard cases made up the gang, Kate being head and shoulders the worst of the bunch. As long as she kept to ordinary rustling the cattlemen overlooked her faults. Later she got to shooting cows and running off the dogies, and then the mob got busy.

IN THE Spring of 1899 a bunch of twenty men rode quietly up to her ranch. The gang, with the exception of Avery and her nephew, were all away. Surrounding the house, part of the crowd covered the three of them from the windows, while others broke in the door. Both Avery and Kate were unarmed, their belts hanging on the wall, so got no chance to do any shooting.

Avery quit cold, and begged, but Kate fought the whole bunch bare-handed and the boy tried to knife one and got a pistol-butt over the head and was out of it.

The two were rushed out to the corral, a wagon-tongue hoisted in the air and both hung with the same rope. It is said that Kate offered to fight the entire mob with one pistol, and was still cursing them until the rope shut her off. The rest of the gang swore vengeance, and in less than a year practically the whole mob had died with their boots on.—FRANK L. SCHOTT.

THERE follows a slightly different version of the passing of "Cattle Kate." Both the names "Avery" and "Averill" are used. And there's also a word on McCoy.

Shoshoni, Wyo.

I note in your last issue that L. B. W. wants to know something about Cattle Kate and some notorious outlaw by the name of McCoy. Jim Averill, who helped run the eighth Standard Parallel in this State, lived on the Sweetwater River, some time in the last of the 80's, with a woman by the name of Ella Watson, who had the nickname of Cattle Kate. She was a courtezan and while living with Averill plied her trade and some of the neighboring punchers and owners paid her for favors received in mavericks.

AVERY also was a land surveyor and knew too much about the choice bits of Government lands which some of the big cow outfits had fenced up. Between these two things the hatred of some of these outfits grew to such an extent that one day when Averill and Ella were going to the then new town of Casper they were ambushed on the road north of the Sweetwater and near the mouth of Dry Creek and both were hung on a tree which was still standing some four years ago.

The required coroner's inquest was held, but the paties were never prosecuted. It was a cowardly and dastardly crime. Cattle Kate was written up in the newspapers in lurid and fanciful colors as a dashing cowgirl, dead shot and a few other things. There was nothing to that but hot air.

As for McCoy the only one answering to the description was Bob McCoy of Thermopolis, who was killed some few years ago under peculiar circumstances. He was shot by unknown parties; his body then dragged to the river edge and a nosebag strapped around his head and then the body as far as the shoulders put under water. Bob was supposed to be pretty swift in the use of a rope. Otherwise he was not a particularly hard citizen.—. —. —.

WOULDN'T it be a sort of good idea for our magazine to have a kind of emblem or sign or whatever you want to call it? An "Adventure, its Mark" affair? Might use it on its stationery some day, and

there are various little purposes for which it might come in handy. Tried it out, for example, on the preceding page. Here it is in large size—a kind of coat-of-arms arrangement. Does it get by?

OUR Camp-Fire is the best agency in existence for collecting hitherto unpublished chanteys, ballads and other sea-songs and rescuing them before they are lost forever. It's another job for us, and one as interesting as it is worth while.

We have been fortunate in getting, to aid us in this work, the friendly cooperation of John F. Lomax, who is perhaps the best authority on this subject. With him as guide and expert we can be sure that what we collect will be assessed at its right and full value.

Whenever any of you sends in a hitherto unpublished chantey or sea-song or a ballad of the Great Lakes or Erie Canal we'll try to have it at our Camp-Fire for the benefit of all of us. And we hope that later on Mr. Lomax will have enough of them to embody in a book for still more permanent keeping.

Of course original productions have no place in this collection.

Some time in the future we might try our hand at collecting unpublished cowboy songs and songs of the old West in general. And perhaps the lumberjack songs some day.

Some of the songs are of course too broad to be printable, but some of these have merits that offset that point and, if you have any of the latter, no doubt Mr. Lomax will be interested in them.

FOLLOWING is a list of the *published* chanteys and songs so far as accessible in the New York Public Library. These we do *not* want. What we are after is those that have not yet been preserved in print.

If you know any that are *not* in the following list, please send them to Mr. Lomax, Y. M. C. A. Building, Austin, Texas, and he'll see that they are properly handled and classified and that the suitable ones come to us for Camp-Fire. If you can send music with words, so much the better, but for most of us that, I fear, will be impossible.

Titles are given in italics; first lines in ordinary letters. They are published in one or more of the following: *Journal of American Folk Lore:* "Old Sea Chanteys," by Bradford & Fogge; "Naval Songs," by S. B. Luce; "Sea Songs and Ballads," by Christopher Stone; "Real Sea Songs," by R. B. Whall in the *Nautical Magazine;* "A Sailor's Garland," by John Masefield; "The Chantey Man Sings," by Wm. Brown Meloney in *Everybody's* for August, 1915.

All Hands on Deck
All hands on deck, the bos'n cries.
As I Was Going
As I was going to Rigamarow
I say so, and I hope so.
Black Ball Line
In the Black Ball Line I served my time.
Black Ball Line
Come all you young fellows that follow the sea—
With a yo, ho—blow the man down.
Blow the Man Down
Blow the man down,
Blow the man down,
Way; Hi; Blow the man down.
Boney
Boney was a warrior,
Oh, aye, oh.
California
Good-by, my love, good-by,
I can not tell you why
I'm off to Californy
To dig the yellow gold.
Also—
Blow, boys, blow!
For Californy O!
We're bound for Sacramento
To dig the yellow gold.
And other forms.

The Camp-Fire

Capstan Bar
Walk her round, for we're rolling homeward,
Heave, my boys together.
Come Roll Him Over
Oho, why don't you blow?
Aha, come roll him over.
Come Roll the Cotton
Come roll the cotton down, my boys,
Roll the cotton down.
Dreadnaught
There's a saucy wild packet,
And a packet of fame.
(*Several forms.*)
Give Me the Gal
Give me the gal can dance fandango
Running down to Cuba.
Hand Over Hand
A handy ship and a handy crew—
Handy, my boys, so handy.
Haul Away
Away, haul away, boys,
Haul away together.
Away, haul away, boys,
Haul away.
Haul on the Bowline
Haul on the bowline
The bully ship's a-rolling!
Haul the Bowline
Haul upon the bowline, the fore and main top bowline.
Haul the Bowline
Kitty is my darling,
Haul the bowline, haul.
High Barbery
There were two lofty ships from England came,
Blow high! Blow low! And so sailed we.
Homeward Bound
Oh, to Pensacola town we'll bid adieu.
(*Used with names of any seaport.*)
Homeward Bound
We're homeward bound this very day
Good-by, fare you well.
I'll Sing You a Song
I'll sing you a song, a good song of the sea—
To my aye, heigh, blow the man down.
And I trust that you'll join in the chorus with me—
Give me some time to blow the man down.
It's Time for Us to Leave Her
Oh, the times are hard and the wages low.
Leave her, Johnny, leave her.
Knock a Man Down
I wish I was a Mobile Bay
Wey, hey, knock a man down.
Let the Bulgine Run
Oh, the wildest packet you can find—
Oh, he! Oh, ha! Are you 'most done?
Is the *Margaret Evans* of the Black X Line.
Clear the rail! Let the Bulgine run.
Liverpool Jack
Oh, Liverpool Jack with your tarpaulin hat,
Amelia, where you bound to?
Long Time Ago
A long, long time and a long time ago—
For me, way, hey, Ohio!
Long Time Ago
I wish to God I'd never been born,
To me way, hay, hay, yah!
Lowlands
I dreamt a dream the other night.
Lowlands, lowlands, hurrah, my John!
Lowlands
I thought I heard the old man say
Lowlands, lowlands my Johnny.
Maid of Amsterdam
In Amsterdam there dwelt a maid—
Mark well what I do say!
or
And her you ought to see!
My Sal
My Sal, she's a 'Badian bright mulatto.
Wa-ay sing Sallie!
Oh, Betsy Baker
Oh, Betsy Baker!
Heigh ho!
Oh, Polly Brown
Oh, Polly Brown, I love your daughter,
Away my rolling river!
Oh, Shake Her Up
Oh, shake her up from down below,
So handy, my boys, so handy!
Ol' Joe
Ol' Joe, bully ol' Joe:
Hi, pretty yaller girl.
Oh, Blow
Oh, blow ye winds, I long to hear you,
Blow, bullies, blow.

Our Anchor We'll Weigh
Our anchor we'll weigh and our sails we will set,
Good-by, fare ye well!
Paddy Come Work on the Railway
In eighteen sixty-three
I came across a stormy sea.
Paddy Doyle
To my
Aye!
And we'll furl!
Aye!
And pay Paddy Doyle for his boots.
Outward Bound
We're outward bound from New York town,
Heave bullies, heave and pawl!
Johnny Boker
Oh, do my Johnny Boker,
Come rock and roll me over.
Poor Old Joe
Old Joe is dead and gone to hell.
We say so, and we hope so!
Ratcliffe Highway (Or any seaport street)
As I was a walking down Ratcliffe Highway,
Away, hay, blow the man down!
Reuben Ranzo
Oh, my poor Reuben Ranzo,
Ranzo, boys, Ranzo.
Rio Grande
I'll sing you a song of the fish of the sea,
Rolling Rio Grande!
Rio Grande
Where are you going, my pretty maid?
Oh, away, Rio.
Rio Grande
I'm bound away this very day!
Oh, you Rio!
Roll and Go
There was a ship, she sailed to Spain,
O roll and go.
Royal Artillery Man
My bleeding fancy man,
My Royal Artillery man,
He—wears—spurs.
Runaway Chorus
What shall we do with a drunken sailor?
Sally Brown
Seven long years I courted Sally
Way! High! Roll and go, oh!
Sally Brown
Oh, Sally Brown of New York City,
Aye! Aye! Roll and go!
Sally Brown
Oh, Sally Brown was a bright mulatto.
Sally Brown
I love my gal across the water.
Aye! Aye! Roll and go.
Santa Anna
Oh, Santa Anna's dead and gone.
Sebastopol
The Crimean War is over now;
Sebastopol is taken.
Shanadore (Shenandoah)
Shanador's a rolling river
Hurrah, you rolling river—
Shanandoah
Shanandoah, I love your daughter,
Away, ye rolling river—
Sometimes
Sometimes we're bound for England
Sometimes we're bound for France.
Heave away, my bullies, heave away.
Shallow Brown
Come get my clothes in order,
Shallow, Shallow Brown.
Shanghai Brown
O, Shanghai Brown he loves us sailors—
Blow, boys, blow.
Storm Along John
Old Stormy he is dead and gone!
To my weigh hey,
Storm along John
Susan on My Knee
'Twas on the twenty-fourth of June
I sailed away to sea.
Tommy's Gone to High Low
My Tommy's gone and I'll go too.
To my very hey hey ajola.
Whisky Johnny
Whisky is the life of man,
Whisky for Johnny!
We're All Afloat
We're all afloat in a very fine clipper,
Blow, boys, blow!

What Do You Think?
Who do you think's the skipper of her?
Blow, boys, blow!
Yankee Ship
Yankee ship come down the river,
Blow, boys, blow!

BALLADS OR FORE-BITTERS

Admiral Benbow
Oh, we sailed to Virginia and then to Fayal.
Ben Backstay
Ben Backstay was a boatman.
Ben Block
Ben Block was a veteran of naval renown.
Billy Taylor
Billy Taylor was a brisk young sailor.
Board of Trade Ahoy!
I'm only a sailor man.
Tradesman would I were,
For I've ever rued the day I became a tar.
Boston
From Boston Harbor we set sail.
Captain Glen
There was a ship, a ship of fame.
Come loose every sail to the breeze
(Title and first line)
Doo Me Ama
As Jack was walking
Through the square.
Female Smuggler
Oh, come rest a while and
You soon shall hear.
Fishers
Oh, a ship she was rigged and ready for sea.
Golden Vanity
I have a ship in the North Country.
Harry Grady and Miss Elinor Ford
In Coursand Bay lying, the
Blue Peter flying.
Henry Martin
In Scotland lived three brothers of late.
Honor of Bristol
Attend you and give ear a while.
I am a brisk and sprightly lad.
Jack the Guinea Pig
When the anchor's weighed
And the ship's unmoored.
Jack Mainmast
Jack Mainmast once got half seas over.
La Pique
'Tis of a fine frigate,
La Pique was her name.
Rolling Home
All hands to man the capstan.
Sailor's Only Delight
The *George Aloe* and the *Sweepstake* too
With hey, with ho, for and a nony no.
Sir Francis Drake
Some years of late, in '68.
Sir Walter Raleigh Sailing in the Netherlands
Sir Walter Raleigh has built a ship in the Netherlands.
Song of the Fishers
Come all ye bold fishermen, listen to me.
Spanish Ladies
Farewell and adieu to you, Spanish Ladies.
Sailor's Resolution
How little do landsmen know.
Shannon and Chesapeake
Now the Chesapeake so bold, sailed from Boston
I've been told.
Will Watch
One day when the wind
From the northward blew keenly.
The Whale
Oh, 'twas in the year of '94
And June the second day.
When I Come Back
When I come back to Bonny Shadwell Dock,
Fol de rol tal do rara folderolla
How the girls will stare at their friend Jack Block!
With his chip cherry chow.
Admiral Benbow's Death
Come all you sailors bold, lend an ear.
A Sailor
A sailor is blythe and bonny, O.
Bold Sawyer
Come all ye jolly sailors, with courage stout and bold.
Brave News from Admiral Vernon
Come, loyal Britons, all rejoice, with joyful acclamation.
Distressed Sailor's Garland
When first I drew the breath of life
'Twas in the merry month of June.
Second of November
It was one November—the second day.

Ballads listed as anonymous by Masefield
Benjamin's Lamentations
Captain Chilver's gone to sea
I Boys, O Boys.
Cap't Bover
Where have you been, my bonny honey?
Dansekar the Dutchman
Sing we seamen now and then.
Fight at Malaga
Come all you brave sailors
That sails on the Main.
Fair Maid's Choice
Being a pleasant song, made of a sailor.
Fight Between Captain Ward and Dover
Strike up, you lusty gallants.
Gallant Seaman's Resolution
A gallant youth at Gravesend lived, a seaman neither rich or poor.
Seaman's Reply
Hark! Hark! I hear the trumpet sound, it calleth me to come away.
Gallant Seaman's Return from the Indies
I am a stout seaman and newly come on shore.
Gallant Seaman's Song at Meeting His Betty
We'll meet, pretty Betty, my joy and my dear.
Greenwich Pensioner
'Twas in the good ship *Rover*
I sailed the world all round.
Honor of Bristol
Attend you and give ear awhile.
Ho for Lubberland
There is a ship, we understand,
Now riding in the river.
John Dory
It fell upon a holy day.
Lass of Lochroyan
Oh, who will shoe my bonny foot.
Lowlands of Holland
My love has built a bonny ship and set her on the sea.
Maydens of London
Come all you very merry London girls that are disposed to travel.
Mermaid
On Friday noon as we set sail.
North Country Collier
At the head of Wear Water
About twelve at noon.
Press Gang
Here's the tender coming
Pressing all the men.
Sailor Laddie
My love has been in London City.
Seaman's Compass
As lately I traveled towards Gravesend
Smuggler
O, my true lover's a smuggler, and sails upon the sea.
Teach, the Rover
Will you hear of a bloody battle?
Salcombe Seaman's Flaunt to the Proud Pirate
A lofty ship from Salcombe came,
Blow high.

Do you know any others? If so, lend a hand in this Camp-Fire work of saving these old chanteys and songs before it is too late. Send to Mr. Lomax direct, Y. M. C. A. Building, Austin, Texas.

ANOTHER definition of the spirit of adventure, though whether it is "biologically considered" I have my doubts. But then, I'm a bit shaky as to just what "biologically considered" means when it comes right down to brass tacks.

Bermuda.

In the March issue I saw a quoted opinion of Jack London on this subject, and the late famous yarn-spinner uttered a thought so widely at variance with my own ideas that I am giving you in brief my conception of the adventure spirit as it has affected and still affects myself.

Curiosity, pure and simple—that's the adventure spirit! Somewhere beyond the limit of physical vision lies the unknown, the supposedly inaccessible. Comes curiosity. Curiosity proves too strong for mental fear, though it may give a sharp jolt to mere physical courage; and out goes the adventurer, bound to satisfy his curiosity even at the cost of his life, even though the object prove after all a will-o'-the-wisp. The adventure lies not in the finding, but in the seeking, while yet the goal remains unseen and unknown. And the adventurer is a great or small adventurer in the proportion by which curiosity conquers fear.

Such is my notion of the spirit which moves so many men to perform otherwise unaccountable actions. I know it is so in my own case. Let some one tell me that there is some place I can not reach, something I can not do, and up rises All Powerful Curiosity. What is it? Where? If foot free, I want immediately to have a go.—A. E. Dingle.

A DAINTY morsel from Henry Oyen of our writers' brigade:

Just noticed in one of the recent numbers of *Adventure* that there's mention of "Liver-Eating Johnson," of the Yellowstone country. Did your correspondent tell you how he got his name? Don't think it was because he had a weakness for "liver and." Far be it from such. I have it straight from a man who hunted with him a few years before he died: Johnson played king to his neck of the country, and there was only one young Indian, a Cheyenne chief, who dared to defy him. Said chief raided and burned Johnson's camp once while Johnson was away at his traps. "The ——!" said Johnson, when he returned and saw the ruins. "I'll eat his liver!" And, tradition saith, he made good the threat.—Oyen.

AS PREVIOUSLY announced, our Camp-Fire buttons are now ready for delivery. I think there's going to be no doubt as to a big demand for them. At this writing the first announcement of their being ready has not reached you, yet requests have been coming in right along, though the askers had only the vague preliminary announcements to go on, without knowing price or date of delivery. As the buttons were delivered to us long before we could notify you in print we have been sending them out to these early seekers. There will be enough for all. Though this first order may be exhausted before long, more will be ordered before it entirely disappears and, now that the die is made, re-orders will not take so long.

The button or badge is small, neat, inconspicuous and yet individual and easily seen. Enamel with gold-washed edgings, round, three-eighths of an inch in diameter, screw-back, with a clinch pin to hold in place. Three fields, blue, brown and green, for sky, earth and sea. The numeral 71 is the only lettering or design of any kind that appears on the badge, 71 being the sum of the letters of "Camp-Fire" when assigned their numerical positions in the alphabet.

Membership in our Camp-Fire is open to any one who has the desire to be a comrade. There is no ceremony of admission. And any member may apply for a badge. They are sent out at cost price, 25 cents covering badge and return postage to any part of the world.

I'm glad the badges are assured of a strong demand. There is a good idea back of their use and the badges themselves will, I think, win favor when you see them. Personally I'll be glad when I can locate a comrade among apparent strangers and I think most of us feel the same way.

IN RESPONSE to a Camp-Fire suggestion, a number of you have written in their own experiences in getting out of the clutches of old Mr. Demon Rum. No preaching, you understand; we're not conducting any temperance crusade. Just plain facts, given on the chance they may be of practical help to other comrades who are trying to cut it out. Here is one of the letters. It is our comrade E. E. Harriman, of our writers' brigade and "Ask Adventure," to whom he refers.

Pasadena, Calif.

For several years, having the restless foot, wandered around the country and very naturally picked up booze. First came malaria, then a morning drink, which soon grew into a quart a day. The fever was not cured, so I visited Hot Springs, Ark., taking four months' water cure. It proved a success, for I have never had the fever since, but the booze appetite remained.

For several years I hit it up pretty hard, then tried to quit, and I guess I swore off several hundred times only to go back again. I never reached the "bum a drink stage," but came very close.

THREE years ago I decided it was either quit or go under, for I am a lunger and have been for twelve years, and booze was not helping me. Knowing I could not stand the pace much longer, I rolled my bed and struck out for Trinity County, Calif., landing in Hyampom, a valley, not a town.

As far as the eye could reach there was nothing but pines and mountains, valleys and streams. The sort of country that lifts a man out of himself, raises him to a higher plane and makes him clean whether he wants to or not. I spent four months in and close to Hyampom. Fishing, hunting and hiking. I forgot about booze, and to this day I have no desire for it and do not drink even beer.

Understand me, I am no anti-booze man, but I have seen some fine men go under from it and I know from experience that old John B. has a fierce kick. He always wins if you stay long enough.

WHILE on the subject let me tell you something about the trip.

Two of us left here on Sept. 16, 1916, by auto and, on arriving in Red Bluff, hired a truck and driver to take us and our outfit to Hayfork, about one hundred and fifty miles. From Hayfork to Hyampom on foot without outfit on mule back, about thirty miles. We walked about twenty miles, I guess, for we rode to the end of the highway about eight miles.

When we reached Hyampom my booze-soaked muscles were screaming with pain. We spent the night at a Mr. Butler's, and early the next morning started for the summit of Hayfork Mountain where we intended camping a few days to enjoy some real good hunting.

Don't think I will say much about that trip, for I always want to go back to bed and rest whenever it comes into my mind. We made it all right and after a short rest took a look at the country.

I'LL never forget the first sunset, and you know this country is noted for its beautiful sunsets, of which I have seen many but nothing to equal that one. Can you imagine hundreds of miles of country standing on end, thickly covered with pine trees and every known color and shade and many unknown covering the whole thing? Can you imagine the west a blaze of color and the east tinted yellow with a great big moon? Well, that is what I saw, only it don't come anywhere near telling you of the wonderful beauty.

I tell you, a man couldn't be anything but clean in this country.

NEVER saw so many deer in my life, or such streams of fish. Rainbow, steel-head and salmon trout. Quail and grouse are positively thick. Believe me, it's a man's country. I am crazy to go back, but can't get enough money together. I work two or three months, then have to rest the same length of time. Some day I hope to collect the correct amount and, *believe* me, I will hike for Trinity, locate a homestead and *Live*.

If you care to use this, hop to it, only please don't use my name.

BY THE way, to come back to the booze question. Tell any chap who wants to quit to go see Mr. Harriman. Just to look at him will make anything on two legs straighten his shoulders and take a brace. He sure is a man's man, and then some. He is *all* man.

If any one ever asks anything about Trinity County let me know. I sure will boost.

Excuse me for taking up so much of your time, but thoughts of Trinity send me back to the trails I dearly love.——— ——— ———.

THE Federal Board for Vocational Education, 200 New Jersey Avenue, Northwest, Washington, D. C., sent us a statement of the many practical helps and services they offer in reeducating disabled soldiers and sailors but there is not space to print them all, concisely stated though they are. Artificial limbs free, free medical treatment after discharge (for disability incurred in service), free vocational training with War-Risk insurance provision covering period of training and period of further disability, help toward suitable positions following training, etc. Fourteen district offices through the country.

If you were disabled in service make sure that you know definitely and in full all the many things the Board will do to help you. Personally I was amazed at the extent of the service offered. But all that service was fully and honestly earned by those in need of it and it would be only childish and wrong to refuse the service because of any mistaken pride. You might just as well refuse the "charity" of a decoration for valor.

THE adventures of our identification-cards in the Great War—if collected what a book they would make! Here is a sample, from a letter written before hostilities ceased:

Warrington, England.

It may interest you to receive a friendly word from one who has carried one of *Adventure's* serial identification-cards in his pocket for many years. The card remains with me yet, but as it is in the safe of this hospital along with other papers of value, Masonic certificates, etc., I can not give you its number.

Nevertheless it has traveled via Canada from Boston, U. S. A., over to the camps of Blighty and the wastes of France, where its bearer has during the past two years alternated between laying rails for France, under General "Jack" Stewart, and dodging "Jerry's" shrapnel, bombs, "flying pigs," and many of the other pleasant surprises "Jerry" entertains our boys with.

Your card was present at the Battle of Vimy, April 1917, at the Cambrai push of November, 1917, in the big retreat of March, 1918, and between times was all over the place in the terrain bounded by Arras, Cambrai, Peronne, Amiens, Paris, Abbéville and the Channel coast. Quite a big territory to cover, embracing nearly all of the ancient domains of Picardy and Artois. "Somme" battlefield it was! Never have Dumas romances seemed so real as when I *saw* Bethune, Le Fère, Beauvais, etc., etc. *ad. lib.*—No. 749285 Sapper ROGER F. GARDENER, 12th Canadian Railway Troops.

SOMETHING for us to be considering. Wouldn't it be a fine thing if we could gradually establish Camp-Fire "stations" or local headquarters all over the map? A place where we could register ourselves or leave word for a comrade who would or might follow later, or run a good chance of meeting other wandering or resident comrades?

Nothing pretentious. Just a "station," which might be in a tobacco-shop or any old place that was reputable. Bar-rooms and such barred. (Oh, yes, I know the objections to barring them, but this matter has to be considered from the general aspect and there are sound reasons for not making bar-rooms our permanent and "official" homes.)

How about it? Yes or no? If yes, what suggestions?

—ARTHUR SULLIVANT HOFFMAN.

SOME close-up data on the James boys from one of us who is in a position to know the facts:

When I read what E. A. Brininstool had written about the James boys I was moved to put my oar in. I was living up there in that part of our country when they tried to rob the Northfield bank. It was Jesse James who shot the cashier. He had gone in the vault and Bob Younger was holding the cashier up with two guns. The cashier, Heyward, saw Jesse pass in, leaped from his stool, slammed the vault door and tried with all his power to turn the combination. Bob jerked him back and opened the door. Jesse came out mad, put his gun against Heyward's head and killed him. Plain, dirty murder.

I KNEW Bill Chadwell very well. Have ridden with him many times when he carried the mail along our highway. Good-natured, obscene roughneck without very many brains. Frank James got hurt twice in that fight. The village blacksmith had a Sharps rifle and he climbed to the roof of his shop, stood behind the square front and killed Bill. Then he plugged Frank in the leg and the same ball killed his horse. Before that the Methodist preacher had come out with a muzzle loading shotgun and filled Frank with chicken-shot, but he had a heavy rubber coat on and it kept the shot from going deeper than just through the skin.

When Frank lost his horse he got behind some boxes and shot from there. As the bunch broke for safety he hobbled out and yelled, "For God's sake, boys, you aren't leaving me, are you?" Then Jesse wheeled and took him up behind.

A funny thing is that a clerk in a store turned that band back three times with an empty .32 caliber gun, by jumping out and throwing down on them as they came galloping by. I knew one of the men in the posse with the sheriff when they found the Younger brothers and Pitts and Miller in the woods. He always insisted that the best man in the posse in point of cool work and fine shooting was a boy of seventeen.

BILL CHADWELL was the only one killed in Northfield. Miller got his in the woods, when Bob and Jim and Cole got punched full of holes. Jim had half his face shot off there. Bill was shot by the Sharps and the ball ranged downward from just below the collar-bone across to the opposite hip. It muxed him up badly inside. Not much left whole in there after it passed.

Bob Ford organized the Merchants Patrol in Los Angeles and ran it for a long time. I might tell you of one of us who served under him, but I won't.

ONE thing I learned when the gang came to Northfield. That was, that I knew plenty of men who could handle a six-gun better than those chaps handled theirs in that fight. This talk about their being crack shots that could snuff a candle or clip a tossed dollar as it flew is all bosh. I shot with one such bandit once and he had nothing on me and acknowledged it. He had such a "rep" that he was hired by Buffalo Bill for three years, as an exhibition rifle expert. Yah! I skinned him twice in contests and had done no practising for two years when we met. Camouflage! Bombast! This great skill attributed to bandits. They simply don't let the other chap have a chance, that's all.

When the gang came to Northfield, they all went into a store kept by old Berkey, a German. He sold them shoes and they took him over to the saloon for some beer. I asked him what he did next day, when the shooting began. He told me.

"Mein Gott! I run me down cellar und lay me mit mein belly in der dirt. I bet you I been lower as dat if dot dirt vas not too hardt to dig mit mein fingers, alretty. Gott, yes! You pet me!"—E. E. HARRIMAN.

HERE are some bits taken from a letter from S. B. H. Hurst concerning his story in this issue. I have, contrary to our custom, not cut out a paragraph speaking a good word for the magazine. Some of you know it already—hundreds of you have reported the same thing, and others may be interested. For, after all, it *is* "our magazine." To a very remarkable degree the men on your side of the editorial desk and the men on our side of it have forgotten that the desk is there and have just sort of gone along together. Not only have we here in the office tried to make the magazine of real service to you besides furnishing amusement, but the rest of you—or the rest of us—have in hundreds of ways and on thousands of occasions helped to make it more useful, more accurate and more entertaining. "Our magazine" is not just an empty editorial phrase and so, once in a while, I feel warranted in passing on to you a bit of good news about our magazine, or some of the friendly words spoken about it, knowing that it will please many of you just as it does us in the office.

Incidentally, don't ever think, just because when we print a letter from one of you and omit from it something you've said in favor of the magazine, that your words didn't make us feel good inside or that we didn't appreciate your taking the trouble to say them.

Seattle, Wash.

YOU ask "Couldn't he chew some opium?" It is rather curious, but no user of opium ever changes his method of taking it. The user of a hypodermic feels sick at the idea of eating morphine, and a smoker must have his pipe. Besides—and this is the real reason—there is always the delightful anticipation of the smoke deferred. You will find that no user of opium will find fault with my story from that standpoint. (I do *not* speak of cocain, mind you.)

THERE is always a source—must be—of all disease, but of course the idea here is only one of those queer notions which some men get, and *M*. takes advantage of it. It may seem strange that so intelligent a man has the idea of a source of T. B., but the best chess player I ever knew startled me with advocating it, with many other queer notions. For instance, he believed he could absorb chlorophill, when any book on organic chemistry would have told him that no animal can absorb it, except some low form of flagellata. I had this man in mind when creating the *composite* character of the *Burra Sahib*. I don't think it hurts the tale.

PHRENOLOGY has been shown to be absurd, but many people still swear by it, and numbers of pseudo scientific men make a living by reading bumps, as you know. Indeed, I have been fool enough to have my own read, when all the time I knew that the morphology of the brain did not indicate as the "professor" said it did.

However, all through I have written from the subjective standpoint of a user of opium—the story is almost a psychological tract on the lapses of an intelligent man under opium—which makes, as you observe, the *Burra Sahib* do and say things which seem childish.—S. B. H. HURST.

P. S.—I collect old books, and it may interest you to know that the second-hand book men here tell me that they hardly ever have a second-hand copy of *Adventure*. As fast as they come in, they are re-bought, while *all* other magazines pile up by the thousand.

HERE'S hoping that this comrade got away for at least a little while on the outward trail. And that he came back satisfied and content again with the cabin and the cats and the garlic:

Oceano, Calif.

Gentlemen of the Camp-Fire: Again I greet you! and this time in gratitude. I who am old have been cheered by your letters and remembrances of the times that were, and before many moons have shone down on the lonesome trail I expect to count coups with at least one Pale-faced warrior, who was and is of my own kind. Huston writes. He is coming! Headed again for the north. Who knows but I will put the pack-saddle on my ancient mule and drift again with him to the northwest, just to camp again on the trails of our youth? Plenty Coups, of the Absaraka; Cut Mouth John of the Klickitat, Spotted Elk of the Sioux (totem of the Bear) or even Washakie of the Shoshones would turn over in their graves and double the horse herders, if they knew that Huston and I were making our medicine again.

OLD? Yes, but our hearts are yet hot. I've got a cabin and some cats and a garden, that grows garlic and dahlias. But, after all, a cabin is only a cabin, and the long trail has no end. We are Pagans "and the Red Gods give us no rest." I know a place in the lava beds of Modoc, where the skeleton of a warrior is hiden in the rocks yet (if some fool sheep-herder has not found him). He is branded between the eyes with a .45 caliber hole. I know a place on the bank of the Rogue River in Oregon where a poor little tenderfoot kid staked out his first placer claim in 1874. And I am grieving tonight to hit the trail in the morning.

If some of you fellows would wrap Huston and his kind up in a blanket and hog-tie 'em, so they couldn't make signs, maybe I might be contented to raise cats and garlic. I've got an ancient mule of the Spanish breed. Some say she is a jennet. But if she is, Pegasus must have been her sire, so if our comrade of the long trail comes, we may sing. HIACK CLATTAWA, COPHA SIAH; CAR SALMON MAMOOK PLAY. NISIKA ISCUM TENAS CUETINS PE, OKOKSUN CLATTAWA SIAH. (Chinook).

Translated:

Harry go far away
Where the salmon play
And we'll have few ponies
When the daylight fades away.

Long live the Camp-Fire.—E. C. ST. CLAIRE.

SLEEP—a word about it from Charles Wesley Sanders in connection with his story in this issue:

Madison, Ohio

SLEEP, which brought trouble to *Haggerty*, has been responsible for many tragic and for some ludicrous things on railroads. In the days before the law limited the hours of work for railroad men, crews would very often be "first out" when they came into a terminal. That is to say, they would have to turn about and make another trip over the road without rest. Nowadays, when an engineer has worked a certain number of hours, he is relieved, no matter where his train happens to be.

When sleep comes to man when he is on railroad duty, it is an overwhelming thing. He feels more as if he had been drugged than as if he were just naturally sleepy. In those circumstances sleep seems to be more powerful than in ordinary circumstances. Perhaps that is because a man knows he must not sleep and therefore wants what he should not have.

I HAVE had some curious experiences with this sleepiness. When I worked in a general office once, I customarily cleared with the Buffalo yards about midnight. The operator at Buffalo, instead of sounding the office call, would say: "G. M. DS." That is, "Good morning, Sanders." I was only a kid and one Fourth of July I didn't go to bed at all. When I got to the office at seven o'clock my lids were heavy. I cleaned up what work there was and went over by the window and sat down in a big chair. Sleep immediately hit me on the point of the jaw.

The next thing I remember I heard Buffalo say, "G.M. DS." That was the only conscious moment I had, so far as I could recall afterward. The next conscious moment came at five o'clock in the morning. Buffalo was "calling his arm off." I answered.

In those days all messages and reports for the general superintendent were copied in a book. Such a report was usually the first thing Buffalo sent. The book lay on the table and written across the page was the word "Buffalo" and the date. Following this a line wabbled down the page for several inches.

"Didn't you get it?" Buffalo asked.

"I didn't," I had to confess.

"Gee!" he said, "I sent you the whole business but I didn't get any O.K. Well, here goes."

I must have risen from the chair by the window, walked over to the table, answered Buffalo, started to write in the book, risen again, and gone back to the chair, while Buffalo, unsuspecting, kept pounding out the report to me.

And I must have done it in my sleep.—C. W. Sanders.

REMEDIES for snake-bite. Frank W. Ryan, seeing the question brought up at Camp-Fire, wrote in giving, from memory, the methods used by Raymond L. Ditmars, Curator of Reptiles, N. Y. Zoological Park, New York City. In order to be sure in so important a matter, I sent Mr. Ryan's letter to Mr. Ditmars and received the following reply:

> Referring to the enclosed would say that it is essentially correct. I am enclosing a booklet that gives some additional information. Abercrombie and Fitch of this city handle a snake-bite outfit.
>
> Antivenomous serum is now used when possible. You will find mention of it in the booklet. It may be obtained from the Pasteur Laboratories of America, 366-8 W. 11th St., New York.
>
> Raymond L. Ditmars.

Our thanks to both Mr. Ryan and Mr. Ditmars and, since the subject is a vital one to any man wandering in snake country, here are some quotations from "Poisonous Snakes of the United States; How to Distinguish Them," by Raymond L. Ditmars—what he calls a bird's-eye view.

Please note that our old Camp-Fire pet and argument, the Gila Monster, is here authoritatively branded venomous. We'll hear more about him later.

THE following is a condensed quotation from the booklet, exact and fairly full, with only minor changes for the sake of connection and with no changes affecting the meaning. The booklet itself can be secured by writing to Mr. Ditmars and enclosing twelve cents.

ONE hundred and eleven species of snakes are found in this country; *of this number seventeen are poisonous.* Besides, there are ninety-seven species of lizards; but of the latter only a single species is venomous and this is the Gila Monster, of the Southwest.

Practically every portion of the United States is inhabited by poisonous snakes. The majority of the species are found in the Southern latitudes, though the few Northern species are so abundant that venomous snakes are actually more common in some sections of Pennsylvania and New York than in the South.

LIST OF NORTH AMERICAN POISONOUS SERPENTS

Elapine Snakes

Common Coral Snake (Elaps fulvius) the Southeast. Sonoran Coral Snake (Elaps eurysanthus), the Southwest.

Crotaline Snakes

1. *The Moccasins*

Copperhead Snake (Ancistrodon contortrix), Eastern U. S. Water Moccasin (Ancistrodon piscivorus), the Southeast.

2. *Dwarf Rattlesnakes*

Massasauga (Sistrurus catenatus) Central Region. Pigmy Rattlesnake (Sistrurus miliarius), the Southeast.

3. *Typical Rattlesnakes*

Timber Rattlesnake (Crotalus horridus), Eastern U. S. Diamond-Back Rattlesnake (Crotalus adamanteus), the Southeast. Prairie Rattlesnake (Crotalus confluentus), Prairie Region. Pacific Rattlesnake (Crotalus oregonus), Pacific Region. Texas Rattlesnake (Crotalus atros), Texas to California. White Rattlesnake (Crotalus mitchellii), the Southwest. Tiger Rattlesnake (Crotalus tigris), the Southwest. Black-tailed Rattlesnake (Crotalus molossus), the Southwest. Price's Rattlesnake (Crotalus pricei), the Southwest. Green Rattlesnake (Crotalus lepidus), the Southwest. Horned Rattlesnake (Crotalus cerastes), the Southwest.

Classification of our Poisonous Snakes

THE North American dangerous snakes may be easily distinguished—except the two Coral snakes, which have a slender body and a head not at all distinct from the neck, in fact, looking precisely like the harmless reptiles. From the typical harmless snakes they differ only in possession of a very short, fixed pair of venom-conducting teeth in the forward part of the upper jaw—and by the absence of a small scale on each side of the head (the *loreal* plate), between the eyes and the nostril. Fortunately, such deceptive-looking reptiles are limited to two species in the United States. As they are peculiarly colored, they may be recognized with little difficulty.

How To Tell the Coral Snakes

BOTH of the species of the *Elaps* inhabit the Southern part of the country. The Common Coral Snake or Harlequin Snake occurs from southern North Carolina to Florida and westward to Texas. It is most abundant in Georgia, Florida, Alabama, and Louisiana. The Sonoran Coral Snake is restricted to Arizona, New Mexico, and northern Mexico. Both of the species are vividly *ringed* with scarlet, yellow, and black—the red and black rings the broadest. Their pattern is wonderfully beautiful, imparting a really artificial aspect, like a gaudy necklace.

The pattern may be given as *broad, alternating rings of red and black, the latter bordered with very narrow rings of yellow.* And here we encounter a difficulty; for several harmless snakes "mimic" these species in displaying exactly the same colors arranged in ring-like fashion. Yet there is one unvarying difference that will always distinguish the dangerous reptile from their innocuous "imitators," *as the yellow rings of the poisonous snakes always border the black rings, while among the non-venomous snakes there are pairs of black rings bordering a yellow one.*

The Coral Snakes are rather secretive in habits and are often plowed up in the fields. They feed mostly upon small species of innocuous serpents.

The Poison Apparatus

THE Crotaline Snakes, the Rattlesnakes, Copperhead, and the Moccasin may be easily told. These snakes do not *sting*. The injury they inflict is a *bite, dealt with a pair of hollow teeth on the upper jaw.* These teeth have an opening at their tip for the ejection of venom. They are exactly like hypodermic needles, and mankind has, in fact, copied the structure of the serpent's fangs in manufacturing that invaluable instrument of medical surgery.

Each fang connects with a gland behind the eye, and this secretes a poison which Nature has intended to be used in purposes of killing the prey—incidentally for self-defense. When the mouth is closed the fangs fold back against the upper jaw.

The venom apparatus is in no way connected with the forked tongue. That organ is used solely for the purpose of feeling; hence it is not a sting.

How to Distinguish the Crotaline Snakes

WE MAY dispose of the Rattlesnakes with a simple suggestion, and that is to *look for the rattle,* a prominent and absolutely unique organ among snakes. Its presence immediately brands the owner.

It is a mistake to think that a poisonous snake may be told by a thick body and a flat, triangular head that is quite distinct from the neck. Many wholly innocuous species have exactly these outlines and many of them are proportionately stouter of body and uglier in appearance than the dangerous Copperhead Snake or Highland Moccasin.

The Moccasin and the Copperhead Snake

THE two North American Moccasins—the Water Moccasin, *Ancistrodon piscivorus* and the Copperhead Snake (Highland Moccasin or Pilot Snake), *Ancistrodon contortrix,* belong, as do the Rattlesnakes, to the subfamily of Pit Vipers—Crotalineo. On each side of the head, *between the eye and the nostril is a deep pit.* Here we have a character by which to determine them immediately. But there are other points: while our harmless snakes have two rows of plates on the under surface of the tail, these two poisonous species have a single row of plates for the greater length of the tail. Our harmless snakes have the pupil of the eye round; the Water Moccasin and the Copperhead Snake have an elliptical—catlike—pupil.

The Moccasin is dull olive, with wide, black transverse bands. It abounds in the swamps and sluggish waterways of South Carolina, Georgia, Florida, Alabama, and Louisiana. The Copperhead Snake is pale, hazel brown; crossing this ground color are rich, reddish-brown bands narrow on the back and very wide on the sides—appearing, when examined from above, to have the outlines of an hour-glass. The top of the head often shows a decidedly coppery tinge, hence the popular name.

Poisonous Snakes in the Eastern States

IN THE New England States and the Middle Atlantic States, there are but two species of poisonous snakes. These are the Timber Rattlesnake and the Copperhead Snake. The Black Snake, Water Snake, Flat-Headed "Adder," Checkered "Adder," and other serpents with formidable titles found in those areas are absolutely harmless.

If we include the Lake Region and the Ohio Valley we must include another poisonous species, the Massasauga, a small rattlesnake of a slaty-gray hue marked with a chain of deep brown blotches.

South of central North Carolina, thence throughout the Gulf States, we find several more venomous species, as follows:

The *Diamond Rattlesnake.* Largest and most deadly of any of the North American serpents. It attains a length of eight feet and is beautifully marked with a chain of yellowish rhombs on an olive ground-color.

The *Pigmy Rattlesnake.* A diminutive, slaty-gray species, closely related to the Massasauga. There are jet-black blotches on the back and a reddish band on the neck.

The *Water Moccasin.* A semi-aquatic species.

The *Coral Snake.* Previously described.

The Timber Rattlesnake and the Copperhead Snake range southward to the northern portion of the Florida peninsula. In the extreme South the Copperhead also extends its range westward to the Rio Grande, in Texas.

Erroneous Theories Concerning Poisonous Snakes

IT IS quite wrong to imagine a poisonous snake springs at an enemy. It never jumps from the ground and seldom strikes more than a third its length. Poisonous snakes never chase an enemy. Their attitude toward man is merely that of self-defense.

It is not necessary for a rattlesnake to coil before striking. It can strike from a crawling position provided the neck can be doubled into an S-shaped loop to lurch the head forward.

It is impossible to render a venomous snake permanently harmless by extracting the fangs, as a number of auxiliary fangs are ready to take the place of the functional pair within a couple of weeks.

Treatment of Snake Bite

WHAT *to Carry in the Field.* Every field naturalist and prospector venturing into regions known to be the lurking places of venomous snakes should carry certain articles to be used in case of accident. These are comparatively simple. Following is a list of them:

A hypodermic syringe; a rubber ligature; several sharp scalpels (or a razor); a jar of antiseptic gauze; material for outside bandage (boiled cheesecloth); a jar of permanganate of potassium (crystals); several tubes of anti-toxin (anti-venomous serum); some strychnine tablets; a flask of whisky.

The entire outfit can be carried in the capacious pockets of an ordinary khaki shooting-jacket, if necessary. The writer speaks from experience.

What to Do if Bitten. Invariably, the injury is upon some part of the arm or leg. *Everything depends upon the promptitude in performing the first two precautions.*

1st. Apply the ligature a short distance above the bite. Thus the ligature should be carried in a pocket that is immediately available, without a second's loss in a fumble.

2nd. Enlarge the punctures by cutting into them, *at least as deep as they are.* Make two cuts over each, these cuts crossing one another. This cutting starts a flow of the poisoned blood, which should be accelerated in every way possible. It is not dangerous to suck the blood away providing there are no cuts or fresh abrasions in the mouth or on the lips. In this way much venom may be drawn from the wounds. If a stream is near by, wash the wounds thoroughly, then bathe them repeatedly in a solution composed of permanganate of potash crystals in water to produce a deep wine color.

If no doctor is near by, the antitoxin should be injected by means of the hypodermic syringe, in some part of the body where it will gain the general circulation—preferably under the skin of the abdomen. In a succeeding paragraph it will be explained where this product may be obtained.

IF CONSTITUTIONAL symptoms develop—weakness and giddiness, a hypodermic injection of strychnine must be administered. As a stimulant, taken in very moderate quantities, brandy is invaluable.

After the wounds have been thoroughly bled and washed with the permanganate, the ligature may be removed, but not until every measure has been employed to draw the venom from the bitten part; these measures including suction and massage.

At this stage there is but one thing to do if that is possible. Journey to the nearest doctor of repute; for grave symptoms, beyond the power of any but a medical man to combat, may possibly develop.

IF A doctor is out of the question, keep your head. You will need to think, and with great care. Take a cathartic. Keep the wounds absolutely clean and remember that tissue that has been weakened by snake poison is peculiarly susceptible to common blood poisoning. Pack small bits of gauze into the wounds to keep them open and draining, then dress over them with gauze saturated with any good antiseptic solution. Keep the dressing saturated and the wounds open for at least a week, no matter how favorable may be the symptoms.

The writer has talked with many men of good, practical reasoning powers, who have been bitten by snakes and entirely recovered, while miles from civilization. They have employed methods similar to those described.

Before leaving the town behind you, consult a good doctor. Learn how to use properly a hypodermic syringe and the amount of strychnine your system will endure.

THE antitoxin, technically known as Anti-Venine, is a foreign product and apparently the best of the so-called antidotes for snake bite, as it is manufactured and does its work along lines well understood and practical. It may be obtained from the agencies of the Pasteur Institute, one of which is situated in New York City.

Once again let the writer advise the sufferer:

Keep your head. Do not give way to despondency. There is every reason why a healthy man should recover, and quickly too, from a bite from any of the greater number of the venomous snakes in the United States. But the proper means to save life should be executed promptly and systematically.

THE THREE AMERICAN LEGIONS

I HAVE just very gladly given my written consent, as a director of the American Legion, Inc., to the use of that name by the national organization of American veterans of the recent war, the "new G. A. R."

Our older readers know that the original American Legion was started by this magazine in the Summer of 1914, received the endorsement of Theodore Roosevelt and Major-General Leonard Wood, was incorporated early in 1915 and, despite entire lack of encouragement and even against direct discouragement from the Wilson administration, went ahead with its work, reached a membership of some twenty-five thousand men trained in war or in some of the trades and professions needed in modern warfare. Military authorities characterized it as the most practical step that had been taken for Preparedness. Every effort was made to prevail upon the Government to take over the organization and develop it into one of our strongest resources for national defense, but there is no need to dwell upon the pacifist attitude of the Administration at that time. It not only refused to take over the Legion's work but peremptorily ordered the Army and Navy officers who were among the Legion's active workers at its headquarters to cease giving it any assistance.

LATER the Legion made many efforts to persuade the National Council for Defense to take over and use its invaluable classified records, with only brief and uninterested refusals as a result. Finally, however, they consented to allow us to deposit our records with them. The Legion, after a fight of several years, realized the Wilson Administration could not be shaken in its determination not to adopt this and other definite Preparedness measures, and, not wishing to go on taking dues from its members in those circumstances, ceased active operations.

Then the war really came, despite those who said there could be no more war for this country. What the Administration could have done through the Legion, carefully and economically through several years, had to be done the other way in a few months.

Then, when it was too late for the nation-wide results that could so easily have been attained, the Administration did use the Legion, the Legion it had held down to twenty-five thousand instead of the two hundred and fifty thousand it might have had in its need. They didn't even let the Legion know it was being of service. Purely by accident we learned that the Ordnance Bureau had had a large force of clerks working from Legion records for months and that other Bureaus were waiting their turn. It wouldn't have been good politics for the Administration to admit its mistake in having refused to make any preparation for the war, to confess that it was being forced to use, after war was upon us, the very machinery it had refused to use when there was time for adequate Preparedness. And, anyhow, it was too busy telling the people what marvelous things it was now accomplishing, things that could have been done far more inexpensively and effectively if they had been done at the right time. But—well, if a private individual gives you a deal like that you mentally take his number and pass him up.

LATER the Legion's duplicate records were offered to those who were desperately seeking skilled labor for ship-building—records giving the names and addresses of men trained to the various special work needed and pledged to respond to a call for their services. There was not even a reply to the letter.

Later the duplicates were offered to the Marine Corps. No blindness or sleepiness there. Very promptly some husky marines appeared with a truck and rumbled off with those store-boxes filled with records.

The main point is that our Legion, against all discouragements and heavy odds, was too soundly practical not to be of decided value when the crisis came and we have reason to be very proud of the organization we of the Camp-Fire originated and built up among ourselves for half a year before it was taken up by all the newspapers of the country and put on a national basis.

THERE was the second American Legion—the Americans who went to France with the Canadians because they couldn't wait any longer for our own country to realize that she should and must fight the Hun. A fine body of men, but not in any way to be confused with our American Legion, the original.

And now the third American Legion is with us, the greatest of them all, and very, very welcome to our name, for there are many of you who belong to both the first and third, and some who belong to all three, and I know that none of you will be any less willing to pass on the name than I am—who, as it happens, first thought of it for our first organization.

The new American Legion is likely to become a tremendous force in national affairs and we of the Camp-Fire have some very special reasons for interest and pride in it.

Good luck to it, and may it become a force for clean democracy.

A WORD from Robert J. Pearsall concerning his story in this issue of our magazine, taken from his letter to me when he first sent in MS.:

Berkeley, Calif.

Herewith "Undue Influence," a rather short tale, but one I think you'll like. You'll observe *John Partridge* appears again, the principal character in "Rogues' End," and the subject of my last letter to you. In my next tale he will be on the China Coast; but I've another man picked for principal character.

Perhaps I'd better say that I got the central idea of "Undue Influence," the use of oxygen as a befuddling agent, from an editorial in the *Scientific American* of April 6, 1912. Indeed, I've made *Partridge* quote that editorial in one paragraph which you'll notice. But I think the unduly stimulating effect of oxygen is commonly known. I remember the propriety of its use by athletes was much discussed a few years ago; but it was commonly condemned as unsportsmanlike and injurious, and barred out along with other drugs.—ROBERT J. PEARSALL.

QUITE a few of you have called our attention to the fact that "The Human Bloodhound," by Captain R. S. Carpenter, which appeared in our Mid-June issue, had previously been published by another magazine under another title with another name as author. A plain break on our part, of course, and naturally we are very sorry it happened.

The only pleasant thing about it is that our readers, with their usual personal friendliness to "our magazine," were prompt to give us the facts and nearly all did so in complete understanding of how such things occur.

One or two, however, accused us flatly of trying to "put something over" on our readers, seeming to have the idea that we had deliberately taken a story from another magazine in order to save buying one. To any one with even a faint understanding of the magazine business, such an idea is ridiculous. There could be no surer way for a magazine to commit suicide than by intentionally following such a policy. Furthermore, our books show that we paid Captain R. S. Carpenter—or at least made out our check to that name—for the story just as we pay for all our other stories. In this issue we have, for the second time in the magazine's existence, republished something from our own pages, with that fact plainly stated and because there was demand from our readers for republication. Once or twice we've quoted from other publications in "Camp-Fire," but always with credit. But never have we knowingly "lifted" anything from any other publication.

I CONFESS these fiery accusers make me sick at the stomach. If they are too crabbed to assign anything but crooked motives to others they might at least use their brains as well as their mouths. "Evidently," says one of these superior beings, "you don't read the other magazines." Of course I don't. Some of them, of course, but how would it be possible for any man to hold down a very full-time job and read *all* the stories in *all* the other magazines, even if he slept only five hours a night, ate no meals and never dreamed of taking any recreation or a bath? Could *you* do it? Could our ready critic do it? Four to five thousand manuscripts a year come into this office. That makes quite a little reading itself even for more than one man. I've been reading our own manuscripts at home till midnight these past several nights. A fine chance I have of reading all the other magazines.

I don't think you've ever found me hesitate to admit my mistakes frankly, but I'm just as quick to fight when anybody tries to hang on me something that is entirely unjust.

All magazines are occasionally victimized by plagiarists. The plagiarists don't last long and very often they get caught at their first attempt, but when they do get away with it there's nothing to do, for either readers or editor, but cuss, blacklist that writer with other magazines, put him behind bars if you can and keep on guarding against them in the future.

I know I don't need to explain all this to most of you, but if there are any more narrow-gage, non-thinking dyspeptics among you I want them to get the facts.

WHY not? I'm not eligible but I'd like to see that club formed. Here is a piece of a letter from Edgar Young the rest of which dealt mainly with details concerning his story in this issue:

Brooklyn.

He has asked me to request you to have a little call put in Camp-Fire for all the trail hitters to register. He is especially anxious to hear from any of the old bunch of "Typical Tropical Tramps," or "TTT'S" that were organized by Ed Burke, at Zacapa, Guatemala, many years ago, and anybody else who has hiked trails in Central and South America. He has made the transcontinental trip from Ecuador to the Amazon, down the Napo, from both Quito and Riobamba, and has walked many trails in Central America.

HE CALLS attention to the fact that Joseph Abner (*Cabrón*) Brown died friendless, without a penny, in a New Orleans hospital. Brown had staked hundreds and wrote a letter to a friend at Huigra, Ecuador, asking for help. This letter was recognized as being from him and opened by the Americans at Huigra, for the party he had written to had gone. They cabled him money which did not reach him before he died. Brown is the only man who is supposed to have gone down through the San Blas Indian country endwise and made the trip alive. He went in from the Canal Zone and came out at Esmeraldas, according to Tropical Tramp tradition. I think we can scare up at least five hundred trail hitters. Their addresses are changing constantly. "Lanky" Moore walked from Lake Titicaca to Sao Paulo, Brazil. Two partners, Hart and James, went in from Manaos, in 1910, to cross from there.

A few words from some of these men might prove interesting dope for Camp-Fire but it is a hard matter to get them to open up with a letter. I know of

several who are here in New York. It might be there is enough of them to start a club of some kind.
EDGAR YOUNG.

I DON'T want to start anything but I want to say something and say it loud. Nothing new. Many of you are thinking the same thing. The Regulars. There's so little printed about them. The papers are filled with columns about the local volunteers and draft men, the noble work they did, their glorious welcomes home. But the Regulars don't even get home as a rule. Most of them are dead or, at this writing in late May, still on duty at the front. They probably won't get any particular welcome when they do get home. They're just Regulars anyhow.

Just the Regulars. Just the backbone of our Army in war and peace. Just the only thoroughly trained soldiers we have. For, even out of the finest material in the world and by the most intensive methods, you can't make a thoroughly trained soldier in six months or a year. Say all you please in praise of our boys who were not Regulars and I'll subscribe to it. But I make this point—they'd have been even better and even more effective if they'd had more training. Among other things it takes years, not months, to instil thorough, absolutely dependable discipline, no matter how good and willing the material. And the lack of such discipline is inevitably measured in the casualty lists if not in the matter of victory versus defeat.

JUST the Regulars. Dig out their war record and see how it stands comparison. Take a look at the recognition they got and see how it does *not* stand comparison.

Oh, yes, they're just the Regulars, but I wish I had a whole hat-store of hats to take off to them. Regulars of Army, Navy and Marine Corps. The Marines, being efficient from cellar to attic, see to it that the public gives them the credit they deserve. The Navy, through no fault of its own, did not see action on so large a scale as did the Army and does not get the recognition it should. But the Army Regulars, the boys who went into the worst there was, did the job as well as any troops that ever lived could do it, and get less recognition than any other kind of fighting-man we've got. They get mine, all of it, and, take our Camp-Fire by and large, I don't think the Regulars will find another bunch who more appreciate what they've done and what they are.

Salute!

ADVENTURE'S new companion magazine, *Romance*, expects to make its appearance this Fall. It wants stories of action, but, being addressed to both men and women, the love-interest will play a more prominent part than it has ever been allowed to do in *Adventure*, but not the kind of love-story that is merely fluff and sugar. Nor will there be any salacious sex appeal.

Like *Adventure*, its field is the whole wide world and its preference is for outdoor stories. *Adventure* seldom uses stories of the future; *Romance* is open to them, as well as to stories of the present and the past.

We're trying to make it a real magazine for real people, and I think I'm safe in saying it's worth a trial by all of you. Its first serial by Joseph Conrad, master of sea-stories, will be looked forward to by all of you who know his work.

CAMP-FIRE buttons now ready. Details given on the following page. From those who have already got theirs come many words of strong commendation and not a single criticism. So I think you're not likely to be dissappointed in the button when you get it.

Though its size is plainly stated, a few voiced pleased surprise over finding it small, neat and tasteful, instead of being big and conspicuous. You can lay three or four of them on a dime. And yet its quiet, simple design is so unique that it stands out sufficiently to serve its practical purpose.

—ARTHUR SULLIVANT HOFFMAN.

Our Camp-Fire came into being May 5, 1912, with our June issue, and since then its fire has never died down. Many have gathered about it and they are of all classes and degrees, high and low, rich and poor, adventurers and stay-at-homes, and from all parts of the earth. Some whose voices we used to know have taken the Long Trail and are heard no more, but they are still memories among us, and new voices are heard, and welcomed.

We are drawn together by a common liking for the strong, clean things of out-of-doors, for word from the earth's far places, for man in action instead of caged by circumstance. The *spirit* of adventure lives in all men; the rest is chance.

But something besides a common interest holds us together. Somehow a real comradeship has grown up among us. Men can not thus meet and talk together without growing into friendlier relations; many a time does one of us come to the rest for facts and guidance: many a close personal friendship has our Camp-Fire built up between two men who had never met; often has it proved an open sesame between strangers in a far land.

Perhaps our Camp-Fire is even a little more. Perhaps it is a bit of leaven working gently among those of different station toward the fuller and more human understanding and sympathy that will some day bring to man the real democracy and brotherhood he seeks. Few indeed are the agencies that bring together on a friendly footing so many and such great extremes as here. And we are numbered by the hundred thousand now.

If you are come to our Camp-Fire for the first time and find you like the things we like, join us and find yourself very welcome. There is no obligation except ordinary manliness, no forms or ceremonies, no dues, no officers, no anything except men and women gathered for interest and friendliness. Your desire to join makes you a member.

CACTUS, diphtheria, Gila Monsters and candy—a word about them all:

San Francisco.

Re diphtheria and cutting the throat. Tell Mr. Hurst not to be too sure they could not breathe through the cut. While in Central America I helped operate on a native that had been in a Saturday-night free-for-all. He had a bullet-hole in him and several knife-cuts, one of them in chest. We had him on the operating-table but could not put him out until one of the boys moistened his hand and clamped it over the knife-cut in his chest.

There were no nurses at hand so we tramps helped the M.D. on his Sunday work, which consists of gun-shot wounds and knife-cuts.

One other case, same place. The Mine Judge's son and another native undertook to show each other who had the most Dutch courage. Result, Judge's son badly cut in neck, wind-pipe nearly cut off, etc., but missed the vein. Other native shot through liver, died. Our doctor saved the Judge's son.

RE GILA MONSTERS. McLaren has color and set OK. They can eat cyanide, etc., also can take a beating with a club that should break every bone in their bodies, and still walk off. Any of you travelers that want to see one, when you land in Frisco go to Third Street, between Mission and Howard. There you will find a Medico at one of the side street corners selling a cure-you-all for a dollar. He has one to get the crowd, and that fellow that was going to send you a skin, well if he does and I ever meet him I'll buy him a drink. The only way to skin a Gila Monster is to pound him to a hamburger and open up and cut and scrape the meat from the skin piece by piece. He is sure a "one-piece combination."

RE the cactus. The one that the Indians and we desert rats (prospectors) chew when we get out of water is called a barrel cactus and is from two to three feet high. I never saw one over three feet high. Its thorns are somewhat flat and curved like a hook. Whereas the one he describes grows to over twenty feet high and has straight round thorns or spines. The barrel cactus is almost all water and is not bitter to taste.

A candy and ice-cream parlor in Phœnix has built up a good business out of cactus candy made from the barrel cactus, cut in squares the size of caramels and sugar sirup cooked.

I too know Cave Creek and the Black Cañon, having "footed" it from Meyer to Phœnix.—G. Hoyt.

SOMETIMES it takes a good while, owing to lack of space, for a question asked at Camp-Fire to get its answer in print, but it's seldom indeed that at least one answer doesn't come in and eventually find its way into our columns. Here, for example, is a reply on the ancient walled cities of Zululand—to me, at least, a fascinating subject:

Oakwood, Mich.

L. V. Roberts, Jr., has asked for information about the mysterious walled cities of Zululand. His question was addressed particularly to actual visitors of that region—in which respect I can not qualify; but having conducted in my own interest a "fireside exploration" which revealed answers to most of his questions, I take the liberty of offering results. Sources of information were old magazines—"Wide World," "Scientific American Supplement," "Golden Argosy" and others, and "Encyclopedia Britannica." To plunder the latter treasure-house an "open sesame" is needed; in this case the key words are *Zimbabwe*, *Rhodesia* (*Archaeology*), *Monotapa Solomon*, *Ophir*, *Africa* (*Roman*). As all this involves extensive research, I present a summary:

ZIMBABWE is a Bantu name, meaning "stone house," used as a generic term for the capital of a chief. The Great Zimbabwe, to which modern usage has affixed the name, is situated in southern Rhodesia, near Victoria, Mashonaland. Discovered in 1868 by Adam Renders; explored by Karl Mauch in 1871; stripped of its romance by D. Randall-MacIver's explorations (1905), which apparently proved the ruins to be the work of Bantus, and established their date as not earlier than 14th or 15th century A. D. The "Elliptical Temple" is an irregular enclosure over 800 feet in circumference; wall in places 30 feet high and 14 feet thick; construction uneven and contour erratic. The "Acropolis" is a high hill, fortified with a completeness and judgment betokening military genius. The "Valley Ruins" appear to have been a trading mart, or abode of visiting merchants who exchanged their goods for gold dust.

Similar ruins are the Inyanga and Niekerk groups, about 250 miles northeast of Zimbabwe. The inhabitants of these northern regions evidently devoted their energies more to agriculture than to gold-seeking, as there are traces of an extensive and well planned irrigation system. The ruins consist of smaller units than those in the south, but their extent is enormous, the Niekerk Zimbabwe covering an area of 50 *square miles*. So much for the archeological evidence—now for the historical.

DUTCH and Portuguese maps, A. D. 1500-1700, designate what is now Rhodesia as the "Kingdom of the Monomotapa." Extent and boundaries appear indefinite, but all accounts of the Portuguese chroniclers agree that the kingdom was large and populous. The Monomotapa, or "Lord of the Water Elephants," seems to have been a sort of emperor under whom ruled numerous petty kings and underlords called *inkosis*. In the dispute with England as to ownership of Delagoa Bay the Portuguese based their claims on a cession by the Monomotapa (1629), whose dominions they declare extended southward *nearly to the Cape of Good Hope!* Stories of a ruling caste of a different race (Arabic strain) are set at rest by Dominican baptismal records, which state that the "powerful king" was a black man. The light complexion of the southern Zulus, who displaced the black aborigines, probably furnished foundation for the rumor.

HOWEVER, it is a historial fact that this progressive race (Bantu), themselves non-seafaring, for centuries carried on trade with merchants who brought goods from the sea-coast. If their knowledge of government, of military tactics and irrigation, and their crude but ambitious building operations, are surprising in an African people, how better account for it than by ascribing it to commercial intercourse with superior races. As to whether the fleets of King Solomon might have secured their ladings of "gold and sandalwood, ivory, apes and peacocks" from the kingdom of the Monomotapa, *vide* Herodotus, who derided the claims of Phenician navigators (600 B. C.) that he had sailed around the southern end of Africa, because they said the sun (in southern solstice) was on their right hand—an obvious impossibility according to the Greek historian. But this same assertion is now taken as proof of truthfulness, since no Phenician of that day could invent a *lie* like that.

Those emissaries of Necho, king of Egypt, were nearly three years on their journey, halting from time to time to reap crops and otherwise forage. It has been suggested that King Necho might have learned of the great sea to the west (Atlantic) from the gold miners of the "water elephant's" realm. The time required for a voyage of Solomon's fleets does not necessarily indicate a more remote "Ophir" than the "Afura" of Rhodesia. Perhaps they, too, stopped off at various places, and possibly they sent expeditions into the interior after peacocks and apes and precious woods. The ivory and fine gold certainly could have been obtained at Zimbabwe. Britannica says several of the ancient gold workings have been rediscovered and are now being operated "with profit."

ABOUT 14 years ago, one explorer (name forgotten by writer) discovered and investigated "King Solomon's Mines," somewhere in Rhodesia. He found remains of buildings showing evidences of civilized handiwork; also objects connected with worship of the "strange gods" of Solomon's latter days. Also, the crucibles of the workers in gold! These crucibles or furnaces, he found, could be peeled off in layers, revealing splashes of gold underneath. The ancient workers, instead of flaking off the precious metal that spilled, had simply smoothed on another layer of cement *whenever the accumulation became excessive*. The account of this discovery appeared in *Wide World Magazine* some time between the years 1905-1912, as I remember, those copies having passed out of my keeping.

In closing, I would suggest that the origin of the name, *Africa* is still open to debate. Ancient maps give it variously as Afer (?), Afur, Afura—the last named form being still attached to the region south of Zimbabwe. Compare with the Biblical Ophir—and draw your own conclusions.

Fiction: "King Solomon's Mines," "She," and other works of H. Rider Haggard; "The White Shield," and "The King's Assegai," by Bertram Mitford.—W. E. KEEVER.

IN CONNECTION with his story in this issue you'll be interested in a letter from Thomas McMorrow, who served in the 53rd Pioneer Infantry. When we took the story we were a bit worried over the difficulty of soldier slang for the uninitiated. Of course all who have been in the Army will find it easy going, as will some who have not, and we've an idea the others will get the meaning of most of it and will have a good time with the tale even if a word here and there is a bit obscure.

New York.

Just landed here from Upton—discharge dated May fourteenth. On the back it says St. Mihiel, Argonne, Meuse.

I was Provost Sergeant in Chablis from January fifth, when we came down from the Argonne, till April sixth, when we started for Brest. That yarn about *Scallan* the merchant was written in our guard-house in snatches after Taps, while my merry men were starting the nightly crap game and lifting the roof with "Silver Threads Among the Gold," and leaning over my shoulder with "Getting out tomorrow's schedule, Sarge? Hey, put me down to take care of the Lion d'Or!"

Soldier slang? Imagine trying to write classic English! Say, I can see our buddies around the Camp-Fire grinning right now at the idea that they don't compree the chatter of the A. E. F.!

YES, some outfits took barrack bags to France. We didn't ourselves, but the bags were there, lots of them. The earlier outfits brought them, I think so. I remember a heap of them lying in a barracks near Les Islettes, and the original of *Scallan* the merchant picking a couple out for his own peculiar purposes. On the level, I haven't overdrawn him a bit—he was one industrious boy, as bold as he was thrifty. He was an acrobat and tumbler by trade. And in the front areas you could carry about anything you had the legs to tote, unless actually going into the lines. My pack consisted of a shelter-half and a blanket, and then as much grub as I could lay hold of. I met one sergeant of Engineers who had no pack at all. "You freeze at night," I said. "I do," he said. "But I'm comfortable in the daytime!"

Well, I tried to give you a yarn from the viewpoint of the doughboy—the grumbling, singing, sinful, soft-hearted kid from the U. S. A. He didn't believe in heroes. He wasn't one himself, and he could lick any guy that claimed to be one—and he Won the War!—Thos. McMorrow.

NO, COMRADE MILLS, once in a while we print letters in praise of *Adventure*, but not very often, and I don't believe we do much blowing ourselves. Yet sometimes a letter like your own seems to come under the head of legitimate information about our magazine and we pass it on to everybody concerned.

Mr. Mills, one of our "Ask Adventure" staff, is editor of the *Feilding Star* in New Zealand.

Feilding, New Zealand.

I have noticed that in the course of my reading of your magazine you are somewhat different. You do not boast *Adventure*. You must have much material with which to do the boasting, for during the short time that I have been one of your "AA" editors I have received words of praise concerning *Adventure!* As an "AA" staffsman, too, I have had much evidence of the cosmopolitanism of your magazine and its world-wide circulation. The latest proof in this direction was furnished only last week:

NEW ZEALAND, like the rest of the world, is in the throes of the influenza epidemic. In this little town where I reside there were calls for volunteers to help the helpless in houses and two temporary hospitals. Two of my daughters answered to the call. One day the younger girl reported to me on her return home at night that amongst the reading matter brought in by the town clerk for those patients who were well enough to read were two copies of *Adventure*. I made a call myself at that hospital two days later (as a newspaper man) and whilst talking to the matron I saw a bundle of books and magazines handed in. In the bundle was a copy of *Adventure*. And this in a country town in New Zealand, the farthest outland on this footstool!

I SHOULD like to add a little about other evidence of the circulation of your magazine. It is just over twelve months since I began to receive "AA" queries concerning New Zealand and the South Sea Islands. To date I have received seventy letters containing about seven times seventy questions. As I intimated in a previous letter to you on this subject, the letters have come from all parts of your own United States. But I have actually received "AA" letters from New Zealand, a town not three hundred miles from my own place of residence. I have discovered for a man in U. S. A. a long-lost chum in New Zealand who actually happens to be an old friend of my own. I have had two "AA" letters from away in the interior of Australia; from the far north region of Canada; from Alaska; from a suburb of Melbourne, Australia; from Assiniboia, Sask.; from Tampico, Mexico; from away up in the highlands of Peru; from the hills region of India; from Havana; from Rezal, Philippines; and from China.

AND some of the letters have discovered for me some highly interesting correspondents, whose gratitude from answers given has prompted them to send me entertaining and worthwhile letters of acknowledgment, so that it has been a genuine pleasure to keep up a correspondence. Busy as my life is —for who, outside of the woman who does her own housework, is busier than a working journalist on a country paper?—I have welcomed these "AA" acquaintances and find these adventurers and would-be adventurers very likable fellows.—Tom L. Mills.

P. S.—So the war is over! Here's congratulations and thanks to the Americans. Christmas and New Year are with you—here's wishing you all of the *Adventure* health and prosperity throughout 1919!

The above letter was written December 2, 1918, and reached us some time well along in January. Here is a bit from an earlier letter:

I have had a number of reminders of the watchfulness of your censor department—with no verdict against me yet. But right here and in this connection I desire to point out the value of your duplicating of replies system. I have under my hand at this writing replies to S. B. Pelton, Smethport, and Jos. P. Lawrence, Bridgeport, both "passed by the military censor," one returned to me marked "Unknown" and the other "Unclaimed." These two casuals owe myself and *Adventure* an apology for dodging the issue.

With regards and best wishes, *Kia Ora!*—TOM. L. MILLS.

Comrades Pelton and Lawrence needn't do any apologizing to the magazine, though possibly they might have saved needless trouble by more care in giving their addresses, but they can get their replies by giving correct—and sure—addresses to Mr. Mills.

I HAVEN'T talked much about our "Ask Adventure" department since it got under way but I can summarize by saying that its practical accomplishment has been splendid and it certainly is established as a permanent feature of our magazine. A number of its editors have gone into the war, which has made some delays and changes, but the department's service has been even better than we hoped.

One phase of it may by some be overlooked. It isn't just a bureau for satisfying idle curiosity. Most of the questions asked are asked for practical purposes and a goodly portion of the answers become decisive factors in the lives of the inquirers. For example, there are quite a few who, with their families, have found new homes and new opportunities through our "Ask Adventure" and very cheerfully give it credit. From the answers printed in each issue you can judge for yourself the important part "Ask Adventure" plays in a good many lives.

WHO will give this comrade the title and words of the song he heard in Tampico?

At Sea.

By a recent edition you were successful in obtaining the words of a tropical recitation for a Camp-Fire comrade, so I am seeking your assistance.

I was struck with a monologue that I heard a few days ago in Tampico, Mexico. The reciter was a Tropical Tramp and vanished after the recitation, so I was unable to get the words. Therefore I appeal to Camp-Fire. The few lines that I recollect are:

"Do you know the road to Chile and the run to Panama?"

"I'll go back to my blue-eyed Saxon girl."

"You can holler 'Gringo——' till your voice grows hoarse."

Please excuse shaking writing, *porque*, I am only half-way 'tween Vera Cruz and New Orleans and the ship has a movement of her own.

I will make for New York after I get to N. O., and my address there will be 355 West 19th Street, New York.

Hoping I get my song, and good luck to Camp-Fire.—JAMES CREANEY.

IT IS just as well to be clear-eyed in reading the news that is daily fed to us. For example, an article of several columns in the New York *Times*, of whose contents the heading gives the meat:

America Was Ready to Win Victory with Artillery, Rifles and Ammunition; The Record of Production; How the War Plants, with a Late Start, Sped Up to the Front of the Race.

All very fine. But the main head-line of the article, though it generally does not happen so in such cases, bursts the bubble by giving the central truth of the whole matter:

OUTGUNNED WORLD WHEN WAR ENDED

When the war ended! Exactly. The richest and greatest country in the world was able to take her full share in winning the war—after the war had been won.

AS A people we Americans generally think very, very well of ourselves, but let us apply our self-conceit with some judgment. Let us swell with just pride over the magnificent way our boys did their part when they got the chance, or half a chance. But let us remember not only how long the United States took to realize it *could* not keep out of the war, and, worse still, how very long it took us to get really into it after we began trying. To put the matter unpopularly, we were caught like a big, rich, soft booby with his mouth hanging open—suddenly confronted with the need to play a man's part without experience, training or the necessary tools.

AND now the Wilson-Baker Administration is feeding the newspapers with pap about what a lot we'd have been able to do, in spite of unpreparedness, if only everything hadn't been all over before we were fully ready. All through the war we had to listen to sugar-coated publicity about how quickly and nobly, under the unprepared Administration, we were doing the things that should have been already done. If a man refuses to go some place at the right time it's small credit to him that he moves quickly and nobly when a forest fire drives him there.

Quickly! Quickly enough to be ready when it was all over.

Who can measure the blood and property that would have been saved to the world if this country had been able to enter the war at anything like full strength? And who is responsible for that bloody cost? For the American blood shed through lack of preparation? The nation as a whole, perhaps, but certainly most of that bloody responsibility rests forever upon the Wilson-Baker Administration. The same Administration concerning whose after-the-war war preparations we are now supposed to read with pride and admiration.

THE propagandists are trying to get us all ready to make the same mistake again. Back to Unpreparedness! Back to the National Guard system, exploded by the actual test. Readiness for the country's defense is not a part of a citizen's duty; let's hire a few people to attend to it and then not train or equip them for the job. There won't be any more war. And all the rest of the foolish stuff.

A league of nations by all means, if we can have one that really lessens the chances of more war. But preferably not an unopen one unopenly arrived at, drawn up by a few autocrats bickering and bargaining among themselves behind closed doors. Good in that it is a first step along the new road, but certainly no such guarantee against future war as would warrant our being again caught unprepared.

So when we read the "news" let's sift out what is facts from what was given being by those whose eyes are on the next election, whether they be Administration politicians or the politicians who are opposed to them. *We must think for ourselves.*

YES, there's very often a good deal of fact back of our magazine's fiction stories. Here's a case in point:

Chicago.

The incident on which Louis Dodge writes his story, "A Fight to a Finish," in the May *Adventure*, occurred at Cebu on the Island of Cebu in the P. I. Some of the boys of the 23rd were stationed outside Cebu. Sergeant Pete Darcy, a very good friend of mine, with two companions were surprised on their way to the town of Cebu by a bunch of Gugus. Pete and one of his companions were killed and cut up horribly with bolos and spears. The other one escaped in the manner Dodge describes by accidentally stumbling into this culvert.

I was in Cebu at the time, having been discharged from the *U.S.S. Boston*, my time in the navy having expired. There were some of the 23rd, the 18th, and some of the Tennessee boys there at the time. I got permission and also a gun and shells from Lieutenant Alexander of the Tennessee company and went out with the boys to square accounts for Pete. We cleaned up, too. I went into Manila Bay with Dewey May first; was discharged the following February at Manila. Went to Iloilo, thence to Cebu, returned to Manila, met some of the 23rd boys in the 11th Cavalry and took on with them in Troop I, 11th Cavalry. Would like to ask Dodge if he knew Joe Branzell or Micky Walsh, both sergeants of the 23rd at Cebu at that time.—F. W. CONNERS.

IF ONLY Captain North would get out of his head the idea that we don't listen eagerly to what he tells us about the Old West and about his brother, the well-known Major North. Talks like this from an old-timer are exactly our meat and we are always hungry. Talk to us again.

I have, contrary to custom, left in this letter the sentence about the new democracy, for it serves as sample of many similar replies indicating a strong and growing interest in right citizenship and its needs. Many Americans are thinking along the same lines. The results will surely show in the long run.

Columbus, Neb.

I see in *Adventure* a letter in Camp-Fire from Mr. E. A. Brininstool, in which he says a friend of his who was with my brother and the Pawnee Scouts is now living in the State of Washington. He didn't give his name or where he lives. I would very much like to know who he is and where he lives, as I thought I was the last white man left of the Scouts.

IN 1864-65 my brother had a company of one hundred Pawnees. He was captain and had a first and second lieutenant of his own choosing that were white men. They went with General Connor into the Powder River country in 1865 where they had several skirmishes and one real battle with the Cheyennes and Arapahoes. Then they came back to Fort Kearney and were mustered out in the Spring of 1866.

The following Winter, 1867, General Auger (who was in command of this department) had him enlist four companies of fifty men each with captain and one lieutenant, white men, for each company. He was allowed to choose his own officers and he had the rank of major. I was captain of one of the companies. That was the year they built the U. P. road from North Platte, Nebraska, to Cheyenne, Wyoming. We were guarding the track layers with one company (which happened to be mine most of the time), and the other companies were camped at different grading camps.

I WAS at Ogallala when a band of Sioux led by a brother of Spotted Tail ran off a herd of mules. My brother and myself with forty men followed them to the North Platte River, recaptured the mules, killed several of the Indians, among whom was Spotted Tail's brother, took ten of their horses and didn't lose a man.

Later that Summer the Indians ditched a train at Plum Creek Station, killed the train crew, burned several of the cars and carried off a lot of stuff. One of our companies was ordered there and the next day after their arrival one of our men came in and said the Indians were coming on the South side of the river. My brother took all of the best mounted men in the company (I believe there were thirty-five of them) and crossed the river and met the Cheyennes under Chief Turkey Leg (one hundred and fifty warriors), killed seventeen of them, took thirty-five horses, one boy and one woman prisoner.

NOT long after that General Sherman, General Harvey and General Auger met the chiefs Spotted Tail and Turkey Leg at North Platte to make a treaty with them. My brother was there and when he entered the tent where they were holding their council Turkey Leg knew him and turning to his interpreter he said:

"Ask this man if he still has the Cheyenne woman and boy prisoners."

My brother told him he had.

Turkey Leg said, "The woman is my wife. Tell him I have some white prisoners I will exchange with him."

Frank told him all right, so he sent a messenger to his camp on Medicine Creek and three days after they brought in two girls and three boys and my brother took the woman and boy up and made the exchange.

WE HAD several more fights with the Indians that Summer, but I must cut them out. We were mustered out in December, 1867. In 1868 there were two companies of scouts. I was not out that year. My brother had the most desperate fight of his whole career that year. But I have made this too long now. They were mustered out that Fall and in February, 1869, three companies were re-enlisted. That year we campaigned with General E. A. Carr. I was with Major Neyes on a Winter campaign when we were caught in a blizzard between the Republican River and the Frenchman's Fork. Fifty men were frozen so they had to have amputations of toes and fingers. Fifty horses and mules were frozen to death. That Summer we fought the Cheyenne Dog Soldiers under Tall Bull at Summit Springs in Colorado, and just about annihilated them. I could tell you of many things that happened that day but dare not try your patience.

WE WERE mustered out late in the Fall and the next Summer two companies were enlisted. This was 1870. We served only five months that year, and were mustered out. The scouts were not called out again till 1876 when we went on the Powder River campaign with General George A. Crook. We were mustered out at Sidney in the Spring of 1877. We had several fights that year and when we were mustered out our men had a lot of horses that we had taken from the enemy and General Crook had allowed them to keep them. The Government furnished them with rations, but wouldn't furnish transportation. So my brother and I went with them across country from Sidney to their reservation in Oklahoma.

I have read over what I have written and am very much inclined toward throwing it in the stove. It is not what I wanted to write at all but I guess I'll let it go. Of course I don't expect you to put it in the Camp-Fire notes as there is altogether too much of it that probably is of no interest to any one but me.

About the first thing I read in *Adventure* is what you say about the new democracy. I am much interested.—CAPT. L. H. NORTH.

AT THIS writing, June second, the German hand has not been disclosed. Possibly it will not be fully disclosed for fifteen or twenty years. But the leopard can not change his spots. A Hun is a Hun. At birth all Germans were systematically taken in hand and molded into Huns.

They say the Huns have learned a lesson. I do not believe. They say the Hun people really desire peace. I do not believe. They say the Hun fangs have been pulled. I do not believe. They say the military clique has lost its grip on the minds of the other Huns. I do not believe. They say Germany can not build herself up into a first-class power again. I do not believe. They say the Huns have given up their idea of world domination. I do not believe. They say that when the Huns sign another scrap of paper they will abide by the signing, either because they are willing to abide by it or because others make them. I do not believe.

It is the same Hun. A year ago we loathed him for his calculated cruelty, maniacal ambition and bestial methods. Now, because we think him whipped, we gradually look upon him more and more tolerantly. But he is the same old Hun. And will remain so, unless a new generation can grow up breathing a different air.

They say he is no longer secretly shaping other peoples to his own purposes by world-wide propaganda. I do not believe.

HERE is a very interesting and new contribution to one of our old discussions:

San Antonio, Texas.

I have become interested in the Camp-Fire discussion of "What is the spirit of adventure, biologically considered?" For a long time I was where I could not obtain magazines conveniently and it is possible that in those months some one said what I have in mind now, but anyway here goes my opinion:

I think the word "adventure" often is confused with the word "experience." Adventure is what is known in biology as play, to a certain extent.

THERE are several basic needs in man—things he *must* do. One is economic, obtaining food and shelter; another is propagation of race and care of young; and yet another is play. All normal people play. They must play for relaxation. The play of civilization is travel, or swinging a golf-club, kicking a football, or it may be the theater, street-corner talk, the club, sewing-bee, riding or skating. It is the getting away from the pressure of living, the reaction from economic struggle.

So far, of course, you do not dispute me.

ACCORDING to my terminology that which we must do to have food and shelter is work, *experience*. That which we do for relaxation is *play*, and out of play comes *adventure*. Adventure is imbued with a sense of a good time, fun, play, success, victory. Experience may be imbued with a sense of hardship, failure, economic harshness.

Let me illustrate. A party of men in an automobile set out from their town to go West in search of land on which they will live and make a living. They have just the needed amount of money. On the road a highwayman holds them up and robs them. They are injured economically. They have not had what we think of as adventure, because the circumstance is attended with misfortune and failure. There has been no play. Therefore what they have passed through is *experience*.

Another party from the same town goes south on a pleasure trip. They likewise are held up. But they hide their money and the robber goes away empty-handed. They are victorious. They can laugh. They have had a play. Therefore, they tell of their startling *adventure*.

Now change the two circumstances slightly.

The land- or home-seeking party hides its money and the robber gets nothing. The party goes on and gets its land. They are successful. They feel good. They laugh about the robber's defeat. What might have been a hardship turns out to be mere play. They tell of their *adventure* under these circumstances.

The pleasure party that goes south is held up. In the affair one of the party is shot and killed by the robber. They no longer have had an adventure but a *terrible experience*. There is no play about it.

SO I get to a point: adventure grows out of the idea of play.

Take two tribes of our cave-time ancestors. One has plenty of food for a few days. They get well fed; their bellies are full and they are well and strong and ready for play. Nearby is a range of mountains and they decide to go just beyond to see what they can see. Over the mountains they meet wild animals, some hunger, flood waters, cold. But all the while they are merely playing. Always they are victorious, though often they just escape by the breadth of a hair—just enough for a laugh afterward. The things that befall them are wonderful adventures.

The other tribe has no food, is half sick. They go over an adjacent range of mountains to find food. They go for an economic reason. There is no fun, no play, in it. They meet ferocious animals and flood water, just as the others did. They suffer. They do not have fun. So there is handed down in that tribe a tale of hardship and killing experience.

So adventure is attended by the idea of play and things that make one good humored and happy.

WHAT sends the average Yankee down into Mexico to join a revolution? It is not often a sense of responsibility, nor of wickedness. It is to have a good time, to be entertained by something new. It, biologically, is the urge in him to go and play, to stretch his muscles and amuse himself by new sights.

A man pines for South Sea beaches. He wants to go there—why? To play—to take it easy, see new things, maybe try himself out now and then in a good red-blooded savage fight.

Of course, economic conditions may take him there, or economic needs may take him down a dark city alley at night. But when he gets back he hasn't had an adventure, has he, unless he can laugh and feel good about it and be amused and rested—as if he had had a good play?

YES, it is the spirit of play that whispers and coaxes and winks and gestures a man over the hills and far away. Or into dangerous dark alleys. Or into lonely houses. For what is adventure but the glamour of play, that hints of the Seven Seas and their lively ports, of strange sights, fine sacrifices, bold daring, of high love and red fighting and sportsmanship that throws back its head and laughs courageously in the face of hell?

Yes, considered biologically, the *spirit* of adventure is play, for adventure *is* play.—BARRY SCOBEE.

SEVERAL other instances of this kind at the front have been reported by Camp-Fire members. And here's hoping that this comrade is out of hospital as sound as ever.

A. E. F.

No, I am not an adventurer—just an ordinary "buck" in the Marines. Am now at Bordeaux in the hospital. Am flat on my back so excuse writing. Have just been reading the *Adventure* of March eighteenth.

Now here is an old story of *Adventure* magazine in a strange place. We went over at 5 A.M. on November first and passed through the town of Bayonville. About a kilometer past the town we stopped and "dug in." Being a temporary stretcher-bearer, I helped carry a wounded man to the First Aid Station now in Bayonville. After disposing of our patient we went into the officers quarters (German officers). In the front room of the first on a large table midst German papers and books was an *Adventure!*

Fish? Maybe so, but, as the fellows say, "Some —— funny things happened in the old war."

Consider myself fairly an old-timer. Been an "Adventurer" since "Gold at Sea" and "The Story of William Hyde."—Pvt. DONALD C. NORRIS, 43rd Co. 5th Regt., U. S. Marines, A. E. F.

HERE is something to be added to the cowboy saddle, described and illustrated by Angus MacManus at our first June Camp-Fire:

Have read friend MacManus's letter in regard to throw-ropes, saddles, etc., and I think he has the right dope. (As I have spent about seven years on the range.) But there is one important item he has not mentioned, neither have I heard of any authors mentioning it in their western stories, and that is the Cinch Buckle or "Hurry up Buckle," as we call it out West.

The latigoe is run from the cinch-ring to the first step of the buckle, then back through the cinch and through the second step of the buckle and is buckled there according to the horse's girth. The top of buckle is merely slipped through the short latigoe-ring. After a cinch buckle is adjusted to a horse he can be saddled or unsaddled in a few seconds by merely drawing up the cinch with one hand and with the other hand slip the top of the buckle through the short latigoe-ring. In unsaddling just draw up the cinch again and slip the buckle out.

The above is used by most riders in the West and I would not be without it.

In regard to a throw-rope I have found a 35-foot length, three strand hard manila 7-16 of an inch to be of the best use.—IRVING BLANK.

THE following from our old comrade Alex. McLaren refers to an inquiry as to what are the real conditions along the Border—are they wild or tame?

Ruby, Ariz.
March 10, 1919.

Well the "long connected guy" is buttin' in again. This time due to a squib in "Camp-Fire" about border conditions. I can throw some light on that small portion of it that is "staked off" by international monuments 130, 131, 132, 133, same being about three miles or so apart (approx in my mind).

FOR the last three years or so things have been somewhat disturbed among cowmen on both sides of the line. The "*Caranzistas soldados*" seem to favor eating gringo beef in preference to the much easier obtained Mex. variety and often cut wires and chase it over from U. S. side. This has been the cause of our otherwise docile cowboys strapping on six-guns and making walking, or rather I should say riding, arsenals out of themselves. Numerous little scraps have been pulled off, but with no very serious effect.

Bad men? Well I don't know how to answer that. We have none of the dime-novel variety, who parade with bowie-knives in their teeth and a multiplicity of firearms adorning their persons, yet this is no different than any other border district where human tempermant is a factor. We have men who would not hesitate to act should the occasion arise that demanded "smokin' things up with the trigger-finger."

OF LATE, during the last few weeks, the most excitement has been by the Mex. troops "ginning" the Yaquis around and latter taking refuge on this side. Only last week right along the boundary line there were a bunch of sixty-odd Yaqui bucks and some ninety Mex. soldiers. The Yaquis were retreating slowly under fire, covering the retreat of their women and children. The Mex. soldiers were firing from eight hundred yards. This was kept up most of a day. One Yaqui in particular, a big fine-looking fellow with a slashing good outfit under him, rode up and down the skirmish-line, brandishing his rifle and yelling in Mex. at the enemy, "Come on, you Carranza ladrones, move up closer! Come to three hundred yards and fight like men!" But the Mex. respects a Yaqui's marksmanship. He knows he counts every cartridge and does not shut his eyes and pull trigger as do many Mex.

Several of these scraps have taken place just below here lately and naturally reports have gone in to military officials hereabout, which has busied the U. S. border troops somewhat. They have picked up straggling Yaquis from time to time, but have killed only one that I know of, and that but a short distance east of my camp.

NOW I am going to say something about the negro soldier, as the subject was opened up in "Camp-Fire" a few issues back. For the last two years that I have been in here I have seen almost daily troopers from D and E Troop, 10th U. S. Cavalry, the same boys who were in Mex. with Pershing. Members of the border patrol, camped but a short walk below my camp. I have had many dealings with them. I have been of service to them and *vice versa*—I guess the biggest debt is in their favor. Now, like all rules, there are exceptions to all classes, and the negro soldier is no exception to that. As a whole, I have found them courteous, gentlemanly, generous, soldierly, and when you consider the uniform they wear, "soldierly" means a whole lot. They are slaves to duty. And, with but one or two exceptions (individual), I have no kick. (I keep chickins!) They are children, but that is no fault of theirs.—ALEX. MCLAREN.

WHEN we began using Hugh Pendexter's tales of the early days of this country I felt it necessary to put up an argument at Camp-Fire to the effect that so long as a man gave us a good story we ought not to mind if he gave us along with it a lot of sound historical knowledge and a better understanding of the making of our country. My remarks were not needed. Few of our stories have been devoured with such eagerness as have these tales of our country's past. There are plenty of real Americans, native-born, who welcome so pleasant a method of learning what our school-books merely skeletonize, and plenty of real Americans, new to our shores, who are glad to learn more of their new country by becoming familiar with her stirring and splendid past.

Here is something from Mr. Pendexter on his two-part novel that begins in this issue:

Norway, Maine.

I have followed the historical outline quite closely, and have sought to give a comprehensive view of the border when Spain played her best cards. The description of McGillivray follows the estimate of historians, and I have put no words in the mouth of this remarkable man that he might not have spoken. Tonpit is a composite picture of two men whom James R. Gilmore, in his "John Sevier," heartily condemns, but who he admits in his preface, are viewed more leniently by others. I have made Tonpit more of a romantic character than either of the two men described by Gilmore. John Watts of course is real, as is Dragging-Canoe and Old Tassel.

On the whole it's a faithful fiction-picture of the time and events and I have taken but few liberties in fictionizing. The Western settlements were disowned and did form the State of Franklin, which existed three years, with Sevier as governor. A most astonishing situation. Sevier never has received the historical distinction his remarkable and intensely patriotic career deserves. He was a Commonwealth builder, a greater Indian fighter than George Rogers Clark, and the most feared man by Indians the border ever produced. Major Hubbard, the "Killer," lived. Jackson, Polcher, Hajason, the girl Elsie, are fiction. But there were many scamps to play the rôles I've fastened on to Polcher and Hajason; and doubtless many young rangers pursuing under similar difficulties as sweet maids as Elsie.—Pendexter.

YOU remember the strange message that was found on the coast of Nova Scotia and sent to Camp-Fire by one of our comrades who wished help in deciphering it? It was sent in perfect good faith by this comrade as you will see by the following letter. And once again it shows how our Camp-Fire brethren are scattered all over the earth, wandering, wandering, wandering, and yet always with us when our council-fire is started and we gather to exchange experiences.

Brooklyn, N. Y.

In 1910, when I was something more of a boy than I am now, I shipped from Bridgetown, Barbados, on the Finnish tramp *Merkador*, Captain Funcke, flying the Russian flag.

SHE hailed from Helsingfors and was owned by an old man there who had never made a trip on her. I and a friend, who is now located in Panama, signed the papers before the Russian consul. We had come across into the West Indies from Central America and were waiting for a chance to ship out for South America. The *Merkador* had brought a load of pyrites from Spain to a U. S. port and had picked up a cargo of lumber in a southern Mississippi port for Rio. She had put in for coal. By a great amount of talk and with the aid of Mr. Spiller, who had recently been located in Colon, we got the captain to agree to take us on at the stipulated rate of one shilling each for the trip. We filled our bunkers and built other bunkers on deck and filled them with coal, for coal was cheaper here than it was in South America and Captain Funcke was a careful man. We sailed from Bridgetown, tilting at an uneasy list from the deck bunkers and the top cargo of lumber we carried.

THERE is a heavy north current up the Brazilian coast and Captain Funcke put far to the eastward to avoid it and save coal if he did not save time, and we were at one time almost in sight of the African coast. However, we never saw land for eighteen days and never sighted a ship until we were near Rio, when we sighted a cattle boat *en route* for England.

Captain Funcke was a fine man who spoke fluent and perfect English. We dined at his table, where he would have dined alone otherwise, on potted fowl, fruit soup and delicacies from every port in the world. We smoked cigars and cigarettes that he had picked up in their native lands and we drank various kinds of wines. Captain Funcke claimed he had not taken a drink of water in eighteen years and he did not take one on this trip. Also he had never been drunk in his life. He drank coffee and wine with his meals and did not drink anything between meals.

HE TAUGHT us navigation, which any man can learn in two weeks, and we taught him the "Harmony Kid roll" with a pair of celluloid dice. He always claimed that if the cruise had been longer we would have owned both ship and cargo. We also read books, talked, played checkers, and contended in acrobatic feats on a horizontal bar the ship's carpenter erected on deck and came off second best in this for the Captain could do the giant swing and other stunts we could not do. On the latter end of the voyage we began the forty-two day fast that we thought was a world's record until we later learned that a man had fasted under guard for *ninety-four* days. In the meantime we did various things to kill the time, for eighteen days is a long time for a landlubber to be at sea. I'll say it is!

ONE of the things we did was to write our names and home addresses on slips of paper and put them in bottles with the request that the finder would write us when picked up. I suppose we used thirty Swedish punch, Spanish wine, or other kinds of bottles for this purpose. One day in searching around for bottles, we came across an old dirty one that had been lying around and was full of dust and cobwebs. The idea came to us to write a message purporting to come from some Captain Kid that would put the natives to searching for treasure on the coast where it was picked up. We hunted up a scrap of dingy paper and, after much consideration and draughting, evolved one that could not be deciphered, my friend making the suggestion to change "POR" to "PAR" and both of us chuckling at the expression "Captain Blackburne," an account of whom we had been reading. The first line was not intended to mean anything except veiled insinuations as to directions and the quick assertion "el venge pirot," or that the pirate was coming and that the writer was acting in great haste. The rest of the message was intended for the chance finder to dope out "Buried some gold" from "Bure Desimgild," and I believe we wrote it in capitals.

THESE are the facts in connection with the mysterious MS. found by some one, I do not know where, and sent to Camp-Fire by I do not know whom. It was intended for some ignorant native and was written to kill a few minutes of a voyage. I certainly never expected to see it crop up through *Adventure*, which was not then in existence, and feel like a boob that it has cropped up. I will give three swift kicks free to any man who has tried to dope it out, and will stand convicted of perpetrating a very silly hoax. It is only that I consider the facts should be made known that I have forced myself to acknowledge my part in this affair and also with the hope that if any of the other bottles were found with my real name and address contained in them that the finders will drop us a line and say where and under what circumstances they were picked up. This might prove of value in showing the distances such objects will drift.—EDGAR YOUNG.

You can see that it was not an easy thing for Edgar Young to write that letter. It was just a prank designed to help while away weary days. All of us play our little games and we may be glad if they are no more harmful than this one. Yet we don't always like to own up to them years afterward, when we've begun to wonder why on earth we played them, and our thanks go to Edgar Young for preferring to own up to that by-gone game rather than to let our Camp-Fire follow a wrong trail.

Most of us, including myself; while we realized the possibility of a hoax, took the matter seriously enough to work over it, so it is up to us to laugh and be cheerfully ready to take up the next one. Better to follow a score of false trails than to miss the right one through fear of making a mistake.

And has any of you found one of the bottles whose message was *not* a hoax?

A WORD from one of our many comrades who have been sojourning in Germany since our troops occupied Hun territory and gave Americans a chance to study the Hun at home and at close range. This particular American was not taken in by the characteristic Hun propaganda for pulling the wool over the eyes of his conquerors and making them think he was a pretty nice chap after all.

And, thank heaven, our boys back from the other side return with less reverence for our political parties and with a keener eye for the country's interest than for a party's interests. Look at the Republican party, for instance, abandoning its usual position and opposing an increased appropriation for the air service merely because the Democratic party had changed *its* usual position and favored the increase. What are the country's interests to the Republican Senators and Representatives if it seems paying party tactics to abandon them? One of the big parties is no whit better than the other, and the Socialist party no better than either of them. Nor is any other of the parties who have been prostituting the country's interests for their own, betraying the trust of the people for the sake of spoils, personal advancement and party interests.

I hope our boys back from service are going to war again, and this time against party politicians and public officials who serve everybody and everything before they serve the public.

Germany, May 26, 1919.

My state of mind on the Hun question is even worse now that I have spent 8 more weeks since I wrote you. I met a lot of Boches who had spent from five to a dozen years in America and some had even taken out their first papers—they gave me even better lines on the question. The snake is only scotched and we must look out. They all want to come to U. S. and of course we will let them. What in —— is our Government doing—scrapping over Democrats and Republicans when they should be re-united on a common policy? —— ——.

A NEW member of our writers' brigade follows Camp-Fire custom and rises and introduces himself on the occasion of his first story in our magazine.

All the same, Algot Lange to the contrary notwithstanding, I'm from Missouri on this sixty-foot snake question. It's quite possible, as Mr. Friel says, that there are some of that length but, like him, I've never seen any (no, I've never been in Brazil) and there seems to be no fully established record of any of that length. This question came up at Camp-Fire years ago. One of you was going to send me a fifty-foot skin but it never arrived. Mr. Ditmars, the reptile specialist of the Bronx Zoo, puts the limit, if I remember rightly, down somewhere in the thirties. I don't say there are no sixty-footers, but—well, let's see one.

Brooklyn.

About the dainty little reptile which figures in this story. The Brazilian *sucuruju* (or *sucuriu*) is the Goliath of snakes—the anaconda, whose scientific name is *Eunectes murinus*. By the way, he should not be confounded with the *surucucu*, which is a very venomous rattler. Their Brazilian names are similar, and they both belong to the same club, but that's about all they have in common. *Sucuruju* is an aquatic boa, haunting the swamps and rivers of the dense tropical forests, where he lies in the water with only his head out, or hangs out on a limb over the water, or lurks along the bank wherever he is likely to find a free lunch. He is said to be the only boa which has a savage disposition. Maybe that's because his belly is so big that he doesn't get a square meal very often.

PERHAPS some of the snakeologists will rise up and tell you that the anaconda is not really a boa, because his snout is covered with plates instead of small scales. All right, let 'em. This tale is not a hair-splitting technical treatise, but a story told by a Brazilian rubber-worker, to whom the "big snake" is a boa, or *sucuruju*. And I dare say some folks, on reading of a 60-footer, will voice the classic remark of the old farmer who went to the circus and saw the giraffe: "——! There ain't no such animal!" All right again. I never saw a 60-footer myself, and I rise to remark that whenever I do I'm going to bust all ancient and modern records for a fast getaway. All the same, I have no doubt that reptiles of this size exist in that particular region. Algot Lange records killing one on the Itecoahy (an affluent of the Javary), which was 56 feet long. He also mentions another, killed by the rubber-workers, whose length was 52 feet 8 inches, and states that the rubber-workers told him the *sucuruju* grew even larger.

While his 56-footer was being skinned he told his men that North Americans would not believe so large a snake existed, and one of them replied in an offended tone:

"Sir, you say your people in the north will not believe we have snakes like this, or even larger. That is an insult to Brazilians. Yet you tell us that in your town Nova York there are *barracaos* (houses) that have thirty-five or even forty stories on top of each other! How do you expect us to believe such an improbable tale as that?"

So there you are. There is no particular reason for supposing that these two snakes mentioned were the largest in South America. The one killed by Lange was coiled in a seven-foot cone on a sand-bar, where it was spied by Lange's men while paddling by moonlight. The *sucuruju*, you know, is a night-feeder.

WHEN the scientific gentlemen assert that no snake grows longer than 35 feet or thereabouts, you must remember that they base their declarations only on the specimens whose existence has been solemnly attested by somebody of their own scientific clan. It is quite obvious that such a leviathan as the gigantic *sucuruju* of the Amazonian headwaters is not likely to come under their observation, since he is seldom seen by white men, and the difficulties in the way of bringing him out of that infernal jungle are almost insuperable. It must also be remembered that all of that vast lowland region extending from the great El Tapado swamps of Bolivia around *via* the Javary to the Amazon is a reptilian paradise, where all conditions are conducive to the development of this form of life to enormous proportions.

I HAVE been told, and believe it to be true, that in those matted swamps there exist strange creatures which the scientific world knows nothing about—grotesque survivals and perversions of prehistoric things without a name. That this is not based merely on Indian tales is indicated to my mind, at least, by the fact that farther north, in Colombia, huge prehistoric animals survived until quite recently. Even science admits this: for A. H. Keane, F. R. G. S., states that "there is reason to believe that some of the huge extinct animals—megatheriums, glyptodons, taxodons, horses of earlier types and mastodons—which formerly abounded in Colombia, survived till comparatively recent times, and in any case were almost certainly associated with primitive man. Mr. R. B. White refers to necklaces from Indian graves made of the molar-fangs of mastodons, "so well preserved that they could scarcely have been fossils." Now if these enormous brutes lived in Colombia until quite recently, when they were wiped out by changing climatic conditions, is there any good reason why huge reptiles should not still be living in the swamp country, where everything favors their survival? In this connection, listen to the incident related by Charles Johnston Post, who passed down the Rio Beni and Madeira from Bolivian gold-diggings:

"THE night before we left Riba Alba an Indian was brought around to tell me an experience. He was a rubber scout who hunted up possible new areas of rubber trees. Somewhere, about a couple of hundred miles back in the interior from this settlement, he had come across the trail of an animal unfamiliar to him—and from his savage infancy such forest lore had been his sole academic curriculum; it was a trail like a snake—but not a snake! It was approximately three feet in width, and there were feet-marks on either side of the trail like a turtle's flippers—but only two. He had not followed it, for he was afraid. About a week later, in the shallow lagoon of one of the great lakes that are known to exist in that part, although no white man has yet penetrated to them, he saw a long neck rise out of the water. And it had a head on it. A snake's neck? he was asked. No, he insisted it was not a snake, he knew snakes. It was a neck with a head on it, something new. Then he fired at it, and it disappeared—and that was all.

"He had described, in the combined circumstances, a possible plesiosaur. What he saw I do not know, but when an Indian wants to romance his animals have the regulation iridescent eyes and spout flames. No combination of two overlapping trails could deceive him; he was adept on animal trails, nor would such a commonplace incident as an overlapped trail stir his imagination. He had never seen a circus poster, or an illustrated treatise on paleontology, but he indicated the existence of some animal closer, at least to the plesiosaur than any known and distant descendant."

OF COURSE, no scientist would ever believe this. He would demand that this thing be photographed, weighed, measured, bottled up, and delivered to him with the seals unbroken, accompanied by a mass of affidavits. Personally, I am willing to believe this Indian saw what he said he saw; I am not especially ignorant or credulous either. Compared with the misshapen monsters which may be still living in that swamp country where the Amazonian rivers rise, a reptile such as an overgrown *sucuruju* is nothing much to worry about. However, if you want to play safe in this snake story, you can chop a few feet off the tail (no pun intended) and make him only as long as eight or nine tall men. Nine 6-foot men would come to 54 feet, which is two feet less than Lange's 56-footer. Personally, I'd rather stand pat on the 10-man length: but do as you please.

There, I've written you quite a long drool in regard to this snake story, and you can doll it up for the Camp-Fire to suit yourself. Hope it doesn't sound like an ill-natured knock at the scientists, for I've met quite a few scientific men and found them mighty fine fellows—in fact, I've belonged to a couple of scientific societies myself. All the same, they're the most skeptical folks in the world.—A. O. Friel.

Since writing the above I've thought of a little change I'd like to make regarding the *surucucú*, which I dismissed with the brief statement that he is only a rattler. As this is likely to make folks think of a little three-foot side-winder, which is not exactly fair to the Brazilian reptile, I'd like to add the *sucuruju* should not be confused with the *surucucu*, whose society name is *Lachesis rhombeatus*, but who is more commonly known as the bushmaster. The latter is not to be sneezed at either, unless the sneezer is at a safe distance from the sneezee. He is a thick, heavy brute, grows to a length of ten feet, and is extremely venomous—sure death within half an hour. The Brazilian names of these two squirmy gentry are similar, and they both move in the highest circles of snakedom, but that's about all they have in common.—A. O. F.

ADVENTURE, biologically considered—what is it? I said that S. B. H. Hurst's theory would have to be barred from further discussion because unsuited and awkward for a general argument of this kind, but I suppose I need not bar out the following on that account since it treats this topic only in a minor way. Also, the other side, as here represented, is entitled to one argument in reply to Mr. Hurst's. And, if I may horn in with my own opinion, I don't believe either sex or food is the answer. Nor do I ever lie down peaceably under the ruling that man is just an animal, though "biologically considered" certainly justifies that treatment of the question.

Detroit, Mich.

I read with interest what S. B. H. Hurst had to say on the subject, and frankly don't agree with him.

I DON'T believe that the impulse which bids us go out to the far places of the earth is for the gratification of the sex interest. Mr. Hurst presents us a picture showing man running after women, which of course he does, but not so much as he does after his first god, gold. In other words, man has two gods, the first being gold and the second woman. Man is an animal (as I think all will agree, after watching events of the last four years) and if we study our "lesser" brethren of the fields, we'll find that the instinct which causes them to go into the next valley is for nothing more nor less than for the food which may be there. That is all the "animals" need—food.

Man having shed his natural covering, needs an artificial coat to keep him warm, needs food and other things to make him comfortable and so must acquire gold (or money) with which to purchase these things. His home town may not offer him the opportunity, so he goes to the next one. It is just as bad, so he goes on to the next, and then to the next until he has been practically all over the continent, and very often goes to the next continent.

I know a young fellow born in India, who went to England, then came here, whose reason for doing so was that he "thought he could do better here."

I have also met quite a few fellows, who I think could be called adventurers, who always say "This town's no good. I'm goin' here or there—and when I make a good stake, believe me, boy, I'm gonna settle down." There is the whole thing—when he makes his stake.

IF WE study the lives of the "great" adventurers we'll find the same thing. It would be hard to convince any one that Drake and Raleigh and their swashbuckling crews, adventurers all, came to the new world for the women it contained. I think most of us will agree that gold was the thing uppermost in their minds. Take our more modern adventurers, Stefansson and Shackleton, and one could hardly accuse them of adventuring into the arctic wastes after the few greasy Esquimaux women to be found there. They go usually because of the reward which is given them on their return.

NOW having said that animals roam in search for food, and man roams in search of that which will bring him food, I think the spirit of adventure is nothing more than the old predatory instinct which bids us to go out and over the hills and into the next valley and have a "look around and see the country" and "mebbe find somethin'."

Of course, I'm basing this on the belief that the man who roams from town to town in search for "something better" is as much an adventurer as he who roams to the out places of the world. Money means more than food and clothing—it means power if we have enough of it, and so we search for it.

Sorry to take up the time if I haven't said anything new.—Allen Stuart Reid.

The Camp-Fire

THE following interesting letter from one of our comrades will be eagerly read by many of you and will undoubtedly bring out some differences of opinion from others of you who know Latin America.

The Argentine, for example. Do the rest of you agree with Dr. Sargent's (Ph. not M.D. or D.D. or D.D.S.) estimate? And do others of you make Honduras your first choice?

My own little personal feeling is that the little old U. S. is a pretty good place itself, with a very wide range of climate, conditions and opportunities. Also, being Americans, don't we owe our country something in the way of standing by her in her development, particularly in these critical times?

Hacienda "La Manuelita,"
Palmira, El Valle, Colombia.

Fellow *Adventure* Readers and Friends: With all good wishes I salute you one and all.

During the past four years I have received from many people, some one hundred and seven to be exact, queries concerning the feasibility of establishing a colony or a home in Latin American lands. These letters came from all sorts and conditions of men and women, viz:

5 women. (These did not state whether married or single.)

11 men. (Who did not state whether married or single.)

65 men with families.

26 single men.

To the most of these I replied; but in a recent mail I received a letter from a relative and four friends (all on active service) asking about the same thing. Therefore I decided to send this letter to *Adventure* and will be only too glad to go into details with any person holding an *Adventure* card with serial number.

In one of his letters to me, the Great American (Roosevelt) said: "Every great war has resulted in a change of population, and incidentally new and powerful states have sprung into existence. The sovereign states to the south of us, offer great opportunities to a man who has the real gumption of the old American pioneer in him. Many people look with increasing suspicion on the acts of the people in power for the moment, and one of the results of the present Great War, in my opinion, will be an increase in immigration to other lands."

A FEW mails ago I received, as stated above, a letter from a near relative, asking all sorts of questions *in re* settling in a tropical country. My relative asked questions enough to fill a pamphlet, while any sort of intelligent replies to them would fill two large volumes, but boiled down the questions were:

Is it possible? Is it practicable? Can money be made? Are the countries healthful? How much capital is necessary? What outfit is necessary? What crops can be grown? What country is the best? How do I get there? Whom shall I write to? Are the people civilized? And others of minor importance.

To the questions Is it possible? Is it practicable? Can money be made? I answer unqualifiedly YES. To the others as follows:

Are the countries healthful? Yes. If a man takes care of himself, behaves himself and takes his quinin, sleeps under a mosquito bar and is not a glutton, he will have nothing to fear ordinarily. If he does not do these things or follow the well-known rules of health for the tropics, he will be sick a goodly portion of the time.

How much capital is necessary? This is a hard question. One man with five hundred dollars to start with and plenty of "gumption" can make a success and a big success, while another man with five thousand dollars will be a miserable failure.

The great secret lies in the patience possessed by the person in question. The only cost attached to the land, say twenty-two hundred acres, is the surveying, and this is very reasonable. The stamped paper required by the courts of all Latin American countries will cost about a dollar—and that will be about all.

The next item of expense is the dwelling and its furnishing. A settler should have hens, geese, ducks, turkeys, pigs, goats, and a couple of good dogs. He will be able to raise in his dooryard, chocolate, sugar-cane, rice, bananas, plantains, yucca, beans, corn, tomatoes, oranges, lemons, pineapples, papayas, squash, and many other tropical fruits and vegetables. The jungle and the forest will supply him with all kinds of game, and the rivers, lakes, and sea with fish, oysters, turtles, etc., and the seashore with salt. Pepper can be grown. The forests supply the lumber or bamboo and roofing for his house and fences, although the latter are not at all necessary if his locality is not settled as would be most likely.

The answer to the question, What are the best crops? really comes in here, so I will answer it at this time. All depends on the altitude and geographic location. In the far south and in the high mountain regions, all the Temperate Zone crops can be raised, but if in the Torrid Zone, and on the coast or in the low lands, the tropical crops hold the attention of the settler.

I have seen colony after colony meet with the most miserable kind of failure and the Red Cross convey them back to the "States" absolutely penniless, but these failures have been due to the general laziness or lack of bodily care (*in re* health) on the part of the settlers. Only too often do the settlers try to do too much at the start. If I were going to settle in the tropics in the highlands, I'd try wheat and sheep; if on the coast, coconuts and, if possible, cattle. The coffee and chocolate crops are excellent for certain places, but they are few and far between and I do not recommend these crops to the new settler. A few chocolate trees will furnish the settler with the very best drink nature gives and consequently should be planted.

The man who goes to a new country in the tropics with a small capital should, after getting his titles to his land and his house erected, begin to plant coconuts and improve, little by little, the land in the immediate vicinity. Build for the future. Then wait for results. The coconut is the big payer and the easiest crop to raise, yet there is a lot to learn about coconut culture, but even the greenest novice from the center of N. Y.

City, who has never seen a blade of wild grass, can, if he has patience, make a success of coconuts. Therefore my reply to the question, What crops can be grown? is: A great many different kinds, but the best is coconuts.

NOW comes the query, What outfit is necessary? That largely depends on the man and his ambition. A personal outfit should always include quinin, a mosquito-bar, a .30-30 Winchester, a .22 Remington, a good machete, a camp cot or navy hammock, a compass, a pocket magnifying glass, a watch, blankets, clothing, hightop boots, colored glasses, Epsom salts, note books, toilet articles, etc. I will be very glad to give any interested person a complete list of my own outfit and the one I sent my relative.

WHAT country is best? This is the most difficult of all the questions. I strongly advise the would-be immigrant to stay away from the Argentine and Colombia, while the Allied citizen is a *persona non grata* in Venezuela. Mexico and Guatemala are not suitable lands in which to settle at the present moment nor will they be until we get a Government in the United States which will look after the citizens of that country abroad. Argentina is full of nothing except hot air and thousands of "white men" seeking employment. Colombia frankly does not want any foreigners to settle except the Germans and is especially bitter against the American. They still hold to the Panama grudge (Note: Panama is still, officially, a part of Colombia). Costa Rica and Salvador have scarcely any public lands. Nicaragua is O K and under American protection, but its people are shy of foreigners, they are suspicious, and so, for my part, I strongly recommend Honduras. Honduras has not a very large population but they are good friends, and always have been, of the American and are seeking settlers from our country. The public lands are excellent and safe and the present Government is more than willing to help. There are none of the obnoxious customs laws that nearly every country on this hemisphere has.

I KNOW of a place in Honduras where there is a huge salt-water lake, some 20 or 30 miles long, and about 1 to 6 miles wide, separated from the sea by a wide strip of land some one-half mile across, which strip is covered with coconut trees. The land side of the laguna has pine trees running down to the laguna's edge and is possessed of a fine salubrious climate. Here are great open grazing lands with thousands of wild cattle. The land is public, the cattle and the coconut trees belong to no one. Here would be an ideal spot for a colony or for a big ranch of several hundred thousand acres. The pine trees and open savanas run directly back to the mountains and there are no bad jungles or swamps near by. It is the best spot I know of in any of the Americas and the editor of this magazine can vouch for the fact that I know Latin America fairly well. I will be glad to inform any private person interested more about this locality, but I can say that I have advised my relative to go there, and if he does I shall probably buy a large tract of land there myself for future profit.

How do I get there? Talk with the nearest ticket agent, either railroad or steamship. If away from either, write to the United Fruit Company at N. Y. City and make inquiries. Better still, write "Ask Adventure." Be sure and enclose your stamp and also tell the editor what country you want information about.

ARE the people civilized? I do not care to answer that question. Some people say yes, others say no, but taking all in all into consideration, I believe that the Peruvian, the Chilean and the Hondurenian are the best of the bunch and of course the higher classes of all these lands are refined, cultured and educated people (accord-cording to their view-points). Personally outside of Colombia, I've no kick coming except with Mexico.

The most important factor in the consideration of any tropical land as a permanent place of residence is the glamor of romance that writers have cast over it. The *first thing to do* is to strike this factor out, root, branch and tendril. There's no romance, absolutely none. The man or the woman who comes to one of these lands to make a home will enter a country as matter of fact and as sordid as his own homeland, the only difference being the climate, the people, and their offspring.

Don't imagine money can be made here easily, it *can't*. You've got to work and work mighty hard, but there's a great success awaiting the worker. The settler who cultivates, or uses his land as it should be cultivated or used, *and who sticks, and who takes care of his health*, can at the end *of five years take a rest for the rest of his life—but five years is the minimum!*

MOST everybody likes to read about the tropical moon, the wonderful palms and flowers, the marvelous productiveness of the soil and the great fortunes amassed, likewise the dark-eyed señoritas and the haughty, but cordial and generous Dons and Hidalgos, but nobody has ever found the latter outside of a novel while the other things have as *ever present attendants—poisonous* snakes, mosquitoes, flies, ants, vines and flowers and most dangerous of all, poisonous water. There are terrible swamps and jungles and in the cities and towns, vice, squalor, and minor political upheavals, but thank heaven and Roosevelt—the day of the revolution is past.

FINALLY, should there be any of the readers of this article who are thinking of going to the Tropics to settle, one word of advice: Go slow. Figure the new game from every angle. Write to the consul-general at the capital of the country in which you intend settling. INVESTIGATE and be sure you know your companions and the man who is the prime mover in your colony scheme. Write the United Fruit Company, write any one you know or know of who is reliable. Get all the data you can. Don't pay any attention whatsoever to *prospectuses, novels, story books, and books of travel.* The writers of the books of travel mean well, but invariably they see a country as their hosts want them to see it, and a man with a well-filled purse and well-filled belly will see things through a different pair of spectacles from the man who is hungry and with but precious little money. I have yet to read a fair-minded book on any part of South America. But I do most heartily recommend any intending settlers to look into the offerings of Honduras. *Stay away from the Argentine. Don't get tangled up to any thing that purports to come from that country. It is a land of rich men and there are mighty few openings for any one. I KNOW as I have a ranch there and know the people like a book.*

The man who wants to build a home for himself, his family and his posterity, should, if he can't do anything at HOME, look into Honduras, and if not satisfied there look into Nicaragua, Peru, Ecuador, Chile, or our very good friend Brazil.

I will be very glad to reply to any questions, if I can, intelligently, made to me by any holder of an *Adventure* card.—J. W. SARGENT.

IMMIGRATION. Won't Congress have sense enough and patriotism enough to stop it at least for a period of years until we can Americanize the millions whom we have already let in and not Americanized or, generally speaking, even tried to Americanize? Are our Congressmen afraid? Of offending Capital? Of losing the "foreign vote"? Think of Americans too cowardly to defend American interests because they fear to lose the "foreign vote"! Patriots? Traitors.

IN CONNECTION with his story in this issue Harold A. Lamb gives us some illuminating glimpses into ancient history:

New York.

"The Rider of the Gray Horse" happens to be a battle-cry of the Rajputs. These gentry were excellent fighters and possessed a great deal of pride.

Early in their history one Rajput prince was chasing another after a battle. As it chanced, they were brothers, and enemies. I think one was Prithvi-Raj. Overtaking his brother, whose horse was done up, instead of killing him he offered his own fresh gray mount. And returned to his C. O. to surrender himself in his brother's place.

This act is significant of the Rajput chivalry in the middle ages. The fact that they took this phrase—"the rider of the gray horse"—for a war-cry shows how highly they held personal honor. Any one who knows of the annals of the Raj understands how jealously this honor was guarded. Chitore was the stronghold of the Raj. Three times it was attacked and taken—twice by Moghuls—and each time, instead of surrendering, the women burned themselves, and the men put on the yellow robes of death, ornamented with pearl necklaces, to fight to the last man.

AS TO the story of Nur-Jahan, this follows history. Being loved by Jahangir, when the latter came to the Mogul throne in 1605, Nur-Jahan's husband, Sher Afghan, was marked for death. Nur-Jahan, who was ambitious and returned Jahangir's love, was likewise marked for destruction by Sher Afghan, the Tiger Lord.

The affair was complicated by the fact that the late emperor, Akbar, father of Jahangir, regarded Nur-Jahan's beauty as dangerous to his son. Akbar had married Nur-Jahan to Sher Afghan to keep her out of Jahangir's hands. When Jalal-Ud-Din Akbar died, it was a case of which member of the eternal triangle could kill the other first.

Jahangir won. Sher Afghan, being under no delusion as to his fate, calmly sabered the official Jahangir despatched to bring him to court, and died sword in hand.

So it happened that Nur-Jahan survived the enmity of Akbar and Sher Afghan. She was little more than a Persian adventuress; but she knew her own mind and possessed the beauty of Helen of Troy. Incidentally she made an excellent queen.

As to the bonpas, the priests of Bon—they were a branch of the lamas known as the black hats. The followers of the Dalai Lama were then known as the yellow hats. The worship of Bon was of a phallic nature—based on magic, and erotic ceremonial. It resembled, and was allied to, that of Kali. Nur-Jahan, being a Mohammedan, was outlawed by both Buddhists and Hindus.—H. A. LAMB.

AS THIS comrade says, I think that those of us who have really hit the trail are not likely to criticize our magazine's stories as "impossible." Mistakes, yes. They are quick to call attention to a mistake by one of our writers, particularly if it is a mistake in local color or custom. But they themselves have seen too many strange things to question the truth of a new thing because it seems strange or improbable on the face of it. And very often, like this comrade, they themselves are familiar with the very incidents that one of our writers has woven into his fiction tale and that seems so "impossible" to one who does not know the facts.

I have long been a member of Camp-Fire and never until recently have I heard any criticism (adverse) of our magazine and this was to the effect that too many of the stories were "impossible." Now I wish to state that in several stories I have had the pleasure of reading in *Adventure* I have found things which I know to be true and there are lots of other stories which read like straightforward facts but with the settings of which I am unfamiliar; perhaps some of the rest of Camp-Fire members know them. You who are familiar with some parts of this little world, how many times have you found stories under the guise of fiction that you knew to be true?

Now the next time you hear one of these mollycoddles knock our magazine just tell him to shake the grass off his feet and go out and see what the world looks like. Ask him if he ever thanked God for water to drink that was so yellow it looked like iron-rust, or if he was ever out in the woods or the swamps with a compass and a gun, or ever been outside of harbors in the fo'castle, or away from the States "on his own." It is the stay-at-home boys to whom these things are impossible, and I hope the editor will edit this enough to permit its being published in Camp-Fire to discourage some who would criticize.—ID. CARD 1649.

QUITE a lot of us in Australia, New Zealand and Tasmania, and here's the good word from a comrade of the last named:

Red Chapel Avenue,
Sandy Bay,
Hobart, Tasmania.

Just a little skite from a Tasmanian "adventurer" who has emerged from the "armchair" and "fireside" stages. I will try to give you an idea of how things are going here from *Adventure's* point of view.

OF TASMANIA'S 26,000 square miles about three-quarters is settled, and about one-quarter (the South-West) is absolutely unsettled. Mention the district to a city-dweller here. He will look wise and patronizingly inform you of "the terrible bleak, bare, uninhabitable, barren, dangerous, etc., etc., western wilds. Newspapers ditto. The old-time explorers must have been very prosaic guys, or else the conditions damped their ardor. Anyway, recently a society has been formed—the National Park Board, which has got a reserve of 27,000 acres, at the "edge of cultivation, at the little border station where the trains run out and stop," to misquote Kip. National Park is supposed to contain every variety of flora and fauna peculiar to Tasmania. In her you get water-falls, fernery, gullies, mountains (or rather, a mountain plateau over 4,000 feet) and mountain lakes, which in time they expect to civilize enough to educate the locals and other tame tourists up to.

MY COBBLER and I have our "happy hunting ground" west of this park, with our jumping-off place at Fitzgerald, 6 miles past the Park Ry. station, and hike south-west. The last holding is 6 miles from Fitz. and the few settlers up to here unanimously agree that when the Deadheads (Government) wake up, they will get wise to the big timber and the mountain mineral country, then they will put a railway through to Port Davey (to a Hoburger, the last place God made), on the S. W. coast.

As far as we know, we are the only two genuine "adventurers" in Tasmania. Instead of grumbling at the wet weather (which is the real wet), we try to get used to the damp. On exploration stakes we have done a little in the original line, having located some falls on the side of one of those "inaccessible" mountains. Director of Tourist Bureau here wants us to take a party out to the falls (which we did not reach, but can locate, where others can't); and on an official report, will try to get a track made to them for the tame tourists.

RE E. C. ROSE'S remarks on Wabbles, they exist here too. There are several in the office where I have hung out for eleven months, and am chucking in March to go surveying. One of these snooped up to me one day when I was running my eye over a typewritten draft of an expedition which I was suggesting to Director of Tourists aforementioned. His piggy little eyes concentrated on the headlines "Proposed Trip to Mount Mueller." Without my permission, the snoop starts to pore through its specs at the draft, while I look down with pity at this smug insect of five foot nil. When it finishes, its first remark is that I have in one place got down "sae level" instead of sea level. Then it looks up, and tries to sneer.

"H'm, you'll be quite an explorer some day," it sniggers.

"Uh-huh!" I grunt, not wasting words.

Re exploration generally, it said: "There's nothing left to explore now, except a little bit of South America."

To this whine, I orated that there was exploration right here in Tasmania, even in the city's back yard. It does not believe me, for does it not say in the official records such and such? And these archives can not lie.

OSMIRIDIUM here boomed a lot last year, and mining generally seems to be keeping its end up, and now a few prospectors are beginning to get out into fresh country. The Government has announced its intention of appointing a Conservator of Forests, somewhat on Californian lines. Perhaps they will, some day.

If you know of any adventurers ever likely to butt in on this isle and wanting to know where to hike to, you could get them to drop a line to either myself, above address, or to my mate J. F. Murray, address 20 Lord Street, Sandy Bay, Hobart, Tasmania, and we would only be too glad to put them on to anything. There are kangaroos, wallaby, badger to get in the wilds, fish stocked at Lake Pedder among the mountains, and now forgotten; there are hundreds of mountains to climb, rivers, lakes, forests, button-grass plains to traverse, panoramas to sketch for artists, volumes for photographic enthusers, little known tracks and shacks, a real miniature paradise.—S. H. LIVINGSTON.

OLD-TIMERS of the West, can any of you shed light on this man Adams and this lost mine?

———, New Mexico.

Can some of the old-timers write me something concerning a certain man named Adams, who originated in California, freighted across the

U. S., was robbed by Indians and finally fell in with a number of men, partly soldiers, and with them was led by a Mexican guide to a very rich gold mine which the Apache Indians had hidden in N. W. New Mexico.

ACCORDING to the best information obtainable, after the party was working in mine Apaches rushed them and killed all in party. Adams and man named Davis were gone looking for party coming bringing chuck for outfit but found them killed also.

Adams and Davis walked from mine to a certain landmark I have located and hid. Saw several Indians pass hunting them. Adams and Davis finally reached Ft. Wingate, where Adams seeing some of the Indians who were in the massacre party, promptly shot them. Hid out for several years and when able to try to return could never follow his trail back to the noted hidden mine.

Victoria, who used to be chief, once offered to take a party to this mine for 100 horses. Party got afraid of Indians and broke up.

It has always been claimed that the Apaches were the only Indians who knew the trail to this mine and always killed any whites coming from there.

Supposed to have been 54 years since Adams was at this mine. One other white man has been there and come back alive, a doctor from Albuquerque, N. M.

Any information about this sent in to Camp-Fire will be greatly appreciated.—M. M. COLEMAN.

HERE'S a sample letter from a sample wanderer:

San Francisco.

I've just finished making a three-year "bumming" tour around the world, touching at England, Egypt, Gallipoli, South Africa, Tasmania, New Zealand, Australia, Tahiti and Hawaii and here I am back in California.

FROM Los Angeles to New Orleans was the first leg of my journey, which I covered in about three weeks *via* the underneath method on passenger trains. Two weeks I stopped over at El Paso, the gambling-houses, race-track and odd characters hanging around being the attractions. From New Orleans to England on a lumbering old mule boat. Passage in twenty days; net proceeds six pounds and a fine collection of cooties. I had left New Orleans with a nickel. Then I made a trip as third baker on *S.S. New York* to New York and back to Liverpool to fatten the bank-roll a bit in order to take in London. Arrived in London with eleven pounds odd and roamed the highways and byways of that grand old city for nearly two months. When broke, I took job as assistant cook on troop ship *Minneapolis*, visited Alexandria, Malta, Gibraltar and Gallipoli, then back to London.

A month later I shipped as second cook on the *Kia Ora*, touched at Dakar, Africa, Cape Town, Hobart, Tasmania and Auckland, New Zealand, where I deserted. Worked there as barman for several months, when, in the war registration, the irregular method of my arrival in the country was revealed to the authorities which resulted in my spending a few weary months in their modern and sanitary gaol. Upon my release, I hopped over to Sydney, Australia, spent nine months there and landed back in California on *S.S. Sierra*, working as second butcher. Five times I attempted to enlist in the British Army. Three times refused because I was an American and twice on the grounds that aboard ship in some capacity was doing a bit and was told to continue in that game. Perhaps you have no idea with what suspicion and prejudice an American was looked upon in England in 1915-16.

THE morning after a Zeppelin raid in London the police visited my room in Camden Town to ascertain whether I had any means of flashing signals out of my window. It seems some time previous a German had been caught in the act of using a mirror and strong light to flash signals and always after that all foreigners were under suspicion. Especially Germans, Belgians and Americans. Yes, sad to relate, many Belgians both in England and Belgium assisted or attempted to assist the enemy.— —— ——.

THE spirit of adventure, biologically speaking? Here's another definition to be added to our growing collection:

Baltimore, Md.

"The spirit of adventure, biologically speaking"—well, it is my impression that, biologically speaking, "there ain't no such animile" as the spirit of adventure.

To my mind the spirit of adventure is not a primal motive force or intention, or anything else of that sort; it is an emotion and pre-supposes a certain amount of mental—if not physical also—detachment from the self-preservation propagation of the species.

I would say that the spirit of adventure is that curiosity that will not be satisfied without knowing from first-hand evidence what lies around the turn in the road and what lies behind the distant hill. It travels always in an atmosphere of its own making; of glamour of romance that is none the less real because science with all of her wonderful apparatus is not able either to weigh it or measure it. And to be the true spirit of adventure, the whole must be bathed in the "light that never shone on land or sea."—C. R. MEREDITH.

SOME interesting words from Farnham Bishop about the facts back of his story in this issue. But how about this "no white man has crossed the San Blas country"? I've an idea that one man did. Who has the final facts? A good many have gone into it and been asked out or at least didn't get across. How about it?

Berkeley, Cal.

As you say, 1892 is a pretty late date for fictitious history. I didn't dare spring the real date: 1900. That year, there was an attempted revolution, a Scotchman at Las Cascadas, and a Colombian regiment wiped out at Matachin, very much as I have told in the story. The Scot—whose name was *not* Cameron—married a Colombian lady and their son told me of his father's exploits.

AFTER the Matachin affair, the Scotchman and his Indians skirmished with the Colombian forces up and down the line of the P. R. R. His proposal that both sides cease firing when the engineer of an approaching train whistled for "Time out" was made in all seriousness, and worked well in practise. His capture of the fort on Monkey Hill, and with it the city of Colon, was also done substantially as in the story.

Then, with his native allies—who were a much more decent lot than the *Sosa* and *Pedregal* of my story—he laid siege to Panama City. The United States naval officer protecting the neutrality of the P. R. R. insisted that the attack be made at a pre-arranged time, after the rolling-stock had been moved to the far end of the railroad yard, which lay between the insurgent position in the suburb of Calidonia and the Colombian barricade at the head of the Avenida Central.

ACCORDING to the Scotchman's son, his father's advice was disregarded by the native members of the insurgent council of war. They decided on a direct frontal attack against barbed wire and machine-guns. The attack was repulsed with great slaughter and the Colombians regained their control of the Isthmus for three years longer.

The San Blas, I believe, had gone back to their own country before that. They had fought for the Scotchman on a cash basis, like American or European soldiers of fortune; also, because he had dealt fairly with them and won their esteem, and finally, because they have never forgotten the treaty of alliance made between the San Blas and the Scotch colonists in Darien at the end of the seventeenth century.

Fever, famine, and the jealousy of the British East India Company brought the Scotch colony, as *Cameron* said, "to an ill end." You can read about that in the history books. What strikes me as more suitable for the "Camp-Fire" is to mention the intangible thing that helped make those San Blas fight for the plantation-owner, and that is the affinity between Scotchmen and Indians. Did you ever hear of a successful Hudson's Bay factor who wasn't Scotch? An Indian said to a friend of mine: "The Scotch are our brothers; they dance like us, and their music is like ours."

BUT because an adventurous war-party of San Blas bucks were willing to fight for a Scotch friend, do not imagine that a Scot, or any other white man would be tolerated in the San Blas country today. No white man has ever gone through it, from Panama to South America, overland, at any period of history. No white man has crossed it from ocean to ocean, by the route Balboa followed four hundred years ago, since a detachment of United States marines and bluejackets marched across there in 1871. There is a thorough understanding between the tribal authorities and the Governor of the Panama Canal, and any armed party of adventurers bent on entering the forbidden territory will be turned back by the Zone Police.

Of course, you can buy a timber or mining concession from the native authorities, either in Bogatá or Panama City. Selling such "scraps of paper" is one of the best things they do. Nominally, the San Blas country is a part of each of the two republics of Panama and Colombia; actually, it is an independent buffer state between them. Neither of those countries has any more real authority over the San Blas than Germany has over Belgium.

I know a man who bought a mining concession, went in, and struck it rich. Then, as he was sitting by his camp-fire, out of the night came silent brown men. Without a word they turned the cooking-pot and every other receptacle in his camp upside-down, and melted back into the jungle. That bit of symbolism, he explained to me afterward, meant that he was to go. He went.

THE San Blas are no weak and helpless "Wards of the Nation." They have plenty of Winchesters, machetes, and grit. Some of them are college-bred, more of them are able seamen. I have heard of them as far afield as Russia. "San Blas" is the name the Spaniards gave them; they call themselves the Tulé, which, like the word "Zulu," means simply "The Men." And they *are* men—up-standing, thoroughbred he-men. For more than four hundred years they have held their own against the white men, and I, for one, hope they may keep on doing so till the end of time.

WHEN I first went down to Panama in 1907 you could still see the old wooden signal-tower in the P. R. R. yards outside Panama City, riddled with bullet-holes during the attack made by the revolutionists in 1900. The American naval officer who umpired the battle would not let the fighting begin until the operator had had plenty of time to get down out of the tower. Rose, the American soldier of fortune who held the bridge over the yards with a machine-gun and broke the insurgent attack, was later a steam-shovelman in the Culebra Cut.

Here is the exact dope on the treaty:

From Chapter V of "The History of Caledonia: or, The Scots Colony in DARIEN, In the West Indies. With an Account of the Manners of the Inhabitants and Riches of the Countrey. By a Gentleman lately Arriv'd. LONDON: Printed and Sold by John Nutt, near Stationers-Hall. MDCXCIX."

"After the Colony had refreshed themselves ashore, and taken all possible precautions against any suddain surpprise, by such fortifications as could be made in so short a time; It was agreed on by all, that it would add much to the security of the enterprise, if they could enter into a League and strict bond of friendship with the *Indians*, whom they knew to be great Enemies of the *Spaniards*, who had endeavoured to extirpate them, but could never prevail, by reason of the invisible paths of the Country. Accordingly, some Deputies were sent out, among whom was *Mr. Paterson*, the chief Projector of the whole design. . . .

" . . . the Deputies . . . arrived in the King's presence, whom they found seated under a tree of an extraordinary bigness, upon a kind of a Throne made of several Logs of Wood, piled neatly one upon another, and covered with a sort of Party-coloured Cloth, which he had purchased from the Spaniards for a great Sum of Gold. He had on his head a Diadem of Gold Plate, about ten inches broad, indented at the top. . . .

"Then *Mr. Paterson*, the First of the Embassy, rose up, and after due reverence, made a short and pithy Speech; the substance of which was, *That they were come from the Uttermost Coast of the World, being the Subjects of a Mighty Prince, to admire his Grandeur, to establish Traffick, and to make a strict League with him against all Enemies whatsoever*. . . .

"Then, by his Majesties Order, a Noble *Indian* stood up, and made a speech, the substance of which was, *That the bearded Men were welcome; that there should be nothing wanting that they could possibly assist them in; that a League should continue while Gold and Floods were in Darien* (an expression used there to signify Perpetuity), *and that they might be assured of it the more, his Majesty would Swear it by his Teeth, and Touching of Lips with his Fingers.*"

THIS is the original version; the expression "While rivers run and gold is found in Darien" has been popular on the Isthmus and elsewhere since Warburton's novel "Darien, or the Merchant Prince" in the fifties.

If you use this in the "Camp-Fire," please don't let the proofreader abolish the lovely spelling and italics of the "Gentlman lately Arriv'd.' Speaking of spelling, the suburb outside Panama City where the last fight of the 1900 revolution occurred is called "Calidonia," with an "i" in the second syllable. This is Spanish spelling; of course, the "Caledonia" where the Scots settled was many miles away, in the San Blas country.—FARNHAM BISHOP.

HERE'S another comrade who agrees, at least in part, with Earl J. Teets as to adventure not being adventure. After writing me the two following letters, though I had expressed no doubts, he sent me some documents establishing his position, giving me other lines upon his training and, incidentally, some interesting information on parachutes.

He speaks of fishing the Stillwater. So have I, for I was a country editor at Troy, Miami County, Ohio, for nearly three years. And I too grew up on family tales of the local Indians, my great-grandfather having laid out what is now Columbus in 1797. It was on his grounds that General Harrison persuaded the chiefs not to join in Tecumseh's rising, and Indians were every-day features of my grandfather's younger days.

AIRPLANES. As they come into general use what are they going to do to adventure's last frontiers? Regions now inaccessible, or accessible only with extreme danger and difficulty, will become easily reachable in a few hours. What jungle so remote that you can be sure you won't, after fighting your way into its depths, be whacked on the head by an empty beer-bottle jauntily heaved overside by some fellow floating by in an airplane?

Lancaster, Pa.

This is J. J. Coughlin, talking, Inspector of Aeroplanes, for the Navy, now down here on temporary duty.

I've had a balloon burn, while half a mile above the ground; came down in parachute. I've had a balloon burst wide open from top to bottom rope; used parachute. The rip-panel blew out of a war-kite, letting the gas out; used parachute. On night patrol, with no lights, in dirigible, over the sea, motor stopped, compelled to drift with wind to uncertain landing, knowing that to land in rough sea was bad enough, but with a two hundred and forty pound depth-bomb loaded with T. N. T. hung under the fusillage, landing at night on the ground was not to be thought of.

OR, HAVE the motor of a sea-plane commence missing fire, when you know the flying-boat will never live in those waves. Or, and the worst ever, be in basket of a war-kite that is being towed by a vessel and have the kite start diving, ending in looping the loop and find yourself and basket sitting on top of the kite.

But I've had no adventures.

When I want thrills, I buy a copy of *Adventure* and read an Indian story by Hugh Pendexter. Where in the world does that man get his Indian dope? I want to know because I wish to purchase a work on the Indians who inhabited the Northwest territory when Mad Anthony licked —— out of them. "Red Sticks," in Mid-September issue, was exceptionally interesting to me, because I was born on the Stillwater Creek mentioned, and as a boy fished the Stillwater for bass, from its source north of Ansonia, Ohio, to its mouth at Dayton, and there are good bass in it yet.

MY MOTHER'S folks were the first French settlers in Darke County, then called the "Black Swamp." Mother has told me that of a night her folks could see from their cabin door the camp-fire of Indians. This was of course after 1795 and the Indians had learned their lesson as taught by Wayne.

Mother told us children many stories of the dangers and hardships endured by her folks while clearing a homestead in that wilderness. Deer were so plentiful her father had seven hanging in the smoke-house at once. A neighboring family lived through one entire Winter on five bushels of turnips and seven bushels of hickory-nuts.—J. J. COUGHLIN.

Lancaster, Pa.

Was, and am, sincere in what I said about Mr. Pendexter's Indian stories. They supply the thrills which the real adventure lacks. Earl J. Teets, was correct; the man who is busy taking care of himself during an adventurous life has no time for thrills. Not because he lacks imagination but because just at the supreme moment his hands, feet and brain are occupied in more important work.

FOR example, suppose you were going to make a triple parachute drop. You arrive at an elevation of three thousand feet, cut away, and the first parachute opens nicely. You then cut away the next one, but she fails to open and must be got rid of at once. So, while you are falling through space like a bat out of ——, there's no time for delicious thrills with that ground covered with buildings and trolley-cars coming up to meet you. You get busy, kick the offending parachute out of the way, tear the next one lose from its fastenings, gently open a fold of its fabric and let the rushing torrent of air going by your ears do the rest with a jerk that brings you up standing.

This is no fiction, it has been done, and will be

again, and that man will read Hugh Pendexter's stories to get thrills.

No imagination? Don't those people know it requires imagination and leisure moments to secure thrills by reading?

OF COURSE, like everybody else, I went through the "Dayton, Ohio, Flood." Counted forty-seven horses drowned before my window. One mule, only his bridle caught on an electric light pole and, with seventeen feet of water under him, he lasted four hours and ten minutes before sinking beneath the water. On Thursday morning at break of day the body of a man, whose upper chest was covered with snow, went bobbing by.

With buildings all around us burning and seventeen feet of water on sidewalk, many people on their knees offering up prayers, in which they beseeched the Almighty to cause the wind's direction to change and drive the fire in the other fellow's direction. We tore out electric lighting fixtures and secured the wire to construct a rope which would enable us to cross an alley and gain another building.

THE only thrill we succeeded in extracting from the Dayton Flood was this: A board, on which a kitten with a blue ribbon around its neck was sitting, came bobbing down that mill-race of a current. From the windows people would call "Kittie, Kittie," and the kitten would mew. Well, that was too much for a drunken guy who sat in the window of a hotel opposite us, so he threw off his clothes, hopped out of the window, swam to the kitten, reached up and, taking the kitten, placed it on his head and with it there swam back to the hotel. And, believe me, the fellow had a hard fight to make it.

HOW'S this? On patrol, looking for submarines, fly one thousand feet above for best view of depths under certain conditions, five hundred at other times, then again two thousand five hundred or three thousand feet. Try at all elevations, just as you would adjust a camera or glass for focus. The sub., we are told, will have appearance of a shadow, long and slim, but a large fish will also produce just such a shadow, so that when you do observe just such a shadow—and here's where you really do get a thrill, thinking of the pleasure of reporting a submarine, sighted and destroyed—you work down and over the spot; it moves; while reaching for wire which releases the depth-bomb you notice it has fins and, instead of a sub., for which you have for so long been looking and praying for a sight, it's a —— fish, and you're so badly disappointed you depress the machine-gun and pour a stream of bullets into him anyhow, and find you have killed a shark which looks to be twenty feet long.

Whales have met same fate, because of their resemblance to the Dutchman.

NOT long since the newspapers told you that, while flying in a fog, two sea-planes collided, one nose-diving, and her crew of three men were lost. But what the papers omitted was this: The crew of second plane immediately landed on spot where first plane disappeared beneath the waves, and one of the crew, name I can't recall, swam around the spot for forty minutes hoping some survivors were afloat in the vicinity, but none appeared. However, the nose of the injured plane did, just came once to the surface.—J. J. COUGHLIN.

PROBABLY it seems a simple matter just to gather together some of the letters that come in from comrades and have the printer put them into type for our Camp-Fire pages. It *is* a simple matter, looking at it that way. It looks easy to me, when I'm not doing it. But every time I start on it there's always a multitude of what are called "details" and often enough it's the smallest of them that take the most time. There's no use trying to explain why or what, because I never know myself till I'm into it.

Add also the fact that everything in "Camp-Fire" has to be timed for two months ahead, since magazines are made up in advance. Also the fact that it's impossible to index the letters waiting for publication, except in a most elementary way, because of their diversity of subject or subjects. And it's no small task to keep track of those that *have* been printed, to know just which issue, already out or in process of making, a certain item appeared in so as to turn back and see its exact relation to a new letter on a similar subject.

Sometimes I remember a letter very distinctly but can not for the life of me recall whether I have just read it myself, or whether it's been sent to the printer and not come down in galleys yet, or is in galleys but not put into page form, or in page form but in the printer's hands, or made up in a number not yet on the stands, or really and finally published and, if so, in what issue. Which means quite some little looking around at records before I can even start.

TAKE the following letter, for example. When I got it out from the drawer where Camp-Fire letters stay till they are ready to go to the printer it was very familiar to me. I recalled that I had written to Mr. Offley, that "Peas River" had never given us his right name or full address, that I'd tried a letter to his pen-name to the town from which his letter came and that I'd never received an answer.

But I couldn't remember for sure whether I had published an inquiry in "Camp-Fire" asking him for name and address. Thought I had, but couldn't be sure. Don't know yet and I'll be hanged if I have time to look back through some twenty issues of "Camp-Fire" to find out.

Also I had an idea the following letter had been published, but it came from the "unpublished" drawer and bears none of the marks of having gone to the printer.

I MENTION it merely as a sample case. It was written March 18, 1918, and must have reached us in April. The hunch that it had been published probably kept it in the drawer. If routine had been adhered to, it could not have been published, for the letter itself had not been to the printer and, being typewritten, no copy would have been made and sent to the printer. But sometimes a stenographer gets mixed and copies a typewritten letter and then any kind of confusion is possible.

You see, a letter may call for quite a few things after it's been read—the outgoing basket on my desk may receive it marked "id," "L. T. o. k.," "L. F.," "Camp," "desk," "A. A.," "copy," "?," "mail," "address," etc., sometimes three or four on one letter. Then, if the stenog——

That's enough. I just pestered you with all this to give you an idea of the detail and time involved so you'd be easy on me and understand that when I make mistakes in these matters I'm not necessarily an idiot. Now I'll quiet down and give the letter I should have published long ago.

And, Peas River, where are you, and who are you? Or will you write to Mr. Offley on the chance of his old address still being good, or trying his Virginia address?

U. S. S. Caesar,
Naval Station, Olongapo, P. I.

The world is certainly "small," the truth of which saying has once again been proved to me by reading, purely accidentally at that, the Camp-Fire in your magazine of March 3, 1918.

On page 180, happening in the most casual manner to open the copy which I had only a few minutes previously purchased in Olongapo, my eyes fell on a letter which on the next page was signed "Peas River." This individual says that he went to Dodge City, Kansas, in '78—went to work for Bob Wright and Jim Langton. My father, then major of the 19th United States Infantry, was at that time in command of Fort Dodge, where I joined him in 1879. In 1881, still at Fort Dodge, although my father had been relieved by Colonel G. O. Haller, of the 23rd United States Infantry, I married Jim Langton's youngest sister (Ena), remaining at old Dodge until a breakdown in health drove me out of Kansas to Southern Texas (Fort Brown, Brownsville). My own life has been a roving one since then, although I have for some time owned a nice home and a business of my own in Charlottesville, Virginia.

I am at all times glad to hear of or from acquaintances—most of whom I flatter myself were friends—of my youth, and I should be delighted to enter into communication with "Peas River." Do you mind helping me to reach him, either by forwarding this letter to him or giving me his name and address?—EDW. H. OFFLEY, Paymaster.

P. S.—When I arrived the first time at Fort Dodge, George Curry, who in later life made such a good name for himself and did such good work wherever he was put, was taking care of Jim Langton's horses, etc. Lordy, Honey! How dis worl' do move and keep on a-movin'!

THE following appeal will, I know, meet with response from Camp-Fire. Theodore Roosevelt still has a warm place in the hearts of most of us, both as a great American and as a man. In general I believe that money should go to the present and the future, not to the past, but in this case it is not easy to withhold tribute, for recognition of his real Americanism will help build us better Americanism in the future.

Roosevelt Memorial Association

The Roosevelt Memorial Association has been formed to provide memorials in accordance with the plans of the National Committee, which will include the erection of a suitable and adequate monumental memorial in Washington; and acquiring, development and maintenance of a park in the town of Oyster Bay which may ultimately, perhaps, include Sagamore Hill, to be preserved like Mount Vernon and Mr. Lincoln's home at Springfield.

In order to carry this program to success, the Association will need a minimum of $10,000,0000, and so that participation in the creation of this memorial fund may be general, it asks for subscriptions thereto from millions of individuals.

Colonel Roosevelt was the greatest American of his generation. He blazed the trail which this nation must travel. Unselfish and sincere in purpose, unswerving in seeking the right and following it, definite and direct in action, with his theory of personal responsibility for wrong-doing and his creed of "the square deal" for all, he gave a lifetime of devoted public service which must stand as an inspiration to the youth of this land for all time. Ardently American, believing profoundly that only through fullest acceptance of America's privileges and responsibilities could the people of this country realize their highest well-being and fulfill their obligations to themselves and to humanity, he set up ideals which it is not only a duty but a privilege to follow.

A memorial to this man will not so much honor him as honor America and the citizens who raise it to him. A contribution to the Roosevelt Memorial will be, in the highest sense, a pledge of devotion to ideal citizenship. Checks may be sent to Albert H. Wiggin, Treasurer, Roosevelt Memorial Association, 1 Madison Avenue, New York City.

WILLIAM BOYCE THOMPSON,
President, Roosevelt Memorial Association,
1 Madison Avenue, New York City.

Our Camp-Fire came into being May 5, 1912, with our June issue, and since then its fire has never died down. Many have gathered about it and they are of all classes and degrees, high and low, rich and poor, adventurers and stay-at-homes, and from all parts of the earth. Some whose voices we used to know have taken the Long Trail and are heard no more, but they are still memories among us, and new voices are heard, and welcomed.

We are drawn together by a common liking for the strong, clean things of out-of-doors, for word from the earth's far places, for man in action instead of caged by circumstance. The *spirit* of adventure lives in all men; the rest is chance.

But something besides a common interest holds us together. Somehow a real comradeship has grown up among us. Men can not thus meet and talk together without growing into friendlier relations; many a time does one of us come to the rest for facts and guidance: many a close personal friendship has our Camp-Fire built up between two men who had never met; often has it proved an open sesame between strangers in a far land.

Perhaps our Camp-Fire is even a little more. Perhaps it is a bit of leaven working gently among those of different station toward the fuller and more human understanding and sympathy that will some day bring to man the real democracy and brotherhood he seeks. Few indeed are the agencies that bring together on a friendly footing so many and such great extremes as here. And we are numbered by the hundred thousand now.

If you are come to our Camp-Fire for the first time and find you like the things we like, join us and find yourself very welcome. There is no obligation except ordinary manliness, no forms or ceremonies, no dues, no officers, no anything except men and women gathered for interest and friendliness. Your desire to join makes you a member.

SINCE all who have written in about it have endorsed the above as a good "coat-of-arms" or emblem for our Camp-Fire, I suppose we may as well consider it adopted. Of course our 71 on its three-colored field is the Camp-Fire badge but this other emblem, which can be satisfactorily reproduced in black and white, will also serve a useful purpose. For example, on a sign in front of one of those "stations."

ONCE more the Gila Monster, our old comrade Alex. McLaren, giving us some further data:

Ruby, Arizona.

In your issue of June third I note that our old friend the Gila Monster has again cropped up in a letter from Mr. Williams. Just who Mr. Williams refers to in his enquiry or challenge, I am in doubt, yet, having been partly instrumental in the starting of this discussion, far be it from me to drop out at this stage of the game. Not being extra familiar with Congress Street and its shops, can not say that I remember seeing one in any of the windows there, and as for the Santa Rita I hardly think our friend Mr. Iager was ever guilty of keeping any of the reptiles in his hotel lobby.

HOWEVER, I have seen a number in captivity, but the most I have seen have been in their native haunts. I found them more numerous in a strip of desert that lies between Cave Creek and the Hassyampa River in Arizona. Another district where I remember seeing a great number is that strip of country in Yavapai Co., Arizona, to the west of the Santa Maria River through to Burro Creek, also between the Santa Maria and the Harqua Hala Mountains.

Just who the party is that mentioned handling the birds I do not know, but believe me when I do it it is at the end of a stick. In one of my

letters I said "breath is said to have a sickening effect, but from personal experience can not say. They snap viciously and poke a stick at one and he will grab the end of it."

I ALSO made the statement that I had tried to kill one with a dose of K C N and had to resort to nitric acid. The reaction that takes place is governed by the condition of the animal's stomach, whether the lining be acid or alkaline.

NOT long since I was in Los Angeles and happened across a man who claimed to be authority on all kinds of reptiles, and I guess he did know something about them as he had a house full of all kinds, and among them several Gila Monsters. He told me that they were said to be very poisonous, but that he thought that the extent of that was in a great measure due to what they were feeding on, an old carcass, for instance. He said that in the course of his experiments with them he had taken one just fresh from the range, where it had possibly been feeding on carrion, caused it to bite a rabbit and that the rabbit died in great agony, but that he had taken that same reptile and fed it for several weeks on clean food, such as eggs, then caused it to bite a rabbit and that same rabbit lived. Now understand, I personally did not see this experiment pulled off, but merely relate it as given me.

Like Mr. Williams I have cowpunched, mined, prospected and hunted for the best part of thirty years, all over the West but particularly in Texas, New Mexico, Colorado, Arizona, California and Nevada, and hotel lobbies have been far-apart luxuries for me.

Well, this would not be a real good Camp-Fire unless there was some argument going on.—ALEX McLAREN.

ADVENTURE'S new comrade, *Romance*, will make its first appearance October twelfth. When you see it on the stands I hope you'll take a look and form your own judgement. In it you'll find stories by some of our own writers as well as stories by some who have never appeared in our pages. I'm not going to toot its horn, but I do want you to form your own opinion and I've an idea that most *Adventure* readers will like *Romance*. I'll be very glad to get your frank, unvarnished judgment after you've read Vol. 1, No. 1. Will you drop me a line when the time comes?

THE following is really a "Lost Trails" inquiry but, being too lacking in detail for brief statement, we are glad to have it here at Camp-Fire. Are any of you any of them?

Ft. Worth, Texas.

Concerning travelers that I would like to find, that I have met with in some of my wanderings around the country, and don't know their names (but they might know me), I would be very glad if you would publish a small synopsis of what I will scribble below. Not all of it, as it would be too much worthless gush, but pickings here and there, enough to make a respectable showing, you know.

ON MY hikes, from Ft. Wayne, Ind., to Erie, Pa., and from Buffalo, N. Y., to Susquehanna, Pa., in 1913, from Portland, Ore., to "Frisco," Calif., in 1914. From "Frisco," Calif., to Seattle, Wash., in 1915. In my trip in 1914 I met a comrade in N. Calif. who had been on a hike for over 17 years, around the world, and had over 6 years more to go, making 23 years all told, and I also met him, in Tacoma, in 1915. In 1915, myself and two others met two fellow travelers in Southern Oregon, I think between Ashland and Medford, who were then hiking around the rim of the U. S. A. on a wager. They had started out, 4 of them, but the other two left for troubles of one kind or another. I think that one of them lost his father in the East. Had quite a chat with them.

I HAVE had quite a good many exciting adventures in every State west of the Mississippi River except N. Dakota; in Old Mex.; along the Border; Canada; on the broad Pacific Ocean, and in six Eastern States, including Ill., Ohio, Ind., Penn., Mich., N. Y. We must not think that all of the exciting times are excluded from the U. S. A. and that they are to be found only in foreign lands, as we are certainly on the wrong side of the fence when we even think so, and if some of the travelers who haven't been over all of the most out-of-the-way places in the U. S. A. will take some of the short cuts in this country, I dare say that they will still find a good many hair-raising and exciting times, that haven't been in print yet. And if any one thinks that this is bosh, let him or her try some of the Western half of this country, or ask some of the more experienced ones, who do know, and they may not be so anxious to tackle the proposition themselves. Have gone a few times postponing my meals, but I have never missed any that I am aware of. Once in the Rockies I went 3 days, once in the Cascades 3 days, and I was 4½ days on the Great American Desert, in western Utah, without sight of anything but sand, and plenty of that, and if I hadn't had a bottle of water I would have been strictly up against it. I could sit down and talk for three weeks and I couldn't tell the same story twice, but that is neither here nor there. I had a monogram in my travels, and some of the travelers must have come across some of them, somewhere, of different colored chalk.

There is, or was, a "Denver-Slim" who was considered a desperate hombre, but I can assure you that I am not the same party, and possibly if I had known of same beforehand, I would have chosen a different cognomen. I was born in Hannibal, Mo., in 1880, but I am just as proud of the fact that I am a citizen, of Texas as I am that I am a Missourian, if Missourians are all considered travelers and can not stop long enough to change their shirts.—CHAS. D. (Denver-Slim) BURNETTE.

The monogram is an arrow running through a circle, with E. and W. or N. and S. at either end, the head labeled "To" and the rectangle at the feather end labeled "From." In the circle below the arrow-shaft is "Denver." Above is something I can't read clearly—looks like "W 175." Perhaps it is "M 175," for 175 miles.

ONE of the things that may make us here in the office white-haired is the matter of foreign words and phrases used in our fiction stories. It seems a simple matter to make sure they are correct. When we don't know ourselves we ask those who do, so far as they are available. But what is to be done when, for example, a critic says so-and-so in a story is not correct Spanish and the author of the story says it is the way Spanish is used in the particular locality where his story is laid? We don't know how all the languages of the world are spoken in all the localities in the world and neither does any one else. When you get a flat contradiction from two authorities both of whom should know, how would you decide which is right?

All the other magazines make mistakes in such matters, but *Adventure* probably has to handle more diverse questions along this line than any two of the others. So you'll have to make allowances and be easy on us.

Here is something from Edgar Young which bears on the subject:

Brooklyn.

I am attaching one of several articles I wrote for the *Editor* a few years ago along the same line. The Spanish language is spelled when correctly used the same in Latin America as in Spain. The difference is in the *idioma* or dialect of the unlettered. There is a slight difference in all these dialects between countries from Mexico all the way south. Chile and Argentine speak the worst dialect. The Peruvians speak perfect Spanish. Written words are the same, when in good Spanish, whether printed in Spain or Latin America, except in joke books which bring out dialects when the mispronounced words are spelt in Spanish letters. What I mean is that it would never do to have an off-colored word of Spanish spelt in English and italicized. The Mexican peon is called a *pelao* (paylow) and the correct Spanish is *pelado* (pay-lah-do), etc.

The language of Brazil is Portuguese and the difference is in the dialect of the spoken language of Brazil, similar to the differences in the English of England and here, the South, and West.

I am familiar with the outstanding points of difference of the Latin American dialects, except the Guianas and as they are a mixture of slave English (from the runaways), French, Portuguese, and Spanish, mixed with local Indian I am not familiar enough to know how they are spelled and pronounced.—EDGAR YOUNG.

THE demand for our metal identification cards continues strong and steady. Indeed, they have met such a practical need that for every one of the free pasteboard cards there are three or four aluminum cards called for at twenty-five cents each. Since the two are exactly the same except as to material and the pasteboard cards are just as good for ordinary pocket purposes, it seems that the heavy call for the metal cards must be mostly from those who go out of the beaten paths and need a card that will stand water and hard wear of all kinds. Some day we'll have the stories of some of those cards.

IF SOME one else wants to present the opposite side of the case with equal brevity, we'll print it for the sake of fairness, but a general discussion of the Jap question, with all the bitterness involved, doesn't seem just the thing for Camp-Fire. Perhaps even the following letter should not appear, but I believe so firmly in the need of excluding *all* immigration from this country until we have really Americanized what we have already that I'm falling for this kick against one of the foreign races even though it praises another. Japanese, Chinese, Germans, English, Italians, Hungarians and all the rest of them, no matter whether good or bad, should be kept out until we have had time to make real citizens out of those already here—and out of ourselves.

A country profits by getting new blood, but not after it has reached the point where what it has of good is imperilled by too many foreigners—and natives—who do not understand the real meaning of Americanism, citizenship and democracy. Exclude the Japanese by all means, but make a clean sweep of it and exclude all other foreigners along with them. Then the Japs can raise no cry of discrimination. And we can have time to set our home in order by building up an America that will have something more worth while to offer the peoples of other nations and that we can keep worth while after sharing it with them.

Taunton, Mass.

Have just finished reading what Wm. M. McCoy tells about his knowing Chinamen, and I want to add my "little bit," especially since I'm all "fed up" on the "bunk" about the Japs.

Though I've never been in China or Japan, I wandered quite a bit through the West, where I came in contact with both Japs and Chinks, and I say, "Me for the Chink." They will, and do, treat a "bo" white, which is more than can be said of the Jap. I have wandered through the West a little, and always found the Chinamen "white" and square, but the Jap just the opposite. In this vicinity the general opinion seems to be that the Japs are everything that is good, but I can't see it, so take this opportunity of blowing off steam.

With best wishes to the Camp-Fire comrades,—F. T. TRACY.

THIS copy of our magazine goes on the stands September eighteen. Two days later, September twenty, *Adventure's* new cousin, *The Home Sector*, makes its first appearance. It is issued by The Butterick Company, but Butterick is the parent company of The Ridgway Company, which issues our magazine, and *The Home Sector* lives on the same floor with *Adventure, Romance, Everybody's, The Delineator, The Designer* and *The Woman's Magazine*, seven of us in all.

A great many of you already know its editors and what they can do in the way of turning out a good publication, for they are the men who turned out *The Stars and Stripes*, the official paper of the A. E. F. They can state their case better than I:

THE HOME SECTOR, which makes its first appearance with this issue, is a weekly magazine designed to serve, inform, interest and entertain the new civilian.

It is dedicated and will be devoted to the four million eight hundred thousand men who served the United States of America in the war against Germany; to the two million who went overseas—above all, to the seventy thousand of them who will never return; to the two million who were waiting on Armistice Day in the camps at home—"the last great reserve army of civilization;" to the half-million more who manned the fleet and the transports, holding open the longest line of communication that an army had ever dreamed of maintaining, holding it open in the face of the blackest menace the seas ever knew.

The new weekly will be conducted by the former editorial council of *The Stars and Stripes*, the official newspaper of the American Expeditionary Forces. A fortnight before peace was signed, that newspaper published its final number and so brought to an end the history of an institution which was born of the needs of the A. E. F. It served those needs according to the lights of the soldiers—almost a squad of privates and two or three dehorned non-coms.—who, chosen from the ranks of outfits already in France, wrote almost all its copy and drew almost all its pictures and who, from first to last, shaped its editorial destinies. Of these men it may be said that they kept the weekly "by and for the soldiers of the A. E. F.," kept it faithful in word and deed to the troops to whom it was dedicated. If it interested the folks at home, if it satisfied the powers at G. H. Q., so much the better. But it was edited to interest and satisfy the men in the ranks.

Now *The Stars and Stripes* has been drawn down, folded up and put away, never to be taken out again unless America embarks on another expedition—a production and an inspiration of the troops, too closely identified with their struggle and their sacrifice to permit of its being brought into the market-place.

But while *The Stars and Stripes* can not and should not be transplanted to civilian life, the journalistic principles which it embodied and the fun-loving, bunk-hating spirit which animated it can be and should be transplanted, and so the men whom chance and war brought together to edit the soldiers' weekly are not now, in their red-chevron days, parting company. They are keeping close formation to edit this new weekly, which will be the better if it can also enlist the aid of those wags and poets who, from dugouts and lousy billets and the great cold base-port barracks, used to send in to *The Stars and Stripes* the things which they thought were funny and the thoughts they had which were beautiful. To be their voice in time of peace as surely as *The Stars and Stripes* was their voice in time of war, that is the ambition of *The Home Sector*.

In this, the home sector, there are no dugouts, no endless streams of guns and rolling kitchens and thumping field-pieces, up to their hubs in muck. There are no lines of helmeted doughboys ready to go over beneath the umbrella of a rolling barrage. The guns and the barrages are in the salvage pile. The equipment for the home sector is a new issue. It knows no rifle, no gas mask, no dungarees, no shirt, flannel, O. D. Its uniform is not uniform—it may be blue serge or mixed tweed, single-breasted or double—and where is the supply sergeant to say no? Indeed, where is the supply sergeant himself? Gone—gone with all the rest of it.

What, then, is left for the nearly five million former service men to bring back with them into the home sector. A belief in their country, for one thing, a belief that, as she was worth fighting and risking life for, so is she worth living for; a belief that there are campaigns yet to be waged to the end that she may be a better country, a power for incalculable good in the newly welded world which every one of us knows must somehow be in the making.

The Home Sector is edited for the five million in the belief that they will want to hear some one talking to them in their own language, that from time to time they will want to hear echoes of the old tent and deck and barrack debates and news from the old haunts, both here and overseas. Through *The Home Sector* they can keep in touch with one another. They can keep in touch with their past, and above all with their future.

Their future! Rich and poor, lettered and unlettered, immigrant and First Families of Virginia, East and West, North and South, they were all pitched in together to make the greatest expedition in the history of the world. And now, though for most of them their own front gates have once again swung to behind them, they have a common denominator. They have in common a new interest in the country they have served. They have a stake in America. No longer mere idle heirs of a great estate built on the toil and sacrifice of their fathers, they have taken over that patrimony and added to it. Does an audience made up of red-chevron men seem a limited audience for a new weekly to address? Why, it is merely to climb on a soap-box and talk to the healthy manhood of this country.

THIS from our comrade Paul A. Strachan will probably make you grin a little:

Riverdale, Md.

The man I was in partnership with, on the Coast, was the owner of a stanch 48-footer, the *Battler*, and a rattling good fishing boat was she. Charley couldn't swim a stroke, and, to cap the climax (no pun intended), he was very, very bald-headed.

In the Sound, near Olalla, Wash., he owned an 80-acre strip bordering the water-front.

AT LOW tide, on one occasion, we hauled the old boat up, he having decided to paint her and scrape her bottom. He got several cans of Marine paint, heavy copper stuff, and, as he was an inveterate blunderer, he proceeded to paint himself in a hole, after applying the brush to the sides, the pilot house and finally the deck space. Up for'ard, with about 10 foot beam, he painted 'round and 'round, till, suddenly, he surprisingly found that he had painted himself into a very narrow spot in the dead-center of the deck.

Meantime, time had passed, and it was then about 5.30 P.M. The tide comes in very suddenly there, and, although we thought we had plenty of clearance, she suddenly came in, with a good strong biff, bang, bowie! Gentlemen, hush! It canted that old boat over to an angle of 45 degrees. Charley had a two-gallon can of paint in his hand. When the deck flopped up, of course he lost his footing, and you can imagine the spectacle of a full-grown man, shooting across a slippery, painted deck and into the water, gathering all the paint to his bosom, so to speak, *en route*, and especially, hanging on to the can for dear life and thus managing to pour its whole contents down over his unprotected pate (his hat having blown off, first crack).

He plumped down into the water, and his two brothers and myself were so paralyzed at the suddenness of the thing that we could do no more than hold tight to stanchions and laugh our fool heads off. Up he came, for the first time, having managed, in some way, to get a corner of the can so fixed on his bean that he looked like a Court Jester to His Majesty, King Nep. We had laughed before, but, when he popped up, we literally exploded with mirth. He went down and came up again, and, this time, his brother, Frank, had wind enough to ask "Want any help, Charley?", to which the latter replied "Gug-gug-go to ——!" and, down he went again. We just had sense enough to realize his plight then, and, next time he came up, I threw him a line and we hauled him out and bailed the water outer his innards.

THE aftermath is even more humorous. The paint stuck to his face and head, giving him the appearance of some cloud effects on Puget Sound. His head, particularly on top, had received a generous dousing, and, what is more, the —— stuff refused to wash off, be scrubbed off, or even sand-papered, although liberal use was made, of all three methods. Now it was his custom to visit cabarets frequently, and, pursuant to habit, he unconsciously walked into the "American" the following Saturday night, and, after he got there, he remembered his pate and refused to remove his hat. After an argument with a waiter, he got up and left.

Ladies, whom he met on the streets, commented on his lack of courtesy. He was also a great booster in the Flynn Health Chautauqua, and, since he religiously practised what he called "Vegetarian-ism" (eating nice mild-cured salmon, howsumever, on the side, declaring that fish wasn't meat), he was booked for an address before the society. I'll never forget that night as long as I live.

In the first place, the chairman presiding was an elderly female whom, instinctively, as soon as you looked at, you'd hem and haw and expectantly wait for her to say, "And, in conclusion, my sisters. . . ."

WELL, anyhow, Charley sneaked up and sat down on the extreme back row, on the platform. (As he dealt in a business way with many of the members, he could not refuse to make his spiel.) After preliminary proceedings, during which he fidgeted and squirmed but still sat, with his hat on, the severe female at the desk arose and announced that Brother Westerman would deliver an address on "Lentils, Their Value as Food Units."

Charley half arose, then sat down again, cast a wild eye around for a possible means of escape, then, resignedly, he made his way, uncertainly, to the center of the stage, STILL WITH HIS HAT ON!

The Chairman looked at him, over her glasses, and pursed up her lips. I can not tell you with what mixed feelings I viewed that audience, for I knew they were in for either a surprise or a disappointment. Anyhow, he nervously cleared his throat and opened his mouth, when there was a sharp rap on the table, and the Lady Chairwoman suggested that "Brother Westerman come to order." He turned around, looked desperately at her and replied, "I'm in order!" and began again.

This time she positively glared at him (I realized then what Kipling meant by "the female of the species, etc.") and, louder, she said, "Would Brother Westerman please come to order AND REMOVE HIS HAT?"

Oh, boy, if I could only describe the conflicting emotions on that man's face! Since it's not in my power, Ill simply tell the finale. He replied again "I AM in order!" but the audience began to yell (the male and younger members at least) "Take it off! Take it off!"

Charley stood there, looking dumbly at them for a moment, then broke into a run for the rear exit. Just as he passed a fat man on one of the middle rows, that individual jumped up, grabbed his hat and snatched it from Westerman's head. Say, can you imagine the yell that went up?—PAUL A. STRACHAN.

OUR magazine has been read for nine years now and one of the things that should please all of us most is that there are so many who have been reading it since the first issue in October, 1910. And of these a large part seldom get more than a few numbers in any one place, for they do not stand still long at a time. Yet they make our magazine part of their regular program, and if they go where there are no magazines, they hunt for the missed issues when they get back. That is one of the reasons why it is so hard to find our magazine on the shelves of the second-hand dealers.

Have I ever told you that only three or four per cent. of our circulation is in subscriptions? And yet, at the times when the circulations of all magazines were falling off hard due to general conditions, our magazine held its own better than almost all the others. When a man joins us he generally sticks. And I think it is quite largely due to the fact that our magazine isn't just a magazine but is more than that—a kind of meeting-place for all of us who like the same kinds of things in life, a meeting-place that somehow brings us into a sort of fellowship among ourselves.

THAT, I judge, is why we have had to order a new supply of our Camp-Fire buttons. You haven't been writing for buttons just because you like the stories in a magazine but because you know that back of the magazine is this fellowship and that the button is a means of helping you recognize, when you happen to meet them, the others who belong to it, those whom you have heard at Camp-Fire or whose stories you have read or with whom you may have had an argument by letter over fire-arms or some Latin-American question or the Old West or some other discussion that has come up. And you are sure that, when you meet one of these men, he may be a very different kind from yourself but will just the same have certain interests in common with you and be worth meeting. He may be a physician or a brakeman, a sailor or a clerk, a college professor or one of our very own gentry of the wandering foot who may be anything else in the world besides. But you will have some things in common and will be glad to shake hands with each other, get acquainted and decide between yourselves just how far along the same road your common interests will carry you.

Those of you not yet familiar with our Camp-Fire buttons will find the data on our "Service Page" and learn that they carry nothing on their face except the number 71, which is obtained by assigning 1 to A, 2 to B, 3 to C and so on and then adding the numbers of the letters of the word "Camp-Fire."

WELL, I was talking about those of you who began with No. 1, Vol. I, and here is one of them. Like most of you, he "always reads 'Camp-Fire' first," as I would myself if I could pick it up off the stands without having read it before. Say, did you ever think of that little point? We here in the office, who are now Wade, Cox, Brace and Hoffman, and the compositors and proof-readers, are the only ones of all of us who can't ever pick up a copy of our magazine and carry it off for some hours of fresh reading. May be I shouldn't say it, but I call it sort of hard luck. Just as a reader I hunted a long time for something like our magazine when there wasn't any such thing, and then when it came into existence I had to be, by one chance out of many millions, one of the fellows who had to sit on the other side of the editorial desk and become unable to pick up a new copy and sit down to some new amusement the way the rest of you can. Well, if I'm ever fired I'll get that much out of it anyway, but I've lost nine years of it already. It may sound like tooting the magazine's horn, but it's true. Sympathize with me a bit and then I'll shut up and let this old-timer talk, an old-timer of only about thirty-one but with quite a bit to talk about just the same.

First saw the light of day in Colon, Panama, June 12, 1888. Father is Cavan County Irish. Mother is Muresco Spanish. (Both living). Lived on an English tramp of which dad was master and part owner. Visited every port of any importance from Petrograd to Rio and from Frisco to the ports of Japan and China, including the Philippines and Hawaiian Islands, Australia and New Zealand.

WENT to school in New Orleans and enlisted in U. S. Army and went to Ft. Wm. McKinley in the —— infantry. After time was out, enlisted in the U. S. Marines in Manila and was sent to Pekin and was a Legation Guard entire hitch. Discharged, came back to God's Country, enlisted in Coast Artillery, finished hitch there and took on four more in U. S. Navy, serving on a destroyer, one year as a gunner's mate after going through ordnance school, Newport, R. I. Later shanghaied to repair ship, then to transport fleet, made several trips to England, France and Italy (saw home of Christopher Columbus in Genoa.)

Transferred to 16-inch gun crew on navy gun mounted on railroad trucks, special design. Held this down until Armistice signed. No thrilling experiences in Navy except shooting up a Haitian town and starting an anti-native riot in Bocaroon, Cuba, during ship's stay in Guantanamo Bay.

TORPEDOED three times in North Sea; lay in freezing water nine hours off the Irish Coast. Had a young war with pro-German Irish in Queenstown, Ireland.

While on leave in Paris (December, 1917) traded uniforms with Highland soldier, fell overboard in Seine River while viewing a "Kultur-buzzard" brought down by French anti-air craft guns (Dec. 24th, 1917.) Also had the pleasure of testing machine-guns on rifle range, Guantanamo Bay,

Cuba, in which I became familiar with Beut-Mercier (Volcano) Lewis, Browning (heavy and light), Colt, Vickers-Maxim; Browning being best in all ways and under all conditions.

Also hold expert marksman medals under old and new Army regulations, with Krag-Jorgensen and Springfield rifles, also with Colt .45 new service revolver and .45 automatic Colt pistol.

At present am radio operator with a first-grade preferred license, also hold a marine engineer's license, second assistant, salt water unlimited tonnage and horsepower.

THIS letter is rather disjointed, to say the least, but guess you can put it all together. Served as artificer, Q. M. sergeant, top-sergeant in infantry; Electrician and master gunner, Coast Artillery; ordnance sergeant or rather gunnery sergeant in the Marines. Served as Captain National Guard in 1914-15. Gunner's mate, special mechanic 1st class, U. S. Navy (obtained marine engineer's license while in U. S. N.) Have had numerous close calls and have been shot at several times but happened to be too good a runner. Have been shot on several occasons. Fell over the side in Japan and just escaped being a meal for shark. Fell into a pen of alligators. These were close shaves, but they only added spice to the sauce of life, so to speak.

Well, I have run my course, so I will spill my mud-hook and pay out a long cable.

With best regards to all of the friends of *Adventure* and Camp-Fire, both old and new.— —— ——.

WE'VE already had a "close up" of our old friend *Magpie Simpkins* and here is one of his old side-kick *Ike Harper*, which same we are glad to see looking so cheerful and so forgetful of the many rough times he has passed through since we first met him. The drawing, of course, is from the hand of W. C. Tuttle.

NOT a chance! Will I find me a fine big boiling kettle of trouble and then with my eyes open deliberately crawl into it? No matrimonial agency for this magazine. Go away. And no lady who thinks she fills the exacting requirements of the comrade who wrote the following letter need address any letter in our care to "——." It sure won't reach him. He's asking for it, of course, and I'd like to help him and probably it would be all right in this one case, but how about the other cases that would immediately come to the fore? Nothing doing.

Our old "Wanted" department, which had to be given up after several years because two or three people put it to wrong uses, would be absolutely trouble-proof in comparison with any kind of attempt at matrimonial negotiations through our magazine. Oh no, nothing doing in *that* line!

But it's an interesting problem this letter presents and one that has, I know, confronted a good many of you at one time or another. Here's the letter. But no ladies need apply.

Mare Island, Calif.

During the several years I've been reading *Adventure* a great diversity of topics have been discussed in Camp-Fire. But, providing this gets into print, I think I'm going to spring a new subject, new, at least to Camp-Fire.

I remember the department of expeditions and employment that used to appear in *Adventure*, until it was found impracticable. And it seems hardly probable that *Adventure* could conduct or would care to conduct, a matrimonial department, because it would fail for reasons similar to those that affected the expedition department.

In an article published in Camp-Fire by a friend of Jack London's, after London's death, it was stated that London's married life had proved that one afflicted (or blessed) with the wanderlust could be happily married and still not have to stifle the craving for adventure and action.

There are doubtless among the readers of Camp-Fire a great many persons, both male and female, who find themselves in the same predicament that assails me. The wanderlust spirit is strong in me. I'm only twenty-six years old, but I've been pretty much on the go since I was seventeen, and there is no diminishing of the desire. Just about equally strong is the desire for a mate. That is natural, of course. But up to the present time I haven't succeeded in finding a woman with whom I think I could be happy. That is because I haven't found a woman who cares to live as I do.

Certainly I do not expect to have everything my

way, but what I'm looking for is a woman who likes the outdoor life and who is willing to travel, whether by Pullman or horseback, steamer or canoe or, if need be, do her thirty miles or better a day on foot. And at the same time I would like her to be equally at home in a lumber camp or a ballroom, and able to eat beans from a tin plate or eat soup correctly.

There are women who like to travel when there are no hardships attending, and there are women who can stand the hardships but wouldn't know what to do with an orange-wood stick. Surely there must be a happy combination of the two. And surely there must be other people looking for a similar combination.

And so it occurs to me that if *Adventure* could devise some method by which its readers might become acquainted that perhaps a great many people might find a solution to similar problems.— —— ——.

HOW many more of you can claim membership in all three American Legions —the original one started by us of the Camp-Fire in the Summer of 1914, the body of Americans at the front in the Canadian service before this country entered the war, and the final and permanent American Legion which is the new G. A. R. That is a proud claim and very few men in the world are entitled to make it, but just the same there are probably a few more of Camp-Fire who have the honor.

Camp "A," Palmer, Oregon.

I have just been reading your article about the "Three American Legions" and it suddenly dawned upon me that I happen to be one of the fortunate ones who can claim membership in all three of them.

I was enrolled as a member of your American Legion and then went to Canada and entered the Canadian service, serving more than two years in every grade from private to captain and then, too battered up for further use, was shipped back home, arriving in New York late in April, 1917. August 2, 1917, I was back in Uncle Sam's uniform (had had twenty years of it before) as a captain of a machine-gun outfit. Served as instructor in that branch and when the Small Arms Firing School was organized at Camp Perry went there as an instructor and remained until the closing of the school.

Tried many times to get back overseas but the "medicos" wouldn't stand for it.

Am now leading the simple life up on top of Larch Mountain and trying to learn something of the logging industry—one of the few things which I had overlooked during my twenty-five years of knocking around.

It may interest you to know that my identification-card No. 540 has been with me through a number of very strenuous years, including the Ypres, Somme and Arras campaigns.

If you happen to run across Edward Cave, kindly convey to him my good wishes and tell him that I am going to write him a letter some time.—HERBERT W. MCBRIDE.

FROM John A. Lomax comes word that he has received interesting letters from some of you in response to the call for old chanteys and sea-ballads that have not yet been collected and preserved in print. Any more of you who know some of these old songs? If so, won't you write to Mr. Lomax, Y. M. C. A. Building, Austin, Texas?

THE suggestion of gradually establishing Camp-Fire "stations" all over the world has aroused enthusiasm and we'll surely have to work out a way to do it and do it right.—A. S. H.

SOMETHING from our old comrade E. E. Harriman concerning Doc Middleton:

For the information and amusement of those who have been hunting up data concerning Doc Middleton I submit the following, gathered at Requa, at the mouth of the Klamath River on the evening of July five. This was told me by the brother-in-law of Jack Welch.

WHEN the head of Doc Middleton was worth one thousand dollars, hot or cold, to the man that brought it in, Jack Welch and Buck Taylor decided to win spending money by finding Doc and persuading him to lie down and be a good dog. They started out quietly, thinking that their object was unknown to any but themselves. They scouted a bit, then made camp one night and cooked their bacon.

They left their guns leaning against a tree and sat down to eat about six feet away. They had barely begun to dish up the bacon when a voice said, "Just move over about ten feet to the left."

They looked and saw a rifle looking at them from a bush and it had a terrible hole in the muzzle. They hesitated a second and the voice grew a little impatient.

"I wouldn't be slow about it either," it said and they moved. Then Doc Middleton came out of the brush, sat down by the fire, ate their nice hot bacon and frying-pan bread, laughed at them and told them to be careful not to hunt Doc again for "the kiotes might get you if you did."

He took all the shells they had and their guns, then told them the guns would be left about a mile away and departed. The boys made up their minds that there were many occupations more congenial for them than hunting Doc Middleton and they never made another attempt.—E. E. Harriman.

IN CONNECTION with his story beginning in this issue Hugh Pendexter gives us some interesting historical data:

Norway, Maine.

I have liberally consulted Alexander Henry's "Journal," edited by the late Dr. Elliott Coues, published by Francis Harper, 1897, for the color and atmosphere of this story. The notes supplied by this celebrated authority on early Western travel more than doubles the value of the "Journal."

HENRY was employed by the North West Company. He built a post at the confluence of the Park and the Red Rivers in 1800-01 and in the following year built the post at the mouth of the Pembina. He was at Pembina largely until 1808. The lower Red River department, of which he was in charge, extended throughout what is now North Dakota and Minnesota as well as north of the international boundary. He was at Pembina in 1804, whereas in my story I have him away and one, *Chabot* (fictitious character) in his place. He visited the Mandans and Minnetarees on the Missouri and the Knife Rivers in 1806, and it is from his journal of that trip, also from Lewis and Clark's Expedition, Chittenden's Am. Fur Trade, H. M. Brackenridge's journal of his Missouri trip in 1811, that I drew my pictures of the Mandans and their neighbors.

GEORGE CATLIN sketched and wrote about these Indians, but, as he was hopelessly pro-Indian and idealized them to the maximum degree, he proves untrustworthy, although his sketches, especially of the river and the village life, have their value. I have utilized the coming of Lewis and Clark in the latter part of the story as an agency operating upon the mind of Le Borgne, the one-eyed war chief of the Minnetarees. L. and C. were at the mouth of the Platte on July 26, 1804, and the news of their coming spread far and wide, and their meager force was increased by rumor into more than a hundred and fifty armed men. The expedition arrived at the Mandan villages in the later part of October.

THE North West Company was the strongest rival of the Hudson Bay Company. It grew out of the old French trade round the upper lakes, and at the end of the French and Indian War was under the control of some energetic Scotch traders of Montreal. These traders acted each for himself until 1783, when they formed the N. W. Co. This combine was made necessary by the shrinkage in profits due to the small-pox epidemic in 1782. The Pond, Pangman & Co., of Montreal, including (Sir) Alexander McKenzie was a rival to the N. W. Pond joined the N.W. Company. In 1787 the N.W. had absorbed this rival. After nearly a decade of great activities and much prosperity, the partners split. Simon McTavish represented one faction, Alexander McKenzie the other. The latter party organized the New N. W. Company, and was invariably known as the X. Y. Company. The only explanation of this name I have been able to find is that the new company took the next two letters following "W" in "N. W." If I remember correctly Chittenden suggests this. (See his "History of the Fur Trade" for details of history of various fur companies.)

Henry speaks of his employers as The "Gentlemen

of the North," and all traders were proud to be known as "Northmen." Henry, by the way, was in at the finish of Astor's Pacific Fur Company, when the N. W. ousted it from the Columbia.

Old Tabashaw was killed by a Sioux war party at Wild Rice River in early Winter of 1807. I have described this character much at Henry pictures him. Concerning the dead buffalos seen floating in the Red River each Spring, and in every western river where the buffalo roamed and ice formed, John McDonnell in his "Journal" says that in May, 1795, he counted 7,360 dead buffalo mired along the banks of the Qu' Appelle River.

The reader should not get the notion I've laid it on rather thick concerning the Indians' drinking bouts. Henry's diary of happenings contains repeated mention of these carousals, attended with horrible maiming and brutal killing, all given with a certain bold-blooded matter of course air. My descriptions of these tragedies are toned down until, compared with the original facts, they seem like some peaceful parlor entertainment.

ESHKEBUGECOSHE, or Flat Mouth, chief of the Pillager Chippewas, was born in 1774 and died in 1860. He was of the Awausee gens, and as a youth travelled and fought much. He lived with the Crees and the Assiniboins, and visited the Missouri tribes in peace and war several times. For some time he lived with the Minnetarees (Hidatsa-Siouan). He was one of Henry's hunters, and while he does not figure at all prominently in the work, history records him as being highly respected both by red and white. He was early impressed by the prophecies of The Skwatawa the Shawnee prophet and twin brother of Tecumseh. He is credited with influencing the Pillagers and other Chippewa bands to cease their practise of poisoning. He refused British wampum belts in 1812. He led the fighting against the Siouan tribes in contesting the matter of ownership of the headquarters of the Mississippi. He was about thirty years old at the time of this story.

LE BORGNE (called by Brackenridge, "The One-Eyed") is similarly described by various early travelers. His perpetual smile was one of his characteristics. According to Brackenridge the woman he killed was the wife of a young warrior, whom he had appropriated and who had returned to her husband. Her mother went mad and pursued Le Borgne as I have described. Henry's account of it pictures her as a young wife unfaithful to him, and makes no mention of the insane woman.

Choke-Cherry, Le Borgne's brother, had three sons, and I mention but one, Chief of the Wolves. Henry bought a batch of white robes and one skin on the Red River in one trade. The calfskin was marked with black round the right eye.

For the sake of speeding-up the action I have forced the coalition of the N. W. and the X. Y. companies a few months. The coalition was completed Nov. 5, 1804, and a Winter express brought word to Henry at the Pembina post Jan. 1, 1805. The combination was made possible by the death of Simon McTavish in July, 1804. Sir Alexander McKenzie, his implacable rival, now had no reason for not returning to the N. W. The new and stronger N. W. was absorbed by the H. B. in 1821.

The Indians I mentioned in the Red River part of the story were hunters for Henry. Black Cat and Big Man, at the lower Mandan villages, also were real characters. The legend of the Qu'Appelle was firmly believed in by Crees and Assiniboins.

Of course the Cheyenne River of the story is not to be confused with the Missouri's tributary of the same name.—HUGH PENDEXTER.

WHO knows about King John? It is Edgar Young asking and he has helped us out so many other times that I hope some of you can return the favor by giving some real facts on this interesting and perhaps mythical character.

I wonder if you could help me through the Camp-Fire in getting something definite about King John. I have heard of him all over South America, from Ecuador, Peru, Argentina and Brazil. According to current report he is a Spaniard, from Spain, who has made himself king of a large tribe of Indians somewhere on the eastern slope of the Andes, ruling them with an iron hand and forbidding entry to foreigners. I have heard so much that I am sure he is not a myth. What I want to know is: Who is this King John? Is he a Spaniard? Who was he in Spain? Why did he leave and how? And when? How did he get to be king? How do you get to his country? This is pure curiosity on my part and I am sure that some man will bob up who really knows something definite.—EDGAR YOUNG.

THE old Cossack, *Khlit*, has been a friend of ours for some time and now H. A. Lamb is introducing us to some new people whom I think you will also come to like. There are more of these tales to come and it may be that after a while *Khlit* may wander down and meet these new people himself. But not for quite a while.

Incidentally, how do you pronounce his name? I always sounded it as if it were spelled "Kleet," but Mr. Lamb tells me it should be pronounced with the "i" short—"Klitt." However, I've known him too long by the former sound and can't make the change comfortably.

A word from Mr. Lamb about these Moguls of the early seventeenth century:

New York.

Tales of *Abdul Dost* deal with the Moguls of India, in the early seventeenth century. Scene of "The Skull of Shirzad Mir" laid in northern hill country of Afghanistan.

AS FOR the skull in question. They were frequently made into drinking cups. A fashion of the time—to have an enemy chieftain's skull on exhibit, ornamented with gold or silver according to the wealth of the possessor.

There's a good deal of history in back of Abdul Dost's tales. Badakshan, home of *Shirzad Mir*, was the backbone of the Mogul kingdom before the great conquerors descended from the hills into

Hindustan and central India. Once in India, the Moguls never returned to their homeland; but they had a great fondness for Kabul and Kashmir, showing it was from politic rather than personal reasons that they favored Delhi and Agra over the hills.

IN THE time of *Abdul Dost* Jahangir was on the throne of India, and Jahangir did not match up to his two great forebears, Baber and Akbar. It was the old story of the fighting conqueror whose descendants became palace figureheads and ruled through women and eunuchs.

Baber was a man's man, and his memoirs are an unbroken tale of fighting, mostly against odds. He won the respect even of his Rajput enemy, Rajah Sanga, who must have been an experienced judge of fighters as he was blinded in one eye, without one arm, lame and with eighty other battle scars. Baber enjoyed picking up two men and carrying them, leaping across the battlements of a rampart. In his own words, the year before he died:

"I swam across the Ganges for amusement. I counted my strokes and found that I swam over in thirty-three; then I took my breath and swam back. I had crossed by swimming every river I met except (until then) the Ganges."

Akbar also was a fine strain of man; and Jahangir displayed flashes of his heritage of courage, will and humor. The Mogul was absolute owner of most of the land within the empire, and when Jahangir took the throne there was a general rush on the part of the *amirs* and *begs* to register their claims. It was a case of first heard, best rewarded. Likewise, the powers at court were of mixed nationality—Rajputs, Persians, Afghans, Uzbeks and Turki-Mohammedans. The Mogul couldn't afford to play favorites. Shirzad Mir was late.

SIR RALPH WEYAND I have drawn from the historical John Mildenhall, or Midnall. Mildenhall sailed from London for Syria in 1599, bearing a letter from Queen Elizabeth to the Mogul. Left Aleppo 1600 for Kandahar. Received at court at Agra about three years later. Portuguese intrigue defeated his efforts to gain trade *firman*. The Portuguese were then firmly dug in at Goa and Surat. They had valuable trade rights, and their priests were in favor at court (owing to the Moguls' policy to countenance every creed).

Mildenhall suspected his interpreter—probably with reason—of a fondness for Portuguese gold, and determined that he must be able to speak Persian in person. Learned Persian in six months, escaped poisoning by his enemies, put some of said enemies out of action, returned to court and argued his own case. Said the Moguls had received little hard cash—although the satellites of the throne had got much—and won his trade concession. The first, I think, granted to an Englishman.

Mildenhall's second chapter doesn't make such good reading. He was, as the chronicle has it, in "an exceeding great rage" at his enemies; bartered his concesssion somehow for money; got together a fortune of $120,000 after returning to Persia; later, changed his religion, turned rogue, and disappeared.

In order to keep the Englishman of the Abdul Dost tales clear of this second chapter, I've rechristened him Sir Weyand and set him on his own; but his adventures follow closely the first part of Mildenhall's career.—H. A. LAMB.

ADVENTURE'S younger brother, *Romance*, will make its appearance October 10th. I don't brag much about our own magazine at Camp-Fire (at least I hope I don't) and I'm not going to brag about its companion magazine, but I want you to give *Romance* the once-over and form your own judgment.

Along with Joseph Conrad, Harris Dickson, Norval Richardson and others you'll find some of the old stand-bys of our own writers' brigade and still others who have appeared in our pages at some time or other. The first number happens to have our writers particularly well represented and, though they will not always be so much to the fore in *Romance*, there will always probably be some of these old friends in every issue. W. Townend, S. B. H. Hurst, Gordon Young and Charles Beadle have stories in the first issue, and others, like William H. Hamby, Eugene P. Lyle, Jr., and Patrick Casey, who have not appeared so regularly in our magazine of late.

A lot of you have been kicking because *Adventure* doesn't appear every week instead of twice a month and I've an idea that the monthly appearance of *Romance* will go a long way toward quieting that kick. Try out Vol. I, No. 1, and decide for yourself whether you are going to be one of the pioneer old-timers on *Romance* as so many of you are proud of being on *Adventure*.

And I'll be glad if you'll give me your honest, straight-from-the-shoulder judgment on *Romance* after you've seen it—stories, decorations, cover and all.

THE following is an extract out of a letter from one of our writers' brigade who has given us as red-blooded, two-fisted, man's stories as any we've ever had in our magazine. He himself has the same characteristics as his stories. Like a good many of the rest of us, he is done with formal religious creeds and dogmas, but knows there is a God and is groping to find Him.

As to the military aspects of the case, well, isn't he right? All credit to our men and officers alike, *but* you can't train either officer or enlisted man thoroughly in the time we tried to do it, even with the best material in the world to work on. It wasn't training that carried our troops to victory, though what training they had was a necessary factor. It was something in the men themselves, and neither training nor equipment nor anything else can be a substitute for it.

—but as I came to the evidence of what Faith can do and has done, I read Paul's words "—through faith subdued kingdoms . . . wrought righteousness. . . . out of the weakness were made strong, waxed valiant in fight, turned to flight the armies of aliens." ! ! ! !

WAS ever a more colossal demonstration than the finish of the World War? America was the materialization of *faith in the might of right*—half-trained and half-led by half-trained officers those fresh-faced Yankee-Bohunk-and-what-not boys went over there chock-full of the subconscious conviction that the Hun was a foul thing to be expunged, saw the beast before them and just naturally went and *got* him. It's the universal testimony of all that veteran troops could never have put it over—would not have tried; but our polyglot doughboys didn't bother about possibilities or tactics, but with the sublime faith of fools and angels just naturally *did it!* Also it is the astounding truth that it was their glorious faith and pep that won the war—Morale! Call it what you will—war-stale Europe had run out of it—our boys were simply polluted with it, flooded those old fields, peopled with the ghosts of centuries of slaughters, with an inundation of the faith that is the essence of power, and God! Who knows what shining hosts marched with them through that stinking mud and wrought the World's Salvation?

I AM free to say that no sermons, no storied chronicles of miracles or monk-wrought spires have ever come so near to showing me the Light.

I don't know that I see it now, but I've had flashes, and am reverently thankful I am living in this age of mighty doings.

But where is our Paul, or Saul of Tarsus?

— —— ——.

A WORD from Robert J. Pearsall concerning his story in this issue:

Berkeley, Calif.

The custom which furnished me with the idea upon which I really built "Silver Sycees"—that of politely forcing a dishonest magistrate to be his own executioner by sending him a "suicide cord"—originated with the Manchus, and really passed with them. Indeed, like a great many other of the old customs, it waned rapidly after the death of the Empress Dowager, Tsi'an, in 1910—possibly partly because she had been so prodigal in dispensing those unwelcome tokens of her regard. There's no reason some of the recipients shouldn't have chosen a getaway instead of death—and, as a matter of history, some did. Also I might say that the Taoist priesthood in China is, taken in general, very much as I've indicated. Of course, there are good priests and bad priests; but I suppose there's no greater fall in the history of religion than that of Taoism. However, it's an influence that the modern Chinese are throwing off fast; and it's only in the western provinces that the Taoist hierarchy are still able to build their power on superstition and ignorance.—ROBERT J. PEARSALL.

THERE has been such enthusiastic response to the suggestion of establishing Camp-Fire stations all over the world that there can be no doubt as to the popularity of the idea. Not a single dissenting voice.

After reading carefully all the letters offering plans and suggestions, I'm going to piece together the outline of a fairly complete plan and then wait for your opinions on it as a whole. Look it over and let me know how you feel about any or all of it.

ESTABLISH as many stations as possible, not only in this country and Canada but all over the world, and keep adding new ones as time goes on, until a wayfaring comrade can find at least one or two of them clear out to the edges of civilization—and maybe beyond. That sounds like a big undertaking, but it isn't.

In the first place a station is not an elaborate affair, costs almost nothing, needs almost no space. It serves these simple but useful purposes:

(1) A mail address for traveling comrades.
(2) A place for getting in touch with other Camp-Fire comrades who may be traveling the same district.
(3) A place for learning the names and addresses of resident Camp-Fire comrades who want to meet wayfaring members.
(4) A place to leave brief bits of information or warning concerning trails, local changes or conditions.
(5) A meeting-place to be designated in advance by comrades traveling different routes.
(6) A registration place where comrades can leave messages or put on record the date of their arrival and departure, destination, route and similar data for the information of friends or acquaintances following after, or for purposes of record only.
(7) An informal local meeting-place for resident members.

NOW see how little is required to make these things possible; a box for letters, a blank record and register book and a sign hung up in front.

Any reputable shop or office can serve as a station. Some of you have already offered your own homes. The owner of course is in all cases the judge of the extent to which his place shall be used, but must furnish a box for letters and have accessible the register book and any names of resident members left with him. That and ordinary courteous treatment and fair dealing are all that is required of him. In return, if he is a shop-keeper he is probably assured of a certain amount of trade he would not get otherwise. Tobacco shops, drug stores, book stores and, in some countries, reputable cafés would seem particularly adapted to the purpose.

One of you has suggested the Y. M. C. A. branches. In private homes the return would lie in meeting wayfaring members to the extent the owner desired. A station is not a lounging place and the owner is sole judge of the amount of hospitality to be extended. Printed rules, furnished by the magazine, could be posted to avoid misunderstandings.

THE sign and register can probably be supplied from this office, since the magazine would incidentally receive advertising through the station system and the house would therefore be justified in expenditure to make the system possible. The sign would be either the Camp-Fire "coat-of-arms" or the design of its button. If the house furnished them, the name of our magazine would also appear.

Stations open to any one who claims to be a member of Camp-Fire—and any one is a member who wishes to be. No one need be an "imposter." And there is nothing but the simple services above outlined that he can get out of it, neither the owner nor any other member being under any obligation whatever to do anything else for him or even to talk with him. Under no circumstances is any member of Camp-Fire obligated by the station system to do any more for another member than he is at present, which is none at all. It remains always a matter of individual choice, barring, of course, the mail and register services of the stations.

No responsibility is assumed by any one for the safety or correct delivery of mail or packages. It is assumed that no one will volunteer for a station unless sufficiently interested to take care of the light duties and that members will use their own judgment as to leaving things for delivery at their own risk.

The register is to be used for brief entries, not for essays or autobiographies. Either names or Identification-Card numbers could be signed.

IF POSSIBLE a simple bulletin-board should be maintained. Residents could post their addresses with a brief statement of the extent of the hospitality they cared to offer, what kinds of wayfarer they were particularly interested in, etc. The board would serve also for trail-notes, tips on local conditions, etc., the owner being free to decline any notice he pleased. Also, to state exactly what is, and what is not, offered by that particular station.

A station may range all the way from a place for a brief, businesslike call to a local club-room for resident and wayfaring members. Reading matter, for both information and amusement, could be left there. There is no end to the development possible if desired by the owner and other resident members. Each station in such matters is a law unto itself.

ANY one can volunteer to provide a station. As many stations in a town as desired. So far as possible a list of them would be published in the magazine; later a small booklet directory could be issued at cost price. Sufficient complaint from members would be ground for discontinuing a station and the discontinuance would be published. (The magazine could not and should not be judge in such cases except in so far as its own interests might be jeopardized; State or district secretaries or boards could perhaps be chosen.) Protection lies in the fact that there is small incentive for any one to assume the light duties of a station unless he is willing to meet them. Also, our wayfarers are not lambs it is easy to fleece or bulldoze. A pledge to accept unquestioningly a discontinuance and to turn in book, mail and sign would be exacted in the beginning.

There's the rough outline. Now come ahead with criticisms and suggestions. Nothing is settled yet and now is the time to say your say.

Meanwhile, all of you ready to offer a place for a station send in the name and address, subject to change of mind if the final plan does not suit you. Please state the general nature of the place offered and give a rough idea of the extent of service and hospitality that would be offered.

It takes a good many words to present the case, but I think it is a simple one. And as easy as it is simple.

IN "PLAIN BLANKET INDIAN" you meet *Bull Judson* for the first time, but Mr. Pladwell arranged for your introduction in a story written before this one. Owing to the w. k. exigencies of laying out an issue, it happens that this later story reaches you first. Some day you'll read "A Teacher of Etiquette" and learn how *Bull Judson* first met up with Gila City. There were quite some doings on that occasion.

And now something as to Gila City itself:

Oakland, Calif.

I'd like to explain Gila City, since it has come to my memory that there is a town called Gila in western Arizona, some miles out of Yuma, and there is also a Gila Bend in central Arizona. It is needless to say, however, that neither of these towns is the city of marble and skyscrapers which appears in *Adventure*.

IT HAS been given me to travel extensively through the West. In this way I have seen many thriving cities and tried to learn their ways. The young Western city is a wonderful thing. You can think up a whole list—El Paso, Yuma, San Diego, Stockton, Fresno, Bakersfield and Reno among them—each a lively, forward-looking, happy, industrious commonwealth with a Board of Trade or a Chamber of Commerce to induce new settlers to share in their benefits, and a Real Estate Board to help them establish homes. They are as up-to-date as any Eastern city of four times the age. In fact, sometimes they are even up-to-dater. They are not bound by traditions.

And yet, among these modern communities, one can find traces of the old West, living alongside the new. It is a study in perpetual contrast.

It was not given me to know the old West, but I find I have learned somewhat the West in transition, with the old and new, perpetually in contrast, sometimes pitifully, sometimes ludicrously, and sometimes wonderfully. It has been therefore, my endeavor to write on things that I know about, and I have found this West as interesting and picturesque as the old must have been, and just as romantic.

I FIND this study in contrasts interesting. Perhaps it brings a new angle into things and persons already established in the public mind. To explain what I mean, take Geronimo, for instance. Here was the vilest old hellion that ever tortured a prisoner or burned a cabin—a grim figure of our Western history. When you think of Geronimo, you think of rifle-fire and bloood-lust and murder, a combination of brutality and picturesqueness.

And yet has it ever occured to any one that Geronimo, before his death and after he had languished in a Federal prison, paid his nickel to the street-car conductor, ate in a Dairy Lunch, put a coin in a phonograph and listened to the music, or skidded about in a taxi or fought with a laundryman because his shirt did not arrive on time? That is another Geronimo—and perhaps his actions in this environment were more interesting, more human, more pathetic, more ludicrous and perhaps more warlike than when he was burning ranches and shooting settlers.

AND so, in Gila City, I am attempting to bring out this new angle to the West, where the ultra-modern and the old-time customs flourish together, and where, perhaps, some old deputy sheriff tells of his gun-fight days to the operator of the wireless station on the site of what was once the sheriff's favorite saloon. The old West still flourishes as such, in places. Men still tote guns, in places. But forty miles from those places, wherever they are, there is probably an Automatic Lunch, a Movie Palace, and an agency for Ultra-plus Suits, made in Chicago and guaranteed to be much snappier than any tailored suit made.

I guess that explains Gila City. It is a symposium of El Paso, Yuma, Bakersfield, et al. In fact, a couple of Gila City stories are based on happenings in those communities. I did not wish to use the real towns because I have forgotten the details of the real towns and could easily be caught up on some misremembered street name or hotel or locality. Hence, Gila City.—E. S. PLADWELL.

MORE about snake-bites—a very interesting use of iodine, as both internal and external remedy. Not because I have any doubt that Mr. Major knows what he is talking about, but merely as a safe rule to follow in general, I want to make it clear that when opinions, recipes, remedies and suggestions are offered at Camp-Fire it does not mean that the magazine endorses them. We are gathered together to exchange opinions and ideas on things that interest us and when one of us talks *he* is talking, not the magazine. The magazine and its editor merely sit and listen like all the rest.

Mr. Major tells of a snake-bite remedy that sounds all right and his own sincerity is evidenced by his carrying iodine himself, but I take it he is merely offering his find for the benefit of Camp-Fire comrades and expecting them to use their own judgment in the matter. Probably it would be wise to get the O. K. of a good physician before trying any remedy in so vital a matter as snake-bite, though it must be borne in mind that most physicians will play safe by refusing to recommend anything of which they have not definite, personal knowledge. Can any of our physician comrades pass on this particular remedy?

Prescott, Arizona.

I have read with much interest the article on American venomous snakes and directions for the treatment of snake-bite and it occurred to me that a simple and easily used remedy might not be an unacceptable addition to what you have already given your readers.

SOME years ago I read an article stating that a doctor with many years' experience in India had successfully used iodine for the treatment of the bites of the cobra and other venomous serpents found there, and that the same thing had been found very effective in the treatment of rattlesnake bite. I copied it, and now, whenever I am in the field, I always carry a small bottle of a strong tincture of iodine, as well as permanganate of potassium crystals, strychnine and nitroglycerine in 1-100-grain pills. The strychnine and nitroglycerine are for the heart, as you are aware. Here is the application of the iodine:

Take internally seven drops of tincture of iodine on sugar. Repeat in one hour. It may be necessary to take more than only two doses. Scarify wound and bathe with a solution of iodine. A tourniquet to stop circulation and the pressing, or sucking, out the blood and contained poison, the same as would ordinarily be done, is also advised.

This is simple, is easily remembered and is easily taken.

The nitroglycerine is to stimulate the heart action the same as the strychnine. It may be taken in 1-50-grain doses at one or two hour intervals, as needed, then reduced.

Glad to see that Mr. Ditmars authoritatively corroborates my previous statement to you that your old friend G. M. is venomous. I have known that to be a fact without question.—CHAS. EDWARD MAJOR.

WILL some of the archeologists among us throw some light on this ancient village whose remains were found by Mr. Brown and his party?

And Mr. Brown adds something about Pat Garrett and Billy the Kid. There are many versions of the capture of the Kid but there is, I think, no doubt as to the fact of Garrett's death.

Chicago.

A number of years ago I was a member of a surveying party, running the lines for the Pecos Valley Railway in southern New Mexico. The Pecos River follows what is evidently an ancient river-bed, a flat-bottom valley ranging from one-half to five or six miles wide, bordered on each side with a mesa or highland fifty to one hundred feet above the valley.

ONE Sunday afternoon four or five of the members of the surveying party were exploring the country around the camp. Wandering along the edge of this mesa one of the boys stepped into a hole, and a hole in such a locality arousing our curiosity, we stopped to investigate it.

We found it to be a circular depression about two feet across and ten or twelve inches deep, with no opening in the bottom. This seemed very odd to us, so we pulled out the grass, dug out two or three inches of dirt and found that our depression was lined with round flint boulders about the size of your fist. In the bottom we found some small fragments of charcoal, from which we deduced that this had once been a fireplace. Still more interested, we cleaned the grass and dirt off around the fireplace and found that the ground for a space of about ten by twelve or fourteen feet around was also paved with the same kind of boulders and that at each corner and in the center on each side there was a sort of soft spot in the ground just outside of the paved space. Digging down into the soft spots fifteen or eighteen inches below the surface of the ground, we found small pieces of rotten wood but were unable to determine the variety. From this we concluded that at one time there had been six posts set up with some sort of a superstructure resting on them for a roof, and perhaps side walls attached.

AS THE soil in this section is a soft loam with a considerable proportion of gypsum mixed in, there are no stones or boulders to be found. Even along the Pecos River, which cuts straight down into this soft soil, you can go for miles without finding any stones. Later we searched the country for eight or ten miles around there without finding any boulders at all like those used for the paving.

Continuing our investigations, we found that there was a regular hamlet laid out there consisting of some twenty houses arranged about thirty feet apart, on each side of a central paved street, with a paved path leading from each house to the street.

There was no timber within fifty miles of this place that would be large enough to make the posts. We found a few imperfect arrow-heads and some small fragments of pottery but not a particle of wood nor any trace of the walls or roofs from which we believed that this village must have been built there one hundred or more years ago.

IN ONE of the recent issues, I read with interest an account of the life, adventures and death of "Billy the Kid."

I was quite well acquainted with Sheriff Pat Garrett, as I was in Lincoln County, New Mexico, while he was sheriff and on several occasions served as his deputy. I have heard from his own lips the account of his *pursuits* of Billy the Kid and of his final and successful raid and the manner in which Billy the Kid was killed, and my recollection of it does not agree at all with the account published.

Pat Garrett was appointed Collector of the Port of El Paso, Texas, by President Roosevelt and is, so far as I know, still living and I would suggest that you get his own account of the demise of "Billy the Kid."—H. W. BROWN.

FROM W. E. Carpenter, Inspector of Police Bureau, Montreal, comes an invitation to us, which, when I first read it, made me grin, thinking perhaps Inspector Carpenter was having his little joke on us. But on second thought I realized he was speaking, not as a member of the police, but merely as a man and Camp-Fire comrade. He wrote in for his Camp-Fire button. The remainder of his letter follows and, I, for one, will surely look him up if ever I get to Montreal, and hope he'll drop in on me if he strikes New York.

Montreal.

This also gives me an opportunity to extend an invitation to all members of the Camp-Fire to call on me any time that they happen to be in Montreal. I may state that Chicago is my home, but have been here since November, 1916, joining the police force a few months later. Will be pleased to have any member call on me, and especially Chicago ones. I was on the beat for a short while, but for the past two years I am in the Inspectors Bureau from 9 A.M. till 5 P.M., where I can be seen any time, and if preferred, they can call up Main 3500 on their arrival, and I will be pleased to meet them any place.—W. E. CARPENTER.

Our Camp-Fire came into being May 5, 1912, with our June issue, and since then its fire has never died down. Many have gathered about it and they are of all classes **and degrees, high and low, rich and poor,** adventurers and stay-at-homes, and from all **parts of the earth. Some whose** voices we used to know have taken the Long Trail **and are heard no more, but they are** still memories among us, and new voices are **heard, and welcomed.**

We are drawn together by a common liking for the strong, clean things of out-of-doors, for word from the earth's far places, for man in action instead of caged by circumstance. The *spirit* of adventure lives in all men; the rest is chance.

But something besides a common interest holds us together. Somehow a real com**radeship has grown up among us. Men** can not thus meet and talk together without **growing into friendlier relations; many a time** does one of us come to the rest for facts **and guidance: many a close personal** friendship has our Camp-Fire built up between **two men who had never met; often** has it proved an open sesame between strangers **in a far land.**

Perhaps our Camp-Fire is even a little more. Perhaps it is a bit of leaven working **gently among those of different station** toward the fuller and more human understand**ing and sympathy that will some day bring** to man the real democracy and brotherhood **he seeks.** Few indeed are the agencies that bring together on a friendly footing so many **and such great extremes as here.** And we are numbered by the hundred thousand now.

If you are come to our Camp-Fire for the first time and find you like the things we like, join us and find yourself very welcome. There is no obligation except ordinary **manliness, no forms or ceremonies, no dues,** no officers, no anything except men and **women gathered for interest and friendliness.** Your desire to join makes you a member.

WE HAVE already had one reply to the inquiry about the ancient ruins of Zululand and now here is an interesting letter along the same lines but centering on other African ruins:

Wheatridge, Colo.

I read W. C. Roberts letters of inquiry with special interest, as it recalled a trip I made through Matabeleland and Mashonaland some years ago. In answer I would say that I know nothing of ruins in Zululand, but over the Plateau of Southern Matabeleland and Mashonaland from Tate to Dhlodholo situated in the Mattoppo Hills about fifty miles southeast of Bulawayo to Fort Victoria are ruins, walls and ancient mining shafts, a few of which I have seen.

THE largest of these, the Zimbabwer ruins, is about fifteen miles from Fort Victoria. It consists of a large round *solid* tower about forty feet high within a circular wall fifteen feet thick near the ground, tapering off at the top to about seven feet. This wall is at least thirty feet high and constructed of roughly chipped granite of a uniform size, about six inches high and twelve inches long, laid upon one another without cement or mortar of any kind. I understand that the towers in other ruins, as in this one, are perfectly solid.

Soap-stone hawks on pedestals were discovered in the ruins; also fragments of bowls with hunting scenes depicted on them. These have been removed to Cape Town Museum. The general impression is that these are of Semitic origin, probably Phenician. The Makalangar natives of that district have a distinctly Arab cast of countenance, having the arched noses and thin lips rarely seen in the Kaffirs. If the natives have any traditions as to the origin of these ruins they keep it to themselves and are in great fear of ghosts.

THE Dhlodholo ruins, though vastly interesting, are not as large as the Zimbabwer. The walls are about twenty feet high.

North of Bulawayo I found a few gold beads in some ruins. It was sixteen years ago since I was through that country and archeologists have in all probability found some clue as to their origin.

I have sometimes wondered if there could be any connection between the soap-stone hawks of the Zimbabwer and the Egyptian goddess Hathor, whose emblem was a hawk and the special goddess of mines.

I don't mean to infer that these crude buildings are of Egyptian origin. But might they not have been built by a servile race who had adopted their religion in part? Just conjecture, that's all.—A. H. GRICOURT.

FROM Thomas McMorrow a word or two concerning his story in this issue:

New York.

I can not put down here a reasoned statement of the causes of "Tub o' Lard." Stories are not written from rigid premises, are they? But I remember *Tub o' Lard's* garden very well. I leaned on its mossy gate and studied its recesses one evening this Spring. I was looking for a bad man who was A. W. O. L. from his regiment and was lying out somewhere along the river. I remember the tremendous stone wall which hedged the garden, a wall that might have turned the stroke of a seventy-five, and the circling paths and flower-beds—no foot of it all but had been lovingly contrived, and the dappled sheet of river that lapped its further side.

IN AMERICA we don't know how to live. We are busy piling up the raw materials, the wealth and the station, tomorrow we will raise an elegant and spacious edifice, and we die in harness and have not joined the first stones of our House of Life. But the French aren't builders. They live contentedly in the gray homes of their fathers. Change agitates them. They have reduced life to a working equation, and do not want to change its terms. They are not adventurers. They pour into your laboring ear a tale of discontent until you ask, "Then you are Bolshevist here?" "No, no, monsieur, we are anti-militarist." Their discontent is with the prospect of change!

So also they like their human relations fixed. They want to know what to think of people. They abhor fluidity. Thus a Boche is a Boche. "But our American Boches have stood by our Government. The American Army has many Boches, and they have been good soldiers." "Do not trust them, monsieur: a Boche is a Boche."

That's about the idea. If there is a more concrete cause of "Tub o' Lard" it is then in the old wife's tales that Madame Mathieu told me as I sat in her dark kitchen of mornings and watched her draw roast rabbits and heaps of laundry and pails of hot water and puddings and such trifles out of a wood-stove as big as the ordinary magician's hat.—THOS. McMORROW.

AN INTERESTING letter, this. I've written to the men he mentions but as yet have had no reply. In several places a dash is substituted for a proper name. The writer is referring to the short article by E. A. Brininstool.

Among other things, I'll admit I was much surprised to learn I had met Billy the Kid in the pages of "Ben Hur" years before I ever heard of him under his workaday name.

U. S. S. *Beaufort*.

Just finished reading the article "Billy the Kid" and certain things in it do not coincide with what I learned of him when I was a boy in New Mexico.

FOR instance, I always heard he was a Tennesseean, born in that State. Again, in the article in question, one would infer that Billy was as black-hearted as they are made. His killing the second guard with a shotgun from the window and the salutary phrase he used are again misapplicable in morality. This guard had been in the habit of befouling Billy's food in a most detestable manner and I have heard that Billy told him just before he shot him that never again would he have the opportunity to commit again the indignities he had perpetrated. Furthermore, the first thing Billy did, when free, was to demand food.

GARRETT, again, was hid from view behind the bedstead and the Kid never saw him till he was almost on top of him. The Kid then turned to his Mexican friends and had got as far as "Who is this?" (speaking in Spanish) when Garrett shot him. The reputation Garrett then earned for unethical gun-play later cost him his life. Garrett tried to collect the full reward for Billy's life but never did, as old General Lew Wallace, who respected the Kid, saw to that.

Your correspondent does not mention that Lew Wallace advertised in all New Mexico papers for Billy to come and see him, which the Kid did and also explained away many lies which had been told of him. Wallace busied himself immediately revoking the territorial reward offered for Billy, "Dead or Alive." It might interest you to know that one of the better characters in "Ben Hur" is a portrayal of Billy in a different atmosphere.

You might write a man named Phillips who lives on a ranch three miles from Alamogordo, N. M., for information. Phillips was a deputy U. S. Marshal just about that time and was, at one time, in a position to arrest Black Jack Ketchem had he known he was wanted.

Also write Oliver M. Lee, of ——, N. M. Lee could give you the straight facts in this case, for while Billy worked for the Chisholms, still the Chisholms were one of the three big cattle men who divided the districts known as the Miller, Chisholm and Lee interests. Chisholm had the Pecos Valley and Lee the Sacramento Valley.

—— could tell a lot, if he wanted, for he was sufficiently mixed up in the Lincoln County War to be immensely relieved when Judge Shepherd disappeared the day after staying at the Pelman ranch. Nothing was found of the Judge's rig but a burnt wheel, and —— himself says he knows nothing about it and the Judge's disappearance is a mystery to him. Shepherd had the documentary evidence on him at the time of his disappearance which was said to be sufficient to hang many, he being on his way to Santa Fé from Lincoln.

—— killed two men while I was there and the tale of one of the attempts to arrest him for the death of one of the men is almost hilarious. Caught at a disadvantage, —— recovered his gun, drove the Deputy under a galvanized water-tank where the

Deputy hid in some dog burrows, and —— then shot the tank full of holes and let 50,000 gallons of water trickle into the holes, the Deputy up to his neck in water and afraid to show his head, while —— went to Alamogordo, surrendered, was bailed, and then returned. These men can give you the facts.—G. B. WILLMAN, Lt. U. S. N. R. F.

HOW do you feel about this suggestion? The use of such words as "How" or "Bayete" would lose value in the regions where they are used for ordinary purposes. The whole idea of a password and grip is up to you.

New York.

Re the "Armorial bearings" of "The House of Adventure," you ask: "Does it get by?" I should say rather. Personally I think it a ripping idea, and the design A 1.

HOW about a password for use when two "comrades" wearing the "71" button meet? To me this would add color to the Camp-Fire camaraderie, as a man might lose his button and it might be found by some one not "of" the clan. This finder might be a delicatessen-store clerk with about as much adventure in him as a tape-worm, and this would take the exclusiveness (that somehow exists despite the fact that there are no dues, no ceremonies of admission, etc.) away from our Camp-Fire.

I suggest something on the order of the Elks' countersign of "Hello Bill,"—say: "Hello Comrade." This is a little used expression, comrade, these days. You might even use some aboriginal greeting of some kind like the Indian "How." To this one might add "Comrade," thus making "How Comrade." Again, we could use the Zulu's royal salute, "Bayete." I don't know whether I have spelled this right or not, you might ask Thomas S. Miller about that.

How about some grip or other, or an unusual hand-shake, say, both chaps putting their right hand on each other's left shoulder, or shaking with the left hand instead of the right?

Of course all this may be screamingly funny and childish, but, dash-it-all, the Masons, I believe, have "stuff" like this, so why not the comrades of the "Camp-Fire"?—LAMBERT TERRY.

SOME time ago we heard W 216 say some interesting things about tropical colonies. Now here is something from Edgar Young on the same subject, differing, as you will see, on a number of points.

I'm no authority on Latin-American colonies but I'm very sure on one point, which Mr. Young also brings out: Before you even make any definite plans apply to the Pan-American Union and others of the very best and surest authorities for guidance on all points. Unless you are pretty thoroughly familiar with Latin-American conditions—and perhaps even if you are—you don't know the colonizing game down there and it's always wise to know any game before you play it. And a game down there is generally not the same as the same game up here.

Brooklyn.

In 1916 the United Fruit Company owned and leased a total of 1,200,450 acres of ground, were operating 2,932 miles of railway and 1,042 miles of tramway. They owned 18,039 head of cattle, 6,009 head of horses, asses and mules, had $50,765,-234.17 (book cost) invested in houses and lands and equipment, had 23 ships in active service. Their earnings from bananas and miscellaneous tropical products (pineapples, citrus fruits, coconuts, cocoa, rubber, etc.) was $8,584,951.85 and from sugar $4,758,034.62, making a total of $13,342,986.47 net income for 1916. The land they had under cultivation was 246,679, and the unimproved 953,771, acres. These statistics were sent me by Mr. Minor C. Keith and are contained in the Seventeenth Annual Report and dated Sept. 30, 1916. I have no doubt they have made as great strides during the past two years as they did the two previous ones before this report, unless the taking of their ships for war use has put them back temporarily.

MR. EARLEY VERNON WILCOX, of the U. S. Department of Agriculture, states in his book "Tropical Agriculture," New York, D. Appleton & Company, 1916, page 37, "In Porto Rico, white men working cooperatively have developed a $3,000,000 fruit industry from nothing in a period of ten years. Moreover, white colonies of fruit and truck growers are prospering in Cuba, particularly in La Gloria, Herradura, and Isle of Pines." This entire chapter which is headed *Economic and Social Conditions* is well worth reading, and, for that matter, the entire book, while dealing particularly with the eastern tropics, is of great use to a man thinking of settling in the tropics of any country. In his bibliography he mentions forty-one other books on the subject he has consulted and a great number of periodicals mostly published in various places in the tropics.

From the two instances I mentioned in the second paragraph, which are not the only ones by any means, it is to be seen that farming the tropics both cooperatively and by stock companies pays big money. The list of companies that have arisen and sold stock and fleeced the public, and the number of cooperative colonies that have failed, are numerous. I suppose it's about like success in all other lines of endeavor. I have heard, but will not vouch for the truth of the statement, that the United Fruit Company was originally started with some money derived from gold that was dug from an old Chiriqui graveyard in Costa Rica. It is within my own tropical experience when it was a struggling little company.

MY CANDID belief is that a company centering on pineapples in Central America could within a few years put the Hawaiian companies out of business, due to two reasons: nearer to market and better pines. The quality of Central American and Panamanian pines is proverbial. Any old canal digger who has been to Toboga Island can vouch for this statement. It is also my candid belief that a company engaging in banana culture in Central America will go broke, for the power of the big business is very great and it is a power in Central American politics that is not to be sneezed at. There are also many unexploited fields that are open such as drugs, tans and dies, spices and flavorings, perfumes, oils, gums, etc., which have been exploited in the Eastern tropics, as well as fiber-producing plants, beverages, tobacco, and many thousand fruits that are delicious but are unknown in this country. The bottom has dropped out of rubber, due to the plantation rubber being raised in the East by British planters, from a few Hevea seeds that were smuggled out of Brazil under false pretenses about forty years ago. They are raising the highest grade of Para rubber on these plantations. Anything that has been done by the Eastern British planters can be duplicated in Central America, and can be exceeded, for Central America is a better climate than India. I have seen black pepper and spices growing on an American farm within a few miles of the canal zone in the republic of Panama.

PEACHES, apples, and other American fruits act peculiarly at sea-level in the tropics but do well at altitudes of from 5,000 feet up. Also American cattle, horses and poultry do not thrive when first imported. An improvement of the native breeds is a better idea. Chickens imported into Panama refused to lay an egg. A man a few years ago went through the tropics buying the best native breeds and at last accounts had 60,000 in Panama which were doing good laying. The best of milk cattle do not give the quantity of milk they do here and the second generation do not grow so large, but the native breeds seem to thrive. My own opinion is that either the zebu or goat is a better milk animal. While in Brazil I noted that the native cattle growers were crossing about a quarter zebu blood through their cattle to avoid native fevers. Pure zebu meat is strong and smells rank, but a quarter-blood is not noticeable.

IT ALL comes to the same thing. A man should read up and find out what has already been proven concerning tropical agriculture before he tries his hand at it and the British methods in India and the American methods in Hawaii are the best ones for him to look into, for he will learn little from the native Central American farmer who is tilling the soil after the Indian methods of his ancestors with a machete, a crooked stick for a plow, and getting his products to market on his own or his peons' back. This does not mean the German, American and English farmers who have settled in these countries, who are farming according to what they have found out was the best way for them. I saw many of them as I walked through the various countries.

Some of these started in on as little as four hundred *billetes* (twenty dollars), got a little patch of ground and got a thatched hut on it and then began hiring the natives to work for them. Wages vary for farm labor. We paid our laborers on the National Railways of Nicaragua between fifteen and twenty-one cents per day and they boarded themselves. We paid locomotive engineers and conductors twenty-four dollars, and telegraph operators and agents from twelve to sixteen dollars American gold per month. This was in 1914 and I do not know what they are paying now. I would say that farm labor as a general thing all over Central America would not average over twenty-five cents per day and would run less if the old rule of giving each family their sack of beans per month was held to. The United Fruit pays top wages to the negroes they import from the West Indies and I believe pay as much as one dollar per day in some places, which is many times more than the negro is used to at home. Any man who labors in the fields is of lower caste and I fail to see why an American should go down there and get out and work except as foreman or manager of the natives when they work so cheap. By doing so he would lose caste in the eyes of the native laborers and native well-to-dos. I am sure I would not do it. I once had a pretty fair four-room house and kitchen built for forty dollars American money. It was thatched on top and the walls were woven of bamboo. I wasn't farming at the time and just had it built to have a quiet place to stay.

I WAS raised on a farm in Virginia and have done quite a bit of farm labor, have worked through the harvest in our own West and in the Argentine, and have been foreman on tropical cane plantations, and have walked through many miles of banana plantations, as well as watching natives farming as I paused to rest when I was traveling, and have worked on many railroads that handled farm products as freight, and after all this I would not know what to say in regard to a tropical colony, except to keep out of low swampy country such as the colonies occupied at Pachuca, Gracias a Dios and San Juan del Norte. Any man who tried to establish a colony of white people on the Mosquito Coast was a fool for the want of sense. The Mosquito Coast (which is not called that on account of the insect *mosquito* but from the name the Spaniards gave the native Indians) runs from Yucatan to Panama and is low and unhealthy, and until it is cleaned up as Colon has been, or as the United Fruit Company cleans up their camps, is no fit place for white men. The town Matagalpa he mentions is on the railroad I was auditor for and is a healthy place. As far as that is concerned the coast of Mexico is the same. A white man does not thrive in a low, swampy, humid place until it has been drained and sanitated, for the mosquitoes keep him full of malaria.

ONE would not speak of Mexico City being enervating if he had ever been there, especially if he was there during the Winter, and a comparison of the temperature of Mexico City with any of our cities will show it to be a better temperature and with less variation than anything we have. Strawberries are for sale every day of the year in Guadalajara. Mazatlan, Guaymas, Salina Cruz, Vera Cruz, San Geronimo, etc., which are on the coast, are enervating, although the temperature rarely exceeds 85° F. And the nights at Mazatlan and Guaymas are cool enough to call for blankets the year round.

Roughly speaking, the temperature falls four degrees for every 1,000 of ascent up the mountains. (Bogota, Colombia, has the most even climate in the world. It's average temperature the year round is 60° F.) This fact holds good all along the high plateau and mountain chain that extends from end to end of Central America, Excellent climates are to be found in San José, C. R., Tegucigalpa, Honduras, the *pueblos* of Nicaragua between Managua and Granada,

Guatemala City, and all the towns, cities and places of the higher country. There are parts of all the Central American countries where mosquitoes are almost unknown. The Pacific side of all Central America averages about half the rainfall of the Atlantic side, even in so short a distance as that between Panama and Colon, and both places are at sea-level. Incidentally there are places in the republic of Panama where the climate is excellent and where cool weather may be found. A good account of tropical climate is given in Chapter I of Mr. Wilcox's book, which is much better than I can give here; also good accounts are given in the monographs distributed by the Pan-American Union, of Washington, D. C. I am quoting both these sources as authentic, both being a part of the U. S. Government and written with no ulterior motive.

ANY Central American country would welcome and help a colony of American farmers. In fact they are doing all they can do to get American farmers interested in their countries. Due to the many frauds that have been put across on the Americans by sharks of various degrees of crookedness, I think the best manner to start a project of this kind would be through the Pan-American Union direct with the Government of the country selected, and in this manner guarantee titles to land, or through some company like Brown Bros. & Seligman, who own a half interest in the National Railways of Nicaragua, run the banks of the country, and own large holdings of property, or other company. I do not know the sentiments of the United Fruit Company on this score, but most of their land is low lying and needed for the purpose they are using it.

I am sure a query from a party large enough to colonize any great tract of land would be taken up by the Pan-American Union and acted upon. They are in touch with conditions at all times and have men on the ground down there who could help anything they backed. This society is what the author meant by the Bureau of Pan-American Republics. It would also be best to get the ideas of their experts on any place and any project intended and act along the lines they suggested. I would much rather suggest them than any individual or set of individuals for fear some one would bob up and do a bit of trimming the unwary. Of course Brown Bros. & Seligman are reliable if they should wish to father a colonization scheme on their holdings.

SO FAR as Mexican colonization is concerned I have seen most all of them at first hand and some of them have done, or were doing, well, before the revolution. I was there during the revolution but have not been back since and do not know how they fared. The Mormons were good colonizers and there were two prosperous colonies located on the Vera Cruz and Pacific Railway and one on the Pan-Americano, south of Tehauntepec. The Mormons go right into it on a native basis and without the speech would be taken for peons.

W. 216 mentions crops and *live stock* being different from ours. Crops are different as to most things, with the exception of some of our cereals, but live stock consists of horses, cattle, sheep and goats, as well as razor-back hogs. India has different cattle, but not our own tropics.

CONCERNING Rex Beach, I suppose Rex would draw the long bow in fiction to make a point, like all the rest of us, but I am pretty sure if he made the statement attributed to him that it was a slip of the pen. I met Mr. Beach at Gatun and at the time he had a tapir's head he had cut from an animal killed by him back in the jungles with a body of Gatun sportsmen. I talked with him for some time, seated on a baggage-truck, concerning the trip I had made overland and he wanted me to go back the same way with him. He was in Panama for some time and I am sure he saw enough banana bushes and rubber trees (in the park in Ancon if nowhere else) to know the difference.

All the colonies W. 216 mentions failed on the Mosquito Coast and well they might.

Compare the death rate of tropical America with that of England, France, and this country per 1,000. About the same per cent.

Bosh! about going in large parties. I am sure that is just the way *I* wouldn't go. What for? As for the *strong* handling the *weak* in a colony of 100, what method are they going to use to enforce discipline, and who is going to back them? The strong and the weak are relative terms and mean nothing until the draw-bar pull of the part of a man's anatomy above the eyes can be measured, and there is no known machine for the purpose yet. Houses should be in line. We are farming and a man should live on his ground, or hire some one else to live on it, and the line would be a long one provided there were many colonists and they had many acres. Live on the ground, say I, and build straw ranchos for Juan and Pedro, Jesus, José, Pancho, Maria and Concha.

My last opinion is that the ideas of W. 216 are a bit hazy.

MARKETING is what put many people on the Isle of Pines out of business. A colony should be large enough to charter their own ship to market direct with this country or raise something they can can and ship when they have a cargo. The methods of the United Fruit on a small scale would succeed. So far as making a living is concerned a man can get that with a bare machete from the day he lands, but money-making means getting the stuff to market and the native markets in Central America, with the exception of Panama, are not very good. South America has much better native markets as a rule. I scarcely think the United Fruit would cooperate with any colony. I use the word "colony" for want of a better one, for I am thinking all the time of independent owners employing native and black help.

I guess that's about all I can crowd into a letter. The opinions of *Adventure's* readers might prove interesting.—EDGAR YOUNG.

WE HAVE met *Zari* in other tales and we already know that L. Patrick Greene knows Africa at first-hand. A word from him in connection with his story in this issue:

Boston.

It might be of interest to the Camp-Fire folks to know that I actually witnessed a "healing" such as I have described in this story. The patient was a native who appeared to be in a very bad way. He had a very high fever and was without doubt on the border of the "land of the Spirits of the Great Great." The witch doctor went through a much more elaborate performance than the one I have described, before giving his patient the magic potion. But, be that as it may, it is a fact that from the time he took the medicine, or (as the witch doctor would have it) from the time the evil spirit was extracted, the man began to get better. The bone was, I remember, the lucky-bone of a chicken!

In the interests of truth I am compelled to add that this particular witch doctor was a "bad actor," and he was afterward sentenced to a long term of imprisonment for attempting to poison one of his patients who had offended him.—L. PATRICK GREENE.

REMEMBER the pictures of a sword in Camp-Fire some months ago—a small sword that my friend Robert J. Smith found in a junk-shop in Piqua, Ohio, back about 1901 and gave to me? Neither he nor I nor any of the numerous people who had seen it during some eighteen years was able to identify it in any way, or even the country or continent from which it came. But Camp-Fire turned the trick at the first try.

After writing me, Mr. Reisenberg, who is a well-known expert on tropical products, came in to see the weapon personally, examined it under a lens and pronounced it undoubtedly genuine.

Does any of you, by any long chance, know how it got into that Piqua shop?

And now Mr. Reisenberg asks a question in his turn. Is there among us any one of the twenty-five men he took on board the *Maria P.* at Kingston, Jamaica, about 1883 or 1884?

Also is there among us any one of the officers and Annapolis naval students who, on a U. S. surveying vessel in the Gulf of Mexico, once gave the *Maria P.* her exact position, as explained in his letter?

New York.

Your sword of which you write and give cut should be very valuable and I would like to see it, to give a better history perhaps than I can write. The small flowers are Edelweis and the large mountain roses which grow on a higher elevation—and smell (the Edelweis does not)—from Salzkammergut through the Tyrol and Carpathians in extinct Austria-Hungary. The word "Bandur" goes far back before the great Napoleon and is connected with the history of Andreas Hofer, the great Tyrolian Patriot who was shot in Mantua, Italy—sacrificed by the then reigning Emperor Francis of Austria.

THE meaning of "Bandur" carried a classification of liberators or fighters of foreign enemies and originally came from Hungary, which especially the figure refers to, with leather (chamois skin) breeches, tiger pelt and the old bow and arrow (similar to those the archers used) and the stiff leather breast-plate. You will find the handle end to be a chamois hoof.

The figure itself dates still further back, more to the time of Maria Theresa, Empress of Austria-Hungary, when the Honveds of Hungary and the Banduren with the help of the Russians saved her from the Turkish invasion. The Banduren were not exactly a class or tribe or association as we have today, but can be likened to our pioneers in this country (for defense against the Indians), choosing their leaders for the time being and retaining their title of Bandur.

"Vivat" is a true original Austrian expression condensed and meaning "Hip, Hip, Hurray!"

I DOUBT if there are many such swords still in existence even in Austria, although I have seen one in an Imperial castle but of a later date on account of the figure being different. What I was told then (that is 50 years ago) was that there were the gunsmiths who also made swords, shaping, tempering and gunbarrel-boring, all by hand. It only could be afforded (where decoration came in) by wealthy mountain farmers. Therefore your sword may have been made for a leader. I wonder how it came over here! A real owner, a descendant, would never have given it up at any price; they were heirlooms.

If you can make an appointment when I could see it and have a magnifying glass handy, I may be able to give you a lead to follow up further into the history of it.

As to the figure's breeches on your sword—they are full length. In the one I saw the breeches were shorter, coming only to the knees, with stockings, indicating an earlier date for yours. Also the other had heavy nailed shoes for mountain climbing, whereas yours has full-length breeches and leather sandals, which proves that yours belongs to the Lower Valley.

IF IT is not infringing too much on your good nature I would like to make a call through the Camp-Fire whether there is any fellow left of the 25 men whom I took with me on the *Maria P.*, an Italian steamer from Kingston, Jamaica, by signing them up to the ship for a shilling a month and taking them to New Orleans as an excuse, all being stranded in Jamaica (and many more) from the French Canal about 1883 or '84. The only way I could take them with me was to have them help look after my banana cargo.

If they remember the adventurous trip we had I would like them to communicate to address below, especially if they remember the dates to refresh my memory.

THE same would apply also to the Annapolis naval students and officers on board a U. S. surveying vessel in the Gulf of Mexico where one evening I was chasing them with the *Maria P.* until they dropped anchor for the night, in order to find out from them where I was. Especially I want to repeat my thanks to the Captain who permitted me to bring the boatswain on board as a witness (being the only one of the crew who could talk a little English) where he so kindly and smilingly explained to us in their big chart-room the exact position we were in just then.

After being their guest for five hours (everybody writing letters) I took with me a couple of mail-bags for the home folks. There were certain reasons I could not take advantage of some of their families' extended invitations for a visit, received at the time.

Some time ago I saw Commander McCounly in Washington, but, although being an extraordinary occurrence, he thought it would be difficult under the circumstances to find the record of the log after so many years without knowing the name of the ship. But I never will forget the *Maria P.* as long as I shall live, even if she is at the bottom of Mediterranean for many years, where she was lost as soon as she got back to her home waters I heard afterward. With best wishes for our Camp-Fire.—F. S. Reisenberg, P. O. Box 468, New York City.

ALL you need do is write the titles and authors' names of the ten stories you consider best, given in order of preference, and mail us the sheet of paper to reach us not later than December thirty-first. If you like, add as many as ten more for honorable mention. You see, the time draws near for our annual vote by readers on the ten best stories published during the year. As in past years, short stories, novelettes, novels and serials are included, poems "Camp-Fire and the other departments are barred out. The issues covered are those dated January 3, 1919, to December 18, 1919, inclusive. Serials only parts of which are contained in these issues are included.

We very sincerely want your cooperation and help in getting for *Adventure* the kinds of story and the authors that a majority of our readers like best. If you know of a better way of furthering this cooperation than is the annual vote by readers, name it, for we are ready to try any legitimate plan that will help register your wishes in the making of the magazine. It's not only common sense to strive for this but it's a lot happier and more comfortable all around if people work together in friendly fashion.

WHILE the departments are excluded from the vote, we'll be more than glad to get suggestions for improving them. Or adding to them, but don't forget that "Letter-Friends" and "Wanted" have already been tried, and, though successful and popular, had to be given up because two or three readers abused them.

And if you have any suggestions concerning the magazine in general or any part of it, by all means send them in. I mean constructive suggestions that will definitely point out ways for improvement. Wherever we can meet your ideas we will, but remember that it is the majority whom we must please and that, while a given plan may please a minority and perhaps us here in the office, if it fails to please the majority it is not warranted.

But the only way to find out what the majority want is for the readers themselves to tell us. And you are one of the readers.

THERE is no doubt about it, "greasers" are not popular in this country and haven't been for many, many years. But are all greasers bad and are all Mexicans greasers? And isn't the seemingly inherent prejudice of northern races against Spanish and other southern blood largely responsible for our feeling about the Mexicans and the Central and South American peoples and, if so, is this prejudice a just judgment? Or merely a lack of understanding due to difference? Certainly the Latin-American opinion of us is a most unflattering and contemptuous one. We consider *their* opinion ill founded; they consider ours the same.

Mexico has been a pollution for some time, but it does not follow that every Mexican or, still less, every one of Spanish blood, is polluted. Spain is half a dozen different peoples, each differing vastly from the others. On this side of the Atlantic Spanish blood has generally been mixed with many others including American. And are all these just greasers and, if so, can it be that all greasers are our inferiors? Hardly.

I don't suppose anything could drop the word "greaser" from our vocabulary but, well, let's have a little more sense about it. For the rest, Miss Trujillo presents the case very well in the following letter.

AS TO the use of Spanish words in our stories I fear Miss Trujillo speaks rather hastily. She can hardly be familiar with all the dialects and colloquialisms of all the various districts between the U. S. and Cape Horn. This criticism is an old story with us and with other magazines; we have never found any authority who could pass on all the local usages of Spanish and it has been found most practical to depend on the writer for knowledge of idiom in the particular district he has chosen for his story and almost always has known personally. It would be easy enough to make all characters in all stories talk perfect academic Spanish, only in real life they wouldn't talk any such thing.

Masquero, New Mexico.

For several years I have been a very much interested reader of your magazine including your "Camp-Fire" department. It has been a great pleasure to me and at the same time I have often felt very much hurt by some of the stories that I have read therein.

TO BEGIN with I suppose that at heart I, too, am an adventurer, at least I like to take my adventures through reading of those stirring things that happen to others. Perhaps it is an hereditary taint for being a lineal descendant of the old Spanish Conquistadores, I suppose that a love of adventure is more or less inherent in my innermost being. And right here rests my complaint against *Adventure* and its writers. I suppose that you would call me Mexican or, as you so often say in your magazine, "Greaser," notwithstanding the fact that my forefathers landed in this country a quarter of a century before the landing of the Pilgrim Fathers and brought civilization and Christianity to this little known part of the Southwest long before it was brought to the Eastern shores of our continent. In fact we are more truly American through long residence of our forefathers than ninety per cent. of those who pride themselves upon their Americanism. Then, too, we are proud, and justly so, of our record of patriotism.

Notwithstanding that we were but recently forcibly adopted into the Union, my native State of New Mexico furnished more soldiers to the Union Army during the Civil War than any other State in the Union according to population. And needless to say the majority of them were native sons bearing Spanish names. And a roster of the New Mexico soldiers during the World War would show a predominating number of native sons bearing Spanish names.

ALTHOUGH almost completely isolated from the rest of the continent for a long period of time, our forefathers kept alive the light of Christianity, continued in almost classical purity the beautiful Spanish language and waged a terrible and continual warfare against the barbarous hordes of Indians that surrounded them on all sides.

During later years they have not enjoyed the benefits of a good school system, as have the citizens of other States but have made good citizens, intelligent to a remarkable degree and, where given the advantage of even a poor school system, have produced some very noble and able citizens.

SO YOU see it is with considerable sadness that we read these tales of adventure that seek to give an incorrect idea of our native Mexican citizens, in much the same way that the entire West was given an unenviable reputation as a bloody ground where Indians, cowboys and cut-throats paraded down the streets of little towns that were in reality more law-abiding than the larger towns of the East where civilization was supposed to be much further advanced.

To term the Mexican people "Greasers" is an insult to every intelligent man, woman or child of Spanish descent, and there are many of them. Another very common mistake is to call us citizens of the United States who happen to be of Spanish descent "Mexicans," since that designation really belongs only to those people who are citizens of Mexico.

ALSO if you would have your writers use intelligent Spanish when attempting to quote Spanish words that they may have chanced to hear, it would add much to the attractiveness of the stories. Like any other language that has long been isolated from its cradle, a great many colloquialisms and incorrect expressions have crept into the language but the "stuff" that is sometimes used by your writers is absolutely ridiculous and used by no person having even a slight knowledge of Spanish or Mexican, if you prefer to call it that.

HAVING been editor, publisher, compositor, reporter and "devil"—should I say "Deviless"?—of a small country weekly for about seven years during my girlhood days, I feel that I have had enough adventure in the way of meeting bills, collecting deliquent subscriptions and placating irate subscribers to entitle me to a seat at the Camp-Fire and a voice in regard to what I like and dislike in the make up of our magazine. Perhaps I am over presumptuous in anticipating woman's suffrage before its final adoption and casting a vote with all the "trimmin's" of an explanation at this time, but feel that my complaint is a just one and my grievance a justifying one.

I would like to have an opinion of other fair-minded readers of your magazine on this subject but shall insist on my feminine prerogative of "having the last word."

Instead of being afraid to sign my name to this little lecture I am proud to do so and respectfully subscribe myself—AURELIA TRUJILLO.

HERE'S an amusing picture of Wild Bill, Buffalo Bill and their cowboys and Indians:

Huntingdon, Pa.

Here is a little side-light on Wild Bill, Buffalo Bill and the crowd of "actors" who filled old Doolittle Hall, at Oswego, N. Y., with gun-smoke and dead Indians on that famous Eastern trip.

Some practical jokers invited the whole outfit to take a boat-ride on Lake Ontario. As a kid I stood on the west pier and saw them returning from an hour of bucking a good-sized sea on the old tug *Maria Melvin* and, believe me, the whole bunch of heroes didn't look the part and I reckon none of them felt it. You could not knock the heads off those white-caps with a six-shooter.—E. E. C. GIBBS.

THE bearers of our identification-cards naturally wander pretty well all over the earth and it would take many pages to recount the adventures all those bearers have gone through—to recount even the cases in which they write in for this reason or for that and incidentally report on their wanderings. But here are a sample few, most of which are rather the adventures of the cards themselves:

Washington, D. C.

Some time in 1914 I sent for an identification card, which I carried until the second day of the Argonne drive last September, when a piece of shrapnel destroyed it. Yes, had it in my blouse! But what I wanted to say, was: I would like to have another card, and the old number destroyed. I am sure that it was fifteen hundred and something. I think fifteen-forty-one. The old card saw some service before it went west, from Mexico to Flanders, and then some.—ALBERT R. FRANCIS.

Pensacola, Florida.

Enclosed you will please find twenty-five cents in stamps, for your identification card in aluminum. I have carried your paper identification card for some four years, which same was sent to the bottom by a Hun U-boat. I do not remember the number, but there is not much chance of any false alarms from that card.—CHARLES ALEXANDER MORINE.

Philadelphia.

I have carried one for some time and during the war was holding card number 7882 (pasteboard).

That little piece of cardboard left the States with me on board the S. S. *Cedric*, November 11, 1917, and landed in Liverpool, England, December 1, '17. Was with me through the training period in France. Entered the trenches "northeast of Toul," to be more exact, the Luneville Sector, February 25, 1918. Left there with me March 21, 1918, and then did a hundred and ten day hitch in the Baccarat Sector. I was carrying it in my left-hand breast pocket on the memorable day of July 14, 1918, when the Dutch made their push east of Rheims toward Chalons-sur-Marne and Paris. It accompanied me at historical Château-Thierry, St. Mihiel, and the Argonne-Meuse, then into Germany where I received card number 10866 (metal), but nevertheless it is still with me and lies in front of me as I write. Its blue surface is turning to yellow, but, believe me, it has always been a good pal and I intend to keep it the rest of my life.—W. A. FULMER.

League Island Navy Yard,
Philadelphia, Pa.

I noticed in my last *Adventure* how one of the cards had traveled in France, etc. I have held one since 1915 which has been over nearly all of the U. S. and since March, 1917, has been on a U. S. submarine along the entire coast of U. S., and a few other places—one dive of 200 feet—and been submerged something over 200 times.

I think they could tell some stories now if some aviator has held one, I guess there aren't many places they haven't been.—J. H. DUNLAP.

The next letter *is* from an aviator, but its adventure is of a different sort.

DuBuque, Iowa.

You recall mailing me a metal card to my New York address November last? It was the means of finding trace of me by an honest gentleman, Mr. C. W. Simonds, of Woodward, Oklahoma.

New York City to Fort Sill, Oklahoma, I lost a wallet containing the card and three fifty-dollar bills. Mr. Simonds found the wallet containing the money and card. By means of the card he located me and returned the money.

My faith in the card and human nature went above par as a result and is still "soaring."—J. W. MCGRATH.

SO FAR as I can remember, this comrade is right—we've never had a single word concerning Liberia at our Camp-Fire, unless it was some incidental mention by Thomas Samson Miller. Well, here it comes at last, and a pigmy elephant to come later:

Humboldt, Sask., Canada.

Although I am a reader for the last two years and although I think that I have seen quite a bit of the world, at least enough to be eligible for Camp-Fire, I had practically made up my mind not to get out of my seclusion, before I would read once about Liberia, or hear through Camp-Fire from one who also "served his term" at the "Pepper Coast."

ONLY once was I tempted to write to you, and that was when a doctor, whose name and address I mislaid in the meantime enquired about the best hunting grounds in West Africa. Do I know them? I should say I do. No game license, no bag limit, no impertinent officials, at least not in the interior, and, oh boy, game! Say, none of the colonies on the West Coast at their best had more game than the "Land of the Lonesome Star." Do you know where the latest discovery amongst the large animals was made, the pigmy hippopotamus? Liberia! Do you know where there is still a discovery due? The pigmy elephant? Guess! I have seen them but I did not have the time and means to bring proofs of their existence, except tusks, all my photos being anchored at the bottom of the Messurado River within two miles of Monrovia through the capsizing of our canoe returning from a seventeen months' ivory hunt.

OH, YES, there is a manuscript lying in my bureau drawer for the last two years, covering our trip, but I am afraid, after the last long *Monty* story, it would seem too much like plagiarism although Tippoo Tib's ivory hoard exists only in fiction and the ivory we were hunting for existed and—we found it. Maybe I will tell you some time about it.

But if ever anybody wants to know something about Liberia, the land of unlimited possibilties, or better, limited impossibilties, send him to me. I will satisfy his thirst of knowledge.—WALTER PETERSON, Box 395, Humboldt, Sask., Canada.

THIS comrade echoes the sentiments of many others when he says it was good to sit in once more at our Camp-Fire after the Great War. Our magazine followed the boys to France as much as it could, even sent a special representative over there to further its distribution, but it was impossible to get it where wanted until the armistice was signed.

Comrade —— may not be what some think of when they say "old-timer" but any man who has given two legs to his country and takes the loss with the spirit this comrade shows will, I know, always have a seat kept for him at our Camp-Fire. And I guess most of us will see to it that the seat is up in the first row.

New York.

To start with, I've been reading the *Adventure* a

good many years now, and am still going strong. I started as a kid. (Here's hoping I remain one for a long while to come.) Have enjoyed it to the sweetest end (The Camp-Fire).

I'm not "aimin'" to break out among the "Old Timers" and try to horn in on their arguments, but I've sure got to sit down and let you folks know how good I feel to be able to be back in the fire-light and listen in on the subjects that are dear to the hearts of men—the great outdoors, romance and adventure.

MAYBE a little of my history will interest you, but compared with the "regulars" it will seem a bit tame. But here goes:

Was twenty-nine years of age last February. Have seen some of the world and in my rambles and picked up some of the lingo of different ports. Am a pretty fair shot, as "shooting" goes.

Was in San Diego, California, 1916, when I thought I had better get into the "Big Red Glow." In doing so I became one of the many John Smiths in the Canadian Ninety-seventh Battalion (American Legion). Managed to get transferred to the U. S. A. E. F. and at the Marne, when a bunch of Jerries tried to come in for a swim, I was hit by a Quick Dick, (one-pounder) during the festivities. Result—lost two perfectly good legs and gained some idea of how a war was carried on. Am out now, and roving around same as usual.

I almost forgot to tell you, Montana claims the honor of my birthplace.

I don't think it would be right to lots of fellows to publish this epistle, for they may have more important things that would interest your readers (may the tribe increase) than this little tale of wo.— —— ——.

Our Camp-Fire came into being May 5, 1912, with our June issue, and since then its fire has never died down. Many have gathered about it and they are of all classes and degrees, high and low, rich and poor, adventurers and stay-at-homes, and from all parts of the earth. Some whose voices we used to know have taken the Long Trail and are heard no more, but they are still memories among us, and new voices are heard, and welcomed.

We are drawn together by a common liking for the strong, clean things of out-of-doors, for word from the earth's far places, for man in action instead of caged by circumstance. The *spirit* of adventure lives in all men; the rest is chance.

But something besides a common interest holds us together. Somehow a real comradeship has grown up among us. Men can not thus meet and talk together without growing into friendlier relations; many a time does one of us come to the rest for facts and guidance; many a close personal friendship has our Camp-Fire built up between two men who had never met; often has it proved an open sesame between strangers in a far land.

Perhaps our Camp-Fire is even a little more. Perhaps it is a bit of leaven working gently among those of different station toward the fuller and more human understanding and sympathy that will some day bring to man the real democracy and brotherhood he seeks. Few indeed are the agencies that bring together on a friendly footing so many and such great extremes as here. And we are numbered by the hundred thousand now.

If you are come to our Camp-Fire for the first time and find you like the things we like, join us and find yourself very welcome. There is no obligation except ordinary manliness, no forms or ceremonies, no dues, no officers, no anything except men and women gathered for interest and friendliness. Your desire to join makes you a member.

SOME more testimony concerning the Custer Massacre, from a comrade who was formerly of the 7th Infantry, which barely missed being in the fight itself.

What Dr. Arnold said about Buffalo Bill was mild enough in tone but, well, takes the general point of view that to a certain degree Buffalo Bill's fame was due, as "Uncle Frank" Huston has put it, to press-agenting. Of course he was press-agented; even his best friends must admit that. But whether it was to a degree that really affected the validity of his claim to fame is another matter and I don't believe we want to start another Drannan discussion at Camp-Fire.

Elyria, Ohio.

I have just been reading about Custer, Buffalo Bill and Calamity Jane. There has been so much bunk written and told concerning Custer, Reno, Buffalo Bill, etc., that I thought it might be that you would like to read a more truthful account concerning those men.

My regiment, the 7th U. S. Infantry, was ordered into the fight where Custer fell, but the order being countermanded, the 7th Cavalry, Custer's command, was ordered into the fight while the 7th Infantry were detailed to guard the wagon-train. Reno was not to blame for the massacre of Custer and his men, for Reno obeyed Custer's orders as well as he could under the circumstances, while Custer, disobeying his own orders, caused the deaths of himself and his men. Custer had been warned for days before that the Indians were out in very great numbers, but, paying no attention to his scouts, he ordered Reno to go down the Little Big Horn a ways, cross over, and, after circling around to the back of the Indians' camp, to fire a signal shot, upon which Custer and his men were to charge upon the camp from the front. Custer, however, bull-headed as ever, never waited for Reno to get back of the camp and fire the signal shot, but dashed right in, when, as Chief Gall said when showing a party over the field in 1886, the Indians were as thick as the leaves of the forest, springing up from the ground and in lots of instances clubbing the cavalrymen off from their horses.

CUSTER went into the fight with long hair, all stories to the contrary, and it is no doubt all bosh about his having committed suicide. He was certainly killed by either Rain-in-the-Face or some other Indian. It was a massacre, all right, for their carbines were mostly fastened to their saddles and, their horses breaking away, they were left with only a few carbines, about a half dozen sabers and their revolvers with which to defend themselves.

In the meantime Reno and his men were surrounded on a hill by Indians, and the 7th Infantry and a small outfit of cavalry, the 8th, if I remember right, rescued Reno and his men. Afterward the 7th Infantry and the 8th Cavalry helped to bury Custer and his men. Reno would have been wiped out with his men if they had not been rescued just in time.

BUFFALO BILL used to scout with my regiment and . . . I used to know Calamity Jane. Calamity Jane was certainly a very noted woman. She was full of life and vigor, and when she looked at a person her eyes would almost bore holes through them.—DR. WILLIAM E. ARNOLD (formerly Musician, Co. B, 7th Infantry, U. S. A.)

A WORD from Harold A. Lamb in connection with his story in this issue:

New York.

A few points about "Said Afzel's Elephant." It may seem improbable that three men could do what Abdul Dost and his friends tackled. In India at that time, however, a noble from the court traveled with a large following of slaves, personal attendants, eunuchs, wives, buffoons, *hafiz*, or poem-readers, bearers, etc.

FEW of such gentry were fighting men by inclination or training. And even today the hillmen of Afghanistan such as the Afridis are excellent combatants when so inclined. At that time tribal warfare was the rule and the hillmen were skilled in weapons. They had to be.

As to Said Afzel. The character of the opium-using poet is not overdrawn. Drugs of varied sort were in general use, and it was the fashion to remain stupefied for certain lengths of time. The Rajputs were addicted to opium in very large quantities. One passage in the memoirs of Baber relates that he kept sober at a drinking party of his friends in order to see what the bout would be like. He watched them drink wine, then change to *bhang* and distilled spirits, ending up with opium and more wine until "they became senseless or began to commit all manner of follies, whereupon I had myself carried out."

A GOOD deal has been written of the treasure of the Moghuls. This was hardly so very great in money, but consisted of enormous quantities of jewels, especially diamonds and rubies, horses, cloth-of-gold, etc. The amount of an amir's treasure measured the number of fighting-men he could buy; hence the possession of a store of riches as in this story was more valuable to an ambitious noble than a small kingdom.—H. A. LAMB.

THANKS to our comrade Ira A. Thompson of El Paso I have a copy of "Poisonous Animals of the Desert," by Charles T. Vorhies, which is Bulletin No. 83 of the Agricultural Experiment Station, College of Agriculture, University of Arizona, Tucson, Arizona. The Bulletins, Timely Hints and Reports of this Station will be sent free to all who apply. Among other things, it seems to give us a final and authoritative decision on our old, old friend, the Gila Monster. It *is* poisonous, but the effects of its bite are variable and there seems to be no established case of the death of a human being from its bite.

Here is Mr. Thompson's letter:

El Paso, Texas.

In your issue of August 18th you list 13 kinds of rattlesnakes.

As Arizona is the home of 11 kinds, I take the liberty to send you this booklet issued by Arizona State University, which states there are 19 known varieties of rattlesnakes, 14 of which inhabit U. S. A. and 11 of these are found in Arizona. My .45 Colt (single-action, if you please) has finished many a rattler.

Re coral snake. A Mexican woman at a mine about 60 miles south of the line lived about 10 or 15 minutes after being bitten by coral snake.

You will also find something about Mr. Gila Monster. Nothing like the bunk one sometimes reads in stories, nor for that matter is it much like the stuff I have handed out to entertain some of the new comers, who as a rule will believe the lies but not the truth.—IRA A. THOMPSON.

And here is a quotation from the Bulletin:

Just one other poisonous reptile belongs to our fauna—the Gila Monster (Heloderma suspectum, cover cut). This and a closely related species, Heloderma horridum, found only in Mexico, are the only poisonous lizards in the world. Absolutely no other lizards (these including the so-called "horned toads") are poisonous. The Gila Monster has poison-glands, but in the lower instead of the upper jaw, the secretion oozing out between the teeth and the lower lips. It has no poison fangs, however, and therefore no definite mechanism for forcibly injecting poison with a stroke as does the rattlesnake. It will snap and bite if irritated, and will cling like a bulldog when it gets hold, and poison may enter the wounds made by its numerous small sharp teeth as a result of the tenacious grip of the animal.

THE effects of its bite are variable, owing doubtless to the imperfect application of the venomous saliva. Though some reports have it that human deaths have resulted from the bite of this animal, these reports are but hearsay and fade away to nothing upon investigation. The writer is indebted to a reputable physician of Tucson who has made considerable effort to authenticate a single case of death caused by the Gila Monster, and has failed to do so. An exhaustive report on "The Venom of Heloderma," by Leo Loeb, published by the Carnegie Institution, as well as the researches of other investigators, shows that the venom produces fatal results in various small animals, such as rats, mice, frogs, guinea pigs, etc. As to effects on man, we find no local data to discountenance the following statement from Loeb's report:

"NO DEATH of a human being has come to our knowledge that can be attributed to the bite of a Gila Monster. A bite from this animal is in man either followed by no symptoms at all or by a local swelling, perhaps extending to the shoulder, if the bite affected the upper extremity. In all the reports concerning the local effect of the bite of the Heloderma in man, mention is made of the rapid appearance of swelling and hemmorrhagic discoloration of the skin at the site of injury. We found that when fresh venom was injected subcutaneously into an animal, no swelling or hemorrhage appeared at the site of injection; and when venom was injected intramuscularly, no hemorrhage was noted. . . . . It is impossible, however, to absolutely rule out mechanical injury as a factor in causing the appearance of these local symptoms when an individual is bitten by a Heloderma. The animal has very powerful jaws and its bite would easily bruise a large area of flesh and skin. When the animal bites it clings tenaciously, and in endeavoring to extricate a wounded part of the injury might easily be increased."

WHETHER potassium permanganate is destructive to Heloderman venom is not determined. Therefore we can not recommend it as of value in case of a bite by this animal. We would only suggest releasing the bitten part as rapidly and yet as coolly and carefully as possible and then seeking a physician, perhaps first inducing some bleeding and then washing the wound with an antiseptic. The venom is not to be regarded as deadly to man, hence there is no need for hysterical fear.

In closing on Heloderma we would suggest that there is no good reason for remorselessly slaying every Gila Monster encountered. Rather should we class it with the road runner and the peccary as unique features of our fauna, a part of the characteristic landscape of Arizona, like the giant cactus among the flora of the State.

Also, in addition to a detailed statement of treatment for snake-bite and poisonous insect bites the Bulletin takes up another subject that has produced much argument—the "hydrophobia skunk." Its conclusion is that there is no particular species of skunk which can be designated as the "hydrophobia skunk," but that skunks are rather more likely to bite sleepers than are coyotes, wolves and dogs and that perhaps a larger proportion of bites from skunks produce rabies. Mr. Vorhies arrives at one "unavoidable conclusion"—in case of skunk-bite take the Pasteur treatment.

WHEN Captain Smith wrote the following letter he was in France. Some of you are sure to give him the information he wants, so will he, when he sees this, kindly give us his home address so I can forward letters to him?

Angers, France.

I noticed in one of your recent numbers a request for a poem from some party, and one of your other readers had supplied him with it, through your Camp-Fire pages. A number of years ago I read a poem called "The Ballad of Boastful Bill" in a book of cow-country ditties, and have never been able to get a copy of it since. All I can remember of it is as follows:

THE BALLAD OF BOASTFUL BILL

At a cow camp on the Gila,
One sweet morning, long ago,
Ten of us was throwed right freely
By a hoss from Idaho.
And it looked as though he'd go abegging
For a man to bust his pride,
Till a-hitching up one legging,
Boastful Bill cut loose an' cried:
"I'm an ornery proposition for to hurt,
I fulfill my earthly mission with a quirt.
I can ride the highest liver
Twixt the Gulf and Powder River,
An' I'll ride this thing as easy as I'd flirt."

If any of you readers can supply the balance of this I would feel obliged. I will watch your Camp-Fire pages for results. Thanking you for your favor. *Adios.*—HERBERT R. SMITH, Capt. Signal Corps.

AS TO water-proof coating, here's a receipt:

Mound House, Nevada.

I see in the last "Ask Adventure" that Mer—(can't recall the name now) gives parrafine and benzine as a waterproofing mixture. I would like to say that beeswax dissolved in turpentine beats this all hollow. I also want to say for the benefit of the uninitiated that *any* waterproofing compound should be applied to canvas in more than one coat for the best result. Far better to take a thinner mixture and use it twice.—JOSEPH GRAY.

IN THE language of the poet, you can search me. Remember the strange manuscript picked up in a bottle on the Nova Scotian coast, which, passed on to

Camp-Fire, brought forth a number of interesting translations? Yes, and remember that Edgar Young confessed he and a friend had thrown it overboard in the South Atlantic as a hoax? Well, that seems to settle it, doesn't it? Only it doesn't. For the original sender writes indignantly that Young's message could not be the one he has because the latter was found before the date on which the hoax was pulled off.

Here's the letter from our Nova Scotian comrade—at least such part of it as it seems right to make public. I pointed out to the writer that Edgar Young's address appears in every issue of the magazine.

——, Nova Scotia.

While not disputing Edgar Young's veracity or intentions, I note that he says he did this in 1910 and I was a miner full grown and earning men's wages at a coal-face at that time. It was in 1909-1911 we Nova Scotia miners had our twenty-two months' strike for U. M. W. recognition.

NOW to the point I can not understand. Edgar Young says he wrote a message purporting to be from Blackburne in 1910. Well, this old chart was found when I was a school kid and I left school when 16, and am 36 years old now. My uncle died in 1894 and he and a chum found this old bottle in 1889. So how does that rhyme with Comrade Young's statement?

It's queer that there are two old —— about the locality of the bay and rivers indicated; also a good clear spring in a line with that tree and the anchorage; also that tree, which I have found and identified—by markings, which are similar to some on the old chart which Edgar Young no doubt can describe. What I can not understand is how he wrote it in 1910 and it was found in 1889, as I have ascertained by going over some files of old letters.

NOW, I'm not boosting this thing for publicity. I'm on the "lone" trail in this thing and have reason to believe that there is a rich find for some one. If, however, Edgar Young can describe that old chart and explain how it was written in 1910 and found in the Fall of 1889; also how I knew of it and took it to the high school principal here when a school kid of 14 or so and was a man of 27 when it was written, that's too psychological for me to comprehend. I would like to get hold of that old account of that pirate Blackburne as I think I've located the old fellow's favorite rendezvous.

I wonder if Edgar Young can tell me where to get it. Also I'd like to correspond with him to see if he can fully describe the locality drawn on that chart in my possession. If his claim is authentic and true, then the whole thing is a hoax perpetrated and invented for the purpose of misleading and deceiving. It certainly accomplished its purpose if so, for I know I've spent hours untold in corresponding about it and had offers to buy it from folks who could decipher part of it and not all (so they said), but were particularly anxious to see the original.

This has been no joke in our family.—— ——.

And here is Edgar Young's reply:

Brooklyn.

The first thing that occurred to me when I read what that fellow had to say about the Capitan Blackburne manuscript was to shut up like a clam. He has his dates wrong and seems set on making a liar out of me. My first decision was to let that MS. remain a mystery and I was advised by a close friend to say nothing about it, even if I had written it. Fate seems to be mixed up in this and I was unable to follow my better judgment and remain silent.

THERE happens to be living proof to support the details I gave you in the former letter. This is the man who was with me and helped concoct the MS. Right here a funny thing comes in. This man and I parted in anger in Nicaragua in 1913 and have not spoken or written each other since. The cause of our disagreement was very slight and I have always kept track of him through others, for he was a true-blue pal, one of the only two I met up with. We made the trip from Colon down the east coast of South America and back up the other side, working in all the countries en route. He remained to work in Ecuador and I came to Panama to work for the Panama Railroad until he arrived. We both went to Nicaragua, where we worked as officials of the National Railways, I as auditor and he as general storekeeper. We separated after some seven months.

He blew up first and came to New York and I blew up later and came to San Francisco. Later he returned to Panama and went into the contracting business and was civil engineer for some Panama Government work. I understand he is now employed by the Panama Railway, or was the last time I asked about him. I am pretty sure he has kept track of me, in fact, I know he has, for a friend has passed along comments he has made on stories of mine that appeared in magazines.

I POSSIBLY owe him an apology for the words passed between us in Nicaragua, for he was really trying to keep me from making a —— fool out of myself, which I later did. But I do not intend to write him an apology now at the present time to get him to uphold a statement in regard to a fool MS. we placed in a bottle in 1910. Even if I did, proof obtained in this manner would be worthless. The best thing I can think of is to run the explanation I have given in Camp-Fire and right with it run the later letter of the man who has the MS. at the present time which makes a liar out of me. I am willing to appear in the rôle he has placed me. I am pretty sure that —— will come forward with a statement if he happens to see the letters, which he no doubt will see. If he does not, I will still be satisfied. However, I feel pretty sure he will not let that fellow put the Kobie on me.

IN THE meantime I have framed the card in a little frame I got at the five-and-ten and have it hanging on the wall over my desk. I remember the exact words that passed when the MS. was written. Part was written by each of us. I made the arrow pointing down stream, —— made the little house in the corner and the anchor. I don't remember whether we showed it to Captain Funcke or not. If we did he may see the discussion and come forward with further corroboration. He will no doubt remember the two strange passengers who refused to eat on the latter end of the voyage and whom he came to visit in the room of the best hotel in Rio after we landed, in company with a ship's chandler of the city.

It may be that some of the shipmates of this man's uncle will write in and state that the dates he has are in error, for they certainly are. I was born in 1883 and I am sure I did not write that before I was six years old. I am saying it was written with a Waterman's fountain-pen bought from the Panama Railroad newsstand at Gatun, of which Mrs. Nolte was in charge, on board the good ship *Merkador* between the 12th and 31st of December, 1910, and thrown overboard between Barbados and Rio.

These are the facts. If proof comes naturally, let it come. I have always been something of a fatalist. I don't know what reason Fate had for making me get mixed up in this. From present circumstances it looks as if she wanted to make a liar out of me. It may be that the MS. —— and I wrote was intended to bring us together after we had split up. *Quien sabe?* and again *Quien sabe?*

RIGHT here I rest my case. If you wish to use this letter, please use blank spaces for the names of —— and ——. For the love of *Miguel*, what reason would I have to claim authorship of a MS. the sea has returned? Don't the editors return enough of them? That's a good one! "Due to the supply of MSS. we have on hand from the Mermen and Mermaids, we herewith return as unavailable, etc."

It has just occurred to me that . . . . . . Let's find out. Let's get some dope on the other bottles that were thrown over at the same time and some of which I am sure have been found. Perhaps the ink, paper, etc., of these other messages contain proof. —*I am telling the truth and have nothing to fear from later developments.*—EDGAR YOUNG.

So there we are—or aren't. As I said in the beginning, you can search me. Two documents instead of one? Perhaps. A scheme to arouse interest and capital in a treasure-hunt? Doesn't sound so on the face of it. Quite a number of possible solutions offer themselves but no one of them proves itself.

But I'm not holding out on you, except, of course, the man's name and address, which he gave me in confidence. I can add only the fact that I never met him and know no more about him than you do, and the minor detail that when Edgar Young first wrote me that he had set that bottle adrift I replied asking whether he were kidding me and was assured that he was not. If the two men have corresponded since the above letters, I have not heard the results. But I'm writing to both and asking, so maybe there'll be more news later.

At least let's hope that Edgar Young's old pal comes across. The kind of man Mr. Young describes would hardly fail to toe the scratch in such a case if it comes to his attention.

OWING to something I don't remember but which was quite likely my own fault, Henry Leverage's introduction to Camp-Fire doesn't reach us in the same issue with our first story from him, but be easy on me and meet him now. If there are any of the old *Karluk* men among us they can write Mr. Leverage in care of this office.

New York.

In introducing myself to the Camp-Fire, I'm going to lie down, fill up my old cord-wrapped pipe, reach for a brand and between puffs, say:

"The Iron Dollar," my first story to sell to *Adventure*, is almost fact. I can see the picture now, coming home to San Francisco. A dirty, sawed-off whaler—twenty-four in the fo'cas'le—and only two American-born among them.

We had beans for all three meals over the period of two months. Beans—topped with salt-horse. The crew started promising certain things which were going to happen to the skipper. They sharpened knives and mentioned the first time they got the old man ashore.

WE LANDED and all hands went with the skipper into the nearest dive—it was called the "Blubber Room" in those days. He bought a round of steam beers, everybody shook hands with him, and he went out—without a knife in his back.

I dug in my dungaree trousers, fished forth a five-dollar gold-piece, and offered to buy a square meal. Twenty-three whalemen followed me into The Home Dairy Restaurant. They glanced at the menu card, coughed, stared at the wall where signs hung inscribed: "Roast-Beef, Very Rare; "Chicken Fricasee"; "Liver and Bacon."

They passed these up, grinned sheepishly, and all ordered baked beans.

The next day I signed off, received an Iron Dollar for eight months' labor, and bade good-by to the sea.

I wonder if any of the Camp-Fire readers were aboard the *Karluk* with Captain McGregor during the season of 1897? I would like to hear from them.—LEVERAGE.

IN SOME of Hugh Pendexter's earlier stories in our magazine we met the Oneidas pretty frequently and now here comes a comrade with their blood in his veins to talk with us. When he wrote, two days before the armistice was signed, he was serving on the U. S. S. *Roanoke*, so you see it has been a long time coming to the surface in our mail-bag. Perhaps by this time he is at the headwaters of the Amazon, according to his desire. But if Walter R. Johnson remembers him and will write him care of this office, Mr. Benton will probably get it sooner or later, for he sits in at our Camp-Fire whenever he's where he can get to it. Or I can forward to the name and address of friend registered for Mr. Benton's identification card.

I omit a small bit of his letter merely because it endorses the idea of a badge for us to wear and that badge has since then been adopted and come into use.

Mr. Benton spells it "Oniedoes," not "Oneidas," and, as his spelling is O.K. in the remainder of his letter, I'm wondering whether that is the French form or whether I'm all wrong as to Oneidas being the same tribe. I'm no wiseacre on our old Indian tribes, despite a strong interest in them.

U. S. S. *Roanoke*.

It has been a good while since I last wrote to you, but, I can not give any account of myself at present, for military reasons, but being a seaman for some years gone, you may be sure "Fritz" has received my calling-cards since we went into the war.

THERE'S one thing I can mention, I believe. About three months ago I was caught in one of the most beautiful ninety-mile gales that ever visited these parts, which shook all the tropic fever I ever contracted out of my bones. It turned the tugs to the beach, chased everything in general to shelter and left me to fight it out with a 36-footer. My boots, slicker and one perfectly good pair of wool socks were missing when I reached my rendezvous. Sorry I can not give a better description of the incident, but any shipmate that has had experience at sea knows how she is when she makes you wish you were a longshoreman instead of a common seafaring man.

AND I noticed also a letter from Mr. Walter R. Johnson, whom I believe I met in Quito, Ecuador, and later in Guacayilla, quite a few years ago, and if my memory serves me right, he offered me a comrade's hand and financial help. Perhaps my looks justified his offer, for at the time my sole possession was a dungarie suit and a suit of serge in the clothing line. But my most carefully guarded secret was 27 English pounds at that date. Four hours previous to our meeting I was beached from the English tramp *Union* for getting too affectionate with a pinch-bar. I was just barely in my teens then, and I haven't grown but one inch and gained four or five pounds since, so perhaps Mr. Johnson would still know me if we chanced to meet again, which I hope will be in the near future.

I may add that I have passed the expert rifle course since that time, and I long for the war's end. I crave a trip far up the headwaters of the Amazon and over the borders of Bolivia. Afterward I still expect to return to the States and become a settled "hombre." But I would be glad to hear from Mr. Johnson, and would appreciate meeting him again very much. I would also like to hear from Mr. Young.

So why not give it a trial? I have met many in my years at sea. The most famous of the places I like to go to (when I call there) is Wilcox's in Colon. I still cast a longing eye and heart in the direction of the San Blas country.

And I may say for the interest of all concerned that I am a half-cast of the famous old tribe of the Oniedoes (as we were called by the French) and now known as part of the "praying Indians" of the North Country, and the other half Scot-English. You may easily guess where my roving blood was picked up, and why it still burns.—LEARNY J. BENTON.

P. S.—I would be glad to hear from any member of Camp-Fire and will answer any inquiries that I can within reason.—L. J. B.

THIS letter was written November 22, 1918, probably reached me a month or so later, and has somehow got out of turn—as often happens—in the mass of good material waiting to be heard at Camp-Fire. I'm sorry for the delay, but the letter has lost none of its interest. Americans serving with the Australians in Egypt and the Holy Land! Of course, but even yet we're not quite used to the mixing up the war gave this old world and its peoples.

Penmanship? What do we care about his penmanship except to be sorry he didn't come through the war-furnace unsinged?

Port Said, Egypt.

I have never written to you before, but would like to join the Camp-Fire gatherings.

I AM serving under the Australian flag, with the Australian Light Horse, the cavalry that has done the great work in Gallipoli Peninsula, Egypt, Sinai, Palestine and Syria. There are many more Yanks serving here in the Australian forces besides me. We are keeping up the name of the dear old States over here.

I have had some great experiences since I left home. I have traveled about the Hawaiian Islands, Society and Cook Islands, the Philippine, Celebes, Borneo islands and knocked about China, Japan, Australia, Ceylon and India. I have seen Gallipoli, all of Egypt, Sinai, Palestine and a good bit of Syria since I have been here. I have had many thrilling adventures in my travels, and was shipwrecked on an uninhabited island in the China Sea for ten days.

Now that the war is over, I will return to America.

I am a lover of tropical countries, and islands, so I intend to do more traveling about looking for adventure, after spending several months with my old folks at home.—Trooper C. H. DETERT, A. I. F., Egypt.

P. S.—Please excuse my penmanship, as my nerves are shattered.

ONE of you suggested the old Indian sign as a kind of greeting or sign for members of Camp-Fire when they meet or when one of them wants to know whether some other fellow is a member. (I suppose there is still need to explain that any one is a member who wishes to be.) I wrote to "Uncle Frank" Huston to be sure of just how the sign is made. He says:

Hand up, palm forward, thumb and fingers joined. You've made the sign often and never knew what it was. Of course, made casually and quickly, the fingers are not always stuck and glued together. Sometimes the hand is not raised above the shoulder; again, level with ear; again, top of head.

So there is the sign if any of you ever care to use it. If you do, you'd better say so, so that we can mention it at Camp-Fire now and then to be sure that all members, new and old, understand what it signifies in our case.

CACTUS, barrel and giant. Some more about it from one of our Southwestern comrades:

Prescott, Ariz.

Just move along a bit, will you, and make room for me to sit next you at the Camp-Fire circle?

IN THE Camp-Fire of your Sept. 3rd issue is a letter which I found interesting and also somewhat a bit in error. The barrel cactus, which is a source of water for the desert wanderer, is quite accurately described by him; the thorns are hooked slightly and are rather more elliptical in cross section than flat, as he describes. These thorns are about 3 in. in length. The cactus grows from 3 to 4 ft. in height. The best way to procure the water it contains is to cut off the top as one cuts the top of a soft-boiled egg when set in an egg-cup, dig out a bowl-shaped hollow, take a long-bladed knife or a clean, sharp stick and jab it up and down in the pulp, thus freeing the water which will accumulate in the bowl prepared. Quite a quantity of refreshing liquor will thus be secured and it is a God-send to the man on the desert whose water supply has been exhausted.

The other cactus he refers to is the giant cactus, properly called saguaro (pronounced in this part of the country and in Mexico "sah-hwar-ro" and generally incorrectly spelled by the story writers). I have seen this cactus attain a height of 40 to 50 ft. in many localities of the Southwest. I am enclosing a photo of a comparatively small one beside which I had my driver stand for a comparison. Being a bit nearer the camera than the cactus, he is a little larger in perspective than his true relative height would be. The other small photo is of a group of young saguaros, which was so unusual an occurrence for the number grouped that I thought the photo worth taking. The large photo is of a young saguaro and behind it is an ocotillo (pronounced "o-ko-teel-yo").

NOW a bit of criticism. If the comrade whose letter I read walked from "Meyer" (Mayer) to Phœnix, he probably took the Black Cañon road, which passes *east* of the Black Cañon proper and between it and the Agua Fria River, crossing the latter at Cañon, where it takes a short turn to the west just below the mouth of the Black Cañon, before continuing its southerly course. I hardly think he would have walked through the Black Cañon unless prospecting for mineral. And *en route* to Phœnix from Mayer he does not get anywhere near Cave Creek, which is quite some miles to the east of the Agua Fria, but he will cross Cave Creek *Wash* after he has got down on to the desert which is a continuation of the Salt River Valley, to the west.—CHAS. EDWARD MAJOR.

PROBABLY there is little need to explain that your delay in getting this issue of *Adventure* and the one before it is due to the printers' strike in New York. Camp-Fire is not the place to discuss the merits of the strike, but I'd like to make clear the fact that if it were not for a conflict between the local Unions and the general organization there would be no delay in getting your magazines to you, this being a Union shop in good standing with the general organization. Perhaps the strike will be over by the time you read this, but in any case you will probably be getting your issues of *Adventure* faster than usual until we catch up with the regular schedule. Don't wait for the usual two-week interval; keep your eye on the stands for the appearance of new issues.

Romance, too, will go through the same kind of hurry-up process.

I'll not bother you with the details, but in order to speed up these delayed issues it was found advisable to substitute the Mid-January and First February issues for the Mid-December and First January issues, with, of course, the exception of the serials and some minor changes. Also another change—since the stories by H. A. Lamb and Robert J. Pearsall are consecutive, they have to be dropped from several issues but will appear as soon as conditions make it possible.

Likewise it was impossible for us to publish in this number the stories promised in the last "Trail Ahead." They will appear in a later issue.

Our "Camp-Fire," too, has had to be changed in minor ways, as have "Ask Adventure" and "Looking Ahead," but, unless I make a slip somewhere in the general confusion, I think these changes will in no way affect your comfort in reading the magazine.

HERE is an extremely interesting suggestion put forward by Edgar Young. He knows the adventurer's needs at first-hand but the value of these books seems plain enough even to the stay-at-home. How do you feel about it?

Brooklyn, New York.

I am passing along an idea that occurred to me. Perhaps there might be some manufacturing stationery comrade of your acquaintance who might like to take it up, or the man who finally makes the large registers for the stations might like it. It's free to any one who likes it, so far as I'm concerned.

IT is a fact that all of us have carried books of some sort and got signatures in them, but nothing especially for this purpose has ever been designed, so far as I know. Every man who drops in here begins to drag out railroad clearances, letters, etc., to establish proof of something or other. A book of the sort along the general lines I have hastily sketched should be very acceptable to all travelers. A great many of us are modest about telling some outlandish thing we have seen in some outlandish place without having proper papers to back it up, and a thing that cuts is to be accused of lying when telling the exact and unvarnished truth.

Books of this kind could be filled and others obtained and used in numerical order. A man could have a just pride in such a record and hand the book down to his children. The numerous foreign and native seal impressions and signatures with autographs of prominent men would also make it interesting.

I AM one of those who claim that adventure has better precedents and records than it has ever been given credit for. All advancement on the face of the earth has been due to it. We Americans can be especially proud of our adventurous forefathers. There are those who, alas, wish to detract from the spirit of adventure. "Rolling stones gather no moss," they claim. This in spite of the fact that the famous hobo A1 owns a large brick building in Pittsburg or somewhere over there, the usual detractor from the name of the roving tribe not having a hundred dollars' bank balance. The rolling stones do gather the moss, lots of it, intellectual and material, when they get ready to. Tom Edison, tramp telegrapher, lights the world, splits one wire into four parts for the telegraph companies, braces them up with phonograph music, and other stunts. Where do they get that stuff?

It's partly up to us to respectabilize adventure and, besides the many of us who are doing it in a didactic and thematic way, this has occurred to me as another method.

A SIZE to fit easily in the coat pocket or roughly about the size of the page I am attaching (4½ × 6 in.) seems to be about right. The printing would jam up closer than the type of this machine I am using. This would leave more room for the seal space and for the remarks spaces at bottom. Two, if not three, such blanks could fill a page.

Without taking much time to inflate on the idea, these books would prove useful:

1. To establish an alibi when arrested on suspicion. (I was arrested in Matoon, Ill., once for a burglary in Paris, Ill., and if the conductor of the freight I came in on had not voluntarily come forward with his story I would possibly have been locked up.)
2. Proof of residence in some place.
3. Record for quick trips by foot, mule, or auto across country.
4. Autographs of famous men.
5. Records of exploration.
6. To produce to newspaper men when asking for publicity in small towns.
7. To prove a man is what he claims to be.
8. As an ad for the magazine when shown and spoken of, etc., etc., etc.
9. To establish records of residence for bond companies when not employed.—EDGAR YOUNG.

One page of Mr. Young's plan for the book contains the following:

One who carries a book of this kind should experience no trouble in obtaining signatures from American or other consuls, postmasters, railroad and steamship agents, mayors or other prominent persons of the city, town, village, hamlet, in which they happen to be, in order to establish beyond doubt a record of travel or exploration. Beyond the outposts of civilization, among Indians and others who are unable to write, the identifying person should be requested to make a thumb-print in the space left for "seal of office" and a tiny pad should be carried for this purpose in a sealed cartridge-shell or other small air-tight container.

Another page contains blanks for the bearer's name, home address, nationality, male or female, weight, height, hair, eyes, complexion, physical marks—a description identification. Also directions as to whom to notify in case of injury or death. Also certified signature, thumb-print and photograph.

Other pages contain (two each) forms for official seals and signatures:

This is to certify that the person whose photograph and signature appear in the front of this book has requested me to witness the fact that he has been here on the above date and I assume no obligation whatever beyond the fact that I have seen him or her in person.

What do you think of this idea? Let's have your opinions and suggestions. In case the plan is put into operation a first step would be to get registered the names of those who would want these books.

AS to the exactness of his story of the killing of Billy the Kid, in an earlier issue, E. A. Brininstool is ready to go to the mat:

Los Angeles, California.

Pat Garrett was killed himself in a manner somewhat after that in which he killed the Kid. This is history. Ask anybody who knows New Mexican and Arizona history. Ask John Poe, banker of Roswell, N. M., who was one of the three men in the party who captured the Kid—and killed him.

As a matter of fact, I will wager Brother Wood $1000 in cash, and put up the money, if my story of the killing of Billy the Kid is not exactly as described by me. And we will leave it to John Poe himself. Poe yet lives and is president of the Citizens Bank of Roswell.—E. A. BRININSTOOL.

IT doesn't seem likely to me that any man who hands out his honest opinions man-fashion at Camp-Fire will get anything but respect, whether all of us agree with his opinions or not. Nor will Mr. Cain, who introduces himself according to our custom on the appearance of his first story in our magazine, fail to find a good many of us who see things as he does, at least in a general way.

South Orange, New Jersey.

YOU ask me to make a bow to the Camp-Fire. I bow. That is easy. But, to tell anything about myself that would interest your readers is something else again. I've been a fat family man so long that it seems to me the only real adventure is getting the rent and keeping the door-step half-way free of bill-collectors. Compared to that, the excitements I have got out of such uneventful voyages as I once made, or by batting about a little in small motor or sail boats—seem mild indeed. Honestly, this mere matter of life and death seems pretty tame to me. Dying doesn't look to me like half the sacrifice or pain of living through some things. And what sort of man is it who would not give his life a dozen times rather than see some others suffer or yield a real principle? I've written a lot of adventure stories. When I get a situation up where the hero and the heroine are sailing through the air about half-way down the thousand-foot precipice, I have to sit back and laugh. What does it matter whether they land on a hay-mound and survive, or hit a rock and go out?

EDITORS have a way of shifting titles on me. I'm calling the story, "A Prejudice Against Suicide," because that was the real idea I had in writing that story. Circumstances broke to keep me from being a clergyman after I had got most of the training for it. My idea is that of obedience to the law, even when it seems to have lost its purpose in an individual case. Here is a man without a chance to live, refusing to save himself the last hours of agony by a crime which, perhaps, few would condemn under the circumstances. The sea setting of the story was a mere detail for conveying the feeling I have that law and right are fixed by a power so much above us that they may not be subverted to special conditions of individuals. Not all the ideas I put into stories come, as this one did, out of the tomes of moral theology; but when I write a story with no idea bigger than living through a peril or series of them, you can figure that I laughed when I wrote it. A man will always be to me so much bigger than his mere physical life that I shall find it funny to take that side of him very seriously. Still—I love funny things. So don't strain your mind too hard trying to find the moral of a yarn with my name at the top of it. There may not be any.

But I am still theologian enough to believe that the real big adventure is that of each one of us in keeping our souls out of hell for the long time after we're dead, and getting and holding the love for the Right and the God that makes Right.

Think I ought to have kept away from the Camp-Fire and stayed in church? Yours for the real adventures.—GEORGE M. A. CAIN.

MANY of you responded to my request for frank and detailed opinions on our new sister magazine *Romance* and I want to thank you sincerely. That kind of opinion helps a lot. Creating a new magazine is not so easy as it sounds and it is perhaps still more difficult for the editor to tell just what it's like after it is created. It's like a writer trying to criticize his own story. In either case a fellow has to turn to outside opinion to find out what's really there.

Your opinions helped in many ways. Of course there were the inevitable differences of taste and judgment. One letter would say "Give us more stories like 'x';" the next would say "All the stories are good except 'x,' which is rotten." But, taking all the letters as a whole, the net result was very valuable guidance for the future.

NATURALLY your letters, being from *Adventure* readers and nearly all men (we find only 15 per cent. of *Adventure's* newsstand sales are to women and girls), they give the point of view of only those who are strong for a man's magazine, and I'm glad to say their verdict is overwhelmingly favorable. But *Romance*, aimed at women as well as men, must appeal to both. I have no such quick ways of getting a verdict from women readers, but, though there has been criticism (not from any of you) that *Romance* is too much like *Adventure*, newsstand reports prove that the other sex must be taking kindly to it. Indeed, the sales indicate that we should have printed a much larger edition to meet the demand.

AND *Romance* has by no means struck its real gait yet. It takes time to shape a new magazine into its final form. Remember how long it's taken to shape our own magazine, and of course there are always some changes and improvements to be made. If *Romance* is good now, it's going to be a whole lot better at the end of a year.

FROM one of our Indian comrades a word about mound-builders and snake-bites:

Eufaula, Oklahoma.

I note a lot about the Indian in your magazine. I am an Indian myself, and have written a great many articles for newspapers; and at one time wrote magazine articles. I don't know if this recommendation would cut any ice with *Adventure* or not, but I believe I could open the eyes of some of the historians of this country on some subjects such as the history of the mound-builders of North America as handed down to me from mouth to ear. I can give a mouth to ear history of the origin of the Red Moon and can relate some stubborn facts about the Medicine Men of the Red Race.

I notice in the *Adventure* several times about the cure for snake-bites. It is no trouble to cure a rattler's bite if one knows what to use, which is very simple. I have a dead-shot cure, an Indian remedy.

If this does not go to the waste basket I may open the eyes of the bunch at the Camp-Fire, by relating some of my ups and downs. I like *Adventure* because its articles have lots of ups and downs in the wilds of American and also foreign lands. As the Red Man always ends his speech, "That is all."—CHARLES GIBSON.

SOME time ago we offered a five years' subscription for the best sub-title or characterizing line for our magazine. There were some hundreds of suggestions after dropping out duplications, and selection was made by a large and rather informal committee. The highest vote went to "Calls Us All" by V. C. Doaslaugh of Oakland, California. "In the World's Four Corners," from Williams F. Hooker of New York, and "The World Between Two Covers," from Daniel Flannery of Hampton, Virginia, ranked next.

I was particularly pleased that many of the suggested lines centered on our magazine's cleanness. Many, of course, featured its appeal to real men; many its educative value. Taken as a whole, the list not only contained many good lines but helped by giving us a clearer understanding of our readers' feelings toward the magazine.

Here in the office we've been trying for years to hit on a characterizing line that would hit the bull's-eye in the exact center. Though my personal opinion doesn't exactly coincide with the general vote, I think "Calls Us All" is better than anything we in the office have ever produced. Whether it can be improved upon and to what extent it shall be used are other questions.

Anyhow, the little contest gave valuable results; every one who contributed has our sincere thanks and we're very glad to put Mr. Doaslaugh down for a five years' subscription.

THE crucifixion of Estevanico, the negro who shared with Cabeza de Vaca ten years of exploration, as set forth in his story in this issue, Captain Rodney states is historical, and his fight with the black stranger of the South is still told in the traditions of the Moqui Indians.

Of the valley *Mercedes* passed through, after having been thrown into the hands of the Indians by the tornado, Captain Rodney says:

> This was the valley of the Santa Cruz River that flows from Mexico, north into Arizona. Coronado left Culiacan in Sonora, passed north through the site of the present city of Nogales; thence to where Tombstone stands. From there he headed about northeast through the White Mountains and Nutriosa to the first of his fabled cities, Hawikuk. At this point he had a battle, drove the Indians away and headed east for the second city, Acoma, where Estevanico had been killed the previous year in a fight, the traditions of which still are told by the Moquis.

WE'RE going to try a new stunt in our magazine. If you don't like it we'll not go on with it, but I've very little doubt about your liking it.

It's this way. Occasionally one of our stories will be called an "Off the Trail" story. There will be a * after its title on the contents page and again at the head of the story itself. That star will be a warning that it is in some way different from the usual magazine stories, perhaps a little different, perhaps a good deal. It may violate a canon of literature or a custom of magazine, or merely be different from the type usually found in this magazine. The difference may lie in unusual theme, material, ending or manner of telling. No question of relative merit is involved.

Remember that when a story is so marked it does not mean that this story is either better or worse than the other stories in the same issue. Merely sort of different. All of you won't always agree with us, of course, as to which stories should be called "Off the Trail." Sometimes we'll have a hard time deciding ourselves. But, as a class, you can safely count on such stories being different from our usual stories and often different from the run of stories in any magazine.

We don't know how many of them there will be. Probably about one every other issue, possibly fewer, improbably more.

There will be one in the next issue.

IN this issue we have our first "Off the Trail" story, as marked by an * and explained in the note on the second contents page. Of course you can't judge the general idea from any one story, but keep your eye on them as they happen to appear and reserve your final opinion until you've seen quite a little bunch of them. There probably won't be more than one every other issue, probably fewer.

And remember that these stories aren't marked to indicate that they're either better or worse than the other stories in the same issues—merely in some way different.

ONE of our identification-tags saved this man's life and he writes to thank us. And it was not his card at that. I'm sorry that he did not give us the number of the tag or even a civilian mail address so that we could have the name of the tag's original owner. I've written Mr. London in care of the British War Office. Anyhow, we're glad one of our cards was of service to him. I think the Yank medico would have cared for him just the same, but if said medico was a member of our Camp-Fire—and heaven knows there are a lot of doctors among our number—the tag may well have got Corporal London some extra care and attention even beyond what any ordinary American would have received.

New York.

Waking up from a sorely needed sleep, I perceived lying on the floor a bright object that I later found out to be an identification-tag issued by *Adventure*.

TEN days later I led a patrol over the top to find information regarding a drive the Germans were going to start for the Channel ports. As the dawn was rising, we had to work mighty quick, my men having lost much time looking for enemy outposts.

At last we succeeded in coaxing a few of the boche to accompany us back, with the aid of our bayonets. Through some carelessness or other I strayed from my men, eventually losing myself in the barren wastes of "No Man's Land," constantly stumbling over the bodies of friends and foes who had "gone West" the evening before.

Presently I sighted a shell-hole and made for it, finding the body of a dead German. I changed clothes with him, mine being muddy and wet and continually adding to my discomfort. As morning appeared I started to crawl for our lines, reaching within a hundred yards of them, when an enemy sniper winged me in the shoulder. After crawling some time I became unconscious.

THE following morning the Yanks broke the Hindenburg Line and one of their medical corps picked me up and, believing me dead, dropped me, but some inner sense told him to examine me more closely. Tearing open my coat, he saw tied around my neck the tag and, taking me for an American, had me taken to the rear, possibly saving my life as the wound was serious.

Later returning to Canada, I was discharged and came to New York, hoping to make it my future home.

I feel it my duty to write you this little story as a token of appreciation for the services rendered by the little tag issued by this magazine, which without the slightest doubt saved my life.—JACK LONDON, Corporal Seaforth Highlanders, 42nd Scottish.

STRONG response to the suggestion of establishing Camp-Fire "stations" keeps coming in. So far as I can, in getting the plan into practical shape, I am guided by the opinions and suggestions that come in from you. I'd like to bring up each point to be voted on democratically by all of you, but if this were done we'd be a year or two in even getting started on our stations.

For example, one of you writes a letter like the following, raising a point that ought to be passed on by all of us, not just by us here in the office. It takes several days to reach me. Suppose I'm able to put aside all other work, read it and get it ready for the printer at once. Then it may have to wait a week or ten days before the printer's schedule brings him to it. To cut matters short, it will reach your eyes in from two to three months. Then you can write in your opinions if you wish, which you may do at once or a week or two after that issue has gone on the stands. It takes anywhere from a few hours to a few days (or even weeks) for the letter to reach me. Again a question of when the printer and I can get to it. Then another two or three months before your argument, which may possibly raise new points in connection with the first, can get before all of you. It's taken somewhere around half a year to get this far along. If further discussion results, add two or three months or more before it can come up again.

THE result is that it would take forever to get anywhere on even one out of many points. The only way to get things moving is for me to act as clearing-house, soak up the various opinions as they come in, follow majority opinion where it shows definitely, use my own judgment where it doesn't, assemble all the points into a whole as best I can and just say to you, in effect: "Here it is, fixed up as well as I can to meet your general opinions. Let's go ahead and try it as it stands. As it goes along we can change it if changes are desired or prove necessary."

I hope you'll bear all this in mind, not only in connection with our stations, but in the case of anything else that comes up in the future or has come up in the past. I have no desire to do the czar stunt, but we're too scattered and it involves too much delay for really democratic methods to be followed. As clearing-house I'm just doing the best I can to make things the way the majority wants them and yet get them into actual operation.

ON the point raised in the following letter I can't quite make up my mind, though I believe the writer's view is the right one. No one else has expressed himself on this point. (If I don't vote on it at all, then there is a "unanimous" vote in its favor.) Suppose we make it a general rule, to be changed later if you wish, that there shall be only one station in towns of thirty thousand or less.

Tucson, Arizona.

I'm strong for your idea of establishing Camp-Fire stations throughout the world wherever convenient. If you had started it up ten or twelve months ago, I could have helped start one at Panama City, but now I'm on the move again and have no idea of where I'll be a month from now. My P. O. Box is about the only thing that won't change.

I would suggest, though, that in a town of ordinary size, like Tucson, with something like twenty-five thousand to thirty-five thousand people, or less, there be only one station. There would be no real *need* for more than one, and the fact that there were two or more might easily lead to a sort of snobbery, if one happened to have a more expensive place than the other. I don't believe our Camp-Firers would be much inclined to that sort of thing, though, so perhaps two or more would be O.K. But in case there were two or more asking to start a Camp-Fire station in the same town or locality, why not ask them to get together and decide on one place, instead of stringing it out over two or three? This of course applies only to medium or small-sized places, or the same locality in a large city. I'd like to see as many stations come into being as there are permanently located Camp-Fire members. If I get a permanent place to hang my hat, you can count me in on it, too.—ROBERT S. GORDON.

ANOTHER of you has suggested that no one be entitled to use a station unless he has either one of our identification-cards or a Camp-Fire button. This is a point I will *not* decide until there's been time to get opinions from the rest of you. It might seem to some only a scheme for forcing people into getting cards or buttons from this magazine—a "foxy advertising stunt" and all that kind of thing. A button or metal card costs you twenty-five cents; most of you know there is no profit in them for us and I can prove it to any doubters. Cardboard cards are given out free, unless you count the two-cent stamp for return postage. Just the same, I'm not going to decide this point till I hear from the rest of you.

For that matter, the whole station scheme can be considered "a foxy advertising stunt." So can the whole "Camp-Fire" scheme, the whole "Ask Adventure" stunt, our identification-cards, buttons, mail-service and "Lost

Trails." Anything whatever that a magazine does is an advertising stunt if it attracts people's interest and attention. Just the same, no one of you is asked to have anything to do with any of them unless he figures out for himself that he can get more out of it for himself than he puts into it.

No, no one has been riding me on this subject. I haven't any grievance—just steering clear of that card or button requirement idea so no one will try to hang something on me.

BUT here's the general idea for stations, subject, always, to changes if desired.

A station may be in any shop, home or other reputable place. The only requirements are that a station shall display the regular station sign, provide a box or drawer for mail to be called for and provide and preserve a sufficiently substantial register book. When there are enough stations to warrant even a small wholesale order this office will furnish the books and signs. (I think I'll be ordering them soon.) No responsibility for mail is assumed by anybody; the station merely uses ordinary care. Entries in register to be confined to name or serial number, route, destination, permanent address and such other brief notes or remarks as desired; each station can impose its own limit on space to be used. Registers become permanent property of station; signs remain property of this magazine, so that if there is due cause or complaint from members, a station can be discontinued by withdrawing sign.

A STATION bulletin-board is strongly to be recommended as almost necessary. On it travelers can leave tips as to condition of trails, etc.; resident members can post their names and addresses, such hospitality as they care to offer, calls for any travelers who are familiar with countries these residents once knew, calls for particular men if they happen that way, etc., notices or tips about local facilities and conditions. Letters to resident members can be posted on this bulletin-board.

Any one who wishes is a member of Camp-Fire and therefore entitled to the above station privileges. (Question of requiring identification-card or Camp-Fire button to be decided later.) Those offering hospitality of any kind do so on their own responsibilty and at their own risk and can therefore make any discriminations they see fit. Traveling members will naturally be expected to remember that they are merely guests and act accordingly.

A station may offer only the required register and mail facilities or enlarge its scope to any degree it pleases. Its possibilities as headqnarters for a local club of resident Camp-Fire members is excellent.

THE following comrades have already come forward with offers of stations even before the plan has been definitely shaped as to details. Camp-Fire owes them its thanks. Until the magazine supplies them with registers and signs they are under no obligation to furnish these, but will doubtless manage temporary substitutes.

Arthur R. Lloyd, 16 Cross Street, Malden, Mass.
Harry J. Lang, 137 South Arlington Street, East Akron, Ohio.
R. L. Hastings, Granville, Vt.
G. L. A. Bleemers (Capt.), United States Reserve Army, Tucson, Ariz.
A. M. Barlow, c/o Jones & Pierce, 609 11th Street, Wichita Falls, Texas.
John Bradford Main, The Junior Yanks, 144 South Wabash Avenue, Chicago, Ill.
A. S. Albert, Albert's Billiard Hall, Ione, Wash.
Mr. and Mrs. M. A. Monsen, Gen. Pet. No. 2, Lost Hills, Calif.
Wm. H. Fagan, 1404 New York Avenue, N. W., Washington, D. C.
Paul A. Buerger, 216 11th Street, Milwaukee, Wis.
G. DeH. Lyon, 91 North Pine Avenue, Albany, N. Y.
Wm. A. Fulmer, 252 South 9th Street, Philadelphia, Pa.

Add your name to the list so that it can be printed for the benefit of Camp-Fire members as soon as possible.

SEVERAL Camp-Fires ago Señorita Trujillo came to us with a frank complaint over the American habit—particularly in magazine stories—of applying the word "greaser" to all Mexicans. The following from E. E. Harriman is perhaps a just analysis of the case:

Los Angeles.

Señorita Aurelia Trujillo, may I have your attention for one moment? As one of the writers who have used the offensive word, allow me to offer an explanation. I would do so respectfully, politely.

I HAVE lived in Los Angeles County, California, almost thirty-four years. I have known many people of Spanish blood in that time, many from Mexico. I know many of whom I never think as "greasers," others to whom no other name seems to apply. Thomas Nelson Page does not feel aggrieved when one alludes to "Gawgie crackahs!" They are not in his class and he is untouched by the allusion.

No Englishman of letters feels hurt when one speaks of "cockneys." Dumas, Balzac, Hugo, would have been unscarified by any allusion to the "Apaches of Paris." The decent element in Mexico is never "greaser" to one who knows. It is the immoral, unregenerate, thievish class that gets the slang name. As one Mexican-born man of Spanish blood called them here, when speaking to me, "the —— Apache element in Mexico."

I SPEAK now of the element all too common among the peon class, with vocabularies principally made up of words and phrases you never heard. The class that packs a knife, even when reduced to shirt, overalls and *sombrero de palmo*. The class that steals as naturally as a snake bites. The class that herds like cattle, with as little regard for the decencies of life, verminous, drunken, diseased and vicious.

I do not refer to the scores and hundreds of Mexican-born and Mexican-bred citizens who are honored for their integrity in this city. I turn from thoroughbred to scrub in humanity as I do in a stock show.

Señorita Trujillo, there are MEXICANS and Mexicans, just as there are AMERICANS and Americans.

SO, Señorita Trujillo, when you read the word "greaser" in the pages of *Adventure*, consider that it is used as we apply the word "hoodlum" in our cities, to the disreputable, not to a people at large.

I might be induced to call a cattle-thief, horse-thief or ladron of any sort a choice collection of names, if I could not talk to him with a Winchester. That would not hit my next neighbor of the same nationality. I was born in Ohio. That is no reason why I should defend Cassie Chadwick. I lived twenty-two years in Minnesota. That does not bind me to defend Doc Ames of Minneapolis.

I think you will find, if you run through the back numbers, that in almost every case where the word is used, it is applied to the lowest class, the criminal element. In that case the shot passes far below you, too far below to hear it strike. Does the bird in the tree give thought to the troubles of the toad? *Es lo mismo* in this case, *señorita*.

Keep your chin up and your eyes away over yonder. Consider that the writer is hitting at a class far below your range. Never flutter a feather, for the shot is not fired at you or yours or at any decent *paisano*. And so *despedida á Dios*, Señorita Trujillo.—E. E. HARRIMAN.

ANOTHER letter about the Old West and its famous characters:

Deming, New Mexico.

During the last year or so I have met several of the genuine "Old-Timer" herd and have made several good friends.

I read the argument in "Camp-Fire" about "Wild Bill." Now, here in Deming lives a person who is going on ninety years of age, by the name of W. F. Gordon. "Navajo Bill," we call him. He knew Kit Carson personally, and I asked him about "Wild Bill." He says, he (W. B.) was the *real stuff*. Gordon says he has seen Wild Bill stand between two telegraph-poles and hit them both at once with his six-shooters. He also said that Hickock and Cody were the two best plainsmen of their day.

I also know Gus Gildea quite well. Perhaps some of the old fellows will recall these names.—E. F. KIERNAN.

A SECOND case of a man who has really been through the San Blas country—the only case, as this comrade claims. Does any one know of still others who really know the interior of this bit of territory so close to the Panama Canal and yet so unknown to white men, so carefully and fiercely guarded from all "foreigners"?

The comrade who sends in the second name was one of the most active men in the United States in building up the first American Legion, 1914–16, the original Legion started by our Camp-Fire for Preparedness and numbering 24,000 to 25,000 men. It is fitting that he should now be on Major-General Wood's staff, for General Wood was one of the Legion's chief sponsors. Unofficially, of course, but in those days before the United States was drawn into the war, it wasn't healthy for an Army officer to advocate Preparedness even unofficially.

THE Administration, though now we hear a great deal about its wonderful preparations for war (said preparations all having suffered from unreadiness and many of them not materializing until the war was over), was in those days very much opposed to any preparations whatsoever, preferring to take the risk of being caught unprepared and paying the bill in delay and needless expense in money and American lives. General Wood was not only clear-sighted but patriotic enough to risk his whole future by doing his utmost to rouse the country to its danger and the need of Preparedness. Despite the Wilson Administration, he did more than any other one man except Roosevelt to awaken Americans to the coming peril. And he had to pay the costs. The logical commander of the A.E.F., he was carefully side-tracked by the Wilson Administration and suffered the humiliation of being denied any kind of command at the front. His only retort was to serve his country to the last ounce of his ability in the subordinate task assigned him at home.

When you write down the heroes of the war write General Wood's name close to the top. He met the hardest test of the soldier and of the citizen and he came clean.

The other day one of you wrote me that he was going to become a Canadian because he had served this country in war and she hadn't treated him right. As a citizen of the United States or of any other country, he, and all similar kickers, would do well to take a lesson from General Leonard Wood in citizenship. We Americans need the lesson that citizenship in a democracy is not merely a matter of "What can I get out of it?" but a matter of obligation, responsibility, duty and unwavering service.

MAJOR JNO. S. BONNER, who sends us the following letter, is a member of the Chicago chapter of the Adventurers' Club, of which Theodore Roosevelt was an honorary member. Several other members or ex-members of General Wood's staff, and General Wood himself, are members of the New York chapter, as are various other Army and Navy officers.

Chicago.

It is a long time since I last had this pleasure, and some interesting events have intervened. It is of no particular importance, but this may serve to advise yourself and the Camp-Fire that I am still casting a shadow and am now serving on Major General Leonard Wood's staff in the Central Department.

Recalling the old days of the American Legion, I am doubtless one among many highly pleased to note your attitude toward the new American Legion, of whom I am which. The new Legion is destined to a great future and will deserve the support which it will receive.

BUT what I really wished to bring to your attention, and the apology for this screed, is a matter which may be of interest to the Camp-Fire. In your last number we were advised that "Cabron" Brown is the one man who successfully toured the San Blas country and emerged all in one piece. The purpose of this letter is to introduce to whomsoever may be interested Captain G. L. Fitz-William, V.C., D.S.O., M.C., late B.R.E., and present sub-chief of the San Blas tribe.

Captain Fitz-William is an American of Texan nativity, though his service in the late unpleasantness was in the British Army, and so far as I can learn he is the one white man who has established friendly relations with the San Blas tribe and is free to come and go and trade among them as he desires. And not only that, but he is a duly and truly prepared and designated sub-chief of the tribe and as such is authorized to sport the carved cane which is emblematic of supreme authority. His record and experience with this little known and hitherto impenetrable tribe dates from 1912.

If the members of the Camp-Fire would be interested in details, including photos, I can readily supply them, as I am now in close touch with Captain Williams and contemplating a visit to that primitive region under his chaperonage.

With sincere personal regards to yourself and all the members of our Camp-Fire.—JNO. S. BONNER, Major U. S. A.

SOME queries and some interesting bits about the Old West. I'm sure any sheriffs and deputies among us will hold their fire as requested. And if they do, I hope we'll hear more from this old-timer.

Arlington, Texas.

After two years of lurking in the shadows, listening to the bunch at the Camp-Fire pow-wow, and now sure "thar ain't no sher-ruffs" at the blaze, I'm going to step into the clearing with a flag of truce waving and ask all deputies to hold their fire while I make an inquiry.

HOW many of the "old buckeroos" remember the following: "Kid Barnet of Mineral Wells"; Tex George Barnes, a "bad" man with the emphasis on the word "bad," mostly of anywhere; "Young Wild" West, last heard of on the Whyle ranch, Tex. (the name sounds like six-cent fiction, but it is his name and he looked the part); Bill Posey, cattle-thief, who was killed at Wichita Falls (killed or captured); Joe Collins of Sam Bassis' gang. If any of you do, please speak up and let us know more of them. I know almost all of their history and knew most of them.

Can any of the Camp-Fire supply the remaining verses? I have forgotten them:

SAM BASS

Sam Bass was born in Indiana,
That was his native home,
And at the age of seventeen
Young Sam began to roam.

He first came out to Texas,
A cowboy for to be,
A kinder-hearted fellow
You hardly ever see.

Sam used to deal in race-stock,
One called the "Denton Mare,"
He matched her in scrub races
And raced her at the fair.

Sam used to coin the money,
He spent it mighty free.
He always drunk red "likker"
Wherever he might be.

Sam had four bold companions,
Four bold and daring lads,
Their names were Richinson, Jackson,
Joe Collins and "Old Dad."

Four bolder, braver cowboys
The Texans never knew;
They whipped the Texas Rangers
And ran the boys in blue.

That is as far as my memory allows me to go with it. It was composed by a "longhorn," many years ago, as "the boys in blue" prove, for they wore the blue then, not khaki.

JUST a few miles from where I am at present located, Sam made one of his daring train hold-ups at Grand Prairie. To stop the train (a Texas and Pacific) they piled cord-wood across the track. The engineer thought he would keep going and knock his way through. They are still picking up parts of his engine.

Sam was full of optimism. The day he was surrounded by a posse of a hundred and fifty strong—he was amid a lot of rocks, fighting them off, when the day became so hot he could hardly stand it.

"Is hell hotter'n this?" he yelled at the posse.

"You'll find out pretty soon," some one answered.

"That's right." Then silence.

"I done sent some of yuh down to welcome me, haven't I?"

No answer.

During the day, the posse claim, he stood erect, looked around and walked over to where a sage-bush afforded a little shade, and there, over a rock, he fought them off until night.

The next morning Sam was gone. Well, I guess I will back out into the shadows again. Good-night.—CHAS. B. MCCAFFERTY.

OUR old friend M. Logie, after going through the great war on the Salonika and Western fronts with the British and our own Army, was keen to get back to "God's country." He liked it but, even shortly after his return, when I saw him for an interesting half-hour or so, he was beginning to fret under the inaction and was busily looking for more excitement. Early in November I had a letter from him, written in Paris. From the following extract you will judge that by the time you read this he will be where things are happening.

Paris.

Have been trying to connect up with one of the new Republics; so far have not been successful, but "never say die." Have met several Americans—old-timers—who are serving with the Lithuanian forces. They have organized a regiment of infantry, composed of all the races and nationalities there are, quite a large percentage being Yanks. Will be a great mix-up when the American Poles and the Lithuanian bunch are opposing one another.

Hope to inform you of success shortly. A great gamble all the same.—MARC LOGIE.

THE CAMP-FIRE
A MEETING-PLACE FOR READERS, WRITERS AND ADVENTURERS

FROM one of our soldier comrades, a Regular since before the war, and with an uncle who has earned the title "old-timer."

Fort Hunt, Va.

I have an old uncle, an old country doctor, who lives in a little town in South Carolina, and he is one of the old-timers. He is about seventy-five years old and fought all through the great war between the States in the S. C. forces and so fought under Lee and was in all the great battles that were fought in Virginia, and he can tell some stories let me tell you.

After the war he went to Mexico and was in the Foreign Legion in the army of Maximilian, was captured at the same time as Maximilian and was condemned to death but escaped and made his way back to the U. S. Then served some time in the Texas Rangers and at last came back to the old home and settled down to the life of a country doctor, in the mountains of S. C.

I HAVE not seen as big snakes as the writer of the story called "The Snake," Mr. Friel tells about, but I have seen snakes in the Philippines very nearly thirty feet long. I saw one that by actual measurement was 27ft. and 4" and nearly as thick in the largest part as the body of a good sized boy. What his weight was I do not know, as we had no means of weighing him, but he was some snake.

I HAVE also been among the head-hunters and they are some pleasant people, let me tell you. Have seen a good many heads that were taken by some of their famous fighters.

I don't know if you recall the fact or not but the head-hunters from northern Luzon—the Bontoc Igorotes I think—made an attack on the Utah Light Battery with bows and beheading-knives, and were very much surprised when they were raked with shrapnel and machine-gun fire. They laid the blame on the Tagalogs and went after them in fine style, and incidentally took many heads of the tribe aforesaid.

Of all the tribes of savages it has been my luck to run up against, and I have dealt with savages nearly all my life, the Moros were the fiercest and, as Kipling says of the Arabs, "He's a poor benighted heathen but a first class fighting man." I saw two of them charge a company of militia and get just about shot to ribbons and never turn a hair. I saw one attach a sentry and the sentry shoved a bayonet through him and at the same time shot him and the Moro pulled himself up on the bayonet and would have cut the sentry down if I had not blown his head off with a .45 revolver. They were the best fighters, barring none, I ever saw.—Wallace S. Sims.

P. S. Red Belts takes me back to ground which I am very familiar with, as I lived in that part of the South for a while when I was a boy. My father was a country doctor and practised in the mountains of S. C., N. C., and Tenn. for nearly forty years and knew well all the stories connected with that part of the country and about Old Nolichucky Jack as well as any man could know them, for his grandfather was one of the men who helped Old Jack Sevier fight Indians, outlaws and Red Coats for many a long year, and lived to be about ninety-eight years old, and left ten sons and eight daughters. So I got all my stories of those times from first hand and some of them were wild let me tell you.—W. S. S.

HERE is some more about the walled cities of Zululand, from Charles Beadle of our writers' brigade who, as you will note, has wandered from the States to Paris:

Paris, France.

Dear Camp-Fire:

W. E. Keever's article on the walled cities of Zululand is particularly interesting to me as I happen to have been in the Niekerk Zimbabwe district—(Inyanga — The Spell: Motokos — The White Frog) and he gives me much information which I did not know. The currently accepted theory there—among whites of course—is that it is the work of the Phenician or else of Arabic origin built or taught by Arab slave raiders from the north.

AS I have seen them and camped among 'em, they covered several acres at a time as if they were the ruins of a small town: triangles and squares of *stone* walls usually about a foot or two high—said conformation suggesting that some crazy giant had been teaching Euclid and illustrating the propositions for the benefit of his pupils. On the tops, too, of kopjes — usually granite and boulder-strewn— were what had been decidedly fortifications: walls remaining breast high with vents for arrows— equally useful for rifles. Upon the side of hills were terraces built up by stone suggesting the terraced vine hills of Greece. On the back of the Inyanga station on a rough kopje was quite an extensive old fortification which we adapted and rebuilt as a fort. "Old workings" of gold mines are all over Rhodesia from Tuli (Big Zimbabwe) in the south to the Ruania River in the North and, as the Britannica says, are now operated with profit.

PERSONALLY I can not swallow the idea that ever the Bantu progressed as far as building these structures or mining as illustrated there. I have almost a conviction that Solomon or some of the Pharaohs sent their people right down through Uganda, etc., to Rhodesia by *land* and not fleets by sea. Certainly in comparatively modern times Arabs from as far north as the White Nile came down through or round Abyssinia as far south as this, slave raiding as they did upon the other side of Africa, Dongola and Barotseland. I think it is quite conceivable that, say, Solomon's parties would establish distant camps as the Romans did where they would teach their native slaves to build houses as they knew them; for certainly they would remain there some time after such a trip, say, from Egypt.

NOW there is no trace that I have ever heard of the Bantu constructing anything like such permanent dwellings. The Baganda were renowned upon discovery — first I think by Burton although I am not sure. Or was it Baker Pasha? — for the fact that they, a Bantu race, made more or less real roads, broad, and with bridges across swamps etc. If such an advanced race of the Bantu existed, where has it disappeared to? And why? Africa is fairly well explored now. There can not remain a sufficiently large area unknown as to provide a safe hiding-place for this super-Bantu tribe—and report of such doings and things would spread for many hundreds of miles. I can not even imagine a plausible theory to account for their having been wiped out. The men who made those ancient dwellings must have been equally advanced in the arts of war.

Another point: the setting of the sites surrounded with fortified kopjes gives quite the sense of men living in an occupied territory. The baptismal records of the Dominicans mentioned by Mr. Keever do not, I think, dispose of the theory of a ruling or a different race for the "powerful king" might well have been a titular king—the Sultan of Morocco at the present moment is Mulai Ali Mohammed (I *think*, for they change so darned quick out there!) but the French are the rulers all the same.

However I wonder whether some one else can put forward a more plausible theory.—CHAS. BEADLE.

TANNING buckskin. The sample enclosed was certainly good, and here is the recipe.

You will notice that Mr. Hendershot mentions Captain Drannan and I pass it on, not to reopen that discussion, but merely because it is one of, I think, two Camp-Fire opinions that back up Drannan's claims, whereas dozens of you have taken the other side.

Los Angeles.

I recently read the receipt for tanning buckskin, which, although it might produce results, is rather too complicated and laborious.

I enclose herewith a sample of buckskin tanned by the following method, which is much the same as used by the Indians, except that they use the brains of the animal instead of oil.

For genuine oil-tanned buckskin:

1. Flesh the skin by removing all flesh adhering to the skin by scraping with a keen but rough-edged knife.

2. Soak in lime-water (not too strong) until hair slips and remove hair. I generally use a curry-comb.

3. After hair is removed, lay skin (flesh down) over a good-sized smooth log, free from bark or other roughness, and remove "grain" (or epidermis) with the back of a draw-knife. To the novice this seems to take most of the hide, but not so, the "grain" merely being the outer part of the skin, which held the roots of the hair.

4. After removing the grain, wad the skin up and soak in neat's-foot oil for two or three weeks. Then wring out and wash in two or three changes of warm (not hot) strong soap-suds.

5. Before skin becomes entirely dry in any part begin working with the hands to keep from stiffening, which will always result (if not worked) on account of the natural glue in the skin.

During the final drying the skin should be "pulled" and worked. This is done by two persons sitting facing each other and grasping the edges of the skin and pulling (not too hard) and slowly revolving skin horizontally. This process keeps the skin to its natural size and shape.

THE enclosed sample was colored yellow by mixing yellow ocher in the last water. I have tanned many buckskins in Wyoming, Utah and Colorado and find this the easiest and simplest; although it is always tedious work to properly make good buckskin.

I am an old mountaineer, surveyor, trapper, cow-punch, rancher, etc., and have some dope on Jim Bridger and King Fisher which I will send in before long.

Have both of Captain Drannan's books and from my knowledge of the country and stories I have heard, am willing to take it for granted that most of the Captain's stories were at least based on facts.—C. A. HENDERSHOT.

CAMP-FIRE will be glad to hear from any of the still living old-timers mentioned by "Uncle Frank" Huston in the following letter.

Uncle Frank served in the Confederate Army. That is why he prays forgiveness for one of his relatives who fought on the other side. Uncle Frank now manages to be a Confederate and just plain American at the same time.

Los Angeles.

Bill Hickok was in Berdan's sharpshooters of the Yank Army enduring of the war. A certain relative of mine, Joe Huston (the original California Joe who went to California with Fremont prior to Mexican War), was also a member (God forgive him), and he and Bill scouted agin us. Neither liking army discipline, somehow got out, I think. Later a German robed himself in skins and called himself California Joe, and some confused him with the true Joe. Confound him.

HICKOK never made up to Cody, Hickok then being in a John L. Sullivan class, as it were, and Cody a pork-and-beaner. I remember Stocking. Cody was press-agented, as they say now. As for Curley, he was not a Crow, but his mother was.

THE Nortons of Wilcox, who were teaming contractors from Santa Fé to Arizona Posts; the Coulter boys of the Arivapa, Tommy Driscol of Marsh & Driscol, La Lagenea Ranche; Frank and his brother Charlie, who was foreman for Marsh and later for Bill Greene of the Cananea Cattle Company. I forget Charlie's and Frank's last names. Their father was a Missourian, and lived around Salinas or Monterey, but you can get their names. Old Marsh himself, though being a German and a runaway sailor at the time, Claus Spreckels, later Sugar King, in Honolulu and Joe Meyers of the *Patrero* left his whaler in San Diego, all three known to each other, all three from some German peasant burgh and all three ship boys. Joe Meyers married a native California woman, and got a big ranch. His sons live there yet. Marsh married a Mexican woman in Tucson (pronounced "Tookson" and *not* "Tooson"). Any of these and hundreds of others could tell you of "Pache days."

Johnny Dobbs (Deuce 2nd notwithstanding) civilian scout at Fort Bowie, shot plumb to —— and pensioned by the Territorial Legislature. His brother, Capt. Dobbs, an ex-Yank Vol. Cav. Capt., who ten years ago ran, with his son, a livery and express in Phœnix. That fat ex-Yank soldier with a German name I have now forgotten, fine fellow, good scout, and also civilian scout at Bowie, who shook hands with me at the post when I left and twenty-five years later walked into my camp in the Temecula Cañon below Fallbrook with Judge Bell, another ex-Yank swaddie, and was surprised to find it was me he was trailing, he being Deputy Game Commissioner (State), and Deputy Sheriff of Riverside. When last in Riverside I went to courthouse to *wau-wau* with him and they said the words so very, very familiar to me of late years "Oh! he's dead."

"Wyinel" don't you get Buck Connor to get some dope from his people, the Bois Brules?

RENO was a brave Yank soldier enduring of the war, but knew nothing of Indians. He did, however, save his command by good sense and bravery, but was made a scapegoat. (Neurasthenic, hysterical women, with pull at Washington.) Had he obeyed Custer's orders his command and the pack-train would be there now with the others.

—— was in Reno's command and, as soon as he could, skipped and joined the Marines in Boston. Later I heard (Oh, 10 or 15 years ago) —— was the postmaster in —— or some such town in New England.

Or ask Larry North.

Say, these fellows that "have read every scrap of information" make me tired. Closet naturalists and book-farmers all. I can't remember names very good nowadays, but old —— used to be postmaster at Whipple Barracks in the old building just above the Q. M. stores and corral and stables if alive (was in 1908) can give you galore of old Arizona days and dozens of others in other places if I could call 'em to mind.

Andy Mills is an expert on Geronimo campaigners and Pache Kid. Andy's P. O. address Willcox.

AND say, did you ever hear of Fort Bliss—old Fort Bliss, old, old Fort Bliss, old, old, old Fort Bliss? Well, the present is the fourth of that name at El Paso del Norte. The other three were around the bend up the river, having been removed a few hundred yards as newly established, but in 90's under a caretaker. First fort obliterated and second two combined as one with S. P. Ry. passing between.

Fort Grant first built of dobe and later moved across the "crick" a few yards to present location. Camp Grant was further north 40 or 50 miles, at junction of Pedro and Arivapa Rivers, and the 5th Cavalry in '71 moved from there to slope of Mount Grahame and built Fort Grant (the first one).

See if you can get the history of the little town of Tubac, between Tucson and Nogales, from the time it was founded in 16 or 17 something. Lord, the bloody times it has seen!

If you have a friend or correspondent in Washington, get him to go to Soldier's House at Rock Creek and ask librarian to let him look over the books, then to Congressional Library and repeat.

Both are mines of information. Now dig.—FRANK HUSTON.

THE missing white race of China. Now there's a subject that smacks loudly of adventure. Harold A. Lamb brings it up and we know from his stories of *Khlit* the Cossack that Mr. Lamb is no stranger to the past of Asia. He and Major Quilty have been corresponding and the following letter from Mr. Lamb is the result. Can any of you throw additional light? And if Dr. Beech is one of us I hope he'll tell us more about the strange people mentioned below.

New York City.

Here's a point I'd like to pass along to the fellow members of Camp-Fire.

MAJOR T. FRANK QUILTY, Constructing Quartermaster, Columbus Quartermaster Interior Storage Depot, Columbus, Ohio, is the man who asks the question. This is the question, quoted from his letter.

"According to recent investigations, the Blond White Race, or Nordics (our race), now confined to Western Europe, at one time spread across Asia as far as the confines of China. The farthest Eastern sub-division was known as the Wu-Suns or Hiung-Nu in Central Asia, referred to in Chinese annals because of their blue eyes, as the Green-Eyed Devils.

"Do you presume there is the slightest trace of the Nordic race left in these regions? Turkestan, according to Madison Grant (of the American Geographical Society), was at one time as blond as Sweden; the shores of the Caspian being, as regards race, as are now the shores of the Baltic. Bactria, 'The Mother of Cities,' has been, within historic times, a distinctively Nordic city."

A PRETTY big question, this. And the more you think of it the more interesting it gets. Did the white race at one time overrun Central Asia? And has it left traces which can be found today? Did the tribes of the great region from the headwaters of the Yenissei to the Indus, from the Caspian Sea to the western border of the desert of Gobi, have white forefathers!

Major Quilty says, in a second letter, that whether Central Asia was ever dominantly Nordic is open to debate. He adds that Bactria was found by Alexander to be inhabited by a distinctively Nordic people. And that there are—he believes—some Nordic traces still to be found in Afghanistan and in Turkestan—quite distinctively in the Mongolized Kirghizes.

NOW, getting down to fundamentals, Madison Grant, who ought to know, explains that the Nordic race, unlike any other, has the long skull, light eyes, and, usually, blond hair. A tall race—that of (in ancient times) the Persians, Phrygians, Gauls, Goths, Franks, Saxons, Angles, Norse and Normans.

It is the adventure race, as Major Quilty says, *par excellence*. And it's interesting to picture to ourselves the ancestors of the Vikings and Celts sweeping across the highlands of Mid-Asia, driving the round-skulled, slant-eyed and stocky races before them.

Madison Grant says this actually happened, between 1200 and 600 B.C. He mentions by way of proof the Aryan languages, Sanscrit and Old Persian, which were established in Northern India and Mesopotamia. Also the fact that remnants of an Aryan language have been found in Chinese Turkestan. (As to this, didn't the explorer Stein find, in the sand-buried cities near Khoten in Chinese Turkestan, traces of a language similar to Sanscrit?)

SO MUCH for language. Madison Grant, from the viewpoint of the scientist, adds: "Some traces of their (Nordic conquerors) blood have been found in the Pamirs and in Afghanistan. . . . It may be that the stature of some of the Afghan hill tribes and of the Sikhs, and some of the facial characteristics of the latter, are derived from this source."

LANGUAGE and history having given us, briefly—they probably have a lot more to say, if some one will point it out—their points, we'll ask the question of the explorers and adventurers.

Marco Polo says a lot about the mythical kingdom in Mid-Asia, of Prester John, the Christian. But this is no mention of an Aryan race. Marco Polo's story shows he saw, or heard of, an Asiatic people or tribe with an immensely wealthy and powerful ruler who may or may not have been a Christian.

Other medieval explorers speak of the "fair faces and tall bodies" of a semi-Tatar tribe situated about the eastern end of the Thian Shan Mountains—the Naimans, I believe. These were not the Kirghiz, mentioned by Grant.

TWO other medieval priests who traveled across the caravan routes past the Pamirs and Chinese Turkestan (as it is now called)—Fra Rubruquis and Carpini, tell of handsome and tall tribes in the interior, but of no race which resembled Europeans. Naturally, the priests did no skull-measuring. Probably it would not have been a safe thing to try on the Central Asian tribesman of the sixteenth century.

In modern times C. A. Sherring, of the Indian Civil Service, in his trips along Tibet and the British borderland, ran across a tribe in the Southern Himalayas, of the Khasia race, which he states, "is certainly Aryan and connected with that branch of the great Aryan race which . . . spread itself over the great Gangetic Valley." (In the Vedic times mentioned above by Grant.)

AND then, out of a clear sky, comes this story of a modern missionary—Dr. Joseph Beech, president of the West China University at Chengtu, who was twenty years in China.

Dr. Beech says he saw "a tribe of good-sized men, who, for all I could see, were exactly like the Bohemians." (Note: Madison Grant states that the modern Bohemians are of the round-skulled races, like the Asiatic Tatars.)

Furthermore, he says: "My friends told me of another tribe which, as one Chinese put it, 'are just like you.' I was not able to visit this people. They live in the district of Sung Pan. It is ten days' journey, or about 300 miles northwest of Chengtu.

"This tribe resembling Anglo-Saxons was described to me as consisting of large, furious men, whose bravery is considered somewhat of a marvel to the Chinese. 'They never run away any more than you do,' my Chinese friend told me. 'They love to fight.'

"I was told the men often fight duels on horseback which recall the duels of the Middle Ages. The duellists start the fight with a discharge of short blunderbusses—so heavy they rest them on a wooden cross attached to the saddle-bow. I judged they were made by native workmen, and rather inefficient weapons, hurling a handful of slugs.

"The second stage of the duel is fought with stones, of which each has a bag. If the bags are exhausted without serious injury, the duellists draw nearer and throw spears tied to the ends of ropes so they can be pulled back and thrown again. Meanwhile the two horsemen are circling around and constantly getting closer.

"In the final stage the antagonists ride up to each other and fight hip to hip with great swords, after the fashion of Richard the Lion-Hearted. The duel always goes to a decision, my Chinese friend told me."

(Has any one ever seen a Central Asian tribesman with a "short blunderbuss," or short gun of any kind?)

DR. BEECH mentions a medieval castle that he saw on the border between China and the tribes country "which was totally unlike Chinese architecture."

Possibly the Chinese friends of Dr. Beech—the Chinese enjoy a good story and are prone to exaggeration—were describing one of the tribes of the mountain Kirghiz, who are good fighters and better horse-thieves. By the way, the Kirghiz tribes are not confined to the steppe around the western Thian Shan. Their *auls* stretch north and east, well across the borders of Mongolia and into Siberia. E. H. Wilson, the naturalist, was ten years in the country around Chengtu and mentions no Aryan-looking tribes.

Dr. Beech is now in this country. Perhaps some one in the Camp-Fire knows him, or his experiences, and can get word to us from him.

PERHAPS some tribes of Aryan descent are to be found in the interior of China, between the Kuan Lung Mountains and the headwaters of the Yang-tze (the Sung Pan Ho and the Ta Ho rivers).

Tibet is rather out of date as the Forbidden Country. The only district of Central Asia not yet visited—to my knowledge—by white explorers is the Kuan Lung region, mentioned above.

The Sung Pan district, of which Dr. Beech speaks, forms the southeastern corner of this region. Wilson went as far as the Chinese military post of Sung Pan, without trouble except from vermin and native curiosity.

Sven Hedin crossed the western boundary of this region, but tells of no unusual tribes—of very few tribes at all, in fact.

Marco Polo must have crossed from Khotan into China proper along the north side of this "blind spot" region. Incidentally, Marco Polo says the khan he christens "Prestre John" lived in this blind spot south of the Kuan Lung. Another strange fact—Mr. Ney Elias says that while on the northeast corner of this blind spot, "An old man called on me at Kwei-hwa-ching who said he was neither Chinaman, Mongol, nor Mohammedan, and lived on ground especially allotted by the Emperor, and where exist several families of the same origin. He said he had been a prince." The tale of the old man was interrupted and Elias was warned against asking questions.

CAN any member of the Camp-Fire shed light on these tribes of Central Asia? Perhaps the English or Oriental men can do so. At present Major Quilty's question is unanswered.—H. A. LAMB.

YOU know, those of you who have written saying good things about the Camp-Fire, and our magazine, that, while I surely appreciate it, I cut this praise out of all such letters when other parts of them are printed. Maybe I've yielded to a particular temptation a half-dozen times in all the years our Camp-Fire has been burning, but there's been almost none of it. It would spoil the whole spirit of our Camp-Fire if it even seemed to be a place for advertising the magazine by printing "words of praise."

And yet today it struck me for the first time that in a way it is an injustice to all the rest of you, for *you* are the Camp-Fire. There couldn't be any without you. And the words of praise are really directed at you.

Also it struck me that none of us except us here in the office (who see all the letters that come in) can have even a faint idea of how very many people swear by our Camp-Fire, of how keen is their interest in it and their loyalty to it. Thousands of letters come in that really ought to be passed on to all of you, for you'd enjoy hearing their kind words and knowing how blamed many of us there are. Not much soft stuff, but the kind of talk you know is meant—all the stronger because it doesn't wallow around in language but says its say briefly, man-fashion, and goes on to something else.

NO, I'M not going to hand out a bunch of it by way of samples. The most important thing is to keep Camp-Fire from even looking like an admiration society or an advertising scheme. But I do want you all to know that there are many thousands more of us than most people think and that there's a whole lot more comradeship and loyalty than appears on the face of the letters when they get into type. Also, that we could fill Camp-Fire many, many times over if we printed all the letters.

If anybody with an ingrowing case of "show me" thinks there's any "hot air" about this, let him come into the office, or delegate a friend to do so, and, without showing any letters whose senders would mind having them shown, I'll give him a look at the day's correspondence, or the letters waiting their turn at Camp-Fire, or letters from the files, and let him make his own estimate from whatever reasonable test *he* thinks is fair. All I ask is that, if he is convinced, he will sign a statement to that effect, let me print it in Camp-Fire over his name and address and agree to answer any of you who might write to find out whether he was a real person or a name faked by me.

There are always some people like that, but I think most of you realize, from the kind of letters we have at Camp-Fire, that there are quite a lot of people sitting around it and that they are its pretty good friends.

Just one thing more. I want to add that a very high percentage of those letters close with hearty good wishes for the Camp-Fire and its members.

ANOTHER letter written a year ago and only just coming to the surface among the other letters waiting to be heard at Camp-Fire. No, it doesn't take a year for most letters to get in. When letters, with interest for Camp-Fire, come in I put them all in one place and draw on them more or less haphazard when getting together material for our twice-a-month meetings. Sometimes I get a systematic streak and dig out the old ones first; sometimes I succumb to the informal and adventurous spirit of our Camp-Fire and just take things as they happen to come. My days are full enough of systematic routine and I know you won't grudge me a rather free and easy time in getting things ready for our meetings. After all, I'm the fellow who has to tend to our chores—usher, janitor, sergeant-at-arms, sort of a toastmaster and so on. Be easy on the hired help.

Camp Upton, N. Y.

The "What Is Adventure?" discussion of the Camp-Fire has my pen hand itching for some time, but it took Mr. Young's answer to Mr. Hatheway to finally compel action.

I LAY no claim to be the final word on the spirit of adventure, but I do know this: It is interesting to spin the yarn about the stove whereon I had a kettle of beans for six hours, and then ate them half raw because that stove—despite mud and dry firewood—sent all the heat up the chimney and the smoke into the cabin. It's interesting to tell the yarn *now*, and to laugh at the idea of being held in that stray cabin by a raging storm, but at the time it wasn't adventure; it was a —— nuisance. And I have noticed that books of adventure—authentic yarns—are mostly written after the events have occurred, while those written during the time and action being recorded present the picture much as a workaday affair.

BUT to return to Mr. Young. When considering his advice for intellectual adventure: "Prowl out beyond the apex end of the triangle of the known into the unknown realms," always remember Punch's advice to those considering marriage: "Don't." You'll find queer things out there, all right, but if it's adventure you're after, try something safe. Such, for example, as going to the zoo and crawling into the grizzly bear's cage, or tickling a mule's heel, or jumping off Brooklyn Bridge. For when hunting the "Me in one" and the—but never mind—the original "one" is in danger of being lost! Them's facts.—WM. A. GOOD.

ANNUAL VOTE

THE last call for our annual vote by readers on the ten best stories published by our magazine during 1919. Voting is an easy matter. Here are the particulars:

ALL you need do is write the titles and authors' names of the ten stories you consider best, given in order of preference, and mail us the sheet of paper to reach us not later than January thirty-first. If you like, add as many as ten more for honorable mention. As in past years, short stories, novelettes, novels and serials are included, poems "Camp-Fire" and the other departments are barred out. The issues covered are those dated January 3, 1919, to December 18, 1919, inclusive. Serials only parts of which are contained in these issues are included.

We very sincerely want your cooperation and help in getting for *Adventure* the kinds of story and the authors that a majority of our readers like best. If you know of a better way of furthering this cooperation than is the annual vote by readers, name it, for we are ready to try any legitimate plan that will help register your wishes in the making of the magazine. It's not only common sense to strive for this but it's a lot happier and more comfortable all around if people work together in friendly fashion.

WHILE the departments are excluded from the vote we'll be more than glad to get suggestions for improving them. Or adding to them, but don't forget that "Letter-Friends" and "Wanted" have already been tried, and, though successful and popular, had to be given up because two or three readers abused them.

And if you have any suggestions concerning the magazine in general or any part of it, by all means send them in. I mean constructive suggestions that will definitely point out ways for improvement. Wherever we can meet your ideas we will, but remember that it is the majority whom we must please and that, while a given plan may please a minority and perhaps us here in the office, if it fails to please the majority it is not warranted.

But the only way to find out what the majority want is for the readers themselves to tell us. And you are one of the readers.

THE following letter was addressed to one of you who had made inquiry through the magazine.

Toledo, Ohio.

Noting your letter for information in the current issue of *Adventure*, would call your attention to the remarkable resources in your line, which may be obtained in Peru, which country I have represented as Consul to the State of Ohio. Any encyclopaedia will give you an idea of the natural resources of that country. The works of Humboldt, which may be consulted at your library, also will give you some remarkable statements as to the natural mineral resources.

PERSONALLY, I have been interested in that country financially and had at one time what was considered the richest placer grounds in the world in area. There are places where two of you, with men to do the hard work of digging and shoveling, can actually pan out several hundred dollars per day, and it is a matter of fact, that the natives in certain districts in Peru are in the habit of spreading across the dry torrents, in Summer, skins of the jaguar, in such a manner that the fur smooths up stream. In other places they spread riffles of stone, a few yards apart, forming what appears to be little fences all around cobble-stones about six inches in diameter.

During the freshets and the thawing of the snows of the Andes Mountains, these rivers swell and then recede again in a few hours. After the rivers become dry the skins are taken up by the natives, dried over a fire and then beat with sticks, which causes gold-dust in flakes to fall on a blanket spread on the ground. The little stone fences and riffles also are then scooped up and gold-dust taken in paying quantities.

As a matter of fact, nearly all of the gold which is now produced in Peru is obtained in this manner by the Indians. No placers are being worked. The educated Peruvians are too lazy to do this work, so that the country is still virgin, as far as prospectors in placers are concerned.

I HAVE personally seen in the north of Peru such an abundance of crude oil that it escapes in some of the small streams flowing into the rivers, staining the waters for miles. There are wells in Peru worked by the British along the coast, some of which are almost built in the surf in the Pacific.

It seems to me that you and your companion would do a thousand times better in the Andes Mountains of Peru, prospecting for gold-dust, or in in the northern district of Peru, prospecting for oil, which can be sold in Panama, where there exists a pipe-line crossing the Isthmus. (See my "Guide to Modern Peru" in your public library). I know India and its conditions and would certainly advise you to try Peru by all means—cheaper, healthier, nearer home and much more profitable.—D. R. A. DE CAIRMONT, M.D.

Since the subject fell within Edgar Young's department of "Ask Adventure" I passed the letter (a copy of which was courteously sent me) on to him. Here is his letter in comment. I do not think he meant to warn me personally against buying gold-mine stock. If he did, my thanks to him for very good advice. I trust, however, that I didn't need it.

Brooklyn, N. Y.

The peculiar part of this letter is that it is absolutely true and its statements can be backed by any one that has traveled in the highlands of Peru. The skins he speaks of are used to catch "flour" gold that is so very light it defies the laws of gravity and would otherwise be lost. The hair on them serves the same purpose that moss does on stones in some of our own rivers. Any old prospector has "moss hunted." By that I mean has gone along some gold-bearing stream tearing off moss from stones and shaking the dust from it into his pan and washing it when he has a panful, using quicksilver to pick the gold from the remaining dust. The other way of putting down cobblestones and building riffles is nothing but making a natural sluice-box in the bottom of a stream and is exactly the same principle as our own placer mining.

THE amount of gold and silver and tin that have been taken from Peru and Bolivia would be almost unbelievable were it not a matter of record and history, and great quantities of them are being taken from there to-day. Even the Cerro de Pasco Copper Company get enough gold from their copper to pay all operating expenses, or that was what I heard when I worked at Cerro. And Peru has nothing on Bolivia. I will have to demur that far.

I suppose you read Doctor Mozans' account of his trip "Along the Andes and Down the Amazon," which was published in the magazines and is now in book form (New York, D. Appleton & Co., 1912). In snatching for a book to uphold this letter's statements I turned to pp. 183 and 184 and find the following:

"The republic (Bolivia) is celebrated for its mines of gold, silver, tin, and other metals, but in no mineral region in the world has 'Nature ever offered to the avidity of man such mines of riches as those of Potosi,' that *preliosa margarita de la Naturaleza*, which, it has been estimated, has produced from two to four billions of dollars. . . . Although it may never be possible to find another Cerro del Potosi in South America, it is, nevertheless, certain that there are untold fortunes awaiting the prospector in Bolivia and Peru. The mines of Cerro de Pasco, Hualgayoc, and Pulacayo, from which many hundred million dollars worth of the precious metals have been taken, give some idea of the immense treasures still awaiting the enterprising miners of the future."

EASTERN Ecuador, Eastern Peru, and Eastern Bolivia are full of gold. All of the Indians that inhabit this country have plenty of dust to trade, which they get about $11 an ounce for in goods at high prices. The Indians of Central America get about $16 and the gold is worth $20 an ounce. *The Pan-American Bulletin* recently published a photo of a nugget picked up in Eastern Boliva, life-size, which occupied a full page. All of the data of the Pan-American Union will back statements in regard to the gold, silver, copper and tin of the countries mentioned, and all literature of these countries will do so without any exception. Humbolt says, and is quoted by Doctor Mozans as follows: "The abundance of silver in the Chain of the Andes is in general such that when we reflect on the number of mineral depositories, which remain untouched, or which have been very superficially wrought, we are tempted to believe that Europeans (Doctor Mozans—, and he might have added the people of the United States) have yet scarcely begun to enjoy the inexhaustible fund of wealth contained in the New World."

HERE'S the big idea. Do not buy stock in placer mines and do not buy stock in any fly-by-night stock companies. A good placer mine does not have to sell stock for the very reason that half a dozen men can get out enough to start any kind of plant they need. The other statement refers to bitter experence that is to be had in any gold-mining country. My advice is go and hunt it for yourself. I am saying this to get in the clear.—EDGAR YOUNG.

THERE has not been time yet to hear from you on the final plans for "Camp-Fire" or *Adventure* stations all over the world.

The strong points of the plan, so far as developed, are its simplicity and elasticity. Almost no outlay is required—a register book, a sign and a box for letters. Each station must have these. It need have nothing else, but on the other hand, it can have a great deal more. That is a question to be decided locally, in each case, by the owner of the shop or home or by the local resident members of our Camp-Fire. It can even be made into a local club with a welcome for traveling members, a center through which members of Camp-Fire can find one another and get acquainted.

Send in your name if you're ready to start a station in your shop or home, or suggest other places for stations.

Our Camp-Fire came into being May 5, 1912, with our June issue, and since then its fire has never died down. Many have gathered about it and they are of all classes and degrees, high and low, rich and poor, adventurers and stay-at-homes, and from all parts of the earth. Some whose voices we used to know have taken the Long Trail and are heard no more, but they are still memories among us, and new voices are heard, and welcomed.

We are drawn together by a common liking for the strong, clean things of out-of-doors, for word from the earth's far places, for man in action instead of caged by circumstance. The *spirit* of adventure lives in all men; the rest is chance.

But something besides a common interest holds us together. Somehow a real comradeship has grown up among us. Men can not thus meet and talk together without growing into friendlier relations; many a time does one of us come to the rest for facts and guidance; many a close personal friendship has our Camp-Fire built up between two men who had never met; often has it proved an open sesame between strangers in a far land.

Perhaps our Camp-Fire is even a little more. Perhaps it is a bit of leaven working gently among those of different station toward the fuller and more human understanding and sympathy that will some day bring to man the real democracy and brotherhood he seeks. Few indeed are the agencies that bring together on a friendly footing so many and such great extremes as here. And we are numbered by the hundred thousand now.

If you are come to our Camp-Fire for the first time and find you like the things we like, join us and find yourself very welcome. There is no obligation except ordinary manliness, no forms or ceremonies, no dues, no officers, no anything except men and women gathered for interest and friendliness. Your desire to join makes you a member.

SOME more about Billy the Kid and Wild Bill from one of us whose letter-head has printed on it: "Wing over Wing; Loop the Loop; Upside Down Flying; Wing Slides; Vertical Drop; Tail Slides; Cork-screw Drop."

HENDERSON, KY.

From 1903 to 1906 I punched cattle in southeastern New Mexico and was acquainted with an old chap, Uncle Pat Brady by name, and he used to tell me stories of old-timers and gunmen he had known. He mentioned having seen Wild Bill Hickok, at San Antone, Texas, two or three times, but stated that he (Wild Bill) seldom came farther south than Abilene, Kansas.

BILLY the Kid, so I was informed, was a product of the Lincoln County war. Eddy, now Carlsbad, N. M., was one of his stamping-grounds. Billy the Kid, so far as I could learn, was the inventor or originator of the trick of presenting his guns butt-forward in token of surrender and at the same time retaining his hold on the gun or guns with his gun-finger through the trigger-guard, then, when his adversary reached for the gun, pivoting it on his gun finger and firing. He was killed at Roswell, N. M., I believe, and, according to Uncle Pat's story, in this manner: Pat Garrett, the sheriff, learning that the Kid had a young Mexican woman that he visited at night, went to the woman's home, made her allow him to lie in bed with her and, when the Kid came into the room, shot him dead without warning.

Several years since Garrett was shot and killed at or near El Paso, Texas, and I have heard a number of old-timers say that he got what was coming to him.—BAXTER ADAMS.

Mr. Adams also sends Camp-Fire a poem, by way of thanks for its having put him on the trail of several old friends, among them Melville Ross, "who was injured while flying for Britain. By the way, do you know where he now is? We both learned flying at the Curtiss land flying-school at North Island, San Diego, California in 1914."

As to the poem, the mule undoubtedly has weak spots of character or disposition but on the whole I think there are many of you who will endorse him as a "real person." One of us has written a poem to him; let the rest of us join in and drink to the mule's best health, even if Prohibition has made it impossible to do so in the way he peculiarly deserves—with something with a kick in it.

An Ode to the Mule

THEY call you a jackass, an onery beast;
  Cuss you and maul you until you're deceased;
Gear you up at early morn,
Working you hard till the sun is gone;
Hitch you on to a heavy load,
Expect you to haul it on any old road;
And all you get at the best of it
Is a "Damn you, Tobe!" or a jerk of the bit.

It's a lucky day when you are tired
If the road is smooth and you don't get mired.

In days now gone when the West was new,
Indians many and settlers few,
When they hauled their freight they depended on
  you.
Now they talk of tractors and motor-cars.
And send you to France to be killed in the wars.
In Flanders fields where heroes fell
They loaded you down with shrapnel shell
And sent you through mud that alone was hell
While all you got at the best of it
Was a "Damn you, Tobe!" or a jerk of the bit.

—BAXTER ADAMS.

I'LL say they are. Of all the peoples our boys met and fought beside in the great war most of them seem to like the Australians and New Zealanders best, with the Canadians almost neck and neck. But I'll say they are. Maybe that's one reason why our boys liked them, being pretty strong themselves when it comes to josh, spoof, bull and otherwise large talk. Just listen to this Australian comrade! But we like him, don't we?

Bowaderry, New South Wales, Australia.

I want to throw my blanket down by your Camp-Fire and hold out my hand and say, "Can I join up?"

HAVING no one to give me a "knock down," I must introduce myself. I'm an Australian, born in the State of New South Wales, and though you might as well try to roll a snow-ball into —— as to get up an adventure like I've read in your magazine, or get a man here to pull a gun on another man—the whole police force together with the relations of the man (to the third and fourth generation) would be on your heels, and you'd be handed a "Kathleen Mavourneen"—it may be for years or may be forever. Yet we're no "Willies" (a term meaning an effeminate man). You remember when the Kaiser unbuckled the belt band of Eternity, we landed at the Dardanelles. My kid, nineteen years of age, fought his way with his mates through that surf and up those hills and made Von der Goltz a liar when he said "It couldn't be done." We never turned our backs in France.

I just mention these things lest you may think us soft because we've not got a notch on our gun, or mixed it in gun-play with a wild and woolly greaser, or got on speaking terms with a grizzly, or stood with a handkerchief in our mouths and a knife in our hands inviting some one to write on a bit of paper what they'd have on their tombstone before they took hold of the other end of a handkerchief. Yet, as I said, we are no Willies. I repeat this lest some chap of the Kit Carson type may want to offer me his hand in holy matrimony.

WE CAN ride, and I've never met the cowboy who could put it over an Australian at the buck-jumping game. In a contest between a cowboy with a lassoo and an Australian who rode at his beast, threw it by the butt of the tail, and hog-tied, the Australian won out with 5 to 3.

While I'm on this buck-jumping business, Angus McManus says there never was such a thing as a trained buck-jumper. Shades of Wallace! I hate to tell a Scot that he handles the truth very carelessly, for our soldiers have nothing but praise for the Scotties with whom they fought in France, but man Angus! I know a trained buck-jumper that will buck nine times out of every five. He travels with a show, and has been at it for the past three years. He can throw the whole Ten Commandments one after another, and the only hope one would have of staying on his back in a park saddle—we bar Mexican saddles and stock saddles with big knee-pads (they're for girls)—would be to cut a nick in his forehead and let him buck through the slit and leave the rider on his hide.

WE'VE got no big game to hunt. Foxes there are in thousands on our stations—ranches you call them. They were introduced by some fool Englishman for sport, and, like the rabbits, they are a curse. We run them down on horse-back (with a gun). Have got five in two hours. Kangaroos there are in thousands, but they are as harmless as lemon squash. Rabbits exist in millions, and shooting them is like taking corn out of a blind parrot's cage. All one has to do is to sit behind a bush, make a noise like a cabbage, and then catch the rabbits as they line up for cabbage.

SO YOU see, we have no adventures to compare with yours over there, and the only long suit I hold to give me a footing at the Camp-Fire is that I'm an Australian. I could tell some yarns—so tame that they'd feed out of one's hand—of our country, of our sheep-dog, that can drive a blow-fly with one wing pulled off into a gun barrel one hundred yards away, or yard newly hatched chickens back into their shell; of our cattle-dogs that can bite twice without letting go; of our trees so tall that it would strain the barrel of a gun shooting at a bird in the top of them; of our horses that can travel fearsome journeys, doing the distance between sunrise and sundown in two and one-half hours, and no short cuts, of our blacks who are such adepts at tracking that they can tell where you spit last week, or track an ant up a corn-stalk; of the come-back boomerangs they throw, of our shearers who can peel the fleeces off so fast and spear the sheep down the "shute" so quickly, an outsider would think they were playing leap-frog.

I could tell of these things, but it wouldn't be like the derring-do deeds in *Adventure*.

However, if you will have me at your Camp-Fire let me know. I may be able to call forth a smile from the men who have seen and done things. In any case good luck.—E. READ.

BY WAY of introducing himself on the occasion of his first story in our magazine, Charles N. Webb tells us something about the real things back of "A Triumphant Journey." When his letter came I ought to have written him and explained that what Camp-Fire really expects when a new man joins our writer's brigade is a personal word about himself, but I failed to do so, so I am to blame, not Mr. Webb, who after all falls into the essential spirit of the occasion.

Lancaster, Wis.

The central incident in "A Triumphant Journey" is not fictitious. It happened nearly as described in a town on the Mesabi range where I was working on an evening paper three years ago. An old-timer gave most of his Winter's wages to aid a brother woodsman who had been crippled in an accident on a logging railroad.

THE old-timers are rapidly disappearing from the woods. The men who went in in the Fall and came out in the Spring, who held their jobs because of physical fitness, and who had the utmost contempt for a man who "toted whisky to the push" are becoming rarer each season. Those I have run across in the logging-camps and the Northern Minnesota towns were mostly camp foremen or, at least, straw bosses. Occasionally one encounters a veteran, like *Patty O'Toole*, who is employed as a common woodsman.

The old-timers I have known were one and all foes of the I. W. W. I was working in the woods when the "Reds" were carrying on a very vigorous agitation which in that immediate section failed to hamper the work of logging to any considerable extent. Later, when I was employed as a reporter, an I. W. W. agitator who called himself the "Timber-beast," did manage to get a few hundred lumber-jacks to leave their work and join him in a demonstration in the town I happened to be in.

The men went back to work in a few days, however, and, as nearly as I could ascertain, the strike was a failure. Whatever reason the lumber-jacks may have had for a strike in the past, it seemed to me that they had the slightest that season when wages were higher than they had been for years and living conditions better.—CHARLES N. WEBB.

STILL another cure for snake-bite. Camp-Fire is always glad to hear these cures, but of course no responsibility is assumed for any of them. We are just a company gathered together, any one of us can offer a suggestion or advice, and all the others listen, each passing judgment for himself and acting accordingly.

Pascagoula, Miss.

There is one remedy for snake-bites which I have not seen mentioned in *Adventure*. It was given me by a California ranchman and miner and vouched for as a sure and speedy cure. He says he always carried a bottle of ammonia and in case he was bitten by a poisonous snake he immediately washed the wound with the ammonia and also put a little of it in water or whisky and drank it. He says he has used that remedy times enough so he knows it is a sure cure and without any after ill effects.—C. E. WALTER.

FROGS. Can you talk to a frog? That surely is a new subject for Camp-Fire. But if comrade Crippen is a liar I belong in the same class, for I know from personal experience that there's something in this frog thing.

VANCOUVER, B. C.

Say, I'd like to tell you something about frogs, but I'm afraid you might think I was having a pipe dream. Did you ever see American bull-frogs that measured twenty inches from nose to tip of hind legs? I had some this big; one was stuffed and on exhibit in the Idaho building at San Francisco fair. Did you ever know frogs could be charmed and coaxed out of the water on to the bank, and that they have a language of their own? I have coaxed up a big bunch out of the moss by making the noise that means something good to eat; then give the signal that means danger, and see them all jump and dive. I guess I better quit before you think I'm lying.—CARLETON F. CRIPPEN.

Several years ago, on an island in the St. Lawrence, about June first I caught a small frog with my hands, held him a few minutes and noticed that he seemed not at all anxious to escape and even to like being gently stroked with the fingers. Getting tired of the game, I tossed him out into the water three or four feet from where I was sitting on my heels on the shore. He started to swim, turned and headed directly back to me. I held out my palm just below the surface of the water and he climbed back on it, stayed a few more moments and finally departed. It happens that I can produce two witnesses. Was it that he liked the warmth of the hand?

This Summer, hunting small frogs for bait, I found half a dozen or so in an old boxed-in spring. Caught one or two and the others went down under the floating moss, perhaps into the mud, the box bottom being broken. I waited; no frogs reappeared. Remembering Mr. Crippen's letter, I took a chance on frog talk. Heaven knows what I said, but I thought it at least sounded like a frog. Apparently they thought the same, for instantly three of them appeared at the surface and became bait. No witnesses. Maybe just coincidence. But next time I want frogs for bait I'll try it again.

I wrote Mr. Crippen my first experience—the second happened later—and finding I believed him, he wrote me a second letter, giving me more detailed data. I put that second letter aside for Camp-Fire and can't lay hands on it now, but it wih appear sooner or later and I'll pass it on.

Laugh all you please, but some time make an experiment or two yourself and see what happens. Doubtless some of you have already done so. If so, be game and stand up with Mr. Crippen and me.

THAT *Adventure* and Camp-Fire draw many of us into personal acquaintanceships or friendships is an old story, but here is "Ask Adventure" doing the same thing among its scattered editors with our writers mixed in—Theodore S. Solomons, Thomas Samson Miller, Arthur Gilchrist Brodeur, Kathrene and Robert Pinkerton, E. E. Harriman. It's a personal and intimate letter, but breathing only good will and friendship and I'm hoping all concerned will not mind my passing it on to their other friends.

BERKELEY, CALIF.

I thought you'd like to know that we had a sort of "A. A." symposium here, just ended this morning.

I've been trying, occasionally, to see Milller, and he me, but we never made it, due somewhat to his migratory habits. Tried to find Harriman when in Los Angeles recently, but—no go. Also always wanted to see the Pinkertons, but never expected to—in the flesh. Likewise, have been struck with Brodeur's Scotch and Norse stuff and wondered what sort of chap, etc. Didn't know he lived on this coast, however.

THIS week have met the whole —— bunch! Isn't that queer? Harriman's booming voice hit me on the phone, first, a week ago. He was talking from the Pinkertons' house. They've been on the coast nine months and been living in Berkeley two. Called on me, but I and my family were on a vacation. All three called, and have seen them since several times. Miller this morning. (He too called while I was away. He's living in 'Frisco, across the bay, now.) Also, two nights ago took dinner with the Pinkertons and Brodeur and his wife and sister-in-law.

I've got a country place up near Yosemite Valley that I can't seem to arrange things to occupy (—— of a sentence, that) of late years, and I'm going to try to get the Pinkertons to live in it for a month or a year or ten years. They are awfully nervous in civilization—hankering for the Canadian pine woods; but I'm off with that Canada stuff for Americans except as a strict outing. For steady consumption the Sierras is more fit and becoming. So we are going to motor thither to-morrow. Pinkerton wants to work in the timber or herd sheep for awhile—says he's gone stale. Nicest people I've met in a coon's age, and we're thrashing out sledcraft problems, the spelling of "Parka" *vs.* "Parkey" (as to which *you* are still from Missouri) and various matters. Also I've been drawing out these "A. A." people on the subject of that peculiar—to say the least—department, getting their views, etc.—THEO. S. SOLOMONS.

WE OWE a debt of gratitude to Hugh Pendexter, not only for his stories of frontier life during the first making of America, but also for his very interesting Camp-Fire chats that make still clearer and more living the actual conditions and customs of those early days and show just how fully his stories follow actual history.

You will note now in this new serial of his, in order not to encroach upon W. C. Tuttle's fiction preserves, he has changed the real name of one of the characters instead of giving us a second *Magpie*. Incidentally these two members of our writers' brigade have become good friends by letter and at last reports were quarreling cheerily because one of them wanted to give the other a present and the other was refusing to accept it because he thought it too valuable. Which is about the only kind of quarrel that is warranted between friends.

WOOTON was born in Virginia, and lived there until seven years old, when his family moved to Kentucky. In 1836 he went to Independence, Mo., and joined a wagon-train owned by the Bents and Col. St. Vrain.

Wooton was better educated than his early companions, having had a good business education. He was nineteen when he went to the plains, and a dead shot. (He shot a mule while standing guard on the Upper Arkansas. A decade before him Carson did the same thing at Pawnee Rock.) Wooton was at Bent's Fort during 1836-37 and made frequent trips to Indian villages. During these two years he had many fights with the Pawnees, who hung about the fort after. hair. In the same period he had many thrilling experiences with the Utes. In fact, his thirty years on the plains as trapper and trader were filled with adventures with various tribes.

In my story I've picked up his life at the close of the old order of things. He opened his toll-road in the Spring of 1866. Road-agents were extremely thick and very busy. Chuckle-luck and his running mate, Magpie, dined with him one morning and then hurried down the south slope of the Pass and held up the coach, much as I have *Chuckle-luck* and *Boy Charlie* do it. Because of W. C. Tuttle's immortal *Magpie* I didn't have the heart to use the name. And, once I invented *Boy Charlie*, I was further tempted to take liberties with Chuckle-luck's finish. As a fact Chuckle-luck and Magpie were shot in their sleep by one Seward, a member of their gang. He loaded the dead bandits into a cart, took them to Cimarron City and collected the one thousand dollars per.

Uncle Dick was perfectly safe at any time in any Arapaho village or camp, just as Jim Hobbs was a prime favorite with the Comanches. Uncle Dick's Arapaho name was Cut-Hand, as given in the yarn. He lived to be ninety years old. In Inman's "The Old Santa Fé Trail" it is stated that Wooton was blind for some time during the latter part of his life, and that a surgical operation restored his sight so that he could gaze once more on the magnificent scenery of the Raton Range. Col. Inman also says the Atchison, Topeka and Santa Fé Railroad named one of its freight locomotives (largest in the world then) "Uncle Dick" in honor of the old mountain man. Wooton and Carson were fast friends.

Little Raven, Yellow Bear, of the Arapahoes, and Satanta (Settainte), of the Kiowas, were real Injuns.

My story was suggested by the original name of the Purgatory, or rather by the story that explains the name. The Purgatory, Le Purgatoire, Picketwire, as it was variously called, was El Rio de las Animas Perditas—The River of Lost Souls. During the time when Spain claimed practically all the Mississippi Valley and Florida, Santa Fé was ordered to open a road to Florida. A regiment of infantry set forth late in the season and passed the Winter on the site of Trinidad. The soldiers were accompanied by their women and children. In the Spring the camp-followers were ordered back to Santa Fé while the regiment marched down the river, which flows for miles through a cañon. Not a single soldier was ever seen or heard of again, says the story.

The duel between *Baptiste* and *Keene* was suggested by Jim Baker's duel with a rival French trader on Green River. They exchanged shots for several hours, retiring to their cabins between shots to drink. Thanks to the whisky, neither was injured. The fight between the Kiowas and Carson's New Mexico troops, and Satanta's playing the bugle, are correctly stated.

The tribal medicine of the Arapahoes consisted of the turtle, the ear of corn and the flat pipe, all of stone. The Kiowas had their *taime* images, the Cheyennes their sacred arrows, the Omahas their large shell, the Creeks their graven metal tablets (said to be relics of De Soto's visit). In fact, nearly every tribe (the Comanche being a notable exception) possessed tribal medicine.—HUGH PENDEXTER.

A WEAK memory for names is one of my strongest points and, even if I'm right as to the first name in this case, it doesn't follow that this comrade is the brother of Patrick and Terence Casey of our writer's brigade, the brother who was one of less than half a dozen survivors of the original Foreign Legion of the French army. I've never seen that Joe Casey, though I've talked with him over the phone and read about him in the papers. The intelligent thing would be to write to the writer of this letter and find out, but it will be more interesting to talk to him at Camp-Fire and then maybe Comrade Casey—or the two of them if there are two—will straighten matters out for all of us.

In any case we're obliged for the poem he sends in, a poem found in the trenches:

New York City.

SIR: The following lines were found in the hands of a young Irish officer, who lay dead in a trench on the Western front in France. An old-time reader of *Adventure*.—JOE CASEY.

Mother

Oh, mother, I am calling from the silence and the darkness,
And I wonder if you'll hear me in your home across the sea.
Oh, mother, darling mother, how I wish that you were near me,
With your arms around my shoulders. and my head upon your knee.

For I'm dying, mother darling, and it's hard to die without you;
So I'd like to hold your hand and hear your voice and see your eyes,
And feel myself a child again, and nestle close beside you,
And say the prayers you taught me to the One above the skies.

There'd be many things to whisper—it's so long since I have seen you;
And you'd gently draw me closer while I told about the fight.
Then, although your heart was breaking, you'd smile and say "My hero,"
And, when you thought me near the end, you'd kiss your boy good night.

Am I selfish, mother darling, to be wanting you so badly?
But there's no one like you, mother, you're just all the world to me.
And I'm not afraid of dying, but I'd face the Valley gladly,
If I knew that you could hear me in your home across the sea.

I must leave you, now, my darling, though I know that you'll be weeping,
But your boy has died for country, and the parting's for a day.
Till we meet again, then, mother, I leave you to His keeping,
And may His love enfold you, and His presence guard your way.

OUR magazine is found in many strange places and sometimes there are interesting stories about how some comrade first met it, or the strangest place in which he has found a copy, or about the most traveled copy he knows.

Toledo, Ohio.

Know how I got my first *Adventure?* Well, I was out in the park with my cousin in the Winter and on a dare I climbed at the top of the "Speedway," a very tall skeleton of wood supporting tracks for a car to run on, and there I found an old copy of the magazine, tattered, torn and wet with slush. Well—that started me.—JACK ORWILER.

YOU will see that "Uncle Frank" is a bit sore. At least he was when he wrote the following quite a while ago; by now the soreness is probably only a memory, if even that. Anyhow Uncle Frank has given us many interesting talks and I imagine none of us will object to his growling a wee bit for once. It isn't a very fierce growl.

LOS ANGELES, CALIF.

"Vieljo" questions my statement re "ropeing." The Dah Kotas and allies did rope. One Anderson was a well-known scout, latter 60's and early 70's and had a squaw some relation to Red Cloud. One of his sons, Andy, then a sergeant in 17th U. S. Inf., was talking to me at Fort MacPherson, Georgia, in 1904 or '05 and laughed when I spoke of "ropeing." "They don't any more," he said, "but I remember when they did."

Now some used a very elaborate system, others a simple thong. Individual taste, you know. But the thong was a symbol, as it were, as a chair tipped up against a restaurant table is also a symbol. Get the point? Ask Captain North. I think he was called Larry, but can't be sure after this lapse of years. No, you don't get me in any argument. Pigs is pigs and facts is facts.

ME, I dunno, not even what I *know*. Remember, "nothing is, only seems, etc?" Now, again I've chewed betel and have just one fang left, but I never chewed betel-nut. The "Camp-Fire" once published something I said on this subject. A native said, "*No, Don Paco* (We), *no se masca betel. Este es areca* (touching nut); "*este* (touching leaf) *es betel.*"

"No, Francis, they do not chew betel; this (nut) is areca and this (leaf) is betel. They called buyo here."

The areca nut, a slice (a nutmeg-looking critter is wrapped in a betel leaf smeared with oyster-shell lime and sometimes a shred of tobacco and chewed reddening lips and saliva and playing hob with teeth, but is claimed to be good for the *estomaca*—"tummy." Mebbe so, mebbe no so, I dunno, but of "ropeing" I do know and so does any old-timer who lived with the Injuns, not merely resided with them.

AT "ISSUES" on receiving a pair of pants the buck would immediately cut the seat and front, converting them into a pair of leggings supported by the waistband. Now stand on your hind legs, you closest naturalists, and say "That's not so," because you mebbe saw one turn 'em over to his squaw to operate on and thought that was all.

I struck the frontier in '66 and left it for good after the big pow-wow in Cheyenne in '81 or '82—forget which. Some one will tell me next that never occurred and that Standing Elk never used to catch the train as it was pulling out and leaving him or that every Injun in sight whooped and howled and yelled and danced in encouragement or derision or pure devilment as Elk bounded for the train and the California-bound homeseekers thought another rising had occurred. Some one will tell me that the Injuns never had free rides on car platforms and steps through a treaty permitting rails to be laid through their reservations.

I'll wake up some day to learn that I never saw an Injun.—FRANK H. HUSTON.

OUR Camp-Fire "stations" have brought in a good many letters of strong endorsement and we have already published a list of those who gave in their names at once, as willing to conduct stations, without waiting for final details to be arranged. Other volunteers have come forward since then, some of them from outside the United States, and more will be speaking up right along.

The holding up of our magazine by the strike has prevented responses from coming in so fast as they would do under normal conditions and the whole plan has thereby been delayed. Help it to make up for lost time by sending in your name for a station and by getting any suitable man you know to do the same.

It's a big idea and will spread rapidly enough once it's well started. Do your part by helping it get a good start. If you are interested in the plan, don't just sit back and wait for other men to start stations for you to use, but do your part too.

HERE'S the general idea for stations, subject, always, to changes if desired.

A station may be in any shop, home, or other reputable place. The only requirements are that a station shall display the regular station sign, provide a box or drawer for mail to be called for and provide and preserve a sufficiently substantial register book. When there are enough stations to warrant even a small wholesale order this office will furnish the books and signs.

No responsibility for mail is assumed by anybody; the station merely uses ordinary care. Entries in register to be confined to name or serial number, route, destination, permanent address and such other brief notes or remarks as desired; each station can impose its own limit on space to be used. Registers become permanent property of station; signs remain property of this magazine, so that if there is due cause or complaint from members, a station can be discontinued by withdrawing sign.

A STATION bulletin-board is strongly to be recommended as almost necessary. On it travelers can leave tips as to condition of trails, etc.; resident members can post their names and addresses, such hospitality as they care to offer, calls for any travelers who are familiar with countries these residents once knew, calls for particular men if they happen that way, etc., notices or tips about local facilities and conditions. Letters to resident members can be posted on this bulletin-board.

Any one who wishes is a member of Camp-Fire and therefore entitled to the above station privileges. (Question of requiring identification-cards or Camp-Fire button to be decided later.) Those offering hospitality of any kind do so on their own responsibility and at their own risk and can therefore make any discriminations they see fit. Traveling members will naturally be expected to remember that they are merely guests and act accordingly.

A station may offer only the required register and mail facilities or enlarge its scope to any degree it pleases. Its possibilities as headquarters for a local club of resident Camp-Fire members is excellent.

THE adventures and travels of some of our identification-cards are certainly worth hearing—this one, for example:

Seattle, Washington.

In reading Camp-Fire of August 3, 1919, I came across a letter by comrade Sapper Roger F. Gardner, No. 749285, 12th Canadian Railway troops, regarding his identification-card and thought perhaps some of the readers of Camp-Fire would be interested in another of the same kind. I have carried my card No. 5476 for a number of years both on land and sea—all of the five extreme Western States, different ports of Alaska. In 1917 I enlisted in the Royal Engineers at Seattle, Washington. Went to Vancouver, B. C.; thence to Montreal; Glasgow; Sandwich, Kent, England; Sierra Leone, West Africa; Cape Colony, S. A.; Bombay, India; Basra, Mesopotamia; through the campaign on the River Euphrates; invalided to Egypt; back to England; Halifax, N. S.; New York, Boston, Chicago, Seattle, and still have it before me as I write, in good condition, proving the good quality of which it is composed. While I and it have not been under fire as often as comrade Gardner, I believe we have wandered more miles together.—E. K. IRVING, No. 554,220, Royal Engrs.

A CALL to Camp-Fire for an old river-driver's song:

Cambridge, Mass.

I wonder if any woodsmen in the Camp-Fire can give me the words to that old river-driver's song "Guy Reed?"—THOS. B. STEWART.

MANY of you will remember *Fulvia*, the warlike Norman girl whose adventures in Sicily gave us a number of stories by Farnham Bishop and Arthur Gilchrist Brodeur. In their novel in this issue we meet her again, and Mr. Brodeur tells us something about the times and conditions in which she lived.

Berkeley, California.

In the decade between 1134 and 1144, Roger of Sicily was engaged in a long and bitter war with the German Emperor, who invaded Italy again and again, and laid waste the greater part of Roger's Italian possessions. Sicily itself was not directly threatened; but it would have been had Roger's cunning as a statesman and his courage as a soldier not robbed the Emperor of the fruits of the German victories. Roger's problem was a two-fold one: he had to stand off the most powerful military state in Europe and at the same time to keep his own possessions in Italy and on the Sicilian island in order. The turbulent Norman barons repeatedly revolted from him; their cities and strongholds were fortified against him, and many of them made common cause with the German enemy. Brigandage flourished, and the King's sword alone kept his oldest possessions faithful.

THE only part of the population on whose fidelity he could count was the Moslem element, the descendants of the very Arab conquerors of Sicily whom Roger's father and uncle had overthrown. By a policy of wise religious toleration Roger won the love of his Mohammedans, who fought in his army abroad and at home, side by side with a few trustworthy Normans, and served the King in all branches of his government.

But Roger, by the extremes to which he went to win the favor of his Moslem subjects, incurred the charge of being a half-hearted Christian and an enemy of the Church. The Pope denounced him for his inactivity in the Second Crusade (1147-9), and he was accused of contributing to its failure by his refusal to take part in the Crusade. Between 1144 and 1149, he was engaged in constant intrigue and negotiation to secure himself against Conrad, the German monarch, who, he knew, would hope to attack him again as soon as the Crusade was over. Conrad made an alliance with Manuel, the

Byzantine Emperor, against Roger; and but for the brilliant naval achievements of George of Antioch, Roger's admiral, the alliance would have declared war on him in 1149, the date in which our story opens. By a daring raid on the Greek coast and Constantinople, George broke the spirit of the alliance and secured the safety of Sicily.

IN THE meantime, between the end of his wars with the Germans and the opening of the Crusade, Roger held a meeting of all the barons under him, at which he browbeat even the most rebellious of his subjects into recognizing his authority. After this, all was quiet in Italy and Sicily both. Brigandage was at an end, and both Christian and Moslem subjects were content. But a fresh danger threatened.

The Berber Abd-el-Mumin, Ibn Tumart's successor as prophet and caliph of the Almohad sect, invaded Spain from Northern Africa and speedily subdued the Almoravid Moorish rulers of the peninsula. After Spain was in their hands, they began nibbling at Roger's possessions on the North African coast, between Tripoli and Barca. George of Antioch held them off for as long as he and Roger both lived; but in 1153 Abd-el-Mumin, who was both caliph and "Mahdi" of his fanatical, heretic sect, took every inch of Sicilian territory in Africa and for a time threatened the island itself. The Almohades were what we should call Unitarian Mohammedans: they declared against worship of saints and of the attributes of Allah, recognizing Allah as one; and they were ascetic in manner of life. The fervor of their faith made them more dangerous than any hashish-doped assassins that ever lived.

WE HAVE taken liberties with historic fact in making them attack Sicily during Roger's life, and in representing them as a peril to the heart of Sicily. That is, we have anticipated their attack four years, and have made it much more serious than it actually was. Of course, *Ian Dhu Mackay* is pure fiction, though the quarrel between Angus Mackay and King David of Scotland for the throne is historical. There were Scots on the Second Crusade; we have merely brought them back *via* Sicily and used them there. The Mackays, in the early twelfth century, were a seafaring clan; their possessions included all of what is now Moray, Ross, Elgin, and Cromarty.

They actually used—like all Highlanders of the time—the huge broadsword; though for purposes of fiction we have had to represent these terrible weapons as shorter than they really were. No one would have believed us if we had told their true size. When I was last in New York, in July, 1916, I saw one of these old Scottish broadswords—the true claymore—in the Metropolitan Museum. It is probably there now, for the skeptical to examine. The sight of it makes one realize what the Scots must have been in those days. The average modern athlete would do well if he succeeded in raising one of these swords as high as his waist.

WHEN the hero arrives in Sicily, we represent him as precipitating the Almohad invasion a little ahead of time, since the Mahdi allows his plans to embrace the killing of *Ian Dhu*. The trouble Roger has to face is no longer one of revolting Norman barons, and *Fulvia's* peril is no longer from outlaws or unscrupulous Normans; but the danger to both is the Mahdi's army and fleet and the revolt he attempts to stir up, through his agents, among the ordinarily loyal Moslem population. We have tried to show the natural struggle between the real loyalty of the native Moslems and their natural tendency to succumb to fanatical teachings.

Roger's inaction in the face of danger is not historic. He was an exceptionally wide-awake monarch. But he was the very man to ignore any peril that came from such a source as secret Almohad intrigue, because of his great confidence in Moslem integrity. He actually did not realize the danger of the Almohad conquest in Spain, and therefore we figured that he would hardly have been willing to accept any but the most startling evidence of intrigue among his Moslems in Sicily.

Christodoulos, the renegade, is the subject of much dispute among historians. Crawford depicts him as a villain and potential traitor; Curtis declares he was a faithful and honest official. Between the two, we have chosen Crawford's account of him; but little is really known about Christodoulos, and we warn you that we may be doing an injustice to him.—ARTHUR G. BRODEUR.

P. S.—You may have some doubts, in examining this story, about the use of divining-rods. The Encyclopædia Britannica states that though an explanation of the working of the rod is impossible, the consistent and repeated success of the instrument in locating water is so certain as to make reasonable doubt impossible.

CERTAINLY there is no slacking of interest in "What is the spirit of adventure, biologically speaking." Here is a definition from one of us who has wandered quite a deal:

MEMPHIS, TENN.

What is the Spirit of Adventure? In approaching the question, "What is the religious sentiment?" Spencer finds two alternatives: the one, that the feeling resulted, along with all other human faculties, from an act of special creation; the other, that it, in common with the rest, arose by a process of evolution, a result of intercourse of the organism with its environment. Observation has convinced me that the Creator accomplishes no thing directly, as we comprehend the word, but, on the contrary, produces an environment which in turn produces the desired result. Therefore, Spencer's two alternatives, to my mind, are only one, for the latter would merely be the process of the former. In other words, the feeling, if produced by "intercourse of the organism with its environment," still would be an act of special creation, the Creator merely employing the environment to register the impressions that would bring the mind to the desired state. Whatever the First Cause, we classify the feeling as a normal human faculty.

Might we not then assume that the Spirit of Adventure is as normal as the other faculties and, *in its office*, is a feeling of Divine origin, designedly responding to the Creator's system of dispersing man—physically, mentally and spiritually—from his original common center for the achievement of the divine purpose, whatever our respective (and respected) ideas upon that purpose may be, and that the getting of food, mates, etc., was and is merely incidental to the achievement of the ultimate purpose?—G. C. RUBLE.

FOLLOWING our Camp-Fire custom, Carl Clausen rises and introduces himself on the occasion of his first story in our magazine:

I was born in Denmark some twenty-odd years before that country was discovered by Doctor Cook. As a people we Danes are a seafaring nation. In every large family there are usually one or more who chose the sea as a livelihood.

I WAS the one of our family to be sacrificed upon the altar of Neptune. For some ten years I knocked about the Western Pacific—Australia, the Fijis, Gulf of Papua, New Zealand and South Africa. I was shipwrecked three times, twice on the coast of New Zealand and once off Delagoa Bay, South Africa.

In that ten years I followed fishing, pearl-fishing, copra-trading, not to mention a fling now and then at land occupations such as opal-miner, gum-digger, structural iron worker, window-cleaner and —opera-singer. In the last-named occupation I got as far as high C and then quit out of consideration for my friend Caruso. He's getting along in years, and I don't like to take a job away from an old man, so I turned my attention to "literature." I'll say, however, if I ever take up singing again, I'll sing like Caruso. I like his method—and salary. Also Mr. Caruso generally sings in a language I don't understand. Singing in a foreign language is so romantic to the audience, and I like my audience to be romantic about me.

I should like very much to know the whereabouts of Robert Burns—no, not the poet; I know where *he* is—but an old shipmate of the same lyrical nomenclature. I saw him last in Graymouth, New Zealand, in 1903. If "Scotty" happens to see this, please address F. A. Jones, 70 Fifth Avenue, New York, who will forward my mail. Also I would like to hear from Dick Tomlinson, last heard of in Moana, New Zealand. If either of these men will jog his memory, they'll recollect a certain trip on foot across New Zealand in 1902.—CARL CLAUSEN.

STILL another bit of testimony to the fact that there is a disease that in rare instances turns Indians white, as presented in one of our stories by Kathrene and Robert Pinkerton:

Blackfoot, Idaho.

I want to say a word about Indians turning white, which some folks seem to doubt, but it sure is a fact. I have seen some myself among the Navahos. An old friend of mine, chief of police Santa Vall—I don't know if that is the right way to spell it—anyway, half his face was white in patches when I last saw him, and he is not the only one I have seen. And it does not pain or trouble them in the least.—L. H. ANDERSON.

A LETTER from a woman comrade with the spirit of adventure—a woman who still "keeps going":

Denver, Colorado.

This is my first letter to Camp-Fire, and I am only a traveler not an adventurer. Being a woman, I stay closer home. Once upon a time—"Tell it not in Gath"—I did actually beat it on a freight train. I rode the rods from Jocatella, Idaho, to Ogden, Utah. Won't my women friends raise their eye-brows when they hear of this! I have been round the world a number of times and still keep going. I keep to the cities and the countries where I can find English-speaking people; then there is no difficulty in working my way.

I have so often seen in Camp-Fire letters the names of boys who have soldiered with my uncle, Col. Robert I.. Hirst, late commander of the Third Infantry.—DOLORES LEIDEN.

HERE is a question from E. E. Harriman of "A. A." and our writers' brigade. He wants information on a snake. Also he gives us an example of what an old-fashioned squirrel rifle could do, with the right man behind it, in the way of good shooting. Were they better marksmen in those days and in America's still earlier days, allowing for difference in weapons?

Now that you fellows have begun to talk about snakes (rather late in the day to bring it up when we've gone dry), I want to ask the bunch to identify a little one for me.

WHEN I was twenty years old I worked for a cousin of Nick Longworth on the north shore of Big Lake, Wright County, Minnesota. I went home Sunday mornings, pulling a heavy skiff two miles across the lake and walking three-fourths of a mile through the woods. Late in the afternoon I would return to my job under Octavius, Junior.

One Sunday afternoon when I was on my way through the woods to reach my boat, sober and in my right mind, I found a little snake on the dead leaves, trying to avoid my number tens. I whipped out my knife, cut a snake-stick and pinned him. He was only about a foot long, no thicker than a pencil, pale blue in color, with copper-colored belly. The anterior two inches of his tail looked exactly like one of the brown thorns from a wild crab-apple tree, dark brown, running off to a needle point. This tail was darting, not whipping, at the stick, just as a scorpion strikes or as a hornet darts his stinger.

I picked a large leaf and held it between stick and tail and he punctured the leaf neatly, making minute round holes that looked wet around the edges. I used a second stick and raised him to a large log for further observation. I took a fresh leaf and bent to get a side view of the action. That tail curved over backward and darted straight through the leaf, sticking into the fresh, green bark of the forked snake-stick at each plunge. It made holes such as a cambric needle might have caused. I killed the creature and left it there.

WHAT was it? Not a jugsnake, since alcohol and I were never intimate. Anyhow, who ever heard of a jugsnake letting himself get caught?

I have always understood that jugsnakes were coy critters, always wriggling just beyond reach of the canes, books, chairs and cuspidors hurled at them.

I have heard wonderful tales of hoopsnakes, but he did not fill the description of a hoopsnake, that product of the imagination run riot. That he was real, an active, wiry, mad little devil I know. That he did use his tail as a weapon, and not with the thrashing, whipping motion of a snake that is merely seeking freedom, I know.

What was he? Wake up, *compadres*, and tell me.—Fraternally, E. E. HARRIMAN.

P.S.—About long shots—my father saw a warrior of the Sioux nation at Greenleaf, Minnesota, in '63, with a bullet-hole in the solar plexus and the bullet stuck in his spine, sent from a Kentucky squirrel rifle of the thirty-to-the-pound type, from exactly one-mile distance.

The commandant of the post testified that he and two lieutenants watched the buck on a bald hill one mile away, with telescopes, while the hunter loaded and fired from a prone position on a sloping plank. The Sioux slumped and the captain sent a detail to bring him in.—E. E. H.

THOUGH this is his second story, not his first, in our magazine, Robert J. Horton follows Camp-Fire custom and introduces himself:

Milton-on-Hudson, N. Y.

Ten years in the newspaper game as all kinds of a reporter, correspondent, rewrite man, copyreader, sporting editor, city editor, telegraph editor, and other kinds of an editor, have instilled in me an abhorrence of the capital *I*. But this seems to be an occasion when the personal pronoun can not be avoided; hence the alibi.

ONE of the first recollections I have of Coudersport, the beautiful little town in north central Pennsylvania, in which I was born, is of a desire to find out what was beyond a hill west of town. Eventually I got to the top of that hill, only to discover that my travels had just begun, for I saw other hills and wanted to know what was on the other side of them. And I'll be doggoned if I haven't been finding out what is on the other side of hills ever since.

It's remarkable how many hills I've encountered; and they keep getting higher!

A MORE or less desultory schooling in a good high school in my home town and a mediocre preparatory school in New Jersey prepared me for my first real job, which was writing advertising in a New York department store. I hate to set this down; it sounds so commercial! But it paid well. I've never hated to tell people about the money I made in the advertising game. That's funny, isn't it?

Right here we may as well get down to cases on one subject—"art." I've listened a lot to the boys with the flowing neckties talking about their "art," but my definition of art is *work*.

Twelve years ago the West called. It seems ages (I'm thirty-four years old) since I boarded the Southern Pacific steamer *Momus* on a New Year's Day bound for New Orleans on my first trip west. I took in Texas, New Mexico, Arizona and California that trip, and "took in" is right.

THEN I broke into the newspaper game. I've worked from Park Row to Market Street and from Houston, Texas, to Great Falls, Montana. I've been out with Roosevelt, Hughes and McAdoo; I was a "war" correspondent on the Border; I was a correspondent for one of our greatest news-gathering agencies at a number of Texas cantonments and just missed going across during the war by a hair; I've "covered" State political conventions, legislatures, speeches, celebrations, floods, wrecks, forest fires, murders, baseball games, fights and most everything else that falls to the lot of news writers and gatherers.

My newspaper experience convinced me of three things:

1. It's a great game and a thankless one;
2. We've got the greatest country on earth and one to be thankful for;
3. People are pretty much the same everywhere and mostly good.

I've held some mighty good jobs, but none for any great length of time. The wanderlust has found me a willing victim. I went West to see the country out there and I saw it. I kept moving around. The old adage has it that "a rolling stone gathers no moss." But if experience and material can be called "moss" for a writer, then I've gathered tons of it. I have sufficient local color alone to decorate several hundred stories and now if I can just convince the editors—but that's another matter, of course. Everything in its place.

I HAVEN'T always been engaged in white-collar occupations, either. As a matter of fact, I don't lean to white collars at all. I'm quite a bit of a roughneck, old tops; and if any of you boys happen along on my camp sometime you'll hear anything but book-talk and see anything but a highbrow.

I've unloaded bricks in Pennsylvania, hopped bells in New Jersey, piled linens in New York, jumped lunch-counter in Kansas, seeded wheat and shocked it and loaded it onto bundleracks and helped thresh it in Montana; I've picked peaches and tomatoes in Utah, cut corn in Idaho, gloomed apples in Washington, and thrown slabs out of a sawmill in Oregon. These are not hard jobs, but if you understood the combination of circumstances which brought them about you would also understand why they are among my most treasured and interesting reminiscences. I mention them merely so you can know that my viewpoint of life in general is not framed by mingling solely in stiff-collar sections.

I've crossed and criss-crossed the West for the past ten years. I've ridden over it in Pullman cars and on top of them, in automobiles, on horseback, and walked miles and miles of it afoot. I love it. And of all the West, I love Montana the best.

Once when my eyes went back on me I beat my way—tramped, hoboed, bummed or whatever you want to call it—from Ogden, Utah, to Seattle, back across the Cascades and down the Columbia to Portland, from Portland to San Francisco, from the Golden Gate to Los Angeles, across the San Bernardino Mountains and Desert to the Imperial Valley and Yuma, across southern Arizona and New Mexico to El Paso, and from there on a cattle train to Kansas City.

I wouldn't take ten thousand dollars for my

experiences on that jaunt. I saw things a man never could see from a Pullman car; heard things that are proving invaluable to me every day. And that trip taught me something I needed very much to learn: It's the little things that count.

I'VE hunted every species of big game in the United States and killed most of them. I've spent months at a time in the mountains of Montana, and I'd have you know that Montana's mountains are not tame. I've fished in practically every great fishing stream in the West; I've been lost in a blizzard, nearly drowned in the ocean, almost killed a dozen times. I've been in jail, too—but not for long.

I took the whole course.

I obtained the material for my first story in Southern California, wrote it in Tucson, Arizona, mailed it in El Paso, giving a Montana address, received the check for it in Kansas City, and was in Omaha when it appeared on the newsstands.

I'D RATHER write about the West than anything I know of; hence "The Gulch of the Lonesome Winds." This is a story written about a locality. The setting is authentic, as the gulch and the "sink hole" exist in the Little Belt Mountains of Montana. The story has no hero and the somewhat weird touch was suggested by the extraordinary effect which the spot had on me while stalking deer there. I've listened to those winds.

This is the first of a series of stories of the high hills which I intend to write and into which I hope to put some of my love for them and portray some of the amazingly interesting characters which abound in them.

I am writing this in the East, but by the time it is published I expect to be in a cabin in the Montana hills. You must know this about me: I claim that the successful man is the *contented* man, whether he is a millionaire leader of industry, or a trapper near some pine-fringed lake. If he is satisfied and contented, then he is a success. Other people may not view him as such, but, after all, isn't success a matter of individuality? Whom does it affect the most?

The story of mine which won the best press notices, brought letters of praise from readers and requests from editors, was laid in the East and concerned an Eastern hero. But it was conceived and written in the Far West.

So maybe my philosophy will work out all right in the Western shack. But whether it does or not, I'll have fresh trout for breakfast, and other game in season. And I can drink in the scent of the pines and flower-splashed meadows and see the moon shining on the peaks. Perhaps you do not realize this, but it is quite a thing just to see the moonlight on the peaks. *I* think so. And if you're ever round my way, drop in; you'll find everything except a lock on the door. So long.—ROBERT J. HORTON.

MORE about Billy the Kid from a comrade whose name is known to a good many of us through his stories. Mr. Poe, to whom I wrote, tells me that his account of the killing was sent to a writer in New York some time ago and as it has probably already found its way into print I have not followed the matter further.

Long Beach, California.

I have just been glancing through your Camp-Fire and can throw some light on the matter of Billy the Kid's death.

TWO years ago I spent some time in Lincoln County, New Mexico, gathering material for my novel "A Man Four-Square." While in Roswell (which, by the way, is not now in Lincoln County) I talked with many people who knew "the Kid"; also in Lincoln and on the Ruidosa I talked with several others. Among those I met was a Mr. Poe (I think John Poe), a banker of Roswell, N. M., and an absolutely reliable man. Mr. Poe was sent out from Texas by the Cattleman's Association to try to stop the rustling that was being done from New Mexico. He cooperated with Garrett, discovered where Billy the Kid was staying, and was with Garrett at the time he shot "the Kid." Later he was Garrett's business partner and succeeded Pat as sheriff of the county, elected to stamp out lawlessness, which he did.

Poe is a modest man and rarely talks of his exploits, but he told me one evening the story of the killing of "the Kid" by Garrett. That story, within a few days, upon being urged by me to do so, he put on paper and had some typewritten copies struck off. One of these he sent to Colonel Goodnight (of the famous buffalo and cattle ranch in the Panhandle, Texas). I know this because when I was at the Goodnight ranch next year Colonel Goodnight handed me the manuscript to read. The story was exactly the same as the one Mr. Poe had told me, and it is undoubtedly the true one, since he was on the porch, within ten feet of both men, though not in the room, when Garrett shot. The only other man in the room was Pete Maxwell, now dead, and Pete was very much on the way out of the room at the moment the shot was fired.

I FOUND persistent rumors in New Mexico to the effect that Billy the Kid was not killed by Garrett but is living on a ranch in Arizona. There is of course no truth in this and it is proabaly due to the fact that Billy has already become a traditional hero like Robin Hood.

Poe's story is in substance like that of Garrett, though details differ. Garrett's story can be read best in Emerson Hough's book, "The Outlaw." There is no occasion whatever for any substantial variations of the account of "the Kid's" death. These are due to writers sending in accounts based on rumor and gossipy details gleaned from casual narrators. One point that has perhaps tended to mix writers is the fact that Garrett captured "the Kid" some months before the time he killed Bonney (the Kid's name). On this occasion his posse shot down some of the Kid's lieutenants. After being convicted of murder Billy escaped, killing his two guards, Bell and Olinger.

Billy the Kid is the most famous outlaw the West has produced, with the exception of Jesse James and possibly one other. Why not get Mr. Poe's story while he is still living? It is short, clear, and entirely accurate.—WILLIAM M. RAINE.

A LETTER from one of use who has no trouble in finding adventure:

Springfield, Mo.

Camp-Fire is like an old pal, but I do not think Camp-Fire is all to the good on the James boys. Have been talking to a man here that knew Cole Younger very well here and in Platte, Nebr., and had worked nights for a week at a time in the same room with them all making them saddles, etc. Will write all I get on them at another time.

When it comes to adventure, say, I step into every new city and street with a feeling of adventure, to stop where the road leaves me, to see strange sights, strange people. It is life—all adventure, every day. A mile or so southeast of here I can find all that Stanley found in Africa; a mile south I can be a guerrilla raider or a member of the K. K. Klan; a mile north I can be Peary at the Pole. It's all adventure if you look at it right.—M. CHARLES CHAMBERLAIN.

WHEN he first sent us the story that appears in this issue and is marked as one of our "Off the Trail" stories, Mr. Hurst was for having it published without any word to indicate whether or not it was to be taken seriously. Finally I persuaded him to let me give you his letter concerning the subject-matter of the story. Personally I do not smile at any seeming improbability in the main idea. I've learned it doesn't pay to smile very broadly at a thing merely because it *seems* improbable. Lots of things, like airships, the World War and the wireless, have come to pass after wiseacres had laughed themselves sick over the idea that there could ever be any such improbable thing. I don't say that the amazing catastrophe described in this story is going to come to pass, but I most certainly don't say it isn't.

Most of us know very little about that subject; a few have made it a real study, but it is entirely possible that the natives of India may have gone much further into the problem than our Western students have yet been able to follow. And if we don't know all about a thing we're taking a big risk in saying that it can or can not accomplish certain things

Fearing that Christian Scientists might object to an underestimate of the effects of their teachings, I submitted the story to Scientists who are well able to give authoritative opinion and found them quite willing to pass over this point because of what may be called the net truth of the tale.

In any case, it seems to us in the office an interesting story quite aside from these points.

Here is an extract from Mr. Hurst's letter:

Seattle, Wash.

This story "The Limit of Conquest," while not a story of war, is just *as true a warning*, although you will consider my fears fantastic. Wells, and many others, including the late Kaiser, have written upon the final war, in which the East vanquishes our civilization. But none of them got the ***straight tip*** that I got.

SOME time ago, I met a high caste native of India, one of those who come to America and make a good thing out of pandering to the craving of silly women, with some fancy religion. We had long talks. He claimed to be Prince something, but his title does not matter. I was astonished at his grasp of every subject we discussed. Among other things, I asked him why the Indian rope trick was no longer performed. It used to be common enough. You know the thing; a fakir unwinds a rope from around his waist, throws it up in the air, where it stands straight up like a pole; then a boy climbs the rope, and disappears or not, as the case may be. I asked this because when the present King of England was in India a large sum of money was offered to any fakir who would do the trick. I forget the amount, but it was far more than a fakir could earn in a dozen lifetimes. Yet not a one came forward. Why? My prince chap smiled at the question. "But it was only an instance of group hypnosis, which your psychologists deny the possibility of, wasn't it?" he asked.

"Yes—but why wasn't it done for the King? Was the crowd too large?"

"The crowd number would have been arranged to suit the fakir—if it is possible to have too large a crowd. No, that was not the reason we decided to stop it."

"Who do you mean by 'we'?"

He grinned that peculiar, irritating grin of the native, "I can not tell you—only we did not wish your psychologists to become believers in group psychology. A few, I believe, do admit its possibilities, but they are rare."

That was the gist of our talk, and the native

seemed sorry he had said so much. You will learn why from my story.

I HAVE made it look as practica. as possible, but it was a job. Of course I was helped by believing what I wrote about—which you won't. We should prepare for this danger, just as we should have gotten ready for the war with Germany. I know I will be called a crazy fool for the warning, or else what I write will be taken for mere fiction. But if—I could bring home the danger—the danger which lies in the East, in which men will not believe until too late. An unseen weapon, the very existence of which is denied by our scientists, is pointed in our direction. Now, read the tale, and call me an imaginative fool, who has allowed a story to get the best of his common sense. Because, at any rate, we will not live to see the final war—at least, I don't think we will.—S. B. HURST.

IF IT were any of the other magazines I worked on before *Adventure* was born I'd not like to ask the readers just voluntarily to help push the magazine. It would seem a bad case of nerve. But I haven't a bit of reluctance in asking Camp-Fire to do just that for *Adventure*. In fact, I'm sorry I didn't think to do it sooner.

I don't mean I'm going to ask anybody to get subscriptions or anything like that. And I don't mean that *Adventure's* circulation is going down and we need help to make it pay. It's not going down. It's going up. And it's paying. But naturally we want it to go up still faster and still higher. We want it to pay all it legitimately can and I make no bones about presenting this matter on that basis. I'm asking a pure favor, not trying to jolly you into something by painting it up to look like something it isn't. It happens that you would gain in a minor way by doing what I ask, but not enough to warrant my putting the matter up to you on that basis at all. I'm asking you to do it because it will increase the magazine's sales and make it pay better.

IT'S just this. Every little while some of you write in quite voluntarily and tell us *Adventure* isn't being carried for sale in such and such a place or that there are not enough copies to supply the demand. Sometimes it is a plain kick—the writer of the letter is sore because he couldn't get the magazine when he wanted it. Sometimes it is merely mentioned incidentally. Sometimes as a favor and kindness to us—and very often the writer says something like "though maybe you aren't interested in such matters" or half-apologizes for speaking of it.

Believe me, we here in the office *are* interested. That's exactly the favor I want to ask of all of you who can spare the time and are willing to take the trouble. *Adventure* sells well when it is put where people can buy it, but that isn't so easy to do as it seems. I used to think it was a simple matter, but I had that idea knocked out of me. The proper distributing of a magazine is a difficult and very complicated business. The newsdealer, the news company and the publisher all stand to gain by the best distribution that can be attained and all work together to attain it, but even that cooperation can't ensure it.

WE WANT *Adventure* on every newsstand where there is a demand for it—in the United States, Canada, Australia and everywhere that there are readers of the English language. We don't want to burden any newsdealer uselessly. Though as *Adventure* is "fully returnable" he doesn't lose if any copies remain unsold. But we do want to be sure that every newsdealer has enough copies so that no one will be unable to get an *Adventure* when he wants it.

That is where you come in, if you will. A newsdealer nearly always knows his own business, but, like all the rest of us, sometimes he doesn't seize on every opportunity to make supply fit demand. Also it is by no means always his fault if he hasn't a magazine when it's called for; the publisher may be responsible, as in the case of the recent strike, or the big machinery of the news company may have slipped a small cog somewhere, or, most likely of all, transportation may not have been what it should. Or he may be sold out on some particular issue of a magazine even though he had ordered the number indicated by previous sales.

We're not trying to hang anything on the newsdealer. It's our business to make satisfactory adjustment with him. But first we must know whether any adjustment is needed. And you are the ones who can tell us. We have our own men in the field but there are a good many newsstands in the world, conditions are changing at each one of them and even ten times as many men couldn't keep track of all the details.

WILL you, then, let us know whenever you have difficulty in getting your copy of *Adventure?* Get the dealer's side of it first and give us the main points of the situation. Your own judgment will indicate the important points and don't forget to be specific so we can locate the dealer by name or exact location or address. *Adventure* appears on the 3rd and 18th of every month; of course the supply will be lower, perhaps exhausted, by the 2nd or 17th, so it is important that you should give us the date of your visit to the news-stand.

And will you let us know if you find a district anywhere in which *Adventure* is not on sale? If you know any one who would carry it, that will help all the more. In short, if you will give us any tips that occur to you on how to perfect our distribution of the magazine we'll be very grateful to you indeed and these tips will certainly get the fullest and most careful consideration. We can hardly ask you to write specially for this purpose, though it will be appreciated if you do, but thousands of you are writing in on other accounts and you could tack on a paragraph or two on this subject. Write it to me personally or to any of us or just to the magazine, but time in handling will be saved if you write direct to J. J. Crowley, Director of News-stand Sales.

THAT'S the favor I want to ask—your friendly cooperation in getting *Adventure* to wherever there is a demand for it. And if it isn't convenient to grant the favor, we'll be just as good friends as we were before. As I said at the beginning, I'd not like to ask this favor if it were a case of any other magazine, but *Adventure's* readers have proved their real friendship for "our magazine." I know I have a friend's right to ask a favor, and you know you have a friend's right to grant it or not, as you see fit, knowing it will be all right either way.

AN extremely interesting reply to Edgar Young's call for information on "King John." Surely a call at our Camp-Fire goes out over all the world and in some nook or cranny, near or distant, is very likely to find at least one man who can answer. And I've an idea there will be some more responses before we're through.

Lindsay, California.

In answer to an inquiry in the October *Adventure* with regard to King John:

The man who is once and again heard of under that name was at one time bosun's mate upon the Liverpool four-mast barque *Silberhorn.* The *Silberhorn* was abandoned at sea some fourteen years or so ago, on fire. She was sighted by an Iquique bound ship some eighty miles southwest of Robinson Crusoe Island; and a search later carried out for her ship's company was fruitless. The fate of the old *Silberhorn* has nothing to do with King John, however.

THIS man's real name was Reuben Sweeny; and he was an immense Liverpool Irishman. There was certainly no Spanish blood in him at all. He was very fair and had remarkably deep blue eyes.

He was a foremast hand on the *Pyrrhenes,* a full rigger that took fire at sea when bound from 'Frisco for a European port. They ran her to Pitcairn Island and on arriving there found that the sea was too high for them to be able to beach her and so, with the ship a smoldering mass beneath hatches and with her decks on the point of breaking out at any moment, they decided to make for Manga Reeva Island, some three hundred miles or so away. The only way that they were able to procure provisions at all was by passing a line under one or other of the men and lowering him into the lazaret, where he groped for whatever he could lay his hands upon in the darkness and smoke. The men who made the dive into the lazaret were as often as not hauled back to deck unconscious from the smoke..

One man who seemed to be quite unaffected by the heat and smoke was Reuben Sweeny, and the mate, as he returned to the deck on one occasion, said to him, "Sweeny, if you weren't Irish you'd ought to have been king of all the niggers."

Sweeny, who was black as any negro and nearly naked, replied with an oath: "By —— mister, it's quittin' the sea that I'm thinkin' of and maybe it's a nigger emperor I'll be."

THE *Pyrrhenes* was at length beached at Manga Reeva, where the crew found the natives almost starving and where there was no food for them. Fortunately in a few days a small schooner took them off. When they lay upon her decks at night there was barely room for a man to put his foot down. They sailed thus for a few days and then had the good fortune to fall in with a steamer bound from the Colonies to 'Frisco and were taken aboard her. If I remember aright it was the *Sierra*—either her or the *Sonoma* or *Ventura* of the same line.

They arrived in 'Frisco just a day or two before the *Silberhorn* sailed from there, bound around the Horn for Falmouth for orders. And a number of the crew of the *Pyrrhenes* shipped with her, among them being Reuben Sweeny.

THIS man had two cronies named Tom Swift and Bloody Quayle. The three of them used to be well known from one end of the world to the other in all the joints along the waterfront. They were all Liverpool Irish and a fighting, cursing, hell-raising trio.

I made a passage at one time with Tom Swift and Sweeny and Quayle from the Columbia to Antwerp. With them in the lead, the crew mutinied at sea, and we had for a while quite a cheery time of it.

Some years after, I was down Fenchurch Street on my way to look for a ship and ran into Tom and Bloody. I asked them where Sweeny was and Tom replied:

"Billy, by ——, that old stiff's gone an' made himself king o' the blighted niggers."

It seemed that the three of them had been upon a packet named the *Blytheswood* that was hove down and lost all her sticks off Valparaiso. She made Valparaiso under jury rig; and there the three of them skipped and went ashore. There is no question that Sweeny is the man in the rôle of "King John." I was a close friend of the second mate of the *Pyrrhenes* and well acquainted with the *Silberhorn*, having made several voyages with her and having corresponded for a number of years with several English sea apprentices who served their time on her. The mate of the *Blytheswood* when she was dismasted and taken into Vallapo for repair was a man named Abel Pengelly and hailed from Bude Haven. I knew him well.

THE three sailors shipped out of Vallapo with a steamer going up the coast, and Reuben Sweeny left her at Callao and thence went inland upon a cruise of care-free devilment. He spoke both French and Spanish fluently, was afraid of absolutely nothing and was, to boot, as strong as a grown bull. He was a splendid singer and carried with him on all his ships an old fiddle.

Swift and Quayle were on the point of cleaning up on me for laughing at them when they told me that he was king of the blacks.

They insisted that they were not kidding at all and so I got busy and looked up by letter my various old shipmates who were in a position to corroborate to any extent their statements.

Both Swift and Quayle saw Sweeny a couple of years after he left them in Callao at the same port and there he tried to persuade them to go up country with him. He told them that he was actually "King o' the damdest gang o' niggers you ever saw" and that he had them where they obeyed every word he spoke on the running jump. He did his utmost to pursuade his old shipmates to go with him. But Tom Swift was at the time much enamored of a woman who lived on Cordova Street, Vancouver, and was heading at the time north to see her and absolutely refused to go. Bloody Quayle was too quarrelsome a man to get along with Sweeny unless Tom Swift were there and so decided to stay with Tom.

IT is now a number of years since I heard of King John. It is, moreover, possible that the "King John" in question may be a descendant of the original, or rather a successor, or possibly a different man entirely and ruling in a different part of the world.

Reuben Sweeny acquired the name of John during a rumpus in some West Coast port where a Dago addressed him as John—meaning that he was a Johnny Bull.

He was rather fat for a deep-water sailor and very square and wide-shouldered. His legs were decidedly bowed, and perhaps as noticeable a feature as any about him was his nose, which was unusually large and not unlike the cartoons that one sees of Ferdinand of Bulgaria.

If you run across him give him my compliments.

How to get to his kingdom I have no idea. He is a man who can go where most other men would be quite unable to follow. And I think that any one trying to find him might have a gay time in doing so.—B. M. ADAMS.

A LINE from W. C. Tuttle of our writers' brigade concerning something that happened when he was hunting partridge:

Spokane, Washington.

Funny thing happened. Jackrabbit hopped out of the stubble, and one of the boys took a shot at it—too far to do much damage. Anyway, the rabbit hopped through a barb-wire fence, caught on one of the prongs, and just about disemboweled itself. One of the bunch started after it, and away went Mr. Jack, across plowed ground, running like ——. In all it must have traveled a mile—without any insides to speak about, and finally crawled into an old coyote den, where we found it, still alive, but with its works all gone. Can you beat that? Any old time that anybody tells you that a rabbit hasn't any guts, you can tell 'em that it don't make any difference—they don't need 'em.—TUT.

SOMETHING more about Doc Middleton, who has already come up at our Camp-Fire, from one of us who knew him personally:

Omaha, Nebraska.

In November *Adventure* I read a sketch By E. E. Harriman regarding a bygone attempt to capture Doc Middleton; and having known Middleton in his later years, I thought it might interest readers to hear something about his death.

TO ME Doc Middleton's noble, rugged features and straight six-foot of sinewy manhood characterized the fast disappearing frontiersman more strikingly than any of the old-timers I ever saw—and I have seen a few.

In the West men are still largely judged by what they are today, and not what they were in the past. What deeds and transgressions Middleton committed during his notorious career as a frontiersman, gambler, outlaw and convict, they were cast into oblivion when the law released its grip upon him and sent him forth once more a free man.

Middleton returned to the Black Hills country, where the good and bad of him was known, and began life as a rancher. In this field he not only won success but, in time, even the honor and respect of his fellow citizens.

Middleton loved horses. He was much interested in racing events. Even in his advanced years he took part in a long-distance race from Chadron, Neb., to Chicago. He did not win.

Middleton also ventured into a saloon business at Ardmore, So. Dak., which eventually proved his undoing. A few years ago he was arrested for some infraction of the liquor law and lodged in jail at Douglas, Wyo. This proved too much for nature. The accumulated injury of a strenuous life wrecked his health, he contracted pneumonia and died in jail, a broken, lonely old man.—J. FRANCIS KOLLER.

THIS comrade is strong for our Camp-Fire buttons, "the open sesame of good fellowship," etc.

Brooklyn, New York.

On the road on my last trip I often wished I had a means of knowing who was who. The only way I had was to meet a fellow and find out through a talk if he was a brother-reader of the magazine and "Camp-Fire" or not. I have met many who belonged and have spent many pleasant hours that otherwise would have been dull. I think the Camp-Fire insignia is a great idea.

AM KNOWN as number 10559 on my metal card, and I have had it read in every language engraved on it. I have covered twenty-eight States not merely across, but up and down and over. I am supposed to be a sign-painter and letterer, and up to date I have got by splendidly. I have had all the ups and downs of the road from A to Izzard, but have never had any adventure worth while to send in for you all to read—at least nothing out of the ordinary.

I will sure be proud to wear a Camp-Fire button, and believe me it will mean *some* to me. I leave New York for the open road next week, *pronto*. I may walk or ride—who knows? The blind if I am broke, the cushions if I am flush.—WILLIAM MAHER.

THE following letter was received by W. A. Sternberg of Tacoma, Washington, and passed on by him to Camp-Fire:

Holbrook, Arizona.

I read your letter in the "Camp-Fire" about Calamity Jane. My husband, when he was in the Indian War and served U.S.A. for nine years and eight months in the 2nd and 3rd Cavalry as sergeant knew her. She was married to her man as she called him. He and she both were (?) of Dutch Henry's. She got up the sights for the band.

MY husband hid her for three days away from the sheriff that had trailed her. He told me that she came to his camp, he being out with some 20 men to trail some Indians, and asked him to protect her. She told him she would reform. Said he to me: "She was a woman, led away and ruined by men. My mother was a woman. I could not refuse." Therefore he hid her for three days, until the sheriff was really gone. Then he gave her a compass and provisions and started her off upon her journey, which was to Deadwood. She had a very fine riding horse. His men did not see her. She told him if ever he needed a friend to write her.

She died after I came to Arizona. My husband was in Texas at that time—I do not remember the place. She was never a real scout. Had a bogus passport, which she lost. I can not write you all. It would take too long. He also gave her some ammunition. Her face was hard from the life she led, but once, when he returned unexpectedly, he found her crying; her face had a different look, then the defiant look returned, which she maintained. Memory bells were chiming, I suppose.

I have written this under a lot of outside noise. Children crying, etc., so please excuse mistakes.—(MRS.) HELEN LAWRENCE THYSING.

DO YOUR share toward adding to the list of Camp-Fire stations all over this country and Canada and, gradually, all over the world. Here's the general idea for stations, subject, always, to changes, if desired.

A station may be in any shop, home or other reputable place. The only requirements are that a station shall display the regular station sign, provide a box or drawer for mail to be called for and provide and preserve a sufficiently substantial register book. When there are enough stations to warrant even a small wholesale order this office will furnish the books and signs.

No responsibility for mail is assumed by anybody; the station merely uses ordinary care. Entries in register to be confined to name or serial number, route, destination, permanent address and such other brief notes or remarks as desired; each station can impose its own limit on space to be used. Registers become permanent property of station; signs remain property of this magazine, so that if there is due cause for complaint from members, a station can be discontinued by withdrawing sign.

A STATION bulletin-board is strongly to be recommended as almost necessary. On it travelers can leave tips as to condition of trails, etc., resident members can post their names and addresses, such hospitality as they care to offer, calls for any travelers who are familiar with countries these residents once knew, calls for particular men if they happen that way, etc., notices or tips about local facilities and conditions. Letters to resident members can be posted on this bulletin-board.

Any one who wishes is a member of Camp-Fire and therefore entitled to the above station privileges. (Question of requiring identification-cards or Camp-Fire button to be decided later.) Those offering hospitality of any kind do so on their own responsibility and at their own risk and can therefore make any discriminations they see fit. Traveling members will naturally be expected to remember that they are merely guests and act accordingly.

A station may offer only the required register and mail facilities or enlarge its scope to any degree it pleases. Its possibilities as headquarters for a local club of resident Camp-Fire members is excellent.

The Camp-Fire

A Free-To-All Meeting-Place For Readers, Writers, And Adventurers

HOOP-SNAKES, snake-bite remedies and General Custer. My personal inclination when anybody mentions hoop-snakes is to cross my fingers, but I'm unable to prove that there is no such thing as a hoop-snake, not having been everywhere all the time. So if the rest of you say there are hoop-snakes, all right, I'll be a believer.

Hollywood, Calif.

Having read the article in "Camp-Fire" on snakes and remedies for snake-bites, I just couldn't help writing a little story, which I hope may help some one.

MANY years of my young life were spent in the West and I have had quite a bit of experience with snakes, also learning of an antidote for snake-bite which I say "can't be beat." The article to which I refer, gave remedies for snake bite, and among other things, gave a list of what "should be carried by every prospector going into snake infested regions." It seems to me that said article must have been written by some one endeavoring to boost the drug-store business.

The best remedy that I have found for snake-bite, or the bite of any insect, is common coal-oil, (kerosene) or else turpentine. My idea is that any one going tramping in snaky regions should carry a small bottle of either the coal-oil or the turpentine. When bitten, the liquid should be poured on to the wound, or sopped on with a cloth.

On the plains in the early days this was the only antidote used by the plainsmen or the stockmen, and was certainly used very effectively. Of course this liquid must be applied at once, the same as any other remedy. All these medicines, syringes, tourniquets, etc. are absolutely unnecessary, if either the coal-oil or turpentine can be obtained.

I can recall one case where a man was bitten on the hand by a rattlesnake, and the only remedy was to suck the bite, spit out the substance, and apply a cud of good old tobacco.

SAW no mention made of the hoop-snake which used to be found in some parts of the Middle West States. This snake would catch its tail in its mouth and roll, like a hoop, hence the name. It was stated on one occasion, that one of these snakes ran against a tree and its poison killed the tree. Has no one heard of the rattle-snake weed, which was used successfully in combating snake bite?

SOMETIME ago, at Camp-Fire, a writer mentioned that Custer had committed suicide, rather than be captured, at the battle of Little Big Horn in 1876. Any one who was acquainted with George A. Custer and knows his history from early life until his death, will say that he would be the last man to take his own life under any circumstances.

Any one who undertakes to belittle Custer's character or reputation as a military leader, in view of his brilliant career as an officer in the War of the Rebellion and as a great leader in the war against the Indians, certainly must have a prejudiced disposition toward General Custer, or envy his remarkable and useful career in the service of the United States Government—BENJ. M. BLOOD.

ANOTHER point of view as to what is the spirit of adventure. The question when originally started at Camp-Fire by Edgar Young was "What is the spirit of adventure, biologically considered?" But there is no reason why we shouldn't discuss it in any of its aspects we please.

U.S.S. *New Mexico.*

Our comrade Barry Scobee claims that the spirit of adventure is play. He points out that if an automobile party were held up and all their available funds taken it would not be adventure, but experience. On the other hand, if they fool the robber and get away with it, they have not had an experience, but an adventure. In my opinion he is wrong both ways. If the auto party that had their money stolen had sold the machine and fought their difficulties in a man's way, and gone on looking for their land, found it and made a home there in spite of auto robbers, etc., they would have been true adventurers.

What is more, there is a little curiosity in adventure, and there must be a little touch of danger. The more, the better. If there is no danger, it is like 2.75, flat.

Light adventure, if there is such a thing, is play, like taking a tour around the world in some finely fitted out passenger ship. Real adventure must have its dangers and hardships, like leaving N. A. for Calcutta on an old tramp with one suit of clothes, a cargo of, say, T.N.T., and subs waiting out off Sandy Hook. All hardships are laughed at when they are over with and one is walking up Broadway well supplied with money and time.

Adventure is waiting with a thrill for the unknown around the corner, and who knows (or cares) the great adventure death?—E. E. MARSH.

IN CONNECTION with his story in this issue we raised a question as to whether a certain expression used by some of the characters was really in use at the time of the story, but is seems as if W. C. Tuttle were justified:

Regarding the slang expression, "I'd tell a man." Now, I don't know how far back that expression dates, but I'd tell a man that it goes back at least fifteen or eighteen years. Perhaps it was the first real slang expression to hit cow-land. The expressions, "I'd kiss a pig," "I'd smoke a lamp," came about the same time.

The first time I ever saw the mooted expression in print was early in about 1900 or 1901. I happened to see the expression and it read so homelike that I read the tale.—TUT.

A REPLY to an inquiry from one of us concerning Adams and his lost mine.

Garrison-on-Hudson, New York.

In the "Camp-Fire" of the *Adventure* of 3rd., October, 1919, I saw a request for information from M. M. Coleman about a man named Adams who had been with others to a very rich gold mine known to the Apache Indians in N. W. New Mexico.

Replying to the inquiry, I will say that I have a story first hand from credible sources concerning a very rich mine known to the Apache Indians of North Western New Mexico but it is a silver mine and is supposed to be within the boundaries of the Jicarilla Apache Reservation. At the present moment I have not my notes on the subject so am quoting from memory and a thorough acquaintance with the story as it came to me.

A MAN named Adams with a party made up of civilians and soldiers were led by an Indian or half-breed guide to an extremely rich silver mine in North Western New Mexico. This party was attacked and wiped out with the exception of Adams and one or possibly two companions who reached safety at a U. S. Army post some distance away. Adams tried to return to the mine on several subsequent occasions but was unable to correctly find his way. Later some whites made a deal with Victorio, who promised to lead them to this mine and started to do so but the party was turned back by a large war party of Apaches. The mine since has not, so far as I know, been reached by whites. Some have tried it, but were all turned back by the Apaches.

When I go West I will get my notes and send you a more thorough account of the story.—AMEDÉE LA V. REYBURN, JR.

A LETTER from a very, very rare bird—a man who used to read our magazine and never even look at "Camp-Fire." But finally he tried it and now is a member in good standing—and a good American. I can't agree that ours is the best governed country in the world, but if it isn't it's *our* fault, yours and mine, for we have the opportunity to make it all it should be. We have democracy to that extent at least—we can make our government register our wishes and opinions, lawfully and without force and riot, if only we *will*. Can't do it just by wishing. It takes work. But we *can* do it if we *will*.

Anyhow, it's our country and its government is as good as we are. And a —— fine country at that.

The "editorial" question he speaks of was a suggestion that, before we go colonizing in other countries, we'd better consider our own country's need of us.

Vancouver, B. C.

I have been an irregular reader of *Adventure* for some time, buying it in preference to other publications when I wanted something that would really rest my tired brain.

I NEVER paid much attention to the "Camp-Fire" section, hardly ever looking at it, until the issue of September 18. Growing tired of reading I threw the book down. It happened to open at the Camp-Fire page and, remaining open, my eye caught a heading and a few more words that interested me, and picking the book up again, discovered that I had lost much by not reading it in the previous issues that had passed through my hands, for it appealed to me at once very strongly, I wanted to be a member and break into the circle.

THAT'S what I am trying to do now, and if my attempt is crude, I hope you will pardon my maiden effort and not kick me out the first time. Among the Camp-Fire contributions, that which interested me most was Dr. Sargent's reply to queries of would-be Latin-American emigrants, and particularly the editorial comment on same. I feel like the editor, and will answer his question most emphatically in the affirmative.

We Americans, especially native-born sons, certainly *do* owe the little old U. S. not only something, but everything.

What wander-bug entices us to leave the land of our birth and seek asylum in foreign lands, when our native land is the most free and best governed country on the face of the globe?

Did you (who have the wanderlust for a new home) ever stop to think why you wish to leave a country where the government is stable, and the people more free than any other nationality, for a country where the majority of the people are ignorant peons?

Why do hundreds of thousands of emigrants come from the eastern continent to find homes and better conditions—people of all nationalities races, and colors?

And nearly all stay; and their native land knows them no more.

Their families grow up and are educated here, and become American citizens; and know no home but the land of the Stars and Stripes.

IT seems to me that the United States has range of climate, productions, topographical and geological conditions, to suit the most fastidious; if they only endeavor to find the conditions they desire within the borders of their native land instead of looking to foreign lands. There is plenty of reliable information to be obtained in regard to all parts, for the asking, and many opportunities, in any vocation; and the best and most reliable source of information (unlike most foreign countries) is from the Government bureaus.

I left my native land (the U. S.—and a native-born citizen too)—thinking to better my condition and environment, but as yet have failed to find the Mecca of my expectations; and while not a groucher by any means, and having no fault to find, if I ever again gain a foothold in the good old U. S., I will stick.—E. B. SAFFORD.

OUR Camp-Fire seems to be gradually exploding the Gila Monster as to the deadly quality of its bite. We have already had some strong evidence from recognized scientific authority and now there comes to Camp-Fire a letter from Dr. H. C. Yarrow, formerly curator of the reptile department at the U. S. National Museum, more commonly referred to as the Smithsonian Institution. This, especially considering the thoroughness of the tests made, would seem by itself, conclusive evidence.

Also note Dr. Yarrow's word of warning concerning permanganate of potash. One of you who claims no scientific knowledge of the subject and bases his statements only on the early day remedies of the Indians and plainsmen, has recently written in similarly discrediting this remedy from the standpoint of practical experience. And one of our physician comrades makes out a strong case proving the tourniquet is the only essential part of the treatment.

The following from Dr. Yarrow is from his series of papers on "Snake Bite and its Antidote." In itself it seems definitely to settle the question of the deadliness of the Gila Monster's poison. The other experiments referred to indicated venomous qualities, but there seems no authenticated case of the poison being the direct cause of a human being's death.

Washington, D. C.

I have read with much interest the discussions in your interesting magazine regarding the Gila Monster and am sending you the results of our experiments at the Smithsonian some years since. The reptile which bit Dr. Shufeldt was one of those whose saliva was used in our tests and you will see by the report which I send you we failed to determine the so-called venomous property of the saliva. In Dr. Shufeldt's case we believe the mental shock caused his symptoms. I have yet to discover an authoritative case of death from the bite of the *Heloderma suspectum* and rather think that, if deaths have occurred, they have been due to the enormous quantities of bad whisky with which the parties were deluged.

Make such use of this report as you see fit.—H. C. YARROW.

P.S. I may add that I have handled a number of Helodermas and have never known them to show a malignant disposition or desire to bite if gently held.

A Word of Warning:

Let no man believe he has a positive antidote to the bites of venomous reptiles in Potassa permanganas. It is a fallacy and has been proved so at the Smithsonian Institution.

BITE OF THE GILA MONSTER

BY DR. H. C. YARROW

ON Feb. 7, 1883, Drs. S. Weir Mitchell and Edward T. Reichart read a paper before the college of Physicians of Philadelphia, entitled, A Partial Study of the Poison of *Heloderma Suspectum Cope*, the Gila Monster, in which the statement was made that after several experiments with the saliva of this reptile, they had come to the conclusion that it possessed strongly venomous properties. This had been suspected by some naturalists, from the fact that this lizard possessed anterior deciduous grooved teeth, which communicated by ducts with large glands near the angle of the lower jaw.

All sort of conflicting reports have been published from time to time regarding this reptile, some observers claiming that it is deadly venomous, others believing it perfectly harmless; in fact, in some parts of the Southwest it was kept as a household pet. Bocourt and Dumeril mention the bad name it has in Mexico, and Sumichrast states that the natives hold it in the utmost terror and consider it more fatal than any serpent. A fowl bitten by it died in twelve hours, with bloody fluid exuding from its mouth, the wound being of a purple tint. A cat bitten was very ill, but recovered, remaining thin and weak. Sir John Lubbock reports that a *Heloderma* sent him killed a frog in a few minutes, a guinea-pig in three minutes. Dr. R. W. Shufeldt, of the United States Army, reports serious symptoms after having received a bite on the right thumb, but no permanent disability followed.

THE writer has for several years endeavored to trace out an authentic account of death resulting from the bite of a Gila Monster, and the following is all the evidence in his possession. The first account was secured through Dr. S. P. Guiberson, of Ventura County, Cal., and is as follows:

"G. J. Hayes, a miner in from the Frazer mine, says that in 1878, or '80 in Tip-Top Mining Camp, Arizona, he saw a Gila monster bite a man by the name of Johnny Bostick, who at the time was under the influence of liquor. That he took hold of the *Heloderma* and shoved his finger at it, and the reptile seized his finger, and its jaws had to be pried open before he could disengage his finger. The *Heloderma* was 22 in. long and lay on the card-table. It was also seen by a man named Lou Smith, and a lot of Italian miners. Immediately Mr. John Bostick drank large quantities of liquor, and from the effects of the bite one side was paralyzed, and he died in about three months, April 19, 1878. I hereby certify that the above statement is correct. (Signed) G. J. Hayes."

Subscribed and sworn to before me, a notary public, this 19th day of April, 1886.—S. P. Guiberson, Notary Public for Ventura county, Cal.

The second affidavit, which follows, differs somewhat from the first but relates to the same individual. The query is, was the *Heloderma* bite the cause of death or was it the whisky so lavishly administered?

State of California, County of Ventura.—R. C. Carleton, who first being duly sworn, deposes and says that he was present at the time, and knows of his own knowledge, that Johnny Bostick, of Tip-Top, Arizona, was bitten by a Gila Monster, from the effects of which he afterward died. That the Gila Monster seized one of the fingers or thumb of the said Johnny Bostick, and that in order to disengage the reptile the boys cut its head off, that deponent thinks it occured in 1883. Subscribed and sworn to this day of December, 1886.—R. C. Carleton. S. P. Guiberson, Notary Public., (A true Copy.)

IN conversing with Dr. F. V. Ainsworth, U. S. A. who has had a large experience in Arizona, upon the subject of the bite of the Gila Monster, he informed the writer that he had heard of a case of death from the bite of this reptile, but that his brother Frank K. Ainsworth was conversant with the details, and he obligingly offered to write and procure full details. From the letter which follows, it will be seen that the case is reported by Dr. G. E. Goodfellow of Tombstone, Arizona, to Dr. Ainsworth:

Tombstone, July 23, 1887.—My dear Ainsworth: I at last am ready to reply to your letter concerning "snakes." The Fairbanks case was as follows: Yeager, about 55 years of age, was in May, 1885, in Fairbanks, Arizona Territory, bitten by a Gila Monster. He, to prove the innocuousness of the beast, put his left thumb and forefinger into its mouth, and he was bitten. He was immediately loaded to the guards with whisky—it happened in a saloon—and he seemed all right, save for a slight numbness and swelling in the hand and arm. He sat down in a chair in the saloon, talked with those around for an hour. The crowd thinning out, he seemed to drop asleep. In about an hour more, the saloon keeper spoke to him, but not making a reply, he was taken hold of and found to be dead. I was sent for, but before I could leave received a second message announcing his death. He was a man addicted to the use of liquor, and so far as I can ascertain had been on a prolonged spree for months. Whether he died of the reptilian poison or a combination of whisky, disease and Gila Monster I can not say.

About four years ago on the lower San Pedro I was informed that a man had been bitten in the foot while in the field and died within three hours. I could neither prove nor disprove the case.

That the Gila Monster is a poisonous lizard can not now be denied. That its bite is fatal uniformly is open to discussion. I have always considered that they were a trifle more poisonous than the scorpion, tarantula and centipede, not even approaching the rattlesnake, and I have been accustomed to regard the bite of the first three mentioned as little worse than the stinging of a bee or wasp. I have known of bee-stings killing, but though I have seen many bitten, and have had a personal experience as well, never have I known of a death to occur from the bite of a scorpion, tarantula or centipede. That they can kill under conditions I am convinced. Very respectfully, G. B. Goodfellow.

These accounts are the only authentic ones the writer has been able to gather, after ten years of constant labor and research.

ON THE other side it may be stated that Mr. Horan, the superintendent of the National Museum, has been bitten several times by this lizard without serious results following.

The first experiment of Mitchell and Reichart was as follows: "About 4 minims (of saliva) was diluted with one-half cubic centimeter of water, and thrown into the breast muscles of a large strong pigeon at 4 25 P.M. In three minutes the pigeon was rocking on its feet and walking unsteadily. At the same time the respiration became rapid and short, and at the fifth minute feeble; at the sixth minute the bird felt in convulsions with dilated pupils, and was dead before the end of the seventh minute. The first contrast to the effect of venom was shown when the wound made by the hypodermic needle was examined. There was not the least trace of local action, such as is so characteristic of the bite of serpents, and especially of the *Crotalidae*. The muscles and nerves responded perfectly to weak induced currents and to mechanical stimuli. The heart was arrested in the fullest diastole, and was full of firm black clots. The intestines looked congested. The spine was not examined." A number of other experiments made by these experienced investigators left no doubt in their minds as to the terribly venomous character of the *Heloderma* saliva.

BEFORE giving notes of the experiments made at the National Museum, it may be well to describe the process by which Drs. Mitchell and Reichart obtained the saliva, and our own. The first consisted in "provoking the reptile to bite on a saucer edge, which it was not disposed to do. When once it had seized the saucer it was hard to pull it away, so powerful was the grip of the lizard's jaws. After a moment a thin fluid-like saliva dripped in small quantities from the lower jaw. It was slightly tinted with blood, due to the violence of the bite, and it had a faint and not unpleasant aromatic odor. The secretion thus collected from the mouth was distinctly alkalin in contrast to serpent venoms, which are all alike acid."

OUR own method consisted in forcing the lizard to bite upon a piece of artist's gum, which being elastic and yielding, did no injury to the teeth and afforded a fair hold. So soon as the saliva appeared to be flowing it was carefully swabbed up with pledgets of absorbent cotton, which were washed out with glycerin, and in this way we had no difficulty in securing all of the fluid needed. It was preserved in glycerin the same as our serpent venom.

The first experiment, Nov. 8, 1887, was as follows:

Nov. 8, 1887—12:17 P.M.—held left hind leg of rabbit to *Heloderma*, which grasped it with his teeth, and held on for three-fourths of a minute, biting fiercely.

1:30 P.M.—Rabbit a little lame, but enjoyed eating as much as before.

3 P.M.—No result so far.

Nov. 9.—Rabbit appears to be perfectly well with the exception of a very slight lameness of the left hind-leg, due to the lacerated wound made by the lizard's teeth.

12:30 P. M.—Held leg of another rabbit near the mouth of a different *Heloderma* from the one used in the former experiment, and irritated the reptile until he took hold. In this case the rabbit's leg was seized several times and bitten to the bone, the reptile being unwilling to let go. There was a copious flow of saliva, which ran over the teeth wounds and was rubbed in by the experimenters, care have been taken to remove the hair from the rabbit's leg. In fact this was done in every case, as it was feared the thick fur might prevent the saliva from reaching the wounds.

3 P. M.—No result.

Nov. 10.—No result.

Nov. 11.—No result except slight lameness.

Nov. 17.— 12:45 P.M.—Injected three minims of solution of *Heloderma* saliva in leg of hen (brown). Respiration somewhat increased, but no other symptoms noticed.

2:30 P.M.—Fowl in about the same condition; respiration slightly increased and breathes with beak partly open.

Nov. 18.—Fowl appears to be entirely recovered.

Nov. 20.—Chicken completely recovered.

In this case the increased respiration was probably due to the fact that the chicken being a very noisy one it became necessary to compress its throat to avoid annoying other workers in the Museum.

Nov. 22—12:19 P.M.—Injected ten minims of solution of *Heloderma* saliva and ten minims of water into left breast of another hen. This chicken was very thin but perfectly healthy, and had been used for two rattlesnake venom experiments with ligature and recovered.

12:25 P.M.—Increase of respiration, wants to lie down, defecates, feathers ruffled.

12:30 P.M.—Panting heavily; peculiar outward and inward movement of rectum; eyes closed and very drowsy.

Nov. 28.—Chicken entirely recovered, and has been so for several days.

12:35 P.M.—Injected 25 minims of solution of *Heloderma* saliza into left leg of another hen.

12:40 P.M.—Hen lying down, respiration quickened, and breathes with mouth open.

2:30 P.M.—Chicken still lying down and breathing fast.

Nov. 29.—11 A.M.—Chicken in same condition as yesterday; will not eat.

Nov. 30.—11 A.M.—Chicken improving; eats a little.

Dec. 1.—11 A.M.—Chicken appears to be all right; eats well.

Dec. 2.—11 A.M.—Chicken entirely recovered.

Dec. 5.—12:15 P.M.—Injected 25 minims of solution *Heloderma* saliva into breast of chicken, same quantity into right leg, same quantity into left leg, making in all 75 minims. In short time. fowl had copious watery discharge *per anum*, with a curious oscillatory movement of that opening.

12:25.—Chicken lying down with its feathers much ruffled.

Dec. 6.—Chicken found dead. This fowl had been used for previous experiments, and was very thin and weak, and it is by no means certain whether the copious diarrhea, probably produced by the glycerin did not cause its death.

Dec. 5.—Forced largest *Heloderma* to bite a chicken on the leg (from which feathers had been removed several times. There was a copious flow of saliva and many lacerated wounds.

Dec. 6.—Chicken seems perfectly well, no swelling or local manifestations whatever.

Dec. 7.—Chicken perfectly well.

Fearing that possibly the glycerin solution of venom (2 drs. of saliva to 6 drs. of glycerin) was too weak or had lost its strength through keeping on Dec. 8 the following conclusive experiment was performed:

12:15 P.M.—Forced open the jaws of the largest and most savage *Heloderma* and collected upon a piece of absorbent cotton from ten to fifteen drops of fresh saliva. An incision was made in the breast of a chicken and the cotton placed in it and allowed to remain.

Dec. 10.—The chicken appears perfectly well; no sign of indisposition or local manifestations whatever. Wound appears to be healing kindly.

Jan. 20, 1888.—Wound in breast has been healed for some time, the cotton remains where it was placed and can be felt encysted under the skin and has produced no injury.

April 4.—The chicken alive and healthy with the cotton still *in situ*.

THIS experiment would seem to show that a large amount of the *Heloderma* saliva can be inserted into the tissues without producing any harm and it is still a mystery to the writer how Drs. Mitchell and Reichart and himself obtained entirely different results. Were it not for the well known accuracy and carefulness of Dr. Mitchell it might be supposed possibly that the hypodermic syringe used in his experiment contained a certain amount of *Crotalus* or cobra venom, but under the circumstances such a hypothesis is entirely untenable. Moreover no local symtoms were manifested as would have been the case had venom been inserted. Both the Gila Monsters were good-sized active specimens, full of vigor, secreting a considerable amount of saliva, and we can hardly suppose that the short captivity they had suffered could have so modified their saliva as to render it innocuous.

AN INTERESTING bit concerning his story in this issue from Farnham Bishop:

Berkeley, California.

I was asked to take part in just such an expedition as the one described—except that there were to be a half a dozen white men in it instead of two, and Mannlichers instead of Winchesters. The Chucunaque had not been consulted beforehand, but the adventurer who hatched up the scheme felt sure of finding a feud between them and the San Blas. He declared his intention of going there anyhow, and then burning our boat behind us—giving Cortez no credit for inventing the stratagem. Then, he declared, the Chucunaque could not drive us out and would accept our offer to help fight their enemies. Maybe they would, and maybe they would have told us to dive off the dock and swim back. It sounded like an exceedingly interesting sort of trip, but he never found the recruits and capital to undertake it. Probably the Zone Police put a spoke in his wheel; they have a way of finding out about such expeditions and stopping them before they start.

As for *Henry Clay*, there is more than one story about an American college graduate coming down to the Isthmus and being greeted by a class-mate wearing a breech-clout and a derby hat.—FARNHAM BISHOP.

THIS man needs our friendly help. The chances are slight that publishing his letter may help him to learn his identity, but every chance is worth taking. At least he wants to hear from us and that much we can do. I regret very sincerely that, in the mass of Camp-Fire letters, his did not get the immediate printing I should have given it, though even so it could not have seen publication for several months after it was written. I only hope his temporary address will see to the forwarding of letters.

If Mr. Stuart sees this and has not already found out who he is, I suggest that he send us his personal description and whatever other facts he can furnish. By publishing these data to the Camp-Fire there is at least a chance worth taking that some one among us may be able to give him a clue. There are, by the usual method of computing a magazine's readers, somewhere around a million who read our magazine, there seem almost none of them who do not read "Camp-Fire"and the vast majority seem to read it first. That makes quite a few to draw on when seeking information or trying to run down a mystery.

I would like very much to enter my name and address for letters from readers of *Adventure.*

I AM a case of "shell shock" causing loss of memory. I have been in this game (just finished) since August 7, 1914, and am at present returning soldiers to their homes and loved ones. I am at present on one of His Majesty's Australian Transports bound for England.

We left Wellington, New Zealand, homeward bound on the 7th day of August, 1919, arriving at Panama September 1, 1919. Passed through canal in seven hours and left Cristobal, C. Z., after coaling, September 2, 1919, to bunker at Newport News, Va.

I am like many another soldier of the French Foreign Legion. I went in to forget and I am afraid now I have forgotten only too well. My birth given at time of enlistment was December 31, 1896, so I am only 23 years of age. I *do* know what my real name is. The suggestion is that I am an American. Evidently all bridges were burnt behind me when I enlisted. My mind is a bit hazy as to a good several things that I seem to have taken part in. But I have the decorations received on the field, some with my name and date engraved on them, so I must have taken part in the sorties. When talking with boys that were with me at the time I seem to remember the incident quite well.

The doctors say memory may (?) come back in time.

I would send for one of your indentification-cards but my address is only temporary. Wishing you the best of luck and open trails I beg to sign—COURAGE STUART, Union Jack Club, Waterloo Rd., London, England.

SEVERAL queries and some interesting bits from one of our Western comrades:

San Diego, Cal.

Can any old adventurer tell us anything about "Port" Stockton, who terrorized Northern New Mexico and Southern Colorado during the latter seventy's and early eighty's? If I am not mistaken he was killed in a pitched battle with a posse in the Animas Valley between Animas Forks (now Durango) and Farmington. I have forgotten the year, but was at that time with the Government Survey, establishing the boundaries of the Navajo Indian Reservation.

I WAS also near the place that "Billie the kid" was killed at the time of the killing, and Pat Garrett was in my camp for more than a week just prior to the climax. Just in this connection I wish to state that a few months ago I met with a man who was for a time "Billie's" chief lieutenant. I was intimately acquainted with him in Las Vegas and east of there. We had a long and (for me) a very interesting conversation about the old times and he told me where John Rudebaugh was about five years ago engaged in the meat-market business. He told me many things which cleared up doubts about certain episodes of Billie's career. I do not mention his name as he is still living hale and active and highly respected.

CAN any one tell what has become of Nellie Cashman, one of the most noted characters of the extreme South-west, 30 to 35 years ago? I was on one expedition which she headed to a Lower California Gold-rush in 1885. I believe she went to the first Klondyke excitement. Heard indirectly that she was running a saloon and gambling-house in San Francisco just before the Quake. I know that at one time she ran a hotel in Nogales, Arizona, and wore a six-gun when she went shopping.

Jerry Burke followed the line of the Atlantic & Pacific (now the Santa Fé) Railroad during construction. He was not a bandit, just the reverse;

nevertheless he did some very neat gun work at Flagstaff before the R.R. got there and was present when Blind Jim and Jim made the big killing.

Is there any reader of *Adventure* that was there? If so I would be pleased to compare notes with him. —PHIL SNODGRASS.

OFTEN in cutting out from a letter for Camp-Fire the parts that contain words of praise for our magazine I find quite a job on my hands to avoid marring the continuity and general bearing of the letter as a whole. The following letter from our comrade Captain James Moorhead begins by stating, more at length, that he likes our magazine because the people in the stories are "real men with good red blood in their veins" and then goes on as quoted below. And a very interesting letter it is.

New York.

. . . To some people that have never been away far from home this might read much like fiction, but in my turn going to sea I often met just with such men as often appear in *Adventure*—men afraid of nothing. Probably I could fill a book on just such a subject as "brave men I have met," especially in the packet ship days in the Western Ocean trade, when the rule was a word and a blow, where there was always continual trouble between men and officers, the sailor as a rule getting the worst end of the deal, but occasionally a good man would crop up in the forecastle able to take care of himself. And when such a man ran against the bucko second mate and got the best of him, he was usually taken aft and the ex-bucko second mate was sent forward, a broken man for the rest of the voyage.

SOME time ago I wrote you a letter on the wreck of the schooner *Kocheko* on the coast of Magdalene Islands, as your characters in the story (I think it was called "Wave Crest," by Samuel Alexander White) were so vivid to me that I really thought I had come in contact with the same men and characters, that the writer of that story had in mind.

Again, in reading November 3rd issue, "Mule Skinner Dynamite," by C. M. Cosby, takes my money. I have many times in the course of my sea life come across just such men as, *Handsome Joe Kerrigan*, *Sheridan* and *Donald McDonald*, especially the latter. So I shall try to depict a few lines on life on board ship in the early sixties, where my hero might be twin brother to your *Donald McDonald*.

IN the early sixties quoted above sailors were a happy-go-lucky lot, tough you might say, but a simple lot of fellows at that, and the first day out from Liverpool or New York was cleaning-up day (especially on packet ships), when the officers measured up the crew to find out just what they measured up to. The men were used to the rough treatment, and if the officers could not carry it out they were looked down upon by Jack, but with all, after the first day out, they were sailors, men who could do anything with a piece of rope or a palm and needle.

Then there was the boss of the forecastle, who was always looked up to, and always got first cut of the old salt hoss when the mess kid came to the forecastle and who got his title by brawn and muscle and remained so until a better man cropped up, and so the happy days went on.

AROUND the latter part of '65 I joined a little full-rigged ship in Liverpool, called the *Lammergeier*, bound to New Orleans with general cargo, and was probably one of the first ships to tow up the Mississippi after the peace was declared. I was only a lad at the time, but although I had seen lively times on board packet ships ere this, I shall never forget the high jinks we had on board this ship, The captain was a Liverpool Englishman, the officers were a mixture of Irish and Scotch, while the crew were full-blooded Irish.

Our carpenter (commonly called Chips) was also a Liverpool man and as fine a built man as you would want to meet, over six feet tall and built in proportion. He was the captain's pet.

In the forecastle was also the pet of the crew, also a fine built fellow as you could meet anywhere, Nat Laughlin, six feet tall, built in proportion, a bunch of muscles and smart as a steel trap.

The officers were a quiet lot and not looking for any trouble with the crew, so all the scrapping was done forward and during the passage from Liverpool to New Orleans. Our friend Laughlin had taken care of most every member of the crew forward and naturally was looked up to as the boss and the pet of the forecastle. What more natural than that Chips, the captain's pet, should look with envy at Laughlin the forecastle pet? And although we made the passage without any friction, we all knew the day would surely come when these two gladiators would meet and settle the supremacy.

WE were laying at the Levee at New Orleans and, after discharging our cargo, began to load cotton for Liverpool. The men who loaded cotton in these days were commonly called Cotton-Jammers, and a pretty lively bunch they were. They very soon came to know of the feeling between these two men, which only needed a spark, which came one Sunday afternoon.

Chips and I were lying on the after hatch, reading, when our friend Laughlin came on board and, passing us where we lay, announced there was no man on board the ship he could not lick, and walked forward.

It only took a few minutes for Chips to think the matter over, when he jumped forward, taking me with him and armed with his adze to see fair play, but Laughlin had gone ashore.

After supper the captain advised his pet to retire and rest and be ready for the fight next morning at daylight.

About 8 P.M. the sailors all returned on board with their champion and, as Chips refused to come out until morning, Laughlin was rubbed down and put to bed by his followers and the fight staged for 6 A.M. Monday morning.

THE news flew like fire along the Levee and you can rest assured we had a real audience as the Cottom-Jammers were out in force. Work on the ships all stopped, to see the great fight on the ship *Lammergeier*. The Levee was black with spectators, so here we had a prize fight on a ship's deck, staged to perfection, seats free, no purse, and—which would be the envy of the sporting fraternity today—no police interference. A marvelous exhibition, carried out to perfection. Of course, if such a thing was attempted today all hands from captain down would be landed in jail.

5.30 A.M., as the second mate called all hands to turn to and wash decks, the mate came out and ordered all work stopped and to get ready for the fight.

Our two gladiators came out on deck ready, naked bodies, light pants, heavy boots, bare knuckles; the officers were back of Chips, sailors back of Laughlin, rubbing him down with a decoction of rum and resin, while the captain took care of his pet, keeping out of sight but passing out a drink and watching the fight.

Timekeepers were arranged and handlers, etc., and the men were placed abreast the mainmast on center of deck, the mate put up his hand and the timekeeper called "Time!" and the ball was on.

FIRST round: Chips led and was followed by Laughlin, both landing heavily. It was give and take even to the end of round.

Second round: Both men sparring for time, Laughlin backing up, Chips following his man, when Laughlin led, landing on Chips' lip and splitting it up badly. First blood for the sailor. Round ended in light sparring.

Third round: After both men sparring for an opening Laughlin led and missed his mark, falling on deck; was immediately up driving Chips back most to break of poop. The round ended with Chips pretty well winded when time was called, the captain passing a drink to his man, while the sailors rubbed their man down carefully each round with rum and resin.

Fourth round: Both men were well matched. It was a rough and tumble fight, and although Chips was badly winded he fought on to the end of the round when time was called. The mate wanted to make it a draw, but as the men insisted their man had the best of it the fight must go on. Time was called again.

Fifth round: Laughlin led off in this round landing on Chips and giving him his first fall, which was a bad one, but he got up before time was called, rushing at poor Laughlin like a mad bull. Laughlin gave way, and as the captain made his appearance on deck to stop the fight, Chips got an opening and landed on Laughlin, lifting him clean off his feet, and when he landed nearly 20 feet away he lit with his cheek on a beef barrel which was setting at the galley door, splitting his cheek open and so the fight was called a draw, Chips and Laughlin going ashore arm in arm, best of friends ever after, neither the best man. They were a sight, Nat Laughlin with his split cheek, and Chips with his split lip, and oh! Boy, what a fight—between two of the best men I have ever seen stripped; and I have seen a lot of boxing since I gave up the sea, but nothing like this, on a ship's deck, no money in it and free for the audience.

MANY years after I had the pleasure of spending an evening at the house of Nat Laughlin in Liverpool. He had married a very nice young lady and settled down to shore life.

During supper we went over old times. I noticed the scar on his cheek and remarked that it still showed up pretty plain. I noticed him winking at me, but did not know I was treading on dangerous ground until his dear little wife spoke up and said: "Just think of it! That mark nearly killed him. It was a topsail halliard block fell on him, but I don't mind the scar as long as his life was saved." I replied, "Yes, Nat, it come very near fixing you."

NOW in closing I might say I call the character *Donald McDonald* a duplicate of Nat Laughlin, A. B. on the good ship *Lammergeier*, a real man from his feet up and every inch a sailor.

I would call your character *Handsome Joe Kerrigon* the duplicate of Jack Irwin, the carpenter, on board the *Lammergeier*, also every inch a man and a master of his trade.

I don't know who I could duplicate for *Sheridans* as we had no peacemaker at this show. However, you must remember your story is fiction while mine is a true story to show that many a true story reads like fiction.—CAPTAIN JAMES MOORHEAD.

P.S. I only put five rounds in this fight, as that was as much as I could remember, it happened so long ago, but the sight is as vivid to me today as if it happened yesterday. I know that these two able-bodied men fought that morning from 6 A.M. until after 7 A.M. and no idle time in hugging, etc., at that.—J M.

CONCERNING his story in this issue Robert J. Pearsall tells us the following about an extremely interesting race of people:

Palo Alto, California.

I really got the idea of this story from my old friend, *Encyclopædia Britannica*, under "Conjuring." The account of "Dr. Pepper's ghost," which Hazard mentions, connected itself up with some speculations I once heard in China concerning the bullet-defying powers of the Boxer chiefs—and that, naturally, with Koshinga. "The Test of the Five Arrows" is optically possible—and I'm really inclined to think that it, or some very similar stunt, was part of the Boxer repertoire.

THE scene is again the land of the Lolos, named by Dr. Thorel the "Black Caucasians" of Asia. A certain Chinese map describes them thus: "The Barbarians of Shama, who, at indeterminate periods, cross the Blue River (the Yang-tse-kiang) to kill, pillage, burn and make captives." But they have other qualities than savagery: for instance, they possess a system of writing peculiar to themselves, and numerous books which no one but themselves can decipher. And they are a strong race, who, though surrounded by Chinese for hundreds of years, have managed to preserve complete racial homogeneousness. Their origin is a matter of dispute, but everything about them speaks of the vigor of a young people. Even their system of society is indicative of youth, being the same system that we find among the most powerful races in the beginnings of history. Perhaps these Lolos should be included in any consideration one gives to the future of the East.—ROBERT J. PEARSALL.

MAKE our chain of Camp-Fire stations not only a success but a big success. Add one or more stations to the chain so that eventually a member of Camp-Fire can wander almost anywhere in the world and yet find friendly men with common interests, where those of us who can not wander can meet those who do.

A station may be in any shop, home or other reputable place. The only requirements are that a station shall display the regular station sign, provide a box or drawer for mail to be called for and provide and preserve a sufficiently substantial register book. When there are enough stations to warrant even a small wholesale order this office will furnish the books and signs.

No responsibility for mail is assumed by anybody; the station merely uses ordinary care. Entries in register to be confined to name or serial number route destination, permanent address and such other brief notes or remarks as desired; each station can impose its own limit on space to be used. Registers become permanent property of station; signs remain property of this magazine, so that if there is due cause or complaint from members, a station can be discontinued by withdrawing sign.

A STATION bulletin-board is strongly to be recommended as almost necessary. On it travelers can leave tips as to conditions of trails, etc., resident members can post their names and addresses, such hospitality as they care to offer, calls for any travelers who are familiar with countries these residents once knew, calls for particular men if they happen that way, etc., notices or tips about local facilities and conditions. Letters to resident members can be posted on this bulletin-board.

Any one who wishes is a member of Camp-Fire and therefore entitled to the above station privileges. (Question of requiring identification-cards or Camp-Fire button to be decided later.) Those offering hospitality of any kind do so on their own responsibility and at their own risk and can therefore make any discriminations they see fit. Traveling members will naturally be expected to remember that they are merely guests and act accordingly.

A station may offer only the required register and mail facilities or enlarge its scope to any degree it pleases. Its possibilities as headquarters for a local club of resident Camp-Fire members is excellent.

PERHAPS the following is one of the most "different" talks we've had from our writers' brigade. Rightly enough, most of them talk very little about their writing but get together with us in the adventure field, so the present letter seems particularly interesting and really leads us into a sort of new adventure. It's partly my fault that Mr. Noel talked along these lines, but I'm glad it is.

And, since I've been headed into talking shop, I'm tempted to gab a bit about what he says about story writing. "If a man has a natural crook for story writing there is little need of formal training." Yes, but what *is* a "natural crook," and how does a man know whether he has it, and what is meant by "formal training"? I haven't anything wise to say about it. Might as well admit that I don't know. I've been with our magazine since it started in 1910, worked before that on five others and on *Romance* since it started last Fall. Also three years on a country newspaper, besides the nearly eighteen on magazines. Used to write fiction for some I didn't work on.

I'VE learned an awful lot, too. Only, unfortunately, most of what I've learned has been in the way of finding out how much I don't know. That's valuable knowledge all right, but lots of times lately I've found myself wondering how other people know so much. (No, this is no sly dig at Mr. Noel. So far as I am competent to judge, I agree with him, with due allowance for various interpretations of terms used. I'm thinking of critics, writers and editors in general.) And I pick up books, critical or analytic, and wonder how any human being can know so much as that about anything. I've managed, after all these years, to end up with only two fundamental theories as to story writing. I won't bother you with them. The point is that so many other people in the game seem to have hundreds instead of only two.

What I don't know is too big a subject to try to put on paper, but as to this thing of a writer's not needing instruction I want to deliver the wise judgment that he does and he doesn't. As Mr. Noel says, doing a thing is the best way to learn how to do it, but you have to make an exception of such things as handling high explosives or running a complicated and delicate piece of machinery. Each writer (and there are probably 109,000,000 of them out of our estimated population of 110,000,000) is more or less a case to himself. All of them, of course, need instruction. But what kind of instruction? A correspondence or college course? Books on the art of story writing? Or just studying for himself the work of those who write best? Or some of each? I can't get much further toward an answer than saying "It all depends." Not only on the man himself but on the *kind* of course or book or writer he turns to.

IN ONE thing surely Mr. Noel is on the right track. Too little instruction is better than too much, if a man has any real ability. And surely no imitation of other writers is infinitely better than a little or much. If you'd read manuscripts by the ten thousand as I have you'd be amazed at the vast number of writers who've been trying to imitate O. Henry, for example. No single one of them can *be* O. Henry, therefore no single one of them can write O. Henry stories. Some can't write any kind of story, but others could write very good ones if only they'd *be themselves* and write their own kind of story.

I HAVEN'T said much, have I? But I warned you in the beginning that I didn't know much. I wouldn't have dragged these matters up to our Camp-Fire if it weren't that I know some of you are interested. Because year after year many letters keep coming in to every editor asking him to tell some one how he or she can learn to write. They might almost as well ask me to tell them how to be happily married. Sometimes I can help them on specific points but the main case seems to me about as I've put it above.

Now let Mr. Noel follow Camp-Fire custom and introduce himself on the occasion of his first story in our magazine:

Pullman, Wash.

I much prefer to read the chatty writing of others in "Camp-Fire," The Meeting Place, to making a contribution to that feast; but there are some few people who seem to know who I am and what I am, so it may do no harm to let others into the secret.

BORN in Iowa, many, many long years ago. "Mercenary Ambitions" is my first published story. Well, I am young, for the older I get the younger I am. Such a paradox can not very well be helped when one is born that way.

Some more: I'm a farmer by qualifications and destiny. It doesn't worry me either. A plain farmer is what I am. I've garnered a good many pumpkins (to me they are punkins) in my time, and loads and loads of corn. And if all the pigs I've brought safely up to bacon-sized hog-hood could be fried together in a big skillet there would be some grease.

In my teens I missed some years of schooling, then at twenty-one or later attended a country school two Winters. Later by insane persistency and much hard work I plowed my way through college.

Once upon a time I homesteaded in South Dakota, lived in a sod house and roamed the prairies. Some life that was! I've taught school, dug ditches (not many) mixed concrete, and—of course farming is my blue ribbon stunt.

ADVENTURES? I'm afraid not. But wait till I consult the dictionary to see how broad the term is. Laying Webster's word aside, I might say that if milking a cow is an adventure some few thousands have fallen to my lot. Matrimony has never crossed my path, so if it is really an adventure, as some who have mixed with it claim, I'm barred there too.

I'm an outlaw when it comes to conventions. The groovers are too uncomfortable for me. Eating soup in a set way has no fascination for me and stiff collars are an abomination in the sight of both mine eyes. I doubt it I have a collar-bone. If I should ever essay to deal in a branch of haberdashery it wouldn't be a collary. My hair would be the bane of my life if I were interested in banes. Though I get a haircut semiperiodically I am continually being identified as a musician, or better still as a retired farmer. When I enter a barbershop to get a haircut the barber begins to prate about crops, the weather, and E-strings, which shows that barbers do not talk shop on all occasions.

MY DESIRE to write originated years ago, as I remember, while I was on the farm in Iowa. Somehow I got infected with writers' bacillus and it has been in my system ever since. There is a theory that when germs enter the system the vital forces begin at once to develop a serum to fight the germs.

The battle rages hot for some time and if the germs come off victorious the human element is laid to rest with certain ceremonies. On the other hand if the victory goes to the serum the germs demobilize according to the terms of the treaty, the human element smiles and the nurse smiles back at him.

Now the fiction germ holds itself indifferent to this theory—at least in my case. At times I had a superficial feeling that the battle was over, that the germs had lost, but down deep in the back of my head (about the region of the parieto-occipital) I knew the fight would be renewed at some time or other. These intuitions have always been verified by ensuing attempts at composition.

ABOUT the writing of "Mercenary Ambitions". I received the stimulus to write the story from reading W. C. Tuttle's account of "Monkeying with Ancestors," a good story which appeared in *Adventure*, June, 1918. After reading Tuttle's yarn, boy-like I had an impulse to write a monkey story. In the midst of fabrication Pete and his group entered a protest. They argued that they were sufficient unto themselves, that there was no sense in bringing in a monkey. So I decided, "out goes he." The whole story is fiction from ear to ear—such fiction as it is.

All told, I've hardly done enough story writing to serve an apprenticeship. Of course I've written several stories, or near stories, or possibly far stories. The most of them are stored away in a shoe-box and the archives of my trunk. Some day I may blow a trumpet and resurrect them.

I've read writings galore on the technique of the short story. And I've taken two courses in story writing in college, but with it all it seems to me that if one has a natural crook for story writing there is little need of formal training. Common sense will soon point out the rules of the game. We learn to do this, that and the other thing by doing them, and I've found out by experience that I can learn to write by writing. I don't claim to have completed the learning; the process is still going on.—James E. Noel.

THERE have been various requests and offers for the original paintings from which *Adventure* covers have been made but they had to be declined because we could hit upon no entirely satisfactory basis or method of sale. We now have a large number of these originals on hand and believe we've found the right way to dispose of them.

On May 1, 1920, all will be offered for sale to the highest bidder and any one may bid. Send in your bid to reach us before that date and state very carefully not only the subject of the painting you want but also the exact date of the issue on which it appeared. Most of these originals cost us one hundred and twenty-five dollars each. They should bring a price of about one-third that figure but each will go to the highest bid. No bid less than ten dollars will be considered. Some of them will probably go for no more than that; for some of them so low a bid will not stand any chance. It is altogether a question of how many others happen to want the same painting and of the recognized market value of the work of the various artists, some of whom have more than a national reputation. All paintings are in good condition, none of them being damaged to an extent to make it unfit for framing.

Size of canvas is usually 30 in. by 21 in; sometimes smaller. A few larger. Exact size can be given in advance if desired.

All are oil-paintings except where indicated.

Packing done by us. Expressed collect and at your risk.

Beginning January 1, 1921, semi-annual auctions of cover originals will probably be held on the first day of January and the first day of June every year. But this is the time to get a chance at all cover originals up to and including the April 18, 1920, issue, which appears March 18.

Covers for the following issues have the word "ADVENTURE" and other, smaller type painted on them: 1911—Feb., Mar., June, July, Aug., Sept.; 1912—Apl., July, Sept., Oct., Dec.; 1913—Mar., Aug., Dec.; 1914—Feb., Mar., Apl.; 1915—Mar.

Covers for Nov. and Jan. 1915, Mid-Apl., 1919, and First Mar., 1920, have the word "ADVENTURE" but no other lettering painted on them.

Covers for the following issues have no lettering at all on them: 1917—Apl., May, First Sept., First Oct., First Dec., Mid-Dec.; 1918—First Jan., First Mar., Mid-Mar., First Apl., First May, Mid-May, Mid-June, Mid-July, First Aug., Mid-Aug., First Sept., First Oct., First Nov., Mid-Nov., First Dec.; 1919—all but First Feb., First Apl., Mid-May, First June, Mid-Oct., Mid-Dec.; 1920—First Jan., First Feb., First Mar., Mid-Mar., First April, Mid-April.

No other covers than these mentioned here are for sale.

IT IS not his first story in our magazine, though the first was a very short one, but Captain Scott's letter was written on that occasion, back in April, 1917, and probably reached us too late to go into that issue, so here it is now:

New York.

I speak with humbleness and would state that many of the experiences sound much worse than they really were. Nature has a wonderful way of bucking you up so that alarming incidents lose much of their terror when faced.

I WAS born in 1882 at Woodstock, Ontario, and was educated at high school and at the Royal Military College which latter is the Canadian "West Point." During peace time I held a commission first in the 22nd Regiment, the Oxford Rifles and then in The Governor General's Foot Guards. From 1908 to 1912 I was abroad installing a new system of marine lighting for the various Governments in Italy, India, Burma, Ceylon and Australia. In 1914, on the outbreak of war, I accepted a commission in the 21st Battalion, Canadian Expeditionary Force, and served with them until they had been in the trenches about half a year when I came home with injured ears *via* the Red Cross.

While doing marine work at Aden I had a near accident with 1500 lbs. of calcium carbide on a barge out in the harbor. Water broke through on to the carbide and started to generate the six or seven thousand cubic feet of acetylene. An explosion of great force was probable and my native workmen all dived into the water with the sharks. As I could not swim as well as the sharks I stayed up and managed to get things under control.

While duck shooting at Karachi my life was attempted by two native boatmen but I saved myself with my automatic pistol.

In a railway compartment between Madras and Calcutta two Bengali natives tried to murder me but, again, my automatic saved the day.

I HAVE had very bad luck at sea. For years something always seemed to happen on board ship. I have run aground off the coast of Australia and I have been there three days at sea without wireless with the hold on fire. I have been stuck on a sand-bar in the mouth of the Hoogli River with a falling tide and not enough boats to take off more than part of the third-class alone. The captain told me that ours was the first boat known to slip off without turning turtle. Even in New York the old *Etruria* of the Cunard Line (now scrapped) once started her engines the wrong way and crashed through two barges ahead of her instead of backing out into the stream. That was the worst voyage I ever made across the Atlantic. Several times I dined in the main saloon in my pyjamas, once with the floor awash with half a foot of water. Needless to say there were no ladies present.

OF COURSE the war remains the greatest adventure of all. For half a year I had a front seat in the greatest show the world has ever seen. And they paid me five dollars and twenty-five cents a day to sit there. Finally my ears gave out and I was sent home. It started with a big shell from a howitzer that nearly got me. The enemy were registering their big guns on our front line and it was before our guns had plenty of ammunition so we could not call for much retaliation. Consequently we had to grin and bear it more or less.

These big shells from howitzers come over very slowly with a whistling sound. They fall almost vertically and, for the last hundred feet, may be seen as a great black dart. When the ground is soft, as it usually is in Belgium, these shells penetrate from five to ten feet before sufficient resistance is encountered to operate the percussion fuse which explodes the shell. I had been getting the men into the "feathers" or shell-shelter trenches and was on some low ground behind the parapet when I heard the ominous whistling of one of these big high explosive shells. It seemed to be coming very near but it was useless to move as I might run into it just as easily as away from it. I saw it enter the ground very close and tried to throw myself flat but the explosion occurred before I could reach the ground and I was spun around in mid-air by the concussion. The edge of the crater was close to where I picked myself up. At first I thought I was more feared than anything else but my side and neck were stiffened and my left ear permanently injured according to the London specialists. Time, however, has done much and, while I still have much noise in my head, I hope to be in uniform once more if the war lasts.—R. T. M. Scott.

OF COURSE he rates a say. Maybe some of you who know Afghanistan may feel like telling him and Camp-Fire in general what you think about it. At this writing it looks as if that country might have quite a lot going on before long.

Elizabethport, New Jersey.

Was reading Camp-Fire this evening and think I have traveled about enough to rate a say in said place. Just got discharged from the Navy last week at San Diego, Cal. I have punched cows from Montana to Mexico and from Death Valley to Oklahoma. Spent a year digging gold in the Klondike. Am rated an excellent revolver shot. Can hit an orange at twenty paces from the hip, drawing and firing. What's the matter with a story about the Klondike or a good tale about Afghanistan? I spent two years there and would like to find out what other people think of it.—H. B. Hanford.

IN THE following, J. Allan Dunn shows us how closely his novel in this issue follows actual history:

Pittsfield, Mass.

Reading over the carbon of "The Long Trail," it seems wise that I should take advantage of "The Camp-Fire" to say a few words that may save discussion or clear up doubt. When a story runs as close to actual history as "The Long Trail," it should be a satisfaction to know that some care has been taken to make it authentic.

I HAVE been happy in authorities, using many biographies of Fremont and, largely, his own "Memoirs." When an autobiography is written as simply as Fremont's, when it gives so generously the full meed of honor and applause to those who assisted a leader, when it describes so fully yet so simply the actions of the field, its mistakes as well as its triumphs, so unostentatiously the thoughts that prefaced and led to such actions, revealing an ambition leavened by faith, a daring and a true manhood enriched with enthusiasm for the project in hand, one can but feel, long before the bulky volume has ended, that one has seen a true revelation of the man—physical and spiritual, a hero despite his modesty, a strong man despite his failings and, above all, a true patriot.

THERE are those who decry Fremont's part in the conquest of California, who belittle his daring by the suggestion of self-aggrandizement. Some things stand clear—that he believed here was a wondrous country belonging by geographical right to the United States—that he was in secret service for the government, at least including the President and Cabinet and those desiring the advance of territorial possession and the protection of American frontiersmen—that his swift strokes saved California to America. As a scientist and an explorer he is unchallenged.

His man-love for Kit Carson was fully returned. Carson (in what is claimed to be the only authentic and approved history of his life, written by Lieut. Col. De Witt C. Peters, U. S. A. at Taos) corroborates in every detail the "Memoirs" of Fremont, and Carson was strong in his defense when Fremont was court-martialed at the instance of General Kearny. That the cause for this unfortunate charge was a jealousy between the two arms of the service, the army and navy, with perhaps a misunderstanding as to the exact standings of General Kearny and Commodore Stockton, is as certain as it is lamentable. To us of the Camp-Fire, Carson's whole-hearted love for Fremont perhaps says all that is necessary.

LET it not be forgotten that Fremont made five expeditions, two at his own expense, that, through stress and danger of weather, of desert, of Indian strife, he accomplished his ends, not least of which was the blazing of the trail for the trans-continental railroad, long one of his ardent dreams.

There have been only one or two men greatly honored and trusted by the Indian tribes, none more so than Fremont, and this by the varied clans from the Atlantic to the Pacific, all of whom hailed him as "The Great White Chief" and with whom he rarely was forced to fight because of his understanding of them, his absolute fairness and his intrepidity.

THE "long trail" is well known to me. From its starting-point, near the present site of Pueblo, over into California, there is none of it that I have not personally traversed. Twenty-five years ago I rode horseback over all that part of it in Colorado and Utah. Later, much of it in California in various ways, all of it in some way.

The language used, the acts performed, wherever Fremont is in action in the story, are, very largely, the actual words of Fremont or his men and, in ninety per cent. of the instances, the actions are absolutely as they occurred. Also when Carson takes up the tale of their Klamath expedition.

AS TO the situation between Mexico, England and the United States at the time, the following history, not always included in our textbooks—if ever in its entirety—may shed some light:

War was threatening because of the coming over of Texas. Mexico sulked and scowled and simmered. Mexico owed England money. California was suggested as payment of the debt and also as a slap in the eye for the American Gringos. England had a fleet at Mazatlan and in the mouth of the Columbia River waiting for the time to claim this possession. America had a squadron at Mazatlan watching England's actions. The *Savannah*, a frigate of 54 guns, the *Portsmouth, Levant, Warren* and *Cyane*, sloops-of-war averaging 24 guns, 32 lbs longs, 68 lbs shell, 42 lbs carronades; the sloop *Erie* with long 18's, the big *Congress* of 60 32 lbs longs, represented us. Ultimately Yankee ingenuity outwitted the British, led them on a false chase to Honolulu, doubled and got first to Monterey where the pusillanimity of Commodore Sloat almost lost us California, until Fremont forced Sloat's hand, ran up the Stars and Stripes and, when the formidable British ships arrived, it was to see the American flag floating proudly and Fremont at the head of his picked troops grimly ready to discuss the matter.

"If," said the British commander later, "if the Stars and Stripes had not been afloat above Monterey I should have infallibly landed and hoisted the Union Jack with all preparations to maintain it." So Mexican intrigue and British desire for a fair land and invaluable harbors was frustrated.

Further, State archives declare that Consul Larkin at Monterey was fully advised that Fremont's mission, while admittedly one of exploration, covered also authority for swift action should war break out. The sending out of Lieutenant Gillespie by the Government, to travel through hostile Mexico, to command assistance from Sloat at Mazatlan, to force marches until he found Fremont in Oregon with the news of war, is proof enough that Fremont acted advisedly and in complete alliance with Washington diplomacy.

HERE is a pertinent piece of history. In the year 1845 a priest, Eugenio Macnamara, was domesticated with the British Legation in Mexico City. He then made application for a grant of land for the purpose of establishing a colony in California. A square league (containing 4428 acres) was to be given each family, and half that amount to each child of a colonist. This territory to be conveyed was around San Francisco Bay, embracing three thousand square leagues and including the whole valley of the San Joaquin. Macnamara agreed to bring a thousand families at the beginning.

I set down here—without comment, save an underlining where he refers to America, that he who runs may read, a portion of his memorial to the Mexican President:

> "I propose, with the aid and approbation of your excellency, to place in Upper California, a colony of Irish Catholics. I have a triple object in making this proposition. I wish, in the first place to advance the cause of Catholicism. In the second, to contribute to the happiness of my countrymen. Thirdly, I desire *to put an obstacle in the way of further usurpations on the part of an irreligious and anti-Catholic nation.*"

Macnamara was landed, from the British frigate *Juno*, of the main fleet under Sir George Seymour, at Santa Barbara, at the critical moment, ripe for the settlement of the grant of land and the passing, with it, of the whole country under British protection.

If he did nothing else, the preservation of the lives of American pioneers by Fremont's prompt actions, is enough to justify him.

FREMONT invariably had a bodyguard of Delaware Indians who slept about his person and tent. On his second expedition—this was his third—Fremont describes the arrangement by the Indian Agent, Major Cummins, to supply him with Delaware hunters. So satisfactory were these that on the next trip Fremont writes:

"From the Delaware Nation twelve men had been chosen to go with me—good hunters and brave men—among them two chiefs, Swanok and Sagundai."

Lieutenant Walpole, British Navy, in his book "Four Years in the Pacific on *H. M. S. Collingwood*," describes these Delawares at Monterey at the time of the arrival of the British Fleet. Carson speaks constantly of their exploits. They "were ever on the war-path, so far as the expedition was concerned, leaving no opportunity untouched of that sort."

IT MAY seem strange to read of any alliance between such savage tribes as the Cheyennes, Arapahoes and Sioux. Much is misunderstood of the existence of pacts and truces between these fierce warriors. Let me quote Fremont's official log of his first expedition.

"The Great Village had been broken up and the tribes were on their ways home. It consisted of Arapahoes, Cheyennes and Oglallah Sioux who had crossed the Platte eight or ten miles below the mouth of Sweet Water intending to regain the Platte *via* Deer Creek. They had been brought together by the bad year."

Again, on the third expedition:

"We met Oglallah Sioux on the way up Bijou Fork to beg horses from the Arapahoes, who were hunting."

As a matter of fact a bad season of drought, with scarcity of game, invariably meant a friendly junction of these tribes for purposes of subsistence. I do not believe the Sioux would ever make truce with the Kiowas, the Comanches, the Snakes or the Osages, but with the Arapahoes and Cheyennes they *did*—and there's an end on't. These three tribes practically shared a hunting territory under elastic conditions little understood to-day. All had far greater scope than is usually understood. The Arapahoes were not confined to any part of what is now Colorado, nor were the Cheyennes, while the Sioux had numerous and widely scattered sub-tribes.

A FREED-NEGRO actually accompanied one of Fremont's expeditions and was well liked by the commander. He later settled and prospered on the Pacific Coast.

AS FOR the gold, Fremont relates that Owens and a man named Breckenridge on occasions called his attention to glittering grains that he set hastily aside without examination as pyrites of iron, or fool's gold. Owens' discovery was in the American Fork. Fremont states that they were far more occupied with the discovery of a good spring, a fine camping-place, a pass in the mountains, the source and flow of a river, than they were with the possibilities of metal in the hills or streams. They were men of single purposes.

I think this is all. I don't want to be prolix. I do want to assure my friends of The Camp-Fire that I have earnestly tried to make my yarn convincing from the historian's, as well as the story-teller's, standpoint.—J. ALLAN DUNN.

A CASE in which our Camp-Fire buttons introduced comrades wandering in foreign lands. I'm even leaving in the post-script. Though I make a business of cutting out things referring to the magazine when I send your letters to the printer for Camp-Fire, this is a mild example of the reports we have at Camp-Fire now and then of strange places where the magazine has been found. I only wish, now, that I had passed on to you the many instances that were reported in letters from the front—of copies begged, stolen and fought for. I remember one of you who was rejoicing because at the end of a scrap over one copy he had emerged with eight pages of a story by W. C. Tuttle.

But on the whole it's better to cut out complimentary things about the magazine before letters go to Camp-Fire. Otherwise some people would think we were merely using "Camp-Fire" to boost the magazine. And anyhow there are a lot of things besides the magazine for us to talk about.

Brooklyn, N. Y.

While in Huelba, Spain, and also in Marseilles, France, I was fortunate to find two Camp-Fire men whom I knew to be such by the buttons in their coats. Of course we got together and made merry, and many a toast was made those nights to Camp-Fire and its members. I tell this to explain my hurry to get my button. I expect to sail for southern waters in a short time and might miss some comrades by being without a button.

With best wishes to Camp-Fire.—JOHN ADAMSON.

P.S. The most welcome thing we got on board was a copy of *Adventure*. A British officer gave it to me when we ran into Gibraltar for fresh water.

WORD from an old Camp-Fire comrade (not Uncle Frank) from whom we haven't heard for some time. He didn't ask me not to use his name, but I thought I'd play safe.

California.

. . . My right eye is gone, and I do not write much. I have taken up the study of Pacific Coast shells as a means of passing the time. . . . but I wish you would tell the writers to not hit a man with the *butt of a pistol*. It is not good form among gun-men. Punch 'em with the muzzle, smash 'em with the barrel, throw the gun at them when emptied. But, for the the love of Mike, never paste a man with the butt. Even in fiction. It's a loss of time, and it isn't done.

As an illustration of what I mean by butts: Once upon a time (1891) one "Moccasin Jake," a deputy marshal in Lusk, Wyo., tried to hit me with the butt of a Colt forty-five. He lost his gun and had to resign, and I got six months in jail for resisting an officer. If he had not changed ends with that "hog-leg" he might have made a winning. As it was we both lost a bet.

ADVENTURE still exists in real life. The other day I went to the village (Oceano) and assisted at Portugal's National Celebration. Had a scrap with an Irishman, got full of Dago Red, and the mule upset me in the lake. Three Greeks rescued me and I arrived at home a sadder, wiser and wetter man.

I am enclosing a photo of the mule aforesaid. She isn't a mule, but a Spanish jennet. Sired by a race horse, and suckled by a jackass of the feminine gender. Most of the time she is a real pal, but, like all the other hybrids, she sometimes tries to find out who the boss is.

You will perceive that I do not use spurs, Spanish bits, nor yet a club. This photo is as real a wild (?) Western scene as often occurs. Most people here have automobiles, but Jane and I are relics of the olden time. The wild West greets the effete East.—
———.

IT'S a good bet that this comrade and Edgar Young will find plenty to back up their opinion. I wonder, sometimes, which is harder and takes more real stuff—wanting to wander and wandering, wanting to wander but sticking in one place through a sense of duty, or wanting to stay in one place but wandering because you have to. I don't know. Am just wondering.

Atlantic City, New Jersey.

Have just finished reading "The No-Good Guy," by Edgar Young, also his answer to W. F. Connolly, Princeton, N. J., and would say that his remarks about the fellows from New Hampshire and Vermont that are found in Central and South America would fit the ones from Massachusetts that get out of their native State.

It struck me as being such a truthful picture of the natives of my own State that I just had to spiel about it. If there is anything that damns a person more than lack of material success in Massachusetts I'd like to know the name of the animal. Of course this is true to a great extent wherever one goes, but nowhere is it stronger than in the old Bay State.

The old adage, "A rolling stone gathers no moss," is true enough, but what would the United States consist of to-day if it wasn't for the rolling stones who pushed out and out and out?

Personally I don't believe that it takes much for a man to stick in one place for years and grind away for a great many times he couldn't go to work anywhere else. But for a man to "blow in" here, there and somewhere else, get a place and hold it down until the wanderlust becomes too strong and repeat time and again I claim only a good man can do it.—F. T. TRACY.

Our Camp-Fire came into being May 5, 1912, with our June issue, and since then its fire has never died down. Many have gathered about it and they are of all classes and degrees, high and low, rich and poor, adventurers and stay-at-homes, and from all parts of the earth. Some whose voices we used to know have taken the Long Trail and are heard no more, but they are still memories among us, and new voices are heard, and welcomed.

We are drawn together by a common liking for the strong, clean things of out-of-doors, for word from the earth's far places, for man in action instead of caged by circumstance. The *spirit* of adventure lives in all men; the rest is chance.

But something besides a common interest holds us together. Somehow a real comradeship has grown up among us. Men can not thus meet and talk together without growing into friendlier relations; many a time does one of us come to the rest for facts and guidance; many a close personal friendship has our Camp-Fire built up between two men who had never met; often has it proved an open sesame between strangers in a far land.

Perhaps our Camp-Fire is even a little more. Perhaps it is a bit of leaven working gently among those of different station toward the fuller and more human understanding and sympathy that will some day bring to man the real democracy and brotherhood he seeks. Few indeed are the agencies that bring together on a friendly footing so many and such great extremes as here. And we are numbered by the hundred thousand now.

If you are come to our Camp-Fire for the first time and find you like the things we like, join us and find yourself very welcome. There is no obligation except ordinary manliness, no forms or ceremonies, no dues, no officers, no anything except men and women gathered for interest and friendliness. Your desire to join makes you a member.

THIS identification-card certainly saw its share of adventures. I was glad to hear from Mr. Hofford. He stopped in at the office to say howdy on his way to England to enlist, a few letters came from him and then none at all, so it was good to learn that he was not among the millions who passed out.

Buff Bay, Jamaica, B. W. I.

My first identification-card—I think number was 180 or about there—I gave to my brother, R. M. Hofford, when he went to France in 1915 and I wrote you and told you to change your records acordingly and send me another card. Which you did. Well, that first card went through the 2nd battle of Ypres (when gas was first used), in 1915. In 1916 it went through the Somme accompanied by the 10th Gordon Highlanders of which my brother was then a 2nd Lieut.

In 1917 he was transferred to Indian army and went to India, later being seconded to the Royal Air Force and being sent to Egypt for instructions. Some time later, after the Armistice, he went through the Egyptian rebellion, patrolled the streets of Cairo in a Ford, with a rifleman on each running-board.

That is the card's history up to date. In a letter recently my brother observed that he still had the card. I wonder how many others have seen as much war service and come through it as unscathed.

My card had an easier time. My two years actual active service were put in in France. I did not get a chance to do much globe-trotting.—W. S. HOFFORD.

IF I remember correctly one of you wrote in and gave G. A. Wells and me the laugh for printing his story about the Canal Zone fight between a tiger and a bull. I think he said there had never been any such fight; that it was all right for fiction but that Mr. Wells oughtn't to have claimed any basis of truth for it. Anyhow, here's a letter from another Camp-Fire member:

Seattle, Wash.

When I got back from France last September I found many *Adventures* in my mail and proceeded to have a good long read. When I arrived to the copy of September 3rd and had started the story "Promoters" by G. A. Wells I said to myself "If I can ever find my war-bag I will be able to show Camp-Fire something that may interest them."

Yesterday I was rummaging about my belongings and gatherings of forty years and ran into my Panama scrap-book and the very thing that I have been looking for. None other than the bill the "Promoters" stuck up the length and breadth of the Zone.

AND that fight! I will never forget it. The bull looked at the tiger and the tiger looked at the bull, neither of them liked the looks of the other and decided to have nothing to do with each other so the tiger started for the crowd and the bull started for the gate. There was sure some excitement for a while. All the Spig police started to fire into the crowd where Mr. "Tigre" was and the crowd did their best to get out of the way of the Cops shooting the tiger. I'll tell the world it sure was some time for about five minutes.

I never did know who promoted the fight but I have a deep and dark suspicion that I could name the gents. The same birds started to put on a football game on Thanksgiving day 1906 and as I had an idea that I knew the game I wanted to play but that is another story and I will leave it to a more gifted typewriter than mine to tell it.

I wonder if Mr. Wells is the same gent that one bright and sunny day in the office of Mr. Zinn of the P. R. R. handed the walking papers to the writer of this note. If so I also wonder if he knew that all of my cash and savings had gone on the wheel a few days before, the Quarto de Novembre, at the Hotel Central, and that I was as flat as a hot cake.—FRANCIS ROTCH, JR.

I sent the letter and the hand-bill advertising the fight to Mr. Wells and here is his reply. And is Jack Odum present? Or "K. C."? They are both "lost trails" so far as Mr. Wells is concerned and he wants to find them. Owes one of them fifty cents.

Concerning the enclosures I want to say that I was very glad to have a look at the hand-bill from Mr. Rotch's scrapbook and hugely interested in his letter accompanying it. I had not seen this hand-bill, though I knew of its existence, thus you can imagine what a treat it was for me to see it in black and white. I am sorry to have to confess to Mr. Rotch that I did not myself see this particular fight. The genesis of the story is this:

LAST year my older brother, who has been a resident of Cuba for the past two or three years in the employ of the Fruit Company, was up here on a vacation. One day we took an all-day hike over the hills. He told me about the vast stores of story material in the Latin-Americas (of which I was aware) and deplored the fact that so little of it was used. (Edgar Young knows how to put it up in readable form, believe me.)

It was my brother who told me about the bull and tiger fight, together with several other incidents I have since worked into stories and had published. The story came to him from one of the original promotors of the fight, a gentleman whose name I do not feel at liberty to disclose without his permission. We agreed that it was story material. My brother has done some story writing on his own account, but he declined to write this story. He told me to use the idea if I wanted it. I did want it, and decided to step in where possibly real writers had feared to tread.

I KNEW the country, the people and customs down there in the Latin-Americas, having done some trekking in that neck of the woods, and thus, with the bare facts of the incident, I thought myself equipped to spin the yarn. I am sure Mr. Rotch and other readers of "Promoters" who were present at that fight will be able to separate the facts from fiction, and also concede the privilege of writers to doctor the facts to make readable fiction. Bald facts make very poor magazine stories and I believe most writers avail themselves of the so-called poetic license.

You will no doubt remember that I originally called this story "The Black Devil." You renamed it "Promoters." But with the given idea that the bull was one tough *hombre* I had to make him live up to his name, which accounts for the strenuousness of his combat with the enemy. As a matter of fact, I have never seen a bull that wouldn't willingly fight man or beast, if he was trained for the ring, and I have seen a number of bull-fights in my day.

AND right here and now I want this opportunity to inform Mr. Rotch that I am not the "onry" cuss he has doubtless been believing me to be. That name under "Promoters" is a sure enough "monicker" and I never knew any other. I am not the gent who handed him his walking papers that day in Mr. Zinn's office, because I don't know Mr. Zinn and never had the pleasure of working on the Canal owing to the jealousy of numerous members of the Commission who turned me down as fast as I asked to be sent there as a valuable laborer for our Uncle Samuel. I think they told me the Canal was already swamped with telegraph operators, and I happened to be an operator.

No, I wouldn't have fired Mr. Rotch for any reason. At an earlier date I did some riding of the rods and panhandling of the main drag myself. I know what it is to be a couple of thousand miles from the roof-tree, broke and friendless. I've straddled the "blind" and stretched the "rattlers" on frequent occasions, and even crawled through the manhole in the tank into four or five feet of cold water in order to make a few miles in a given direction.

I've been staked too often (and have staked others) not to know what it means to a man down on his luck. There's a fellow by the name of Jack Odum, for instance, of Peru, Ind., to whom I'm greatly obliged for a lift. Met him in a Chink restaurant in Tucson, Arizona, rode north to Kansas City with him, and there we parted and I've heard neither hide nor hair of him since. I often wonder whether he remembers that late afternoon when the thermometer hovered about zero and we hoofed it across the frozen Canadian River into Logan, a cow town, because the railroad bridge was down.

I'D ALSO like to meet that little gink called "K. C." with whom I spent a night in jail in East St. Louis, having been picked up by a plain clothes man because some poor devil happened to be murdered by a gang of bums in the railroad yards. When the judge turned us loose next morning with a warning to get out of town K. C. tried to convince me that it was good stuff to help him crack a crib that night, and I was so down-and-out and dispirited he almost succeeded. And to show he had a heart the kid handed me fifty cents and said good-by. I owe him fifty cents with generous interest.

No, I am not a crook; I never committed a real

crime in my life, unless you want to call robbing melon-patches and stealing pies from the corner bakery crimes. I'm merely the hard luck guy who helps officious dicks and bulls to run up a record for efficiency. But I think a certain plain clothes man whom his partner called "Jim" has cause to remember me from the fact that I swore to bring suit against the city of Louisville because he wrongly pinched me for looking like a man who had stuck up a street-car that morning and pilfered the fare-box.

No indeed, I didn't tie a can to Mr. Rotch. I've been struck that way myself so often I'd have staked him to a year's free "flop and chuck" before turning him out into the cold. Anyhow, I don't think he should have blown all his cash on the wheel. If he had the consistent bad luck I did he would realize that fate didn't cut him out to get something good without working like a Turk to get it, though I have still another brother who pulled down several hundred gold Costa Rica because of his uncanny ability to pick the lucky number.—G. A. Wells.

Lastly, here is the bill itself, with the display type. Also without changing the spelling of the original. Also without a bit of text that was torn off the bottom:

THRILLING SENSATION—ONCE ONLY!—FIGHT TO DEATH BETWEEN A TIGER AND A BULL—ORIGINAL ACT IN EUROPE, NEVER SEEN IN AMERICA

As all probabilities of victory are with the Bull, those having killed the togers whemover they have fought, there will only be ONE OPPORTUNITY to witness the extraordinary fight.

At Cocoa Grove Grounds!

To facilitate the public and to avoid speculation, the tickets will be sold at the office of the "Panama Journal," 6th Street, No. 57. Telephone No. 68.

Prepare yourselves to see whart you have never seen and will never see again!

Look up the Programmes.

ESPECTACULO SENSACIONAL
POR SOLO UNA VEZ

Duelo a muerte entre un TIGRE y un TORO

Acontecimiento raro en Europa Y nunca visto en America

Como todas las probabilidades deltriunfo estan de parte del toro, pues siempre que se ha dado este espectaculo en Europa, eltoro ha matado al tigre, solo habra una sola fuucion.

El Circo do Cocoa Grove se esta refaccionando convenientemente para la eficaz comodidad de los espectadores.

En prevision de que se agoten las entradas y para evitar la especulacion de revendedores, la Empresa ha resuelto poner desde ahora a la venta en la Oficina de la Administracion del periodico "Diario de Panama," las mencionades localidades.

El espectaculo tendra lugar el 19 de los corrientes. Pronto circularan

A WORD from H. A. Lamb concerning an interesting custom that figures in his story in this issue:

A word on the "bracelet-brother" custom of the Rajputs, from Colonel Tod, annalist of Rajasthan. The custom is quite ancient, and has more than once played an important part in the wars of central India.

"The Rajput lady sends a bracelet either by her handmaid, or the family priest, to the knight of her choice. With the *rakhi* she confers the title of adopted brother; and, while its acceptance secures to her all the protection of a cavalier servant, scandal itself never suggests any other tie to his devotion. He may hazard his life in her service, and yet never receive a smile in reward.

"No honor is more highly esteemed than that of being the *rakhi band bhai* or "bracelet-bound-brother" of a princess."

The bracelet was generally sent when the woman in question was in distress, in warfare. Naturally, the *rakhi* usually passed between Rajput and Rajput; but at least on one occasion—that of Humayon, mentioned in the story—the bracelet was bestowed on a man of another race. There is no reason why an Englishman of this period could not have been selected as a brother in arms, inasmuch as the choice was determined more by the courage and known fighting ability of the man than by rank or caste.—H. A. L.

HERE are some sportsmen across the sea who want to shake hands with their fellows in the United States and Canada. They've been reading our "Ask Adventure" and know that it and Camp-Fire will put them in touch with canoeists on this side. Natural conditions over here make canoeing an individual rather than a club matter, except in crowded districts, but here's a welcome to these men who took to the canoe not because it stood waiting for them, but because they saw its possibilities and went after them.

Biddenham, Bedford, Eng.

I believe it will be of interest to canoeists and boating men in general in America to hear of the revival of the British Canoe Association which is being very vigorously proceeded with. As doubtlessly the case in America there is a real revival of interest in canoeing and out-of-door life, and our great endeavor is to encourage and foster this in every way. Not enjoying the fine facilities of America, the sport had somewhat languished here prior to the war, but now the outlook is a very different one. Before very long we hope to have the pleasure of a canoe cruise in the States.

IT WILL always be a great pleasure to hear from American well-wishers and supporters particularly now at the outset. American canoeists visiting Great Britain can depend on a warm welcome and every assistance.

To still further our common aims we are about to produce an attractive illustrated *Cruising and Canoeing Journal* on up-to-date lines in which, besides the Continental news, we hope to make American notes a special feature. For this purpose the editor will welcome contributions, canoeing stories, cruises, club notes, etc., as well as subscribers. For the same purpose, and also for the cruising and canoeing bibliography in process of compilation, sendings of canoeing and cruising literature, magazines and cuttings will be gratefully received.

With best wishes and hearty greetings from the enthusiastic canoeists of the Old World to their canoeing cousins of the New.—E. J. GORDON SPENCER, F. R. G. S., Hon. Sec'y.

FOLLOWING Camp-Fire custom, Gregory Mason rises and introduces himself on the occasion of his first story in our magazine. When he said "If I had only a month to live" he said it. But why risk the other twenty-nine or thirty days?

New York.

You ask me into the warmth of your "Camp-Fire," your "meeting-place for readers, writers and adventurers," and I am glad to come in. As a reader and adventurer I come confidently enough, but as a writer I come with some diffidence. For I have a confession to make. Although I have been making my living by writing since graduating from college eight years ago my story in this issue, "French Heels and Bobbed Hair," is the first piece of fiction I ever wrote.

I am certainly to be congratulated, as is any man who sells his first story right off the bat. *Adventure* is certainly to be congratulated also. Think of what a distinction it will be thirty years from now when the world is echoing with appreciations of the great American Joseph Conrad—think of what a distinction it will be for the editor of *Adventure* to be able to boast that he had the taste and acumen to buy the great man's first story! How he will be envied by other editors! What fabulous offers he will turn down for that thumb-worn original manuscript!

SPEAKING seriously, though, to you who may take the trouble to read the yarn, the writer imagines that those of you who may like it will like the same things in it which he mostly likes. It was not so much his interest in the man and woman—although he hopes they behave naturally and convincingly enough—as it was his interest in their background, in the great stage on which they move, which impelled the writer to produce this tale. Mexico—do you love it?—come in then, their's always room for one more in the club-of-the-nuts-who-love-Mexico. Mexico—who would spoil it by intervention, Americanize it? With the exception of Alaska, Australia, India and America-south-of-Panama I have seen most of the good places in the world. The North Woods, the Yangtse valley, the African veldt, the coast of Japan—each has its charm, but where is anything to equal Mexico, varicolored as a *serape* and unpredictable as TNT? If I knew I had only a month to live I could think of nothing better to do with it than to cross the Rio Grande, get a bronco under me, point him south and give him his head.—GREGORY MASON.

THIS comrade, apparently, is an American who has been serving a dozen years or more in the British Army. He wants to get into touch with his friends back home. Incidentally he mentions two fairly well traveled copies of our magazine.

Meerut, India.

A few weeks ago two copies of *Adventure* magazine were handed on to me by a comrade in the regiment. They are in a very delapidated condition, several pages from the front and back being missing.

I should be very pleased to hear from some one in America, as I have lost touch with a number of friends at home. This is the result of a long absence, because I have been away nine years. I enlisted in the 21st Lancers at the age of 15½ years, as a bandsman. Served three years in England, two in Egypt, and seven in India, and have been on active service in three frontier campaigns. I expect to be demobilized about April, 1920.—FREDERICK J. SAMWAYS, No. 259, Private, 21st Empress of India's Lancers, British Cavalry Lines, Meerut, United Provinces, India.

NEARLY a year since this letter was written, but that doesn't hurt it any.

California Camp, Ruby, Arizona.

Things getting very tight on the Border. Have a detail of D Troop, 10th Cav., at my camp. Sergeant Black—he's well named; lives up to his name in complexion—came up around camp the other day.

"Seen any Carranza troops across the fence lately, Sergeant?" I asked.

"Yes, sah, dey's twenty-five of dem comic opera soldiers over there," he answered.

"Well," said I, "you have eight in your patrol, so you are just even."

"Lawdy, Lawdy, boss, dat's right! Three to one makes it just right!" he answered, grinning from ear to ear.

THE pack-train which serves the detail at my camp also serves several other outposts along the line. The other day they got a new one loaded with forage and rations from Arivaca. They went to this outpost and on starting to return to Arivaca with the train light (nine pack-mules and two saddles-mules) they got into the wrong cañon, traveled for some miles and come to a *ranchito*.

They were informed they were in Mexico, that the hills were full of soldiers and that they would lose their whole outfit. They started back; had gone but a short distance when they were fired on. But shots fell short; then from another direction came shots going over them. By this time one of the packers was in the lead, riding as fast as his mule could carry him, the pack-train behind and the other packer bringing up the rear. The Mex. after them on foot and mounted; then they tried to cut them off on a flat plain with a "flivver" full of Mex. *soldados*, but hard riding got them to the Line. As they neared the Customs gate at Sabase the Mex. custom officer ran out yelling "Alto! Alto!" but the lead packer said. "To —— with you and your 'alto'," and through they went.

In five minutes every cavalryman on the patrol

at the Sasabe post was mounted and ready for action, some fourteen of them, and itching to tackle the some two hundred and fifty Mex. soldiers on the other side.

That shows the spirit of them individually and collectively. This episode, like many similar ones down here, escaped the press. Excuse this long harangue but must get it off my system.—ALEX. MCLAREN.

OUR Camp-Fire button will help us fix at least one date in our minds:

Dawson, North Dakota.

The figures "71" have a peculiar significance for me as it was in "71" that I first became a resident of the U. S. I will never forget the impression of ruin and desolation in Chicago when I passed through the city early in November of that year, and saw smoke still issuing from some of the ruins of the big fire. I have seen Calamity Jane's name mentioned several times in Camp-Fire. I had a drink with the old girl in August, 1882, in Bob McKee's saloon in Billings, Mont. She was on a mild spree and set 'em up to the house. She had a small ranch at the time on the Rosebud.—J. A. COULTER.

THE story by Arthur O. Friel in this issue is the first of several dealing with the same characters, each story entirely complete in itself. In these tales the rubber-hunters wander into new territory.

IN ONE of Mr. Friel's stories in our magazine he made one of his characters say "If all of you Americans can shoot like him, *senhores*, it is no wonder that your army won the great war in Europe." An Australian comrade cuts it out and sends it in with a bitter protest and much abuse of Mr. Friel, me and Americans in general. I'm strong for Australians and this particular one is probably a good fellow, but if all Australians and all Americans hunted as hard for trouble as he does, the two countries would be at war. There have been several other similar outcries from English, Canadians or Australians, all with nothing more to kick about than this case.

It all strikes me as silly and childish. In the present case it is foolish to hold any author or editor personally responsible for what any character in a story says to another character. If a story is any good, a character speaks out of his own mouth, not the author's. Why worry because an imaginary Portuguese or Indian in South America thought Americans won the war?

AS TO the general question of "Who won the war?" What's the use? There are, of course, Americans who think we did most of it, but there are also English who think they did most of it, Canadians who think they were the only real boys, Australians, French, Italians and so on who think the same. Why get excited about what any of them says?

I think most Americans feel about as follows: We did our part well, in spite of unpreparedness, graft and inefficiency, and the war might be going on yet if we had not come in. But we were very late in coming in. A good many of us think we were far too late in coming in. And we didn't amount to much at the front for a year after we did come in. Indeed, there wouldn't have been anything left to come in to if the French, English, Italians and other Allies had not been bearing the brunt of the war for years before we even started.

We became effective at the front at the final crisis, as it happened. We happened to be the added weight that swung the pendulum the right way. In that sense we did win the war. But in the broader sense we did not do so any more than did the English, French or Italians. Suppose any one of them had dropped out when we came in. If we had had time we might have been able to fill the gap and still have enough force to provide the needed additional weight. And we surely would have tried. But if one of the Big Allies had dropped out when we first came in, April, 1917, the Huns would have won before we could have furnished enough trained troops to take a respectable part in the defeat.

THE truth is that each of the big countries actively arrayed against Germany won the war, in the sense that each was necessary to anything like an immediate victory. We let the others carry most of the burden through most of the struggle, but, once really started, we did our part with the best and it happened that our part came at a time to turn the scale.

Why sit around and squabble like children over "who won the war"? There are squabbling, bragging children of all nationalities; this country has no monopoly on them. But why let them worry us?

As a nation I think we are proving our country neither a squabbler nor a braggart. We are not bragging over the fact that we are not and have not been among those squabbling over the spoils of war. We may have been slow in giving, but when we did give we gave all we had as fast as we could give it. And we are not asking for any of the material rewards.

WHEN you of other nations sneer at our slowness remember that in our place you would probably have been no quicker to join in. Nor, when started, would you, remote from the actual scene and direct pressure, have joined in more whole-heartedly and earnestly. Perhaps, some of you, not so much.

When you of other nations sneer at our penny-politician Senate, at our note-writing President, at our mixed blood, our inconsistencies, our commercial ideals and all the other things you find to sneer at, often with good cause, do not stop there in the foolish idea that you have been talking about America. That is only part of America, and only the surface part. If there were no more to us than that we should have gone to perdition long ago.

There is something else here. Something else that, down underneath all these other things, is the real America. We ourselves are not always sure just what it is. And the surer we are, the less we like to talk about it. Let us call it our idealism. It is always there. All our materialism and commercialism have not crushed it. All the inflow of unabsorbed alien blood has not been able to wash it away. And now, stirred by world events, it will grow stronger, not weaker.

I can not prove my case. I do not care to try. You of other nations must learn for yourselves, if you are able to learn.

BUT I can say this: During the war hundreds and hundreds of our boys wrote to me, wrote in the comradeship our Camp-Fire has engendered and wrote as freely and frankly as the censorship would permit. They were of all kinds, all degrees, all classes. Some were fresh-faced boys, some hardened adventurers. Their letters joked and joshed, the war and the whole world were taken jauntily, sometimes impudently, sometimes indifferently.

And yet that which is the real America broke through. Sometimes *via* a joke, sometimes bursting in grimly, sometimes as brief matter of fact, sometimes an unconscious hint. But it broke through. Because it was there and because it was too big and strong to be held down by even the greatest effort of suppression.

No matter what real or professed causes brought about the war, no matter what political, commerical and diplomatic strings might be tugging at the nations, no matter what these boys themselves might pretend was making them fight, the vast majority of them were fighting for nothing in the world but an ideal. And they were in very deadly earnest about it.

SO WERE men of other nations. But the comparison is slightly in our favor, for you must remember that with the European nations and their territorials fighting meant self-preservation. Our boys, their own land and its territories safe from direct, immediate disaster, went across the world to find the fighting.

You of other nations, we credit you, too, with ideals. Do as much for us.

Try to realize that, no matter what the crimes and blunders of our politicians, no matter what the accusations hurled against us, there is that among the body of the people that entitles us to hold our head erect. As nations go, we have walked a clean path.

"A READER" in Toledo, Ohio, sent us the following newspaper clipping, saying "It may be that some of the old-timers may recall some experiences they had with this fellow or in the country where he lived."

Dies Keeping Secret of Big Diamond Field

Upington, South Africa—"Scotty" Smith has just died here—a name more widely known in South Africa than any save that of the great Cecil Rhodes himself.

With him died the last relic of thrilling, melodramatic frontier days.

And he carried to the grave the secret of the "lost diamond mines of the Kalahari district." He died stubbornly refusing to reveal the site of untold wealth.

Notorious and picturesque—onetime desperado, fugitive, diamond adventurer and cattle runner—Scotty Smith was a sort of a combination of American Jesse James, Australian Stingaree and Mexican Villa.

FOR a quarter of a century he kept Boer farmers in a constant reign of terror, wielded a rule of fear among natives and kept the government out of breath trying to capture him.

Coming with the Smithsonian-Universal African expedition to Upington, seven hundred and sixty miles north of Cape Town, on the edge of the Kalahari desert—a vast, waterless tract extending a thousand miles further north—we heard about Scotty Smith on every hand.

Unluckily he died a few days before we reached Upington. He was seventy-three years old and for twenty years had lived a peaceful, blameless life on a small farm here. He had wiped out old scores by notable work in the British intelligence service during the Boer war.

His real name was George St. Ledger Lennox, and he is said to have come from a ducal family of England. When he came here about the time of the Kimberly diamond rush in 1870 he speedily got into trouble and gave the name of "Scotty Smith," which has clung to him ever since.

IN THE 80's he was convicted of gun running in the Basuto war, and once he was tried for murder at Kimberly. But he always escaped.

While hiding from his pursuers in the Kalahari, the outlaw is said to have discovered a rich diamond field. But he steadfastly refused to tell its location —prefering to forfeit wealth rather than share it with the government.

Scotty railed against the law—which was, and still is that sixty per cent. of newly discovered diamond fields automatically becomes the property of the government.

He either had to take forty per cent. or nothing. For he couldn't work the mines and market the diamonds without governmental consent. So he chose nothing—and he lived the rest of his life in veritable poverty.

YES, our identification-cards have come in handy on quite a few occasions. If we could get a big map of the world and stick a pin in it marking every spot where a bearer of a card was at some given moment it would make an ordinary pincushion look empty.

The other day one of our comrades in service died at a camp in this country. For some unknown reason, there was nothing to identify him except one of our cards, and the military authorities had to apply to our office for name of next friend. (We have never agreed to notify a next friend by wire but have always done so except in cases where the element of time was of little importance.)

Los Angeles, California.

I have held on to one of your identification-cards for the last four years, which by the way was the only mark I had to identify me while I served nineteen long dreary months in foreign waters in a guncrew on a packet which made six knots on the Suicide Run, namely down the Bristol Channel across the English and through the Bay of Biscay. Well, I am still going and the card is with me.—O. SHREMP.

SOMETHING about Kit Carson's famous ride. When Mr. Sleeper's letter came in I sent it to Hugh Pendexter in Maine. Here are the two letters:

Boston, Mass.

As I am very much interested in horses and horsemanship I almost invariably save items pertaining to the subject for my scrapbook. Whenever it is possible to do so I have the story verified before pasting in the book. In this case the story is related as an incident in the life of Kit Carson as told in "Captains of Adventure," by Roger Pocock. It is as follows:—

"It was during the California campaign that Carson made his famous ride, the greatest feat of horsemanship the world has ever known. As a despatch rider, he made his way through the hostile tribes, and terrific deserts from the Missouri to California and back, a total of four thousand, four hundred miles. But while he rested in California, before he set out on the return, he joined a party of California gentlemen on a trip up the coast from Los Angeles to San Francisco. Two of the six men had a remount each, but four of them rode the six hundred miles without change of horses in six days. Add that, and the return to Kit Carson's journey, and it makes a total of five thousand six hundred miles. So, for distance, he beats world records by one hundred miles, at a speed beyond all comparison, and in face of difficulties beyond all parallel."

I have no idea as to where Mr. Pocock got his dope, but it sure was some riding if true.—MYRON O. SLEEPER.

Norway, Maine.

I should assume Pocock's account of Carson's ride is correct. I have read it either in Peters' or Abbot's biography of him. I haven't the details at hand, but so far as I go I am correct, according to my notes.

SEPT. 15, 1846, Carson with fifteen men started overland from Los Angeles with despatches for Washington. Urged to make trip in sixty days. No trouble till within two days' journey of Copper Mines, New Mexico, when met hostile Apaches but succeeded in trading for fresh horses. Oct. 16 met Gen. Kearny's army. Kept Carson as scout and guide, sending despatches on by other men. Oct. 18, Carson began guiding army from Rio del Norte, N. Mex., and Dec. 3 reached Warner's Ranch, Cal.

Later Carson went to Washington and President Polk commissioned him lieutenant in rifle corps. Returned across the Plains with despatches and at Fort Leavenworth picked up escort of fifty men. Left all but sixteen of his escort at Santa Fé, ran into three hundred Indians on Virgin River, and bluffed them. Reached California, O. K. and was sent back with despatches to Washington. Before starting back learned U. S. Senate refused to confirm his commission. Took long trip just the same.

AT THIS time, all the time of the Washington-to-California trip the Comanches were at war with the U. S. Their allies, Apaches and Kiowas, were very hostile. Point of Rocks, near Rockies, one of most dangerous spots on the route. Apaches were operating under their most famous war-chief, Chico Velasques, who wore fringe of Mexican fingerbones on one legging and American digits on other.

Without examining the source of these notes I can't give distances or time consumed. I know the ride through hostile territory was a world-beater for spead, endurance and danger involved.—PENDEXTER.

"THE Old Chisholm Trail." Who has a copy of it? W. H. Taylor, Mulino, Oregon, is the comrade inquiring.

FROM Barry Scobee an interesting Camp-Fire talk in connection with his story in this issue:

San Antonio, Texas.

My story, "Road Signs and a Nose-Ring," grew out of my observation of the men in the mountain region of southwest Texas being keen readers of spoor. I had not been in that country long when, one day, I was driving in a car with a citizen along a cañon road. After a period of silence he remarked desultorily:—

"Wonder what's wrong with that feller?"

"What feller?" I asked, looking hastily along the trail and even into the broken cañon walls to see the object of his regard.

"Ugh!" he grunted in disgust like an Indian. "I mean that man ahead of us with a rickety wagon, a leaky water-keg, a horse and a mule."

I scanned the trail some more. "I don't see anybody," I finally admitted, feeling chagrined at my blindness.

"Look at the road!" he bellowed, nodding once to the ground ahead of the rapidly moving car.

Properly humbled, I gazed at the dusty trail sliding back under the automobile. Presently I made out the snaky tracks of a wobbly wheel, but nothing more.

"Why do you think there is something wrong?" I asked.

"Stopped twice. Once he cut a piece off a rope. Harness busted, I reckon. We'll see pretty soon."

And sure enough we came presently to an outfit that answered the description as if my companion had seen it beforehand, which he had not. A Mexican was in the act of tying up his harness with a rope.

I was considerably impressed, and afterward I began to watch the road as I traveled. I never learned to read spoor as well as the old timers by a great deal, but I did acquire knowledge enough to appreciate their ability. Of course, their feats never equal what the Australian trackers do, but yet I think they have merit.

READING ground signs is a necessity with these cattlemen, for at roundup times they must track some stock about the mountains to find it else lose it from their herds. Practically every ranchman can tell whether a wolf, bear or deer has crossed a trail as he drives over the country. He does this instinctively and unconsciously, just as a townsman will glance up at the city hall clock and observe the time without thinking of what he is doing. Even the younger generation is not lacking in the ability to read the country's spoor, as this incident will show:

In my story I speak of Mount Livermore and, in another place, of wild cattle coming down from the mountains. These wild animals are ones that have strayed away from the herds, become afraid of men, and reverted to a state of undomesticity like deer. There is one of superfame called "The Wild Steer of Livermore." It is so wild and wily that few have ever seen it, and is thought by many persons to be a myth. I know a ranch foreman and two young men sons of a ranchman who saw the big white-faced beast once and trailed him ten miles by his spoor. They pretty well covered Livermore mountain following the trail, and if you knew how rocky that mountain is, how dry and hard the soil where there is soil, you would understand that these three men did a bit of unusual work in sticking to the trail for so many miles.

So from these facts grew my story.

IT MAY be interesting to tell a little thing concerning Bear Gap which I heard the other day. The ranchman who owns this next-to-highest mountain in Texas has hunted bear on Livermore many times. He said that the bears—species, Mexican brown—when scared up by hunters always race for the great crater of the extinct volcano, go to the westerly side and make their way down Bear Gap. The gap is as precarious as I have made it appear in the story, yet bruin gets through and hits for the thick brush of Goat Cañon or for more impassable mountain sectors.

MOUNT LIVERMORE seems to have been a "high spot" among the Indians. The first woman to make the ascent of it was Mrs. S. M. Janes, now, I believe, of Deming, N. M. That was several years ago. She accompanied her brother and other men to the very top of the little peak, which in the story I liken to the head of an Indian hatchet. The object of the trip was to investigate a rock monument topping the peak. This was six or eight feet high, or higher, with a base probably six by eight feet. (I have forgotten exact measurements.) Digging under it, the party unearthed something like two thousand perfect arrow heads, all of them small, finely cut, beautiful. Some were not an inch long; few, if any, longer than that. Indianology sharks have examined this remarkable collection and are at a loss to name the origin of it. The monument was destroyed so that scientists failed to see its architecture.

I understand that there is ground for believing the peak was a temple of sun-worshipers—Indians so ancient that their history was forgotten by the hordes of Redskins who flowed down from the North, a stream of extermination, and who preceded even the earliest tribes of American Indians known to archeology.

The pit from which the arrowheads—made of fine flint and obsidian—were taken has had its dust sifted and dug in for years, without more heads being found, but when I was on the peak I had the remarkable good fortune to find an arrowhead, not an inch in length, lying on a flat rock at the edge of the pit, in plain sight! I wanted one so much that when I first saw it I thought it an hallucination.—BARRY SCOBEE.

DON'T forget to come across in doing your share toward starting our chain of Camp-Fire stations. If you are not in position to offer a station yourself, try to interest some one who can. A station can be maintained with very little effort and practically no expense.

A station may be in any shop, home or other reputable place. The only requirements are that a station shall display the regular station sign, provide a box or drawer for mail to be called for and provide and preserve a sufficiently substantial register book. When there are enough stations to warrant even a small wholesale order this office will furnish the books and signs.

No responsibility for mail is assumed by anybody; the station merely uses ordinary care. Entries in register to be confined to name or serial number, route destination, permanent address and such other brief notes or remarks as desired; each station can impose its own limit on space to be used. Registers become permanent property of station; signs remain property of this magazine, so that if there is due cause for complaint from members, a station can be discontinued by withdrawing sign.

A STATION bulletin-board is strongly to be recommended as almost necessary. On it travelers can leave tips as to conditions of trails, etc., resident members can post their names and addresses, such hospitality as they care to offer, calls for any travelers who are familiar with countries these residents once knew, calls for particular men if they happen that way, etc., notices or tips about local facilities and conditions. Letters to resident members can be posted on this bulletin-board.

Any one who wishes is a member of Camp-Fire and therefore entitled to the above station privileges. (Question of requiring identification-cards or Camp-Fire button to be decided later.) Those offering hospitality of any kind do so on their own responsibility and at their own risk and can therefore make any discriminations they see fit. Traveling members will naturally be expected to remember that they are merely guests and act accordingly.

A station may offer only the required register and mail facilities or enlarge its scope to any degree it pleases. Its possibilities as headquarters for a local club of resident Camp-Fire members is excellent.

AS ANNOUNCED in the last Camp-Fire, the originals of all *Adventure* covers, up to and including the one for this issue, with the exception of those already disposed of, will be offered at auction May 1st. Send in your bid to reach us before that date and state very carefully not only the subject of the painting you want but also the exact date of the issue. Any one may bid. No bid of less than ten dollars considered; most of these paintings cost us one hundred and twenty-five dollars each. Packing done by us and expressed at your risk. Express charges collect.

Beginning January 1, 1921, semi-annual auctions of cover originals will probably be held on the first day of January and the first day of June every year. Bids may be sent in any time. But this is the time to get a chance at all cover originals up to and including the present issue, with the exception of those previously disposed of. A list of the available originals appeared in the last Camp-Fire. No covers for the issues of 1916 are available. Very few before that. Most of those after that year and up to the present issue.—A. S. H.

THE CAMP-FIRE

A MEETING-PLACE FOR READERS, WRITERS AND ADVENTURERS

ONE of our old-timer comrades tells us something about a long shot at the Adobe Wall fight:

Austin, Colorado.

I read an article by Louis G. Mullikin about killing an Indian one and one-half miles at the Adobe Wall fight. The facts are that a bunch of Indians were having a powwow just a little over 1,700 yards up on a hill and Wm. Dixon knew the range and took a shot at the crowd and killed a young Comanche chief. I have forgotten his name. The shot was fired from a Sharps big fifty, 800 grains of lead. Don't know how much black powder. That was the old big fifty; the new ones came out in 1876, shot 800 grains of lead—that was the new big fifty. They could kill over a mile. Wm. Dixon died in Oklahoma about eight years ago. Do you know where I could get the story by Alfred Henry Lewis?—JAS. W. STELL (Moccasin Jim*).

*That was the name I went by in the '70's on the Buffalo Range.

THIS letter gets me where I live. I commend it to such of our Australian comrades as have been worried by such Americans as claim for this country all the glory of having "won the war." This letter does not even touch upon that point, but it says something else that I wish all Australians and all other foreigners could get clearly in their minds.

Still more, I wish that all Americans could get it clearly in their minds. It would comfort them and give them strength.

THE letter is far from a preachy letter but what it says at the end is something far too big to be passed by as merely interesting.

The point I mean is this: The *heart* of America is sound. We—and the foreigners—look at our dirty politicians, at fiddling, shifty, corrupt "statesmen" and public officials, at greedy, callous business men, the careless rich, the sullen trouble-maker, at the graft among us, at classes struggling selfishly, at the mistakes our nation makes within and without its territorial limits, and naturally things look ugly and hard and cheap and disgusting. But the *heart* of America is sound.

If there is much to be ashamed of, yet there is vastly more to stir our pride and to strengthen our confidence in the future. If our house needs cleaning, still it is a house that is *worth* cleaning.

OUR national reputation would be a better one if it were the many, instead of the few, who guide the national destiny. For the mass of the American people are sound in heart. Despite all careless adulteration, despite all false surface ideals, despite all our sins and stupidities, despite all outward signs, despite everything, still there is that in the mass of us that, when driven, rises to say "Thus far and no farther."

I do not mean Fourth of July patriotism. Nor is it a question of morals. It is, I think, too fundamental for easy definition. Perhaps its elements are manliness and independence of spirit and brain; a reliance on facts, combined with a susceptibility to ideals; an instinct of cleanness, and a belief in fair play. Whatever it is, it is there. Buried very deep sometimes, but there.

THAT is our best insurance that what changes must be made in our political and economic conditions will be made by reasonable methods, not by an orgy of force. And I wish that many of those who are belatedly sending out propaganda to combat the Bolshevist propaganda could understand this thing. If they did, they would send out less frothy, sickening stuff, fewer platitudinous appeals to Fourth of July patriotism. They would see that to beat the Bolshevist propaganda they must use propaganda that is more sound, more true, more fair, more open, more based on common sense—would see that cheap and slushy appeals, ignorance, lies, and distortion and suppression of facts are things that should be left entirely to the Bolshevists, since the user of them is surely doomed in the end.

They would see, too, that if a cause is to make permanent headway in the heart of the American people it must not only be presented on a horse-sense basis but must also play fair even with an opponent that does not play fair.

YESTERDAY I read a full newspaper page of utter slush, one of a series using paid advertising space for propaganda against Bolshevism. That particular mess of pap was devoted solely to picturing the very, very horrible rich man who secretly supports the Bolshevist movement with his check-book. If the Bolshevists can turn out anything more cheaply sensational, more sickeningly sentimental, more wholly based on a tawdry appeal to brainless emotion, I sincerely hope they will. For nothing could hurt Bolshevisn more in the long run. That page of slush was so bad that I almost wondered whether the Bolshevists might not be paying for it in order to discredit the sound cause it purported to support. Certainly the writers of it, whoever they may be, have never had even a glimpse of the real heart of America if they expect it to respond to that kind of piffle and slobber.

The case of our democracy against Bolshevism is sound and sane and strong. It is only injured by using pap and piffle.

I HADN'T meant to talk so much. Let's have the letter.

It brings up a question for discussion, a question I wonder hasn't come up before—"Where does the West begin?"

Battle Creek, Michigan.

I have a few questions to ask and a few observations to pen and perhaps I had better start the discussion by telling something about myself first.

I WAS born in San Francisco and spent the first seventeen years of my life in California and the neighboring State of Oregon. At seventeen I went East to attend school and remained there until my graduation from a New England university at the age of twenty-two. The next two years found me in the Northwest States (Oregon and Washington) engaged in the lumber business. A wanderlust which had been mine since the days of my first long pants led me to sever my connection with the lumber firm and, with half the savings of two and one half years, I went East and embarked for Europe with the intention of traveling that continent a la Bayard Taylor. I did, although my travels were not attended with the literary success which was deservedly his. But I wrote and walked and worked for eighteen months in Europe. I vagabonded from Andalusia, Spain, to Moscow, Russia, and then, retracing my steps as far as Prussian Silesia, journeyed south through Hungary and the Balkans, finally landing at Constantinople.

From that city I continued my vagabond journey to Greece, etc., and in Alexandria went broke. This rather unhappy condition gave me the opportunity of learning how it feels to work one's passage on a British (or any other) steamer, but, as such ship was bound for England and not for the East, I was compensated for my hardships by finally arriving in a country whose language (Oh! blessed tie of language!) was my own. The next four months I spent in the tight little isle, going no further afield from London than the Cheviot Hills, an excursion which embraced a three weeks' tramping in a country whose rural loveliness can not be beaten anywhere in the world.

UPON my return to my native land, Boston being the port which gave me my first glimpse of America after my nearly two years' absence, I made up my mind to *know* the United States as well as my tramp had made me know not a few of the European countries, and with this intention planted firmly in my mind I started a vagabond journey from the Hub to the Golden Gate. The season was late Spring and I had twenty-five dollars in my pocket. I arrived in the Golden State in the early Autumn, sans the twenty-five dollars but with an accumulation of knowledge anent my native country (which few save tramps and commerical travelers have) and a wanderlust which has been my constant companion ever since. Oh! the sweetness of an American Summer in our Northern States! If one wants to *know* America—and to know her is to love her better—let him "hoof it" for a month through any of our States and especially any one of the North Central States in June or September.

SINCE that far off Summer I have been in every State of the Union, save two. I have traveled on foot, the "box car" route, by *le chemin de fer* as a *bona fide* passenger and—but why go on? Suffice to say that I *know* America, know her as only a fellow who has been of the genus hobo American can. I know her great heart, know her inherent soundness, know the differences which mark her various sections. It is concerning this last that I wish to intrude some questions and pen some observations. New York City people assume that the West begins at an imaginary line running from Buffalo to Pittsburgh and extends from that imaginary line clear to the Pacific Ocean. Others believe that Chicago is the dividing point between the East and West. Still others say Kansas City is the first really Western city. Can *Adventure* readers settle the question, "Where does the West begin?" Also is the Pacific Ocean the ending of the West or are the Cascade and Sierra Nevada Mountains? California is not Western in the same sense as North Dakota, is it?

AND is New Mexico Western or Southern? Also how many distinct sections has the United States in the opinion of your readers? There have been many writers who have written minutely on the personality of various American cities, but few who have attempted a discussion of the personality of the various States, and yet (the world over) cities are ever more similar to each other than are the communities which comprise them. We label vast communities Southern, Northern, Western, but forget that such definitions of sections are at best vague.

For instance take the most distinct section of our country—the South—and compare the old and aristocratic (I use the word in the best sense) State of Virginia with the young and mighty State of Texas. There is small similarity between the two save an aversion to the negro as a race (not as an individual).

New England, as the smallest distinct section, might be said to have more or less uniform characteristics, but there is very little similarity between industrial Rhode Island and rural Maine. And the people are different, as a hundred-mile walk in both those States would quickly disclose.

Take the States of Ohio and Indiana, twin States as far as the maps go, and a walk through them would disclose many differences between the people of these two splendid Mid-West (or is it Mid-East?) States.

OUR novels, for the most part, deal with the rural Far West or New York City. New York City, being ultra feminine, is usually pictured as a place where unusually beautiful girls abound and where masculine virtue is wanting. Every New York novel has a precocious and amazingly beautiful heroine and a few pursuing males (of the Continental type, mustaches, etc.) and the wealthiest or least unworthy wins her. Result, from the Appalachian Mountains to the Pacific Ocean the bulk of people believe New York men are weak, silly and "sissy," and that New York City is made up of elderly men and elderly young men (if I may use such a term) who pursue innocent and unusually beautiful "girls." New England novels are usually pale and lifeless affairs picturing New Englanders as they might have been once but certainly are not now. The Western novels are complimentary enough to both hero and heroine, but many of them are a little too strong on that "where a man's a man" stuff.

I am a Westerner, a big fellow standing six feet two inches and weighing (after a good supper) about two hundred pounds, but I know that all our *men* are not found in the West and that moral, mental, and physical bigness is not the product of any particular section but is common to our soil as a whole. I know there are fops in New York City, but there are more fops in the pages of novels having a New York setting than are to be found on Broadway and Fifth Avenue. Thank goodness, *Adventure* trades with novelists whose brain children are not emasculated creatures of a disordered fancy but he-man and she-woman, the like of which can be found in any section of the United States, from Maine to California. All of your stories are not of the same caliber, of course, but the vast majority of them paint the real men and women of this country and see the best side of American life, and believe me that best side is second to none in the world.

AND now for my observations, observations which have been gleaned from a topsy-turvy, routs about life in this and other lands, observations which have been perhaps rounded out by my almost three years in the Canadian Army (June, 1916, to Jan., 1919) and twenty-two months in France. And I want to say here that our brothers to the North are men in every sense of that word; big, wholesome, splendid fellows who are working out their destiny (and a great destiny it will be, too) in a way befitting their splendid land and their splendid stock. Wherever I am in the future, in my own country or in the far-flung spaces of the world, the Canadian will always seem my brother because of my knowledge of him, because I was a part of his country, aye, a part of him, during the grand, sad days which have now passed into history.

I can not answer the question "Where does the West begin?" which I have put to your readers. If the words of the beautiful poem are true—"Where men's hearts grow a little kinder," then I should say it starts anywhere five miles beyond the limits of the larger cities, for take it from an itinerant farm-hand, a hobo (if you will), the heart of rural America is very kind and that applies to New England as well as the South and far West. We all have our favorite States, and mine without a moment's hesitation are California and Oregon, but as far as kindness (among the rural people) is concerned it would be a toss-up between any two of the forty-eight.

I THINK that of all the States, Kentucky, Virginia and California have the most distinct personalities, or perhaps it would be better to say that in those States there seems to be developed among the people the greatest degree of State consciousness, if I may use such a term. Texas, Pennsylvania, Indiana, and a large number of the Southern States have this to a degree also, and the young States of the Northwest and the States of the industrial East seem to have the least State consciousness.

I believe that central and western New York belong to what is termed the Middle West rather than to the East—Buffalo surely is as Western (?) as Cleveland, and the few remaining New York cities southwest of Buffalo seem more Western. Maine, except the extreme southern tip, is radically different from all other New England States, or so I have always found. Florida is far less Southern (as we understand the term) than any of her near neighbors, indeed in many ways less Southern than Maryland.

WHAT foolish observations these! And yet as I have traveled about the country I have tried to taste the different flavors of the various sections and States, to understand their separate personalities, to interpret their peculiarities, and if one doubts that such exist I advise him to take a three-hundred-mile tramp through any two of them and then write his impressions.

The (many times) weary pilgrimages of my youth have netted me a knowledge of America (the United States) which I could not have got in any other way, and this knowledge of my own country has given me such a love for her and such a belief in her ultimate destiny that all the Bolshevists in the world could not change my ardor for, and belief in, this country and her ultimate destiny. The heart of America is sound and that inherent soundness will tide her over these troublesome times. And if any Camp-Fire reader wants to know and respect and love and believe more firmly than ever in the United States, let him take up his knapsack and walking-stick and tramp the highways and the by-ways of this mighty land. Go in the early Spring or the harvest time, start in the East or West or South or North, tramp anywhere from two hundred to eight hundred miles, and you will learn the real America, and mayhap see her soul—ANDREW MACCRUM.

A QUERY at Camp-Fire by Frank Huston as to where some of the old Western scouts were buried brought him the following from James W. Stell, an old-timer who was interested in getting into touch with Uncle Frank. Our Camp-Fire gatherings not only bring to light many bits of interesting information concerning the Old West but incidentally forge quite a few links in a chain that serves to connect many of the scattered old-timers with one another.

Austin, Colo.

Saw your notice in *Adventure*, requesting the burial places of old scouts. Here are a few that I know about.

Jim Bridger died in Westport, Mo., in the early 70s, Texas Jack in Leadville, Colo., in 1879, Spotted Jack in Reynolds, Texas, in 1877, Capt. Chas. Christie in Monte Vista, Colo., Oct., 1916, Hurricane Bill in Tombstone. Ariz., about 1880, Jack Stillwell in Cody, Wyo., about 1881. I will find out about more and let you know. Where did you run the range? I used to hunt buffalo out of Dodge City, Kansas, in the early 70s.

I would like to hear from you. We may have reminiscences in common, which would be of mutual interest.

Yours for the olden times.—JAS. STELL (Moccasin Jim).

WORD from our old comrade Major Robert W. Foran, of our writers' brigade and one of the founders of the Chicago Chapter of the Adventurers' Club. You'll remember his occasional letters, also, during his long service in the Mesopotamian campaign. Back in November he wrote from London that he had been given further extension of sick leave until December first and expected then to be permanently invalided out of the British Army as unfit.

Fortunately, while his physical condition puts some limit upon climatic conditions, he is still able to do a man's work and is getting more fit instead of less so. Perhaps we shall be hearing from him later in Mesopotamia, South Africa or his old stamping ground, British East. Also he's getting back into the writing game and we may be having some more stories from him.

In any case, here's good luck to him.

BECAUSE it would not, for various reasons, fit just right into our schedule at times when we were starting a new serial, "Wulfhere" has been in our safe since 1918 and it was then that Mr. Higginson gave us the following by way of introducing himself to Camp-Fire according to our custom, for neither he nor I foresaw that so much time would elapse before the story saw print. What he says, however, is no less interesting for the delay:

Port Dalhousie, Ontario, Canada.

THERE is an old saying, "He may lie boldly who comes from afar." Now in speaking of my life as I am asked to do, I might tell of hair-raising adventures, miraculous escapes from certain death, perilous trips and voyages in southern climes or amid Arctic icebergs, of dangers among giant Patagonians or African pigmies, etc., etc., but I do not speak of these things because in the first place space here would not permit, and in the second place both my conscience and my profession would protest loudly against any such juggling with facts. Unfortunately, or fortunately as the case may be, my life has contained more ventures than adventures. I have even tried my hand at "perpetual motion," but gave that up when my father informed me that I could as soon hope to raise myself off the floor by taking hold of the seat of my trousers. My venture into the realm of invention produced several interesting things that would have been great successes *if*—but they all went the way of the perpetual motion machine, so I gave up this line of business and turned my hand to short story writing. I wrote a dozen or more, and came very near to having one of them published once, but didn't have the twenty-six dollars required by the editor, who must have been as hard up as I was. Then I settled down to write a long story, finished it, and had it accepted by ADVENTURE.

SO FAR I have told very little of my life. There is not much to tell. I was born some few years ago in a small town with a big name in Eastern Ontario, Canada. When a boy at school I received a silver medal for good conduct; I was always rather ashamed of that distinction, I don't quite know why. When eighteen years of age I went to college in Toronto. I could tell of some gruesome adventures while there, in my Freshman year. Finally I graduated, in '98, with honors, but all in the class who passed at all passed with honors, so there was nothing to brag about. With an M. A. degree and two or three years more of training I took up my profession which I still practise with indifferent success. I married about twelve or thirteen years ago—I've forgotten the date. That was another venture that proved a success. I have three children, two girls and a boy. Eight years ago I entered the 20th Halton Regiment and hold a captaincy in it. It is through no fault of mine that I have not yet been overseas.

IN MY story "Wulfhere," I have tried to describe events as they took place in the stirring Saxon times in England when Penda the Strong strove to make himself master of the whole land, and to set up again the old heathen gods in the place of the religion of Christ. He was a man of wonderful parts, this Penda, and his son Wulfhere inherited all his good gifts while he lacked his father's evil qualities. The main facts of the story are gathered from Bede's History, the Anglo-Saxon Chronicle, both written in Saxon times, and from Geoffrey of Monmouth, Florence of Worcester, William of Malmsbury, Henry of Huntingdon, who wrote in the 12th century.

Green in his "History of the English People" speaks of Penda as "a man of whom we would willingly know more." I have endeavored in this narrative to give some account of this Mercian king who made things so lively for England in his day.

HE WAS indeed a marvelous man. Beginning as a mere chief of a petty tribe on the upper Trent, he rose gradually in power through sheer ability and strength of purpose, till before his death he was the most powerful and most feared of all the kings of his time in England. First he subdued the smaller kingdoms about him; then, uniting with Cadwallo of Wales, he defeated and slew Edwin the great king of Northumbria. Oswald, Edwin's successor, he defeated and slew at Mesafeld, and he expelled Kenwal of Wessex from his kingdom. Ecgric, Sigebert, and Anna, successive kings of East Anglia, fell before him and their whole race was practically exterminated. Penda stood supreme in England. Then at Winwedfield Penda himself was slain, and his kingdom crumbled till only one small province, that of the Middle-Angles left in the hands of Peada, Penda's son, was all that remained of the once mighty kingdom of Mercia.

The task of rebuilding his father's fallen house was the task that Wulfhere, Penda's third son, undertook, and with the help of his father's great captains, Immin, Eafa and Eadbert, so completely accomplished.

IT IS the story chiefly of Wulfhere that I try here to tell. Most of the incidents in the tale are true, if the old Chronicles are to be believed. Most of the persons mentioned, too, are actual historical characters, *viz.*, Penda and Burgenhild his mother, and Cyneswithe his wife; Eadbert, Immin and Eafa his captains; Edwin, Osric, Eanfrith, Oswald, and Oswy of Northumbria; Sigebert, Ecgric and Anna of the East Angles; Elgiva or Ermengild, Wulfhere's wife; Aidan also, and Brian and Cadwallo, and Pellitus the Wizard, and others.

The tale is at least as true to history as "Ivanhoe" or "Hereward the Wake" or "Harold." If there is much war and slaughter in the story, let the reader remember those were strenuous times. In Penda's days not much else of importance happened.—A. B. HIGGINSON.

A HAND-SHAKE for this old-timer comrade who after all these years at last comes forward from his listening seat at Camp-Fire to entertain us with a brief outline of his eventful life. Maybe some of you who live in Sacramento might like to look him up and get acquainted at first hand. We'll forward a letter addressed in our care.

Sacramento, California.

I've been for years—since 1913—a reader of *Adventure* and now after all this time I'm going to join the dear friends around the Camp-Fire.

A FEW words of introduction may be in order. I am sixty-two years young—born February 24, 1857, of Irish-American parents. I've wandered pretty well all over this old sphere from Vladivostok to Bombay and Singapore, Manilla, Batavia (Java), fairly well all over Australia and the many islands included in that name. Besides being even more at home in our own good old U. S. A. and our full grown neighbor—Canada, besides considerable in old Mexico.

Was for nineteen months one of the thousands employed on the Panama Canal—and "take it from me, she's some ditch."

Have been lost in the West Australian bush; was one of the crew of the steamer *Queen* when she burned at sea, six hundred miles off Talinisok Point, Oregon. I've been lost three days on a burned over prairie in Montana; and have "put in" three years as lieutenant of North Borneo. Native Constabulary.

EVEN at my present age I feel the return of the wanderlust. At present I'm a mere porter in a restaurant, and though I'm not foolish enough to think myself any better than my job, still I can but long sometimes for the good old days that were.

Like most in whom the wanderlust burns strongest, I've saved practically nothing—my home a lodging-house room; all my belongings could be contained in a small trunk and a suit-case.

I've neither wife, chick nor child to worry over, or to worry over me, and am likely to "hit the trail" again any day. I long for the free out-of-doors again, to know more that I'm free to come and go as I please and where I please.—JAMES D. MOORE.

P. S. Just a few words afterthought! Would like to meet at the Camp-Fire some one who was acquainted with Western Kansas—say Wallace, Sheridan, Logan or Grove counties, during the late '70's and early '80's.

I lived at Grinnell, Grove Co., Kansas, from '79 to 1886, and when we moved there the "God's Acre" contained thirty-six graves; the occupants of same all died with their boots on except one woman and two babies.

SOME very interesting advice on snake-bites, from a California physician. As stated before, any seemingly intelligent remedy is eligible to a hearing at Camp-Fire, but no responsibility is assumed for any of them. It's up to each of us to listen and form his own judgment. There is, however, at least one big point for this remedy—it could be tried in situations where it was impossible to get drugs.

California.

In reading Camp-Fire I see some controversy *re* snake-bite treatments, and can not refrain from butting in. All the treatments given are useful, as is that recommended by Mr. Ditmars in his "Poisonous Reptiles, etc.," of the desert. But most of the measures are unnecessary, confusing and tend to make the excitable loose time.

THE following case was reported by me, and published in the *Clinical Notes Journal* of the American Medical Association about five years ago. I forget the date fully. At present all I wish to give is the principle involved.

A child about six years of age was bitten by a Mississippi ground rattler (Sistrurus crotalidae) on toes. Could see only one fang puncture. Made four or five incisions through skin surrounding puncture. Put on tourniquet handsbreadth above knee. Put on poultice of wet cotton into which had been mixed paste made of powdered boric acid and water. Every fifteen minutes for six hours tourniquet was loosened till leg resumed healthy pink appearance (usually in about twenty seconds) after which tourniquet was tightened enough to stop arterial circulation for another fifteen minutes.

At end of six hours removed poultice. The toe I had incised (the one showing the fang-mark) was normal in appearance except for incisions which were clean and clear. Toe next was twice normal size, inflamed, and on one side showed a black patch beneath the gray skin. In the center of the skin over black patch was a puncture. On breaking skin the black patch proved to be an area of digested tissue (flesh) about the consistency of rotted meat, and when scooped out with spoon left a hemispherical depression. In short, that toe had been punctured by the snake fang and had been overlooked so far as local treatment was concerned. As evidenced by the very sharp line of demarkation between the digested flesh and inflamed flesh, it was evident, however, that the spread and absorption of the venom had been completely checked as soon as the tourniquet was applied on the thigh, and that thereafter the venom exerted its cytolytic and toxic action entirely locally.

In this case I had the interesting experience of seeing two venom injections of the same venom of same strength, in the same individual at same time and under same conditions, but one was treated both with tourniquet and locally, while one was untreated except by tourniquet. The toxic or venom of the sistrurus is, weight for weight, more deadly than the venom of the rattle-snake (Crotalus horridus). At the end of eight hours after the bite was received the child was running about the yard, apparently no worse for his adventure. The accident occurred in my yard and tourniquet was applied within four minutes of the bite.

FROM the foregoing, as well as from reading up a good deal on the actual evidence in the recorded investigations of snake-bite, I am here to state that the essential in the treatment is to get the tourniquet on at once, and tight enough. The rest is refinement of technique. If one likes permanganate, strychnin, nitroglycerin, iodin, ammonia, digitalis, whisky, aromatic spirits of ammonia, tobacco-juice, gunpowder, saltpeter, etc., and doesn't take too much or too many of them at once, I can see no objection to them, and they undoubtedly calm the minds of that class which demands that everything possible be done. But they are unessential. If the tourniquet is properly applied, it will stop the spread and action of injected or applied permanganate as certainly as it stops the spread and action of the venom. And it does it at once. It is a law of physics that when two solutions of crystallines are brought in contact with each other, or are separated only by a colloid, then there is a flow of fluid from the solution of lesser specific gravity into the solution of greater specific gravity. For this reason in all local intoxications, from felons to snake-bites, I believe in and have practised with uniform success incising the skin freely and then applying a poultice of greater specific gravity than the blood. In the case of this boy boric acid and the salt crystaloid were used for this purpose, and at the end of six hours all the venom had been drawn through the incisions into the poultice, as evidenced by the non-imflamed condition of the treated puncture. Common table salt, epsom salts, Glauber's salts, sal-hepatica, sugar, bichloride of mercury, or any other crystaloid would have been equally effective if used in sufficient strength of concentration and kept wet—not moist, but wet. *Vide* elementary physics, chapters on "Osmosis."

The above of course applies to snake-bites of the extremities, or to over 98 per cent of all bites. Bites of the body are best treated by permanganate injected into the fang marks at once, and by heart stimulants, and free purgation. They are serious however treated.

If the fang happens to have pierced a large vein and injected a fair dose of venom directly into the blood stream, prayer is about as effective a treatment as any, and is seldom very satisfactory in its efficacy. The patient is usually dead in thirty or forty minutes unless antivenom can be administered, of course. The injection of specific antivenom does away with necessity of all other treatment, but is rarely possible.

NOW the above is off my chest and I feel better. You may use it in any way you choose, but I prefer not to have my name appear in print. If you wish to refer any private inquiries to me, or give any name to private inquirers, do so.

I spend six months out of most years in the hills or deserts, on sea or stream, and believe you will be doing my less specifically informed fellow time-killers and chance-takers a service by telling them how simple the treatment of venom may be: (1) Tourniquet tight enough to prevent bleeding when skin is cut, kept tight for fifteen minutes, then loosened till blood flows, then tightened again, and repeat for six hours. (2) Thick poultice of table salt, over incision through fang-marks. That's all.— ——— ———.

Camp-Fire is not the place for advertising peace-time drives, but the country, especially since the war, owes a big debt to the Salvation Army and I think you'll agree to an exception in this one case.

The Salvationists are now most of them back at their peace-time posts. The appeal that they are to make to the country at large May 1 to 10 is for the sinews of that warfare which the Salvation Army has waged without ceasing since its inception—the warfare against wickedness, poverty, sickness and distress.—A. S. H.

THIS time, with no apologies whatever, I pass on to you a letter telling what one comrade did to get a copy of our magazine. I leave it to you whether I ought to have suppressed it merely because praise of the magazine is usually kept out of Camp-Fire. Me, I couldn't resist. If no one else will join me, I'll give Chew Tobacco a rising vote of thanks all by myself.

Mr. Webb, at the time of writing, was general agent of The Liberty Amusement Co., Ltd.

En Route.

There has never been, nor ever will be, a magazine that will take a-hold of the real American adventurer like *Adventure*. That is made up with stories by real old live he-men to be read and appreciated by the peregrinate he-men of the world. On our little show we have many admirers of *Adventure*—real he-men, too. Among these are two fancy ropers and experienced cowmen, who have herded on our own Western frontiers and punched in the South and Central American cow-countries.

ONE of these fellows looks forward to the arrival of *Adventure* stronger than myself, and that is going some. Only a few days since we were playing a stand in which we were water-bound; no trains were running, nôr any likelihood of one running in another week. *Adventure* was due on the newsstands. The nearest newsstand was thirty-two miles away, which would have been easy to reach by mail, through the train news-agent or telephone, had we adequate train service. What does this monkey do? He stands the strain for two days, and, lo, one morning I notice him saddling his best mount.

"Where to, Chew Tobacco?" I asked.

"Aw, I want something to read, and these —— birds in this strip of country only know a newspaper and their Bible."

"But, Chew Tobacco, the nearest newsstand of any importance is thirty-two miles south, and the whole country is under water for miles. Anyway, what will you find when you get there?"

"*Adventure*, by ——!" was the prompt rejoinder. "It was due out two days 'fore this —— flood came, and I'm going to have her or bust a lung swimming after it." And, with that he swung into his saddle and was gone.

LATE that night, or rather early the following morning, I heard an awful commotion outside my stateroom door on board the sleepers.

"Who's there?" I called.

"Chew Tobacco Wallace, you rummy-head! Who'd you reckon was here; and furthermore, he's got your *Adventure*. So just unroll your carcass from the downy-down, old hoss, and make a dive for the poke, taking therefrom the full amount of twenty cents. I'm pretty well tuckered out and the pinto is worse; but I knew you'd be just plum' anxious to see her. That's why I make all this fuss, you old feather-bed wallower."

Well, he was about right. I was "just plum' anxious" to see the magazine. I always am. But think it over. This fellow—a man of the great outdoors, and one who has been a tramp in many climes—rode over a dangerous route to the tune of sixty-four miles to get our favorite magazine. He rode, and he and his horse were compelled to swim in many places in the thirty-two there and thirty-two miles back. That shows the old "take a-hold" stuff—eh, what?—THOMAS WEBB.

AN ARGUMENT. Go it easy, comrades. Camp-Fire is sure the place for difference of opinions, but—well, words have a trick of appearing a bit harder on paper than they're meant. We're all friends together and we'll all have to watch so that our words will sound as friendly from the printed page as if we could all talk together personally. Now and then Uncle Frank Huston lets go with a wallop but we all have known and liked him for a long time, he's old enough to be a daddy to most of us and, well, he's Uncle Frank and that's enough.

Unfortunately, for lack of space, we had to omit the drawings this time, though they were entirely good and clear enough for reproduction.

Arapahoe, Wyoming.

Have read Irving Blank's letter regarding the so called "Hurry Up Buckle." I hardly like to dispute the word of a man that has spent about seven years on the range, but right here is where I will have to go on record as saying that one Irving Blank has his wires twisted. In the first place no self-respecting cow waddie is caring to risk his neck any more than is necessary, and he would sure be doing it were he to use a takleberry buckle.

Then on the other hand, according to friend Blank's letter he must saddle and mount his horse from the Injun side, and saddle him in a way that would make a "common hand" ashamed of himself.

While I am not much of an artist I have tried to make the diagrams plain enough to show what I am driving at. As any one can see, a man can hardly work a "hurry up buckle" on the "short latigo ring," to quote friend Blank. At least he can't if he is plum' cold sober' and is a cow hand as he claims to be.—GEORGE ORMOND.

ON THE occasion of his first story in our magazine Lee Hooper, following Camp-Fire custom, stands up and introduces himself:

Beaufort, N. C.

A sketch of my life would be, in my opinion, sadly out of place in the company of adventurous histories such as I have so frequently read in "Camp Fire," but if such a sketch can bring me closer, even in spirit, to those interesting men who write for you, it will be a pleasure to give it to you.

BORN in Alabama, I spent my earlier years in that State until I went to Virginia to college. I was one of a brave troop that made the welkin howl on the night when the United States declared war on Spain, but after a firm word from a very matter-of-fact professor I recall our evaporating patriotism even to this date. My other adventures there consisted in sundry death-grapples with mathematics. I took the count when I tackled history, Greek, Latin, and such studies, so I came to the belated conclusion that I was cut out for a civil engineer. I still labor under that delusion.

My travels have taken me as far north as Canada, and in the other direction to the tropics, where I spent about eight years, most of the time on the Panama Canal. I have moved around considerably in southern seas, but have never met a pirate or found a buried treasure or had any other kind of adventure out of the ordinary run of incidents. I might have had a fight with a boa-constrictor once in Costa Rica but for the fact that he saw me first; I nearly killed a tiger once on a tiger hunt in Colombia. I saw him first.

My occupation is building highways, and I have done that for the better part of my mature years, or more exactly, for twenty years, and I get my adventures usually at second-hand.—LEE HOOPER.

SOME more about the Gila monster, from one of our comrades who had some rough luck in Mexico:

El Paso, Texas.

I just happened to see Mr. Alex McLaren's letter in Camp-Fire (regarding Gila Monsters), and will say this much. I think the man he speaks of as living in Los Angeles and having a house full of reptiles is full of hop as regards to Gila Monster not being poisonous when fed on eggs and other clean food. For I have held a few Gila Monsters in captivity myself and I tried the rabbit experiment too, and I'll tell the wide, wide world that if a Gila had been fed on honey and ambrosia I would not let him bite me for a speckled pup. Because the Gila I experimented with had had nothing but eggs for over three months and when he bit that said rabbit poor bunny cashed in in about five or ten minutes more or less. Mr. McLaren also says that the breath is said to have a sickening effect but from personal experience can not say. I can say that there is only one thing that is any more sickening than a Gila's breath and that is two of 'em.

As for handling a Gila, it is simple. Just grab him by the neck as you would a snake and he is your meat. Only be darned careful about that said breath, for it smells just like a Gila looks, and when that is said it's all said.

He also speaks of Cave Creek, Arizona. I wonder if he means the Cave Creek between Rodes, New Mexico, and Paradise, Arizona?

I LOST all I had in Cananea, Sonora, Mexico, in 1916. The folks were living there then a while. I was driving a truck for Tio Samuel with Mistah Pershing in pursuit of the elusive Mr. Villa, and while I was engaged in this pleasing pastime the cholos went "Hermantile" at Cananea and undertook the cleaning out of all the Gringoes.

Well, to make a long story short, the folks had to *laigasen* (beat it) between suns and all my books, clothes and everything I cared a darn for including a .45 Colt, Bisley model Six, went to help La Patria. —ALBERT LEFITZGERALD.

AS TO the bears in "Wulfhere" Mr. Higginson gives us the following:

Port Dalhousie, Ontario, Canada.

Frank Finn, F. Z. S. author of "The Wild Beasts of the World," a work that may be found in most public libraries, tells many interesting things about bears, their intelligence, etc. The polar bear, the largest of the tribe, uses great ingenuity in attacking seals, even to covering his black nose with his white paw to escape detection as he approaches his prey. In the Zoo he will skilfully peel an orange with his claws, or make a current in the water with his paw to draw a floating object towards him, or open a coconut by flinging it against the bars of his den. "Old Sam," a polar bear that died in the London Zoo in 1903, would put a piece of his rations just outside the bars of his den, then hide just behind the stone wall where he would be invisible to persons coming by. These persons thinking to do the bear a good turn would push the piece of food inside the den with their canes or umbrellas, when a great paw would suddenly dart out and these articles would be snatched from their grasp and made unfit for future use. This was a common trick of Old Sam, and one which he seemed to enjoy thoroughly.

THE polar bears prowl oftentimes in companies. The female bear alone hibernates. They eat fish, seals and whale meat, and more than one case of man-eating has been reported against them by arctic explorers.

Even as early as Viking times bear-baiting was a favorite amusement, and both white and brown bears were used. One old-time author tells of a certain church falling down one Sunday while the people were at the bear-baiting, remarking, quaintly, "Now if those people had been at Church when they should have been at the Bear-baiting they would have been killed."

Male polar bears have been mated with brown bears and hybrids produced. These have been in turn mated with both polar and brown bears and with other hybrids and cubs have been born. There are specimens of such hybrids in the London Zoo and in a German Zoo, all of them fertile.

THE bear though clumsy in appearance will in a fair race outrun any man. They are exceedingly quick too with their paws and jaws. They will kill and eat cattle and even horses, and young pigs are esteemed by them a great delicacy. Most of us have seen bears do many extraordinary tricks, such as standing on their heads, catching skilfully a pole thrown into the air, tossing and catching a ball, standing on a large ball and rolling it across the platform, drinking out of a bottle, dancing, etc, all at the command of the trainer.—A. B. HIGGINSON.

ANOTHER my-first-copy-of-*Adventure* story, the promise of the story of one of our "Id." tags and a letter that is characteristic of the dyed-in-the-wool adventurer:

New York.

That metal tag which I received from you in 1917 or '18 while at Chicago has been with me through some hard corners and sometime I am going to write you a full account of them. I read my first story in *Adventure* in France, 1915, while trying to forget the mudholes and Flanders. I was wounded at the battle of Vimy Ridge, in April, 1917, and shortly after discharged. If I belonged to the great majority of sensible humans I would settle down and stay in one place for a while, but as it is I am constantly on the go.—JOHN PAUL JONES.

P. S. I am heading for Central America the first of December. Can you get my card to me before that? Thanks.

A WORD from E. E. Harriman concerning his story in this issue:

Los Angeles.

Missionary Bill is a conglomerate, made up from an intimate and varied acquaintance with numbers of naval seamen. I have met him in various guises and in many places. In lake ports in several coast cities, ashore in Los Angeles, on the decks of destroyers, cruisers and battleships. I saw three of him go overboard after an old lady who fell between a lighter and the *Colorado* and there was less than the time of a swift wink between the three splashes.

I HAVE seen a number of him walking city streets, on shore leave with his matey, hearty, good-tempered, kindly, generous, but a fighting terror when some fool trod on his sensibilities. I have talked with him hundreds of times in all sorts of places and I have long wished to let others see *Bill* from both sides, with some slight emphasis laid on the kindly generosity which is strong in his nature.

Limey, his undersized matey, is drawn from life. He talks just the same on a destroyer deck as he does in the story. He looks just as diminutive when he walks, swaggeringly, beside my two hundred pound, six foot three son, as he does beside Bill. And his favorite name for that son is always "You bloomin' big 'ippo!"

He bets his "bloody spukes" on a crap game or scraps an insulting landsman with just the same terrier-like intensity.

THE salient point in *Bill's* makeup is his generously kind spirit and that he has shown to me in a hundred ways. Impudent, bullying little Limey backs him up and abets him, just as far as his duty to "the missus" will let him. I wrote the story because I like a "gob" so darned well that I want every one else to like him, too.

We had 1,300 of him ashore here in one day and only four arrests for disorderly conduct. "—— it!" said one. "We're your guests!"

This short and emphatic sentence, I maintain, gave a reason in full for the good behavior of the 1,300 men.

The battle scene on Main Street is fiction, but its cause is not. We had an Austrian here at the opening of the great war who tried the same tactics shown by the ex-bosun. There was no great fight. An ambulance carried him off for repairs, that was all.

The ride in the patrol wagon is historic. I know the hero of that very well indeed. Only George threw off two officers and the drivers without any help and drove back to the central station alone.

I reckon that is about all there is to say, except that I hope you Camp-Fire boys will like *Bill*.—E. E. HARRIMAN.

A COMRADE in Burma writes in about one of Edgar Young's South American stories and Mr. Young gives interesting information concerning wart fever:

Yenangyaung, Upper Burma.

When the story "The Son of a Fool" came out I went to one of the boys who know Peru like the palm of his hand and asked him about the wart fever. Well, he told me all about the time that the epidemic hit that bunch up on the railroad bridge and he also claims that there is a cure for it, which can be procured from the Amazon River Indians over east of the Andes. But he said he had never heard of the wart fever having been in Lima or Callao.—HILAND MCREATH SMITH.

Brooklyn, N. Y.

Have read with interest the quotation from the letter of Mr. Hiland McReath Smith, Upper Burma.

The following is about all that is officially known about Wart Fever, unless something has been definitely learned during the past two years:

UNDER *Warts* in Encyclopedia Britannica occurs this statement: "A peculiar form of wart known as *verrugas* occurs endemically in the Andes. It is believed to have been one of the causes of the excessive mortality from hemorrhages of the skin among the troops of Pizarro. Attention was called to it in 1842 by Dr. Archibald Smith."

In the Standard Dictionary under *Verrugas* (Lat. *Verruca*, wart) they give the definition in these words: "An endemic disease peculiar to Peru, characterized by ulcerous vascular tumors on the surface and mucuous membranes that become confluent and exhaust the patient by prolonged suppuration and frequent hemorraghes: due to a special bacillus."

The International Dictionary puts it in this form: "*Verrugas*—(Sp. *Verrugas*, warts). An endemic disease occuring in the Andes in Peru characterized by warty tumors which ulcerate and bleed. It is attended with febrile symptoms and is probably due to a special bacillus and is often fatal. Called also Oroya Fever, Peruvian Warts, etc." Attention is also called to framboesia, a tropical disease of the West Indies and Africa.

NOW as to what knowledge I have of it from first hand: Back in 1911 or '12 I came up the coast and over to Lima with just about enough money to buy a package of cigarets. I hit the Cerro de Pasco general office in the Sun Life Building on Calle Union for a pass to Cerro de Pasco in order to look up a job of work. They gave me a ticket to Oroya and a pass from there up to the mines. The road up to Oroya is not their line but belongs to the Central of Peru. The conductor on the Peru Central was a white haired old granddaddy of an American who had helped build the road. When he learned I was also a railroad man he came and sat in the seat with me and talked to me all the time he was not engaged in collecting tickets. He pointed out the Veraguas Bridge, which, due to the scourge of wart fever that annihilated the American and native forces during construction, has come to be locally known as Verrugas Bridge, or Puente de Verrugas, "Wart Fever Bridge." It is at Kilometer 84 and is 575 feet high. If the kilometers are numbered from Callao, which I think they are, this would make it about 70 kilometers from Lima, or about 45 miles. On this same line the altitude 90 miles from Lima is about 3,000 feet. From there on it shoots right up the mountains. However, according to these figures the Wart Fever Bridge is something between sea level and 3,000 feet.

HE TOLD me that several thousand were killed by the fever during the construction of the bridge and that it was abandoned several times on this account. He said it was so virulent that if a man even walked over the bridge and got above the water of the river he was smitten. According to his report three American doctors came down to study the cause and put up tents near the bridge and all died within a short time. He said he had tasted the water of the river and that it was acrid and bitter and could not even be used for making tea. He said he had confined his drinking to *pisco* and *chica*, native whisky and wine, when near the neighborhood of the bridge with his work-train.

I took most all he said with a small grain of salt but was able to corroborate his story after I arrived in Cerro de Pasco. I believe it was 1,800 men who died at the bridge and how many laborers died in the other camps is unknown. His statement that "thousands died" can be accepted literally. He also told me about Meiggs and his work of locating and building a railroad which is regarded as one of the most wonderful in the world, about the runaway (which I verified) which run down the mountain, killed eleven men on a bridge, and then jumped into the cañon below, and many of the incidents I narrated in "The Streak of Lean."

I WORKED for a time in Cerro and when I came out I heard they had another scourge of verrugas down on the lower end of the Peru Central R. R. We took on passengers down to a station after we began hitting the lowlands at the base of the mountains which is something like 5,000 feet. I believe they took on passengers at a couple of stations below there. The last passenger they let on was an Italian lady accompanied by a young Indian girl servant who carried a hen in her arms. Then they locked the doors and "highballed" through to Lima, neither taking on nor letting off passengers. I looked out the window to get an eye-full and saw signs of much distress in many of the small towns as we came through, doing about 20 miles an hour, or less, for we had to kill time to keep on the schedule, which allowed for numerous stops.

The country was a flat, desert valley, with a small town here and there along the railroad. I noticed that each little village had one or two Chinese stores and that the local officials had put out yellow flags on many houses. In one or two I saw them hauling away dead in carts. I am pretty sure that I saw signs of the plague in the last village before we struck Lima and on the outskirts of Lima I saw armed men maintaining the quarantine. Further, from personal observation and questioning—for I was interested from personal motives as I did not want the plague—I learned that there were a few cases in Lima and that one American, a tobacco merchant, had died in Callao with it, and that another man, a German, had died on a boat en route to Panama. I made numerous inquiries as to the effect of the disease from two American doctors and from a missionary from Baltimore, Md., a Mr. Pohl, of the Seven Day Adventist Faith. All seemed to say that there was a chance of recovery so long as none of the warts bursted inwardly and assured me that the mortality was high enough to be startling. I used this with other true incidents from other places and all the story can be upheld by taking parts from three or four countries, including plague-ridden Guayaquil.

I HAVE asked frequent questions about wart fever and I have told several scientific men about it. Dr. Samuel of Louisville, Ky., was greatly interested and wanted to go down and study it at first-hand. I also told the surgeons in the Panama Canal Hospitals as much as I knew, and I believe I have spoken to you about it. So far as I know the bacillus *has not yet been segregated*, in spite of the statement in the dictionary to that effect; neither has the carrier been found. Numerous surmises have been made. Gnats have been suspected, flies, even toads, but, at last accounts I had, nothing definite had been learned. Not only does this fever prove to be endemic to Peru, but endemic to this particular valley of Peru and this particular river, and I might almost say endemic to the lower portion of the river, although the water of the upper river is shunned by the Indians who call it "Verruga Water" and say it gives wart fever. All accounts agree that it is bitter and unfit to drink. It may be that the secret of this fever and its transmission will yet be found to be some abrasive or astringent chemical which evaporates from the river as it passes through the desert country of the lowlands at the base of the Andes. We can only surmise, and I, for one, would like to know just what causes this peculiar and deadly disease.

NOW I have never heard of this fever on the upper Amazon and will go on record as saying that it does not exist on the eastern slopes endemically, from questions I have asked and all books I have read of men who have explored this country (and

I have missed few in the past five years). Cancer-giving flies exist on the eastern slopes. I saw a Mr. Ross at Cerro de Pasco who was bitten between the eyes while on a trip down the eastern slopes and whose face was almost entirely eaten away when I talked with him in the club house at Cerro. A collection was being taken up at the time to send men with Mr. Ross back to some tribe of Indians who were supposed to possess a poultice of herbs that would cure him. I have learned since that he had waited too long and that they were unable to help him when he finally went, and I believe Dr. Ivans, a Cerro de Pasco camp doctor who lived at Sayville, L. I., told me he died soon after I left Cerro.

THE fact that no wart fever is to be found on the Upper Amazon would probably "knock Mr. Hiland McReath Smith's 'cure' for it for a goal" if allowed to remain as I have stated it. However, as he has been light on me, I will assist him. According to the report of two Americans who made the trip from the Cauca Valley of Colombia across the Andes and down the Putumayo River to Iquitos (The Putumayo, the Devil's Paradise," T. Fisher Unwin, 1912), they encountered a settlement of Incas on the upper headwaters of the rivers. There are doubtless many such settlements. Our old Camp-Fire comrade Walter R. Johnson spoke of seeing similar people and a man who wrote the Camp-Fire in answer to his letter also mentioned them. Lange spoke of seeing Indians with typical Jewish features among the Mangeromas.

The Incas, according to my notion, were descendants of the ancient Persians. The type has disappeared from the civilized portion of Peru, Bolivia and Ecuador. I looked in vain for an "Inca type" and found him not. It is possible that the Spaniards worked few of these highly intelligent men to death, with thousands upon top of thousands of miles of unexplored territory across the mountains. Walter Johnson firmly believes they have a capital with all the splendor of ancient Cuzco back in the unexplored forests of Ecuador, Peru, or Brazil, and I believe he is right now searching for it. The Incas had their "holy city," a custom probably brought from Persia. A man coming from Cuzco was given deference by a man going to it. Possibly at one of the small outposts of their new country they heard of the ravages of the plague in what had been their former homes. Having had it to deal with for hundreds of years they possibly knew a cure, for they farmed this valley of Peru. I saw the terraces they made in this same valley and the remains of their houses of stone. It is quite likely they were as far advanced in medicine as they were in science and mathematics and politics (they had done away with poverty and crime).

THEY possibly knew how to cure and prevent verrugas as they knew how to temper that copper head I saw in the glass case at Cerro de Pasco and as "healing the sick" is a part of their religion they possibly sent word that they knew the cure when they heard of the scourge. Or, to be less visionary, the cure possibly got handed down through the Quichuas, the subjects of the Incas, Kings of Peru. Those old Indian cures are usually good. They were using Hot Springs, Arkansas, in this country for the curative effects of hot water and our Indians were dopes when compared with such highly civilized and cultured people as the Incas. There's the loop-hole for Mr. Smith. Tell him to inform his friend that there have been other scourges of the verrugas and a couple since I was there. The Peruvian Government, and the Pan-American Union may not say that verrugas was ever in Lima and Callao. But I know what I saw. I guess his friend was down there before my time ——fire, haven't I made this a long one!
—EDGAR YOUNG.

ONCE Harold Lamb, of our writers' brigade, made a statement in a letter that caused me to ask just what he meant. In his reply he put the whole thing concisely in a nut-shell. Without making comparisons between our magazine and others, I think that what he says is true. It does give a living, intimate panorama of our country's development, thanks to the fact that our writers as a class know the material and atmosphere they use in their stories.

Here is the bit from Mr. Lamb's letter:

New York.

I think my claim that *Adventure* unfolds the story of national development is *bona fide*. Page for page, no other magazine that I know of draws the picture that *Adventure* draws of American growth all along the line from the pioneer to the lumber boss.—HAROLD LAMB.

SOMETHING about homesteading and free range conditions in connection with his story in this issue from William M. McCoy:

Los Angeles.

I've known and observed my share of homesteaders, white, black and all shades in between, and I have never seen one make a success who did not have his vision of a home, a sort of mirage to which he could turn his eyes. He might not have called it that, but he had it, and he had to fight every day to make it come true just as the wop does in this yarn. Homesteading is a real adventure these days, and it is a game which assays a much higher percentage of broken hearts than it does dreams come true. One reason, of course, is that the man with money enough to buy a farm does not homestead. It is the chap with little money and consequently little equipment who endures privation, isolation, and all sorts of things a pioneer must face, in order to win a home on the land.

I RECENTLY returned from a swing of a thousand-odd miles through the desert, both tamed and untamed. In one very interesting valley not far from California, Arizona and Nevada I spent a couple of weeks. This is all free range country, and there are three outfits in the vicinity. One of them is a very large affair, which we'll call the Bar-B's, which is not its name. Their riders are all

Indians or breeds, and fights over water are common. This outfit have perhays a dozen section foremen each one with his riders occupying a section headquarters. The other two outfits are smaller, but all white. The valley has an elevation of more than four thousand feet, there is good grazing, the land is good, and about a score of settlers, perhaps more, have taken up homesteads there.

The Bar-B's have tried to drive every one of them out, but the other two outfits side with the settlers. The day I landed a cattle-water war broke out between the Bar-B crew and the other cattlemen. The next day a woman settler went away from her home for a while, and when she came back every vestige of her house had disappeared. Before dark the nearest section headquarters of the Bar-B outfit mysteriously burned to the ground, and while the general foreman was investigating this, his own house burned down.

At daylight on the third morning of my stay armed cowboys took possession of the water-holes in "our" end of the valley, and began cutting out Bar-B cattle, gathering them into bunches of scores or hundreds and stampeding them north. There was a grand mêlée of riding, roping, and bowling, and plenty of excitement for a time. Every one, even small boys and women, were packing guns. The water-holes were guarded night and day. The Indian riders came down in force, but their bluff didn't work. I was at the water-hole when they showed up, and when the old white riders—all the young ones were away in the Army—rode out to meet them I would have bet anything in the world to one that there was going to be real trouble. But the Indians and breeds lost their nerve, and those old bow-legged, gray-haired lizards turned them around and sent them back with instructions to stay there. So you see there is still something doing once in a while in the free range country.—William M. McCoy.

Our Camp-Fire came into being May 5, 1912, with our June issue, and since then its fire has never died down. Many have gathered about it and they are of all classes and degrees, high and low, rich and poor, adventurers and stay-at-homes, and from all parts of the earth. Some whose voices we used to know have taken the Long Trail and are heard no more, but they are still memories among us, and new voices are heard, and welcomed.

We are drawn together by a common liking for the strong, clean things of out-of-doors, for word from the earth's far places, for man in action instead of caged by circumstance. The *spirit* of adventure lives in all men; the rest is chance.

But something besides a common interest holds us together. Somehow a real comradeship has grown up among us. Men can not thus meet and talk together without growing into friendlier relations; many a time does one of us come to the rest for facts and guidance; many a close personal friendship has our Camp-Fire built up between two men who had never met; often has it proved an open sesame between strangers in a far land.

Perhaps our Camp-Fire is even a little more. Perhaps it is a bit of leaven working gently among those of different station toward the fuller and more human understanding and sympathy that will some day bring to man the real democracy and brotherhood he seeks. Few indeed are the agencies that bring together on a friendly footing so many and such great extremes as here. And we are numbered by the hundred thousand now.

If you are come to our Camp-Fire for the first time and find you like the things we like, join us and find yourself very welcome. There is no obligation except ordinary manliness, no forms or ceremonies, no dues, no officers, no anything except men and women gathered for interest and friendliness. Your desire to join makes you a member.

UNDOUBTEDLY this comrade will get most of the information he seeks. What one can't supply, another can. Doubtless, too, there are books on the subject and their titles will be welcome.

Ft. Worth, Texas.

For many long months I have puzzled over a most curious beauty spot in Texas and am coming to the Camp-Fire for help as others have before me.

DOWN in Concho County there is a little town by the name of Paint Rock that gets its name from huge boulders grotesquely painted, located in the bluffs. These rocks are situated about ten miles from Paint Rock and about a mile and a half from where the Concho River empties into the Colorado. The cliffs are about forty-five feet high. All over them are painted, in blood-red, astonishing and puzzling designs left by the Indians.

And although centuries have passed since being placed there, the designs are as bright and noticeable as ever. An outline resembling a church surmounted by a cross is recognizable. A drawing that looks like a ship is also to be seen. Two immense hands are clearly discernible. Another design would seem to represent a boy riding a buffalo. Most conspicuous of all are the moon and sun designs. Others are so queer and so grotesque as to be nothing short of monstrosities.

DO ANY of the Camp-Fire know of any old-timer who lived in this part? Or any one who has knowledge of its history? Do you think these Indians were sun-worshipers? I would surely like to discover the paint formula of theirs. A buffalo-hunter first heard of these cliffs from friendly Indians whom he encountered. They told of cliffs of fire, and claimed that these bluffs gave forth smoke and fire for months at a time. His curiosity aroused, he proceeded with them and was shown the Paint Rock Cliffs. Since last September abundant amount of oil has been discovered there, which leads me to believe that the "Cliffs of Fire" were nothing more than petroleum seeps afire. Some one let me have an opinion on this.—CHAS. McCAFFERTY.

OUR "Ask Adventure" editors don't claim to know it all, nor can they tell all they know in a single letter. They, and we office editors, are merely trying to give our people all the information we can manage to do, so we are glad to have Comrade

Erickson give some more data to our comrades from Washington, D. C., and Honduras. Also data on a district from an aviator's point of view is particularly welcome for naturally that is not part of our regular stock in trade, though one or two of our "AA" editors happen to have had aviation experience.

New York.

I don't believe it's customary for those in the flickering shadows at the outer circle of the Camp-Fire to attempt any further information to that given by those in the limelight in answer to the various questions asked in "Ask Adventure." If so, I'm going to break the precedent—if I'm allowed—so here goes:

THERE are two questions to which I might be able to add a few enlightening remarks; one, that of Captain H. F. Rothery of Washington, D. C., concerning the Florida Everglades; the other, Chas. E. Borden of Tela, Honduras, C. A., regarding Yucatan county, Mexico.

Personally I'm not an an adventurer, though some day I hope to qualify—Scandinavian blood, you see. The only things I can recount with any thrill are: when four and one-half years old sat on top of a five story washpole; at two years, ran away from home; at twelve, pulled out of the Hudson when sinking for the third time. Later, having my clothes frozen on me when the cake of ice I was drifting on in Great South Bay broke through and I had to swim for it; getting cured of "side-car pullmaning" which I had till then conducted on an extensive scale by getting locked up for two days; a load of salt-and-pepper for stealing apples in a farmer's orchard. While at sea, saw two ships blown up by "Fritz" and wished myself torpedoed, just for the experience of it. Passed Cape Hatteras Lightship as she was sinking from a U-boat shot. Mere escapades, those, compared to my latest and best—flying. Lived in the Florida Everglades for six months. Boasted no pilot (I was trained for an aerial gunner) could get me sick by stunting. Was given a chance to make my boast good—five consecutive loop-the-loops, and I counted nineteen "Immelmans" (which are still worse for the stomach) before I "threw up." Lord knows how many followed—I was too sick to die.

HOWEVER, by habitation in, and flying over them, I naturally know a little of the Everglades. I know of no place in the U. S. which has better, more enjoyable weather during the months of November to June. In the Summer, insects resembling muchly in body and bite the mosquito are numerous around dampy spots. Their bodies are small but their legs make them resemble spiders. They are not so voracious as they are pesky.

The Seminole Indians now number less than five hundred. Of the many I have seen, only one man and his wife and child ever bore the semblance of cleanliness. They are more or less of a dark yellowish color and look ugly. However reticent they are toward whites they will not harm one unless in a quarrel or in self-defense. They are a shiftless lot, the women doing most of the work. Their favorite color is plaid, the men wearing knee-length skirts of calico or gingham. I have seen only two who wore shoes and socks. A number of white women have interested themselves in the welfare of the remaining Seminoles and often make trips to their camps in the 'Glades to teach their women. A white man can best make himself understood by gestures and signs.

THERE is a State Drainage Canal which runs from Lake Okeechobee due south to the Miami River which empties into the Bay of Biscayne at Miami. Down this canal the Indians pole their way in their long canoes to Miami where they trade their wares. For any one purposing a trip I would suggest the use of this canal. It is about fifty feet wide and thirteen feet deep half its length north to where a dredge is still at work deepening it to thirteen feet clean through to Lake Okeechobee which is some seventy odd miles north of Miami and west of Palm Beach. I have caught more fish in this canal in an hour than a large family could eat in a week (these I threw back again because I couldn't use more than two or three of them). Alligators abound in this canal. I have bathed and washed clothes amongst a bunch of them without being molested and thus from personal observation must say they will not attack any one unless they are angered or bothered. I have seen a man, single-handed and unaided except by a rope, capture a seven-foot alligator and walk away with him thrown over his shoulder.

RATTLESNAKES are the only things, that to me, take the joy out of the Everglades. They are too numerous to suit me. A fine motorboat trip would be from Tampa down the Gulf of Mexico to the mouth of the Caloosahatchee River (about fifteen miles south of South Boca Grande) past Fort Myers and into Lake Okeechobee cruising southeast along its banks until the canal is reached and drifting down it south to Miami. The Chamber of Commerce, Miami, Florida, will be glad to give important data about Dade and other county waterways. The Everglades soil is of the finest black muck and at the low land prices is a fine farm investment. The canal lends an easy access to market. Sisal growing is rapidly becoming an important industry in Florida. Let me add a warning to hunters. The rare and beautiful plumaged birds of the Everglades are protected by the State under heavy penalty of long jail sentences. The hunting around Lake Okeechobee can not be beaten.

AS TO friend Borden. I take it, being that he is at Tela, he is in the offices of the United Fruit Company and therefore has a pretty good knowledge of Spanish, which is necessary for a well-paying job in Progresso. The chief product is sisal, the export of which is controlled by the Commission Reguladora de Hennequen. The exporters must ship through the above, therefore there are no independent exporters. While Merida is the larger city, Progresso is the seaport.

The Commission Reguladora is owned by the Mexican Government and as far as I know is operated in Yucatan only and circulates its own money. A recent order that came to my notice through my connection with the Ward Steamship Company (where, incidentally, I handle the Progresso and Merida Agency accounts) worded as follows: "Effective in Yucatan, Mexico, November 15th, 1919. The Commission Reguladora Mercado de Hennequen, the Chamber of Commerce, Hemp Growers and the Governor agree to liquidate Commission Reguladora paper money, formerly two pesos for one dollar U. S. Currency, and fixing in the meantime the rate of exchange at four pesos to One American Dollar. After November 15, pesos will cease to exist." It isn't quite clear to me yet just what this portends. As a parting tip—Steamship agents' salaries are somewhat in excess of seven thousand dollars a year, and competent agents are hard to get. Let me know how you make out.— HERMAN E. ERICKSON.

IN A letter beginning with some news about his friend Alaska Jack, Carleton F. Crippen writes concerning Wild Bill Hickok and then gives us the following:

Vancouver, Canada.

Another one of our old timers who is still living, or at least was when I saw him last in San Francisco in 1915, is Diamond Field Jack Davis. I saw his name mentioned in "Riley Grannan's Last Adventure."

When the author wrote about Jack saying "Knick, old boy, you mustn't talk that way. Guns are made to blow the other feller's brains out," he certainly was quoting Diamond Field from first-hand. "Old boy" was one of Diamond Field's favorite ways of speaking to a friend, and I believe he was a friend of every man who was in hard luck. He was so generous he gave away two fortunes, one made in Alaska, and another in Nevada, and later lost a fortune in Mexico, after escaping from thirty Mexicans when they were about to stand him and two companions against a stone wall to be shot.

DIAMOND Field Jack, to my notion, is one of the biggest-hearted men who ever lived, although he was a gunman and had several notches on his guns; and like Wild Bill there are some who will print him as a blackguard when he passes on to the long trail. Jack's good nature and willingness to help others often made him the goat. This was the case in the killing for which he was sentenced to be hung in Idaho. Governor Hunt who pardoned him was the brother of my old friend Tom Hunt whom I have written of before. Jack's pardon by Governor Hunt was made a political issue by the opposing party, and naturally the opposing party condemned Jack as a cold-blooded murderer.

Hunt, Diamond Field, myself and others intended taking the oldest stage coaches to the Fair in 1915 and run them with old long-haired drivers, but the jitneys scored us out, and since then I have lost track of Jack. Undoubtedly, when Old Jack passes on, his memory will be brought up at Camp-Fire, as he is a character known from South America to Alaska.—CARLETON F. CRIPPEN.

WHO can supply this comrade with a copy of the poem she wants?

Balboa Heights, C. Z.

I read the talks about the Camp-Fire with much interest, recalling my own good times about the camp-fires in the Rocky Mountains. Such memories serve to lighten the burden of life in cities and settled sections.

I WOULD like to ask a favor of the members. About four years ago there appeared a poem in one of the newspapers in Washington, D. C., the theme of which was the farewell of a cowboy to his chum who is going East for a visit. The first line is "And so, farewell." It recalls their rides together, morning, noon and night, the howls of the wolves, etc., speaks of the call of the mother to all, "And Mother East is calling you, I know," but after a while it will all pall and he will return and everything will be fine "When we ride the range together, you and I."

I used the poem for a reading (I am a public reader) but lost it some way and have forgotten much of it. If any one can furnish me with a copy, I shall be most grateful.

That hidden gold-mine of the Apaches always holds the interest. I have been trying to get my mother to write to you what she learned of it while at San Carlos, Arizona.—CECILE CARTER.

FOLLOWING Camp-Fire custom, Alexander Hull rises and introduces himself on the occasion of his first story in our magazine:

Newberg, Oregon.

Your custom is mighty jolly. I've always enjoyed the last few pages of the magazine. "Enjoy" perhaps shouldn't be the word for pages so fraught with the stuff of life and death, with grim "lost" and "missing" notices. The potential fictional possibilities of those items have seemed to me tremendous. If one had the inside story of half a dozen of them, there might be material enough for a life's work. I take that aspect of it, because I take fiction seriously. As an interpretation of life—that protean, apparently insoluble problem. Still, if every man contributes his bit of data, and his quota of experience, honestly, telling the truth of it as he sees it, maybe in the end we shall get somewhere with the riddle.

THE adventure streak—rather late in life, for I am thirty—is rather strong in me. It sounds strange to say that, when most of them have been vicarious. I wish I had something spectacular to offer in the way of adventures. I've seen more or less of life, of course, but mainly in its more civilized aspects; I've touched the shadowy border half a dozen times by the fever route, and once or twice have been in more or less physical danger—but that's all, and there's no thrill in it for any one else.

At any rate, greetings and good will I can send you—and do.

"THE Better Head" was purely and simply a brain-child. My knowledge of the South Seas is not a first-hand one, though, considering the number and quality of the second-hand sources I've consulted, it may not be such an inaccurate knowledge after all. I shall be young enough to admit that I liked the story, I enjoyed writing it—although I've written and sold quite a lot of tales—as much as anything I ever turned out. I liked the irony of it. I liked the old head-hunter. And I was fond of the enterprising young native of the last paragraphs, who had so little to do with the rest of the story. There is a certain simplicity about the native mind that is tremendously attractive, I think.

WE'RE likely, for reasons of our own, to overrate the Caucasian. After all, analyzed according to the light that is in him, I don't think that he shines too brightly, particularly when you judge him by the reactions that take place when he's placed in juxtaposition with the natives. He has, of course, a constructive ability and trend of character that the others lack, and he's more alert mentally because his world is vastly more complex and demands alertness, and, failing to get it, promptly serves disaster.

Of course, the reason that the white men of this story appear to such disadvantage is because they were simply "bad eggs," whereas the natives were, by Papuan standards of their day, upright and moral men. A head-hunter isn't particularly terrible if you take the trouble to study him in the light of his race, his past and his beliefs. *Nganoni*, in his way, was a very good man, I take it. An accident of birth and environment and time made him a head-hunter. In Athens he might have chiseled at the bas-reliefs of the Parthenon. In Gotham he might have been a mural painter or an interior decorator. The white head-bargainer, of course, was either amoral, or a homicidal degenerate. In any case, he was a misfit, and quite as valuable hanging over the fire of *Nganoni's* devil-devil house in the serene high hills as anywhere else.

THE story came into my mind all at once, full-blown—I don't know how—in the latter part of 1918. I think that's all I can say about it—unless some indulgent reader should happen to want to ask about it, or criticise it, in which case I will do my best.—ALEXANDER HULL.

P. S. I was born in 1887 in Columbus, Ohio, attended the public schools of that city, Muskingum College, and the University of Pennsylvania. I've been on the coast here for a bit over ten years, am professionally (until I began writing a few years ago, at least) a musician. A number of my compositions have been published. I am at the head of the Music Department of Pacific College at Newberg. In the last four years I have sold and had published some seventy short stories.—A. H.

CONCERNING an Asiatic race that figures in some of the stories of his series Robert J. Pearsall tells us the following:

Palo Alto, Calif.

The Lolo territory is, I believe, entirely new in fiction—and almost new in Western knowledge. Its Asiatic appellation is "the land where the Chinese do not go." When I was in China it had been penetrated only once, by the D'Ollone expedition, about 1907. I remember I once conceived the idea of attempting it myself, in company with another young fellow who was the son of a missionary and as enterprising a chap as ever roved. However, that went the way of many other good plans. But I knew the country roundabout—where "Ghost Ruled" was really laid—pretty thoroughly, from some experience and much study. And everything is as I've written it, including the element of superstition. The Lolos do come down to raid the Chinese villages—and perhaps sometimes they have been assisted by some such trickery as I described.—ROBERT J. PEARSALL.

HERE are the results of the readers' vote on the ten most popular stories in *Adventure* during 1919. As in previous years, we give also the ten ranking next in the vote. (S) stands for "serial," (N) for complete "novel," (n) for complete novelette, those unmarked being short stories.

Of course a vote of this kind is only a partial expression, being cast by only a minority of the total number of readers, but nevertheless it is both interesting and decidedly useful in helping us in the office fill the magazine with the kinds of story our readers like best.

The vote on the relative value of fiction and the various departments was so scattering that we have not tabulated the results. "Camp-Fire" ran very strong, with "Ask Adventure" a good second. But no formal vote was needed to show that "Camp-Fire" is a favorite.

		Vote
1	LYNCH LAWYERS (S) *William Patterson White*	5,921
2	FROM BEHIND MASKS (S) *Gordon Young*	4,867
3	SAVAGES (S) *Gordon Young*	4,557
4	RIDER OF THE GRAY HORSE (n) *Harold Lamb*	3,999
5	ON THE TRAIL OP TIPPOO TIB (S) *Talbot Mundy*	3,751
6	SHRIEK OF DÛM (N) *Talbot Mundy*	3,565
7	RED BELTS (S) *Hugh Pendexter*	3,087
8	MULE-SKINNER—DYNAMITE (n) *C. M. Cosby*	3,069
9	THE HELLION (n) *Earl Ennis*	2,728
10	THE SLOTH *Arthur O. Friel*	2,604
11	THE BOSS OF MIRAGE (n) *E. S. Pladwell*	2,046
12	CARSON OF TAOS (N) *Hugh Pendexter*	2,029
13	BORN TO BE HANGED—BUT (n) *Gordon Young*	2,015
14	GO-AHEAD DAVIE (N) *Hugh Pendexter*	1,953
15	SALT OF THE SEA (S) *J. Allan Dunn*	1,829
16	GENTLEMEN OF THE NORTH (S) *Hugh Pendexter*	1,767
17	DOOM OF THE GODS (N) *Arthur Gilchrist Brodeur*	1,519
18	STAR OF EVIL OMEN (n) *Harold Lamb*	1,457
19	MAN TO MAN (S) *Jackson Gregory*	1,271
20	THE SNAKE *Arthur O. Friel*	1,225

Because shorter stories labor under a disadvantage in a vote of this kind, those under 20,000 words are listed separately, those under 10,000 being marked with a *.

STORIES UNDER 20,000

	Story	Author	Vote
1	THE HELLION	*Earl Ennis*	2,728
2	THE SLOTH *	*Arthur O. Friel*	2,604
3	THE SNAKE *	*Arthur O. Friel*	1,225
4	THE DEATH OF ZARI *	*L. Patrick Greene*	1,209
5	LOCAL OPTION IN LOCO LAND *	*W. C. Tuttle*	1,178
6	THE SPIDER *	*Arthur O. Friel*	1,116
7	THE STREAK OF LEAN	*Edgar Young*	1,054
8	FLAT BEHIND THE EARS	*Norman Springer*	1,041
9	THE SON OF A FOOL *	*Edgar Young*	1,023
10	THE LURE OF THE LODE *	*Stephen Chalmers*	999
11	SILVER SADDLE	*Everett Saunders*	992
12	WHILE RIVERS RUN *	*Farnham Bishop*	961
13	ROOF OF THE WORLD	*Harold Lamb*	937
14	BUMPS	*S. B. H. Hurst*	931
15	GODFATHER TO SATAN'S KITCHEN *	*Hapsburg Liebe*	878
16	COLOR OF HIS BOOTS *	*W. C. Tuttle*	868
17	CONVERGING TRAILS *	*Edgar Young*	782
18	PARIAHS OF PIPEROCK *	*W. C. Tuttle*	775
19	PROMOTERS	*G. A. Wells*	651
20	MERELY BRUTE *	*George L. Catton*	620

Bear in mind the vote during the coming year and be marking down your favorites as you go along. The next vote will be on the stories that appear in the issues from First January 1920 to Mid-December 1920 inclusive. No qualifications are required for voting—only that you read at least one copy of the magazine. We want to get what you consider to be the ten best stories of the year, but if you want to vote for more than this number, or for less, all well and good. Be sure to make up your list with the best story first, second best second, etc.

YES, a good many subscribers to this magazine have had a pretty raw deal in failure of the magazine to reach them regularly and on time. And we've been late very often in getting it on the stands. The worst of it is that we can't do much to help it, for most of the trouble is not our fault. Our Circulation Department makes mistakes like all other human beings, but if there were no trouble except what is due to their mistakes our circulation troubles since last Fall would be comparatively insignificant.

You can get part of the answer by casting back on your own personal experience these past months in the matter of mail gone astray. You don't always know about mail sent you that didn't arrive or mail sent by you that didn't arrive, but probably you've detected enough cases to know that mail service has not been up to par for some time. It has been so bad here that the Merchants' Association of New York has finally secured a Congressional investigation.

EXPRESS service, which covers part of the distribution to subscribers, has been at least equally sad here in New York. Being unable to handle their work on the usual basis, the express people imposed condition upon condition, which were met by us at great trouble and expense, until they finally stated they were unable to handle our shipments at all! Our company, with its parent company the Butterick, being next to the largest express shipper in New York City, were naturally hard hit, but even that knock-out blow was met. With trucks hired at one hundred dollars a day (bear in mind that all other New York shippers were up against the same difficulties) we hauled our various magazines across the Hudson and out to small towns in New Jersey not affected by the local congestion and shipped from there.

Incidentally this last stunt had its amusing and cheerful side. Express company agents got a percentage bonus on increased business in addition to salary. The percentage seemed to increase with the smallness of the town and the lack of promise of much increased business. Well, our big trucks began rolling in upon little commuting stations in Jersey. I like to picture the local agents' eyes bulging with surprise and joy at this wholly unexpected and very, very large increase of their local business—and bonus. To the express officials who promptly appeared at our offices the next morning our man in charge replied blandly, "Yes, and it will be a —— sight more today. Wait till we get things really started."

ADD to these little matters the other little matter of the strike of the local printers here last Fall. You and we have been paying the bill ever since—in the sad delay of all issues until, as already explained, we finally had to cut the Gordian knot by omitting our two May issues entirely in order to get back on schedule. Oh, believe me, we in the office have been having our own troubles. No one suffers more from such delays than do we.

DID I ever tell you that two of our issues were printed in Boston in our attempts to make up time lost by the strike? Sounds simple enough. It wasn't. At the same time our own plant was working full time on other issues. Don't get me started on telling *our* troubles.

But bear them in mind when inclined to cuss over delays in subscriptions and on newsstands. Conditions are by no means ideal yet at this writing in April. Picture our Circulation Department struggling against all the piled up troubles, for most of which they are in no way to blame.

Call out, by all means, whenever your magazine fails to reach you as it should. If you don't, we shan't even know about your trouble to rectify it. But don't forget that we have quite a little job on our hands, that we are not the ones most to blame for these troubles and, most of all, that we are the ones who suffer most from them and are doing all we can to remedy matters.

I WANT to thank very particularly those of you who responded to my appeal for reports of places where ADVENTURE should be on sale but wasn't and of insufficient supply to particular newsstands. That kind of friendly tip is more than appreciated and is invariably acted upon as quickly as conditions permit. Please keep on sending in those tips about our magazine.—A. S. H.

IT LOOKS as if most of you were as much in a "show me" attitude on hoop-snakes as I am. You don't seem to be rallying to the job of proving that hoop-snakes exist. Yet here is Comrade Quinby backing them again and, having known him a long time by correspondence, I have too much respect for his veracity and good sense to pass lightly over what he says.

Graniteville, South Carolina.

Certainly you can publish anything I wrote you about snakes, although I am sorry you seem inclined to doubt the veracity of some of my friends. I am afraid we will have to class you as a doubting Thomas. I'll bet that when you were a kid you did not believe in Santa Claus, nor fairies, goblins nor nuthin'. And I expect that, being a grown man, you don't even believe in ghosts. Well, I believed in all of them, and still believe in some of them to-day.

But in all seriousness, I am sure that the hoop-snake as I wrote you exists, not from personal knowledge, for I admit I am not curious about seeing one, but because I know the parties who told me about them. I understand that there is a variety known as the horn-snake which strikes with its tail. But so far as I know, it does not roll as a hoop.—JAS. L. QUINBY, JR.

THOUGH his talk did not reach us in time for his first story in our magazine, "The Out-of-Dates" in Mid-March, Captain Frank H. Shaw now follows Camp-Fire custom and introduces himself along with his novelette in this issue:

Though born in an inland manufacturing town in Yorkshire, I heard the call of the sea when quite young. Seafaring as a profession was frowned on by those responsible for my future, and medicine was strongly urged as a career, but the craving to be up and away on wide waters was too strong to be overcome and after much argument my desires were gratified.

AT SIXTEEN years of age, I went to sea, in a tramping "windjammer," a three-masted barque, which took me round the world three times in four years, and showed me every phase of the sea. It was a hard life—bitter hard in places—and I suppose I must have wondered a thousand times what inherent madness it was that prompted me to take service afloat. It showed me the world, however, and the ways of ships on the sea. Particularly did these four years teach me much of the ways of men upon the ships; and this learning stood me in good stead in after years.

One great fact was borne in upon me: the surprising lack of knowledge, amongst a people that owes its very existence to the sea, of the conditions of sea-life, and the beauty, the majesty and the terror of the sea. I had in those days no thought of ever being in a position to endeavor to attempt to interpret the realities for the understanding of those who had not seen with their own eyes, but I suppose I must have stowed away impressions and recollections subconsciously; and, hard though the days and months in sailing ships were, I would not have missed a single one of them.

BUT I got out of this windjammer life as soon as it could be managed. A' hankering after the rumored greater comforts of steamboat life, perhaps. I passed the second mate's examination and proceeded to sea in cargo-carrying steamers! South America and North America were my beat for two or three years; examinations were passed as they came due; and I was lucky enough to secure an extra-master's certificate of competency when about twenty-three, passing with honors, and at what was then a fairly early age. By this time I considered I had learnt a lot about the humbler side of seafaring and, introduced by my extra certificate, I went in for the Atlantic ferry. The following years were good ones and certain U. S. cities became familiar places to me. I might have taken command of an American yacht, but already the hankering after written expression was beginning to assert itself.

I TRIED my 'prentice hand at a story of the sea—the actual narrative of the mutiny that figured as its central feature had been told me by an old skipper who had taken part in the adventure.

Sometimes I read that first story again and wonder that any editor ever risked his professional reputation by publishing it. It was without form and void; it was a solid block of writing, ungainly and lacking construction; but it must have possessed some quality of which I was ignorant, for it was accepted and published. I suppose men have been less delighted at discovering a gold-mine than I was when I heard this surprising bit of news. But it altered my life's course completely. The day I saw my own work in print opened out vistas of a new heaven and a new earth. I resolved that I would endeavor to become the mouthpiece of such men as used the sea. An ardent Kiplingite, I vowed to "paint the thing as I saw it." It was not until later that I realized that many people don't want to read of a brutal thing as it really is but as they would like to think it was.

Leisure was a scant possession on the Atlantic ferry, but every spare minute at sea was devoted to writing of the sea. In port I made friends with American newspaper men and I believe I learned a lot regarding my own language and its possibilities from them. And always there was an ever-growing desire to settle down to real writing, to put everything I had into the task. Conflicting with this desire was the old sea maxim—learned in sailing ships—that a man should never let go with one hand until he'd got a secure grip with the other. The sea promised a livelihood; literature was as yet an untried jackstay. So there was nothing to do but plod on at sea, and plod on with the pen—or, to be quite frank—with the typewriter.

I GOT a story accepted in America; another in England. After some eighteen months I discovered that I had doubled my seafaring income by the work of my imagination. Also there were matrimonial hankerings: a girl there was who said that she'd no real desire to be a widow for eleven full months of every year, which is what a sailor's wife really is.

I bade good-by to the sea for a year, and settled down to make a business of writing. If I failed, there was always the sea to go back to, and the promise of a living wage. But I found that I didn't need to go back to sea. Little by little my stories found favor with the editors that link the Bristish reading public with the author. I received letters—from sailors—saying that my stories were salt-water personified; the real thing. One letter I treasure struck me as being a real compliment. The story it dealt with had to do with a delicate piece of seamanship performed under great difficulties. The root idea of the story was to show up in some degree the parsimony of certain ship owners. They had stored their ship with cheap gear. In the middle of the operation I was describing, the rope on which everything depended carried away and the labors of a week were wasted. Said my forecastle correspondent, in dealing with the matter:

"When I read about that rope parting, I sang out: 'Stand from under!" That was one of the pats on the back that make a man realize he is getting hold of his trade.

Since then I have had many letters, approving of or questioning details of seamanship; and the fact grew upon me that I was, to some extent, achieving my set ambition—I was explaining the sea, its ships and its men, to laymen, to the satisfaction of seamen.

CAME then a sea-novel. It got hold, but was far from being a best-seller. An eminent English firm of magazine-publishers wrote asking for work, much work. They got it. They must have liked it, for they asked for more. On the strength of growing success, I married; but I was afraid the sea might call me back; and, cowardliwise, I went and hid in the English Lakeland. More books were written, with varying success. My last book before the war broke out was "The Haven of Desire"—an honest attempt to portray sea-life as it was and is.

I HAD my own opinions concerning a man's duty to his country, and when the war broke out, I was holding a captain's commission in a Territorial unit. I was actually in uniform when the war-clouds broke and mobilization followed swiftly. Now, a man can not be a soldier and an author at the same time, if he wants to be good at either trade. It would have been an easy matter to secure a comfortable, leisurely Staff job, or employment in the Propaganda Department. Instead, I went with my division to France—soldiering had won. It meant a struggle for the family at home to keep their heads above water, but they agreed with me: it was up to every man of a serving age to throw his full weight into the scales.

After a while, however, siege warfare grew monotonous; a desire for greater activity possessed me. I contrived to transfer to the Royal Flying Corps, and served as pilot and flight commander in that Corps in France for a year. I was about twice the average age, but it was an interesting and an exciting experience. And by this time the old-time love of adventure, which had taken me to sea some twenty years and more before, was itching in my veins. I made up my mind to see as many phases of the war as could be seen so long as such seeing could be reconciled with my desire to do the very best I could do for the country. I studied wireless telegraphy and Secret Service work, and took a hand in dealing with the Zeppelin menace. It was all very interesting work, and, I flatter myself, useful work, too—for the country.

BUT somehow the sea kept calling. The years of vagabondage were not yet done. I came across a Navy man; took him for a joy ride along the British front. We discovered a common interest in the sea; he expressed surprise that I, a trained sailor with good qualifications, was content to be soldiering. Later, he wrote from the Admiralty, London, making suggestions and offers. Normally it was about as easy for a man to transfer from Army to Navy as it was for a camel to navigate a needle's eye; but I found the right strings to pull and almost before I realized what had happened, I discovered myself a full-pledged naval officer, busy on great waters in one of the carefully hidden "mystery ships."

I was battering about the Mediterranean in a tiny Italian coasting brigantine when the Armistice was declared, but that simple coaster was in reality a very efficient submarine-killer, heavily armed and heavily manned.

THUS, throughout the war, I contrived to see three dimensions—land, air and sea. I was a fighter more than a spectator; but I was able to store up a valuable assortment of varied experience and when I returned to the matter-of-fact existence of a writer again I was prepared to swamp the reading world with thrilling narratives. I found, as many another writer has found, that the reading world was nauseated with war. But this stock-in-trade of actual experiences should come in useful when the historical interest of war comes to its own.

Anyhow, battering about the seas in tiny sailing ships taught me much more than ever I had known before of the sea and the ships upon it: it revealed to me beauties, terrors and majesties never before comprehended. So I do not grudge these varied years.—FRANK H. SHAW.

AS TO the ancient ruins in the Pecos Valley concerning which a comrade inquired at Camp-Fire:

Bellingham, Wisconsin.

H. W. Brown inquires in Camp-Fire about the ruins of ancient Indian structures found in the Pecos Valley of New Mexico. Perhaps I can throw a trifle of light on the subject.

I AM somewhat familiar with such Indian remains in the Pecos Valley along its upper waters in Texas and southward across the mountains and upland plains to the Rio Grande—say 160 miles north and south. Have been over the ground a good many times and frequently have seen the sort of relics Mr. Brown surmised to be a fireplace.

Those which I am familiar with are fireplaces, in a sense, but are called "mescal pits." They are where the Indians, fairly modern tribes, roasted the succulent head or heart of the sotol, which I take to be a low-growing species of the palm. I believe also the yucca head was sometimes roasted. But the sotol contained a juice that when roasted and allowed to ferment slightly turned alcoholic. Eaten or sucked, they supplied an orthodox drunk, putting a buck to sleep for a good many hours. The yucca, I believe, was more of a food, like cabbage.

MESCAL is made today and smuggled over the Rio Grande, though I understand it is not a genuine mescal, and the boys who buy it from the bootleggers call it sotol. It is about the same stuff the Indians made in the pits.

I have seen scores of the pits. They consist of a depression scooped out a foot or so deep and six to twelve feet in diameter. All that I have seen appeared to have been circular when made. There was no central hole two feet or so deep, as Mr. Brown speaks of. The pits were saucer-like. I have no doubt what Mr. Brown refers to is about the same thing, if they were in a country that grows sotol, and I have seen sotol in that region of New Mexico.

THERE are a good many signs of ancient Indian village remains in the region I mentioned above and in the New Mexico country Mr. Brown speaks of. From an investigation of one near Fort Davis, Texas, a hundred miles or so from the New Mexico corner, I, and others better informed, judged them to be the ruins of Indian villages made previous to the time of the modern historical Indians—the Comanches and Apaches—perhaps by the immediate predecessors of the Apaches. This would set a date for their use back about 300 years.

THE presence of such a pit in the region that Mr. Brown described, if no sotol grew there, would be accounted for by the probability that sotol might have grown there 500 years or so ago. In a region with such scant rainfall as it has, the wood at the sides, evidently used at one time for a roof support, might endure five centuries. Mescal pits are frequently found in Texas far from fuel, from water and shelter, but seldom if ever far from plenty of stone. Usually they are where sotol still grows, but sometimes are where it appeared to grow centuries ago.

The Mescalero Apaches, now held on a small reservation in New Mexico, once roamed all this region in question. The word "mescalero" means mescal-maker. The forefather tribe of the Mescalero Apaches was the Tobosos. The Tobosos were given to roasting and fermenting sotol—making mescal. And it is considered most probable that they are responsible for the mescal pits and that they roamed the Southwest 300 years ago back to 500 or 600 years ago.—BARRY SCOBEE.

A WORD from Harold Lamb concerning his story in this issue:

New York.

MOST of us are familiar with the Hindu custom of *suttee*. It prevailed until stamped out by the British—and they had a hard time doing it—in the middle of the last century. Not all of us, perhaps, are aware of the religious significance of the act—the burning of a widow on the funeral fire.

It seems that the widows—often several in number—believed that their voluntary death insured themselves a higher life, according to the doctrine of the transmigration of souls. Thus, if they died in this manner seven times, they became perfect. Most of the women went to the funeral pyre voluntarily, and displayed extraordinary courage. But the Brahmans always had along an orchestra of horns and cymbals to drown the cries of the victim, in case the woman's strength gave way under the ordeal. Also, the priests had long poles ready, to prevent any attempt to escape from the pyre.

AS TO those who did escape the *suttee*, Francois Bernier, the French physician who wandered over India during the seventeenth century, says:

"I have been often in the company of a fair idolater who contrived to save her life by throwing herself upon the protection of the scavengers (*halalkhors*) who assemble on these occasions, when they learn that the intended victim is young and handsome, that her relations are of little note, and that she is to be accompanied by only a few of her acquaintance.

"Yet the woman whose courage fails at the sight of the horrible apparatus of death, and who avails herself of the presence of these men to avoid the impending sacrifice, can not hope to pass her days in happiness, or to be treated with respect.

"Never again can she live with the Hindus; no individual of that nation (religion) will at any time or under any circumstances, associate with a creature so degraded, who is accounted utterly infamous and execrated because of the dishonour which her conduct has brought upon the religion of the country. Consequently she is ever afterward exposed to the ill-treatment of her low and vulgar protectors.

"There is no Moghul"—(meaning, probably, Mussulman)—"who does not dread the consequences of contributing to the preservation of a woman devoted to the burning pile, or who will venture to offer an asylum to one who escapes from the fangs of the Brahmans. But many widows have been rescued by the Portuguese."

I'm not sure that Mohammedan women were burned, but often slaves were sacrificed with their mistress. The girl of the tale, being a Mohammedan, was not bound to the Hindu ritual.

As for *Abdul Dost*, he was hardly a man to be influenced by the power of the Brahmans. And *Khlit* conducted himself upon the favorite phrase found in U. S. Army instructions—"as circumstances may direct."—HAROLD LAMB.

NOW here's a letter I wish I had dug out of our cache long ago, for it gives practical information I know some of you want. Written shortly after the Armistice. He was serving on the same boat with Patrick Casey of our writers' brigade.

U. S. S. Sub-Chaser 73
Section Base, Cape May, New Jersey.

In Camp-Fire I saw a request for information as to museums and collectors which was referred to the readers. I can help somewhat; I'm (or was) a collector and I have been more or less connected with several museums.

TO BEGIN with, by far the finest natural history collection in the country is in the National Museum at Washington. This museum, however, does not employ collectors, as its collections are kept up by private gifts and by the Biological Survey.

The Smithsonian Institution, however, does employ collectors and send out expeditions—most famous of these was Roosevelt's East African Expedition. Its collections go to the National Museum.

After the National Museum in Washington come the Academy of Natural Sciences of Philadelphia, the American Museum of Natural History in New York, the Museum of Comparative Zoology of Harvard at Cambridge. These have collections of varying worth—that is, they specialize in different things.

THE Academy of Natural Sciences does not send out collectors. Its staff does the collecting.

The American Museum is now doing more extensive collecting than any other museum in the country, and it is in a position to carry on the more adventurous and continued sorts of work. Roosevelt's South American Museum, Chapin and Lang's seven-year expedition to the interior of the Congo, which brought back nineteen Okapi examples.

The Howard Museum is specializing in the zoology of the West Indies and South America.

THE Carnegie Museum at Pittsburgh, the Peabody Museum of Yale at New Haven, the museum of the Brooklyn Academy are institutions which are either doing more special or more local work and which have not the collections of the larger institutions. Many of the colleges have museums; practically none, however, send out collectors. Cornell is an exception; there they specialize in North American fauna. In the Middle West the Museum of the University of Michigan, the Field Museum at Chicago and the Museum of the University of Indiana do more than local work. In the West the Museum of the California Academy of Sciences at San Francisco and the Museum of Vertebrate Zoology of the University of California at Berkeley are far and away ahead of the rest, though most of the State Universities have museums.

The San Francisco Museum deals with Western animals and with animals of Eastern Asia.

TO SUM up—The big five are the National Museum, the American Museum, the Museum of Comparative Zoology, the Academy of National Sciences and the Field Museum.

I know little of foreign museums.

I should refer your correspondent to the Naturalist's Directory, the new edition of which is now being compiled. The old edition is in any good library.

Possibly your correspondent wished to know about Eastern Asia. Two museums contain almost all the material from Eastern Asia in this country—those at Washington and San Francisco. Mr. Allen Owston's store at Yokohama, and his stock, brought in by native collectors, has provided many of the rarest animals.

As to myself, I am a collector of reptiles and Amphibians, or rather I was, for I am on Sub-chaser 73 off Cape May, on the same boat with Pat Casey, one of *Adventure's* authors.—EMMETT DUNN.

WHO knows about this Nebraska stone wall apparently built in ancient times?

Birmingham, Alabama.

Who among the Camp-Fire readers know of or have seen the hidden or lost stone wall located in a wash-out or dry cut, two and a half miles north of Chadron, Dawes County, Nebraska? A portion of the wall is to be seen on both banks of the washout, of which I am sending two pictures taken twenty-three years ago.

THE rocks of which the wall is built are of sandstone, one and a half foot wide, two and a half feet long, if I remember correctly. I spent a great deal of time searching and probing around that wall and washout, where I herded cows for six Summers in that vicinity, but all I discovered was the fact that the wall was there and must have been for ages, as in the hard, rock-like clay of the washout could be found petrified turtles, snail-shells, pieces of jaw-bones with teeth of different animals, also joints of snakes and fish. Now that was twenty-three years ago and I am anxious to know if since that time anything has been done to discover why the wall was built, by whom, and when, where, was the sandstone for the wall brought from, as there is none in the surrounding country.

Do any of the readers know Billie the Bear, a pioneer cowboy? Also Red Jacket, a well known character of pioneer days of the West?—C. A. M.

SOME time ago the following newspaper clipping was sent in to Camp-Fire by G. M. Allen of Florence, Arizona. I passed it on to E. E. Harriman, and his opinion follows the newspaper article. Stories of buried treasure have a fascination for most of us, but, when it comes down to the cold, hard, practical question of what are the chances of really finding the treasure, then—well, that's something else. Mr. Harriman's letter was written a year ago, when he was wandering around a bit. Have there been any developments since then?

What is believed to be the first clew to the reputed buried treasures of the padres of the Tumacacori mission, built by Spanish Jesuits high up in the Tumacacori Mountains, less than three hours journey from Tucson, has been discovered by Frank Pinkley, custodian of the ruins. It is the gateway to the mission cemetery. From this gateway, it is said, the plans and maps left by the padres start to outline the way to the buried gold and silver.

The Tumacacori Mission was built near what are believed to be the ruins of one of the Seven Cities of Cibola. Scattered over the long, red mesa surrounding the mountains, are large numbers of hieroglyphic boulders, which, say the modern Indians, Aztecs placed there to mark the hiding-place of another great treasure hidden in the neighborhood. This is said to consist of 2050 burro-loads of white silver and 905 burro-loads of gold and silver.

The entire region is said to show evidences of rich mineral deposits, which, declare those who have inspected the mountains, doubtless led the padres to build their missions.

IN THE sides of the mountains lie the ruins of many dwellings, while on the top, carved from solid rock, is the Aztec god standing guard over the silent city.

Nearby, on a large flat rock, are the stone basins that held the bleeding hearts of the victims sacrificed to appease the wrath of the stone image. Hundreds of these sacrifices are said to have been made each year.

There are five of these ancient villages in the vicinity of Tucson and two immediately across the Mexican border in Sonora. Some say they are the seven cities referred to by the conquistador, Cabeza de Vaca.

A newer city, that of Tubac, meaning "Ruined House," stands near the mission, but little is known of the life there.

Ten acres of land on which the Tumacacori mission was located have been deeded to the United States Government and the plot now is known as the Tumacacori national monument. It is under the direction of Frank Pinkley, who also supervises the mysterious Casa Grande ruins near Florence.

Samoa, California.

Regarding the buried treasure in the Tumacacori Mountains, the information seems rather nebulous. It is quite possible that the padres did bury a large treasure around there. Two years ago a puncher, looking for strays in a like place in Graham County, found a shovel sticking out of a tree and under it discovered treasure to the value of about $400,000, according to the papers. This story was corroborated by the mother of the man who found the treasure, in a personal letter to me.

I HAVE never been able to discover that any man had any thing like accurate directions or maps for relocating this treasure. I have heard of it many times and have talked with a number who have been in that section. As far as I could learn, the directions in existence are incomplete and vague. It is possible that Pinkley's discovery may complete them to such an extent that a discovery may be made later.

As for the Aztec treasure, I "hae ma doots" about the hieroglyphic stones being there for any such purpose as stated. They are a great deal more likely to have some religious significance, or they may tell of some events in the history of these strange people. They may prove, when translated, as unsatisfactory as the brass plate in the old story. It held strange characters, scratched on with a sharp point. Treasure trove stories set many to eager endeavors to secure a translation. At last they found a man who read the scratches.

"This belongs to Jan Van Voort. Damn the man that steals it," said the brass, in old Dutch characters.

Now let some one read the hieroglyphics.—E. E. H.

COLONEL JAMES BOWIE. Yes, he ought to provide some interesting Camp-Fire talks. Mr. Pendexter of course gave our inquiring comrade what data he had, but the subject is too big for one man to cover thoroughly nor can any one man easily collect all the scattered data that an inquiry to Camp-Fire can produce.

Bakersfield, California.

Some time ago I wrote you with reference to Colonel James Bowie, one of the Alamo victims, and you told me you were referring my query to Mr. Pendexter. You stated that in case Mr. Pendexter could not help me, you would try to present my case to Camp-Fire—and I am herewith asking you to redeem your promise.

BRIEFLY stated, the matter stands thus: The redoubtable Colonel—to whom I bear a distant relation—figured largely in the history of the Southwest generally, and particularly in the days of Texas' struggle for independence. That period should be rich in material for the man of literary tendencies; likewise, the lives of such men as Bowie, Crockett, Travis, et al., read pure adventure to us of modern days.

It is my idea that among the old-timers of Camp-Fire there must be at least a few who possess, in one way or another, facts and scraps of information concerning the life of Bowie which would make mighty interesting Camp-Fire talk—besides being of considerable value to his unworthy relative. There are very few people who are unacquainted with the bowie-knife—how many Americans know anything at all of its originator?—HUGH J. BOWIE.

IF YOU have character, will-power, strength of mind, horse-sense and other things like that, you'll carefully refrain from reading the following from Romaine H. Lowdermilk until after you've read his story in this issue. If you don't, it will give away the outcome of the story in advance.

I'll bet you don't take my advice.

Wickenburg, Arizona.

SAY, have you ever been broke? Haw, ask the Camp-Fire that! Of course you have. If you haven't you've likely missed something enjoyable. To the true adventurer being broke is simply the "broad" that lets you into the realm of more adventure. If a fellow's broke, or going broke, or just getting over being broke, he's bound to be going through something "different." And it's these "different" moments that make up the high-lights you like to remember in moments of reminiscence.

WELL "me" and "Al" were broke—worse than broke. We were broke and in debt when we sold "Major Action" to what we thought was a sucker. Maj was the only horse we had that could do us any good in fast company but he wasn't any good unless he could run in the mud! And we just couldn't find any mud for him to run in. Three race-meetings, one right after the other, without a single day of mud! Ordinarily a boy with a "string" of racing horses thinks he's in luck as long as the tracks are dry, but with us it was different; we craved something soft that'd give our "mudder" a chance.

We didn't think we were having a funny time—not then we didn't. We didn't crack any jokes with our prospective buyer, either. And by the way it was a woman who bought our horse, instead of *Tondy*. We wheedled her to buy. We talked her into buying Maj. The next day it rained! (Fact was too strange for fiction so I made 'em irrigate the track. "Al" said it looked like somebody had helped the rain along with ditch-water, anyhow.) Yes sir, it rained! The track floated, oozed and burbled. Old Maj, taking advantage of that slush, pounded out a mile with a jolt that shook ten thousand berries into our "sucker's" nifty little change-cup. How'd she know it was going to rain? She'd played a "hunch"!—ROMAINE H. LOWDERMILK.

IT TAKES a long time to get things started when we have to communicate through the magazine and it takes several months for a communication to reach print after it reaches this office. But there has been real progress in the matter of our Camp-Fire "Stations" and we can open our list with twenty-seven Stations and eight others who have written in that they are interested but have not yet definitely undertaken a station, seven of them in Canada, one in Cuba and one in the Philippines. The Canada stations run from Vancouver to Prince Edward Island and in this country the States represented are Michigan, Oregon, Pennsylvania 2, California 4, New York 3, Massachusetts, New Jersey, Washington 3, Wisconsin, Maine 2, Ohio, Illinois, Texas, Vermont, Indiana, Iowa and District of Columbia. California heads the list, with Washington and New York second. (I don't know where my own home is going to be after October first or I'd add it to the list. Meanwhile and anyhow the office does service as a Station.)

The list follows: Those not yet definitely representing Stations are marked with a star:

CANADA—Vancouver, B. C. C. Plowden, B. C. Drafting & Blue Print Co.
Burlington, Ontario. Thos. Jocelyn.
The Post Weekly, Deseronto. Harry M. Moore.
Dunedin, P. E. Island. J. N. Berrigan.
Norwood, Manitoba. Albert Whyte, 172½ De Meurons St.
*Toronto, Ontario. W. de H. Hammond, 1302 Ossington Ave.
*New Toronto. E. Sheetz, Box 391.

CALIFORNIA—Oakland. Lewis F. Wilson, 1036 Thirtieth St.
Lost Hills. Mr. and Mrs. M. A. Monson, care of Gen. Pet. No. 2.
San Bernardino. Mrs. R. Souter, 275 K St.
Santa Monica. Col. Wm. Strover, Westlake Military School.

CUBA—Havana. R. N. Faries, Dominquer 7 Cerro.

DISTRICT OF COLUMBIA—Washington. Fagan's Cigar Store, 1404 New York Ave. N.W.

INDIANA—Connersville. Norba William Guerin, 112 East 18th St.

ILLINOIS—Chicago. John Bradford Main, care of The Junior Yanks, 144 S. Wabash Ave.

IOWA—*Bettendorf. Lloyd Royer.

MAINE—Bangor. Dr. G. E. Hathorne, 70 Main St.
* Carroll L. Houghton, 71 South St.

MASSACHUSETTS—Malden. Arthur R. Lloyd, 16 Cross St.

MICHIGAN—Marquette. T. Mitchell, Box 864, G. P. O.

NEW JERSEY—Caldwell. Charles A. Gerlard, P. O. Box 13.

NEW YORK—N. Y. C. Robt. V. Steele, Care of American Legion, 19 West 44th St.
Jamestown. W. E. Jones, 12 Fairview Ave.
*Ilion. Ross Travis, 7 Rand St.

OHIO—East Akron. Harry J. Lang, 137 South Arlington St.

OREGON—Marshfield. F. J. Webb, 200 Market Ave.

PENNSYLVANIA—Philadelphia. Wm. A. Fulmer, 252 S. 9th St.
Philadelphia. Alfred A. Krombach, 4159 N. Eighth St.

PHILIPPINE ISLANDS—Ft. Wm. McKinley, Rizal. Marc Guissard, Cpl. 10th Service Co., Signal Corps.

TEXAS—Wichita Falls. A. M. Barlow, P. O. Box 51.

VERMONT—*Granville. R. L. Hastings.

WASHINGTON—Republic. A. E. Beaumont, Box 283.
Ione. A. S. Albert, Albert's Billiard Hall.
Seattle. *Col. C. D. Smyth, Gen. Del.

WISCONSIN—Madison. Frank Weston, Room 9, Tenny Bldg.

Signs are being printed. Various designs have been suggested but none seems better or has more support than the simple design of our Camp-Fire badge. Underneath it on the sign will be in smaller size the one word "*Adventure*," arranged as it appears on our covers. This, of course, is advertising for the magazine. I think it's been proved that we keep the Camp-Fire and its whole spirit free from use for advertising purposes, but in this case, since the house is to pay for the signs and record-books, it seems only fair that they should get what advertising value there is from the one modest word on the sign. Also its use there seems natural and legitimate. If any Station-Keeper objects to it, he can cut it off.

THESE Stations are going to grow in number. The services they perform, though simple ones, are valuable and much needed. It is understood that each Station Host or Keeper is the sole judge of the nature and extent of the hospitality offered, the only things being required of him being displaying the sign, keeping the register or record-book, and a box for mail to be called for or forwarded at the sender's risk. Those of us who wander will bear in mind that, in using a Station, we are not enforcing rights but accepting hospitality.

Send in your name for a Station. Those of you who have wandered in your day will find here an easy way of renewing old times, hearing again at first hand of once familiar places, of meeting or hearing from old friends. Those of you whom circumstances prevent from wandering can, through a Station, meet those who do the things they themselves would like to do and can gather personal news of the world's far corners.

Here is the definite statement of the Station idea. It is understood, of course, that the Stations do not belong to this magazine but so far as any one besides the Station Host himself is concerned, to Camp-Fire in general, nor has this magazine any responsibility for them. Our magazine figures in this only as the mouthpiece of the Camp-Fire at large. It will supply, free, the signs and books and will print from time to time the list of Stations, dropping from the "official" list any that on complaint from Camp-Fire seem prejudicial to the best interests of Camp-Fire and the Station plan as a whole.

A station may be in any shop, home or other reputable place. The only requirements are that a station shall display the regular station sign, provide a box or drawer for mail to be called for and provide and preserve a sufficiently substantial register book. When there are enough stations to warrant even a small order this office will furnish the books and signs.

No responsibility for mail is assumed by anybody; the station merely uses ordinary care. Entries in register to be confined to name or serial number, route destination, permanent address and such other brief notes or remarks as desired; each station can impose its own limit on space to be used. Registers become permanent property of station; signs remain property of this magazine, so that if there is due cause of complaint from members, a station can be discontinued by withdrawing sign.

A STATION bulletin-board is strongly to be recommended as almost necessary. On it travelers can leave tips as to conditions of trails, etc., resident members can post their names and addresses, such hospitality as they care to offer, calls for any travelers who are familiar with countries these residents once knew, calls for particular men if they happen that way, etc., notices or tips about local facilities and conditions. Letters to resident members can be posted on this bulletin-board.

Any one who wishes is a member of Camp-Fire and therefore entitled to the above station privileges (Question of requiring identification-cards or Camp-Fire button to be decided later.) Those offering hospitality of any kind do so on their own responsibility and at their own risk and can therefore make any discriminations they see fit. Traveling members will naturally be expected to remember that they are merely guests and act accordingly.

A station may offer only the required register and mail facilities or enlarge its scope to any degree it pleases. Its possibilities as headquarters for a local club of resident Camp-Fire members is excellent.

AS YOU may have noticed, H. A. Lamb now signs Harold Lamb to his stories. Same man. Just wanted to use a signature that would make him less likely to be confused with other writers named Lamb. Which is a sound idea, though there's always some small loss in changing from one signature to another.—A. S. H.

THE CAMP-FIRE
A Meeting-Place for Readers, Writers and Adventurers

WITH the opening of his new serial in this issue Hugh Pendexter gives us of Camp-Fire some interesting facts about the times in which the story is laid. As you know already, Mr. Pendexter's stories are more than stories. They're education—the rare kind of education that's pleasant in the getting and the most worth while when got. What most school books do to American history is a sin and a shame. And a bore. Perhaps most of us, as children and adults, have a natural interest in history and a real liking for it. A dose of school history and school histories generally kills at least part of that interest. Mr. Pendexter gives us, first of all, stories, but with them and in them he gives us real history—the living, breathing life of past times.

Norway, Maine.

On the monument erected to James Bridger by Maj. Gen. Grenville M. Dodge is the following inscription:

1804—*James Bridger*—1881.
Celebrated as a hunter, trapper, fur trader and guide.
Discovered Great Salt Lake 1824, *the South Pass* 1827.
Visited Yellowstone Lake and Geysers 1830.
Founded Fort Bridger 1843.
Opened Overland Route by Bridger's Pass to Great Salt Lake.
Was Guide for U. S. Exploring expeditions, Albert Sidney Johnston's army in 1857, *and G. M. Dodge in U. P. surveys, and Indian campaign* 1865-66.

Although his long life was replete with invaluable services, Bridger left no written word of his adventures. Mention in the story of early boyhood, when at the age of ten he bought and operated ferry boat at St. Louis, is a fact. At 13 years of age he was apprenticed to Phil Cromer to learn the blacksmith's trade. At the age of 18 he hired out with Ashley for the Rockey Mountains trip. That expedition went up the Missouri to the Yellowstone and lost a boat loaded with $10,000 worth of goods. The land party keeping abreast of the boats lost their horses to "friendly" Indians. They built a fort at the mouth of the Yellowstone and spent the Winter hunting and exploring. Bridger was at the Aricara village fight in the Spring of 1823, and in August of that year went under command of Andrew Henry back to the Yellowstone, two of the band being killed by Indians on the way.

THIS fort was abandoned that Fall and a new site selected at the mouth of the Powder. Bridger was sent with others to Green River by Etienne Prevost, and discovered South Pass late in the Fall of 1823. The Prevost party trapped the Green, Wind and other streams, and wintered 1823-24 in Cache valley on the Bear River.

How Bridger came to discover the Great Salt Lake is correctly given in the story. And it is also recorded as a fact by Gen. Dodge in his sketch of Bridger that the party believed it an arm of the Pacific till it was further explored in 1825. Ashley sold the Rocky Mountain Fur company in July, 1826, to Smith (Jedediah S.), Jackson & Sublette.

Bridger trapped for them until 1829-30, Kit Carson being his companion that season.

THE first wagons used on the Oregon Trail were those taken out by Sublette in the Spring of 1830. They (ten wagons, five mules to each) left St. Louis April 10th, and arrived at the Wind River rendezvous July 16. The first wheeled vehicle to cross the plains north of the Santa Fé route was Ashley's six-pounder cannon, which he took to Utah Lake in 1826.

In August, 1830, the Rocky Mountain company again changed hands, with Bridger one of the most influential partners. It is supposed that Bridger first saw the Yellowstone Lake and Geyser during this year. He described the wonderful region to every one he talked with, but not until some thirty years later was the region explored.

In the Spring of 1831 Bridger and Sublette started with their outfit for the Blackfoot country and lost their horses to the Crows. This theft despite the fact Bridger was a great friend of the Crows. Bridger recovered the horses and all the Crows' poines to boot.

SILK hats cut the price of beaver down to two dollars a pound. Kit Carson in the Southwest knew the beaver days were over. Jim Bridger also realized it, and the Rocky Mountain Fur Company dissolved in 1834. From 1833 to 1840 Bridger handled trapping parties for the A. F. C. west the Big Horn River. In 1843 he built Fort Bridger on a tributary of the Black Fork of Green River. Here came the trail through Bridger's Pass, both for the overland immigrant and the Mormon, whether traveling by the North or South Platte routes.

Bridger lived there until 1857, when he leased the property to the United States, the formal lease being signed by Gen. Johnston's quartermaster, the rental being six hundred dollars a year. Gen. Dodge in his sketch of Bridger says none of the rental was ever paid, although thirty years later the Government paid six thousand dollars for "improvements" on the land.

IN 1856 he had much trouble with the Mormons, his buildings being destroyed by fire, and he barely escaping death. He estimated the stock and merchandise of which he was robbed, or otherwise lost, to be of the value of one hundred thousand dollars. In 1850 he settled at Little Santa Fé, Jackson Co., Mo. He spent his Summers on the plains and in the mountains. In 1862 the Government asked him to act as guide in the Indian campaign. In 1865-66 he guided Gen. Conger's column from Fort Laramie to Tongue River. Capt. E. H. Palmer, of that expedition, tells how Bridger saw smoke fifty miles away with naked eye while the general could see nothing with powerful glasses. Two days later Pawnee scouts reported an Indian village on the Tongue, the smoke of which Bridger had claimed to have seen. Capt. Palmer says Bridger remarked, "These —— paper-collar soldiers telling me there wasn't any smoke!"

In 1869 Bridger was guide for Capt. Raynolds, assigned to explore the country around Yellowstone Park. He was with him a year and a half. Bridger died July 17, 1881, 77 years of age. Gen. Dodge says his fame rests on the part he bore in exploring the West, that he had no equal as a guide, that the topography of the whole West was mapped out in his mind, that he could describe and draw an intelligent map of any region he ever visited, even though he visited it but once.

JIM Baker practically lived his life in the mountains with various Indian tribes. He was Illinois born and bid good-by to civilization when eighteen years old. His first employment, according to Inman, was with the A. F. C. He was thoroughly imbued with the superstitions and beliefs of the Indians, overfond of whisky at times, generous to imprudence, unacquainted with the sensation called fear. He was famous as a mountaineer, hunter and trapper, a friend of Carson, Bridger, Wooton, Hobbs, Beckwourth, and many others of the old time mountain men. His views on the Indian, as given in Chapter 7, are quoted by Inman in his "Old Santa Fé Trail." His fight with two half grown grizzly bears is too well known to be more than mentioned.

KENNETH McKENZIE, *the* King of the Missouri, was the greatest trader ever employed by the A. F. C. From the beginning of his ventures in fur-trading John Jacob Astor showed a strong partiality for men who had been taught in the H. B., the N. B., or the X. Y. Z. schools in Canada. McKenzie's opening up the Blackfoot trade through Jacob Berger was a master stroke. While bourgeois at Fort Union he ruled as dictator and was host to several famous travelers, such as Audubon, Catlin (he drew a picture of Fort Union showing three bastions) and Prince Maximilian. McKenzie had James Kipp build Fort McKenzie at the mouth of the Marias, it being the first fort established for the Blackfeet. Gauche fought the Piegans here in August, 1833. The steamer arriving at Fort Union on June 24, 1834, brought an express to McKenzie, announcing Astor's retirement from the A. F. C., Pierre Chouteau, Jr., and Company being his successors. Fort Union was commenced by McKenzie in 1829. His theory was to stop all opposition by breaking and crushing it. In the story I advanced the time of the famous distillery. It was operated in 1833-34.

FATHER DE SMET in his "Western Missions and Missionaries" says of Gauche, "Crafty, cruel, deceitful. A bad Indian in every sense of the word, his life was full of horrors." Charles Larpenteur, who commenced as whisky-clerk at Union and worked up to bourgeois, speaks of him as "This great perverted genius." And says he was infamous as a secret poisoner (see "Forty Years in the Fur Trade").

Fort William, named after William Sublette, was built just below mouth of Yellowstone, two and a half a miles from Fort Union as an Opposition. It lasted a year and was bought out by the A. F. C. Fort Buford was built on this site in 1866 when Fort Union went out of business. Gauche, through some whim, refused to bring his Winter trade to Fort Union the Fall of 1833, but took it to the new fort. There were five hundred Indians and their squaws, all drunk, says Larpenteur, and kept locked in so they could not go to Union. This was the first big chief the Opposition succeeded in getting away from the A. F. C., and this victory, of course, was only a transient one. It was in March, 1836, that Gauche with three hundred warriors jumped thirty lodges of drunken Blackfeet, massacred them and took three hundred ponies. Gauche died at Fort Union in the Autumn of 1843 after being soundly whipped by the Aricaras.

THE Deschamps are worse than I have painted them, and the Rem family no better. Gardepied killed Deschamps at the fort in July 1836. An A. F. C. man took a pipe of peace and made peace between the Deschamps and the Rems, the latter having abetted Gardepied in the killing. In the Fall Rem's two sons-in-law were killed by Blackfeet on Milk River, and the Deschamps family planned revenge on their weakened foes. Old Mother Deschamps urged her sons to avenge the death of their father. They promptly killed old Jack Rem, declared war on his people and also on the whites in Fort Union. Ten of the company's men demanded guns of Larpenteur, and he gave them out, also a cannon. The Deschamps were living in Old Fort William, which had been rebuilt nearer Fort Union. The fight went on all day. Old Mother Deschamps was shot while standing in the door and holding a peace-pipe. François was killed in the bastion, being out of ammunition and suffering from a broken wrist. In all eight of the family were killed. The company lost two men.

PINAUD killed Blair while employed as hunter at Cabanne's Post. He was acquitted, although the murder was deliberate. But the A. F. C. would not send down witnesses as it would reveal their liquor traffic with the Indians. (See Chittenden's "History of Navigation on the Missouri.") I don't know what became of Pinaud, but being a worthless cuss I've taken the liberty to kill him off.

The most important post on the Missouri from 1812 to 1823 was Fort Lisa, named after its founder, Manuel Lisa, pioneer trader. It was located five miles below the old Council Bluffs, or one mile above Cabanne's.

The Benton-Lucas duels were August 12 and September 27, 1817. The Biddle-Pettis duel was fought at a distance of five feet, Pettis being very near-sighted. This was on August 27, 1831.

The death of the bull from hydrophobia, and the biting of Goerge Holmes by mad wolves, is related by Larpenteur. Alexander Henry in his "Journal" also speaks several times of mad wolves and of their persistency in entering tents.—HUGH PENDEXTER.

ANOTHER old letter out of our pile that is waiting for Camp-Fire. Some of you will remember how, through various comrades, we kept track for a while of the old whaler *Morning Star*. Here she is again in this letter written "somewhere in France" probably toward the end of 1918. In a way, I'm glad I don't try to handle our Camp-Fire letters in the order they're received, not only because it would be more complicated than it seems but because it lends an added interest to dip into our store of letters and lift out one, for example, written back when the whole world was at war.

U. S. A. T. —— ——.

I am quartermaster in U. S. A. T. and a great lover of sailing ships, especially whalers. I saw your article about the old *Morning Star*.

I KNOW the old *Morning Star* well, and I sailed with Captain Arey, an old-timer who sailed in her years ago. At the time I knew her she lay at an old storage dock in Providence, R. I., and I was aboard her, looking round. She was to be used in a motion picture, I heard. Last Summer I saw her in Brooklyn at the Red Hook dock, or near there. She was schooner-rigged (three-masted) and her boat cranes and after deckhouse were gone, but I knew her at once. The name was still painted across the square old stern between the batteries.

I know the *C. W. Morgan*, the *Hicks*, *Bertha*, *Swallow*, *Viola*, *Greyhound* and a few more, and am waiting for the war to knock off so I can go to New Bedford and see the model of the old *Lagoda*. If you print any more articles about the old girls I hope to run foul of them. I see one at sea occasionally, but they don't hang around the steamer tracks much, so a tramp doesn't get to see many.—GEO. A. GALE.

P. S.—I am also a painter of ships and cowpunchers when I'm ashore for a spell (which is not very often) and have painted several whaling scenes, which partly explains my interest in the old-timers. I have been to sea as sailor and quartermaster since November, 1915, so have seen a little deep-water time. Was in the A. H. line running to South America in the *Luckenbach* to Colon, and for the last year have been running across for the Army Transport, carrying stores to the boys *over there*, or *over here* as the case now is.

Have a brother in the army here, "Somewhere in France."—S. A. G.

YOU can't blame this comrade. He's talking about my initials used as signature to most of my letters. Probably I couldn't read 'em myself if I didn't know what they are, but I've already explained why I sign with them and no man can explain why I write so badly. The following letter was written December 7, 1918. Found it as I dug down into a pile of letters to Camp-Fire.

U. S. S. Arkansas.

Now, pard, what's your handle? You just dash a few letters down and Lord only knows what it means. Now the next time you send a line put your handle at the end.

You see, we were on a mine-sweeper last week and the crew—near took the long trail. Yes, we were sweeping mines when I spotted one right ahead of us. Talk about your fun! Say, it looked like we were all going up for a minute. Believe me, it's no fun being out here in the wastes of nowhere when you're picking the darn things up. The trenches might be bad, but it hasn't got anything on this outfit.

Well, I'll knock off now, send regards to all the old-timers.—C. F. LESKEALIS (TEXAS CHARLES).

THIS old-timer of the West "comes across" handsomely with pictures of the past for Camp-Fire. Mr. Hooker lives in New York now, editor of the *Erie Railroad Magazine*, but he lived a full life before ever he settled down in the metropolis.

NEW YORK.

Here is something *in re* "Wild Bill," and others.

WHY not get some one who knows the details to tell the story of John Finnerty's ride from the Custer battlefield to a telegraph office? He scooped the world in his report to the old Chicago *Times* (Wilbur F. Storey's paper) and, at that, the news was not published until several days after the battle —nearly the 1st of July, 1876. I think the battle was on June 25th.

I think some of your correspondents hesitate about signing their letters with their real names, for publication, because they feel, as I do, that after the lapse of nearly half a century it is impossible to give correct dates and other facts. I, myself, have discovered that many things are not as clear as they might be. Take "Wild Bill's" marriage, for example: I have always been of the opinion that he married Madam Lake (then the premier woman horseback rider) in Cheyenne or Omaha. However, if I tried to locate the place or the time I'd have to guess.

Madam Lake, in 1876, was with "Cooper & Bailey's Ten Allied Shows in One," which starred Madam Lake. The show played in Omaha, Neb., Red Oak, Mt. Pleasant, Albia, Ottumwa and Burlington, Iowa, that year. It was in Burlington on July 4, 1876, and was caught in a big cyclone that day. Some of its cars were blown off the tracks.

Madam Lake was with the C. & B. show that day, and later, either at Monmouth or Galesburg, Ill., was thrown, her saddle padding slipping. Even the so-called "bareback" riders have a level pad arrangement, sometimes. I don't believe "Wild Bill" was with the show, but it seems to me he had been married to the madam some time before that.

Madam Lake was a wonderful horsewoman, with or without a saddle.

I'm telling you this to show you how time obliterates or twists our minds. I have tried hard to connect a whole lot of events of those old days, but can't do it; consequently I (and no doubt others) hesitate about going into them over our own signatures.

WHEN the C. & B. show was at Albia (Iowa) there was a "hey rube" battle with a gang of miners who tried to pull down the tent. Two or three citizens were killed and Mr. Bailey, I remember, had to go back next year to a trial. If old "Tody" Hamilton was on earth he could—perhaps—tell us all about it, and I am sure could clear up any mystery about "Bill" and Madam Lake; but he's dead like most of the fellows of that period. And those who are alive—or think they are—are some of 'em just walking around. Maybe I'm one of the latter but believe me, I'm still a live wire, even though I admit I would possess a wonderful brain if it didn't leak just a little once in a while when ye olde times are up for discussion.

ONE issue of ADVENTURE interests me greatly because it contains so much from so many sources about "Wild Bill" Hickok, General Custer and others of the once wild and wooly West. But in reading what your entertaining Camp-Fire contributors say and then going over some of the published things I have written about events on the Wyoming and Western Nebraska frontier, I reach the positive conclusion that some of us old fellows are sometimes terribly mixed in our dates. However, I am positive of one thing, viz.: I met "Wild Bill" every day for a number of weeks in Cheyenne during the beginning of the Black Hills gold excitement, and had many conversations with him. (I was in Wyoming before the gold strike in the Hills.)

He was to me—then a youth of 17, but of man's size—a curiosity that I could hardly keep away from. Even then there was a considerable dispute among the bullwhackers (of which I was one)as to whether he was a coward or a brave man. To me he seemed to be a little of each, and I will tell you why. In the first place, at that time (1875, I think) his eyesight had begun to fail him, and he gave that as a reason for not accepting a challenge to a duel at ten paces made by a small-sized California *buccaro* with whom he had a dispute either in McDaniels' Variety Theater or Jack Allen's Gold Room. The last-named was a combination hurdy-gurdy, variety show, beer-jerker's "palace" and gambling hall—faro, twenty-one, roulette, stud, etc.

MY FIRST meeting with "Bill" was in the Gold Room. I sat (as a mere piker) at the faro table, on a wooden chair. Pat Gorman (footnote No. 1) and a man known as "Big Ed" were running the game, Gorman dealing and "Big Ed" holding down the lookout chair. A bow-legged Texan was keeping cases. Chairs were set close together around the table, and every one of them was occupied, some of the time by two players, one standing on the rung, while others were reaching over heads and through gaps between players to place their bets (and few of them were the 25 cent white chips like mine) for it was, as we say nowadays, some game—what the gamblers used to call a *snap*. (The word *snap* not used in the sense of present day.) That is to say, some one outside the "house" (meaning Allen) had put up $25,000 or some other sum, and taken charge with the "lid off," meaning, of course, no limit to bets. I was a piker at the rate of from 25 cents ("two bits") to $2.00 a bet, following as best I could the bettors who seemed to be winning.

SUDDENLY just as I had "cashed in" and made up my mind to quit—ahead of the game, and with a fortune for me at that time of nearly $100—I felt a slight movement of my chair. A new deal had just begun, all bets were placed, and two or three "turns" made by Gorman, but I had made no wager on any one of the thirteen spades in the lay-out. So really I was due to "come in" or get out; and if, just at that moment "Bill" Hickok hadn't lost patience with me and pulled the chair out from under me, I would have quietly risen and gone over (probably) to the "21" game run by the famous Madam Mustache (footnote 2), a Frenchwoman with a small black mustache, and lost all I had taken from the "tiger." Instead, Bill's quick move caused me to sit down on the floor. He made some remark—I think, "Oh, give some one else a chance,"—and I, knowing him by sight, readily (and hastily) departed to the street, thus, no doubt, saving what I got out of the "snap" from the till of the Madam or the stud game running on the other side of the dance floor.

A day or two later I met "Bill" on the street and he smiled, stopped and said a whole lot of nice things, not forgetting to say several times that he didn't intend to hurt me and hoped he hadn't. He called me "Kid," put his hand on my shoulder and said, "Remember, I'm no enemy of yours."

THIS meeting made me like "Bill," but later on, as I got better acquainted, I couldn't help dislike him on account of some of the stories he told me about himself and what he did to poor Mormon women who, hitched like cattle, some years before, were hauling their effects from Nauvoo, Ill., to Brigham Young's promised land in Utah. Perhaps he lied, but he told circumstantial tales that were horrible in their detail.

A LITTLE later, either in '75 or early in '76 the authorities (or a vigilance committee) at Cheyenne, in an attempt to rid the town of "bad men," tacked notices on telegraph poles containing a list of names of men, headed by "Bill" Hickok, ordering them to leave town within forty-eight (or some other number of) hours.

And here is where "Bill" showed himself not to be a coward, for he not only refused to leave Cheyenne but, with a bowie knife, cut his own name out of the lists. This is no report that I heard—*I saw him do it.* Moreover, he stayed in town for a condiderable length of time after the period stipulated in the notice. Finally, however, he went to Custer City, then the chief town in the Black Hills, and was soon after murdered (footnote 3) by McCall (was it in 1877?)

IF MY estimate of "Wild Bill" Hickok is worth anything, I am willing, in the interest of history and to help straighten out the record, to give it. It is this: He was a man of nerve, and had, as city marshal of Abilene (I think) kept the town in fairly good order for those times, and in doing it was obliged to scatter quite a bit of lead among the garroters, then the pest of every camp along the K. P. Of course, he killed a number of men, and when he blew into Cheyenne on the big stampede to the "hills," after Gordon's wagon-train had been held up by Uncle Sam in the Bad Lands west of Fort Pierre at the request of the Interior Department, he was just a plain gambler and, I believe, not a very successful one and with but little money. I doubt if he owned a horse, something nearly every one had in those days (and blankets), although I have a faint recollection of seeing him emerge from Tracey's corral a-straddle one fine-looking sorrel and gallop off toward Fort D. A. Russell. Tracey's corral (and barn) were located on the outskirts of Cheyenne on the Laramie trail and our camp was on Crow Creek not far away in plain sight of Russell and Camp Carlin. For all I know, "Bill" was then headed for Custer, though some one may rise up and say he rode like a prince to that point in Johnny Slaughter's stage, à la Horace Greeley and Mark Twain.

THERE are several things I do not want to do, and do not intend to do:

1. Put myself forward as an authority on "Wild Bill" or as his biographer.
2. Give the impression that I ever was a pal of his, or
3. Try to give the Camp-Fire fellows an impression of myself that would be unjust (to me) by telling them of the faro incident, because
4. I wasn't then, haven't been since, am not now, and never will be a professional gambler. But—
5. In "them days" nearly every one on the frontier, especially youthful adventurers like myself, took a whirl at games of chance. (I've played a little penny ante since!)

I *know* this will shock some of my old lady friends, but as I am well into the 60's, and haven't a hair on my head that isn't white, and now live a somewhat prosaic life as a magazine editor (even in New York) I do not hesitate to sign my full name below, middle name and all, although if, when Cheyenne was humming, I had spelled out my middle name, I almost know some one would have taken a shot at me and I wouldn't be here to scribble this reminiscent gossip.

HERE are a few old-timers (of Wyoming when it had the word "Territory" added) who could add much to Camp-Fire discussion—former Mayor David S. Rose, of Milwaukee, (footnote 4) Willard A. Van Brunt (footnote 5), now in Los Angeles, Calif., who hunted buffalo in western Nebraska and Kansas, and others. Mr. Rose, like myself, Gorman, the faro dealer, and one or two more I might mention, went to Wyoming to die with the "con" as they called it, but "Dave" Rose and "Bill" Hooker are both alive and kicking and long past the three-score mark!

AS TO General Custer. Please let me say that in the several years I spent in Wyoming—at Cheyenne, Medicine Bow, Fort Fetterman, Fort Laramie, and at Red Cloud and Spotted Tail agencies, Sydney, Neb., old Sherman station on the U. P. (in the lower Black Hills) and at Laramie City, I always heard him spoken of as the best friend the citizens had in the Army. He was a very plain and agreeable man among the scattered populations, and greatly admired because he was a real fighter.

There was, almost always, ill feeling between the "buck" soldiers and the men who piloted the prairie schooners to and fro between the railroad and the outlying forts and Indian agencies. The army, however, was made up mostly of good men from top to bottom, and I couldn't understand why there was such ill-feeling. Of course, a bullwhacker or other citizen who misbehaved on a military reservation—and sometimes off it—went to the guard-house without much ceremony except being disarmed, and, if obstreperous, prodded with a bayonet or belabored with a saber. For there was no civil law in the North Platte country, and none to speak of sometimes down toward the Colorado line. The bullwhacker with his sombrero, his greasy buckskin trousers, and his revolvers and butcher-knives, long hair and nearly always bearded face, while usually a pretty decent chap at heart, was not, as I can understand now, a man that an army officer would be apt to invite to dinner, although they sometimes drank together at Post Sutler Tillotson's bar at Fetterman, but not often.

HERE is a quotation from the chapter headed "Bill Hickok, City Marshal," in my book, "The Prairie Schooner," published in 1918:

" 'Wild Bill' Hickok was perhaps the best-known 'character' in Cheyenne in the '70's. He was a ministerial-looking person, but was not a confidence operator. [Like 'Canada Bill' (footnote 6) mentioned in a previous paragraph.] He was just a plain gambler, but he managed to escape the halter every time he put a notch in his gun. 'Bill' killed no one in Cheyenne; in fact, his days there were quiet and (in comparison with those in Kansas) prosy. His killings were all done at the time the K. P. was being built from the Missouri River to Denver. When he was in Cheyenne he was on his last legs—had begun, as they say nowadays, to slow up. Nevertheless he was feared by a great many, owing to his reputation, although among certain classes it was understood that he had lost his nerve. . . . Many deeds, however, that have been laid at his door, and others that he bragged about, were never committed. It has been estimated that he murdered all the way from fifteen to thirty men, but most of these were killed while he was marshal."

MY IMPRESSION is that "Bill" Hickok's real career of killing ended in Kansas. In fact, I am positive of it. Where it began I don't know. Anyway, he was perfectly tame when I knew him, and even playful, as I have endeavored to illustrate by relating the faro-table incident in which I played such an important rôle; though I think if I had resented his action he would have at least pulled his gun.

IN THE evening of my life I return almost daily in my thoughts to those wild days of my youth when life seemed of little value, when sowbelly and beans tasted better than they do now; when a cootie was not a cootie but a grayback, and when no real man in my class would admit he was not entertaining at least a few hundred; when I couldn't sleep in a regular bed under a roof without a real sense of suffocation; when to be wet to the skin all day long—and perhaps all night in the bargain—never even started a cold; when I slept in the open, with the great dome of heaven, its twinkling stars and one blanket or buffalo robe all that was above me, and the thermometer below zero—or at least when high proof whisky froze, for we had no thermometers; when we slept peacefully with as many thicknesses of canvas wagon covering or blankets or gunny-sacks as we could find, *under us*; when four A.M. was the hour to rise and yoke up seven pairs of oxen and string them out into the Bad Lands or into a mountain pass, or around a "break neck"—or, but now I'm wandering, and so I'll close with the verse the good old buffalo hunter, Willard A. Van Brunt, quoted to me in a letter not long ago:

"I'm growing fonder of my staff,
I'm growing dimmer in my eyes,
I'm growing fainter in my laugh,
I'm growing deeper in my sighs;
I'm growing careless in my dress,
I'm growing frugal with my gold,
I'm growing wise—I'm growing—yes,
I'm growing old."

Sincerely,
William Francis Hooker.

Footnotes to the above

1. Gorman died, I was told by his brother Tom, a few years ago at Gunnison, Colo., where he ran a hotel, I believe.
2. Madam Mustache was a Parisian, and at the time mentioned there were men and women in Cheyenne from every quarter of the globe.
3. When "Bill" was shot he was sitting with his back to a door, something he never would do in Cheyenne; and his assassin came upon him unawares.
4. Mr. Rose is practising law in New York City and represents big Western oil interests. He is hale and hearty and not long ago buried a pal of the early days at Tucson, when there was no one else to buy a coffin.
5. Mr. Van Brunt is one of the largest manufacturers of agricultural implements in the Northwest, at Horicon, Wis., now retired, I believe. He once entered a Comanche Indian camp alone, at night, and recovered a stolen horse. The Comanches were *en route* north to fight the Sioux.
6. "Canada Bill" was a famous three-card-monte man who cut a wide swath when history was making on the U. P. and in Cheyenne, and he is worth a chapter from some one who knew him well.—W. F. H.

A WORD from Edgar Young on his Off-the-Trail story in this issue. Some of us in the office had queried whether a man would really be rash enough to throw away his shoes in such circumstances.

Brooklyn, N. Y.

Perhaps I could state many things that would make the whole story appear more plausible from my own experience in the tropics about people remaining well through visitations of the plagues. I do know of several who went down from this country to Panama in the early days and who never even took one dose of quinine. An old timer, Mr. Wade, the trainmaster at Gatun for the I. C. C., and his wife never were sick from malaria or any other cause. I do know this, for he used to try to argue to me that it was Christian Science that did it, but my opinion is that it's luck as much as anything else. Incidentally, I saw this horrible plague in Guayaquil and was the only passenger who came on the *Quito* when she made her first trip to Balboa. I was hemmed in there and could not leave and saw enough horrors to do me the rest of my life. A close personal friend went insane and wasn't right in his head when I saw him the last time in Panama.

But all these things are, as they say in Spanish, *poco importa*, and the story must tell the thing itself.

ONE thing I stand on: No one in New York can instruct me on going barefooted in the jungle. Ninty-nine out of a hundred wear no shoes in the tropics, their use being confined to generals in the army and people of the higher walks of life. About the first thing that occurs to a man when he gets in mud half-way to his knees is to strip off his shoes. I pulled mine off and lost one after I had tied it on my pack, which rendered the other useless, and my partner and myself actually (not fictitiously, mind you) walked a couple of hundred miles of beach and jungle trail. Ouch! I cringe when I think of it.—Edgar Young.

THE following comrade was one of several who sent in newspaper clippings stating that Captain Clifford W. Sands, another Camp-Fire comrade, received the D. S. C. for saving the lives of three of his men during heavy fighting in the Argonne. You will remember that Sands bore the title of general as a result of Central American activities. In this letter the writer is merely coming forward to do his share in our Camp-Fire talks and to promote the general feeling of friendliness. He also has some interesting things to say about guns, but gun talk belongs more especially in "Ask Adventure."

Seattle, Washington.

I have often thought of doing my bit in the Camp-Fire pages, but nothing very exciting ever seemed to happen to me, except once. A friend and I *did* meet Kid Curry and his gang on the north fork of Grand River about eighty miles north of the Black Hills, South Dakota. It would have been a forced horse-trade as far as we were concerned if our broncks were not as tough looking as theirs.

The day before they had robbed the Belle Fourche Bank, killing the cashier. They loped around that part of the country for quite a while, and next turned up in South America and were cutting up quite a few didos down there.

I worked for Jim Browning on his ranch on the Little Missouri near Camp Crook. A good many old-timers would know him, as in early days himself and partner, a man by the name of Wringrose, ran a general store in Deadwood, S. D. So long.—C. L. Martin.

FOLLOWING Camp-Fire custom, Clay Perry stands up and introduces himself on the occasion of his first story in our magazine:

Pittsfield, Mass.

Well, fellows, this is the way it was: I was born in about the center of the U. S. A. and always wanted to go West and grow up with the country, but, instead, I stuck to the Middle West and grew up anyhow and then came East and lived up in the Berkshires.

Biographically speaking, the story of my life, so far, might be run off into a real moving picture and although I've never been so guilty—or happy—as to draft a scenario, here goes, for the amusement, I hope, of the Camp-Fire Circle:

"FROM THERE TO HERE"

A travelog in five reels

PART ONE

(Flicker, flicker) "The Farmer's First-born"—A potato farm in Badger Township, Waupaca County, Wisconsin. Father, mother, grandpa, horses, cattle, dog, chickens, sand and potatoes.

PART TWO

"*The Lay Preacher's Son*"—City of Waupaca. Sand-paved streets, potato warehouses, Dane's Hall, trolley-line to Old Soldiers' Home where father played bass drum in the band; court-house square with hitching-rails all round it.

PART THREE

"*The Ordained Minister's Son*"—Princeton; Poles and Poverty and a little church (flicker) Eureka (you couldn't find it on the map—you get there by river-steamer or stage-coach from Oshkosh); school and church. (Flicker) Elo (harder to find that Eureka). Mostly country, district school, trains don't stop, throw off mail and grab it on from a mail-crane; more church.

(Flicker) Hortonville-Junction town, county fair, camp-meeting, more church. (Flicker) Oconto Falls, pulp and paper mills, river, logs, timber-jacks, river-rats, Peerless tobacco, log-running, near-drowning, more church (Hero becomes janitor) (Flicker)

Shawano-Menominee Indian reserve, fire-water (genuine brand, made out of drug-store alcohol diluted at the pump by Chief Red Nose and his braves) "Whoeee! Ki, ya, ya!" And more church and Junior League—also love. (Flicker on) Fondulac, more poverty and much more church and Junior and Epworth League, shredded wheat biscuits for breakfast, dinner and supper, camp-meeting, a job on a farm, plenty to eat and less church (Flicker) Oakfield. Back to the country, high school, barley harvest, another sweetheart, a job singing in the choir (more church and prayer-meeting).

(Flicker-flicker) Weyauwega—By the mill-pond where the bull-heads bite; graduation and another love affair ('til death, this time). More church, official position (assistant postmaster twenty-five dollars a month). Traveling for the town promoter who had space to sell in county fair premium books.

(Flicker, flicker, flicker)

PART FOUR

"The College Stude"—Lawrence College, Appleton, coeducational, sectarian (Methodist). Ye Gods, more church and even chapel on week-days. Waiting on sixteen sisters in ladies' dormitory to earn my grub. (Flicker, flicker) The family flits from Weyauwega to Union Grove (I said this was a moving picture) Sugar-beets, cabbages and new-mown hay and cattle and R. L. S. and Ibsen on rainy Sundays (very little church).

(Flicker) Milwaukee, trucking freight, peddling Kickapoo Indian hand-bills, nabbing a job at the Y. M. C. A., to tend a fruit-farm over the Winter where grandma cooks pancakes that stick to your ribs and Our Hero reads his eyes out by kerosene light.

(Flicker) Back to Union Grove in the Spring and set up farm machinery and land a job weighing sugar-beets at Corliss Junction where there's plenty of time to translate the "Iliad" between loads.

(Flicker) to Waldo whence the family hath removed and try to sell contracts to farmers to raise sugar-beets—and translate the "Iliad" anyhow.

(Flicker) to Lawrence in mid-Winter and become a jovial Junior and fall in love with a sweet girl graduate in June.

(Flicker) back to Waldo and sell books on a bicycle. Much money! (Almost three hundred dollars.)

(Flicker) Back to college and sit up nights with the weakly weekly, of which Our Hero has been elected editor, and fall out of love.

(Flicker) On to Menasha and get sick with the wanderlust and (flicker) on to Milwaukee and from Milwaukee to Boston by trolley and (flicker) back to Springfield, Mass., and break into the newspaper game and fall in love again and—

(Flicker) Banished to the Berkshires and can't stand it any longer so (flicker) to Hartford, Conn., with the lady and get married (not in church but by a minister).

PART FIVE

(Flicker) Domesticity in two rooms and a type-writer desk and a chafing-dish.

(Flicker) to three rooms and a gas-stove. "It's a girl."

(Flicker) to four rooms.

(Flicker) to six rooms and a furnace and "It's a boy, this time."

(Flicker) to seven rooms, "Another boy."

(Flicker) to New York to fix the editors. "It's another girl."

(Flicker) Our Hero in desperation buys an eight-room house, hen-coop, dog-yard and typewriter of his own and proceeds to prostrate his genius before magazine editors. *Selah.*—CLAY PERRY.

HERE'S a man who fell out of a ship and scalped himself without any permanent bad effects:

Cranford, New Jersey.

Regarding scalping which is so often discussed. A longshoreman named Oscar ——(?), while opening the port of a ship in the winter of 1915 in New York harbor slipped and fell overboard, striking the port on his way down. Fortunately for him the ice was so jammed between the ship and the float that he lay there until we got him up, when I saw his scalp was hanging over one shoulder. It was as pretty a piece of work as could be done by a surgeon. I examined the skull for a fracture and, finding none, drew back the scalp in place and held it there until proper attention could be given. He returned in about two weeks, none the worse for either the fall, scalping or immersion. One had to look closely to find the scar. He continued working until he hit the trail West, since which time I have not heard of him, but I feel sure that neither the lead from the port or the filthy water of our beautiful Hudson ever affected his health any more than it did the growth of his hair which, I had ample time to observe, was quite normal.—L. J. SCHAEFER.

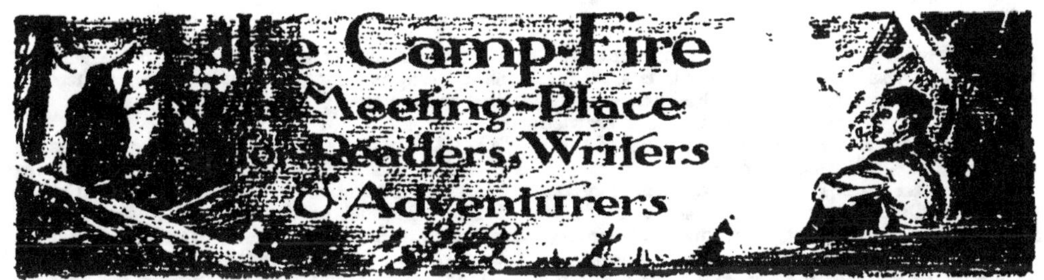

Our Camp-Fire came into being May 5, 1912, with our June issue, and since then its fire has never died down. Many have gathered about it and they are of all classes and degrees, high and low, rich and poor, adventurers and stay-at-homes, and from all parts of the earth. Some whose voices we used to know have taken the Long Trail and are heard no more, but they are still memories among us, and new voices are heard, and welcomed.

We are drawn together by a common liking for the strong, clean things of out-of-doors, for word from the earth's far places, for man in action instead of caged by circumstance. The *spirit* of adventure lives in all men; the rest is chance.

But something besides a common interest holds us together. Somehow a real comradeship has grown up among us. Men can not thus meet and talk together without growing into friendlier relations; many a time does one of us come to the rest for facts and guidance; many a close personal friendship has our Camp-Fire built up between two men who had never met; often has it proved an open sesame between strangers in a far land.

Perhaps our Camp-Fire is even a little more. Perhaps it is a bit of leaven working gently among those of different station toward the fuller and more human understanding and sympathy that will some day bring to man the real democracy and brotherhood he seeks. Few indeed are the agencies that bring together on a friendly footing so many and such great extremes as here. And we are numbered by the hundred thousand now.

If you are come to our Camp-Fire for the first time and find you like the things we like, join us and find yourself very welcome. There is no obligation except ordinary manliness, no forms or ceremonies, no dues, no officers, no anything except men and women gathered for interest and friendliness. Your desire to join makes you a member.

FROM Arthur O. Friel, who has a story in this issue, comes an interesting report on an animal supposed to have survived from the prehistoric past. Have any Camp-Fire members run across anything else in this line?

Brooklyn.

Here's an interesting thing. At least it's interesting to me, and I think it will be to the rest of the Camp-Fire gang.

Some months ago, in connection with my story, "The Snake," I orated regarding the probability of survivals of prehistoric reptiles in the swamps of the Amazon region. In the course of said oration I quoted Charles Johnston Post as relating this narrative by an Indian rubber scout:

"SOMEWHERE about a couple of hundred miles back in the interior from this settlement (Riba Alta, on the River Madeira) he had come across the trail of an animal unfamilar to him. It was a trail like a snake—but not a snake. It was approximately three feet in width, and there were feet-marks on either side of the trail like a turtle's flippers—but only two. About a week later, in the shallow lagoon of one of the great lakes that are known to exist in that part, although no white man has yet penetrated to them, he saw a long neck rise out of the water. And it had a head on it. A snake's neck? he was asked. No, he insisted it was not a snake, he knew snakes. It was a neck with a head on it, something new. Then he fired at it, and it disappeared—and that was all.

"He had described, in the combined circumstances, a possible plesiosaur."

WELL, now comes a clipping from the Boston *Globe*, sent me by an old pal in Massachusetts, which announces the discovery of the plesiosaur's big brother—a brontosaurus—in the Congo. Nope, not fossil remains, but a real live one. Here it is:

"MONSTER OF THE PREHISTORIC AGE FOUND ALIVE IN AFRICA

"A brontosaurus has been found alive in the Congo, according to a news item accredited to M. Capell, a Belgian explorer. Scientists are leaving for Africa from every country to try to find the thought-to-be extinct monster which is now supposed, the last of his race, to be wandering about the land and waterways of the interior of Africa.

"Walter Winans of Baltimore, the explorer, who now is too old for active work, believes the find is true and, if he were younger, he says he would join the hunters who will attempt to capture the creature alive. He says the brontosaurus is a reptile, practically a crocodile, with a snake-like neck. It was practically a crocodile once, he says, and crawled on its belly when on land, although many of them had straight legs and used them.

"The Brontosaurus Excelsus is a member of the dinosaur family and grew, in prehistoric times, to the length of sixty feet. Although apparently stupid it possessed a great deal of cunning and used its long neck to spy above the reeds and ferns upon the approaching enemy. It is supposed to be more or less amphibious in its habits, feeding upon aquatic plants. Its remains have generally been found where the animal had evidently become mired in swamps and on the margins of lakes and rivers. Each track made by the creature in walking occupies one square yard in extent."

ALL of which just goes to show that in the little-known parts of our old earth there may be weird things rambling around even today—things which only the chap who wanders away from the beaten path is ever likely to see.—A. O. F.

THE following letter was dated December 19, 1917. Knowing that an adventurer like the man who wrote that letter, and anything he might have to say to us, would be very warmly welcomed at Camp-Fire, I wrote asking for permission to pass his letter on to you and saying how glad we'd be to hear from him further. But there was no reply, perhaps because the only address given was the name of a city in Texas. Quite likely when he wrote he meant the letter for Camp-Fire, but, having no definite assurance on this point, I did not print it. But it's too good to lose and I venture to use it now, without giving the writer's name.

The letter he refers to was, you may remember, one objecting to our publishing stories by Hapsburg Liebe because the name was, or sounded, German. You may remember, too, that, Mr. Liebe's Americanism—of birth and ancestry as well as of spirit—was very thoroughly established, though our magazine would not have discriminated against any German-named or German-born loyal American. I couldn't myself very well, having a German name of my own, though it's several centuries away from Germany.

Just finished reading "The Cross at Purgatory Fork," by Liebe. Some time ago you had a communication from some kind of a cuss, who evidently thinks he is an American, asking you to discontinue Mr. Liebe's stories. Had you done so I and lots of others would have quit reading *Adventure* instantly, but of course you did not. Even had Mr. Liebe been born in Germany and was at present a loyal American he would be, in my estimation at least, entitled to as much consideration, at least, as we who have been here since this country was first settled.

WHO am I to express an opinion on a subject like this? Only a descendant of Ezekiel Hopkins who came over in the Mayflower and was the first commander of the American Navy (see U. S. History). Also of Stephen Hopkins, a signer of the Declaration of Independence, from Rhode Island. Am a civil engineer and just got back from South America, where I have been for twelve years. Helped survey the "Big Ditch," am a Civil War veteran (C. S. A. with Quantrell), and a Captain of Cuban Cavalry, during and before the Spanish American War. Will be 70 years old the 8th of March. Enlisted with Quantrell on my 15th birthday (March 8, 1863), served under Maximilian in Mexico as lieutenant of cavalry till he was killed in '67. Took up civil engineering and have been pretty much of a rover ever since. Am surveying auto roads at present in Louisiana and Texas. Put in some time as a scout in the U. S. A. in the '70s and again in '85 marched overland with the 5th Cavalry from Fort Fetterman, Wyo., to Fort Reno, Ind. Ter. Knew Frank Gruard, "Capt. Jack" Crawford and Ben Clark well and some time in the future may have something to say about them, and others of the old West.— —— ——.

OUR old friend the Gila monster is led forward again, because the following letter is from an authoritative source and because it contains a general appeal for accurate field study of wild life in America. As you know, the Vorhies and Ditmars authorities referred to below are among those already heard at Camp-Fire.

American Museum of Natural History
Seventy-seventh Street and Central
Park West, New York.

Your letter requesting information in regard to the Gila Monster has been referred to me. In view of the large amount of valuable literature concerning the Gila Monster we can safely make definite statements about its bite. I will try to answer briefly your several questions:

1. *Coloration.* There are two species of Gila Monster which differ from each other considerably in color. *Heloderma suspectum* of southern Arizona and New Mexico has the head and body marbled with black and a pale tone which may be salmon, pink, white or pale yellow. *Heloderma horridum* of Mexico has the upper and lower surfaces black or dark brown with scattered spots of bright yellow.

2. *Poison.* You were correct in assuming that the breath of the Gila Monster is harmless while the bite is poisonous. The bite, however, is only mildly poisonous. Loeb, Van Denburgh and other writers (see below) deny the existence of a single authoritative record of the death of a man due to the bite of the Gila Monster. Still a recent statement has come to my attention of a showman in very poor health who died as the direct result of the bite of a Gila Monster. This record comes from very good sources.

3. *Fights with other reptiles.* The Gila Monster has been found to be very pugnacious in captivity.

There is at least one record of its having killed a non-poisonous snake. Data on the habits of the Gila Monster *in the field* are much to be desired.

4. *Remedy for the bite.* The poison of the Gila Monster is never injected deep into the flesh. The poison glands although homologous to those of the rattlesnake appear as true salivary glands on the floor of the mouth, while the teeth are not specialized for injecting the poison. If care is exercised in removing the animal so that the wound is not a jagged one, and if the wound is then carefully washed first with water and later with a saturated solution of permanganate of potash, no serious results should follow.

More detailed information in regard to the Gila Monster may be obtained from the following publications.

Vorhies, C. T.—1917—Poisonous Animals of the Desert. University of Arizona, Agricultural Exper. Station, Bulletin No. 83, p. 366.

Loeb, Leo, and others—1913—The Venom of Heloderma, Publ. Carnegie Inst., Washington, No. 177.

Van Denburgh, J. & Wight, O. B.—1900—On the Physiological Action of the Poisonous Secretion of the Gila Monster (Heloderma suspectum). Amer. Journ. Phys. Vol. 4, No. 5, pp. 209-238.

Ditmars, R. L.—1907—The Reptile Book, New York, pp. 169-177.

I am sure that not only the authorities of this Museum but science in general would appreciate any effort you could make to instill into your readers accurate observation of wild life in the field. The English have for many years distinguished themselves by their *intelligent* explorations. The British do not guess at the names of the animals they observe; they send specimens for identification to their British Museum. Why should not the Americans have the same loyalty toward, and secure the same benefits from, the American Museum that the British do from the British Museum?—G. K. Noble, Assistant in Herpetology.

IF AMONG us is Billy Law, New Zealander, here is a friend inquiring for him, a Britisher who is strong for our West:

Yokohama, Japan.

I am rather cocksure that any attempt to apologise for trying to creep alongside your Cheerful Blaze will be disqualified. Here, I must confess, that I've only just hit on the trail of your magazine.

My experiences out West, from California to Alaska, are typical of many of your Camp-Fire correspondents especially those of Mr. E. S. Pladwell—more so as regards his mining stunts.

Leaving dear old England at the age of 19, a very raw Britisher with qualifications as an assayer, I failed to make good as far as the financial aspect is concerned, but I have a lot to thank the wide-open glorious West for—a most liberal and practical education of life. One soon finds his level there.

MY MANY little adventures include a cheap but cold ride on the ore-cars from Rossland to Northport soon after Christmas of 1901. You couldn't buy a job on Red Mountain that Winter. Fell dead off to sleep in the Owl Saloon at N'port while my partner, the more enterprising half of the firm, indulged in a clean little game of poker. I take my hat off to Pearce, the proprietor. He was a real good sport. After a few shifts in the smelter we freighted most of the way to Spokane. Side-tracked twice, even after paying the brakey a couple of dollars. Cold! Oh my! I can hear my teeth chattering even now. Wintered in Spokane. Quite a good burg, by the way, for free-lunches. Failing an attempt on Denver, we freighted for the Coast and, judging from others, including professionals, we seem to have been exceedingly lucky on this ride particulary in getting through the Cascade Tunnel without any serious set-backs or, rather, throw-outs. Somewhere near Snohomish, in company with three others, we made our first attempt on the blind baggage. My! It was some going, but alas! for twelve miles only. Through a mistake of one of the crowd we landed on the depot side and face to face with the train boss. Tableau!

The excitement of this particular trail practically ended at the Everett Smelter (P. S. R. Co's) Arsenic Plant then in charge of one Little Billy, a big burnt Cousin Jack. It is almost quite superflous to mention that we were broke.

"Don't 'e sweat, boys." This to my pard and self. Just fancy a boss deigning to extend such instructions. Well, we soon discovered that he had indeed whispered words of real wisdom. Six days at the flues, shifting crude arsenic, including one lay-off, and then, *quantum sufficit.* I may as well emphasize that on starting we were in tip-top condition *re* health.

Pay: two dollars and seventy-five per shift of nine hours, though I believe my memory errs on the generous side. There was a bait offered of an extra two bits on lasting a couple of weeks or over, but I would much like to hear of the guy who accomplished this record. Really, one can hardly term this a sporting offer of the management.

APART from my profession, other side issues were: mucking (quite an art if done properly), hammer and drill, chuck tending, topman, assistant engineer and fireman, blacksmith's helper, prospecting, with a slight change as cook on a tug, and deckhand.

Six years of real solid apprenticeship to Life, and even if it were really possible, I would not part with these experiences for pounds sterling, gold dollars or pieces of eight.

DIGRESSING somewhat: I am thoroughly in accordance with Mr. W. H. Bambury. Caste, cliques and snobbery seem to be an everlasting curse of the Britisher, and here in Yokohama we have it typically exemplified. Rope 'em at about the age of twenty and turn 'em loose out West with no remittance seems to me a good cure, at least, it took it all out of your humble, though he never lost his self respect oı pride in the land of his birth and could generally put up a fair average scrap when required.

I wonder if any of your readers were ever located on Texada Island, B. C.? I was there on and off from 1900 to 1904 with a farewell visit in July, '06. Implanted in my memory is that picturesque little limestone cove in Marble Bay, the magnificent view of the mainland from our shack and the Clark-Russell sunsets. A most charming spot for work and play.

From out of the Copper Queen, Cornell and Marble Bay properties came some very pretty specimens of bornite and peacock copper ore. From a freak sample of matte from the one-horse smelter at Van Anda, in the form of a metalic moss, I obtained two guineas (ten dollars) from the British Museum.

Gifted literary one could have written quite a readable volume on the humor and pathos of this little community alone, and all through the West it would seem to be the same interesting and absorbing atmosphere.—ALFRED H. CLARKE.

P. S. I would welcome any news of Billy Law, a cheery New Zealander, one time foreman at Van Anda, T. I.

A CALL for inside dope on Pondoland from a New England comrade:

Hartford, Connecticut.

The Camp-Fire seems to be a great place for clearing up mysterious and peculiar things, so I am hereby taking the liberty of presenting something to the members, in the hope that some information may be gleaned from a discussion of the subject around the Camp-Fire.

Where is Pondoland? Is it "closed," if so, why? What is there, if it exists? Please note the above word "closed."

I HAVE a friend, an Englishman, one of the confoundedly tight-mouthed kind, who is a veteran of the Boer war. One day in a fit of talkativeness he told me of Pondoland. The tale he told me was bald enough, but from what I could gather this land is very rich in minerals, precious stones, etc.

To use his own words, "I saw with my own eyes enough copper ore to make the Guggenheims look poor if it were developed."

It seems at the close of the war he and another trooper endeavored to enter Pondoland. They succeeded and gained valuable information. Later they tried to enter again, but were prevented by the British authorities. A third time they tried with the same result. The fourth attempt failed and they were told they would be shot on sight if they tried again.

My friend became discouraged and came to America, but his friend tried to enter a fifth time and was killed in a running fight with the constabulary.

Here the tale ends, but what is the reason for this section of Africa being closed?—JOHN L. WHITE.

THE Custer Massacre mystery—a statement that seems solid and to the point. Usually it is not easy to point definitely to the deaths and destruction caused by graft or by neglect or betrayal of the trust of a public office. Here the trail is clear and straight and blood-red, as the following letter from our comrade of the writers' brigade, Arthur D. Howden Smith, sets it forth.

We are too used to graft and to public officers who are traitors to their trust to be much impressed or to see clearly the terrible costs to us as a people. Also, as a people, we've never been definitely taught why graft and betrayal of public trusts are treason and more blackly criminal than crimes against an individual. Never having been taught the real meaning of individual citizenship in a democracy, we are unable to see what graft and neglect or betrayal of public office really are.

WE SHOULD have been having these things taught to us from six years of age on up. Just as we have been taught that it is wrong to rob or betray an individual. It would not have made us perfect citizens, any more than the teaching we've had makes us perfect individuals, but the first is as worth doing as the second. At the least it would have restrained the very large portion of us who would not rob an individual but who consider robbery or misuse of public funds merely a natural perquisite of public office—who betray a public trust often without even realizing they are betraying anything or anybody, yet who are trustworthy in dealing with individuals.

And what are we going to do from now on? Just continue letting American children grow up without any real understanding of their individual, personal obligation and responsibility as citizens of the American democracy? Change to some other form of government and find that it, too, is made ineffective in its attempt at practical democracy because it is built out of the same ignorant and crooked-viewed citizens? Or shall we make our present form of government what it should and can be made by building it out of citizens who *are* citizens?

THE people must control. But the people must be *fit* to control. Democracy is neither a form nor a practise of government. It is a state of mind, an attitude and practise of a people, principles and the daily application of those principles. Democracy is in the minds of the people. It can not be suddenly created by any change in form of government nor by anything else. Democracy is a growth. The only way to hasten that growth is by education. The only kind of education equal to the task is *systematic, organized, definitely directed* education. The only way to establish that kind of education is to establish it. Why don't you get on the job? Waiting for some one else to do it? Aren't you as much an American citizen as any one else is? Are you just a parasite?

Democracy and citizenship should be regularly taught in every school in the land. The first thing a democracy should teach is democracy. Our democracy teaches everything else.

BEFORE we come to Mr. Smith's letter I want to say that I do not like to publish any instance of bad faith by our Government, which means by the American people. We do not stand for the scrap of paper idea and we are ashamed when we find that our representatives have ever committed us to it. But that shame is good for us. We'll be less likely to permit such a thing again if we have already blushed under that dishonor. I do not like to publish the instance below, nor to admit that it is not the only similar case in our dealings with the Indians, but I should like still less not to publish it.

Washington, D. C.

I don't often intrude myself into the Camp-Fire—in fact, I don't think I ever did it before—but in the Dec. 3rd issue of *Adventure*, just out, I notice another addition to the mass of misinformation about the Custer Massacre. The writer, I believe, was a Dr. Arnold, who states that he was a member of the Seventh Infantry, which, with the Seventh Cavalry, Custer's regiment, was included in Terry's column designated for operations against the Sioux and allied Cheyenne hostiles in the Little Big Horn country. Now, as you probably know, I am not a Westerner and was not even born at the time of Custer's last fight. But I do like to study history, and the story of the battle on the Little Big Horn is one of the most dramatic in our frontier history. Also, it is one of the most ill-used, in that gradually as time has passed a mist of mistaken or false or partly erroneous accounts of it have been circulated.

LIKE most historical controversies it is rather a simple matter when you strip it to the bare bones of fact. To begin with, the known facts establish quite conclusively that neither Custer, Reno nor Benteen was at fault or was guilty of disobedience of orders. The attacks upon Custer's memory sprang out of the controversy in which he had become involved with President Grant. It does not reflect credit upon Grant's fairness or political astuteness. Briefly, Custer had found that horse-feed was being issued to his regiment which had been sent West by the Indian Bureau for use on the reservations, but had been sold on the side by the so-called "Indian Ring" to Army contractors, as graft. He called the attention of the War Department to this; the Democratic opposition in Congress seized upon the incident to attack the Interior Department which was headed by a protégé of Grant's; and almost before poor Custer knew it he had become involved in a very mucky political row.

Grant took Custer's action as a personal affront and for a time refused to permit Custer to join his regiment, then under orders to operate against the Sioux. He relented, under pressure, but retaliated by replacing Custer in command of the Little Big Horn column with Terry. Custer felt hurt by Grant's conduct, but he was not the sort of man to risk his regiment or his reputation in a rash action. His whole record as a cavalry commander proves him to have been not only dashing but exceptionally sagacious. The truth was that Custer—and with him that wily veteran, Crook, and Terry, Custer's immediate superior—was misinformed by the Indian Bureau as to the number of hostiles in the field.

WHEN the unrest of the Sioux—a justly founded unrest, too—was stirred by the incroachments of white prospectors in the Black Hills country of the Dakotas, which had been set aside by the United States as a part of their reservation, the Indian Bureau appealed for troops to round up the bands which had begun straying from the reservations with the coming of the Spring of 1876. In reply to inquiry from the military authorities, the Indian Bureau reported that there was a total of 3,000 Indians off the reservations. This, according to the usual computations, meant from 600 to 800 braves. The military expeditions set on foot to round up these bands were formed and given instructions to operate in accordance with the supposition that the forces opposed would be as reported by the Indian Bureau. Actually, there were intended for the field some three or four times as many soldiers as Sioux warriors, if the Indian Bureau's figures were correct.

But—and this is all-important in judging Custer—after the Little Big Horn disaster, the first move of the military was to insist upon the taking of a careful census on the reservations affected. It was found that at the Red Cloud agency, instead of 12,873 Indians there were 4,760; at Spotted Tail, instead of 9,610 there were 3,315; at Cheyenne River, instead of 7,586 there were 2,2800; at Standing Rock instead of 7,322 there were 2,305. There were 25,800 Indians off the reservations, which the Indian Bureau had never counted, a total force of about 30,000, allowing for hostiles from other agencies and tribes. There were at least 5,000 braves in the field. It was figured afterward that there were not less than 3,000 picked warriors with Sitting Bull at the Little Big Horn. Some Indians and white men think this is an under-estimate.

TERRY sent Custer up the Rosebud, with very loosely-defined orders. The general plan of campaign was for Custer to get above the encampment the Indians were supposed to have on the Little Big Horn, while Terry, with the slower-moving infantry, came at them from below. But if Custer saw a good opportunity to strike he was not to wait for Terry. Neither Custer nor Terry dreamed there were enough Indians in the field to bother the Seventh cavalry, whose twelve troops were probably nearly 700 strong. The main thing was to cripple the hostiles before they had a chance to get started, kill as many braves as possssible and run off their stock and burn their stores and teepees.

Custer started on the afternoon of June 22 and marched twelve miles up the Rosebud. The next day he advanced 33 miles, incidentally striking a lodge-pole trail which Major Reno of the Seventh had scouted several weeks before. On the 24th Custer followed this trail 28 miles further, camping at 9:30 o'clock that night. A council of war was held and, after canvassing the situation, Custer decided to strike off from the Rosebud across the divide into the valley of the Little Big Horn, where it was now apparent, the trail led. At 11 o'clock the Seventh took up the march. There was a halt at two o'clock in the morning of the 25th for daylight which came about five o'clock. Then the advance was resumed. The first hostiles were seen about eight o'clock.

CUSTER'S plan of operations was to take five troops, himself, down the valley of the Little Big Horn. Captain Benteen, with three troops, was to move forward to certain bluffs, from which it was supposed he would be able to charge into the Indian village on Custer's left. Major Reno, with three troops, was to cross the river and move up the other side so as to take the hostiles in rear. Captain Macdougal with his troop, was detailed to guard the pack-train. This was a perfectly sound plan and would have worked—had there been less than a thousand braves to fight, or perhaps even if there had been less than 2,000.

AFTER leaving Reno, Custer disappeared. Only two of his men came back. One was Trumpeter Martin who was sent back to Benteen with a message for him to join Custer as soon as Custer gained some idea of the odds against him—although even then he had no idea that he had practically the entire fighting strength of the Sioux in opposition. The other was Curley, the Crow scout, who escaped in the mêlée by letting down his hair in Sioux fashion and donning a Sioux blanket. What happened to Custer was pieced out afterward from the corpses of his men and from the accounts given by Indians who participated in the fight.

IT SHOULD be said, in the first place, that Benteen was obliged to abandon the route laid out for him, after a good deal of time had been wasted in a detour. When he got back to the valley of the Little Big Horn Reno was in trouble, and it was only by joining forces with each other and picking up the pack-train and escort that they were able to stand off the hordes that rode around them. Custer was already dead, but of this neither Reno nor any of the officers knew. In fact, they took it for granted that Custer had ridden clear. They simply hung on until the morning of the 27th, when Terry's column came up and relieved them. They suffered very heavily.

THIS was what happened to Custer: he advanced something more than three miles down the river, keeping behind the crests of the bluffs as much as possible out of sight of the Indians down in the valley. Then he swung in towards the river. Evidently, this was when he gained his first real grasp of the size of the village. Already he was under fire and his men were falling. Indians were pouring down through all the ravines and gulleys. But he turned, his column still in good order, and retreated inland about three-quarters of a mile. Here Calhoun's troop were detailed as rear-guard to stand off the pursuit. They were found in a regular skirmish line, body next to body, carbines cuddled to cheek, where they had died, fighting to the last.

About a mile farther back the pursuit became so bitter that the remaining four troops dismounted and formed line, Yates's troop in the center on a small ridge; Keogh's on the left; Smith's on the right of Yates's and Tom Custer's in the right center, where it was probably intended to serve as a reserve and horse-guard. Custer's men, for the most part, died in this position, in regular ranks, and Custer, standing on the ridge with Yates, was among the first to fall.

SITTING BULL, fighting with splendid strategy, launched a mass of braves against Keogh, smashed him, flanked the left of the line and drove off the spare mounts of all except a few of Tom Custer's and Smith's troops. The soldiers' horses gone, the rest was simple for the Indians. They simply rode over the Seventh, their total losses, according to their own figures—which included the attack on Reno and Benteen—about thirty-five men. Those of Tom Custer's and Smith's troops who got away with their horses retreated toward the river bank, but Sitting Bull threw a screen of warriors behind them and, hemmed in, they died in a dwindling circle—probably the origin of the myth that Custer and the whole five troops fought in a ring. There was no time to form a ring, no dominant position they could have seized upon.

THIS is a very sketchy account of the battle of the Little Big Horn. Custer's friends very foolishly attacked Reno for not coming to Custer's rescue. Reno had no reason to suppose that Custer had gotten into trouble. Also it would have been suicide for him to have attacked the 900 warriors who were attacking him while some 2,000 or more were wiping out Custer's detachment. And as has been said, Reno took it for granted, from the very number of Indians who were occupied with him, that he was bearing the brunt of the action and that Custer either had retired or had been driven off. It was not until after Terry had come up and the scouts were sent out on the morning of the 27th that the bodies of Custer and his men were found.

Likewise partisans of Reno made the mistake of retaliating upon Custer's memory. Grant did not hold them back. The real fault lay upon the shoulders of the corrupt gang of men who were grafting on the Indians, betraying the trust the Government had reposed in them, robbing the people of the United States as well as their Indian wards and too busy with their sordid, contemptible pursuit of pelf to keep track of the Indians they were supposed to look out for.

Incidentally, and by way of final word, it is sad but true that Custer and all his men died in a rotten cause, a cause which was nothing less than carrying out by main force the determination of the United States to compel the Sioux to accept the repudiation of our treaty promises to them. Talk of scraps of paper: The history of our intercourse with the Indians is full of them.—ARTHUR D. HOWDEN SMITH.

P. S. There probably was not a saber in

Custer's command. Mrs. Custer says he never used one on the plains. Our cavalry used the six-shooter by preference—it was six times as effective.

HOOP-SNAKES and joint-snakes. The former I confess I'd always thought were purely imaginary, used for "stringing" the credulous, but certainly I don't *know* that there is no such animal. Nor do I know anything about joint-snakes. And now one of us, whom I believe sincere and whose word I would not question, testifies to both of them. Any others who can bear witness?

Graniteville, South Carolina.

Some moths ago some one rose on his hind legs and through the Camp-Fire gave vent to some expressions on the Gila Monster. I am not acquainted with the critter in question, and am not anxious to be. Will leave a discussion of *their* merits and demerits to those who are acquainted with *them* and *their* peculiarities. However, he did not stop there but villainously slandered two of our Southern pets by declaring that the joint-snake and hoop-snake do not exist.

NOW I was raised, as most Southern boys were, with negroes for some of my playmates. In that way I imbibed a good bit of their superstitions, and many a night went to bed frightened by the tales of "hants" and dreamed all sorts of horrible things. But among the tales they told were tales of joint and hoop-snakes. As I grew older many of these tales faded from my mind; others I dismissed as being improbable, among these the snake takes. Yet today I consider these tales true.

I have never seen a hoop-snake, but I have it upon reliable authority that they do exist. I have it from men who have seen them and killed them. It seems to be a rare variety. From what I can learn it has a projection on its head, which is uses to strike with; it seems to be somewhat of a thorn shape, broad and heavy across the base and tapering to a curved point and is very deadly. It takes its tail in its mouth, or wraps it around its head and rolls like a hoop over the ground and at a very rapid rate. I knew of one case when a boy chased by one of these snakes ran behind a tree, and the snake hit the tree and drove its horn in it. The snake was killed and a few days later the tree began to die. I had this from several parties, and all of unimpeachable veracity. I have also heard of it from others.

AS TO the joint-snakes, I know they exist having seen and helped kill two of them. Both that I saw were small, about three feet long, and green striped. I saw one hit with a tiny switch, and it flew into eight pieces. We kept quite and the pieces began to hop about and, being boys, not scientists we could not stand it. We buried the head and threw the tail in the creek.

The other was a somewhat similar occurrence. This time one of the boys picked up a piece of the snake and you could snap it, just as though it was a piece of brittle wood. It seemed to be nothing but joints, each fitting so far into the other joint. It did not make a smooth break, the part next the head having a rounded hollow in it, and the other part being a rounded projection. After breaking the two parts, they were stuck back together and seemed as though the snake was one piece. We killed this one in the same manner.

AS TO large snakes, I will believe most anything I hear. Have seen snakes here, two or three of them at least fifteen feet long. So why should they not grow to an extreme size in tropical countries? However, I don't like them. The only time I ever get close to a snake is when I do not know it. For instance, I killed a copper-headed moccasin that had crawled in bed with me *one time* while out in the country. I was waked by it crawling over my body, put my hand on its head before I knew it. Killed it because I was so scared I did not know what else to do. It threw it out of the window and the next day the people with whom I was stopping told me what kind it was and what a narrow escape I had.—JES L. QUIMBY, JR.

WHO can help this comrade to mummify the snakes that bit him? He's perfectly right in taking a sort of special interest in them.

E. Mauch Chunk, Pa.

Some time ago, while I was rambling around, I had some narrow escapes from death due to snake-bite. Being a greenhorn in a strange land and sort of bewildered, that is how they come to get ahead of me. Twice I was bit by rattlers, but on both occasions I captured the snake alive and only saved my life by slitting the arm and leg. Now the information I'm after is: Can you direct me to either a member of the Camp-Fire (or non-member) who can petrify those rattlers for me? After the experience I had with them it would be an unforgivable sin to skin them and throw the insides away. I want them as well as the outside. —JOSEPH F. PAYOR, 320 South St.

ORIGINALLY "L'Atlantide" was scheduled as a complete novel for this issue. After it was all set in type and made up in pages outside complications arose and, to accommodate its future book publisher and the literary agent through whom it had been purchased, we made it a two-part story. It was a most unusual case and involved a lot of rearranging but I'll spare you the details.

The main point is that it made us give you a story in two parts that we thought you'd enjoy more if read all at one sitting. Also it cost a very appreciable amount in money, time and delay. Legally we were entitled to publish it as planned, but it would have worked hardship—or what they feared would be a hardship—on others and we felt that if you were here to decide you'd be as willing to make a bit of a sacrifice as we were.—A. S. H.

The CAMP-FIRE

A MEETING-PLACE for READERS, WRITERS and ADVENTURERS

HERE is a letter Theo. S. Solomons wrote to me when he sent us his story appearing in this issue:

Berkeley, California.

May 21st, 1919, you wrote: "Once you wrote me about stories that gave real life instead of sacrificing it to the conventions of fiction. We're planning later on to do a stunt that would open up a chance right away for just this kind of story—the kind that is pretty sure to be refused by all magazines at present."

I AM slow but sure. I have selected the backbone of a story I once wrote, or thrice wrote, rather, and I guess I could have written it thrice times thrice without ever getting it published. You—to quote just one editor—said: "splendid material, but—it isn't organized right." No wonder. I took this "real life" rescue from the rotting glairice of a Klondike lake and dressed it up in a darn fool plot—just lugged or "drug" the plot in and threw it on top of the incident. I thought this would be a good thing for a first experiment in real life adventure—the kind I can't write diatribes against and anent and inflict them on you! Hey, what?

Now this is garnished just a little. It is from 95 to 98 per cent. FACT. I saw what I say I saw—minus the embellishment. That's neither here nor there however, for I haven't that invidious species of personal integrity that would stay my hand from *making up* real (!) stuff like this. My seven-year-old does it, so whine ell shouldn't I? This story is long for the matter in it. But that's part of the experiment, which—this time—is in the way of a very detailed picture to enhance life-likeness, graphicness, movingness.—THEO. S. SOLOMONS.

Our New Type

THIS number is thinner and has fewer pages than previous numbers. The paper shortage does it. But please note very carefully that *there is just as much in it as before*. The new type does it. If you understand just what we and all other magazines are up against I think you'll say that we've done the best that could be done for you our readers. For we're giving you just as much as you got before and we're doing it simply by changing to another type, a standard-sized type, exactly the same size *Everybody's* has used for years. And if you'll look back over magazines in general you'll find that a large number of the best ones have been using this size right along. So we're not "handing" you anything in making the change.

Our old type was a ten-point, the new is nine-point. (The smaller type used in Camp-Fire is eight-point; that on the Service Page and in the standing matter at the head of "Ask Adventure" is six-point.) But that small change from ten to nine enables us to save one-sixth of the amount of paper used and, believe me, that means a tremendous lot these days when paper is not only very high but hard to get at any price. And yet, if you will count or estimate the exact number of words of fiction in this issue and compare it with the number in previous issues, you will find that it is practically the same.

WITH ten-point type and 192 pages we averaged about 127,000 words of fiction per issue; with the new nine-point type and 160 pages I think you'll find, allowing for the varying size of "Camp-Fire," that you're getting just as many words of fiction as before. I'm writing this before the stories for this issue have all come down from the printer in type and I can't be any more exact than above until we have that definite testimony in hand, but the printers and we have been doing some close estimating, the change wasn't decided upon until we were convinced it could be made without cutting down the amount of your reading-matter and, so far as we can tell, you're just as likely to get a bit more as a bit less.

THIS paper shortage is real. Some one may be holding up a supply somewhere but that doesn't help *us* any, and the main cause seems to be that from 1917 on there hasn't been enough timber cut or enough mills operated. War, transportation, labor troubles, all these have been factors. If you have any doubts of the shortage, watch all the other magazines and note that, in one way or another, most or all of them are suffering as we are. Indeed, we are comparatively in good shape.

I'm not going to whine about our troubles, but I want you to understand them. If you do, you'll know that we are doing the best we can by you. I've already told you about our difficulties from transportation conditions. So far there is little improvement. And it makes us particularly sore that we can't get our magazines distributed on time, regularly, to all points and in sufficient quantity, for never before has the demand been so strong. That is pretty well proved by the fact that, in spite of everything, our magazine's circulation is going up steadily and has already reached a point far higher than ever before. If we can get anything like normal outside conditions, it looks as if we'd probably perform the little stunt of doubling our circulation in the present period of twelve months.

Meanwhile, well, like all other magazines, we're having our troubles. It's costing us work, worry, money and loss of entirely possible circulation. But, as instanced by this type change, we're trying to handle things so that our readers will keep on getting all we can give them.

SOME information and a query from Farnham Bishop in connection with his story in this issue:

Berkeley, California.

The double-barrelled cannon and its crazy projectile are no products of the imagination. Mr. Francis Bannerman has the gun in his store at 501 Broadway, New York. Only it is iron, not bronze, and was designed by a Southerner during the Civil War. It was tried out in the presence of the local Home Guard and the beauty and chivalry of the town. The missile behaved as in the story—danced all over the place, chased everybody off the premises and finally wound itself around a tree. I read about it years ago in some newspaper, saw a half-tone of the gun in Mr. Bannerman's catalogue, and thought it was a sad pity it was never used in action. I moved the scene to Mexico because our Yank and Reb grandfathers didn't stampede easily, and there was mighty little comedy about their battles.

Perhaps some Southern reader of the Camp-Fire could oblige with the name of the inventor of the double-barrelled gun and of the place where it fired its first and last shot.—FARNHAM BISHOP.

ANOTHER comrade, whom some of us have seen with Buffalo Bill's Wild West back in 1883-4 or later with Fore augh's Circus and Wild West or other companies, stepping out in defense of Wild Bill Hicock as marshal, scout and Indian-fighter, gives interesting details concerning his death and the fate of his killer:

New York City.

I saw a letter to the Camp-Fire signed by a man writing under the name of "Deuce." From the tone of his letter he doesn't have much use for Wild Bill. In fact, in some of his statements he is away off. He claims that Wild Bill was never a scout or Indian-fighter. I would advise "Deuce" to read the book, "Boots and Saddles," in which General George Custer states that Wild Bill was one of his best and most reliable scouts. If Wild Bill was with Custer during the Indian wars of Western Kansas he could not be hanging around Springfield, Mo., at that time drinking whisky.

HE ALSO goes on to say that Wild Bill never made good as a marshal of any of the towns. How is it that, when Wild Bill cleaned up a town of all the bad men, other towns would send for him to come and clean up their towns? If such was the case I can't see where "Deuce" gets to think of Wild Bill being a four-flusher, as in that time towns in that part of the country would not have a man as marshal unless he would make good.

HE ALSO states that Wild Bill killed a cowboy by the name of McCall, a brother of Jack McCall that afterward killed Wild Bill. I will say from well-known facts that Jack McCall had no brother.

In the Spring of 1876 Charlie Utter (Colorado Charlie) was fitting out his outfit in Cheyenne, Wyo., to go to the Black Hills with freight. Wild Bill was in town, and Charlie Utter asked him to take the trip with him. About this time a noted character drifted into Cheyenne. A woman known by the name of Calamity Jane. A woman well known to be without fear of any kind. Hearing Colorado Charlie was going to Deadwood, made arrangements to go along. Jack McCall was one of the drivers in the outfit.

AFTER the outfit arrived in Deadwood, McCall lost all of his money gambling, and he would go to Wild Bill for money. Of course McCall could go to camp to eat and sleep, but at that Wild Bill would lend him a little spending money now and then. It was then rumored around Deadwood that the law-abiding people were going to make Wild Bill marshal. This so worked up the thieves and crooked gamblers that they set out to find a man to do away with Wild Bill, as they knew if ever he became marshal that he would run the thieves out of town and make the crooked gamblers half-way behave themselves. The only man they could find to do the job was this same Jack McCall. As Wild Bill knew him, he would have the best chance.

ONE day, while Wild Bill was sitting in a card-game, McCall came in and stepped behind Wild Bill. Wild Bill looked at him as he did so, saw who it was, and went on playing. McCall waited for about a minute, pulled his gun and shot Wild Bill through the back of the head, the ball going through his head and coming out of the face, hitting the table and breaking a mirror in back of the bar. Wild Bill's head fell forward, and before his head hit the table, he had dropped his cards, threw both of his hands on to his six-shooters and had them half-way out of the holster. McCall turned his gun on to the crowd and backed to the door and then made a run for a horse that stood saddled at the back. In his hurry to mount, the saddle turned and he fell to the ground. Before he could get up the crowd caught him.

As there was no court of justice in Deadwood, he was given what was called a Miner Trial, and during the trial McCall stated that Wild Bill had killed his brother at Hays City, Kansas, and that that was the first chance he had of getting even with him. As the miners take for their text, "An eye for an eye, a tooth for a tooth," that cleared him. McCall was given five hours to leave town. He walked outside the court and on the street there stood a horse all saddled and bridled. On the saddle was hanging a six-shooter, a belt of cartridges and a Winchester rifle. He mounted and waved his hand to the crowd and hit the trail toward Custer City.

AT THIS time Colorado Charlie was up at Gayville, looking after some business, so he did not hear of the killing of Wild Bill for some hours after the trial. When he did he dropped all business and took up the trail of McCall. McCall never stopped until he reached Custer City. In the first saloon he went into for a drink he started to boast that he had killed Wild Bill the day before in Deadwood. The marshal of Custer City at that time was an old friend of Wild Bill's, from Hays City, Kansas, and he placed him under arrest. A little over an hour later Colorado Charlie came in and offered to guarantee to the marshal that five minutes after McCall was loose he would never bother anybody else. McCall was afterward taken to Yankton, there given a fair trial, and hung for the killing of Wild Bill.

Now if "Deuce" wants to take the trouble to look up the records of that trial, he will see that one of the sisters of McCall while on the stand testified that she had no other brother but the prisoner, and that knocked the Deadwood evidence out.

"DEUCE" also stated that Wild Bill aped the manners of Buffalo Bill. You must stop and think that, as Wild Bill was almost ten years older than Buffalo Bill, Buffalo Bill could only have been a boy at that time. So I do not think there could have been much apeing done.

After the killing of Wild Bill, Calamity Jane got drunk, rode up and down the streets of Deadwood, dressed in buckskin, telling the people that had anything to do with the killing of Wild Bill what she thought of them, also California Joe when he got back from Mead City, where he had been after some Indians that had stolen some stock.—"SETH" HATHAWAY.

THE Incas. Edgar Young advances an interesting theory, giving considerable information along the way. I wonder how much we "civilized" Americans could learn and profit from the old Incas' system of government. Note, too, the similarity to the system of Tens (and higher decimal units) advanced in "Looking Ahead for Democracy" some time ago. Until I read Mr. Young's letter, however, I had not heard of the Inca system, being only faintly familiar with the Inca civilization.

Brooklyn, N. Y.

Walter Johnson tells me that some one wrote in and tried to make it appear that he and I did not know what we were talking of when we mentioned Incas. This got away from me while I was working for the War Department. I never saw it.

IF ANY one should bob up with an idea like that, turn him loose on me. I am quite familiar with the *accepted* version of Inca history and government from Manco Capac and Mama Ocllo, first Inca and his sister-wife, who appeared mysteriously upon the shores of Lake Titicaca, down to and through the conquest. I say *accepted* version because a man with half an eye can see that the accounts given by the conquerors themselves are tissues of lies inspired both by the Church and the Spanish Government. We are asked to believe that 162 Spaniards slew 20,000 Indians in one day and other such incongruities. Garcilasso de la Vega, a half-breed Inca, was living in Spain at the time he wrote his history, and we may be sure that nothing crept into his account that was not strictly censored.

The only truth I have ever run across was contained in the dying confession made to Philip II by one of the last of the conquistadores, which has come to light recently, in which he says the Incas were better people than the Spanish conquerors, that not a thief or immoral woman existed among them, and that there was no poverty.

IT IS a fact that there was *a race* of Incas, rulers of the Indians. The empire took in all of Ecuador, Peru, Bolivia and a great part of Chili. The capital was at Cuzco, and the empire was divided into four parts from there: Chinchay-suyu, to the north; Anti-suyu, to the east; Colla-suyu, to the south; and Cunti-suyu, to the west. Each of these four parts was ruled by a viceroy, under whom were officers ruling over 1,000, 500, 100, 50 and 10, all Incas. There were many other *tucuyricocs*, or inspectors, directly under the chief ruler in Cuzco, who went around seeing that the others ruled correctly. The entire Inca realm was called Ttahuantin-suyu. They were living in a state of perfect Socialism when Pizarro arrived and I am quite sure offered little resistance when he captured their emperor, on the pretext of inviting him to dinner, and held him for ransom. The ransom amounted to $17,000,000. The room in which it was collected is still intact. The priest who accompanied Pizarro gave Atahualpa the choice of embracing Christianity and being choked to death or not doing so and being roasted alive. This was after he had been promised his freedom if he collected the gold for them. Atahualpa took the former course to "shuffle off."

IN DIGGING back through ancient Persian history before the battle of Marathon (490 B. C.) when Persia (or Irania) was master of Western Asia I have come upon data which solves the mystery of the first two Incas. I wish I had time to work this up. It is original so far as I am concerned and I have arrived at it by using common sense. I am surprised that it has been overlooked all this time. I have been trying for many years to place the country from which these first two Incas came, for I am not a very strong believer in the supernatural. The trouble has been that men have been misled into thinking the first Incas came there a few hundreds of years before the Spaniards themselves arrived. This has been caused by the exact data that was given in the Indian traditions, and is very simple to explain: the traditions were handed down from one to the other teachers of the people by the means of knotted cords and were understudied and learned verbatim and according to my belief came down in this manner from about 300 B. C. The only thing we have to do is to get one of the wise men concerning ancient Persian history turned loose on the Inca question and it will soon be cleared up.

Here's the tradition: (I didn't mean to go into this stuff)—

MANCO Capac and Mama Ocllo suddenly appeared (full grown) in a cradle in Lake Titicaca. They found the Indians (who yet speak the *lingoa geral* of all other South-American Indians) living in caves, holes in the ground, and otherwise like wild animals and tame beasts (similar to the way the Fuegians yet live). They said their father, the Sun, had sent them to teach and rule the Indians. Manco Capac carried a long rod of gold and, followed by the Indians and accompanied by his sister-wife, he started out looking for a likely spot to begin his empire. Arriving at what was later Cuzco, he stuck this rod in the ground, out of sight, and said that would be the city he would found.

He began teaching the Indians how to make clothes for themselves, to cultivate the ground, domesticate the native animals, and live like rational human beings. (Bear in mind the *andenes*, or terraces, which they made on the mountain sides, and those of parts of China). His wife began teaching the women how to weave cloth, make clothes for themselves, cook, and run the household. The traditions say they did these things and they must have done so, for when the Spaniards arrived they found them living in houses built of stone of which the equal is not now to be found in the whole world, blocks of stone fitted together without the use of mortar so close that a knife-blade can not be inserted, and some of them of such colossal size as to stagger the imagination with the amount of work required to hew them out and get them in place.

He knew the value of gold and had it collected into a public treasury. If it was not a matter of history how much gold the Spaniards sent back from this place it would be unbelievable the amount they had. And the amount they didn't get was possibly more, for when the Inca sacerdotes saw that the Spaniards were gold-hungry and were without honor they threw great quantities of it in the lakes and otherwise disposed of it, thinking to rid themselves of the invaders.

From these two began the race of Incas, kings of the many tribes of Indians who were to be found in those countries, raising an inbred race, for they did not allow the Indians to marry into the royal blood, and ruling by love and service.

The rod of gold that Manco Capac carried was possibly a sword of bronze and the manner in which he buried it might have to do with his former history.

USING a grain of salt with the narration of Garcilasso de la Vega (for he was the son of a Spanish conqueror by an Inca princess, educated in a Catholic school, and living in Spain at the time he wrote his account, which he claims he got from the lips of a learned Inca at Cuzco when he was a boy), we can piece together and visualize the entire Inca rule down to the conquest. One fact I get that has been overlooked. Manco Capac and Mama Ocllo were dressed in a peculiar fashion and had *very large ears*. Ever since I read about those large ears I have been studying ancient portraits and history for peculiar headdress or ear-rings that would make one appear to have large ears. I drew as many as fifty books at a time from the large libraries here and in New York and studied the old prints and pictures of people, and images of them carved on stone monoliths, and went over the collections of old idols and statues in the museums. It never occurred to me that people existed who had those large ears. I have located them on both ancient Indian (of India) and ancient Persian portraits and pictures of statues, which proves that the old Medes, Persians, Bactrians and Parthians, the group being Iranians, and the ancient Indians (of India) were of a common origin. This fact is accepted by men learned in the history of these two races.

ALL right. The ancient Iranians and Indians (of India) descended from a common stock. And of this common stock came also Manco Capac and Mama Ocllo, the first two Incas. The avesta, or bible, of the Iranians with its Ahura-mazda (god) and Angra-mainu (devil) is that of a religion refined from the pure sun-worship of the people who went before. It is the book from which our own Bible was taken almost literally, with changes so slight as to be negligible. Back behind our Bible we find the avesta, and back behind the avesta was the religion to which Manco Capac belonged.

The word "insha" and its meaning in the avesta is worthy of notice. In rough words it means "a history of rule." The hyphenated words in it are so similar to some words and names that descended from the Incas as to be startling. Many names, especially of places, in the highlands of Peru, Ecuador, Bolivia and other countries where the Incas held sway are not of Quichua origin, nor of any other Indian language origin, but words foreign to their language, and compared with Iranian words and Hindu words, making allowances for distortion by handing down by tradition through unfamiliar tongues, are very interesting.

Also CUZCO WAS A HOLY CITY. A man who had been to Cuzco and was coming away was considered superior to one on his way to the city. Does this shed any light? The strings of knotted cords that Manco Capac taught the Indians to preserve their traditions with were the same knotted cords he had seen his own people using to do the same thing in his own country, and one look at a string of Catholic beads will send the imagination flying back to their origin. The Inca religion and the Catholic religion were *one and the same thing* but one several generations ahead of the other, caused by Inca inbreeding and the natural stupidity of the people they ruled, but far ahead in devotion and sincerity. A man leaving home in the Inca empire had only to leave a stick across his door to show that he was not at home and no one would enter even if he had things within of great value. "And when they saw that we had thieves among us they despised us."

Here is the mystery solved:

LOOK on any globe of the earth and note the two strong currents that leave the China, and even present Persian, coast and cross the Pacific and wash the west shores of Peru and Northern Chili. A boat, even a small one, if it got in that current and nothing happened to it would finally arrive on the west coast of South America. And one did arrive there. I can see Manco Capac and his wife describing it in *sign language* after they had climbed the mountains and woven a small boat to cross Titicaca in, looking for populated country. They stood there and the Indians came and regarded them as great curiosities. They signed that they came far, far, from the west (pointing) and at the little boat they had made, and at the water of Lake Titicaca and made rocking motions that they had come all the way in a boat.

Here's the way Garcilasso de la Vega got it from the lips of an old Inca when he was a boy (Mozans' translation).

"Our Father, the Sun, seeing the human race in the condition I have described, living like wild beasts, without religion or government or towns or houses; without cultivating the land or clothing their bodies, for they knew not how to weave cotton or wool to make clothes, living in caves or clefts in the rocks, or in the caverns under the ground, eating the herbs of the field, and roots and fruit, like wild animals, also human flesh. . . . With these commands and intentions our Father, the Sun, placed his two children in the lake of Titicaca, which is eighty leagues from here, and he said to them that they might go where they pleased, and that, at every place where they stopped to eat or sleep, they were to thrust a scepter of gold into the ground, which was half a yard long and two fingers in thickness. . . ."

INASMUCH as Manco Capac could not talk to them he had to resort to sign language. Visualize the signs one would have had to make to explain the many things he had to tell, his trip and his religion. He is said by the traditions to have ruled about forty years, and probably was never able to explain fully in their own simple language, and possibly his own children were unable to explain when they ruled after him. Perhaps his own language was primitive enough. Yet we have two leaks. He was a man of marvelous genius and if we had his verbatim account it might prove enlightening. The Spaniards killed the wise men who spoke the story to the multitude in the temples from the knotted cords, *quipus*, and Garcilasso de la Vega, the boy, whose mother was an Inca princess, heard the story at second-hand from one who had heard it told long before when he was young. And he had been educated in the religion of his father, the alien conqueror, and was doubtless more in sympathy with his father's people than with the noble race from which he descended on his mother's side, for he left and went to Spain and lived there the rest of his life without coming back. — —— with him!

Here's to Manco Capac and Mama Ocllo, first adventurers to reach these shores, who began a reign of love and service, the like of which has never been known before or since on the face of the earth, man and woman with hearts of purer gold than that which now lies buried in the bottom of Lake Titicaca.—EDGAR YOUNG.

A FEW curiosity-exciting words from Romaine H. Lowdermilk about his story in this issue. And about the can.

Wickenburg, Ariz.

I must lay bare a fact that will forever destroy my chances for becoming the President of the United States. Simply this: I've been in the can. You know, you Adventurers, how easy it is to get into the can. Well, I got there too. I'm not going to commit myself by telling the grand total of my trips to the shady spot, nor enlarge on the various trivial offenses contributing toward those pleasant hours of indolence. I'll merely say that when I began "Thees Eees the Hombre" I was there.

Seems like most folks who have enjoyed a sojourn in the resounding belly of a stationary "tank" think they could—and should—write a story about it. Well, I thought that way too. So I began, but before I got very far along I could see my Ms. was simply a document chock full of state's evidence against me. So I shifted the scenery a little, brought on new actors, turned the spot-light just as far away from my own alleged misdeeds as the stage setting would permit and now you're the audience who, by the simple act of purchasing this copy of *Adventure*, have bought the ticket that lets you see the show. I hope you'll like it. It's a hard job to write a short-story and I have expended much labor to make this one both interesting and true to life. I've not overdrawn nor lied about anything. But people, I sure left out a lot!—ROMAINE H. LOWDERMILK.

WE'VE already discussed South American shrunken heads. Thanks to one of us, here's another look-in on the subject from the une 29, 1918, issue of the *West Coast Leader* of Lima, Per :

The West Coast Leader
Calle Boza 830, Lima, Peru.
P. O. Box 1265

Mr. J. M. Mercer of W. R. Grace & Co. has requested me to forward you the attached *West Coast Leader* containing the story of a reported "head-factory" at Guayaquil. The Guayaquil merchant referred to in the story is a man by the name of ——, I believe, who is well known in that port and has an established business. —— told the story to a friend of mine and declared that he had been inside the "factory" and had seen the heads in question.—C. N. GRIFFIS, Manager.

The "Head Factory" of Guayaquil

"And if you doubt the tale I tell,
Go where the South Pacific swell," etc.
—*Kipling.*

The curious and grewsome art of shrinking an adult human head to approximately one-fourth its normal size has long been one of the minor mysteries of the Amazon basin. This art or craft has been regarded as the exclusive secret of a certain tribe or tribes of Indians dwelling on the northern tributaries of the upper Amazon. Guayaquil on the West Coast and Para on the East Coast have been the principal tidewater markets for these uncanny objects—the human head shrunk to a miniature with long hair hanging down.

You can pick them up in jeweler's shops in Lima mounted on a small stick, but they will cost you anywhere from 20 to 50 pounds sterling. The manner in which these heads are shrunk, as far as we are aware, no scientist has attempted to explain. Even the question of whether the bones are first taken from the head or whether the bones are likewise shrunk is a moot point, with the evidence more in favor of the boneless theory than otherwise.

In connection with these heads we have recently received what is apparently authentic information that, while astounding in character, is not lacking in points of probability.

Going up Coast on a *calatera* a few weeks ago, our informant chanced to meet a Guayaquil merchant and in the course of conversation the subject of heads came up. Whether on the East or West Coasts, it may be noted, these heads are always bobbing up in conversations just as they bob up in shop windows. They are irrepressible jacks-in-the box and they smack of the Amazonian wilderness, reed huts, sluggish brown rivers crawling like snakes through jungle that is dark at noonday. Your carefully groomed tourist balancing one on the tip of his fingers over the counter of a shop in Lima is fascinated by that impish, silent head—because it harps back through the ineradicable savage strain within him to the dusk of centuries when his own ancestors howled about wood-fires at night and a man-head swinging on a stick or string was the finest possession obtainable in all the world.

Leaving the philosophy of heads, however, and returning to our story, the Guayaquil merchant offered to secure for his acquaintance a fine specimen of the shrunken head if he desired one for the small sum of 15 or 20 pounds sterling. "But," said he, "this particular head you might not regard as legitimate. In fact, the great majority of heads marketed on this coast nowadays fall into the same class. I will tell you why. Among the minor industries of Guayaquil we have a head-factory!

"That will sound a somewhat crazy statement to you. But I know it as a matter of fact, for I have visited the place. The man who shrinks these heads may have learned the secret from the Indians of the interior or he may not. I went to his place one day and he led me back into a rear room where he pulled out a large tin can and emptied it out on the floor. There must have been forty or fifty of these shrunken heads in the can. He told me that he did the shrinking himself.

"He secured the heads from dead bodies, paupers, or perhaps through the intermediary of body-snatchers. Then he boiled them in a certain secret preparation for three or four days. At the end of that time the shrinking process was completed. He mounted them and obtained good prices.

"At the present time, however, he told me the head market was poor. Owing to the war, perhaps. It is a difficult business to handle. You must exercise a certain secrecy in securing your raw materials and in marketing the product. Moreover, you must not overload the market. It's a limited market and must be watched carefully.

"While the merchant was talking I bent down and picked up one of the heads and looked at it, for though the skin was browned there was a very startling resemblance to A——, an old friend of mine who used to work on the Guayaquil & Quito Railway. He died a year and a half ago from yellow fever and as far as we knew had been decently buried. I could not get that resemblance out of mind, and later asked the head manufacturer and merchant if he would loan me this particular head. I had a friend who might wish to buy it. He readily assented and I carried the head over to the G. & Q. offices, where it was passed around among the men who had worked with A——. To a man they declared it was A——'s head. I took the head back. There was no absolute proof, of course, and we didn't want to make a public scandal over the matter. It would not have done poor old A—— any good to have his head fought over in a Guayaquil court like a band of Borneo wild men.

"Now that's my story. You may believe it or not, but I tell you that I saw the forty or fifty heads with my own eyes."

A WORD from Roy P. Churchill about *Stormy* in his story in this issue. Also Mr. Churchill is starting a new bit of slang. It looks good. Let's see how far it will get.

Santa Barbara, California.

Another *Stormy Jones* yarn. I like *Stormy* myself. I found him sitting well back in a half-dark conning tower on board the *Minneapolis*, scrubbing clothes. It was soon after the armistice and everybody else on the ship wanted to know when in the —— they were going to be released, to get back to the dear old soda-fountain and the farm. What worried *Stormy* was that there were not enough days to go round to do all the things he had booked. Thought maybe he might have to ship over to get them all in. In other words, *Stormy* was the potential "thirty-year man," the kind of Navy man who, when the time came, trained forty or fifty or a hundred to their jobs in the war. They made some of them full lieutenants and they got away with the job.

And so there is *Stormy* as I saw him.

Hope you like the "Gong-Beater." It means, of course, a hot-air merchant and a spreader of the good old bull, and if these expressions are passé, why not gong-beater?—Roy P. Churchill.

FROM one of us whose adventures began before the war:

U. S. S. *Lake View*.

I was spending part of my time in the powder mills (mostly DuPont's at Carney's Point, N. J. Any old-timer will know Slim of C Line Plant No. 1) and part on the sea. I have been on English horse boats as seaman and have seen on one trip two mutinies, and while going through the sub-zone (then five hundred miles from the English coast) had a drunken crew of horsemen breaking bottles against the bulkhead and raising ——. We were running without any lights, and a full lookout. Then I have (during the war) been on a ship in mid-ocean with a fire on board, and all hands fighting it for their life. I have seen a torpedo just miss the stern of the ship on which I was armed guard (Gun's Crew) and hit the ship just abaft us. I have seen ships shooting rockets so that they could see the sub to fire at it. That's just a few things, but some day I will tell more about having buildings blown up and seeing men running around, their clothes afire and run till they drop dead. I have seen a blending tower blow up and take twenty men with it.—John T. Welsh.

A LETTER from an old-timer of the West telling us more about one of the famous characters of early days:

Los Angeles, Cal.

I have just had the pleasure of reading Mr. Brininstool's story about Tom Smith, but he told only a few of his many good and brave deeds. In July and August, 1868, I was at Green River, Wyoming. The U. P. Railroad was at Bills Creek. The advance population was made up of all kinds of people. The town of Green River made up from tents to a few adobe houses—sporting girls, gamblers, a few merchants, and thieves to beat the band. Robbery and murder were the main business night and day.

TOM SMITH was made city marshal. He talked to a crowd of over two thousand people. He told them that they must not expect any mercy when they were caught in a crime—that he was not a gun-man or a prize fighter, but he was marshal and would protect innocent people from abuse. Jack Briston, a drunken gun-man, gave a yell and started for Smith, but Smith gave him such a punch that he had to be carried away that night. Jo Bean got busy in a dance-tent. Smith told him to go to his camp, as Bean was a noted prize-fighter. That was too much to take and right there they went at it. Smith won, but it was a hard fight. Then Smith made Bean a help-mate. The two worked together and the town was quiet for a few days.

Patsy Marly came in and challenged Bean to fight. In the talk Patsy Marly called Smith some name, and Smith won another fight. Big Bennet, a prize-fighter, got after them all for a fight; he got one with Jim McQuire. Then, when the crowd broke into the ring, Tom Smith got busy and stopped the fight. Bennet told Smith he was standing in with the crowd for popularity. That made Smith call him down and Smith cleaned Bennet out.

Then some of the very worst came in from the grading camp and for a month a perfect hell was kept up. In August the town started to move forward to Bear River; there the big fight occurred. Smith went over their breastworks and took out a desperado; Smith got shot and was taken to a hospital.

THAT was the last heard from him until he was made marshal of Abilene.

Smith found many good people to back him, but he never waited for any pal to go ahead. He always beat them to it. He was a quiet, easy talking man, never drinking, never seen dancing in the dens. His weight was about 165 pounds, very slim, dark eyes and hair, polite to all—even to those rough-necks in and around the dance-houses.

I have never seen his equal for bravery. I understood he was struck by an ax in the hands of a thief when Smith was handcuffing a man. I always had a kind feeling for him. His principles were of the very best in mankind—he deserved a monument. He was a man among men.—CLARK B. STOCKING.

The Camp-Fire

A Meeting-place for Readers, Writers and Adventurers

OUIJA-BOARDS and Piperock and W. C. Tuttle and Tut's own experiences with a ouija-board:

Hollywood, California.

Did you ever monkey with one of those ouija-boards? I did. I have an old friend, who is a helpless invalid, and he owns a ouija-board. Of course he doesn't believe in it any more than I do, but we used to work it for amusement.

THE first message it gave me was this: "Go to ——!" We set the date for the end of the war, the disposition of the kaiser, the price of beans and where we would go on the Fourth of July. We asked it for an opinion of the League of Nations, and it told us to go to ——.

We absolutely proved that we could—without forcibly moving the thing—make it spell what we wished, just by thinking of the answer. We would ask a question that neither of us could answer or even guess at, and the thing was unable to spell anything except a jumble of letters. We made one good test. We asked the board to tell us the color of the sweater my wife was knitting. My wife thought "blue" while I concentrated on "green." That board spelled out BGLRUEEEN, after hard labor. The color of that sweater was gray. Then the board got sore and refused to talk any more. Said we were a lot of —— fools, with no respect for the dead. This statement was mentally spoken by our invalid friend.

Anyway, I thought Piperock might fall for it—and they did.

Best regards to everybody and good luck.—W. C. TUTTLE.

THE following letter was written more than a year ago and I think Mr. Brockway is no longer in Cuba, but dope about lost mines is always interesting though very seldom are the lost mines found.

Marianao, Cuba.

It was my good fortune to be one of the pioneers in the construction of the old Atlantic and Pacific Railway nearly all the way from the Rio Grande to the Needles, Calif. We put in the original waterworks at Peach Springs and went into the Grand Cañon of the Colorado through Diamond Wash. Have been in the Cañon at two other points farther north. This was in '81-2. We had an old time photographer with us, Ben Wittick, who took several fine views in the Cañon. He used the old wet plate process and I can tell you it was some job to pack his outfit across the river and up side cañons.

IN '81 I was in charge of a large rock quarry at Quirino Cañon near Honcks Tank, and near the Arizona-New Mexico State line. We found at this place any quantity of small garnets—in ant-hills, brought up by the ants. I have always thought that we missed a big thing as I believe good sized stones can be found there by sluicing; the ants could handle only the small ones. I have seen 2- and 3-carat size stones brought in by the Indians, found in the washes, during the rainy season. I sent some of these large stones to St. Louis and had them cut and polished—and they were fine as any ruby. Here is something worth investigating, but I do not suppose will interest any one, as we all seem to be eternally looking for adventure and treasure in some far-off inaccessible country and overlook good things right under our noses.

MY MINING partner, a Mr. James N. Taylor, and myself with Navajo John made a trip in the Fall of '82 from Honcks Tank to Navajo Mountain—going by way of Kearns Cañon and the Moynoi town, and to the very summit of Navajo Mountain. The view of the cañon country from this mountain summit is unsurpassed. You can see the entire Marble Cañon, the junction of the San Juan and Colorado Rivers at the base of the mountain—you can see away up in the Green River country in the misty distance, and the whole range of the Rockies in the State of Colorado unfolds itself in a magnificent panorama. We saw and visited several cliff-dwellings at the approaches and side cañons of this mountain. Of course we were looking for a lost mine; and I want to give you a little history of this lost mine, as I often wonder if it has ever been found, or if any of the old outfits that went into this same country—one from Prescott, Arizona, and another from Pueblo, Colorado—are still among the living.

We had pretty good evidence that such a mine existed, as previously I had prospected and camped out with an old-timer, Lorenzo Lawrence, who was one of the Prescott party, on Mount Taylor in New Mexico; also the story told us by Navajo John, who, by the way, could talk his own language, also perfect Spanish and English—he had been stolen when a boy by the Rio Grande Mexicans, raised by them and when a young man got over into Texas and worked several years for American cattlemen. Therefore as a guide his services were very valuable.

THE lost mine story is as follows. An old renegade American by the name of Austin had lived among the Navajos and Pi-Utes in the Navajo Mountain country, and used to make a trip yearly to Durango, Colorado, always taking out a few loads of rich silver ore which he sold in Durango. This fact was well known by the old settlers. Austin (am not so sure of the name) struck up a friendship in Durango, with a man by the name of McLain who on one occasion was taken to the mine by a roundabout way and over hidden trails.

The ferry at the crossing of the San Juan River was kept by an old man by the name of Smith who had a grown-up son. McLain conceived the idea of going back into that country and jumping the old man's mine—while Austin was in Durango. Austin got wind of what was going on and lit out, taking the young son of Smith with him as a witness to the legal location of the mine. By this time the Indians got incensed at Austin's bringing of white men into the country, and on their way out both were killed, at the Black Butte. We were shown their graves by Navajo John. Their animals escaped and went to Kearns Cañon. Tom Kearn told us himself that he followed their trail back and found and buried the bodies at the base of the Black Butte. McLain had reached this place about that time on his way to the mine and got scared out and made his way back to Durango.

HE AFTERWARDS organized an outfit in Prescott and went in there to find the mine, but the Indians were too bad to do anything and the outfit broke up and scattered.

He also organized an outfit in Pueblo, Colorado—if I remember rightly—which consisted of 52 men, well armed and equipped. They got to Navajo Mountain by the only accessible trail, which leads up to a beautiful mesa several miles across, and one of the most beautiful landscapes I have ever seen. The Indians had their return cut off and they forgot their way back across the mesa. We saw several places where they had built up defensive breastworks. They finally reached the rim of the mesa on the north side and blasted a trail so they could get down off the mesa on the San Juan side, in the Pi-Ute country, and in this way escaped the Indians and got out of the country. And the mine was still a lost mine.

If any of these old-timers who were on these raids are still alive, we would like to hear them tell the story of these expeditions.—WM. BROCKWAY.

FROM Romaine H. Lowdermilk a few words about one of the characters in his story in this issue. Also a word as to whether we still have real cowboys.

Wickenburg, Arizona.

Does anybody around the Camp-Fire this evening believe that cowgirls (or cowboys) are getting to be a rather scarce article? Well, I don't want to take up a lot of time trying to prove they're thick, but I'd like to assure you that if you get out in the Cow Country of Western United States you'd be amazed to learn how plentiful they are. In support of these statements I'll suggest that doubters attend some of the numerous annual "Stampedes," or Frontier Day Celebrations, held at many different towns in the Cow Country. Here, barring professional movie and Contest hands, you'll see hundreds of real rangemen who make their living riding horses and "punching" cattle. As long as cattle run on the Western ranges we'll have cowboys and cowgirls and these cow chasers of to-day are just as slick with the rope and as handy with the broncs as they were fifty years ago, and they're breaking old records every year.

But to get back to cowgirls. *Della Greathouse* is taken from real life—something I seldom do. But this real *Della* is such a fine example of all the brave, womanly, wholesome girls of the West, who, being ranch-raised, still love the life of the open places thought they are as at home in the cities as many of their metropolitan sisters. This original *Della*, besides being a wonderful horsewoman, puts on a nurse's costume and holds her own in any man's hospital; She puts on a cook apron and looks (and acts and produces) like a real cook; she puts on an evening gown and—Oh, Boy! Nor has she ever seen the front end of a movie camera.—ROMAINE H. LOWDERMILK.

DON'T FORGET our annual vote by readers on the ten best stories published by our magazine during 1920. Voting is an easy matter. Here are the particulars:

ALL you need to do is write the titles and authors' names of the ten stories you consider best, given in order of preference, and mail us the sheet of paper to reach us not later than December thirty-first. If you like, add as many as ten more for honorable mention. As in the past years, short stories, novelettes, novels and serials are included, poems, "Camp-Fire and the other departments are barred out. The issues covered are those dated January 3, 1919, to December 18, 1919, inclusive. Serials only parts of which are contained in these issues are included.

We very sincerely want your cooperation and help in getting for *Adventure* the kinds of story and the authors that a majority of our readers like best. If you know of a better way of furthering this cooperation than is the annual vote by readers, name it, for we are ready to try any legitimate plan that will help register your wishes in the making of the magazine. It's not only common sense to strive for this but it's a lot happier and more comfortable all around if people work together in friendly fashion.

WHILE the departments are excluded from the vote, we'll be more than glad to get suggestions for improving them. Or adding to them, but don't forget that "Letter-Friends" and "Wanted" have already been tried, and, though succesful and popular, had to be given up because two or three readers abused them.

And if you have any suggestions concerning the magazine in general or any part of it, by all means send them in. I mean constructive suggestions that will definitely point out ways for improvement. Wherever we can meet your ideas we will, but remember that it is the majority whom we must please and that, while a given plan may please a minority and perhaps us here in the office, if it fails to please the majority it is not warranted.

But the only way to find out what the majority want is for the readers themselves to tell us. And you are one of the readers.

The Camp-Fire

ONE of you asked for the full text of a poem some of whose lines had stuck tight in his mind. Doubtless others of you also will remember it, for it is that kind of poem. It was published by *McClure's Magazine* of January, 1899, and by the courtesy of that magazine and its late editor, Charles Hanson Towne, we reprint it here in full.

The Regular Fighting Man

by **James Barnes**

THERE'S always a cheer for the volunteer,
There's ever a welcoming host,
The wide land stretches a greeting hand—
Glad hail from the hill to the coast!
There's none but will vaunt the deeds he's done—
Let us praise him and pledge him high!

But the fighting man who serves for pay,
The public passes by.

Who rushed the lines on San Juan hill?
Who at Caney fought alone?
The enlisted regular fighting man—
The soldier—bred to the bone!
Who bore the big brunt of the battle front?
Should we speak it below a breath?
The enlisted regular fighting man,
Who cheered as he charged to death!

Who he was, the public seldom knows—
Who he is, it does not care—
Just Private Blank of the ——ty-third,
Recruited from God knows where!
Just "a man—" (Built up on a soldierly plan
For a place that he's shaped to fit.)
Just a name put down on a muster-roll;
Yes, numbered and stenciled from shirt to soul—
And he doesn't object a bit!

No; he takes it all as it all may come,
And it's more of work than play—
From the goose-step into the awkward squad—
Then into a trench some day.
He answers "Sir" to his officer,
He watches his sergeant well,
And if things they happen to rub him wrong,
He can not run home and tell!

For "The Army" spells his name for Home,
And "The Post" proves his abode;
And he's taught his company manners there,
Up to: "Numbers! Ready! Load!"
Oh, he gets his fill of the family drill,
And they train his hand and eye!
Till he stands or moves and questions not—
Let his captain know the "why."

For the service adopts the enlisted man,
And he's treated as a child!
And he's cautioned how to mind his health
In tones not overmild.
Oh, he's bound to go and do just so;
But when things are at the worst,
He learns that the men with the shoulder-straps
Are thinking of him first!

From the colonel down to the officer lad,
They share his fare and lot,
And they train his trigger finger right
And his feet to falter not;
For war's a trade for which tools are made
Out of names on a muster-roll;
And the soldier's a bound-to-obey machine,
With a human heart and soul!

He asks for no praise as a patriot,
He lays claim to no laurel wreath,
Tho' he's proud of his nation and regiment
And the flag that he fights beneath!
He "serves for pay," they were wont to say.
But before an advance began:
"A trench or a height to be taken?
Where's the regular fighting man!"

God keep in the breast of the Nation's sons
The soul of the volunteer;
Let there always be men when the country calls
To join in the great "We're here!"
And to God be thanks that we've men in the ranks
Let the lines be black or white—
The men at arms who stand on guard
To keep the flag in sight!

(By Courtesy of *McClure's Magazine*)

CONCERNING those interesting professional murderers of whom we've all heard, and in connection with his novelette in this issue, Harold Lamb gives us some facts that are doubtless new to most of us:

New York City.

Most of us have had experience with thugs of various kinds. And we are still alive and kicking. Not many of us know about the *thags* of India.

THEY were not dacoits—as the British Government supposed until Seringapatam and 1799—nor were they organized gangs of robbers and murderers. Rather, they were murderers and robbers, the one thing always coming before the other. They were professional men, law-abiding and harmless except in this one respect, and they took immense pride in their profession.

This pride was not religious pride; and the thags were not essentially Kali-worshippers, I think. In fact nearly half were Mohammedans. Kali was a kind of tutelary deity and a certain percentage of spoil gained from the murders by *thaggi* was set aside as a propitiary offering to the goddess.

Regarding these Mohammedans Captain Sleeman—who devoted a lifetime to stamping out *thaggi* in India in the nineteenth century and failed of complete success—says a curious thing. He asked some condemned *thags* whether the taking of life was not proscribed by the law of the prophet. The answer was that the victims of the *thags* were without doubt pre-destined to die. In slaying them the Mohammedan *thags* only aided destiny and hence were guiltless of bloodshed.

ANOTHER general misbelief among us is that the *thags* murdered Europeans. They very rarely did so, unless necessary. When one member of a band of travelers had been killed by these hereditary students of death, it was a law of their cult that all members of the party must meet a like fate. Nor did they kill women, not from any reverence for woman as a sex but because it was generally considered unlucky. They went entirely by omens. Many a traveler on the highway was saved when in company with *thags* by a snake crossing the road from the wrong side.

It was a curious profession, this, and very skillfully conducted. Estimates of the known deaths by thags run as high as fifteen hundred a year in Central India alone. And the actual deaths were many more, for the simple reason that the *phansigars*—stranglers—rarely left any evidence of their work. Those who were condemned to death attended to the matter themselves, knotting the halter rope under their right ear, and jumping off into oblivion—perhaps actuated by the rigid caste of the profession and also by firm conviction that to be hanged by the hand of a *chumar* was unendurable.

AND it is one of the curiosities of human life that these devotees of human death never held themselves to be criminals. The son followed the trade of the father. Wives sometimes never knew their husbands were *phansigars*. The young lads who were—as they termed it—"hard-breasted" enough to be given a *rumal*, or strangling noose, were as proud as an English youth of the same age upon whom knighthood had been conferred.

During *Khlit's* time the *thags* were powerful and usually unmolested. They were rich, and an established part of the community. In the "Masterpiece of Death" Khlit, who was a warrior by profession and a believer in the merits of a fair fight with bare weapons when a fight was necessary, meets some members of this cult.

Sleeman archives. What I meant was this: "The peculiar customs of *thaggi* appearing in the tale have the confessions of the stranglers themselves and testimony before Captain Sleeman for authority."

THIS comrade says he "sure is an admirer of Camp-Fire." It's just his kind that make our Camp-Fire worth while. And yet I'll bet it never occurred to him that he was really admiring himself. Some of us talk and some of us don't, but it isn't the talking alone that makes Camp-Fire.

Let's all get together and wish him out of that bed and back on his two feet, as husky as ever.

Lima, Ohio.

—but have never written before, as I handle a rope or six-gun much better than a pen. Have drifted over about all of the Border from the Big Bend to the Pacific and have tried my hand at about everything, from busting bad ones to picking canteloupes in Imperial Valley and hunting our knife-wielding brothers for Uncle Sam.

Have just returned from a ten months' visit to the land of Vins Rouge and Blanc. Was in the little arguments at the Argonne, St. Mihiel and Mouse-Argonne. But it looks as if I am due to occupy a bed in place of a saddle for some time as a result of disabilities received.

Would say a word about guns. The new .45 caliber D. A. Colts, adopted by Uncle Sam, that handles the .45 automatic cartridge, is sure some gun. With best wishes to *Adventure* and Camp-Fire.—Frank Porter, 785 St. Johns Ave., Lima, Ohio.

NO, I didn't quote the Britannica to that effect, as the following letter addressed to me states, but some one did at Camp-Fire, and this comrade offers a theory as to divining-rods that sounds solid enough for the encyclopedia:

Capon Springs, West Virginia.

You quote Encyclopædia Britannica as saying that the discovery of underground water courses by divinging rods "can not be explained."

The explanation is simple:

Damp earth is a conductor. Dry earth is not. The soil above underground streams is damp. Magnetic currents follow this damp earth and "water witches" are peculiarly susceptible to magnetic influences; are often men mentally unbalanced because of this susceptibility. Q. E. D.—Will Atkinson.

FROM Patrick Casey an interesting talk in connection with his serial beginning in this issue. What can other Camp-Fire members tell us as to whether there is a real Japanese secret society called Toyama?

San Francisco.

"Toyama" was built practically out of a sentence. That sentence was the opening one. For years it had been running through my mind. It struck me as quite novel. To begin a story with it, particularly an adventure-mystery story, would be to begin where most stories of this type end—with the finding of the treasure. In "Toyama" the finding of the treasure is accomplished in the first sentence and whatever of adventure and mystery may be in the story hinges on the reason for that treasure and its eventual disposition.

IN CONVEYING the party of Americans south on board a former submarine-chaser, I but used a type of craft with which I became familiar during two years' naval service in the recent war. Even the transformation of the war-craft into more or less of a pleasure ship was living within the law of probabilities. To-day you may buy one of them for something like twenty-thousand dollars.

When I read such intelligence in the newspapers, I can not help but recall that time, following Armistice Day and the anticipated release from active service of my skipper, when the *S. C. 73* was about to be given into my entire keeping and I was told, by high authority and with much grim injunction for caution, that I was to be responsible for nothing less than one hundred and fifty thousand dollars of Government property. And to-day the same craft, dismantl d of her guns, will sell for twenty-thousand dollars! It is my opinion that the gasoline engines aboard, three in number and capable of generating over six hundred horsepower, are alone worth that price in any market. Add to that the steel frame and bulkheads which rib this type of craft and have caused her staunch weathering qualities to be everywhere acknowledged, and you may have food for thought.

MARIQUITA'S story is an attempt to visualize the havoc wrought by the unrest in Mexico. The idea of the army trunk containing the missing military funds was suggested by the arrest in this city of a former Mexican paymaster on the charge of absconding with over sixty-thousand dollars from the coffers of Carranza. The truth is that the paymaster was detected and identified through the peculiar color of his eyes; they were a distinct green in hue. It might have been realistic to have given *Dicenta* those green eyes, but I feared the truth in this case would sound too much like fiction for my readers to swallow.

The intrusion of the party of Japanese into "Toyama" utterly upset all plans. Here was color, mystery, high romance! I was carried away. Thereafter, to a large extent, the story wrote itself.

THERE was that incident of the little Japanese girl, once she had landed from the foul schooner, removing her sandals and short white socks, and dabbling her feet in the tepid water. Her actions then—her giggles, the play of sunlight on cheeks and throat, the very picture of her silken kimono and glossy hair—were such as I had observed, years before, at a swimming-pool back of my rooms in Nuuanu Avenue of Honolulu.

I'll tell you about it. It was a Sunday, moistly hot, nothing to do but run out, perhaps, to Waikiki or the Pali. A fellow guest of the hotel, a civil engineer from Boston, suggested that the two of us walk through the unkempt field behind the building to where, he said, he had discovered a swimming-hole of the natives.

We found it after a little journeying. A tiny stream rippled down from the hills and dropped, in a miniature waterfall, over a great rock. In the course of many years the constant falling of the water had worn away the rock below into a perfect basin, a dozen yards in diameter and brimming with cold clear water.

THERE were all sorts in and around the basin—full-blooded Kanakas, hapa-haoles, squat Portuguese women in native Mother Hubbards, and boys, Japanese and Hawaiian, who looked like wriggling tadpoles in the water. I saw one Hawaiian man approach the pool on crutches. One of his legs was lamed, not permanently but as if it had been injured slightly in the course of his daily toil. At the brink of the pool he cast aside the crutches, lowered himself into the water, and swam.

It was a shock. He was more fish than man. But truly the water was more his element than the land, not entirely from environment, but also from that birthright handed down to him from his seafaring ancestors—those Polynesians who, in the remote past, set out in their great war-canoes from the islands south of the Line, from New Zealand and Samoa, and discovered in turn the Society Group, the Marquesas and Hawaii.

While we sat there, watching the swimmers, three Japanese women, scrupulously clean and dainty in their Sunday kimonos and obis, approached from up the cañon. They paused behind us, with many trebly giggles, to dabble their feet in the stream. The two older women had only to remove their straw sandals, but the youngest one was bothered further by short white socks with a separate hood for the great toe.

I can see her now, standing atop a black slippery rock and dabbling gingerly one yellow foot after the other in the chilly water. She was dressed with unusual richness, her sandals of felt, not straw, and her kimono a beautiful shimmer of silk. She never looked toward us, but her incessant giggles showed plainly that she was aware of our presence. It is that Japanese flirt I have attempted to describe in the person of *O Haru San*.

THE basis for the secret society "Toyama" was furnished by the evidence gathered by the police of Washington, D. C., when they investigated, some time ago, the murder of three Chinese Educational Commissioners to this Government. The theory, adduced from the evidence, was that word had been flashed from the Far East that a particular Chinese mission was a menace to the successful conclusion of certain peace terms, then being made in Paris, and that the agents of a powerful Oriental secret society, called "Toyama," had been sent to Washington to shadow and kill the members of that mission.

When the society's agents reached Washington, however, they made a fatal blunder. There were three Chinese missions in the capital at that time. One had charge of the administration of Chinese Government funds voted for the use of her students in this country. The second was in control of the funds returned by the United States from the indemnity paid by China on account of the Boxer outrages, and also used for educational purposes.

The third mission was the one marked for extinction. It was political in character, being engaged in issuing propaganda that was designed to impress upon the people of the United States the charge that Japan was striving, in the then pending peace settlements, not alone to gain control of all the former German islands of the Pacific but also to secure an ineluctable grasp upon China.

BY STRANGE coincidence, the chairmen of the two latter missions bore the same surname. The Boxer Indemnity Commission, known as the Tsing Wau Mission, was headed by Dr. T. T. Wong, while another Wong, Dr. C. T. Wong directed the energies of the political commission.

The agents of "Toyama" made a fatal mistake. They wiped out the wrong mission. The chances are they had naught to guide them in their killing but the name of the chairman of the marked commission. They killed the three members of the innocent and educational Boxer Indemnity Commission in the stead of the members of the damaging political mission. And the political mission went merrily on issuing its propaganda.

I quote from a newspaper account of the affair:

"In the mysterious 'Toyama,' Japan is believed to have a hideous agency which never hesitates to wreak vengeance upon those who oppose or obstruct her imperialistic doctrines. It is said that the society is composed of a group of powerful business interests which use terrorism to force the policy of the island empire along the line they believe best."—PATRICK CASEY.

BY THE time you read this, Harry E. Wade, who has become good friends with so many of you during the more than six years he has been one of Adventure's editors, will no longer be a member of our staff. I am glad to say that he goes to a position so good that it more than justifies him in leaving us, but his loss will be felt here none the less on that account. I'm glad to say, too, though I suppose it is unnecessary, that in leaving the office he does not leave our Camp-Fire nor end his interest in the magazine. Or the friendships he has formed during these half-dozen years.

I know that your good wishes will follow him into his new work and that you, too, will miss him in your intercourse with the magazine.

"Ask Adventure," which is one of the things that has been particularly in his charge, will now be in Mr. Noyes' hands, as will most of Mr. Wade's other work, and we are lucky in that Mr. Noyes is almost as thoroughly identified with *Adventure's* career. Indeed, he was with our magazine before Mr. Wade, leaving to our regret, to accept an opportunity that could not be passed by, and, when Mr. Wade was in the Army, came back to us to fill his place. For some time past both have been working side by side here in the office.—A. S. H.

DID Kit Carson have any brothers or sisters? It's one of our oldest comrades asking.

California.

Did Kit Carson have any brothers or sisters? Much ancient history has been discussed in the Camp circle in the past and I would ask some of our own historians to riddle me this riddle. In a recent San Francisco daily newspaper I saw an account of the sale of a piece of property said to have formerly been owned by Lindsay Carson, a brother of the famous Kit Carson.—G. L. C.

BECAUSE Camp-Fire can't keep up with the many letters waiting to be heard, the following welcome from one woman comrade to another is long in being heard. I like the idea of such a welcome. There are a surprising number of women comrades among us and, perhaps because they are *not* the type who carry out the tradition about woman's talking proclivities, we hear from them too seldom. Well, if they won't talk more to all of us it's particularly good to have them get chummy among themselves and to make new women comrades feel that there is a special place for them among us. They're the right stuff or they wouldn't be here or even want to be.

Castine, Maine.

May I be permitted to welcome a woman comrade when she sits in at the Camp-Fire? I mean Dolores Leiden, whose letter came out in the February 18th issue.

OUR brothers haven't the monopoly of the spirit of adventure, though they have been more generously endowed with the physical strength and independence to put their spirit over. That is quite as it should be, too. But there are those of us who have the feminine blood royal of adventure coursing in our veins and who have been able to take advantage of it. I have met a number in my own wanderings over the face of this earth, and it's always interesting to read of such. It is particularly interesting to see a letter from one in the Camp-Fire; for we aren't quite so used to "speaking in meeting" as are our brothers.

I CAN'T recall exactly where I saw my first copy of *Adventure*, but I think I found it several years ago in a bunch of old periodicals left on an English tramp steamer in the Indian Ocean. I've been a constant reader since then, and Camp-Fire generally comes first in order of reading.

I haven't "beaten it on a freight train," as has Dolores Leiden, but I have circled the globe several times and ridden on coal-cars in Borneo. Also, I've seen some strange places and lived with strange people—some of them so-called pagans. Do you know where Perim is? Did you ever order iced tea at the Club House there? There was a time in my life when I could sleep comfortably on a ledge of rock, with my husband's boots for a pillow and the sky for a cover. That period has passed, but I am hoping to make soon another extended tour of the Oriental countries and the South Seas, when I shall be ready to take whatever falls to my lot.

ANOTHER thing I was glad to see in the Mid-February issue was Mr. Huston's *correct* remarks regarding the betel leaf and *areca* nut. I've sported *areca* palms—upon which the nut grows—in my back yard and have several "buyo" boxes on my possession. I don't use them, excepting as curios.

I want to endorse Mr. Hoffman's middle-class union, and to end by saying: as the plant is urged towards the light, so the human soul is urged towards "something better farther on," the earthly manifestation of which is the spirit of adventure—may this spirit never grow less!—GRACE P. T. KNUDSON.

A FEW words from Roy P. Churchill in connection with his story in this issue:

Santa Barbara, California.

Adventure is getting so many new readers that it is about time I was making a bow again. I hope the older members of Camp-Fire remember the first bow I made with a Navy yarn, and that the memory has been kept somewhat green by those that have come along since. A sailor usually says few words about a marine and those words so full of pep that editors use an upper-case dash instead of letters. But this feeling isn't quite so bad just now so soon after they have been fighting Germany instead of each other, and so I know you will pardon a Gob for writing real respectful about leathernecks. Even making them the heroes and giving them the best of it. They do get the best of it, now and then, at that —ask any marine. So the story, "Tell It to the Marines."

Tony Rierson was suggested by the California-Spanish boys who crowded into the Navy during the war. Some of them are as dark as their Moorish ancestors, and some of the families own so much land they can't get over it in a day's ride. They made real sailors, too. *Mickey Dolan* is the kind of marine that the Gobs are always after because they want to be as good as *Mickey*. The setting is a seaport in Mexico where a couple of sailors were put in jail not so many years ago, and where the rescue party failed. The rescue in the story did not really come off, because *Mickey Dolan* wasn't there to take the chance, but I am sure that most any reader will agree that *Mickey* is not to be blamed for that.—Roy P. Churchill.

THE Australian comrade who cheerily handed us some tall tales of his country—not to fool us but to get the grins—has stirred several of you to replies of one kind or another. But here is one from a Yank who's knocked about Australia a bit himself and sort of likes it:

Jennings, Okla.

Just chuck your old swag into the Camp-Fire ring, old chappie, and welcome. You will always find the latch-string hanging outside around my shack to any brother from under the Southern Cross.

I have wallabied some myself in old New South and South Australia and from there clear on back west o' sunset. "Adventure!" Why, "mon dear," Australia is slopping over with it. I put in six solid months in Australian adventures back in the never-never and up and down the ranges of the old blue mountains where the horizon is always hid in a blue haze, without going out to civilization to get a shave or hair-cut. When Billy and I landed back in old Penrith out of the Waragamba, Coxes River and Cowmung Cañons the sidewalks hurt our feet.

I AM going to ask you a question. Do you know where Cowmung Mountain is? There is gold not far from there and pay stuff too. You probably will smile when I say gold, because Australia has gold every place. I can pan gold dust up the Parramata or out at Wooloomooloo, but when I say gold I mean it. The same as I say there is oil here under the house I live in. Two hundred yards from where I am writing this we brought in a well at two hundred and twenty barrels an hour. Billy and I buried our gold-pan, pick, etc., not far from Cowmung Mountain below a milky quartz reef cropping out of the mountain that is pay stuff. We were strangers with nothing but whiskers and experience and that would not tunnel a shaft under a mountain very far. I have eaten wanga pigeon and galors with the blacks in camps in the Murray and Darling Rivers country and could throw a boomerang, punt a dugout and whack a whole caravan of camels on their knees and make them kneel for their burdens. Now laugh, —— it, and say there is another Yankee Blowhard. I suppose you are right at that.

No, I did not say "I guess" and "calculate." You are right, pardner. Just some of us do.

I KNOW something about how your shearers work too. There is close competition for the position of "ringer"—a man is only a roustabout that can not pass the hundred mark in the shank of the afternoon and then clip more wool from then on until "nock off" time than I could in three moons.

I have toasted my toes on the mourners' benches around Circular Quay, swapping jaw-tackle with the old salts and "larricans" when I was o' blooming graft, or lolled on the grass in the Botanic Gardens. Man, I was pulled up by the hair of the head in a part of the U. S. A. where even New Yorkers think there is nothing but redskins, rattlesnakes and roaring cow-punchers, but if I want adventure I will roll up my swag and wallaby up into central Australia where the blacks think a pale face the finest stew under the old Southern Cross.

I have been reading your "Lost Trails" from some years past, hoping to be able to throw a life-line to some old salt adrift or stand in my stirrups and wave my sombrero at some rangler unseated.

I am producing oil now, but for the other fellow. I have lakes, tanks and more lakes of it, all worth three dollars a barrel. There is one more adventure for me and that is the oil game and that is to produce oil for some man or company that will pay me more money for the interest I take. *Kia Ora!*—Jack Weber.

P. S. At one A.M. this morning gas from the flow-tank of the two hundred and twenty barrel well settled around a drilling well three hundred feet distant, causing an explosion, burning the driller and tool-dresser to death, and igniting the oil in the tank. As I write this, the oil from the well is burning as fast as it flows from the well. We will set another tank and lay another 5-inch line to it to handle the oil until the fire is extinguished.

The queerest part of the accident is that the rig where the crew were burned did not ignite. Both men after catching fire jumped into a lake of burning oil. We managed to get one out, but he was past recognition.—J. W.

PROBABLY more than any other general magazine *Adventure* has given its readers living, breathing but historically accurate pictures of our country's early history. One of our novelettes in this issue gives us such a picture of an event in American history that is probably unknown to many of us. A year or so ago, reading "Old Times in the Colonies" to my ten-year-old boy (from the same volume I had devoured as a kid) I came upon a brief account of the amazing journey made by Cabeza de Vaca and his companions. It had left no mark on my memory but at once it became evident that it was tremendously dramatic material for our magazine.

Writing about it to Mr. Scobee, I bumped into the strange coincidence that he had already been getting historical data on this expedition and was putting it into shape for a story.

Let him tell you about it from the point of view of actual history:

Bellingham, Washington.

The journey of Cabeza de Vaca and his three companions across the Western Continent is one of the big events in earliest American history, taking place nearly 400 years go. Since they were the first Europeans to cross our own mainland, much interest is attached to it by historians.

NOT much is known of the journey, and still less of the travelers' route. De Vaca was the chronicler. He kept no notes and wrote his book nine or ten years after some of the events occurred, which accounts in part for the lack of information. Also, the places he touched had no names, or at least no names that he used. The only names that he used and which we recognize to-day were Florida and the two west Mexico towns, Culiacan and San Miguel.

Thus we have no data concerning the route except what can be deduced, and historians have been giving differing opinions for decades.

It is not disputed that the expedition touched and landed on the west coast of Florida, traveled northward by land, afterward built small barges and coasted westward. Where they landed, however, is the point at which the scholarly disputes begin. Bancroft believes they sailed past the mouth of the Mississippi River and perhaps were cast ashore on what is now Galveston Island. That is the idea I have carried out in my story.

EVEN greater differences exist as to the land route of the four. Some writers say they were as far north as the Arkansas and Canadian Rivers. This seems to have been successfully refuted, and a route much farther south established as the actual one, as nearly as history will ever establish it, perhaps. This southernmost route has been suggested by Judge O. W. Williams of Fort Stockton, Texas, who, more than likely, is the only scholar to obtain his knowledge from the field in person. He traces it by vegetation, fruits and animals that de Vaca mentions.

For example: The wanderers lived from early Summer to Fall, each year, on prickly pears or tunas. These, it seems, can be had in such abundance and for such long periods only in a belt extending from somewhere south of San Antonio to the mountain region, running in a northwesterly direction.

Further, de Vaca does not speak of buffalo until he has gone far west, or northwest, of the coast where he stayed seven years. It is true that the southern limit of the bison range was in the locality of the San Antonio and Nueces Rivers, and four hundred years ago was farther north than that.

SO THERE are two pretty nearly conclusive pointers that de Vaca was in South Texas. That he was not south of the Rio Grande is shown also by vegetation mentioned, and by the fact that he does not mention the "River of Palms," as having been crossed. Also, he speaks of farming *in temporalis* (not his words but his meaning), on a river between mountains. That without doubt was at Presidio, Texas, on the Rio Grande, for they still farm, and seemed to have always farmed *in temporalis* there—that is without irrigation except what the flooding river affords.

So by fruits and vegetation, by buffalo present and absent at different places, and by a river and farming, de Vaca's route has been established accurately, to my mind.

I take credit, but give all to Judge Williams. I mention the matter because it is new to print and is historically interesting and of value.

I SHOULD say, approximately speaking, that the land route of the adventurers lay from what is now Port Lavaca on the Texas coast to San Antonio, to Rock Springs, to Sheffield, to Fort Stockton and thence southwestward through the mountains.

In my story I have in mind San Pedro springs at San Antonio, six blocks from my home, when I write of the camp where the four found the white girl.

It might be interesting to remark parenthetically that buffalo never went in herds west of the Pecos River in Texas. There are indications that not more than a half-dozen ever entered the country west of that stream, and those few were stragglers or lost members of the herds. This fact is hard to explain, unless it was that the buffalo instinctively kept away from a drouth country.

THERE is one point of which I am cognizant and of which I never have seen historical mention—perhaps because it was not significant. The Spaniards of the expedition in question seemed to have desired to establish a settlement on the River of Palms. Historians, I understand, "believe" this to have been the Rio Grande. Undoubtedly it was, and my proof, or evidence rather, is this—

Six miles down the river from Brownsville, Texas, at the very southernmost point of Texas, is a natural, or wild, palm grove. It covers, as I recall, about two hundred acres, and would have been a tremendous place for a settlement because of the rich soil and attractive environments. I believe the earliest explorers along that coast must have gone a few miles up the Rio Grande—ten or fifteen—and found that grove, from which they named the river.

AS TO my story wherein a woman of the fleet warns the leader that all who go on a land expedition will vanish from the earth like smoke, I wish to say that it is a fact, according to de Vaca, that the ten women of the fleet did take new husbands as soon as the expedition started inland. This will make plain Narvaez's supersitions, since the other Spaniards were so superstitious.

De Vaca himself, I have deduced after a careful study of his book, was an old woman sort of man, though he was devoutly religious and loyal to his church and king. But he takes all credit for the success of the journey and makes his companions out to be more or less numbskulls. He tells much of his healing the Indians by religious power, and accounts largely for the success of the journey by that.

The journey contributed little to American history in the sense of giving information. Nor was it important in that it led to further explorations. It is important and interesting chiefly in that it was the first journey across the American mainland by Europeans.—BARRY SCOBEE.

THANKS to Edgar Young, here is an interesting letter about Tiburon and a King John. Mr. Young says "The King John he refers to is not the one I was asking about and I am beginning to give up hope of ever hearing anything concerning mine." However, this other King John is interesting in himself. And maybe there'll yet be some of you to bob up with dope about King John No. 1.

Steubenville, Ohio.

DEAR MR. YOUNG: Just picked up a copy of a Nov. 3rd, 1919, *Adventure*—one copy that I unfortunately missed owing to the printers' vacation and the resultant scramble for them when they finally did show up on the news-stands.

I NOTE in Camp-Fire that you are hunting for a King John, supposed to be a Spaniard and the ruler over a tribe of uncivilized Indians.

I know of one King John; he may and he may not be the one you are hunting for, *quien sabe?* My King John, or Juan Thomas as he chooses to call himself, hangs out on Tiburon Island in the Gulf of California. I had the pleasure several years ago of visiting Tiburon Island and it was there that I first met His Royal Highness.

It seems that several years ago the Seris, the present inhabitants of Tiburon, captured several Papago Indians and among them was a husky little kid. This little boy became the natural leader of the tribe in later years and was made ruler of the island. For his mate he picked a young Spanish girl who had been captured by his Seris as she was traveling from Guaymas to Hermosillo. King John is the son of this Papago Indian and the Spanish girl. Several years after the girl's capture, a Mexican punitive expedition visited the island and offered to take her back to her people in Guaymas. Owing to the fact that her face had been tattooed in the Seri fashion and the miserable life that she led, she decided to stay on the island for the rest of her days.

CREDENTIALS. Yes, old Juan has the official papers all right. Around his neck in a canvas sack he has a dilapidated letter from the Prefect of Hermosillo acknowledging Juan Thomas to be the king of Tiburon and holding him responsible for their good behavior.

As I have said before, Mr. Young, he may be the bird you are hunting for. The facts are somewhat alike, your description and mine, but still he may not be the man. It was just because nobody else in the later issues of *Adventure* spoke up that I decided to give you my dope, as you have at all times shown me the greatest courtesy and kindness. For this reason I hope you can get some line on the old boy. At least Tiburon Island can be eliminated if somebody else writes in about this same King John.—J. W. PREBLE, JR.

THANKS to the huge accumulation of letters for Camp-Fire, the following has been held until the service offered becomes limited in time. But there's still a chance, and the spirit back of the offer is in any case too fine not to be passed on.

9, West Bolton Gardens,
In Old Brompton Road,
London, S. W. 5, England

If the following will be of any service to our fellow members of Camp-Fire I know you will not mind the time I'm taking.

NO DOUBT many Camp-Fire fans will be coming across this Summer, and any whom I can help in any way within my abilities I shall be glad to have them call for help just as they would do at any regular Camp-Fire. I would offer to take a Station were it not that I expect to leave for the States some time early in December, in the meantime this address and myself are at the service of any of the Gang. I know London and certain parts of these Islands fairly well, also a little about Paris, so I may be able to be of assistance; besides, I shall more than enjoy meeting any of the Camp-Fire following, so the offer is not all one-sided.

Just a bit about myself so you may know that I'm safe to recommend: am a physcian, of St. Augustine, Fla., doing special work here in nerve and mental cases; served from June, 1916, to Aug., 1919, with the Medical Corps, U. S.; discharged as a Lt. Col.; was with the 77th Division of New York City from Oct., 1917, until March, 1919, as Commanding Officer of the 302 Sanitary Train; most any of that Division will know me.—JAMES BURNIE GRIFFIN, M. D.

SOMETHING from Charles Beadle about the facts back of his novelette in this issue:

Paris, France.

This yarn was suggested by a real episode perpetrated by a bunch of the British South-African Police who came down to Beira on leave got in a mix-up and actually put the police in their own jail and then played Old Harry with the town. The torturing stunt is not in the least exaggerated, nor the possibilities on the Beira railway. It's great, that rail. Coming down from Beira, our train pulled up in the open veldt. Got out to see what was up. A Scotch engineer and the Irish conductor had worked up a dispute *en route* and, with the passengers forming a ring, fought it out. Then we continued peaceably. Another time some one spotted a lion. We stopped the train and everybody joined in the hunt—for some hours, for we didn't get him after all.—CHARLES BEADLE.

HEY, Ulysses! You Yank who floated over from North and South America to New Zealand and Australia and were the goat in the strike at Erewhon, are you sitting among us at this meeting? I think we'd all like to meet you— if we haven't already—and I know Tom L. Mills of the *Feilding Star* and our "Ask Adventure" will particularly want to hear from you again.

Feilding, New Zealand.

At the moment when he stood over me by the side of my table here in faraway Feilding I was absorbed in reading a proof-slip, for the last afternoon edition was going to press. It was when I had handed the proof to the waiting devil that I first observed the stranger.

"The editor?"

"Yes."

"Tom L. Mills, of *Adventure*?"

"The same again," said I, as I rose to the occasion. He put out his hand, and we shook mutually.

"Got time to talk?"

"Why, sure—shoot!"

"That's fine," said he; "just like a little piece spoken from home."

There was only the suggestion of anything U. S. about his appearance or his speech. But he was mighty interesting. The surprise however, was in the opening of the interview. It wasn't a fraternal or a lend-me-a-dollar-call. It started on a business basis, and ended in an up-and-down-the-earth chat that opened out a long vista of an adventurous life. And thus my caller began:

"I came in to see if a fellow Adventurer had got the right dope about that strike up at Erewhon. I don't want Tom Mills to fall in. I want your paper to get the straight of it. Have you?"

"Spill what you know about it, and I'll indicate where we disagree," said I; "but I might as well say right here that I know the trouble began and ended at the cook-house door."

"Say, now you've got the exact straight dope!"

exclaimed the wanderer with enthusiasm. "And I might as well tell you now that I was the goat for that strike—which is why you get a call from me here in your town."

CERTAINLY he was some distance away from the scene of the trouble to which he referred, and he must have traveled all night to reach Feilding, for the strike was well up the Main Trunk line. It was in the Erewhon freezing meat works, and three hundred men walked out without a moment's notice because eighty men were not being properly fed at their boarding-house. They went out on Saturday morning, and they were back on their job on the following Monday morning—all but the Adventurer, who called upon me that very Monday afternoon. He had been fired in the bad old way—not because he had moved the resolution which sent a deputation to the chairman of directors of the company to state the grievances, but because "there was no longer any work" for him—although the season had only just opened. He was the goat, but a cheerful one. "I don't mind it a bit so long as the other seventy-nine get proper grub from now on as the result of the strike," was his philosophic and altruistic way of looking at the sequel.

HAVING disposed of the business side of the call and thanked him for his interest in seeing that my paper had gotten the true inwardness of the trouble, I put to him the question that had been running through my mind:

"What brought you to this, the uttermost end of the earth?"

"Oh, that was simple. I met up with a New Zealander in Brazil some time ago, and he told me that there were only two countries that were fit for white democrats and adventurers to wander over to, and those were New Zealand and Australia. And here I am on my way."

AND here is the Odessey of this modern Ulysses, as told over the editorial table with the passing to and fro of numerous passports, certificates, letters, testimonials and other documents to prove the progressive statements in his narrative:

He is forty-four years young to-day—he had been a wanderer up and down and across the earth since his fifteenth year, when he ran away from home in one of the States. He shipped to England, stayed there awhile, and then crossed to South America, went back to the North, and then worked his way due south some more. He knew every part of South America, from Mexico right away to the Magellan Straits—yes, sir! Had the best of good words to say about the real southern folks, whose virtues and weaknesses were summed up in one word: Hospitality. If you offer to pay for a meal: "What's the matter with my hospitality, *señor*—don't it suit you?" "Oh, but I must recompense you!" "Ah, but, *señor*, some day I may call at your home!" And there you have South America—the real S. A. You could take it from Edgar Young, too. He knew the South—not all of it accurately, but ninety-five per cent. of accuracy, which was a good assay.

Honduras? Yes—here was a letter to which a story was attached. See that signature? Note the initials. There's a German camouflage in the signature. "I exposed it—and my services were no longer required! Well, well. I got that diplomatic letter from the enemy in the midst—and then I gave him a clean knock-out punch on the jaw by way of receipt. I had only to cross the road to get another job. Oh, there's lots of work for a husky white man 'way down in those southern republics. For he is the only one that will work—and get the native to work, in a land that only plays at work and makes hard work of passing the time away."

Peru? Now, there was a fine and large and open country for any man who had red blood in his veins and wanted to get on in this world. Peru? Yes, he would remember Peru. Oh, yes, there was bite as well as Peruvian bark. (He had a fine wit, this wanderer.) It was down there that he worked in one of the mines controlled by one Hearst of New York. It was down there that the Germans got in some fine work for their Fatherland.

PANAMA? He was away back behind and beyond the Zone, miles away from the next white man, when he heard first about the outbreak of the Great War. And thereby hangs a funny tale. The news of the outbreak had come to him in a letter from a friend up in the States. Amongst the gangs he was bossing at the time were two British-born negroes. Holding out the letter, he called to one of them, a Jamaican:

"Say, Sambo, lookahere! There's a —— big war on. Germany is fighting your England, has blown London to bits, and they've killed your King and Queen!"

Sambo was goggle-eyed and tongue-tied with the horror of it. When he got control of his vocal mechanism again he gasped. "Good Gollymity! You don't say, Massa Jack! Fight England—yes. Blow up Lunnon—why, yessir! But you go kill the King and Queen—no sir, not atall! That's a —— lie, Massa Jack—a very —— lie! Whyfore, if they-all was to go kill the King and Queen, why"—and here he and the other blacks let out raucous yells of laughter—"why, that would be the end of the world! We would all be dead 'uns—Sambo and Massa Jack and the King and the Queen and every —— one of us all!"

And amid a shout of laughter Ulysses waved his hand in a large gesture of farewell, and said he would "be on his way," and I haven't seen his breeziness since.—Tom L. Mills.

THIS is about the death of an old friend, for Camp-Fire has for years followed the waning fortunes of the famous old whaler *Morning Star*. I like to think, with Mr. Mitchell, that her death was really a rescue.

Bridgeport, Connecticut.

Quite some time ago I wrote you in regard to the whereabouts of the brig *Morning Star*. Your answer was that you had already been informed as to her whereabouts At that writing I was in the Navy and being a sailorman am quite interested in the sailing ships of the past. At present I am with the Lake Torpedo Boat Co., in the capacity of rigger.

I LATELY inquired about her brief stay as a "mother-ship" for the Lake Co.'s subs. The *Morning Star* was brought to Bridgeport in the Spring of 1914, (if I remember right) and all her spars and rigging unshipped, and had engines installed, and, from what I can learn, wasn't a success.

Later she was sold to a company down No'folk way, and used as a lighter of some sort. But, she didn't last long as a lighter, as she was caught in a blow off the Virginia Capes and sunk laden with coal.

But I can hazard a guess old Father Neptune took her to his domain rather than see her used for that purpose. As no doubt you can recall, she was one of the finest and most famous of our old whalers. I am writing and offer you a small souvenir which I dug up the other day. It is very small, yet no doubt you will appreciate it, not for its face value, but because of the days when all rope for standing and running rigging was spun by hand. This souvenir is a piece of gear called in the olden days "pear" and was used in laying up strands as it was from a spinning "jenny." The fiber was laid up by hand into what is termed yarn. The yarn was then laid up again in strands, and then lastly laid up into the line proper. All this was done by hand by aid of the "jenny."—P. H. Mitchell.

IT IS pleasing to note that the French Academy conferred the Grand Prix de Roman upon Pierre Benoit's "L'Atlantide," which appeared in English in the Mid-August and First-September issues of Adventure. Its first publication in this country.

IN ARTHUR O. FRIEL'S story in this issue there recurs a pun on a proper name. The pun is really dependent upon the English translation of a common noun—a darned common one, not upon the Portuguese for that word. Hence a problem which we put up to Mr. Friel. Here's his letter. As you'll see, we decided to let it run as it stands.

I'll admit that this time I've used "literary license" in order to make a laugh. The Portuguese word is *barriga*. It's a pretty safe bet, however, that 99% of our readers won't know this, and that the others won't give a rip. I've noticed that most folks, given a choice between meticulous precision and a chance to snicker, will reach for the snicker and let precision go hang.

However, if you think it's really essential, I'll fix it up somehow. I haven't yet had time to figure on it, though, and right now it looks as if I'd have to use an ax—chop out the humor at that point. To me it seems that the story would lose more than it would gain by this operation. . . .

The custom of confining a girl when she reaches womanhood is quite wide-spread among the Amazonian Indians, particularly at the head-waters; and it is nothing uncommon for a girl to be kept in her cage until she bleaches out and becomes sickly—in fact, some of them die from it.—Arthur O. Friel.

While we have more stories by Mr. Friel in our safe, there are not likely to be any more for some time, I'm sorry to say, as he has temporarily given up writing for other work. Later, however, I'm hoping he will take up the pen again and, if he does, I think he'll be writing for our magazine.

A COMRADE who signs himself only "A Canadian" wants to know where he can get a true history of Jesse James and his gang and similar information about Billy the Kid. It happens that there are other Canadians and anyhow I haven't much use for anonymous letters, however innocent. If a comrade doesn't want his name printed, that's his right, but he ought at least to give me some name and address where a letter will reach him. Otherwise I'm forced to ignore his request or to take Camp-Fire space from perhaps more interesting material and then take more Camp-Fire space to print a reply. If any of you want to send the information he asks, I'll try to find space for it, but I make no more definite promises than that. Of course "A Canadian" was only thoughtless, but it doesn't follow that we have to pay the bill.—A. S. H.

Our Camp-Fire came into being May 5, 1912, with our June issue, and since then its fire has never died down. Many have gathered about it and they are of all classes and degrees, high and low, rich and poor, adventurers and stay-at-homes, and from all parts of the earth. Some whose voices we used to know have taken the Long Trail and are heard no more, but they are still memories among us, and new voices are heard, and welcomed.

We are drawn together by a common liking for the strong, clean things of out-of-doors, for word from the earth's far places, for man in action instead of caged by circumstance. The *spirit* of adventure lives in all men; the rest is chance.

But something besides a common interest holds us together. Somehow a real comradeship has grown up among us. Men can not thus meet and talk together without growing into friendlier relations; many a time does one of us come to the rest for facts and guidance; many a close personal friendship has our Camp-Fire built up between two men who had never met; often has it proved an open sesame between strangers in a far land.

Perhaps our Camp-Fire is even a little more. Perhaps it is a bit of leaven working gently among those of different station toward the fuller and more human understanding and sympathy that will some day bring to man the real democracy and brotherhood he seeks. Few indeed are the agencies that bring together on a friendly footing so many and such great extremes as here. And we are numbered by the hundred thousand now.

If you are come to our Camp-Fire for the first time and find you like the things we like, join us and find yourself very welcome. There is no obligation except ordinary manliness, no forms or ceremonies, no dues, no officers, no anything except men and women gathered for interest and friendliness. Your desire to join makes you a member.

THIS is where I catch it hard. Quite a lot of you lambasted me for printing one of Talbot Mundy's stories in *Romance* instead of in *Adventure*. The funny part of it is that some of you also lambasted me for printing any of Mr. Mundy's stories in *Adventure*. One of you wrote that he always tore out a Mundy story before beginning to read a copy of *Adventure*. (I tell this because I know Mr. Mundy well enough to know he'll only chuckle when he reads it.) In other words, I'm damned if I do and damned if I don't. Can't possibly suit all of you. Best I can do is to let you take turns in cussing me.

And there's another similar predicament in this matter of using Mr. Mundy's story in *Romance*. *Adventure* has always printed some stories with some women and some love-interest in them, but it's never let the love-interest be the first interest and it has always made a point of having part of the stories in each issue entirely free from any love-interest. During the past year some of you wrote in complaining because, they said, there was getting to be too much love-interest in the book. (One —— fool even indulged in idiotic speculations as to my personal affairs on the theory that they were the cause of the change. He figured I'd fallen in love. Just as another —— fool once figured I was a woman-hater and hardened cynic because there wasn't enough soft stuff in the magazine to suit him. Please note this—Whatever my personal feelings and affairs happen to be, any time I get to editing the magazine according to them I'll lose my job and be fully entitled to lose it. I've managed to hang on as an editor for some twenty years and, whatever other mistakes I've made, I haven't made *that* one.)

WELL, to go back, quite a number of you complained that there was getting to be too much love-interest in the magazine. We here in the office talked it over. Hadn't noticed it ourselves, but, if that many readers had, it was time we did. (Incidentally, the others concerned don't choose stories according to the thermometer of their personal hearts any more than I do.) Going back over the magazine we couldn't notice any marked change but there did seem to be fewer of the rough-and-ready kind than before and, whatever happens, we want to keep *Adventure* primarily a man's magazine.

Stories have a tricky way with them. No one has ever been able to explain why they run in streaks and bunches. Why, do you suppose, do Latin-American stories, for example, come in in large number for a year or two, then stop suddenly and come scarcely at all for a year or two? For several years we scoured around hard for snow country stories and could get almost none. Then for three or four years more came than we could use. For the past year or two they've been scarce again. Same kind of thing holds for sea stories, detective stories, mining stories, all kinds of stories except bad stories. And every time some particular kind of story gets plentiful or scarce in the magazine, somebody writes in and cusses the editor and accuses him of taking bribes, being a fool, cutting throats, or something like that. Take my advice, consider a long time before you become an editor!

WELL, we office people mean well enough in spite of the fact that there are thousands and thousands of readers who can do the job a whole lot better than we can. "All right," said we, "if there are even symptoms of the stories running too much to the love-interest, we'll get right on the job of changing things. It'll take quite a while before the change can show in the magazine, but we're now on our way."

One of the things we did was to take out of *Adventure's* inventory a few stories with strong women-interest or love interest and transfer them to *Romance*, which has no objection to them. Among them was Talbot Mundy's story, though the time element also figured here, for reasons over which we had no control, and *Romance* could use it sooner that *Adventure*. And now comes along comrade Irwin and clubs me over the head for doing it. Some of you fellows who kicked about too many love-interest stories in *Adventure*, it's really up to you to step forward and take care of comrade Irwin.

Here's his letter:

Philadelphia.

You are now going to hear some "Honest to God" criticism.

YOU have been disloyal to your trust. You have been absolutely dishonest with the many old, tried and true friends of *Adventure*. You have robbed the readers and subscribers of *Adventure* of that which belonged to them just as much and as sure as though you sneaked in the night and stole their birthright.

Adventure does not belong to you or the management of the Ridgway Company; it belongs to the thousands of subscribers, old and new.

When you announced the coming of *Romance* we rejoiced with you and wished you success. Yes, we the band of loyal friends joined with you in pulling for the young brother, but we never imagined for one single minute that you would rob *Adventure* to promote *Romance*.

YOU stole Mundy, Conrad, Buck, Young and others—deliberately stole them. *Monty* and his friends belong to *Adventure*. You know it and we know it. Oh; but you have raised —— among your friends of *Adventure*, and that is not all. You are numbers behind in *Adventure*. You present difficulties, paper-shortage, strikes, transportation etc., but your *Romance* is on the book stands and we old *Adventure* readers can go hook and wait.

I dare you to publish this as it stands and invite a fair and just criticism. The shadow for the substance—it's pitiable.

Don't misunderstand me. I buy and read *Romance*, but for goodness' sake let it stand on its own bottom, live or die on its own merit, don't rob the readers, the "Old-Timers," the people that made *Adventure* such a success.—W. Y. IRWIN.

INCIDENTALLY, I don't see anything very "daring" in publishing his letter. I don't think he has much of a case, and, if he has, I'm willing to take my medicine. Only it would be a whole lot easier for me if all the doctors agreed on the same treatment instead of contradicting one another.

Conrad, for example, never appeared in *Adventure*. Consequently I didn't steal him from there. Nor has Buck been in *Adventure* since its earliest years. And Mundy, Young and "others"—does friend Irwin think we don't "allow" our writers to appear in other magazines, even those not published by other houses? True, some of them are distinctly identified with *Adventure*, but I'm proud to say that the identification is by their own free will and that not one of them has ever had any pressure put on him to keep him away from other markets. Hasn't Mr. Irwin noticed that most writers appear in more than one magazine? Gosh, what a life an editor leads!

And we've been giving *Romance* the advantage over *Adventure* in distributing it? Nope. Never once, to the best of my knowledge. Comrade Irwin overlooks the fact that *Adventure*, being issued twice as often, is twice as hard to distribute in these days when transportation doesn't transport. Same holds as to paper shortage and catching up two months lost by strike. We cuss and do the best we can for each of them and cuss, and that's all we can do.

I'VE talked a lot but I haven't half covered the ground. That's the trouble, and please note it. A magazine looks like a simple matter —all the editor has to do is to get some good stories and put 'em in it and there you are. I wish it were like that, but it isn't. When you see something wrong with our magazine, criticize it, by all means. We honestly want your criticism. But don't, on the strength of that something that seems wrong to you, do any of these things:

(1) Don't forget that there are other readers and that they may like what you dislike.

(2) Don't forget that there may be many factors and conditions of which you ha e no knowledge.

(3) Don't be sure that the editor is necessarily a fool and a crook. Maybe he is, but give him the same chance a murderer gets—a chance to prove his innocence before he is condemned.

AND now, to be quite serious, don't get the idea that our readers treat me badly. They certainly do not. If there is a whack now and then, for every whack there are a score of hand-shakes, even some pats on the back, though I like the hand-shakes better. But there are hundreds of thousands of you and among that number there are bound to be a few who are inclined to cuss instead of criticize, to blame before they consider. And sometimes, when I get cussed for doing and for not doing the same thing at one time, I have to grin and cuss a little and tell the rest of you my troubles.

Also, *Romance* doesn't make me turn a cold shoulder to *Adventure*. I like *Romance* and I'm trying to build it into the best magazine I can, but it, like all other magazines, is not *Adventure*. It can never bring me the friends *Adventure* has brought me and still brings me.

SOME of the things Mr. Irwin says in his letter I like very much. "*Adventure* does not belong to you or the management of the Ridgway Company; it belongs to the thousands of subscribers, old and new." I think, and hope, that this is true. If it is, I'm very proud that I've helped build up a magazine that is something more than a magazine. And I like Mr. Irwin's fierce loyalty to our magazine, begging him to believe that I am fully as loyal to it as he is. If there's anything he thinks still needs explanation I'll try to make it clear to him if he'll drop into the office some time when he's in New York. Also, I appreciate his friendly help, and that of the rest of you, in helping launch our younger brother magazine. Friends that you can count on are worth while. I had to whack back in self-defense, but I like Mr. Irwin the better for his letter.

ABOUT Sam Bass and Gus Gildea from an old-timer comrade who knew them both:

Everett, Washington.

This is my first attempt to appear at your Camp-Fire but I can answer a few questions asked.

ANSWER first to comrade E. F. Kernan of Demming, New Mexico. Yes, I was personally acquainted with Gus Gildea. He lived at Brackett or Fort Clark and was a deputy sheriff of Maverick County. In '79 or '80 he went west to New Mexico and while there became involved, in some trouble and was shot crosswise through the mouth, which left a hideous scar on both cheeks. He didn't stay long in New Mexico but came back to Fort Clark and while there the Southern Pacific was being built. He scouted the Devil's River and Pecos country as a deputy sheriff. He was a small man but was not afraid. Not a bad sort of a fellow. While a gun-man, I would not consider him in the class of desperado. He gambled but who didn't on the front in those days?

NOW for the question from comrade Chas. B. McCafferty of Arlington, Tex. I knew Sam Bass and was within a few miles of him when killed. He was killed at Round Rock, Tex. in the early eighties by a Ranger. I was there on date and went immediately to Round Rock, but he was dead when I arrived. The Legislature was in session at Austin, only a short distance away, and they adjourned and with the Governor came to Round Rock.

Sam and two others came down to rob a country bank and stopped at Round Rock, tying their stock in an alley that a blind alley led out of or a cross alley from the Main street to the long alley. They went into a store with their pistols on and that had a bar in the rear. The deputy marshal of Round Rock went in to disarm them and Sam shot him and the three ran for their horses. Sam was behind and just as he ran in the side alley a Ranger who happened to be stopping over night, showed up and shot Sam through the body with a Winchester. He made good to his horse and rode out about three miles, got off beside the road and a farmer or milkman came along and he called him and sent word to town for them to come and get him. The authorities would hardly believe him when he told them he was Sam Bass.

I knew all of the gunmen of those times; was within four feet of Ben Thompson and King Fisher when they were killed in Jack Hines' old place in San Antonio. I don't remember the balance of song. Good night.—H. P. WHARTENBY.

YES, I believe most of us think of a bully as a coward. But here is something from G. A. Wells about the strange and contradictory character that figures in his story in this issue:

New Albany, Indiana.

There will no doubt be one or more readers of this story who remember the man whom I have called in to serve as the model for "*Devil" Jackson*. If they do, they will realize that I have been rather faithful in drawing his character. I am inclined to believe that I have given him a shade the better of it, making him appear less a wolf and more a lamb.

IF EVER there was a half-tamed savage he was it. He was as bad and worse than I have shown him in the story. And yet it is paradoxical that a better-hearted fellow never lived that I know of. He would think nothing of giving you the shirt off his back if he thought you needed it more than he did.

He was afraid of nothing. He was a first-class

bully, and, in view of the courage he shows in the story, that may seem strange, for we generally assume bullies to be cowards. At least I do. *Jackson*, which was not his name, seemed to take delight in maltreating and abusing the weaklings aboard; but at the same time he wouldn't take water from any man, big or little. He'd stand up and take what was coming to him until he couldn't stand up any longer, then, as I said in the story, laugh at you.

NOW the incident of *Jackson's* knocking the pin from the shackle in order to let the chain slip never happened to my knowledge; that is pure fiction. But *Jackson's* model, this man I knew, did perform a service for other men no less hazardous. And the incident of fact was directly responsible for the present story.

Leaving Manila for Japan we ran into one big blow a hundred miles or so off the northwest coast of Luzon. I do not hesitate to say that that was the worst storm I have ever experienced, and I have been through a cyclone that wiped out a quarter of a city of twenty thousand population.

Naturally there was some damage to the ship. For one thing, the pole of the foremast (corresponding to the topgallant mast in square-rigged sailing ships, I believe) cracked short off at the cap and toppled over. Nothing supported it but a few weak stays and halyards and a splinter of the pole itself. If these gave way, down would come the wreckage to kill somebody and do more damage to the ship.

NOW on a ship at sea with the waves running mountain high and the wind howling past at a hundred miles an hour the deck itself is no place for absolute safety. And, that being true will you please imagine yourself under the circumstances crawling inch by inch up a mast that sways from twenty to forty degrees from the perpendicular like a gigantic pendulum inverted? Unless you know something of the sea and of ships it will be hard for you to imagine anything like that.

Further imagine that part of the way to your goal at the top of the foremast you must ascend by a finicky Jacob's-ladder that swings you about in dizzying circles and jerks the daylights out of you. If the gods have deserted you, you get smashed against the mast with sufficient force to break every bone in your body, or else you are pitched overboard into a raging sea from which you will never emerge.

UNDER such circumstances ships' officers do not like to command men, so they ask for volunteers. You've heard of an entire ship's company stepping forth as one man to volunteer to blow up the hulk in the middle of the channel to the harbor and block the enemy. Let me say for the hazard of this particular job of clearing away the wreckage of that pole that I didn't notice anybody breaking his neck to be at it, though there were any number of courageous men in the crew.

It was a cinch, however, that the wreckage must be cleared away. The pole was threshing about high above the deck like a huge flail, threatening at any moment to break away of its own accord and come smashing to the deck.

IT WAS *alias "Devil" Jackson* who volunteered for the job. Preparing himself with a knife and an ax, up he went, hanging by his eyebrows half the time, and we below wondered how long he could stick it out. Several times in the West I have tried to ride broncs and have managed to stay aboard just long enough to know what it was like to be shipwrecked. I can imagine how the man up on the mast felt at that time. After all of half an hour he had the wreckage cut away and, under the most amazing difficulties rove lines so that the pole could be lowered away to the deck with safety.

And let me say in passing that this man eventually drew a sentence in naval prison for some dirty trick or other.—G. A. WELLS.

EXCEPT for the fact that E. B. is a woman I'd at once cry a warning against comrades fighting over the various snake-bite remedies that have been advanced. Everybody has a right to suggest his remedy or to warn against other remedies, but those of us who are just listening are all supposed not to adopt any remedy until it has been absolutely established as safe and effective.

Humboldt, Arizona.

I have just finished reading Mr. Major's letter in "Camp-Fire" and I must write you or just naturally explode. As a warning to any one who would be tempted to use his "snake-bite" remedy.

IODIN is good to cauterize any wound and a good disinfectant but strychnin and nitroglycerin are too dangerous drugs to be used with too much familiarity by the laity. He advises nitroglycerin and strychnin to be given in conjunction and in doses of one-fiftieth of a grain. The most any physician will order at one time is one-thirtieth of a grain. Now with his repeat in two hours he will have his patient taking one-twenty-fifth of a grain and that is a poisonous dose. Not only that, but he would have the dosage repeated ad infinitum. The best thing to do with strychnin and nitroglycerin is to leave them alone.

PERMANGANATE of potassium or K Mn O, he does not tell what to do with and *that* is your only safe remedy. Ten cents' worth of potassium permanganate crystals will cure a hundred snake-bites.

Method: Apply a tourniquet above the wound; take a sharp clean knife and pass blade through a flame enough to destroy bacteria, and make two deep incisions horizontally and laterally of the bite; after it bleeds freely rub in a few crystals of kmnoy. If you are a great distance from a doctor, ease the tourniquet about once every two hours, let the blood flow well, then stop it. The reason for this is that the tourniquet presses the arteries together and also the nerve endings, and they might glue together and therefore refuse to grow and mend with the severed tissue, and cause a local paralysis and a difficult wound to heal.

Really two hours is an awful long time to leave a tourniquet tight. To ease you should let the blood flow freely enough to show that circulation is unimpeded, this applies to all wounds where a tourniquet is needed.

In snake-bites everybody knows that the tourniquet is used to prevent the poison from going into the circulatory system, and that it should be applied between the wound and heart, preferably about four inches above wound.

WHEN Michael J. Phillips sent us a story this year he had me guessing. Was Michael J. in California the M. J. Phillips of Michigan who years ago was a member of our writers' brigade? Of course he could easily have moved to California and, less likely, could have changed his exact signature, but we'd been friendly in the old days and it didn't seem likely he'd just fire in a manuscript without even a hello note attached. And, though there'd been years for improvement, Michael J. was a whole lot better writer than M. J. But I looked up M. J.'s signature, identified the two as one and wrote him.

He confessed in his reply that he'd grinned when he sent me the story—wanted to see how long it would take me to recognize him. The old-timers among you will join with me in welcoming him back. And some of you will remember that once we ran "Talks to Readers" by our writers, long talks with headings over 'em instead of the less formal ones we have now. We discontinued the long ones from lack of space, but several of them were left over and were too good to lose, so they have been carefully preserved.

Among them was one by M. J. Phillips. When he appeared as Michael J., I decided you'd agree with me that it was so good that space could go hang. Also it was about the sensations of being under fire in the Spanish War, written before the World War added some new sensations to the experience, and I figured that those of you who'd been in the trenches of Europe would have a particular interest in the Spanish War experience, especially those of you who'd served in both wars.

AND Mr. Phillips has added some later notes to what he wrote somewhere about 1911 or 1912. He lives in Santa Barbara now and puts in part of his time as telegraph editor of the *Daily News*. He was a major for eight or nine years in the Michigan National Guard and served on the Border in 1916. As to the late war he tells me, "I had a half-hour argument with Secretary Baker in which I set forth why I should go with combatant troops, but he won it, which I suppose is fair enough."

Nine or ten years ago the man in charge of the destinies of *Adventure*—the same man who is editor to-day—asked me to write a little something about certain experiences of mine. He had bought some of my stories, which were published in the *Adventure* of that day, and so I obliged. Here it is:

"UNDER fire"—has a sort of promising, suggestive, exciting sound, doesn't it? How many of the *Adventure* readers and writers have been under fire? I don't mean in the figurative sense, in politics or business or friendly argument, but really under fire, with the fellows on yonder hill making as strenuous an effort to "get" you as you are making to "get" them? Well, I have, and the sensations are as suggestive and as exciting as the title indicates.

And then some, to descend to the vernacular. If a man could describe truthfully and fully just what he feels when he hears the bullets fired in anger whistling overhead, he would outrank Shakespeare and Zola and all the rest of the clan. To attempt to set it down in every-day English—why, it's useless, that's all. Either it sounds tame and colorless, or it seems like the wildest imaginings of "Old Sleuth" or "Deadwood Dick."

I "got mine" in 1898 in Cuba. It is thirteen years ago, but the remembrance is as clear and distinct as it was on the first day of July when "Commence firing!" was sounded all along the attacking line. I was in a volunteer regiment, and we were told off to make a demonstration against Fort Aguadores, which was the extreme right of the Spanish fortifications about Santiago. I was considerably under voting age, as were many of my comrades, and we were wild to "get at 'em."

WE HAD landed a few days before at Siboney, which is a harbor a few miles up the coast from Guantanamo, where the Marines made their historic stand, and fired the first shots of the war. Our first camp was in a coconut grove, our second on a sandy plateau above the village. There was a narrow-gage railroad running up the coast from an iron mining town beyond Siboney—Juragua—to Santiago, and the morning of the first we loaded into ore-cars and were taken up to within a couple of miles of Aguadores.

We unloaded and formed against the side of the cliff, with a solid wall of rock on one side, and the deep blue sea dashing restlessly almost at our very feet on the other. They called for sharpshooters to go ahead and scout, and five of us from our company—C—were among those to volunteer. We shed our haversacks, blanket rolls and canteens, shifted our cartridge belts, which weighed heavy with the big, old-fashioned .45-70 lead bullets, and started forward.

In perhaps an hour the eighteen volunteers, in charge of a lieutenant, had gained the crest of a hill across the San Juan River from the fortifications. Our hill was perhaps five hundred feet high. On our left was the ocean, with a big warship and three busy little gunboats lying offshore in a wide half-circle. In front and a little to our left was the long-legged bridge which crossed the estuary a quarter of a mile wide, where the San Juan ran down to the sea. This bridge, which bore the railroad tracks, was intact except for a fifty-foot span, where the Spaniards had blown it up with dynamite.

TO GO back a little: We had been warned to "Beware of the bridge!" by the fragment of the fleet that had nosed along up-shore with us. The message was delivered by megaphone from the little *Gloucester*, Commander Richard Wainwright, recently retired, commanding officer. I never knew what seamanship meant till I saw that little cockleshell come dancing in gaily until within half a rifle shot from shore. The surf was thunderous and rolling high; the water was silvered by the foam which surrounded scores of saw-toothed rocks. It did not seem to the landlubbers ashore that a rowboat could pick its way through that deadly tangle; but—hats off to gallant Wainwright—on she came like a fine lady crossing a ballroom floor until a sailor, hanging perilously in the prow, had shouted that the bridge was mined, and dangerous. Then she backed and twisted and dodged her way to open water again.

WELL, to get back to our muttons, and the description of the panorama that was spread out before us. In the left foreground was Fort Aguadores—grim and gray and massive, the colors of Spain hanging limply in the bright morning sunlight from a tall staff all but over the water. The railroad ran through a deep cut between the fort proper and the barracks, evidently burrowed into the hillside. Above on the right, near the military crest of the hill, was a raw yellow rifle-pit, newly dug. Even in our inexperience we knew that was all a bluff; it was too conspicuous. Three of us who lay behind the same log presently discovered a real rifle pit, pretty well masked, and two-thirds of the way down the hill. And our excitement grew when we saw a Spanish soldier standing on the top of this pit, watching the maneuvers of the fleet.

WE DISCUSSED the range in whispers and decided the gentleman, in his blue and white cotton uniform which harmonized perfectly with the vivid landscape, was about 800 yards away. We set the sights, got comfortable positions, and waited for the word. Presently when the troops and the ships were ready the word came.

We fired. Our friend on top of the pit threw up both hands and plunged forward. We traced his fall by tiny white blurs which his hands made, and the arc described by his yellow straw hat. We had all taken careful aim and fired together, to make sure of "getting" him.

How does it feel to kill a man? To tell the truth, one's conscience doesn't seem to be fussed about it at all. My sensations were: Elation over our good aim; satisfaction at having drawn first blood; and a sort of heady excitement and an itching of the trigger-finger. We looked eagerly for another one.

AND then, suddenly and sickeningly, everything changed. They began firing at us!

The first bullet said *P-ss-st!* It didn't seem to be more than six inches from my head. I ducked. Two or three came with that rushing, mysterious, urgent sound. I ducked quickly for each one of them. Then one whined hungrily a good ways over head. But my neck worked automatically for that one, too. Funny thing about bullets. You dodge; that's all there is to it. You may not want to; you may reason to yourself, as I did, that the bullet that you hear is not one that hits you, and the danger is over when it hisses or hums.

But reason and instinct don't couple up. Along comes another, and you pay your usual tribute of respect.

I began to get scared with that first bullet; and the feeling increased for an hour or more. There was nothing pretty about the sensation. It was nauseating, degrading, horrible. One's brain pictured what would happen if one's cringing body stopped a red-hot messenger of death. One's stomach protested sickeningly as though it were alone in an express elevator in a twenty-story building, detached from the rest of the body, but retaining its sensitiveness, and the elevator was running away, up and down, up and down the shaft.

WE FIRED, regularly at first, and then more sparingly. We were armed with black-powder, single-shot Springfields, and a dense cloud of smoke neatly indicated our positions to the Spaniards, who fired high-power Mausers that left no telltale smoke behind; with each discharge of the Springfield, there would be a little cluster of hisses and whines and cracks all about us. The crack came from the passage of the high-power bullet through the air. We didn't know that; we supposed they were firing explosive bullets and that they were breaking to pieces near by.

That added a few more layers to the pyramid of fear. It was bad enough, I thought, to be drilled decently by a bullet that didn't bungle the job. But to stop an explosive, and be torn and rent—Ugh! It was awful.

THE pyramid of panic was yet to come, though we didn't know it. We had noticed a heavily laden ore-car on the track, between the fort and the garrison, at the bottom of the deep cut on the Spaniards' side of the river. No one knew what it meant. But after things had warmed up, a field piece barked, and a shell whistled over our heads. Leaves and branches fell upon us—I forgot to say the hill was heavily wooded—and we all but burrowed into the rocky hill with our fingers. Great ——! Did you hear that? They had big guns—cannons!

Fear had reached the peak. A bullet was bad enough; an explosive bullet was horribly worse;

but a shell—a shell that left you a thing of red, dismembered fragments! Oh, they couldn't be cruel enough to try to kill a chap with shells!

We learned later that that first one exploded in the center of a company and tore it to pieces, killing three and mangling a half-dozen others.

I LAY there on the hill, clammy, bathed in cold sweat, deadly sick, firing automatically and carefully when ordered to do so. All the time I saw, not the wild green hillside and the gray fort and the sparkling water and our four ships lying out there, but my home back in the good old United States. I would have given honor, wealth, youth and strength to be back there, up in the hayloft in the barn or under the bed. Those were the two places of refuge that occurred to me. And mixed with that fear that turned my bones to water—the man who first wrote that knew what fear was—was one thought, one shred of satisfaction, one un-Christian, unholy, gloating remembrance: "Well, —— 'em, if they get me in a minute, I got one of them first!"

The bullets kept coming; so did the shells. Luckily for us and unluckily for the poor devils behind us they couldn't get our range. They tilted the piece to get the shells over the ore-car, and that sent the shells over our heads. Occasionally one came low enough to tear a path through the tree-tops and shower us with more wreckage. But we never knew when they were going to discover their mistake, back her up a bit, and rake the face of that hill as one rakes the lawn.

DID you ever hear a shell? The song of the shell is the bloody, relentless, savage spirit of war personified. The boys of '61 tell me they put words to the song: "Which one, which one, which one?"

The sound would strike terror to the very soul of one who did not know what it meant—a visitor from another planet where war is unheard of. It is a whine and a roar and a growl all mixed up. And the old-timers knew what they were about when they claimed the shells said, "Which one?" For there is a stealthy, questing note to it.

Meanwhile our ships had opened up, and by the time they got to hammering Aguadores good, we were over the worst of the fear. Boom! One of those gunboats would roar, with an incredible, deafening explosion; we could see the batlike flitter of the shell in flight, and then a cloud of dirt, a few score branches of trees and a pall of pulverized masonry as the missile exploded. The *New York* lay back of the line, and at irregular intervals, with a racket that rocked the eternal hills, would hurl a great shell into the city of Santiago, six or eight miles away. These big fellows we could see plainly.

STRANGELY enough, my feelings toward our own men on the war vessels were almost as bitter as toward the Spaniards. There they were, comfortably out at sea, in no danger of being hurt—the Spaniards devoted all their attention to us—merely indulging in target practise, while any minute we might be snuffed out. I witnessed the incident, now historic, where one of the gunboats signaled for permission to take a wallop at the Spanish flag. "Three tries," said the commanding officer aboard the *New York*. I suspect he was a gentleman of sporting proclivities.

The first shell struck at the base of the staff, and we looked out in astonishment as the roll of cheers from the fleet came out to us. The second missile tore a strip out of the barred red and yellow. We cheered with the jackies at that.

Everybody stopped what he was doing to watch and wait. Even the Spaniards let that accursed field piece cool for a bit.

Boom! and we all yelled madly. The flagstaff quivered, swayed, and fell into the sea!

MY DELIGHT in the feat was tempered by a fierce hatred for a jackie on board the gunboat from which the shells had sped. Clad all in white, he sat on the rail, smoking. As the gunboat let go each time, the vessel rolled from the explosion until first one rail and then the other was all but in the water. My enemy seemed about to wet his feet with each alternate dip. When the staff came crashing down, he snatched off his white canvas hat with one hand and jerked the pipe from his mouth with the other, to wave them wildly above his head.

"Yell, you double-dashed idiot, you!" I gritted. "If you were up here, dodging bullets, you wouldn't be so blamed enthusiastic." That a man could sit there, carefree and placid, and applaud a good shot as he would applaud an act that pleased him in the theater, while I was in mortal danger, struck me as the height of effrontery. Even yet I am surprized at the resentment that surges over me as I think of that saucy tar.

I THINK that it was about at this time that the fear began to subside. I analyzed my feelings a bit afterwards—and ever since I have had the most profound respect for public opinion. Had I been alone, I would have scuttled away like a rabbit. But when the thought of retreat occurred to me up there, I knew it was impossible. It was utterly out of the question. "What would they say back home if I ran away?" I asked myself, and buckled to it, perspiring coldly, firing when ordered to do so, scared sick, but sticking to my job—because public opinion wouldn't let me do anything else.

The man next to me rolled over just then, with a surprized, silly smile. He was from another company, a bunch of "rookies" we called them because they were not National Guardsmen but had been recruited for the war. We patronized and bothered them. "Well," I demanded impatiently, "what's the matter with you?"

"Why—I'm shot," he said, still with that smile. He was. The bullet had ripped through his gunstock and through his leg. "What'll I do?"

"Can you crawl?"

"Yes, sure."

"Well, crawl," I said. "Don't stand up either. They've cut away the brush along the path and have the range on this hill. You crawl or slide, down to the bottom. Do you want me to go with you?"

"Naw," he said carelessly, "I can make it."

I was glad of the answer; I was afraid of getting plugged going down that cut-over path; and, to my intense surprize, there was another feeling. I didn't want to quit my post. I was still afraid, but the fear had pulled its ugly head back into its scales a little further. I was master of it now.

WE STAYED up there eight hours, and I came down with one regret. A spent bullet whined past me as we retreated stoopingly to the path, and stuck in a sapling—just stuck there. Another man from my company was a step ahead of me, and got that Mauser bullet. He wears it on his watch chain. I think a hundred dollars would be a small price for that bullet.

Into our little ore-cars we piled again and were chugged back to Siboney. We were white-faced, and weary beyond belief; and our hands trembled as if we were palsied. But a great change had taken place in us. We had gone to the front boys—eager, thoughtless boys. We came back with just a suspicion of a swagger. We had faced death, and were men. We had been under fire, and had taken our part in the heat and the dust of the day. We were of the tumult and the shouting. We had seen history made and helped to make it. We had been *under fire!*

Here is the later word added by Captain Phillips:

Santa Barbara, California.

HOW thin and pale and weak that experience must seem to the men who went through the hell of the Argonne or Château-Thierry only a few short months ago! But it was real and vivid to me then. And though the Spanish War wasn't much of a brawl, measured by modern standards, the death-rate per capita was just as high as any in history: Precisely one per individual.

Speaking of the world war, I am thinking seriously of organizing a society or two on account of it. The one that looms largest in my thoughts will be called The Order of Those Who Almost Got Across.

I was a captain in the Air Service. I accepted my commission from a personal friend on the express understanding that I was to go overseas—quickly. I went to Camp Sevier, South Carolina, and was there put in command of a battalion of troops, a thousand of them, with overseas orders in my pocket. We went down to Garden City together and for a month they were the joy of my heart. I liked them, and I think they liked me. We soldiered together and won various compliments, deserved by them, for cleanliness and soldierly ability and discipline and willingness.

AND then came an order transferring me to Washington, and they went over without me. They professed to think at Washington that I had had administrative experience. I drew a nice golden-oak desk, a stenographer, a wire waste-basket and a filing-cabinet. And there I stayed until the war was over and three months besides. Most of the time I was company neither for man nor beast.

Service on this side was not without its compensations and excitements. There was the time when I unmasked and arrested the man who talked like a German spy, and may only have been an infernal fool. There was the other time when we went up in a free balloon and escaped death by drowning only to have the big gasbag explode over our heads, and we escaped death by burning, all in the same afternoon. There were various other occasions when I took responsibility and bought and sold and decided and ordered on my own, while hardened regulars, caught in the meshes of red tape, sat back and wondered in awe. But I was only a reserve officer, so my file in Personnel in Washington meant nothing in the future, and theirs did. It was great stuff if you didn't weaken, there in Washington.

THE other organization I propose to effect some day is the Society of Those Who Almost Got Promoted. My file of papers, recommending a majority, were in the Adjutant-General's Office with a few thousand others when the armistice was signed. I will never be able to decide whether the blamed war stopped too soon or not soon enough.

I am living in California, now, and spend a good many afternoons trying to make a golf ball go where you aim it. Usually it doesn't, but when it does—oh, man! Ain't it a 'grand and glorious feelin'?—MICHAEL J. PHILLIPS.

And that Jackie on the gunboat that got the Spanish flag, is he by any chance sitting around our Camp-Fire? If so, please come forward. All is forgiven.

IT'S proved. I've always maintained that Americans are just as good liars as Australians, New Zealanders or any other darned people. Remember the cheerful ones an Australian comrade handed us some time ago? Read this:

Chicago, Illinois.

In reading over Camp-Fire I was much amused at incidents E. Read, Esq., states to show how intelligent the dogs of Australia are.

While I do not, for one moment, wish to have it thought that the Australian dog is not the smartest canine in all the world, I nevertheless wish to show that there are other dogs in this world which also have some sense of reasoning. I am referring here to the dogs encountered in some parts of the Philippine Islands.

IN CERTAIN rivers of the Philippines there are numerous crocodiles; and that crocodiles are very fond of dog-meat is a thing that has been found out long ago by the Philippine canine. That dogs are in the habit of crossing rivers, much for the same reason that the proverbial hen crosses the road, is a fact which the crocodile has learned.

But here is where the wise dog wisdom comes in. The dog knows that every time he crosses a river he runs the risk of being snapped up by a crocodile. He also knows that the crocodile is so greedy and anxious that the mere bark will draw the crocodiles, even as a dinner-bell the farm hands. Mr. Dog therefore, when he has found the place where he wishes to cross the river, runs along the bank away from this place and when he is quite a distance away he sets up a most unearthly howl.

Immediately the news that a dog is on the bank is voiced throughout the crocodile colony and immediately they all proceed hither in anticipation of one grand mouthful. When Mr. Dog is certain that all the crocodiles from the neighborhood are gathered before him, he, quick as a wink, turns tail, runs to the place selected for crossing and is on the other side before the disappointed crocodiles are really aware that they have lost a titbit.

IT HAS also come to my knowledge that in certain instances where Mr. Dog has a number of polite and accommodating dog friends, that these dog friends will do the barking so that Mr. Dog can cross the river in perfect safety and ease.

I have been further informed, on good authority, that, in a number of instances where the dogs have been so well acquainted with the woods that they knew almost every tree, when Mr. Dog was alone and in a great hurry to cross the river he would leap into the river and swim to the other side while the trees barked excessively.

Maybe the readers of the Camp-Fire have been in the Philippines and can substantiate the above statements.—O. HANSEN.

AS YOU see, there's quite a good deal of fact behind Ferdinand Berthoud's story in this issue:

Bridgeport, Connecticut.

The story isn't exactly what you'd call a story, though. I simply wrote down a sequence of real happenings just as I'd write a letter. The Maxim Hotel is real; Jack Moore was the man's real name, but as he's successfully kicked the bucket years ago that doesn't matter much. The captain was real—Captain Windley, who marked out the line of demarcation between Damaraland and Bechuanaland. Even the eye-glass was real and was not affected. Incidentally I never have been able to understand why custom should ridicule a man who had the nerve to wear one eye-glass when only one eye was bad instead of wearing two.

The sale by auction of the four women was a real happening too, and quite a usual one. When I had got that far with the writing I was at a loss to know how to give the story the necessary twist to end it up so just finished it in the quick way as you read. Little though the amount of love was that I put into it, I felt somewhat ashamed of even that. A fellow who was in the interior of Africa "on his own" when he was barely seventeen years old may be sentimental enough to bust but he hates to show it.—FERDINAND BERTHOUD.

AN ACCOUNT of the killing of Billy the Kid from one who was practically an eye-witness:

Frisco, Colorado.

I have been reading a lot of accounts of the killing of "Billy the Kid." Will try and give you the straight of it, as I remember it pretty clearly although it is a long while ago.

I WAS riding for the Holt outfit and was down to Pete Maxwell's looking for horses. I was watering my string just about daylight when Billy rode around the corral. He was all in. They were hunting him all over —— and back. His gang was pretty well busted up and the Kid was hiking for the Panhandle where there was a bunch of bad ones hiding out.

The Kid was plum tuckered out, so was his pony, and he felt safe for a little while at Maxwell's. Maxwell knew Billy and carted out a couple of Mexican women to get breakfast. Some folks said Maxwell sent word to Garrett that Billy was at the ranch, but don't you believe it, for Billy wasn't at Pete's place an hour before Garrett came over the divide north of the ranch. He kept the out-building between him and the houses, let his pony in the corral and crawled around the house to the front. He listened a minute and could hear Billy and Pete talking and was sure they were not looking for anybody.

PAT pushed open the door and stood for a second, for the room was kind of dark yet. Billy didn't know Garrett and pulled a gun, asking Pete, "*¿Quien est está?*" twice. Before Maxwell could say a word Pat fired. Maxwell bolted through a door at the back of the room and over the corral fence. Garrett didn't wait, but ran around the corner of the house and behind the well where he crouched down with his gun over the curb waiting to see if Billy would show up. After waiting about fifteen minutes Pat hollered to old Mother Rimoldi, an old Mexican woman, and gave her some money to go and see if Billy was in the room. She pushed open the front door, gave a look and beckoned to Pat.

Billy was sitting on the floor, his back against the door Pete had run out of, with a gun in each hand, dead. He had dragged himself across the room after he was shot, so he could guard the front door.

If Pat hadn't beat it the Kid would likely got him. He could have killed Pat if he hadn't waited to see who he was. The Kid was a bad *hombre*, but Garrett was sure leary of him and didn't take a chance.

WAYNE BRAZEL, a rancher about twenty-three years old, killed Pat Garrett last of April, 1908 or '09.

Dudley Garrett, Pat's son, filed information charging Brazel with murder at Las Cruces N. M. Brazel got bail and I left there that Summer and I never knew what was done to him.—B. W.

THE San Blas Indians and their country have always seemed to me to hold particular interest. Especially the question of how many white men have ever succeeded in crossing that bit of the Isthmus. Here is something from our comrade of "A.A." and our writers' brigade, E. E. Harriman:

Los Angeles.

I see that the San Blas country is under discussion again. Well, I am very well acquainted with another "sole and only" who has been across the San Blas country. Al Corson was for years a freight-train conductor and was the big man in a wreck in the Royal Gorge, where a member of his crew was pinned down by the feet, with a big boiler on the bank above him, ready to roll him flat at a little jostle. Al built up a pair of skids that held the boiler well above the victim, rolled the boiler over him into the river and chopped the man free at his leisure. And the guy was practically unhurt.

LATER in life Al and a pard, Jack, were desirous of crossing the San Blas country. They had a mule who was unusually averse to braying and they had reason to be thankful. They entered a pass and climbed quietly. At the crest they saw two Indians asleep under a low tree and went past, holding their breath. The mule never said a word.

Farther on they found a young buck across a big rock, nearly dead from loss of blood. He had chopped a big hole in his instep with a machete in cutting a big, tough vine. They stopped the blood, bound up his wound and heaved him up on the mule, after dosing him with a stiff jolt of aromatic spirits of ammonia.

After plodding for several miles they saw a village and they were seen even sooner, for here came a motley throng, armed with bows, clubs, spears and primitive muzzle-loading guns. Al punched the young buck and told him to "sit up and *hablar* to these folks. Tell 'em what we did for you, *paisano*."

The gang met them and one old warrior, who sported ten thousand wrinkles to the square foot, lowered a long-bladed spear in an effort to learn how far it was through a white man anyhow. Al gave the buck another poke and yelped at him rather sharply. He sat up groggily, waved one hand while he braced with the other, and said half a dozen words that sounded like a cow with a turnip in her throat. The gang turned into an escort of honor at once.

THOSE two boys traveled to the village in state, and the chief, who proved to be the father of the slashed boy, gave them everything he could think of in the way of accommodations, sent a runner ahead to the next village, which passed the word on in a sort of "fiery cross" style. Al and Jack passed through the entire country and came out on the hither side, feasted, escorted in honor, petted and made much of.

If any one of *Adventure's* readers wishes to know more about this, let him write to Al Corson, Calexico, California. The last I heard of him he was in the train dispatcher's office there. He told me this yarn while I was in his room in this city, three years ago. He said that he was allowed absolute freedom to roam at will among the old villages and through the woods, but the chief sent an escort of two men with him everywhere, because, as he said, "I know you, but others don't."

When they met a strange native the escort talked to him and the stranger promptly bowed to Al and moved on, satisfied. There you have it, as it was told to me.— E. E. HARRIMAN.

WHEN I first read Harold Lamb's story, "The Masterpiece of Death," in the Mid-Sept., issue my brain was shipwrecked on the mixture of "thag," "thug," "thuggi," "thaggi." So I wrote Mr. Lamb for help and here's his reply. I admit I passed the buck to Mr. Noyes as to whether we'd use an "a" or a "u." I refused to look at those words again and don't even know which he chose.

You see, any magazine has to adopt one system of spelling and stick to it, despite awkward exceptions that will arise under any system. We happen to use the Standard Dictionary in this office and now and then the spellings grieve Mr. Lamb (and others).

How come? Highbinders and gunmen are called "thugs" in this country. We derived the word from England, *via* India where a curious assassin-robber fraternity called itself thags (singular, thag). The cult or science of the murderers is known as thaggi, just as the cult of masons is known as masonry. (The word thuggi was a slip on my part.)

If you must give the Standard its pound of flesh, spell 'em thug, thugs and thuggi. The "a" I think is correct, if you look on the word as a quotation from the native language. That's just what it is—in the story.

But if we spell thag "thug" we should write Jagannath as "Juggernaut." As to this last, I've seen it spelled at least twelve ways by the authorities. Why not write down all the variations, put 'em in a hat on separate slips of paper and let the foreman of the composing-room draw one?—HAROLD LAMB.

IN HOT weather I seem to make more mistakes than usual. And I can make enough in zero weather. The following, written by Mr. Lamb for you of Camp-Fire, should of course have appeared with "The Bride of Jagannath" in our First August issue. It was my mistake that did it. Here, too, there is a reference to the vexed question of spelling.

I think we all have an idea that the Hindus were and are accustomed to throw themselves under the wheels of the car of Jagannath, to be crushed to death. I had. But the idea seems to be as wrong as our way of spelling Jagannath—Juggernaut.

The British officials in the Orissa sector investigated the matter and found that deaths of worshipers under the wheels of the giant car were limited to two or three a year, at the annual festival. And these victims were usually very sick men who chose this way of ending their misery, believing, of course, that such an end would be blessed.

And many hundreds—in fact, several thousands, if the records are to be believed—died annually at these festivals. They perished from want, hunger and thirst; from the pressure of the crowd about the car. The most devout gave all their available possessions to the priests of Jagannath at the temple, saving nothing to utilize on their return journey.

Also, these Hindus gave more than they had. That is, they signed bonds to make over their homes, farms or houses and goods to the priests. These bonds were invariably honored, even if the signer died of want on the home journey.

AS TO Vishnu worship, as exhibited in the festivals of Jagannath, there are two sides to the picture. Most religions have these two sides. The one we know best is the Siva worship, the shrine devoted to the All-Destroyer, the god that is best pleased by the sight of blood. Here we have the words of the apostle Vallabha Swami urging pleasure and luxury and the abandonment to the senses, just as we have Epicurus, and perhaps certain abbots of monastic orders of another age.

Turning the picture over, we see the gosain Chaitanya and read his splendid words that "life is the gift of God." This worshiper of the brighter Vishnu held that sanctity was gained by "warrior ascetics" through privation and self-denial, that all religions can save man's spirits by *bahkt*—faith.

Yet in the temple of Jagannath food was offered at intervals throughout the day to the lips of the grotesque wooden gods, and then eaten—or rather the best of it was eaten—by the priests. Jagannath also was outfitted with false arms and a nose and various garments for his yearly appearance in public. And this half-trunk of wood, ornamented with an extensive wardrobe and preceded by naked woman worshipers, was the deity of the car who cost the lives of thousands of men a year. Such is the strength of a traditional idea.

In "The Bride of Jagannath" there are two men from the opposite sides of the picture. The ritual of the bride, and the hideous means by which the prophecy was voiced through her is substantially as it existed in the early seventeenth century—and later. It is taking a liberty—as members of the Camp-Fire who are acquainted with Benares know—to place the car festival in one of the minor temples of the northern districts, but the festival, whether with the car or not, was held in these places.

CONTRIBUTIONS to the Bull Dog Lake Public Library are now in order. And if the spirit back of all libraries (and back of all our public and semi-public institutions) were like the spirit back of the B. D. L. P. Library this continent would be a whole lot better place to live in.

Winnipeg, Man.

Last Summer up on Bulldog Lake, in the Rice Lake gold-mining district of Manitoba, Canada, I made camp at the head of the lake. There was an old lard-pail, tightly covered, hanging on a bush in plain sight, at the beginning of the portage. I was curious and, on removing the cover of the pail, found a four months' old copy of *Adventure* with a note reading:

> NOTICE. This is the Bull Dog Lake Public Library. Please read, replace, recover, and hang up for the next fellow.
> BILL REDSOLVE.

Several other names had been written on the cover by prospectors who had read, so I sat up in my tent 'most all night reading, signed my name, and restored the magazine to the can, together with another and later issue taken from my own pack. So now we have two books in our library.—A. I. MACNAMEE.

The Camp-Fire

A Meeting-Place for Readers, Writers and Adventurers

A WORD from Robert J. Pearsall concerning his novelette in this issue:

San Diego, California.

The belief upon which *Koshinga's* plot is based, that Lao-Tse, founder of Taoism, and Gautama, the first of the Living Buddhas, were really one and the same individual, is actually held by a great many Chinese, including scholars. Since the two were contemporaneous, the time element can't be invoked to deny that belief. And the basic principles of the two religions are very much the same—also their modern decadence. The story is that Lao-Tse left China by way of the Sacred Pass I've mentioned (which pass is now actually filled up with the Gobi sand), thence through Tibet to India, where he established Buddhism, and that he was on his way back to China when he was translated. The difference in the names of the two religions and the two characters is attributed to difference in language. And, of course, religious Asia is always on tiptoe for another reincarnation of Buddha—which, according to this story, would also be a reincarnation of Lao-Tse. Also I will state again that the Ko Lao Hui is an actual society, or *tong*, constituted much as I've described in this and previous stories, which has played a large part in China's past and may play a larger part in her future—ROBERT J. PEARSALL.

THE article referred to by our Tennessee comrade was unfortunately too long to reproduce at Camp-Fire but maybe some of you can give us some first-hand information:

Langdon, N. D.

I'm strong for Camp-Fire because it's hallowed by the presence of great men. Then, too, I believe that it's a fundamental love of nature that "birds of a feather flock together." But the most useful thing about the Camp-Fire, apart from the information, is that when I meet a stranger who appeals to me I show him the Camp-Fire. And by their actions ye shall know him. Nuf said about this sort of thing.

I was born in the mountains of eastern Tennessee, consequently didn't get much "book learning," but in tramping round old "ma" earth I've been gathering up a little knowledge here and there and find archeology a wonderfully interesting study.

In the March 18, 1920, issue, Mr. Pendexter refers to a newspaper article describing the finding of red-blooded mummies in Grand Gulch, Utah. I'm enclosing this article, hoping you may give us a little more authentic dope on the subject.—MORRELL REED.

FROM E. S. Pladwell a brief word concerning his story in this issue:

Oakland, California.

The story follows fact almost word for word, although the hero of the original is a Piute over in Nevada. As a Piute is worse than an Apache by at least five layers of dirt, I decided to add class and romance to the tale by elevating the hero into an Apache, who at least has been known to bathe, although of course not intemperately—E. S. PLADWELL.

FOLLOWING Camp-Fire custom Lynn Montross rises and introduces himself not on the occasion of his first story in our magazine, but with the appearance of his second. "In the Dark" was in our Mid-August issue.

Chicago, Illinois.

Introducing myself as a writer is a short task. My story, "In the Dark," is the first fiction yarn I've ever put over, indeed one of the first I've ever tried. It's based on an experience of my own overseas when I became a pal of an Australian by meeting him each night in a dark dugout. I'm writing to him yet but don't have much idea what he looks like—never saw him in the day.

As a human being I haven't much more to my credit than as a writer. In 24 years I've been hobo, university student, newspaperman and doughboy and have found tints of adventure in each of these occupations. There is, I'm pretty sure, some adventure to be found 'most any old place.

I am at present an editor on a newspaper and a Chicagoan by adoption and firm conviction.

I esteem this chance to break into print in "Camp-Fire" just as much as seeing my first fiction yarn in type. I can't imagine any more delightfully human and informal meeting-place. My hope is that I can live up to the pace already set and be of service some way or other—LYNN MONTROSS.

The Camp-Fire

HUGH PENDEXTER certainly gives us good measure. In addition to his stories themselves he nearly always tells us of Camp-Fire some interesting things about the times in which his stories are laid. Most of us like American history when a real human passes it to us. The following about his serial beginning in this issue:

Norway, Maine.

It is now known that Michael Cresap, so long blamed for the massacre of Logan's relatives and friends at Baker's Bottom, was in Red Stone at the time Joshua Baker and Daniel Greathouse, aided by a score of neighbors, killed the Indians when the latter came across the Ohio from their village on Yellow Creek. The accusations against Cresap made by Thomas Jefferson in his "Notes on Virginia" to the effect "A man infamous for the many murders he had committed on these injured people," was eliminated from the edition of 1800. Cresap was the son of Thomas Cresap, a noted Indian-fighter. The son was a trader, and although thirty-two years old at the time of Dunmore's war, was not famous as an Indian-fighter. In June, 1775, he marched 130 Maryland riflemen to Cambridge. That Fall he was taken sick and started for home. He died in October and was buried in Trinity churchyard, New York City, near the door of the north transept. Greathouse died of the measles in 1775.

IN 1774 Logan's home was at Old Chillicothe (modern Westfall) on the west bank of the Scioto, Pickaway County, Ohio. According to the evidence supplied by Frantz Mayer and others it would appear that Logan's sister, and possibly one other relative, were killed in the massacre, but his wife was not murdered; nor were his children, for he had none. Logan believed Cresap led the band of murderers and, after hostilities began, left a letter at a raided cabin in which he asked him why he had killed "my people." Logan was intemperate and after his removal to the Ohio he became a slave to drink, and in 1780 was killed by a nephew while returning from Detroit to the Ohio.

BALD EAGLE was killed by Hacker, Scott and Runner, and set adrift with a piece of journey-cake between his teeth, on the Monongahela. In the story I have him drifting down the Cheat. Crabtree killed Cherokee Billy, brother of Oconostota, as pictured in the story. The magistrates offered a reward of fifty pounds, and Dunmore of one hundred pounds, for Crabtree's arrest, but he was unmolested by the border men. Patrick Davis's cabin on Howard's creek was about the site of modern White Sulphur Springs. The route taken by Morris in crossing the mountains, when he rode to Salem, is practically the same as the road from White Sulphur Springs to Dunlap's Creek, and not far from the line of the Chesapeake & Ohio Railroad. Governor Dunmore's complaint to Morris about the restless spirit of the frontiersmen was expressed by him in a letter to Earl Dartmouth, Colonial Secretary, in defending his course on warring against the Shawnee and other tribes.

I BELIEVE that somewhere in the story I have used the term "gunmen" in designating the number of warriors possessing fire-arms. If so it need not be considered an anachronism because of its modern use in designating a "gangster." As early as 1710 the French and English spoke of the Cherokee warrior armed with guns, as "gunmen."

BOONE was gone 62 days on his trip with Stoner to recall the surveying parties from the Falls of the Ohio. He traveled more than 800 miles, found the different bands and sent, or brought, them home. One authority has it that out of the 62 days he took enough time to build himself a log cabin on a likely spot of Kentucky land which appealed to him. It may be of interest to know that Benjamin Logan made one of the longest, swiftest, most arduous and dangerous trips ever accomplished by a white man traveling through a primeval forest when during the Revolutionary War he broke through an Indian blockade of Logan's fort in Kentucky and went for ammunition to the Holston. In all, he covered more than 200 miles, took back the ammunition, and did it in ten days. Because of the savages it was necessary for him to pick a route where no white man ever traveled before.

COUSIN'S death while wearing the scarlet coat was suggested by the death of Lieutenant John Frogg, of Staunton. He is described as being young, handsome and very gallant and fond of display. After the battle he was found with five dead savages heaped above his body.

Colonel Andrew Lewis was criticized by the unthinking because he remained behind the firing-line instead of leading his men against the savages. Washington evidenced his appreciation of him by urging his appointment as commander-in-chief of the Continental army. Lewis was modern in his methods and realized that his place was where he could control his forces. He sacrificed a spectacular, pictorial part in order to win the battle.

CORNSTALK kept the peace he swore to Dunmore until 1777, although part of the Shawnees were strongly opposed to it. In '77 he went to Point Pleasant and notified the settlers he might be forced into war by his people. In recognition of his manliness in taking this course the settlers seized him and his son Ellinipsico and held them as hostages. They were murdered in retaliation for the death of a white hunter, and the Shawnees kept to the war-path until 1794.

BLACK HOOF, or Catahecassa, was born near the present Winchester, Ky., in 1740. He was active during the greatest period of activity of the Shawnees against the whites and was considered to be one of their greatest war-chiefs. He was at Braddock's defeat, Point Pleasant, the defeats of Harmar and St. Clair. When the British agents succeeded in stirring up Tecumseh to make war on the United States Black Hoof succeeeded in restraining the greater part of the Shawnees. He died at Wapakoneta, Ohio, in 1831.

A hollow log was used by the Indians in an attack on Wheeling in 1781. They had captured a boat loaded with cannon-balls, sent from Fort Pitt to the Falls of the Ohio. They bound their wooden cannon with chains, and several were killed by the explosion.

Of the three white men who fought with the Indians at Point Pleasant, Collet was killed and his body identified by his brother; Ross returned to the settlements; Ward took an Indian wife and was killed in a fight in which the whites were led by his own brother, James Ward.

Colonel William Christian moved to near Louisville, Ky., in 1785. He married a sister of Patrick Henry. On April 9, 1786, he was mortally wounded by Indians. Because of the wounds received at Point Pleasant Colonel William Fleming was disabled for active service during the Revolutionary War, but was invaluable in organizing the frontier defense, as a member of the privy council, and in opposing Cornwallis' invasion while acting as governor. He died as the result of his wound in August, 1795.

Inasmuch as I have mentioned James Robertson, the "father of Middle Tennessee," who was a sergeant at the battle of Point Pleasant, it may be of interest to note that out of 250 men in his settlement of Nashville 229 died by violence inside of twelve years.

AMONG the sources of information used in building the story are:

Thomas Jefferson's "Notes on Virginia;" "Dunmore's War," compiled from the Draper manuscripts in the Library of Wisconsin Historical Society and edited by Thwaites and Kellogg; Withers' "Chronicles of Border Warfare," edited by Thwaites; "Virginia, its History and Antiquities," by Henry Howe; "Annals of the West," by Jas. H. Perkins; Gilmore's "Rearguard of the Revolution;" Shaler's "Kentucky;" A. S. Clark's "History of the Mississippi Valley;" James Hall's "Tales of the Border;" Dunbar's "History of Travel in America;" "Critical History of the United States," edited by Winsor; Helen A. Smith's "The Thirteen Colonies;" Roosevelt's "Winning of the West;" Doddridge's "Settlements and Indian Wars;" John Fiske's "The American Revolution."—HUGH PENDEXTER.

INDIANS turning white. Here's more about it and the possibility of still more, as I've written to Father Gagnieur as Mr. Cook suggested:

Houghton, Michigan

J. H. Anderson of Blackfoot, Idaho, has a note in "Camp-Fire" that got me started again. It must be more than a year since I started out to get for the brothers the real facts regarding "The-Disease-That-Turns-Indians-White—" it started with a story by the Pinkertons, didn't it?

FIRST, let me say that while the condition exists it is no more a disease than baldness or the loss of teeth in old age. The old Indian just naturally begins to turn white but never lives long enough to complete the transformation. I have lived among Indians or close to them all my life—the Chippewas, Ojibwas or Ochipwes or whatever Hugh Pendexter wants to call them. And they all begin to turn white when they get old. At the Indian reservation at Assinins in Baraga County, Mich., there is a full-blood named Pete Shelafoe, whose hands are as white as mine, and I am of the Norse type of Irish.

But what I started to tell you was this:

I wrote the Rev. Father William Gagnieur, S. J., Sault Ste. Marie, Mich., the only remaining Jesuit missionary among the Indians of Northern Michigan. He ought to know the Indian ideas on this subject. The Michigan Historical Society considers him the foremost authority on the Michigan Indian. He has lived among the Indians so long that he has grown somewhat like them, at least in the matter of shyness. He has promised to investigate the matter for me—did so a year ago. I hate buck-passers, but I have a hunch that Father Gagnieur will not bother with me, and for that reason I suggest that Camp-Fire write him at the address given. This is a worth-while subject for investigation and the good father probably would take more of an interest if asked by a stranger. The buck has passed.—L. P. COOK.

OHIO Arabians would naturally be an interesting problem. The following was written to Gordon McCreagh with permission to pass it on to Camp-Fire. There was more in the letter, but as it might make a certain Ghurka feel a bit uncomfortable, it's omitted.

Steubenville, Ohio.

Say, did you ever hear of an Arabian named Mohammed Ali (a very common name I'm sure, but wait), who claimed to have been brought to this country by Grover Cleveland as his valet, spent two years in Harvard University, head effendi on Roosevelt's expedition to Africa (I saw Roosevelt's letter of recommendation)? Head man on Buffalo Jones' African expedition who went there to lasso wild animals and the man who was the recognized leader of the Arabian laborers around Buffalo, N. Y., and Youngstown, Ohio.

I MET him when I was working in the employment office of the Youngstown Sheet and Tube Co. He stands about six feet, weight about one hundred and sixty-five pounds, very dark brown complexion with typical Arab features, *viz.*, thin, high arched nose, clear eyes, thin lips, etc. He was a fine dresser and looked like a million dollars when he was dressed up. Nothing showy, but more like a well to do white man. I gave him a job as head fireman on the boilers in the middle of July and he liked it so well that he went back to Buffalo, N. Y. and brought back with him over three hundred Arabs.

Of course they all wanted work as fireman. They didn't mind the heat and as we had a hard time getting men for that job in Summer time we were glad to get them. I had always liked them and was a particular friend of Mohammed Ali's, so they always brought their troubles to me. And if I didn't have my hands full!

We had a labor camp for white laborers and also a camp for the negroes we imported from the South. I was not at the office the day the men were assigned to their quarters, but one of the fellows assigned them to the camp where the negroes lived. Well, the next day we had ——. The entire three hundred refused to live with the negroes and wanted to live with the white men. "We are white, Tjack," Mohammed said to me and bared his chest and he *was* white there. So I, in my youthfulness told them I would fix them up and assigned the entire bunch to the white laborers camp. Then I got ——. The whites were Slovaks, Bulgarians, Greeks and Finns and they chased the Arabians out of the camp after a pitched battle.

WELL, there I was, with my Arabians on hand. All I could hear in the office that day was, "Preble's Arabians!" "What are we going to do with them." "King (the camp boss) says they won't eat their bacon in the morning." "Sure, they're niggers, look at their black hides." "No, they ain't, look at their faces." I sure did have a pleasant time with the waiting-room in the office crowded with three hundred wild Arabs all clicking and gurgling Arabic at once.

It was simple the way I settled it. We had almost completed a new labor camp and I promised them if they would stay with the negroes another day or two or find rooms for themselves for a short time that they could have the new camp. In addition I promised them I would have a little mosque built for them to pray in. That last part was a masterpiece, as I knew that, no matter how wild and bloodthirsty they seemed, they were always outwardly deeply religious. Well, after they had moved in their new quarters and had been fixed up all right I could have been king among them. They were eternally buying me cigars, cigarets and bringing me presents such as scarabs, and once a small nargileh or water-pipe. I asked one of their priests one day for a copy of the Koran in the original Arabic and after promising him I would take a bath, clean all up and put on my best clothes before I even touched it he promised to get me one. That was the only time any of them ever broke their promise to me, for I never got it. I hardly expected to get the Koran from them, but asked to see if I could.

THEY even got to eating bacon. Can you beat it? I knew the Koran taught them they could eat it when they were starving, so I told one of their priests, Moussa Sulayman, they sure would starve if they didn't eat it, so eat it they did. I was always welcome in the morning or any time they held services in their mosque, and I was the only man that was welcome. All I had to do was take off my shoes and kneel down with the rest of them and face the east. I got so I could say, "Allah il aha illa Allah. Mahmud rasul Allah" with the best of them.

I got Mohammed Ali a job in the English Army as interpreter for their Holy Land campaign, and I later enlisted and have never seen him since.—J. W. PREBLE, JR.

WHAT I once told Camp-Fire about calling frogs to the surface by a crude imitation of their croaking was told in entire good faith, but it was only one instance and, like Mr. Schaefer, I'm ready to believe it may have been coincidence. It certainly surprized me at the time, though I recovered in time to collect the frogs for bait. (Never got a strike on one of them!) I'm writing this in June and maybe soon I can get another chance to experiment at the same place, though not with the same frogs. If I do and get any results worth reporting I'll certainly do so. Also I'll be glad to hear from Mr. Schaefer as to his experiences this Summer.

How many of you are good enough naturalists to compute correctly the length of this boa from the size of the piece of skin?

Cranford, New Jersey.

Do you honestly think you can call frogs from the bottom of a brook to come up for bait or was it just coincidence? I am asking this as an honest question and not in a derisive sense, for the first thing that comes to mind is how far through water can sounds, made above it, travel. I can not recall ever having heard any made above when swimming completely submerged.

I BELIEVE frogs, like all animals with vocal chords, have distinct calls, but they must be out in the air to hear them from other species. I also know, as a boy, I could go to a frog-pond and by walking softly and making, what I believed, a sound that imitated a frog, I could get a mess to eat. I have tried to teach the trick to my own boy, but either my step is heavy or the call is off key or else I give the danger signal (unknowingly) or else I just plumb don't know how, but I do know that all the frogs within a mile jump into the water and stay there. Then by keeping very quiet for quite a while they again poke their heads out and I can get a couple, if I am quick enough. Anyhow your correspondent, ably assisted by yourself, brings up a question that is worth trying out. If I get results will be pleased to let you know, but we will both have to wait until the good old summertime rolls around once more.

To go back a few numbers *in re* the length of snakes. A friend of mine has a piece of a Boa-imperator's skin that is eight feet five inches long at present. At two feet from the head end it is ten inches wide of which 7½ inches are colored. The "spot" at this distance being broken, I can not give dimensions. At forty inches from the head the skin is also ten inches wide of which seven and one-half inches are also colored. The "spot" here being six and one-half inches long by one and one-half inches wide. There is a spot twenty-six inches from head end which is five inches by one and one-half inches. The length of the tail is twelve inches and the body at the base four inches wide. At three feet from the head, or rather, beginning at that point, the fourth and fifth spots both measure five and one-half by one and one-half inches. I know this is very incomplete, but thought the size might be computed from it.—L. J. SCHAEFER.

ABOUT the Custer massacre. And a bit of comfort for any comrades who are bald-headed:

Birmingham, Alabama.

I have read with much interest the many articles and letters in Camp-Fire, and noting our friend Huston's letter referring to Gen. Custer and Maj. Reno wish to add my contribution.

I was employed for about two years by A. I. Colton, who was a courier under Custer, and his story of the battle of the Little Big Horn and causes leading thereto follows:

NOT long before the battle, a man whose name had been forgotten, deserted from Custer's command, but afterward, being chased by hostile Indians, fled to the traveling column for protection. As he rode up, General Custer and his brother Tom pulled their pistols and shot the deserter.

This news reached the War Department, and Custer learned that a court martial was imminent, so he conceived the plan of breaking the Sioux in order that the offense might be condoned.

His plan, as has so often been stated, was to make an attack and Major Reno was to make a flank attack after the battle was under way. Had this attack been delivered, there is little doubt in the minds of those familiar with the Indian methods of fighting that the plan would have been successful, in spite of the overwhelming numerical superiority of the Indians, as even the Sioux, who were acknowledged to be the best ot the plains Indians, were averse to a hand-to-hand battle in mass.

IF ANY other Camp-Fire readers have heard this version, I would be glad to know it, for, though I have heard it from several sources in my life among the Indians and old-timers, it has never appeared in print, so far as I know.

So far as Major Reno's defection is concerned, I have been told various stories—that he was lost in the hills and arrived too late, that he simply quit and deliberately failed to follow orders, etc., but evidence was as corroborative of one story as the other.

I ALSO wish to add a humorous touch to the story of the Canby Massacre as told me by Jake Riddle himself, while I was living among the Modocs in 1896.

Meacham was entirely bald, and when the Indian who had knocked him down with a club attempted to scalp him, he found an unexpected obstacle, as there was absolutely no way to get the scalp loose. After exhausting all means at his disposal, he finally attempted to pull it off with his teeth, but was interrupted by Jake's shout that the soldiers were coming. As a matter of fact, they were not coming, this being only a ruse on his part.—O. D. WILSON.

HERE is some interesting dope from one of our old-timers, about Sam Bass and Wild Bill. And an inquiry about Luke Short.

Arlington, Texas.

I'm stepping up to the blaze once more to ask a few questions and let a little light on the "Wild Bill" discussion.

FIRST: Do any of the herd know of Luke Short? I knew one Luke Short well here in Ft. Worth, years ago while at the White Elephant saloon and would like to know if the stories about a Luke Short and two other men that hit the trail to Dodge City, Kansas, while the rule of the lawless elements had the best of the decent and put the crime wave down in one night, are true and if by chance this Luke Short came from Texas way, so I can learn if it was my friend.

IN RE "Wild Bill" Hickok. Wild Bill was a white man and acted like one. He was the upholder of the law every time.

One day Bill was lured to a cabin out of town and was attacked by six greasers. Bill used a knife in the fight and next morning there were six newly dug graves occupied by six sons of Mexico.

In re to the fellow Bill-shot and killed on the Square, I would like to say Bill gave the man as fair a chance as I would ask a man for and did not shoot him down without a chance as some one stated at Camp-Fire. Bill and this man, who seemed inclined to be boastful, engaged in a game of stud poker. The man won every hand. Bill kept still and said nothing until he detected the fellow's trick then said: "You're cheating."

The fellow blew up, cursed Bill and dared him to fight. Bill told him that he didn't want to kill him but if he would give his (Bill's) watch (which had been last stake) back to him he would not harm him.

The fellow refused, boasting that on the next day, at twelve o'clock, he would be on the Square and to show them he was not afraid of Wild Bill, he would proclaim the hour when it rolled around.

The next day he fulfilled his boast. Bill killed him, then, turning to the crowd, asked: "Any of you gentlemen object?"

No one did.

ONE night I met Sam Bass while camping in Trinity River bottoms about ten miles below Dallas, Texas, when he walked into camp. I was just fifteen years of age and was hauling lumber from Dallas to Rockwall which town my father was late mayor of. Sam stayed all night with me and I did not know who he was until he was about to depart the next morning, when he said: "Son, if any one asks if you have seen Sam Bass, you haven't. Understand?"

I almost fell off the wagon.

About nine o'clock I met a posse. The sheriff stopped me and asked: "Sonny, have you seen a young fellow with long black hair, riding a white stallion, around here?"

Somehow I just couldn't set the law-hounds on the kid's trail and I pointed in the opposite direction he had taken. "Yes, sir," I said "he went that way." Turning about, they rode away in the direction I had indicated.

A few months later Sam and four other men, whom I took to be Joe Collins, Rickinson, Jackson and "Old Dad," rode up to the fence that circled the field wherein I was ploughing. They asked a few questions, then Sam offered me a drink of whisky. I refused it saying, "No, thanks. Mother doesn't allow me to drink."

Sam looked at me and said: "That's right, son, mind your Ma," then added, "I wouldn't be where I am to-day, if I had minded mine."

One of the fellows, the oldest one, coughed and changed the subject.

I've often wondered how many other young fellows that, like Sam, have "gone wrong in the making" and been pursued and dogged and hounded by the grim hand of the law, have voiced these same words: "If I had only minded mother."

SAM was hanged, shot, snake-bit and drowned all at one time and then the young rascal popped up again. A mob got him once and hanged him. In a blood-thirsty frenzy some of them began shooting at his suspended body. A shot broke the rope and his body fell and rolled off into the river. From the place his body had struck a large rattlesnake was seen to wiggle away. They dragged the river but couldn't find his body.

A farmer asked one of the returning mob if Sam was really dead.

"If he ain't, he ought to be," he replied. "He was shot, hanged, snake-bit and drowned."

Sam later said his falling body must have stunned the snake, and that when he struck the water it revived him. Coming to the surface, he found himself under a pile of driftwood where he remained until night-fall, then escaped.

Sam is buried at Round Rock, near Austin, Texas.—CHAS. B. McCAFFERTY.

MAYBE this will make a certain low-voiced Westerner blush and cuss, but, after all, you can't really shoot people for saying complimentary things and I don't believe he'll go gunning after E. E. Harriman for writing the following, or me for printing it. In it, Mr. Harriman has unblushingly advertised a particular motion-picture show, but the idea back of that show deserves any free advertising it gets.

Los Angeles.

I have just returned from calling on Bill Tilghman, scout, plainsman, United States marshal, State senator, sheriff, peace officer, police chief of Oklahoma City, Indian fighter, buffalo hunter and gunman for the law.

BILL is well set up, solid, a good height, square shouldered, mild and low voiced. He believes that the young men and boys need to see wild Western shows that do not idealize the ruffian and outlaw. So he has written and filmed a story—"The Passing of the Oklahoma Outlaws."

Bill has made some history in Oklahoma and he is fully able to do more along that line. Take one look into his quiet face and you know that he is a safe one to tie to, if you are straight, but a bad one to buck if you are crooked.

BILL lifted the lid of a low, flat-topped trunk and waved a hand for me to look within. There lay fifteen revolvers, with barrels all the way from five inches to nine inches in length. He has had them polished and heavily plated with gold and silver. Some were gold throughout. Some had gold barrels and silver ornaments. Some had gold cylinders and silver barrels. There were pearl handles and ivory handles, wood handles in light color and wood handles in dark color.

"This gun shot my hat off," remarked Bill, handing me a short, thick Colt. "This one is the gun Bill Doolin, king of the Oklahoma outlaws, packed when I took him in. This is the one Henry Starr used. Here is one that was carried for a long time by Frank James."

So he went through the list till he came to a long, slim, old style Colts that had been built for powder and ball.

"My old partner packed that in the early days," he said, with much gentle feeling in his tone. Then paused and his eyes looked as though he were remembering days of long ago.

BILL looks like a man whom you would just naturally tell your real troubles to, but to whom you would never spill the little fool things. He gives the impression that he would hand out "chuck" to a hungry chap as naturally as he would clamp the spurs into a bad bronc. He is just the epitome of the Far West at its very best, generous, kindly, firm, cool, daring, loyal and strong. I saw Bill Tilghman but this one time, but I am ready to put my money on him. Furthermore—if I were in a scrap, with right on my side, and Bill Tilghman were within reach—I would never worry about my back being kept clear.

AWAY back in 1884, in southern Kansas, it was my fortune to have a quiet, low voiced man with eyes that resembled Bill's, come up to me, put his hand on my arm and say "You're all right. I'm with you."

I noticed indications of marked respect on the part of bystanders and after the quiet man had passed on one of them informed me as to his past history. I did not get the name and have wondered many times since that date who the quiet man was. Bill told me today. "Why, that was McCluskey! Sure! He was down there then and you have described him to a hair. Mighty quiet, but mighty deadly at times. Killed a-many."

They told me in Kansas that the quiet man had fourteen notches on his gun, or the right to that many. I wonder how many times we pass by mild looking, quiet men who are really the ballast that keeps the ship on an even keel, never suspecting that they are anybody worth a look.

"I want the young folks to understand just how low and ornery and mean the life of an outlaw is," says Bill. "My play is written with a purpose—an idea back of it—and that is just it, to show the real thing in a way to take the shine off outlawry. Discourage the fools that get a notion it is smart and desirable."—E. E. HARRIMAN.

THIS comrade was one of those who called our attention to a slip we'd let one of our writers' brigade make as to the habits of high explosive. And he added the following about rattlers:

Durango, Colorado

I want to buy into the rattlesnake game with this: Southwest of Cripple Creek is Rattlesnake Gulch. Rock rattlers—short and thick. They never rattle until they strike or are struck. Have been in there off and on for twenty years and this statement is the result of personal experience and inquiry. Would be glad to hear whether such rattlers are know elsewhere. Last man who doubted my word broke record for backward standing jump when he straightened up from cutting a small quakie for a snake club and exchanged coy glances with a nine rattle snake not three feet away—less then length of snake. That snake did not rattle even when shot at and closely missed twice by a .22. Blind? No. Any time during snake season they fail to "ring da bell." Somebody explain it.—FRED B. MORRIS.

HERE'S a "my first *Adventure*" story from a comrade who is now settled down in army life:

Fort Bliss, Texas.

I'd like to tell you that in my hoboing days 1912-1914, I traveled over Ill., Wis., Minn., No. Dak., Mont., W. V., Mo., and saw some awful things. One day in 1913 I wanted to go from Harve, Mont., to Seattle, but took the wrong train to Great Falls, Mont. About sixteen miles from old Fort Benton the train which I was riding on ran into a local freight, killing one fireman and piling about seven cars one on top of the other. Later a passenger train came along, two swell dudes got off the train and, as I was the only one not doing anything, they started to ask questions. I gave them some awful hard-luck stories, which ended in them buying me a swell feed and giving me one of your magazines. That was the first *Adventure* I read.—ALBERT TRAXLER, Cook Wagon Co., No. 14.

THOUGH it should have appeared with his story "Heart of the Yankee," in an earlier issue, the following letter from Barry Scobee, who has another story in this issue, brings up an interesting point as to the Mexican attitude toward Gringos and especially toward the Texas Rangers:

Bellingham, Washington.

There's no special "inside" stuff in connection with my story, "Heart of the Yankee." I had been wanting to make a story about the "bonus hunter" of the Southwest country. There are such, some of them ready to take a big chance for a big find in the vacant land. Also it had been rolling around in my mind that scrap of knowledge most Texans—I'm not a Texan, however—will say is plumb branded—in fact, namely, that the Mexicans think Funston and Pershing drew out of Mexico because they got afraid of what the Mexican Government and the Mexican army were going to do to them. "The Gringos," thinks the Mexican peon in his naive way, "are afraid of us." (And in a heart-to-heart confession with himself, he will add, "It is a good thing the Texas ranger is between us and the *Americanos*." You see, the ignorant and easy going, and most of the time pretty good *hombre* south of the Rio Grande, thinks, or seems to, that the ranger is just a little bit different breed from the regular gringo. They stand in terror of the ranger.) So I put the two foregoing ideas together and made a story. I am fond of the characters in it because they are like a lot of men I know.—BARRY SCOBEE.

THE following suggestion from one of you is right in line with plans we've been turning over for several years. Our house does not publish books but we've been trying to work out a way of getting "Ask Adventure" material into book form for the benefit of our readers. Others of you have brought up the matter and some day, when the paper shortage is a thing of the past, transportation facilities have become dependable again and labor conditions have become stable, we expect to put it through.

Some book house ought to jump at the chance. There is not only a decided demand but those books would be unique in that they would have the *most perfect editing and compiling in the world*, for that work would not be done by editors but by *the buyers themselves*. I mean that the exact material is already selected and each bit of it labeled with its relative value and relative space needed simply by the number of questions that have called each particular bit into existence. If there were ten inquiries from readers calling for one answer and five hundred calling for another, it is easy to determine at once how much relative space in the book each should occupy. The actual inquiries from readers are an almost perfect index as to just what should go into a book and nearly all our "Ask Adventure" experts have for several years been saving their questions and answers with this end in view.

HOW many books should there be? How shall the material be divided into books? By district or by subject or by both or part one way and part the other? Bound in cloth or paper? What arrangement should be made with the book publisher? Turn the whole thing over to him and let him sell you the books direct, we carrying a list of them in "A. A."? The magazine is not looking for any large profits for itself in the matter, but our "A. A." experts should get some authors' profits from it. It's not so simple and easy as it looks, particularly the arranging with a book house, but it seems well worth doing.

Let's hear from you. We not only want advice but the more exactly we know what you want, the simpler it will be to work out the problem.

I AGREE with the Texas comrade, whose letter follows, as to "Camp-Fire," "Ask Adventure" and our other departments being at least the most distinctive part of our magazine. I know you, our readers, like the stories and, as against the stories of other magazines of our general type, I think we at least hold our own. But in "Camp-Fire," "Ask Adventure" and the other departments we have something no other magazine in the world has. "I always read 'Camp-Fire' first" is so usual an expression in your letters that it's become a matter to be expected. (And I never get tired of hearing it.) Luckily we can have both stories and departments, but I honestly believe that, if we had to have only one or the other, a readers' vote would be very strongly in favor of keeping the departments and letting the stories go.

Yet there would be many who wanted the

stories and very few who would vote to drop the stories if we didn't have to. And if we're going to have stories at all we have to have a considerable number of them to make it a story magazine, one that can hold its own or better with any of the others. So when it comes to dropping some of them each issue in order to give more space to the departments you have to do quite a little considering.

JUST the same, what we in the office are trying to do is to turn out just the kind of magazine you readers want. Which is not just philanthropy on our part, but plain business and hard common sense, though I guess you know, too, that we want to please you just because we want to.

If we could get a sufficiently heavy vote from you to be thoroughly representative of the wishes of all of you on whether to drop some stories out of each issue and take more space for the departments, we'd certainly adopt the course indicated by that vote. But there's one factor that makes me doubt the fairness of that vote. Maybe I'm wrong, but I have a hunch that if a man is a department fan at all he's likely to be a very rabid one; it gets him where he lives. While if he's a story fan, he may like the stories better than those of any other magazine, yet isn't so likely to get "het up" about it. That is, the department fan is more likely to take the trouble to send in his vote than is the story fan. There is also the point that many readers never write to any magazine about anything, though I'll tell the world there are fewer of them on our magazine than on any other I know. These, though they might have strong preferences, would not be heard from or represented in the voting.

I'd like to have a full vote from you. Or even a fairly full one. Maybe later we can print a blank form in the magazine that can be torn out and mailed in. Then we'd have a pretty good idea as to whether to cut down on stories and enlarge on departments. Will you be thinking it over?

Now for our Texas comrade and the matter of "Ask Adventure" books:

Burkburnett, Texas.

I would like to make a suggestion in regards to the Camp-Fire of *Adventure*. I have bought or secured every issue obtainable since volume one, number one, and it is my opinion that "Camp-Fire" and most of all the "Ask Adventure" section are the greatest drawing cards you have, not merely from an advertising and circulation point of view but from a matter of service.

I WOULD suggest that you obtain copies of all queries written in to the different departments together with the replies and what further information was vouchsafed by the editor. Have them bound with convenient references and indexed and sold at nominal price. They could either be put up in the form of pamphlets or separate countings or conditions or bound together in one large volume. To publish each and every one would of course cause a great amount of repetition and unnecessary printing besides robbing the volume of correctness and making the whole most uninteresting. This however, could be done away with by a little intelligent editing. You know that nearly every question asked can be and possibly has been answered in three or four different ways, by collecting all together it would be of more service to the readers and also relieve the editors from covering the some ground over and over again.

My idea would be to gather all information queries, etc., in one volume which could be bound well and cheaply. Then if necessary have separate pamphlets printed covering each country, section, or condition such as Eastern U. S., Western U. S., Gold mining, trapping, etc. Titles to be published in "Camp-Fire."

THOSE desiring information on a given subject could look up title in "Camp-Fire," send for whichever seem to apply and then, if further information is desired, could write in to editor. This would enable a man to get all information at once, give him a chance to look over other opportunities he perhaps hasn't thought of and would eliminate over half your correspondence.

The whole volume would be for those who do not know just what they want or are merely curious and interested in such matters.

I believe it would be well to enlarge "Ask Adventure" even at the expense of a story or two. Nine-tenths of the readers, I think, turn to this before looking at the rest of the book. Stories can be had anywhere, but this is something new and interesting.—C. P. THOMAS.

FOLLOWING Camp-Fire custom, A. W. Callisen stands up and introduces himself on the occasion of his first story in our magazine:

Rosebank, Staten Island, N. Y.

It is hard to write about oneself—and then the very things one might tell would seem fulsome and simply bore one's audience. Yet I have had many real story-book adventures by sea and by land, belonged to the alpine club and did a lot of climbing, almost losing my life on a glacier, and a lot of similar stuff. I work it into my stories, but in my case it is truth not fiction.

But by far my most interesting experiences have been my friendships—in many instances very close ones—with interesting men. Roosevelt and I were boys together, my father's country place being at Oyster Bay. I know and have known intimately such men as Kipling, Lord Brice, Dean Howells, Peary, Stanley, von Helmholtz, John Bigelow and his son Poultney, John Hay, Fighting Bob Evans and a host of others. I know Oscar Strauss, Herbert Hoover and George Wickersham; I have known Grover Cleveland, and know Wilson and Taft.

MY PRELIMINARY bow before the Camp-Fire audience is a rather perturbed one, as to most I am an unknown quantity, for although the author of many stories short and long, they have usually been of a nature which unfitted them for this particular magazine.

I wish I could begin this narrative, as so many of my brothers of the quill have done, by tales of early struggles, poverty and ultimate triumph, but am obliged to confess that I was born with a silver spoon in my mouth (or at least a heavily plated one) my father being considered a rich man in his day. Thus I started in life with all the dreadful handicap this statement implies—believe me there is no heavier one—yet lacking every element of dramatic interest. We had a big town house with a lot of servants, a charming country place on Long Island, and frequently traveled to Europe and elsewhere. As a boy I was pretty well wrapped up in cotton and guarded at all points. I attended the best private school of my day, later entered college, and ultimately spent several years at a foreign university. On returning home I joined some good clubs, played polo and la crosse, and became an expert yachtsman. Had learned to shoot, ride and pull an oar as a kiddy.

My view of life was as false as possible, and I was about as fit to take care of myself if dumped into a cold, unsympathetic world as a callow sparrow three days old. Yet there must have been a latent sport somewhere deep down in my constitution, perhaps the heirloom of my maternal grandfather, a hardy old New York shipping merchant of the fast-sailing clipper period, foı one day I grew tired of it all and announced to my father that I proposed to go to sea. He, being a sensible man, did not oppose me, and I shipped as foremast hand on a fine bark of 600 tons.

In this way I saw much of the world, and, what was far better, learned to view life from another angle and ceased to bow down to false gods. After my college days I made other voyages and the love of travel has remained with me ever since.

ABOUT this time I took a crack at politics in the old Twenty-second, the so-called silk stocking district, with Teddy Roosevelt, Douglas Robinson, Ernest Crosby and other young friends. We thought we could reform the universe, but found it a tough job. Still we did good work for six or seven years, showing plenty of enthusiasm and lots of good will, and we learned many useful lessons and another side of life. While still a young man my father did me the greatest possible service by losing his fortune, and I quickly came down to stern realities. I tried my hand at various occupations, taught school, for I had not alone received a good education but always had the knack of getting along with boys.

Finally I drifted into magazine work and in time became an editor, but some twelve years ago the lure of the land took possession of me, I bought a one-hundred-and-ten-acre farm in New Jersey and started to farm on a business basis, and I believe I am one of the few city-bred men that ever made a success of it.

AS FOR stories, I have written them ever since I was a kiddy, though with frequent interruptions. On my farm for instance I worked all Summer in the fields just like any other farm hand, but the long Winter afternoons were devoted to writing, and where else could one work under more congenial surroundings? The great log fire crackling on the hearth with five or six sleeping dogs for silent companionship and, without, the snow-clad fields, purple woodlands and distant hills kissed by the early Winter sunset. "The Worm that Turned," was written by this Winter fireside. I abandoned this wholesome life with a sigh to take up war work and now I ply my pen again, stories, scenarios, whatnot—am always at it.—A. W. Callisen.

NORDICS, racial deposits and survivals, blond beasts and Western China—something more in the discussion Harold Lamb and Major Quilty started. Our comrade needn't have apologized for his spelling. We're not holding any spelling-bee at Camp-Fire. I'm no great shakes as a speller myself, but we have a dictionary and I can generally fix the other fellow up if he happens to need it, though, even so, I slip a cog now and then. If you have something that will interest the rest of us, fire away. Forget about spelling and grammar and such. If there's any bunch in the world that won't judge a man by his "literary" attainments, it's this bunch at our Camp-Fire.

McGill, Nevada.

I have been watching your smoke quite a while now, but never could catch up with you till tonight. Your outfit looks good to me, and if none of you have any objections I would like to come in, and sit down by the fire, and listen to the yarns. And furthermore, if all present agree, I want to travel a ways along the trail in your company since we all seem to be headed in the same general direction.

NOW I shall not make a long story of the fires I built back behind along the trail—some of those old fires seemed to me at the time to cast their glow over the entire section, but I have since found out that the light was only reflected back to me from the granite walls of the narrow cañon through which I was passing when night overtook me. Be that as it may, those fires are dead and many winds have scattered their ashes.

I guess we have all camped at pretty much the same places, and drunk from the same springs and panned the same gulches, so it would ill beseem me, a stranger, basking in your warmth and listening to the strange tales of your many adventures by land and sea, to sit here and babble of the few commonplace experiences that have befallen me.

I JUST now overheard Harold Lamb and Major Quilty on the other side of the fire discussing the probability of the Nordic invaders who overran Western China between twelve hundred and six hundred years before Christ, having left descendants in that section who have retained the Nordic racial characteristics, light hair, blue eyes, and tall stature.

Now I haven't got Mr. Grant's book, "The Passing of the Great Race," to refer to at the present time and there is no public library at this place, but if I remember correctly, Mr. Grant tells us, and History and Tradition prove, that the Nordic race swept over Europe and Western Asia from their home in the North in wave after destructive wave, ravaging and destroying every people that dared oppose them.

THE Nordics founded kingdoms and empires from the Pillars of Hercules to the Red Sea. Waves of yellow-haired and blue eyed giants washed down through Turkestan and Persia and flowed through the passes of the Hindu-Kush into India. Now, whenever the Nordics invaded a country and conquered it they forced their language and customs on the original inhabitants and always in a few generations, if there were no fresh infusion of Nordic blood, the people of the country—in whose veins flow quite as much Nordic blood as there is blood of the Alpine, Mediterranean, Mongolian or whatever race the conquered people originally belonged to—have again returned both physically and mentally to what the original inhabitants were before the invaders set foot in their country.

Madison Grant says: "The conquered breeds out the conquerer."

One might search through the width and breadth of many countries that the Nordics conquered and overran for centuries and the only way or reason you would have for thinking "The Blond Beast" had passed that way would be by the language and customs of the people.

SO IT seems to me, as I sit here by the fire (now I am free to admit that all I know on the subject is what I have read), that the chances would be pretty slim of finding any of the Nordics breeding true to type after being in contact with a people of such strong racial characteristics for so many centuries. For we know that the long-headed, dark skinned Mediteranean has always replaced him in a few generations wherever the climate is favorable for that race, even in the British Isles which heretofore have always been overwhelmingly Nordic; also the Alpine is encroaching on him everywhere in Central Europe.

Pardon my keeping you up so late. (And, Mr. Editor, I beg that you will overlook the fearful and wonderful way I have spelled some of my words.) I will bid you all good night.—HOMER CHALLENGER.

IT IS not his first story in this issue, but Charles T. Davis' letter introducing himself to Camp-Fire, as per our custom, came a little too late to appear in our Mid-September issue which contained "Tartarin of Trouble Creek." So here we meet him now:

Denver, Colorado.

I thank you sincerely for the invitation to draw up to the Camp-Fire, on the outskirts of which I have sat, as a reader, since the first blaze was started years ago. I feel that the position of listener best suits me, for, in view of the brave accounts I have heard around the fire, I can find no tales that could compete. Of myself, there is little of interest to write. I might even condense my autobiography to the extent that once was done in a census report: "Born—yes. Parents—Two. Business—Rotten."

More specifically, I was born in Dardanelle, Arkansas, an Arkansas River town under the shadow of a range of the Ozarks. Since then I have traveled more or less up and down the country and have been in, over or through practically all the ranges from the Alleghenies to the Rockies, inclusive.

I know my own Ozarks best—through fishing trips and other outings into their depths, and, as a reporter for the *Arkansas Gazette*, through assignments to cover revenue raids, etc. I might have had adventures on some of these expeditions, only they didn't advent. One time I went in with two machine-gun squads to break up an armed resistance to the draft which had resulted in two pitched battles with a sheriff's posse and the killing of a posseman. The punitive expedition was a ghastly nightmare of endless hiking and after a week of it the mountaineers surrendered without resistance. Another time I was "war correspondent" with a revenue raid in force, one of the most extensive ever staged in the mountains of the Southwest. Eleven men were arrested and brought out without the firing of a shot.

I lay claim to knowing something about conditions in the mountains, but I readily admit that I could not give anything like an authoritative character estimate of mountaineers as a genus, nor do I believe any one else can. I have found mountaineers individually quite as variant as city people, or Easterners, Westerners or Southerners. I believe I have taken occasion to refer to the hospitality of mountain folk in everything I ever wrote about them. I still believe this to be one of their salient characteristics—that welcome or aid awaits every inoffensive wayfarer wherever night or necessity overtakes him in the hills. And yet—last Summer my father and I loaded our tent, commissary, guns and fishing tackle on to a flivver and bored into the heart of the Arkansas Ozark foothills, twenty miles from anywhere. When we started home several days later the flivver refused to fliv, and, when all other first-aid measures failed, I crawled across a couple of mountains to where one of the native free-holders was plowing in his more or less vertical cornfield. Without the slightest question he left the plow in the furrow, and with the mules came to the rescue. After a short tug the flivver's heart action resumed, and the rescuer bade us a cordial god-speed. But the next time he came to town he presented my father with a bill for three dollars for "drayage."

Another special characteristic I have always noticed among mountain folk is not usually brought out in the average mountaineer story. It is a kindly, dry wit, and it is usually based on a keen and accurate observation and a quick sense of the ridiculous.

Concerning *Tartarin*, he is a composite character. I never knew him all in one piece, but various parts of him exist all the way from the Cumberlands to the Ozarks. I own a rifle which used to belong to the gun-loving part of him.—CHARLES T. DAVIS.

CONCERNING his story in this issue a word from Arthur O. Friel:

Brooklyn.

The test of the tucandeira which the American hero of this tale has to undergo is quite widespread among the tribes of the southern rivers tributary to the Amazon. Its details differ with different tribes, but its essentials are the same—the proving of manhood by enduring the torments of these huge ants, which have been kept for a time in fiber cylinders or hollow palm-logs, through which the victim has to pass his arms. Sometimes he also has to go to each hut and do a sort of clog-dance while being bitten, but I have dispensed with that in this instance as being unnecessary and also detracting somewhat from the dignity of the white man.—ARTHUR O. FRIEL.

SOMETHING about comrade Harriman's snake or one something like it. Can any of you identify it?

Minneapolis, Minnesota.

Referring to Mr. E. E. Harriman's account of seeing a small snake which struck with its tail, rather than whipping it, when pinned to the ground.

Last Summer on the Sauk River, Minn., I saw a snake of this description, about a foot long, very thin and of a dark blue hue on top. I remember the bottom to be more of a strawberry rather than copper color.

I killed him with a stick, so can not say whether he used his tail for striking, although his slender body writhed in a peculiar way. His general appearance and quickness made me cautious or might have studied him alive.

This is the only specimen I ever saw. Have asked several people about it, but no one seemed to know of such a snake or else made some reference to the time before July 1st, 1919.

A person will see many strange things in the woods, but this snake seemed out of place for this part of the country and that is what made me curious.—L. G. ZESBAUGH.

ANOTHER new member of our writers' brigade follows the old Camp-Fire custom on the occasion of his first story in our magazine.

Seattle, Wash.

Until I began to review my own history, that I might stand up and introduce myself at the Camp-Fire, it never occurred to me that perhaps for once in my life I was among my own kind. I have been a railroad and commercial telegrapher, a wireless operator, an electrician, a Navy bluejacket, newspaper reporter, and, yea, even city editor of a metropolitan daily. Seems as though I had been a sort of adventurer all my life, without suspecting it.

I WAS born in a Wisconsin backwoods village, (not in a log cabin, however), and I am convinced now that my nativity determined that I should roam the world in search of adventure, for I never found one in the home town after fifteen years of trying. When I learned telegraphy, I felt that my opportunity to still hunt the unusual had arrived. Yet, although I "boomed" through State after State, and worked for eighteen different railroads in two years, I regarded the result of my pursuit as vain. Four years in the Navy, during which I combed the odd corners of the Orient—and my water trail was 46,000 miles long—without ever catching up in my chase, so I thought. Then came years as a newspaper man—leg-work, police reporter, general assignments, feature writing, city editor—and I became so blasé that I possibly met the elusive sprite many times without recognizing her true identity. And I guess that's the way with every adventurer.

Looking back now, I recall being in a landing party that succored the consulate party of a beleaguered village on the Yangste during the Chinese revolution. Then, too, a drizzly night on a side street in Shanghai, when the plop-plop of my 'ricksha man's sandals was the only sound that broke the stillness; how a dark form appeared suddenly, steel gleamed under the dim street light, and my 'ricksha man flinched, thereby becoming the only person who ever saved my life, for right behind us was another 'ricksha with two of my shipmates, and the would-be assailant did not stop to strike again. Likewise, there were the fights we had on Ship Street in Hong Kong, with men from the foreign fleets, and the typhoon in the Yellow Sea, which jammed our rudder and held us in the trough, helpless, for hours. All near-adventures, yet lacking something, it seems.

FICTION writing, I began one night at sea during a particularly tedious mid-watch in the wireless room. Yet it was nearly five years later that I sold my first story. Doubtless I would have sold one sooner, had I applied myself harder.

But if I never found the kind of adventure I sought, it is likely that I never will, because my wife tells me that hereafter I'll do my adventuring in the pages of my stories and not elsewhere. And there are two other reasons that lend strength to her argument; you married adventurers will understand what I mean when I say their clothes cost something scandalous these days.—KENNETH GILBERT.

AS STATED before, Edgar Young started something when he asked "What is the spirit of adventure, biologically speaking? I'm out of my depth, as I've frequently been before in this discussion, but the water's fine if you can swim:

Cleveland, Ohio.

Though I have been a reader of *Adventure* since its beginning, I have never written to you. Not that I didn't enjoy it—the Camp-Fire is the club-like atmosphere of thinkers and doers—but that I was not moved to write until Edgar Young's query and Richard H. McDonald's admirable answer stirred my ambition.

ADVENTURE is the essence of life. That is why a magazine like *Adventure* appeals. It enlarges the field of ideas for the average man, who is generally forced by circumstances, or his own inclination, to a circumscribed arena for his experience. History is a record of the adventures experienced by the human race. Though the story is thrilling when relating the deeds of crowds—Romans, Greeks, the Bible People and the modern nations, it becomes absorbing when it tells of individuals. Who has not among your readers imagined himself into the personality of an interesting fictionized character or a historical hero? Alexander, he who sighed for more worlds to conquer; who would not be proud of the glory of Napoleon without his butchery, or the deeds of a Bismarck without being responsible for the German nuisance?

Most people are contented to reach the five thousand dollars a year class, but the adventure of reaching a million interests Americans. Roosevelt was a beau ideal in the ramification his adventures took. His naturalist expedition to South America, where he discovered the "River of Doubt," might be interesting as a story of travel to some, to others his ideas in regard to some of the strange animals would be the most absorbing adventure. Darwin's "Origin of Species" as a biological adventure made the world sit up, while nowadays we are more interested in adventuring among machinery and invention.

EVERY one is an adventurer. Even he who never cares to wander far from his own fireside. Wadsworth, in celebrating a tea-pot, disclosed the intimate life of small and ordinary things. The electrons that form the existence of a grain of sand, constitute the sidereal universe; though our limited human ideas measure their importance small to the great. The reason for adventure is to find new ideas, and we become adventurous in proportion as we become bored with the ideas already known, and are eager to seek.

Thus adventure is an emprise for ideas. The young man who is in love, and fondly imagines the old, old story of the incomparable she, is constantly renewing a very old experience, and always very new, and if their tastes incline, they can spend a life-long in the study of the erotic psychology. But to the more robust the familiar bores, and then away to other worlds!

The journey to other worlds is most tedious and so thankless that it does not appeal to the generality of poeple; these worlds, numerous as the stars, have each their idea experience to teach. But the most difficult, the most forbidding, is to adventure in the ideas about the Ruler of all these worlds: God.—Louis Siegel.

FROM Buck Connor comes some interesting data as to who killed General Custer. As I wrote Mr. Connor's name just now it came to me with a sort of sudden surprise that I've never met him. Of course I knew I hadn't, but after you've been friends with a man by letter for a number of years you sort of lose sight of the fact that you've never laid eyes on him. I'd hate to lose the friends Camp-Fire has brought me but whom I've never seen and I imagine quite a good many of you can say the same thing, for Camp-Fire has a way of getting us acquainted among ourselves even if we can't all really sit down together.

By the way, it would be some sitting, that! There must be a million of us. And right there's a little problem for the mathematically inclined among us—if you build a fire, how much ground will if take for a million people to sit down around it and how big a fire will it take to be seen by all? And how far back will the first row have to sit to keep from getting singed? Might make allowance for aisles, too. If there were no aisles, how long would it take the assemblage to disperse? How far into the gathering could a human voice carry distinctly? Come forward, statistics experts, and tell the rest of us about it.

Here is Buck Connor's letter:

University of New Mexico,
Albuquerque, New Mexico.

Here is a clipping I have dug up that will set at rest many little arguments relative to the man who killed Custer. I myself have heard many tales on the reservations—generally handed out by the knowing ones (?) concerning the man who actually gave General Custer the long sleep. Some claimed it was an Ogallala named Ocshilla Tonka (Big Boy) who put General Custer on the trail that leads West. But this seems authentic.

It might be well to publish it in Camp-Fire, and then we will see if Uncle Frank comes out of the brush with a shot or two. I have a lot of respect for Uncle Frank, and his talks of the Injuns are interesting. I happened to have a heap smoke and long pow-pow with him last season—he's there and no mistake.—Buck Connor.

WHEN I wrote to Mr. Connor to get the date of the clipping he replied as follows:

Albuquerque, New Mexico.

About the Rain-In-The-Face clipping. That thing has been smothered for years among my "trash" and I just ran across it when I sent it on to Mr. Wade. It is at least twenty years old, and that alone makes it more valuable, because time and fading memory have not warped or distorted the facts of the case. If you note how many different versions there are of Billy the Kid and other notorious characters to-day so many have a different story, and each one assures us that his own is the gospel. I learned while with the Sioux that one Injun named Big Boy (Ocshilla Tonka) had killed General Custer, and afterward ate a piece of his heart. But it was hard to substantiate the story. Personally, I feel inclined to accept the clipping as authentic.—Buck Connor.

THIS is the clipping:

Milwaukee, Wisconsin.

The *Sentinel's* special correspondent at Miles City, Montana Territory, telegraphs to-night a sensational matter in the shape of a statement by Rain-In-The-Face, the Indian Chief who killed General Custer in the memorable Indian fight of June 21, 1876.

FROM that day to this there has been a mystery hanging about the affair, from the fact that not a man of General Custer's little band escaped death to tell the story of their fate, and the historian has no other source from which to fill the page than the horrible imagination which clustered around the dead and mutilated bodies of the gallant commander and his troops, heightened by the memories of the smoldering ruins of the Indian village to capture which they paid the penalty of their recklessness with their lives.

WHILE the correspondent was in the merchandising house of Mr. J. J. Graham, at Fort Keogh, three Indian Chiefs, Rain-In-The-Face, Two Roads and Spotted Eagle—who surrendered to General Miles last Spring—came in, as is their custom, being encamped only two miles away, on Tongue River, for the purpose of conversation with Mr. Wm. M. Courtenay, the clerk and interpreter of the establishment, in whom the Indians religiously believe. Mr. Courtenay was reading Wittaker's Life of Custer, and in turning the leaves of the book one of the Indians caught sight of his own picture, which he immediately recognized. They then took the book from Mr. Courtenay, and found all their portraits, but exhibited very little emotion of pleasure or otherwise, until one of them turned a page and the picture of General Custer was revealed.

AT THIS Rain-In-The-Face became greatly excited, going through all the gyrations of the war dance, and giving the Sioux war-whoop at the top of his voice. After he had got through with his wild demonstration, but still exhibiting the greatest anger, he struck the picture with his hand and, with a demoniac sneer on his face, exclaimed in the Sioux tongue: "I killed him. I made many holes in him. He once took my liberty. I took his life. I am glad I did." On being told by a by-stander that General Custer was still living, Rain-In-The-Face became very violent, and hissed between his teeth: "Your tongue is forked," which is the Sioux figure for "you lie."

Continuing he said: "I visited his body after the battle. I cut him open. I ate part of his liver. I am glad I killed him. He was bad to my people. He kill many warriors."

It is a superstition among the Sioux that by eating the liver of a valorous victim the warrior so eating obtains all his cunning and prowess. This is the first authentic account of General Custer's death ever given.

THIS letter was written over two years ago, April 6, 1918, and the writer said that in about two years he expected to be back from his second trip to the Jivero county. Perhaps he is back now; if so, I know Camp-Fire will be eager to hear all he's willing to tell us. Meanwhile I've sent a letter to the permanent address he gave, with no reply as yet.

Houston, Texas.

I see some of the readers are interested in and looking for facts, of the Jivero Indians of Ecuador and Peru. So perhaps the little I know of them will be of interest.

HAVING been born with the wanderlust and a preference for the trails that lead far from the white man's road, consequently among the places I have passed is the country of the Jiveros.

I left Guayaquil in February of 1916 *via* Santa Rosa and Loja, over the Andes to the Zamora River (and returning left the Jivero country the latter part of February, 1917). Looking for placer gold. The Jivero country begins just over the Andes, at an altitude of about 900 meters, on the headwaters of the Rio Santiago, which includes the Zamora, Pauti, Pastaca and Morona, with numerous tributaries, and extends south to the Marañon and Amazon, and west I don't know just how far, but not to the Napo.

I STARTED in there with two partners, but they lost their nerve (and who could blame them) before we reached the frontier of the Jivero country. However, I went on alone and was very glad later that they went back, as it is a poor place for a man unless he knows something of the traits of the savage people. That I still carry my own head goes to show that I had no trouble with them. I attended some of their dances, feasts, etc., learned enough of their language to get by with some 80 or 100 words when I try to count them. Some of the Jiveros on the edge of their country speak some Spanish, but in the interior none.

They live in houses built in the form of an ellipse. I have seen a number 200 feet long 50 to 75 feet wide and 25 to 80 to the peak. Walls are of split churta purlius and rafters of bamboo and thatched with leaves which are cured with smoke. One half of the house belongs to the women and woe to the man who enters at the wrong door. Several families sometimes live in one house. They are polygamists. Cook their food in earthenware pots which they make themselves. I can not believe with Mr. Young that they are cannibals. Though the Chunclis are, who inhabit the country of the Ucayali and Huallaga Rivers, and there may possibly be some to the north of the Amazon in Ecuador.

I PRIZE the friendship of the Jiveros very highly. Among them a number of chiefs. Had many invitations to go on head-hunting expeditions but, needless to say, I had other work to do that I could not neglect. Also the German Mr. Young speaks of went into the country for the express purpose of learning the process of reducing the heads, which he no doubt learned, but not in a manner that left him able to impart the knowledge to the world. And that same process I had complete control of my curiosity in regard to it. The heads are taken in battle, the same as our North American Indians took scalps, though the head of the vanquished is not always taken. The taking of the head signifies defiance to the friends of the dead. I have heard many theories as to the process but I know nothing about it myself. It is a secret carefully guarded by the people.

I did have a couple of the heads, which are difficult to procure at present. There were two sold in Duran last year.

THE nearest towns to the Jivero country are Sigsig and Indanca, on the Pauti River; Loja, on the head of the Zamora, and Gualaquiza, all in Ecuador.

Will be glad to give any further information I have, and may have a lot more two years hence, as I intend to go back into that country the latter part of the present year.

There are many interesting facts concerning the Jiveros, but as I'm a much better prospector than writer, will let it go at this.—G. S. VERBECK.

YOU probably know by this time that the publication of our younger brother *Romance* has been suspended until times get better. Here is the statement given to readers.

OF COURSE if we had been wizards we could, in the Winter of 1918, when the publication of *Romance* was decided upon, have foreseen just what general conditions would be at the beginning of the Winter of 1920. But, like most other people at that and other times, we weren't wizards. So now, with *Romance* passing its first birthday successfully and well squared away for an even more satisfactory second year, the ax of General Conditions falls upon our undeserving neck.

You all know what General Conditions are. The particular General Conditions that press hardest in this case are the paper shortage, the badly deranged transportation system and the high cost of labor. The whole magazine field suffers under the pressure and inevitably gives ground in one way or another, but it is hardest on the young little magazines who have not yet had time to become adults. *Romance* will go into a state of suspended animation.

Just that. For *Romance* has proved its ability to succeed and, when General Conditions become normal and it is once more possible to secure all the paper needed and to get a magazine distributed so that buyers can buy it, why then we expect to bring *Romance* to life again and go on where we left off.

So, when you find yourself realizing that G. C. have struggled back to normal, whenever that may be, take a look at the news-stands to see whether *Romance* is not again in its old place.

We are sorry that we must say even *au revoir*, for we here in the office have not only enjoyed making the magazine but have found you pleasant company along the way. And we are sorry that we can not give you at once the good things we had gathered. There were so many we were particularly eager to pass on to you. We shall keep those we may, but, in fairness, we can hold for indefinite publication only such as our authors are willing to leave on that basis.

Those of you who are regular subscribers have already been notified by mail and your accounts adjusted.

And so it remains only to say the *au revoir*, to voice again our hope that the G. C. will hurry back to normal and to thank you very sincerely for your pleasant comradeship along the way.

ARTHUR S. HOFFMAN.

The last instalment of the serial by Beatrice Grimshaw, "The Terrible Island," therefore did not reach *Romance* readers through the magazine. So that they may not be disappointed we have had this last instalment specially printed on loose sheets which we will supply gratis on request.

Let me delay long enough to answer any question that may have arisen in your minds as to the effect upon *Adventure* of our having had to tuck its younger brother away until general conditions become normal. *Adventure* had the advantage of starting when general conditions were settled, and the further advantage of building slowly and very solidly. When the stress came it was full grown and husky. It has to face the same conditions all other magazines must face but, as comparative news-stand reports show, *Adventure* has a strength that will carry it as far as internal strength can carry any magazine. If *Romance*, just learning to walk, had to be put to bed till times get better, that makes *Adventure's* chances for paper just so much better. *Adventure* is now realizing the benefits of its solid foundations and it wants you, who helped make it, to know this.

Indeed, it relieves the paper shortage to such an extent that we are now able to restore the pages we were compelled to take from *Adventure* and, beginning with the issue dated January 3, 1921, our magazine goes back to one hundred and ninety-two pages and the old ten-point type. In other words, we are carrying out our purpose of giving you all that general conditions allow us to give. We were forced to drop thirty-two pages and, in order not to cut down the actual amount of reading you would receive, to change to a smaller type. But the instant the pressure relaxes enough to make it possible we put the magazine back on the old basis.

As to the future, until general conditions become more settled we do not dare make any promises, except one, for the future of all magazines is too uncertain. The one promise we can and do make is to give you the most and best we are able. We can also give you the assurance that little old *Adventure* is likely to come through the fire as little singed as any of them.—A. S. H.

INDEX TO AUTHORS

Miller, Thomas S.* *(June 3, 1918)*
Montross, Lynn *(November 18, 1920)*
Moore, Harry *(June 18, 1918)*
Nichols, T. *(April 3, 1918)*
Orczy, Baroness *(May 18, 1919)*
Partridge, Edward Bellamy *(March 18, 1918)*
Perry, Clay *(August 3, 1920)*
Pladwell, E.S. *(May 3, 1919)*
Pope, William H. *(March 18, 1919)*
Ramsaye, Terry *(March 3, 1919)*
Rice, Louise *(September 3, 1918)*
Rittenberg, Sidney *(February 3, 1918)*
Sanders, Charles Wesley *(April 3, 1919)*
Scobee, Barry *(April 18, 1919)*
Scott, Kingsbury *(June 3, 1918)*
Scott, R.T.M. *(April 3, 1920)*
Shaw, Stanley *(May 18, 1918)*
Shryer, William A. *(January 18, 1918)*
Slocombe, Herbert *(May 3, 1918)*
Utter, Robert Palfrey *(February 18, 1919)*
Wall, R.N. *(February 3, 1919)*
Webb, Charles N. *(February 18, 1920)*

* Reprinted from 1911.

www.ingramcontent.com/pod-product-compliance
Lightning Source LLC
Chambersburg PA
CBHW081131300726
48982CB00005B/924
9781618277282